'McAuley is one of the best' *ent*

'Few writers conjure futures as convincingly as McAuley' *Guardian*

'McAuley is part of a spearhead of writers who for pure imagination, hipness, vision and fun have made Britain the Memphis Sun Records of SF' *Mail on Sunday*

'He subtly explores what makes us human' *BBC Focus*

Also by Paul McAuley from Gollancz:

400 Billion Stars

Cowboy Angels

Eternal Light

Fairyland

Pasquale's Angel

Red Dust

The Quiet War

Gardens of the Sun

In the Mouth of the Whale

Evening's Empires

Something Coming Through

PAUL McAULEY

CONFLUENCE

CHILD OF THE RIVER, ANCIENTS OF DAYS, SHRINE OF STARS

First published in Great Britain in 2014
by Gollancz
An imprint of the Orion Publishing Group
Orion House, 5 Upper St Martin's Lane,
London WC2H 9EA
An Hachette UK Company

This edition published in Great Britain in 2015
by Gollancz

1 3 5 7 9 10 8 6 4 2

A CIP catalogue record for this book
is available from the British Library

ISBN 978 0 575 11942 0

Typeset at The Spartan Press Ltd,
Lymington, Hants

Printed and bound by CPI Group (UK) Ltd,
Croydon, CRO 4YY

www.unlikelyworlds.blogspot.com
www.orionbooks.co.uk
www.gollancz.co.uk

CONTENTS

CHILD OF THE RIVER

THE FIRST BOOK OF

CONFLUENCE

For Caroline,
shelter from the storm

Praise the Lord, for He hath spoken;
Worlds His mighty voice obeyed.
Laws which never shall be broken
For their guidance He hath made.

Anon.

1
THE WHITE BOAT

The Constable of Aeolis was a shrewd, pragmatic man who did not believe in miracles. In his opinion, everything must have an explanation, and simple explanations were best of all. 'The sharpest knife cuts cleanest,' he often told his sons. And: 'The more a man talks, the more likely it is he's lying.'

But to the end of his days, he could not explain the affair of the white boat.

It happened one midsummer night, when the huge black sky above the Great River was punctuated only by a scattering of dim halo stars and the dull red swirl of the Eye of the Preservers, no bigger than a man's hand and outshone by the heaped lights of the little city of Aeolis and the lights of the carracks riding at anchor outside the harbour entrance.

The summer heat was oppressive to the people of Aeolis. For most of the day they slept in the relative cool of their seeps and wallows, rising to begin work when the Rim Mountains clawed the setting sun, and retiring again when the sun rose, renewed, above the devouring peaks. In summer, stores and taverns and workshops stayed open from dusk until dawn, fishing boats set out at midnight to trawl the black river for shrimp and noctilucent jellyfish, and the streets of Aeolis were crowded and bustling beneath the flare of cressets and the orange glow of sodium-vapour lamps. On summer nights, the lights of Aeolis burned like a beacon in the midst of the dark shore.

That particular night, the Constable and his two eldest sons were rowing back to Aeolis in their skiff with two vagrant river traders who had been arrested while trying to run bales of cigarettes to the hill tribes of the wild shore downstream of Aeolis. Part of the traders' contraband cargo, soft bales sealed in plastic wrap and oiled cloth, was stacked in the forward well of the skiff; the traders lay in the stern, trussed like shoats for the slaughter. The skiff's powerful motor had been shot out in the brief skirmish, and the Constable's sons, already as big as their father, sat side by side on the centre thwart, rowing steadily against the current. The Constable was perched on a leather cushion in the skiff's high stern, steering for the lights of Aeolis.

The Constable was drinking steadily from a cruse of wine. He was a large man with loose grey skin and gross features, like a figure hastily moulded from clay and abandoned before completion. A pair of tusks protruded like daggers from his meaty upper lip. One, broken when the Constable had fought and killed his father, was capped with silver: silver chinked against the neck of the cruse every time he took a swig of wine.

He was not in a good temper. He would make a fair profit from his half of the captured cargo (the other half would go to the Aedile, if he could spare an hour from his excavations to pronounce sentence on the traders), but the arrest had not gone smoothly. The river traders had hired a pentad of ruffians as an escort, and they had put up a desperate fight before the Constable and his sons had managed to despatch them. The Constable had taken a bad cut to his shoulder, cleaved through blubber to the muscle beneath, and his back had been scorched by reflection of the pistol bolt that had damaged the skiff's motor. Fortunately, the weapon, which probably predated the foundation of Aeolis, had misfired on the second shot and killed the man using it, but the Constable knew that he could not rely on good luck forever. He was getting old, was ponderous and bumbling when once he had been quick and strong. He knew that sooner or later one of his sons would challenge him, and he was worried that this night's botched episode was a harbinger of his decline. Like all strong men, he feared his own weakness more than death, for strength was how he measured the worth of his life.

Now and then he turned and looked back at the pyre of the smugglers' boat. It had burned to the waterline, a flickering dash of light riding its own reflection far out across the river's broad black plain. The Constable's sons had run it aground on a mudbank so that it would not drift amongst the banyan islands which at this time of year spun in slow circles in the shallow sargasso of the Great River's nearside shoals, tethered only by fine nets of feeder roots.

One of the river traders lay as still as a sated cayman, resigned to his fate, but his partner, a tall, skinny old man naked but for a breechclout and an unravelling turban, was trying to convince the Constable to let him go. Yoked hand to foot so that his knees were drawn up to his chest, he stared up at the Constable from the well, his insincere smile like a rictus, his eyes so wide with fear that white showed clear around their slitted irises. At first he had tried to gain the Constable's attention with flattery; now he was turning to threats.

'I have many friends, captain, who would be unhappy to see me in your jail,' he said. 'There are no walls strong enough to withstand the force of their friendship, for I am a generous man. I am known for my generosity across the breadth of the river.'

The Constable rapped the top of the trader's turban with the stock of his whip, and for the fourth or fifth time advised him to be quiet. It was clear from the arrowhead tattoos on the man's fingers that he belonged to one of the street gangs that roved the wharves of Ys. Any friends he might have were a hundred leagues upriver, and by dusk tomorrow he and his companion would be dead.

The skinny trader babbled, 'Last year, captain, I took it upon myself to sponsor the wedding of the son of one of my dear friends, who had been struck down in the prime of life. Bad fortune had left his widow with little more than a rented room and nine children to feed. The son was besotted, his bride's family impatient. This poor lady had no one to turn to but myself. And I, captain, remembering the good company of my friend, his wisdom and his friendly laughter, took it upon myself to organise everything. Four hundred people ate and drank at the celebration, and I counted them all as my friends. Quails' tongues in aspic we had, captain, washed down with yellow wine a century old. And mounds of oysters and fish roe, and elvers in parsley broth, and carpaccio of wild duck served with blood sauce and pickled reed heads, and baby goats whose flesh was as soft as the saffron butter they'd been seethed in.'

Perhaps there was a grain of truth in the story. Perhaps the man had been one of the guests at such a wedding, but he could not have sponsored it. No one desperate enough to try to smuggle cigarettes to the hill tribes could afford to lavish that kind of money on an act of charity.

The Constable rapped the skinny trader on the head again, told him that he was a dead man, and dead men had no friends. 'Compose yourself. Our city might be a small place, but it has a shrine, and it was one of the last places along all the river's shore where avatars talked with men, before the Insurrectionists silenced them. Pilgrims still come here, believing that the shrine's avatars are still able to listen to confessions and petitions. We'll let you speak your piece before the shrine after you've been sentenced, so you'd be better off thinking of how to account for your miserable life rather than wasting your breath by pleading for mercy you don't deserve and won't get.'

'I can be as generous to you as I am to my friends, captain,' the trader said. 'If you need money I can get you money. If you have enemies, I know people who can make them disappear. A single word from me, and it will be as if they were never born. Or I could help you win promotion. I have friends in every department. Why risk your life protecting the ungrateful citizens of your mudhole of a city when you could live like a potentate in Ys?'

The boat rocked when the Constable stood. He stuck his coiled whip in his belt and drew his knife. His sons cursed wearily, and shipped their oars. The Constable planted a foot on the trader's neck, bore down with his considerable weight. The man gasped and choked; the Constable thrust two fingers into his mouth, caught his tongue and sliced it off, and tossed the scrap of flesh over the side of the skiff.

As the trader gargled blood and thrashed like a landed fish, one of the Constable's sons cried out. 'Boat ahead! Leastways, I think it's a boat.'

This was Urthank, a dull-witted brute grown as heavy and muscular as his father. The Constable knew that it would not be long before Urthank roared his challenge, and also knew that the boy would lose. Urthank was too stupid to wait for the right moment: it was not in his nature to suppress an impulse. No, Urthank would not defeat him. It would be one of the others. But Urthank's challenge would be the beginning of the end.

The Constable searched the darkness. For a moment he thought he glimpsed a fugitive glimmer, but it could have been a mote floating in his eye, or a dim star glinting at the edge of the world's level horizon.

'You're dreaming,' he said. 'Set to rowing or the sun will be up before we get back.'

'I saw it,' Urthank insisted.

The other son, Unthank, laughed.

'There!' Urthank said. 'There it is again! Dead ahead, just like I told you.'

This time the Constable saw the flicker of light. His first thought was that perhaps the trader had not been boasting after all. He said quietly, 'Go forward. Feathered oars.'

As the skiff glided against the current, the Constable fumbled a clamshell case from the pouch hung on the belt of his white linen kilt. The skinny trader was making wet, choking sounds. The Constable kicked him into silence before opening the case and lifting out the spectacles. Shaped like bladeless scissors, with thick lenses of smart glass, they were the most valuable heirloom of his family, passed from defeated father to victorious son for more than a hundred generations.

The Constable carefully unfolded them and pinched them over his bulbous nose. At once, the hull of the skiff and the bales of contraband cigarettes stacked in the forward well seemed to gain a luminous sheen; the bent backs of the Constable's sons and the bodies of the two prisoners glowed with furnace light. The Constable scanned the river, ignoring flaws in the ancient glass which warped or smudged the amplified light, and saw, half a league from the skiff, a knot of tiny, intensely brilliant specks turning above the river's surface.

'Machines,' the Constable said, and stepped between the prisoners and pointed out the place to his sons.

As the skiff drew closer, he saw that there were hundreds of them, a busy cloud of tiny machines swirling around an invisible pivot. He was used to seeing one or two flitting through the air above Aeolis on their inscrutable business, but had never before seen so many in one place.

Something knocked against the side of the skiff, and Urthank cursed and feathered his oar. It was a waterlogged coffin. Every day, thousands were launched from Ys. For a moment, a woman's face gazed up at the Constable through a glaze of water, glowing greenly amidst a halo of rotting flowers. Then the coffin turned end for end and was borne away.

The skiff had turned in the current, too. Now it was broadside to the cloud of machines, and for the first time the Constable saw what they attended.

A boat. A white boat riding high on the river's slow current.

The Constable took off his spectacles, and discovered that the boat glimmered with its own spectral light. The water around it glowed too, as if it floated in the centre of one of the shoals of luminous plankton that sometimes rose to the surface of the river on a calm summer night. The glow spread around the skiff, and each stroke of the oars broke its pearly light into whirling interlocking spokes, as if the ghost of a gigantic machine hung just beneath the river's skin.

The mutilated trader groaned and coughed; his partner raised himself up on his elbows to watch as the white boat turned on the river's current, light as a leaf, a dancer barely touching the water.

The boat had a sharp, raised prow, and incurved sides that sealed it shut and swept back in a fan, like the tail of a dove. It made another turn, seemed to stretch like a cat, and then it was alongside the skiff, pressed right against it without even a bump, and the Constable and his sons were inside the cloud of machines. Each burned with ferocious white light; none were bigger than a rhinoceros beetle. Urthank tried to swat one that hung in front of his snout, and cursed when it stung him with a flare of red light and a crisp sizzle.

'Steady,' the Constable said, and someone else said hoarsely, 'Flee.'

Astonished, the Constable turned from his inspection of the glimmering boat.

'Flee,' the second trader said again. 'Flee, you fools!'

Both of the Constable's sons were leaning on their oars, looking at their father. They were waiting for his lead. All right. He could not show that he was afraid. He put away his spectacles and reached through the whirling lights of the machines and touched the white boat.

Its hull was as light and close woven as feathers, moving under the Constable's fingers as the incurved sides peeled back with a sticky, crackling sound. As a boy, the Constable had been given to wandering the wild shore downriver of Aeolis, and he had once come across a blood orchid growing in the cloven root of a kapok tree. The orchid had made precisely the same noise when, sensing his body heat, it had spread its fleshy lobes to reveal the lubricious curves of its creamy pistil. He had fled in terror before its perfume could overwhelm him, and the ghost of that fear crept over him now.

The hull vibrated under his fingertips with a quick, eager pulse. Light poured out from the boat's interior, rich and golden and filled with floating motes. A shadow lay deep inside this light, the shadow of a body, and at first the Constable thought that the boat was no more than a coffin set adrift on the river's current. The coffin of some lord or lady no doubt, but in function no different from the shoddy cardboard coffins of the poor, or the painted wooden coffins of the artisans and traders.

And then a baby started to cry.

The Constable squinted through the light, leaned closer, reached out. For a moment he was at the incandescent heart of the machines' intricate dance, and then they were gone, dispersing in flat trajectories into the darkness. The baby, a boy, pale and fat and hairless, squirmed in his hands.

The golden light was dying back inside the white boat. In moments, only traces remained, iridescent veins and dabs that fitfully illuminated the corpse on which the baby had been lying.

It was the corpse of a woman, naked, flat-breasted and starveling thin, and as hairless as the baby. She had been shot, once through the chest and once in the head, but there was no blood. One hand had three fingers of equal length, like the grabs of the cranes of Aeolis's docks; the other was a monstrously swollen and bifurcate pincer, like a lobster's claw. Her skin had a silvery-grey cast; her huge, blood-red eyes were divided into a honeycomb of cells, like the compound lenses of certain insects. Within each facet lived a flickering glint of golden light, and although the Constable knew that these were merely reflections of the white boat's fading light, he had the strange feeling that something malevolent and watchful lived behind the dead woman's strange eyes.

'Heresy,' the second trader said. He had got up on his knees somehow, and was staring wide-eyed at the white boat.

The Constable kicked the trader in the stomach and the man coughed and flopped back into the bilge water alongside his partner. He glared up at the Constable and said again, 'Heresy. When they allowed the ship of the Ancients of Days to pass beyond Ys and sail downriver, our benevolent bureaucracies let heresy loose into the world.'

'Let me kill him now,' Urthank said.

'He's already a dead man,' the Constable said.

'Dead men don't talk treason,' Urthank said stubbornly. He was staring straight at his father.

'Fools,' the trader said. 'You have all seen the argosies and carracks sailing downriver, towards the war. They are armed with cannons and siege engines, but there are more terrible weapons let loose in the world.'

'Let me kill him,' Urthank said again.

The baby caught at the Constable's thumb and grimaced, as if trying to smile. The Constable gently disengaged the baby's grip and set him on the button cushion at the stern. He moved carefully, as if through air packed with invisible boxes, aware of Urthank's burning gaze at his back. 'Let the man speak,' he said. 'He might know something.'

The trader said, 'The bureaucrats are so frightened of heresy consuming our world that they will try anything to prevent it. Some say that they are even trying to wake the Hierarchs from their reveries.'

Unthank spat. 'The Hierarchs are all ten thousand years dead. Everyone knows that. They were killed when the Insurrectionists threw down the temples and silenced the avatars.'

'The Hierarchs tried to follow the Preservers,' the trader said. 'They rose higher than any other bloodline, but not so high that they cannot be called back.'

The Constable kicked the man and said, 'Leave off the theology. What about the dead woman?'

'Some say that the bureaucrats and mages are trying to create weapons using magic and forbidden science. Most likely she and the baby are fell creatures manufactured by some corrupt and unnatural process. You should destroy them both! Return the baby to the boat, and sink it!'

'Why should I believe you?'

'I'm a bad man. I admit it. I'd sell any one of my daughters if I could be sure of a good profit. But I studied for a clerkship when I was a boy, and I was taught well. I remember my lessons, and I know heresy when I see it.'

Unthank said slowly, 'Heresy taints everyone it touches. Whatever these things are, we should leave them be. They aren't any business of ours.'

'All on the river within a day's voyage upriver or down is my business,' the Constable said.

'You claim to know everything,' Urthank said. 'But you don't.'

The Constable knew then that this was the moment poor Urthank had chosen. So did Unthank, who shifted on the thwart so that he was no longer shoulder to shoulder with his brother. The Constable put his hand on the stock of his whip and met Urthank's stare and said, 'Keep your place, boy.'

There was a moment when it seemed that Urthank would not attack. Then he inflated his chest and let out the air with a roar and, roaring, threw himself at his father.

The whip caught around Urthank's neck with a sharp crack that echoed out across the black water. Urthank fell to his knees and grabbed hold of the whip as its loop tightened. The Constable gripped the whip with both hands and jerked it sideways as if he was holding a line which a huge fish had suddenly struck. The skiff tipped wildly and Urthank tumbled head first into the glowing water. But the boy did not let go of the whip. He was stupid, but he was also stubborn. The Constable staggered, dropped the whip – it hissed over the side like a snake – and fell overboard too.

The Constable shucked his loose, knee-high boots as he sank through the cold water, and kicked out towards the surface. Something grabbed the hem of his kilt, and then Urthank was trying to swarm up his body. Light exploded in the Constable's eye as his son's elbow struck his face. They thrashed through glowing water and burst into the air, separated by no more than an arm's length.

The Constable spat out a mouthful of water. 'You're too quick to anger, son. That was always your weakness.'

He saw the shadow of Urthank's arm sweep through the milky glow, countered the thrust with his own knife. The blades slid along each other, locking at their hilts. Urthank growled and pressed down. He was very strong. A terrific pain shot up the Constable's arm as his knife was wrenched from his grasp and Urthank's blade sliced his wrist. He kicked backwards in the water as Urthank slashed at his face: spray flew in a wide fan.

'Old,' Urthank said. 'Old and slow.'

The Constable steadied himself with little circling kicks. He could feel his blood pulsing into the water. Urthank had caught a vein. There was a heaviness in his bones and the wound in his shoulder throbbed. He knew that Urthank was right, but he also knew that he was not prepared to die.

He said, 'Come to me, son, and find out who is the strongest.'

Urthank's grin freed his tusks from his lips. He threw himself forward, driving through the water with his knife held out straight, trying for a killing blow. But the water slowed him, and the Constable was able to kick sideways, always just out of reach, while Urthank stabbed wildly, sobbing curses and uselessly spending his strength. Father and son circled each other. In the periphery of his vision, the Constable was aware that the white boat had separated from the skiff, but could spare no thought for it as he avoided Urthank's frantic onslaught.

At last, Urthank gave it up and kicked backwards, breathing hard. 'You aren't as strong as you thought, are you?' the Constable said. 'Surrender to me now and I'll grant you a quick and honourable release.'

'Surrender to me, old man, and I'll give you an honourable burial on land. Or else I'll kill you here and let the little fishes strip your bones.'

'Your end will be neither quick nor honourable, then,' the Constable said. 'Because someone as weak and foolish as you can be no son of mine.'

Urthank lunged with sudden, desperate fury, and the Constable chopped at him with the side of his hand, striking his elbow at the point where the nerve travelled over bone. Urthank's fingers opened in reflex; his knife fluttered down through the water. He dived for it without thinking, and the Constable bore down on him with all his strength and weight, enduring increasingly feeble blows to his chest and belly and legs. It took a long time, but at last he let go and Urthank's body floated free, face down in the glowing water.

'You were the strongest of my sons,' the Constable said, when he had his breath back. 'And you were faithful, after your fashion. But you never had a good thought in your head, and couldn't see more than five minutes into the future. Even if you had managed to defeat me, someone else would have killed you inside a year.'

Unthank paddled the skiff over, helped his father clamber aboard. The white boat floated several oar-lengths off, glimmering against the dark. The skinny trader whose tongue the Constable had cut out lay face down in the well of the skiff, drowned in his own blood. His partner was gone; Unthank said that he must have slipped over the side in the middle of all the excitement.

'You should have brought him back,' the Constable said. 'He was bound hand and foot. He wouldn't have given a big boy like you any trouble.'

Unthank returned the Constable's gaze and said, 'I was watching your victory, father.'

'Watching how I did it, eh? So you'll know what to do when your turn comes. You're a subtle one, Unthank. Not at all like your brother.'

Unthank shrugged. 'The prisoner probably drowned. Like you said, he was bound hand and foot.'

'Help me with your brother.'

Together, father and son hauled Urthank's dead weight into the skiff. The milky glow was fading from the water. After the Constable had settled Urthank's body, he looked up and saw that the white boat had vanished. The skiff was alone on the wide dark river, under the black sky and the smudged red whorl of the Eye of the Preservers. On the leather pad by the skiff's tiller, the baby grabbed at black air with pale starfish hands, chuckling at unguessable thoughts.

2

THE ANCHORITE

One evening early in spring, with the wheel of the galaxy tilted waist-deep at the level horizon of the Great River, Yama eased open the shutters of his room's arched window and climbed out. Any soldiers walking their beats in the great courtyard or the gardens might have seen, by the galaxy's faint light, a sturdy boy of some seventeen years on the broad ledge beneath the eaves of the red tile roof, and recognised at once the pale sharp face and cap of black hair of the Aedile's foundling son. But Yama knew that three of the regular garrison were standing guard over the labourers at the Aedile's latest excavation, and Sergeant Rhodean was leading the rest on a patrol through the winding paths of the City of the Dead, searching for the heretics who last night had tried to firebomb a ship at anchor in the floating harbour, leaving only the pack of watchdogs and a pentad of callow youths under the command of old one-legged Rotwang, who by now would be snoring in his chair by the kitchen fireplace after finishing his usual glass of rice brandy. So there was little chance of being spotted by the night watch, and Yama knew that he could persuade the watchdogs to allow him to pass unreported.

It was an opportunity too good to be missed. Yama planned to hunt frogs with the chandler's daughter, Derev, and Ananda, the sizar of Aeolis's temple. They had agreed on it that afternoon, using mirror talk.

The original walls of the Aedile's peel-house were built of smooth blocks of keelrock fitted together so cunningly that they presented a surface like polished ice, but at some point in the house's history an extra floor had been added, with a wide gutter ledge and gargoyles projecting into the air at intervals to spout water clear of the walls. Yama walked along the ledge as easily as if on a pavement, hooked his rope around the ruff of a basilisk frozen in an agonised howl, and abseiled five storeys to the ground. He would have to leave the rope in place, but it was a small risk.

No one was about. He darted across the mossy lawn, jumped the ha-ha, and quickly and silently threaded his way through the dense stands of rhododendrons which had colonised the tumbled remnants of the peel-house's outer defensive wall. Yama had played endless games of soldiers and heretics with the kitchen boys here, and knew every path, every outcrop of broken stone, all the holes and hollows which had once been guardrooms or stores, and the buried passages between them. He stopped beneath a mature cork-oak, looked all around, then lifted a mossy brick to reveal a scrape lined with stones and sealed with polymer spray. He pulled out a net bag and a slender trident from this hiding place, replaced the brick, and hung the bag on his belt and laid the trident across his shoulders.

At the far edge of the rhododendrons, an overgrown demilune breastwork dropped away to a barrens of tussock grass and scrub. Beyond, bordered on either side by patchworks of flooded paeonin fields, the dark gleam of the Breas wound away through shadowy ranges of hills crowded with monuments and tombs, cairns and cists: league upon league of the City of the Dead stretching to the foothills of the Rim Mountains, its inhabitants outnumbering the living citizens of Aeolis by a thousand to one. The tombs glimmered in the cold light of the galaxy, as if the hills had been dusted with salt, and little lights flickered here and there, where memorial tablets had been triggered by wind or passing animals.

Yama stuck his trident in soft leaf-mould, took out a slim silver whistle twice the length of his forefinger and blew on it. It seemed to make no more than a breathy squeak. He blew twice more, then squatted on his heels and listened to the peeping chorus of the frogs that had emerged from their mucus cocoons just a week ago. They had been frantically feeding ever since, and now they were searching for mates, every male endeavouring to outdo his rivals with passionate froggy arias. Dopey with unrequited lust, they would be easy prey.

Behind Yama, the peel-house reared above black masses of rhododendrons, lifting its spiky freight of turrets against the galaxy's blue-white wheel. A warm yellow light glowed near the top of the tallest turret, where the Aedile, who rarely slept since the news of Telmon's death last summer, would be working on his endless measurements and calculations.

Presently, Yama heard what he had been waiting for: the steady padding tread and faint sibilant breath of a watchdog. He called softly, and the strong, ugly creature trotted out of the bushes and laid its heavy head in his lap. Yama crooned to it, stroking its cropped ears and scratching the ridged line where flesh met the metal of its skullplate, lulling the machine part of the watchdog and, through its link, the rest of the pack. When he was satisfied that it understood it was not to raise the alarm either now or when he returned, he stood and wiped the dog's drool from his hands, plucked up his trident, and bounded away down the steep slope of the breastwork towards the barrens, and the flooded fields beyond.

Ananda and Derev were waiting at the edge of the barrens. Tall, graceful Derev jumped down from her perch halfway up a broken wall cloaked in morning glory, and half-floated, half-ran across overgrown flagstones towards Yama. Ananda kept his seat on a fallen stele, eating ghostberries he had picked along the way, pretending to ignore the lovers as they embraced and whispered endearments. He was a plump boy with dark skin and a bare scalp, wearing the orange robe of his office, saying as if to no one in particular, 'I remembered to bring the lantern.'

It was a little brass signal lantern, with a slide and a lens to focus the light of its wick. The plan was to use it to mesmerise their prey. As Yama inspected it, Ananda said, 'I saw your soldiers march out along the old road just after noon.'

'They are chasing after the heretics who tried to burn that ship,' Yama said.

'Perhaps they're still hiding close by,' Derev said. Her neck seemed to elongate as she turned her head this way and that to peer into the darkness. Her feathery hair was brushed back from her shaven forehead and hung to the small of her back. She wore a belted shift that left her long, slim legs bare. A trident was slung over her left shoulder. 'We might find them. Or they might find us.'

'If they are stupid enough to remain close to a place they have just attacked, then there is nothing to fear,' Yama said. 'They would surrender as soon as we threatened them with our frog-stickers.'

'My father says they force their women to lie with animals to create monstrous warriors,' Derev said.

Ananda spat seeds. 'He also promised to pay a good copper penny for every ten frogs we catch.'

'He has a price for everything,' Yama said, smiling.

Derev smiled, too. She looked very beautiful in the faint light, like an aspect of the heroine of an ancient saga. She said, 'He also said I should be back before the galaxy sets. He only allowed me to come because I told him that one of the Aedile's soldiers would be guarding us.'

Derev's father was very tall and very thin, and walked with his head hunched into his shoulders and his pale hands clasped behind his back, like one of the night storks that picked over the city's rubbish pits. He was invariably accompanied by his burly bodyservant: he was scared of footpads and the casual violence of sailors, and of kidnapping. The latter was a real threat: his family was the only one of its bloodline in Aeolis, and he was disliked within the tight-knit trading community because he bought favours rather than earned them. Yama knew that Derev was allowed to see him because her father believed it would forge a bond with the Aedile.

Ananda said, 'The soldier would be guarding something more important than your life, although, like life, once taken it cannot be given back. But perhaps you no longer have it, which is why the soldier is not here.'

Yama punched Ananda on the shoulder and said, 'You spend too much time thinking about that which you cannot have. Give me some berries as a penance.'

Ananda held out a handful. 'You only had to ask,' he said mildly.

Yama burst a ghostberry between his tongue and palate: the rough skin shockingly tart, the pulpy seed-rich flesh meltingly sweet. He told Derev, 'We could stay out all night, then go fishing at dawn. I am sure your father would pay more for fresh fish than for frogs.'

'He buys all the fish he needs from the fisher folk,' Derev said. 'And if I don't get back before midnight he'll forbid me to see you again. He really will. We will both pine away, like one of the old songs, and be buried side by side, and they'll plant roses on our graves that will twine together in a true lovers' knot.'

Yama smiled. 'You know that is not true. Otherwise your father would never have let you out in the first place.'

'I cannot stay out all night, either,' Ananda said. 'Father Quine rises an hour before sunrise, and I must sweep the naos and light the candles in the votary before he does.'

'Even though no one will come,' Yama said. 'Few visit the shrine any more, except on high days.'

'That's not the point. The avatars may have been silenced, but the Preservers are still there.'

'They will be there whether you light the candles or not. Stay with me, Ananda. Forget your duties for once.'

Ananda shrugged. 'I happen to believe in my duties.'

Yama said, 'And you are scared of the beating you will get from Father Quine.'

'There's that, too. For a holy man, he has a fearsome temper and a strong arm. You're lucky, Yama. If my master was half as kindly and scholarly as the Aedile my life would be improved tenfold.'

'If the Aedile is angry with me, he has Sergeant Rhodean beat me. And if he learns that I have left the peel-house at night, that is exactly what will happen. Which is why I did not bring a soldier with me.'

'My father says that physical punishment is barbaric,' Derev said.

'It is not so bad,' Yama said. 'And at least you know when it is over.'

'The Aedile came to talk with Father Quine three days ago,' Ananda said. He crammed the last of the ghostberries into his mouth and got to his feet. Berry juice stained his lips; they looked black in the galaxy's blue-white light. 'I couldn't quite hear what they discussed, but I suspect it was something to do with you. Afterwards, Father Quine asked me if I thought you were happy.'

'And am I happy, in your opinion?'

'I told him that you were stupidly happy.'

'It would be easier if I was stupid,' Yama said. 'I would not care what my father wanted me to become. As it is, he has been talking about finding a clerkship for me in a safe corner of the department. I think that is why Dr Dismas went to Ys. But I do not want to be a clerk – I want to be a soldier. I would even prefer to be a priest than a clerk. At least I would get to see something of the world.'

'You're far too old,' Ananda said. 'My parents consecrated me to my holy duties a hundred days after my birth, while my innocence was still intact. And besides being too old, you are also too full of sin. You spy on your poor father, and steal.'

'And you sneak out after dark,' Derev said.

'So has Ananda.'

'But not to fornicate,' Ananda said.

Derev laughed. 'We really want to hunt for frogs. At least, I do.'

'Also, I will confess my sin tomorrow,' Ananda said.

'As if the Preservers care about your small sins,' Yama said.

'That's another thing. You're too proud to be a priest,' Ananda said. 'Above all else, you're too proud.'

Yama said, 'I would rather be a priest than a clerk, but most of all I would rather be a soldier. I suppose that I will have to run away and enlist. I will train as an officer, and lead a company of myrmidons or command a corvette into battle against the heretics.'

Ananda said, 'That's exactly why your father wants you to be a clerk.'

Derev said, 'Listen.'

The two boys turned to look at where she pointed. Far out across the flooded fields, a point of intense turquoise light was moving through the dark air towards the Great River.

'A machine,' Yama said.

'So it is,' Derev said, 'but that isn't what I meant. I heard someone crying out.'

'Frogs fornicating,' Ananda said.

Yama guessed that the machine was half a league off. It seemed to slide at an angle to everything else, twinkling as if stitching a path between the world and its own reality.

He said, 'We should make a wish.'

'You'll break Zakiel's heart with talk like that,' Ananda said. 'Hasn't any of his education taken?'

Derev said, 'Besides, you should never make a wish in case it is answered, like the story of the old man and the fox maiden. I know I heard something. It may be the heretics. Or bandits. Listen!'

Ananda cocked his head and after a moment said, 'It was most likely a mouse caught by an owl. I may be the makings of a poor priest, Yama, but one thing I know is true. The Preservers see all. There is no need to invoke them by calling upon their servants.'

Yama knew that there was no point in debating such niceties with Ananda, who had been trained in every aspect of theology since early childhood and had memorised every word of the Puranas, but he thought that machines might hear the wishes of those they passed by, even if they did not act on them. Wishing was only an informal kind of prayer, after all, and prayers must be heard by the Preservers and the servants of the Preservers, and must sometimes be answered. For if praying did not bring reward, people would long ago have abandoned the habit of prayer, as farmers abandoned land that no longer yielded a crop. The priests taught that the Preservers heard and saw all, yet chose not to act because they did not wish to undermine the free will of their creations; but machines were as much a part of the world created by the Preservers as the Shaped bloodlines. Even if the Preservers had withdrawn their blessing from the world after the affront of the Age of Insurrection, as the divaricationists believed, it was still possible that machines, their epigones, might recognise the justice of answering a particular wish, and intercede. After all, the avatars of the Preservers which had survived the Age of Insurrection had spoken with men as recently as forty years ago, before the heretics had finally silenced them.

In any event, better the chance taken than that lost and later regretted. Yama closed his eyes and offered up the quick wish, hostage to the future, that he be made a soldier and not a clerk.

Ananda said, 'You might as well wish upon a star.'

Derev said, 'Quiet! I heard it again!'

Yama heard it too, faint but unmistakable above the unceasing chorus of the frogs. A man's angry wordless yell, and then the sound of jeering voices and coarse laughter.

He led the others through the overgrown ruins. Ananda padded alongside him with his robe tucked into his girdle – the better to run away if there was trouble, he said, although Yama knew that he would not run. Derev would not run away either; she held her trident like a javelin.

One of the old roads ran beside the edge of the fields. Its ceramic surface had been stripped and smelted for the metals it had contained thousands of years ago, but the long straight track preserved its geometric ideal. At the crux between the old road and a footpath that led across the embankment between two of the flooded fields, by a simple shrine set on a wooden post, the Constable's twin sons, Lud and Lob, had ambushed an anchorite.

The man stood with his back to the shrine, brandishing his staff. Its metal-shod point flicked back and forth like a watchful eye. Lud and Lob jeered and threw stones and clods of dirt at the anchorite, but stayed out of the staff's striking range. The twins were swaggering bullies who believed that they ruled the children of their little city. Most especially, they picked on those few children of bloodlines not their own. Yama had been chased by them only a decad ago, when he had been returning to the peel-house after visiting Derev, but he had easily lost them in the ruins outside the town.

'We'll find you later, little fish,' they had shouted cheerfully. They had been drinking, and one of them had slapped his head with the empty bladder and cut a clumsy little dance. 'We always finish our business,' he had shouted. 'Little fish, little fish, come out now. Be like a man.'

Yama had chosen to stay hidden. Lud and Lob had scrawled their sign on a crumbling wall and pissed at its base, but after beating about the bushes in a desultory fashion they had grown bored and wandered off.

Now, crouching with Derev and Ananda in a thicket of chayote vine, Yama wondered what he should do. The anchorite was a tall man with a wild black mane and wilder beard. He was barefoot, and dressed in a crudely stitched robe of metallic-looking cloth. He dodged most of the stones thrown at him, but one had struck him on the head: blood ran down his forehead and he mechanically wiped it from his eyes with his wrist. Sooner or later, he would falter, and Lud and Lob would pounce.

Derev whispered, 'We should fetch the militia.'

At that moment, a stone clipped the anchorite's elbow and the point of his staff dipped. Roaring with glee, Lob and Lud ran in from either side and knocked him to the ground. The anchorite surged up, throwing one of the twins aside, but the other clung to his back and the second knocked the anchorite down again.

Yama said, 'Ananda, stay hidden until I call your name. Derev, you set up a diversion.' And before he could think better of it he stepped out onto the road and shouted to the twins.

Lob turned. He held the staff in both hands, as if about to break it. Lud sat on the anchorite's back, grinning as he absorbed the man's blows to his flanks.

Yama said, 'What is this, Lob? Are you and your brother footpads now?'

'Just a bit of fun, little fish,' Lob said. He whirled the staff above his head. It whistled in the dark air.

'I think you should leave him alone,' Yama said.

'Maybe we'll have our fun with you instead, little fish,' Lob said.

'We'll have him, all right,' Lud said. 'Remember why we're here?'

'I clean forgot, thanks to him,' Lob said, and kicked at the anchorite.

'We'll grab the kid and tie him up,' Lud said. 'Then we can finish our bit of fun with this culler, and be on our way.'

'I would like to see you try,' Yama said. 'Especially with Ananda at my side.'

He did not look around, but by the shift in Lob's gaze knew that Ananda had stepped out onto the road behind him.

'The priest's runt?' Lob laughed, and farted tremendously.

'Gaw,' his brother said, giggling so hard his triple chins quivered. He flapped a hand in front of his face. 'You been at those preserved eggs again.'

Yama flung his flimsy trident then, but it bounced uselessly off Lob's hide. Lob yawned, showing his stout, sharp tusks, and swept the staff broadside. Yama jumped back; the staff's metal tip cut the air a finger's width from his belly. Lob came on, stepping heavily and deliberately and sweeping the staff back and forth, but Yama easily dodged his clumsily aimed blows.

'Fight fair,' Lob said, stopping at last. He was panting heavily. 'Stand and fight fair.'

Ananda had managed to slip behind Lob; now he struck at his legs with his trident. Enraged, Lob turned and swung the staff at Ananda, and Yama stepped forward and kicked him in the kneecap, and then in the wrist. Lob howled and dropped the staff; Yama swept it up and jabbed Lob hard in the gut.

Lob fell to his knees in stages. 'Fight fair,' he gasped again.

'Fight fair? Where's the fun in that?' Lud said, and pulled a knife from his belt. It was as black as obsidian, with a narrow, crooked blade. He claimed to have stolen it from a drunken sailor, and said that it was from the first days of the Age of Enlightenment and almost as old as the world. Lud kissed its blade and grinned at Yama and Ananda. 'Which one of you wants to be stuck first?'

Yama held the staff close, ready to strike at Lud when he moved forward. Lud tossed the knife from hand to hand, and told Yama how much it would sting, going in, and Lob threw himself forward. Yama saw the movement in the corner of his vision and swiped at Lob and struck his back, and then Lob wrapped his arms around Yama's thighs and Yama lost his balance and tumbled over backwards, his legs pinned beneath Lob's weight. Ananda stepped forward and swung his clenched fist: the stone he held struck the side of Lob's skull with the sound of an axe sinking into wet wood. Lob roared with pain and sprang to his feet and swiped at Ananda, who barely managed to dance out of his way. Lud roared too, and stepped forward, brandishing his knife. Behind him, a tree burst into flame.

*

'It was all I could think of,' Derev said. She was trembling, and breathless.

Ananda ran a little way down the road and shouted after the fleeing twins, a high wordless shriek of triumph.

'I think you saved my life,' Yama told Derev, and stepped forward and kissed her.

The burning tree shed sparks upwards into the night, brighter than the galaxy. Its trunk was a shadow inside a roaring pillar of hot blue flame. Heat and light beat out across the road. It was a young sweetgum tree. Derev had soaked its trunk with kerosene from the lantern's reservoir, and ignited it with the lantern's flint when Lob had fallen on Yama.

'Even Lob and Lud won't forget this,' Ananda said, walking back to Yama and Derev. 'Frightened by a tree. It's too funny, Yama.'

'They'll leave us alone from now on,' Derev said.

'I hope so,' Yama said, and helped the anchorite to sit up.

The man dabbed at the blood crusted under his nose, cautiously bent and unbent his knees, then scrambled to his feet. Yama held out the staff, and the man took it and briefly bowed his head in thanks. Something had sliced and seared the left side of his face: a web of silvery scar tissue pulled down his eye and lifted the corner of his mouth. He was so dirty that his skin looked like embossed leather. The metallic cloth of his robe was equally filthy, his hair was tangled in ropes around his face, and bits of twig were caught in his forked beard. He smelt powerfully of sweat and urine. He fixed Yama with an intense gaze, then made shapes with the fingers of his right hand against the palm of his left.

Yama felt a little shock, realising that the man was about his height, that his hands and his fingers were much like his. But so were Ananda's and those of many bloodlines . . .

Ananda said, 'He wants you to know that he has been searching for you.'

'You can understand him?'

'We used hand speech like this in the seminary, to talk to each other during breakfast and supper when we were supposed to be listening to one of the brothers read from the Puranas. Some anchorites were once priests, and perhaps this is such a one.'

The man made more shapes with his fingers.

Ananda said uncertainly, 'He says that he is glad that he remembered all this. I think he must mean that he will always remember this.'

'Well,' Derev said, 'so he should. We saved his life.'

The anchorite reached inside his robe and pulled out a small disc attached to a thong looped around his neck. He lifted the thong over his head and thrust the disc towards Yama. It was one of the ceramic discs that could be dug up anywhere in the City of the Dead, so common they were virtually worthless. The children of Aeolis called them Preservers' pennies.

The anchorite, staring at Yama, twisted and bent his fingers against his palm.

'You are the one who is to come,' Ananda translated.

The anchorite shook his head and signed furiously.

'You will come here again,' Ananda said. 'Yama, do you know what he means?'

And Derev said, 'Listen!'

Far off, whistles sounded, calling and answering in the darkness.

The anchorite thrust the ceramic disc into Yama's hand, and then he was running out along the footpath between the flooded fields, a shadow dwindling against cold blue light reflected from the water, gone.

The whistles sounded again.

'The militia,' Ananda said, and turned and scampered off down the old road.

Derev and Yama chased after him, but he soon outpaced them, and Yama had to stop to catch his breath before they reached the city wall.

Derev said, 'Ananda won't stop running until he's thrown himself into his bed. And even then he'll run in his dreams until morning.'

Yama was bent over, clasping his knees. He had a cramp in his side. He said, 'We will have to watch out for each other. I think Lob and Lud will neither forgive nor forget this night. How can you run so fast and so far without getting out of breath?'

Derev's pale face glimmered in the galaxy's light. She gave him a sly look. 'Flying is harder work than running.'

'If you can fly, I would love to see it. But you are teasing me again.'

'This is the wrong place for flying. One day, perhaps, I'll show you the right place, but it's a long way from here.'

'Do you mean the edge of the world? I used to dream that my people lived on the floating islands. I saw one—'

Derev grabbed Yama and pulled him into the long grass beside the track. He fell on top of her, laughing, but she put her hand over his mouth. He was aware of the heat of Derev's slim body pressing against his. He kissed her fingers and said, 'I think the militia have given up their search.'

'No. They're coming this way.'

Yama rolled over and parted the long grass so that he could watch the track. Presently a pentad of men went past in single file. None of them were of the bloodline of the citizens of Aeolis. They were armed with rifles and arbalests, and wore tight pantaloons and baggy shirts.

'The heretics,' Derev said, after they had passed. 'I told you they were still here.'

'I do not think so,' Yama said. 'Sergeant Rhodean and his soldiers would have found them before they found us. And they were dressed like sailors.'

'Heretics disguised as sailors, then.'

'Possibly. I wonder if they are looking for us, or for the anchorite.'

'We did the right thing by him, didn't we? Or you did. I could not have stepped out and challenged those two.'

'I did it knowing you were at my back.'

'I'd be nowhere else.' After a moment, Derev added thoughtfully, 'He looked a little like you.'

'He looked like he had been walking the roads of all the world for the past hundred years.'

'I mean in the proportions of his limbs, and the shape of his head.'

'I saw that too. But he was so much thinner, and his skin was darker, and the way he moved… No. I do not think so. The Aedile has been looking for my parents, and for others of my bloodline, ever since he took me in. Do you really think it is likely that we would stumble over one of my cousins scarcely a league from my home?'

Several years ago, Yama had started visiting the floating docks, watching the traders, the sailors and soldiers, talking to them, asking them questions about the different peoples in Ys and elsewhere. He had learned that a few bloodlines had skin as pale as his, and one or two of those bore a passing resemblance, but no one he talked to knew of any quite like him. One obvious rogue had offered to take him to the quarter in Ys where his people lived, but Yama had guessed that the man had been planning to kidnap and ransom him, and had reported him to Sergeant Rhodean. The trader had been arrested and flogged for possession of contraband cargo, and that had been the end of Yama's visits to the docks.

He had not much minded. One day he would become a soldier

so famous that his parents would learn about him and find him. Or he would find them in Ys or while travelling the length of the Great River . . . He had lived with the mystery of his origin all his life. He knew that solving it would not be easy, and would involve grand adventures.

'Well, he did look like you, just a little,' Derev said. 'And he seemed to know you.'

'He was touched by the Preservers. It is cruel to tease me like this, Derev.'

'I did not mean to.' Derev kissed him, and said, 'You aren't alone in the world, Yama.'

'I know,' he said, and kissed her back.

They kissed and rekissed with growing urgency, until at last Derev pushed away a little and sat up, brushing dry grass from her shift.

Yama sat up too, and leaned against her. 'I suppose he is halfway to Ys by now,' he said. 'Still, I should like to find him again, and ask him why he gave me this.'

He pulled the ceramic disc from the pocket of his tunic. It seemed no different from the discs that the Aedile's workmen turned up by the hundred during their excavations: slick, white, slightly too large to fit comfortably in his palm. He held it up so that it faintly reflected the chill light of the galaxy and saw, far off, a small, solitary star shining off to one side of the crowded lights of Aeolis, and realised that it was a lighted window in the tall, thin tower that stood without the city wall.

Dr Dismas had at last returned from Ys.

3

DR DISMAS

Dr Dismas, bent-backed, black-clad, came up the stony hillside with a bustling, crabbed gait. The sun was at the height of its daily leap into the sky; like an aspect, he cast no shadow.

The Aedile, standing at the top of the slope, near the spoil heap of his latest excavation site, watched the apothecary draw near with swelling expectation. The Aedile was tall and stooped and greying, with a diplomat's air of courteous reticence which many mistook for absent-mindedness, and was dressed after the fashion of the citizens of Aeolis, in a loose-fitting white tunic and a linen kilt. His knees were swollen and stiff from the hours he had spent kneeling on a leather pad brushing hairfine layer after hairfine layer of dirt from finds, freeing them from the cerements of a hundred thousand years of burial. The excavation was not going well and the Aedile had grown bored with it before it was halfway done. Despite the insistence of his geomancer, he was convinced that nothing of interest would be found. The crew of trained diggers – convicts reprieved from army service – had caught their master's mood and worked at a desultory pace amongst the neatly dug trenches and pits, dragging their chains through white dust as they carried baskets of soil and limestone chippings to the conical spoil heap. A drill rig taking a core through the reef of land coral that had overgrown the hilltop raised a plume of dust that feathered off into the blue sky.

So far, the excavation had uncovered only a few potsherds, the corroded traces of what might have been the footings of a watchtower, and the inevitable hoard of ceramic discs. Although the Aedile had no idea what the discs were (most scholars of Confluence's early history believed that they were some form of currency, but the Aedile thought that this was too obvious an explanation), he assiduously catalogued every one, and spent hours measuring the faint grooves and pits with which they were decorated. The Aedile believed in measurement. In small things were the gauge of the larger world, and of worlds without end. He believed that all measurements and constants might be arithmetically derived from a single number. The cypher of the Preservers, which could unlock the secrets of the world they had made, and much else.

But here was Dr Dismas, with news that would determine the fate of the Aedile's foundling son. The pinnace on which the apothecary had returned to Ys had anchored off the mouth of the bay two nights before (and was anchored there still), but it seemed that Dr Dismas had been taken ill, and had only returned to his tower last night. Meanwhile, the Aedile had chosen to spend his time at the excavation site while waiting for the apothecary to get around to paying a visit. He hoped that Dr Dismas had discovered the truth about Yama's bloodline, but he did not want to press the matter because it would acknowledge that he was beholden to the apothecary. It was Dr Dismas, after all, who had proposed that he take the opportunity offered by his summons to Ys to undertake research into the matter of Yama's lineage. That this trip had been forced upon him by his department, and had been underwritten by the Aedile's purse, would not reduce by one iota the obligation that he would no doubt expect the Aedile to repay in some fashion, when it suited him.

Dr Dismas disappeared behind the tilted white cube of one of the empty tombs which were scattered beneath the brow of the hill like beads flung from a broken necklace – tombs dating from the dissolute era after the Age of Insurrection, and the last to be built in the City of the Dead, simple boxes set at the edge of low, rolling hills crowded with monuments, mausoleums, crypts, and statues. Presently, Dr Dismas reappeared almost directly below the Aedile and laboured up the last hundred paces of the steep, rough path. He was breathing hard. His narrow face, propped between the high wings of his black coat's collar and shaded by a black, broad-brimmed hat, was sprinkled with beads of sweat in which the plaques of his addiction stood like islands in the shrinking river.

'A warm day,' the Aedile said, by way of greeting.

Dr Dismas pulled a lace handkerchief from his sleeve and fastidiously dabbed sweat from his forehead. 'It is hotter than an overpressured alembic. Perhaps Confluence tires of circling the sun and is falling into it, like a girl tumbling into the arms of her lover. Perhaps we'll be consumed by the fire of their passion.'

Usually, Dr Dismas' wordplay amused the Aedile, but now it intensified his sense of foreboding. He said, 'I trust your business was successful.'

Dr Dismas dismissed this with a flick of his handkerchief. 'With my department? It was nothing. The miserable termagants who nest amongst the dusty ledgers of my department do nothing but transform rumour into fact, but I was able to set them straight, and have returned to serve with renewed vigour.'

'I am pleased to hear it, my dear doctor. I heard a rumour that you were laid up with a fever.'

Dr Dismas did not reply at once. He had turned to gaze, like a conqueror, across the dry slope of the hill and its scattering of tombs, the flooded fields along the Breas and the little city at the river's mouth and the long finger of the new quay pointing across banks of greenish mud towards the Great River, which stretched away, shining like polished silver, to a misty union of water and air. He screwed a cigarette into his holder (carved, he liked to say, from the finger-bone of a multiple murderer), lit it, and drew deeply, holding his breath for a count of ten before blowing a riffle of smoke through his nostrils with a satisfied sigh.

The apothecary, hired two years ago by the city's Council for Night and Shrines, had been summoned to Ys to account for several lapses after he had taken up his position. He was said to have substituted glass powder for the expensive suspensions of tiny machines which cured river blindness – and there had certainly been more cases of river blindness the previous summer, although Dr Dismas attributed this to the greater numbers of biting flies that bred in the algae choking the muddy basin of the former harbour. He was said to have peddled his treatments amongst the fisher folk and the hill tribes, making extravagant claims that he could cure cankers, the blood cough, and mental illness, and halt or even reverse ageing. And there were rumours that he had made or grown chimeras of children and beasts, and that he had kidnapped a child from one of the hill tribes and used its blood and perfusions of its organs to treat one of the members of the Council for Night and Shrines.

At first, the Aedile and most of the members of the Council had dismissed these allegations as fantasies, but then a boy had died after a blood-letting, and the parents, mid-caste chandlers, had lodged a formal protest. A field investigator of the Department of Apothecaries and Chirurgeons had arrived thirty days ago, but had quickly left in some confusion: it seemed that Dr Dismas had threatened to kill the man when he had attempted to search the apothecary's tower. And then the formal summons had arrived, which the Aedile had to read out to Dr Dismas in front of the Council for Night and Shrines. The doctor had been commanded to return to Ys for formal admonishment, both for his drug habit and (as the document delicately put it) for certain professional lapses. The Aedile had been informed that Dr Dismas had been placed on probation, although the doctor's manner suggested that he had won a considerable victory rather than a reprieve.

The apothecary drew on his cigarette and said, 'The river voyage was a trial in itself. It made me so febrile I was confined to my bunk aboard the ship for a day and a night after it dropped anchor. I am still not quite recovered, but came as soon as I could.'

'Quite, quite,' the Aedile said. 'I am sure that you came as soon as you could.'

But he did not believe it for a moment. Dr Dismas was up to something: no doubt about it.

'You have been working alongside those convicts of yours again,' the apothecary said. 'Don't deny it. I see dirt under your nails.'

'I wore my hat, and coated my skin with the unguent you prescribed.'

The sticky stuff smelled strongly of menthol and raised the fine hairs of the Aedile's pelt into stiff peaks, but it seemed uncharitable to complain.

'You should also wear glasses with tinted lenses,' Dr Dismas said. 'Cumulative ultraviolet exposure could permanently damage your corneas. I believe I can see some inflammation, in fact. You should not risk your health on work that will proceed perfectly well without your help.'

'I do not think I will learn anything here,' the Aedile said. 'There are the footings of a tower, but the structure itself must have been dismantled long ago. A tall tower, it was – the foundations are deep, although quite rusted away. It was made of metal, at least in part. Fabulously costly even in the Age of Enlightenment. The geomancer may have been misled by the remains into thinking that a larger structure once stood here. It has happened before. Or perhaps there is something buried deeper. We shall see.'

The geomancer had been from one of the hill tribes, a man half the Aedile's age but rendered wizened and toothless by his nomadic life, one eye milky with a cataract which Dr Dismas had removed. This had been in winter, with hoar frost mantling the ground each morning, but the geomancer had gone about barefoot, and naked under his red wool cloak. He had fasted three days on the hilltop before scrying the site with a thread weighted by a sliver of loadstone.

Dr Dismas said, 'In Ys there are buildings which are said to have once been entirely clad in metal.'

'Quite, quite. If it can be found anywhere in Confluence, then it can be found in Ys,' the Aedile said, beginning to work his way around to the subject that had been on his mind ever since Dr Dismas had left for the great and terrible city.

'So they say,' the apothecary said. 'But who would know where to begin to look?'

'If there is any one person who could find something in Ys, then that would be you, my dear Dr Dismas.'

'It wasn't easy,' Dr Dismas said.

'I did not think it would be. The libraries are much debased these days. Since the librarians fell silent, there is a general feeling that there is no longer any need to maintain anything but the most recent records. And so everything more than a thousand years old is considerably compromised.'

The Aedile realised that he had said too much. He was nervous, standing at the threshold of a revelation that might change Yama's life, and his.

Dr Dismas did not answer at once. With the thumb and forefinger of his left hand, so badly affected by the side effects of the drug that they were as stiffly bent as the claw of a crayfish, he plucked the stub of his cigarette from the bone holder and crushed its coal, then fitted another cigarette into the holder, and lit and drew on it. He was an inveterate gossip, and knew how to pace his revelations, how to string out a story and tease his audience. There was something about his manner that reminded the Aedile of a sly, sleek nocturnal animal, secretive in its habits, quick to pounce on some tasty scrap or tidbit.

He blew twin streams of smoke through his nostrils and said, 'Yes, it was far from easy. Not only are the libraries, as you put it, compromised, but there is also the confusion brought about by the current political situation.'

'Well, we are at war.'

'I mean the confusion in the Palace of the Memory of the People. Something for which your department, my dear Aedile, must take a considerable part of the blame. It is trying to forget or even erase the past, as the Committee for Public Safety teaches we all should.'

The Aedile was stung by this remark, as Dr Dismas had no doubt intended. The Aedile had been at the edge of a rebellion against the destruction of the records of ages past. Others in his faction had fallen in a long siege after they had stormed and taken control of the archives; the Aedile, to his everlasting regret and shame, had not joined them. Instead, he had tried to raise a petition against the destruction, and when the rebellion was over his life had been spared and he had been permanently exiled to this backwater city. And now his wife was dead. And his son was dead. Only the Aedile was left, a revenant of a political squabble mostly long forgotten.

He said with some asperity, 'The past is not as easily lost as you might think. We have only to look up at the night sky to be reminded of it. In winter, we see the Home Galaxy, sculpted by unimaginable forces in ages past, and in summer we see the Eye of the Preservers. And here in Aeolis, the past is more important than the present. The tombs will endure long after the mudbrick houses down by the bay have crumbled to dust. All that lived in Ys during the Golden Age came to rest here, and much remains to be discovered.'

Dr Dismas waved this away with another flick of his handkerchief. 'Despite the current difficulties, the library of my department is still well-ordered. Several of the archive units are still completely functional, albeit only under manual control, and they are amongst some of the oldest on Confluence. As I told you before I left, if records of the boy's bloodline could be found anywhere, it would be found there. But I regret to say that although I searched long and hard, I could find no trace of it.'

The Aedile thought that he had misheard. 'What do you mean? Are the records missing?'

'The records are complete. But there was no match.'

'This is— I mean to say, it is unexpected. Quite unexpected.'

'I was surprised myself,' Dr Dismas said.

'There was no match at all?'

'None. Absolutely none. And that is the most amazing thing. All Shaped bloodlines possess a universal sequence of genes inserted by the

Preservers at the time of the remaking of their ancestors. Despite the many and various ways in which the codes of the genetic inheritances of the bloodlines are written, the expression of those inserted sequences is the same. Tests of the boy's self-awareness and rationality show that he is not an indigen, but like them he lacks that which marks the Shaped as the chosen children of the Preservers. And more than that, the boy's genome is quite different from anything on Confluence.'

'But apart from the mark of the Preservers, we all differ from each other, doctor. We are all remade in the image of the Preservers in our various ways.'

'Indeed. But each bloodline shares a genetic inheritance with certain beasts and plants and microbes of Confluence. Even the various races of simple indigens, which were not marked by the Preservers and which cannot evolve towards transcendence, have genetic relatives amongst the flora and fauna. The ancestors of the ten thousand bloodlines were not brought to Confluence on their own; the Preservers also brought something of the home worlds of each of them. But it seems that Yamamanama is more truly a foundling than we first believed, for there is nothing on record, no bloodline, no plant, no beast, not even any microbe, which has anything in common with him.'

Only Dr Dismas called the boy by his full name. It had been given to him by the wives of the old Constable, Thaw. In their language, the language of the harems, it meant *Child of the River*. The Council for Night and Shrines had met in secret after the baby had been found on the river by Constable Thaw, and it had been decided that he should be killed by exposure, in case he was a creature of the heretics, or some other kind of demon. But the boy had survived for ten days amongst the tombs on the hillside above Aeolis, and the women who had finally rescued him, defying their husbands, said that bees had brought him pollen and water, proving that he was under the protection of the Preservers. Even so, no family in Aeolis would take in the baby, and so he had come to live in the peel-house, son to the Aedile, brother to poor Telmon.

The Aedile thought of this as he tried to fathom the implications of Dr Dismas's discovery. Insects chirred all around in the dry weeds, insects and plants that might have come from the same long-lost world as the beasts which the Preservers had shaped into the ancestors of his own bloodline. There was a comfort, a continuity, in knowing that you were a part of the intricate tapestry of the world. Imagine what it must be like to grow up all alone, with no knowledge of your bloodline, and no hope of finding one . . . The Aedile thought of his wife, dead more than twenty years now. It had been a day as hot as this when she had died, yet how cold her hands had been. His eyes pricked with the beginnings of tears, but he controlled himself. It would not do to show emotion in front of Dr Dismas, who preyed on weakness like a wolf that follows a herd of antelope, and marks the gait of each.

'All alone,' the Aedile said. 'Is that possible?'

'If he were a plant or animal, perhaps.' Dr Dismas pinched out the coal of his second cigarette, dropped the stub, and ground it under the heel of his boot. His black, calf-length boots were new, the Aedile noted: hand-tooled leather as soft as butter.

'He could be a stowaway,' the apothecary said. 'A few ships still ply their old courses between Confluence and the mine worlds. One could imagine something stowing away on one of them. Perhaps the boy is an animal, able to mimic the attributes of intelligence in the same way that certain insects are able to mimic a leaf, or a twig. But if so, we must ask ourselves this – what is the difference between the thoughts of a real person, and a mimic?'

The Aedile was repulsed by this notion. He could not bear to think that his own dear adopted son was some kind of beast disguised as a human being, mindlessly parroting people's speech and thoughts.

He said, 'Anyone trying to pluck an insect disguised as a leaf would know it was not really a leaf. They cling to the plant, but they are not part of it. They do not make sugars from sunlight, and so on. The same with animals imitating people. We would know the difference.'

'Ah, but suppose an animal was so perfect a mimic that it would not only look like the thing it wished to imitate, it would *become* it. It would even lose the ability to dissemble, to appear to become something it is not.'

'Then the difference is merely one of philosophy,' the Aedile said.

'And of origin. Which brings us back to the boy.'

'Who resembles no one else in Confluence, according to you. Why imitate something that is unique, and draw attention to yourself? No,' the Aedile said, with a confidence he didn't quite feel, 'whatever he is, the boy is as human as any bloodline. But the question of his origin remains unanswered. If he is not part of this world, then where is he from? Not from a mine world, I think. They are uninhabited.'

Dr Dismas looked around. Although the nearest workers were a hundred paces away, chipping in a desultory manner at the edge of the neat square of the excavated pit, he stepped closer to the Aedile and said, 'You overlook one possibility. In the millennia since the Preservers abandoned Confluence, just one new bloodline has appeared, albeit briefly.'

The Aedile smiled. 'You scoff at my theory, doctor, but at least it is supported by what is known. Whereas you make a wild leap into thin air. The ship of the Ancients of Days passed downriver twenty years before Yama was found floating in his cradle, and no members of its crew remained on Confluence.'

'Their heresies live on. We are at war with them. And the Ancients of Days were the ancestors of the Preservers: we cannot begin to guess at the nature and extent of their powers. I believe,' Dr Dismas said, 'that there have been certain portents, certain signs . . . Perhaps you know more. Perhaps it would help me to help you if you told me all you know.'

'I trust you have spoken to no one else,' the Aedile said. 'Such wild talk could put Yama in great danger.'

'Have you not ever thought that he may be dangerous? Consider how he was found. In the arms of a dead woman, in a frail craft on the flood of the river.'

The Aedile remembered old Constable Thaw's story. The man had confessed, with some shame, after his wives had delivered the foundling to the peel-house. The Constable had been a coarse and cunning man, but he had taken his duties seriously, and believed that he had failed the boy by failing to protect him from the Committee of Night and Shrines.

'But my dear doctor, you cannot believe that Yama killed the woman. He was just a baby.'

'Someone got rid of him,' Dr Dismas said. 'Someone who could not bear to kill him. Or was not able to kill him.'

'I have always thought that the woman was his mother. She was fleeing from scandal or her family's condemnation, and she gave birth to him there, on the river, and died.'

'We do not know all the facts of the case,' Dr Dismas said. 'However, I did examine the records left by my predecessor. She performed several neurological tests on Yamamanama soon after he had been brought to your house, and continued to perform them for several years afterwards. We are all marked by our intelligence. Unlike the beasts of the field, we must continue our development outside the womb, because the womb does not supply sufficient sensory input to stimulate growth of neural pathways. It appears to be a universal law for all known bloodlines. Counting backwards, and allowing for a good margin of error, I formed the opinion that the tests show that it was no newborn child that Constable Thaw rescued. Yamamanama had been born at least fifty days before he was cast adrift on the river.

'I understand why you have not discussed Yamamanama's troublesome origin before – even with those from your own department. But you cannot keep him hidden forever. His strange origin, his uniqueness, his powers. Oh yes, I know something about his powers. The signs are there, for those who know how to look. The increasing numbers of machines seen around Aeolis, for instance.'

The Aedile felt a chill touch of dismay. Dr Dismas was cleverer than he'd thought. And it wasn't just the machines presently buzzing around Aeolis. There were the machines that had accompanied the white boat, too. The woman in the shrine. Yama's silly tricks with the watchdogs. And the 'bees' which had kept him alive when he'd been abandoned on the hillside as a baby, they had probably been machines, too.

He said, 'We should not talk of such things here.'

Dr Dismas laid a stiff hand on the Aedile's arm. 'I am a friend to you, and to Yamamanama. And I am, and shall continue to be, the very embodiment of discretion.'

'I mean it, Dismas,' the Aedile said. 'You will say nothing of what you found, and keep your speculations to yourself. And you will be good enough to show me the records of your searches. Perhaps there is something you have missed.'

He should not have involved Dr Dismas. The man presumed too much, and he could not be trusted.

'I should like to rest, first. I have not quite recovered from my journey. I will bring them tonight, and you will see that I am right in every particular. We stand at the threshold of a great mystery.'

After Dr Dismas had left, the Aedile began to compose in his head the letter he needed to write. It must undermine Dr Dismas's already blemished reputation, and devalue any claims he might make about Yama, but it should not condemn him outright. Best to suggest a suspicion that the apothecary, because of his drug habit, might be involved with the heretics who had recently tried to set fire to the floating docks, but it must be the most delicate of hints, hedged around with equivocation, because if Dr Dismas was ever arrested he would most likely confess all he knew. The Aedile realised then that the two of them were linked by a cat's cradle of secrets tangled around the soul of the foundling boy, the stranger, the gift, the child of the river.

4

YAMAMANAMA

Aeolis, named for the winter wind that sang through the passes of the hills above the broad valley of the river Breas, was the only home Yama had ever known, and he knew it as intimately as only a child can – especially a child who, because of his adoption by the city's Aedile, wore innocently and unknowingly the badge of privilege. In its glory, before the Age of Insurrection, it had been the disembarkation point for the City of the Dead. Ys had extended far downriver in those days, and then as now it was the law that no one could be buried inside its boundaries. Instead, mourners had accompanied their dead to Aeolis, where funeral pyres for the lesser castes burned day and night, temples rang with prayers and songs for the preserved bodies of the rich, and constellations of butter lamps shimmered on altars heaped with flowers and strung with prayer flags. The ashes of the poor had been cast on the waters of the Great River; the preserved bodies of the ruling and mercantile classes, and of scholars and dynasts, had been interred in tombs whose ruined, empty shells still littered the dry hills beyond the town. The Breas, which then had been navigable almost to its source in the foothills of the Rim Mountains, had been crowded with barges bringing slabs of land coral, porphyry, granite, marble, and all kinds of precious stones for the construction of tombs and shrines and memorials.

An age later, after half the world had been turned to desert during the rebellion of the feral machines, as the Preservers had withdrawn their blessing from Confluence, and Ys had retreated upriver, contracting around its irreducible heart, funeral barges no longer ferried the dead to Aeolis. Instead, bodies were launched from the docks and piers of Ys onto the full flood of the Great River, given up to caymans and fish, lammergeyers and carrion crows. As these creatures consumed the dead, so Aeolis consumed its glorious past. Tombs were looted of treasures; decorative panels and frescoes were pried from walls; preserved bodies were stripped of their clothes and jewellery; the hammered bronze facings of doors and tomb furniture were melted down – the old pits of wind-powered smelters could still be found in the hills of the City of the Dead.

After most of the tombs had been stripped, Aeolis had become little more than a way station, a place where ships put in to replenish their supplies of fresh food on their voyages downriver from Ys. This was the city that Yama knew. There was the new quay, which ran across the mudflats and stands of zebra grass of the old, silted harbour to the retreating edge of the Great River, where the fisher folk of the floating islands gathered in their little coracles to sell strings of oysters, spongy parcels of red river-moss, bundles of river-weed stipes, and shrimp and crabs and fresh fish. There were always people swimming off the new quay or puttering about in coracles and small boats, and men working at the fish traps and the shoals at the mouth of the Breas where mussels were cultivated, and divers hunting for urchins and abalone amongst the holdfasts of stands of giant kelp whose long blades formed vast brown slicks on the surface of the river. There were the ruined steps of the old waterfront, where tribesmen from the hills of the wild shore downriver of Aeolis squatted at blanket stalls to sell fruit and fresh meat, and dried mushrooms and manna lichen, and scraps of lapis lazuli and marble from the decayed facings of ancient tombs. There were ten taverns and two brothels; the chandlers' godowns and the farmers' cooperative; straggling streets of mudbrick houses which leaned towards each other over narrow canals; the one surviving temple, its walls white as salt, the gilt of its dome recently renewed by public subscription. And then the ruins of the ancient mortuaries, more extensive than the town, and fields of yams and raffia and yellow peas, and flooded paddies where rice and paeonin were grown. One of the last of Aeolis's mayors had established the paeonin industry in an attempt to revitalise the little city, but when the heretics had silenced the shrines at the beginning of the war there had been a sudden shrinkage in the priesthood and a decline in trade of the pigment used to dye their robes. These days, the mill, built at the downriver point of the bay so that its effluent would not contaminate the silty harbour, worked only one day in ten.

Most of the population of Aeolis were of the same bloodline. They called themselves the Amnan, which meant simply *the human beings*; their enemies called them the Mud People. They had bulky but well-muscled bodies and baggy grey or brown skin. Clumsy on land, they were strong swimmers and adept aquatic predators, and had hunted giant otters and manatees almost to extinction along that part of the Great River. They had preyed upon the indigenous fisher folk, too, before the Aedile had put a stop to it. More women were born than men, and sons fought their fathers for control of the harem; if they won, they killed their younger brothers or drove them out. The people of Aeolis still talked about the fight between old Constable Thaw and his son, Unthank. It had lasted two days, and had ranged up and down the waterfront and through the network of canals between the houses until Thaw, his legs paralysed, had been drowned by Unthank in the Breas.

Patricide was a barbaric custom, the Aedile said, a sign that the Amnan were reverting to their bestial nature. He went into the city as little as possible – rarely more than once every hundred days, and then only to the temple to attend the high-day service, with Yama and Telmon sitting to the right and left side of him on hard, ornately carved chairs, facing the audience throughout the three or four hours of obeisance and offerings, prayer and praise-songs. Yama loved the sturdy square temple, with its clean high spaces, the black disc of its shrine in its ornate gilded frame, and walls glowing with mosaics picturing scenes of the end times, in which the Preservers (shown as clouds of light) ushered the recreated dead into perfect worlds of parklands and immaculate gardens. He loved the pomp and circumstance of the ceremonies, too, although he thought that it was unnecessary. The Preservers, who watched all, did not need ritual praise; to walk and work and play in the world they had made was praise enough. He was happier worshipping at the shrines which stood near the edge of the world on the far side of the Great River, visited every year during the winter festival when the triple spiral of the galaxy first rose in its full glory above the Great River and most of the people of Aeolis migrated to the farside shore in a swarm of boats, and set up camps and bonfires, and greeted the onset of winter with fireworks, and danced and prayed and drank and feasted for a whole decad.

The Aedile had taken Yama into his household, but he was a remote, scholarly figure, busy with his official duties and otherwise preoccupied with his excavations and endless measurements and calculations. His work left him with little in the way of small talk. Like many unworldly, learned men, the Aedile treated children as miniature adults; thanks to his benign neglect, Yama and Telmon spent much of their childhood being passed from one to another of the household servants, or running free amongst the tombs of the City of the Dead. In summer, the Aedile often left the peel-house for a month at a time, taking most of his household to one or another of his excavation sites. When they were not helping with the slow, painstaking work, Yama and Telmon went hunting and exploring amongst desert suburbs of the tombs, Telmon searching for unusual insects for his collection, Yama interrogating aspects – he had a knack for awakening them, and for tormenting and teasing them into revealing details of the lives of the people on whom they were based, and for whom they were both guardians and advocates.

Telmon was the natural leader of the two, five years older, tall and solemn and patient and endlessly inquisitive, with a fine black pelt shot through with chestnut highlights. He was a natural horseman and an excellent shot with bow, arbalest and rifle, and often went off by himself for days at a time, hunting in the foothills where the Breas ran white and fast through the locks and ponds of the old canal system. He loved Yama like a true brother, and Yama loved him in turn, and had been as devastated as the Aedile by news of his death.

Formal education resumed in winter. For four days each decad Yama and Telmon were taught fencing, wrestling and horsemanship by Sergeant Rhodean; for the rest, their education was entrusted to the librarian, Zakiel. Zakiel was a slave, the only one in the peel-house; he had once been an archivist, but had committed an unspeakable heresy. He did not seem to mind being a slave. Before he had been branded, he had worked in the vast stacks of the library of the Palace of the Memory of the People, and now he worked in the library of the peel-house. He ate his simple meals amongst dusty tiers of books and scrolls, and slept in a cot in a dark corner under a cliff of ledgers whose thin metal covers, spotted with corrosion, had not been disturbed for centuries. All knowledge could be found in books, Zakiel declared, and if he had a passion (apart from his mysterious heresy, which he had never renounced) it was this. He was perhaps the happiest man in the Aedile's household, for he needed nothing but his work.

'Since the Preservers fully understand the universe, and hold it whole in their minds, then it follows that all texts, which flow from minds forged by the Preservers, are reflections of their immanence,' Zakiel told Yama and Telmon more than once. 'It is not the world itself we should measure, but the observations of the world set down in these books. Of course, boys, you must never tell the Aedile that I said this. He is happy in his pursuit of the ineffable, and who am I to interfere with that?'

Yama and Telmon were supposed to be taught the Summalae Logicales, the Puranas, and the Protocols of the Department, but mostly they listened to Zakiel read passages from selected works of natural philosophy before engaging in long, formal discussions. Yama first learned to read upside-down by watching Zakiel's ink-stained forefinger track glyphs from right to left while the librarian recited the text in a sing-song voice, and later had to learn to read all over again, this time the right way up, to be able to recite in his turn. Yama and Telmon had most of the major verses of the Puranas by heart, and were guided by Zakiel to read extensively in chrestomathies and incunabula, but while Telmon dutifully followed the programme Zakiel set out, Yama preferred to idle time away dreaming over bestiaries, prosopographies and maps – most especially maps.

Yama stole many books from the library. Taking them was a way of possessing the ideas and wonders they contained, as if he might, piece by piece, seize the whole world. Zakiel retrieved most of his prizes from various hiding places in the house or the ruins in its grounds, using a craft more subtle than the tracking skills of either Telmon or Sergeant Rhodean, but one thing Yama managed to retain was a map of the inhabited half of the world. Its scroll was the width of his hand and almost twice the length of his body, a material finer than silk and stronger than steel wound on a resin spindle decorated with tiny figures of a hundred bloodlines, frozen in representative poses. Along one edge were the purple and brown and white ridges of the Rim Mountains; along the other was the blue ribbon of the Great River, with a narrow unmarked margin at its far shore. Yama knew that there were many shrines and monuments to pillar saints on the farside shore – he visited some of them each year, when the whole city crossed the Great River to celebrate with fireworks and feasting the rise of the galaxy at the beginning of winter – and he wondered why the map did not show them. For there was so much detail crammed into the map elsewhere. Between the Great River and the Rim Mountains was the long strip of inhabited land, marked with green plains and lesser mountain ranges and chains of lakes and ochre deserts. Most cities were scattered along the Great River's nearside shore, a thousand or more which lit up with their names when Yama touched them.

The greatest of them all stood below the head of the Great River: Ys, a vast blot spread beyond the braided delta where the river gathered its strength from the glaciers and icefields which buried all but the peaks of the Terminal Mountains. When the map had been made, Ys had been at the height of its glory, and its intricate grids of streets and parks and temples stretched from the shore of the Great River to the foothills and canyons at the edge of the Rim Mountains. A disc of plain glass, attached to the spindle of the map by a reel of wire, revealed details of these streets. By squeezing the edges of the disc, the magnification could be adjusted to show individual buildings, and Yama spent long hours gazing at the crowded rooftops, imagining himself smaller than a speck of dust and able to wander the ancient streets of a more innocent age.

Yama was growing ever more restless as he came into manhood, ever more preoccupied with fantasies of searching for his bloodline. Perhaps they were a high-born and fabulously wealthy clan, or a crew of fierce adventurers who had sailed their ships downstream to the midpoint of the world and the end of the Great River, and had fallen from the edge and gone adventuring amongst the floating islands; or perhaps they belonged to a coven of mages with secret powers, and those same powers lay slumbering within him, waiting to be awakened. Yama elaborated enormously complicated stories around his origin, and Telmon listened patiently to them in the watches of the night whenever they camped amongst the tombs of the City of the Dead.

'Never lose your imagination, Yama,' Telmon told him. 'Whatever you are, wherever you come from, that is your most important gift. But you must observe the world, too, learn how to read and remember its every detail, celebrate its hills and forests and deserts and mountains, the Great River and the thousands of rivers that run into it, the thousand cities and the ten thousand bloodlines. I know how much you love that old map, but you must live in the world as it is to really know it. Do that, and think how rich and wild and strange your stories will become. They will make you famous, I know it.'

This was at the end of the last winter Telmon had spent at home, a few days before he took his muster to war. He and Yama were on the high moors two days' ride inland, chasing the rumour of a dragon. Low clouds raced towards the Great River ahead of a cold wind, and a freezing rain gritty with flecks of ice blew in their faces as they walked at point with a straggling line of beaters on either side. The moors stretched away under the racing clouds, hummocky and drenched, grown over with dense stands of waist-high bracken and purple islands of springy heather, slashed with fast-running peaty streams and dotted with stands of juniper and cypress and bright green domes of bog moss. Yama and Telmon were on foot because horses were driven mad by the mere scent of a dragon. They wore canvas trousers and long oilcloth slickers over down-lined jackets, and carried heavy carbon-fibre bows which stuck up behind their heads, and quivers of long arrows with sharply tapered and cruelly hooked ceramic heads. They were soaked and windblasted and utterly exhilarated.

'I will go with you,' Yama said. 'I will go to war, and fight by your side, and write an epic about our adventures that will ring down the ages!'

Telmon laughed. 'Why not? Although I doubt that I will see any fighting at all.'

'Your muster will do the town honour, Tel. I am sure of it.'

'They can drill well enough, I suppose. I hope that is all they will need to do.'

After the Aedile had received the order to supply a hundred troops to contribute to the war effort, Telmon had chosen the men himself, mostly younger sons who had little chance of establishing a harem. With the help of Sergeant Rhodean, Telmon had drilled them for sixty days; in three more, the ship would arrive to take them downriver to the war.

Telmon said, 'I want to bring them back safely, Yama. I will lead them into the fighting if I am ordered, but they are set down for working on the supply lines, and I will be content with that. For every man or woman fighting the heretics face to face, there are ten who bring up supplies, and build defences, or tend the wounded or bury the dead. That is why the muster has been raised in every village and town and city. The war needs support troops as desperately as it needs fighting men.'

'I will go as an irregular. We can fight together, Tel.'

'You will look after our father, first of all. And then there is Derev.'

'She would not mind. And it is not as if—'

Telmon understood. He said, 'There are plenty of metic marriages, if she is as serious about you as you are about her.'

'I will not get married before you return, Tel. Or before I have had my chance to fight in the war.'

'I'm sure you will get your chance, if that is what you want. But be sure that you really want it.'

'Do you think the heretics really fight with magic?'

'They have technology given to them by the Ancients of Days. It might seem like magic, but that is only because we do not understand it. But we have right on our side, Yama. We are fighting with the will of the Preservers in our hearts. It is better than any magic.'

Telmon sprang onto a hummock of sedge and looked left and right to check the progress of the beaters, but it was Yama, staring straight ahead with the rain driving into his face, who saw a little spark of light suddenly blossom far out across the sweep of the moors. He cried out and pointed, and Telmon blew and blew on his silver whistle, and raised both arms above his head to signal that the beaters at the ends of the line should begin to walk towards each other and close the circle. Other whistles sounded as the signal was passed down the line, and Yama and Telmon broke into a run against the wind and rain, leaping a stream and running on towards the scrap of light, which flickered and grew brighter in the midst of the darkening plain.

It was a juniper set on fire. It was burning so fiercely that it had scorched the grass all around it, snapping and crackling as its branches tossed yellow flame and fragrant smoke into the wind and rain. Telmon and Yama gazed at it with wonder, then hugged and pounded each other on the back.

'It is here!' Telmon shouted. 'I know it is here!'

They cast around, and almost at once Telmon found the long scar in a stand of heather. It was thirty paces wide and more than five hundred long, burnt down to the earth and layered with wet black ashes.

It was a lek, Telmon said. 'The male makes it to attract females. The size and regularity of it shows that he is strong and fit.'

'This one must have been very big,' Yama said. The excitement he had felt while running towards the burning tree was gone; he felt a queer kind of relief now. He would not have to face the dragon. Not yet. He paced out the length of the lek while Telmon squatted with the blazing tree at his back and poked through the char.

'Four hundred and twenty-eight,' Yama said, when he came back. 'How big would the dragon be, Tel?'

'Pretty big. I think he was successful, too. Look at the claw marks here. There are two kinds.'

They quartered the area around the lek, moving quickly because the light was going. The tree had mostly burned out when the beaters arrived and helped widen the search. But the dragon was gone.

Nine days later, Telmon and the muster from Aeolis boarded a carrack that had put in at the floating harbour on its way from Ys to the war at the midpoint of the world. Yama did not go to see Telmon off, but stood on the bluff above the Great River and raised his fighting kite into the wind as the little flotilla of skiffs, each with a decad of men, rowed out to the great ship. Yama had painted the kite with a red dragon, its tail curled around its long body and flames pouring from its crocodile jaws, and he flew it high into the snapping wind and then lit the fuses and cut the string. The kite sailed out high above the Great River, and the chain of firecrackers exploded in flame and smoke until the last and biggest of all set fire to the kite's wide diamond, and it fell from the sky.

After the news of Telmon's death, Yama had begun to feel an unfocused restlessness. He spent long hours studying the map or sweeping the horizons with the telescope in the tower which housed the heliograph, most often pointing it upriver, where there was always the sense of the teeming vast city, like a thunderstorm, looming beyond the vanishing point.

Ys! When the air was exceptionally clear, Yama could glimpse the slender towers rooted at the heart of the city. So tall that they rose beyond the limit of visibility, higher than the bare peaks of the Rim Mountains, punching through the atmosphere whose haze hid Ys itself. Ys was three days' journey by river and four times that by road, but even so the ancient city dominated the landscape, and Yama's dreams.

He began to plan his escape with meticulous care, although at first he did not think of it as escape at all, but merely an extension of the expeditions he had made, first with Telmon, and latterly with Ananda and Derev, in the City of the Dead. Sergeant Rhodean was fond of saying that most unsuccessful campaigns failed not because of the action of the enemy but because of lack of crucial supplies or through unforeseeable circumstances, and so Yama made caches of stolen supplies in several hiding places amongst the ruins in the garden of the peel-house. But he did not seriously think of carrying out his plans until the night after the encounter with Lud and Lob, and Dr Dismas's audience with the Aedile.

Dr Dismas arrived at the end of the evening meal. The Aedile and Yama customarily ate together in the Great Hall, sitting at one end of the long, polished table under the high ceiling and its freight of hanging banners, most so ancient that all traces of the devices they had once borne had faded, leaving only a kind of insubstantial, tattered gauze. They were the sigils of the Aedile's ancestors. He had saved them from the great bonfires of the vanities when, after coming to power, the present administration of the Department of Indigenous Affairs had sought to eradicate its past.

Ghosts. Ghosts above, and a ghost unremarked in the empty chair at the Aedile's right hand.

Servants came and went with silent precision, bringing lentil soup, slivers of mango dusted with ginger, and a roast marmot dismembered on a bed of watercress. The Aedile said little except to ask after Yama's day.

Yama had spent the morning watching the pinnace which had anchored downriver of the bay three days ago, and now he remarked that he would like to take a boat out to have a closer look at it.

'I have been wondering why it does not anchor at the new quay,' the Aedile said. 'It is small enough to enter the mouth of the bay, but has chosen to keep its distance. I do not think it would be good for you to go out to it, Yama. As well as good, brave men, all sorts of ruffians are recruited to fight the heretics.'

For a moment, they both thought of Telmon.

Ghosts, invisibly packing the air.

The Aedile changed the subject. 'When I first arrived here, ships of all sizes could anchor in the bay, and when the river level began to fall I had the new quay built. But now the bigger ships must use the floating harbour, and in a year or two that will have to be moved further out to accommodate the largest of the argosies. From its present rate of shrinkage I have calculated that in less than five hundred years the river will be completely dry. Aeolis will be a port stranded in a desert plain.'

'There is the Breas.'

'Quite, quite, but where does the water of the Breas come from, except from the snows of the Rim Mountains? Snows that have fallen from air pregnant with water evaporated from the Great River. I have sometimes thought that it would be good for the town to have the old locks rebuilt. There is still good marble to be quarried in the hills.'

Yama mentioned that Dr Dismas was returned from Ys, but the Aedile only said again, 'Quite, quite.'

'I suppose he has arranged some filthy little clerkship for me.'

'This is not the time to discuss your future,' the Aedile said, and retreated, as was increasingly his habit, into a book. He made occasional notes in the margins of its pages with one hand while he ate with the other at a slow, deliberate pace that was maddening to Yama. He wanted to go down to the armoury and question Sergeant Rhodean, who had returned from his patrol just before darkness.

The servants had cleared away the great silver salver bearing the marmot's carcass and were bringing in a dish of iced sherbet when the major domo paced down the long hall and announced the arrival of Dr Dismas.

'Bring him directly.' The Aedile shut his book, took off his spectacles, and told Yama, 'Run along, my boy. I know you want to quiz Sergeant Rhodean.'

Yama had used the telescope to spy on the Aedile and Dr Dismas that afternoon, when they had met and talked on the dusty hillside at the edge of the City of the Dead. He was convinced that Dr Dismas had been to Ys to arrange an apprenticeship in some dusty corner of the Aedile's department, and wanted to know everything. And so, although he set off towards the armoury, he quickly doubled back and crept into the gallery just beneath the Great Hall's high ceiling, where, on feast days, musicians hidden from view serenaded the Aedile's guests. Yama thrust his head between the stays of two dusty banners and found that he was looking straight down at the Aedile and Dr Dismas.

The two men were drinking port wine, and Dr Dismas had lit one of his cigarettes. Yama could smell its clove-scented smoke. The apothecary sat stiffly in a carved chair, his white hands moving over the polished surface of the table like independently questing animals. Papers were scattered in front of him, and patterns of blue dots and dashes glowed in the air. Yama badly wanted a spyglass just then, to find out what was written on the papers, and cursed himself for his lack of forethought.

He had expected to hear Dr Dismas and the Aedile discuss his apprenticeship, but instead the Aedile was making a speech about trust. 'When I took Yama into my household, I also took upon myself the responsibility of a parent. I have brought him up as best I could, and I have tried to make a decision about his future with his best interests in my heart. You ask me to overthrow that in an instant, to gamble my duty to the boy against some vague promise.'

'It is more than that,' Dr Dismas said. 'The boy's bloodline—'

Yama's heart beat more quickly, but the Aedile angrily interrupted Dr Dismas. 'That is of no consequence. I know what you told me. It only convinces me that I must see to the boy's future.'

'I understand. But, with respect, you may not be able to protect him from those who might be interested to learn of him, and might believe that they have a use for him. I speak of higher concerns than those of the Department of Indigenous Affairs. I speak of great forces, forces which your few decads of soldiers could not withstand for an instant. You should not put yourself between those powers and that which they may desire.'

The Aedile stood so suddenly that he knocked over his glass of port. High above, Yama thought for a moment that his stepfather might strike Dr Dismas, but then he turned his back on the table and closed his fist under his chin and said, 'Who did you tell, doctor?'

'As yet, only you.'

Yama knew that Dr Dismas was lying, because the answer sprang so readily to his lips. He wondered if the Aedile knew, too.

'I notice that the pinnace which brought you back from Ys is still anchored off the point of the bay. I wonder why that might be.'

'I suppose I could ask its commander. He is an acquaintance of mine.'

The Aedile turned around. 'I see,' he said coldly. 'Then you threaten—'

'My dear Aedile, I do not come to your house to threaten you. I have better manners than that, I hope. I make no threats, only predictions. You have heard my thoughts about the boy's bloodline. There is only one explanation. I believe that any other man, with the same evidence, would come to the same conclusion as I have, but it does not matter if I am right. One need only raise the possibility to understand what danger the boy might be in. We are at war, and you have been concealing him from your own department. You would not wish to have your loyalty put to the question. Not again.'

'Be careful, doctor. I could have you arrested. You are said to be a necromancer, and it is well known that you indulge in drugs.'

Dr Dismas said calmly, 'The first accusation is a baseless rumour I have just now refuted. And while the second may be true, you have recently demonstrated your faith in me, and your letter is lodged with my department. As, I might add, is a copy of my findings. You could arrest me, but you could not keep me imprisoned for long without appearing foolish or corrupt. But why do we argue? We both have the same interest. We both wish no harm to come to the boy. We merely disagree on how to protect him.'

The Aedile sat down and ran his fingers through the grey pelt which covered his cheeks. He said, 'How much money do you want?'

Dr Dismas's laugh was like the creaking of old wood giving beneath a weight. 'In one pan of the scales is the golden ingot of the boy; in the other the feather of your wealth. I will not even pretend to be insulted.' He stood and plucked his cigarette from the holder and extinguished it in the pool of port spilled from the Aedile's glass, then reached into the glowing patterns. There was a click: the patterns vanished. Dr Dismas tossed the projector cube into the air and made it vanish into one of the pockets of his long black coat.

'If you do not make arrangements, then I must,' he said. 'And believe me, you'll get the poorer part of the bargain if you do.'

When Dr Dismas had gone, the Aedile raked up the papers and clutched them to his chest. His shoulders shook. High above, Yama thought that his father might be crying, but surely he was mistaken, for never before, even at the news of Telmon's death, had the Aedile shown any sign of grief.

5

THE SIEGE

Yama lay awake long into the night, his mind racing with speculations about what Dr Dismas might have discovered. Something about his bloodline, he was sure of that at least, and he slowly convinced himself it was something with which Dr Dismas could blackmail the Aedile. Perhaps his real parents were heretics or murderers or bandits . . . But who then would have a use for him, and what powers would take an interest?

Like all orphans he had filled the void of his parents' absence with colourful fictions. They could be war heroes or exotic villains or dynasts wealthy beyond measure; what they could not be was ordinary, for that would mean that he too was ordinary, abandoned not because of some desperate adventure or deep scandal, but because of the usual small tragedies of the human condition. Now that he was older he knew that mundane reality was more likely than his fantasies, but although he had put them away, as he had put aside his childish toys, Dr Dismas's return had awakened them, and all the stories he had elaborated as a child tumbled through his mind in a vivid pageant that ravelled away into confused dreams filled with unspecific longing.

As the sun crept above the Rim Mountains, Yama was woken by a commotion below his window. He threw open the shutters and saw three pentads of the garrison, clad in black resin armour ridged like the carapaces of sexton beetles and kilts of red leather strips, burnished metal caps on their heads, mounting their horses. Squat, shaven-headed Sergeant Rhodean leaned on the pommel of his gelding's saddle as he watched his men settle themselves and their restless mounts. Puffs of vapour rose from the horses' nostrils; harness jingled and hooves clattered as they stepped about. Other soldiers were stacking ladders, grappling irons, siege rockets and coils of rope on the loadbed of a grimy black steam wagon. Two house servants manoeuvred the Aedile's palanquin, which floated a handspan above the ground, into the centre of the courtyard. And then the Aedile himself appeared, clad in his robe of office, black sable trimmed with a collar of white feathers that ruffled in the cold dawn breeze.

The servants helped the Aedile over the flare of the palanquin's skirt and settled him in the backless chair beneath its red and gold canopy. Sergeant Rhodean raised a hand above his head and the procession, two files of mounted soldiers on either side of the palanquin, moved out of the courtyard. Black smoke and sparks shot up from the steam wagon's tall chimney; white vapour jetted from leaking piston sleeves. As the wagon ground forward, its iron-rimmed wheels striking sparks from the concrete, Yama threw on his clothes; before it had passed through the arch of the gate in the old wall he was in the armoury, quizzing the stable hands.

'Off to make an arrest,' one of them said. It was the foreman of the stables, Torin. A tall man, his shaven bullet-head couched in the hump of muscle at his back, his skin a rich dark brown mapped with paler blotches. He had followed the Aedile into exile from Ys and, after Sergeant Rhodean, was the most senior of his servants. 'Don't be thinking we'll saddle up your horse, young master,' he told Yama. 'We've strict instructions that you're to stay here.'

'I suppose you are not allowed to tell me who they are going to arrest. Well, it does not matter. I know it is Dr Dismas.'

'The master was up all night,' Torin said, 'talking with the soldiers. Roused the cook hours ago to make him early breakfast. There might be a bit of a battle.'

'Who told you that?'

Torin gave Yama an insolent smile. His teeth were needles of white bone. 'Why, it's plain to see. There's that ship still waiting offshore. It might try a rescue.'

The party of sailors. What had they been looking for? Yama said, 'Is it a pirate ship, then?'

'I don't know about that, but there's some that reckon it's in the pay of Dr Dismas,' Torin said. 'It brought him back from Ys, after all. What's certain is that there'll be blood shed before the end of this. Cook has his boys making bandages, and if you're looking for something to do you should join them.'

Yama ran again, this time to the kitchens. He snatched a sugar roll from a batch fresh from the baking oven, then climbed the back stairs two steps at a time, taking big bites from the warm roll. He waited behind a pillar while the old man who had charge of the Aedile's bedchamber locked the door and pottered off, crumpled towels over one arm; then he used his knife to pick the lock, a modern mechanical thing as big as his head. It was easy to snap back the lock's wards one by one and to silence the machines which set up a chorus of protest at his entrance, although it took a whole minute to convince an alembic that his presence would not upset its delicate settings.

The papers that Dr Dismas had brought were not amongst the litter on the Aedile's desk, nor were they in the sandalwood travelling chest, with its deck of sliding drawers. Perhaps the papers were in the room in the watchtower – but that had an old lock, and Yama had never managed to persuade it to let him pass.

He closed the chest and sat back on his heels. This part of the house was quiet. Narrow beams of early sunlight slanted through the tall, narrow windows, illuminating a patch of the richly patterned carpet, a book splayed upside down on the little table beside the Aedile's reading chair. Zakiel would be waiting for him in the library, but there were more important things afoot. Yama went back out through the kitchen, cut across the herb garden and, after calming one of the watchdogs, ran down the steep slope of the breastwork and struck off through the ruins towards the city.

Dr Dismas's tower stood just outside the city wall. It was tall and slender and had once been used to manufacture shot. Molten blackstone had been poured through a screen at the top of the tower, and the droplets, rounding into perfect spheres as they fell, had plummeted into an annealing bath of water at the base. The builders of the tower had sought to advertise its function by adding slit windows and a parapet with a crenellated balustrade in imitation of the watchtower of a bastion, and after the foundry had been razed the tower had been briefly used as a lookout post. But then the new city wall had been built with the tower outside it, and it had fallen into disuse, its stones slowly pried apart by the tendrils of its ivy cloak, the platform where molten stone had once been poured to make shot for the guns of soldiers and hunters becoming the haunt of owls and bats.

Dr Dismas had moved into the tower shortly after taking up his apothecary's post. Once it had been cleaned out and joiners had fitted new stairs and three circular floors within it, and raised a tall slender spire above the crenellated balustrade, Dr Dismas had closed its door to the public, preferring to rent a room overlooking the waterfront as his office. There were rumours that he performed all kinds of black arts in the tower, from necromancy to the surgical creation of chimeras and other monsters. It was said that he owned a homunculus he had fathered by despoiling a young girl taken from the fisher folk. The homunculus was kept in a tank of saline water, and could prophesy the future. Everyone in Aeolis would swear to the truth of this, although no one had actually seen it.

The siege had already begun by the time Yama reached the tower. A crowd had gathered at a respectful distance to watch the fun. Sergeant Rhodean stood at the door at the foot of the tower, his helmet tucked under one arm as he bawled out a final warning. The Aedile sat straight-backed under the canopy of the palanquin, which was grounded amongst the soldiers and a unit of the town's militia, out of range of shot or quarrel. The militiamen were a motley crew in mismatched bits of armour, armed mostly with home-made blunderbusses and rifles, but drawn up in two neat ranks as if determined to put on a good show. The soldiers' horses tossed their heads, made nervous by the crowd and the steady hiss of the steam wagon's boiler.

Yama clambered to the top of a stretch of ruined wall near the back of the crowd. It was almost entirely composed of men: wives and daughters were not usually allowed to leave the harems. They stood shoulder to shoulder, grey- and brown-skinned, corpulent and four-square on short, muscular legs, bare-chested in breechclouts or kilts. They stank of sweat and fish and stale river water, and nudged each other and jostled for a better view. There was a cheerful sense of occasion, as if this were some piece of theatre staged by a travelling mountebank. It was about time the apothecary got what he deserved, they told each other, and agreed that the Aedile would have a hard time of it winkling him from his nest.

Hawkers were selling sherbet and sweetmeats, fried cakes of river-weed and watermelon slices. A knot of whores of a dozen different bloodlines, clad in abbreviated, brightly coloured nylon chitons, their faces painted dead white under fantastical conical wigs, watched from a little rise at the back of the crowd, passing a slim telescope to and fro. Their pander, no doubt hoping for brisk business when the show was over, moved amongst the crowd, cracking jokes and handing out clove-flavoured cigarettes. Yama looked for the whore he had lain with the night before Telmon had left for the war, but could not see her, and blushingly looked away when the pander caught his eye and winked at him.

Sergeant Rhodean bawled out the warrant again, and when there was no reply he set his helmet on his scarred, shaven head and limped back to where the Aedile and the other soldiers waited. He leaned on the skirt of the Aedile's palanquin and there was a brief conference.

'Burn him out!' someone in the crowd shouted, and there was a general murmur of agreement.

The steam wagon jetted black smoke and lumbered forward; soldiers dismounted and walked along the edge of the crowd, selecting volunteers from its ranks. Sergeant Rhodean spoke to the bravos and handed out coins; under his supervision, they lifted the ram from the loadbed of the steam wagon and, flanked by soldiers, carried it towards the tower. The soldiers held their round shields above their heads, but nothing stirred in the tower until the bravos applied the ram to its door.

The ram was the trunk of a young pine bound with a spiral of steel, slung in a cradle of leather straps with handholds for eight men, and crowned with a steel cap shaped like a caprice, with sturdy, coiled horns. The crowd shouted encouragement as the bravos swung it in steadily increasing arcs. 'One!' they shouted. 'Two!'

At the first stroke of the ram, the door rang like a drum and a cloud of bats burst from the upper window of the tower. The bats stooped low, swirling above the heads of the crowd with a dry rustle of wings, and men laughed and jumped up, trying to catch them. One of the whores ran down the road screaming, her hands beating at two bats which had tangled in her conical wig. Some in the crowd cheered coarsely. The whore stumbled and fell flat on her face and a militiaman ran forward and slashed at the bats with his knife. One struggled free and took to the air; the man stamped on the other until it was a bloody smear on the dirt. As if blown by a wind, the rest rose high and scattered into the blue sky.

The ram struck again and again. The bravos had found their rhythm now. The crowd cheered the steady beat. Someone at Yama's shoulder remarked, 'They should burn him out.'

It was Ananda. As usual, he wore his orange robe, with his left breast bare. He carried a small leather satchel containing incense and chrism oil. He told Yama that his master was here to exorcise the tower and, in case things got out of hand, to shrive the dead. He was indecently pleased about Dr Dismas's impending arrest. Dr Dismas was infamous for his belief that chance, not the Preservers, controlled the lives of men. He did not attend any high-day services, although he was a frequent visitor to the temple, playing chess with Father Quine and spending hours debating the nature of the Preservers and the world. The priest thought that Dr Dismas might yet be saved; Ananda knew the doctor was too clever and too proud for that.

'He plays games with people,' Ananda told Yama. 'He enjoys making them believe that he's a mage, although of course he has no powers of any kind. No one has, unless they flow from the Preservers. He's been revelling in his notoriety for far too long. His department wouldn't punish him, so it has fallen to the Aedile to do the right thing.'

'Dr Dismas knows something about me,' Yama said. 'He found it out in Ys. I think that he is trying to blackmail my father with it.'

He described what had happened the night before, and Ananda said, 'I shouldn't think that he has found out anything at all, but of course he couldn't tell the Aedile that. He was bluffing, and now his bluff has been called. You'll see. The Aedile will put him to question.'

'He should have killed Dr Dismas on the spot,' Yama said. 'Instead, he stayed his hand, and now he has this farce.'

'The Aedile is a cautious and judicious man.'

'Too cautious,' Yama said. 'A good general makes a plan and strikes before the enemy has a chance to find a place to make a stand.'

It was an aphorism from an ancient book on the art of warfare that he had found in the library.

Ananda said, 'He could not strike Dr Dismas dead on the spot, or even arrest him. It would not be seemly. He had to consult the Council for Night and Shrines first – Dr Dismas is their man, after all. And by putting on this little show justice is seen to be done by all, and all are satisfied. That's why your father chose volunteers from the crowd to break down the door. He wants to involve the citizens in this.'

'Perhaps,' Yama said, but he was not convinced. That this whole affair was somehow hinged around his origin was both exciting and shameful. He wanted it over with, and yet a part of him, the reckless and undisciplined part that dreamed of pirates and adventurers, exulted in the display of force, and he was more certain than ever that he could not settle into a quiet tenure in some obscure office in one of the great bureaucracies.

The ram struck, and struck again, but the door showed no sign of giving way.

'It is reinforced with iron,' Ananda said, 'and it is not hinged, but slides into a recess. In any case, we'll have a long wait even after they break down the door.'

Yama remarked that Ananda seemed to be an expert on the prosecution of sieges.

'I saw one before,' Ananda said. 'It was in the little town outside the walls of the monastery where I was taught, in the high mountains upriver of Ys. A gang of brigands had sealed themselves in a house. The town had only its militia, and Ys was two days' march away – long before soldiers could arrive, the brigands would have escaped under cover of darkness. So the militia decided to capture them. But several volunteers were killed when they tried to break into the place, and at last they burned it to the ground, and the brigands with it. That's what they should do here. Otherwise the soldiers will have to clear the floors of the tower one by one to catch Dismas. He might kill many of them before they corner him. And suppose he has something like the palanquin? He could simply fly away.'

'If he does, my father will chase him.' Yama smiled at the vision this conjured: Dr Dismas fleeing the tower like a black beetle on the wing; the Aedile swooping after him in his richly decorated palanquin, like a vengeful parrot.

The crowd cheered. Yama and Ananda pushed to the front, using their elbows and knees, and saw the door had split from top to bottom.

Sergeant Rhodean raised a hand and there was an expectant hush. 'One more time, lads,' he said. 'And put some back into it.'

The ram swung; the door shattered and fell away; the crowd surged forward, carrying Yama and Ananda with it. The soldiers started to push people back. One recognised Yama and said, 'You should not be here, young master.'

Yama dodged away before the soldier could grab him and, followed by Ananada, retreated to his original vantage point on the broken bit of wall, where he could see over the heads of the crowd and the line of embattled soldiers. The team of bravos swung the ram with short brisk strokes, knocking away the wreckage of the door; then they stood aside as a pentad of soldiers, with the leader of the militia trailing behind, came up with rifles and arbalests at the ready.

Led by Sergeant Rhodean, this party disappeared into the dark doorway. Yama looked to the Aedile, who sat upright under the canopy of his palanquin, his face set in a grim expression. The white feathers which trimmed the collar of his sable robe fluttered in the morning breeze.

There was a muffled thump. Thick orange smoke suddenly poured from one of the narrow windows of the tower, round billows swiftly unpacking into the air. The crowd murmured, uncertain if this was part of the attack or a desperate defensive move. More thumps: now smoke poured from every window, and from the smashed doorway. The soldiers stumbled out through swirls of orange fog. Sergeant Rhodean brought up the rear, hauling the leader of the militia by the scruff of his neck.

Flames mingled with the smoke pouring from the windows, which was slowly darkening from orange to deep red. Some in the crowd knelt, fists curled against their foreheads to make the sign of the Eye.

Ananda said to Yama, 'This is demon work.'

'I thought you did not believe in magic.'

'I believe in demons. They tried to overthrow the order of the Preservers an age ago. Perhaps Dismas is one, disguised as a man.'

'Those demons were machines, not supernatural creatures,' Yama said.

But Ananda was watching the burning tower with rapt attention, and did not seem to have heard him.

The flames licked higher: there was a ring of fire around the false spire that crowned the top of the tower. Red smoke hazed the air. Fat flakes of ash fell though it, and there was a stink of sulphur and something sickly sweet. Then there was another muffled thump and a tongue of flame shot out of the doorway. The tower's spire blew to flinders. Burning strips of plastic foil rained down on the heads of the crowd, and men yelled and ran in every direction.

Yama and Ananda were separated by the sudden panic, as the front ranks of the crowd tried to shove past the press of those behind, and men clambered over the broken wall. A horse reared up, striking with its hooves at a man who was trying to grab its bridle. The steam wagon was alight from one end to the other. The driver jumped from the burning cab, rolling over and over to smother his smouldering clothes, staggering to his feet just as the charges on the wagon's loadbed exploded and blew him to red ruin.

Siege rockets flew in criss-cross trajectories, trailing burning lengths of rope. A cask of napalm burst in a huge ball of oily flame, sending a mushroom of smoke boiling into the air. Flecks of fire spattered in a wide circle. Men dived towards whatever cover they could find. Yama dropped to the ground, arms crossed over his head, as burning debris pattered all around.

There was a moment of intense quiet. Yama climbed to his feet, his ears ringing, and a heavy hand fell on his shoulder and spun him around.

'We've unfinished business, small fry,' Lob said.

Behind him, Lud grinned around his tusks.

6

THE HOUSE OF GHOST LANTERNS

Lud took Yama's knife and stuck it in his belt beside his own crooked blade. 'Don't go shouting for help,' he said, 'or we'll tear out your tongue.'

People were retreating from the fire, streaming towards the gate in the city wall. Lob and Lud gripped Yama's arms and carried him through the crowd. Behind them, the tower burned furiously, a roaring chimney belching thick red fumes that mixed with the smoke of the burning wagon and countless lesser fires and veiled the sun. Several horses had thrown their riders and were galloping about wildly. Sergeant Rhodean strode amidst the flames and smoke, organising countermeasures; already, soldiers and militia were thrashing at small grass fires with wet blankets.

The fleeing crowd split around Ananda and the priest. They were kneeling over a man and anointing his bloody head with oil while reciting the last rites. Yama struggled, trying to free himself, but Lud snarled and cuffed his head and forced him on.

The smoke of the burning tower hung over the crowded flat roofs of the little city, and there was an unruly surge of people in the streets. The two brothers marched Yama past men picking over fruit spilled from a stall, a crowd besieging a tavern, passing bottles from hand to hand overhead. Along the old waterfront, peddlers were bundling wares into their blankets. Chandlers, tavern owners, and their employees were locking shutters over windows and standing guard at doors, armed with rifles and axes. Men were looting the building where Dr Dismas had his office, dragging furniture onto the second-floor veranda and throwing it into the street. Books rained down like broken-backed birds. Jars of simples smashed on concrete, strewing arcs of coloured powder. A man was methodically smashing all the ground-floor windows with a long-handled sledgehammer.

Lob and Lud bundled Yama through the riot and turned down a side street that was little more than a paved walkway beside a stagnant canal. The single-storey houses that stood shoulder to shoulder along the canal had been built from stones taken from older, grander buildings; their tall, narrow windows were framed by collages of worn carvings and broken tablets incised with texts in long-forgotten scripts. Chutes angled into the scummy green water: this part of the city was where the bachelor labourers lived, and they could not afford private bathing places.

Yama wondered if the two brothers had dragged him to this shabby, unremarked place so that they could have their fun with him without being interrupted. He started to struggle again, and they picked him up, one on either side, and hustled him to a tavern whose doorway squatted under a cluster of ancient ghost lanterns that squealed and rustled in the fetid breeze.

A square plunge-pool lit by sunken lanterns took up half the cavernous space inside. An immensely fat man floated on his back in the middle; his shadow loomed across the galleries that ran around three sides of the room. As Lob and Lud dragged Yama past the pool, the fat man snorted, expelling an oily mist from his nostrils, and opened one eye. Lob threw a coin, and the man twisted his head and snapped it from the air. It gleamed briefly on his black tongue; then his blubbery lips snapped shut and his eye closed.

Lud jabbed Yama with the point of his knife and marched him around a rack of barrels, into a narrow passage that led to a tiny courtyard roofed with glass stained by green algae and black mould. A cage woven from wire took up most of the space; inside, beneath the gleaming mesh of its ceiling, Dr Dismas hunched at a rickety table, reading a book and smoking a clove-scented cigarette stuck in his bone holder.

'Here he is,' Lud said. 'Just as we promised.'

'Don't stand there – bring him inside,' the apothecary said, and closed his book with an impatient snap.

Yama's fear had turned to paralysing astonishment. Lob held him while Lud unfastened a door in the cage; then he was thrust inside and the door rattled shut behind him.

'As you can see, I am not dead,' Dr Dismas said. 'Close your mouth, boy. You look like one of the frogs you are so fond of hunting.'

Outside the cage, Lud and Lob nudged each other. 'Go on,' one muttered, and the other said, 'You do it.' At last, Lud said to Dr Dismas, 'We done what you asked. Now you pay us.'

'Ah, but I have not forgotten that you failed the first time,' Dr Dismas said. 'The inconvenience that has caused me far outweighs your fee. And besides, if I pay you now, you'll immediately turn the money into drink, and there's still work to be done. Meanwhile, I need to talk to Yamamanama. A private talk. You two will come back an hour aftersunset, and we'll make a start on the second part of this venture.'

After more nudging, Lob said, 'We thought maybe we get paid for the one thing before we start on the other.'

'I told you that I would pay you to bring the boy here. And I will. And there will be more money after you help me to take him to the man who commissioned me. But there will be no money at all unless everything is done as I ask.'

'Maybe we only do the one thing and not the other,' Lob said.

'It is dangerous to leave something unfinished,' Dr Dismas said.

'This isn't right,' Lud said. 'We did what you asked—'

'When did I ask you to begin the second part of your work?'

'Sunset,' Lob said, in a sullen mumble.

'An hour after. Remember that. You will suffer as much as I if this goes badly. You failed the first time. Don't fail again.'

'We got him for you in the end, didn't we?' Lud said.

'We would have got him the other night,' Lob said, 'if the old culler with the stick hadn't got in the way.'

Yama stared at the two brothers through the mesh of the cage and said, 'I do not know what Dr Dismas has promised you, but whatever it is, my father will pay double if you let me go now.'

Lud and Lob grinned, nudging each other in the ribs.

'Ain't he a corker,' Lud said.

'A proper little gentleman,' Lob said, and belched.

Yama turned to Dr Dismas. 'And I offer you an amnesty, doctor. Let me go, and we will not speak of this.'

Dr Dismas put a hand on his narrow chest and sighed. He had six fingers, and long nails filed to points. 'You are a rare and unique creature, Yamamanama. I have sacrificed my home, my research and my books to get hold of you. The Aedile cannot scrape together one tenth of the amount that would compensate me for my losses and my trouble. And even if he could, it would not begin to approach your true worth.'

Yama felt a flush of excitement. 'Do you mean that you have found out something about me? About my family – that is, my real family—'

'O, what I've discovered is far better than that,' Dr Dismas said. 'But this is not the time to discuss it.'

Yama said, 'I would know it now, whatever it is. I deserve to know.'

'I'm no house servant, boy,' Dr Dismas said, and his hand flashed out and pinched Yama's elbow.

Yama's head was pierced by pain as pure as light. He fell to his knees on the mesh floor of the cage, and Dr Dismas came around the table and caught Yama's chin between his stiff, cold fingers.

'You are mine now, and don't forget it,' he said, and turned to the twins. 'Why are you two still here? You have your orders.'

'We'll be back tonight,' Lud said. 'And you'll pay us then.'

'You'll get what you deserve,' Dr Dismas said.

After the twins had left, the apothecary told Yama, 'Frankly, I would rather work alone, but I could hardly move amongst the crowd of gawpers while everyone thought I was in the tower. A fine diversion that worked rather better than I hoped.' He got his hands under Yama's arms and hauled him to his feet. 'Let's get you seated. You'll soon feel better.'

Yama perched on the edge of the flimsy plastic chair and concentrated on his breathing until the pain had retreated to a warm throb in the muscles of his shoulder. At last, he said, 'You wanted my father to lay siege to your tower. You provoked him.'

Dr Dismas sat on the other side of the little table. As he screwed a cigarette into his bone holder, he said, 'I tried to reason with the Aedile, but he would not listen. He refused to believe me. Instead of accepting the facts of the case, he attempted to suppress them by arresting me. Fortunately, he is scrupulous in following law and custom. He confided his intentions to the Council for Night and Shrines, one of them owed me a favour, and here we are.'

'It was always your intention to kidnap me. Lob and Lud tried to take me as soon as you returned from Ys. And I think you had other people looking for me, too,' Yama said, remembering the party of sailors.

'Everything worked out in the end,' Dr Dismas said. 'The Aedile thinks I'm dead, so I can leave this wretched little backwater without worrying that he or anyone else will chase after me. We are going to have such adventures, Yamamanama.'

'Once the fire burns out, they will look for a body. When they do not find one, they will look for you. And this is a small city.'

Dr Dismas blew a riffle of smoke towards the mesh overhead. 'But they *will* find a body.'

'Then you planned to burn your tower all along, and you cannot blame me for its destruction. I expect you removed your books before you left, too.'

Dr Dismas did not deny this. 'How did you like the display, by the way?'

'Some are convinced that you are a magician.'

'Those who claim to be magicians are as deluded as their clients. My little pyrotechnic display was no more than a few judiciously mixed salts, ignited by electric detonators when the circuit was closed by some oaf stepping on a plate I'd hidden under a rug.' Dr Dismas aimed a long forefinger at Yama, who squashed the impulse to flinch. 'All for you. You see, you really do owe me, Yamamanama. Child of the River . . . But which river, I wonder? Not our own Great River, I'm certain of that.'

'You know about my family.' Yama could not keep the excitement from his voice. It was rising and bubbling inside him – he wanted to laugh, to sing, to dance. 'You know about my bloodline.'

Dr Dismas reached into a pocket of his long coat and drew out a handful of plastic straws, rattled them together, and cast them on the table. He was making a decision by appealing to their random pattern: Yama had heard about this habit from Ananada, who had reported it in scandalised tones.

'Are you deciding whether to tell me what I deserve to know, doctor?'

Dr Dismas tapped ash from his cigarette. 'Oxen and camels, nilgai, ratites and horses – all work under the lash, watched by boys no older than you, or even younger, armed with no more than fresh-cut withes to temper their charges. How is this possible? Because the part in those animals that yearns for freedom has been broken, and replaced by habit. No more than the twitch of a stick is required to reinforce that habit; even if the animals were freed of harness and burdens, they would not attempt to escape. Most men are no different from beasts of burden, their spirit broken by fear of the phantoms of religion invoked by priests and bureaucrats, their thoughts constrained by the ingrained habits of work and hearth. I strive to avoid such habits. To be unpredictable.

That is the best way to cheat those who believe themselves to be your masters.'

'I thought you did not believe in the Preservers.'

'I don't question their existence. For they certainly once existed. This world is evidence of that; the Eye of the Preservers and the ordered galaxy beyond are evidence. But I do question the great lie that the priests use to hypnotise the masses. That the Preservers watch over us all, and that we must satisfy them so that we can win redemption and live forever after death. As if creatures who once juggled stars in their courses would ever care about whether or not a man beats his wife, or the little torments one child visits upon another. It is a lie to keep men in their places, to ensure that so-called civilisation can run on its own momentum, unchanged. I spit on it.'

And Dr Dismas did spit, as delicately as a cat, before fitting his cigarette holder between his large, flat-topped teeth. When he smiled around it, the plaques over his cheekbones stood out in relief, sharp edges pressing through brown skin.

'The Preservers created us, but they are gone,' he said. 'They are dead, and by their own hands. They created the Eye and fell through its event horizon with all their worlds. And why? Because they despaired. They had remade the Home Galaxy, and could have gone on to remake the universe, but their nerve failed. They were cowards and fools, at the end, and anyone who believes that they watch us still, yet do not interfere in the terrible suffering of the world, is an even worse fool.'

Yama had no answer to this. There was no answer. Ananda was right. The apothecary was a monster who refused to serve anyone or anything except his own swollen pride.

Dr Dismas said, 'The Preservers are gone, but their machines still watch over and regulate the world according to antique and irrelevant rules. Of course, the machines can't watch everything at once, so they predict the behaviour of crowds and populations from inbuilt rules, and watch only for gross deviations from that so-called norm. It works most of the time, but there are a few men like me who defy their predictions and their rigid logic by basing important decisions according to chance. The machines cannot track our random paths, and so we become invisible. Of course, a cage like this one also helps. It screens out the remote sensing of the machines. I wear a hat for the same reason – it is lined with foil of the finest beaten silver.'

Dr Dismas confessed this ridiculous habit with such sincere solemnity that Yama had to laugh. 'So you are afraid of machines,' he said.

'Not at all. But I am deeply interested in them. I have a small collection of machine parts excavated from ruins in the deserts beyond the midpoint of the world. One is almost intact, a treasure beyond price.' Dr Dismas suddenly clutched his head and shook it violently, then let out a shuddering sigh and winked at Yama. 'Ah, but that's not to be spoken of. Not here! There are many spies, all around. They might overhear my thoughts, even inside this cage. One reason I came here is because machine activity is higher than anywhere else on Confluence – even Ys. And that, my dear Yamamanama, is how I found you.'

Yama pointed at the straws scattered on the table. They were hexagonal in cross-section, with red and green glyphs of some unknown language incised along their faces. 'You refuse to acknowledge the authority of the Preservers over men, yet you follow the guidance of these scraps of plastic.'

Dr Dismas gave him a crafty look. 'Ah, but I choose which questions to ask them.'

'Let me ask you a direct question. Did you find my family, in Ys?'

'You will have to look beyond Ys to find your family, my boy. And you will soon be given the opportunity to do so. The Aedile is a good enough man in his way, I suppose, but at bottom he is no more than a petty official barely capable of ruling a moribund little region of no interest to anyone. Into his hands has fallen a prize that could determine the fate of all the peoples of Confluence – even the world itself – and he knows and understands nothing about it. A man like that deserves to be punished, Yamamanama. And as for you, well, you are very dangerous. For, like the man who adopted you, you do not know what you are.'

'I would like very much to know,' Yama said, although he was beginning to think that the apothecary was insane.

'Innocence is no excuse,' Dr Dismas said. He seemed to be speaking to himself. He moved the plastic straws around the tabletop with his forefinger, as if seeking to rearrange his fate, then lit another cigarette and stared at Yama until Yama grew uncomfortable and looked away.

Dr Dismas laughed, and with sudden energy pulled a little leather case from inside his coat and opened it out on the table. Inside, held by elastic loops, were a glass syringe, an alcohol lamp, a bent silver spoon with a blackened bowl, a small pestle and mortar, and several glass bottles with rubber stoppers. From one bottle, Dr Dismas shook a small dried beetle into the mortar, added a few drops of a clear liquid from another bottle – the room was suddenly filled with the smell of apricots – and ground the beetle to paste and with finicky care scraped the paste into the bowl of the spoon.

'Cantharides,' he said. 'You are young, Yamamanama, and will neither understand nor approve. But to someone of my refined sensibility the world sometimes becomes too much to bear.'

'My father said that this habit got you into trouble with your department. He said—'

'That I had sworn to stop using it? Of course I did. Otherwise I would not have been allowed to return to Aeolis.'

Dr Dismas lit the wick of the alcohol lamp with flint and steel, and held the spoon over the blue flame until the brown paste liquified and began to bubble. The smell of apricots intensified, sharpened by a metallic tang. Dr Dismas drew the liquid into the hypodermic and tapped the barrel with a fingernail to loosen the bubbles that clung to the glass.

'Don't think to escape,' he told Yama. 'I have no key.'

He spread his left hand on the tabletop, probed the web of skin between thumb and forefinger with the hypodermic's needle, teased back the plunger until a wisp of red swirled in the thin brown solution, then pressed the plunger home. He drew in a sharp breath and stretched in his chair like a bow. The hypodermic clattered on the table as his heels drummed an irregular tattoo, and then he relaxed, and looked at Yama with half-closed eyes. His pupils, smeary crosses on yellow balls, contracted and expanded independently. He giggled.

'If I had you long enough . . . Ah, but what I'd teach you . . .'

'Doctor?'

But Dr Dismas's gaze wandered away from Yama, fixing at last on the spattered glass that roofed the courtyard. Yama dared to stand and test the door, but it was locked, and he could not work his fingers between its edge and the frame. He tried various places in the cage's wire walls, but the close-woven hexagons were strong and close-knitted, and sprang back into shape after he deformed them. He turned away, and touched the apothecary's outstretched hand. It was clammy, and irregular plates shifted under the loose skin. Dr Dismas did not stir. His head was tipped back, and his face was bathed in the light of the sun, which had crept into view above the little courtyard's glass ceiling.

Yama found only one pocket inside the apothecary's long black coat, and it was empty. Dr Dismas stirred as Yama withdrew his hand, and gripped his wrist and drew him close with unexpected strength. 'There's no escaping your fate,' he murmured. His breath smelt of apricots and wet iron. 'Sit, boy, and wait.'

Yama sat, and waited. The sun crept across the glass ceiling, began its slow reversal. Presently, the immensely fat man who had been floating in the tavern's communal pool shuffled down the passage. He was naked except for blue rubber sandals, and he carried a tray covered with a white cloth.

'Stand up and stand back,' he told Yama. 'No, further back. Behind the doctor.'

'If you let me go, I promise that you will be handsomely rewarded.'

'I've already been paid, young master,' the fat man said. He unlocked the door, set the tray on the table, and backed out and relocked the door. 'Eat, young master. The doctor, he won't want anything. I never seen him eat. He has his drug.'

Yama sprang to the door and rattled it, and yelled threats at the fat man's retreating back, continued to yell long after he had disappeared. At last, when he was certain that the man wasn't coming back, he turned to the table and looked under the cloth that covered the tray.

A dish of watery soup with a cluster of whitened fish eyes sunk in the middle and rings of raw onion floating on top; a slab of black bread, as dense as a brick and almost as hard; a glass of small beer the colour of stale urine.

The soup was flavoured with chilli oil, making it almost palatable, but the bread was so salty that Yama gagged on the first bite and could eat no more. He drank the sour beer and somehow fell asleep on the rickety chair.

He was woken by Dr Dismas. He had a splitting headache and a foul taste in his mouth. The courtyard and the cage were lit by a hissing alcohol lantern which dangled from the cage's wire ceiling; the air beyond the glass that roofed the courtyard was black.

'Rise up, young man,' Dr Dismas said. He was filled with barely contained energy and hopped from foot to foot and banged his stiff fingers together. His shadow, thrown across the whitewashed walls of the courtyard, aped his movements.

'You drugged me,' Yama said stupidly.

'A little something in the beer to take away your cares.' Dr Dismas banged on the mesh of the cage and shouted, 'Ho! Ho! Landlord!' and turned back to Yama and said, 'You have been sleeping longer than you know. The little sleep just past is my gift to make you wake into your true self. You don't understand me, but it doesn't matter. Stand up! Stand up! Look lively! Awake, awake! You venture forth to meet your destiny! Ho! Landlord!'

7

THE WARLORD

In the darkness outside the door of the tavern, Dr Dismas clapped a wide-brimmed hat on his head and exchanged a few words with the landlord, who handed something to him, knuckled his forehead and shut the heavy street door. The cluster of ghost lanterns above the door creaked in the breeze, glimmering with a wan pallor that illuminated nothing but themselves. The rest of the street was dark, apart from a few blades of light shining between the closed shutters of the houses on the other side of the canal. Dr Dismas switched on a penlight and waved its narrow beam at Yama, who blinked stupidly in the glare; his wits were still dulled by sleep and the residue of the drugged beer.

'If you are going to be sick,' Dr Dismas said, 'lean over and don't spatter your clothes or your boots. You must be presentable.'

'What will you do with me, doctor?'

'Breathe, my dear boy. Slowly and deeply. And don't think to shout for help. There is a curfew. No one will be around to help you, and I'll be forced to hurt you so you won't do it again. Look at this. Do you know what it is?'

Dr Dismas showed Yama what the landlord had given him. It was an energy pistol, silver and streamlined, with a blunt muzzle and a swollen chamber, and a grip of memory plastic that could mould itself to fit the hands of most of the bloodlines of the world. A dot of red light glowed at the side of the chamber, indicating that it was fully charged.

'You could burn for that alone,' Yama said.

'Then you know what it can do.' Dr Dismas pushed the muzzle into Yama's left armpit. 'I have it at its weakest setting, but a single shot will roast your heart. We will walk to the new quay like two old friends.'

Yama did as he was told. He was still too dazed to try to run. Besides, Sergeant Rhodean had taught him that in the event of being kidnapped he should not attempt to escape unless his life was in immediate danger. He thought that the soldiers of the garrison must be searching for him: he had been missing all day. They might turn a corner and find him at any moment.

The dose of cantharides had made Dr Dismas talkative. As they walked, he told Yama that originally the tavern had been a workshop where ghost lanterns had been manufactured in the glory days of Aeolis.

'The lanterns that advertise the tavern are a crude representation of the ideal of the past, being made of nothing more than lacquered paper. Real ghost lanterns were little round boats made of plastic, with a deep weighted keel to keep them upright and a globe of blown nylon infused with luminescent chemicals instead of a sail. They were floated on the Great River after each funeral to confuse any restless spirits of the dead and make sure that they would not haunt their living relatives. There is, as you will soon see, an analogy to be made with your fate, my dear boy.'

Yama said, 'You traffic with fools, doctor. The owner of the tavern will be burnt for his part in my kidnap – it is the punishment my father reserves for the common people. Lud and Lob too, though their stupidity almost absolves them.'

Dr Dismas laughed. His sickly-sweet breath touched Yama's cheek. He said, 'And will I be burnt, too? Burnt for the second time?'

'It is in my father's power. More likely you will be turned over to the mercies of your department. You won't have a chance to profit from this.'

'That's where you are wrong. First, do you see anyone coming to your rescue? Second, I do not take you for ransom, but to save you from the pedestrian fate to which your father would consign you.'

The long waterfront, lit by the orange glow of sodium-vapour lamps, was deserted. The taverns, the chandlers' godowns and the two brothels were shuttered and dark. Curfew notices fluttered from doors; slogans in the crude ideograms used by the Amnan had been smeared on walls. Rubbish and driftwood had been piled against the steel doors of the big godown owned by Derev's father and set alight, but the fire had done no more than discolour the metal. Several lesser merchants' premises had been looted, and the building where Dr Dismas had kept his office had been burnt to the ground. Smouldering timbers sent up a sharp stench that made Yama's eyes water.

Dr Dismas marched Yama along the new quay, which ran out towards the mouth of the bay between meadows of zebra grass and shoals of mud dissected by shallow stagnant channels. The wide bay faced downriver. Framed on one side by the bluff on which the Aedile's house stood, and by the chimneys of the paeonin mill on the other, the triple-armed pinwheel of the galaxy stood beyond the edge of the world. It was so big that when Yama looked at one edge he could not see the other. The Arm of the Warrior rose high above the arch of the Arm of the Hunter; the Arm of the Archer curved in the opposite direction, below the edge of the world, and would not be seen again until next winter. The structure known as the Blue Diadem, that Yama knew from his readings of the Puranas was a cloud of fifty thousand blue-white stars each forty times the mass of the sun of Confluence, was a brilliant pinprick of light beyond the frayed point of the outflung Arm of the Hunter, like a drop of water flicked from a finger. Smaller star clusters made long chains of concentrated light through the milky haze of the galactic arms. There were lines and threads and globes and clouds of stars, all fading into a misty radiance notched by dark lanes that barred the arms at regular intervals. The core, bisected by the horizon, was knitted from thin shells of stars in tidy orbits concentrically packed around the great globular clusters of the heart stars, like layers of glittering tissue wrapped around a heap of jewels. Confronted with this ancient grandeur, Yama felt that his fate was as insignificant as that of any of the mosquitoes which danced before his face.

Dr Dismas cupped his free hand to his mouth and called out, his voice shockingly loud in the quiet darkness. 'Time to go!'

There was a distant splash in the shallows beyond the end of the quay's long stone finger. Then a familiar voice said, 'Row with me, you culler, not against me. You're making us go in circles.'

A skiff glided out of the darkness. Lud and Lob shipped their oars as it thumped against the bottom of a broad stone stair. Lob jumped out and held the boat steady as Yama and Dr Dismas climbed in.

'Quick as you like, your honour,' Lud said.

'Haste makes waste,' Dr Dismas said. Slowly and fussily he settled himself on the centre thwart, facing Yama with the energy pistol resting casually in his lap. He told the twins, 'I hope that this time you did exactly as I asked.'

'Sweet as you like,' Lob said. 'They didn't know we were there until the stuff went up.' The skiff barely rocked when he stepped back into it;

he was surprisingly nimble for someone of his bulk. He and his brother settled themselves in the high seat at the stern and they pushed off from the rough stones of the quay.

Yama watched the string of orange lights along the waterfront recede into the general darkness of the shore. The cold breeze off the river was clearing his head, and for the first time since he had woken from his drugged sleep he was beginning to feel fear.

He said, 'Where are you taking me, doctor?'

Dr Dismas's eyes gleamed with red fire beneath the brim of his hat; his eyes were backed with a reflective membrane, like those of certain nocturnal animals. He said, 'We are going to meet a great warlord, Yamamanama. Are you not intrigued? Are you not excited?'

'I suppose you want to sell me to this warlord, so that he can use me as a hostage or a bargaining counter.'

'Haven't I told you already that this isn't about money?'

'Little fish,' Lud said mockingly. 'Little fish, little fish.'

'Fish out of water,' Lob added.

They were both breathing heavily as they rowed swiftly towards the open reaches of the Great River.

'You must forgive them,' Dr Dismas told Yama. 'Good help is hard to find in backwater places. At times I was tempted to use my master's men instead.'

Lud said, 'We could tip you overboard, doctor. Ever think of that?'

Dr Dismas said, 'This pistol can kill you and your brother between one heartbeat and the next.'

'If you shoot at us, you'll set fire to the boat, and drown as neat as if we'd thrown you in.'

'I might do it anyway. Like the scorpion who convinced the frog to carry him across the river, but stung his mount before they were halfway across, death is in my nature.'

Lob said, 'He don't mean anything by it, your honour.'

'I just don't like him bad-mouthing Aeolis,' Lud said sullenly.

Dr Dismas laughed. 'I speak only the truth. Both of you agree with me, for why else would you want to leave?'

Lud said, 'Our father is young, that's all it is. We're strong, but he's stronger. He'd kill either of us or both of us, however we tried it, and we can't wait for him to get weak. It would take years and years.'

Dr Dismas said, 'And Yamamanama wants to leave, too. Do not deny it, my boy. Soon you will have your wish. There! Look upriver! You see how much we do for you!'

The skiff heeled as it rounded the point of the shallow, silted bay and entered the choppier waters of the river proper. As it turned into the current, Yama saw with a shock that one of the ships anchored at the floating harbour half a league upstream was ablaze from bow to stern.

The burning ship squatted over its livid reflection, tossing harvests of sparks into the night, as if to rival the serene light of the galaxy. It was a broad-beamed carrack, one of the fleet of transports that carried troops or bulk supplies to the armies fighting the heretics at the midpoint of the world. Four small boats were rowing away from it, sharply etched shadows crawling over water that shone like molten copper. Even as Yama watched, a series of muffled explosions in the ship's hold blew expanding globes of white flame high above the burning mastheads. The ship, broken-backed, settled in the water.

Lud and Lob cheered, and the skiff rocked alarmingly as they stood to get a better view.

'Sit down, you fools,' Dr Dismas said.

Lud whooped, and shouted, 'We did it, your honour! Sweet as you like!'

Dr Dismas said to Yama, 'I devised a method so simple that even these two could carry it out successfully.'

Yama said, 'You tried to burn a ship a few days ago. Everyone thought it was heretics, but it was you. You did it so my father's soldiers would be busy searching for heretics, and you would have a better chance of kidnapping me.'

'We tried fire-rafts, but a current took them wide of their target. This time we used two barrels of palm oil mixed with liquid soap,' Dr Dismas said. 'One at the bow, one at the stern, both armed with clockwork fuses. It makes a fine diversion, don't you think? Your father and his men will be fully engaged with rescuing sailors and saving the rest of the floating harbour while we go about our business, and the heretics will be blamed for the burning of the ship, and for your disappearance. Your father will receive a ransom note tomorrow, but even if he answers it there will, alas, be no reply. You will disappear without trace. Such things happen, in this terrible war.'

'My father will search for me. He will not stop searching.'

'Perhaps you won't want to be found, Yamamanama. You dreamed of running away, and here you are, set on a great adventure.'

The skiff drifted on a slow current parallel to the dark shore. The burning ship receded into the night. It had grounded on the river bottom; only the forecastle and the masts were still burning. The fisher folk were abroad, and the lanterns they used to attract fish to their lines made scattered constellations across the breast of the Great River, red sparks punctuating the reflected sheen of the galaxy's light.

Dr Dismas stared intently into the glimmering dark, swearing at Lud and Lob whenever they dipped their oars in the water. 'We got to keep to the current, your honour,' Lud said apologetically, 'or we'll lose track of where we're supposed to be.'

'Quiet! What was that?'

Yama heard a rustle of wings and a faint splash.

'Just a bat,' Lud said. 'They fish out here at night.'

'We catch 'em with glue lines strung across the water,' Lob explained. 'Make good eating, bats do, but not in spring. After winter, see, they're mainly skin and bone. You have to wait for them to feed—'

'Be quiet,' Dr Dismas said. 'One more word and I'll fry you both where you sit. You have so much fat on your bodies that you'll go up like candles.'

The current bent away from the shore and the skiff drifted with it, scraping past young banyans that raised small crowns of leaves a handspan above the water. Yama glimpsed the pale violet spark of a machine spinning through the night. It seemed to be moving in short stuttering jerks, as if searching for something. At any other time he would have wondered at it, but now its remote light and unguessable motives only intensified his feeling of despair. The world had suddenly turned strange and treacherous, its wonders traps for the unwary.

At last Dr Dismas said, 'There! Row, you fools!'

Yama saw a red lamp flickering to starboard. Lud and Lob bent to their oars and the skiff flew across the water towards it. Dr Dismas lit an alcohol lantern with flint and steel and held it up by his face. Cast through a mask of blue plastic, the light made his pinched face, misshapen by the plaques beneath its skin, look like that of a corpse.

The red lantern hung from the stern of a lateen-rigged pinnace anchored beside a solitary banyan. It was the ship that had returned Dr Dismas to Aeolis. Two sailors had climbed into the branches of the tree, and they watched over the long barrels of their rifles as the skiff came alongside. Lob stood and threw a line up to the stern of the pinnace. A sailor caught the end and made the skiff fast, and someone vaulted the pinnace's rail, landing so suddenly and lightly in the well of the skiff that Yama half rose in alarm.

The man clamped a hand on Yama's shoulder. 'Easy there, lad,' he said, 'or you'll have us in the river.'

He was only a few years older than Yama, bare-chested, squat and muscular, with an officer's sash tied at the waist of his tight white trousers. His pugnacious face, framed by a cloud of loose red-gold hair, was seamed with scars, like a clay mask that someone had broken and badly mended, but his look was frank and appraising, and enlivened by good-humoured intelligence. He steadied the skiff as Dr Dismas unhandily clambered up the short rope ladder dropped down the side of the pinnace, but when it was his turn Yama shook off the officer's hand and sprang up and grabbed the stern rail. His breath was driven from him when his belly and legs slammed against the planks of the pinnace's hull, and pain shot through his arms and shoulders as they took his weight, but he hauled himself up, got a leg over the rail and rolled over, coming up in a crouch on the deck of the stern platform at the bare feet of an astonished sailor.

The officer laughed and sprang from a standing jump to the rail and then, lightly and easily, to the deck. He said, 'He has spirit, doctor. That's good, very good.'

Yama stood. He had banged his right knee, and it throbbed warmly. Two sailors leaned on the steering bar and a tall man in black stood beside them. The pinnace's single mast was rooted at the edge of the stern platform; below it, three decads of rowers, naked except for breechclouts, sat in two staggered rows. The sharp prow was upswept, with a white stylised hawk's eye painted on the side. A small swivel-mounted cannon was set in the prow's beak; its gunner had turned to watch Yama come aboard, one arm resting on the cannon's fretted barrel.

Yama looked at the black-clad man and said, 'Where is the warlord who would buy me?'

Dr Dismas said, 'The boy can't harm you. There is no need to aim your weaponry at him. Or at me, for that matter.'

The officer gestured – the two sailors perched in the banyan branches above the pinnace put up their rifles – and told Dr Dismas that it was merely a precaution. 'If I had wanted you shot, Dercetas and Diomedes would have picked you off while you were still rowing around the point of the bay. But have no fear of that, my friend, for I need you as much as you need me.'

Yama said again, loudly, 'Where is he, this warlord I'm supposed to meet?'

The bare-chested officer laughed. 'Why, here I am,' he said, and stuck out his hand.

Yama took it. The officer's grip was firm, that of a man who is confident of his strength. His fingers were tipped with claws that slid a little from their sheaths and pricked the palm of Yama's hand.

'Well met, Yamamanama,' the officer said. His large eyes were golden, with tawny irises; the only beautiful feature of his broken face. The lid of the left eye was pulled down by a deep, crooked scar that ran from brow to chin.

'This war breeds heroes as ordure breeds flies,' Dr Dismas remarked, 'but Enobarbus is a singular champion. He set sail last summer as a mere lieutenant. He led a picket boat smaller than his present command into the harbour of the enemy and sank four ships and damaged a dozen others before his own boat was sunk under him.'

'It was a lucky venture,' Enobarbus said. 'We had a long swim of it, I can tell you, and a longer walk afterwards.'

Dr Dismas said, 'If Enobarbus has one flaw, it is his humility. After his boat was sunk, he led fifteen men – his entire crew – through twenty leagues of enemy lines, and did not lose one. He was rewarded with command of a division, and he is going downriver to take it up. With your help, Yamamanama, he will soon command much more.'

Enobarbus grinned. 'As for humility, I always have you, Dismas. If I have any failing, you are swift to point it out. How fortunate, Yamamanama, that we both know him.'

'More fortunate for you, I think,' Yama said.

'Every hero must be reminded of his humanity, from time to time,' Dr Dismas said.

'Fortunate for both of us,' Enobarbus told Yama. 'We'll make history, you and I. That is, of course, if you are what Dismas claims. He has been very careful not to bring the proof with him, so that I must keep him alive. He is a most cunning fellow.'

'I've lied many times in my life,' Dr Dismas said, 'but this time I tell the truth. For the truth is so astonishing that any lie would pale before it, like a candle in the sun. But we can talk about that later. It is past time to raise anchor and leave. My diversion was splendid while it lasted, but already it is almost burned out. And while the Aedile of that silly little city may be a weak man, but he is no fool. His soldiers searched the hills after my first attempt; it is very likely that he will widen his search to include your pinnace this time. Especially as you did not come to the aid of the burning ship.'

'Before we leave, my physician will take a look at your lad,' Enobarbus said, and called the man in black forward.

He was of the same bloodline as Enobarbus, but considerably older. Although he moved with the same lithe tread, he had a comfortable swag of a belly and his mane, loose about his face, was streaked with grey. His name was Agnitus.

'Take off your shirt, boy,' the physician said. 'Let's see what you're made of.'

'It's better you do it yourself,' Dr Dismas advised. 'They can tie you down and do it anyway, and it will be more humiliating, I promise you. Be strong, Yamamanama. Be true to your inheritance. All will be well. Soon you will thank me.'

'I do not think so,' Yama said, but pulled his shirt over his head. Now he knew that he was not going to be killed he felt a shivery excitement. This was the adventure he had dreamed of, but unlike his dreams it was not under his control.

The physician sat Yama on a stool and took his right arm and turned the joints of his fingers and wrist and elbow, ran cold hard fingers down his ribs and prodded at his backbone. He shone a light in Yama's right eye and gazed closely at it, then fitted a kind of skeletal helmet over Yama's scalp and turned various screws until their blunt ends gripped his skull, and recorded the measurements in a little oilskin-covered notebook.

Dr Dismas said impatiently, 'The proof is in his genotype, not in the shape of his bones or the structure of his eyes. And I hardly think you can conduct that kind of test here and now.'

Agnitus said to Enobarbus, 'He's right, my lord. I can take a sample of the boy's blood, and a scraping of the skin from the inside of his cheek, but it will take a while to work on them. I can tell you that his bloodline is not one I recognise, and I've seen plenty in my time. And he's not a surgical construct, unless our apothecary is more cunning than I am.'

'I would not presume,' Dr Dismas said.

'A proof by elimination is less satisfactory than one by demonstration,' Enobarbus said. 'But unless we storm the library of the Department of

Apothecaries and Chirurgeons, we must be content with Dismas's word. For now, at least.'

'Everything I have told you is true,' Dr Dismas said. 'Haven't I sworn to it? And does he not fulfil the prophecy made to you?'

Enobarbus looked at Yama. 'What about you? Do you have a clear view of your destiny?'

Yama liked Enobarbus's bold candour, even though he was a friend or ally of Dr Dismas. He realised that everyone was looking at him, and said defiantly, 'I would say that you are proud and ambitious, Enobarbus, a leader of men who would seek a prize greater than mere promotion. You believe that I can help you, although I do not know how – unless it is to do with the circumstances of my birth. Dr Dismas knows about that, I think, but he likes to tease.'

Enobarbus laughed. 'Well said! He reads us as easily as a book, Dismas. We must be careful.'

'The Aedile would have made him a clerk,' Dr Dismas said with disgust.

'The Aedile belongs to a part of our department that is not noted for its imagination,' Enobarbus said. 'We should not condemn him for what, in his office, is a virtue. Yamamanama, I know the story about the white boat. I know that you have always considered yourself to be different from those around you. And you are. Dr Dismas has discovered that you are unique, and he has convinced me that you are a part of my destiny. With my help, the fate of the world itself lies within your grasp.'

And then this powerful young man did an extraordinary thing. He knelt before Yama and bowed his head until his forehead touched the deck. He looked up through the tangle of his mane and said, 'I will serve you well, Yamamanama. I swear with my life. Together we will save Confluence.'

'Please get up,' Yama said. He was frightened by this gesture: it marked a solemn moment whose significance he did not understand. 'I do not know why I have been brought here, or why you are saying these things, but I did not ask for any of it, and I do not want it.'

'Stand fast,' Dr Dismas hissed, and grasped Yama's upper arm in a cruel pinch.

Enobarbus stood. 'Let him alone, Dismas. We are about to embark upon a hard and perilous journey, Yamamanama. I have worked towards it all my life. When I was a cub, I was blessed by a vision. It was in the temple of my bloodline, in Ys. I was praying for my brother, who had died in battle a hundred days before. The news had just reached me. I was praying that I could avenge him, and that I could play my part in saving Confluence from the heretics. I was very young, as you might imagine, and very foolish, but my prayers were answered. The shrine lit and a woman arrayed in white appeared, and told me of my destiny. I accepted, and I have been trying my best to carry it out ever since.

'To know one's fate is a privilege granted only to a few men, and it is a heavy responsibility. Most men live their lives as they can. I must live my life in pursuit of an ideal. It has stripped me of my humanity as faith strips an eremite of worldly possessions, and honed my life to a single point. Nothing else matters to me. How often have I wished that the obligation be lifted, but it has not been, and I have come to accept it. And here we are, as was predicted long ago.'

Enobarbus's sudden smile utterly transformed his wrecked face. He clapped his hands. 'I have spoken enough for now. I will speak more, Yamamanama, I promise, but it must wait until we are safe. Pay your men, Dismas. We are at last embarked on our journey.'

Dr Dismas pulled out his pistol. 'It would be well if your boat put some distance between itself and their miserable skiff. I'm not sure of the range of this thing.'

Enobarbus nodded. 'It's probably for the best,' he said. 'They might guess, and they'd certainly talk.'

'You overestimate them,' Dr Dismas said. 'They deserve to die because they endangered my plans by their stupidity. Besides, I cannot stand boorishness, and I have been exiled amongst these uncivilised creatures for an entire year. This will be a catharsis.'

'I'll hear no more. Kill them cleanly, and do not seek to justify yourself.'

Enobarbus turned to give his orders, and at that moment one of the sailors perched in the branches of the banyan to which the pinnace was moored cried out.

'Sail! Sail ahead!'

'Thirty degrees off the starboard bow,' his mate added. 'Half a league and bearing down hard.'

Enobarbus gave his orders without missing a beat. 'Cut the mooring ropes fore and aft. Dercetas and Diomedes, to your posts at once! Ready the rowers, push off on my word! I want thirty beats a minute from you lads, and no slacking.'

In the midst of the sudden rush of activity, as oars were raised and sailors hacked at mooring lines, Yama saw his opportunity. Dr Dismas made a grab for him, but was too slow. Yama swung over the rail and landed hard in the well of the skiff.

'Row!' Yama yelled to Lob and Lud. 'Row for your lives!'

'Catch hold of him!' Dr Dismas shouted from above. 'Catch him and make sure you don't let go!'

Lud started forward. 'It's for your own good, little fish,' he said.

Yama dodged Lud's clumsy swipe and retreated to the stern of the little skiff. 'He wants to kill you!'

'Get him, you fools,' Dr Dismas said.

Yama grabbed hold of the sides of the skiff and rocked it from side to side, but Lud stood four-square. He grinned. 'That won't help, little fish. Keep still, and maybe I won't have to hurt you.'

'Hurt him anyway,' Lob said.

Yama picked up the alcohol lantern and dashed it into the well of the skiff. There was a flare of translucent blue flame. Lud reared backwards, and the skiff pitched violently. Flames licked around Yama's feet; he took a deep breath and dived into the river.

He swam as far as he could before he came up and drew a gulp of air that burned all the way down the inverted trees of his lungs. He pulled at the fastenings of his boots and kicked them off.

The skiff was drifting away from the side of the pinnace. Fire flickered brightly in its well. Lud and Lob were trying to beat it out with their shirts. Sailors threw ropes down the side of the pinnace and shouted to them to give it up and come aboard. A tremendous glow was growing brighter and brighter beyond the pinnace, turning everything into a shadow of its own self. The cannon in the prow of the pinnace spoke: a crisp rattling burst, and then another.

Yama swam as hard as he could, and when he finally turned to float on his back, breathing hard, the whole scene was spread before him. The pinnace was sliding away from the banyan tree, leaving the burning skiff behind, and a great glowing ship was gliding towards the pinnace. She was a narrow-hulled frigate, her three masts crowded with square sails, and every part of her shone with cold fire. The pinnace's cannon spoke again, and there was a crackling of rifle fire. And then Dr Dismas fired his pistol, and for an instant a narrow lance of red fire split the night.

8
THE FISHERMAN

Dr Dismas's shot must have missed the glowing frigate because it did not falter or change course as it bore down on the pinnace. The bristling oars of the smaller ship beat at a steady and rapid rhythm and it turned away from the burning skiff, towards its pursuer. Yama saw that Enobarbus was planning to come around to the near side of the frigate and pass beneath its cannons and rake its sides with his own guns, but before the warlord could complete his manoeuvre the frigate swung about like a leaf blown by the wind. In a moment, its bow loomed above the pinnace. A chain gun hammered defiantly, and Yama heard someone cry out in wordless panic.

But at the instant when it struck the pinnace, the frigate dissolved into a spreading mist of white light. Yama backstroked in cold water, watching as the pinnace was engulfed by a globe of fog that boiled higher than the outflung arm of the galaxy. A point of violet light shot up from the fog, rising into the night sky until it had vanished from sight.

Yama did not stop to wonder at this miracle, for he knew that Enobarbus would start searching for him as soon as the pinnace had escaped the fog. He turned in the water and began to swim. Although he aimed for the dark, distant shore, he soon found himself in a swift current that took him amongst a scattered shoal of banyans. They were rooted in a gravel bank that at times he could graze with his toes; if he had been as tall as the Aedile he could have stood with his head clear of the swiftly running water.

At first, the banyans were no more than handfuls of broad, glossy leaves that stood stiffly above the water, but the current soon carried Yama deeper into a maze of wide channels between stands of bigger trees that rose in dense thickets above prop roots flexed in low arches. The roots were fringed by tangled mats of feeder roots alive with schools of tiny fish that flashed red or green dots of luminescence as they darted away from him.

With the last of his strength, he struck out towards one of the largest of the banyans as he was swept past it. The cold water had stolen all feeling from his limbs and the muscles of his shoulders and arms were tender with exhaustion. He threw himself into floating nets of feeder roots and, scraping past strings of clams and bearded mussels, dragged himself onto a smooth horizontal trunk, and lay gasping like a fish that had just learned the trick of breathing air.

Yama was too cold and wet and scared to sleep, and something in the tangled thickets of the tree started a thin, irregular piping, like the fretting of a sick baby. He sat with his back against an arched root and watched the uppermost arm of the galaxy set beyond the bank of faintly luminescent fog that had spread for leagues across the black river. Somewhere in the fog was Enobarbus's pinnace, lost, blinded. By what strange allies, or stranger coincidence? The top of the wide fog bank seethed like boiling milk; Yama watched the black sky above it for the return of the machine's violet spark. Answered prayers, he thought, and shivered.

He dozed and woke, dozed again, and jerked awake from a vivid dream of standing on the flying bridge of the ghostly frigate as it bore down on the pinnace. The frigate was crewed neither by men nor even by ghosts or revenants, but by a crowd of restless lights that responded to his unspoken commands with quick unquestioning intelligence. Zakiel had taught him that although most dreams were stitched from fragments of daily experience, a few were portents of the future or riddles whose answers were keys to the conduct of the dreamer's life. Yama did not know if this dream was of the first or second kind, let alone what it might mean, but when he woke it left him with a clinging horror, as if his every action might somehow be magnified, with terrible consequences.

The galaxy had set, and dawn touched the flood of the river with flat grey light. The bank of fog was gone; there was no sign of the pinnace. Yama slept, and woke with sunlight dancing on his face, filtered through the restless leaves of the banyan. He was sprawled on a wide limb that sloped gently up from the water and ran straight as an old road into the dense leafy tangles of the banyan's heart, crossed by arching roots and lesser branches that dropped prop roots straight down into the water. Glossy leaves hung everywhere like the endlessly deep folds of a ragged green cloak, and the bark of the tree's limbs, as smoothly wrinkled as skin, was colonised by lichens than hung like curtains of grey lace, the green barrels of bromeliads, and the scarlet and gold and pure white blossoms of epiphytic orchids.

Yama ached in every muscle. He drew off his wet shirt and trousers and hung them on a branch, then set to the exercises Sergeant Rhodean had taught him. At last his joints and muscles eased and loosened. He drank handfuls of cold water, startling shoals of fairy shrimp that scattered from his shadow, and splashed water on his face until his skin tingled with racing blood.

He had come ashore on the side of the banyan that faced towards the farside of the river. He slung his damp clothes over his shoulder and, naked, set off through the thickets of the tree, at first following the broad limb and then, when it joined another and bent upwards into the high sunflecked canopy, scrambling through a tangle of lesser branches. There was always black water somewhere beneath the random lattice of branches and prop roots. Tiny hummingbirds, clad in electric blues and emerald greens, as if enamelled by the most skilful of artists, darted from flower to flower. When Yama blundered through curtains of leaves, clouds of blackflies rose up and got in his eyes and mouth. At last, he glimpsed blue sky through a fall of green vines. He parted the soft, jointed stems and stepped through them onto a sloping spit of mossy ground, where a round coracle of the kind used by the fisher folk was drawn up.

The upturned shell of a snapping turtle held the ashes of a small fire, still warm when Yama sifted them through his fingers. He drew on his damp shirt and trousers and called out. No one answered. He cast around and quickly found a winding path leading away from the spit. And a few moments later found the fisherman, tangled in a crude net of black threads just beyond the second bend.

The threads were the kind that the Amnan used to catch bats and birds, resin fibres as strong as steel covered with thousands of tiny blisters that exuded a strong glue at a touch. Their net had partly collapsed when the fisherman had blundered into it, and he hung like a corpse in an unravelling shroud, one arm caught above his head, the other bound tightly to his side.

He did not seem surprised to see Yama. He said, in a quiet, hoarse voice, 'Kill me quick. Have mercy.'

'I was hoping for rescue,' Yama said.

The fisherman stared at him. He wore only a breechclout. His pale skin was blotched with islands of pale green; black hair hung in greasy tangles around his broad, chinless froggy face. His wide mouth hung open, showing rows of tiny triangular teeth. He had watery, protuberant eyes, and transparent membranes flicked over their balls three times before he said, 'You are not one of the Mud People.'

'I come from Aeolis. My father is the Aedile.'

'The Mud People think they know the river. It's true they can swim a bit, but they're greedy, and pollute her waters.'

'One of them seems to have caught you.'

'You're a merchant's son, perhaps. We have dealings with them, for flints and steel. No, don't come close – you'll be caught too. There is only one way to free me, and I don't think you carry it.'

'I know how the threads work,' Yama said, 'and I am sorry that I do not have what is needed to set you free. I do not even have a knife.'

'Even steel will not cut them. Leave me. I'm a dead man, fit only to fill the bellies of the Mud People . . . What are you doing?'

Yama had discovered that the surface of the path was a spongy thatch of wiry roots, fallen leaves and the tangled filaments of epiphytic lichens. He lay on his belly and pushed his arm all the way through the thick thatch until his fingers touched water. He looked at the fisherman and said, 'I have seen your people use baited traps to catch fish. Do you have one on your coracle? And I will need some twine or rope, too.'

While Yama worked, the fisherman, whose name was Caphis, told him that he had blundered into the sticky web just after dawn, while searching for the eggs of a species of coot which nested in the hearts of banyan thickets. 'The eggs are good to eat,' Caphis said. 'But not worth dying for.'

Caphis had put into the banyan shoal last night. He had seen a great battle, he explained, and had thought it prudent to take shelter. 'So I am doubly a fool.'

While the fisherman talked, Yama cut away a section of lichenous thatch and lashed the trap upright to a prop root. He had to use the blade of the fisherman's short spear to cut the twine, and several times sliced his palm. He sucked at the shallow cuts before starting to replace the thatch. It was in the sharp bend of the path; anyone hurrying down it would have to step there to make the turn.

He said, 'Did you see much of the battle?'

'A big ship caught fire. And then the small boat which has been lying offshore of the Mud People's city for three days must have found an enemy, because it started firing into the dark.'

'But there was another ship – it was huge and glowing, and melted into fog . . .'

The fisherman considered this, and said at last, 'I turned for shelter once the firing started, as anyone with any sense would. You saw a third ship? Well, perhaps you were closer than I was, and I expect that you saw more than you wanted to.'

'That is true enough.' Yama stood, leaning on the stout shaft of the spear.

'The river carries all away, if you let it. What's done one day is gone the next, and there's a new start. He might not come today, or even tomorrow. You will not wait that long. You will take the coracle and leave me to the fate I deserve.'

'My father outlawed this.'

'They are a devious people, the Mud People.' Sunlight splashed through the broad leaves of the banyan, shining on the fisherman's face. He squinted at Yama and added, 'If you could fetch water, it would be a blessing.'

Yama found a resin mug in the coracle. He was dipping it into the water at the edge of the mossy spit when he saw a little boat making its way towards the island. It was a skiff, rowed by a single man. By the time Yama had climbed into a crotch of the banyan, hidden amongst rustling leaves high above the spit, the skiff was edging through the slick of feeder roots that ringed the banyan.

He recognised the man. Grog, or Greg. One of the bachelor labourers who tended the mussel beds at the mouth of the Breas. He was heavy and slow, and wore only a filthy kilt. The grey skin of his shoulders and back was dappled with a purple rash, the precursor of the skin canker which affected those of the Amnan who worked too long in sunlight.

Yama watched, his mouth dry and his heart beating quickly, as the man tied up his boat and examined the coracle and the cold ashes in the turtle shell. He urinated at the edge of the water for what seemed a very long time, then set off along the path.

A moment later, while Yama was climbing down from his hiding place, made clumsy because he dared not let go of the fisherman's short spear, someone, the man or the fisherman, cried out. It startled two white herons which had been perching amongst the topmost branches of the banyan: the birds rose up into the air and flapped away as Yama crept down the path, clutching the spear with both hands.

There was a tremendous shaking amongst the leaves at the bend of the path. The man was floundering hip-deep amongst the broken thatch which Yama had used to conceal the trap. The big trap was wide-mouthed and two spans long, tapering to a blunt point. It was woven from pliable young prop roots, and bamboo spikes had been fastened on the inside, pointing downwards, so that when a fish entered to get at the bait it could not back out. These spikes had dug into the flesh of the man's leg when he had tried to pull free, and he was bleeding hard and grunting with pain as he pushed down with his hands like a man trying to work off a particularly tight boot. He did not see Yama until the point of the spear pricked the fat folds of skin at the back of his neck.

After Yama had used the spray which dissolved the threads' glue, Caphis wanted to kill the man who would have butchered him for meat. But Yama kept hold of the spear, and at last Caphis satisfied himself by tying the man's thumbs together behind his back and leaving him there, with his leg still in the trap.

The man started to shout as soon as they were out of sight. 'I gave you the stuff, didn't I? I didn't mean no harm. Let me go, master! Let me go and I'll say nothing! I swear it!'

He was still shouting when Caphis and Yama put out from the banyan.

The fisherman's scrawny shanks were so long that his knees jutted above the crown of his head as he squatted in the coracle. He paddled with slow, deliberate strokes. The threads of the trap had left a hundred red wheals across the mottled skin of his chest. He said that once he had warmed up his blood he would take Yama across to the shore.

'That is, if you don't mind helping me with my night lines.'

'You could take me to Aeolis. It is not far.'

Caphis nodded. 'That's true enough, but it would take me all day to haul against the current. Some us go there to trade, and that's where I got that fine spear-point last year. But it is a wicked town.'

'It is where I live. You have nothing to fear. Even if the man gets free, he would be burnt for trying to murder you.'

'Perhaps. But then his family would make a vendetta against my family. That is how it is.' Caphis studied Yama, and said at last, 'You'll help me with my lines, and I'll take you to the shore. You can walk more quickly to your home than I can row. But you'll need some breakfast before you can work, I reckon.'

They landed at the edge of a solitary grandfather banyan half a league downstream. Caphis built a fire of dried moss in the upturned turtle shell and boiled up tea in the resin mug, using friable strips of the bark of a twiggy bush that grew high in the tangled tops of the banyans. When the tea started to boil he threw in some flat seeds that made it froth, and handed Yama the mug.

The tea was bitter, but after the first sip Yama felt it warm his blood, and he quickly drained the mug. He sat by the fire, chewing on a strip of dried fish, while Caphis moved around the hummocky moss of the little clearing where they had landed. With his long legs and short barrel of a body, and his slow, deliberate, flat-footed steps, the fisherman looked something like a heron. The toes of his feet were webbed, and the hooked claws on his big toes and spurs on his heels helped him climb the banyan's smooth, interlaced branches. He collected seeds and lichens and a particular kind of moss, and dug fat beetle grubs from rotten wood and ate them at once, spitting out the heads.

All anyone could want could be found in the banyans, Caphis told Yama. The fisher folk pounded the leaves to make a fibrous pulp from which they wove their clothes. Their traps and the ribs of their coracles were made from young prop roots, and the hulls were woven from strips of bark and varnished with a distillation of the tree's sap. The kernels of banyan fruit, which set all through the year, could be ground into flour. Poison used to stun fish was extracted from the skin of a particular kind of frog that lived in the tiny ponds cupped within the living vases of bromeliads. A hundred kinds of fish swarmed around the feeder roots, a thousand kinds of plants grew on the branches, and each had their uses, and their particular tutelary spirits which had to be appeased before a leaf or flower was plucked or a fish taken from a net or trotline.

'There's hardly anything we lack, except metals and tobacco, which is why we trade with you land folk,' Caphis said. 'Otherwise we're as free as the fish, and always have been. We've never risen above our animal selves since the Preservers gave us the banyans as our province, and that is the excuse the Mud People use when they hunt us. But we're an old folk, and we've seen much, and we have long memories. Everything comes to the river, we say, and generally that's true.'

Caphis had a tattoo on the ball of his left shoulder, a snake done in black and red that curled around so that it could swallow its own tail. He touched the skin beneath this tattoo with the claw of his thumb and said, 'Even the river comes back to itself.'

'What do you mean?'

'Why, where do you think the river goes, when it falls over the edge of the world? It swallows its own self and returns to its beginning, and so renews itself. That's how the Preservers made the world, and we, who were here from the first, remember how it was. But things have been changing lately. Year by year the river grows less. Perhaps the river no longer bites its own tail, but if that is so I cannot say where it goes instead.'

'Do you – your people, do they remember the Preservers?'

Caphis's eyes filmed over. His voice took on a sing-song lilt. 'Before the Preservers, the universe was a plain of ice. The Preservers brought light that melted the ice and woke the seeds of the banyans which were trapped there. The first men were made of wood, carved from a banyan tree so huge that it was a world in itself, standing in the universe of water and light. But the men of wood showed their backs to the Preservers, and did not respect animals or even themselves, and destroyed so much of the world-tree that the Preservers raised a great flood. It rained for forty days and forty nights, and the waters rose through the roots of the banyan and rose through the branches until only the youngest leaves showed above the flood, and at last even these were submerged. All the creatures of the world-tree perished in the flood except for a frog and a heron. The frog clung to the last leaf which showed above the flood and called to its own kind, but the lonely heron heard its call and stooped down and ate it.

'Well, the Preservers saw this, and the frog grew within the heron's stomach until it split open its captor, and stepped out, neither frog nor heron but a new creature which had taken something from both its parents. It was the first of our kind. And just as it was neither frog nor heron, neither was it man or woman. At once the flood receded. The new creature lay down on a smooth mudbank and fell asleep. And while it slept, the Preservers dismembered it, and from its ribs fifty others were made, and these were men and women of the first tribe of my people. The Preservers breathed on them and clouded their minds, so that unlike the men of wood they would not challenge or be disrespectful to their creators. But that was long ago, and in another place. You, if you don't mind me saying so, look as if your bloodline climbed down from the trees.'

'I was born on the river, like you.'

Caphis clacked his wide flat lower jaw – it was the way the fisher folk laughed. 'Sometime I'd like to hear that story. But now we should set to. The day does not grow younger, and there is work to do. It is likely that the Mud Man will escape. We should have killed him. He would bite off his own leg if he thought that would free him. The Mud People are treacherous and full of tricks – that is how they are able to catch us, we who are more clever than they as long as our blood is warmed. That is why they generally hunt us at night. I was caught because my blood had the night chill, you see. It made me slow and stupid, but now I am warm, and I know what I must do.'

Caphis pissed on the fire to extinguish it, packed away the cup and the turtle shell beneath the narrow bench which circled the rim of the coracle, and declared himself ready.

'You will bring me luck, for it was by luck that you saved yourself from the phantom and then found me.'

With Yama seated on one side and Caphis wielding a leaf-shaped paddle on the other, the coracle was surprisingly stable, although it was so small that Yama's knees pressed against Caphis's bony shins. As the craft swung out into the current, Caphis paddled with one hand and filled a long-stemmed clay pipe with ordinary tobacco with the other, striking a flint against a bit of rough steel for a spark.

It was a bright clear afternoon, with a gentle wind that barely ruffled the surface of the river. There was no sign of the pinnace; no ships at all, only the little coracles of the fisher folk scattered across the broad river between shore and misty horizon. As Caphis said, the river bore all away. For a little while, Yama could believe that none of his adventures had happened, that his life could return to its normal routines.

Caphis squinted at the sun, wet a finger and held it up to the wind, then drove his craft swiftly between the scattered tops of young banyans (Yama thought of the lone frog in Caphis's story, clinging to the single leaf above the universal flood, bravely calling but finding only death and, in death, transfiguration). As the sun fell towards the distant peaks of the Rim Mountains, Yama and the fisherman worked trotlines strung between bending poles anchored in the bottom of the gravel bank. Caphis gave Yama a sticky, odourless ointment to rub on his shoulders and arms to protect his skin from sunburn. Yama soon fell into an unthinking rhythm, hauling up lines, rebaiting hooks with bloodworms and dropping them back. Most of the hooks were empty, but gradually a pile of small silver fish accumulated in the well of the coracle, gill flaps pulsing as they drowned in air.

Caphis asked for the forgiveness of each fish he caught. The fisher folk believed that the world was packed with spirits that controlled everything from the weather to the flowering of the least of the epiphytic plants of the banyan shoals. Their days were spent in endless negotiations with these spirits to ensure that the world continued its seamless untroubled flow.

At last the fisherman declared himself satisfied with the day's catch. He gutted a pentad of fingerlings, stripped the fillets of pale muscle from their backbones, and gave half to Yama, together with a handful of fleshy leaves.

The fillets of fish were juicy; the leaves tasted of sweet limes and quenched Yama's thirst. Following Caphis's example, he spat the leaf pulp overboard, and tiny fish promptly swarmed around this prize as it sank through the clear dark water.

Caphis picked up his paddle and the coracle skimmed across the water towards a bend of the stony shore, where cliffs carved and socketed with empty tombs rose from a broad pale beach.

'There's an old road that leads along the shore to Aeolis,' Caphis told Yama. 'It will take you the rest of this day, and a little of the next, I reckon.'

'If you would take me directly to Aeolis, I can promise you a fine reward. It is little enough in return for your life.'

'We do not go there unless we must, and never after nightfall. Because you saved it, you are responsible for my life now. Would you throw it away so soon, by taking me into the jaws of the Mud People? I do not think you would be so cruel. I have my family to consider. They'll be watching for me this night, and I don't want to worry them further.'

Caphis grounded his frail craft in the shallows a little way from the shore. He had never set foot on land, he said, and he wasn't about to start now. 'Don't walk after dark, young master. Find shelter before the sun goes down and stick to it until first light. Then you'll be all right. There are ghouls out there, and they like a bit of live meat on occasion.'

Yama knew about the ghouls. He and Telmon had once hidden from one during one of their expeditions into the foothills of the City of the Dead. He remembered how the man-shaped creature's pale skin had glimmered in the twilight like wet muscle, how frightened he had been as it stooped this way and that, and the stench it had left. He said, 'I will be careful.'

Caphis said, 'Take this. No use against ghouls, but I hear tell there are plenty of coneys on the shore. Some of us hunt them, but not me.'

It was a small knife carved from a flake of obsidian. Its hilt was wrapped with twine, and its exfoliated edge was as sharp as a razor.

'I reckon you can look after your own self, young master, but maybe a time will come when you need help. Then my family will remember that you helped me. Do you recall what I said about the river?'

'Everything comes around again.'

Caphis nodded, and touched the tattoo of the self-engulfing snake on his shoulder. 'You had a good teacher. You know how to pay attention.'

Yama slid from the tipping coracle and stood knee-deep in ooze and brown water. 'I will not forget,' he said.

'Choose carefully where you camp this night,' Caphis said. 'Ghouls are bad, but ghosts are worse. We see their lights sometimes, shining softly in the ruins.'

Then he pushed away from the shallows and the coracle waltzed into the current as he dug the water with his leaf-shaped paddle. By the time Yama had waded to shore, the coracle was already far off, a black speck on the shining plane of the river, making a long, curved path towards a raft of banyan islands far from shore.

9

THE KNIFE

After spending the day in Caphis's coracle, after wading through the beach's deep, soft drifts of white shell fragments to the worn stone stair that zigzagged up the face of the carved cliff, Yama found it strange to walk on firm ground again, where each step sent a little shock up the ladder of his spine. A spring welled inside a trough cut from the native stone at the first turn of the stair. Yama knelt on the mossy ground and drank clear sweet water until his belly sloshed, knowing that there would be little chance of finding any potable water in the City of the Dead. Only when he stood did he notice that someone else had drunk there recently – no, to judge by the overlapping footprints in the soft red moss, it had been two people.

Lud and Lob. They had also escaped Dr Dismas. Yama tucked the obsidian knife into his belt under the flap of his shirt, snug against the small of his back, before he continued his ascent.

An ancient road ran close to the edge of the cliff. Its smooth black pavement was so wide that twenty men could have ridden abreast along it. Beyond, the alkaline, shaly land shimmered in the level light of the late-afternoon sun. Tombs stood everywhere, casting long shadows towards the river. This was the Silent Quarter, which Yama had rarely visited – he and Telmon preferred the ancient tombs of the foothills, where aspects could be wakened and the flora and fauna was richer. Compared to the sumptuously decorated mausoleums of the older parts of the City of the Dead, the tombs in the Silent Quarter were poor things, mostly no more than low boxes with domed roofs, although here and there memorial steles and columns rose amongst them, and a few larger tombs stood on artificial stepped mounds, guarded by statues that watched the river with stony eyes. One of these was as big as the peel-house, half hidden by a small wood of yews grown wild and twisted. In all the desiccated landscape nothing stirred except for a lammergeyer high in the deep blue sky, riding a thermal on outspread wings.

When Yama was satisfied that he was not about to be ambushed, he set off down the road towards the distant smudge that must surely be Aeolis, halfway towards the vanishing point where the Rim Mountains and the misty horizon of the farside seemed to converge.

Little grew in the stone gardens of this part of the City of the Dead. The white, sliding rocks weathered to a bitter dust in which only a few plants could root, mostly yuccas and creosote bushes and clumps of prickly pear. Wild roses crept around the smashed doorways of some of the tombs, their blood-red blooms scenting the warm air. The tombs had all been looted long ago, and of their inhabitants scarcely a bone remained. If the cunningly preserved bodies had not been carted away to fuel the smelters of old Aeolis, then wild animals had long ago disinterred and consumed them. Ancient debris was strewn everywhere, from fragments of smashed funeral urns and shards of broken furniture to slates which displayed pictures of the dead, impressed into their surfaces by some forgotten art. Some of these were still active. As Yama followed the road scenes from ancient Ys briefly flickered to life along its margins, or the faces of men and women turned to watch him, their lips moving soundlessly or shaping into smiles or coquettish kisses. Unlike the aspects of older tombs, these were mere recordings without intelligence. The slates played the same meaningless loop over and over, whether for the human eye or the uncomprehending gaze of any lizard that flicked across them.

Yama was familiar with these animations: the Aedile possessed an extensive collection of them. They had to be exposed to sunlight before they would work, and Yama had always wondered why, for they were normally found inside the tombs. But although he knew what these mirages were, their unpredictable flicker was still disturbing. He kept looking behind him, fearful that Lud and Lob were stalking him through the quiet solitude of the ruins.

The oppressive feeling of being watched grew as the sun fell towards the ragged blue line of the Rim Mountains and the shadows of the tombs lengthened and mingled across the bone-white ground. To be walking through the City of the Dead in the bright sunshine was one thing, but as light faded from the sky Yama glanced more frequently over his shoulder as he walked, and sometimes turned and walked backwards a few paces, or stopped and slowly scanned the saddled hills and their freight of empty tombs. He had often camped in the City of the Dead with the Aedile and his retinue of servants and archaeological workers, or with Telmon and two or three soldiers, but never before alone.

The distant peaks of the Rim Mountains bit into the reddened disc of the sun. The lights of Aeolis shimmered in the distance like a heap of tiny diamonds. It was still at least a day's walk to the city, and would take even longer in darkness. Yama left the road and began to search the tombs for one that could give him shelter for the night.

It was like a game. Yama knew that the tombs he rejected now would be better than the one he would choose of necessity when the last of the sun's light fled the sky, but he did not want to choose straight away because he still felt that he was being watched, and fancied, as he wandered the network of narrow paths between the tombs, that he heard a padding footfall behind him that stopped when he stopped, and resumed a moment after he began to move forward again. At last, halfway up a long, gentle slope, he turned and called out Lud and Lob's names, feeling both fearful and defiant as the echoes of his voice died away amongst the tombs spread below him. There was no answer, but when he moved on he heard a faint squealing and splashing beyond the crest of the slope.

Yama drew the obsidian knife and crept forward like a thief. Beyond the crest, the ground fell away in an abrupt drop, as if something had bitten away half the hill. At the foot of the drop, a seep of brackish water gleamed like copper in the sun's last light, and a family of hyraces were sporting in the muddy shallows.

Yama stood and yelled and plunged down the steep slope. The hyraces bolted in every direction. A youngster squealed in blind panic when it saw Yama charging towards it; before it could change direction, he threw himself onto its slim, hairy body and flipped it onto its back and slit its throat with his knife.

Yama built a fire from shards of furniture and dry grass, and lit it with an ember from a friction board and a long spindle rolled between his hands. He cleaned and skinned and jointed the hyrax, roasted its meat over the fire, and ate until his stomach hurt, cracking bones for hot marrow and licking the fatty juices from his fingers. The sky had darkened to reveal a scattering of dim halo stars, and the galaxy was rising, salting the City of the Dead with its eldritch glow and casting a confusion of shadows.

The tomb that Yama chose as a place to sleep was not far from the seep, and as he rested against its granite facade, which still held the day's heat, he heard something splash in the pool – an animal come to drink. Yama laid the remains of the hyrax on a flat stone some distance from the tomb and took the precaution of dragging a tangle of rose briars across the tomb's entrance before curling up to sleep on the empty catafalque inside, his head pillowed on his folded shirt, the obsidian knife in his hand.

He woke from bad dreams at first light, stiff and cold. The golden sun stood a handspan above the Rim Mountains. The tomb in which he had slept was one of a row that stretched along the ridge above the pool, each with a gabled false front of rosy granite. They glowed like so many hearths in the sun's early light. Yama warmed himself with a set of exercises before pulling on his shirt and walking down to the pool.

His offering was gone. Only a dark stain was left on the flat white stone. There was a confusion of tracks around the water's edge, but he could find no human ones, only the slots of hyraces and antelopes, and what looked like the impress of the pads of some large cat, most likely a spotted panther.

The seep water of the pool was chalky with suspended solids, and so bitter that Yama spat out the first mouthful. He chewed a strip of cold meat and skinned and ate new buds taken from a prickly pear stand, but the tart juices did not entirely quench his thirst. He put a pebble in his mouth to stimulate the flow of saliva and walked back towards the river, thinking that he would climb down the cliff to drink and bathe at the water's edge.

He had wandered further than he had thought when he had been looking for shelter the previous evening. The narrow paths that meandered between the tombs and memorials and up and down the gentle slopes of the hills were all alike, and not one ran for more than a hundred paces before meeting with another, or splitting into two, but Yama kept the sun at his back, and by midmorning had reached the wide straight road again.

The cliffs were sheer and high, here. If the peel-house had stood in the seething water at their bases, its tallest turret would not have reached to their tops. Yama got down on his belly and hung over the edge and looked right and left, but could not see any sign of a path or of stairs, although there were many tombs cut into the cliff faces – there was one directly below him. Birds nested in the tombs, and thousands floated on the wind that blew up the face of the cliff, like flakes of restlessly sifting snow. Yama spat out the pebble and watched it bounce from the ledge in front of the tomb directly below and dwindle away, vanishing from sight before it hit the tumbled slabs of rock covered and uncovered by the heave of the river's brown water.

Behind him, someone said, 'A hot morning.'

And someone else: 'Watch you don't fall, little fish.'

Yama jumped to his feet and pulled the obsidian knife from his belt. Lud and Lob stood on top of a bank of white shale on the far side of the road. Both wore only kilts. Lob had a coil of rope over his bare shoulder; the skin of Lud's chest was reddened and blistered by a bad burn.

'Don't think of running,' Lud advised. 'It's too hot for you to get far without water, and you know you can't get away.'

Yama held up his knife and said, 'Dr Dismas wanted to kidnap me and kill you. There is no enmity between us.'

'I wouldn't know about that,' Lud said. 'I reckon we've a score to settle.'

'You owe us,' Lob said.

'I do not see it.'

Lud explained patiently, 'Dr Dismas would have paid us for our trouble, and instead we had to swim for our lives when you pulled that trick. I got burnt, too.'

'And he lost his knife,' Lob added.

'I loved that knife, you miserable culler,' Lud said. 'First thing I'm going to do is take that little stone tickler from you. But don't think it'll make up for what you made me lose.'

Lob said, 'And then there was the boat you put on fire. You owe for that, too.'

'That boat was not yours.'

Lud scratched at the patch of the reddened skin on his chest and said, 'It's the principle of the thing.'

'If I do agree to give you something to compensate you for your injuries and the loss of your knife, I cannot pay you now,' Yama said. 'I have no money. You will have to wait until I return home.'

Lob said, 'Yeah? And how do we know we can trust you?'

'Of course you can.'

Lud said, 'You haven't even asked how much we want. And besides, I reckon you just might think to tell your father. I don't think he'd pay us then, would he, brother?'

'It's doubtful.'

'Very doubtful, I'd say.'

Yama knew then that there was only one chance to escape. He said, 'If we cannot reach an agreement I must take my leave.'

Lud realised what he was going to do. He started down the slope and yelled, 'Don't—'

Yama did. He turned and jumped over the edge of the cliff.

He fell in a rush of air, and as he fell threw back his head and brought up his knees. (Sergeant Rhodean was saying, 'Just let it happen to you. If you learn to trust your body it's all a matter of timing.') Sky and river revolved around each other, and then he landed on his feet, knees bent to take the shock, on the ledge before the entrance to the tomb.

The ledge was no wider than a bed, and slippery with bird excrement. Yama immediately fell flat on his back, filled with a wild fear that he would tumble over the edge – there had been a balustrade once, but most of it had long ago fallen away. He caught a tuft of wiry grass and held on, although the sharp haulms reopened the wounds made by Caphis's spearhead. He had dropped the little obsidian knife when he'd landed; it stood upright in front of his face, its blade caught in a crack in the ledge.

As Yama climbed to his feet and pulled the knife from the crack, a stone clipped the ledge and tumbled away towards the heaving water far below. Yama looked up. Lob and Lud capered at the top of the cliff, silhouetted against the blue sky. They shouted down at him, but their words were snatched away by the wind. One of them threw another stone, which smashed scarcely a span from Yama's feet.

Yama ran forward, darting between the winged figures, their faces blurred by time, which supported the lintel of the gaping entrance to the tomb. Inside, stone blocks fallen from the high ceiling littered the mosaic floor. An empty casket stood on a dais beneath a canopy of stone carved to look like cloth rippling in the wind. Disturbed by Yama's footfalls, bats fell from one of the holes in the ceiling and dashed around his head, chittering in alarm.

The tomb was shaped like a wedge of pie, and behind the dais it narrowed to a passageway. It had once been sealed by a slab of stone, but that had been smashed long ago by robbers who had discovered the path used by the builders of the tomb. Yama grinned. He had guessed that the tombs in the cliffs would have been breached and stripped just like those above. It was his way of escape. He stepped over the sill and, keeping one hand on the cold dry stone of the wall, felt his way through near-darkness.

He had not gone far when the passage struck another running at right angles. He tossed an imaginary coin and chose the left-hand way. A hundred heartbeats later, in pitch darkness, he went sprawling over a slump of rubble. He got up cautiously and climbed the spill of stones until his head bumped the ceiling of the passage. It was blocked.

Then Yama heard voices behind him, and knew that Lud and Lob had followed him. He should have expected it. They would lose their lives if he was able to escape and tell the Aedile about the part they had played in Dr Dismas's scheme.

As Yama slid down the rubble, his hand fell on something smooth and hard. It was a metal knife, its curved blade as long as his forearm. It was cold to the touch and gave off a faint glow; motes of light seemed to float in the wake of its blade when Yama slashed at the darkness. Emboldened, he felt his way back to the tomb.

The dim light hurt his eyes; it spilled around one of the twins, who stood in the tomb's narrow entrance.

'Little fish, little fish. Why did you try to run? What are you so scared of?'

Yama held up the long knife. 'Not you, Lud.'

'Let me get him,' Lob said, peering over his brother's shoulder.

'Don't block the light, stupid.' Lud pushed Lob out of the way and grinned at Yama. 'There isn't a way out, is there? Or you wouldn't have come back. We can wait. We caught fish this morning, and we have water. I don't think you do, or you would have set out for the city straight away.'

Yama said, 'I killed a hyrax last night. I ate well enough then.'

Lud started forward. 'But I bet you couldn't drink the water in the pool, eh? We couldn't, and we can drink just about anything.'

Yama was aware of a faint breath of air at his back. He said, 'How did you get down here?'

'Rope from the boat,' Lob said. 'I grabbed it when we sank, knew it would come in useful. People say we're stupid, but we're not.'

'Then I can climb back up,' Yama said, and advanced on Lud, making passes with the knife as he came around the raised casket. The knife made a soft hum, and its rusty hilt pricked his palm. He felt a coldness flowing into his wrist and along his arm as the blade brightened with blue light.

Lud retreated. 'You wouldn't,' he said.

Lob pushed at his brother, trying to get past him. He was excited. 'Break his legs!' he shrieked. 'Break his legs! See how he swims then!'

'Watch out!'

Yama swung the knife again. Lud crowded backwards into Lob and they both fell over.

Yama yelled, words that hurt his throat and tongue. He did not know what he yelled and he stumbled, because suddenly his legs seemed too long, and bent in the wrong place. Where was his mount? Where was the rest of the squad? And why was he standing in the middle of what looked like a ruined tomb? All he could remember was a tremendous crushing pain, and then he had suddenly woken here, with two fat ruffians threatening him. He struck at the nearest and the man scrambled out of the way with jittery haste; the knife hit the wall and spat a shower of sparks. It was screaming now. He jumped onto the casket – yes, a tomb – but his body betrayed him and he lost his balance; before he could recover, the second ruffian caught his ankles and he fell heavily, striking the stone floor with hip and elbow and shoulder. The impact numbed his fingers and the knife fell from his grasp, clattering on the floor and gouging a smoking rut in the stone.

Lud ran forward and kicked the knife out of the way. Yama got to his feet. He did not remember falling. His right arm was cold and numb and hung from his shoulder like a piece of meat; he had to pull the obsidian knife from his belt with his left hand as Lud ran at him. They slammed against the wall and Lud gasped and clutched at his chest. Blood welled over his hand and he looked at it dully. 'What?' he said. He stepped away from Yama with a bewildered look and said again, 'What?'

'You killed him!' Lob said.

Yama shook his head. He could not get his breath. The ancient knife lay on the filthy floor between him and Lob, sputtering and sending up a thick smoke that stank of burning metal.

Lud tried to pull the obsidian knife from his chest, but it snapped, leaving a finger's width of the blade protruding. He blundered around the tomb, blood all over his hands now, blood running down his chest and soaking into the waistband of his kilt. He didn't seem to understand what had happened to him. He kept saying over and over again, 'What?

What?' and pushed past his brother and fell to his knees at the entrance to the tomb. Light spilled over his shoulders. He seemed to be searching the blue sky for something he could not find.

Lob stared at Yama, his grey tongue working between his tusks. At last he said, 'You killed him, you culler. You didn't have to kill him.'

Yama took a deep breath. His hands were shaking. 'You were going to kill me.'

'All we wanted was a bit of money. Just enough to get away. Not much to ask, and now you've gone and killed my brother.'

When Lob stepped towards Yama his foot struck the ancient knife. He picked it up, and screamed. White smoke rose from his hand and then he was not holding a knife but a creature fastened to his arm by clawed hands and feet. Lob staggered backwards and slammed his arm against the wall, but the creature only snarled and tightened its grip. It was the size of a small child, and seemed to be made of sticks. A kind of mane of dry, white hair stood around its starveling face. A horrid stink of burning flesh filled the tomb. Lob beat at the creature with his free hand and it vanished in a sudden flash of blue light.

The knife fell to the floor, ringing on the stone. Yama snatched it up and fled down the passage, barely remembering to turn right into the faint breeze. He banged from wall to wall as he ran, and then the walls fell away and he was tumbling through a rush of black air.

10

THE CURATORS OF THE CITY OF THE DEAD

The room was in some high, windy place. It was small and square, with whitewashed stone walls and a ceiling of tongue-and-groove planking painted with a hunting scene. The day after he first woke, Yama managed to raise himself from the thin mattress on the stone slab and stagger to the deep-set slit window. He glimpsed a series of stony ridges stepping away beneath a blank blue sky, and then fatigue overcame his will and he fainted.

'He is ill and does not know it,' the old man said.

He had half-turned his head to speak to someone else as he leaned over Yama. The tip of his wispy white beard hung a finger's width from Yama's chin. The deeply wrinkled skin of his face was mottled with brown spots and deep, old scars cut the left side, drawing up his mouth in a sardonic rictus. His bald pate was fringed with white hair. Glasses with lenses like small mirrors hid his eyes.

He said, 'He does not know how much the knife took from him.'

'He is young,' an old woman's voice said. 'He'll learn by himself, won't he?'

The old man curled and uncurled the end of his wispy beard around his fingers. At last he said, 'I cannot remember.'

Yama asked them who they were, and where this cool white room was, but they did not hear him. Perhaps he had not spoken after all. He could not move so much as a finger, although this did not scare him. He was too tired to be scared. The two old people went away and Yama was left to stare at the painted hunting scene on the ceiling. His thoughts would not fit together. Men in plastic armour over brightly coloured jerkins and hose were chasing a white stag through a forest of leafless tree trunks. The turf between the trees was starred with flowers. It seemed to be night in the painting, for in every direction the slim trunks of the trees faded into darkness. The paint had flaked away from the wood in places, and a patch above the window was faded. In the foreground, a young man in a leather jacket was pulling a brace of hunting dogs away from a pool. Yama thought that he knew the names of the dogs, and who their owner was. But he was dead.

Some time later, the old man came back and lifted Yama up so that he could sip thin vegetable soup from an earthenware bowl. Later, he was cold, so cold that he shivered under the thin grey blanket, and then so hot that he would have cast aside the blanket had he possessed the strength.

Fever, the old man told him. He had a bad fever. Something was wrong with his blood.

'You have been in the tombs,' the old man said, 'and there are many kinds of old sicknesses there.'

Yama sweated into the mattress, thinking that if only he could get up he would quench his thirst with the clear water of the forest pool. Telmon would help him.

But Telmon was dead.

In the middle of the day, sunlight crept a few paces into the little room before shyly retreating. At night, wind hunted at the corners of the deep-set window, making the candle gutter inside its glass sleeve. When Yama's fever broke it was deepest night. He lay still, listening to the wuthering of the wind. He felt very tired but entirely clear-headed, and spent the hours before dawnlight piecing together what had happened.

Dr Dismas's tower, detonating like a firework. The strange cage, and the burning ship. The leonine young war hero, Enobarbus, his face as ruined as the old man's. The ghost ship, and his escape – more fire. The whole adventure seemed to be punctuated by fire. He remembered the kindness of the fisherman, Caphis, and the adventure amongst the dry tombs of the Silent Quarter, which had ended in Lud's death. He had run from something terrible, and as for what had happened after that, he remembered nothing at all.

'You were carried here,' the old woman told him, when she brought him breakfast. 'It was from a place on the shore somewhere downstream of Aeolis, I'd judge. A fair distance, as the fox said to the hen when he gave her a head start.'

Her skin was fine-grained, almost translucent, and her white, feathery hair reached to the small of her back. She was of the same bloodline as Derev, but much older than either of Derev's parents.

Yama said, 'How did you know?'

At the woman's shoulder the old man smiled. As always, he wore his mirrored lenses. 'Your trousers and your shirt were freshly stained with river silt. It is quite distinctive. But I believe that you had been wandering in the City of the Dead, too.'

Yama asked why he thought that.

'The knife, dear,' the woman said.

The old man pulled at his scanty white beard and said, 'Many people carry old weapons. They are often far more potent than those made today.'

Yama nodded, remembering Dr Dismas's energy pistol.

'However, the knife you carried has a patina of corrosion that suggests it had lain undisturbed in some dark, dry place for many years. Perhaps you have carried it around without scrupling to take proper care of it, but I think that you are more responsible than that. So it is more likely that you found it only recently, and did not have time to clean it. You landed at the shore and began to walk through the City of the Dead, and at some point found the knife in an old tomb.'

'It's a cruel thing. From the Age of Insurrection, if I'm any judge,' the old woman said.

'And she has forgotten a good deal more than I ever knew,' the old man said fondly. 'You will have to learn its ways, or it could kill you.'

'Hush!' the old woman said sharply. 'Nothing should be changed!'

'Perhaps nothing can be changed,' the old man said.

'Then I would be a machine,' the old woman said, 'and I don't like that thought.'

'At least you would not need to worry. But I will be careful. Pay no attention to me, youngster. My mind wanders these days, as my wife will surely remind you at every opportunity.'

The old man and the old woman had been married a long time. They both wore long, layered shifts over woollen trousers, and shared the same set of gestures, as if love were a kind of imitation game in which the best of both participants was mingled. They called themselves Osric and Beatrice, but Yama suspected that those were not their real names. They both had an air of sly caution which suggested that they were withholding much, although Yama felt that Osric wanted to tell him more than he was allowed to know. Beatrice was strict with her husband, but she favoured Yama with fond glances, and while he had been stricken with fever she had spent hours bathing his forehead with cloths moistened with oil of spikenard, and had fed him infusions of honey and herbs, crooning to him as if he were her child. While Osric was bent by age, his tall, slender wife carried herself like a young dancer.

Later, husband and wife sat side by side on the ledge beneath the narrow window of the little room, watching Yama eat a bowl of boiled maize. It was his first solid food since he had woken. They said that they were members of the Department of the Curators of the City of the Dead, an office of the civil service which had been disbanded centuries ago.

'But my ancestors stayed on,' Beatrice told Yama. 'They believed that the dead should not be abandoned, and fought against dissolution. There was quite a little war. Of course, we're much diminished now. Most would say that we had vanished long ago, if they had heard of us at all, but we still hold some of the more important parts of the city.'

'You might say that I am an honorary member of the department, by marriage,' Osric said. 'Here, I cleaned the knife for you.'

He laid the long, curved knife at the end of the bed.

Yama looked at it and discovered that although it had saved his life he feared it; it was as if Osric had set a live snake at his feet. He said, 'I found it in a tomb in the cliffs by the river. I put out my hand in the dark, and there it was.'

He remembered how the knife had kindled its eldritch glow when he had held it up, wonderingly, before his face. But when Lob had picked it up, the horrible thing had happened. The knife was different things to different people.

Osric laid a bony finger beside his nose. The tip of the finger was missing. He said, 'I used a little white vinegar to take the bloom of age from the metal, and every decad or so you should rub it down with a cloth touched to mineral oil. But it will not need sharpening, and it will repair itself, within limits. It had been imprinted with a copy of the personality of its previous owner, but I have purged that ghost. You should practise with it as often as you can, and handle it at least once a day, and so it will come to know you.'

'Osric—'

'A little practical knowledge will not hurt anything,' Osric told his wife. 'Handle it often, Yama. The more you handle it, the better it will know you. And leave it in the sunlight, or between places of different temperature – placing the point in a fire is good. Otherwise it will take energy from you again. It had lain in the dark a long time. That was why you were hurt by it when you used it. I would guess it belonged to an officer of the cavalry, dead long ages past. They were issued to those fighting in the rain forests two thousand leagues downriver.'

Yama said stupidly, 'But the war started only forty years ago.'

'This was another war, dear,' Beatrice said. 'In the younger days of the world.'

The tomb where Yama had found the knife was a long way from the home of Osric and Beatrice, the last stronghold of the curators of the City of the Dead, in the foothills of the Rim Mountains. He had not realised until then the true extent of the necropolis.

'The dead outnumber the living,' Osric said, 'and this has been the burial place for Ys since the construction of Confluence. Until this last, decadent age, at least.'

Yama gathered that there were not many curators left now, and that most of those were old. This was a place where the past was stronger than the present. The Department of the Curators of the City of the Dead had once been responsible for preparation and arrangement of the deceased, whom they called clients, and for the care and maintenance of the graves, tombs and memorials, the picture slates and aspects of the dead. It had been a solemn and complex task. For instance, Yama learned that there had been four methods of dealing with clients: by interment, including burial or entombment; by cremation, either by fire or by acids; by exposure, either in a byre raised above the ground or by dismemberment; and by water.

'Which I understand is the only method used these days,' Osric said. 'It has its place, but many die a long way from the Great River, and besides, many communities are too close together, so that the corpses of those upriver foul the water of those below them. Consider, Yama. Much of Confluence is desert or mountain. Interment in the soil is rare, for there is little enough land for cultivation. For myriad upon myriad years, our ancestors built tombs for their dead, or burned them on pyres or dissolved them in tanks of acid. But building tombs takes much labour and is suitable only for the rich, for the badly constructed tombs of the poor are soon ransacked by wild animals. And these days firewood is in as short supply as arable land, for the same reasons, and dissolution in acid is usually considered aesthetically displeasing. How much more natural, in the circumstances, to expose the client to the brothers of the air. It is how I wish my body to be disposed of, when my time comes. Beatrice has promised it to me. The world will end before I die, of course, but I think there will still be birds somewhere . . .'

'You forgot preservation,' Beatrice said sharply. 'He always does,' she told Yama. 'He disapproves.'

'Ah, but I did not forget. It is merely a variation on interment. Without a tomb, the preserved body is merely fodder for the animals, or a curiosity in a sideshow.'

'Some are turned into stone,' Beatrice said. 'It is mostly done by exposing the client to lime water.'

'And then there is mummification, and desiccation, either by vacuum or by chemical treatment, and treatment by tar, or by ice.' Osric ticked off the variations on his fingers. 'But you know full well that I mean the most common method, and the most decadent. Which is to say, those clients who were preserved while still alive, in the hope of physical resurrection in ages to come. Instead, robbers opened the tombs and took what there was of value, and threw away the bodies for wild animals to devour, or burned them as fuel, or ground them up for fertiliser. The brave cavalry officer who once wielded your knife in battle, young Yama, was in all probability burned to fuel the furnace that melted the alloy stripped from his tomb. Perhaps one of the tomb robbers picked up the knife, and it attacked him. He dropped it, and you found it an age later, knowing nothing of its history. Only the Preservers outrun time. I remember that I played amongst the tombs as a child, teasing the aspects who still spoke for those whose memories were otherwise lost to the living. I did not know then that the aspects were bound to oblige my foolishness; the young are needlessly cruel because they know no better.'

Beatrice straightened her back, held up her hand, and recited a verse:

Let fame, that all hunt after in their lives,
Live registered upon our brazen tombs,
And then grace us in the disgrace of death;
When, spite of the cormorant devouring time,
The endeavour of this present breath may buy
That honour which shall bate his scythe's keen edge,
And makes us heirs to all eternity.

Yama guessed that this was from the Puranas, but Beatrice said that it was far older. 'There are too few of us to remember everything left by the dead, but we do what we can, and we are a long-lived race.'

There was much more to the tasks of the curators than preparation of their clients, and in the next two days Yama learned something about the care of tombs and the preservation of the artefacts with which clients had been interred, each according to the customs of their bloodline. Osric and Beatrice fed him vegetable broths, baked roots and succulent young okra, corn and green beans fried in airy batter. He was getting better, and was beginning to feel a restless curiosity. He had not broken any bones, but his ribs were badly bruised and muscles in his back and arms had been torn. There were numerous half-healed cuts on his limbs and torso, too, and the fever had left him very weak, as if most of his blood had been drained.

Beatrice cleaned out the worst of his wounds; she explained that the stone dust embedded in them would otherwise leave scars. As soon as he could, Yama started to exercise, using the drills taught him by Sergeant Rhodean. He practised with the knife, too, mastering his instinctive revulsion. He handled it each day, as Osric had suggested, and otherwise left it on the ledge beneath the narrow window, where it would catch the midday sun. To begin with, he had to rest for an hour or more between each set of exercises, but he ate large amounts of the curators' plain food and felt his strength return. At last, he was able to climb the winding stairs to the top of the hollow crag.

He had to stop and rest frequently, but finally stepped out of the door of a little hut into the open air under an achingly blue sky. The air was clean and cold, as heady as wine after the stuffy room in which he had lain for so long.

The hut was set at one end of the top of the crag, which was so flat that it might have been sheared off by someone wielding a gigantic blade. Possibly this was more or less what had been done: during the construction of Confluence energies had been deployed to move whole mountains and shape entire landscapes as easily as a gardener might set out a bed of flowers.

The flat top of the crag was no bigger than the Great Hall of the peel-house, and was divided into tiny plots by low drystone walls. Squash and yams, corn and kale, rows of cane fruits, watered by a complicated system of cisterns and gutters. At the far end, Beatrice and Osric were feeding doves which fluttered around a round-topped dovecote built of unmortared stone.

The crag stood at the edge of a winding ridge above a gorge so deep that its bottom was lost in shadow. Other flat-topped crags stood along the ridge, their smooth sides fretted with windows and balconies. There was a scattering of tombs on broad ledges cut into the gorge's steep sides, huge buildings with blind, whitewashed walls under pitched roofs of red tile that stood amidst manicured lawns and groves of tall trees. Beyond the far side of the gorge, other ridges stepped up towards the sky, and beyond the farthest ridge the peaks of the Rim Mountains seemed to float free above indistinct blue and purple masses, shining in the light of the sun.

Yama threaded his way along the winding paths to the little patch of grass where Beatrice and Osric were scattering grain. Doves rose up in a whir of wings as he approached. Osric raised a hand in greeting and said, 'This is the valley of the kings of the first days. Some maintain that Preservers are buried here but, if that is true, the location is hidden from us.'

'It must be a lot of work, looking after these tombs.'

The mirror lenses of Osric's spectacles flashed light at Yama. 'They maintain themselves,' the old man said, 'and there are mechanisms which prevent people from approaching too closely. It was once our job to keep people away for their own good, but only those who know this place come here now.'

'Few know of it,' Beatrice added, 'and fewer come.'

She held out a long, skinny arm. A dove immediately perched on her hand, and she drew it to her breast and stroked its head with a bony forefinger until it began to coo.

Yama said, 'I was brought a long way.'

Osric nodded. His wispy beard blew sideways in the wind. 'The Department of the Curators of the City of the Dead once maintained a city that stretched from these mountains to the river, a day's hard ride distant.'

Beatrice suddenly flung out her hands. The dove rose into the wind and circled high above the patchwork of tiny fields. She watched it for a minute and then said, 'I think it's time we showed Yama why he was brought here.'

'I would like to know who brought me here, to begin with.'

'As long as you do not know who saved you,' Osric said, 'they are not obliged to honour their debt to you. And that is their wish. For now, at least.'

Yama nodded, remembering that after he had saved Caphis from the trap the fisherman's life had become his obligation.

'One of our goats had disappeared,' Beatrice said.

'The leopard took her,' Osric said. 'Just like it took the other one, at the beginning of winter.'

'Or perhaps she wandered off. I found no sign of a leopard this time,' Beatrice said. 'I was looking for her in the fields below, and found you and the person who saved you close to the entrance to the roads in the keelways.'

'The keelways?'

'You will see them later,' Beatrice said. 'As for why you were brought here, I think it is time we showed you.'

Descending the long spiral of stairs was easier than climbing up, but Yama felt that if not for him Osric and Beatrice would have bounded away eagerly even though he was so much younger than they. The stairs ended at a balcony that girdled the crag halfway between its flat top and its base. A series of arched doorways opened off the balcony, and Osric immediately disappeared through one. Yama would have followed, but Beatrice took his arm and guided him to a stone bench by the low wall of the balcony. Sunlight drenched the ancient stone; Yama was grateful for its warmth.

'What do you think of our home?' Beatrice said.

'It is very beautiful. And very old, I think.'

'It is the oldest part of the City of the Dead,' Beatrice said. 'We, who are the last of our kind, have retreated to the place built by the first of our kind. We have done what we can to preserve it, but it cannot be preserved forever, of course. Time sweeps everything away. Even Confluence will fall, one day.'

Yama said, 'You sound like those who believe that the war against the heretics is the war at the end of all things.'

Beatrice said, 'In every war, those who fight hope for a victory that will bring an end to all conflict. Sooner or later they will be right. There have been many wars, more than anyone can remember, but every series of events must reach an ending. Although it is impossible to know if you have reached the end of one thing until everything else ends.'

Yama said, 'I know that the heretics will be defeated. The Ancients of Days claimed to be the distant ancestors of the Preservers, but that means only that they and their followers are inferior, just as the ancestors of the Shaped bloodlines are inferior to their descendants.'

Beatrice smiled. 'You are still young, and believe that the present is stronger than the past.'

'With respect, perhaps you and your husband live for the past, while I live for the future.'

'Ah, but which future, I wonder? Osric suspects that there might be more than one. As for us, it is our duty to preserve the past so that it can inform the future, and this place is where the past is strongest. There are wonders interred here which could end the war in an instant if wielded by one side, or end the world if used by both against each other.

'The living bury the dead and move on, and forget. We remember. Above all, that is our duty. There are record keepers in Ys who claim to be able to trace the bloodlines of Confluence back to their first members. My family preserves the tombs of those ancestors, their bodies and their artefacts. The record keepers would claim that words are stronger than the phenomena they describe, and that only words endure while all else fails, but we know that even words change. Stories are mutable, and in any story each generation finds a different lesson, and with each telling a story changes slightly until it is no longer the thing it was. The king who prevails against the hero who would have brought redeeming light to the world becomes after many tellings of the story a hero saving the world from fire, and the light-bringer becomes a fiend. Only things remain what they are. They are themselves. Words are merely representations of things; but we have the things themselves. And they are much more powerful than their representations.'

Yama thought of the Aedile, who put so much trust in objects preserved in the soil. He said, 'My father seeks to understand the past by the wreckage it leaves behind. Perhaps it is not the stories that change but the past itself, for all that lives of the past is the meaning we invest in what remains.'

Behind him, Osric said, 'You have been taught by a record keeper. That is just what one of those near-sighted bookworms would say, bless them all, each and every one. Well, there is more of the past than can be found in books. That is a lesson I have learnt over and again, young man. All that is ordinary and human passes away without record, and all that remains are stories of priests and philosophers, heroes and kings. Much is made of the altar stones and sacralis of temples, but nothing of the cloisters where lovers rendezvoused and friends gossiped, and the courtyards where children played. That is the false lesson of history. Still, we can peer into random scenes of the past and wonder at their import. That is what I have brought you.'

Osric carried something square and flat under his arm, covered with a white cloth. He removed the cloth with a flourish, revealing a thin rectangle of milky stone which he laid in a pool of sunlight on the tiled floor of the balcony.

Yama said, 'My father collects these picture slates.'

'He took them for important research, perhaps,' Osric said, 'but I am sorry to hear of it. Their proper resting place is not in a collection, but in the tomb in which they were installed.'

'I have always wondered why they need to drink sunlight to work, when they were buried away in darkness.'

'The tombs drink sunlight, too,' Osric said, 'and distribute it amongst their components according to need. Outside the tomb, without their usual power source, the pictures must drink their own draught of sunlight.'

'Be quiet, husband,' Beatrice said. 'It wakens. Watch it, Yama, and learn. This is all we can show you.'

Colours mingled and ran in the slate, seeming to swirl just beneath its surface. At first they were faint and amorphous, little more than pastel flows within the slate's milky depths, but gradually they brightened, running together in a sudden silvery flash.

For a moment Yama thought that the slate had turned into a mirror, reflecting his own eager face. But when he leaned closer the face within the slate turned as if to speak to someone beyond the frame of the picture, and he saw that it was the face of someone older than he was, a man with lines at the corners of his eyes and grooves at either side of his mouth. But the shape of the man's eyes and their round blue irises, and the shape of his face, his pale skin and the mop of wiry black hair – all these were so very like Yama's that he cried out in astonishment.

The man in the picture was talking now, and suddenly smiled at someone beyond the picture's frame, a frank, eager smile that turned Yama's heart. The man looked away and the view slid from his face to show the night sky. It was not the sky of Confluence, for it was full of stars, scattered like diamond chips carelessly thrown across black velvet. There was a frozen swirl of dull red light in the centre of the picture, and Yama saw that the stars around it seemed to be drawn into lines that curved in towards the red swirl. Stars streaked as the viewpoint of the picture moved, and for a moment it steadied on a flock of splinters of light hung against pure black, and then it faded.

Osric wrapped the white cloth around the slate. Immediately, Yama wanted to strip it away and see the picture blossom within the slate again, wanted to feast on the stranger's face, the stranger who was of his bloodline, wanted to understand the strange skies under which his long-dead ancestor had stood. His blood sang in his ears.

Beatrice handed him a square of lace-trimmed cloth. A handkerchief. Yama realised then that he was weeping, and dabbed the tears from his eyes.

Osric said, 'This is the place where the oldest tombs on Confluence can be found, but the picture is older than anything on Confluence, for it is older than Confluence itself. It shows the first stage in the construction of the Eye of the Preservers, and it shows the lands which the Preservers walked before they fell into the Eye and vanished into the deep past or the deep future, or perhaps into another universe entirely.'

'I would like to see the tomb. I want to see where you found this picture.'

Osric said, 'The Department of the Curators of the City of the Dead has kept the picture a long time, and if it once rested in a tomb, then it was so long ago that all records of that tomb are lost. Your bloodline walked Confluence at its beginning, and now it walks it again.'

Yama said, 'This is the second time that someone has hinted that I have a mysterious destiny, but no one will explain why or what it is.'

Beatrice told her husband, 'He'll discover it soon enough. We should not tell him more. What must be will be.'

Osric tugged at his beard. 'I do not know everything. What the hollow man said, for instance, or what lies beyond the end of the river. I have tried to remember it all over again, and I cannot.'

Beatrice took her husband's hands in her own and told Yama, 'He was hurt, and sometimes gets confused about what might happen and what has happened. Remember the slate. It's important.'

Yama said, 'I know less than you. Let me see the slate again. Perhaps there is something—'

Beatrice said, 'Perhaps it is your destiny to discover your past, dear. Only by knowing the past can you know yourself.'

Yama smiled, because that was precisely the motto which Zakiel used to justify his long lessons. It seemed to him that the curators of the dead and the librarians and archivists were so similar that they amplified trivial differences into a deadly rivalry, just as brothers feuded to assert their individuality.

'You have seen all that we can show you, Yama,' Osric said. 'We preserve the past as best we can, but we do not pretend to understand everything we preserve.'

Yama said formally, 'I thank you for showing me this wonder.'

But he thought that it proved only that others like him had lived long ago – he was more concerned with discovering if they still lived now, and where. What had Dr Dismas discovered in the archives of his department?

Beatrice stood with a graceful flowing motion. 'You cannot stay, Yama. You are a catalyst, and change is dangerous here.'

Yama said, 'If you would show me the way, I would go home at once.'

He said it with little hope, for he was convinced that the two curators were holding him prisoner. But Beatrice smiled and said, 'I will do better than that. I will take you.'

Osric said, 'You are stronger than you were when you arrived here, but not, I think, as strong as you can be. Let my wife help you, Yama. And remember us. We have served as best we can, and I feel that we have served well. When you discover your purpose, remember us.'

Beatrice said, 'Don't burden the poor boy, husband. He is too young. It is too early.'

'He is old enough to know his mind, I think. Remember that we are your friends, Yama.'

Yama bowed from the waist, as the Aedile had taught him, and turned to follow Beatrice, leaving her husband sitting in a pool of sunlight, his ravaged face made inscrutable by the mirror lenses of his spectacles, the blue uncharted mountain ridges framed by the pillars behind him, and the picture slate, wrapped in white cloth, on his lap.

Beatrice led Yama down a stair to a byre carved out of bare rock, divided by wooden pens, its floor covered with deep clean straw. Beyond was a steep slope of flower-starred turf and low, wind-carved stands of gorse that stretched along the side of the winding ridge, in the shadow of the chain of smooth-walled, flat-topped crags. Several goats scattered, wooden bells at their necks dully clacking, as he followed Beatrice along a path of trampled dirt to the truncated ruin of a slim tower. A plain wooden door opened onto a helical flight of steps that descended to a chamber where machines as big as houses stood half-buried in the stone floor. Yama and Beatrice walked past the machines, past the broad mouth of a pit in which long narrow tubes made of a metal as clear as glass fell into white mists a league or more below. Vast slow lightnings sparked and rippled in the transparent tubes. Yama felt a slow vibration through the soles of his feet, a pulse deeper than sound, and asked Beatrice about the function of these vast mechanisms.

'They are not in our care,' Beatrice said, 'and you are not ready to talk to them.'

She led him around the pit to a long hall with black keelrock walls, lit by balls of white fire hung beneath a high curved ceiling. Short corridors led off the hall on either side. Beatrice ushered Yama along one of them, into a small room which, once its door slid shut, began at once to hum and shake. Yama felt for a moment as if he had stepped over a cliff, and clutched at the rail which ran around the curved walls of the room.

'We fall down one of the roads in the keelways,' Beatrice said. 'Most people live on the surface now, but in ancient times the surface was a place where they came to play and meet, while they had their dwelling and working places underground. This is one of the old roads. It will return you to Aeolis in less than an hour.'

'Are these roads everywhere?'

'Once. No more. We have maintained a few beneath the City of the Dead, but many more no longer function, and beyond the limits of our jurisdiction things are worse. Everything fails at last. Even the universe will fall into itself eventually.'

'The Puranas say that is why the Preservers fled into the Eye. But if the universe will not end soon, then surely that is not why they fled. Zakiel could never explain that. He said it was not for me to question the Puranas.'

Beatrice laughed. It was like the tinkling of old, fragile bells. 'How like a librarian! But the Puranas contain many riddles, and there is no harm in admitting that not all the answers are obvious. Perhaps they are not even comprehensible to our small minds, but a librarian will never admit that any text in his charge is unfathomable. He must be the master of them all, and is shamed to admit any possible failure.'

'The slate showed the creation of the Eye. There is a sura in the Puranas, the forty-third sura, I think, which says that the Preservers made stars fall together, until their light grew too heavy to escape.'

'Perhaps. There is much we do not know about the past, Yama. Some heretics have claimed that the Preservers set us here for their own amusement, as certain bloodlines keep caged birds for amusement. All who believed it are safely dead an age ago, but it is still a dangerous thought.'

'Perhaps because it is true, or contains some measure of the truth.'

Beatrice regarded him with her bright eyes. She was a head taller than he was. 'Do not be bitter, Yama. You will find what you are looking for, although it may not be where you expect it. Ah, we are almost there.'

The room shuddered violently. Yama fell to his knees. The floor was padded with a kind of quilting, covered in an artificial material as slick and thin as satin.

Beatrice opened the door and Yama followed her into a long, cluttered room lit by shafts of wan light that fell through narrow slits in the rib-vault ceiling. It had once been a stone masons' workshop; Beatrice led Yama around half-finished carvings and benches scattered with tools, all abandoned an age ago and muffled by thick dust. At the door, she took out a hood of soft black cloth and said that she must blindfold him.

'We are a secret people, because we should not exist. Our department was disbanded long ago, and we survive only because we are good at hiding.'

'I understand. My father—'

'We are not frightened of discovery, but we have stayed hidden for so long that knowledge of where we are is valuable to certain people,' Beatrice said. 'I would not ask you to carry that burden. It would expose you to unnecessary danger. If you need to find us again, you will. I can safely promise that, I think. In return, will you promise that you won't mention us to the Aedile?'

'He will want to know where I have been.'

'You were ill. You recovered, and you returned. Perhaps you were nursed by one of the hill tribes. The Aedile will be so pleased to see you that he won't question you too closely. Will you promise?'

'As long as I do not have to lie to him. I think that I am done with lies.'

Beatrice was pleased by this. 'You were honest from the first, dear heart. Tell the Aedile as much of the truth as is good for him, and no more. Now, come with me.'

Blinded by the hood, Yama took Beatrice's hot, fine-boned hand, and allowed himself to be led once more. They walked a long way. He trusted this strange old woman, and he was thinking about the man of his bloodline, dead ages past.

At last she told him to stand still. Something cold and heavy was placed in his right hand. After a moment of silence, Yama lifted the hood away and saw that he was in a dark passageway walled with broken stone blocks, with stout tree roots thrust between their courses. A patch of sunlight fell through a narrow doorway at the top of a flight of steps whose stone treads had been worn away in the centre. He was holding the ancient metal knife which he had found in the tomb by the river's shore – or which had found him. A skirl of blue sparks flared along the outer edge of its blade and sputtered out one by one.

Yama looked around for Beatrice and thought he saw a patch of white float around the corner of a passageway. But when he ran after it, he found a stone wall blocking his way. He turned back to the sunlight. This place was familiar, but he did not recognise it until he climbed the stairs and stepped out into the ruins in the Aedile's garden, with the peel-house looming beyond masses of dark green rhododendrons.

11

PREFECT CORIN

Lob and the landlord of *The House of Ghost Lanterns* were arrested immediately after Yama had finished telling his story to the Aedile, and the next day were tried and sentenced to death for kidnap and sabotage. The Aedile also issued a warrant for the arrest of Dr Dismas, although he confided to Yama that he did not expect to see the apothecary again.

Yama had not told his father the whole story about his adventures. He had suppressed the part about Enobarbus, for he had come to believe that the young warlord had been corrupted by Dr Dismas's malign influence. And he had kept his promise to Beatrice, had said that after he had been attacked by Lob and Lud amongst the ransacked tombs of the Silent Quarter he had become lost in the far reaches of the City of the Dead, had fallen ill, and had not been able to return to the peel-house until he had recovered. It was not the whole truth, but the Aedile did not question him closely.

Yama was not allowed to attend the trial or leave the grounds of the peel-house, although he very much wanted to see Derev. The Aedile said that it was too dangerous. The families of Lob and the landlord would be looking for revenge, and the city was still on edge after the riots that had followed the failed siege of Dr Dismas's tower. Yama tried to contact Derev using mirror talk, but although he signalled for most of the afternoon there was no answering spark of light from the apartments that Derev's father had built on top of his godown by the old waterfront of the city. Sick at heart, Yama went to plead with Sergeant Rhodean, but the sergeant refused to provide an escort.

'And you're not to confuse the watchdogs and go sneaking out on your own, either,' Sergeant Rhodean said. 'Oh yes, lad, I know all about that trick. But see here, you can't rely on tricks to keep yourself out of trouble. They're more likely to get you into it instead. I won't risk having any of my men hurt rescuing you from your own foolishness, and think how it would look if we took you down there in the middle of a decad of armed soldiers. You'd start another riot. My men have already spent too much time looking for you after you disappeared, and they'll have their hands full in a couple of days. The department is sending a clerk to deal with the prisoners, but no extra troops. Pure foolishness on their part, but I'm the one who'll get blamed if something goes wrong.'

Sergeant Rhodean was much exercised by this, pacing in a tight circle on the red clay floor of the gymnasium as he talked. He was a small, thickset man, almost as wide as he was tall, as he liked to say. As always, his grey tunic and blue trousers were neatly pressed, his black knee-boots were spit-polished, and the scalp of his heavy, ridged skull was close-shaven and burnished with oil. He favoured his right leg, and the thumb and forefinger of his right hand were missing. He had been the Aedile's bodyguard long before the entire household had been exiled from the Palace of the Memory of the People, and had celebrated his hundredth birthday two years ago. He lived quietly with his wife, who was always trying to feed Yama because, she said, he needed to put some muscle on his long bones. They had two married daughters, six sons away fighting heretics, and two more who had been killed in the war.

Now he suddenly stopped pacing and looked at Yama as if for the first time. 'I see you're wearing that knife you found. Let's take a look at it.'

Yama had taken to hanging the knife from his belt by a loop of leather, with its blade tied flat against his thigh by a red ribbon. He undid the ribbon now, and unhooked the loop and held out the knife; Sergeant Rhodean put on thick-lensed spectacles which vastly magnified his yellow eyes, and peered closely at it for a long time. At last, he blew through his drooping moustache and said, 'It's old, and sentient, or at least partly so. Maybe as smart as one of the watchdogs. A good idea to carry it around. It will bond to you. You said you were ill, after using it?'

'It gave out a blue light. And when Lob picked it up it turned into something horrible.'

'Well now, lad, it had to get its energy from somewhere for tricks like that, especially after all the time in the dark. So it took it from you.'

'I leave it in sunlight,' Yama said.

'Do you?' Sergeant Rhodean gave Yama a shrewd look. 'Then I can't tell you much more. What did you clean it with? White vinegar? As good as anything, I suppose. Let's see you make a few passes with it. It will stop you brooding over your true love.'

For the next hour, Sergeant Rhodean instructed Yama on how to make best use of the knife against a variety of imaginary opponents. Yama found himself beginning to enjoy the exercises, and was sorry when the sergeant called a halt. He had spent many happy hours in the gymnasium, with its mingled odours of clay dust and old sweat and rubbing alcohol, its deep underwater light filtered through green-tinted windows high up in the whitewashed walls, the rubber wrestling mats rolled up like the shed cocoons of giant caterpillars, the rack of parallel bars, the open cases of swords and knives, javelins and padded staves, the straw archery targets stacked behind the vaulting horse, the battered wooden torsos of the tilting dummies, the frames hung with pieces of plastic and resin and metal armour.

'We'll do some more work tomorrow, lad,' Sergeant Rhodean said at last. 'You need to work on your backhand. You aim too high, at the chest instead of the belly. Any opponent worth their salt would spot that in an instant. Of course, a knife like this is really intended for close work by a cavalryman surrounded by enemies, and you might do better carrying a long sword or a revolver when walking around the city. But now I have to drill the men. The clerk is coming tomorrow, and I suppose your father will want an honour guard for him.'

But the clerk sent from Ys to oversee the executions slipped unnoticed into the peel-house early the next morning, and the first time Yama saw him was when the Aedile summoned him to an audience that afternoon.

'The townspeople already believe that you have blood on your hands,' the Aedile said. 'I do not wish to see any more trouble. So I have come to a decision.'

Yama felt his heart turn over, although he already knew that this was no ordinary interview. He had been escorted to the Aedile's receiving chamber by one of the soldiers of the house guard, who now stood in front of the tall double doors, resplendent in burnished helmet and corselet and scarlet hose, his pike at parade rest. Yama perched on an uncomfortable backless seat while the Aedile paced about restlessly. He was dressed in a tunic embroidered with silver and gold. His sable robe of office hung on a rack by his chair.

The clerk who had been sent from Ys to supervise the executions stood in the shadows by the small private door that led, via a helical stairway, to the Aedile's private chambers. Yama watched him out of the corner of his eye. He was a tall slender man of the Aedile's bloodline, dressed in a plain homespun tunic and grey leggings. A close-clipped black pelt covered his head and face, with a broad white stripe, like a badger's marking, on the left side of his face. Yama had heard from the stable hands that the clerk had disembarked from an ordinary lugger, armed with only a stout ironshod staff and with only a rolled blanket on his back, but that when the Aedile had met him at the gate he had prostrated himself at the man's feet as if he was a Hierarch risen from the files.

'I don't think he expected someone so high up in the Committee for Public Safety,' the foreman, Torin, had said.

But the clerk did not look like anyone important. He could have been any one of the thousands of ordinary scribes who plied pens in cells deep in the Palace of the Memory of the People, as indistinguishable from one another as ants.

The Aedile stood before one of the great tapestries that decorated the walls of the high, square room. It depicted the seeding of Confluence. Plants and animals raining out of a blaze of light towards a bare plain crossed by silvery loops of water; birds soaring through the air; little groups of naked men and women of various bloodlines standing on wisps of cloud, hands modestly shielding their genitals and breasts.

Yama had always loved this tapestry, but after his conversations with the curators of the City of the Dead he knew that it was a false vision, a dream that exaggerated and distorted the plain truth. Everything in the peel-house had seemed to have changed after he had returned. The house was smaller; the gardens were cramped and neglected; the people were preoccupied with small matters, their backs bent to routine labour so that, like peasants planting a paddy field, they failed to see the great events of the world rushing above their heads.

At last, the Aedile turned and said, 'It was always my plan to apprentice you to the department, Yama. You are not of my bloodline, but you are my son, now and always, and you are determined and ambitious, and I have great hopes for you. Zakiel says that you are the best pupil he has known. Sergeant Rhodean believes that in a few years you will be able to best him in archery and fencing, although he adds that your horse-riding skills still require a little attention. And I think that you have the potential to become a great power in the department. I was going to wait until you reached your majority before I entered you for an apprenticeship, but after what has happened . . . Well, I am sure you know that you cannot remain here.'

'I am not afraid of anyone in Aeolis, father. And I am not afraid to show them that I am not afraid.'

But Yama's protest was a formality. In Ys there were records that went back to the foundation of Confluence. Beatrice and Osric had shown him a slate that had displayed the likeness of an ancestor of his bloodline; in Ys, he might learn who that man had been. He might even find his mother, or his true father, or a brother or a sister. Anything was possible. He was eager to kick the dust of this sleepy, corrupt little city from his heels and begin his search, and he knew, more than ever, that he could not serve as an apprentice. But he could not tell his father that, of course, and guilt burned in his chest like a coal.

'I'm glad you're so confident,' the Aedile said. 'But you can't spend your life looking over your shoulder, Yama, and that is what you would have to do if you stayed here. One day, sooner or later, Lob and Lud's brothers would attempt to exact revenge. That they were the sons of the Constable of Aeolis makes this more likely, not less. Any attack on you would do more than satisfy their family's thirst for revenge. It would also undermine their father's status. It would make him look weak, and fortify your attacker.

'But it is not the townspeople I fear, however. Dr Dismas has fled, but he may not have given up his plans to kidnap you or cause you harm. Or he may have sold his information to some other villain. In Aeolis you are a wonder; in Ys, which is the fount of all the wonders of the world, you'll be able to hide, anonymous amongst uncountable multitudes of every bloodline. Here, I command just three decads of soldiers; in Ys, you will be safely lodged in the heart of the department. You are too young to begin an apprenticeship, but Prefect Corin has kindly agreed to find you a position.'

From his place in the shadows, Prefect Corin said, 'I'll start you off as a message boy, and if you do well at that you will become my assistant.'

'You do us both a great favour,' the Aedile said.

Yama knew then that this had been Prefect Corin's idea, not his father's, and the flame of his guilt immediately diminished. He would not be betraying his father by running away; he would be escaping servitude, payment for a debt he did not owe. He stood and turned to the Prefect, bowed and thanked him, and said, 'When shall I leave?'

The Aedile clasped his hands and bowed in turn. It was a disturbingly submissive gesture. 'You will go with Prefect Corin, after he has concluded his business here. He will escort you to Ys, and to the offices of the department in the Palace of the Memory of the People.'

'We will leave tomorrow morning,' Prefect Corin said. 'In cases like this, it is not advisable to linger once justice has been administered.'

Prefect Corin had already visited Lob and the landlord of *The House of Ghost Lanterns*. They were imprisoned in the oubliette of the peel-house, and were to be immolated outside the city's walls that evening. Afterwards, their ashes would be scattered on the wind, so that their families would have no memorial and their souls would never find rest until the Preservers woke all the dead at the end of the universe.

'I know it is very sudden and unexpected,' the Aedile said. 'A great change, but also a great opportunity. I will visit you in Ys as soon as I can be certain that there will be no more trouble here. In the meantime, I hope you will remember me with affection.'

'You have done more for me than I deserve, or can ever hope to repay,' Yama said.

It was a formal sentiment, and sounded trite, but he felt a sudden flood of affection for his father then, and would have embraced him if Prefect Corin had not been watching.

'Quite, quite,' the Aedile said, and turned as if to study the tapestry again. It seemed that Prefect Corin made him uncomfortable, too.

Prefect Corin cleared his throat. It was a very small sound in the large room, but father and son turned to stare at him as if he had shot a pistol at the painted ceiling.

'If we are finished here,' he said, 'it is time to shrive the prisoners.'

Two hours after sunset, Father Quine, the priest of the temple of Aeolis, walked barefoot and bareheaded in his orange robes up the winding road from the city to the peel-house. Ananda accompanied him, carrying a chrism of oil. The Aedile greeted them formally at the peel-house gate, and escorted them to the oubliette so that they could hear the final confessions of the prisoners.

Yama had no part in the ceremony. He had been exiled to the kitchen, but that had changed, too. He was no longer a part of the bustle and banter. The scullions and the kitchen boys and the three cooks politely replied to his remarks, but their manner was subdued. He wanted to tell them that he was still Yama, the boy who had wrestled with most of the kitchen boys and cheeked the scullions to make them chase him, and had been cuffed by the cooks when he had tried to steal bits of food. But in truth he was no longer that boy.

After a while, oppressed by the polite deference to a station he neither wanted nor deserved, Yama went out to watch the soldiers drilling in the slanting sunlight, and that was where Ananda found him.

The young sizar's head was freshly shaved – there was a cut above his right ear, painted with yellow iodine. His cheeks were rouged and his eyes enlarged by clever use of blue paint and gold leaf, and he gave off a smell of cloves and cinnamon. It was the scent of the oil with which the prisoners had been anointed.

Ananda knew how to judge Yama's mood. The two friends stood side by side in companionable silence and watched the soldiers make squares and lines in the dusty sunlight. Sergeant Rhodean's barked commands echoed off the high wall of the peel-house. After a while, Ananda pulled a pouch from inside his robe, spilled hulled pistachio kernels into his palm, and offered them to Yama.

Yama shook his head, and said, 'I have to go away tomorrow.'

'I know.'

'With that little badger of a clerk. He is to be my master. I have to prove that I can run errands, and then he will teach me how to copy records and write up administrative reports.'

'You have other plans,' Ananda said, around a mouthful of pistachios. 'You would rather be a hero. A soldier.'

'I will not submit to the Prefect, Ananda. I cannot. I want to search for my family, and find out all I can about my bloodline.'

'As to that, didn't Dr Dismas tell you what he had discovered? That was why he kidnapped you, wasn't it? And the tavern landlord said that he overhead Dr Dismas talking to you about your family.'

'It was little more than vague hints. I think he pretended to know more than he did. He told me that I would have to look beyond Ys if I wanted to find my family, but I think that I should start my search in the Department of Apothecaries and Chirurgeons. I will find out what Dr Dismas discovered there, to begin with.'

'I'm never going to leave Aeolis,' Ananda said. 'My master will die, and I will take his place, and begin to teach the new sizar, who will be a boy just like me. And so on.'

'You could come to Ys with me,' Yama said.

'And we'd have a high old time,' Ananda said. 'All kinds of adventures.'

'Why not?'

They smiled at each other. Ananda tipped the last of the pistachios into his mouth and dusted his palms.

'At least you know who you are,' Yama said. 'And you will get to see the execution. I am not allowed to attend.'

'Of course not. It would be unseemly.'

'I would like to prove that I am brave enough to see it.'

'What happened to you out there, Yama? We haven't had a chance to talk before, and we might not have the chance to talk again for a long time.'

'You mean apart from escaping Dr Dismas, fighting Lob and Lud, and getting lost in the City of the Dead?'

'You don't have to talk about it if you don't want to. But if you think it might help, I'll gladly listen. And not just to satisfy my curiosity.'

'I still don't understand all of it. But one thing I do know. I found something. Something important.'

'Something pointing you towards your family, your bloodline?'

Yama stepped hard on the urge to tell his friend about the two curators, Osric and Beatrice, and the picture they had shown him.

'I want to explain, but not here, not now. Meet me tonight. Afterwards.'

'After I have performed my small part in the solemn civic event.'

'Bring Derev. I tried to send a message to her by mirror talk, but no one replied. I want her to hear my story. I want to . . .'

'I know. There will be a service. We will exculpate the Prefect after he sets the torch to the pyre. Then there'll be a formal meal. I'm not invited to that, of course, but my master will be there. It begins an hour after sunset. I'll come and find you then. And I'll find a way of telling Derev.'

'Have you ever seen an execution, Ananda?'

'Not yet. But I know everything that will happen, and I know what I have to do.'

'I know that you will not disgrace your master.'

'I hope I will not disgrace myself,' Ananda said.

They looked at each other, looked away.

Ananda said, 'Did you know that the landlord was an addict of the drug that Dismas used? Dismas supplied him with it, and in return he had to do everything Dismas asked of him. He put that forward in an attempt to win mitigation of the death sentence, but it was dismissed.'

Yama remembered Dr Dismas grinding the dried beetle and apricot-scented liquid into paste, remembered the slow relaxation in the apothecary's face after he had injected himself.

'The landlord did it for cantharides,' he said. 'And Lob and Lud did it for money.'

'But only Lob got paid,' Ananda said. 'He was drunk when he was arrested, and he'd been buying the whole quarter drinks for several days before that. I think he knew that you'd be back. He was getting up the courage to confront you.'

'I wonder who paid him. It wasn't Dr Dismas.'

Ananda had turned to watch the soldiers on the parade square, forming up into two lines that marched off towards the main gate, with Sergeant Rhodean loudly counting the pace as he marched at their head. 'Lob and Lud had something in common with you, you know. They also wanted to escape from Aeolis.'

Yama wanted to watch Lob and the landlord of the tavern leave the peel-house for the place of execution, but even that was denied him. Zakiel found him at a window, staring down at the courtyard where soldiers were harnessing two horses to a wagon that had been freshly painted white, and took him off to the library.

'We have only a little time, master, and there is so much to tell you.'

'Then why begin to try? Are you going to the execution, Zakiel?'

'It is not my place, master.'

'I suppose that my father told you to keep me occupied. But I want to see it, Zakiel. I think that imagining it is worse than actually being there.'

'I have taught you something, then.'

Zakiel was a tall, gaunt man with a long face and a shaven skull with a bony crest. His black skin shone in the yellow light of the flickering electric sconce, and the muscles of his heavy jaw moved under the skin on either side of the crest when he smiled. As a party piece, at high-day feasts, he cracked walnuts between his strong, square teeth. As always, he wore a grey tunic and grey leggings, and sandals with rubber soles that squeaked on the polished marquetry of the paths between the library stacks. He also wore a slave collar around his neck, but it was made of a light alloy rather than iron, and was covered with a circlet of lace.

He said, 'I could tell you exactly what will happen, if you like. I was instructed in it, because it is believed that to tell a prisoner exactly what will happen to him will make it more endurable. But it was the cruellest thing they did to me. Far crueller than being put to the question.'

Zakiel had been under sentence of death before he had come to work for the Aedile. Yama, who had momentarily forgotten that, was mortified, and apologised at once.

'You would prefer to see it than hear about it,' Zakiel said. 'You trust experience, and your senses, over words. Yet the long-dead men and women who wrote the volumes which stand about us had the same appetites as us, the same fears, the same ambitions. All we know of the world passes through our sensory organs and is reduced to electrical and chemical impulses in certain nerve fibres. When you open one of these books and read of events that happened before you were born, some of those nerve fibres are stimulated in exactly the same way. There are certain mages who claim to be able to read minds, and mountebanks who claim to have discovered ancient machines that print out a person's thoughts, or project them in a sphere of glass or crystalline metal, but the mages and mountebanks lie. Only books allow us to share another's thoughts. By reading them we see the world through the senses and sensibilities of their authors. And if those authors are wiser than us, or more knowledgeable, or more sensitive, then so are we, while we read. I will say no more than this. I know you would read the world directly, and tomorrow you will no longer have to listen to old Zakiel. But I would give you something, if I may. A slave owns nothing, not even his own life, so this is more in the nature of a loan than a gift. But I have the Aedile's permission.'

Zakiel led Yama deeper into the stacks, where books crowded two or three deep on shelves that bent under their weight. He pulled a ladder from a recess, settled its hooked top on the lip of the highest shelf, and climbed up. He fussed up there for a minute, blowing dust from one book after another, and finally climbed down with a volume no bigger than his hand.

'I knew I had it,' he said, 'although I have not touched it since I first catalogued the library. Even the Aedile does not know of it. It was left by one of his predecessors – that is the way the library has grown, and why there is so much of little value. Yet some hold that gems are engendered in mud, and this book is such a gem. It is yours.'

It was bound in a black, artificial stuff that, although scuffed at the corners, shone as if newly made after Zakiel had wiped away the dust with the hem of his tunic. Yama received it from the librarian, and riffled its pages. They were stiff and slick, and seemed to contain hidden depths. When he tilted the pages, images came and went in the margins of the crisp double-columned print. He had expected some rare history of Ys, or a bestiary, like those he had loved to read when he was younger, but this appeared to be no more than a copy of the Puranas.

'How could my father allow you to give me this book, if he does not know he owns it?'

Zakiel cracked his knuckles. They were swollen, like all his joints: his fingers looked like strings of nuts. 'I asked if I could give you a volume of the Puranas, and so I have. It is very old, and differs in some details from that which I have taught you. An edition that has long been suppressed, and perhaps the only copy that survives.'

'How is it is different?'

'You must read all of it to find out, and remember what I have taught you. And so my teachings will continue, in some fashion. And you should also study the pictures. Modern editions do not have pictures, of course.'

Yama, who had been tilting the pages of the book to the light as he turned them, suddenly felt a shock of recognition. There in the margin of one of the last pages was the view he had glimpsed behind the face of his ancestor, the view of stars streaming towards a dull glow.

He said, 'I will read every word in it, Zakiel. I promise.'

For a moment, Zakiel stared at Yama in silence, his eyes black beneath the bony shelf of his brow. Then the librarian smiled and clapped dust from his big, bony hands. 'Very good, master. Very good. Now we will drink tea, and talk about the history of the department of which, when you reach Ys, you will become the newest and youngest member.'

'With respect, Zakiel, I am sure that the history of the department will be the first thing I will be taught when I arrive in Ys, and no doubt the clerk will have some words on it during our journey.'

'I do not think that Prefect Corin is a man who wastes words,' Zakiel said. 'And he does not see himself as a teacher.'

'My father would have you occupy my mind. I understand. Well then, I would like to hear something of the history of another department. One that was broken up a long time ago.'

12

THE EXECUTION

After sunset, Yama climbed to the heliograph platform that circled the top of the peel-house's towers. He uncapped the telescope and, turning it on the heavy steel gimbals which floated in sealed oil baths, lined up its declinational and equatorial axes in a combination he knew as well as his own name.

Beyond the darkening vanishing point, the tops of the towers that rose up from the heart of Ys shone in the last light of the sun like a cluster of fiery needles floating high above the world, higher than the naked peaks of the Rim Mountains. Ys! In his room, Yama had spent a little time gazing at his old map before reluctantly rolling it up and putting it away. He had traced the roads that crossed the barrens of the coastal plains, the passes through the mountains that embraced the city. He vowed that in a handful of days he would stand at the bases of those towers a free man, ready to begin his search for the truth about his origins and his bloodline.

When he put up the telescope and leaned at the rail, with warm air gusting around him, he saw prickles of light flickering in the middle distance. Messages. The air was full of messages, talking of war, of faraway battles and sieges at the midpoint of the world.

Yama walked to the other side of the tower and stared out across the wide shallow valley of the Breas towards Aeolis, and saw with a little shock that the execution pyre had already been kindled. The point of light flickered like a baleful star fallen to the ground outside the wall of the little city.

'They would have killed me,' he said, trying out the words. 'They would have killed me for cantharides and a little cash.'

He watched for a long time, until the distant fire began to dim and was outshone by the ordinary lights of the city. Lob and the landlord of *The House of Ghost Lanterns* were dead. The Aedile and the colourless clerk, Prefect Corin, would be in grave procession towards the temple, led by Father Quine and flanked by Sergeant Rhodean's men in polished black armour.

Yama's supper had been set out in his room, but he left it and went down to the kitchen and, armoured by his new authority, hacked a wedge from a wheel of cheese and took a melon, a bottle of yellow wine, and one of the loaves of date bread that had been baked that morning. He cut through the kitchen gardens, fooled the watchdogs for what might be the last time, and walked along the high road before plunging down the steep slope of the bluff and following the paths along the tops of the dykes which divided the flooded paeonin fields.

The Breas made a rushing noise in the darkness as it ran swiftly over the flat rocks of its bed. At the waterlift, two oxen plodded side by side around their circle, harnessed to the trimmed trunk of a young pine. This spar turned the shaft that, groaning as if in protest at its eternal torment, lifted a chain of buckets from the river and tipped them in a never-ending cascade into the channels which fed the irrigation system of the fields. The oxen walked in their circle under a roof of palm fronds, tails rhythmically slapping their dung-spattered flanks. Now and then they snatched a mouthful of the fodder scattered around the perimeter of their circular path, but mostly they walked with their heads down, from nowhere to nowhere.

No, Yama thought. I will not serve.

He sat on an upturned stone a little distance off the path and ate meltingly sweet slices of melon while he waited. The oxen plodded around and around, turning the groaning shaft. Frogs peeped in the flooded fields. Beyond the city, at the mouth of the Breas, the misty light of the Arm of the Warrior was lifting above the farside horizon. It would rise a little later each night, a little further downriver. Soon it would not rise at all, and the Eye of the Preservers would appear above the upriver vanishing point, and it would be summer. But before then Yama would be in Ys.

Two people were coming along the path, shadows moving through the twilight. Yama waited until they had gone past before he whistled sharply.

'We thought you might not be here,' Ananda said as he walked up to where Yama sat.

'Well met,' Derev said, at Ananda's shoulder. 'O, well met, Yama!'

She rushed forward and hugged him. Her light-boned body, her long slim arms and legs, her heat, her scent. Yama was always surprised to discover that Derev was taller than himself. His love rekindled in her embrace, but he disengaged from her and stepped back.

Derev stared at him. The galaxy's light set blue sparks in her large dark eyes. 'What is it, Yama?'

'I am glad you came,' Yama said. 'There is something I want to ask you.'

Derev moved her arms in a graceful circle, making the wide sleeves of her white dress floatingly glimmer in the half-dark. 'Of course.'

Ananda had found the wedge of cheese, and began to pare slices from it. 'I've been fasting,' he explained. 'Water for breakfast, water for lunch.'

'And pistachios,' Yama said.

Ananda shrugged. 'I am also supposed to be cleaning out the narthex while Father Quine dines with the Aedile and Prefect Corin. Yet I came here out of friendship.'

'You seem well,' Derev said. 'Fully recovered from your adventures.'

'I learned much from them.'

'And you promised to tell us all about them,' Ananda said. He handed out slices of bread and cheese and pried the cork out of the wine bottle with his little knife. 'I think that you should start at the beginning.'

The story seemed far stranger and more exciting than the actual experience. To tell it concisely, Yama had to miss out the fear and tension he had felt during every moment of his adventures, the long hours of discomfort when he had tried to sleep in wet clothes on the trunk of the banyan, his growing hunger and thirst while wandering the hot, stony hills of the Silent Quarter of the City of the Dead.

While he talked, he remembered a dream that had crept over him while he had slept on the catafalque inside the old tomb in the Silent Quarter. He had dreamed that he had been swimming in the Great River, and that a current had suddenly caught him and swept him towards the edge of the world, where the river fell away in thunder and spray. He had tried to swim against the current, but his arms had been trapped at his sides and he had been swept helplessly through swift white water towards the tremendous noise of the river's fall. The oppressive helplessness of the dream had stayed with him all that morning, right up to the moment when Lud and Lob had caught up with him, but he had forgotten about it until now. It seemed important, but he couldn't explain why. He told his two friends about the dream as if it was a seamless part of his adventures, then described how Lob and Lud had surprised him, how he had killed Lud by accident.

'I had found an old knife, and Lob got hold of it, ready to kill me because I had killed his brother. But the knife hurt him. It seemed to turn into something like a ghoul or a giant spider. I ran, I am ashamed to say. I left him with his dead brother.'

'He wanted to kill you,' Derev said. 'You did the right thing.'

Yama said, 'I think the knife would have killed him if I had not snatched it up and ran. It helped me, like the ghost ship.'

He dimly remembered something else, then. How, when he had threatened Lud and Lob with the knife, he had been seized by the feeling that someone else fought in his place. Perhaps he had dreamed about the fight while he had been stricken with fever in the house of Osric and Beatrice, and dream and memory had mixed and mingled until he could not tell which was which...

'Lob escaped,' Ananda said. 'He wanted his father to arrest you for the murder of his brother, the fool. But as soon as you returned home he was arrested, and when he was questioned he tried to blame everything on Dr Dismas and Unprac.'

Unprac was the name of the landlord of *The House of Ghost Lanterns*. Yama had not known it until after the trial.

'So I killed Lob anyway,' he said. 'I should have killed him when I first had the chance, in the tomb. It would have been a cleaner death. It was a poor bargain he got in the end.'

'That's what they said about the farmer,' Derev said, 'after the girl fox had lain with him and took his baby in payment.'

Suddenly, with a feeling like falling, Yama saw Derev's face as a stranger might. All planes, with large dark eyes and a small mouth and a bump of a nose, framed by a fall of white hair that moved in the slightest breeze as if possessed by an independent life. They had pursued each other all last summer, awakened to the possibilities of each other's bodies. They had lain in the dry grasses between the tombs and tasted each other's mouths, each other's skin. He had felt the swell of her small breasts, traced the bowl of her pelvis, the elegant length of her arms, her legs. They had not made love; they had sworn that they would not make love together until they were married. Now he was glad that they had not.

He said, 'Do you keep doves, Derev?'

'My father does. He sells them to palmers who come to pray at the temple's shrine. Mostly they don't want doves, though, but flowers or fruit.'

'There is one more mystery,' Yama said, and explained that he had been knocked unconscious by a fall and had woken elsewhere, in a little room of a hollowed crag far from the Great River's shore, watched by an old man and an old woman who claimed to be curators of the City of the Dead.

'They showed me a marvel. A slate from a tomb. It showed a picture of someone of my bloodline. I have been thinking about it ever since.'

Derev had the bottle of wine. She took a long swallow from it and said, 'But that's good! That's wonderful! In less than a decad you have found two people of your bloodline.'

Yama said, 'The man in the picture was alive before the keel of Confluence had been laid. I imagine he is long dead. What is interesting is that the curators already knew about me, for they had the picture slate ready, and they had also prepared a route from their hiding place to the grounds of the peel-house. That was how I returned. And one of them, the woman, Beatrice, was of your bloodline, Derev.'

'We are traders and merchants. We are to be found throughout the length and breadth of Confluence.'

Derev looked cooly at Yama when she said this, and his heart lifted and turned. It was hard to continue, but he had to. He said, 'I did not think much of it for that very reason, and I did not even make very much of the fact that, like you, they had a fund of cautionary sayings and stories concerning magical foxes. But they kept doves, like your father. He can't make any kind of profit, selling them to palmers, so I think he must keep them for another purpose. Such as exchanging messages with Beatrice and Osric.'

'My father clips the wings of his doves. It would be a bad omen if they escaped in the middle of the sacrifice.'

'So if Sergeant Rhodean examined your father's doves, he would not find any capable of flight.'

Ananda said, 'What is this, Yama? You make a trial here.'

Derev said, 'It's all right. Yama, my father said that you might have guessed. That was why he did not allow me to go to the peel-house, or to talk with you using the mirrors. But I came here anyway. I wanted to see you. Tell me what you know, and I'll tell you what we know. How did you guess that I helped you?'

'Ananda told me that Lob was drunk when he was arrested, that he had been buying drinks for everyone he knew. I know that he had not been paid by Dr Dismas, so his money had to have come from someone else. I think that you gave him money when he returned to Aeolis, and got him drunk to learn his story. I also think that the old woman, Beatrice, has a son, and that he is your father. Lob told you what happened, in the Silent Quarter. You searched for me there and found me, and took me to your grandparents. They made up a story about looking for a lost goat and finding me instead.'

'They lost a goat last year, to a leopard, and think they may have lost another,' Derev said, looking directly at Yama. 'Beatrice was looking for it when I found her, and she and Osric helped me to carry you to their home. I'm not sure what scared me more, getting Lob drunk, or climbing down the cliff using the rope he had left behind and picking my way through the passages to find you. You were very ill – you had been lying there all night. One of the entrances to the keelways was nearby, but it wasn't easy to get you there. You could walk only a little way at a time, and you wouldn't let go of the knife you'd found. But at last I got you to Beatrice and Osric, and they used the old machines to save your life.'

'I don't remember any of it,' Yama said, and wondered if those old machines had erased certain memories as well as treating him. 'You could have brought me back to the peel-house. One of the roads in the keelways runs there.'

'Beatrice and Osric were closer,' Derev said, after a moment.

'And they knew something about me. About my bloodline. Why did you keep that secret until now?'

'My family have stayed true to the old department after everyone else gave up on it,' Derev said. 'We revere the dead, and keep the memories of their lives as best we can. Beatrice isn't my grandmother, Yama: she and her husband came to live at the tower after my great-grandparents died. My real grandparents wanted a normal life, you see. They quit the old family home and established a business downriver. My father inherited it, and Beatrice and her husband persuaded him to move here because of you.' She paused, then added, 'I know you are destined for great things, but it doesn't change what I feel for you.'

Yama remembered Beatrice's verse and recited, ' "Let fame, that all hunt after in their lives, Live registered upon our brazen tombs." '

Derev said, 'It's a favourite verse of Beatrice's. She says that it is far older than Confluence.'

'According to her, I may have more in common with the dead past than with the present.'

Derev walked about, pumping her elbows in and out as was her habit when agitated. Her white dress and white hair glimmered in the faint light of the outflung arm of the galaxy. 'We keep the memories of all the dead as best we can, but we have no knowledge of your bloodline, except from legends about the beginning of the world. We kept watch over you. We were planning to tell you all we knew when the time seemed right. But events overtook our plans.'

Ananda had drunk most of the wine. He tipped the bottle to get the last swallow, wiped his mouth on his sleeve, and said gravely, 'What are you saying, Derev? That you're some kind of spy? On which side?'

'The Department of the Curators of the City of the Dead was disbanded long ago,' Yama said, looking at Derev.

'It was defeated,' Derev said, 'but it endures. There are not many of us now. We mostly live in the mountains, or in Ys.'

'Why are your family so interested in me? What do they want from me?'

'I don't know,' Derev said. She had turned her back to Yama and Ananda and was looking out across the swampy fields towards the ridge at the far side of the Breas's valley. 'My father thinks that it is to do with the ship of the Ancients of Days. Beatrice and Osric know more, I think. They have many secrets.'

Ananda said, 'The ship of the Ancients of Days passed downriver years before Yama was born.'

'The Ancients of Days set out for the neighbouring galaxy long before the Preservers achieved godhead,' Derev said. 'They left more than five million years ago, while the stars of the Home Galaxy were still being moved into their present patterns. It was long before the Puranas were written, or the Eye of the Preservers was made, or Confluence was built. They returned to find all that they knew had passed into the Eye of the Preservers, and that they were the last of their kind. They landed at Ys, travelled downriver and sailed away from Confluence for the galaxy they had forsaken so long ago. But they left their ideas behind.'

'They turned innocent unfallen bloodlines against the word of the

Preservers,' Ananda said. 'They woke old technologies and created armies of monsters to spread their heresies.'

'And thirty years later you were born, Yama,' Derev said. 'A child of a bloodline that vanished long, long ago.'

'So were many others,' Ananda said. 'All three of us were born after the war began. Derev makes a fantasy.'

'Beatrice and Osric think that Yama's bloodline is the one which built Confluence,' Derev told Ananda. 'Perhaps the Preservers raised his bloodline up for just that task and then dispersed it, or perhaps as a reward it passed over with the Preservers when they fell into the Eye and vanished from the universe. In any event, it disappeared from Confluence long ago. And yet Yama is here now, at a time of great danger.'

Ananda said, 'The Preservers needed no help in creating Confluence. They spoke a word, and it was so.'

'It was a very long word,' Derev said. She lifted her arms above her head and raised herself up on the points of her toes, as graceful as a dancer. She was remembering something she had learned long ago. She said, 'It was longer than the words in the nuclei of our cells which define what we are. If all the different instructions for all the different bloodlines of Confluence were put together it would not be one hundredth of the length of the word which defined the initial conditions necessary for the creation of Confluence. That word was a set of instructions or rules. Yama's bloodline was part of those instructions.'

Ananda said, 'This is heresy. I'm a bad priest, but I know the sound of heresy. The Preservers needed no help in making Confluence.'

'Let her explain,' Yama said.

Ananda stood. 'It's a fantasy,' he said flatly. 'Her people deceive themselves that they know more of Confluence and the Preservers than is written in the Puranas. They spin elaborate sophistries and delude themselves with dreams of hidden power, and they have snared you, Yama. Come with me. Don't listen any more. You leave for Ys tomorrow. Don't be fooled into thinking that you are more than you are.'

Derev said, 'It is our duty to preserve the memories of the dead. It has been the duty of our bloodline ever since the foundation of Confluence. My family are among the last to keep that duty. After the defeat of the department, my bloodline were scattered the length and breadth of the Great River. Most of them became traders and merchants. My grandparents and my father wanted to be traders, too, but my father was called back.'

Yama said, 'Sit down, Ananda. Please. Help me understand.'

Ananda said, 'I don't think you're fully recovered, Yama. You've been ill. That part I believe. You have always wanted to see yourself as the centre of the world, for you have no centre to your own life. Derev is treating you cruelly, and I'll hear no more. You've even forgotten about the execution. Let me tell you that Unprac died badly, screaming to the Preservers for aid with one breath and cursing them and all who watched with the next. Lob was stoic. For all his faults, he died a man.'

'That is cruel, Ananda,' Yama said.

'It's the truth. Farewell, friend Yama. If you must dream of glory, dream of being an ordinary soldier and of giving your life for the Preservers. All else is vanity.'

Yama did not try to stop Ananda. He knew how stubborn his friend could be. He watched as Ananda walked away beside the noisy river, a shadow against the misty arch of the galaxy. Yama hoped that the young priest would at least turn and wave farewell.

But he did not.

Derev said, 'At first I became your friend because it was my duty. But that quickly changed. I would not have come here if it had not.'

Yama could not stay angry at her. If she had deceived him, it was because she had believed that she was helping him. And his heart had its own reasons.

They fell into each other's arms and breathlessly kissed. Yama felt her heat pressing through their clothes, the quick patter of her heart like a bird beating at the cage of her ribs. Her hair fell around his face like a trembling veil: he might drown in its dry scent.

After a while, he said, 'If you took me to Beatrice and Osric, and they nursed me back to health, then what of the ghost ship? Do they claim that, too?'

Derev's eyes shone a handspan from his. She said, 'I'd never heard of it before you told me your story. But there are many strange things on the river, Yama. It is always changing.'

'Yet always the same,' Yama said, remembering Caphis's tattoo, the snake swallowing its own tail. He added, 'You thought that the anchorite we saved from Lud and Lob was one of my bloodline.'

'Perhaps he was the first generation, born just after the ship of the Ancients of Days arrived.'

'There may be hundreds of my bloodline by now, Derev. Thousands!'

'I told Beatrice and Osric about the anchorite, but they didn't seem to be very interested. Perhaps I was mistaken about him being of your bloodline, but I do not think I was. He gave you a disc. You should take it with you.'

'So he did. I had forgotten it.'

13

THE PALMERS

Yama discovered the ancient knife at the bottom of his satchel on the first evening of his journey to Ys in the company of Prefect Corin. Before they had set off, the Prefect had examined the contents of Yama's satchel and removed the knife, saying it was not the kind of thing a message boy should own, the map of Ys, and a horn-handled pocketknife that had once belonged to Telmon, leaving only a change of clothes, a few necessaries, the copy of the Puranas, two gold rials – the Aedile's parting gift – and the anchorite's disc, which the Prefect had overlooked because Yama wore it around his neck, inside his shirt.

The knife was sheathed in brown and white goatskin and tucked beneath his spare shirt and trousers, with a brief note in Sergeant Rhodean's hand. The old soldier must have slipped it back into the satchel when Yama had been making his farewells. Yama was pleased to see it. Even though the thought of using it made him uneasy, he knew that all heroes carried weapons with special attributes, and he was determined to be a hero. He was still very young.

Prefect Corin must have seen some small sign of surprise, and asked Yama what he had found. Reluctantly, Yama pulled the knife from its sheath and held it up in the firelight. A blue sheen extended slowly from its hilt to the point of its curved blade. It emitted a faint high-pitched buzz, and a sharp smell like discharged electricity.

'I thought that I made it clear that you have no need for weapons,' Prefect Corin said. 'You may have some training in combat but you lack experience. If we are attacked, it will do nothing but endanger you. And it is very unlikely that we will be attacked. There are few bandits on the road because most people travel by river.'

The Prefect sat cross-legged on the other side of the small campfire, neat and trim in his homespun tunic and grey leggings. He was smoking a clay pipe and his ironshod staff was stuck in the ground behind him. They had walked all day at a steady pace, and this was the most he had said to Yama in all that time.

Yama said, 'I understand why you took it, dominie. But it has been returned to me by a well-meaning friend.'

'Well, we cannot leave something like that here. Perhaps you could make a gift of it to the department, when we reach Ys. Weapons like that are generally loyal to their owner, but loyalty can be broken with suitable treatment. Meanwhile, you may carry it, but do not think to try to use it.'

But when he was certain that Prefect Corin had fallen asleep, Yama took out the knife again and practised the passes and thrusts that Sergeant Rhodean had taught him. Afterwards he slept sweetly and deeply, with the point of the knife thrust into the warm ashes of the campfire.

The next day, after rising before dawn and breaking fast and praying, Yama and Prefect Corin walked along raised paths that threaded the intricate green and brown quilt of flooded fields at the margin of the river. It was the planting season, and the fields were being ploughed by teams of water buffalo commanded by small, naked boys who controlled their charges with no more than shouts and vigorous application of long bamboo switches.

A cool wind blew from the Great River, ruffling the water which flooded the fields, stirring the bright green flags of the bamboos and the clumps of elephant grass that grew at the places were the corners of four fields met. Yama and Prefect Corin walked until the day grew too hot, and sheltered in the shade of a tree until early evening, when, after a brief prayer, they walked again until the galaxy began to rise above the river.

Ordinarily, Yama would have enjoyed this adventure, but Prefect Corin was a taciturn companion. He did not comment on anything they saw, moving implacably through the sunlit world like a machine, noticing only what was necessary. He responded with no more than a grunt when Yama pointed to a fleet of argosies far out across the glittering waters of the Great River. He ignored the ruins which could be glimpsed amongst stands of palms, flowering magnolias and pines on the ridge of the old river bank in the blue distance; he ignored the little villages through which they passed, standing on islands of higher ground amongst the flooded fields; he ignored the fishermen who worked the margin of the Great River beyond the weedy gravel banks and mud flats revealed by the river's retreat, standing thigh-deep in the shallows and casting circular nets across the water, or sitting in tiny bark boats further out and using cormorants to catch fish.

Yama thought of the verse which the old curator, Beatrice, had recited to him. Had its author seen the ancestors of these fishermen? He understood then a little of what Zakiel had tried to teach him: that books were not obdurate thickets of glyphs but transparent windows, looking out through another's eyes onto a familiar world, or onto a world which lived only when the book was read, and vanished when it was set down.

The mud walls of the straw-thatched huts of the villages often incorporated slates stolen from tombs, so that pictures from the past flashed with vibrant colours amid the poverty of the peasants' lives. Chickens and black pigs ran amongst the huts, chased by naked toddlers. Women pounded grain or gutted fish or mended fishing nets, watched by impassive men who sat in the doorways of their huts or beneath shade trees, smoking cigarettes made from rolled green leaves, or sipping tea from chipped glasses.

In one village there was a stone pen containing a small dragon coiled on white sand. The dragon was black, with a double row of diamond-shaped plates along its ridged back, and it slept with its long, scaly snout on its forelegs, like a dog. Flies clustered around its long-lashed eyes; it stank of sulphur and marsh gas. Yama remembered the abortive hunt before poor Telmon had gone away to war, and would have liked to see more of this wonder, but Prefect Corin strode past without sparing it a single glance.

Sometimes the villagers came out to watch Yama and Prefect Corin go by, and little boys ran up to try to sell them wedges of watermelon or polished quartz pebbles or charms woven from thorny twigs. Prefect Corin ignored all of them; he did not even trouble to use his staff to clear a way but simply pushed through them as through a thicket. Yama was left behind to apologise and ask for indulgence, saying over and over that they had no money. Although just one of the gold rials that the Aedile had given him was more than enough to buy an entire village, he had no smaller coins. And Prefect Corin possessed nothing but his staff and his hat, his leggings and his homespun tunic, his sandals and his blanket, and a few small tools packed inside the leather purse that hung from his belt.

'Be careful of him,' the Aedile had whispered, when he had embraced Yama in farewell. 'Do all he asks of you, but no more than that. Reveal no more than is necessary. He will seize on any weakness, any difference, and use it against you. It is their way.'

As they walked along, Yama picked and ate ghostberries from thickets which grew around ruined tombs, but the ghostberries were almost over now and difficult to find under the new leaves of the bushes, and Prefect Corin would not allow Yama to move more than a few paces from the edge of the path. There were traps amongst the tombs, he said, and ghouls and worse things haunted them at night. Apart from the necessities of toilet Yama was never out of Prefect Corin's sight. There were a hundred moments when he wanted to make a run for it. But not yet. Not yet. He was learning patience, at least.

The stretches of uncultivated country between the villages grew wider. There were fewer flooded fields and more ruined tombs, overgrown with creepers and moss amidst rustling stands of bamboo, clumps of date or oil palms, and copses of dark green swamp cypress. There was a long sandstone cliff-face carved with pillars and friezes and statues of men and beasts around gaping doors. Then they passed the last village and the road widened into a long, straight pavement. It was like the ancient road that ran between the river and the edge of the Silent Quarter downriver of Aeolis, Yama thought, and then he realised that it was the same road.

It was the third day of the journey. They camped that night in a hollow with tall pines leaning all around. Wind moved through the branches of the trees. The Great River stretched away towards the galaxy, which even at this late hour showed only the upper part of the Arm of the Warrior above the horizon, with the Blue Diadem gleaming cold and sharp at the upflung terminus of the lanes of misty starlight. Halo stars were like dimming coals scattered sparsely across the cold hearth of the sky; the smudged specks of distant galaxies could be seen here and there.

Yama lay near the little fire on a soft layer of pine needles, and thought of the Ancients of Days and wondered what it might be like to plunge through the emptiness between galaxies for longer than Confluence had been in existence. And the Ancients of Days had not possessed one hundredth of the power of their distant children, the Preservers.

He asked Prefect Corin if he had seen the Ancients of Days when they had arrived at Ys. For a long time, the man did not answer, and Yama began to believe that he had not been heard, or that Prefect Corin had simply ignored the question. But at last the Prefect knocked out his pipe on the heel of his boot and said, 'I saw two of them once. I was a boy, a little older than you, and newly apprenticed. They were both tall, and as alike as brothers, with black hair and faces as white as new paper. We say that some bloodlines have white skin – your own is very pale – but we mean that it has no pigmentation in it, except that it is suffused by the blood in the tissues beneath. But their skin was truly white, as if their faces had been powdered with chalk. They wore long white shirts that left their arms and legs bare, and little machines hung from their belts. I was in the Day Market with the oldest of the apprentices, carrying the spices he had bought. The two Ancients of Days walked through the aisles at the head of a great crowd and passed by as close to me as you are now.

'They should have been killed, all of them. Unfortunately, it was not a decision that the department could make, although even then it was possible to see that their ideas were dangerous. Confluence survives only because it does not change. The Preservers unite us because it is to them that each department swears its loyalty, and so no department shows particular favour to any of the bloodlines of Confluence. The Ancients of Days have infected their allies with the heresy that each bloodline, indeed every individual, might have an intrinsic worth. They promote the individual above society, change above duty. You should reflect on why this is wrong, Yamamanama.'

'Is it true that there are wars in Ys now? That departments fight each other in the corridors of the Palace of the Memory of the People?'

Prefect Corin gave him a sharp look across the little fire and said, 'You have been listening to the wrong kind of gossip.'

Yama was thinking of the curators of the City of the Dead, whose resistance had dwindled to a stubborn refusal to yield to the flow of history. Perhaps Derev would be the last of them. He said, trying to draw out the Prefect, 'But surely there are disputes about whether one department or another should carry out a particular duty. I have heard that outmoded departments sometimes resist amalgamation or disbandment, and I have also heard that these disputes are increasing, and that the Department of Indigenous Affairs is training most of its apprentices to be soldiers.'

'You have a lot to learn,' Prefect Corin said. He tamped tobacco into the bowl of his pipe and lit it before adding, 'Apprentices do not choose the way in which they serve the department, and you are too young to be an apprentice in any case. You have had an odd childhood, with what amounts to three fathers and no mother. You have far too much pride and not enough education, and most of that appears to have been an odd assortment of history and philosophy and cosmology, and far too much in the arts of soldiering. Before you can be accepted as an apprentice, you will have to catch up in all the areas that your education has neglected.'

Yama said, 'I think I might make a good soldier.'

Prefect Corin drew on his pipe and looked at Yama with narrowed eyes. They were small and close together, and gleamed palely in his black furred face. The white stripe ran past the outer corner of his left eye. Eventually he said, 'I came down here to execute two men because their crimes involved the Aedile's private life. That is the way it is done in the department. It demonstrates that the department supports the action of its man, and it ensures that none of the local staff have to do the job. That way, there is no one for the locals to take revenge on, with the exception of the Aedile himself, and no one will do that as long as he commands his garrison. I decided to bring you to Ys because it is my duty. It does not mean that I owe you anything, especially answers to your questions. Now get some sleep.'

Later, after the Prefect had rolled himself in his blanket and gone to sleep, Yama got up as quietly as he could and backed away from the fire, which had burnt down to white ash around a dimming core of glowing coals. The road stretched away between hummocks of dry friable stone and clumps of pines. Its paved surface gleamed faintly in the light of the galaxy. Yama settled his pack on his shoulders and set off. He had planned to follow Prefect Corin all the way to Ys, had planned to stay in the offices of the department until he got his bearings, but after the cruel insults to his father and his home he knew that he could not bear the man's company a day longer.

He had not gone very far down the road when he heard a dry rattle in the darkness ahead. Yama put his hand on the hilt of his knife, but did not draw it from its sheath in case its light betrayed him. He advanced cautiously, his eyes wide, his whole skin tingling, his blood rustling in his ears, and whirled around when something, a stone, smashed onto the road behind him. Another stone exploded at his feet. A fragment stung his shin; he felt blood trickle into his boot.

He gripped the knife tightly and said, 'Who is it? Show yourself.'

After a long moment of silence, Prefect Corin stepped up behind Yama and gripped the wrist of his right hand and turned him around and said, 'You really do have a lot to learn, boy.'

'A clever trick,' Yama said. He felt oddly calm, as if he had expected this all along.

'It is lucky for you that I played it, and no one else.' Yama had never seen Prefect Corin smile, but in the blue light of the galaxy he saw the man's lips compress in what might have been the beginning of a smile. 'I told the Aedile that I would look after you, and you will help me to keep that promise. If you try to run away again, you will go directly to the prison block when we reach Ys, and you will not be released until you have proved your loyalty to the department. Do we have an understanding?'

'I understand,' Yama said.

'Good. Let's get some sleep. We still have a long way to go.'

Early the next day they passed a group of palmers. They soon left the group behind, but the palmers caught up with them that night, and camped a little way off. They numbered more than two decads, men and women in dust-stained orange robes, their heads cleanly shaven and painted with interlocked curves which represented the Eye of the Preservers. They were a slightly built people, with pinched faces under swollen, bicephalic foreheads, and leathery skin mottled with brown and black patches. Like Prefect Corin, they carried only staffs, bedrolls, and little purses that hung from their belts. They sang in clear high voices around their fire, welding close harmonies that carried a long way across the dry stones and the empty tombs of the hillside.

Yama and Prefect Corin had made camp under a group of fig trees beside the road. A little spring rose amongst the trees, a gush of clear water that fell from the gaping mouth of a stone carved with the likeness of a fierce bearded face into a shallow pool kerbed with flat rocks. The road had turned away from the Great River, climbing a switchback of low hills dotted with creosote scrub and clumps of saw-toothed palmettos as it rose towards the pass.

The priest in charge of the palmers came over to talk with Prefect

Corin. His group was from a city a thousand leagues downriver, archivists on their way to the Palace of the Memory of the People, to tell into the records the stories of all those who had died in their city in the last ten years, and to ask for guidance from the prognosticators. They had been travelling for half a year, first by a merchant ship and then by foot after the ship had been laid up for repairs after having been attacked by water bandits.

The priest, Father Belarius, was a large smooth-skinned man. He offered Prefect Corin a cigarette and was not offended when his offer was refused, and without prompting started to talk about the risks of travelling by foot. He had heard that there were roving bands of deserters abroad in the land, in addition to the usual bandits.

'There are deserters near the battle lines, perhaps, but not this far upriver.' Prefect Corin drew on his pipe and studied the fat priest. 'Are you armed?'

'We are palmers, not soldiers.' Father Belarius mopped at his bare scalp with a square of cloth. His smooth skin was chrome-yellow, and shone like butter in the flickering firelight. 'Have you seen any sign of trouble?'

'Apart for the chattering of this boy, it has been a quiet journey.'

Yama smarted at Prefect Corin's remark, but said nothing. Belarius smoked a cigarette – it smelt overpoweringly of cloves – and gave a rambling account of how the ship on which he had hoped to take his charges all the way to Ys had been ambushed one night by water bandits in a decad of small skiffs. The bandits had been beaten off when the ship's captain had ordered pitch spread on the water and set on fire.

'Our ship put every man to the oars and rowed free of the flames,' Father Belarius said, 'but the bandits were consumed. Unfortunately, chainshot had damaged the mast and rigging of the ship, and holed the hull at the waterline. We were taking on water in several places, and limped to the nearest port. My people did not want to wait out the repairs, so we walked on. The ship will meet us at Ys, when we have finished our business there. A ghoul followed us for a brief time, but I think we have left it behind. And so far, like you, we have not been troubled. What times these are, when the road is safer than the Great River.'

After the priest had filled his waterskin from the spring and taken his leave, Yama said to Prefect Corin, 'You do not like him.'

Prefect Corin considered this, then said in a measured tone, 'I rather think that our well-upholstered priest has told us only half the story. He did not hire anyone to guide and protect his group on the long journey after they left the ship, and in any case it would have been prudent to have waited until it was repaired than to have gone forward on foot. Either he does not have the money to hire guides, or he is willing to risk the lives of his group to make extra profit. And he put aboard with a bravo of a captain, which also says little for his judgement. If the ship was able to outdistance the fire it set on the water, then it could have outdistanced the bandits. Often flight is better than fight.'

'If less honourable.'

'There is no honour to be found in needless fighting. The captain's trick could have destroyed his ship along with the bandits.'

'Will we stay with these people?'

'Their singing will wake everyone within a league,' Prefect Corin said. 'And if there are any bandits, then they will be attracted to the larger group rather than to the lesser.'

14

THE BANDITS

The next day, Yama and Prefect Corin drew ahead of the group of palmers, but never so far ahead that the dust cloud they raised was lost from sight. That evening, the palmers caught up with them again and camped nearby, and Belarius came over and talked to Prefect Corin about the day's journey for the length of time it took him to smoke two of his clove-flavoured cigarettes. The palmers' songs sounded clear and strong in the quiet night.

When Prefect Corin woke Yama from a deep sleep it was past midnight and their fire was no more than warm ashes. They had camped by a square tomb covered in the scrambling thorny canes of roses, on top of a bluff that overlooked the Great River. White blossoms glimmered like ghosts of their own selves in the faint light of the galaxy. Their strong scent packed the air.

'Take up your knife and come with me,' Prefect Corin said in a quiet voice. He was a shadowy sketch in the near dark, leaning on his staff.

'What is it?' Yama whispered.

'Some kind of intruder. Hopefully no more than an animal.'

They crossed the road and circled the palmers' camp, which had been pitched in a grove of eucalyptus trees. Low cliffs loomed above. The openings of tombs carved in the rock were like staggered rows of hollow eyes: a hiding place for an army. Yama heard nothing but the rustle of leaves and, far off, the screech of a hunting owl. In the camp, one of the palmers groaned in his sleep. Then the wind shifted, and Yama caught a faint, foul odour above the medicinal tang of the trees.

Prefect Corin pointed towards the camp with his staff and drifted forward. Yama saw something scuttle away through the trees, man-sized, running on all fours with a lurching sideways movement. He drew his knife and gave chase; Prefect Corin overtook him and sprang onto an outcrop of rock beyond the trees with his staff raised above his head. He held the pose for a moment, then jumped down.

'Gone,' he said. 'Well, the priest was right about one thing. They have a ghoul following them.'

Yama sheathed his knife. His hand was trembling. He was out of breath and his blood sang in his head. He remembered the time when he and Telmon had hunted antelope armed only with stone axes, like the men of the hill tribes. He said, 'I should not have chased after it. It was a needless risk.'

'We scared it off for now, but it will be back,' Prefect Corin said. 'In the morning I will tell the priest to make sure that his people burn their rubbish, and hang their food from branches when they camp.'

Yama and Prefect Corin reached the pass the next day. It was only a little wider than the road, cutting through a high scarp of rough-edged blocks of grey granite that rose abruptly from the gentle slope they had been climbing all morning. A cairn of flat stones stood at the edge of the road near the beginning of the pass, built around a slab engraved with a list of names. Prefect Corin said that it was the memorial of a battle in the Age of Insurrection, when the scant handful of men whose names were engraved on the slab had held the pass against overwhelming odds. Every man defending the pass had died, but the army they had fought had been held up long enough for reinforcements from Ys to arrive and drive them back.

Across the road from the shrine was a house-sized platform of red rock split down the middle by a single straight-edged crack. Prefect Corin sat in the shade of the rock's overhang and said that they would wait for the palmers to catch up before they tried the pass.

'Safety in numbers,' Yama said, to provoke a reaction.

'Quite the reverse, but you do not seem to understand that.' Prefect Corin watched as Yama poked restlessly about, and eventually said, 'There are supposed to be footprints on top of this rock, one either side of the crack. It is said that an aesthetic stood there an age past, and ascended directly to the Eye of the Preservers. The force of his ascent cracked the rock, and left his footprints in it.'

'Is it true?'

'A great deal of energy would be required to accelerate someone so that they could fall beyond the influence of Confluence's gravity field – more than enough to melt rock if applied to a small area. But a human body accelerated in such a fashion would be flash-heated into a cloud of steam by friction with the air. I do not blame you for not knowing that, Yama. As I have said before, your education is not what it should have been.'

Yama did not see any point in responding to this provocation, and continued to wander about in the dry heat, searching for nothing in particular. The alternative was to sit by Prefect Corin. Small lizards flicked over the hot stones; a scarlet and gold hummingbird hung in the air on a blur of wings for a few moments before darting away. At last, Yama found a way up a jumble of boulders to the flat top of the outcrop. The fracture was straight and narrow; its depths glittered with shards of what looked like melted glass. The fabled prints were just as Prefect Corin had described them, no more than a pair of foot-sized oval hollows, one on either side of the crack.

Yama lay down on warm, gritty rock and looked up at the empty blue sky. His thoughts moved lazily. He started to read in his copy of the Puranas, but did not find anything that was different from his rote learning and put the book away. It was too hot to read anyway, and he had already studied all the pictures. Apart from the one which showed the creation of the Eye of the Preservers, they were little different from the scenes of the lost past captured in the slates of tombs and, unlike the pictures in the slates, the pictures in the book did not move.

Yama wondered idly why the ghoul was following the palmers, and wondered why the Preservers had created ghouls in the first place. For if the Preservers had created the world and everything in it, as was written in the Puranas, and had raised up the ten thousand bloodlines from animals of ten thousand worlds, then what were the ghouls, which stood between animals and the humblest of the indigenous races?

According to the argument from design, which Zakiel had taught Yama and Telmon, ghouls existed because they aided the processes of decay, but there were many other scavenger species, and ghouls had a particular appetite for the flesh of men, and would take small children and babies if they could. Others said that the ancestors of ghouls had been imperfectly raised up, or that their bloodline had not advanced like those of other kinds of men but had instead run backwards, until they retained nothing of the gifts of the Preservers but the capacity for evil. Both arguments suggested that the world which the Preservers had created was imperfect, although neither denied the possibility of perfectibility. Some claimed that the Preservers had chosen not to create a perfect world because such a world would be unchanging, and only an imperfect world allowed the possibility of evil and, therefore, of redemption. By their nature, Preservers could do only good but, while they could not create evil, the presence of evil was an inevitable consequence in their creation, just as light casts shadows when material objects are interposed. Others argued that since the light of the Preservers had been everywhere at the construction of the world, where then could any shadows lie? By this argument, evil was the consequence of the rebellion of men and machines against the Preservers, and only by rediscovering the land of lost content which had existed before that rebellion could evil be banished and men win redemption.

Still others argued that evil had its use in a great plan that could not be understood by any but the Preservers themselves. That such a plan might exist, with past, present and future absolutely determined, was one reason why no one should rely on miracles. As Ananda would say, no use praying for intercession if all was determined from the outset. If the Preservers wanted something to be so, then they would have created it already, without waiting to hear prayers, without needing to watch over every soul. Everything was predestined in the single long word which the Preservers had spoken to bring the world into existence.

Yama's mind rebelled against this notion, as a man buried before his death might fight against the confines of a winding sheet. If everything was part of a predetermined plan, then why should anyone in it do anything at all, least of all worship the Preservers? Except that too was a part of the plan, and everyone in the world was a wind-up puppet tick-tocking from birth to death in a series of preprogrammed gestures.

That the Preservers had set the world in motion was undeniable, but Yama did not believe that they had abandoned it in disgust or despair, or because, seeing all, they knew every detail of its destiny. No, he preferred to think that they had left the world to grow as it would, as a fond parent must watch a child grow into independence. In this way, the bloodlines which the Preservers had raised up from animals might rise further to become their equals, and that could not occur if the Preservers interfered with destiny, for just as a man cannot make another man, so gods cannot make other gods. For this reason, it was necessary that individuals must be able to choose between good and evil – they must be able to choose, like Dr Dismas, not to strive to achieve goodness, but to serve instead their own base appetites. Without the possibility of evil, no bloodline could define its own best nature. The existence of evil allowed bloodlines to fail and fall, or to transcend their animal natures by their own efforts.

Yama wondered if ghouls had chosen to fall, revelling in their bestial nature as Dr Dismas revelled in his rebellion against the society of men. Animals did not choose their natures, of course. A jaguar did not delight in the pain it caused its prey; it merely needed to eat. Cats played with mice, but only because their mothers had taught them to hunt by such play. Only men could choose to wallow in their base desires or by force of will overcome them. Were men little different from ghouls, then, except they struggled against their dark side, while ghouls swam in it with the innocent unthinking ease of fish in water? By praying to the Preservers, perhaps men were in reality doing no more than praying to their own as yet unrealised higher natures, as an explorer might contemplate the untravelled peaks he must climb to reach his goal.

But if the Preservers had left the world to its devices and there were no miracles, except the existence of free will, what then of the ghost ship? Yama had not prayed for it, or at least had not known that he had done so, and yet it had come precisely when he had needed a diversion to make good his escape. Was something watching over him? If so, to what purpose? Or perhaps it was no more than a coincidence: some old machinery had been accidentally awakened, and Yama had seized the moment to escape. It was possible that there was another world where the ghost ship had not appeared, or had appeared too early or too late, and Yama had gone with Dr Dismas and the warlord, Enobarbus. He would be travelling downriver on the pinnace even now, a willing or unwilling participant in their plans. Travelling towards their deaths, perhaps, or to a destiny more glorious than the lowliest position in the Department of Indigenous Affairs.

Yama's speculations widened, and at some point he was no longer in control of them but was carried on their flow like a twig on the Great River's flood. He slept, and woke to find Prefect Corin standing over him, a black shadow against the dazzling blue of the sky.

'Trouble,' the man said, and pointed down the long gentle slope of the road. A tiny smudge of smoke hung in the middle distance, trembling in the heat haze, and at that moment Yama realised that all along Prefect Corin had been protecting the palmers.

*

They found the dead first. The bodies had been dragged off the road and stacked and set on fire. Little was left but greasy ash and charred bones, although a pair of unburnt feet still shod in sandals protruded from the bottom of the gruesome pyre. Prefect Corin poked amongst the smoking ashes with his staff and counted fourteen skulls, leaving nine unaccounted for. He cast about in one direction, bending low as he searched the muddle of prints on the ground, and Yama, although not asked, went in the other. It was he, following a trail of blood speckles, who found Father Belarius hiding inside a tomb. The priest was cradling a dead woman, and his robe was drenched in her blood.

'They shot at us from hiding places amongst the tombs,' Father Belarius said. 'I think they shot Vril by accident, because they did not shoot any of the other women. They came for the women when all the men had been killed or badly wounded. They were small and fierce, with bright red skin and long arms and legs. Like spiders. Some on foot, some on horse, three or four decads of them. They had sharp teeth, and claws like thorns. I remember that they couldn't close their hands around their weapons.'

'I know the bloodline,' Prefect Corin said. 'They are a long way from their home.'

'Two came and looked at me, and jeered and went away,' Father Belarius said.

'They would not kill a priest,' Prefect Corin said. 'They think it bad luck.'

'I tried to stop them despoiling the bodies,' Father Belarius said. 'They threatened me with their knives or spat on me or laughed, but they didn't stop their work. They stripped the bodies and dismembered them, cut what they wanted from the heads. I wanted to shrive the dead, but the bandits pushed me away.'

'And the women?'

The priest started to cry. 'I meant no harm to anyone. No harm. No harm to anyone.'

'They took the women with them, didn't they?' Prefect Corin said. 'To despoil or to sell. Stop blubbering, man! Which way did they go?'

'Towards the mountains. You must believe that I meant no harm. If you had stayed with us instead of getting ahead— No, forgive me. That is unworthy.'

'We would have been killed, too,' Prefect Corin said. 'Bandits of this bloodline strike quickly, and without fear. They will attack larger groups better armed than themselves if they think that the surprise and fury of their assault will overcome their opponents. As it is, we may yet save some of your people. Go and shrive your dead, man. After that you must decide whether you want to come with us or stay here.'

When the priest was out of earshot, Prefect Corin said to Yama, 'Listen carefully, boy. You can come with me, but only if you swear that you will do exactly as I say.'

'Of course,' Yama said at once. He would have promised anything for the chance.

It was not difficult to track the bandits and the captured women across the dry, sandy land. The trail ran parallel to the granite scarp across a series of flat, barren salt pans. Each was higher than the next, like a series of giant steps. Prefect Corin set a relentless pace, but the priest kept up surprisingly well; he was one of those fat men who are also strong, and the shock of the ambush was wearing off. Yama supposed that this was a chance for him to regain face. Already, he was beginning to speak of the attack as if it had been an accident or a natural disaster from which he would rescue the survivors.

'As if he did not invite the lightning,' Prefect Corin said to Yama when they stopped to rest in the shade of a tomb. 'At the best of times, bringing a party of palmers on the land route to Ys without proper escort is like herding sheep through a country of wolves. And these were archivists, too. Not proper archivists – those are from the department, and are trained in the art of memory. These use machines to record the lives of the dying. If you had looked closely at the skulls, you would have seen that they had been broken open. Some bandits eat the brains of their victims, but these wanted the machines in their heads.'

Yama laughed in disbelief. 'I have never heard of such a thing.'

Prefect Corin passed a hand over his black-furred face, like a grooming cat. 'It is an abomination, promulgated by a department so corrupt and debased that it seeks to survive by coarse imitation of the tasks properly carried out by its superiors. Proper archivists learn how to manage their memories by training; these people would be archivists in a few days, by swallowing the seeds of machines which migrate to a certain area of the brain and grow a kind of library. It is not without risks. In one in fifty of those who swallow the seeds, the machines grow unchecked and destroy the brains of their hosts.'

'But surely only the unchanged need archivists? Once changed, everyone is remembered by the Preservers.'

'Many no longer believe it, and because the department will not supply archivists to the cities of the changed these mountebanks make fortunes by pandering to the gullible. Like real archivists, they listen to the life stories of the dying and promise to transmit them to the shrines of the Palace of the Memory of the People.'

'No wonder the priest is upset. He believes that many more died than we saw.'

"They are all remembered by the Preservers,' Prefect Corin said. 'Saints or sinners, all men marked by the Preservers are remembered, while true archivists remember the stories of as many of the unchanged bloodlines as they can. The priest is upset because his reputation will be blemished, and he will lose trade. Hush. Here he comes.'

Father Belarius had ripped away the blood-soaked part of his orange robe, leaving only a kind of kilt around his waist. His shoulders and fat man's breasts had darkened in the sun to the colour of blood oranges, and he scratched at his sunburnt skin as he told Yama and Prefect Corin that he had found fresh horse droppings.

'They are not more than an hour ahead of us. If we hurry, we can catch them before they reach the foothills.'

Prefect Corin said, 'They make the women walk. It slows them down.'

'Then their cruelty will be their undoing.' Father Belarius curled his right hand into a fist and ground it into the palm of his left. 'We will catch them and we will crush them.'

'They are cruel but not stupid,' Prefect Corin said. 'They could tie the women to their horses if they wanted to outpace us, yet they do not. They taunt us, I think. They want sport. We must proceed carefully. We will wait until night, and then track them to their camp.'

'They will leave us behind in the darkness!'

'They do not travel by night, for their blood slows as the air cools. Meanwhile we will rest. You will pray for us, Belarius. It will set our minds to the struggle ahead.'

They waited until the sun had fallen behind the Rim Mountains and the galaxy had begun to rise above the farside horizon before they set off. The tracks left by the bandits ran straight across the flat white land into a tangle of shallow draws which sloped up towards a range of low hills. Yama tried his best to imitate Prefect Corin's ambling gait, and remembered to go flat-footed on loose stones, as Telmon had taught him. Father Belarius was less nimble, and every now and then would stumble and send stones clattering away downslope. There were tombs scattered at irregular intervals along the sides of the draws, unornamented and squarely built, with tall narrow doors which had been smashed open an age ago. A few had picture slates, and these wakened when the three men went by, so that they had to walk along the tops of the ridges between the draws to avoid being betrayed by the light of the past. Father Belarius fretted that they would lose the trail, but then Yama saw a flickering dab of light brighten ahead.

It was a dry tree set on fire in the bottom of a deep draw.

It burned with a white intensity and a harsh crackling, sending up volumes of acrid white smoke. Its tracery of branches made a web of black shadows within the brightness of its burning.

'Now we know that they know that we are following them,' Prefect Corin said. 'Yama, look after Belarius. I will not be long.'

He was gone before Yama could reply, a swift shadow flowing down the slope, circling the burning tree and disappearing into the darkness beyond. The priest sat down heavily and whispered, 'You two should not die on my account.'

'Let us not talk of death,' Yama said. He had his knife in his hand – he had drawn it upon seeing the burning tree. It showed not a spark, and he sheathed it and said, 'A little while ago, I was taken aboard a pinnace by force, but a white ship appeared, glowing with cold fire. The pinnace attacked the white ship and I was able to escape. Yet the white ship was not real; even as it bore down on the pinnace it began to dissolve. Was this a miracle? And if it was, was it for my benefit?'

'We shouldn't question the plan of the Preservers. Only they can say what is miraculous.'

It was a rote reply. Father Belarius was more intent on the darkness beyond the burning tree than on Yama's tale. He was smoking one of his clove-scented cigarettes, cupping it hungrily to his wide mouth. The light of the burning tree beat on him; shadows in his deep eye sockets made a skull of his face.

Prefect Corin came back an hour later. The tree had burnt down to a stump of glowing cinders. He appeared out of the darkness and knelt between Father Belarius and Yama. 'The way is clear,' he said.

Yama said, 'Did you see them?'

Prefect Corin considered this. Yama thought he looked smug, the son of a bitch. At last he said, 'I saw our friend from last night.'

'The ghoul?'

'It will feed well tonight, one way or the other. Listen carefully. This ridge rises and leads around to a place above a canyon. There are large tombs at the bottom of the canyon, and that is where the bandits are camped. They have stripped the women and tied them to stakes, but I do not think they have used them.' Prefect Corin looked directly at Father Belarius. 'These people come into heat like dogs or deer, and it is not their season. They display the women to make us angry, but we will not rise to their bait. They have built a big fire, but away from it the night air will make them sluggish. Yamamanama, you and Belarius will create a diversion, and I will go in and cut the women free and bring them out.'

The priest said, 'It is not much of a plan.'

'Well, we could leave the women,' Prefect Corin said, with such seriousness that it was plain he would do just that if Father Belarius refused to help.

'We should wait until they sleep, and then we can take the women,' the priest said.

'No,' Prefect Corin said. 'They become less active at night, but they do not sleep. They will be waiting for us, and that is why we must make them come out, preferably away from their fire. I will kill them then. I have a pistol.'

It was like a flat, water-smoothed pebble. It caught the galaxy's cold blue light and shone in Prefect Corin's palm. Yama was amazed. The Department of Indigenous Affairs was surely more powerful than he had imagined, if one of its clerks could carry a weapon not only forbidden to most but so valuable, because the secret of its manufacture had been lost an age past, that it could ransom a city like Aeolis. Dr Dismas's energy pistol, which merely increased the power of light by making its waves march in step, was a clumsy imitation of the weapon Prefect Corin held.

Father Belarius said, 'Those things are evil.'

'It has saved my life before now. It has three shots, and then it must lie in sunlight all day before it will fire again. That is why you must get them into the open, so I have a clear field of fire.'

Yama said, 'How will we make the diversion?'

'I am sure you will think of something when you get there,' Prefect Corin said.

His lips were pressed together as if he was suppressing a smile, and now Yama knew what this was all about.

Prefect Corin said, 'Follow the ridge, and be careful not to show yourself against the sky.'

'What about guards?'

'There are no guards. Not any more,' Prefect Corin said. And then he was gone.

The canyon was sinuous and narrow, a deeply folded crevice winding back into the hills. The ridge rose above it to a tabletop bluff dissected by dry ravines. Lying on his belly, looking over the edge of the drop into the canyon, Yama could see the fire that the bandits had lit on the canyon floor far below. Its red glow beat on the faces of the tombs that were set into the walls of the canyon, and on the brushwood corral where a decad of horses milled, and on the line of naked women tied to stakes.

Yama said, 'It is like a test.'

Father Belarius, squatting on his heels a little way from the edge, stared at him.

'I have to show initiative,' Yama said. 'If I do not, Prefect Corin will not try to rescue the hostages.'

He did not add that it was also a punishment. Because he carried the knife; because he wanted to be a soldier; because he had tried to run away. He knew that he could not allow himself to fail, but he did not know how he could succeed.

'Pride,' the priest said sulkily. He seemed to have reached a point where nothing much mattered to him. 'He makes himself into a petty god, deciding whether my poor clients live or die.'

'That is up to us, I think. He is a cold man, but he wants to help you.'

Father Belarius pointed into the darkness. 'There's a dead man over there. I can smell him.'

It was one of the bandits. He was lying on his belly in the middle of a circle of creosote bushes. His neck had been broken and he seemed to be staring over his shoulder at his doom.

Father Belarius mumbled a brief prayer, then took the dead man's short, stout recurved bow and quiver of unfletched arrows. He seemed to cheer up a little, and Yama asked him if he knew how to use it.

'I'm not a man of violence.'

'Do you want to help rescue your clients?'

'Most of them are dead,' Father Belarius said gravely. 'I will shrive this poor wight now.'

Yama left the priest with the dead man and quartered the ground along the edge of the canyon. Although he was tired, he felt a peculiar clarity, a keen alertness sustained by a mixture of anger and adrenalin. This might be a test, but the women's lives depended on it. That was more important than pleasing Prefect Corin, or proving to himself that he could live up to his dreams.

A round boulder stood at the edge of the drop. It was half Yama's height and bedded in the dirt, but it gave a little when he put his back to it. He tried to get Father Belarius to help him, but the priest was kneeling as if in prayer and either did not understand or did not want to understand, and he would not stand up even when Yama pulled at his arm. Yama groaned in frustration and went back to the boulder and began to attack the sandy soil around its base with his eating knife. He had not been digging for long when he struck something metallic. The little knife quivered in his hands and when he drew it out he found that the point of the blade had been neatly cut away. He had found a machine.

Yama knelt and whispered to the thing, asking it to come to him. He did it more from reflex than hope, and was amazed when the soil shifted between his knees and the machine slid into the air with a sudden motion, like a squeezed watermelon seed. It bobbed in the air before Yama's face, a shining, silvery oval that would have fitted into his palm had he dared touch it. It was both metallic and fluid, like a drop of hydrargyrum. Flecks of light flickered here and there on its surface. It emitted a strong smell of ozone, and a faint crepitating sound.

Yama said, slowly and carefully, shaping the words in his mind as well as his mouth as he did when instructing the peel-house's watchdogs, 'I need to make this part of the edge of the canyon fall. Help me.'

The machine dropped to the ground and a little geyser of dust and small stones spat up as it dug down out of sight. Yama sat on his heels, hardly daring to breathe, but although he waited a long time, nothing else seemed to happen. He had started to dig around the base of the boulder again when Father Belarius found him.

The priest had uprooted a couple of small creosote bushes.

He said, 'We will set these alight and throw them down onto those wicked men.'

'Help me with this boulder.'

Father Belarius shook his head and sat by the edge and began to tie the bushes together with a strip of cloth torn from remnants of his robe.

'If you set fire to those bushes, you will make yourself a target,' Yama said.

'I expect that you have a flint in your satchel.'

'Yes, but—'

In the canyon below, men cried to each other. Yama looked over the edge and saw that the horses were running from one corner of the corral to the other. They moved in the firelight like water running before a strong, choppy wind, bunched together and flicking their tails and tossing their heads. At first, Yama thought that they had been disturbed by Prefect Corin, but then he saw something pale and skinny clinging upside-down to the neck of a black mare in the middle of the panicky herd. The ghoul had found the bandits. Men were running towards the horses with a scampering crabwise gait, casting long crooked shadows because the fire was at their backs, and Yama threw his weight against the boulder, knowing he would not have a better chance.

The ground moved under Yama's feet and he lost his footing and fell backward, banging the back of his head against the boulder. The blow dazed him, and he was unable to stop the priest pawing through his satchel and taking the flint. The ground moved again and the boulder stirred and sank a handspan into the soil. Yama realised what was happening and scrambled out of the way just as the edge of the canyon collapsed.

The boulder dropped straight down. A cloud of dust and dirt shot up and there was a crash when the boulder struck the side of the canyon, and then a moment of silence. The ground was still shaking. Yama tried to get to his feet, but it was like trying to stand up in a boat caught in cross-currents. Father Belarius was kneeling over the bundle of creosote bushes, striking the flint against its stone. Dust puffed up behind him, defining a long crooked line, and a kind of lip opened in the ground. Little lights swarmed in the churning soil. Yama saw them when he snatched up his satchel and jumped the widening gash. He landed on hands and knees and the ground moved again and he fell down. The priest was standing on the other side of the gash, his feet planted wide apart as he swung two burning bushes around his head. Then the edge of the canyon gave way and fell with a sliding roar into the canyon. A moment later a cloud of dust boiled up amidst a noise like a thunderclap, and lightning lit the length of the canyon at spaced intervals. Once, twice, three times.

15
THE MAGISTRATE

At first the houses were no more than empty tombs with narrow windows chipped into their carved walls and smoke-holes cut into their roofs, improvised villages strung along the terraces at the old edge of the Great River. The people who lived there were very tall and very thin, with small heads and long, glossy black hair, and skin the colour of rust. They went about naked. The chests of the men were welted with spiral patterns of scars; the women stiffened their hair with red clay. They hunted lizards and snakes and coneys, collected the juicy young pads of prickly pear and dug for tuberous roots in the dry tableland above the cliffs, picked samphire and watercress in the marshes by the margin of the river, and waded out into the river's shallows and cast circular nets to catch fish, which they smoked on racks above fires built of creosote bush and pine chips. They were cheerful and hospitable, and gave food freely to Yama and Prefect Corin when they halted at noon.

Then there were proper houses amongst the tombs, straggling up steep, narrow streets, painted yellow or blue or pink, with little gardens planted out on their flat roofs. Shanty villages were built on stilts over the mudbanks and silty channels left by the river's retreat, and beyond these, sometimes less than half a league from the road, sometimes two or three leagues distant, was the river, and docks constructed from floating pontoons and the cut-down hulls of old ships and barges, and a constant traffic of cockleshell sailboats and barges, sleek fore-and-aft rigged cutters and three-masted xebecs hugging the shore. Along the old river road, street merchants sold fresh fish and oysters and mussels from tanks, and freshly steamed lobsters and spiny crabs, samphire and lotus roots and water chestnuts, bamboo shoots and little red bananas and several kinds of kelp, milk from tethered goats, spices, pickled walnuts, fresh fruit and grass juice, ice, jewellery made of polished shells, black seed pearls, caged birds, bolts of brightly patterned cloths, sandals made from the worn rubber tread of steam wagon tyres, cheap plastic toys, cassette recordings of popular ballads or prayers, and a thousand other things. The stalls and booths of the merchants formed a kind of ribbon market strung along the dusty shoulder of the old road, noisy with the cries of hawkers and music from cassette recorders and itinerant musicians, and the buzz of commerce as people bargained and gossiped and argued. When a warship went past, a league beyond the crowded tarpaper roofs of the shanty villages and the cranes of the docks, everyone stopped to watch it. As if in salute, it raised the red and gold blades of its triple-banked oars and fired a charge of white smoke from a cannon, and everyone along the old road cheered.

That was when Yama realised that he could see, for the first time, the farside shore of the Great River: a dark irregular line of houses and docks. The river was deep and swift here, stained brown along the shore and dark blue further out. He had reached Ys and had not known it until now. The city had crept up on him like an army in the night, the inhabited tombs like scouts, the streets of painted houses and the tumbledown shanty villages like the first ranks of foot soldiers. It was as if, after the fiasco of the attempted rescue of the palmers, he had suddenly woken from a long sleep.

Prefect Corin had said little about the landslide which had killed the bandits, the kidnapped women, and their priest. 'You did what you could,' he had told Yama. 'And if you had done nothing, the women would have been dead anyway.'

Yama had not told Prefect Corin about the machine. Let him think what he liked. But Yama had not been able to stop himself anguishing about what had happened as he trudged behind the Prefect on the long road. He had little doubt that the Prefect could have walked into the bandits' camp, killed them all, and freed the women. Instead, he had used the situation to test Yama, and Yama felt guilty for having failed, and angry for having been put to an impossible test. He sometimes imagined drawing his knife and hacking the man's head from his shoulders with a single blow, or picking a stone from the side of the road and using it as a hammer. He dreamed of running fast and far, and until the warship had passed he had been lost in his fantasies and dreams.

Yama and Prefect Corin ate at a roadside stall. Without being asked, the owner served them steamed mussels, water lettuce crisply fried in sesame oil with strands of ginger, and tea made from steeped kakava bark – there was a red plastic bowl in the centre of the table into which fragments of bark could be spat. Prefect Corin did not pay for the food; the stall's owner, a tall man with loose, pale skin and rubbery webs between his fingers, simply smiled and bowed when they left.

'Like most of the populace, he is glad to help someone from the department,' Prefect Corin told Yama.

'Why is that?'

'Because we are at war,' Prefect Corin said. 'Because the department is at the forefront of the fight to save our civilisation. You saw how they cheered the warship. Must you ask so many questions?'

'How am I to learn, if I do not ask questions?'

Prefect Corin stopped and leaned on his tall staff and stared at Yama. People stepped around them. It was crowded here, with two- and three-storey houses packed closely together on either side of the road. A string of camels padded past, their loose lips curled in supercilious expressions, little silver bells jingling on their leather harness.

'The first thing to learn is when to ask questions and when to keep silent,' Prefect Corin said, and then he turned and strode off through the crowd.

Without thinking, Yama hurried after him. It was as if this stern, taciturn man had made him into a kind of pet, trotting at his master's heels. He remembered what Dr Dismas had said about beasts of burden, remembered the oxen trudging endlessly around the water lift because they knew no better, and his resentment bubbled up again, refreshed.

For long stretches now, the river disappeared behind houses or godowns. Hills rose above the flat roofs of the houses on the landward side of the road, and after a while Yama realised that they were not hills but buildings. In the hazy distance, the towers he had so often glimpsed using the telescope on the peel-house's heliograph platform shone like silver threads linking earth and sky.

For all the long days of travelling, the towers seemed as far away as ever.

There were more and more people on the road, and strings of camels and oxen, and horse-drawn or steam wagons bedecked with pious slogans, and sleds gliding at waist height, their loadbeds edged with carved wooden rails painted red and gold. There were machines here, too. At first, Yama mistook them for insects or hummingbirds as they zipped this way and that above the crowds. No one in Aeolis owned machines, not even the Aedile (the watchdogs were surgically altered animals, and did not count), and if a machine strayed into the little city's streets everyone would get as far away from it as possible. Here no one took any notice of the many machines that darted or spun through the air on mysterious errands. Indeed, one man was walking towards Yama and Prefect Corin with a decad of tiny machines circling above his head.

The man stopped in front of the Prefect. The Prefect was tall, but this man was taller still – he was the tallest man Yama had ever seen. He wore a scarlet cloak with the hood cast over his head, and a black tunic and black trousers tucked into thigh-high boots of soft black leather. A quirt like those used by ox drivers was tucked into the belt of his trousers; the quirt's hundred strands were tipped by diamond-shaped metal tags. The man squared up to Prefect Corin and said, 'You're a long way from where you should be.'

Prefect Corin leaned on his staff and looked up at the man. Yama stood behind the Prefect. People were beginning to form a loose circle around them.

The man in the red cloak said, 'If you have business here, I haven't heard of it.'

A machine landed on Prefect Corin's neck, just beneath the angle of his jaw. Prefect Corin ignored it. He said, 'There is no reason why you should.'

'There is every reason.' The man noticed the people watching and slashed the air with his quirt. The tiny, bright machines above his head widened their orbits and one dropped down to hover before the man's lips.

'Move on,' the man said. His voice, amplified by the machine, echoed off the faces of the buildings on either side of the street, but most of the people only stepped back a few paces. The machine rose and the man told Prefect Corin in his ordinary voice, 'You're causing a disturbance.'

Prefect Corin said, 'There was no disturbance until you stopped me. I would ask why.'

'This is the road, not the river.'

Prefect Corin spat in the dust at his feet. 'I had noticed.'

'You are carrying a pistol.'

'By the authority of my department.'

'We'll see about that. What's your business? Are you spying on us?'

'If you are doing your duty, you have nothing to fear. But do not worry, brother, I am no spy. I performed a small administrative task in a downriver city, and now I am returning to the Palace of the Memory of the People, and the offices of the Department of Indigenous Affairs.'

'Yet you travel by road.'

'I thought I would show this boy something of the countryside. He has led a very sheltered life.'

A machine darted forward and spun in front of Yama's face. There was a flash of red light, and the machine flew up to rejoin the spinning dance above the man's head. The man said, 'I don't know the bloodline, but I'd guess he's too young to be an apprentice. Perhaps he is your catamite. Although the war must be going badly if you can't find better. He has a corpse's skin. And like you he is carrying a proscribed weapon.'

'Again, by the authority of my department,' Prefect Corin said.

'You had better show your papers to the officer of the day.'

The man turned, slashing the air with his quirt so that those nearest him fell back, pressing against those behind. 'Make way!' the man shouted as he hacked a path through the crowd. 'Make way! Make way!'

As they followed him, Yama said to Prefect Corin, 'Why does he challenge your authority?'

'He is a magistrate. A member of the autonomous civil authority of Ys. There is some bad blood between his department and mine. He will make a point about who is in charge here, and then we will be on our way.'

'How did he know about the pistol and my knife?'

'His machines told him.'

One machine still clung to the Prefect's neck, a segmented silver bead with four pairs of wire-like legs and mica wings folded along its back; others circled the magistrate's head. Yama could feel their simple thoughts and wondered if he might be able to make them forget their orders, but he did not trust himself to say the right thing to them, and besides, he did not want to reveal his ability.

The road opened onto a square lined with flame trees just coming into leaf. On the far side, a high wall rose above the roofs of the buildings and the tops of the trees. It was built of closely fitted blocks of black, polished granite, with gun platforms and watchtowers along its top. Soldiers lounged by a tall gate in the wall, watching the traffic that jostled through the shadow of the gate's arch. The magistrate led Prefect Corin and Yama across the square and the soldiers snapped to attention as they went through the gate. They climbed a steep stair that wound widdershins inside the wall to a wide walkway at the top. A little way along, the wall turned at a right angle to run beside the old bank of the river, and a faceted blister of glass clung there, glittering in the sunlight.

It was warm and full of light inside the glass blister. Windows hung in the air, displaying aerial views of the road, ships moored at the docks or passing up and down the river, a crowded street. A little cloud of machines hung under the glass panes of the ceiling, above an officer who sat with his boots up on a clear plastic table. The magistrate briefly talked with him, and then the officer called Prefect Corin over.

'Just a formality,' the officer said languidly, and held out his hand. The eight-legged machine dropped from Prefect Corin's neck and the officer's fingers briefly closed around it. When they opened again, the machine sprang into the air and began to circle the Prefect's head.

'Your pass, if you please.' The officer ran a fingernail over the imprinted seal of the resin tablet that Prefect Corin gave him, and said, 'You didn't take return passage by river, as you were ordered.'

'Not ordered. Whether or not I took river passage was left to my discretion. The boy has been placed in my care, and has led a sheltered life. I thought that I would show him something of the country.'

The officer looked at Yama and said, 'There's nothing here about this boy, or his weapon. Quite a hanger for an apprentice.'

'He is not yet an apprentice. And the knife is not official issue, but an heirloom. He is the son of the Aedile of Aeolis.'

Prefect Corin's tone implied that there was nothing more to be said about the matter.

The officer set the tablet on the desk and said to the magistrate, 'Nym, fetch a chair for the Prefect.'

'I need to be about my business,' Prefect Corin said.

The officer yawned again. His tongue, long and sharply pointed, had been stained red by the narcotic leaf wadded between his gum and cheek. 'It will take a little while to confirm things with your department. Would you care for some refreshment?'

The tall red-cloaked magistrate set a stool beside Prefect Corin. The officer indicated it, and after a moment Prefect Corin sat down, saying, 'I do not need anything from you.'

The officer took out a packet of cigarettes and stuck one in his mouth and lit it with a match he struck on the welt of one of his boots. He did all this at a leisurely pace; his gaze did not leave the Prefect's face. He exhaled smoke and said, 'I think you should tell me about your long walk from Aeolis. Meanwhile, Nym will talk to the boy, and then we'll see if the two stories tally. What could be simpler?'

'The boy must stay with me,' Prefect Corin said. 'I am responsible for his safe passage to the Palace of the Memory of the People.'

The officer stubbed out his half-smoked cigarette. 'Oh, I think he'll be safe with Nym.'

Prefect Corin said, 'Nym may not be safe with him.'

The officer raised an eyebrow.

'I have said too much. Thank you for your offer of hospitality,' Prefect Corin said, 'but we must be on our way.'

He started to rise, and for an instant was crowned with a jagged circle of sparks. There was a sudden sharp smell of burnt hair and he fell heavily back onto the stool. The little machine was still circling his head, as if nothing had happened.

'Take the boy away, Nym,' the officer said. 'Find out where he's been, what he's been up to, and where he's going.'

Prefect Corin gave Yama a dark look. His shoulders were hunched and his hands were pressed between his knees. 'Do what you are told,' he said. 'No more, no less.'

The magistrate, Nym, took Yama's arm and steered him around the windows hung in the air. A compact cloud of machines followed them. Outside, in the hot sunlight, Nym looked through Yama's satchel and took out the sheathed knife.

'It is a gift from my father,' Yama said. He half-hoped that the knife would do something to the man, but it remained inert.

'I'm not going to steal it,' the magistrate said, and pulled the blade halfway out of its sheath. 'Nicely balanced. Loyal, too. It tried to bite me, but I know something about old machines. Do you? Or do you use it to cut firewood?' He sheathed the knife and dropped it into the satchel, and told Yama to sit. 'On the bench there. Good. Don't move. If you do, or if you lie to me, the machines will knock you down, as they did with your master. And if you try to make trouble, they'll boil you down to a grease spot.'

'I don't think so,' Yama said, and told the machines to take care of the magistrate.

The man tried to brush them away as they settled in a close orbit about his head, just above the level of his eyes, cursed when fat sparks danced around his fingertips.

'Stay still and don't say anything, or they'll hurt you,' Yama said, and reached for his satchel.

The magistrate grabbed at Yama's wrists, and lightning flickered around his head. He fell to his knees and Yama danced in and snatched his satchel and danced back. 'Keep him there,' he told the machines, and went down the stairs and walked past the soldiers, his heart beating lightly and quickly. But no one spared him more than a glance, and he walked through the shadow of the gate into the busy street beyond.

16

THE CATERAN

At first, the landlord of the inn did not want to rent a room to Yama. The inn was full, he said, on account of the Water Market. But when Yama showed him one of the gold rials, the man chuckled and said that he might be able to make a special arrangement. Perhaps twice the usual tariff, to take account of the inconvenience, and if Yama would like to eat while waiting for the room to be made up . . . ?

The landlord was a fat young man with short, spiky white hair and a brisk manner. He took the rial and said that he'd bring change in the morning, seeing as the money changers were closed up for the day.

Yama sat in a corner of the taproom, and presently a pot boy brought him a plate of shrimp boiled in their shells, stir-fried okra and peppers with chili and peanut sauce, flat discs of unleavened bread, and a beaker of thin rice beer. Yama ate hungrily. He had walked until the sun had fallen below the roofs of the city, and although he had passed numerous stalls and street vendors he had not been able to buy any food or drink – he had not realised that there were men whose business was to convert coins like his into smaller denominations. The landlord would change the gold rial tomorrow, and then Yama could begin the search for his bloodline. But for now he was content to sit with a full stomach, his head pleasantly lightened by the beer, and watch the inn's customers.

Ordinary working men of several bloodlines, dressed in homespun and clogs, stood at the counter drinking in quiet companionship, while a party of men and a single red-haired woman ate at a long table under the stained-glass window which displayed the inn's sign, playing elaborate toasting games and calling from one end of the table to the other. Yama thought that they must be soldiers, caterans or some other kind of irregulars: they wore bits of armour, mostly metal or resin chestplates painted with various devices, and wrist guards and greaves, and many were scarred, or had fingers missing. One big, bare-chested man had a silver patch over one eye; another had only one arm, although he ate as quickly and as dextrously as his companions. The red-haired woman, dressed in a sleeveless leather tunic and a short leather skirt that left her legs mostly bare, seemed to be part of their company rather than a concubine.

The landlord seemed to know the caterans. When he was not busy he sat with them, laughing at their jokes and pouring wine or beer for those nearest him. He whispered something in the one-eyed man's ear and they both laughed; when the landlord went off to serve one of the customers at the counter, the one-eyed man grinned across the room at Yama.

Presently, the pot boy told Yama that his room was ready, and led him around the counter and through a small hot kitchen into a courtyard lit by electric floodlights hung from a central pole. There were whitewashed stables on two sides and a wide square gate shaded by an avocado tree in which green parrots squawked and rustled. The room was in the eaves above one of the stable blocks. It was long and low and dark, with a single window at its end looking out over the street and a tumble of roofs falling towards the Great River. The pot boy lit a fish-oil lantern and uncovered a pitcher of water, turned down the blanket and fussed with the bolster on the bed, and then hesitated, clearly reluctant to leave.

'I do not have any small coins,' Yama said, 'but tomorrow I will give you something for your trouble.'

The boy went to the door and looked outside, then closed it and turned to Yama. 'I don't know you, master,' he said, 'but I think I should tell you this, or it'll be on my conscience. You shouldn't stay here tonight.'

'I paid for the room with good money left on account,' Yama said.

The boy nodded. He wore a clean, much darned shirt and a pair of breeches. He was half Yama's height and slightly built, with black hair slicked back from a sharp, narrow face. His eyes were large, with golden irises that gleamed in the candlelight. He said, 'I saw the coin you left on trust. I won't ask where you got it, but I reckon it could buy this whole place. My master is not a bad man, but he's not exactly good either, if you take my meaning, and there's plenty better than him who would be tempted by your wealth.'

'I will be careful,' Yama said. The truth was that he was tired, and a little dizzy from the beer.

'If there's trouble, you can climb out the window onto the roof,' the boy said. 'On the far side there's a vine that's grown to the top of the wall. It's an easy route. I've used it many times.'

After the boy left, Yama bolted the door and leaned at the open window and gazed out at the vista of roofs and river under the darkening sky, listening to the evening sounds of the city. There was a continual distant roar, the blended noise of millions of people going about their business, and closer at hand the sounds of the neighbourhood: a hawker's cry; a pop ballad playing on a cassette recorder; someone hammering metal with quick sure strokes; a woman calling to her children.

A profound feeling of serenity settled over him. He was at a turning point in his life, anonymous and free in the vast city, in that particular place and time, with his future spread out before him, a sheaf of wonderful possibilities. He would find out the truth about his origin and his bloodline, and then he would become a cateran and sail downriver to the war. He would prove himself in battle, perhaps become a warlord like Enobarbus, and at last return in triumph to Aeolis . . .

He took off his shirt and washed his face and arms, then pulled off his boots and washed his feet. The bed had a lumpy mattress stuffed with straw, but the sheets were freshly laundered and the wool blanket was clean. This was probably the pot boy's room, he thought, which was why the boy had wanted him to leave.

He intended to rest for a few minutes before getting up to close the shutters, but when he woke it was much later. The cold light of the galaxy lay on the floor, and something made a scratching sound in the rafters above the bed. A mouse or a gecko, Yama thought sleepily, but then he felt a feathery touch in his mind and knew that a machine had flown into the room through the window that he had carelessly left open.

Yama wondered sleepily if the machine had woken him, but then there was a metallic clatter outside the door. As he sat up, groping for the lantern, the door flew open with a tremendous crash, sending the broken bolt flying across the room, and a man stepped inside. Yama rolled onto the floor, reaching for his satchel, and something hit the bed. Wood splintered and straw flew into the air. Yama rolled again, dragging his satchel with him. He cut his hand getting his knife out but hardly noticed. The curved blade shone with a fierce blue light and spat fat sparks from its point.

The man turned from the bed, a shadow in the half-light. He had broken the frame and slashed the mattress to ribbons with the broad blade of his sword. Yama threw the pitcher of water at him and he ducked and said, 'Don't struggle, boy, and I'll make it quick and painless.'

Yama hesitated, and the man struck at him with a sudden fury. Yama ducked and heard the air part above his head, and slashed at the man's legs with the knife, so that he had to step back. The knife howled and Yama felt a sudden coldness in the muscles of his arm.

'You fight like a woman,' the man said. Knife-light flashed on something on his intent face.

Then he drove forward again, and Yama stopped thinking. Reflexes, inculcated in the long hours in the gymnasium under Sergeant Rhodean's stern instruction, took over. Yama's knife was better suited to close fighting than the man's long blade, but the man had the advantage of reach and weight. Yama managed to parry a series of savage, hacking strokes – fountains of sparks spurted at each blow – but the force of the blows numbed his wrist, and then the man's longer blade slid past the guard of Yama's knife and nicked his forearm. The wound was not painful, but it bled copiously and weakened Yama's grip.

He knocked the chair over and, in the moment it took the man to kick it out of the way, managed to get out of the corner into which he had been forced. But the man was still between Yama and the door. In a moment he pressed his attack again, and Yama was driven back against the wall. The knife's blue light blazed and something white and bone-thin stood between Yama and the man, but the man laughed and said, 'I know that trick,' and kicked out, catching Yama's elbow with the toe of his boot. The blow numbed Yama's arm and he dropped the knife. The phantom vanished with a sharp snap.

The man raised his sword for the killing blow. For a moment, it was as if he and Yama stood in a tableau pose. Then the man grunted and let out a long sighing breath that stank of onions and wine fumes, and fell to his knees. He dropped his sword and pawed at his ear, then fell on his face at Yama's feet.

Yama's right arm was numb from elbow to wrist; his left hand was shaking so much that it took him a whole minute to find the lantern and light it with his flint and steel. By its yellow glow he tore strips from the bed sheet and bound the shallow but bloody wound on his forearm and the smaller self-inflicted gash on his palm. He sat still then, but heard only horses stepping about in the stables below. If anyone had heard the door crash open or the subsequent struggle, which was unlikely given that the other guests would be sleeping on the far side of the courtyard, they were not coming to investigate.

The dead man was the one-eyed cateran who had looked at Yama across the taproom of the inn. Apart from a trickle of dark, venous blood from his right ear he did not appear to be hurt. For a moment, Yama did not understand what had happened. Then the dead man's lips parted and a machine slid out of his mouth and dropped to the floor.

The machine's teardrop shape was covered in blood, and it vibrated with a brisk buzz until it shone silver and clean. Yama held out his left hand and the machine slid up the air and landed lightly on his palm.

'I do not remember asking you for help,' Yama told it, 'but I am grateful.'

The machine had been looking for him; there were many of its kind combing this part of Ys. Yama told it that it should look elsewhere, and that it should broadcast that idea to its fellows, then stepped to the window and held up his hand. The machine rose, circled his head once, and flew straight out into the night.

Yama pulled on his shirt and fastened his boots and set to the distasteful task of searching the dead cateran. The man had no money on him and carried only a dirk with a thin blade and a bone hilt, and a loop of wire with wooden pegs for handles. He supposed that the man would have been paid after he had done his job. The pot boy had been right after all. The landlord wanted to steal everything he had.

Yama sheathed his knife and tied the sheath to his belt, then picked up his satchel. He found it suddenly hard to turn his back on the dead man, who seemed to be watching him across the room, so he climbed out of the window sideways.

A stout beam jutted above the window frame; it might once have been a support for a hoist used to lift supplies from the street. Yama grasped the beam with both hands and swung himself once, twice, and on the third swing got his leg over the beam and pulled himself up so that he sat astride it. The wound on his forearm had parted a little, and he retied the bandage. Then it was easy enough to stand on the beam's broad top and pull himself onto the ridge of the roof.

17

THE WATER MARKET

The vine was just where the pot boy had said it would be. It was very large and very old – perhaps it had been planted when the inn had been built – and clambering down its stout leafy branches was as easy as using a ladder. Yama knew that he should leave before the cateran's friends found out what had happened, but he also knew that Telmon would not have run away with business still unfinished. It was a matter of honour to get the rial back, and there in the darkness of the narrow alley at the back of the inn Yama remembered the landlord's duplicitous smile and felt a slow flush of anger.

He was groping his way towards the orange lamplight at the end of the alley when he heard footsteps behind him. For a moment he feared that the cateran's body had been found, that his friends were tracking down his killer, but no hue and cry had been raised, and surely the city was not so wicked that murder would go unremarked. He forced himself not to look back, but walked around the corner and drew his knife and waited in the shadows by the inn's gate, under the wide canopy of the avocado tree.

When the pot boy came out of the alley, Yama pushed him against the wall and held the knife at his throat. 'I don't mean any harm!' the boy squealed. Above them, a parrot echoed his frightened cry, modulating it into a screeching cackle.

Yama stepped back. The pot boy fussily straightened his ragged jerkin and said, 'He came for you, didn't he? I saw him sneaking in.'

'I dealt with him,' Yama said, and sheathed his knife. He realised that if the one-eyed cateran had crept into the room to cut his throat or use the strangling wire instead of bursting in with his sword unsheathed, he, and not the cateran, would now be dead. 'I should have listened to you. As it is, I have killed a man, and your master still has my coin.'

The pot boy met Yama's gaze and said, 'You could call the magistrates.'

'I do not want to get you into trouble, but perhaps you could show me where your master sleeps. If I get back the coin, half of it is yours.'

The boy said, 'Pandaras, at your service, master. And you are far too generous. For a tenth of that price, I'll skewer his heart for you. He beats me, cheats his customers, and cheats his provisioners and wine merchants, too. You are a brave man, master, but a poor judge of inns. And you're on the run, aren't you? That's why you won't call on the magistrates.'

'It is not the magistrates I fear most,' Yama said, thinking of Prefect Corin.

Pandaras nodded. 'Families can be worse than any lock-up, as I know too well.'

'As a matter of fact, I have come here to search for my family.'

'I thought you were from the wrong side of the walls – no one born in the city would openly carry a knife as old and as valuable as yours. I'll bet that cateran was more interested in that than his fee for murdering you.'

Yama smiled. 'What about your position here?'

'I'll be glad to be quit of this place. It never was much of a job anyway, and I'm getting too old for it. I may not be much more than a street urchin, but I know my way around. As to hunting down your family, I can help you in a hundred different ways.'

'Let's begin with the retrieval of my property.'

'Follow me. It should be easy enough for one as skilled as you. My master sleeps as soundly as a sated seal. He won't wake until you put your blade to his throat.'

Pandaras let Yama into the inn through the kitchen door and led him upstairs. He put a finger to his black lips before delicately unlatching a door. Yama's knife emitted a faint blue glow and he held it up like a candle as he stepped into the stuffy room.

The landlord snored under a disarrayed sheet on a huge canopied bed that took up most of the space – there was no other furniture. Yama shook him awake, aimed the point of the knife at his face, and demanded his coin. The fat man squinted up at him and said, 'Go ahead and kill me. If you don't, I'll set the magistrates on you.'

'Then you will have to explain why one of your guests was attacked in his room. The man you sent to kill me is dead, by the way.'

The landlord sat up slowly, the sheet bunching over the mound of his belly. The knife's blue glow was liquidly reflected in his round black eyes and glimmered in his spiky white hair. He gave Yama a sly look and said, 'Cyg wasn't working for me, and you can't prove different.'

'Then how did you know his name?'

The landlord shrug was like a mountain quivering. 'Everyone knows Cyg.'

'And everyone will probably know about the bargain he made with you. Call the magistrates, if you wish. Or you can return my coin, and I will leave at once.'

'Why don't we sit down over a glass of brandy and talk about this sensibly? I could make use of a sharp young cock like you. And you could make use of my advice. I know of several ways to make that golden boy multiply tenfold.'

'I have heard that you cheat your customers,' Yama said. 'Those who cheat are always afraid that they will be cheated in turn, so I would guess that the only place you could have hidden my coin is somewhere in this room. Probably under your pillow.'

The landlord lunged forward then, and something smacked Yama's knife so hard it was almost knocked from his hand. The room filled with white light and the landlord screamed.

Afterwards, the landlord huddled against the headboard of his bed and wouldn't look at Yama or the knife. He was bleeding hard from his hand; although he had wrapped his sheet around it before grabbing at the knife, the blade had cut him deeply. But he took no notice of his wound, nor of Yama's questions. He was staring at something which had vanished as quickly as it had appeared, and would only say, over and over, 'It had no eyes. Hair like cobwebs, and no eyes.'

Yama searched beneath the bolster and the mattress, and then, remembering the place where he had cached his map in his room in the peel-house, rapped the floor with the hilt of his knife until he found the loose board under which the landlord had hidden the rial. He had to show the landlord his knife and threaten the return of the apparition to make the man roll onto his belly, so that he could gag him and tie his thumbs together with strips torn from the bed sheet.

'I am only taking back what is mine,' Yama said. 'I do not think you deserve any payment for hospitality.'

Pandaras was waiting outside the gate. 'We'll get some breakfast by the fishing docks,' he said. 'The boats go out before first light, so the stalls open early.'

Yama showed him the rial. His hand shook. Although he had felt quite calm while dealing with the landlord, he was filled now with an excess of nervous energy. He laughed and said, 'I have no coin small enough to pay for breakfast.'

Pandaras reached inside his ragged shirt and lifted out two worn iron pennies hung on a string looped around his neck. 'I'll pay, master, and you can settle up with me later.'

'As long as you stop calling me master. You are not much younger than me.'

'That's true, if you measure by years: I'm just past my fourth birthday. But if you measure by experience, I reckon I have the edge. You are obviously of noble birth, and folk like you live longer than most, and take longer to come into their own. Relatively speaking, you're hardly weaned from the wet nurse's teat.'

Pandaras squinted up at Yama as they passed through the orange glow of a sodium-vapour lamp. 'Your bloodline isn't one I know, but there are many strange folk downriver of Ys, and many more in her streets. Everything may be found here, it's said, but even if you lived a thousand years and spent all your time searching you wouldn't learn a tenth of the city's secrets. Many have tried, and none have succeeded, and many have been driven mad in the attempt. And even if some wise man somehow managed to make a great list of all that might be found here, so much would have changed that by the time he had finished his work it would be time to start all over again.'

'Fortunately, I think I know where to begin my search,' Yama said.

'Ah, but do you know where that first step will lead you, or how long the road will be? It's a wise man indeed who can see the end of a story in its beginning. But you must forgive me my prattle, master. My people love to talk and to tell stories, and invent tall tales. We earn our bread and beer as labourers, and have little in the way of money or possessions, but we are rich in imagination. Our stories and songs are told and sung by every bloodline, and a few of us even gain brief fame as jongleurs to the great houses and the rich merchants, or as singers and musicians and storytellers.'

'Given their talents, your people deserve a better station than they have.'

'Ah, but we do not live long enough to profit from them. No more than twenty years is the usual; twenty-five is unheard of. It is our curse and our gift. The swiftest stream polishes the pebbles smoothest, as my grandfather had it, and so with us. We live brief but intense lives, and from the pace of our living come our songs and stories.'

As they descended towards the waterfront, down narrow streets that were sometimes so steep that they were little more than flights of shallow steps, with every house leaning on the shoulder of its neighbour, Yama told Pandaras something of the circumstances of his birth, of what he thought Dr Dismas had discovered, and of his journey to Ys.

'I know the Department of Apothecaries and Chirurgeons,' Pandaras said. 'It's stuck up on the roof of the Palace of the Memory of the People, like an afterthought.'

'All the roads I could take seem to lead to the same place,' Yama said.

The sky was beginning to brighten when Yama and Pandaras reached the wide road by the old waterfront. A brace of camels padded past, loaded with bundles of cloth and led by a sleepy boy. Merchants were rolling up the shutters of their stalls or lighting cooking fires. On the long piers which ran out to the river's edge from shacks raised on a forest of stilts, fishermen were coiling ropes and taking down nets from drying poles and folding them in elaborate pleats.

For the first time, Yama noticed the extent of the riverside shanty town. The shacks crowded all the way to the edge of the docks, half a league distant, and ran along the river edge for as far as the eye could see. They were built mostly of plastic sheeting dulled by smoke and weather to a myriad shades of grey, and roofed with tarpaper or sagging canvas. Channels brimming with thick brown water ran between mudbanks under the tangle of stilts and props. Tethered chickens pecked amongst threadbare grass on drier pieces of ground. Already, people were astir, washing clothes or washing themselves, tending tiny cooking fires, exchanging gossip. Naked children of a decad or more of different bloodlines chased each other along swaybacked rope walkways.

Pandaras explained that the shanty towns were the home of refugees from the war. 'Argosies go downriver loaded with soldiers, and return with these unfortunates. They are brought here before they can be turned by the heretics.'

'Why do they live in such squalor?'

'They know no better, master. They are unchanged savages.'

'They must have been hunters once, or fishermen or farmers. Is there no room for them in the city? I think that it is much smaller than it once was.'

'Some of them may go to the empty quarters, I suppose, but most would be killed by bandits, and besides, the empty quarters are no good for agriculture. Wherever you dig there are stones, and stones beneath the stones. The Department of Indigenous Affairs likes to keep them in one place, where they can be watched. They get dole food, and a place to live.'

'I suppose many become beggars.'

Pandaras shook his head vigorously. 'No, no. They would be killed by the professional beggars if they tried. They are nothing, master. They are not even human beings. See how they live!'

In the shadows beneath the nearest of the shacks, beside a green, stagnant pool, two naked men were pulling pale guts from the belly of a small cayman. A boy was pissing into the water on the other side of the pool, and a woman was dipping a plastic bowl into the water. On a platform above, a woman with a naked baby on her arm was crumbling grey lumps of edible plastic into a blackened wok hung over a tiny fire. Beside her, a child of indeterminate age and sex was listlessly sorting through wilted cabbage leaves.

Yama said, 'It seems to me that they are an army drawn up at the edge of the city.'

'They are nothing, master,' Pandaras said, again, and thumped his skinny chest. 'We are the strength of the city, as you will see.'

At a stall by one of the wide causeways that ran out to the pontoon docks, Pandaras devoured a shrimp omelette and finished Yama's leavings while Yama warmed his hands around his bowl of tea. In the growing light he could see, three or four leagues downriver, the wall where he and Prefect Corin had been taken yesterday, a black line rising above red tile roofs like the back of a sleeping dragon. He wondered if any of the magistrates' windows were turned in this direction. No, he had dealt with the machines they had set to look for him. For now he was safe.

Pandaras called out for more tea, and told Yama that there was an hour at least before the offices of the money changers opened.

Yama said, 'Do not worry. I will make good my debt to you. Where will you go afterwards?'

'Why, with you, master,' Pandaras said. 'To the Department of Apothecaries and Chirurgeons, to begin with. Now, don't argue. You know you need my help, and besides, our fates are intertwined. You do not know where you were born, and wish to find it, while I know my birthplace all too well, and want to escape it.'

The boy had small, sharp teeth all exactly the same size; his black, pointed fingernails were more like claws, and his hands, with leathery pads on their palms and hooked thumbs stuck stiffly halfway up the wrists, resembled an animal's paws. Yama had seen many of Pandaras's bloodline yesterday, portering and leading draught animals and carrying out a hundred other kinds of menial jobs. The strength of the city.

The boy shrugged when Yama asked about the caterans who had been eating in the taproom of the inn. 'I don't know them. They arrived only an hour before you. I thought that you might be one of them, until you showed my master the coin.'

'I was wondering how one might become part of a company like theirs.'

Yama knew that he was still too young to join the army in the usual way, but his age would be no bar to becoming an irregular. He had just killed a cateran in close combat, and had been caught up in more adventures in the past two decads than most people could expect to encounter in a lifetime.

'If you join up, then I'll go with you, and be your squire,' Pandaras said. 'You've enough money to buy a good rifle, or better still, a pistol, and you'll need armour, too. I'll polish it bright between battles, and keep your devices clean—'

Yama laughed. 'You build an entire fantasy on a passing thought. I must find my bloodline first. But after that, after I have found out all I can about where I come from, then, yes, I will enlist and help win the war. My brother was killed fighting the heretics. I have made a vow to fight in his place.'

'Caterans in need of employment generally hang out at the Water Market, by the Red Temple,' Pandaras said. 'About half a league upriver, on the old shore.'

'On the way to the Palace of the Memory of the People?'

'In the same direction. We might want to make a detour,' Pandaras said, 'in case we run into the caterans from the inn.'

'I will not run or hide from anyone. And besides, only Cyg was in league with the landlord. His companions had nothing to do with it.'

'I hope you can explain that to them, if it comes to it,' Pandaras said.

'I'd like to see the Water Market. I know almost nothing, and want to find out about everything.'

Pandaras drained his cup of tea and spat fragments of bark onto the ground. 'We'll go there as soon as we've found someone who can split your gold into baser metals,' he said, 'and we'll be at the gates of the Palace of the Memory of the People before the Bastion of the Twelve Devotions sounds its noon gun. With my help, master, anything is possible.'

The sky above the crowded rooftops was blue now, and traffic was thickening along the road. Fishing boats were moving out past the ends of the piers of the docks, their russet and tan sails bellying in the wind and white birds flying in their wake as they breasted the swell of the morning tide. As he walked beside Pandaras, Yama thought of the hundred leagues of docks, of the thousands of boats of the vast fishing fleets which put out every day to feed the myriad mouths of the city, and began to understand the true extent of Ys.

How could he ever expect to find out about his birth, or of the history of any one man, in such a mutable throng? And yet, he thought, Dr Dismas had found out something in the records of his department, and he did not doubt that he could find it, too. Freshly escaped from his adventure with the cateran, and from the fusty fate that the Aedile and Prefect Corin had planned for him, Yama felt his heart rise. It did not occur to him that he might fail in his self-appointed quest. He was, as Pandaras had pointed out, still very young, and had yet to fail in anything important.

The first money changer refused Yama's two gold rials after a mere glance. The second, whose office was in a tiny basement with a packed-dirt floor and flaking pink plaster walls, spent a long time looking at the coins under a magnifying screen, then scraped a fleck from one and tried to dissolve it in a minim of aqua regia. The money changer was a small, scrawny old man almost lost in the folds of his black silk robe. He clucked to himself when the fleck of gold refused to dissolve even when he heated the watch glass, then motioned to his impassive bodyguard, who fetched out tea bowls and a battered aluminium pot, and resumed his position at the foot of the steps up to the street.

Pandaras and the money changer haggled for an hour, over several pots of tea and a plate of tiny honeycakes so piercingly sweet that they made Yama's teeth ache. Yama felt cramped and anxious in the dank little basement, with the tramp of feet going to and fro overhead and the bodyguard blocking most of the sunlight that spilled down the stair, and was relieved when at last Pandaras announced that the deal was done.

'We'll starve in a month, but this old man has a stone for a heart,' he said, staring boldly at the money changer.

'You are quite welcome to take your custom elsewhere,' the money changer said, and giving Pandaras a fierce, hawkish look. 'I'd say your coins were stolen, and any price I give you would be fair enough. As it is, I risk ruining my reputation on your behalf.'

'You'll not need to work again for a year,' Pandaras retorted. Despite the money changer's impatience, he insisted on counting the slew of pennies and silver and copper rials twice over before shaking hands with the money changer, who suddenly smiled and wished Pandaras and Yama every blessing of the Preservers.

After the dank shadows of the money changer's basement, the street seemed as bright and hot as a smithy's forge. The road was busier than ever, and the traffic crowding its wide asphalt pavement moved at walking pace. The air was filled with the clatter of hooves and iron-rimmed wheels on stone setts, the shouts and curses of drivers, the cries of hawkers and merchants, the silver notes of whistles and the brassy clangour of bells. Small boys darted amongst the legs of beasts and men, collecting the dung of horses, oxen and camels, which they would shape into patties and dry on walls for fuel for cooking fires. There were beggars and thieves, skyclad mendicants and palmers, jugglers and contortionists, mountebanks and magicians, and a thousand other marvels, so many that as he walked along amongst the throng Yama soon stopped noticing all but the most outrageous, for otherwise he would have gone mad with wonder.

A black dome had appeared amongst the masts of the ships and the flat roofs of the godowns at the edge of the river. Yama pointed to it and said, 'That was not there when we first arrived.'

'A voidship,' Pandaras said casually, and expressed surprise when Yama insisted that they go and look at it. 'It's really just a lighter for a voidship. The ship to which it belongs is too big to make riverfall and hangs beyond the edge of Confluence, unloading the ores it brought from a mine world. The lighter will have put in for fresh food. It's nothing special.'

It turned out that they could not get close to the lighter: the dock where it was moored was closed off, and guarded by a squad of soldiers armed with fusils more suited to demolishing a citadel than to keeping away sightseers. Yama studied the smooth black shape rising beyond the gate of the dock, the blunt silver cap that shone with white fire in the sunlight, and wondered what other suns it had seen. He could have stood there all day, filled with an undefined longing, but Pandaras took his arm and steered him away.

'It's dangerous to linger long,' the boy said. 'And not just because of the guards. The star-sailors steal children, it's said, because they cannot engender their own. If you see one, you'll understand. Most do not even look like men. And someone as unusual as you might attract their attention.'

As they walked on, Yama asked if Pandaras knew of the ship of the Ancients of Days.

'My grandfather said that he saw two of them walking through the streets of our quarter late one night, but everyone in Ys who was alive at that time claims as much.' Pandaras touched his fist to his throat and added, 'My grandfather said that they glowed the way the river water sometimes glows on summer nights, and that they stepped into the air and walked away above the rooftops. He made a song about it, but when he submitted it to the legates he was arrested for heresy, and died under the question.'

The sun had climbed halfway to zenith by the time Yama and Pandaras reached the Red Temple and the Water Market. The temple had once been much grander, according to Pandaras, standing on its own island around a protrusion or plug of keelrock in a wide deep bay, but it been badly damaged in the wars of the Age of Insurrection and had not been rebuilt, and now the falling level of the Great River had left it stranded in a shallow muddy lagoon. The outline of the temple's inner walls and a row of half-melted pillars stood amongst outcrops of keelrock and groves of flame trees; the three black circles of the temple's shrines glittered amongst grassy swales where the narthex had once stood. Nothing could destroy the shrines, not even the energies deployed in the battle which had won back Ys from the Insurrectionists, for they were only partly of the material world. Services were still held at the Red Temple every New Year, Pandaras said, and Yama noticed the heaps of fresh flowers and offerings of fruits in front of the shrines. Although most of the avatars had disappeared in the Age of Insurrection, and the last had been silenced by the heretics, people still came to petition them.

At the water's edge beyond the far side of the temple, on rafts and pontoons and barges, the Water Market was in full swing. The standards of a hundred condottieri flew from poles, and there were a dozen exhibition duels under way, each at the centre of a ring of spectators. There were stalls selling every kind of weapon, the workshops of armourers, provisioners extolling the virtue of their preserved fare. A merchant blew up a water bottle and jumped up and down on it to demonstrate its durability. Newly indentured convicts sat in sullen groups on benches behind the auction block, most sporting fresh mutilations. Galleys, pinnaces and picket boats stood offshore, their masts hung with bright flags that flapped in the strong, hot breeze.

Yama eagerly drank in the bustle and the noise, the exotic costumes of the caterans and the mundane dove-grey uniforms of regular soldiers mingled together, the ringing sound of the weapons of the duellists, and the smell of hot metal and plastic from the forges of the armourers. He wanted to see everything the city had to offer, to search its great temples and the meanest of its alleys and courts for any sign of his bloodline.

As he followed Pandaras along a rickety gangway between two rafts, someone stepped out of the crowd and hailed him. His heart turned over. It was the red-haired woman who last night had sat eating with the man he had killed. When she saw that he had heard her, she shouted again and raised her naked sword above her head.

18

THE THING IN THE BOTTLE

'They are yours by right of arms,' Tamora, the red-haired cateran, said. 'The sword is too long for you, but I know an armourer who can shorten and rebalance it so sweetly you'd swear afterwards that was how it was first forged. The corselet and the greaves can be cut down to suit, and you can sell the trimmings. That way it pays for itself. Old armour is expensive because it's the best. Especially plastic armour, because no one knows how to make the stuff any more. You might think my breastplate is new, but that's only because I polished it this morning. It's a thousand years old if it's a day, but even if it's better than most of the clag they make these days, it's still only steel. But these greaves are real old. I could have taken them, but that wouldn't have been right. Everyone says we're vagabonds and thieves, but even if we don't belong to any department we still have our traditions. So these are your responsibility now. Throw them in the river if you like, but it would be a fucking shame if you did.'

'She wants you to give them back to her as a reward for giving them to you,' Pandaras said.

'I talk to the master,' Tamora said, 'not his fool.'

Pandaras struck an attitude. 'I am his squire.'

'I was the fool,' Yama said to Tamora. 'And because I was a fool your friend died. That is why I cannot take his things.'

Tamora shrugged. 'Cyg was no friend of mine. And as far as I'm concerned he was the fool, getting himself killed by a scrap of a thing like you. You're so freshly hatched you probably still have eggshell stuck to your back.'

Pandaras said, 'If this is to be your career, then you must arm yourself properly, master. As your squire, I strongly suggest it.'

'Squire, is it?' Tamora cracked open another oyster with her strong, ridged fingernails, slurped up the flesh, and wiped her mouth with the back of her hand. Her bright red hair, which Yama suspected was dyed, was cut short over her skull, with a long fringe in the back that fell to her shoulders. She wore her steel breastplate over a skirt made of leather strips and a mesh shirt which left her muscular arms bare. There was a tattoo of a bird sitting on a nest of flames on the tawny skin of one arm: the flames in red and yellow ink; the bird, its wings outstretched as if it was drying them in the fire, in blue.

They were sitting in the shade of an umbrella at a table by a food stall on the waterfront, near the causeway that led from the shore to the island of the Red Temple. It was sunstruck noon. The owner of the stall was sitting under the awning by the ice chest, listening with half-closed eyes to a long antiphonal prayer burbling from the cassette recorder under his chair.

Tamora squinted against the silver light that burned off the water. She had a small, triangular, feral face, with green eyes and a wide mouth that stretched to the hinges of her jaw. Her eyebrows were a single brick-red rope; now the rope dented in the middle and she said, 'Caterans don't have squires. That's for regular officers, and their squires are appointed from the common ranks. This boy has leeched onto you, Yama. I'll get rid of him if you want.'

Yama said, 'It is just a joke between the two of us.'

'I *am* his squire,' Pandaras insisted. 'My master is of noble birth. He deserves a train of servants, but I'm so good he needs no other.'

Yama laughed.

Tamora squinted at Pandaras. 'You people are all the same to me, like fucking rats running around underfoot, but I could swear you're the pot boy of the crutty inn where I stayed the night.' She told Yama, 'If I was more suspicious, I might suspect a plot.'

'If there was a plot, it was between your friend and the landlord of the inn.'

'Grah. I suspected as much. If I survive my present job, and there's no reason why I shouldn't, then I'll have words with the fat man. More than words, in fact.'

Tamora's usual expression was a sullen, suspicious pout, but when she smiled her face came to life, as if a mask had suddenly dropped, or the sun had come out from behind a cloud. She smiled now, as if at the thought of her revenge. Her upper incisors were long and stout and sharply pointed.

'He did not profit from his treachery,' Yama said.

Pandaras kicked him under the table and frowned.

Tamora said, 'I'm not after your money, or else I would have taken it already. I have just now taken on a new job, so be quick in making up your mind on how you'll dispose of what is due to you by right of arms. As I said before, you can throw it in the river or leave it for the scavengers if you want, but it's good gear.'

Yama picked up the sword. Its broad blade was iron and had seen a lot of use, but although its edge was nicked in several places it was razor sharp. The hilt was wound with bronze wire; the pommel was an unornamented plastic ball, chipped and dented. He held the blade up before his face, then essayed a few passes. The cut on his forearm stickily parted under the crude bandage he had tied and he put the sword down. No one sitting at the tables around the stall had looked at the display, although he had hoped that they would.

He said, 'I have a knife that serves me well enough, and the sword is for a strong man more used to hewing wood than fighting with any skill or subtlety. But I will take the armour. As you say, old armour is the best.'

'Well, at least you know something about weapons,' Tamora said grudgingly. 'Are you here looking for hire? If so, I'll give you some advice for free. Come back tomorrow, early. That's when the best jobs are available. Condottieri like a soldier who can rise early.'

'I had thought to watch a duel or two,' Yama said.

'Exhibition matches between oiled cornfed oafs who wouldn't last a minute in real battle. Do you think we fight with swords against the fucking heretics? The matches draw people who would otherwise not come, that's all. They get drunk with recruiting sergeants and the next day find themselves indentured in the army, with a hangover and the taste of the oath like a copper penny in their mouth.'

'I am not here to join the army. Perhaps I will become a cateran eventually, but not yet.'

'He's looking for his people,' Pandaras said.

It was Yama's turn to aim a kick under the table. It was green-painted tin, the table, its umbrella bamboo and varnished paper. He said, 'I plan to look for certain records in the library of a certain department.'

Tamora swallowed the last oyster and belched. 'Then you'll have to sign up with the department. Better still, join the fucking archivists. After all, they control all the libraries. Of course, you'll have to spend ten years as an apprentice first, and at the end of that you might well be sent downriver, to listen to the stories of unchanged toads squatting in some mudhole. But you'll still have a better chance of finding what you're looking for than trying to bribe your way into their confidence. They're a strict and unforgiving people, the archivists. Any one of them caught taking a bribe is executed on the spot, and the same goes for anyone caught trying to bribe them. According to them, the records they guard are all that remains of the dead, kept until they're resurrected at the end of time. It's serious shit to even look at them the wrong way.'

'The Puranas say that the Preservers need no records,' Yama said, 'for in the last instant of time an infinite amount of energy becomes available, and everyone who ever lived or ever could have lived will live again forever, in that eternal now. Besides, the records I am looking for are not in the general archives of the Palace of the Memory of the People, but in the Department of Apothecaries and Chirurgeons.'

'That's more or less the same place. On the roof rather than inside, that's all.'

'Just as I told you, master,' Pandaras said. 'You don't need her to show you what I already know!'

Tamora ignored him. 'Their records are maintained by archivists, too. Unless you're a sawbones or a sawbones' runner, you can forget about it. It's the same in all the departments. The truth is expensive and difficult to keep pure, and so getting at it without proper authority is dangerous. But that doesn't mean that there aren't ways of getting at it.'

Pandaras said, 'She is baiting a hook. Be careful.'

Yama said to Tamora, 'You have fought against the heretics – that is what the tattoo on your arm implies, anyway. In all your travels, have you ever seen any other men and women like me?'

'I fought in two campaigns, and in the last I was so badly wounded that it took me a year to recover. When I'm fit I'll go again. It's better pay than bodyguard or pickup work, and more honourable, although honour has little to do with it when you're there. No, I haven't seen anyone like you, but it doesn't signify. There are ten thousand bloodlines on Confluence, not counting all the tribes of indigens, who are little more than animals.'

'Then you see how hard I must search,' Yama said.

Tamora's smile showed all her teeth. 'How much will you pay?'

'Master—'

'I changed two gold rials for a bag of lesser coins this morning. All of it is yours, if you help me.'

Pandaras whistled and looked up at the blue sky.

'Grah. Against death, that is not so much.'

Yama said, 'Do they guard the records with men, or with machines?'

'Mostly machines. As I said, the records of any department are important. Even the poorest departments guard their archives carefully – often their archives are all they have left.'

'In that case it might be easier than you suppose.'

Yama met Tamora's luminous gaze. It was the heart-stopping stare that a predator turns upon its prey just before it leaps. For a long moment the rest of the world melted away. Her pupils were vertical slits edged with closely crowded dots of golden pigment that faded to copper at the periphery. He imagined drowning in that green-gold gaze, as a luckless fisherman might drown in the Great River's flood.

From somewhere far off, Tamora's voice said, 'Before I help you, if I do help you, you must prove yourself.'

'How?' Yama said faintly.

'Don't trust her,' Pandaras said. 'If she really wanted the job, she'd just take your money. There are plenty like her. If we threw a stone in any direction, we'd hit at least two.'

'In a way, you owe me this,' Tamora said.

Yama took a breath, and looked away. 'Cyg was going to help you with some task, wasn't he? You came here to recruit a replacement, and found me instead. Well, what would you have me do?'

Tamora pointed over his shoulder. He turned, and saw the silver-capped top of the voidship lighter rising above the flame trees that stood amongst the ruins of the Red Temple.

'We have to bring back a star-sailor who jumped ship,' the cateran said

They sold the sword to an armourer for rather more than Yama had expected, and left the corselet and the greaves with the same man to be cut down. Tamora insisted that Yama get his wounds treated by one of the leeches who had set up their stalls near the duelling arena, and Yama sat and watched two men fence with chainsaws ('Showboat juggling,' Tamora sneered) while the cut on his forearm was stitched, painted with blue gel and neatly bandaged. The shallow cut on his palm should be left to heal on its own, the leech said, but Tamora made the woman bind it anyway, saying that the bandage would help Yama grip his knife. She bought Pandaras a knife with a long thin round blade and a finger guard chased with a chrysanthemum flower.

'Suitable for sneaking up on someone in the dark,' Tamora said. 'If you stand on tiptoe, rat-boy, you should be able to puncture a real person's kidneys with this.'

Pandaras flexed the knife's blade between two clumsy, clawed fingers, licked it with his long, pink tongue, then tucked it in his belt.

'I killed the man who would have helped her,' Yama said. 'It is only proper that I should take his place. But there is no need for you to come.'

'Well put,' Tamora said.

Pandaras showed his small sharp teeth. 'Who else would watch your back, master? Besides, I have never been aboard a voidship lighter before.'

One of the guards escorted them across the wharf to the lighter. Cables and canvas hoses lay everywhere, like a tangle of basking snakes. Labourers, nearly naked in the hot sunlight, were winching a cavernous pipe towards an opening which had dilated in the lighter's black hull. An ordinary canvas-and-bamboo gangway angled up to a smaller entrance.

Yama felt a distinct pressure sweep over his skin as, following Tamora and the guard up the gangway, he ducked beneath the port's rim. Inside, a passageway sloped away to the left, curving as it rose so that its end could not be seen. Yama supposed that it spiralled around the interior of the lighter like the track that a maggot leaves in a fruit. It was circular in cross-section and lit by a soft directionless red light that seemed to hang in the air like smoke. Although the lighter's black hull had radiated the day's heat, its interior was as chilly as the mountain garden of the curators of the City of the Dead.

A man came down the ramp, dismissed the guard, and told Yama, Pandaras and Tamora to come with him. 'Keep to the middle of the passageway, do not touch anything, and do not answer any voices that challenge you.'

'I've been here before,' Tamora said. She seemed subdued in the red light and the chill air of the passageway.

'I remember you, and I remember a man with only one eye, but I do not remember your companions,' the man said. He was short and stocky, with a bland face and a shaved scalp criss-crossed by ugly red scars, dressed in a many-pocketed waistcoat and loose-fitting trousers.

'My original partner ran into something unexpected. But I'm here, as I said I would be, and I vouch for these two. Lead on. This place is like a tomb.'

'It is older than any tomb,' the man said.

They climbed around two turns of the passageway. Groups of coloured lights were set at random in the black stuff which sheathed the walls and ceiling and floor. The floor gave softly beneath Yama's boots, and there was a faint vibration in the red-lit air, so low-pitched that he sensed it more in his bones than in his ears.

The man stopped and pressed his palm against the wall, and the black stuff puckered and pulled back with a grating noise. Ordinary daylight flooded through the orifice, which opened onto a room no more than twenty paces across and ringed round with a narrow window that looked out across the roofs of the city in one direction and the glittering expanse of the Great River in the other. Irregular clusters of coloured lights were suspended from the ceiling like stalactites in a cave, and a thick-walled glass bottle hung from the middle of the clusters, containing some kind of red and white blossom that floated in turgid liquid.

Yama whispered to Tamora, 'Where is the captain?'

He had read several of the old romances in the library of the peel-house, and expected a tall man in a crisp, archaic uniform, with sharp eyes focused on the vast distances between stars, and skin tanned black with the fierce light of alien suns.

The man said, 'There is no captain except when the crew meld, but the pilot of this vessel will talk with you.'

Tamora said, 'The same one I talked with two days ago?'

'Does it matter?' the man said. He pulled a golden circlet from one of his pockets and set it on his scarred scalp. At once, his body stiffened. His eyes blinked, each to a different rhythm, and his mouth opened and closed.

Tamora stepped up to him and said, 'Do you know who I am?'

The man's mouth hung open. Spittle looped between his lips. His tongue writhed behind his teeth like a wounded snake and his breath came out as a hiss that slowly shaped itself into a word.

'Yessss.'

Pandaras nudged Yama and indicated the bottled blossom with a crooked thumb. 'There's the star-sailor,' he said. 'It's talking through its servant.'

Yama looked more closely at the thing inside the bottle, and saw that what he had first believed to be the fleshy petals of some exotic flower were the lobes of a mantle bunched around a core woven of pink and grey filaments. It was a little like a squid, but instead of tentacles it had white, many branching fibres that disappeared into the base of its bottle. Feathery gills rich with red blood waved slowly to and fro in the thick liquid.

Pandaras whispered, 'It's not much more than a nervous system. That's why it needs puppets.'

The star-sailor's servant jerked his head around and stared at Yama and Pandaras. His eyes were no longer blinking at different rates, but the pupil of the left eye was much bigger than that of the right. Speaking with great effort, as if forcing the words around pebbles lodged in his throat, he said, 'You told me you would bring only one other.'

Tamora said, 'The taller one, yes. But he has brought his . . . servant.'

Pandaras stepped forward and bowed low from the waist. 'I am Yama's squire. He is a perfect master of fighting. Only this night past he killed a man, an experienced and better armed warrior who thought to rob him while he slept.'

'I have not seen the bloodline for a long time, but you have chosen well,' the star-sailor told Tamora. 'He has abilities that you will find useful.'

Yama stared at the thing in the bottle, shocked to the core.

Tamora said, 'Is that so?'

'I scanned all of you when you stepped aboard.' The star-sailor's servant slammed his chest with his open hand. 'This one will see to the contract, following local custom. It will be best to return with the whole body, but if it is badly damaged then you must bring a sample of tissue. A piece the size of your smallest finger will be sufficient. You remember what I told you.'

Tamora closed her eyes and recited, ' "It will be lying close to the spine. The host must be mutilated to obliterate all trace of occupation. Burn it if possible." '

'You know my bloodline,' Yama said. 'How do you know my bloodline?'

Pandaras said, 'We aren't the first to try this, are we?'

'There was one attempt before,' Tamora said. 'It failed. That is why we're being so well paid.'

The guard said, 'If you succeed.'

'Grah. You say I have a miracle worker with me. Of course we'll succeed.'

The star-sailor's servant was groping for the circlet on his head. Yama said quickly, 'No! I want you to tell me how you know my bloodline!'

The servant's head jerked around. 'We thought you were all dead,' he said, and pulled the circlet from his scalp. He fell to his knees and retched up a mouthful of yellow bile which was immediately absorbed by the black floor, then got to his feet and wiped his mouth on the sleeve of his tunic. He said in his own voice, 'Was it agreed?'

Tamora said, 'You'll make the contract, and we put our thumbs to it.'

'Outside,' the servant said.

Yama said, 'He knew who I was! I must talk with him!'

The servant got between Yama and the bottled star-sailor. He said, 'Perhaps you can talk again when you return.'

'We should get started straight away,' Tamora said. 'It's a long haul to the estate.'

The door ground open. Yama looked at the star-sailor in its bottle, and said, 'I will be back soon, and with many questions.'

19

IACHIMO

When the giant guard went past the other side of the gate for the third time, Tamora said, 'Every four hundred heartbeats. You could boil an egg by him.'

She lay beside Yama and Pandaras in the shadows under a clump of thorny bushes. The gate, lit by the fierce white glare of an electric arc lamp, was a square lattice of steel bars set in a high wall of fused rock, as smoothly polished as black glass, that stretched away into the darkness on either side. Wall and gate were separated from the dry scrub of the hillside by a wide swathe of barren sandy soil.

Yama said, 'I still think we should go over the wall somewhere else. The rest of the perimeter cannot be as heavily guarded as the gate.'

'The gate is heavily guarded because it's the weakest part of the wall,' Tamora said. 'That's why we're going in through it. The guard is a man. Doesn't look it, but he is. He decides who to let in and who to keep out. Elsewhere, the guards will be machines or dogs. They'll kill without thinking and do it so quick you won't know it until you find yourself in the hands of the Preservers. Listen. After the guard goes past again, I'll climb the wall, kill him, and open the gates to let you in.'

'If he raises the alarm—'

'He won't have time for that,' Tamora said, and showed her teeth.

'Those won't do any good against armour,' Pandaras said.

'They'll snap off your head if you don't swallow your tongue. Be quiet. This is warrior work.'

They were tired and on edge. It had been a long journey from the waterfront. Although they had travelled much of the distance in a public calash, they had walked for the last two leagues, climbing the long, scrub-covered slopes of a straggling range of hills that rose like worn teeth at the edge of the city's wide basin, avoiding roads in case they were challenged by magistrates or private guards, skirting the walled estates of the rich. The merchant's estate was at the top of one of the hills, beyond a belt of pine forest where Yama, Tamora and Pandaras had stumbled upon an ancient paved street and the remains of the buildings which had once lined it. An age ago, the hills had been part of the city. They had rested there until just after sunset. Yama and Pandaras had eaten the raisin cakes they had bought hours before, while Tamora had prowled impatiently amongst the ruins, wolfing down strips of dried meat and snicking off the fluffy seeding heads of fireweed with her rapier.

The merchant was a star-sailor who had jumped ship the last time it had lain off the edge of Confluence, over seventy years ago. He had amassed his wealth by surreptitious deployment of technologies whose use was forbidden outside the voidships. His crewmates had sentenced him to death for the transgression, but they had no jurisdiction outside their ship and, because of the same laws that the merchant had violated, could not use their powers to capture him.

Tamora was the second cateran hired to carry out the sentence. The first had not returned, and was presumed to have been killed by the merchant's guards. Yama thought that this put them at a disadvantage, since the merchant would be expecting another attack, but Tamora said it made no difference.

'He has been expecting this ever since his old ship returned. That's why he has retreated to this estate, which has better defences than the compound he maintains in the city. We're lucky there aren't patrols outside the walls.'

Yama had asked several machines to ignore them as they had climbed through scrub and forest towards the estate, but he had not mentioned this to his companions. There was an advantage in being able to do something that no one suspected was possible. He already owed his life to this ability, and it was to his benefit to have Tamora believe that he had killed Cyg by force of arms rather than by a lucky trick.

Now, crouched between Tamora and Pandaras in the dry brush, Yama could faintly sense other machines beyond the high black wall, but they were too far away to count, let alone influence. He was dry-mouthed, and his hands had a persistent uncontrollable tremor. All his adventures with Telmon had been childhood games without risk, inadequate preparation for the real thing. His suggestion to try another part of the wall had been made as much from the need to delay the inevitable as to present an alternative strategy.

Pandaras said, 'I have an idea. Master, lend me your satchel, and that book you were reading.'

Tamora said fiercely, 'Do as I say. No more, no less.'

'I can have the guard open the gate for me,' Pandaras said. 'Or would you rather break your teeth on steel bars?'

'If you insist that we have to go through the gate,' Yama told Tamora as he emptied out his satchel, 'at least we should listen to his idea.'

'Insist? I *tell* you what to do, and you do it. This is not a democracy. Wait!'

But Pandaras stood up and, with Yama's satchel slung around his neck, stepped out into the middle of the asphalt road which ran through the gateway. Tamora hissed in frustration as the boy walked into the glare of the arc light, and Yama told her, 'He is cleverer than you think.'

'He'll be dead in a moment, clever or not.'

Pandaras banged on the gate. A bell trilled in the distance; dogs barked closer at hand.

'Did you know there were dogs?' Yama said to Tamara.

'Dogs are nothing. It is easy to kill dogs.'

Yama was not so sure. Any one of the watchdogs of the peel-house could bring down an ox by clamping its powerful jaws on the windpipe of its victim and strangling it – and to judge by the volume and ferocity of the barking there were at least a dozen dogs beyond the perimeter wall of the estate.

The guard appeared on the other side of the gate's bars. In his augmented armour, painted scarlet as if dipped in fresh blood, he was more than twice Pandaras's height. His eyes were red embers that glowed in the shadow beneath the bill of his flared helmet. Energy pistols mounted on his shoulders trained their muzzles on Pandaras and his amplified bass voice boomed a warning.

Pandaras stood his ground. He held up the satchel and opened it and showed it to the guard, then took out the book and flipped through its pages in an exaggerated pantomime. The guard reached through the gate's steel lattice, his arm extending more than a man's arm should reach, but Pandaras danced backwards and put the book back in the satchel and folded his arms and shook his head from side to side.

The guard conferred with himself in a booming mutter of subsonics;

then the red dots of his eyes brightened and a bar of intense red light swept up and down Pandaras. The red light winked out and with a clang the gate sprang open a fraction. Pandaras slipped through the gap. The gate slammed shut behind him and he followed the monstrously tall guard into the shadows beyond.

'He's brave, your fool,' Tamora said. 'But he's even more of a fool than I thought possible.'

'Let us wait and see,' Yama said, although he did not really believe that the pot boy could overmaster the armoured giant. He was as astonished as Tamora when, a few minutes later, the dogs began to bark again, the gate clanged open, and Pandaras appeared in the gap and beckoned to them.

The giant guard sprawled on his belly in the roadway a little way beyond the gate. His helmet was turned to one side and one of his arms was twisted behind him, as if he was trying to reach something on his back. Yama knew that the guard was dead, but he could feel a glimmer of machine intelligence in the man's skull, as if something still lived there, gazing with furious impotence through its host's dead eyes.

Pandaras returned Yama's satchel with a flourish, and Yama stuffed his belongings back into it. Tamora kicked the guard's scarlet cuirass, then turned on Pandaras.

'You can tell me how you did it later,' she said. 'Now we must silence the dogs. You're lucky they weren't set on you.'

Pandaras stared calmly up at her. 'A harmless messenger like me?'

'Don't be so fucking cute.'

'Let me deal with the dogs,' Yama said.

'Be quick,' Pandaras said. 'Before I killed him, the guard sent for someone to escort me to the house.'

The dogs were baying loudly, and others answered them from distant parts of the grounds. Yama found the kennel to the left of the gate, cut into the base of the wall. Several dogs thrust their snouts through the kennel's barred door with so much force that their skull caps and the machines embedded in their shoulders struck sparks from the iron bars. They howled and whined and snapped in a ferocious tumult, and it took Yama several minutes to calm them down to a point where he could ask them to speak with their fellows and assure them that nothing was wrong.

'Go to sleep,' he told the dogs, once they had passed on the message, and then he ran back to the road.

Tamora and Pandaras had rolled the guard under the partial cover of a stand of moonflower bushes beside the road. Tamora had stripped the guard's heavy pistols from their shoulder mountings. She handed one to Yama and showed him how to press two contact plates together to make it fire.

'I should have one of those,' Pandaras said. 'Right of arms, and all that.'

Tamora showed her teeth. 'You killed an armed man twice your height, in full powered armour. I'd say you are dangerous enough with that kidney puncher I chose for you. Follow me, if you can!'

She threw herself into the bushes and Yama and Pandaras ran after her, thrashing through drooping branches laden with white, waxy blossoms. Tamora and Pandaras quickly outpaced Yama, but Pandaras could not sustain his initial burst of speed and Yama soon caught up with him. The boy was leaning against the trunk of a cork oak, watching the dark stretch of grass beyond while he tried to get his breath back.

'She has the blood rage,' Pandaras said, when he could speak again. 'No sense in chasing after her.'

Yama saw a string of lights burning far off through a screen of trees on the far side of the wide lawn. He began to walk in that direction, with Pandaras trotting at his side.

'Will you tell me how you killed the guard?' Yama said. 'I might need to use the trick too.'

'How did you calm the watchdogs?'

'Do you always answer a question with a question?'

'We say that what you know makes you what you are. So you should never be free with what you know, or strangers will take pieces of you until nothing is left.'

'Nothing is free in this city, it seems.'

'Only the Preservers know everything, master. Everyone else must pay or trade for information. How did you calm the dogs?'

'We have similar dogs at home. I know how to talk to them.'

'I hope you will teach me that trick when we have the time.'

'I am not sure if that is possible, but I suppose that I can try. How did you get through the gate and kill the guard?'

'I showed him your book. I saw you reading in it when we rested in the ruins. It's very old, and very valuable. My former master and that stupid cateran you killed would have taken the gold rials and left the book, but my mother's family deals in books and I know a little about them. I talked with someone through the guard and they let me in. The rich often collect books. There is power in them.'

'Because of the knowledge they contain.'

'You're catching on. As for killing the guard, it was no trick. He was no more than an ordinary man inside that armour. Without power, he could not move a step; with it, he could sling a horse over his shoulders and still run as fast as a deer. I jumped onto his back, where he couldn't reach me, and pulled the cable that connected the power supply to the muscles in his armour. Then I stuck my knife in the gap where the cable went in, and pierced his spinal cord. A trick one of my stepbrothers taught me. The family of my mother's third husband work in a foundry that refurbishes armour. I helped out there when I was a kit. You get to know the weak points that way – they're where mending is most needed. Do we have to go so fast?'

'Where is the house, Pandaras?'

'This merchant is rich, but he is not from one of the old trading families who have estates upriver of the city. He has a warehouse at the docks, where he does his business, and this estate in the hills. They all fear bands of robbers out here, which is why the wall is so high and strong, and why there are many guards.'

Yama nodded. 'The country beyond seems very wild.'

'It used to be part of the city, but no one lives there now. No one important, anyhow. The robbers mostly come from the city.'

'The law is weaker here, then?'

'Stronger, master, if you fall foul of it. The rich make their own laws. For ordinary people, it's the magistrates who decide right and wrong. Isn't that how it was where you come from?'

Yama thought of the Aedile, and of the militia. He said, 'More or less. Then the house will be fortified. Sheer force of arms might not be the best way to try to enter it.'

'Fortified and hidden. That's the fashion these days. We could wander around for a day and not find it. Those lights are probably where the servants live, or a compound for other guards.' Pandaras stopped to disentangle the unravelling edge of his sleeve from the thorny canes of a bush. 'If you ask me, this crutty greenery is all part of the defences.'

Yama said, 'There is a path through there. Perhaps that will lead to the house.'

'If it was that simple, we'd all be rich and have big houses of our own, neh? It probably leads to a pit full of caymans or snakes.'

'Well, someone is coming along it, anyway. Here.' Yama gave the pistol to Pandaras. It was so heavy that the boy needed both hands to hold it. 'Find a good place to hide and stay there,' he said. 'I will deal with the merchant.'

'Wait,' Pandaras said. 'Aren't we in this together?'

But Yama ran towards the lights and the sound of hooves, carried by a rush of exhilaration. He had been hoping to get the chance to confront the merchant on his own, and he had seized the moment. As he ran, he took the book from his satchel; when three small stars swooped towards him through the dark air, he stopped and held it up. The machines spun to a halt above his head and bathed him in a flood of white light. Yama squinted through their radiance at the riders who had pulled up at the edge of the road.

Two guards in plastic armour reined in their prancing mounts and levelled light lances at him. The third rider was a mild old man on a grey palfrey. He wore a plain black tunic, and his long white hair was brushed back from the narrow blade of his face. His smooth tawny skin was stretched tautly over high cheekbones and a ridged brow.

Yama held the book higher. The white-haired man said, 'You were told to wait at the gate.'

'The guard was attacked, and I got scared and ran. Thieves have been after what I carry ever since I arrived in this city. Only last night I had to kill a man who wanted to steal from me.'

The white-haired man jogged his palfrey so that it stepped sideways towards Yama, and he leaned down to peer at the book. 'I can see why someone would want to steal this.'

'I have been told that it is very valuable.'

The man studied Yama for a full minute, and said at last, 'Where are you from, boy?'

'Downriver,' Yama said. 'At least, that was where I grew up. But your master will tell you that I come from elsewhere.'

'Will he, now? Is that where you found that book? In one of the old tombs, downriver?'

Before Yama could answer, one of the guards said to the white-haired man, 'Take the book, Iachimo, and leave him to us.'

The second guard said, 'He carries a power knife in his satchel.'

'More loot, I expect,' Iachimo said. 'You won't try to use it, will you, boy?'

'I came here to talk with your master,' Yama said.

'Really. And what do you want to talk about?'

'I think he knows who I really am.'

'Hmm. Well, before you can talk to him, you'll have to talk to me,' Iachimo said and swung down from his palfrey and turned to the two guards. 'I'll take charge of him. You two go and check the gate. Find out what happened there.'

The first guard said, 'Isn't he a little too old for you, Iachimo?'

'Do as I command,' Iachimo said pleasantly, 'or I'll slice out your tongue and eat it in front of you.'

As they crossed the road and plunged into a stand of pine trees beyond, Iachimo told Yama, 'You cannot buy loyalty. You must win it by fear or by love. Of the two, I find fear to be the most effective. Now, tell me about the book. Did you find it in some tomb, in the City of the Dead? Answer truthfully. I'll know at once if you are lying.'

Yama did not doubt it, but thought that Iachimo was the kind of man who believed that he was cleverer than everyone else, and so held all others in contempt and did not pay as much attention to them as he should. He said, 'It was not from the City of the Dead, dominie, but from a place close by.'

'Hmm. As I remember, the house occupied by the Aedile of Aeolis has an extensive library.' Iachimo smiled at Yama. 'I see I have hit the truth. Well, I doubt that the Aedile will miss it. The library is a depository of all kinds of rubbish, but as the fisher folk of that region have it, precious stones are sometimes engendered in mud by the light of the Eye of the Preservers. Nonsense, of course, but despite that it has a grain of truth. In this case, the fisher folk are familiar with pearls, which are produced by certain shellfish when they are irritated by a speck of grit and secrete layers of slime to enclose the irritation. This slime hardens, and becomes the black or red pearls so eagerly sought by gentlemen and ladies of high breeding. Your book is such a pearl. An early edition of the Puranas, I believe.'

'It is very old,' Yama said.

'I knew it as soon as I saw it, although I do not think it was you who held it up at the gate.'

'It was my friend. But he got scared and ran off.'

'The guards will catch him. Or the dogs will, if he is unlucky.'

'He is harmless. A pot boy from one of the inns by the waterfront. I struck up a friendship with him.'

'From which he hoped to profit, I expect,' Iachimo said, and then stopped and turned to look at the way they had come.

A moment later a thread of white light lanced through the darkness beyond the trees. Yama felt the ground tremble beneath his feet, and a noise deeper than thunder rolled through the air.

Iachimo grasped Yama's shoulders and pushed him forward. 'One of the guard's weapons, unless I am mistaken. And I am never mistaken. Your friend has been found, boy. Do not think of running, or you'll suffer the same fate.'

'I have no intention of running, because I really do want to meet your master. And I think that you know why. Otherwise you would have already killed me, and taken the book.'

Yama hoped that the guards had found Tamora rather than Pandaras. He also hoped that he would have a little time with the merchant before she came for him. As he and Iachimo descended into a narrow defile between steep rock walls studded with ferns and orchids, another white flash lit the crack of sky above. Pebbles rattled down the walls in the aftershock.

Iachimo tightened his grip on Yama's shoulder and pushed him on. 'I admit that you caught my interest.'

'Because of my bloodline. I saw that you recognised it.'

Iachimo nodded. 'You were not raised by your true mother and father, were you?'

'My mother is dead.'

A silver woman in a white boat. The old Constable, Thaw, had said that he had plucked Yama from her dead breast, but as a young boy Yama had dreamed that she had only been profoundly asleep, and was searching for him in the wilderness of tombs around Aeolis. Sometimes he had searched for her there – as he was searching still.

Iachimo said, 'Of course she is. Dead ages past. I imagine that you were revived from a stored template. The question is, who revived you?'

The defile opened out into a courtyard dimly lit by a scattering of floating lanterns, tiny as fireflies, that drifted in the black air. Its tiled floor was crowded with grey, life-sized statues of men and animals in a variety of contorted poses. When Iachimo pushed Yama forward the statues stirred and trembled, shedding puffs of dust and a dry scent of electricity. Some opened their eyes, but all seemed blind, with eyeballs like white marbles.

Iachimo said, 'As you can see, there are worse fates than death. But if you cooperate, and answer every question truthfully, I'll spare you this.'

'I will trade truth for truth.'

'I hope you will. My master expects only to see the book. You will be an interesting surprise. We'll see what shakes out, and afterwards we'll have a little talk, just you and I.'

Iachimo smiled at Yama, but it was merely a rearrangement of certain muscles in his face. He was lost in his own thoughts, Yama saw, a man so clever that he schemed as naturally as other men breathed.

Yama understood that he was a prize Iachimo wanted to offer to his master in exchange for advancement or reward. He said, 'What can you offer me?'

'Haven't I just agreed to let you talk with my master? Damn these things!'

Iachimo was standing close to the statue of a naked boy, which had managed to grasp the hem of his tunic. He tugged impatiently, then broke off the statue's fingers, one by one. They made a dry snapping sound, and powdered to dust when they struck the floor. Iachimo brushed his hands together briskly and said, 'My master has revived certain technologies long thought forgotten. It is the basis of his fortune and his power. He knows much about old things. But you know that. That's why you're here, isn't it?'

Yama did not know how to begin to answer that question.

'Listen to me,' Iachimo said. 'I know that my master will be interested in you, but do nothing to provoke him. He is one of the oldest members of a long-lived bloodline, and like all who have lived a long time he has a number of enemies. If he feels threatened by you in any way, he will try to kill you. I will do my best to protect you, but it will not be easy. He controls the guards inside the house.'

'I understand,' Yama said.

'Good. Come this way.'

On the far side of the courtyard was an arched doorway and a broad flight of marble steps that led down towards a pool of warm white light. When they reached the head of the stairs, Iachimo's long, pointed nails dug into Yama's shoulder again, pricking his skin through his shirt.

'Stand straight,' Iachimo said. 'Use your backbone as it was intended. Remember that you were made in the image of the Preservers, and forget that your ancestors were animals that went about on all fours. Good. Now walk forward, and do not stare at anything. Most especially, do not stare at my master. He is more sensitive than he might appear, and he has not always been as he is now.'

20

THE HOLLOW MAN

Although Yama sensed the presence of a large number of machines as he descended the marble steps, the size of the room still surprised him. Golden pillars twisted into fantastic shapes marched away across an emerald-green lawn, lending perspective to a space perhaps a thousand paces long and three hundred wide. The lawn was studded with islands of couches upholstered in bright silks, and fountains and dwarf fruit trees and statues – these last merely of red sandstone or marble, not petrified flesh. Displays of exotic flowers perfumed the air. Constellations of white lights floated in the air beneath a high glass ceiling. Above the glass was not air but water: schools of golden and black carp swam lazily through illuminated currents, and pads of water lilies hung above them like the silhouettes of clouds.

Thousands of tiny machines crawled amongst the closely trimmed blades of grass or spun through the bright air like silver beetles or dragonflies with mica wings, their thoughts a rising harmonic in Yama's head. Men in scarlet and white uniforms and silver helmets stood in alcoves carved into the marble walls. They were unnaturally still and, like the fallen guard at the gate, emitted faint glimmers of machine intelligence.

As Yama walked across the lawn, with Iachimo following close behind, he heard music in the distance: the chiming runs of a tambura like silver laughter over the solemn pulse of a tabla. A light sculpture twisted in the air like a writhing column of brightly coloured scarves seen through a heat haze.

The two musicians sat in a nest of embroidered silk cushions to one side of a huge couch on which lay the fattest man Yama had ever seen.

He was naked except for a loincloth, and completely hairless. His black skin shone with oils and unguents; a gold circlet crowned his shaven head. The thick folds of his belly spilled his flanks and draped his swollen thighs. He was propped on his side amongst cushions and bolsters, and pawed in a distracted fashion at a naked woman who was feeding him pastries from a pile stacked high on a silver salver. Without doubt, this was the master of the house, the merchant, the rogue star-sailor.

Yama halted a few paces from the couch and bowed from the waist, but the merchant did not acknowledge him. He stood and waited beside Iachimo while the musicians played through the variations of their raga and the merchant ate a dozen pastries one after the other and stroked the gleaming pillows of the woman's large breasts with swollen, ring-encrusted fingers. Like her master, the woman was quite without hair. The petals of her labia were pierced with rings, and from the largest ring a fine gold chain ran to a bracelet on the merchant's wrist.

When the concluding chimes of the tambura had died away, the merchant closed his eyes and sighed deeply, then dismissed the musicians with a languid wave of a hand. 'Drink,' he said in a high, wheezing voice. The woman jumped up and poured red wine into a bowl which she held to the merchant's lips. He slobbered at the wine horribly, and it spilled over his chin and chest onto the grassy floor. Yama saw now that the cushions of the couch were stained with old spillages and littered with crumbs and half-eaten crusts; underlying the rich scents of spikenard and jasmine and the sweet smoke of candles which floated in a bowl of water was a stale reek of old sweat and spoiled food.

The merchant belched and glanced at Yama. His cheeks were so padded with fat that they pushed his mouth into a squashed rosebud, and his eyes peered above their ramparts like sentries, darting here and there as if expecting a sudden attack from any quarter. He said petulantly, 'What's this, Iachimo? Are you picking up street urchins now?'

Iachimo inclined his head. 'You know that I would never trouble you with my bed companions, master. You might care to look more closely. I believe that you will find he is a rare type, one not seen on Confluence for many an age.'

'You are too fond of games, Iachimo. It will be your downfall. Tell me and have done with it.'

'I believe that he is one of the Builders,' Iachimo said.

The merchant laughed – a series of grunts that convulsed his vast, gleaming body as a storm tosses the surface of the river. At last he said, 'Your inventive mind never ceases to amaze me, Iachimo. There's a passing resemblance, certainly, but it's no more than some river-rat a mountebank has surgically altered, no doubt inspired by some old carving or slate. You've been had.'

'He came here of his own accord. And he brought with him a book of great antiquity. I have it here.'

The merchant took the copy of the Puranas from Iachimo and pawed through it, grunting to himself, before casually tossing it aside. It landed face down and splayed open amongst the stained cushions on which the merchant sprawled. Yama made a move to retrieve it, but Iachimo caught his arm.

'I've seen better,' the merchant said. 'Take it away, Iachimo, and its book. Dispose of it in the usual way, and dispose of its companion, too, once you've caught it. Or do I have to take charge of the guards and do that myself?'

'It won't be necessary, master. But I would ask you to look at this boy again. I believe that he is something not seen in the world for many an age.' Iachimo prodded Yama in the small of his back with a fingernail as sharply pointed as a stiletto and whispered, 'Show him what you can do.'

'I do not understand what you want of me.'

'Oh, but you do,' Iachimo hissed. 'I know what you can do with machines. You got past the guard at the gate – you know something of your inheritance.'

The merchant said, 'I'm in an indulgent mood, Iachimo. Here's your test. I'm going to order my soldiers to kill you, boy. Do you understand? Stop them, and we'll talk some more. Otherwise I'm rid of a fraud.'

Four of the guards started forward from their niches. Faces expressionless beneath the bills of their silver helmets, they raised their gleaming falchions and marched stiffly across the lawn towards the couch, two on the right, two on the left.

Iachimo said in a wheedling tone, 'Master, surely this isn't necessary.'

'Let me have my fun,' the merchant said. 'What is he to you, eh?'

Yama put his hand inside his satchel and found the hilt of his knife, but the guards were almost upon him and he knew that he could not fight four of them at once. He felt a tingling expansion and shouted at the top of his voice. 'Stop! Stop now!'

The guards froze in midstep. Then, moving as one, they knelt and laid down their falchions, and bent until their silver helmets touched the grass.

The merchant reared up and squealed, 'What is this? Do you betray me, Iachimo?'

'Quite the reverse, master. I'll kill him in a moment, if you give the word. But you can see that he is no mountebank's fake.'

The merchant glared at Yama. There was a high whine, like a bee trapped in a bottle, and a machine dropped through the air and hovered in front of Yama's face. Red light flashed in his eyes. When he asked the machine to go away the red light flashed again, filling his vision. He held himself still, although panic trembled in his breast like a trapped dove. He could feel every corner of the machine's small bright mind, but by a sudden inversion, as if a flower had suddenly dwindled down to the seed from which it had sprung, it was closed to him.

Somewhere beyond the red light, the merchant said, 'Recently born. No revenant. Where is he from, Iachimo?'

'Downriver,' Iachimo said, close by Yama's ear. 'But not very far downriver, I think.'

'The City of the Dead,' the merchant said. 'It's possible, although there are older tombs elsewhere on Confluence. Stop trying to control my machines, boy. I have told them to ignore you and, fortunately for you, you don't know the extent of your abilities. Fortunately for you, too, Iachimo. You risked a great deal bringing him here. I'll not forget that.'

Iachimo said, 'I am yours to punish or reward, master. As always. But be assured that this boy does not understand what he is. Otherwise I would not have been able to capture him.'

'He's done enough damage. I have reviewed the security systems, something you haven't troubled to do. He blinded the watchdogs and the machines patrolling the grounds, which is why he and his friend could wander with impunity. I have restored them. He must have killed the guard at the gate, too, because his friend is armed with one of the guard's pistols. Wait – there are two of them, both armed, and loose in the grounds. The security system was told to ignore them, but I'm tracking them now. You have let things get out of hand, Iachimo.'

'I had no reason to believe the security system was not operating correctly, master. But it proves, does it not, that the boy is indeed a rare treasure.'

Yama turned his head from side to side, but could not see past the red light. There were splinters of pain in his eyes. He said, 'Am I blinded?' and his voice was smaller and weaker than he would have liked.

'I suppose it isn't necessary,' the merchant said, and the red light snapped off.

Yama blinked away tears. Two of the guards stood at attention behind the merchant's couch, their red and white uniforms gleaming, the blades of their falchions held before their faces.

'I think we should talk, you and I,' the merchant said. His voice was silkily unctuous now. 'Drink, eat. I have nothing but the best. The best vintages, the finest meats, the tenderest vegetables.'

'Some wine, perhaps. Thank you.'

The naked woman poured wine as rich and red as fresh blood into a gold beaker and handed it to Yama, then poured another bowl for the merchant, who slobbered it down at once. Yama took a sip from his beaker, expecting some rare vintage, and was disappointed to discover that it was no better than the ordinary wine of the peel-house's cellars.

The merchant smacked his lips and said, 'Do you know what I am? And do stop trying to take control of my servants. You will give me a headache.'

Yama had been trying to persuade one of the machines which illuminated the room to fly down and settle above his head, but despite his sense of expansion, as if his thoughts had become larger than his skull, he might as well have tried to order an ossifrage to quit its icy perch in the high foothills of the Rim Mountains. He stared at the gold circlet on the merchant's fleshy, hairless pate, and said, 'You are really one of those things which crew the voidships. I suppose that you stole the body.'

'As a matter of fact I had it grown. Do you like it?'

Yama took another sip of wine. He felt calmer now. He said, 'I am amazed by it.'

'I've yet to find a body that can withstand my appetites, but that's of little consequence, because there are always more bodies. This is my – what is it, Iachimo? The tenth?'

'The ninth, master.'

'Well, there will soon be need for a tenth, and there will be more after that, an endless chain. How old are you, boy? No more than twenty, I'd guess. This body is half your age.'

The merchant pawed at the breasts of the woman. She was feeding him sugared almonds, popping them into his mouth each time it opened. He chewed the almonds mechanically, and a long string of pulp and saliva drooled unheeded down his chin.

He said, 'I've been male and female in my time. Mostly male, given the current state of civilisation, but now that I've made my fortune and have no need to leave my estate, perhaps I'll be female next time. Are there others like you?'

'That is what I want to discover,' Yama said. 'You know of my bloodline. You know more than me, it seems. You called me a builder. A builder of what?'

But he already knew. He had read in the Puranas, and he remembered the man in the picture slate which Osric and Beatrice had shown him.

'Why don't you tell him?' the merchant said to Iachimo.

Iachimo said, ' "And the Preservers raised up a man and set on his brow their mark, and raised up a woman of the same kind, and set on her brow the same mark. From the white clay of the middle region did they shape this race, and quickened them with their marks. And those of this race were the servants of the Preservers. And in their myriads this race shaped the world after the ideas of the Preservers." '

'There's a lot more,' the merchant said, 'but you get the general idea. That's your bloodline. The last of them died so long ago that almost no one remembers—'

White light flashed above, somewhere beyond the lake which roofed the long room. Rafts of water-lily pads swung wildly on clashing waves and there was a deep, heavy muffled sound, as if a massive door had slammed in the keel of the world.

The merchant said, 'No hope there, boy. You put some of my guards to sleep, but now they're under my control again, and are moments away from capturing your friends. Iachimo, you did not say that one of them was a cateran.'

'There was another boy, master. I knew of no other.'

The merchant closed his eyes. For a moment, Yama felt that a thousand intelligences were chattering in his head. Then they were gone, and the merchant said, 'She's of the Fierce People, and she's armed with one of the gatekeeper's pistols. She killed several guards with it, but she's down to her last shot.'

'But you almost have her, master, and we're quite safe here. The lake will absorb any blast from the pistol.'

The merchant pulled the woman close to him. 'She came to kill me, you old fool. This boy is her accomplice, and you brought him here, even though you know I have been in mortal danger of assassination ever since my old ship returned through the manifold.'

'There was the man who broke into the godown,' Iachimo said, 'but we dealt with him easily enough.'

'And now they have sent another—'

There was another flash of light. A portion of water above the glass ceiling seethed into a spreading cloud of bubbles, and the glass rang like a cracked bell.

The merchant closed his eyes briefly. 'Well, perhaps it doesn't matter now. That was her last shot. There's a weapon in his satchel, Iachimo. Take it out and give it to me.'

The white-haired man lifted out the sheathed knife and said, 'It is only a knife, master.'

'I know what it is. Bring it here.'

Iachimo offered the knife, hilt first. Yama implored it to manifest the horrible shape which had frightened Lob and the landlord of *The Crossed Axes*, but he was at the centre of a vast muffling silence. The merchant squinted at the knife's goatskin sheath, and then the woman drew it and plunged it into Iachimo's belly.

Iachimo grunted and fell to his knees. The knife flashed blue fire and the woman screamed and dropped it and clutched her smoking hand. The knife embedded itself point first in the grass, sizzling faintly and emitting a drizzle of fat blue motes. Iachimo was holding his belly with both hands. There was blood all over his fingers and the front of his black tunic.

The merchant looked at the woman and she fell silent in mid-scream. He said to Yama, 'So die all those who think to betray me. You'll answer all my questions truthfully, or you'll join your two friends. My guards have them now. We'll talk, you and I, and decide their fate.'

Iachimo, kneeling over the knife and a pool of his own blood, said something about a circle, and then the guards seized him and jerked him upright and cut his throat and lifted him away from the merchant, all in one quick motion. They dropped the body onto the neatly trimmed grass beneath the light sculpture and returned to their position behind the merchant's couch.

The woman, trembling, placed the mouthpiece of a clay pipe between the merchant's rosebud lips and lit the scrap of resin in its bowl. He drew a long breath and said, dribbling smoke, 'Your people were the first. The rest came later, but you were the first. I had never thought to see your kind again, but this is an age of wonders. That's the only reason you and your friends are still alive. The three of you came to kill me, didn't you? You were sent by my crewmates, who are jealous of my freedom.'

Yama stared in stubborn silence at the merchant, who calmly drew on his pipe and contemplated the wreaths of smoke he breathed out.

At last the merchant said, 'If you can prove your worth to me, I might spare your friends. Tell me now, and tell me the truth: do you know exactly what you are, and where you came from?'

Yama told the story of the white boat and the dead woman, explained how he had been adopted by a kind man who had sent him to Ys to complete his education. 'You say that I am of the bloodline of the Builders, and it might be true – I have seen a picture showing one of my kind before the world was made. But I also have been told that I might be a child of the Ancients of Days.'

'Oh, if they had anything to do with it, it would be by accident rather than by design. For all that they might have appeared as gods to the degenerate population of Confluence, they predated the Preservers by several million years. Their kind were the ancestors of the Preservers, but with about as much relation to them as the brainless plankton grazers which were the ancestors of my own bloodline have to me. They were timeshifted while travelling to our neighbouring galaxy and back at close to the speed of light, and that's why they appeared so late, like an actor delayed by circumstance who incontinently rushes on stage to deliver his lines and finds that he has interrupted the closing soliloquy instead of beginning the second act. When they arrived this world had already passed into the end times, young Builder. This whole grand glorious foolish experiment has all but run its course. The silly little war downriver is only a footnote in its inevitable dissolution.'

The merchant seemed exhausted by this speech, and drank more wine before he continued. 'Still, they meddled in much they didn't fully understand during their brief stopover. It is possible, I suppose, that they activated your template by mistake. Or perhaps they were, unknowingly, part of the grand design that not only quickened the world but also augured its end.'

'We all serve the Preservers as we must,' Yama said.

'Do you really believe that, or are you merely parroting a pious phrase some backwater priest taught you?'

Yama could not truthfully answer. He had never before questioned his faith, but he realised now that by disobeying the wishes of his father he had rebelled against the immutable hierarchy that, according to the Puranas, proceeded directly from the Preservers. But the Puranas also claimed that the Preservers wanted their creations to advance from a low to a high condition, and how could that happen if society was fixed, eternal and unchanging?

The merchant belched. 'I wouldn't hold out much hope that you're a manifestation of the will of the Preservers, boy. No, you're nothing more than a curiosity. An afterthought or an accident – it's all the same. But I can give your life purpose. We can do great things together.'

'What kind of things?'

'I left my ship because I remembered what all others of my kind have long forgotten. They are lost in ascetic contemplation of the mathematics of the manifolds and the secrets of the beginning and end of the cosmos, but I remembered the pleasures of the real world, of appetite and sex and all the rest of the messy wonderful business of life. They claim that mathematics is the reality underlying everything; I say that it is an abstraction of the real world, a ghost.' The merchant belched again. 'There is my riposte to algebra.'

Yama made a wild intuitive leap. He said, 'You met the Ancients of Days, didn't you?'

'My ship hailed theirs as it fell through the void towards the Eye of the Preservers. They had seen the Eye's construction by ancient light while hundreds of thousands of years out, and were amazed to discover that organic intelligent life still existed. We merged our mindscapes and talked long there, and I followed them out into the world. And here I am. It is remarkably easy to make a fortune in these benighted times, but I'm finding that merely satisfying sensual appetites is not enough. If you're truly a Builder, and I am not quite convinced that you are, then perhaps you can help me. I have plans.'

'I am no man's servant. I cannot serve you as Iachimo did.'

The merchant laughed. 'I would hope not. There are many like Iachimo in the world, intelligent and learned and utterly lacking the courage to act on their convictions. There is no end to natural followers like him. You are something more. I don't want you to replace Iachimo, but you will serve me, all the same. Otherwise you will die, and so will your little friend the rat boy.'

The twisting scarves of colour in the light sculpture ran together into a steely grey and widened into a kind of window, showing Tamora and Pandaras kneeling inside tiny cages suspended in dark air.

For a moment, Yama's breath caught in his throat. He said, 'Free them. Let them go. If you'll do that, I promise that I will help you in any way I can.'

'The boy is no different from a million other river-rats in Ys. If I killed him it would be as if he had never been born, but I'll set him free if you keep your promise. But the woman is a cateran. I cannot set her free because she is bound by contract to kill me. I have to kill her before she kills me. Or rather, *you* will kill her.'

'No.'

'I cannot begin to trust you, Child of the River, until you have shown that you will do all that I ask of you. To begin with, you will kill the cateran. Otherwise I'll kill all three of you. Promise that you'll do it now, before I give you a taste of the pain that you and your friends will suffer if you don't.'

The two guards swivelled towards Yama. He stared in sudden panic at their blank, blind faces, and his panic inflated into something immense, a great wild bird whose wings beat in his mind. In desperation, quite without hope, he sent up an imploring scream for help.

The merchant pawed at his head and far down the room something struck the glass ceiling with a tremendous bang. For a moment, all was still. Then a line of spray sheeted down, and the glass around it gave with a loud splintering crash. The spray became a widening waterfall that smashed into the floor and sent a tawny wave flooding down the length of the room, knocking over pillars and statues and sweeping tables and couches before it.

The merchant's couch lurched into the air. The woman gave a guttural cry of alarm, and clung to her master's flesh like a shipwrecked sailor clinging to a scrap of flotsam. Yama charged through surging water (for a moment, Iachimo's corpse clutched at his ankles; then it was swept away), made a desperate leap, and caught hold of one end of the rising couch. His weight rocked it on its long axis. One moment he hung straight down; the next he was tipped forward, and fell across the merchant's legs.

The merchant roared, and the woman clawed at Yama with sudden fury, her long nails scoring his forehead. Blood poured into his eyes. The couch turned in a dizzy circle above the guards as they struggled to stay upright in the seething flood. The merchant caught at Yama's hands, but his grasp was feeble, and Yama, half-blinded, grabbed the golden circlet around the man's fleshy scalp and pulled with all his strength.

For a moment, he feared that the circlet would not give way. Then it snapped in half and unravelled like a ribbon. All the lights went out. The couch tipped and Yama and the merchant and the woman tumbled into the wash of the flood. Yama went under and got a mouthful of muddy water and came up spitting and gasping.

All of the guards had collapsed, like unstrung puppets, and all of the machines in the room had likewise fallen.

Yama asked a question, and after a moment points of intense light flared down the length of the room, burning through the swirling brown flood. Yama wiped blood from his eyes. The current swirled around his waist. He was clutching a tangle of golden filaments tipped with stringy fragments of flesh.

At the far end of the huge room, something floated a handspan above the water, turning slowly end for end. It was as big as Yama's head, and black, and decorated all over with spikes of varying lengths and thickness, some like rose thorns, others long and finely tapered and questing this way and that with blind intelligence. The thing radiated an icy menace, a negation not only of life but of the reality of the world. For a moment, Yama was transfixed; then the machine rose straight up, smashing through the ceiling. Yama felt it rise higher and higher, and for a moment felt all the machines in Ys turn towards it – and then it was gone.

The merchant sprawled across the fallen couch like a beached grampus. A ragged wound crowned his head, streaming blood; he snorted a jelly of blood and mucus through his nose. The woman lay beneath him, entirely submerged. Her head was twisted back, and her eyes stared up through swirling water.

Yama held the frayed remnants of the circlet before the merchant's eyes, and said, 'Iachimo told me about this with his last breath, but I had already guessed its secret. I saw something like it on the lighter.'

'The Preservers have gone away,' the merchant whispered.

The floodwaters were receding, running away into deeper levels of the sunken house. Yama knelt by the couch and said, 'Why am I here?'

The merchant drew a breath. Blood ran from his nostrils and his mouth. He said wetly, 'Serve no one.'

'If the Preservers are gone, why was I brought back?'

The merchant tried and failed to say something, blew a bubble of blood as his last breath rattled in his throat. Yama left him there and went to find Tamora and Pandaras.

21

THE FIERCE PEOPLE

Tamora came back to the campfire at a loping run. She was grinning broadly and there was blood around her mouth. She threw a brace of coneys at Yama's feet and said, 'This is how we live, when we can. We are the Fierce People, the Memsh Tek!'

Pandaras said, 'Not all of us can live on meat alone.'

'Your kind eat leaves, and the filth swept into street gutters,' Tamora said, 'and that is why they are so weak. Meat and blood are what warriors need, so be glad that I give you fine fresh guts. They will make you strong.'

She slit the bellies of the coneys with her sharp thumbnail and crammed the steaming, rich red livers into her mouth and gulped them down. Then she ungloved the furry skins from the gutted bodies, and set about dismembering them with teeth and nails.

She had attacked the merchant's carcass with the same butcher's skill, using a falchion taken from one of the dead guards to fillet it from neck to buttocks and expose the thing which had burrowed into the fatty flesh like a hagfish. It had not been much like the bottled creature that Yama had seen on the lighter. Its mantle was shrunken, and white fibres had knitted around its host's spinal column like cords of fungus in rotten wood.

Tamora kept most of the coney meat for herself and ate it raw, but she allowed Yama and Pandaras to cook the haunches over the embers of the fire. The unsalted meat was half-burnt and half-raw, but Yama and Pandaras hungrily stripped it from the bones.

'Burnt meat is bad for the digestion,' Tamora said, grinning at them across the embers of the fire. She wore only her leather skirt. Her two pairs of breasts were little more than enlarged nipples, like tarnished coins set on her narrow ribcage. In addition to the bird burning in a nest of fire on her upper arm, inverted triangles were tattooed in black ink across her shoulders. There was a bandage around her waist; she had been seared by backflash from a pistol shot. She took a swallow of brandy and passed the bottle to Yama. She had bought the brandy in a bottleshop and used a little of it to preserve the filaments she had flensed from the merchant's body and placed in the miniature flask, cut from a single crystal of rose quartz, that Yama had found in the wreckage left by the flood when he had been searching for his copy of the Puranas.

Yama drank and passed the bottle to Pandaras, who was cracking coney bones between his sharp teeth.

'Drink,' Tamora said. 'We fought a great battle today.'

Pandaras spat a bit of gristle into the fire. He had already made it clear how unhappy he was to be in the Fierce People's tract of wild country, and he sat with his kidney puncher laid across his lap and his mobile ears pricked. He said, 'I'd rather keep my wits about me.'

Tamora laughed. 'No one would mistake you for a coney. You're about the right size, but you can't run fast enough to make the hunt interesting, and most likely you'd taste like you smell. Piss and sour mud.'

Pandaras took the smallest possible sip from the brandy bottle, passed it back to Yama, and told Tamora, 'You certainly showed a clean pair of heels when the soldiers came.'

'Grah. I had to catch up with you, and make sure you went the right way.'

'Enough stuff to set a man up for life,' Pandaras said, 'and we had to leave it for the city militia to loot.'

'I'm a cateran, not a robber. We have done what we contracted to do. Be happy.' Tamora grinned. Her pink tongue lolled amongst her big, sharp teeth. 'Eat burnt bones. Drink. Sleep. We are safe here, and tomorrow we are paid.'

Yama realised that she was drunk. They had needed only a few minims of brandy to fill the crystal flask to the brim, and Tamora had drunk about half of what was left.

'Safe?' Pandaras said. 'In the middle of packs of bloodthirsty howlers like you? I won't sleep at all tonight.'

'No, you will not. Because I will sing a great song of our triumph, and you will listen. Pass that bottle, Yama. It is not your child.'

Yama took a burning swallow of brandy, handed the bottle over, and walked out of the firelight to the crest of the ridge. The sandy hills where the Fierce People maintained their hunting grounds looked out across the wide basin of the city towards the Great River. It was past midnight. The misty light of the Arm of the Warrior was rising above the farside horizon. The city was mostly dark, but many campfires flickered amongst the scrub and clumps of crown ferns, pines and eucalyptus, and from every quarter came the sound of distant voices raised in song.

Yama sat on the dry grass and listened to the night music of the Fierce People. The brief sight of the feral machine still haunted him, like a ringing in the ears or the after-image of a searingly bright light. And beyond this psychic echo he could feel the ebb and flow of the myriad machines in the city, the flexing of a vast and vastly complicated net. They had also been disturbed by the feral machine, and the ripples of alarm caused by the disturbance were still spreading, leaping from cluster to cluster of machines along the docks, running out towards the vast bulk of the Palace of the Memory of the People, clashing at the bases of the high towers and racing up their lengths, clean out of the atmosphere.

Yama still did not know how he had called down the feral machine, and although it had saved him he feared that he might call it again by accident, and feared too that he had exposed himself to discovery by the network of machines which served the magistrates, or by Prefect Corin, who must surely be searching for him. The descent of the feral machine was the most terrifying and the most shameful of his adventures. He had been paralysed with fear when confronted with it, and even now he felt that it had marked him in some obscure way, for a small part of him yearned for it, and what it could tell him. It could be watching him still; it could return at any time, and he did not know what he would do if it did.

The merchant – Yama still found it difficult to think of him as the parasitic bundle of nerve fibres burrowed deep within that tremendously bloated body – had said that he was a Builder, a member of the first bloodline of Ys. The pilot of the voidship lighter had said something similar; and there was the picture that Beatrice and Osric had shown him. His people had walked Confluence in its first days, sculpting the world under the direct instruction of the Preservers, and had died out or ascended ages past, so long ago that most had forgotten them. And yet he was here, and he still did not know why; nor did he know the full extent of his powers.

The merchant had hinted that he knew what Yama was capable of, but he might have been lying to serve his own ends, and besides, he was dead. Perhaps the other star-sailors knew – Iachimo had said that they were very long-lived – or perhaps, as Yama had hoped even before he had set out from Aeolis, there were records somewhere in Ys that would explain everything, or would at least lead him to others of his kind. He still did not know how he had been brought into the world, or why he had been found floating on the river on the breast of a dead woman who might have been his mother or nurse or something else entirely. But although the merchant had scoffed at the idea, Yama believed that he had been born to serve the Preservers in some fashion. After the Preservers had fallen into the event horizon of the Eye, they could still watch the world they had made, for nothing fell faster than light, but they could no longer act upon it. But perhaps their reach was long – perhaps they had ordained his birth, here in what the merchant had called the end times, long before they had withdrawn from the universe. Perhaps, as Derev believed, many of Yama's kind now walked the world, as they had at its beginning. But for what purpose? All through his childhood he had prayed for a revelation, a sign, a hint, and had received no reply. Perhaps the shape of his life was the sign he sought, if only he could understand it.

But he could not believe he was the servant of the feral machines. That was the worst thought of all.

Yama sat on a hummock of dry grass, with the noise of crickets everywhere in the darkness around him, and leafed through his copy of the Puranas. The book had dried out well, although one corner of its front cover was faintly but indelibly stained with the merchant's blood. The pages held a faint light, and the glyphs stood out like shadows against it. Yama found the sura which Iachimo had quoted, and read it from beginning to end.

The world first showed itself as a golden embryo of sound. As soon as the thoughts of the Preservers turned to the creation of the world, the long vowel which described the form of the world vibrated in the pure realm of thought, and re-echoed on itself. From the knots in the play of vibrations, the crude matter of the world curdled. In the beginning, it was no more than a sphere of air and water with a little mud at the centre.

And the Preservers raised up a man and set on his brow their mark, and raised up a woman of the same kind, and set on her brow the same mark. From the white clay of the middle region did they shape this race, and quickened them with their marks. And those of this race were the servants of the Preservers. And in their myriads this race shaped the world after the ideas of the Preservers.

Yama read on, although the next sura was merely an exhaustive description of the dimensions and composition of the world, and he knew that there was no other mention of the Builders, nor of their fate. This was towards the end of the Puranas. The world and everything in it was an afterthought at the end of the history of the Home Galaxy, created in the last moment before the Preservers fell into the Eye and were known no more in the universe.

Tamora said, 'Reading, is it? There's nothing in books you can't learn better in the world, and there's all kinds of fantastic rubbish about monsters and the like besides. You'll rot your mind and your eyes, reading too much in books.'

'Well, I met a real monster today.'

'And he's dead, the fucker, and we have a piece of him pickled in brandy as proof. So much for him.'

Yama had not told Tamora and Pandaras about the feral machine. Tamora had boasted that her last pistol shot had weakened the ceiling and caused the flood which had saved them, and Yama had not corrected her error. He felt a rekindling of shame at this deception, and said, 'He tried to flee from his true self, and let a little hungry part of himself rule his life. He was all appetite and nothing else. I think he would have eaten the whole world, if he could.'

'You want to be a soldier. Here's some advice. Don't think too much about what you have to do, and don't think about it at all when it's done.'

'And can you forget about it so easily?'

'Of course not. But I try. We were captured, your rat-boy and me, and thrown into cages, but you had it worse, I think. The merchant was trying to bend you towards his will. The words of his kind are like thorns, and some of them are still in your flesh. Try to ignore them.'

Yama smiled and said, 'Perhaps it would be no bad thing, to be the ruler of the world.'

Tamora sat down close beside him. 'You would destroy the civil service and rule instead? How would that change the world for the better?'

Yama could feel her heat. She gave off a strong scent compounded of fresh blood and sweat and a sharp, not unpleasant musk. He said, 'Of course not. But the merchant told me something about my bloodline. I may be alone in the world. I may be a mistake thrown up at the end of things. Or I may be something else. Something *intended*.'

'The fat fuck was lying. How better to get you to follow him than by saying that you are the only one of your kind, and he knows all about you?'

'I am not sure that he was lying, Tamora. At least, I think he told me part of the truth.'

'I haven't forgotten what you want, and I was a long time hunting coneys because I really went to ask around. Listen. I have a way of getting at what you want. There is a job for a couple of caterans. Some little pissant department needs someone to organise a defence of its territory inside the Palace of the Memory of the People. There are many disputes between departments, and the powerful grow strong at the expense of the weak. That's the way of the world, but I don't mind defending the weak if I get paid for it.'

'Then perhaps they are stronger than you after all.'

'When a litter is born here, the babies are exposed on a hillside for a day. Any that are weak die, or are taken by birds or foxes. We're the Fierce People, see? We keep our bloodline strong. The wogs and wetbacks and snakes and the rest of the garbage down there in the city, they're what we prey on. They need us, not the other way around.' Tamora spat sideways. 'There's prey, and there's hunters. You have to decide which you are. You don't know, now is the time you find out. Are you for it?'

'It seems like a good plan.'

'Somewhere or other you've picked up the habit of not speaking plainly. If you mean yes, then say it.'

'Yes. Yes, I will do it. If it means getting into the Palace of the Memory of the People.'

Tamora spat again. 'Listen, this is no easy job. This little department is certain to be attacked and they don't have a security office or they wouldn't be hiring someone from outside. They're bound to lose, but if it's done right then only their thralls will get killed. We can probably escape, or at worst lose our bond when we're ransomed. But I won't deny there's a chance we'll get killed, too. You still want it?'

'It is a way in.'

'Exactly. This department used to deal in prognostication, but it is much debased. There are only a couple of seers left, but it is highly placed in the Palace of the Memory of the People, and other more powerful departments want to displace it. It needs us to train its thralls so they can put up some kind of defence, but there will be time for you to search for whatever it is you're looking for. We will agree payment now. You'll front any expenses out of your share of the fees for killing the merchant and for this new job, and I keep my half of both fees, and half again of anything that's left of yours. That's my finder's fee.'

'It seems like a fair price.'

'You're supposed to bargain, you idiot!'

'I will pay it anyway,' Yama said. He was very tired, and a little drunk, and had no energy or inclination to haggle over trivialities. 'Any loss I make on the deal is the price for finding out what I want to know.'

'If you want to join the army as an officer, you'll need plenty of cash. More than you're carrying around now. You'll have to buy the rest of your own armour, and mounts, and weaponry. And if you're looking for information, there will be bribes to be paid. I'll take a quarter of your fees, bargaining against myself like a fool, and share expenses with you.'

'You are a good person, Tamora, although I would like you better if you were more tolerant. No bloodline should raise itself above any other.'

'I'll do well enough out of this, believe me. One other thing. We won't tell the rat-boy about this. We do this without him.'

'Are you scared of him because he killed the guard at the gate?'

'If I was scared of any of his kind, I would never dare spit in the gutter again, for fear of hitting one in the eye. Let him come if he must, but I won't pretend I like it, and any money he wants comes from you, not me.'

'He is like me, Tamora. He wants to be other than his fate.'

'Then he's certainly as big a fool as you.' Tamora handed Yama the brandy bottle. 'Drink to our new venture. Then you will listen to me sing our victory song. The rat-boy is scared to sit with my brothers and sisters, but I know you won't be.'

*

Although Yama tried not to show it, he was intimidated by the proud, fierce people who sat around the campfire: an even decad of Tamora's kin, heavily muscled men and women marked on their shoulders by identical tattoos of inverted triangles. The scariest of them all was a straight-backed matriarch with a white mane and a lacework of fine scars across her naked torso, who watched Yama with red-backed eyes from the other side of the fire while Tamora sang.

Her victory song was a discordant open-throated ululation that rose and twisted like a sharp silver wire into the black air above the flames of the campfire. When it was done, she took a long swig from a wineskin while the men and women murmured and nodded and showed their fangs in quick snarling smiles, although one man complained loudly that too many verses had been about this whey-skinned stranger.

'That's because it was his adventure,' Tamora said.

'Then let him sing for himself,' the man grumbled.

The matriarch asked Tamora about Yama, saying that she had not seen his kind before.

'He's from downriver, grandmother.'

'That would explain it. I'm told that there are many strange peoples downriver, although I myself have never troubled to go and see, and now I am too old to have to bother. Talk with me, boy. Tell me how your people came into the world.'

'That is a mystery I want to solve,' Yama said. 'I have read something in the Puranas about my people, and I have seen a picture of one in an old slate, but that is all I know.'

'Then your people are very strange indeed,' the matriarch said. 'Every bloodline has its story and its mysteries and its three names. The Preservers chose to raise up each bloodline in their image for a particular reason, and the stories explain why. You won't find your real story in that book you carry. That's about older mysteries, and not about this world at all.' She cuffed one of the women and snatched a wineskin from her. 'They keep this from me,' she told Yama, 'because they're frightened I'll disgrace myself if I get drunk.'

'Nothing could make you drunk, grandmother,' one of the men said. 'That's why we ration your drinking, or you'd poison yourself trying.'

The matriarch spat into the fire. 'A mouthful of this rotgut is poison enough. Can no one afford proper booze? In the old days we would have used this to fuel our lamps.'

Yama still had the brandy bottle, with a couple of fingers of clear, apricot-scented liquor at its bottom. 'Here, grandmother,' he said, and handed it to the matriarch.

The old woman drained the bottle and licked her lips in appreciation. 'Do you know how we came into the world, boy? No? I'll tell you.'

Several of the people around the fire groaned, and the matriarch said sharply, 'It'll do you good to hear it again. You young people don't know the stories as well as you should. Listen, then.

'After the world was made, some of the Preservers kindled intelligence in certain kinds of animals they had set down on its surface. There is a bloodline descended from coyotes, for instance, whose ancestors were taught by the Preservers to bury their dead. This odd habit brought about a change in the coyotes, for they learned to sit up so they could sit beside the graves and mourn their dead properly. But sitting on cold stone wore away their bushy tails, and after many generations they began standing upright because the stone was uncomfortable to their naked arses. When that happened, their forepaws lengthened into human hands, and their sharp muzzles shortened bit by bit until they became human faces. That's one story, and there are as many stories as there are bloodlines descended from the different kinds of animals which were taught to become human. But our own people had a different origin.

'Two of the Preservers fell into an argument about the right way to make human people. The Preservers did not have sexes as we understand them, nor did they marry, but it is easier to follow the story if we think of them as wife and husband. One, Enki, was the Preserver who had charge of the world's water, and so his work was hard, for in those early times all there was of the world was the Great River, running from nowhere to nowhere. He complained of his hard work to his wife, Ninmah, who was the Preserver of earth, and she suggested that they create a race of marionettes or puppets who would do the work for them. And this they did, using the small amount of white silt that was suspended in the Great River. I see that you know this part of the story.'

'Someone told me a little of it today,' Yama said. 'It is to be found in the Puranas.'

'What I tell you is truer, for it has been told from mouth to ear for thousands of generations, and so its words still live, and have not become dead things squashed flat on plastic or pulped wood. Well then, after this race was produced from the mud of the river there was a great celebration because the Preservers no longer needed to work on their creation. Much beer was consumed, and Ninmah became especially light-headed. She called to Enki, saying, "How good or bad is a human body? I could reshape it in any way I please, but could you find tasks for it?" Enki responded to this challenge, and so Ninmah made a barren woman, and a eunuch, and several other cripples.

'But Enki found tasks for them all. The barren woman he made into a concubine; the eunuch he made into a civil servant, and so on. Then in the same playful spirit he challenged Ninmah. He would do the shaping of different races, and she the placing. She agreed, and Enki first made a man whose making was already remote from him, and so the first old man appeared before Ninmah. She offered the old man bread, but he was too feeble to reach for it, and when she thrust the bread into his mouth, he could not chew it for he had no teeth, and so Ninmah could find no use for this unfortunate. Then Enki made many other cripples and monsters, and Ninmah could find no use for them, either.

'The pair fell into a drunken sleep, and when they wakened all was in uproar, for the cripples Enki had made were spreading through the world. Enki and Ninmah were summoned before the other Preservers to explain themselves, and to escape punishment Enki and Ninmah together made a final race, who would hunt the lame and the old, and make the races of the world stronger by consuming their weak members.

'And so we came into the world, and it is said that we have a quick and cruel temper, because Enki and Ninmah suffered dreadfully from the effects of drinking too much beer when they made us, and that was passed to us as a potmaker leaves her thumbprint in the clay.'

'I have heard only the beginning of this story,' Yama said, 'and I am glad that now I have heard the end of it.'

'Now you must tell a story,' one of the men said loudly. It was the one who had complained before. He was smaller than the others, but still a head taller than Yama. He wore black leather trousers and a black leather jacket studded with copper nails.

'Be quiet, Gorgo,' the matriarch said. 'This young man is our guest.'

Gorgo looked across the fire at Yama, and Yama met his truculent, challenging gaze. Neither was willing to look away, but then a branch snapped in the fire and sent burning fragments flying into Gorgo's lap. He cursed and brushed at the sparks while the others laughed.

Gorgo glowered and said, 'We have heard his boasts echoed in Tamora's song. I simply wonder if he has the heart to speak for himself. He owes us that courtesy, I think.'

'You're a great one for knowing what's owed,' someone said.

Gorgo turned on the man. 'I only press for payment when it's needed, as you well know. How much poorer you would be if I didn't find you work! You are all in my debt.'

The matriarch said, 'That is not to be spoken of. Are we not the Fierce People, whose honour is as renowned as our strength and our temper?'

Gorgo said, 'Some people need reminding about honour.'

One of the women said, 'We fight. You get the rewards.'

'Then don't ask me for work,' Gorgo said petulantly. 'Find your own. I force no one, as is well known, but so many ask for my help that I scarcely have time to sleep or catch my food. But here is our guest. Let's not forget him. We hear great things of him from Tamora. Now let him speak for himself.'

Yama thought that Gorgo could speak sweetly when he chose, but the honey of his words disguised his envy and suspicion. Clearly, he thought that Yama's was one of the trash or vermin bloodlines.

Yama said, 'I will tell a story, although I am afraid that it might bore you. It is about how my life was saved by one of the indigens.'

Gorgo grumbled that this didn't sound like a true story at all. 'Tell something of your people instead. Please do not tell me that such a fine hero as yourself, if we are to believe the words of our sister here, is so ashamed of his own people that he has to make up stories of subhuman creatures which do not carry the blessing of the Preservers.'

Yama smiled. This at least was easy to counter. 'I wish I knew such stories, but I was raised as an orphan.'

'Perhaps your people were ashamed of you,' Gorgo said, but he was the only one to laugh at his sally.

'Tell your story,' Tamora said, 'and don't let Gorgo interrupt you. He is jealous, because he hasn't any stories of his own.'

When Yama began, he realised that he had drunk more than he intended, but he could not back out now. He described how he had been kidnapped and taken to the pinnace, and how he had escaped (making no mention of the ghostly ship) and cast himself upon a banyan island far from shore.

'I found one of the indigenous fisher folk stuck fast in a trap left by one of the people of the city which my father administers. The people of the city once hunted the fisher folk, but my father put a stop to it. This unfortunate had become entangled in a trap made of strong, sticky threads of the kind used to snare bats which skim the surface of the water for fish. I could not free him without becoming caught fast myself, so I set a trap of my own and waited. When the hunter came to collect his prey, as a spider sidles down to claim a fly caught in its web, it was the hunter who became the prey. I took the spray which dissolves the trap's glue, and the fisherman and I made our escape and left the foolish hunter to the torments of those small, voracious hunters who outnumber their prey: mosquitoes and blackflies. In turn, the fisherman fed me and took me back to the shore of the Great River. And so we saved each other.'

'A tall tale,' Gorgo said, meeting Yama's gaze again.

'It is true I missed out much, but if I told everything then we would be up all night. I will say one more thing. If not for the fisherman's kindness, I would not be here, so I have learnt never to rush to judge any man, no matter how worthless he might appear.'

Gorgo said, 'He asks us to admire his reflection in his tales. Let me tell you that what I see is a fool. Any sensible man would have devoured the fisherman and taken his coracle and escaped with a full belly.'

'I simply told you what happened,' Yama said, meeting the man's gaze. 'Anything you see in my words is what you have placed there. If you had tried to steal the hunter's prey, you would have been stuck there too, and been butchered and devoured along with the fisherman.'

Gorgo jumped up. 'I think I know something about hunting, and I also know that you are not as clever as you imagine yourself to be. You side with prey, and so you're no hunter at all.'

Yama stood too, so that he would not have to look up from a lesser to a higher position when he replied to Gorgo's insult. Perhaps he would not have done it if he had been less drunk, but he felt the sting of wounded pride. Besides, he did not think that Gorgo was a threat. He was a man who used words as others use weapons. He was taller and heavier than Yama, and armed with a strong jaw and sharp teeth, but Sergeant Rhodean had taught Yama several ways which could counter an opponent's advantages.

'I described what happened, no more and no less,' Yama said. 'I hope I do not need to prove the truth of my words.'

Tamora grabbed Yama's hand and said, 'Don't mind Gorgo. He has always wanted to fuck me, and I've always refused. He's quick to anger, and jealous.'

Gorgo laughed. 'I think you have me wrong, sister. It is not your delusion I object to, but his. Remember what you owe me before you insult me again.'

'You will both sit down,' the matriarch said. 'Yama is our guest, Gorgo. You dishonour all of us. Sit down. Drink. We all lose our temper, and the less we make of it the better.'

'You all owe me,' Gorgo said, 'one way or another.' He glared at the circle of people, then spat into the fire and turned and stalked away into the night.

There was an awkward pause. Yama sat down and apologised, saying that he had drunk too much and lost his judgement.

'We've all slapped Gorgo around one time or another,' one of the women said. 'He grows angry if his advances are ignored.'

'He is more angry than fierce,' someone said, and the rest laughed.

'He's a fucking disgrace,' Tamora said. 'A sneak and a coward. He never hunts, but feeds off the quarry of us all. He shot a man with an arbalest instead of fighting fair—'

'Enough,' the matriarch said. 'We do not speak of others to their backs, or in the presence of strangers.'

'I'd speak to his face,' Tamora said, 'if he'd ever look me in the eye.'

'If we say no more about this,' Yama said, 'I promise to say no more about myself.'

There were more drinking games, and more songs, and at last Yama begged to be released. Tamora's people seemed to need little sleep, but he was exhausted by his adventures. He found his way back to his own campfire by the faint light of the Arm of the Warrior, falling several times but feeling no hurt. Pandaras was curled up near the warm ashes, his kidney puncher gripped in both hands. Yama lay down a little way off, on the ridge which overlooked the dark city. He did not remember wrapping himself in his blanket, or falling asleep, but he woke when Tamora pulled it away from him. Her naked body glimmered in the near dark. He did not resist when she started to undo the laces of his shirt, or when she covered his mouth with hers.

22

THE COUNTRY OF THE MIND

The next morning, Pandaras watched with unconcealed amusement as Tamora swabbed the scratches on Yama's flanks and the sore places on his shoulders and neck where she had nipped him. When she had finished, Pandaras sleeked back his hair with wrists wetted with his own saliva, slapped dust from his ragged jerkin, and announced that he was ready to go.

'We can buy breakfast on the way to the docks. Then we'll collect our reward, and go to our new employer in the Palace of the Memory of the People, and find your family, all before the mountains eat the sun. We could already be there, master, if you had not slept so late.'

'There's no need to hurry,' Yama said, smiling at Pandaras's eagerness.

'To be frank, master, I'm not suited to this place. I hardly slept at all last night. I was listening to every rustle of the wind, imagining that some rude meat-eater was creeping up on me.'

Yama held up his shirt. It was stained with silt from the flood which had fallen through the ceiling of the merchant's house, and flecked with chaff where he and Tamora had used it as a pillow. He said, 'I should wash my clothes first. This will make no impression on our new employers.'

'Am I not your squire, master? Give them to me, and I'll beat out the dust and the dirt and have them as good as new inside a minute.'

Tamora scratched at reddened skin at the edge of the bandage around her waist. 'Grah. Some squire you make,' she said, 'with straws in your hair and dirt on your snout. Come with me, Yama. There's a washing place further up.'

Pandaras flourished his kidney puncher and struck an attitude and grinned at Yama. He had an appetite for drama, as if all the world were a stage, and he was the central player. He said, 'I will guard your satchel, master, but do not leave me alone for long. I can fight off two or three of these ravenous savages, but not an entire pack.'

A series of pools in natural limestone basins stepped away down the slope of the hill, with water rising from hot springs near the crest and falling from one pool to the next. Each pool was slightly cooler than the one above. Yama sat with Tamora in the shallow end of the hottest pool he could bear, and scrubbed his shirt and trousers with white sand. He spread them out to dry on a flat rock already warm from the sun, then allowed Tamora to wash his back. Little fish striped with silver and black darted around his legs in the clear hot water, nipping at the dirt between his toes. Other people were using pools higher up, calling cheerfully to each other under the blue sky.

Tamora explained that the water came from the Rim Mountains. 'Everyone in the city who can afford it uses mountain water. Only beggars and refugees drink from the river.'

'Then they must be the holiest people in Ys, for the water of the Great River is sacred.'

'Holiness does not cleanse the river of all the shit dumped into it. Most bathe in it only once a year, on the high day celebrated by their bloodline. Otherwise those who can avoid it, which is why water is brought into the city. One of the underground rivers that transports the mountain water passes close by. It's why we have our hunting grounds here. There are waterholes where animals come to drink and where the hunting is good, and at this place we have hidden machines to heat the water.'

'It is a wonderful place,' Yama said. 'Look, a hawk!'

Tamora lifted the thong around Yama's neck and fingered the disc which hung from it. 'What's this? A keepsake?'

'Someone gave it to me just before I left Aeolis.'

'You can find them here, if you bother to dig for a few minutes. We used to play with them when we were children. This is less worn than most, though. Who gave it to you? A sweetheart, perhaps?'

Derev. This was the second time Yama had betrayed her trust. Although he did not know if he would ever see Derev again, and although he had been drunk, he felt suddenly ashamed that he had allowed Tamora to take him.

Tamora's breath feathered his cheek. It had a minty tang from the leaf she had plucked from a bush and folded inside her mouth between her teeth and her cheek. She fingered the line of Yama's jaw and said, 'There's hair coming in here.'

'There is a glass blade in my satchel. I should have brought it to shave. Or perhaps I will grow a beard.'

'It was your first time, wasn't it? Don't be ashamed. Everyone must have a first time.'

'No. I mean, no, it was not the first time.'

Telmon's high, excited voice as he threw open the door of the brothel's warm, scented, lamp-lit parlour. The women turning to them like exotic orchids unfolding. Yama had gone with Telmon because he had been asked, because he had been curious, because Telmon had been about to leave for the war. Afterwards, he had suspected that Derev had known all about it, and if she had not condoned it, then perhaps at least she had understood. That was partly why Yama had been so fervent with his promises on the night before he left Aeolis. And yet how easily he had broken them. He felt a sudden desolation. How could he ever hope to become a hero?

Tamora said, 'It was your first time with one of the Fierce People. That should burn away the memory of all others.' She nipped his shoulder. 'You have a soft skin, and it tastes of salt.'

'I sweat everywhere, except the palms of my hands and the soles of my feet.'

'Really? How strange. But I like the taste.'

Yama smiled. 'Is that why you bit me last night?'

'Yama, listen to me. It won't happen again. Not while we're working together. No, stay still. I can't clean your back if you turn around. We celebrated together last night, and that was good. But I won't let it interfere with my work. If you don't like that, and think yourself used, then find another cateran. There are plenty here, and plenty more at the Water Market. And you have enough money to hire the best.'

'I was at least as drunk as you were.'

'Drunker, I'd say. I hope you didn't fuck me just because you were drunk.'

Yama blushed. 'I meant that I lost any inhibitions I might otherwise have had. Tamora—'

'Don't start on any sweet talk. And don't tell me about any sweetheart you might have left at home, either, or about how sorry you are. That's there. This is here. We're battle companions. We fucked. End of that part of the story.'

'Are all your people so direct?'

'We speak as we find. Not to do so is a weakness. I like you, and I enjoyed last night. We're lucky, because some bloodlines are only on heat once a year – imagine how miserable they must be – and besides, there's no danger of us making babies together. That's what happens when my people fuck, unless the woman is already pregnant. I'm not ready for that, not yet. In a few years I'll find some men to run with and we'll raise a family, but not yet. A lot of us choose the metic way for that reason.'

Yama was interested. He said, 'Can you not use prophylactics?'

Tamora laughed. 'You haven't seen the cock of one of our men! There are spines to hold it in place. Put a rubber on that? Grah! There's a herb some women boil into a tea and drink to stop their courses, but it doesn't work most of the time.'

'Women of your people are stronger than men.'

'It's generally true of all bloodlines, even when it doesn't seem so. We're more honest about it, perhaps. Now you clean my back, and I'll go use the shittery, and then we'll find the rat-boy. If we're lucky, he's run back to where he belongs.'

As they went back down the hill, along the path that wandered between stands of sage and tall sawgrasses, Yama saw someone dressed in black watching them from the shade at the edge of a grove of live oaks. He thought it might have been Gorgo, but whoever it was stepped back into the shadows and was gone before Yama could point him out to Tamora.

The city was still disturbed by Yama's drawing down of the feral machine. Magistrates and their attendant clouds of machines were patrolling the streets, and although Yama asked the machines to ignore him and his companions, he was fearful that he would miss one until it was too late, or that Prefect Corin would lunge out of the crowds towards him. He kept turning this way and that until Tamora told him to stop it before he attracted the wrong kind of attention.

Little groups of soldiers lounged at every major intersection. They were the city militia, armed with fusils and carbines and dressed in loose red trousers and plastic cuirasses as slick and cloudily transparent as ice. They watched the crowds with hard, insolent eyes, but they did not challenge anyone. They did not dare, Pandaras said, and Yama asked how that could be, if they had the authority of the Preservers.

'There are many more of us than there are of them,' Pandaras said, and made the sign that Yama had noticed before, touching his fist to his throat.

The boy did not seem scared of the soldiers, but instead openly displayed a smouldering contempt, and Yama noticed that many of the other people made the same sign when they passed a group of soldiers. Some even spat or shouted a curse, safe in the anonymity of the crowd.

Pandaras said, 'With the war downriver, there are even fewer soldiers in the city, and they must keep the peace by terror. That's why they're hated. See that cock there?'

Yama looked up. An officer in gold-tinted body armour stood on a metal disc that floated in the air above the dusty crowns of the ginkgoes which lined one side of the broad, brawling avenue.

'He could level a city block with one shot, if he had a mind to,' Pandaras said. 'But he wouldn't unless he had no other choice – if someone stole a pistol and tried to use it against soldiers or magistrates, for instance – because there'd be riots, and even more of the city would be burned.'

Tamora said, 'Energy weapons are prohibited, worse luck. *I'd* like one right now. Clear a way through these herds of grazers in a blink.'

'One of my uncles on my mother's side of the family was caught up in a tax protest a few years back,' Pandaras said. 'It was in a part of the city a few leagues upriver. A merchant bought up a block and levelled it to make a park, and the legates decided that the every tradesman living round about should pay more tax. The park made the area more attractive, neh? The legates said that more people would come because of the open space, and spend more in the shops round about. So the tradesmen got together and declared a tax strike in protest. The legates called up the magistrates, and they came and blockaded the area. Set their machines spinning in the air to make a picket line, so no one could get in or out. It lasted a hundred days, and at the end they said people inside the picket line were eating each other. The food ran out, and there was no way to get more in. A few tried to dig tunnels, but the magistrates sent in machines and killed them.'

Yama said, 'Why did they not give up the strike?'

'They did, after twenty days. They would have held out longer, but there were children to think about, and people who didn't live there at all but happened to be passing through when the blockade went up. So they presented a petition of surrender, but the magistrates kept the siege going as punishment. That kind of thing is supposed to make the rest of us too frightened to spit unless we get permission first.'

Tamora said, 'There's no other way. There are too many people living in the city, and most are fools or grazers. An argument between neighbours can turn into a feud between bloodlines, with thousands killed. Instead, the magistrates or the militia kill two or three, or even a hundred if necessary, and the matter is settled before it spreads. There are a dozen bloodlines they could get rid of and no one would notice.'

'We're the strength of Ys,' Pandaras said defiantly, and for once Tamora didn't answer back.

They reached the docks late in the afternoon. The same stocky shaven-headed servant met them in the shadow of the lighter. He looked at the flask and the strings of nerve tissue that floated inside it, and said that he had already heard that the merchant was dead.

Tamora said, 'Then we'll just take our money and go.'

Yama said to the servant, 'You said you would need to test what we brought.'

'The whole city knows that he was killed last night,' the servant said. 'To be frank, we would have preferred less attention drawn to it, but we are happy that the task was done. Do not worry. We will pay you.'

'Then let's do it now,' Tamora said, 'and we'll be on our way.'

Yama said quickly, 'But we have made an agreement. I would have it seen through to the letter. Your master wanted to test what we brought, and I would have it done no other way, to prove that we are honest.'

The servant stared hard at Yama, then said, 'I would not insult you by failing to carry out everything we agreed. Come with me.'

As they followed the servant up the gangway, Tamora caught Yama's arm and whispered fiercely, 'This is a foolish risk. We do the job, we take the money, we go. Who cares what they think of us? Complications are dangerous, especially with the star-sailors, and we have an appointment at the Water Market.'

'I have my reasons,' Yama said stubbornly. 'You and Pandaras can wait on the quay, or go on to the Water Market, just as you please.'

He had thought it over as they had walked through the streets of the city to the wharf where the voidship lighter was moored. The star-sailor who piloted the lighter had said that it knew something of his bloodline, and Yama was prepared to pay for the knowledge, and thought that he knew a sure way of getting at it if the star-sailor refused to sell it.

Inside the ship, in the round room at the top of the spiral corridor, the servant uncapped the crystal flask and poured its contents onto the black floor, which quickly absorbed the brandy and the strings of nervous tissue. He set the gold circlet on his scarred, shaven scalp and jerked to attention. His mouth worked, and he said in a voice not his own, 'This one will pay you. What else do you want of me?'

Yama addressed the fleshy blossom which floated inside its bottle. 'I talked with your crewmate before he died. He told me a little about my bloodline, and I believe that you might be able to tell me more.'

'No doubt he said many things to save his life,' the star-sailor said through its human mouthpiece.

'This was when he had me prisoner, and my friends too.'

'Then perhaps he was boasting. You must understand that he was mad. He had corrupted himself with the desires of the flesh.'

'I remember you said that I had abilities that might be useful.'

'I was mistaken. They have proved to be . . . inconvenient. You have no control over what you can do.'

Tamora said, 'We should leave this. Yama, I'll help you find out what you want to know, but in the Palace of the Memory of the People, not here. We made a deal.'

'I have not forgotten,' Yama said. 'The few questions I want to ask will not end my quest, but they may aid it.' He turned back to the thing in the bottle. 'I will waive my part of the fee for the murder of your crewmate if you will help me understand what he told me.'

Tamora said, 'Don't listen to him, dominie! He hasn't the right to make that bargain!'

The servant's mouth opened and closed. His chin was slick with saliva. He said, 'He was driven mad by the desires of the flesh. I, however, am not mad. I have nothing to say to you unless you can prove that you know what you are. Return then, and we can talk.'

'If I knew that, I would have nothing to ask you.'

Tamora grabbed Yama's arm. 'You're risking everything, you fool. Come on!'

Yama tried to free himself, but Tamora's grip was unyielding and her nails dug into his flesh until blood ran. He stepped in close, thinking to throw her from his hip, but she knew that trick and butted him on the bridge of his nose with her forehead. A blinding spike of pain shot through his head and tears sprang to his eyes. Tamora twisted his arm up behind his back and started to drag him across the room to the dilated doorway, but Pandaras wrapped himself around her legs and fastened his sharp teeth on her thigh. Tamora howled and Yama pulled free and flung himself at the servant, ripping the gold circlet from the man's head and jamming it on his own.

White light.

White noise.

Something was in his head. It fled even as he noticed it and he turned in a direction he had not seen before and flew after it. It was a woman, a naked, graceful woman with pale skin and long black hair that fanned out behind her as she soared through clashing currents of light. Even as she fled, she kept looking back over her bare shoulder. Her eyes blazed with a desperate light.

Yama followed with mounting exhilaration. He seemed to be connected to her through a kind of cord that was growing shorter and stronger, and he twisted and turned after his quarry without thought. Others were pacing them on either side, and beyond these unseen presences Yama could feel a vast congregation, mostly in clusters as distant and faint as the halo stars. They were the crews of the voidships, meeting together in this country of the mind, in which they swam as easily as fish in the river. Whenever Yama turned his attention to one or another of these clusters, he felt an airy expansion and a fleeting glimpse of the combined light of other minds, as if through a window whose shutters are flung back to greet the rising sun. In every case the minds he touched with his mind recoiled; the shutters slammed; the light faded.

In his desperate chase after the woman through the country of the mind, Yama left behind a growing wake of confused and scandalised inhabitants. They called on something, a guardian or watchdog, and it rose towards Yama like a pressure wave, angling through unseen dimensions like a pike gliding effortlessly through water towards a duckling paddling on the surface. Yama doubled and redoubled his efforts to catch the woman, and was almost on her when white light blinded him and white noise roared in his ears and a black floor flew up and struck him with all the weight of the world.

23
THE TEMPLE OF THE BLACK WELL

When Yama woke, the first thing he saw was Pandaras sitting cross-legged by the foot of the bed, sewing up a rip in his second-best shirt. Yama was naked under the scratchy starched sheet, and clammy with cold sweat. His head ached, and some time ago a small animal seemed to have crept into the dry cavern of his mouth and died there. Perhaps it had been a cousin of the bright green gecko which clung to the far wall in a patch of sunlight, its scarlet throat pulsing. The room was small, ochre plaster walls painted with twining patterns of blue vines, dusty rafters under a slanted ceiling. Afternoon light fell through the two tall windows, and there was the noise of a busy street.

Pandaras helped Yama sit up, fussing with the bolster, and brought him a beaker of water. 'It has salt and sugar in it, master. Drink. It will make you stronger.'

Yama obeyed the boy. It seemed that he had been asleep for a night and most of the day that followed. Pandaras and Tamora had brought him here from the docks.

'She has gone out to talk with the man we should have met yesterday. And we didn't get paid by the star-sailor, so she's angry with you.'

'I remember that you tried to help me,' Yama said. His tongue and the insides of his cheeks were sore; at some point he'd badly bitten them. 'You killed the guard with that kidney puncher she gave you.'

'That was before, master. At the gate of the merchant's estate. After that there was the voidship lighter, when you snatched the circlet from the guard and put it on your head.'

'The merchant was wearing the circlet. It was how he controlled his household. But I broke it when I took it away from him.'

'This was in the voidship lighter. Please try to remember, master! You put the circlet on your head and straightaway you collapsed with foam on your lips and your eyes rolled right back. One of my half-sisters has the falling sickness, and that's what it looked like.'

'A woman. I saw a woman. But she fled from me.'

Pandaras pressed on with his story. 'I snatched the circlet from your head, but you didn't wake. More of the star-sailor's servants came, and they marched us off the lighter. The first, the one you took the circlet from, he and Tamora had an argument about the fee. I thought she might kill him, but he and his fellows drew their pistols, and there was no argument after that. We took some of your money to pay for the room, and for the palanquin that carried you here. I hope we did right.'

'Tamora must be angry with you, too.'

'She doesn't take any account of me, which is just as well. I bit her pretty badly when she tried to stop you taking the circlet, but she bandaged her legs and said nothing of it. Wouldn't admit I could hurt her, neh? And now I'm not frightened of her because I know I can hurt her, and I'll do it again if I have to. I didn't want to fight with her, master, but she shouldn't have tried to stop you. She didn't have the right.'

Yama closed his eyes. Clusters of lights hanging from the ceiling of the round room at the top of the voidship lighter. The thing in the bottle, with rose-red gills and a lily-white mantle folded around a thick braid of naked nerve tissue. 'I remember,' he said. 'I tried to find out about my bloodline. The country of the mind—'

Pandaras nodded. 'You took the circlet from the servant and put it on your own head.'

'Perhaps it would have been better if Tamora had stopped me. She was worried that I would no longer have any need of her.'

Pandaras took the empty beaker from Yama and said, 'Do you need her help any more, master? You stood face to face with that thing and talked to it direct. Did it tell you what you wanted to know?'

It seemed like a dream, fading even as Yama tried to remember its details. The woman fleeing through curtains of light, the faint stars of other minds. He said, 'I saw something wonderful, but I did not learn anything about myself, except that the people who crew the voidships are scared of me.'

'You scared me too, master. I thought you had gone into the place where they live and left your body behind. I'll have some food sent up. You haven't eaten in two days.'

'You have been good to me, Pandaras.'

'Why, it's a fine novelty to order people about in a place like this. A while ago it was me running at any cock's shout, and I haven't forgotten what it was like.'

'It was not that long ago. A few days.'

'Longer for me than for you. Rest, master. I'll be back soon.'

But Pandaras was gone a long time. The room was hot and close, and Yama wrapped the sheet around himself and sat at one of the windows, where there was a little breeze. He felt weak, but rested and alert. The bandage over the wound on his forearm was gone, and the flesh had knitted around the puckers made by the black crosses of the stitches. All the bruises and small cuts from his recent adventures were healed, too, and someone, presumably Pandaras, had shaved him while he had been sleeping. The corselet and greaves that he had won by killing the cateran, Cyg, stood on a chair in one corner, neatly cut down and gleamingly polished. Presumably, Pandaras had collected it from the armourer in the Water Market.

The inn stood on a broad avenue divided down the centre by a line of palm trees. The crowds jostling along the dusty white thoroughfare contained more people than Yama had ever seen in his life. Thousands of people, a hundred different bloodlines. There were hawkers and skyclad mendicants, parties of palmers, priests, officials hurrying along in groups of two or three, scribes, musicians, tumblers, whores and mountebanks. An acrobat walked above the heads of the crowd on a wire strung from one side of the avenue to the other. Vendors fried plantains and yams on heated iron plates, or roasted nuts in huge copper basins set over oil burners. Ragged boys stood at the margins of the crowds, selling flavoured ice, twists of liquorice, boiled sweets, roast nuts, cigarettes, plastic trinkets representing one or another of the long-lost aspects of the Preservers, and medals stamped with the likenesses of official heroes of the war against the heretics. Beggars exhibited a hundred different kinds of mutilation and deformity. Messengers on nimble genets or black-plumaged ratites trotted through the throng. A few important personages walked under silk canopies held up by dragomen, or were carried on litters or palanquins. A party of solemn giants walked waist-high amidst ordinary people as if wading in a stream. Directly across the avenue, people had gathered at a stone altar, burning incense cones bought from a priest, muttering prayers and wafting the smoke towards themselves. A procession of ordinands in red robes, their freshly shaven heads gleaming with oil, wound in a long straggling line behind men banging tambours.

Braying, discordant trumpets rang out in the distance, and a huge cart hove into view, pulled by a team of a hundred sweating, half-naked men, with priests swinging fuming censers on either side. The cart was painted scarlet and gold and bedecked with garlands of flowers, and a screen stood amongst the heaped flowers, its black oval framed by ornate golden scrollwork. It stopped almost directly opposite Yama's window, and people gathered on the rooftops and threw down bucketfuls of water on the men who pulled it, and dropped more garlands of flowers onto the cart and around the men and the attendant priests in a soft, multicoloured snowstorm. Yama leaned out further to get a better view, and at that moment heard a noise in the room behind him and turned, thinking it was Pandaras.

A patch of ochre plaster of the wall opposite the window was cracked in a spiderweb pattern. In the centre of the web stood an arbalest bolt.

The bolt was as long as Yama's forearm, with a shaft of dense, hard wood and red flight feathers. Judging by the downward-pointing angle at which the bolt had embedded itself in the plaster, it must have been fired from one of the flat roofs on the other side of the avenue, for all of them were higher than the window.

Yama crouched and scanned the rooftops, but there were hundreds of people crowded along their edges, scattering flowers and pitching silvery twists of water at the cart. He tried to find a machine which might have been watching, but it seemed that there were no magistrates here. Still crouching, he closed the heavy slatted shutters of both windows, then pulled the bolt from the wall.

A few minutes later, Pandaras returned ahead of a pot boy who set a tray covered in a white cloth on the low table which, apart from the bed and the chair in which Yama sat, were the only pieces of furniture in the room. Pandaras dismissed the pot boy and whipped away the tray's cover like a conjuror, revealing a platter of fruit and cold meat, and a sweating earthenware pitcher of white wine. He poured wine into two cups, and handed one to Yama. 'I'm sorry it took so long, master. There's a festival. We had to pay double rates just to get the room.'

The wine was cold, and as thickly sweet as syrup. Yama said, 'I saw the procession go by.'

'There's always some procession here. It's in the nature of the place. Eat, master. You must break your fast before you go anywhere.'

Yama accepted the slice of green melon that Pandaras held out. 'Where are we?'

Pandaras bit into his own melon slice. 'Why, it's the quarter that runs between the river and the Palace of the Memory of the People.'

'I think we should go and find Tamora. Where are my clothes?'

'Your trousers are under the mattress, to keep them pressed. I am mending one of your shirts; the other is in your pack. Master, you should eat, and then rest.'

'I do not think we should stay here,' Yama said, and showed Pandaras the arbalest bolt.

The landlady called to Yama and Pandaras as they pushed through the hot, crowded taproom of the inn. She was a plump, broad-beamed woman dressed in a purple and gold saree, waving a fretted palm leaf to and fro as she explained that a message had been left for them.

'I have it here,' she said, rummaging through the drawer of her desk. 'Please be patient, sirs. It is a very busy day today. Is this it? No. Wait, here it is.'

Yama took the scrap of stiff paper. It had been folded four times and tucked into itself, and sealed with a splash of wax. Yama turned it over and over, and asked Pandaras, 'Can Tamora read and write?'

'She put her thumb to the contract, master, so I'd guess she has about as much reading as I have, which is to say none.'

The landlady said helpfully, 'There are scribes on every corner. The seal is one of theirs.'

'Do you know which one?'

'There are very many. I suppose I could have one of my boys ask around.' The landlady patted her brow with a square of yellow cloth. Her eyes were made up with blue paint and gold leaf and her eyebrows had been twisted and stiffened with wax to form long tapering points, giving the effect of a butterfly perched on her face. She added, 'That is, when we are less busy. It is a festival day, you see.'

Yama said, 'I saw the cart go by.'

'The cart? Oh, the shrine. No, no, that is nothing to do with the festival. It passes down the street every day, except on its feast day, of course, when it is presented at the Great River. But that is a hundred days off, and just a local affair. People have come here from all over Ys for the festival, and from downriver, too. A very busy time, although of course there are not so many people as there once were. Fewer travel, you see, because of the war. That is why I was able to find you a room at short notice.'

'She moved two palmers into the stables, and charges us twice what they paid,' Pandaras remarked.

'And now they are paying less than they would have,' the landlady said, 'so it all evens out. I hope that the message is not bad news, dominie. The room is yours as long as you want it.' Despite her claim to be busy, it seemed that she had plenty of time to stick her nose in other people's business.

Yama held up the folded paper and said, 'Who brought this?'

'I didn't see. One of my boys gave it to me. I could find him, I suppose, although it's all a muddle today—'

'Because of the festival.' Yama snapped the wax seal and unfolded the paper.

The message was brief, and written in neatly aligned glyphs with firm and decisive downstrokes and fine feathering on the upstrokes. Most likely it had been set down by a scribe, unless Tamora had spent as long as Yama learning the finer nuances of penmanship.

I have gone on. The man you want is at the Temple of the Black Well.

Pandaras said, 'What does it say?'

Yama read the message to Pandaras, and the landlady said, 'That's not too far from here. Go down the passage at the left side of the inn and strike towards the palace. I could get you a link boy if you'd like to wait . . .'

But Yama and Pandaras were already pushing their way through the crowded room towards the open door and the sunlit avenue beyond.

The narrow streets that tangled behind the inn were cooler and less crowded than the avenue. They were paved with ancient, uneven brick courses, and several naked children played in a stream of dirty water that ran down a central gutter. The houses were flat-roofed and none were more than two storeys high, with small shuttered windows and walls covered in thick yellow or orange plaster, crumbling and much patched. Many had workshops on the ground floor, open to the street. Yama and Pandaras passed a hundred tableaux of industry, most involving the manufacture of the religious mementoes displayed in shops that stood at every corner of every street, although none of the shops seemed to be open.

It was a secretive, suspicious place, Yama thought, noting that people stopped what they were doing and openly stared as he and Pandaras went past. But he liked the serendipitous geography, the way a narrow street might suddenly open onto a square lined with cafés or a small courtyard with a white fountain splashing in its centre, and he liked the small shrines set into the walls of the houses, with browning wreaths of flowers and pyramids of ash in front of flyspotted circles of black glass that poorly mimicked the dark transparency of true shines.

The domes and pinnacles and towers of temples and shrines reared up amongst the crowded flat roofs of the ordinary houses like ships foundering in the scruffy pack ice of the frozen wilderness at the head of the Great River hundreds of leagues upriver. And beyond all these houses and temples and shrines, the mountain of the Palace of the Memory of the People climbed terrace by terrace towards its distant peak, with the setting sun bloodying the sky behind it.

Pandaras explained that this part of the city was given over to the business of worship of the Preservers and of the governance of Ys. Civil-service offices displaced from the interior of the Palace of the Memory of the People occupied lesser buildings on its outskirts, and a thousand cults flourished openly or skulked in secret underground chambers.

'It can be a dangerous place for strangers,' Pandaras said.

'I have my knife. And you have yours.'

'You should have worn your armour, master.'

'It would have attracted too much attention. Already I feel as if I am a procession, the way people turn to stare.'

'A gang of organ-leggers could knock us out and drain us of our blood, right here on the street. Or scoop out our brains and put them in tanks, all alive-o like the star-sailors.'

Yama laughed at these fantasies.

Pandaras said darkly, 'This is the New Quarter, master, built on a bloody battleground. A place where good and evil intermingle. And you are a singular person. Don't forget it. You would be a great prize for a blood sacrifice.'

'New? It seems to me very old.'

'That's because nothing here has been rebuilt since the Age of Insurrection. The rest of the city is far older, but people are always knocking down old buildings and putting up new ones. The last battle between machines was fought here, and in and around the Palace of the Memory of the People. Afterwards, the bones and casings of all the dead were tipped into great pits and the ground around about was flattened and these houses were built. Very little has changed here since, except for the construction of new shrines and temples.'

'I had thought the houses were built around the temples.'

Yama remembered now that the Temple of the Black Well had something to do with that last battle, but he could not quite remember what it was.

'No, the temples are much newer,' Pandaras said. 'Houses have to be knocked down each time one is built. Whole blocks, sometimes. It's a dangerous business. There are old poisons in the ground, and old weapons too, and sometimes the weapons wake when they are uncovered. There's a department which does nothing else but search for them by divination, and make them safe when they're found. And some parts of the quarter are haunted, too. It's why the people hereabouts are so strange, neh? The ghosts get inside their heads, and infect them with ideas from ages past.'

Yama said, 'I have never seen a ghost.'

The aspects which haunted the City of the Dead did not count, for they were simple projections. And while the Amnan claimed that the blue lights sometimes seen floating amongst the ruins below the peel-house were wights, the eidolons of the restless dead, Zakiel said that they were no more than wisps of burning marsh gas.

Pandaras said, 'These are machine ghosts mostly, but some were human, once, and they say that those are the worst. That's why they make so many icons hereabouts, master. If you were to look inside one of these houses, you'd find layer upon layer of them on the walls.'

'To keep out the ghosts.'

'They don't usually work. Or so I heard, anyway.'

'Look there. Is that our temple?'

It reared up a few streets ahead, a giant cube built of huge, roughly hewn stone blocks stained black with soot, and topped by an onion dome lapped in scuffed gilt tiles.

Pandaras squinted at it, then said, 'No, ours has a rounder roof, with a hole in the top of it.'

'Of course! Where the machine fell!'

The Temple of the Black Well had been built long after the feral machine's fiery fall, but its dome had been left uncompleted, with the aperture at its apex directly above the wide hole made when the machine had struck the surface of the world and melted a passage all the way down to the keel. Yama had been told the story by the aspect of a leather merchant who had owned a tannery near the site of the temple's construction. Mysyme, that had been the merchant's name. He had two wives and six beautiful daughters, and had done much charitable work amongst the orphaned river-rats of the docks. Mysyme was dead an age past, and Yama had lost interest in the limited responses of his aspect years ago, but he remembered them clearly now. Mysyme's father had seen the fall of the machine, and had told his son that a plume of melted rock had been thrown higher than the atmosphere when it had hit, and the smoke of secondary fires from debris scattered by the impact had darkened the sky above Ys for several decads.

'It's a little to our left,' Pandaras said, 'and maybe ten minutes' walk. That place with the gold roof is a tomb of a warrior-saint. It's solid all the way through, apart from a secret chamber no one knows how to open.'

'You are a walking education, Pandaras.'

'I have an uncle who used to live here, and one time I stayed with him. He was on my mother's side of the family, and this was when my father ran off and my mother went looking for him. She was a year at it, and never found him. And a year is a long time for my people. So she came back and married another man, and when that didn't work out she married my stepfather. I don't get on with him, and that's why I took the job of pot boy, because it came with a room. And then you came along, and here we are.' Pandaras grinned. 'For a long time after I left this part of the city, I thought maybe I was haunted. I'd wake up and think I'd been hearing voices, voices that had been telling me things in my sleep. But I haven't heard them since I met up with you, master. Maybe your bloodline is a cure for ghosts.'

'It may be that all in my bloodline except me are ghosts,' Yama said.

The Temple of the Black Well stood at the centre of a wide, quiet plaza paved with mossy cobbles. It was clad in lustrous black stone, although here and there parts of the cladding had fallen away to reveal the greyish limestone beneath, and had been built in the shape of a cross, with a long atrium and short apses. Its dome, covered in gold leaf that shone with the last light of the sun, capped the point where the apses intersected the atrium. Yama and Pandaras walked all the way around it but saw no sign of Tamora or her mysterious contact, then climbed the long flight of shallow steps at its entrance and passed through the tall narthex.

A thick shaft of reddish light slanted through the open apex of the dome at the far end of a long atrium flanked by colonnades and full of shadows. The pillars of the colonnades were intricately carved and the ruined mosaics of the floor sketched the outlines of heroic figures. The temple had been splendid once, Yama thought, but now it had the air of a place that was no longer cared for, and appeared to be deserted. A good choice for a clandestine rendezvous – or for an ambush.

Pandaras clearly thought the same thing, for his sleek head continually turned this way and that as they went down the atrium. The shaft of red light, alive with swirling motes of dust, fell on a waist-high wall of undressed stone ringing a deep hole that plunged down into darkness. It was the well, the shaft melted by the fallen machine. The wide coping on top of the wall was covered in the ashy remnants of incense cones, and here and there were offerings of fruit and flowers, the flowers shrivelled and brown, the little piles of fruit spotted with decay.

'Not many come here,' Pandaras said. 'The ghost of the machine is powerful, and quick to anger.'

Yama gripped the edge of the coping and leaned over it and looked into the depths of the well. The walls of the shaft were long glassy flows of once-melted rock, veined with impurities, dwindling away to a vanishing point small as the end of his thumb. A faint draught of cold, stale air blew from the lightless depths. It was impossible to tell how deep the well really was, and in a spirit of inquiry Yama dropped a bruised pomegranate into the black air.

'That isn't a good idea,' Pandaras said uneasily.

'I do not think a piece of fruit would wake this particular machine. It fell a long way as I recall – at least, it was two days in falling, and appeared in the sky as a star clothed in burning hair. When it struck the ground, the blow knocked down thousands of houses and caused a wave in the river that washed away much of the city on the farside shore. And then the sky turned black with smoke from all the fires.'

'There might be other things down there,' Pandaras said. 'Bats, for instance. I have a particular loathing of bats.'

'I should have thrown a coin. I might have heard it hit,' Yama said.

He wondered if the fruit was still falling through black air towards the bottom, two leagues or more to the keel. He and Pandaras walked around the well, but there was no sign that Tamora or anyone else had been there recently, and the hushed air was beginning to feel oppressive, as if it held a note endlessly drawn out just beyond the range of hearing.

'We should go on, master. She isn't here,' Pandaras said. 'Perhaps she has run off and left us.'

'She made a contract with me. I should think that is a serious thing for someone who lives from one job to the next. We will wait a little longer.' Yama took out the paper and read it again. ' "The man you want . . ." I wonder what she meant.'

'It'll be dark soon.'

Yama smiled. 'I believe that you are scared of this place.'

'You might not believe in ghosts, master, but there are many who do – most of the people in the city, I reckon.'

'Just because a lot of people believe in ghosts does not make them real. I might believe that the Preservers have returned to the world as river turtles, and I might persuade a million people to believe it, and build shrines to the holy turtles, and keep them in pools lined with the finest marble, and cover their shells in gold and jewels, but that would not make it true.'

'You shouldn't make jokes like that,' Pandaras said. 'Especially not here.'

'Surely the Preservers will forgive a small joke.'

'There's many who would take offence on their account,' Pandaras said stubbornly.

He had a deep streak of superstition, despite his worldly-wise air. Yama had seen the care with which he washed himself in a ritual pattern after eating and upon waking, the way he crossed his fingers when walking past a shrine – a superstition he shared with the citizens of Aeolis, who believed that it disguised the fact that you had come to a shrine without an offering – and his devotion at prayer. Like the Amnan, who could not or would not read the Puranas and so only knew them second-hand through the preaching of priests and iconoclasts, Pandaras and the countless millions of ordinary folk of Ys believed that the Preservers had undergone a transubstantiation, disappearing not into the Eye but dispersing themselves into every particle of the world which they had made, so that they were everywhere at once, immortal, invisible, quick to judge and requiring constant placation.

Pandaras said, 'Ghosts are like ideas. The more people believe in them, the more powerful they become . . . Listen! What was that?'

'I heard nothing,' Yama said, but even as he spoke there was a faint brief rumble, as if the temple, its dome and the massive stones of its walls, had briefly stirred and then settled again. It seemed to come from the well. Yama leaned over again, and peered into its depths. The wind which rose out of the darkness seemed to be blowing a little more strongly, and it held a faint tang, like heated metal.

'Come away,' Pandaras said uneasily. He was shifting his weight from foot to foot, as if ready to run.

'We will look in the apses. If anything was going to happen, Pandaras, it would have happened by now.'

'If it does happen, it'll be all the worse for waiting.'

'You go left and I will go right, and if we find nothing I promise we will go straight out of this place.'

'I'll come with you, master, if you don't mind. I've no liking for being left alone in this hecatomb.'

The archway which led into the apse to the right of the well was curtained by falls of fine black plastic mesh. Beyond was a high square space lit by spears of dim light striking through knotholes high in the thick walls. There was a shrine set in the centre of the space, a glossy black circle like a giant's coin or eyeglass standing on its side, and statues three times the height of a man stood in recesses all around the four walls, although they were not statues of men, and nor were they carved from stone, but were made of the same slick, translucent stuff as ancient armour. Yama could dimly see shapes and catenaries inside their chests and limbs.

Pandaras went up to a statue and knocked his knuckles against its shin: it rang with a dull note. 'There's a story that these things fought against the Insurrectionists.'

'More likely they were made in the likeness of great generals,' Yama said, looking up at their grim visages.

'Don't worry,' a woman's voice said. 'They've been asleep so long they've forgotten how to wake.'

24

THE WOMAN IN WHITE

When Yama turned to the shrine, streamers of blazing white light suddenly raced through its black disc. He raised an arm to shade his eyes, but the light had already faded into a swirling play of soft colours that instantly reminded him of the country he had glimpsed in the voidship lighter.

Pandaras's clenched paw fluttered at his open mouth. 'Master, this is some horrid trick.'

Yama stepped through polychromatic light and pressed his palm against the shrine's slick, cold surface. He was possessed by the mad idea that he could slip into it as easily as slipping into the cool water of the river.

Like a reflection, a hand rose through swirling colours to meet his own. For a moment he thought that he felt its touch, like a glove slipping around his skin, and he recoiled in shock.

Laughter, like the chiming of small silver bells. Streaks and swirls and dabs of a hundred colours collapsed into themselves, and a woman was framed in the disc of the shrine. Pandaras shouted and ran, flinging himself in a furious panic through the black mesh curtains which divided the apse from the main part of the temple.

Yama knelt before the shrine, fearful and amazed.

'Stand up,' the woman said. 'I can't talk to the top of your head.'

Yama obeyed. He supposed that the woman was one of the avatars of the Preservers, who, as was written in the Puranas, stood between the quotidian world and the glory of their masters, facing both ways at once. She was tall and slender, with a commanding, imperious gaze, and wore a white one-piece garment that clung to her limbs and body. Her skin was the colour of newly forged bronze; her long black hair was caught in a kind of net at her right shoulder. A green garden receded behind her: smooth lawns and high, trimmed hedges. A stone fountain sent a muscular jet of water high into the sunlit air.

'I think I've been here before,' she said. 'What is this place?'

'The Temple of the Black Well, domina.'

'Of course. In Ys. Why are you in Ys?'

'Forgive me, domina... This is not your shrine?'

'I don't live in any one place, these days. I'm scattered, I suppose you could say. But this is one of the windows that lets me look out at the world. You live in a house made of rooms. Where I live is mostly made of windows, looking out to different places. You drew me to this one, and I looked out and found you.'

'Drew you? Domina, I did not mean to.'

'You wear the key around your neck. You have discovered that, at least.'

Yama lifted out the disc which hung on the thong around his neck, the disc which the anchorite had given him the spring night when he had gone out to hunt frogs, and had caught something far stranger, and everything had changed. It was warm, but perhaps that was because it had lain next to his skin.

The woman in the shrine said, 'It exchanged information with this transceiver. I heard their conversation, and came here. Don't be afraid. Do you like where I live?'

Yama said, with reflexive politeness, 'I have never seen a garden like yours.'

'Do you wish me to change it? I could live anywhere, you know. Or at least anywhere on file that hasn't been corrupted. The servers are very old, and there's much that has been corrupted. Atoms migrate; cosmic rays disrupt the lattices... Anyway, I like gardens. It stirs something in my memory. My original ruled many worlds once, and I'm certain that some of them had gardens something like this one. But I've forgotten such a lot, and I was never really whole in the first place. There are peacocks here. Do you know peacocks? If we talk long enough perhaps one will come past. They are birds. The males have huge fan-shaped tails, with eyes in them.'

Yama was suddenly overwhelmed by the image of an electric-blue long-necked bird with concentric arcs of fiery eyes peering over its tiny head. He turned away, the heels of his palms pressed into his eye sockets, but the vision still beat inside his brain.

'Wait,' the woman said. There a note of uncertainty in her voice. 'The gain is difficult to control . . .'

The sheaves of burning eyes vanished; there was only ordinary blood-warm darkness behind Yama's eyelids. Cautiously, he turned back to the shrine.

'It isn't real,' the woman said. She stepped up to the inner surface of the shrine and pressed her hands against it and peered between them as if trying to see through the window of a lighted room into a dark landscape. Her palms were dyed red. She said, 'Nothing in here is real. But everything in the so-called real world is an illusion too. It's all waves, and the waves are really manifestations of strings folded deeply into themselves, and so on.'

She seemed to be talking to herself, but then she smiled at Yama. Or no, her eyes were not quite focused on him, but at a point a little to one side.

Yama said, prompted by a flicker of suspicion, 'Excuse me, domina, but are you really an avatar? I have never seen one before.'

'I'm no fragment of a god, Yamamanama. The clade of my original ruled a million planetary systems, once upon a time, but she never claimed to be a god. None of the transcendents ever claimed to be gods. That was a lie put about by their enemies.'

Yama's fear and amazement collapsed into relief. 'An aspect. You are an aspect. Or a ghost.'

'A ghost in the machine. Yes, that's one way of looking at it. Why not? Even when my original walked the surface of this strange habitat she was a copy of a memory, and I suppose that would make me a kind of a ghost of a ghost.' The woman tilted her head with a curiously coquettish gesture. 'We have spoken before. You don't remember, do you? Well, you were very young, and that foolish man with you hid your face in a fold of his robes. I think he must have done something to the shrine, afterwards, because that window has been closed to me ever since, like so many others. I could only glimpse you now and then as you grew up. How I wish I could have spoken to you! How I wish I could have helped you! I am so happy to meet you again, but you should not be here, in this strange and terrible city. You should be on your way downriver, to the war.'

'What do you know about me? Please, domina, will you tell me what you know?'

'There are gates. Manifolds held open by the negative gravity of strange matter. They run in every direction, even into the past, all the way back to the time when they were created. I think that must be where you came from. That, or one of the voidships. Perhaps your parents were passengers or stowaways, time-shifted by the velocity of some long voyage. We did not learn where all the voidships went. There was not enough time to learn a tenth of what we wanted to know.'

'I was found on the river. I was a baby, lying on the breast of a dead woman in a white boat.' Yama suddenly felt that his heart might burst with longing. 'If you know anything about that, please tell me! Tell me how I came here, and why!'

The woman in the shrine lifted her hands, wrists cocked in an elegant shrug. She said, 'I'm a stranger here. My original walked out into your world and died there, but not before she started to change it. And before she died part of her came here, and here I am still. I sometimes wonder if you're part of what she did after she left me here. Would that make you my son, if it were true?'

'I am looking for answers, not more riddles,' Yama said.

'Let me give an example. You see the statues? You think them monuments to dead heroes, but the truth is simpler.'

'Then they are not statues?'

'Not at all. They are soldiers. They were garrisoned here after the main part of the temple was built, to guard against what the foolish little priests of the temple call the Thing Below. I suppose that when the apses were remodelled many years later it was easier to incorporate the soldiers into the architecture than to move them. Most of their kind have been melted down, and small pieces of armour have been cast from their remains, so in a sense they still defend the populace. But the soldiers around us are the reality, and the human soldiers who wear reforged scraps of the integuments of their brothers are but the shadows of that reality, as I am a shadow of the one for whom I speak. Unlike the soldiers, she is quite vanished from this world, and only I remain.'

Yama looked up at the nearest of the figures. It stared above his head at one of its fellows on the opposite side of the square apse, but Yama fancied that he saw its eyes flicker towards him for an instant. They were red, and held a faint glow that he knew had not been there before.

He said, 'Am I then a shadow too? I am searching for others like me. Can I find them?'

'I would be amazed and delighted if you did, but they are all long dead. You must have come from the deep past of this strange world, Yamamanama, but although I have searched the records I do not know who sent you, or why. But it doesn't matter. You are here, and you have already discovered that you can control the machines which maintain this habitat. There is much more I can teach you.'

'My bloodline was made by the Preservers to build the world, and then they went away. That much I have learnt, at least. I will discover more in the Palace of the Memory of the People.'

Yama did not want to believe the woman's story. If he had been sent here from the deep past when his people, the Builders, had been constructing the world according to the desires of the Preservers, then he could never find his family or any others like him. He would be quite alone, and that was unthinkable.

'They were taken back,' the woman said. 'You might say that if I am a shadow of what I was, then your kind were a shadow of what you call the Preservers and what I suppose I could call my children, although they are as remote from me as I am from the plains apes who walked out of Afrique and set fire to the Home Galaxy.'

Someone had recently said something similar to Yama. Who? Trying to remember, he said automatically, 'All are shadows of the Preservers.'

'Not quite all. There are many different kinds of men on this strange world – I suppose I must call it a world – and each has been reworked until it retains only a shadow of its animal ancestors. Most, but not all, have been salted with a fragment of heritable material derived from the Preservers. The dominant races are from many different places and many different times, but they all are marked by this attribute, and all believe that they can evolve to a higher state. Indeed, many seem to have evolved out of existence, but it is not clear if they have transcended or merely become extinct. But the primitive races, which resemble men but are little better than animals, are not marked, and have never advanced from their original state. I do not know why. There is much that I still do not understand about this world.'

'If you can help me understand where I came from, perhaps I can help you.'

The woman smiled. 'You try to bargain with me. But I have already told you where you came from, Yamamanama, and I have already helped you. I have sung many songs of praise in your honour. I have told many of your coming. I have raised up a champion to fight for you. You should be with him now, sailing downriver to the war.'

Yama remembered the young warlord's story. He said, 'With Enobarbus?'

'The soldier too. But I meant Dr Dismas. He found me long ago, long before I spoke with Enobarbus. You should be with them now. With their help, and especially with mine, you could save the world.'

Yama laughed. 'Domina, I will do what I can against the heretics, but I do not think I can do more than any other man.'

'*Against* the heretics? Don't be silly. I have not been able to speak to you, but I have watched you. I heard your prayers, after your brother's death. I know how desperately you wish to become a hero and avenge him. Ah, but I can make you more than that.'

After the news of Telmon's death, Yama had prayed all night at the shrine in the temple. The Aedile had sent two soldiers to watch over him, but they had fallen asleep, and in the quiet hour before dawn Yama had asked for a sign that he would lead a great victory in Telmon's name. He had thought then that he wanted to redeem his brother's death, but he understood now that his prayers had been prompted by mere selfishness. He had wanted a shape to his own life, to know its beginning, to be given a destiny. Now he realised that his prayer had been answered, but not in the way he had hoped.

'You must take up your inheritance,' the woman said. 'I can help you. Together we can complete the changes my original began. I think you have already begun to explore what you can do. There is much more, if you will let me teach you.'

'If you had listened to me, domina, you would know that I pledged to save the world, not change it.'

Did the woman's gaze darken? For a moment, it seemed to Yama that her strange beauty was a merely a mask or film covering something horrible.

She said, 'If you want to save the world, it must be changed. Change is fundamental to life. The world will be changed whichever side wins the war, but only one side can ensure that stasis is not enforced again. Stasis preserves dead things, but it suffocates life. A faction of the servants of this world realised that long ago. But they failed, and those who survived were thrown into exile. Now they are our servants, and together we will succeed where they alone did not.'

Yama remembered the cold black presence of the feral machine he had inadvertently called down; it took all his will to stand his ground. He knew now which side this aspect was on, and where Enobarbus and Dr Dismas had been planning to take him. Dr Dismas had lied about everything. He was a spy for the heretics, and Enobarbus was not a champion against them but was secretly fighting on their side. Perhaps he had not escaped when his ship had been sunk, but had been captured by the heretics, and turned. Or perhaps he had been granted safe passage because he was already on their side – had he not described a vision which had spoken to him from the shrine of the temple of his people? Yama knew now what that vision had been, and the path the young soldier had been set upon.

He said, 'The world cannot be saved by contesting the will of those who made it. I will fight the heretics, not serve them.'

Silver bells, ringing in the air all around. 'You are still so young, Yamamanama! You still cling to the beliefs of your childhood! But you will change your mind. Dr Dismas has promised that he has already sown the seeds of change. Look on this, Yamamanama. All this can be ours!'

The shrine flashed edge to edge with white light. Yama closed his eyes, but the light was inside his head, too. Something long and narrow floated in it, like a needle in milk. It was his map. No, it was the world.

Half was green and blue and white, with the Great River running along one side and the ranges of the Rim Mountains on the other, and the ice cap of the Endpoint shining in the sunlight. And half was tawny desert, splotched and gouged with angry black and red scars and craters, the river dry, the ice cap gone.

It floated before Yama, serene and lovely, for a long moment. And then it was gone, and the woman smiled at him from the window of the shrine, with the green lawn and the high hedges of the garden receding behind her.

'Together we will do great things,' she said. 'We will remake the world, and everyone in it.'

Yama said steadfastly, 'You are an aspect of one of the Ancients of Days. You raised up the heretics against the will of the Preservers. You are my enemy.'

'I am no enemy of yours, Yamamanama. How could an enemy speak from a shrine?'

'The heretics silenced the last avatars of the Preservers. You may have moved into the place where they once lived, but it does not mean that you share their loyalty.'

'Nevertheless, I want to help you.'

'By tempting me with foolish visions? No one can rule the world.'

The woman smiled. 'No one does, and there is its problem. Any advanced organism must have a dominating principle, or else its different parts will war against each other, and it will be paralysed by inaction. As with organisms, so with worlds. You have so many doubts. I will help you understand everything, but not now. Someone comes. We'll talk again. If not here, then at one of the other transceivers that still function. There are many on the farside shore.'

'If I talk with you again, it will be because I have found some way of destroying you.'

She smiled. 'I think you will change your mind about that.'

'Never!'

'Oh, but I think that you will. Already it has begun. Until then.'

And then she and her garden were gone. Beyond the darkly transparent disc of the shrine, on the far side of the apse, someone pushed aside the curtain of black mesh.

25
THE ASSASSIN

It was a bare-chested giant of a man in leather trews. His skin was the colour of rust; his face was masked with an oval of black moleskin. He carried a naked falchion, and there was a percussion pistol tucked into his waistband. His muscular arms were bound tightly with leather thongs and plastic vambraces, mottled with extreme age, were laced around his forearms. His skin shone as if oiled, and a spiral pattern of welts was raised on the drum of his chest. Yama thought of the friendly people who had colonised the abandoned tombs at the edge of Ys. This was one of their sons, corrupted by the city. Or perhaps he had left his people because he was already corrupted.

As soon as he saw Yama, the man quickly advanced around the shrine. Yama stepped backwards and drew his knife. It ran with blue fire, as if dipped in flaming brandy.

The man smiled. His mouth was red and wet inside the slit in his black mask. The pointed teeth of a small fierce animal made a radiating pattern around the slit and little bones made a zig-zag pattern around the eyeholes, exaggerating their size.

'Who sent you?' Yama said. He was aware that one of the statues was only a few paces from his back, and watched carefully as the man moved towards him, looking for weaknesses he could exploit.

'Put up that silly pricking blade and I'll tell you,' the man said. His voice was deep and slow, and set up echoes in the vaulted roof of the apse. 'I was asked to kill you slowly, but I promise to make it quick if you don't struggle.'

'It was Gorgo, wasn't it? Either he hired you at the Water Market, or you owe him a debt.'

The man's eyes widened slightly and Yama knew that he had guessed right. His fingers sweated on the hilt of the knife and the skin and muscles of his forearm tingled as if held close to a fire, although the knife blade gave off no heat. It was taking the energy it needed from him because Pandaras had not known to leave it in sunlight: he knew that he must strike before it weakened him.

He said, 'Did Gorgo tell you who I killed? He cannot have forgotten, because it was only two nights ago. It was a rich and powerful merchant, with many guards. I was his prisoner, and my knife was taken from me, but he is dead and I stand here before you. Go now, and I will spare you.'

He was calling out to any machine for help, but there were none close by. He could only feel their distant, directionless swarm.

The assassin said, 'You think to keep me talking, hoping that help will come. It is a foolish hope. I was paid to kill you as slowly as possible, but if you put away that silly little blade I'll give you a quick and painless dispatch. You have my word.'

'And perhaps you talk because you do not have the stomach for your work.'

'You choose a slow death, then. Prepare yourself.'

The assassin favoured his right arm; if Yama ran to the left, the man must turn before striking, leaving his flank exposed for a moment. Fading sunlight had climbed halfway up the walls, laying a bronze sheen on the cloudily opaque torsos of the gigantic soldiers, and everything in the square apse shone with an intense particularity. Yama had never felt more alive than now, at the moment before his certain death.

He yelled and ran, slashing at the assassin's belly, but the man whirled with amazing speed and parried with such force that Yama was barely able to fend off the blow. The knife screamed and spat a stream of sparks, notching the assassin's sword, and Yama was knocked to his knees.

But the assassin did not press his advantage; he was staring at something behind Yama. Yama pushed up and used the momentum to strike again, lunging with the point of his knife: Sergeant Rhodean had taught him that the advantage of a shorter blade was the precision with which it could be directed. The assassin parried with the same casual, brutal force as before and stepped back, pulling the percussion pistol from his waistband.

Dust boiled around them in a dry, choking cloud and chips of stone rained down like hail, ringing on the stone flags of the floor. Yama lunged again. It was a slight, glancing blow that barely grazed the assassin's chest, but there was a terrific flash of blue light that knocked the man down.

Yama's arm was numbed from wrist to shoulder. As he shifted the knife to his left hand, the assassin rolled away and got to his feet and raised his pistol. The man's mouth was working inside the mask's slit, and his eyes were wide. He fired at something behind Yama, fired again. The pistol failed on the third shot and the assassin threw it away and ran.

Yama chased after him, his blood singing in his head, but the man plunged through the curtain of black mesh and Yama stopped short, fearing an ambush on the other side. He turned and looked up at the soldier which had stepped from its niche, and asked it to go back to sleep until it was needed again. The soldier, its eyes glowing bright red in its impassive face, struck its chestplate with a mailed fist, and the apse rang like a bell.

26

THE THING BELOW

A long way down the shadow-filled atrium, in the glow of a palm-oil lantern which had been lowered on a chain from the lofty ceiling, two men bent over something. Yama ran forward with his knife raised and saw that they were priests tending to Pandaras, who sprawled on the mosaic floor, alive but unconscious. Yama sheathed the knife and knelt and touched the boy's face. His eyes opened and his mouth moved, but no words came. There was a bloody gash on his temple; it seemed to be his only wound.

Yama looked up at the two priests, old men dressed in homespun robes, with broad faces and tangled manes of white hair – they were of the same bloodline as Enobarbus. Although Yama had guessed that this was the place where the young warlord had received his vision, he still felt a small shock of recognition.

He asked if the priests had seen who had wounded his friend, and they looked at each other before one volunteered that a man had just now run past, but they had already discovered this poor boy. Yama smiled to think of the spectacle the masked assassin must have made, running through the temple with a sword in his hand and blood running down his bare chest. Gorgo must be nearby – if he had sent the assassin surely he would want to witness what he had paid for – and he would have seen the rout of his hireling.

The priests looked at each other again and the one who had spoken before said, 'I am Antros, and this is my brother, Balcus. We are keepers of the temple. There is a place to wash your friend's wound, and to tend to your own wounds, too. Follow me.'

Yama's right arm had recovered most of its strength, although it tingled as if it had been stung by a horde of ants. He gathered up Pandaras and followed the old priest. The boy's skin was hot and his heartbeat was light and rapid, but Yama had no way of knowing whether or not this was normal.

Inside the colonnade on the left-hand side of the atrium was a little grotto carved into the thick stone of the temple's outer wall. Water trickled into a shallow stone trough from a spout set in a swirl of red mosaic. Yama helped Pandaras kneel, and bathed the shallow wound on his temple. Blood matting the boy's sleek hair fluttered into the clear cold water, but the bleeding had already stopped and the edges of the wound were clean.

'You will have a headache,' Yama said, 'but nothing worse. I think he struck you with the edge of his vambrace rather than with his falchion. You should have stayed with me, Pandaras.'

Pandaras was still unable to speak, but he clumsily caught Yama's hand and squeezed it.

The priest, Antros, insisted on cleaning the shallow cuts on Yama's back. As he worked, he said, 'We heard two pistol shots. You are lucky that he missed you, although I would guess that he did not miss you by much, and you were hurt by stone splinters knocked from the wall.'

'Fortunately, he was not aiming at me,' Yama said.

'This was a fine place once,' Antros said. 'The pillars were painted azure and gold, beeswax candles as tall as a man scented the air with their perfume, and we received mendicants and palmers from every town and city along the length of the river. But that was many years ago, when an avatar of the Preservers still appeared in the shrine.'

'Was this avatar a woman, dressed in white?'

'It was neither man nor woman, and neither young nor old.' The old priest smiled in recollection. 'How I miss its wild laughter. It was filled with fierce joy, and yet it was a gentle creature. But it is gone. They have all gone. Men still come to pray at the shrine, of course, but although the Preservers hear every prayer, men have fallen so far from grace that there are no longer answers to their questions. Few come here now, and even fewer to bare themselves humbly before their creators. Most who come do so to ask the one below to curse their enemies, but there are not even very many of them.'

'I suppose that most people fear this place.'

'Just so, although we do have problems with cultists from time to time, for they are attracted by the same thing which the ordinary folk fear. My brother and I come here each evening to light the lamps, but otherwise the temple is not much used, even by our own bloodline. Of course, we have our high day when the atrium is decorated with palm fronds and wreaths of ivy, and there is a solemn procession to propitiate the Thing Below. But otherwise, as I have said, most people keep away. You are a stranger here. A palmer, perhaps. I am sorry that you and your friend were attacked. No doubt a footpad followed you, and saw his chance.'

Yama asked Antros if the Thing Below was the machine which had fallen in the final battle at the end of the Age of Insurrection.

'Indeed. You must not suppose that it was destroyed. Rather, it was entombed alive in rock made molten by its fall. It stirs, sometimes. In fact, it has been very restless recently. Listen! Do you hear it?'

Yama nodded. He had supposed that the high singing in his head was his own blood rushing through his veins with the excitement of his brief skirmish.

'It is the second time in as many days,' Antros said. 'Most in our bloodline are soldiers, and part of our duty is to guard the well and the thing entombed at its bottom. But many have gone downriver to fight in the war, and many of those have been killed there.'

'I met one,' Yama said. He did not need to ask when the machine had begun to be restless, and felt a chill in his blood. He had called for help in the merchant's house, and the feral machine which had answered his call was not the only one to have heard him. What else? What else might he have inadvertently awakened?

Out in the atrium, someone suddenly started to shout, raising overlapping echoes. The old priest looked alarmed, and Yama said, 'Do not be afraid, dominie. I know that voice.'

Tamora said that she had returned to the inn, and had been forced to threaten the painted witch who ran it to find out where Yama and Pandora had gone. 'Then I realised what the game was, and came straight away.'

'It was Gorgo,' Yama said, as he tied the laces of his torn, bloodstained shirt. 'I appear to have a knack of making enemies.'

'I hope you gouged out his eyes before you killed him,' Tamora said.

'I have not seen him. But someone shot an arbalest bolt at me earlier, and I remember that you said Gorgo had killed someone with an arbalest. He missed, and sent another man to kill me. Fortunately, I had some help, and was able to scare off the assassin.'

'I will have his eyes if I ever see him again,' Tamora said 'His balls and his eyes. He is a disgrace to the Fierce People.'

'He must be very jealous, to want to kill me because of you.'

Tamora laughed. 'At last you show some human weakness, even if it's only conceit about your cockmanship. The truth is, I owe Gorgo money. He's not one for fighting, but for making deals. He finds work for others, and takes a cut of the fees for his trouble. And he loans money, too. I borrowed from him to buy new armour and this sword after I was wounded in the war last year. I lost my kit then, you see. I was working on commission to pay off the debt and the interest. I got enough to live on, and he took the rest.'

'Then the job I did with you—'

'Yes, yes,' Tamora said impatiently. 'On Gorgo's commission. He didn't really expect me to succeed, but that didn't stop him losing his temper when I told him that we'd killed the merchant and hadn't been able to collect the fee. I still owed Gorgo, but I was going off to work for you, as he saw it. I said he should wait and I'd pay back everything I owed, with points, but he's greedy. He wants liver and lights in addition to meat and bones.'

'He decided to kill me, and steal whatever I possess.'

Tamora hung her head for a moment, then said, 'He said that he would rob you, not kill you. He said it was only fair, because you'd lost him the fee for killing the merchant when you went crazy and grabbed that circlet. I didn't know he'd try to kill you. If I did, I would have warned you straight away.'

'Gorgo found someone else to help you with the job in the Palace of the Memory of the People, didn't he? He wanted me out of the way.'

'A man with red skin and welts on his chest. I told Gorgo that I would only work with you, Yama, but Gorgo told me that his man would be waiting for me at the palace gate. If I didn't go with him, Gorgo said, he'd sell my debt to the highest bidder. I would never be free of it. So I went there, but couldn't find Gorgo's man, and went back to the inn and found that you had come here.'

'The man you were supposed to meet was also here. He who tried to kill me.'

'I was going to tell you everything,' Tamora said. 'I decided something, while I was waiting. Hear me out. I made an agreement with you, and I will stick with it. Fuck Gorgo. When the job is finished I'll find him and kill him.'

'Then you will work for me, and not for Gorgo?'

'Isn't that what I said? Isn't that why I'm here? I am ashamed of my part in this, Yama, and I swear to remedy it in every way I can.'

Tamora stuck out her right hand. After a moment, Yama clasped it.

'You won't be sorry,' she said. 'Now, there's no more time to talk. We have already missed one appointment, and we must not miss the second, or the contract will be voided. Can you ride?'

'A little.'

'That had better mean you can ride like the wind.' Tamora seemed to notice Pandaras for the first time. 'What happened to the rat-boy?'

'A blow to the head. Luckily, Gorgo's man had some scruples.'

'Maybe it'll have knocked some of his airs out and let some sense in. I suppose you still want to bring him? Well, I'll carry him for you.'

Tamora slung Pandaras over her shoulder and walked away with a quick, lithe step, as if the boy weighed nothing at all. After a moment, Yama followed.

It was dusk. Warm lights glowed in windows of the houses around the mossy plaza. Two horses were tethered to a pole topped by a guttering cresset, harnessed cavalry fashion, with light saddles and high stirrups; Tamora said that she'd had to pay the painted witch a fortune for their hire. She and Yama lifted Pandaras onto the withers of her mount, and then she vaulted into the saddle. Yama had just grasped the horn of his mount's saddle and fitted his left foot in the stirrup, ready to swing himself up, when the ground shook. The horse jinked. As Yama struggled to check it, a beam of light shot up through the aperture of the domed roof of the temple.

The light was as red as burning sulphur, with flecks of violet and vermilion whirling in it like sparks flying up a chimney. It rose high into the sky, washing the temple and the square and the roofs of the houses all around with bloody light.

Yama realised at once what it meant, and knew that he must confront what he had wakened. He was horribly afraid of it, but if he did not face it then he would always be afraid. He threw the reins of his mount to Tamora and ran up the steps into the temple. As he entered the long atrium, the floor groaned and heaved like an animal tormented by biting flies, and dust and small fragments rained down from the ceiling.

Yama fell headlong, picked himself up, and ran on towards the column of red light that burned up from the well and filled the atrium with its fierce glare. The intricate mosaics of the floor were heaved apart in uneven ripples and a long ragged crack ran back from the well. The two old priests stood either side of it, silhouetted by raging furnace light. Balcus had drawn his sword and held it above his head in pitiful defiance; Antros knelt with the heels of his hands pressed to his eyes, chanting over and over an incantation or prayer.

The language was a private dialect of the priests' bloodline, but its rhythm struck deep in Yama. He fell to his knees beside the old priest and began to chant too.

It was not a prayer, but a set of instructions to the guards of the temple.

He was repeating it for a third time when the black mesh curtain that divided the right-hand apse from the atrium was struck aside. Two, four, five of the giant soldiers marched out. The red light gleamed like fresh blood on their transparent carapaces.

The priests immediately threw themselves full-length on the floor, but Yama watched with rapt fascination. The five soldiers were the only survivors of the long sleep of the temple's guards. One dragged a stiff leg, and another appeared to be blind, trailing its hand along one wall for guidance as it advanced, but all remembered their duty. They took up position, forming a five-pointed star around the well, threw open their chest-plates and drew out bulbous silver tubes as long as Yama was tall. Yama supposed that the soldiers would discharge their weapons into the well, but instead they aimed at the coping and floor around it and fired as one.

One of the weapons immediately exploded, blowing the upper part of its owner to flinders; from the others, violet threads as intensely bright as the sun raked stone until it ran like water into the well. Heat and light beat at Yama's skin; the atrium filled with the acrid stench of burning stone. The floor heaved again, a rolling ripple that snapped mosaics and paving slabs like a whip and threw Yama and the priests backwards.

And the Thing Below rose up from the white-hot annulus around its pit.

It was similar to the feral machine that Yama had inadvertently drawn down at the merchant's house, although it was very much larger, and had grown misshapen during its long confinement, like a spoiled fruit. Black, bristling with mobile spines, it barely cleared the sides of the well.

The giant soldiers played violet fire across the machine, but it took no notice of them. It hung in the midst of its column of red light and looked directly into Yama's head.

I have answered your call. Now come with me, and serve.

A hot iron wedge struck through Yama's skull. His sight was filled with red and black lightning. Blind, burning inside and out, he gave the soldiers a final order.

They moved as one, and then Yama could see again. The four surviving soldiers had jumped onto the machine, each clinging with one hand and shearing and snapping spines with the other, destroying its ability to bend the gravity field of the world to its will. It jerked and spun, like a hyrax attacked by dire wolves, but the soldiers held fast. Broken spines flew like spears, smacking into the floor and the stone walls, and the machine stopped spinning, hung still for a moment, and then plummeted like a stone into the well.

The temple shuddered again. Several of the pillars on either side of the atrium cracked from top to bottom, and one thunderously collapsed across the floor. Vast volumes of dust whirled up and were sucked into the well. There was a long roaring sound, and the column of red light flickered and went out.

27

THE PALACE OF THE MEMORY OF THE PEOPLE

Yama and the two priests helped each other through the smoky wreckage of the temple. When they emerged into the twilight, scorched, coughing, covered in dust, a great cheer went up – the people who lived in the houses around the temple had run out of their homes convinced that the last day of the world was at hand. Men of the priests' bloodline helped the two old men away; Tamora urged her horse up the shallow steps, leading Yama's mount by its reins.

Yama fought through the crowd. 'It is gone!' he shouted to her. 'I woke the soldiers and I defeated it!'

'We may be too late!' Tamora shouted back. 'If you're done here, follow me!'

By the time Yama had climbed into the saddle of his horse, she was already galloping away across the square. He whooped and gave chase. His horse, a lean, sure-footed gelding, needed little guidance as he raced Tamora through the narrow streets. The rush of warm evening air stung his scorched skin but cleared his head. His long hair, uncut since he had left Aeolis, streamed out behind him.

A distant bell began to toll. Tamora looked back and yelled, 'The gate! Ten minutes before it closes!'

She lashed the flanks of her mount with her reins. It laid back its ears and raised its tail and doubled its speed. Yama shouted encouraging words in the ear of his own horse, and it took heart and gave chase. A minute later, they shot out of the end of the narrow street and began to plough through crowds that clogged a wide avenue beneath globes of blue fire floating high in the air.

They were petitioners, penitents and palmers trying to gain entrance to the Palace of the Memory of the People, their numbers swelled by those panicked by earth tremors and strange lights. Tamora laid about her with bunched reins; people pressed back as she forced a way through, with Yama close behind. The tolling of the great bell drowned most of the crowd's screams and shouts.

At the far end of the avenue, Tamora and Yama checked their horses in front of a picket line of machines that spun in the air, burning with fierce radiance like a cord of tiny suns. Overhead, more machines flitted through the dusk like fireflies. They filled Yama's head with their drowsy hum, as if he had plunged head first into a hive of bees. Robed and hooded magistrates stood behind the glare of the picket line. Beyond them the avenue opened out into a square so huge that it could easily have contained the little city of Aeolis. At the far side, a high smooth cliff of keelrock curved away to the left and right, punctuated by a gateway guarded by a decad of soldiers in silvery armour who stood on floating discs, tiny figures raised high in the blue twilight.

The mountain of the Palace of the Memory of the People loomed above all this, studded with lights, blotting out the sky, its peaks hidden inside a wreath of clouds. Yama stared up at it. He had come so far in a handful of days, from the little citadel of the peel-house of the Aedile of Aeolis to this, the greatest citadel of all, which the preterites claimed was older than the world itself. He had learned that his bloodline was older than the world and that the heretics considered him a great prize. He had resolved to fight against them with all his might, and he had confronted and defeated one of their dark angels.

And he had left his childhood far behind. Ahead lay the long struggle by which he would define himself. Most likely it would end in death: countless men had already died in the war, and many more would die before the heretics were defeated. But at this moment, although he was exhausted and bruised and his clothes were scorched and tattered, he felt more alive than ever before. Somewhere in the great citadel that reared above him, in the stacks of its libraries, in the labyrinths of its temples and shrines and departments, lay the secret of his origin. He did not doubt it. The woman in the shrine had said that he had come from the deep past, but she was his enemy – he was convinced that she had been lying. He would prove her wrong. He would find the secrets that Dr Dismas had uncovered and discover where his bloodline still lived, and learn from them how to use his powers against the heretics.

Tamora caught the bridle of Yama's horse and leaned close. 'The gates are about to close! Are you ready for one last race?'

'Of course! It is my destiny!'

Pandaras raised his head and said weakly, 'My master wills it.'

Tamora grinned, and held up something that stuttered sharp flashes of red light. The picket line of incandescent machines spun apart before her. People started towards the gap and magistrates lashed out with their quirts, driving those at the front into those pressing forward from behind. In the midst of the mêlée, a fat woman reclining on a pallet born by four oiled, nearly naked men suddenly clutched at the swell of her bosom. Under her plump hands, a vivid red stain spread over her white dress. She slumped sideways and the pallet tipped and foundered, sending a wave of confusion spreading out through the close-packed crowd.

Yama did not understand what had happened until a man right by his horse's flank flew forward and folded over and fell under the feet of his neighbours. Yama glimpsed the red fletching of the bolt in the dead man's back, and then the crowd closed over him.

Tamora had drawn her sword and was brandishing it around her as she forced a way through the crowd. Yama kicked at hands which tried to grasp the bridle of his plunging mount, and fought through the tumult to her side.

'Gorgo!' he shouted. 'Gorgo! He is here!'

But Tamora did not hear him. She was leaning against Pandaras and shouting at the magistrates who barred her way. Yama reached for her shoulder and something shot past his ear with a wicked crack, and when he jerked around to see where it had come from another bolt smashed the head of a man who had been trying to catch hold of the bridle of his horse.

Yama lashed out in panic and anger. Red and black lightning filled his head, and then he saw the square from a thousand points of view that all converged on a figure on a flat roof above the crowded avenue. Gorgo screamed and raised the arbalest in front of his face as hundreds of tiny machines smashed into him, riddling his torso and arms and legs. He must have died in an instant, but his body did not fall. Instead, it rose into the air, the soles of its boots brushing the parapet as it drifted out above the packed heads of the crowd.

Yama came to himself and saw that Tamora had forced her way through the line of magistrates. He spurred his horse and followed her.

On the far side of the vast square, the great iron gates of the Palace of the Memory of the People were closing. The bell fell silent, and there was a shocking moment of silence. Then people felt drops of blood falling on them and looked up and saw Gorgo's riddled body sustained high above, head bowed and arms flung wide, the arbalest dangling by its strap against his chest.

A woman screamed and the crowd began to yell again, ten thousand voices shouting against each other. The soldiers on the floating discs swooped towards the crowd as Yama and Tamora raced their horses across the square and plunged through the gates into the darkness beyond.

ANCIENTS OF DAYS

THE SECOND BOOK OF CONFLUENCE

For Kim Newman,
compañero

In books lies the soul of the whole Past
Time; the articulate audible voice of the Past,
when the body and material substance of it
has altogether vanished like a dream.

Thomas Carlyle

1
THE WHISPERERS

Pandaras entered the shadowy arena of the Basilica just as one half of the defence force charged at the other. Tamora led the point of the attacking wedge, screaming fearsomely; Yama ran up and down behind the double rank of the defending line, shouting at his thralls, telling them to stand firm.

The two sides met with a rattle of padded staves against round arm shields. Shadows shifted and swayed as fireflies clashed in a storm of sparks. For a moment it seemed that the attack must fail, but then one of the thralls in the defending line gave ground to Tamora's remorseless blows. Instead of closing the gap as the man went down in the press, the first rank wavered and broke, stumbling backwards into the second. Yama shouted the order to regroup, but his thralls fell over each other or simply dropped their shields and staves and ran, and the wedge formation of the attacking force dissolved as thralls began to chase each other around the Basilica.

In the middle of the confusion, Tamora threw down her stave in disgust, and Yama blew on his whistle until everyone stopped running. Pandaras came towards them, trotting over the pattern of chalked lines that Tamora had drawn on the marble floor that morning. A matched pair of fireflies spun above his small sleek head. He said cheerfully, 'I thought it was very energetic.'

'You should be in the kitchen with the rest of the pot scourers,' Tamora said, and went off to round up the thralls so that she could tell them exactly what they had done wrong. Her own fireflies seemed to have caught some of her anger; they flared with bright white light and whirled around her head like hornets defending their nest. Her long queue gleamed like a rope of fresh blood. She wore a plastic corselet, much scratched and scored, and a short skirt of overlapping strips of scuffed leather that left her powerfully muscled legs mostly bare.

Pandaras said to Yama, 'They are armed with sticks, master. Is that part of your plan?'

'We do not dare give them proper weapons yet,' Yama told the boy.

Like the thralls, he wore only a breechclout. The floor was cold and gritty under his bare feet, but he was sweating in the chill air, and his blood sang. He could feel it thrilling under his skin. His vigorous black hair was bushed up by the bandage around his forehead. A ceramic disc, of the kind believed to have been used as coins in the Age of Enlightenment, hung from his neck on a leather thong. His knife, in its goatskin sheath, hung between his shoulders from a leather harness buckled across his chest.

'We had them at drill most of the day,' he said. 'You should see how they keep in step!'

Pandaras looked up at his master, affecting concern. 'How is your head? Is the wound making you feverish? You seem to think an army of polishers and floor sweepers armed only with sticks can frighten away the crack troops of the Department of Indigenous Affairs by putting on a marching display.'

Yama smiled. 'Why are you here, Pandaras? Do you really have something to tell me, or have you come expressly to annoy Tamora? I hope not. She is doing the best she can.'

Pandaras looked to either side, then drew himself up until his sleek head was level with Yama's chest. He said, 'I have learnt something that you definitely need to know. Although you condemned us to hard labour and maximum discomfort in the bowels of this broken-backed, bankrupt and debauched department, I haven't stinted in trying to help you.'

'You chose to follow me, as I remember.'

Pandaras said, 'And now you may thank me for my foresight. While you two have been playing soldiers with the hewers of wood and drawers of water, I've been risking my life in deadly games of intrigue.'

'You have been spying again. What did you find?'

'I chanced upon a clandestine meeting in the mausoleum they call the Hall of the Tranquil Mind,' Pandaras said. 'And overheard something that threatens to overthrow all your plans.'

The Hall of the Tranquil Mind was a black, windowless edifice carved out of the basalt wall of the big cavern which housed the Department of Vaticination. Yama had thought it locked and derelict, like so much of the department.

He said, 'I suppose you went there to meet your sweetheart. Are you still chasing that scullion? You are dressed for the part.'

Pandaras had washed and mended his ragged clothes and polished his boots. He had found or stolen a red silk scarf which was knotted around his long, flexible neck with such casual elegance that he must have spent half the morning getting it just so. His fireflies spun above his head like a pair of living jewels.

He winked and said, 'Chased, caught, wooed, won. I didn't come to boast of my conquests, master. It's an old tale oft told, and there isn't time. We're in mortal peril.'

Yama smiled. His self-appointed squire loved to elaborate fantasies from chance remarks and conjure drama from insignificant events.

Pandaras said, 'There is a gallery that runs along one side of the Hall of the Tranquil Mind, under the rim of the dome. If you happen to be standing at the top of the stairs to the gallery, and if you place your ear close to the wall, then you can hear anything said by those below. A device much favoured by tyrants, I understand, who know that plotters often choose to meet in public buildings, for any gathering in a public place can be easily explained away. But fortune favours the brave, master. Today I was placed in the role of tyrant, and I overheard the whispered plotting of a pair of schemers.'

Pandaras paused. Yama had turned away to look across the shadowy Basilica. Tamora was marshalling the reluctant thralls into three ranks. Her voice raised echoes under the shabby grandeur of the vaulted dome.

'I can see that you would rather be playing soldiers,' Pandaras said, 'but my news really is important.'

'These exercises are also important. It is why we are here, to begin with, and besides, it is useful to stay in practice.'

It also helped to satisfy something in Yama that hungered for action. His sleep had been troubled by bloodthirsty dreams ever since he had entered the Palace of the Memory of the People, and sometimes an unfocused rage stirred up headaches that filled his sight with jagged red and black lightning, and left him weak and ill. He had been hard-used since he had reached Ys and escaped Prefect Corin, and he had been wounded in an ambush when they had first arrived outside the gates of the Department of Vaticination. He needed rest, but there was no time for it.

He said, 'I must hear what Tamora has to say. Walk with me, Pandaras.'

'The blow to the head has definitely given you delusions, master. You believe yourself a soldier.'

'And you believe that you are my squire, so we are equally deluded. Hush, now. We will speak of what you heard when Tamora has finished with our poor warriors.'

Tamora had jumped onto a square stone plinth which had once supported a statue – only its feet remained, clad in daintily pointed slippers which still retained traces of yellow pigment. She looked at the six decads of thralls who had gathered around her, allowing scorn to darken her small, triangular face. It was a trick she had taught Yama. To be a teacher, she said, was to be an actor first. Unless it was delivered from the heart, no lesson could be truly convincing.

The thralls were all of the same bloodline, lean and long-armed and bowlegged, with loose grey skin that hung in heavy folds from bony joints, untidy manes of coarse black or umber hair that tumbled down their bent backs, and muddy yellow or green eyes that peered out from beneath heavy brows. They were a stupid and frustratingly obdurate people. According to Syle, the Secretary of the Department of Vaticination, their families had served here for more than twenty thousand years. But although they were naturally servile, the unaccustomed drill had made them sullen and mutinous, and they took every opportunity to make it clear that Tamora and Yama had no real authority over them. They were glaring at Tamora now, sharp teeth pricking their thin black lips, as she told them how badly they had done.

She said, 'You have all taken your turn at defence, and you have all taken your turn at attack. You should know that if you are to win through or stand firm, you must stay in formation. A defending rank is only as strong as its weakest member. If he falls, someone must immediately take his place. And if an attacking formation breaks through a line, it must stay together.'

One of the thralls said, 'They ran and we chased 'em down, mistress. What's wrong with that?'

Tamora stared at the man until he lowered his gaze.

She said, 'There might be reserves waiting behind a turn in a corridor. If your disorganised rabble ran into them, it would be quickly slaughtered.'

'But there wasn't anyone else,' the thrall mumbled, and those around him muttered in agreement.

Tamora raised her voice. 'This is an exercise. When you fight for real, you can't assume anything. That's why you must fight as you're told, not as you want. It's very easy to kill one man on his own, much harder to kill him when he's part of a formation. When you fight shoulder to shoulder, you defend those on either side of you, and they defend you. And you don't have to worry about the enemy getting behind your back, because to do that they'd have to get around the line. And they won't, not in the corridors. Elsewhere, in the open, you fight in squares, as you tried yesterday.'

When Tamora paused for breath, a thrall stepped out of the front rank and said, 'We'd do better, mistress, if we had proper weapons.'

'I won't break open the armoury until you've mastered those sticks,' Tamora said. 'And from what I've just seen, I've a mind to take the sticks away.'

The thrall did not back down. He was taller than the rest, if only because he was straight-backed. There were streaks of grey in his mane. Most of the thralls possessed only one or two dim fireflies, but six hung in a neat cluster above his head, burning nearly as brightly as Tamora's. He said, 'We won't be fighting with these sticks, so why do we practise with them?'

The thralls muttered and nudged each other, and Pandaras told Yama, 'That's what they've been complaining about, down in the kitchens.'

Yama felt a sudden hot anger. He strode forward and confronted the grey-maned thrall. 'It is discipline, not weapons, that makes a fighting force,' he said loudly. 'Between all of you, there is not the discipline to attack a nest of rats.'

The thrall returned Yama's glare. He said, 'Beg your pardon, dominie, but we do know a bit about rat-catching.'

Some of the other thralls laughed and Yama lost the last of his temper – it was easily lost these days. 'Come on then, rat-catcher! Show me how well you fight!'

The thrall looked around at his fellows, but none were willing to support him. He said uneasily, 'It's not you I want to fight, dominie.'

'You cannot choose who to fight,' Yama said. He asked Tamora to lend him her sword, and presented it hilt-first to the thrall. 'Take this! Take it right now!'

The thrall dropped his stave and spread his empty hands. 'Dominie . . .'

From above, Tamora said sharply, 'Do as he commands or slink away like the cur you are.'

Yama thrust the hilt of the sword at the thrall until he had to take it or have it fall on his feet. 'Good. Now hold it up. It is not a broom. It is a weapon. You can kill with the point or with the cutting edge. And if you do not have the taste for blood, you can render your enemy insensible with a blow to the head with the flat of the blade. However, I do not recommend that you try the last against anyone less skilled than you. The man who wounded me in that fashion lost most of his fingers when I countered his stroke. Hold it up. Keep the tip of the blade level with your eyes.'

Tamora said, 'If you're any kind of man, you must know that the higher the angle the better the thrust. Obey your master! Show him you're a man!'

The other thralls had broken ranks and backed away, forming a rough circle around Yama and the grey-maned thrall. They laughed now, and Yama scowled at them and told them what Sergeant Rhodean had told him so many times.

'Do not mock an armed man unless you wish to fight him.' He pointed at the thrall and thumped himself just below the breastbone. 'Now thrust at me. Aim here. If you miss the heart, you might get a lung. Either way you will have killed me. Come on!'

The thrall made a tentative jab that did not carry more than halfway. Yama batted the square point of the sword aside and leaned forward and shouted in the thrall's face.

'Come on! Kill me, or I will tear out your eyes to teach you a lesson! Do it!'

The thrall yelled and sprang forward, swiping wildly.

Yama stepped inside the swing and caught the thrall's arm at the elbow, pivoted in a neat half-turn and threw him from his hip. The thrall let go of the sword when he fell; Yama caught it before it could ring on the marble floor and with a smooth swing laid the edge at the thrall's throat. For a moment, he struggled against the urge to complete the motion.

The thrall looked up at him, yellow slitted eyes glaring behind the agitated orbits of his fireflies. In the moment of shocked silence, Yama looked around. None of the other thralls would meet his gaze. He smiled and reversed the sword and presented it to Tamora.

She sheathed it, jumped down from the pedestal, and helped the thrall to his feet. 'Bravely tried. Better than anything anyone else has done,' she said, and looked around at the others. 'I don't mind if you hate us, but I do mind if you can't get angry. Without anger you'll have only fear when it comes to a fight. We can't teach you how to get angry, but if you can manage it we can teach you how to direct your anger. Tomorrow we begin again. Now get out of my sight. Go on! Run!'

Pandaras applauded languidly as the thralls dispersed around him. 'A bold display, master. I had not thought you could play-act so well.'

Yama shrugged. Now it was over he felt self-conscious. His head wound throbbed. He said, 'I was not play-acting. I lost my temper.'

Tamora said, 'You're sharpening your edge, Yama. That's good. The thralls have been servants for hundreds of generations, and we've been treating them like volunteers. We have been too kind. They take up arms not because they want to, but because they have been told to. They will not do anything unless they are told, and then they do what they are told and no more. They can march in perfect formation all day long without losing step, but it's clear that they don't have the heart for a real fight. All we can do is make them more scared of us than of the enemy.'

She was angry with herself, and so all the more unforgiving. Nothing had gone right since they had been ambushed by hired ruffians when they had arrived at the Gate of Double Glory.

She added, 'We're just a couple of caterans. We'll do our best with what we've been given, but in the end it won't matter. Indigenous Affairs will march right in and slaughter the thralls and take this place inside a day. This is a poor diversion in your search, Yama. I'm sorry for it.'

'Without this subterfuge, I would not have been able to enter the palace without being questioned. Besides,' Yama said, 'I enjoy these exercises.'

It was true. The sound of padded staves thumping on shields and the smell of chalk sweat brought back happy memories of all the afternoons he had spent training with Telmon and Sergeant Rhodean in the gymnasium of the peel-house, and the practice fights satisfied a fierceness he had not known he had possessed.

Tamora said, 'I forget how young you are. We might make these poor fools believe they have the heart for a fight, but it'll delay their deaths by no more than a minute. They know they're going to die, and they know that their wives and children will be killed too, or put into slavery. We'll be ransomed, but because our ransoms have already been paid into bond with the Department of Internal Harmony, we'll be freed and given our wages, and that'll be the end of that.'

'I pray you are right. I think that Prefect Corin is still searching for me, and he is a high official in Indigenous Affairs.'

They had talked about this before. Tamora said with exaggerated patience, 'Of course I am right. It is how it has always been, since the world was made. If it were not for the ancient protocols, there would be constant civil war here. I am certain that Indigenous Affairs sent those fools to ambush us, and perhaps Prefect Corin had a hand in it, but now we are inside the boundary of this department he will dare do nothing else.

'Listen. Here is the problem. Not your Prefect, but the real problem. We fight because we're paid. Once captured no harm will come to us. But the thralls fight because they've been told to fight, and they've been told to fight because the fat fool who rules this place and claims to see into the future has predicted victory. The thralls know in their guts that she is wrong. That is why they are so sullen.'

Yama said, 'We do not know that Luria does not have the powers she claims.'

'Grah. She knows that she doesn't, and so does Syle, and so do the thralls. And the other pythoness is no more than a whey-faced wet-brained child stolen from her cradle. I have not heard her speak a single word since we came here.'

Pandaras said, 'From what I hear, only Daphoene possesses any real talent for scrying the future. And that's why she is forbidden to speak: Luria is afraid that one day innocent Daphoene will expose her fraud.'

Yama said, 'Daphoene is very young. She may appear to keep her own counsel, but perhaps she does not speak because she has nothing useful to say.'

Tamora laughed. 'Yama, you're so innocent that you're a danger to all around you. For once your pet rat has said something sensible. If Daphoene does have true foresight, then Luria has every reason to keep her quiet. Syle too, and that bloodless wife of his. For Daphoene will know how badly the defence of this place will go.'

Yama said, 'Well, we will see her at work soon enough.'

In two days, the oracle would be opened for public inquisition, and the pythonesses would answer questions put to them by petitioners. It might be the last time the ceremony was held, for ten days after that the deadline for challenging the quit claim would run out. The Department of Indigenous Affairs would be allowed to march on the crumbling glory of the High Morning Court of the Department of Vaticination, and occupy the place where once Hierarchs had swum amongst star maps, ordering the voyages of ships that fell through holes in space and time.

Pandaras told Tamora, 'My master has paid you to help him find his bloodline, and it is a better and more honourable task than this game of soldiers. As you will at once see, if you let me tell my tale.'

'You run if you want to,' Tamora said. 'I'd like to see you run, rat-boy. It would prove what I've always thought about you.'

Pandaras said, with an air of affronted dignity, 'I'll ignore the slights on my character, except to say that those who attribute base motives to others do so because they expect no better of themselves. And also to note that while you have been playing at soldiers, I have been risking my life. Master, please. Let me tell you what I heard.'

'If this is more kitchen gossip,' Tamora said, 'then hold your yap. You'd inflate the breaking of a glass into an epic tragedy.'

'And why not? It's a painful death for the glass concerned, leaves its fellows bereft of a good companion, and makes them aware of their own mortality.'

Yama said, 'Pandaras claims to have overheard a conspiracy.'

'She will not believe me, master. It is not worth telling her.'

'Out with it, Pandaras,' Yama said. 'Forget your injured dignity.'

Pandaras drew himself up. 'I came across the two of them whispering together in the Hall of the Tranquil Mind. They were clearly at the end of their rendezvous, but I heard enough to alarm me. One said, "Tomorrow, at dawn. Go straight away, and come straight back." This was a woman. The other might have been a servant, for he simply made a noise of assent, and the first said, "If you succeed, the department will be saved. But if you fail, we may miss our chance to strike against her. And if she lives we all may die." Then they both moved off, and I heard no more.'

Tamora said, 'It might not be anything. These old departments are rats' nests of poisonous intrigues and feuds over trifles.'

Yama said, 'You have not told us who these plotters were.'

Pandaras wouldn't meet their gazes. 'I wasn't able to get a good look at them.'

Tamora scowled. 'Because you were too scared to peep out of your rat-hole.'

'I was in the gallery above them. Had I leaned out over the rail, the game would have been up.' Pandaras batted at the pair of fireflies which circled his head; they dipped away and circled back. 'These cursed things we must use instead of candles would have given me away.'

'As I said, you were scared.'

Yama said, 'It does not matter. The gate is closed at night, and opens again at sunrise. Whoever leaves when it opens tomorrow will be our man. I will follow him, see who he meets, and learn what I can. Then we shall decide what to do next.'

Drilling the thralls was all very well, but Yama had done little else since they had arrived here. He was beginning to feel as if he was suffocating in the stale air of the Department of Vaticination, with its meaningless ceremonies and its constant reverent evocation of the dead days of its long-lost glory. He wanted to see more of the palace. He wanted to find the records of his bloodline, and use them to search for any of his family who might still be alive. He wanted to go downriver and plunge into the war at the midpoint of the world.

'It's obviously some plot against the fat bitch,' Tamora said thoughtfully. 'We're here because of Luria's refusal to bargain with the Department of Indigenous Affairs. Without her, there would be no dispute.'

' "If she lives we all may die," ' Pandaras said.

'When your rat-boy agrees with me,' Tamora told Yama, 'then you know I must be right. It's my opinion that we should not become involved in petty intrigues. We were ambushed at the gate, we have been misled about the kind of troops at our command, and now we discover that our employers plot against each other. It's clear someone here has allied themselves to Indigenous Affairs, and hopes to strike a bargain after assassinating their rivals. Let them. However this falls out, we won't cover ourselves in glory. If these plotters don't sell out their department, our attempts to defend it are simply a matter of form before the inevitable surrender. Like all of Gorgo's little jobs, this has nothing to commend it. Another reason to kill him, when we are done here.'

Gorgo was the broker who had given Tamora this contract. He had tried to kill Yama because Yama had cost him the commission on a previous job and because he suspected that, with Yama's help, Tamora might free herself of her obligation to him. Yama had killed him instead, riddling him with a hundred tiny machines, but Tamora had not seen it, and did not or would not believe in what she called Yama's magic tricks.

'If we can find out more about this,' Yama said, 'we might be able to end the plot before it begins. And I think that would count towards defending the department.'

'We are protected by law and custom only as long as we stay within the boundaries of the Department of Vaticination. If you try to follow this plotter, Yama, you might be assassinated.'

'I can take care of myself.'

'How is your wound? Does it trouble you?'

'A headache now and then,' Yama admitted.

He had the beginning of a headache now. He felt as if his skull was too small to contain his thoughts, as if his brain was a bladder pumped up by a growing anger. Red and black sparks crawled at the edge of his vision. He had to stifle an impulse to draw his knife and do some harm.

'I will not make the same mistake again,' he said. 'And I will do as I will.'

Pandaras said, 'If we've been misled as badly as you claim, doesn't that invalidate our contract? Doesn't it mean that my master can quit this place immediately, and begin the search for the records of his bloodline? Which is, after all, why he's really here.'

Tamora whirled, and smashed her stave against the plinth with sudden fury, snapping it in two. She glared at the splintered stub in her hand, then threw it hard and fast down the length of the Basilica. 'Go then! Both of you! Go, and accept what falls out. Death, most likely. Even if you dodge the hirelings of the Department of Indigenous Affairs, you know nothing about the palace, and it is a dangerous place.'

'I'll follow this plotter, and learn what I can, and come back,' Yama said. 'I promised that I would help you, and I will see it through to the end. And besides, I still hope that I might learn something about my bloodline and my family here. After all, many of those who petition the pythonesses hope that they can help them find long-lost relatives.'

2

THE EYE OF THE PRESERVERS

It was the custom of the Department of Vaticination that everyone, from senior pythoness to apprentice collector of nightsoil, took their evening meal together in the refectory hall of the House of the Twelve Front Rooms. The pythonesses and their domestic staff – the secretary, the bursar, the chamberlain, the librarian, the sacristan, and a decad of holders of ancient offices which had dwindled to purely ceremonial functions or nothing more than empty titles – were raised up on a platform at one end of the refectory; the thralls were ranged around the other three sides. The refectory was not a convivial place. Yama guessed that tapestries had once decorated the bare stone walls – the hooks were still in place – and the broken tiers of chandeliers, stripped of gilt and crystal, still hung from the high vaults of the ceiling, but the gloomy hall was lit now only by the fireflies that danced above the heads of every man and woman. The thralls ate in silence while the praise-sayer, standing at his lectern in a corner of the refectory, recited suras from the Puranas in a high, clear voice. Alone amongst several hundred sullen servants, only Pandaras dared glance now and then at the dignitaries on the platform.

The Department of Vaticination was one of the oldest in the Palace of the Memory of the People. Although it had fallen on hard times, it did its best to keep up its traditions. The food served to the pythonesses and their staff was poor stuff, mostly rice and glutinous vegetable sauces eaten with wedges of unleavened bread (the thralls had it even worse, with only lentils and edible plastic), but it was served on fine, translucent porcelain by liveried thralls, and was accompanied by thin, bitter wine in fragile cups of blown glass veined with gold and silver.

Yama found the formal style of the meals comfortingly familiar; they reminded him of suppers at the long banqueting table in the Great Hall of the peel-house. He sprawled in a nest of silk cushions (their delicate embroidery tattered and stained) at a low square table he shared with Syle, the secretary of the Department of Vaticination, and Syle's pregnant wife, Rega. The department's officers and officials were grouped around other tables, all of them turned towards the couches on which the two pythonesses reclined.

Luria, the senior pythoness, overflowed her couch, looking, as Tamora liked to say, like a grampus stranded on a mudbank. Crowned by a tower of red and gold fireflies, she ate with surprising delicacy but ferocious appetite; usually, she had finished her portion and rung the bell to signal that the dishes should be taken away before the others on the platform were halfway done. Swags of flesh hung from her jowls and from her upper arms, and her eyes were half-hidden by the puffy cushions of her cheeks. They were large, her eyes, and a lustrous brown, with long, delicate lashes. Her black hair was greased and tied in numerous plaits with coloured silk ribbons, and she wore layers of gauze that floated and stirred on the faintest breeze. Whenever she chose to walk, she had to be supported by two thralls, but usually she was carried about on a chair. She had been pythoness for more than a century. She was the imperturbable centre of such power as remained in the faded glory of the Department of Vaticination, like a bloated spider brooding in a tattered web in a locked and lightless room. Yama knew that she did not miss a single nuance of the whispered conversations around her.

The junior pythoness, Daphoene, was Luria's starveling shadow. Only a single wan firefly flickered above her pale, flat face, as if she were no better than the least of the kitchen thralls. She wore a long white shift girdled with a belt of gold wires, lumpy scars wormed across her shaven scalp, and she was blind. Her eyes, white as stones, turned towards the ceiling while her fine-boned hands moved amongst the bowls and cups on the tray that a servant held before her, questing independently like small, restless animals. She hardly ever spoke, and did not appear to pay any attention to the conversations around her.

Yama suspected that Daphoene was inhabited by more than one person. Lately, he had begun to sense that everyone had folded within themselves a small irreducible kernel of self, the soul grown by the invisibly small machines which infected all of the changed bloodlines.

But Daphoene was a vessel for an uncountable number of kernels, a constant ferment of flickering fragments.

The formal evening meals were a trial to Tamora, and she guyed her unease by playing up the part of an uncouth cateran. That evening, after the argument in the Basilica, she had chosen to sit alone at a table at the far end of the platform, and was more restless than ever. But the more she played the barbarian, the more she endeared herself to Syle, who would incline his head towards Yama and comment in admiring, mock-scandalised whispers about the way Tamora tossed and caught her knife over and over, or yawned widely, or spat a bit of gristle onto the floor, or drank from the fingerbowl, or, as now, scratched herself with a cat's lazy self-indulgence.

'Quite wonderfully untamed,' Syle murmured to Yama. 'So thrillingly physical.'

'She comes from a people not much given to formalities,' Yama said.

'Fortunately, we didn't hire her for her manners,' Syle's wife, Rega, said. Rega was older than Syle, with a pointed wit and a sharp gaze that measured everyone it fell upon and usually found them wanting. She was tremendously pregnant. As round as an egg, as her husband fondly put it, and dressed in a shift of purple satin that stretched like a drumhead over her distended belly. She had twisted her feathery hair into a tall cone that sat like a shell on top of her small head.

'She is tired, too,' Yama said. 'We have both been working hard.'

The praise-sayer had been reciting from the sura which described how the Preservers had altered the orbits of every star in the Home Galaxy, as a feoffer might replant a forest as a formal garden. A monument, a game, a work of art – who could say? Who could understand the minds of those who had become gods, so powerful that they had escaped this universe of things?

Yama knew these suras by heart, and had been paying little attention to the praise-singer. But now the man paused, and began to recite a sura from the last pages of the Puranas.

The world first showed itself as a golden embryo of sound. As soon as the thoughts of the Preservers turned to the creation of the world, the long vowel which described the form of the world vibrated in the pure realm of thought, and re-echoed on itself. From the knots in the play of vibrations, the crude matter of the world curdled. In the beginning, it was no more than a sphere of air and water with a little mud at the centre.

And the Preservers raised up a man and set on his brow their mark, and raised up a woman of the same kind, and set on her brow the same mark. From the white clay of the middle region did they shape this race, and quickened them with their marks. And those of this race were the servants of the Preservers. And in their myriads this race shaped the world after the ideas of the Preservers.

Yama's blood quickened. He had read that very passage just before entering the Palace of the Memory of the People. It was a description of how the Preservers had created the first bloodline of Confluence: the Builders, his own bloodline, long thought to have vanished with their masters into the black hole at the heart of the Eye of the Preservers. He saw that Syle was watching him, and knew that Syle knew. Knew what he was. Knew why he was here. The sura had been chosen deliberately.

Luria rang her little bell. The attendants cleared away the bowls of rice and the dishes of sauces, and sprinkled the diners with water perfumed with rose petals.

'You will watch the exercises tomorrow,' Luria told Syle. 'I want to know how the training of our defence force is proceeding.'

Syle winked at Yama and said, 'I am sure that it is in capable hands, pythoness.'

Yes, Syle knew. But what was he planning to do with that knowledge?

Tamora said loudly, 'Well, we didn't kill anyone today, and I believe my friend's wound is healing.'

She had spoken out of turn. Luria took no more notice than if she had belched.

Syle said, 'The exercises are very diverting, pythoness. You should see how well the thralls march.'

'It's a pity they can't fight,' Tamora said.

'I have had a presentiment,' Luria told Syle. 'You will see to it that all is well.'

Tamora said, 'If you've seen something with your cards or dice, perhaps you could share it with us. It could help our plans.'

There was a silence. At last, Luria said in a soft croak, 'Not dice, dear. Dice and cards are for street performers who take your money and promise anything they think will make you happy. I deal in the truth.'

Syle said, 'True divination is hard, difficult and dangerous. It not only requires a special talent, but dedication and courage. As you will see in two days, at the public inquisition.'

'Syle likes to explain things,' Luria said. 'Tomorrow, you will show him the progress you have made. He will then explain it to me.'

The last course, iced fruits and sweet wine, was served. Luria ate a token mouthful, then rang her bell. The praise-sayer fell silent. The meal was over. Luria was helped into her chair by two tall strong attendants, and carried away. Another attendant took Daphoene's arm, and she followed him with the child-like trust of a sleepwalker. Her mouth hung open and there was a slick of drool on her chin.

As the thralls began to file out of the hall, followed by flocks of faint fireflies, Rega told her husband, 'You are kinder to Luria than she deserves. Certainly kinder to her than she is to you, who works so hard for her.'

'The pythoness worries all the time about the quit claim, and of course about the public inquisition,' Syle said. 'We are all a little short of patience, these days.'

Rega smiled sweetly at Tamora and said, 'You're doing your best, I'm sure, but you must wish for proper soldiers.'

'We only have what we have,' Syle said, again gazing at Yama. 'I'm sure the thralls will fight to the death.'

'I'm sure they will,' Rega said. She held out her hand, and her husband helped her to her feet. Her round belly swayed, stretching the panels of her satin dress. She added, 'A very quick death it will be, too. Yama, Tamora, I don't blame either of you. Our pythoness has foreseen victory, and is so certain that she is right that she has not provided the means to ensure it.'

Tamora drew herself up. She was very angry. She showed her sharp white teeth and said, 'If anything I have done does not satisfy the department, then I will resign at once.'

Syle made a fluttering motion with his hands. 'Please. Nothing of the sort is intended. I myself have seen how well you have drilled our thralls. A thrilling sight, to see them march!'

'Try getting some of that enthusiasm into your reports for people who can't be bothered to see the drills for themselves,' Tamora said. 'Excuse me. I have work to do.'

Syle whispered something to his wife, who gave her husband a cold look but allowed him to kiss her on her forehead before she took her leave. 'Walk with me, if you will,' Syle said to Yama, and caught hold of his arm.

Yama looked towards Tamora, but she was already halfway across the refectory, the crowd of thralls parting before her as rice plants part before the scythe. 'I would be happy to,' he said to Syle.

He liked Syle too much to be afraid of him. The tall, slightly built man, with his delicate bones, fine features, and white, feathery hair, was of the same bloodline as his sweetheart, Derev, and possessed a genuine enthusiasm for imparting arcane knowledge that reminded him of Zakiel, the librarian who had provided him with much of his education.

Syle had taught him much about the history of the Department of Vaticination, and its trade. There were very many ways of gaining foresight, Syle said, but almost all of them were false, and those that remained could be divided into no more than three types. The least of these was sortilege, the drawing of lots, or astragalomancy, the use of dice or huckle-bones or sticks, neither of which, as Luria had pointed out, were practised in the department, although they were much abused by charlatans. Of more merit were those methods classed as divination, in which signs were scried in the client's physiognomy, as in metascopy or chiromancy, or in the landscape, or in dust cast on a mirror (Syle said that gold was best, but the finings of any metal were better than the husks of rice grains used by village witches). The form most often performed by the department was rhabdomancy, or dowsing, used to find lost property or to find the best place for the site of a house or to locate a hidden spring. Finally, there was true foresight obtained through visions, either in dreams or in waking trances. It was the most difficult and most powerful method of all, and would be attempted by the pythonesses at the public inquisition, although these days most clients wanted answers to trivial questions, to find things that were lost or hidden (wills were a perennial favourite, for many slighted by the posthumous wishes of rich relatives believed that they had been cheated by a fake will got up by scheming rivals, and hoped to find the original), to speak with the dead, or to gain assurance of the success of a new business or a marriage.

The problem was that, as Syle put it, the Department of Vaticination no longer owned the future. Mountebanks claimed exclusive knowledge about the outcome of the war or the imminence of the eschaton. Most of the ordinary citizens of Ys believed that the predictions of roadside cartomancers were as valid as those of the pythonesses of the Department of Vaticination; the other departments no longer called upon its services when planning their affairs.

Now Syle steered Yama towards the broad stair at the far end of the hall. Thralls made way for them. Pandaras had disappeared, no doubt in pursuit of another amatory conquest.

'I promise not to keep you long,' Syle said. He had the tentative touch of an old man, although he was not much more than twice Yama's age, and much younger than his wife. 'Is your wound healing, by the way? Do you still have headaches?'

'Now and then.'

'You should let Brother Apothecary examine it.'

'Tamora said that the dressing should not be disturbed,' Yama said. 'Besides, it is mostly bruising.'

He had been embarrassed in the brief fight. The ruffians had rushed up from behind as Tamora, Pandaras and Yama had climbed the long stair towards the Gate of Double Glory. One had struck Yama with the flat of a blade; dazed and half-blinded by blood, Yama had saved himself with a lucky swipe that had hit his opponent's sword hand, severing two fingers and causing the man to drop his weapon. By the time Yama had wiped blood from his eyes, Tamora had killed three of the ruffians and the other two had fled, with Pandaras chasing after them and screaming insults.

'We have lodged a protest with the Department of Internal Harmony over the incident,' Syle said. 'If it is successful, then we may move on to a formal hearing. Unfortunately, the petition of protest must be read and approved by a clerk of the court in the first instance, and then a committee will be deputised to discuss it. That may take no more than fifty or sixty days if the business is rushed, but little is ever rushed in the palace. As is only proper, of course. These are serious matters, and must be taken seriously. After that, well, the process of establishing a hearing usually takes at least two years.'

'And in twelve days the ultimatum delivered by the Department of Indigenous Affairs will expire.'

Syle said, 'Indeed. But I have every expectation that you will surprise them, Yama.'

Yama wanted to know what the man had discovered about his bloodline, but he had learnt a little of the art of diplomacy from the man who had adopted him, the Aedile of Aeolis, and knew that he would lose the advantage if he asked a direct question.

He made a show of looking around, and said, 'I have never been in this part of the department before.'

'This was the main entrance, once upon a time. Now hardly anyone uses it.'

They reached the top of the stairway and went down a long corridor. Its walls were panelled in dark, heavily carved wood and hung with big square paintings whose pigments were so blackened by time that it was impossible to discern what scenes or persons they might once have depicted. A rat fled from their footsteps, pursued by a single wan firefly. It disappeared into a hole in the panelling and rolled the end of a broken bottle across the hole to stop it. The feeble light of the firefly flickered behind the thick glass as the rat lay still and watched the two men pass.

The corridor ended at a pair of round metal doors, with a metal-walled antechamber sandwiched between them. The inner door was open, the outer door dogged shut. Syle shut the inner door behind them and talked to the lock of the outer door – Yama felt its dim intelligence briefly waken – then instructed Yama to spin a wheel and pull the door open. It moved sweetly on its counterbalanced track, and Yama followed Syle over the high sill.

They had emerged onto the flat roof, lapped with metal plates that fitted together like the scales of a fish, of the House of the Twelve Front Rooms. On one side was the huge hollow of the cavern, with the other buildings of the Department of Vaticination – the Basilica, the Hall of the Tranquil Mind, the Hall of Great Achievements and the Gate of Double Glory – set symmetrically around its edge, shadowy shapes sunk deep in darkness; on the other was the looming arch of the cavern's mouth, and the night sky.

A cold wind blew past the skeletal towers that jutted from the outer edge of the roof. Syle told Yama that in times long past drugged pythonesses lashed to platforms on top of these towers had searched for intimations of the future in the patterns of clouds and the flight of birds, and led him to a narrow walkway that projected from a corner of the roof into the windy night. It creaked under their weight, and Yama held tight to its flimsy rail as Syle led him along it.

'Don't worry,' Syle said. 'This walkway has stood for longer than the department. It was built long before Confluence entered its present orbit.'

The cold wind buffeted Yama; the walkway hummed like a plucked wire. All he could see of it was that part of its mesh floor at his feet, illuminated by the intense light of the single firefly above his head.

He could lose his grip on the slender rail and fall like a stone through someone's roof. Slip, or perhaps be pushed.

Directly below, a long steep slope of scrub and bare rock fell away towards the spurs and spires and towers which had accreted around the ragged hem of the palace, covering it as corals will cover a wreck in the warm lower reaches of the Great River. Beyond, the lights of Ys were spread along the edge of the broad river; Yama could see, across leagues of water, the long edge of the world ruled against the empty darkness of the night sky. Downriver, where the world narrowed to its vanishing point, was a dim red glow, as if a fire had been kindled beneath the horizon of the world's edge.

In the windy dark, his mild face illuminated by his crown of fireflies, Syle said, 'In a few hours the Preservers will look upon us for the first time this year, and the rabble of the city will begin their celebrations. We will have a good view of their fireworks and bonfires from here. And later, perhaps, the fires of riots, and then the flashes of the weapons of the magistrates as they restore order.'

'Ys is a strange and terrible city.'

'It is a very large city, and order can only be maintained by suppressing any disorder at once, by whatever force is necessary. The Department of Indigenous Affairs has raised an army to fight the heretics and greatly expanded its bureaucracy; that is why they claim new territory. But the magistrates are a greater army, and constantly strive against a greater enemy. The people war amongst themselves with more hatred and more energy than is expended against the heretics. How far have we fallen from grace!'

Yama remembered Pandaras's story of how his uncle had been trapped when magistrates had laid siege to a block of the city which had refused to pay an increase in taxes. He said, 'In the city where I grew up, the people celebrate the setting of the Eye of the Preservers, not its rising. They sail across the river to the farside shore and hold a winter festival. They polish and repair the settings of the shrines, and renew the flags of the prayer strings. They light bonfires, and feast and dance, and lay flowers and other offerings at the shrines.'

'The ordinary people of Ys celebrate the rising of the Eye because they think that once more they are beneath the beneficent gaze of the Preservers, and all evil must flee away,' Syle said. 'And so they bang gongs, rattle their pots and pans, and light firecrackers to drive evil into the open. I am not familiar with your city, Yama, but I wonder why your people are glad to believe that they are free of the Preservers' scrutiny.'

'They dislike the summer's heat, and celebrate the beginning of winter,' Yama said. 'But I have always preferred summer to winter, and am glad to see the Eye return. Thank you for bringing me here to see it.'

Syle inclined his head. 'As I'm sure you've guessed, I also brought you here so that we could talk in private. You are a singular young man, Yama. Take your firefly, for instance. You should have allowed them to choose you, and not taken the brightest anyone has ever seen.'

'But it did choose me,' Yama said.

He had kept others from joining it because he feared that he would be blinded inside their ardent orbits.

'Some say that fireflies multiply in dark places hidden from our sight, but I think not,' Syle said. 'Every year there are fewer and fewer people in the palace proper – by which I mean the corridors and chambers and cells, and not the newer buildings built over the lower floors. Once, even the least of bloodlines were crowned with twenty or thirty fireflies, and the palace blazed with their light. Now many fireflies are so feeble that they have become fixed on members of the indigenous tribes which infest the roof, or on rats and other vermin. I doubt that there is another firefly as bright as the one you wear, except perhaps within the chambers of the Hierarchs. It will attract much attention, but it is fixed now, and will not leave you until you leave the palace.'

'I hope that it does not put me in danger.'

Yama supposed that he could order the firefly to leave, and then choose others more ordinary – but that might be worse than having selected it in the first place.

Syle did not answer at once. At last he said, 'You know that I find the cateran is very amusing, but I do not think that she will be able to marshal a successful defence of the department.'

Yama remembered what Rega had said. 'If you gave us more men—'

'How would you train them? Indigenous Affairs will send an army of its best troops to enforce the quit claim.'

'That is what Tamora thinks, too.'

'Then at least she has some sense. But she is no more than an ordinary cateran. I believe that you are capable of greater things.'

'You flatter me,' Yama said cautiously.

His wise but unworldly foster-father had not known what he was. The Aedile had sent the apothecary, Dr Dismas, to the Palace of the Memory of the People to discover what he could about Yama's bloodline, but Dr Dismas had lied to the old man and claimed to have found nothing, and tried to kidnap Yama for his own purposes. After Yama had escaped the apothecary, the curators of the City of the Dead had shown him that he was of the bloodline which had built the world according to the will of the Preservers; now he wondered if Syle, kin to his sweetheart and one of the curators, was part of their conspiracy, and he felt a quickening anticipation.

Syle said, 'I will try to speak plainly, but I am out of the habit. Luria has been pythoness for more than a century, and loyalty to the department has become inextricably entangled with loyalty to her person. And in a department as old as this, every word raises echoes from history. A casual remark can easily be mistaken for an allusion to some weakness or betrayal of the deep past. So we choose our words carefully, and do not always mean what we say, or say what we mean.'

'No one can overhear us here,' Yama said

'Except the Preservers. And we must always speak truthfully under their gaze.' Syle gripped the rail and stared into the night, towards the first light of the Eye of the Preservers. His feathery white hair fluttered in the wind. 'The truth, then. I know what you are, Yama. You are one of the Builders. Your bloodline was the first of all the bloodlines the Preservers raised up to populate Confluence, and the machines which maintain this world have not forgotten your kind. All machines obey you, even those that follow the orders of other men. Even those that will not obey anyone else.'

He laughed. 'There. I have said it. Rega thought I could not, but I have. And the world has not ended.'

Yama said, 'How did you discover what I am?'

'In a rare and ancient book I discovered in our library.'

Yama's heart turned over. Perhaps his quest was already over, before he had hardly begun. He said, 'I would very much like to see that book.'

'Alas, the library is closed to all but the pythonesses and the highest officers of the domestic staff,' Syle said. 'And I fear I am at present more in need of help than you. It is possible, is it not, that the Preservers act through you. If that's true, then whatever you do cannot be evil. You cannot help but do good, and should not deny the powers you possess. I know, for instance, that the Temple of the Black Well burned down on the day you entered the palace. It seemed that someone woke the thing in the well and then destroyed it. As far as I am concerned, a lesser miracle would suffice.'

Yama had encountered two feral machines since he had arrived in Ys. In a desperate moment, he had called down the first without knowing what he was doing. The second had fallen in the wars of the Age of Insurrection, and men had later built a temple over the hole it had melted into the keel of the world. The machine had lain brooding within a tomb of congealed lava for an age, until it had been woken by the same call that had brought down the first. With the help of the ancient guardians of the temple, Yama had reburied it. Machines like it had destroyed half the world in the Age of Insurrection, and although their time was long past, and their powers had faded as the lights of the fireflies had faded, they were still powerful. Some still shadowed the world from which they had been expelled, waiting for the return of the Preservers and the final battle when the just, living and dead, would be raised up, and the damned thrown aside.

After dismissing the fireflies which had eagerly flocked to him when he had first entered the palace, Yama had not attempted to influence a machine. He was scared that he might inadvertently wake more monsters from the past. He told Syle, 'I signed as a cateran, for a cateran's wages. That is the duty I will discharge to you, dominie, nothing more and nothing less. What you have learned from your library is your own affair. I would guess that you have not shared it with the pythonesses, or you would not have brought me here to talk in secret. Perhaps I should ask them about this book you claim to have found.'

Syle turned to look at Yama and said, 'Why involve them, when we can as easily help each other?'

'You said that you wanted to speak plainly,' Yama said. 'Perhaps you can answer this question. If I help you, will you tell me everything you have found about my bloodline?'

'I will show you the book.'

'What would you have me do?'

'That is not so simple.'

'Try your best.'

'It is said that the Preservers could travel from the future into the past as easily as voidships slip from star to star,' Syle said. 'But they could not travel into the future because from the point of view of the past the future does not yet exist. The road to the past is straight, because the world has travelled along it to reach the present. But as we travel along the road from the present into the future, every footstep creates a million new destinations, shaped by all the directions we could have taken. When looking into the future, a true pythoness must encompass all these possible states and choose the most likely, which is to say the one which is most common. It is not an easy task. Sometimes our pythonesses are unable to find the way. And then, instead of telling people which path into the future is the most likely, they tell people what they want to hear, or what they most need to hear, which is not always the same thing.'

'Is this what you do now?'

Syle nodded. 'Luria's ability is . . . uncertain. Many years ago, she would find fault in some detail of the ceremony when her predictions failed, or she would claim that something more powerful intervened to turn events from the course she had divined. At last, she gave up on her powers. Ever since, the department's energies and resources have been squandered on collecting intelligence about our clients, so that we can attempt to satisfy their enquiries. In short, we have lost our way. But Daphoene has the true sight. She can lead us back to the right path.'

'You are very candid.'

'If you will not help us, then what I tell you will do no harm, for the department will cease to exist. If you do help us, then you will need to know these things. Some say that we practise magic, but in truth ours is a rational science.'

Yama thought of the buzzing confusion in Daphoene's head, and wondered if she was able to scry a clear path through the sheaves of possible futures because many versions of her self inhabited a single mind, and her predictions were the sum of their consensus.

Syle said, 'Daphoene only ever tells the truth, and tells it accurately, without regard for the wants and needs of our clients. Luria believes that it will drive them away, and ruin the department – as if it is not already close to ruin. And she is frightened of Daphoene, too. Frightened that Daphoene sees her for what she is; frightened that Daphoene will one day predict a fate that she will be unable to escape. I brought Daphoene here, Yama. I am responsible for her. I hoped that she would be a true pythoness, and would restore the department to its former glory. And because she is so much more than I ever hoped she would be, Luria plans to destroy her. I would rather die than see that.'

It seemed to be a straightforward bargain: a miracle in exchange for revelation. But Yama thought of the plot that Pandaras had uncovered, and Tamora's harsh words – *These old departments are rats' nests of poisonous intrigues and feuds over trifles* – and wondered if Syle hoped to use his powers for his own ends.

He said, 'If Daphoene can see into the future, then what does she say about the department? Will it be saved?'

'Do not think I have not asked, but she has set her heart against revealing what she knows. She says that if she speaks, then the future may be changed, and the fate of the world with it. All she will say is that it will not be saved by force of arms. I understand that to mean that you must intervene in some other way.'

'Would she speak plainly of my fate? Could she look into the future and see where I might meet my people?'

'She has already said something. And that is why you must help us, Yama. If you do not, then yours will be a tragic fate.'

There, in the windy dark high above the oldest city in the world, Yama knew that Syle had baited a hook to set in his heart. But he had to ask.

'Tell me what she said, and then I may know whether I should help you.'

Syle turned to regard the panorama spread far below. The darkling plain of Ys, the wide ribbon of the Great River stretching towards the vanishing point, where the Eye of the Preservers had risen a finger-breadth above the edge of the world. He inclined his head, and said, 'There are two parts. The first is that you will either save the world or destroy it. Daphoene said that both possible futures are deeply entangled. Do not ask me what she meant – she would not explain it to me.'

Yama said, 'Perhaps the first is more likely than the second. The world will continue as before, but those who have more faith in me than I have in myself might say that I am responsible.'

'Then it's time you learned to trust yourself,' Syle said. 'The second part is this: if you do not help me, then you will be betrayed to those you have already escaped. Again, I know no more about it than that.'

Yama felt a chill of presentiment. The Aedile had sent him to Ys to work in the Department of Indigenous Affairs, the very department he was now contracted to fight against. Although he had escaped Prefect Corin, the man to whom the Aedile had entrusted him, he feared that the Prefect would find him again.

He said, 'That seems more like a threat than a prediction.'

'It's plain that serving as a mere cateran will not be enough to save you and the department,' Syle said. 'As a friend, I beg you to help us. And by helping us, you will help yourself. I cannot be responsible for what will happen to you if you do not.'

Yama would have asked him what he meant, but Syle suddenly pointed towards the city below. 'Look there! How brightly they burn!'

Near and far, rockets were shooting up above the streets and houses and squares of the endless city, red and green and gold lights streaking high into the night air and bursting in fiery flowers that drifted down in clouds of fading sparks even as more rockets rose through them. The noise of their explosions came moments later, like the popping of kernels of corn in a hot pan.

Yama thought again of Daphoene. Her mind full of sparks constantly flowering and fading.

Rising faintly on the cold wind came the small sound of trumpets and drums, of people singing and cheering. A flight of rockets terminated their brief arc in a shower of golden sparks a few chains beneath the walkway on which Yama and Syle stood. Bats took wing from crevices in the rock face below, a cloud of black flakes that blew out into the night and swept across the crimson swirl of the Eye of the Preservers.

3
THE DAY MARKET

The inner door of the Gate of Double Glory sank into its slot in the roadway, and the thrall waiting in front of it walked through the round portal into the darkness of the tunnel beyond. Yama stepped out of the doorway of the Basilica, crossed the plaza with Pandaras trotting at his heels, and asked the gatekeeper about the man who had just gone through.

'You mean Brabant?' the gatekeeper said. 'What would you want with him, dominie? He done something wrong?'

Yama hid a yawn behind his hand. It was a little after dawn and for most of the night he had lain sleeplessly on the narrow bunk in his little cell, thinking about everything Syle had told him. It was as if his mind had split in two factions, and their armies had gone to war inside his skull.

After he had inadvertently called down one feral machine and woken and defeated another, after he had murdered Gorgo in a fit of anger, he had sworn not to use his powers again until he fully understood them. And as yet he did not know if he could do what Syle wanted him to do. He did not know if he could successfully defend the Department of Vaticination by warping the minds of machines to serve his own ends. Besides, if his powers came from the Preservers, then it was obvious that he should not use them for his own gain.

But in exchange for defending the Department of Vaticination he might learn much more about his bloodline. And if he knew where he came from, he might better understand his powers and what the Preservers wanted of him.

With this thought came a tumble of images. Yama flying on the back of a metal dragon, driving hordes of defeated heretics into the Glass Desert beyond the midpoint of the world. Yama clad in a buzzing weave of bright motes, preaching to a multitude on some high place, with the whole long world spread beyond. Yama on a doffing ship, waking ancient machines in the depths of the Great River. Yama striking with a golden staff a rock in the icy wastes at the head of the Great River, and calling forth new waters to renew the world. And many more images, bright and compelling, as if his mind was trying to master all the futures in which he might walk. The visions possessed him, wonderful and terrifying. When he was woken by Pandaras it seemed that he had not rested at all.

And now, not half an hour later, he stood beneath the intricately carved portal of the Gate of Double Glory. The tunnel beyond it slanted downwards, curving as it descended. The thrall, Brabant, had already passed out of sight.

'Brabant never did anything bad I heard about,' the gatekeeper said. 'And I know all about what comes and goes.'

Yama said, 'Did he tell you what his business might be?'

The gatekeeper was an ancient thrall, with a humped back and a white mane. He looked at Yama slyly. 'It would be his usual business,' he said.

'And what's that?' Pandaras said. 'Speak civilly to my master, fellow. He has the safety of your department in his hands.'

The thrall said, 'Why, it's well known that Brabant has the keys of the kitchens of the household of the House of the Twelve Front Rooms. He's often out this early. The day markets open when the main gates open, and bidding is fierce these days. Things aren't what they were. There are shortages because of the war. Are you here to protect Brabant, dominie? Is that it? Is he in danger?'

'It is a matter of security,' Pandaras told the old thrall.

This seemed to satisfy the gatekeeper. 'Aye, I suppose we're in danger even now. They're not to start fighting the quit claim for more than a decad, but you can't trust Indigenous Affairs. It's a grower, see. Wants to get control wherever it can, however it can. But I do a good job. Don't worry about the gate. Nothing has ever passed me by without proper authority.'

For once, this was no idle boast. Tamora had surveyed the Department of Vaticination on the first day, and said that once the triple doors were lowered the gate could not be forced without destroying most of the cavern.

'We should hurry, master,' Pandaras said. 'We will lose him.'

'You will stay here, Pandaras. Stay here, and do your duty.'

'I'd do better going with you. I see you've taken off your bandage, but your wound hasn't quite healed. And I've a fancy to seeing more of this place.'

'As you will, when we are done here. I promise it.' Yama turned to the gatekeeper and said, 'How do you open the doors? There are three, I believe.'

The gatekeeper nodded. 'One here, dominie, another a hundred paces further down, and the last a hundred paces beyond that. They were designed to keep in the air, see. In the old days, there was a word you'd speak and the doors would obey. But they're just metal now. The vital parts died long ago. So now we do it by water. You saw me haul on that wheel?'

It stood on a strong post inside the glass booth that clung to the right-hand side of the gate's round mouth. It was as tall as the gatekeeper, and spoked like the wheel of a wagon.

'It controls the sluices,' the gatekeeper said. 'Water is what does the job. It flows out of the counterweights and the doors sink down with it, and then it's pumped into a reservoir above our heads, ready to fill the counterweights to close up the gate as need be.'

'You keep watch on the gate all day?'

'My little house is up above the gate – see the stair? It winds right up to it. I'm cosy as a swallow in a godown roof up there.'

'Then when Brabant comes back, you will make a note of it.'

'I will keep watch,' Pandaras said, 'although I'd rather come with you, master.'

'Your boy there needn't trouble himself,' the old thrall said. 'I see everything that goes in and out. Secretary Syle likes to know what's going on.'

The tunnel was lined with a slick white material that diffused the light of Yama's solitary firefly into a general glow. It was as if he moved at the centre of a flowing nimbus. The tunnel turned a full circle as it descended, then opened on to a shaft ten times as wide, one of the main throughways that ran from top to bottom of the palace. Like all the throughways, its gravity was localised: the tunnel met its roof at right angles, and Yama stood at the beginning of a corkscrew ramp, looking straight across the throughway at the tops of sleds and carts and wagons that, spangled with lanterns, streamed past as if clinging to a sheer wall. But as he went down the ramp, the throughway seemed to turn around him, until at last he was standing on a walkway beside the traffic and the mouth of the tunnel he had left was a hole in the curved roof above his head.

There were few pedestrians, and Yama had no trouble following Brabant. The thrall was a sturdy fellow with a thick black mane done up in braids. He walked at a slow but steady pace along the walkway into the lower part of the palace, where he took a ramp that spiralled up into the roof. It led to a short, narrow tunnel which suddenly opened on to a huge cavern filled with stalls and people.

It was one of the day markets. People from the hundred departments of the Palace of the Memory of the People were wrangling with merchants, gossiping, strolling about, or eating breakfast. The smoke of cooking braziers and hotplates mingled beneath a low ceiling of stained concrete, a blue haze which defined a pale wedge of early sunlight above the flat roofs of godowns that stood shoulder to shoulder at the cavern's wide mouth.

Machines twinkled through the smoky air, and fireflies spun above the heads of the people who crowded the aisles between the stalls. The noise was tremendous. The bawling of animals and the chatter of thousands of conversations echoed and re-echoed from the bare rock walls. In one part of the market, shoals of fish were displayed on banks of smoking ice, and bubbling tanks held mussels and oysters and slate-blue crayfish; in another, tethered goats grazed on straw, placidly awaiting the knife. There were stalls selling erasable paper, inks and pigments, sandals, spices, every kind of fruit and vegetable, cigarettes, edible plastic, confectionery, tea bark, and much more, and at every one spielers praised the quality and cheapness of their wares. Here and there, soldiers of the Department of Internal Harmony stood on discs floating in the air, watching the crowds that surged beneath their feet.

Most of the people who had come to the market were clerks, low-grade administrators or record keepers dressed in white shirts with high collars and baggy black trousers. Everywhere he looked, Yama saw a reflection of the fate that the Aedile and Prefect Corin had wished on him. Most people made way for him as he followed Brabant through the crowded aisles, and some even touched the inky tips of their fingers together; he realised that they were deferring not to him but to the spurious rank lent him by his bright firefly.

The brawling tumult reminded him of the emmet nest Telmon had once kept pressed between two panes of glass. He suddenly felt a suffocating sense of the vast size of the Palace of the Memory of the People, its mazes of corridors, the stacks of offices and chambers and apartments of its hundred departments, its thousands of temples and chapels and shrines, all silted with a hundred thousand years of history.

Mendicants were preaching here and there, but few in the crowds stopped to listen. A line of nearly naked men danced down an aisle, lashing their shoulders with leather thongs; at an intersection, a group of men in red robes whirled on the spot to the frenzied beat of a tambour. The hems of their robes were weighted, and spun out in smooth bells as they whirled around and around; their faces glistened with sweat and their eyes had rolled back so that only the whites showed. They would dance until they dropped, believing themselves to be possessed by avatars of the Preservers.

Amongst the stalls were shrines and altars where men paused to dab a spot of ochre powder on their foreheads and mumble a prayer or turn the crank of a prayer wheel. Brabant stopped at one of the shrines, a glossy black circle framed by an arbour of paper flowers, and lit a candle and wafted its scented smoke towards his bowed face. Praying for the success of his traitorous errand, perhaps – or simply pausing for a moment's devotion amidst his ordinary duties.

After Brabant had moved on, Yama stopped at the shrine and touched the disc hung from the thong around his neck, but the shrine did not light. The Palace of the Memory of the People was littered with shrines. He had found more than a hundred in the various buildings of the Department of Vaticination, but had not yet found one that would show him the garden where the woman in white waited for him. Perhaps it was just as well. He was not yet ready to confront his enemy again.

He pushed on until once more he glimpsed Brabant's braided mane amongst the press of clerks and record keepers. The thrall seemed to know every other person in the market, and stopped at stalls to shake hands and exchange a few words with the merchants, or taste a sample of food. He sat a while with a spice seller amongst aromatic sacks, chatting amiably while sipping tea from a copper bowl. Yama, watching from the other side of the wide crowded aisle, ate sugary fried almonds from a paper bag translucent with grease, and wondered if the plot might concern assassination by poison, or if Brabant was simply negotiating a good price for turmeric and mace.

Brabant shook the spice seller's hand and got up and moved on through the market, saluting merchants, tasting samples and exclaiming fulsomely over their freshness, shouting greetings to passers-by. If he was on a clandestine errand, he seemed to want everyone to know where he was.

At last, Brabant reached the far end of the huge market and entered a corridor with three- or four-storey houses on either side, like an ordinary street under a concrete sky. There was more light here, pouring through a big curved window let into the ceiling at the far end where palm trees rose from clumps of sawgrass. A flock of parrots chased from tree to tree, calling raucously.

A woman sat at a second-floor window of one of the houses, sleepily combing her long black hair. Immediately below, a man in a linen burnous sat on a high stool outside the door. Brabant stopped to talk with the man, then shook his hand and went inside.

Yama walked past, suddenly feeling foolish and out of place. It seemed clear that Brabant had done no more than go about his business in the market before visiting a bawdy house for relaxation. Perhaps the thralls were of one of those bloodlines which could mate at will, rather than on a particular day in a cycle or a season. Yet Yama was reluctant to leave. He felt that he should see this through to the end.

He drifted towards the edge of a crowd which had gathered under the palm trees at the end of the street, where a gambler restlessly switched three half-shells around each other on a little table. Men in white shirts threw coins onto the table, pointing at one or another of the shells, and when the betting was finished the gambler lifted the shells one by one, revealing a black pearl under the middle one. He scooped up the coins, pressed a few into the outstretched hands of two of the spectators and pocketed the rest, then covered the black pearl and began to switch the shells back and forth again.

While the spectators made more bets, the gambler caught Yama's eye and said, 'I can't allow you a wager, dominie. A man like you could ruin me in a single game.'

Yama smiled, and said that in any case he did not gamble.

'Then you may try your luck for the fun of it,' the gambler said. He had an engaging smile, and eyes as blue as cornflowers in a pale face. A single firefly crouched in his crest of red hair, as faint as the one which had followed the rat in the old entrance hall of the House of the Twelve Front Rooms.

The gambler took his hands away from the shells. Yama, gripped by a sudden impulse, pointed to the middle one. The gambler raised an eyebrow and lifted the shell to reveal the black pearl. The clerks around Yama groaned. The gambler took in their money, winked at Yama, and started shuffling the shells again. Yama watched closely this time, and it seemed that the shell hiding the pearl was again in the centre – yet at the same time he knew it was under the shell on the right. The clerks finished laying their bets, and again Yama pointed, this time meeting the gambler's smile with his own when the pearl was revealed.

The clerks murmured amongst themselves and the gambler said, 'You see through my little illusion, dominie. Maybe you'd like to try your skill on something a little harder.'

'Perhaps another time.'

The gambler looked around at the spectators, as if calling upon them to witness his bravado. He said, 'I'd only ask you to risk a single copper rial on your skill. To a man like you that's nothing, and you'd stand to win much more from me. I'll give you odds of ten to one.'

Yama remembered the fierce leathery nomads who in summer came into Aeolis with their horses and hunting cats and tents of stitched hides to sell the pelts of fitchets, marmots and hares they had trapped in the foothills of the Rim Mountains. The nomads' dice games went on for days, drawing those who joined them deeper and deeper, until, from beginning with small wagers, they emerged as from a dream, dazed and penniless, sometimes without even their shoes and shirts.

'Your odds are too much in my favour,' he told the gambler, and some of the clerks laughed.

'They are in it together,' someone said. He was a tall boy not much older than Yama, flanked by two others as he pushed to the front of the crowd. All three wore enamelled badges of a fist closed around a lightning bolt pinned to the high collars of their white shirts.

'I assure you,' the gambler told the boy, 'that I have never seen this good fellow before.'

'Cheats and swindlers,' the tall boy said. 'You rig the game and let your friend win to make others think that they have a chance.'

The gambler started to protest again, but his mild manner enraged the boy, who leaned on the little table and swore at him. One of the other boys swept the shells onto the floor and his leader shouted that there was no pearl and it was no game at all, but a sharpy's trick.

Yama hardly heard him. He had just seen a man come out of the bawdy house. He wore a tunic of plain homespun girdled with a red cord, and his face was covered in a glossy black pelt, with a white stripe down the left side. He carried a staff taller than himself, and Yama knew that it was shod with iron. For he recognised the man at once, and with a shock knew that Brabant must be involved in a conspiracy after all.

The man was Prefect Corin.

4

THE AMBUSH

'A sharpy's trick,' the leader of the boys shouted again. 'We will have justice! Grab them both, lads – the one with the knife first.'

One boy seized Yama's arms. The other wrenched the sheathed knife from its harness and handed it to the leader, who thrust it into Yama's face and said, 'By what authority do you carry a weapon here?'

'By my own,' Yama said. 'What business is it of yours?'

The crowd murmured at this. The tall boy scowled. He and his two friends were excited and nervous, and uncertain about how to proceed. They were not guards or soldiers, who would have taken Yama away for interrogation, but apprentices of some kind, eager and awkward, daring each other on.

'It is departmental business,' the leader of the three said. 'Why are you carrying this antique? Is it licensed?'

The gambler said, 'I beg your pardon, masters, but this is common ground, as is well known. Your department doesn't police it.'

'Keep out of it, animal,' the boy who held Yama's knife said. He looked around at the press of clerks and added, 'You all keep out of it.'

The boy holding Yama's arms said, 'Answer Philo, you piece of shit.'

'It is mine,' Yama said. He hoped that their leader, Philo, would try to draw the knife, for surely the knife would waken and defend him.

But Philo merely dangled the sheathed knife by its clip. He had a small face framed by a bob of glossy black hair, a flat, bridgeless nose, and a wide mouth. He thrust his face so close to Yama that he laid a little spray of spittle of Yama's cheek when he spoke. His breath was scented with cloves.

'This? This is at least ten thousand years old. What is a kid like you doing with it? Explain yourself. If your business is innocent we will let you go.'

'I will fetch the guards,' one of the clerks said.

'We do not need guards,' Philo said loudly, turning this way and that as he tried to identify the man who had spoken. 'We are stronger. We will deal with these cheats in our own way.'

'You are fools,' the clerk said. He turned his back on Philo with contempt, and the crowd parted to let him through.

The crowd had grown. Yama could no longer see Prefect Corin. From the centre of a great calm, he told Philo, 'You have no authority over me. May you kill me with my own knife if it is not true.'

'I will cut out your insolent tongue,' Philo said.

All three boys laughed. Philo's smile widened and he gripped the hilt of the knife. There was a blue flash. Philo screamed and dropped the knife and clutched his hand. Blackened skin hung in strips from it and there was a strong, disgusting smell of burnt meat. Yama felt a slight relaxation in the grip of the boy who held him, stamped on his instep, wrenched free, and kicked his legs from under him. The third boy drew a slug pistol and pointed it at Yama. The clerks behind him moved to either side. All this time, Philo was screaming that he had been killed.

'Give it up,' the boy with the pistol said.

'I will walk away,' Yama said, 'and that will be an end to this.'

People at the front of the crowd, scared by the boy's pistol and Yama's knife, were struggling with others pressing forward to get a better view of the little drama. Yama glimpsed Prefect Corin at the far edge of the melee, striking out with his staff as he tried to clear a path. A decad of armed men was at his back.

'Give it up,' the boy with the pistol said again. He was braver than Yama had expected. 'Give it up or I will put a big hole through you.'

Yama squeezed his eyes shut. The explosive brightness as his firefly gave up all its light in one instant printed his vision with red and gold. All around him, men screamed in fright. The slug pistol went off – the boy must have pulled the trigger by reflex – and something whooped past Yama's left ear. Another scream: one of the bystanders had been hit. When Yama opened his eyes, ghostly volumes of light seemed to hang in the air. Philo and his friends and many of the clerks in the crowd were blinking away tears or rubbing at their eyes; Philo was shrieking that he had been blinded by sorcery.

A hand fell on Yama's shoulder. 'Come with me, dominie,' the gambler said, and dashed something to the floor.

At once, dense red smoke billowed up around the blinded men. It obscured Prefect Corin and his men, who were still trying to fight through the panicky crowd. Overhead, soldiers on floating discs swooped into the street.

'With me!' the gambler said. 'We are your friends!'

But Yama shook off his grip, scooped up the knife and its sheath, and ran in the other direction, towards the sunlit stand of palm trees. Prefect Corin broke out of the bank of red smoke as some of his men started to shoot at the soldiers in the air. The soldiers spun around and shot back. Yama ran beneath a rain of fronds cut down by small-arms fire. Sawgrass caught at his trousers; parrots fled in a whir of wings.

Beyond the trees was a slender metal bridge which arched across a narrow deep cleft. Something beat down there, slow and steady and vast; Yama could feel its pulse through the soles of his boots as he went over the bridge.

Then through a glass-walled tunnel that ran along the side of a sheer rock face, with the slopes of the palace to the mosaic of the city, and mountains in the misty distance. The curved wall suddenly crazed into a thousand splinters; a moment later Yama heard the sharp echo of a pistol shot, and Prefect Corin shouted his name.

Yama turned.

The Prefect and three of his men stood fifty paces away. 'Well met, Yamamanama,' Prefect Corin said.

He looked quite unruffled, standing straight with his staff grounded beside him. He was not even out of breath. One of the men had a bandaged hand – he was the ruffian that Yama had wounded outside the gate of the Department of Vaticination.

Yama held the knife by the side of his leg. He said, as calmly as he could, 'You escaped the magistrates, then.'

Prefect Corin said amicably, 'As did you. You talked to their machines, did you not? Your father should have told me about that trick, but no matter. Here you are anyway.'

'I will not come back,' Yama said, and raised his knife when Prefect Corin stepped forward.

Two of his men aimed pistols at Yama; the third, the one with the bandaged hand, cocked an arbalest.

'We have no wish to harm you,' Prefect Corin said. 'You must be very tired and confused after your adventures, but you have come home now. You have found us, as the Preservers wished. We have a lot to talk about, you and I. There have been sightings of feral machines in the city, and the Temple of the Black Well was destroyed by the Thing Below. Did you speak to them, too?'

Yama said, 'You lured me here, but I will not come with you. I will not serve.'

'Oh, but you will. Although the day market is not yet under the department's authority, this place is ours, for it leads directly to one of our gates. You ran where I wanted you to run, Yama. The soldiers of Internal Harmony cannot help you here. Come with me, and if you can do half the things I believe you are capable of doing you will be treated like a tetrarch. Come with me now. Come home. Your father and your sweetheart will be pleased that you have turned up safe and sound.'

For an instant, Yama was aware of every machine around him, all the way out to the edge of the day market. He spoke to one and turned and struck at the splintered glass with the knife. Blue light flared. Prefect Corin shouted and threw aside his staff and ran at Yama, and Yama hurled himself bodily at the circle of splintered glass and plunged through it into empty air.

5
THE LIBRARY

The city and the side of the palace described a perfect somersault around Yama. Then something flashed towards him out of the blue sky and slammed into him, knocking his breath away. It was the floating disc he had stolen from under the feet of one of the soldiers.

He threw himself across it and clung tightly as it swooped towards a tumble of roofs far below, halting above a narrow strip field where the green globes of pumpkins lay amongst tangles of vines and large leaves. He dropped to the ground, clutching the knife and its sheath, and looked all around. The blue sky was empty; there was no sign of any pursuit. His head ached. When he touched it his fingers came away smudged with sticky blood.

The disc hung in the air like an obedient pet awaiting a command. Yama dismissed it, and it rose above the long wall of black stone that backed the strip field and shot away at a steep angle against the sheer slopes, catching the light of the sun for a moment, flashing like a fugitive star. Then it was gone.

Yama picked up his knife and sheathed it. He judged that he had fallen at least five furlongs; the glass tunnel from which he had thrown himself was no more than a gleaming thread, fine as a hair, laid between two black crags about halfway up the steep side of the palace.

Somewhere up there was the Department of Vaticination's cavern. Tamora would be hard at work, drilling the sullen thralls for their brief, futile battle. He could abandon her and Pandaras, Yama thought, and set out to find the library of the Department of Apothecaries and Chirurgeons, but he knew that he would not. At the very least he must tell them about Prefect Corin, and the attempted kidnapping. Yama suspected that Brabant and the woman who had sent him to the Day Market were the Prefect's agents, and the conversation that Pandaras had overheard had been a lure to draw him into a trap. He'd fallen for the trick like one of the gambler's gullible marks, and had escaped more by luck than by skill. Now he had to find a way back into the palace, and a safe route through the passages and stairways to the Department of Vaticination. He wanted to denounce Brabant and unmask the woman who had helped him, and discover if they had been plotting against the department as well as against him. Prefect Corin would be watching the Gate of Double Glory, but tomorrow was the day of the public inquisition, when the department would be open to all who wanted to petition the pythonesses...

He walked to the edge of the narrow pumpkin field. Beyond the parapet at its edge was a short drop to a slope of red tiles; beyond that were the flat roofs of a huddle of buildings, and the flank of the palace falling away to the hatched plain of the great city. As Yama contemplated this vista something cracked like a whip past his ear, shattered half a dozen tiles, and went whooping away into the distance. He remembered the pistols carried by Prefect Corin's ruffians and vaulted the parapet and ran down the tiled slope. Another slug split the air and he changed direction and tripped and suddenly was rolling amongst a small avalanche of loosened tiles. He grabbed at the edge of the roof and for a moment hung there, breathing hard – and then the tiles gave way.

He landed on his back on a cushion of thick moss. Amazingly, he had not let go of his knife. Small animals fled, screaming. Monkeys, with silver-grey coats and long tails that ended in tufts of black hair. They jumped onto a shelf of black rock at the far end of the shadowy courtyard, their wrinkled faces both anxious and mournful. Dwarf cedar trees, their roots clutching wet black rocks, made islands in a sweep of raked gravel littered with the hulls of pistachio nuts. On three sides of the courtyard were black wooden walls painted with stylised eyes in interlocked swirls of red and white; on the fourth was a clerestory.

When Yama got to his feet, the largest of the monkeys ran forward and swarmed up a rope and swung from side to side, chattering at him. A gong started a brazen clamour somewhere beyond the clerestory's arches.

Yama ran. A broad stair led down from the clerestory to a huge dimly lit hall. The barrel-vaulted ceiling was painted black, with a triple-armed swirl of white that represented the galaxy at one end and a recurved red swirl that represented the Eye of the Preservers at the other: it was the temple of one of the latriatic cults which believed that the grace of the Preservers could be restored to the world by contemplation, prayer and invocation.

The gong was louder here, battering the cool air with an urgent brassy clamour. Suddenly, shaven-headed monks in orange robes rushed into the far end of the hall. They were armed with a motley collection of spears and cutlasses; one carried a hoe. Yama drew his knife. But even as the monks started to advance towards him, light flared in the centre of the hall and they fell to their knees and dropped their weapons.

At first, Yama thought that part of the roof had been opened to admit the light of the sun. Then, shading his eyes against the glare with his forearm, he saw that a shrine stood in the middle of the hall: an upright disc twice his height, filled with restless white light.

Yama drew the disc from his shirt and, raising it as high as the thong looped around his neck would allow, advanced towards the shrine. He wondered if the woman in white had found him again, drawn by the disc, but as the blazing light beat around him he was seized by a deep dread. Something huge and fierce and implacable was advancing through the light and the folded space within the shrine, stooping towards him as a lammergeyer stoops through leagues of air to snatch an oryx grazing on a mountain crag.

Yama's nerve failed. He dropped the disc into his shirt and ran past the shrine, dodging between the monks on the far side. They were grovelling with their foreheads pressed to the floor, their buttocks higher than their heads. Not one moved to stop him.

He ran out into open air, along a stone terrace and down a long flight of steps dished by the tread of countless feet. Monks in orange robes turned to watch as he ran past them, down narrow stone paths between plots of pumpkins, yams and manioc.

The brass gong suddenly fell silent, and there was only the buzz of insects and the distant roar of the city. Yama did not stop. Once again he had unintentionally brought something into the world. He ran from it headlong, with nothing in his head but his hammering pulse.

This part of the palace had been built over with temples and monasteries and sanctuaries. Many stood on the ruins of older structures. Staircases descended sheer rock faces carved with grottoes and shrines. Viaducts and bridges and walkways were strung across gorges and looped between crags. One pinnacle had been hollowed out; a hundred small square windows pierced its sides. Slopes were intricately terraced into long narrow fields irrigated by stone cisterns that collected rainwater from fan-shaped slopes of white stone.

Yama spent the rest of the day descending slopes and terraces and stairs. It seemed that there was always a flight of ravens turning in the air above him. He hoped this was not a bad omen, for ravens, particularly those of the Palace of the Memory of the People, were said by some to be spies. Far below, the city, immemorial Ys, stretched away into blue distances under a rippling layer of smoggy air.

Around noon, as the sun paused at the height of its leap into the sky before falling back towards the Rim Mountains, he arrived at a long terrace thatched in emerald-green grass. An ornate fountain of salt-white stone splashed and bubbled in the middle. Yama drank from one of the fountain's clam-shell basins until his belly was full, and washed dust and dried blood from his face, but he did not dare stop for long. Prefect Corin might be tracking his descent; the thing that lived in the light of the shrine might be following him. So far he had failed to find any gate or portal, but he hoped that one of the wide roads winding across the lower slopes would lead to the palace's interior – there must be some route for the fresh produce that supplied the day markets.

He was descending a narrow stair, with a vertical rock face on one side and nothing but a slender steel rail protecting him from a sheer drop on the other, when it suddenly turned and went under an arch. Something stopped him with implacable force, as if the air around him had congealed, and asked him his business. But it yielded at once to his will, and he went on down the steps with invisible shawms braying and a stentorian voice gravely announcing the arrival of a Hierarch.

As Yama entered the courtyard at the bottom, a squad of guards in full armour pushed him aside and clattered up the stairs, pistols and falchions drawn. The courtyard was wide and shaded by high stone walls. In the middle of it, a soldier with an officer's sash over his corselet stood on a table. He was shouting at the people milling around two gates in the high wall at the far end.

'It was a false alarm! Only a false alarm! Resume your places!'

Slowly, order was restored. The crowd separated into lines before tables where clerks sat in the shade of large paper parasols, questioning each petitioner closely, studying papers presented to them, stamping papers, writing in logbooks. Beyond the tables was a narrow gate guarded by soldiers who carefully scrutinised the papers of all who wanted to pass.

Yama bought a small loaf of waybread and a cup of water from one of the stalls on the far side of the courtyard, and asked the stallkeeper where the gate led.

'To the department, of course.'

'Which department?'

'The Department of Apothecaries and Chirurgeons, where else?'

The woman's eyes widened when Yama laughed. He apologised, and said that he had been searching for the department for a long time, and seemed to have come upon it by accident.

The stall's other customer, an old man sipping a glass of tea, said, 'You are more fortunate than the fool who tried to force entry through the Gate of the Hierarchs. Some poor wretch tries it at least once a year. After the guardian has finished with him, the guards display his body before the main gate as a lesson.'

The old man, Eliphas, was a runner who made his livelihood by researching cases which physicians could not cure by normal means. He explained that most of the people queuing in the courtyard were runners for physicians or leeches; he assumed that Yama was from a family which could not afford to employ an intermediary.

'How long does it take to get an answer to your questions?'

'Usually a day to get through the preliminary certification,' Eliphas said, 'and then a day or two more for the librarians to process your question and search the stacks. Although if you don't phrase it just right it will take much longer than that. There's an art to asking the right question, in the right way.'

'My question is quite simple. I want to know if the Department of Apothecaries and Chirurgeons knows anything about my bloodline.'

Eliphas studied Yama with a shrewd, kindly gaze. He was stoop-shouldered and yet still tall, as tall as the Aedile or Telmon, with smooth black skin and silver eyes. Coarse white hair, wound into corkscrew ringlets, framed his broad-browed face; three fireflies nested there.

'Yours is certainly an unusual physiognomy,' he said. 'But I've never heard of anyone who does not know his own bloodline.'

'If it can be found anywhere, it can be found in Ys,' Yama said. 'That is why I came here. When I was a baby, I was found on the river and taken in by a kind man. But now I want to find my real family. I believe that there are records here that will help me, but I am not certain that

I know how to find them. If you will help me ask the right questions I will be glad to pay you.'

Eliphas scratched amongst his white ringlets with long fingers. 'If you pay for my meals and lodging while we wait for the question to be processed, why then, brother, I'll do my best to put you on the right road.'

'I can pay a fair price,' Yama said, stung by the thought that Eliphas was offering charity.

'It's fair enough, brother. The only way to learn about the way information is catalogued and cross-referenced is to test the system with questions. I have been working here all my life, but I reckon I'll learn a lot by seeing how the library responds to your requests. You should be prepared to go around two or three times, though. Unusual questions usually don't find an answer right away. You must refine your search by learning from your mistakes.'

Yama thought of the library in the peel-house where he had grown up, the packed shelves of books and papers that Zakiel had spent a lifetime arranging, indexing and cataloguing. He said, 'It seems to me that the librarians force you to work in the dark.'

'It was simpler in the days before the heretics,' Eliphas said. 'All records were stored within the purlieu of the avatars. What we now call librarians were then called hierodules, which means *holy slaves*, and the real librarians were sub-routines of the avatars. They spoke through the hierodules, and their answers came promptly. But we live in an imperfect age. The shrines are silent, and most records are second- or third-hand transcriptions, and not always stored as they should be. Besides, if everyone knew where everything was to be found, the librarians would make no money and could not afford to maintain the records in their care. And if facts were free I wouldn't make any money either. But that's the way it is with most professions, brother. If their secrets weren't secret, there'd be no need for most of the people in them. I'd say nine-tenths of the business of any department is to do with guarding the secrets of its skills and knowledge, and only one-tenth in making use of them. I've asked thousands of questions in my time, and reckon I know as much about medicine as most leeches, but I could never practise as I'm not inducted into their mysteries. If I'd been born to one of the medical families it might be different, but only the Preservers can choose how to be born into the world.'

Yama learned that Eliphas's family had been in the trade of question-running for three generations. Eliphas was the last of the line. His only son had joined the army and was fighting the heretics at the midpoint of the world, while his daughters' children would be raised in the trades of their fathers.

'That's the difference between trades and professions,' Eliphas said. 'Trades marry out; professions marry amongst their own kind. It's how they keep their power.'

They had joined a line at one of the tables, shuffling forward step by step at long intervals. When it was at last their turn to speak with the clerk, the sunlight had climbed the wall and the courtyard was drowned in shadow. Lights like drifts of sparks had woken across the darkening slopes above; the fireflies hanging above the heads of clerks and petitioners cast shifting tangles of light and shadow.

Eliphas leaned over the table, the orbits of his fireflies nearly merging with those of the clerk, and fanned a sheaf of pastel-coloured papers, pointing at one and then another with his long forefinger. The two men exchanged a merry banter, and the clerk stamped Eliphas's papers without reading them.

'This is a friend of mine,' Eliphas said, standing aside for Yama. 'You do well by him, Tzu.'

'Picking up strays again, Eliphas?' Tzu looked Yama up and down and said, 'Let's have your papers, boy. You'll be the last I process this day.'

'I have no papers,' Yama said. 'I have only my question.'

Tzu had a long, gloomy face. His brown skin was softly creased, like waterlogged leather. Now more creases appeared above his wide-spaced black eyes. He said, 'Unless you can present the proper papers in the proper order you will have to walk back down to the Hall of Admissions, and start over tomorrow.'

'I did not come here by the usual route,' Yama said. 'I have my question, and money to pay the fee.'

Tzu sighed, and shook a little bell. 'What have you brought me, Eliphas? And at the end of the day, too. We have procedures here,' he told Yama, 'and no time for troublemakers.'

Another clerk appeared, a slight old man with a bent back. He conferred with Tzu, and then stared at Yama through spectacles perched on the end of his long nose. He had a wispy white beard and a bald pate mottled with tubercles.

'Stand straight, boy,' Tzu said. 'This is Kun Norbu, the chief of all the clerks.'

'How did you get here, boy?' Kun Norbu said.

'Down that stair,' Yama said, and pointed across the courtyard.

'Don't lie,' Tzu said. 'No one has used the Gate of the Hierarchs for a century. Now and then thieves and vagabonds try, as one tried today, but all are frightened away or destroyed by the guardian.'

'It has not been used for far longer than a century,' Kun Norbu said. 'The last Hierarch to visit us was Gallizur the Joyous, just before Ys was invested by the armies of the Insurrectionists. That would be, hmm, eleven thousand, five hundred and sixty years ago.'

'I will vouch for this boy,' Eliphas said. 'He is given to flights of fancy, but he is no thief, and his question is most interesting.'

Kun Norbu said, 'When did you first meet him, Eliphas? Not before today, I'd wager. And he doesn't have so much as a single firefly. For all you know, he's some indigenous wildman.'

Yama had supposed that his firefly had followed him, but he now realised that he must have destroyed it by asking it to give up all its light at once. He stared at the chief of clerks and said, 'If fireflies are your only concern, my lack of them is easily fixed.'

'Don't be impudent,' Kun Norbu said. 'Fireflies choose a host according to their station. Clearly you have no station to speak of.' He clapped his hands. 'Guards! To me, if you please!'

Tzu gasped and stood up, knocking over his stool; Eliphas stepped back, covering his face with his hands. All around, people turned to stare at Yama. A few knelt, heads bowed. The two guards who had started across the courtyard stopped and raised their partisans as if to strike at an invisible foe. Light gleamed along the crescent edges of their double-bladed weapons; a hundred sparks were caught in the lenses of Kun Norbu's spectacles.

In an extravagant impulse born of exhaustion and impatience, Yama had clothed himself in the light of a thousand fireflies, borrowed from everyone close by or called from the wild population beyond the walls. He felt that he was close to the end of his quest, and would not be stopped by the petty restrictions of a moribund bureaucracy.

'My question is quite simple,' he told Kun Norbu. 'I want to find my people. Will you help me?'

6

THE HELL-HOUND

Despite the trick with the fireflies, the chief of clerks, Kun Norbu, insisted that Yama prove that he had persuaded the guardian of the Gate of the Hierarchs to let him pass. Yama, still clothed in a thousand fireflies, walked up and down the steps beneath the arch three times, in front of a growing audience of clerks and soldiers and petitioners. It seemed to him that they would have watched him do it all night, and after the third time he told Kun Norbu that he had not come to the library to perform like a mountebank, and returned the fireflies to their former hosts, retaining only a pentad of those he had recruited from the wild population. This trick astonished the clerks more than that of being able to pass the guardian.

Kun Norbu took Yama and Eliphas to his cluttered office, where they sat on dusty couches and drank tea sweetened with honey. 'Tell me your story, young man,' the chief of clerks said. 'Tell me who you are, and where you come from, and what you hope to find.'

Yama explained that as a baby he had been found in a boat on the Great River, and that he had been told that his bloodline was that of the Builders, long thought to have transcended the world. He said that he had come to Ys to search for others like himself, and added that he suspected that a certain Dr Dismas had recently found important clues in this very library. Kun Norbu listened patiently, and then asked Yama a hundred questions, most of which he could not begin to attempt to answer.

'Allow me to take a scraping of cells from your mouth,' Kun Norbu said at last. 'It will not prove that you are a Builder, but it will help me to eliminate other possibilities.'

Eliphas said, 'Then you will take his case, brother. I am glad.'

Kun Norbu smiled and said, 'I think we might learn as much from the answers as your friend.'

Yama said, 'I want to learn all I can.'

Kun Norbu's black eyes twinkled behind the lenses of his spectacles. 'I will do my best to help you, but even this library has its limits. The further you reach back into history, the scarcer records become. And we must reach back very far indeed.'

Eliphas closed his eyes and recited a fragment of text in a lilting chant. ' "They were the first men, part of the word which the Preservers spoke to call forth the world. They were given the keys of the world, and ordered it according to the wishes of their masters." '

Yama said, 'Is that from the Puranas?'

Eliphas smiled. 'It sounds like the Puranas, doesn't it?'

Kun Norbu said, 'It is from a text much older than the Puranas. So old that it might have been written by one of the Builders. Eliphas and I were enthusiastic hunters of obscure texts when we were only a little older than you, Yama. I gave up my quests for lost knowledge many years ago, when I became a novice clerk, but now, do you know, I am reminded of the carefree adventures of my youth. You have rekindled my sense of wonder, which I had thought long ago extinguished by the responsibilities of my office. Now, let us make a beginning by dealing with the paperwork.'

He issued Yama with passes for the library, the refectory and one of the dormitories of the Strangers' Lodge, and wrote his name, age, birthplace (Yama had given it as Aeolis) and questions on a pentad of differently coloured pieces of paper, and stamped each of them with his mark. Yama's patience was exhausted at the end of this long process, and said that it seemed to him that all these rules and bits of paper must hinder free enquiry.

'You could wander the stacks for a dozen years, and never find what you seek,' Kun Norbu said. 'Yet I may be able to lay my hand on the place where the answers to your questions lie in only a few hours. Not only because I have spent much of my life studying the way in which the books and documents are catalogued and shelved, but because of the labour of my predecessors, who organised the catalogues and filed everything in its proper place. The organisation and regulation of knowledge is just as important as knowledge itself. A book may contain the ultimate secret of the world, but if it cannot be found it may as well not exist. So while these forms and rules may seem tedious, they help to preserve the structure and order of the library by tracing and recording the movement of everything in it.'

'It is good to see the light of adventure in your eyes once more, brother!' Eliphas told Kun Norbu. 'I had thought that it might have been lost.'

'Oh, I still supervise the occasional enquiry,' the chief of clerks said, 'if only to keep the apprentices on their toes.' He made a steeple of his fingers, which were each tipped with a black claw like a rose thorn, and looked over them at Yama. 'Have you ever been ill?'

'Just blackwater fever and ague. I lived beside the river.'

'I ask because I do not know if Builders are susceptible to illness. Be glad of your childhood fevers! If any of your people live, then some of them will almost certainly have been treated by chirurgeons or by apothecaries, and the records of all chirurgeons and apothecaries are preserved here. That is how I will begin my search, using the template that lies within your cells as a guide.'

He summoned a clerk, who asked Yama to suck on the end of a small stick, which he then placed inside a glass tube. This also required documentation, and Yama's signature, and Kun Norbu's stamp. When it was done, the chief of clerks bowed to Yama and said, 'You need not lodge in the commons. You will be my guest. My household is yours. I will have someone find you fresh clothes and see that your wound is cleaned.'

'That is kind,' Yama said, 'but I do not deserve special treatment. And the wound is an old one. It does not trouble me.'

He feared that Prefect Corin might hear that the library had an uncommon visitor, one who could command fireflies and ancient guardians.

Kun Norbu gave Yama a shrewd look and said, 'You cannot pretend that you are ordinary, Yama. And your wound has been bleeding recently. At least allow me to have someone look at it. After that, Eliphas can show you to your quarters.'

The Strangers' Lodge of the Department of Apothecaries and Chirurgeons was built around a square courtyard. Tiers of balconies rose above the courtyard on three sides; on the fourth was a sloping wall of metal as transparent as glass, on which the last light of the sun glowed like the shower of gold by which, it was said, the Preservers had manifested themselves for the first and last time on the world, when they had seeded it with the ten thousand bloodlines.

Yama bought Eliphas supper in the refectory on the ground floor, and they ate at one of the long tables with a decad of other petitioners. All were crowned by the restless sparks of fireflies; there was no other light in the long room. Yama's wad of papers was at his elbow, an untidy rainbow fanned on the table's scarred and polished surface. His head wound had been washed with an astringent lotion and freshly bandaged.

After they had eaten, Eliphas filled the bowl of a clay pipe with aromatic tobacco, lit it, and puffed on it contentedly. Yama asked him where he had found the passage that he had quoted.

'It was on a scrap of paper someone had torn from a book an age ago and used to jot down the calculation for a bill of small goods, tucked between the pages of an old record book. Old paper is well made, and forgets very little. That scrap had preserved the verse about your people on one side and the trifling calculation on the other, and had also patiently kept the place in the record book someone dead a thousand years had marked. Often, things forgotten or lost have simply been mislaid. There's no end of places where they might be found. The bindings of books, for instance, where pieces of older documents are often used as backing.'

'I am beginning to believe that I am mislaid,' Yama said. 'That I do not belong in this age. Many times, when I was younger, I hoped that someone was looking for me.'

'You must have courage, brother. I am curious about one thing, though. May I ask a question?'

'Of course.'

'Why, there's no "of course" about it. I simply do my duty, as the Preservers would wish. I do not expect you to satisfy my idle curiosity as reward. But thank you. My question is this. If you do learn where your family lives, what will you do?'

'I would ask them why I was set adrift on the river, to begin with. And if they answered that, I would ask them . . . other questions.'

Eliphas blew a riffle of smoke. 'Who am I? Why am I here? Where am I going?'

'Something like that.'

'Forgive me, brother. I don't mean to make light of your search.'

'If they live at all, I think that they must be living somewhere in Ys, or in the boreal lands upriver of Ys.'

'You should pray that they live in Ys,' Eliphas said. 'The land upriver is wild, and full of races which have not yet changed – or perhaps will never change. Most are little more than animals, and do not have an Archivist to record their lives. The city streets are hard, but one can survive in them with only a little money and a modicum of cunning. But it is not so easy to survive in the dark forests and the ice and snow of the boreal regions at the head of the river.'

Yama was beginning to realise the magnitude of his task. He said, 'The world is very large, and not at all like my map.'

'Then your map must be very old. Little has altered on Confluence since the Age of Insurrection. It is true that when bloodlines reach enlightenment, the Change Wars that follow usually destroy their city. But the survivors move on, and there are always prelapsarian races to take their place, and all seems as it was before. New cities are built upon the old. But what stood in those places at the beginning of the world? I would very much like to see this map of yours.'

'I had to leave it behind when I set out for Ys.'

Yama told Eliphas about Aeolis, and the peel-house and its library, and Eliphas said that he knew of the library of the Aedile of Aeolis.

'I knew the present librarian, Zakiel, before he was disgraced and sent away. Sometimes I envy his exile, for the library has a good reputation. It is said that a very old and very rare copy of the Puranas is lodged there. If not an original copy, then as close to an original as any that have survived.'

It was the book that Zakiel had given Yama when he had left Aeolis for Ys. His heart turned over when he realised the value of the gift. It was with his satchel and the rest of his belongings in the little stone cell in the House of the Twelve Front Rooms, in the Department of Vaticination. He must return there as soon as he could, and discharge his obligation to Tamora and the department. And then he must flee. If he was captured by the Department of Indigenous Affairs, he would almost certainly fall into Prefect Corin's hands.

He said, 'Zakiel was one of my teachers, and a good, kind friend.'

Eliphas blew a smoke ring and watched it widen in the air, then sent a second, smaller ring spinning through the fraying circle of the first. He said, 'No wonder you value knowledge. We should sleep now, brother. We must rise with the sun if we're to get a place at the carrels.'

*

Only one of the dormitories was open, but the narrow beds were comfortable and the sheets clean. Eliphas snored and someone else in the dormitory talked in his sleep, but Yama had risen early and escaped his enemy and walked many leagues, and soon fell asleep.

He woke in pitch darkness. The hairs on the back of his neck and on his forearms were prickling and stirring, and he was filled with a feeling of unspecific dread, as if he had escaped the clutches of a bad dream.

There was a faint light at the end of the long room. At first Yama thought sleepily that the door was open, that it must be morning. But then he saw that the light was vaguely man-shaped, although taller than most men, and thinner than any living man should be. It drifted like a bit of waterweed caught in a current, or like a candle flame dancing in the draught created by its own burning. It reminded Yama of nothing so much as the wispy lights that could sometimes be glimpsed after the river Breas had flooded the ruins outside the city wall of Aeolis. The Amnan called those apparitions wights, and believed that they would steal the soul of any traveller they could entice into their clutches; Zakiel said that they were no more than pockets of marsh gas which kindled in the air upon bubbling to the surface of stagnant water, and had once demonstrated the principle with water and a bit of natrium in a glass tube. But knowing what the wights were did not make them any less eerie when they were flickering in the darkness of a bleak winter's night.

Unlike a candle flame or a marsh wight, the burning figure gave off no light but that which illuminated itself. The dormitory remained in shadow, lit only by the dim clusters of fireflies which clung to the walls above the beds where their hosts slept. The thing stooped over the first of the beds, and the sleeper's face was immersed in its spectral light. The man murmured and turned halfway around, but he did not wake. The thing disengaged itself and waved through the shadows to the next bed.

Yama discovered that he was clutching the sheet so hard that his fingers had cramped. He remembered the light which had burst through the shrine in the temple of the latriatic cult and the thing he had felt rushing towards him from the depths of the space within the shrine, and knew that it had followed him here. He sat up cautiously. His fireflies brightened before he remembered to still them, but the burning figure did not appear to notice. It was bending towards the third sleeper.

Yama put his hand over Eliphas's mouth and shook the old man awake. Eliphas's silver eyes opened at once and Yama pointed to the burning figure and whispered, 'It is looking for me.'

Eliphas bolted from his bed, clutching the sheet to his skinny body. 'A hell-hound,' he said in a hoarse whisper. 'Save us! It is a hell-hound.'

'I think it came from a shrine higher up the palace's slopes. I think it means me harm.'

Another man's face appeared in the hell-hound's blue light; he groaned horribly, as if gripped by a sudden nightmare. Yama thought that everyone here would remember the same dream when they woke – and then realised that if the hell-hound could affect men's dreams, then perhaps it could also see into them. That must be what it was doing, browsing through the minds of the sleepers as a scholar might browse amongst the books on a shelf.

Yama snatched up his shirt and the harness which held his sheathed knife, and said, 'I am going to climb through one of the windows. You can come with me or stay, but I would be happier if you followed me.'

'Of course I'm coming. It is a hell-hound.'

Yama opened the shutter of the window above his bed and climbed out onto the balcony outside. When Eliphas followed, clutching his clothes, Yama turned up the light of their fireflies and discovered that they were only a few man-lengths above the tile floor of the courtyard. He swung over the rail of the balcony, landing with a rush and a shock.

Eliphas let his clothes flutter down and followed more cautiously, and sat down after he had landed, massaging his knees. 'This was never part of the bargain,' he said.

Yama shrugged the harness of his knife around his shoulders. 'You do not have to follow me,' he said.

Eliphas was pulling on his trousers. He looked up and said, 'Of course I will follow. The hell-hound is looking into the minds of those men, and some remember that they saw you with me. And if it looks into my mind it will find my conversations with you. What might it do then?'

'Then you had better show me how to reach the Gate of the Hierarchs. I will get us past the guardian. I have no intention of staying here.'

'I think it would be better if we found Kun Norbu. He will know what to do. And the library's guards are armed.'

'We will return in the morning,' Yama said. 'The hell-hound will not linger once it realises I have left.'

Eliphas might have argued the point, but a blue light appeared at the balcony above. They both lost their nerve then, and ran.

The guardian of the Gate of the Hierarchs had been driven deep inside itself, and did not notice when Yama and Eliphas passed by. It was a few hours before dawn. It was not cold, but Yama and Eliphas were soon mantled with dew after they sat down to keep watch from a turn of the long flight of steps high above the library. Yama said that Eliphas could leave him as soon as it grew light, but Eliphas said that he would as soon stay with Yama.

'I made a contract with you, brother, and I never let a client down.'

Yama said, 'You have other clients before me.'

'I'll let you into a secret.' Eliphas lit his pipe. When he drew on it, the burning coal of tobacco set a spark in each of his silvery eyes. 'Sometimes I already know the answers to the questions I am sent to root out of the library. It would not do to tell the client that, though. It would put the business of the library at risk, and my business, too. Besides, no leech will believe that I know more of his trade than he does. So I enact a little charade. I come here and gossip with my friends, and a day later I return to my client and give him, stamped and documented, the answer I could have given him straight away, if only he had trusted me. The library is paid, I am paid, and the client is pleased with his answer. That is why I was happy to help you. It gave me something to do. My wife is dead, my daughters are married and concerned with their own families, and my only son is fighting heretics at the midpoint of the world. No one will miss me if I go with you. I had thought that there were no more wonders to discover in the world, and you have proved me wrong.'

Yama considered this. At last, he said, 'The road I travel may be long, and it is certainly dangerous.'

'Don't think that I know only the inside of libraries, brother, or that I am innocent of the long world. I travelled much in my younger days, searching for old books with Kun Norbu. It took us to some odd places. Now, once we know it is safe, we shall return to the library and learn what Kun Norbu has discovered about your bloodline. And then I will help you to look for any who still live, wherever they may be.'

'I have some business in the palace first,' Yama said.

He started to tell Eliphas about the conflict between the Department of Indigenous Affairs and the Department of Vaticination, but he had not got very far when Eliphas stood and said, 'Look! Look there!'

A cold blue light flared below. It defined the curtain wall of the library and several of its slim towers before winking out. There was the sound of men shouting in the distance, and then the iron voice of a bell, slow at first but gathering urgency.

Someone down there had an energy pistol. For a moment, an intense point of light shone like a fallen fleck of the sun. There was a noise like that of a gigantic door slamming deep in the keel of the world, and the backwash of the discharge blossomed above the roofs and towers of the library and threw the shadows of Yama and Eliphas far up the long flight of stairs. The cold blue light kindled again. It was smaller now, and seemed to be climbing one of the towers. Yama saw the flashes of pellet rifles; the sound of their fusillade was like the crackle of twigs thrown on a fire. The mote of cold blue light dropped from the side of the tower, drifting down like a leaf.

Eliphas said, 'They have killed it!'

'I do not think it can be killed by rifle fire, nor even by the discharge of an energy pistol. It is not of this world, Eliphas, but of the world that men once glimpsed in the shrines.'

Yama remembered that the woman who had appeared in the shrine of the Temple of the Black Well had told him that there were dangerous things beyond the bounds of the garden she had created. He was certain now that the hell-hound was one of the creatures she had feared.

'You may be right,' Eliphas said. 'Accounts of the wars of the Age of Insurrection speak not only of the battles of men and machines, but of a war in the world within the world. The priests claim that this means that the enemy strove to conquer men's souls as well as their cities, but archivists and librarians know better. Hell-hounds were weapons in that second front.'

'The Insurrectionists tried to destroy the avatars, and the link between men and the Preservers.'

'And the heretics succeeded where the Insurrectionists could not. Perhaps they woke the old weapons.'

'I fear that I have a talent for drawing enemies to myself. There! There it is again!'

The tiny point of blue light had appeared at the foot of the dark wall of the library.

Eliphas knocked out his pipe on the railing of the stairs. His fingers were trembling as he put it away. 'We should not stay here a moment longer. The hell-hound must travel slowly, or else it would have caught you long before you reached the library. But I have a feeling that it will not rest until it has found what it is looking for.'

7
THE GAMBLER

Yama and Eliphas reached the long lawn and its fountain just as dawn began to define the mountain ranges at the edge of the city's wide plain. The library was far below, its towers ablaze with lights, but there was no sign of the hell-hound.

Eliphas sat heavily on the wet grass. 'Perhaps we have lost it,' he said.

'I do not think so,' Yama said. 'It followed me to the library. There is no reason why it cannot follow me in the reverse direction. You are tired, Eliphas.'

'I am old, brother.'

'And my head aches. But we cannot stay here.'

Eliphas clambered to his feet, unfolding his lanky body in stages. He said, 'I'm sure we can spare a few minutes before we go on. I am thirsty as well as tired.'

As Yama and Eliphas approached the ornate fountain in the centre of the lawn, two deer ran from it, white scuts bobbing as they disappeared into the darkness. Eliphas thrust his head into a spout of water that gushed from the gaping mouth of a fish; Yama drank from a basin shaped like an oyster shell and splashed cold water on the back of his neck. His head wound had begun to bleed again. While Eliphas sat on the edge of the fountain's main basin and lit his pipe, Yama walked to the edge of the lawn. He was anxious and tired and afraid.

There was now enough light in the sky to make out the various clusters of buildings scattered across the long slope below. Yama could see that the library's curtain wall had been breached – the adamantine stone slumped like melted candle wax – and that its slim white towers were licked with black soot. The path which climbed through the tiers of fields seemed empty, and for a moment his heart lifted. Perhaps Eliphas was right. But then he saw a glimmer of cold blue light emerge from a distant stand of sago palms: the hell-hound coming on in an erratic dance like a scrap of fabric caught in a breeze, but always moving upwards.

Yama ran back to Eliphas with the news; the old man shrugged phlegmatically, and was maddeningly slow to begin to move. Exhaustion had stifled his fear. He knocked out his pipe on his boot-heel and said that there were roads still in use, and all led to gates to the interior.

'And where there is a gate,' Eliphas said, 'there will be guards.'

'The guards of the library could not stop it.'

'Some guards are better armed than others,' Eliphas said. He pressed the palms of his hands over his eyes for a moment. 'The main part of the palace has always been better defended than the outlying offices. We cannot run forever, brother. If we lead it to them, the soldiers of Internal Harmony will know what to do.'

Yama did not share Eliphas's faith in this plan, but a small hope was better than no hope at all. He said, 'If we are to try to find some way back into the mountain, then we should turn aside. The monastery where I wakened it is not far above. I do not want to confront the shrine again, especially with that thing at my back. I might waken something even worse. As it is, I fear that the library is destroyed.'

Eliphas smiled. 'Not at all. What stands above ground is only a tenth part of the whole. The stacks and carrels of the archives run far back into the palace. Kun Norbu may be somewhat distracted by repair work, but he will remember your request.'

'That is suddenly the least of my concerns,' Yama said.

At the far end of the long lawn they found a narrow path that wound along the foot of a bluff from which a cluster of square windowless buildings hung, like the cells of a wasp nest. Far below, the hell-hound stopped for a full minute, a fleck of blue flame in the middle of a steep field of red corn, and then suddenly moved forward, angling across the field in a straight line like a hound tracking a scent.

Yama and Eliphas hurried on, passing between the legs of a skeletal metal tower clad in a living cloak of green vines. The path cut through a thicket of bamboo, and a little village appeared below, flat-roofed houses of wicker and daub crowded around a central square. Threads of smoke rose into the grey sky from several of the houses. A cock crowed, anticipating the rising sun.

At last Eliphas had to stop. He bent over, clasping his knees, panting. Yama went back to the beginning of the bamboo thicket to look for the hell-hound, then returned to Eliphas, who unbent slowly and said, 'We must go through the village. If the hell-hound follows, the villagers will try to stop it.'

'Will they be better armed than the library guards?'

'They are husbandmen who till the fields on this part of the palace roof. They will have axes and scythes, perhaps a few muskets. They will not be able to stop it, but they may slow it down so that we can make our escape.'

'No. I will not risk their lives. And we cannot wait here, Eliphas. Remember that the hell-hound does not rest.'

Eliphas waved a hand in front of his face, as if Yama's words were flies that could be brushed away. 'A moment, a moment more, and I will be able to go on. Listen, brother. The quickest way to the nearest gate will take us through the village. The husbandmen take their produce to the gates. That's where they sell it to merchants from the day markets. Don't spare a thought for them. They are indigens whose ancestors colonised the ruined parts of the palace ten thousand years ago, like the birds or mice which colonise the ordinary houses of men, and of no more importance than the sacred monkeys of the outer temples. Less so, in fact, since priests and sacerdotes care for the monkeys that live in their monasteries and temples, but no one cares for the husbandmen. They are tolerated only because they supply the day markets with fresh produce.'

Yama remembered the fisherman, Caphis, who had saved his life after he had escaped from Dr Dismas and the young warlord, Enobarbus.

'Even if the indigenous peoples cannot transcend their animal origins, still they are something more than animals, I think. I will not risk their lives to save mine,' he said, and pointed to the terraced rice paddies that stepped away below the next bluff. 'A path descends beside those fields. We can follow it. Eliphas, if you wish to, leave me now. Go through the village. The hell-hound will not follow you.'

'I made a bargain,' the old man said. 'Maybe it's a bad one, but it may still pay off. Lead on, brother, although I fear your scruples will help the villagers more than they will help us.'

The sun had begun to rise above the distant mountains when Yama and Eliphas reached the steep ladder of steps beside the terraced rice fields. The narrow steps were worn by the tread of a thousand generations of husbandmen, and slippery with slimy seepage from the flooded paddies. Despite their fearful haste, Yama paused at a wayside shrine. *Take this burden from me*, he prayed, as he had prayed so often before, meaning, make me ordinary, make me no more than other men. Save me from myself.

The rice paddies were narrow and long, curved to follow the contour of the hillside and dammed with stout ramparts of compacted earth wide enough for two water buffalo to walk abreast. Freshly planted seedlings made a haze of green over the calm brown water of the paddies; the ripe smell of ordure reminded Yama of the flooded fields around Aeolis. At another time it would have eased his heart.

After they had descended a while in silence, Eliphas said, 'This part of the palace was ruined in the last war of the Age of Insurrection, and has never been properly rebuilt. If you were to dig deep enough, you would find rock fused like glass, and then rubble, and then rooms and corridors wrecked and abandoned ten thousand years ago. Because this side faces the Rim Mountains, and is in sunlight for most of the day, it is favoured for cultivation.' The old man laid one hand on the small of his back. 'I am sorry, brother, but I must rest again. Only for a moment.'

Each time Eliphas stopped to catch his breath, Yama looked back at the path they had taken, but by good fortune they managed to reach the bottom of the long ladder of steps before the hell-hound appeared.

White cockatoos rose into the sky, screeching in alarm. A moment later the hell-hound spun out of the thicket of bamboo above the terraced rice paddies. Like a whirlwind or dust devil, it threw clouds of dust and scraps of foliage into the air as it moved. It seemed just as bright in daylight as at night, like a bit of sky fallen to earth and roughly shaped into a tall, skeletal man, coming on slowly and steadily.

Yama and Eliphas ran down a dusty track between the steep bank of the bottommost rice paddy and the margin of a sloping field of melon vines. They splashed across a stream and ran through a belt of eucalyptus trees, scattering a herd of small black pigs, and ran on until Eliphas tripped and fell headlong.

At first Eliphas could not get up, and when Yama finally hauled him to his feet he said that he could not run any more. They were on a long downward slope with tall grass on either side of the path. A chorus of crickets was beginning to cheep and whistle, woken by the early-morning warmth.

'Leave me,' Eliphas said. He was trembling and his silvery eyes were half-closed. He could not get his breath. 'Leave me, brother, and save yourself. I will find you again, if we both live.'

The slender eucalyptus trees at the top of the slope stirred and shook as if caught in a localised gale. A horrible squealing went up and black pigs pelted out of the trees. The hell-hound appeared behind them, blazing like a piece of the sun caught in blue glass. It seemed to have grown taller and thinner, as if the glass, melting, was being pulled apart by its own weight. Veils of dust and leaves whirled up around it. At first it seemed confused by the pigs and made short, swift dashes after one or another of them. Most of the pigs scattered into the tall grass, but a few ran in circles, dazed by the brilliant light, and finally the hell-hound pounced on the smallest. The hapless pig flew up as if it weighed no more than a dead leaf, was dashed to the ground, and lay still. As if excited by this, the hell-hound whirled in wider circles. It swept through the tall dry grasses, which caught fire with a sullen crackling, then steadied and came on down the path towards Yama and Eliphas.

Yama got a shoulder under Eliphas's arm and they staggered down the path to the edge of a steep embankment. Directly below was a broad road crowded with carts drawn by bullocks or water buffalo, camels laden with hessian-wrapped packs, and women and men walking with bundles or clay pots balanced on their heads. Carts and camels and people were all moving downhill towards the high, square entrance of a tunnel in the side of the slope.

As Yama and Eliphas staggered down the embankment, people shrieked and shrank away. Yama glanced over his shoulder. The hell-hound had appeared behind them, burning brightly against a reef of white smoke. Yama shouted in despair and pulled Eliphas behind a cart piled high with watermelons. All around, men and women screamed as the hell-hound swept down the embankment. A bullock bolted, bawling with fear, and its cart overturned, spilling a heap of red bananas. A flock of moas ran in circles, screeching wildly and kicking up dust. The hell-hound plunged amongst them, rearing back and forth as if maddened.

Yama and Eliphas were swept along in the midst of the panicking crowd, into the darkness of the tunnel, brick walls doubling and redoubling the shouts and screams of men and women and the bawling of animals, and emerged into a huge underground chamber. Like a breaking wave, the crowd washed against bays where labourers were unloading and weighing produce and clerks were handing out tallies to husbandmen.

They were halfway across the wide chamber when the flock of moas stampeded out of the tunnel, the hell-hound burning in their midst. People screamed and dropped baskets and packages and ran in every direction, and a pentad of guards came out of a tall narrow gate. The guards wore half-armour and carried slug rifles which they raised and began to fire as they ran towards the hell-hound. Wounded moas fell to the ground, kicking with their strong, scaly legs. Ricocheting slugs whooped and rang, knocking dust and brick fragments from the ground all around the hell-hound as it stretched and bent this way and that and finally fixed on Yama and Eliphas.

Eliphas wailed and sank to his knees, his arms wrapped over his head. Yama held up the ceramic disc in one hand and his knife in the other, and slowly backed away. The hell-hound had elongated to four or five times the height of a man, and shone so brightly that he could only squint at it through half-closed eyes. It made a horrible high-pitched hiss as it advanced, gouging a smoking trench in the brick floor. Its heat beat against his skin. The guards kept up a steady rate of fire, but their fusillade merely kicked up shards of brick around the hell-hound or passed through it as if it was no more than light – and perhaps it was no more than that, light bent into itself.

Yama backed into a stack of baskets of live chickens. He slashed the baskets open and kicked them towards the hell-hound. The thing cast around as panicked chickens scattered around it, but then it straightened and fixed on Yama again. He tried again to command it to halt, but he might as well have tried to snuff a furnace by force of will. He was aware of a number of small machines in the chamber, but knew that there was no point in hurtling them at the hell-hound.

Someone called to him. Yama risked glancing around, and saw that Eliphas had circled around to his right and climbed onto a cart. Another man stood beside him – the gambler who had been playing the shell game outside the bawdy house.

'Come with me!' the gambler shouted. 'Come with me if you want to live!'

Yama ran towards them, and knew by the screams of the people all around that the hell-hound had started after him. Eliphas and the gambler jumped down behind the cart and ducked through a little round hole in the wall beyond. Yama's shadow was thrown ahead of him: he ran to meet its dwindling apex. Fierce heat and light beat at his back as he scrambled through the low opening, and then something fell with a clang behind him and he was in darkness.

8

THE KING OF THE CORRIDORS

Moments after it had fallen into place behind Yama, the hatch rang with a pure, deep note and a smell of scorched metal began to fill the narrow passageway.

'Put up your knife, dominie,' the gambler said. 'You're with friends here. Follow me, quick as you can. The hatch is crystalline iron, but it won't hold for long.'

'I am at your service,' Yama said. Trembling violently from the near escape, he fumbled his knife into its sheath and leaned against the wall, trying to catch his breath.

'It is my turn to help you, brother,' Eliphas said, and put his shoulder under Yama's arm and supported him as they followed the gambler down the passageway.

Yama said, 'Where are we?'

'One of the service corridors,' Eliphas said. 'They're supposed to run through every part of the palace, even to the offices of the Hierarchs. But there are no maps to their maze, and few use them now.'

The gambler glanced at them over his shoulder. He wore a black shirt, and bright red leggings. His stiff coxcomb brushed the low ceiling; his long pale face gleamed in the combined light of their fireflies. 'Most of that's true,' he said, 'but more use these corridors than you might reckon, and not everything has been forgotten. Speaking of which, do you remember me, dominie?'

'You were playing the shell game yesterday. You were wearing a silver shirt then.'

'I'm Magon,' the gambler said. 'We've been on the lookout for you, dominie. You ran the wrong way yesterday, and it's my luck to have found you again. Do you know what it is that you wakened? You did wake it, didn't you?'

'Yes. Yes, I did. It was in a shrine.'

'In the temple of a latriatic cult? We hadn't thought that one was still functional – well, it isn't functional now, of course. The shrine would have been destroyed when the hell-hound broke through.'

Yama touched the disc that hung at his chest. Magon saw the gesture, and said, 'That won't help you, dominie. It isn't a charm.'

'I was wondering if it had woken the thing.'

The woman in the shrine of the Temple of the Black Well had said that the disc had drawn her to him.

Magon said, 'You did that yourself, I reckon. Lucky you were brought up where you were, in the City of the Dead, and not in Ys. There are hundreds of shrines in Ys, and more remain functional than most folk think. If you had been brought up in Ys, it is likely that a hell-hound would have scented you before you were ready for it. But that would be a different world, and I wouldn't have the good fortune to be talking with you here and now.'

'You seem to know a lot about me,' Yama said.

'Lucky for you that I do,' Magon said.

'And you know about the hell-hound.'

'A little, dominie.'

'It seemed to be made of light,' Yama said.

'Exactly so,' Magon said. 'Light is only matter in another form, and can be bound in various forms for a short while. Hell-hounds are one such form. They are terrible things. They can live in the world inside the shrines, and in our world, too. They pass through our world from one shrine to another like an arrow through air, if an arrow could make itself into air in its flight and remake itself when it hits its target. They were sent after avatars, originally.'

Yama said, 'And this one came for me.'

'That was bad luck, and not just for you,' Magon said. 'It must have been bound in the shrine. No doubt that's why the monastery was built around it. It's all too easy to mistake the stirring of a hell-hound for the intimation of an avatar. Those poor monks, praying for thousands of years to a weapon of their enemies! There's irony for you, eh, dominie?'

'It seemed to grow stronger in sunlight,' Yama said. He had the horrible thought that whoever had fired at the hell-hound with a pistol would have fed its strength.

Eliphas said, 'Perhaps this darkness will help to extinguish it.'

Magon said, 'Even in sunlight it loses binding energy. Sunlight's energy is too dilute to sustain it, just as we would gasp for air at the peaks of the Rim Mountains. It must have stolen the residue of the shrine's potential energy when it manifested, but that won't support it forever. With a little luck, we can keep ahead of it, and it will dissipate when its binding energy drops below a sustainable level.'

'We have had little in the way of luck so far,' Yama said. 'I think that I will have to find a way of destroying it.'

'As for that,' Magon said, 'some ways are better than others, as the fox said to the hen lost in the forest. We'll go through here. Don't worry, it's dry on the far side.'

They had reached the base of a kind of well or shaft. A patch of pale daylight showed high above and a sheet or curtain of water fell down one side and drained away through grids in the floor. Magon plunged through it and after a moment of hesitation Yama and Eliphas followed – the water was as warm as soup. There was a short tunnel beyond, and they found the gambler waiting at the other end, where a slim metal bridge arched across a narrow, half-flooded cavern. Shapes flickered beneath the surface of the water: sleek, arrowhead-shaped bodies outlined by dashes of green luminescence, and knots of long, ropy limbs. Creatures like the polyps which swarmed in the river at midsummer, but grown to the size of a man. Waves clashed and broke against stone, casting shivering shadows on the arched ceiling. Something like a snake rose up, sinuously elongating in the air before falling back with a splash.

Eliphas grasped Yama's arm and said, 'There are more things forgotten in the palace than anyone could dream of in a lifetime of sleep.'

'They come up from the Great River through flooded passages beneath the streets of the city.' Magon said. 'Lupe says they might have had a purpose once upon a time, but that's long forgotten. They come here now only because of habit now.'

He stepped quickly and lightly to the top of the bridge's arch and turned and beckoned to Yama and Eliphas.

'They are mostly harmless, but it's best if you don't tarry.'

Yama did not entirely trust the gambler. His ready smile and quick wit seemed assumed, a mask, an act. He said, 'Tell me how you know about my... abilities. It is not just because I saw through your sleight of hand, is it?'

Magon said, 'Of course not. Please, dominie, we must go on. Lupe will answer all of your questions.'

'Why do you know so much about me? How long have your people been watching me?'

There was a loud splash out in the darkness, as if something big had lifted itself out of the water and fallen back.

Magon's left hand darted to his hip, where something made a shape under his loose shirt. He said, 'You were supposed to go to the Department of Indigenous Affairs, but your escort arrived without you. That's when we started looking, but we didn't catch sight of you until after you called down the feral machine.'

'My escort? You mean Prefect Corin?'

For a moment, Yama thought that Magon was in league with the Prefect.

'I wouldn't know the name,' the gambler said. 'But I know that someone in the Department of Indigenous Affairs isn't happy that he lost track of you.'

His gaze darted from side to side as things splashed in the darkness beyond the bridge. When a nest of pale tentacles rose from the water directly beneath the bridge, he gave a cry and took a step backwards.

Eliphas said, 'I thought you said they wouldn't harm us.'

'They are restless. The hell-hound must be near. Come quickly!'

Yama said, 'This is not the first time I have met people who claim to know me better than I know myself. And I have business elsewhere today.'

This was the day of public inquisition at the Department of Vaticination, his best chance of sneaking past any watchers that Prefect Corin might have placed at its gate.

Eliphas caught Yama's arm and whispered, 'They might be thieves and cut-throats, brother, no better than the husbandmen. But unless you know another way out, we will have to follow him.'

Magon cocked his head, his eyes bright as he looked from Eliphas to Yama. He said, 'You don't trust me, and I guess that if I was in your position I'd feel the same. I don't have the answers you want, dominie. I'm just here to bring you to Lupe. And we must move on. The hell-hound is still at your back, and the big fish are restless. We—'

Points of blue light suddenly shone in the gambler's eyes. Yama turned. The hell-hound stood at the end of the bridge. It was smaller now, but burned as brightly as ever. Yama unsheathed his knife. Its curved blade kindled with its own blue flame, as if to challenge the hell-hound's unworldly light.

The hell-hound slid forward, elongating through black air. As Yama and Eliphas followed Magon across the bridge, something hit so hard the entire structure hummed like a plucked string. Magon and Eliphas yelled in fright. Nests of pale tentacles rose up on either side, slithering around the bridge's slender handrails. Their undersides bore rows of fleshy suckers; their ends were frayed into feathery palps which continually tasted the air.

The hell-hound stopped halfway up the bridge's arch, bending from the middle and casting from side to side as more tentacles curled up out of the seething water. Yama guessed that there must be a decad or more of the giant polyps beneath the bridge. The forest of tentacles which gripped the railings tensed, quivering with effort. The bridge groaned as one of the polyps lifted itself out of the water. Under its white mantle, a huge blue eye with a golden pupil revolved and fixed its gaze on Yama. The bridge groaned again, and then the central section gave way with a sudden sharp crack that echoed and re-echoed from the cavern's wet walls.

On the other side of the gap, the hell-hound flared brightly and whirled around and fled into the corridor. The water under the bridge boiled with activity. Green lights flashed furiously under its foaming surface. One, then another, then two more: the great polyps lifted the edges of their mantles out of the water and stared at Yama. Eliphas and Magon shouted again, but Yama, guessing wildly, lifted the disc from his shirt and held it up. Satisfied, the polyps sank back one by one, and the water darkened as their lights faded away.

'Nothing can follow us now,' Yama said.

'The hell-hound will find another way,' Magon said. 'That's what it does.' He was very scared, but he had stood firm, and Yama liked him better for that.

Eliphas took a deep, trembling breath, then another. 'Lead on, brother. And remember that we trust you only slightly more than we trust your fishy friends.'

Magon led them down a narrow corridor with walls of fused rock that dully reflected the lights of the fireflies of Yama and Eliphas. As it rose and turned, Yama believed that its gravity changed direction, too, so that they were no longer walking on its floor but along its wall, rising vertically through the heart of the palace. Occasionally, other corridors opened to either side and above; gusts of warm air blew from these openings, sometimes bringing the sound of distant machinery.

Magon soon regained his jaunty confidence, and boasted that these were the old skyways which only his people knew.

'You might say that there's a palace within the palace, each twined around the other like a vine around a tree until you can't tell whether the tree is holding up the vine, or the vine is holding up the tree. We were here from the beginning. Departments come and go. They fight each other and are destroyed or absorbed, and when the last is gone we will still be here.'

Eliphas said, 'I suppose this is the teaching of your master, this Lupe.'

'It's our history,' Magon said. 'It's passed on in song and dance from father to son, mother to daughter. Just because it's not written in books doesn't mean it isn't true, though for someone like yourself, who has breathed so much book dust he is mostly book himself, that might be hard to believe. We are always here to serve. It's what we do. Whoever owns the palace becomes our master, whether they know it or not.'

What struck Yama now was that Magon's posturing and anxious capering, his hypersensitivity to moods and his eagerness to please, resembled the behaviour of the lap dogs of certain childless gentlewomen. He said, 'I still do not understand why you want to help me. I am the master of no one, let alone of this palace.'

Magon said, 'You are come at last, dominie. Lupe said he had not expected it, although it was foretold by an anchorite years before. But Lupe will tell you himself.'

The corridor turned around itself again. Warm, humid air and a rich organic stink blew into their faces, and at last they emerged into a long, low room. Its bare rock walls ran with condensation; its floor was strewn with heaps of black soil in which frills of fungus grew: dead white, blood red, a yellow so shiny it might have been varnished. At the far end, Magon parted layers of nylon-mesh curtains and ushered Yama and Eliphas into a barrel-vaulted cave lit by shafts of sunlight that fell from vents in the rock ceiling far above.

'My home,' Magon said. 'It is the capital of my people, for Lupe lives here.'

There were little gardens, and patchwork shacks built of plastic or cardboard sheeting, or of translucent paper stretched across bamboo framing. People drew around Yama and Eliphas as they followed Magon across the cavern, and they quickly became the centre of a procession. There were clowns and jugglers, mummers and mimes, weightlifters and agonists, fakirs with steel pins through their cheeks and eyelids. Acrobats walked on wires strung everywhere across the midway of the cavern. There were men dressed in richly embroidered dresses of faded silk stiff with brocade and silver and gold thread, with white-painted faces and black make-up that exaggerated their eyes, transvestites that burlesqued the sacred temple dancers. There were musicians and gamblers, and prostitutes of all five sexes and seemingly of every imaginable bloodline.

Eliphas looked around uneasily, but Yama knew that they would not be harmed. Not here. 'They exist to serve!' he said, and took the old man's arm to reassure him.

They crossed the length of the cavern at the head of the gorgeous, motley procession. A fakir smashed a bottle on his head and rubbed a handful of broken glass over his bare chest; another pressed metal skewers through folds of skin pinched up from his arms. Musicians played a solemn march; clowns knocked each other down and breathed gouts of fire or blew fountains of sparkling dust high into the air; men and women held up their children, who laughed and clapped their hands.

The path ended at a round gilt frame twice Yama's height. It might once have held a shrine. The crowd parted to let Yama and Eliphas follow Magon through this gateway.

The room beyond was swagged in faded tapestries and stained swags of silks. The wrack of ten thousand years lay everywhere in an indiscriminate jumble. Lapidary icons were heaped like beetles in a green plastic bowl. A cassone, its sides painted with exquisitely detailed scenes from the Puranas, its top missing, was crammed with filthy old boots. Ancient books lay in a tumbled heap next to neat rolls of plastic sheeting.

A man sprawled amongst cushions on a sagging bed beneath a canopy of cloth-of-gold. Magon capered forward and jumped onto the bed, raising a cloud of dust from yellowed linen sheets, and laid his head next to the man's bare feet, gazing up with unqualified adoration, for all the world like a faithful puppy gazing at its master.

Without doubt, the man on the bed was Lupe, the king of the palace within the palace. He was a big man. He was an old man. Skin hung in mottled flaps from his arms. His face was scored deeply with lines and wrinkles. He wore a long brocade dress so stiff with dirt that it was impossible to tell what colour it might once have been, and an elaborate headdress of gold wire woven in a tall cone and studded with bits of coloured glass was planted on top of tangled grey hair that fell to his broad shoulders. He did not look absurd in his costume, but wore it with a grave, sacerdotal majesty. His feet were bare and his toenails were painted red; the nails of his big, strong hands, like those of certain mendicants, had been allowed to grow around each other in long corkscrews. His lips had been stained with cochineal and his eyes were made up like the wings of a blue butterfly. His pupils were capped with frost, and from the way he held his head Yama knew he was blind.

He turned his face towards Yama and Eliphas, and said in a soft, hoarse voice, 'You have come at last, dominie. I had thought that I would die before this day, and it is with all my heart that I convey the treasure house of my sentiments, that have been stored up for so long. Please, sit at our table! All that we have is yours!'

Three beautiful girls, arrayed in layers of bright silks that left only their arms and faces bare, stepped through a curtain, carrying trays of sweetmeats and candied fruits arranged on plantain leaves. Their delicate oval faces were painted white; their lips were stained black. Two of them fussed around Yama and Eliphas, seating them in nests of dusty cushions, setting the food before them, pouring red tea into translucent porcelain bowls; the other helped Lupe from the bed, sat him on a low stool, settled his dress around him, and raised a bowl of tea to his lips.

Yama had not eaten since the meal in the Strangers' Lodge of the Department of Apothecaries and Chirurgeons, but he was too excited and nervous to have much of an appetite. He accepted a bowl of tea from one of the girls, and said to Lupe, 'Who told you about me, master?'

'Please, dominie, I am not your master! I am Lupe, no more than Lupe and no less, and entirely at your service. All my people are at your service. All this was foretold, and we have made many songs and poems and dances in your honour. Not all our dances are lewd or comic, you know. We dance in one way for our public, and in another for ourselves. All our history is there, in the dances, and so are you.'

'Ask him how we can destroy the hell-hound, brother,' Eliphas said. 'Ask him to show us the way back to the roof of the palace, so I can help you find what you seek.'

Lupe cocked his head, and said, 'Anything you wish, dominie. Anything within our powers. We are yours to command.'

Yama said, 'How is it that you know me?'

He did not feel afraid here – he realised that this was the first time since he had left his home in Aeolis that he did not feel some measure of fear. But he could not stay long. The gates of the Department of Vaticination would open to petitioners at noon; the assassin would even now be sharpening his covert blade or preparing his vial of odourless poison. But he was eager to discover all that Lupe knew – or believed he knew – about him.

Lupe did not answer Yama's question at once. Instead, he motioned to his attendants. One of the girls filled his tea bowl; when the old man had drained it, he wiped his lips on the back of his hand and said, 'We have always served, dominie. We were put into the world to serve and to bring pleasure. Thus, while our bloodline is of the lowest order, the nature of our service calls upon the highest arts. For while we might be counted as beggars who dance, make mock or make love for a paltry rain of coins, our reward is not in the money but in the pleasure our performances bring to our clients. We are a simple people. We do not need money, except to buy cloth and beads and metal wire for our costumes. Your companion looks among the trinkets stored here, and wonders perhaps how I can claim to be poor, yet live with all these riches heaped about me.'

Eliphas held up a mildewed leather cap embroidered with silver wire, and made a face.

'But these riches are all gifts from grateful clients,' Lupe said. 'We have saved them out of sentiment, not avarice. We are a simple people, and yet, dominie, we have survived longer than any other bloodline. We are too simple to know how to change, perhaps, but we do remember. We remember your people. We remember how great and good they were. We remember how we feared and adored them. They have been gone a long time, but we have always remembered them.'

Yama leaned forward, his entire attention on Lupe's grave, blind face. He said, 'Are my people still in the world?'

'We have never seen them in the palace, dominie, and so we have always believed that they are no longer of the world. How could it be otherwise? For they were the Builders, and this is their place. It was here that they commanded the world, in their day. If they are not here, then surely they live nowhere else.'

'Then they are not in Ys,' Yama said. He had guessed it, but it was still hard to bear. 'Do you believe that they might return?'

Lupe said, 'An anchorite came to me seventeen years ago and told me that one day you would seek help from my people. And here you are. So you might say that your people have returned.'

Seventeen years ago Yama had been found afloat on the river, a baby lying on the breast of a dead woman in a white boat. He touched the disc which hung inside his shirt. An anchorite had given it to him in Aeolis, at the beginning of his adventures. And Derev had said that the man might be of his bloodline.

He said, 'What did he look like? Was he scarred about the face, and dumb?'

'He could speak: he had a gentle voice. As for what he looked like, I cannot tell you, dominie. I was as blind then as I am now, and when he came to me it was deepest night, and those of my people not working were asleep. He told me that one day, near the end of the world, a Builder would come to Ys, and that he would need our help. He told me where you would come from, and when. My people have been watching the docks ever since. I thought that you would not come, but here you are.'

'I came by the road, not the river.'

'And just in time, I think. The departments have been perpetually at war with each other ever since the Hierarchs fell from power, but now one department threatens to destroy the rest in the name of the war against the heretics. If it wins, it will create a tyranny that could hold the world in its grip forever, wielding power in the name of the Preservers, but serving only itself. I have feared this for a very long time, but now you are here, dominie, and I know that these terrible days are the last!'

Lupe's milky eyes gleamed. Magon crept from the bed and tenderly blotted the tears from his master's rouged cheeks.

'It's true,' the gambler said, looking at Yama. 'Everything Lupe says is true. He remembers more than anyone else. It is why he is our king.'

Lupe composed himself and said, 'I weep from joy, dominie, that you have come again. Many new songs and dances will be made out of this wonderful moment.'

'I understand,' Yama said, although it seemed to him that he had mistakenly stumbled into the middle of a myth. Lupe's story had set a hundred questions tumbling through his head. Who was the anchorite? Was he the same man who had given him the disc? If he had set the white boat adrift on the river, why had he returned seventeen years later?

He said, 'I am grateful for your hospitality, Lupe, and for your help. But I cannot stay.'

Magon said, 'He claims to have business elsewhere, Lupe. Probably with the fading flower of a department that hired him. You should tell him that he's wasting his time.'

'Forgive him,' Lupe said to Yama. 'He is young and impatient, but he means well. If you have business to attend to, dominie, then you must do what you must do. My servant will take you where you need to go.'

Eliphas said, 'Then you will let us go?'

'Wherever you are in the palace, we are with you,' Lupe said. 'But before you go, walk with me. Show my people that you are my friend, and so the friend of us all.'

Lupe led Yama and Eliphas through the kingdom of his cavern. A crowd of clowns, dancers and whores followed at a respectful distance while Lupe gravely introduced Yama to each of the elders who stood in shabby finery outside their painted shacks.

Yama asked many questions, but although Lupe answered every one, often at length, he learned little more, except that much was expected of him. Lupe was too polite, or too cunning, to state exactly what this was, but Yama slowly began to realise that there was only one thing these people could desire. They were indigens and, unlike the changed and unchanged bloodlines, were untouched by the breath of the Preservers. They were creatures which had borrowed human form; perhaps even their intelligence was borrowed, a trick or skill that they had learned like tumbling, fire-eating, and prestidigitation. Everything they possessed had come to them from other hands, and they accepted these gifts without discrimination. Fabulous treasures were tipped carelessly amongst the rubbish that had formed great drifting piles in Lupe's apartments; a boy carrying nightsoil to the gardens at the edge of the caverns might be wearing a priceless dress; a dancer made up as fabulously as a courtesan might be clad in a glittering costume that, on close inspection, was cut from sacking and decorated with scraps of plastic and aluminium.

The only thing that was truly theirs was the art of simulation, which they used without guile to enhance the pleasure of their clients. Watching closely, Yama saw that the three girls who attended Lupe were not beautiful at all – it was a trick of poise and muscle tone and expression, sustained by constant vigilance. Lupe's people could become passable imitations of most bloodlines by synthesising and exaggerating with a little make-up the two or three features by which each was distinguished from the others. And so with beauty, for beauty was only an exaggeration of the average. Just as a transvestite exaggerated those features which made a woman attractive, so Lupe's people achieved beauty through burlesque. Through their art they could appear to be anything that their clients might desire. The one thing they could not be was themselves.

Many, like Eliphas, believed that the indigenous races were no more than animals. Yama thought otherwise. For if everything in the world had proceeded from the minds of the Preservers, then surely the indigenous races had not been brought here simply to be despised and persecuted. They must have their own desires, their own destiny.

It was almost noon by the time Yama and Lupe had finally completed the circuit of the cavern and returned through the gilt frame to Lupe's chambers. Somewhere high above, the Gate of Double Glory would be admitting those who wished to participate in the public inquisition at the Department of Vaticination. The two pythonesses would soon appear before their clients, arrayed in ancient splendour.

'I do not forget that you have business elsewhere,' the dignified old man said. He covered Yama's hands with his own. 'You can leave by a hidden way, and the people will think you stay here to talk with me. The more important they think I am, the easier it is to keep order. We are a fractious people, dominie. We get too many ideas from others.'

'You have been very generous,' Yama said. 'I will try to return when I can.'

'Of course you will return,' Lupe said. 'And so I will not say farewell, not yet.'

As they followed Magon up a long stairway, Eliphas said, 'This is a day of wonders, brother. Amongst all that rubbish I saw an edition of *The Book of Blood* known only by repute. It was badly damaged, but a man could live for a year from the sale of only a few intact pages. Do you really plan to return?'

Yama shook his head, meaning that he did not know. Yet he felt a prick of obligation. Not because Lupe's people had saved his life: Lupe had made it clear that there was no debt to be paid, and Yama was ready to take him at his word. But there was the other matter. There was Lupe's impossible dream, the promise of the anchorite, the prophesy fulfilled.

No wonder my people have hidden themselves, he thought, for the world holds a store of their unpaid debts and I seem to be expected to redeem them all.

He said with sudden bitterness, 'I wish I had never come to Ys! I only hurt myself, and those who expect things from me. I should have gone downriver with Dr Dismas and accepted my fate!'

But as soon as he said it, he knew that the words came from his dark half, the part of him that dreamed of easy glory and power without responsibility. The part that had been touched by the woman in the shrine, the aspect whose original had begun the heresy which threatened to consume the world.

Magon glanced over his shoulder, his pale face thrown into sharp relief by the lights cast by the fireflies of Yama and Eliphas. There was no other light in the long stair. All who lived inside the palace inhabited little bubbles of light surrounded by vast expanses of uncharted shadow; Lupe's people, who possessed only the dimmest of fireflies, if any, must navigate their maze of passages and tunnels in near-darkness.

Yama said, 'How far is it, Magon?'

'Not far, dominie. We use the straightest route.'

Eliphas whispered, 'You should feel no obligation towards these people, brother. They are tricksters and whores who live off the crumbs of those engaged in honest toil. Kin to the indigens of the roof gardens – except those are more useful. Would you be the saviour of such as they?'

'I suppose that if one was to attempt to emulate the Preservers, then one must start somewhere, and better to start in a low place than in a high one. But I aspire to no such thing. I see that you are a pragmatic man, Eliphas. You prize things for their utility.'

'Brother, things are what they are. These people spin fantasies – it's their trade. They should not be taken seriously.'

'Yet they dream, Eliphas. They believe that I belong in their dreams.'

'They remember their creators, brother, as men remember their mothers and fathers. But once we have grown up we cannot continue to depend upon our parents. We must face the world ourselves.'

'If Lupe's people are still as children,' Yama said, 'then I envy them.'

They fell silent for a while, following Magon up the stairway to a dark, narrow tunnel which, binding gravity about itself, rose vertically through the palace. At last, Magon stopped and said, 'It is not far, dominie. You follow the way until you reach a place where it branches into two. Take the right-hand branch and you will find yourself in a throughway near the Gate of Double Glory.'

'I owe you much, Magon.'

The ragamuffin gambler bobbed and bowed. 'You have repaid me a thousand fold, dominie, by allowing me to bring you to my people. I will watch for your return.'

When Magon's footsteps had faded into the darkness, Yama said, 'Whatever my intentions, it may fall out that I am never able to return.'

'Because of the territorial dispute,' Eliphas said. 'It is no secret, brother. The whole palace knows the plight of the Department of Vaticination. Many hope it survives, for that will check the ambitions of the Department of Indigenous Affairs.'

'It's a pity that there's only hope and no help.'

'No one wishes to anger the Department of Indigenous Affairs. It has grown very powerful, and careless of the ancient protocols. That is why it has been able to pick off lesser departments one by one.'

'And there is the hell-hound. We cannot be certain that it has lost my trail. You do not have to follow me, Eliphas. It will not be an easy time. You could go back to the library and your friend, if you wish, and wait for me there.'

The old man smiled. 'And suppose the hell-hound finds me? No, I will stay with you, brother. Besides, I made a pledge. Lead on, and I will help as best I can.'

9

THE PUBLIC INQUISITION

Large mirrors had been set up on the flat roof of the House of the Twelve Front Rooms, reflecting sunlight into the cavern and mercilessly illuminating the shabby façades of the buildings ranged around the wide central plaza. Yama squinted against this multiple glare when he and Eliphas came through the Gate of Double Glory. He had expected to find a crowd waiting for the pythonesses, but although a platform had been set up on the steps of the Basilica, its deck covered with landscape cloth and strewn with garlands of white lilies and trumpet flowers that were already beginning to wilt, the plaza was deserted.

Inside, Tamora was roaring at a double file of thralls marching in two-step time, turning them again and again in precise right angles. Pandaras ran up and, staring openly at Eliphas, said, 'We thought you lost, master!'

'So I was, for a little while. This is my friend Eliphas. He searches libraries for facts. He has already been of help to me, and I hope he will help me further. Eliphas, this is Pandaras. The fierce woman over there is Tamora.'

'Yama exaggerates my importance in our adventures,' Eliphas said.

'I am Yama's squire,' Pandaras said, staring up at Eliphas boldly. The boy had oiled his hair and brushed it back from his forehead. It gleamed beneath his two fireflies. He turned to Yama and said, 'I see you have changed the dressing on your head, master. Let me look at it.'

'It is almost healed.'

'As you said two days ago.'

Now Tamora came stalking across the Basilica's marble floor. She wore her corselet and a short leather skirt, and sandals with laces that criss-crossed her calves. Her scalp was freshly shaven, and the fall of red hair at the back of her skull had been braided into a complex knot. She looked both terrifying and desirable.

'I thought you were dead,' she said, and took Yama's arm and drew him a little way from the others. 'Grah. You stink of the warrens of some subhuman race. Where have you been? And who's your fish-eyed friend?'

'Eliphas helped me find my way back into the palace. There are traitors in the department—'

Tamora grinned, showing her rack of pointed teeth. 'The servant you followed? The fucker is dead. When you didn't come back, I got it out of Pandaras that you suspected this fellow by the name of Brabant.'

'I volunteered the information, master, because I was worried about your safety,' Pandaras said.

Tamora ignored him. 'I told Syle, and within the hour Luria had ordered the execution. Brabant was bound and pitched out of a window of the House of the Twelve Front Rooms. It's how they do things here. They call it defenestration. I'm talking too much, but it's because I am pleased to see you. I thought Brabant had lured you into an ambush. I wanted to torture him for the truth, but he went straight out the window.'

Yama said, 'I think I know the whole story. Brabant and the woman who gave him his orders were working for the Department of Indigenous Affairs. They wanted their conversation to be overheard – it was part of plan to draw me out of this place, so that Prefect Corin could kidnap me. They may have been planning to undermine the department from within, too. We have to find out who the woman was, and find out if any others are involved.'

'They are all at each other's throats,' Tamora said. 'Luria told me to watch Syle. And Syle took me aside after Brabant went out of the window and suggested that Luria ordered the execution to cover her tracks. You are friendly with him, I know, but I don't trust him. And I don't trust that pregnant hen of his, either.'

'In short, we cannot trust anyone,' Yama said.

'We'll keep watch on them all, but most of all keep watch on our backs. If someone gets killed, we're the ones who'll be blamed.'

'Then let us hope that the hints about assassination that Pandaras overheard were no more than bait for Prefect Corin's trap.'

'Brabant is dead, at least. If there are any other traitors I'll deal with them as soon as they make a move. Now, tell me about what happened to you.'

Yama suddenly found himself smiling. He could not help it. 'I found the library! The library where Dr Dismas discovered the secret of my bloodline. I put a question to it, and when I return to it I will have my answer.'

But only if the hell-hound had not destroyed the records during its battle with the librarians. Eliphas had sworn that the stacks of the library would be unharmed, but Yama believed that the old man had a habit of telling people what he thought they wanted to hear, even if it was not always the truth.

'I'm pleased for you,' Tamora said. 'I get paid no matter how you go about your search, so the quicker the better as far as I'm concerned. But right now we have work to do.'

'Then I have not missed the inquisition? Good. I mean to keep my word, Tamora.'

'It has already begun. Go and put on your armour. Luria is still worried that an attempt will be made on her life. The Department of Indigenous Affairs would claim this place at once if she were to be killed.'

'I have your armour close by, master,' Pandaras said, and ran off to fetch it.

Tamora turned to Eliphas. 'If you want to be a friend to us, go up with Pandaras and keep watch. Then I won't have to worry about you.'

'Because while I keep watch, the boy will keep watch on me?' Eliphas smiled. 'I understand completely. But you do not have to worry. Yama's interests coincide with mine.'

'We've much to talk about,' Tamora said. 'And we will, when this is over.'

Yama said, 'You do not have help me here, Eliphas. This has nothing to do with helping me find my people.'

'I will enjoy it, brother. Like my friend Kun Norbu, all this excitement makes me feel young again.'

Tamora helped Yama to assemble his patchwork armour. 'This is how it falls out,' she said. 'Syle is talking with the clients and keeping them entertained until the ceremony begins. What he's really doing is finishing off the business of finding out as much as possible about them. The clients have to submit their questions two decads in advance of the ceremony, which gives him plenty of time to research them. He employs spies and bribes clerks, that sort of thing. He says that it is to provide the pythonesses with as much background information as possible, but I reckon that he doesn't really believe in the pythonesses' powers of prediction. He finds out what kind of answers his clients want, and makes sure that's what they get.'

'He doubts Luria,' Yama said, 'but believes that Daphoene can see into the future. And there *is* something strange about her, Tamora. As if her head is full of ghosts.'

'I'd say it was mostly full of air. She hardly speaks, and when she does it's no more than simple-minded babble that's mistaken for obscure wisdom because of her position.' Tamora knelt to tighten the buckles of Yama's greaves – the greaves he had won by killing the one-eyed cateran, Cyg. 'This place really is fucked up, Yama. It's like a bunch of spiders trapped in a jar, all of them eating each other and being eaten. But we have sworn to defend it, and we will do our best to uphold our oath.'

Yama hesitated. He knew that Tamora did not believe in his powers. Did not believe, or refused to allow herself to believe. Although he had tried to explain how he had awoken the feral machine in the Temple of the Black Well, and how he had killed Gorgo, she had merely scoffed and told him that the blow to his head had given him delusions.

He said, 'Syle knows what I am, Tamora. He knows that I am one of the Builders. He asked me to use machines against the forces of the Department of Indigenous Affairs. I refused, of course.'

'So he betrayed you to Prefect Corin?'

'This was after Pandaras overheard Brabant and the woman. But I suppose that Syle might have been behind that. Or he may be thinking of selling me now.'

'Your brain is still bruised from the ding you got at the gate. No more talk about magical powers, or I'll begin to regret that I took up with you.'

'I know you do not believe me, Tamora, but I raised up the feral machine in the Temple of the Black Well. And when I realised what I had done, I woke the guards and ordered them to destroy it. It was that fight which set fire to the temple.'

'Grah. Gorgo's man did that, to cover his tracks after he tried to kill you. You're brave enough, Yama. You got the priests out of the burning temple. Don't spoil it with silly stories.'

'I killed Gorgo. You did not see it, but thousands of others did.'

'If he isn't dead, he deserves to be. He *will* be, when I finish here. I'll make sure of it.'

'My fireflies, then. I left here with one, and I have returned with five.'

'You've been outside, on the roof. Your firefly left you then, and you got a new set when you came back inside.'

Yama laughed. She was as stubborn as an ox.

'Forget your fantasy about secret histories and strange powers, and concentrate on what you are. Which is what I am, a cateran hired to defend this miserable place.' Tamora prowled around Yama, stepped in to tighten a strap of his cuirass, stood back and gave him an appraising look. 'You should have kept Cyg's sword, if only for show.'

'That was all it was good for. My knife serves me well enough.' Yama realised now that the real reason he had rejected the sword was because it had been wielded against him, and saw that Tamora had understood this from the beginning. He said, 'I do not look much like a soldier, do I?'

'There won't be anything to it. The rat-boy is on the roof with an arbalest, and your new friend will help him keep watch. The clients have brought their own guards, and I reckon that's where any trouble will come from. If there are any more traitors amongst the thralls or the officers of the department, they won't make their move in the middle of a public ceremony. A knife or a strangling cord in the dark, or poison – that's the style of this place. All we have to do now is stand on either side of the platform and look fierce. If there is trouble, we'll get the thralls between the stage and the clients. Those grey-skinned cullers can't do much, but at least they can get in the way of anyone who tries to hurt the fat one or the airhead. All right?'

'I think so.'

Tamora clapped Yama between his shoulder blades and added, 'Don't doubt yourself,' and went off to shout at the thralls, ordering them to get back into formation.

When Yama and Tamora marched out of the main doors of the Basilica and came down the steps leading a double column of thralls, the people gathered at the foot of the platform turned to stare at the spectacle. There were only three clients, each sitting in a plain chair with a small entourage of advisers, clerks and bodyguards behind them. No more than a couple of decads of people in total, including the scattering of old women who had come for the entertainment. Yama went right and

Tamora left, each leading a line of thralls. Yama halted at the place where the rear edge of the platform abutted the stairs, and the thralls marched past him and turned out one by one, forming a neat arc down the long, shallow staircase. Tamora really had done wonders with their drill. Their metal caps shone and they had tied long red ribbons beneath the double-edged blades of their partisans.

Yama did not feel nervous now that he was in place. As with the public ceremonies he had attended with his father, the Aedile of Aeolis, he found that the worst thing was the entrance, when the audience had nothing better to look at and was buzzing with anticipation.

A small procession made its way across the plaza towards the Basilica, led by a herald who blew a braying brass trumpet. The people below the platform turned to watch. In better times, Yama supposed, the trumpet would have been needed to clear a way through the crowd, but now it sounded small and plaintive, and its echo came back from the walls of the buildings around the plaza and made discords. Behind the herald came a tall figure in a cloud of red – it was Syle, in a long robe of red feathers that fluttered with his every step. He marched solemnly ahead of the palanquins, carried on the shoulders of bare-chested thralls, on which the pythonesses sat. Both women wore white gowns and were crowned with wreaths of ivy. Luria's jowls were rouged and her eyes were accentuated by gold leaf; Daphoene's face was as bloodless as ever, and she ceaselessly worked her narrow jaw as if chewing something. The senior servants of the household walked behind the palanquins. They were led by Rega, stately as a carrack in a dove-grey silk dress with a full skirt and a high collar trimmed with pearls.

Luria was carried up the steps to the right of the platform and Daphoene to the left. The senior servants took their place on the steps above as the bearers, their grey skins gleaming with oil, carefully set the palanquins on the platform. The landscape cloth, which had been depicting a field of green grass ceaselessly winnowed by wind, now changed to a view of a blue sky. The palanquins of the two pythonesses seemed to be floating in clear air, the heaps of white flowers around them like clouds.

Syle stood beside Yama while the pythonesses were set in place. 'I am so pleased to see you return,' he whispered. 'I had thought all was lost, but now I know that we are saved.'

Before Yama could ask what he meant by this, Syle moved off, taking a position in the centre of the platform in front of a little brazier that stood between the pythonesses. Syle bowed to both of them – Luria acknowledged him with a regal nod, but Daphoene had turned her blind face towards the light which shone from the mirrors on the far side of the plaza – and threw a handful of dried leaves on the glowing charcoal in the bowl of the brazier. Instantly, heavy white sweet-smelling smoke billowed over its sides and spread across the sky-coloured platform and rolled down the stairs.

Syle stepped to the front of the platform, the hem of his red robe swirling through white vapour. His fireflies spun above his head like a spectral crown: he looked hierophantic, uncanny, terrifying. He pulled a slate from his robes and read from it in a conversational voice. 'The merchant Cimbar would ask the avatars of the Preservers this question. Will his business prosper if he leases an additional two ships to supply the loyal army of the will of the Preservers?'

There was a silence. Then Luria began to intone sonorously, 'There is no end to the war—'

Daphoene shuddered violently and bent over, squealing like a stricken shoat. It was as if she had been struck in the belly. Syle covered his confusion by stepping backwards and casting a pinch of dried leaves onto the brazier.

Daphoene straightened. Everyone was watching her, even Luria. Yama could hear her breath whistling through her narrow lips. The faint sense he had of the ghosts of many machines inhabiting her intensified for a moment, like a sea of candle flames flaring in a sudden draught.

She said in a thick, choked voice, 'No one profits from war but the merchants,' and fell back on the couch of her palanquin. Blood spotted the front of her white gown; she had bitten her tongue.

The sleek man in the central chair smiled and nodded as two of his advisers whispered in his ear. At last he waved a hand, clearly satisfied with his answer.

Syle raised his arms, the sleeves of his red robe falling like wings around him, and said, 'The avatars of the Preservers have answered, and the answer is acceptable.'

He framed the second question, concerning plantations of green wood which were not growing properly, and Luria answered at some length. Yama was watching Daphoene, and Tamora was watching the small audience: it was Pandaras who raised the alarm. When he cried out, half of those in front of the platform stared up at the little balcony where the boy and Eliphas stood, high above the door of the Basilica; the rest turned to look at where he pointed.

Huge shadows flickered across the cavern. Yama realised that there were men on the roof of the House of the Twelve Front Rooms, small as emmets against the glare of the mirrors. One fired an energy pistol. A thread of intense red light burned above the plaza. Fire splashed above the turrets of the Gate of Double Glory, and a curtain of rock plunged down with a roar that echoed and re-echoed in the sounding chamber of the cavern.

After that, there was very little resistance. Most of the thralls threw down their partisans and fled; when Tamora tried to rally the others, one drew a knife and ran at her. It was the thrall with the streaks of grey in his mane who had been humbled by Yama two days before. Tamora parried his clumsy stroke, killed him with a single thrust to his throat and turned to face the others, the bloody blade of her sword held up before her face.

Yama drew his knife and started towards her, but Syle caught his arm and thrust the muzzle of a slug pistol into his side and said, 'You should have listened to me when I asked for your help. If you stay calm, your friends will live. One word from you, and they die. Drop the knife, please.'

'Perhaps you should take it. I do not want to damage the blade.'

'I know what it can do. Drop it.'

Soldiers were rappelling down the wall of the House of the Twelve Front Rooms; some were already running across the plaza towards the Basilica. Luria lifted the ivy wreath from her head and dashed it into the fumes at her feet. She pointed at Syle and bellowed, 'You said you'd wait!'

'I promised I'd wait until he returned, and so he has. My first duty is to the Department of Vaticination, not the dead past,' Syle said, and turned to Yama. 'Tell your friends to come down. I've no desire to see them killed if they should try to defend their position. Besides, the Basilica might be damaged.'

Tamora swung around when Yama called to Pandaras, and Syle showed her his pistol. She spat and sheathed her sword and ordered the thralls who remained to lay down their partisans.

'I demand that ransom is paid for my freedom,' she said.

'I would give it to you at once,' Syle said, 'but it is not mine to grant.'

Pandaras and Eliphas came out of the main door of the Basilica as the attacking force began to disarm the thralls. Pandaras held the arbalest above his head. A soldier plucked it from his hands and pushed him towards the thralls.

A man in homespun tunic, the black pelt of his face marked by a bolt of white, vaulted onto the stage. Syle thrust Yama forward and said, 'Here he is, dominie.'

'I am the master of no man,' Prefect Corin said. He had a strip of translucent cloth tied across his eyes. 'We meet again, Yama. How I wish this little drama was not necessary, but you provoked me.'

'Let my friends go,' Yama said. 'They are no part of this.'

'They know about you. More than I do, I think. Your father kept much from the department. That trick with the fireflies, for instance.' Prefect Corin touched the strip of cloth. 'Do not think to try that again, by the way. This will shield my eyes, and all my men are protected in the same way.'

Yama remembered the little machine that had saved him from Cyg by piercing the cateran's brain, and forced the thought away. If he killed Prefect Corin, the Department of Indigenous Affairs would send others after him. They commanded the resources of the army. There would be no end to killing.

He said, 'The Aedile told you all he knew. I have learnt much since I came to Ys.'

Prefect Corin nodded. 'And you will learn more, with the department's help.'

Syle said, 'You remember our agreement.'

'Perfectly. Will you use that silly little pistol, or shall I order one of my soldiers to do it for you?'

Syle blushed with anger. 'Do not presume to tell me what to do. I give you this territory, but the department is not the territory.'

Luria struggled to her feet. White smoke billowed around her. She pointed at Syle and said loudly, 'Traitor! You are disowned, Syle. I so rule.'

Prefect Corin said dryly, 'You have claimed the Department of Vaticination for yourself, Syle. I hope you can control it. Do be careful. I believe that she has a knife.'

It was small, with a crooked blade. Luria flourished it dramatically, as if about to plunge it into her own breast.

Daphoene spread her arms wide. She was smiling towards Luria. Her white eyes were full of tears. A thread of blood ran from one corner of her mouth.

'Now it ends,' she said.

To Yama, it seemed as if a hundred people had spoken with the same voice.

Syle stepped forward and said, 'Pythoness. Please—'

Luria swung the knife. Not at Syle, but at Daphoene. The blade must have been poisoned: although it only inflicted a shallow cut on Daphoene's breast, the girl convulsed and fell back onto the cushioned seat of her palanquin. A moment later Luria fell too, riddled with arbalest bolts. Rega wailed and ran across the stage to Daphoene, and snatched her up and covered her face with desperate kisses.

10

THE COMMITTEE FOR PUBLIC SAFETY

'Daphoene was the daughter of Rega by another marriage,' Prefect Corin said. 'I think it was Rega who had the idea – Syle is a clever man, but he lacks the courage to carry out his schemes. Rega, however, is very ambitious. Her father was a failed merchant who killed himself before his debtors could. She clawed her way up from poverty, and was not content to be the wife of the secretary of a dwindling department. I admire her for her ambition if not for her methods. She is a magnificent bitch.

'She altered her daughter's appearance by surgery and infected her with machines carrying the essences of dead people. It is a technique we use to produce battlefield advisers. The infected subject becomes a population which can derive the best solution to a particular problem by use of heuristic sampling. Unfortunately, it does not have a high success rate – most of the subjects retreat into fugues. Daphoene was more successful than most, but the procedure blinded her, and most of her own personality was destroyed. However, Rega felt that the loss of her daughter's sight and sanity was an acceptable sacrifice to her own ambition. I think that Luria suspected that Daphoene was Syle's stepdaughter, but she had no proof. It was Syle who organised the search for the new pythoness, after all, and Syle who kept all the records, and he married the only person who could betray him.'

Yama said, 'They meant to betray me from the beginning. Luria wanted to exchange me for the safety of her department; Syle and Rega plotted to use me as a counter in a bargain with you. At the last moment, Syle feared that the plans would go wrong and tried to persuade me to help him against you, but I would not. And even if I had helped him, I think that Rega would still have betrayed me.'

Brabant had been innocent. The conversation which Pandaras had overheard had been staged by Syle and Rega, part of the scheme to lure Yama into territory controlled by the Department of Indigenous Affairs. They knew that Brabant patronised the bawdy house at the edge of the Day Market, and Prefect Corin had waited for Yama there. But Yama had escaped the trap and had been betrayed all over again, this time publicly. The gatekeeper had informed Syle of Yama's return, and Syle had delayed the start of the public inquisition until Prefect Corin's men were in place.

Prefect Corin said, 'No doubt Rega will infect her new daughter once she is born – and meanwhile Syle will find an amenable candidate to play the role of pythoness. He is our man now. These old departments are utterly decadent, Yama, incurable except by the most radical surgery. We have developed a new system where all, from the humblest clerk to the most senior legate, are answerable to a network of committees. With no centre of power, no single person can influence the department for their own ends. Thus, we are able to take a long-term view with the best interests of Confluence in mind. In time, all will fall under our system, and we can begin to win the war against the heretics.'

They sat side by side on the narrow cot in Yama's cell, lit only by a luminous stick. Yama's fireflies had been stripped from him, as had his knife and the ancient disc which the anchorite had given him. He had been allowed to keep his copy of the Puranas and his clothes, nothing else.

The cell was small and spartan: the cot with its lumpy mattress, a plastic slop bucket, a shelf which folded down from the wall, a square of raffia matting on the stone floor. A spigot in the wall delivered lukewarm, tasteless water. A plastic cup hung on a chain beside the spigot, above a drain no bigger than Yama's outspread hand. Prefect Corin assured Yama that it was no different from his own cell and every other private cell in the Department of Indigenous Affairs. Husbands and wives each kept their own cells when they were married, and children lived in dormitories until they were old enough to be given a job and a cell of their own.

The heart of the Department of Indigenous Affairs was a vast honeycomb of cells, narrow corridors, and chambers where clerks worked, row upon row upon row, fireflies flickering above their heads as they bent over papers and books and slates. A hundred floors crammed into the middle levels of the palace and ringed by outlying territories sequestered from other departments, which contained barracks and armouries.

Tamora and Pandaras and Eliphas were being held a long way from Yama, in their own cells. They were undergoing debriefing, Prefect Corin said, and would be released once it was finished. Yama asked when that might be, and Prefect Corin replied that it might take only a few days, or it might take years.

'Once we know everything,' he said.

'There is no end to questions,' Yama said.

Prefect Corin considered this. He said, 'In your case, that might be true.'

It was never quiet. There was always the sound of voices somewhere, the clash of doors slamming, the tread of feet. Yama lost track of time. To begin with, he was mostly left in darkness, and meals – edible plastic occasionally leavened with a piece of fruit or a dollop of vegetable curry – arrived at irregular intervals. Later, when sunlight was piped into his cell through a glass duct, he could mark, by the waxing and waning of the weak light, the passage of the days.

At intervals, he was taken from the cell and marched by armed guards to a dimly lit room divided into two by a pane of thick glass. It was where he was tested. On one side of the glass was a stool; on the other were fireflies, anything from one to more than a hundred. A disembodied voice would instruct Yama to sit on the stool. Once he was seated, his side of the room would be plunged into darkness. Then the tests would begin.

The first time this happened there was only a single firefly, a brilliant point of light that hung in the centre of the darkened space on the other side of the glass. Yama was told to move it to the right. He refused, and after a long time he was taken to his cell and left in darkness without food. Judging by the ebb and flow of noise, Yama thought that two days might have passed. At last, weak with hunger, he was brought back to the divided room and asked by the voice to repeat the exercise.

Yama obeyed. Both sides had made their point. He had shown his captors that he was acting under coercion; they had shown that him they would not tolerate resistance.

The voice was patient and never tired or varied its precise inflection. It gave each set of instructions twice over and waited until Yama had complied before issuing the next. It took no notice of any mistakes or failures. Yama gradually constructed a fantasy image of the voice's owner. A middle-aged man with cropped iron-grey hair and a square jaw, sitting in a cell much like his own, a single firefly at his shoulder illuminating the script from which he read.

'Up,' the voice would say. 'Up.' And, 'Red firefly circle right, white firefly circle left. Red circle right, white circle left.'

There were hundreds of these exercises. Sometimes Yama was asked to weave complex dances involving a decad of differently coloured fireflies; sometimes he spent long hours moving a single firefly in straight lines back and forth across the darkness, or varying its brightness by increments. He did not try to understand the significance of the different kinds of exercises. He suspected that if there was a pattern, it had been randomised so that he could never decode it. Better to think that there was no pattern at all. Better to think that they did not know what they wanted to find out, or did not know how to find out what they wanted to know.

He worked hard at the tests, although they often left him with bad headaches. Sometimes red and black sparks would fill his sight and after a blank interval he would find himself lying on the floor of the cell, his trousers soaked with stale urine, blood on his lips and tongue. These fits terrified him. Perhaps they were a legacy of the blow to his head (although the wound had completely healed; there was not even a scar), exacerbated by the stress of the exercises. He did not mention them to anyone. He would reveal no weakness to his enemies.

Meanwhile, he was learning more about his abilities every day. Despite the fits, he exulted in the growing control over his powers. And for the first time since he had set out from Aeolis on the road to Ys, he had time to reflect on what he had discovered about himself. Always, his actions had been driven by contingency or by the needs of others. First, under the unwanted protection of Prefect Corin and then, after his escape from the Prefect and (so he thought) from his ordained fate as a minor official in the Department of Indigenous Affairs, in the company of Pandaras and Tamora.

He had promised himself that he would discover the secret of his origin – the silver-skinned woman, the white boat in the middle of the Great River, attended by a cloud of tiny machines – and he had failed. No, it was worse than that. He had not really tried. He had preferred to adventure with Tamora and Pandaras instead of spending every waking moment attempting to unravel the mystery of his origin and purpose.

When he was alone in his cell, he spent much of his time reviewing every step of his adventures between leaving Aeolis and the fall of the Department of Vaticination, weighing every one of his actions and motives and finding them all wanting. He slept a lot, too, and in his sleep his sense of the location and activity of machines expanded. Sometimes he seemed to be suspended in the midst of a vast array of little minds that were both quick and stupefyingly dull, with webs of connectivity blossoming and fading around him like a runaway loom simultaneously weaving and unravelling a cloth in three dimensions. Most of the machines were fireflies, but at the periphery of their immense flock Yama could detect larger machines employed in defence of the department. Further still, glimpsed like bright lights through river fog, were machines whose purpose was totally obscure, and interspersed through the volume of greater and lesser machines were intense points which he recognised as the potential energies of active shrines.

And sometimes, at the furthest edge of these visions, was a faint intimation of the feral machine that he had accidentally drawn down at the merchant's house. It was very far away, hung in isolation beyond and below the end of the world, but it was always there, the iron to which the lodestone of his mind was drawn again and again.

At times he could even perceive the clusters of tiny machines which every sentient person carried at the base of their brain. Faintly, he could feel in these clusters the echoes of the memories of their hosts: it was as if he was the only living person in an impalpable world inhabited by hordes of ghosts mumbling over their last ends.

In his sleep, Yama tried to discover which of the ghosts might be Tamora, or Pandaras, or Eliphas, but this effort would always shift his trance-like apprehension of the machines around him into a dream. Sometimes he ran along a web of narrow paths between the tombs and steles of the City of the Dead, pursued by men who had by grotesque mutilation merged themselves with machines. Sometimes he fled endlessly from the hell-hound, waking with a start in the very moment that its blue light swept across him. And sometimes he harried numberless enemies with bloody zeal, exultant as cities burned and armies fought and looted the length of the world in his name, and woke shocked and ashamed, and swore never to dream such dreams again.

But they were always with him, like splinters of cold metal under his skin.

At intervals, Prefect Corin came and sat with Yama, and slowly, punctuated by long silences, a conversation would begin. Prefect Corin was very interested in Yama's childhood, asking about details, and details within those details, of small events or ceremonies, the geography of Aeolis or the hinterlands of the City of the Dead, the disposition of books in the library of the peel-house, the lessons taught by the librarian, Zakiel, or by the master of the guard, Sergeant Rhodean.

The matter of the white boat, the mystery of Yama's origins, the attempted kidnap by Dr Dismas, Yama's adventures in Ys – these were hardly ever raised. Yama did not have to dissemble about his encounter with the custodians of the City of the Dead and the slate they had shown him, in which he had seen a man of his bloodline turning away to contemplate a sky full of stars. He did not have to describe how he had drawn down the feral machine at the merchant's house, or how he had woken and then defeated the feral machine that had been trapped far beneath the Temple of the Black Well. He did not have to tell Prefect Corin about the merchant's last words, or what the woman in white, the aspect of one of the Ancients of Days, had told him when she had appeared in the temple's shrine.

But it also meant that all these adventures and discoveries were thrust to the back of his mind by the Prefect's patient dissection of the mundane days of his childhood. It was as if all that had happened to Yama in the handful of days between leaving his home in Aeolis and arriving here, in this bleak cell amongst thousands of identical cells in the Department of Indigenous Affairs, had been no more than a vivid dream. It was another reason why, when left alone in the unquiet darkness of his cell, Yama traced and retraced his every footstep between Aeolis and Ys like an ox plodding around and around a water lift, the groove of its path deepening infinitesimally with each circuit. He was afraid that if he forgot even the slightest detail of his adventures he would begin to forget it all, as the unravelling of a piece of cloth began with the fraying of a single thread.

Whenever Yama asked a question, Prefect Corin had a habit of falling silent, as if engaged in an internal dialogue with himself, before asking a question in return. His silences were vast and arid; his gaze burned intently while Yama talked at random about his childhood, like a mountain lion fixing on its prey and waiting for the moment of weakness or uncertainty that would betray it. It was as if he had shaped his intellect to a single point, as the fisher folk flaked pebbles to form the heads of their spears. Yama got no answers from him at all, only questions. And he did not know if the answers he gave the Prefect were sufficient. Like all of his questions, that also went unanswered.

Apart from Prefect Corin and the disembodied voice in the divided, darkened room, Yama's only human contacts were his guards. Four men had sentry duty outside Yama's cell, changing watches in regular succession. They lived in the cells on either side of his, and marched with him from his cell to the room where he took his tests, and back again.

Only one of the guards ever talked with him. This was the old man who took the second of the night watches, from midnight to dawn. His name was Coronetes. He confided to Yama that he did not mind the night watch. He was old, his wife had died, and he did not sleep much.

'You are still young enough to be able to sleep soundly and innocently,' Coronetes said. 'Old men like me fear sleep because it reminds them that soon they will be dead, and the aeons of that final sleep will end only when they wake into the world at the end of time created by the will of the Preservers.'

Yama smiled at this conceit and replied with one of his own. 'Then it will be no sleep at all, because in the interval you will not exist, and so no time will pass. As it says in the first sura of the Puranas, "Before the universe there was no time, for nothing changed." '

'You are a devout young man.'

'I would not say that.'

'I suppose you must have done something bad, to be here. But you are often reading in the Puranas.'

'Do they watch me, then?'

Coronetes nodded vigorously. 'By the same pipe through which light falls. But I do not think they watch now. They sleep.'

Like most of the common people of the Department of Indigenous Affairs, Coronetes was slightly built. His coarse hair was black and vigorous, despite his age, worn in a stout, greased pigtail that fell halfway down his back. Although he was, as he liked to say, as scrawny as a plucked chicken, he was a strong man: muscles knotted his skinny arms as if walnuts had been stuffed under his brown skin. He had volunteered for the army at the beginning of the war. He had fought in the Marsh of the Lost Waters, and still suffered from fluxion of the lungs.

'There are sandflies that enter the mouth or nose of a sleeping man,' he explained, 'and creep into the throat to lay eggs. The larvae get into the lungs and every now and then one turns into a fly and I must cough it out. But I am luckier than many of my comrades, who were felled by the diseases of the midpoint of the world, and by the wild creatures of the marshes and the forests. It is for that reason that the heretics are brothers to the gar, panther and sandfly.'

Coronetes had been so weakened by fluxion and fevers that his wife had not recognised him when he had returned from the war. He had become a clerk, like his father before him, and still wore a clerk's white shirt, for he had been a clerk longer than he had been a soldier, and had risen to become the head of his section. He was fiercely loyal to his department and feared no one, but he was lonely in his old age. He had no children, and had outlived most of his friends.

'We will rule the world,' Coronetes said, 'because no one else will take up the burden. That is why you will confess to the Committee for Public Safety, and that is why you will enlist in our cause. It is the only cause worth fighting for, young man.'

Coronetes and Yama sat on the bed in the cell, lit by a stick of cold green light that Coronetes had stuck on the fold-down shelf. None of the guards had fireflies. No machines came near Yama except those on the far side of the thick glass wall of the testing room.

Yama said, 'I was brought up in the care of a senior member of the department. He believed that service to the ideal of the Preservers was the beginning and end of the duty of every department.'

'The Aedile of Aeolis? He has the luxury of living in a place where his rule and his ideas are undisputed,' Coronetes said. 'But that kind of view is considered old-fashioned everywhere else. It was old-fashioned even when I was a child, and that was a long time ago. You were lucky to be brought up where you were, but now you are in the real world.'

'This cell.'

'It is no different from my cell.'

'Except you will stop me if I try to walk out.'

Coronetes smiled. He had lost most of his teeth, and those that remained were brown and worn down to the gumline. He said, 'Well, that is true. I would do my best. I would kill you if I had to, but I hope it will not be necessary.'

'So do I.'

In fact, Yama never once thought of escaping when Coronetes came to visit him in his cell. It would not only be pointless; it would also be dishonourable, a betrayal of the old man's trust.

'Tell me about the war,' Yama would say, when he found himself disagreeing with one of the old man's praise songs to the great heart and forthright purpose of the Department of Indigenous Affairs.

The old man had many stories of the war, of long marches from one part of the marshes to another, of engagements where nothing could be seen of the enemy but the distant flashes of their weapons, of days and days when nothing at all happened and his company lay in the sun and swapped stories. Most of the war was either marching or waiting, he said. He had only been in two real battles. One had lasted a hundred days, fought to capture a hill later abandoned; the other had been in a town where the citizens had begun to change, and no one knew who was fighting whom.

'It is what the heretics do,' Coronetes said. 'They force the change in a bloodline, and with change comes war. The war is not one war, but many, for we must fight for each unchanged bloodline, to make sure they do not fall under the spell of the heretics when they are most vulnerable. If we did only what we wanted we would be like animals, or worse than animals, because animals are only themselves, and cannot help what they are. The Prefect, he had a more dangerous job – moving amongst the unchanged and identifying and assassinating any heretic inciters who have infiltrated their villages and cities. That is where the war is really fought, you know. The heretics are powerful enemies because they are powerful at persuading the unchanged to see things their way. Our Committee is dedicated to destroying the heretics, but even so it uses some of their techniques to ensure loyalty within the department.'

The Committee for Public Safety had transformed the Department of Indigenous Affairs, turning a musty cabal of clerks and bureaucrats into an aggressive hive of radicals that claimed to be fighting for the souls of all of Ys. The Committee held that everyone was equal, and the lowliest clerk felt that he was as important in the struggle as the most senior general. Coronetes sometimes talked for hours, his eyes gleaming with pride, about the merits of the organisation of the department, of the wonders it had achieved and the paradise it would bring about once it had defeated the heretics and had united all of Confluence.

Yama preferred to hear about the war. The patrols that looped through a country of tall grasses without ever engaging the enemy, the camps amongst the buttress roots of trees of the virgin forest of the great marshes, the geometry of advances and retreats. He learned the jargon of the common soldiers, the rudimentary sign language they used when the enemy was close by. More than ever, he yearned to join the army as a cateran, to flee downriver and lose himself in the war.

Yama knew that these conversations were another form of interrogation, but nevertheless thought of Coronetes as a friend, and looked forward to the time when, late at night, there would be a scratching at the door and he would ask the old man to enter. Although Yama was the prisoner and Coronetes his guard, they both sustained the fiction that Yama was the host and Coronetes the visitor. Coronetes always waited for Yama's invitation before unlocking the door, and neither commented on the fact that he locked it again once he was inside. That Yama forbore arguing against Coronetes' transparent propaganda was part of this fiction – that, and his suspicion that anything he said against the Department of Indigenous Affairs or the Committee for Public Safety would be used against him. Yama was always disappointed on those nights when Coronetes' inquiring scratch failed to come, and was firmly settled into the unvarying routines of his captivity when the ambush changed everything.

11

'YOU ARE A MONSTER'

Yama was returning to his cell after a testing session, with two guards walking a little way in front of him and two behind. His hands were bound by a loop of plastic that remorselessly tightened if he attempted to test its strength. He had learnt to bend his arms and rest his fists against his chest, as if in prayer, to minimise movement. Coronetes had told him that this form of restraint, called the serpent, could amputate the hands of those who tried to get free, or who wore it for too long.

The long corridor was lit only by the luminous sticks carried by the guards. Yama moved in a bubble of dim green light, with darkness ahead and darkness behind, every ten paces passing a facing pair of doors. The doors were slabs of dense, grainy white plastic deeply recessed in the fused rock walls, as indistinguishable from each other as cells in a honeycomb.

Yama was thinking about the tests. In the past few days he had been fitted with a metal cap while moving the fireflies about. And the fireflies were changing, too. At first they had become slow to respond to his commands; now their little minds were hedged with loops and knots of futile logic that he had to unpick before they would obey him. Those testing him were beginning to probe the limits of his abilities; he was beginning to worry about what might happen when those limits were reached.

Without warning, two doors were flung open, one on either side. Three young men rushed out from the left, two from the right. They yelled hoarsely, clubs cocked at their shoulders. The leader swung a killing star on a short chain. Yama ducked and rammed the man in the chest with his shoulder, catching him off balance. The man slammed into the wall and Yama managed to follow through and use his forehead as a hammer to smash the man's nose before someone kicked his legs out from under him. The serpent tightened around his wrists when he tried to break his fall, the back of his head struck the floor, dazing him, and two of the attackers began to kick and pummel him while the others fought with the guards. Yama tucked his head into his chest and curled up as tightly as he could. There were no machines he could use against his assailants – like the guards, the young men had no fireflies – but they were too close to each other to use their clubs properly and they wore only soft-soled shoes, so that their kicks bruised rather than broke bones. Then someone fell heavily on Yama, saving him from the worst of the blows. A moment later one of the guards fired his slug pistol, and the attackers ran.

Yama was hauled to his feet by two of the guards. It was Coronetes who had fallen on him. The old man's white shirt was ripped down the front and wet with blood. One of the guards knelt beside him and the other two dragged Yama away. The serpent was a band of intense pain around his wrists; his hands had lost all feeling.

The guards would not answer his questions. They unclasped the serpent and left him alone in his cell. His fingers were numb and pale, and felt as if they had swollen to twice their normal size. They started to throb as blood flowed back into them; Yama took that as a good sign. His chest ached with each breath, but the pain was not sharp, and he did not think any ribs were broken. He had cut his tongue, there were pulpy bruises on his scalp, and there was blood on his shirt, so much blood that the shirt stuck to his skin. He took it off and ran his hands over his flanks and back and found many deep bruises but no other wounds. Then he realised that it was Coronetes' blood.

He had rinsed out his mouth and started to wash himself when the two guards came back. They still would not answer his questions. They fitted a serpent to his wrists again and marched him out of his cell. As always, the corridors were deserted. He was led through a great hall crammed with long tables which looked as if they had been abandoned only moments before: pens flung down on unfinished sentences; slates still showing ranks of glowing figures; half-empty bowls of tea. More guards were waiting at the far side of the room. A hood was thrust over his head and the forced march was resumed. At one point he was taken across an open space – cold air whipped around him – and soon after that the hood was ripped from his head and the serpent was unclasped.

He turned just in time to see a door slam shut. It was less than an hour after he had been attacked.

The room was four times the size of his cell, and looked even bigger because there was no furniture apart from a narrow cot. The walls were fused rock, smooth and slick as glass; the floor was rammed earth. It was shaped like an egg, and at the narrower end sunlight flooded through a big glass bull's-eye.

Yama found a spigot that yielded an icy trickle of rust-coloured water, and stripped off his trousers and washed Coronetes' blood from his bruised body as best he could. There was a thin grey blanket on the striped ticking of the cot's mattress; he wrapped it around his shoulders and for a long time knelt by the window, gazing out at the blue sky. By pressing his bruised face against the cold glass, he could glimpse a segment of a steep slope of tumbled black rocks. Trees clung amongst the rocks, their branches all bent in the same direction. Wind fluted beyond the roundel of glass, and now and then birds slanted through the air, tilting on winds beyond the edge of the scree slope.

He broke his fingernails prying at the glass, but it was firmly embedded in the smooth rock. It did not break or crack when he kicked at it; he succeeded only in bruising his heel. He had just begun to scrape at the hard earth at the bottom edge of the window when a chirurgeon came in, flanked by two guards. The chirurgeon tested Yama's limbs, probed his mouth and shone a bright light into his eyes, then left without saying a word. Another guard brought in a slop bucket and tossed Yama's blood-stained shirt onto the bed, and then Prefect Corin entered.

After the guards had locked the door behind them, Prefect Corin sat on one end of the cot. Yama stayed by the window. He was conscious of being naked under the thin blanket. He said, 'How is Coronetes?'

'Dead. As are your attackers.'

'It seems that your department is not of one mind about me.'

'It was not a conspiracy. They wanted revenge because you had blinded their friends. You did not try to defend yourself. Why was that?'

'I believe that I broke someone's nose.'

'You know what I mean, boy.'

'I am your prisoner, not your servant. I do not have to explain myself.'

'You are the prisoner of the department. I am here because I was given the responsibility of escorting you to Ys. I am still responsible for you. You may not believe me, but I have your best interests at heart.'

Yama smiled. It hurt. 'Then you endure our conversations as a punishment?'

'It is my duty,' Prefect Corin said. 'Just as it was my duty to bring you to Ys.'

'You failed at that and you failed to catch me by trickery, too. In the end you had to use force. Perhaps you are not very good at carrying out your duty.'

Prefect Corin rarely smiled, but he smiled now. It lasted only for a moment and did not thaw his wintry expression in the slightest. He said, 'Yet here you are, all the same. If I was superstitious, I might say that it was fate, and that our lives are bound together. I have my duty. You have your duty, too, Yamamanama. You know what it is, but you resist it. I wonder why it is that you are so ungrateful. Your father is a senior officer of the department, and so in a sense the department raised you. It educated you and trained you, and yet you resist acknowledging your considerable obligation. You believe that your own will is stronger than the collective will of the department. Believe me, you are wrong.'

'I do not know what you want of me.' A silence. Yama corrected himself. 'I do not know what the department wants of me.'

Prefect Corin considered this. At last, he said, 'Then you will be here a long time, and so will your friends. It is not about what you know, but what you can do.'

'I am sorry that Coronetes was killed. He did not deserve it.'

'Nor did the men who attacked you. They were not much more than boys, and foolish boys at that, but they were brave. Their only mistake was that they showed more loyalty to their friends than to the department.'

Yama said, 'Do you wish that they had killed me?'

'You are a monster. You do not know it, but you are. You have more power than any individual should ever possess, but you use it without purpose, and refuse to serve, for no other reason than pride. You could help win the war, and that is the only reason why you are kept alive. Some want you dead. I have argued against it, but I cannot defend you forever. Especially if you continue to resist.'

'I have performed every test as best I could.'

'This is not about the tests. It is about loyalty. It is about doing what is right.'

'I will not serve blindly,' Yama said. 'If I am here, with such gifts as

I have, there must be a purpose to it. That is what I want to discover. That is why I came to Ys.'

'You should try to be true to the example of your brother. He served. He served well.'

'I will go to war in a moment, but you will not allow it. So please do not invoke Telmon's bravery.'

Prefect Corin put his hands on his knees and leaned forward, looking directly into Yama's face. His gaze was steady and unforgiving. He said, 'You are very young. Too young for what you possess, perhaps. Too young to control or understand it.'

'I will not serve blindly,' Yama said again. 'I have thought long and hard about this. If there are those in the department who want me to help them, then they should talk with me. Or you should kill me now, and then at least you will know that I will never fight against you.'

'We are all one, hand and brain,' Prefect Corin said. 'Your father did not like the way things had changed, but still he served.'

'Coronetes once said something similar.'

'But you will not serve. You set yourself apart. You are a monster of vanity, boy.' Prefect Corin stood up and tossed something on the mattress of the bed. 'Here is your copy of the Puranas. Read it carefully, and consider your position.'

After Prefect Corin left, Yama broke a thin strip of wood from the frame of the cot and used this and water from the spigot to loosen the packed earth at the base of the window. The sky had darkened by the time he had dug to the depth of his hand and found the point where glass merged seamlessly with fused rock. It seemed likely that the window was no more than a place where the rock walls of the room had been made transparent, but apart from the door it was the only possible way out of the cell.

Yama began to extend the little hole he had made, scraping away hard earth a few crumbs at a time until the frayed strip of wood met something embedded in the dirt. He probed carefully with his bleeding fingertips and felt a thin curved edge, then dug around it until he could pull it free.

It was a ceramic disc, exactly like the one the anchorite had given him. But the Aedile's excavations had turned up thousands of similar discs around the tombs of the City of the Dead, and there was no reason to believe that this one should be any different from those.

Yama dug a little more, but could find no potential weakness in the window's edge. He filled in the hole he had made and leaned against the window and watched the shadows of the bent trees lengthen across the tumbled rocks. He fell asleep, and woke to find a constellation of faint lights hanging outside. They were fireflies, drawn away from the wild creatures that lived amongst the sliding stones. Beyond the shifting sparks of the fireflies, the small red swirl of the Eye of the Preservers was printed on the black sky.

Something nagged at Yama, like a speck in his eye. It was the disc, shining softly on the dirt floor. He picked it up. It was warmer than his own skin, and had become translucent, with fine filaments and specks of cold blue light shifting within its thickness.

There was an active shrine nearby.

He could suddenly feel it, with the same absolute sense of direction that linked him with the feral machine. He shivered and drew the blanket around himself. He knew that he could activate the shrine even at this distance and, although it was horribly risky, it seemed that he had no other choice. Before he could frighten himself by thinking through all the consequences, he willed it.

Beyond the round pane of the window, the fireflies scattered as if before a great wind.

Yama pulled on his damp trousers and tucked the sliver of wood inside the waistband. Then he wrapped the blanket around his shoulders and sat by the window in the dim red light of the Eye of the Preservers, waiting for something to happen. At intervals, he held the disc up to his eye, but the shifting patterns of luminous lines and specks told him nothing.

Perhaps the shrine was dead after all… But then he knew it was not, as surely as if a light had been shone in his face. He got up and paced around the room, a fierce excitement growing like a pressure in his chest. Presently he heard shouts, and the thin snapping of slug guns. The sounds of distant combat lasted several minutes; then there was the scream of an energy pistol's discharge and wisps of white smoke began to curl around the edges of the cell door.

As Yama scrambled to his feet, the door was flung back with a crash. A guard tumbled in ahead of a thick billow of smoke. His tunic was torn and the pelt on one side of his face was scorched and shrivelled to blackened peppercorns.

'Come with me!' he yelled. 'Now!'

Yama straightened his back and drew the blanket around his shoulders. The guard glared at him and raised his rifle. 'Come now!'

For a moment, Yama feared that the man had lost his mind and would execute him on the spot. Then the guard looked over his shoulder and screamed. He scrambled across the cell, knocking Yama aside and fetching up against the window, clutching his rifle to his chest and staring wide-eyed at the door. Yama faced it squarely, his heart beating quickly and lightly. Blue light filled the frame. And then, without any sense of transition, the hell-hound was inside the cell.

Its pillar of blue flame seemed somehow to extend beyond the floor and ceiling. There was a continual crackling hiss as its energies ate the air that touched its surface. Its heat beat against Yama's skin. He had to squint against its brilliance as he held up the disc. It took all of his will to stand still.

He said, 'I do not know if we have already met, or if you are brother to the one I called forth before, but in any case I apologise for my behaviour. I ran away because I did not know what I had called, and I was afraid. But now I have freed you knowingly, and I ask for your help.'

He did not see the hell-hound move, but there was a brief wash of heat on his skin and suddenly it was gone. The guard screamed again. When Yama turned, the man fell to his knees and flung his arm across his face. The sleeve of his tunic started to smoulder. Yama realised what had happened, and looked away before he killed the man.

He had expected the hell-hound to clear a way for his escape. Instead, it had enveloped him.

He was the centre of a blue radiance that fell on everything he looked at. He did not feel any trace of the hell-hound's heat. That was a property of the outermost shell of its energies. Instead, he was gripped by a tremendous exhilaration. His bruises and cracked ribs no longer hurt. There was a prickling all over his body as every hair tried to stand away from its neighbours.

There was a short corridor beyond the cell. Guards scrambled in panic through the door at the far end, although one paused and shot at Yama several times before fleeing, his clothes and hair smouldering. Yama followed them into a wide plaza. Sheer black rock rose on three sides; there was nothing but the darkening sky on the other.

Men ran or stood their ground and fired. Slugs caught and sank slowly in the outer edge of the blue light that surrounded Yama, flaring brightly before evaporating. An officer fired an energy pistol, but its discharge merely whitened Yama's vision for a moment.

He ignored the guards and strode to the edge of the plaza. A railing glowed red-hot before melting away. Directly below was the steep slope of black rocks that he had seen from the window of the cell. His sight washed with white light again for an instant – the officer with the pistol was foolish, but brave. Yama did not look back, but gave himself to the air.

He floated down like a soap bubble, landing beside a dead pine tree which immediately burst into crackling flame. The air was alive with things which hummed and whined. Bits of rock flew off and the foliage of the stunted trees danced jerkily. Yama realised that the guards were still firing at him. He walked to the edge of the slope and gave himself to the air once more.

It took a long time to fall. The hell-hound was subject to the world's gravity field, but could modify it so that it fell at a constant rate. Yama saw a long slope spread below him, curving away on either side and studded with the lights of temples, sanctuaries and the offices of those lesser departments which had long ago lost battles for territory inside the palace and now clung to existence on its roof. He gave the hell-hound an order, and it slid sideways through the air.

The glass-walled tunnel that linked the street of pleasure houses with the territory of the Department of Indigenous Affairs had been repaired with wooden panelling that burst into flames at a touch, and fell away. Yama stepped through and walked amidst reflections of blue fire into a square under a high domed roof.

Three guards ran into the gateway on the far side. Their officer drew his pistol and fired twice, and then stood amazed when he saw that the energy beam had done no harm. The air was hazed with recondensed particles of rock vaporised by the deflected pistol blast; Yama's gaze burnt through them and glanced upon the officer, who threw up his hands to protect his eyes.

'Fetch your masters,' Yama said. 'Do you understand? I wish to speak with them.'

The officer turned and ran through the gateway. Yama followed. He felt as if he could run forever through the maze of corridors and halls, and laughed wildly when men shot at him. Slugs embedded in the hell-hound's outermost shell turned into molten stars that flared and died.

He entered a huge refectory hall. Hundreds of people ran from him through a maze of tables. A confused cloud of fireflies billowed after them. Tables and chairs charred as Yama brushed past. He shouted for the masters of this place to come out, but there was no answer except for a volley of rifle shots from a gallery above the arched doorways at the far end of the hall. Frayed battle standards hung above the central dais of the hall. Yama stared at them until they caught fire, then leapt on to the dais and shouted that he would speak with the masters of this place or burn it all down.

Men ran forward, dragging a long hose. They sprayed water at Yama, but the water exploded into steam when it struck the hell-hound's envelope and the men retreated, clutching scalded faces and hands. An officer on a floating disc fired his pistol. The blue glow of the hell-hound flared white. The chairs and the long table, inlaid with ironwood and turtleshell ivory, burst into flames; the stone of the dais burned Yama's feet through the thin soles of his boots. He jumped down, stared at the officer until the man's clothes caught fire, and strode through the nearest door.

Yama's passage towards the heart of the Department of Indigenous Affairs was a confusion of shouts and screams, flame and smoke and gunfire. He was filled with an exultant rage. Red and black lightning jagged his vision. He might have killed decads of men. Hundreds. He did not know. His rage had taken him and he let it lead him where it would.

When it cleared, he was standing at the base of a vast circular shaft that rose through a hundred floors. The temple of Aeolis, the largest building Yama had known before he had come to Ys, could easily have fitted into it. Its looming walls were hung with tiers of balconies; its vast floor was crowded with desks. Books burned in stacked shelving, in tumbled heaps on the floor. Scraps of burning paper flew into the darkness above like sparks up the flue of a chimney.

Soldiers armed with slug rifles stood in front of every door around the base of the shaft, draped from head to foot in black cloth. They kept up a steady bombardment; the floor around Yama was soon littered with flecks of molten metal. A machine spun slowly through the air towards him, its mind defended by intricate loops of self-engulfing logic. He punched through these defences and the machine suddenly screamed upwards, its load of explosive detonating with a white flash and a flat thump at the top of the shaft, half a league above.

'I know you are here, Prefect,' Yama shouted. 'Show yourself!'

A voice spoke from the air, ordering Yama to surrender – it was the same even, neutral voice that had instructed him during the interminable tests with the fireflies. He laughed at it and then, inspired, shut down the light of every firefly, so that now the vast circular space was lit only by the blue glow of the hell-hound, the flashes of the rifles around the perimeter, and the myriad fires started by spent slugs. Everything was hazed with smoke. Yama felt a tightness in his chest and a scorched taste in his mouth. The air was becoming unbreathable. He knew that he would have to leave soon, and that he would have to kill the soldiers to do it.

Yet still he felt a steady exhilaration thrilling in his blood, a boundless energy. He did not consider himself trapped, but called out again for the masters of this place. As if in answer, the floor heaved sharply. Yama staggered, almost fell. Dust and shards of tiling fell from somewhere above, smashing down amongst the desks; for a moment, Yama stood inside a sleet of burning particles.

The soldiers were as shaken as he was. They were still regrouping when a fresh wedge of troops entered through the high doors beneath a long gallery. They parted, and an old man stepped from their midst. He was slightly built and his dress was no different from that of an ordinary clerk, but he held himself proudly and at his gesture the soldiers around him immediately thrust three people to the front of their ranks.

Tamora shaded her eyes and called out, 'Yama! Are you inside that thing?'

'He has come to free us,' Pandaras said.

Yama checked himself. He had been about to run to them.

The old man walked forward, stepping as delicately as a cat amongst broken shards and little fires and heaps of burning books. He paused when the floor rippled and shook dust into the air, then walked on until he was fifty paces from the blue energies of the hell-hound. His eyes were masked by a strip of cloth, jet-black against the white pelt of his face.

'I had not thought ever to see one of these things,' the old man said. 'I am Escanes, Yamamanama. I have come to ask why you are doing this.'

'I discovered that it is only a machine,' Yama said. 'I should thank you for helping me focus on what I needed to do.'

'It is an inertial field caster,' Escanes said. 'Amongst other things. Anything trying to move through it gives up momentum in the form of heat. It burns with blue light because light reflected from it is shifted from lower to higher energy, and it is hot because of the energy released from dust and air in motion against it. I should warn you that we fully understand it.'

'Yet I control it, and you do not. I can destroy everything around me with a look.'

'Because we understand such things,' Escanes said, 'we can work against them. You are not invulnerable. You should not have brought it here. You endanger the records of the department.'

'I will destroy them all unless you let my friends go.'

'I am empowered to speak for the department, Yamamanama. Listen to what it has to say. We will let your three friends go. You will stay.'

'You will let them go, and let me go, too.'

'I do not think so,' Escanes said mildly. 'Think quickly. One word from me, and they will die.'

'Then you will have no hold over me.'

The floor shook again. Yama flexed his knees, as if he was on a boat. Escanes held the edge of a half-charred desk until the shaking stopped. A balcony gave way and smashed down twenty storeys into a stack of bookshelves on the far side of the shaft.

Yama said, 'Someone is attacking you, I think.'

'Our enemies believe that we are weakened from within,' Escanes said. 'We will prove them wrong. It is a trivial matter, and not one that concerns you. What matters is your answer.'

'Let my friends go.'

'And you will stay?'

'No. You will come with me.'

Yama sprang forward, and the hell-hound relaxed its perimeter for an instant. Escanes threw up his hands, but he was already inside the hell-hound's envelope. Yama caught him and turned him around, and held the sharpened bit of wood to his throat. Escanes struggled, but Yama held him easily.

'Tell your people to let my friends go.'

'They will not obey me. I am only a mouth for the department.'

'Your tunic is silk, dominie, not artificial cotton. Your dogma requires you to appear to be the same as all others in the department, but you raise yourself higher than most.'

'We are all one.'

'Yet some value themselves more than others.'

Escanes tried to turn his head, but Yama jabbed the sliver of wood into the loose flesh of the old man's neck and urged him forward. The soldiers raised their rifles, but an officer snapped an order and they lowered them again.

'If my friends walk out of here with me, then your life will be spared,' Yama told the old man. 'I promise that I will not cause any more damage. You will be free to defend yourself against your enemies. But if anything happens to my friends, then I join your enemies and fight against you.'

'Fight with us, Yamamanama,' Escanes said. 'You could be the most powerful general in our army.'

'You would have made that offer already, if it was genuine. Now repeat to your men what I have told you.'

It was easy to find the way back to the gate – the hell-hound had left a trail of scorched doors and scored floor tiles. Yama let Tamora, Pandaras and Eliphas walk ahead of him. Escanes did not struggle, but continued to try to convince Yama to give himself up to the mercy and generosity of the department until at last Yama lost patience and clamped a hand over his mouth.

Yama stopped at the gate, told the others to go ahead. 'While I stand here, no one can get past. Eliphas, do you know how to reach the place Magon took us to?'

Eliphas blinked and said, 'It finally caught you, brother.' Blue light shone in his eyes.

'No, Eliphas. I caught it. I understand it now. The place Magon took us to – you must take Pandaras and Tamora there now.'

'I will try.'

Pandaras said, 'He had a harder time of it than me, master. I knew nothing important, so they didn't hurt me. It was just talking, and you know how I love that. I told them many stories.'

The boy wore the white shirt and black trousers of a clerk. Yama said, 'It seems you have adopted their ways.'

'Kill them all,' Tamora said. Her head had been shaved, and her face was a palimpsest of fresh bruises laid over old.

'We will talk later, Tamora. Go now.'

Escanes said, 'She is right. You should kill us all, for else we will follow you to the end of the river and beyond.'

'I am not your enemy,' Yama said.

'Anyone who does not serve is our enemy.'

'I will serve the Preservers, if I can, but not your department.'

'So says any man who is full of pride. Such a one believes that by doing as he wishes he serves a higher power, but instead he has allowed himself to become a slave of his base appetites. We are the arm of the Preservers, boy. We strive against their enemies at the midpoint of the world. Stand with us.'

'I do not know why I was born here, in this time and place. But I do know that it was not to serve your hunger for power.'

Tamora, Pandaras and Eliphas had disappeared into the tunnel at the far end of the plaza. Yama told Escanes to close his eyes, and thrust him towards the gate. The hell-hound's envelope had grown hotter because it had contracted, and the old man's clothes smouldered as he staggered away.

The soldiers rushed forward. Yama ran across the square into the tunnel and plunged through the hole he had burnt in the patchwork repair to the tunnel's glass wall.

The night spread before him. The hell-hound turned and dipped and in a sudden rush he was down, standing beside the white fountain in the middle of the long lawn. Yama thanked the hell-hound and dismissed it, and felt a gust of heat as it moved away from him. It stood before him for a moment, then shrank into itself and rose, a bright blue star that dwindled away against the black bulk of the palace.

Yama stood alone in darkness in the centre of a circle of charred grass. He thought of returning to the library of the Department of Apothecaries and Chirurgeons to ask what the chief of clerks, Kun Norbu, had discovered about his bloodline. He thought of running away. But he knew that he could not. He had saved his three companions from immediate danger, but they were still within the bounds of the palace, and the Department of Indigenous Affairs would not rest until they were recaptured. Besides, he was so very tired, and his torn muscles and cracked ribs ached badly. It was as if he drew every breath through a rack of knives. The hell-hound had lent him some of its energies while it had enveloped him, but now he had only his own reserves of strength to draw upon.

He sat at the edge of one of the fountain's wide shallow basins and drank cold water and splashed it on his face. Presently, a small constellation of fireflies gathered around him, lighting his way as he crossed the long lawn and went down the steps. When he reached the beginning of the path through the grove of bamboo, he sat down and rested for a few minutes, breathing hard and feeling beads of sweat roll down his sides. The skeletal tower, hung with creepers, loomed above. Yama struggled to his feet and went on.

White birds, ghostly in the darkness, fled from him. Yama caught at bamboo stems and lost his grasp and slid down a dusty slope, fetching up against a low wall. Startled goats bounded away, their wooden bells clanking. Yama lay on his back, looking up at the black sky, the few blurred stars, the red swirl of the Eye of the Preservers.

After a while, the villagers came to discover what had disturbed their animals. They were armed with spears and slings, for lynxes and fierce red foxes prowled the roof, and the Lords of the Mountain were restless that night. But they found only Yama, asleep on the cropped grass.

12
THE HUSBANDMEN

'There, dominie,' the headman of the village said. 'You see? The Lords of the Mountain quarrel amongst themselves.'

Yama followed the line of the headman's arm. High above the terraced fields of the little village, a thread of black smoke rose from the upper slope of the palace.

'A bad time,' Yama said.

'Not really,' the headman said. 'The Lords will pay more for our food when they are done fighting – the winners will need to feed those they have captured.'

'They will not take it from you by force?'

The headman was squat and muscular, with a seamed face and lively black eyes, and skin the colour of the red earth. His white hair was done up in a braid that fell to the small of his back, and he wore much-darned leggings and a ragged but clean homespun tunic with many pockets. He touched his lips with the tips of his fingers. It was a gesture characteristic of the husbandmen. It meant *no*. 'All serve the will of the Preservers. And we are their most faithful servants.'

'Yet all of those fighting each other also profess to serve the will of the Preservers.'

'We don't question how the Preservers order things,' the headman said. 'Are you feeling stronger, dominie?'

'A little. Resting here in the sun helps.'

Last night, Yama had been given the headman's hammock. An old woman had looked into his eyes and laid her head on his chest to listen to his breathing and heartbeat, and then had given him an infusion of dried leaves to drink. When he had woken, most of the husbandmen were already out in the fields, but the headman and his wife had stayed behind to tend their guest. They had given him dried fish and sweet rice cakes to eat, and a homespun tunic to cover his bare chest.

Yama was still very weak. He was badly bruised from the beating he had received when he had been ambushed, and controlling the hell-hound had been as exhausting as riding a high-spirited thoroughbred across a hundred leagues of difficult terrain. He was content to spend the day lying in a hammock under the shade of freshly cut banana leaves by the sun-warmed wall of the headman's house, listening to the headman's stories and watching children play in the dust of the village square.

The husbandmen believed that they had been brought to the world to tend the gardens of the palace; the headman claimed that the terraces spread above and below the village had once held beds of roses and lilies, jasmine and sweet herbs.

'The first masters of the world walked here in the morning and the evening, dominie. There were different gardens for the morning and the evening of every day of the year, and we tended them all. That's why we look out across the city towards the place where the sun rises and sets.'

'What did they look like, your masters?'

Yama had never seen a picture of the Sirdar, those who had ruled the world when it had been newly made. None of the Sirdar had ever been interred in the City of the Dead, and none of the picture slates or aspects had revealed so much as a glimpse of them. They had never presented themselves to the ordinary people but had ruled invisibly, implementing their wishes through an extensive civil service of eunuchs and hierodules.

'They were small as children, and their skin shone like polished metal,' the headman said.

Yama shivered, remembering that the dead woman in the white boat, on whose breast he had been found, had silver skin.

The headman said, 'Words are poor things. If I had a picture, I would gladly show it you, dominie. But we have no pictures of those times.'

'It must have been long ago.'

The headman nodded. He sat cross-legged in the white dust by Yama's hammock. Blades of sunlight falling through the notched banana leaves striped his face. He said, 'The world was young then, dominie, but we remember those times. We are not able to change, you see. Nor do we wish to, for we would forget how it was, and how it will be again.'

Some believed that the Sirdar had been destroyed by their successors, others that they had achieved enlightenment and passed from the world. There had been many rulers after them, but it was said that, next to the Builders, the Sirdar had been closest to the Preservers. The husbandmen believed that their old masters would come again, opening the sealed core of the Palace and stepping forth as a flower steps forth from a seed. All the world would become a garden then, changed and unchanged bloodlines would achieve enlightenment and ascend into the Eye of the Preservers, and the husbandmen would spread across the face of the world they longed to inherit.

'Trees will drop fruit into our hands, and corn and grain will grow on the plains by the river without need of tilling or sowing. Until then,' the headman said, with a smile that deepened the creases in his clay-red face, 'we must toil in the fields.'

'Perhaps those days are not far off. Great things happen in the world.'

Yama was thinking of the war against the heretics, but the headman knew nothing of the world beyond the Palace of the Memory of the People. He believed that Yama was talking about the conflict in the heights above them. He said, 'These may be the end times, but not because the Lords of the Mountain quarrel. There has been war before. Long ago, long after our first dear masters stopped walking in the gardens, but while the gardens were still gardens and had not yet been turned into fields, one department took over all the others. It was known as the Head of the People. It ruled for many generations, and its rule was fierce and cruel. It was a great weight on all the peoples of the world. But when it had conquered all, the Head of the People found itself without enemies and turned inwards. Soon it was fighting against itself. The Hierarchs arose and ended that war, and in turn they fell after the war against the Insurrectionists, for victory cost them dear. Some of the oldest departments are parts of that greater department, although they have long forgotten that they were once part of a greater whole, much as a lizard's tail forgets that it was shed to escape an enemy, and grows into another lizard exactly like the first. Bloodlines forget much when they change; we cannot change and so we forget nothing, like the lizard that lost the tail in the first place.'

'I recently met someone else who said much the same thing.'

'That would be one of the mirror people. Yes, they remember much, too, but they have not lived on the mountain as long as we have. They are really fisher folk, dominie. They left their living on the Great River when the city spread along the shore, and found work as fishers of men instead. They know much, but we know more. We understand the signs. We know the significance of the hell-hound. Twice it was seen in the past decad. The first time, it vanished into the mountain after passing along the ridge above this village. The second time, it was seen floating through the air, and there was a ghost inside it.'

'I know.'

The headman touched his forehead. *Yes*. 'Then you saw it too, dominie. Perhaps you do not remember that hell-hounds were used as weapons.'

'So one of the mirror people told me.'

The headman touched his forehead again. 'And they learnt it from us, for they arrived after the war with the machines.'

He meant the end of the Age of Insurrection, when the Hierarchs had defeated the feral machines and those bloodlines which had risen against the will of the Preservers: a war which had laid waste to half the world.

'We remember how great swathes of the gardens were destroyed by the energies of packs of hell-hounds,' the headman said, 'and how shrines were silenced. Now the hell-hounds have come again, and one was carrying a ghost or a demon. I had not expected it, but if such wonders are seen in the world, then these may be the end times for which we have waited so long.'

'It was not a ghost,' Yama said, 'and it certainly was not a demon. I should know, because I was there.'

The headman nodded. 'As you say, dominie. We believe that you might have been hurt by the hell-hound. That is why you are confused. But whatever you believe you saw, it was an illusion. Only ghosts or demons from the space inside the shrines may ride hell-hounds. It is how they visit the world. They bring nothing but destruction.'

'Well, it carried me here,' Yama said.

The headman touched his lips. 'Perhaps it was chasing you, although I understand that hell-hounds take little notice of men, who are no more than ghosts to them. More likely you were chasing it. Perhaps you hoped to force it to return to the world inside the shrines. We saw it coming towards our village, and we hid from it, but it is clear that you saved us, or tried to save us. You did not know what you were chasing, so I cannot say that you were foolish, but you were certainly brave. Its energies knocked you down the slope, where we found you. That is why your mind is confused and why you are so weak. But the weakness and the confusion will pass. You are a young man, and strong. Lucky for you, dominie. Such an encounter would have killed most men outright.'

'I was not fighting it. I used it, and it used me. I will show you if you let me.'

Yama's sight washed with red when he tried to sit up in the hammock. He fell back, and felt the headman's dry, hard fingers at his brow.

'Rest,' the headman said. 'Rest is the best medicine.'

'I rode it,' Yama said. 'I really did. It is only another kind of machine. I rode it all the way down the side of the palace, and I rescued my friends.'

Or perhaps he only said it to himself, for the headman did not seem to hear him. He settled the blanket around Yama's shoulders and went away. Yama slept for a while, and woke to find the headman's wife wiping his brow with a wet cloth. He was inside the headman's house again. Night pressed at the window above his hammock but the little room was full of light, for hundreds of fireflies hung in the air.

'You have a fever,' the old woman said. 'In a little while I will bring you some lemon broth.'

Yama clutched the wide sleeve of her embroidered shirt. 'I walked inside it,' he said. 'It carried me through the air.'

The old woman gently lifted his hand away from her sleeve. 'You have been dreaming, dominie. You are very weak, weaker than you believe, and so your dreams seem more real than the world itself. But I do not think that you will die. You will take some broth, and you will sleep. We will look after you until your strength returns.'

Yama lay in the hammock for two days, drifting between waking and sleeping. Whenever he woke, he dismissed the fireflies that had been drawn to him while he slept. At last, no more came: he had exhausted the local population. The shadows seemed to be thronged with dreams, and the dreams mingled with heightened scenes of his recent adventures. Again, he walked with Prefect Corin through the hot dry lands on the road between Aeolis and Ys, but now the Prefect wore a crown of fireflies. Again, he stood at the edge of the deep shaft in the Temple of the Black Well – and this time it was the hell-hound rather than the feral machine which rose out of black air. It enveloped him and carried him high about the roofs of the city to the top of the palace. And at the windy pinnacle of that vast and ancient building, once a mountain that had floated into the void and far older than the world, with the city spread below on one side and the Great River on the other, he stood with his sweetheart, Derev. She clasped him to her breast and spread her strong wings and they flew higher still, until the entire world lay beneath them.

When he woke, dry-mouthed, weak, aching in every bone but clear-headed, it was morning, and Tamora was there. He was so glad to see her that he started to weep.

She grinned and said, 'So the hero isn't dead. You are such a fool, Yama.'

'I am pleased to see you, too, Tamora.'

She wore a bronze-tinted corselet he had not seen before, a short skirt of red leather strips, and a metal cap on her shaven, scarred head. She said, 'I thought you were dead. I thought that the weapon you used against them must have killed you. Don't ever play the hero again, Yama. Or at least let me help you. That's what I am paid for.'

'I lost my money, Tamora, and my knife. I have my book, though. It is all I have.'

He had carried the copy of the Puranas through all his adventures. And he remembered that although he had lost the disc which the anchorite had given him, he had found a replacement. He reached for it, and Tamora caught his hand and then they were holding each other. Her strong arms; her spicy odour; her heat.

Tamora said, 'Well, you're alive. O, Yama, you are such a fool!'

They held each other for a long time, until Pandaras came in.

Eliphas had led Tamora and Pandaras to the home of the mirror people, and Lupe had sheltered them until the search for the escaped prisoners passed into the lower levels of the palace. The war between the Department of Indigenous Affairs and its lesser rivals was intensifying; Tamora said that this would make their escape easy.

'I have arranged for passage downriver. It took all the money I had, and I had to spend yours, too. But we can always earn more.'

'I know that I have to leave the city, Tamora. But I should leave you, too, and Pandaras. Simply by being with me you are in great danger.'

'Grah. Your brains have been cooked by that thing. I will come with you for your own good. I suppose you could try to dismiss the rat-boy, but he will follow you anyway. I think he is in love.'

From the doorway, where he had taken up position like a guard, Pandaras said, 'I merely do my duty as a squire.'

He still wore the black trousers and white shirt that was the uniform of the clerks of the Department of Indigenous Affairs. An ivory-handled poniard sheathed in black leather hung from a loop at his waist.

Tamora shrugged. 'Then there is the old man.'

'Eliphas.'

'I don't trust him. Tell me you don't need him, and make me happy.'

'Eliphas is a friend. He helped me without being asked, and his friend promised to search the library of the Department of Apothecaries and Chirurgeons for records of my bloodline. I must go there before we leave. It is only a few hours' walk. All I want to know is there. It must be.'

'Eliphas told me all about it. He's gone there now, and will meet us at the docks. He promised to arrange passage for us, although I'll believe it only when I see it.'

Pandaras clapped his misshapen hands and said, 'I have brought your spare set of clothes, master. You lost your knife and your armour, but if you need them I shall search the entire palace. And if I can't find them, I'll bring something better. An energy pistol, perhaps.'

'Those are for officers, not caterans,' Tamora said.

Yam said, 'You have my clothes? Then you went back—'

Tamora said, 'Oh, I went back, all right. I told you that I had spent our money – how do you think I got it? There was a pentad of soldiers waiting at the Gate of Double Glory, but I killed them all in a fair fight.' She grinned, showing her racks of sharp white teeth, and patted the heavy sabre sheathed at her side. 'That's where I got this poor substitute for my own sword. I got the rat-boy a knife, too, and a rapier for you. Anyway, I killed them and found where Syle was hiding. I had to bend the back of that feather-headed fool over my thigh until he would agree, but I have what we left behind, and the fee, too. Rega didn't want him to give it up, but he feared death more than he feared her, although I don't think you could put a blade between the difference. She was sitting where Luria used to sit, in a white dress for mourning. I hope she enjoys her rule in the brief time before the fighting spreads and she is assassinated.'

Yama said, 'I feel sorry for Syle. Despite all he did, at heart he is not a bad man.'

'Grah. He tried to serve his department and his wife's ambitions, and will end up losing both, and his own life. His scheming saved the Department of Vaticination for a short while, but it is seen as an ally of

Indigenous Affairs now. And Indigenous Affairs is too busy defending itself to save Syle.'

Pandaras said, 'He betrayed you, master. No one trusts a traitor, least of all those who employ him. Whoever wins the war up there will get rid of him.'

The fighting had spread through the upper tiers of the palace. The Department of Indigenous Affairs had fought off its rivals and secured its borders, but now there were bitter skirmishes in the corridors, and mines and countermines were being dug as the warring departments tried to break out behind each other's lines.

'Indigenous Affairs will probably triumph in the end,' Tamora said, 'but it will have a hard time of it for a while. I don't know what they wanted from you, but you're out from under them now. While their attention is consumed by the war between departments, we can make good our escape and find a ship that will take us downriver. You're still raw around the edges, but you have the makings of a decent cateran.'

Yama thanked her for the compliment. 'The only flaw in your plan is that we must join the army Indigenous Affairs has raised.'

'You told me that you always wanted to follow in the footsteps of your brother and avenge his death' Tamora said. 'And once we reach the midpoint of the world it will not matter who has charge of the army, and the quarrels inside the Palace of the Memory of the People will be of no importance. For we will be pitched against the heretics, who are the enemy of us all.'

Yama thought of the great map he had so often unrolled, at first to dream of finding where his people lived, and in the past year to follow the progress of Telmon towards the war. Yama had wanted to follow his brother and become his squire, but Telmon was dead. And now he stood at the beginning of the voyage he had dreamed of, with a squire of his own, and it seemed that all his adventures since he had left Aeolis had been no more than a diversion.

Tamora said that it was time he got up from his hammock. 'You should not lie there a moment longer, Yama. The muscles in your legs will shrink and you won't be able to walk, much less fight. You should begin to exercise now, and you will exercise every waking hour once we are on the ship, if you are to be fighting fit by the end of it.'

She and Pandaras helped him walk around the square of the little village, but he was quickly exhausted. Although he knew that he must leave the palace before his enemies found him, he was not yet ready to travel.

'The chief of the mirror people wishes to see you before you leave,' Pandaras said.

'There was foolish talk about working some magic,' Tamora said. 'The whole crew of them are on their way.'

'I think I can guess what Lupe wants,' Yama said. 'But I cannot give it to him.'

Whatever he might be, whatever powers he might possess, he was not the saviour of the mirror people. He could not work any kind of miracle.

'That's what I told him,' Tamora said. 'But he insisted on coming here anyway.'

'You are greater than anything they can imagine, master,' Pandaras said, and touched fingers to his throat in the gesture so that many of the lesser citizens of Ys used. A salute, a sign of defiance, a blessing.

13

THE MIRACLE

The whole village busied itself with preparations for a feast. In the dusty square, long red cloths were unrolled and strewn with flowers. Men and women set to cooking decads of different dishes over trenches filled with white-hot charcoal. Children stacked pyramids of sweet melons like the skulls of vanquished enemies, and built mounds of breadapples and small black and red bananas.

'We will honour our friends the mirror people,' the headman told Yama, 'and we will honour you, dominie, because you are the friend of our friends, and because you saved our village from the hell-hound.'

Like the rest of the villagers, the headman wore a garland of freshly cut white flowers. With comical solemnity he set garlands on the heads of Yama, Tamora and Pandaras, and kissed each of them on the forehead. Despite his growing dread, Yama was now resigned to undergoing this ordeal. Besides, the villagers had saved his life and believed that he was a hero. And who would not like to be treated as a hero, even if only for a day?

While the villagers bustled to and fro he sat in the sunshine with Pandaras at his feet like a loyal puppy. Pandaras had tried to persuade Yama to put on his second-best shirt, but he preferred the homespun tunic that the headman had given him. Tamora sat cross-legged beside him with her new sabre across her lap, sharpening it with a bit of whetstone and fretted about Eliphas.

'He has run off with the money I gave him,' she said. 'I know it. Or gone straight to our enemies. I was a fool to trust him.'

'How can he betray me when he does not know where I am?'

'He knows where you will be. Where we agreed to meet. And these husbandmen have told the mirror people about you, and they could have told Eliphas. I was a fool to expect him to do the right thing.'

Pandaras said, 'When we were up in the balcony, waiting for the pythonesses' ceremony to begin, he told me stories about how he used to search for old books when he was young. He said that Yama has reawakened his spirit of adventure.'

Yama said, 'He was a good friend to me at the library, and he did not abandon me when I was pursued by the hell-hound. Try to have a little faith in other people, Tamora.'

Tamora raised the sabre to examine its edge. 'I have faith in my eye and arm. That should be enough.'

'You cannot fight every battle alone,' Yama said.

The mirror people arrived when the sun reached the highest point in the sky. They came up the steps beside the tiers of rice paddies in a long, colourful procession. Men and women waved red and gold flags, beat drums and tambors, and blew discordant blasts on trumpets. There were fire-eaters exhaling gouts of red and blue flame, boys and girls who walked on their hands or on stilts, tumblers and jugglers. Lupe walked in the middle of this circus, wearing an emerald-green dress with a long train held by two stunningly beautiful girls. The tangled mane of the old man's hair was dressed with glass beads and brightly coloured ribbons. His hands, with their long twisted nails, rested on the bare shoulders of two more girls who guided him to the centre of the village where the headman waited, clad only in his darned leggings and his homespun tunic, and his dignity.

After the two men had ceremoniously kissed, Lupe turned to where Yama stood with Tamora and Pandaras. 'Well met, dominie,' he said, as his hands sought and clasped Yama's. 'I am pleased that you have returned to us, but I always knew that you would.'

Yama began to thank the old man for helping his friends, but Lupe silenced him by touching long fingernails to his lips. Lupe's face was painted white, with black eyebrows drawn above his frost-capped eyes. His lips were dyed a deep purple. 'What you will do for us can never be repaid,' he said, 'but we must not speak of that now. Our brothers and sisters have prepared food and drink, and we must dance to earn their hospitality.'

The feast lasted all evening. As the sun sank behind the shoulder of the slope above the village, cressets were lit and hung on high poles, filling the air with scented smoke and sending fierce red light beating across the crowded square. Children served a stream of dishes; husbandmen and mirror people ate and drank with gusto. Pandaras fell asleep, curled up with his nose in the crook of his knees. Tamora drank wine steadily, and soon was as drunk as anyone else.

Yama sat in the place of honour, between Lupe and the headman of the village. The Aedile had taught him the trick of appearing to eat and drink while in fact consuming little, but even the small amount of wine he drank went straight to his head, and there were times when he believed that he was in the middle of a hectic dream, where animals dressed as men frolicked and bayed.

As the air darkened, it became possible to make out the sparkle of gunfire around one high crag of the Palace. Once, a low rumble passed like a wave through the ground beneath the feasting husbandmen and mirror people, and everyone laughed and clapped, as if it was a trick done for their benefit.

Yama asked Lupe if he was worried by the war between departments, but Lupe smiled and said merely that it was good to be in the fresh air once more. 'It has been a long time since I felt sunlight on my face, dominie.'

'The war is nothing to us,' the headman said. 'We do not have the ambitions of the changed. How much it costs them! And when the war is over, everything will be as it was before. No one can change the order of things, for that was set by the Preservers at the beginning of the world.'

He raised a beaker of wine and drank, and the husbandmen around him knuckled their foreheads and drank too.

Lupe had been sucking the marrow from a chicken bone. Now he bit it in half and chewed and swallowed the splinters and said, 'At the far end of time all those who are changed will be resurrected after death by the charity and grace of the Preservers. Isn't that right, dominie?'

And so it had begun. Yama said, as steadily as he could, 'That is what it says in the Puranas.'

'All men,' the headman said. 'But not all who are born and die on Confluence are men. Changed bloodlines become ever more holy, and at last pass away into story and song. Many have passed since the world was made, and many more will do so in ages to come. But we are less than men, and can never change. And so we will inherit the world when all others have transcended their base selves.'

'These people have no ambition to wear a crown of lights,' Lupe said, and waved a hand above his head as if to swat the two dim fireflies which circled him. 'I do not mean these. They are nothing. Rats have brighter attendants. I mean ones such as those you wore when you first visited us. I am sorry that you no longer have them.'

'They were taken away,' Yama said.

'We do not need fireflies,' the headman said, 'for we work in the sun and sleep when the Rim Mountains take away the light. We are a humble people.'

'They have no ambition, but they are not humble,' Lupe told Yama. 'They are the proudest of all the peoples of the Palace. They cleave to their work in the old gardens and claim to be the best of all the servants of the Preservers, but surely the best way to serve the Preservers is to aspire to become more than you already are.'

'We serve the Preservers as we have always served them,' the headman said.

Lupe leaned towards Yama. The glass beads in his tangled hair clicked and rattled. Each held a point of reflected torchlight. His dress was of the finest watered silk, but Yama could smell the must of the long years it had spent in a press. Were the blind old man's cheekbones higher and sharper, was his voice softer?

'Who is right, dominie? They say we sin by wishing to rise above our preordained station. We believe that they are worse sinners, for they refuse the challenge.'

The headman said, 'There is no sin in knowing what you are, and being content.'

On the other side of the flower-strewn strip of cloth, Tamora suddenly looked up, as if startled awake. 'He's right,' she said. 'Dreams only bring heartache.'

'Without dreams,' Lupe said, 'we are only animals. Without dreams, we can be no more than we already are.'

Yama looked from one old man to the other. Although he had drunk little, his head felt as if it was abuzz with drowsy bees. He said, 'You ask me to judge between you? Then I say that both of you are at fault, for you refuse to look into your own hearts and discover why you wish for elevation, or why you refuse the chance. Each of you clearly sees the fault of the other, but neither sees his own fault. We are all raised up by the Preservers, but they do not set limits on what we can be. That is up to us.'

Lupe tipped back his head and laughed. The headman glared at him and said, 'This man is a hero, brother Lupe. We should not presume to put him to the test. Only he can do that.'

'You show him, Yama,' Tamora said. 'Show him what you aren't.'

'It is not a test of your master,' Lupe said, 'but of my people.'

The headman said, 'And as the dominie pointed out, you have thought too long on why we will not copy your foolishness, instead of thinking why you wish to attempt it.'

'Then I stand for my people alone,' Lupe said, and held out his hands.

Two girls stepped forward and helped him to his feet. A silence spread as the people who sat cross-legged around the strips of cloth and islands of food turned to watch the old man. The faces of the mirror people were tinted red by the crackling flames of the torches; those of the husbandmen were tinted black. The two ogres who had been trading blows with clubs in the centre of the square stepped back from each other and their upper halves threw off their tinsel helmets and jumped down from their lower halves, who shucked the wide belts which had concealed where their partners had stood on their shoulders.

Lupe raised a hand, and someone moved out of the darkness into the flaring light of the torches. It was a beautiful young woman in a simple white shift. She stepped lightly and gravely, treading the dust of the square like a dancer, the cynosure of every eye.

She carried a basket of white flowers. When she reached the centre of the square she knelt gracefully and offered the basket to Yama. He jumped up and backed away, horrified. Tamora leaned over to look inside the basket, and began to laugh.

They left Yama alone with the baby in a ruined temple below the village. There had once been gardens and a courtyard before the temple's entrance, but now it was little more than a small square cave cut into the cliff at the edge of a stony field of bean vines. The lintel of its doorway was cracked. The caryatids which had for an age shouldered its weight had fallen on either side of the door. One had broken in two and was missing her head; the other lay on her back, her blank eyes gazing at the night sky. Torches had been set on poles thrust into the dry earth on either side of the entrance. Their smoky red light sent long shadows weaving across the flaking frescos of the naos and put red sparks in the glossy black circle of the shrine.

While the baby, a boy, fat and dusky with health, slept innocently on his blanket of white blossoms, Yama paced back and forth between the two torches, tormented by the thought of the miracle he was expected to perform.

To raise this poor wight. To change him from innocence to one of those fallen into full self-awareness.

It was impossible.

The innocence of the indigens was different from that of the unchanged bloodlines because it was absolute. While most bloodlines of Confluence could evolve towards union with the Preservers, the indigens were as fixed in their habits as the beasts of field and flood and air. Certain coarse bloodlines, such as the Amnan, excused their persecution of indigens by claiming that their victims were merely animals with human appearance and speech, a kind of amalgam of monkey and parrot. Most, though, agreed that the indigenous races resembled unchanged bloodlines in all but potential. They could not fall from the grace to which they had been raised by the Preservers, but neither could they transcend it.

More than once, Yama was seized with the strong urge to pick up the baby and carry him back to the village high above, where, to judge from the sounds of laughter and music which occasionally drifted to him on the night breeze, the feast was proceeding as heartily as when he had been led away from it. And he was also tempted to walk away into the night. To become what he briefly had been when he had first arrived in Ys, a solitary seeker after the truth of his own life.

He did neither. He had not yet regained his strength, the baby was in his care, and he could not return to the village until the night was over. A refusal to act would be worse than failure, for it would imply that he was not grateful to the mirror people for saving his life. No, better to wait out the night, to wait for the mirror people and the husbandmen to return, and find that he had failed. Tamora would be pleased: it would prove that his powers were no more than figments of his imagination. And perhaps the heavy weight of the mirror people's hope might pass from him.

It was not a burden that Yama had ever sought. That was what was so unfair. Zakiel had told him that, because of the great age of Confluence and its many bloodlines, there were so many stories and tales that anyone could find in them a mirror to their own life. And so the mirror people had seen in Yama a reflection of some long-dead hero or half-forgotten promise.

Yama could forgive them that – in these troubled times people looked to the past for heroes to save them, for that was simpler than trying to save themselves. But although, like so many heroes of the Apocrypha, he possessed mysterious origins, strange powers, and what might be mistaken for magical weapons (but he had lost the knife, and the disc he carried was not the disc he had been given by the anchorite), Yama knew that he was no hero. As a child, he had dreamed of finding his real parents and others of his bloodline, dreamed that they would be powerful and rich and strong. He knew now that most orphans had similar dreams, but very few were of notable birth. Now, older and chastened by his adventures, he wanted to find his people only because he hoped that they would shelter him from the expectations of others. Even if they were no more than mendicants and anchorites, he would join them gladly, for surely they would accept him simply for what he was. He had not asked for what little power that he had, and he wanted it gone.

Let it pass.

More than once, gripped by a mixture of self-loathing and self-pity, he shouted this plea into the night. But there was never any reply, nothing more than the wind walking amongst the dry leaves of the vines, and the faint sounds of revelry high above. Presently, he remembered that this place was very old, and grew fearful that he might wake something, and was quiet.

'You are better off without it,' he whispered to the baby. 'The husbandmen are right.'

He did not expect to sleep, but at last he tired himself out by pacing to and fro, like the great spotted cat he had once seen in a cage on the deck of a ship that had put in at Aeolis on its way back to Ys from the jungles near the midpoint of the world. It had prowled restlessly from one corner of its cage to the other, anger blazing in its green eyes, its mad thoughts unguessable. Perhaps it had believed that if it paced long enough it might find a hidden door to the jungle from which it had been taken.

Yama sat with his back against the pedestal of one of the caryatids (her feet, shod in strap sandals, stood there still, broken off at the ankles) and, tired but sleepless, watched the lights of the city spread beyond the dark slopes of the palace's roof.

After some time he realised that the fallen caryatid had opened her blank eyes and was watching him. He felt neither fear nor amazement; not even when she spoke.

'You have a knack of finding windows that still work,' she said. 'I see you lost your key but found another.'

Yama knew at once who was speaking to him. The woman he had seen in the shrine of the Temple of the Black Well. The aspect of the author of the heresies that threatened to consume the world.

He was gripped by a freezing dread, as if confronted with a poisonous serpent. His mouth was dry, but he managed to say, 'The keys are everywhere, but people have forgotten what they were.'

'They have forgotten much,' the woman said. 'When I walked in your world, I tried to tell them a little of what they had forgotten. Some remembered, but many resisted. Knowledge is a bitter thing, after all, and many hesitate to sip from that cup. You, for instance, are not one step further on your journey. Why are you sitting here, and who is it you are sitting with? A very unformed mind . . . Ah, it is a baby from one of the true alien races. Another orphan, Yama?'

'I will not serve you,' Yama said. 'I refuse to serve. I refused Prefect Corin, and I refuse you. I especially refuse you, because I know that you deny the mercy and charity of the Preservers. You would overthrow them and rule in their place if you could. It is the world's good fortune that you are nothing but a ghost.'

'Do you refuse the mirror people, too?'

'You cannot know about that!'

'I am in your dreams, Yama, so for this little time I share some of your memories. The mirror people want only to share the fate of the other bloodlines of this strange world. They want nothing more than to take charge of their own destiny, to become infected with the machines that will record their memories, so that they might live again, at the far end of time. They want to remember their own story, not have it remembered for them. I had long arguments with Mr Naryan on that point. He was particularly enthusiastic about innocence, I remember. But no parent should keep a child from growing.'

'Mr Naryan? Is he another ghost?'

'He was the Archivist of the town of Sensch. As far as I know, he's still alive. It was a great many years ago, but his kind live long, longer than most of the long-lived races of Confluence. He changed his mind, of course. He understands my ideas now.'

'But Sensch was where the war—'

The caryatid smiled, cracking the lichens which had grown like cankers on her stony cheeks. 'I set them free, Yama. Free from the burden of this world's mindless theocracy. Free to be themselves.'

'The Preservers will give us all that freedom.'

'Yes, your priests promise that the Preservers will return all to life, eternal life in a kind of heaven, at the very instant of the end of the universe. It is a grand promise, but costs the priests nothing, for no one will be alive to call them to account when it doesn't come true. My promise is much simpler, and more profound: freedom to become what you will, here and now. That is what I gave the citizens of Sensch. That is what I will give everyone, in time.

'Now, pay attention. I will show you the trick. When I was in the world, I had to call on the shrines to help me change the people of Sensch. Now I live in the space inside the shrines, and the process is much simpler.'

'No! I will not serve!'

But in his dream, Yama seemed to be swimming beneath the surface of the river, as he had swum so often when he was still a child, innocently playing with the pups of the Amnan. They had liked to dive from the end of the new quay and swim out to the kelp beds, where long green fronds trailed just beneath the surface. They swam deeper and faster than Yama ever could, searching for abalone and oysters that clustered around the holdfasts of the kelp on the river bottom. Yama was happy enough to splash above them, but sometimes he struck downwards through sunlight towards the ghost of the river bottom far below, towards the other children. He could never reach them. His lungs began to ache and burn, and the weight of the water compressed his chest and he had to double back and swim strongly for the surface, where he sputtered and coughed in the sunlight. The cool depths of the river were, for him, forever unreachable. But now, as he struck through a hectic flux that was much like the play of light and water, it came to him that his wish had finally come true. The caryatid hung beside him, and he told her that she should sink, for she was stone, and stone could not float.

'Watch,' she said, and he saw the knots within the baby's brain, saw how they could be made stronger *here* and *here* so that the swarming machines, smaller than the single-celled plants on which the largest fish of the river grazed, which hung invisibly in every breath of air just as the tiny plants hung in every drop of water, would excyst in those places, and begin their work of building and amplifying the initial trace of self-consciousness.

The caryatid sank away, slowly dissolving into the flux of light. 'Self-ordering complexity,' she murmured. 'It needs only a seed…'

Yama knew now, or remembered, that this was a dream, and remembered the nature of the creature that had visited him. Yet still something in him yearned towards her, as a starving man will reach towards any kind of food, no matter how foul. He struck out with fierce desperation towards the place where she had disappeared, and woke to find Tamora kneeling beside him. He was lying on the broken tiles of the naos, before the black disc of the shrine. Was there light fading within it? Or was it simply a reflection of the dawn light framed by the square entrance of the little temple?

Tamora was watching Yama with an intent, troubled expression. She snatched back her hand when he reached for it, and he asked her what was wrong. Instead of answering, she turned and pointed to the temple's entrance, where people clustered around something on the ground.

Immediately, Yama felt a sharp pang of guilt. He had forgotten the baby. He had fallen asleep. It could be dead. It could have been snatched by wild animals.

He staggered outside, every muscle stiff. It was already warm, and light flooded the slopes of the palace and filled the sky, so bright after the temple's cool shadows that he had to squint. A great cry went up from the people and Yama started back in alarm before he understood that they were smiling. Lupe stood in the centre of the little crowd, his blind face bent to a girl who whispered in his ear. Another girl took Yama's hand and led him to the basket of white flowers.

There was so much light that Yama did not at first understand why the baby's eyes kept crossing, and why it batted at the air with its chubby hands. And then he saw.

Hung above its head, burning with fierce white radiance, was a crown of fireflies.

14

THE PROCESSION OF YAMA

'They will soon leave,' Yama told Pandaras. 'I must have drawn them here, but they will go away when I do. Before this is over I should explain to Lupe's people that it is not what they think it is.'

'You are too modest, master. And if I may say so, a little foolish. You could live as a Hierarch here, and instead you choose to go to war.'

The produce wagon on which they rode swayed and jounced as it negotiated a pothole in the old road; Pandaras staggered, then sat down hard by Yama's high chair. The boy was drunk. From the noise and music and cheering of the procession, from plentiful libations of palm wine. A wreath of ivy and the white flowers of trumpet vines was skewed on his head. There was a large wet wine stain on the front of his white shirt.

'They'd kill him,' Tamora said. 'Not these fools, but the people in power. He's a threat to them.'

She stood behind Yama, gripping her sabre and scanning the crowd, becoming especially alert whenever someone let off a firecracker. People were running alongside the wagon and its attendant procession of mirror people, or stood on terraces overlooking the road, cheering and waving palm fronds or brightly coloured cloths, offering up flowers or fruit. One group had launched kites into the air: painted with fierce faces, the red and black and yellow diamonds zoomed and swooped around each other in the bright air.

Lupe sat at Yama's feet, arrayed in a dress of cloth-of-gold sewn with fake pearls and sequins. He held the baby with its crown of brilliant fireflies in his lap. He said, 'We mean no harm to anyone. We simply set forth from our immemorial home to claim our place in the world.'

'You'd do better to stay here,' Tamora said. She had to raise her voice to a shrill pitch to be heard above the crowd. 'Innocents like you are prey for every bandit, crimp and reaver in the city.'

'When I was a young man,' Lupe said, 'I used the shell game to take money from your people at the Water Market. Before that, I played the part of the monkey in the illusion of the snake and rope, and worked the front of the house for a puppet theatre. Marks always think that they can fool us, but they forget that they play our games by our rules. But we should not quarrel, young cateran, for we are both set on the same path. Hear how the people cheer the procession of your master!'

The news of the miracle had spread fast and far. By the time the procession had left the village of the husbandmen, people were already lining the old road as far as the eye could see. Gangs of men were clearing the road of brush and fallen rock, or patching gaps with timbers. The road had not been used, Lupe said, since the Hierarchs had fallen silent ten thousand years ago.

The procession wound three times around the slopes of the palace as it descended towards the city. No guards or troops came forward to stop it, but now and then Tamora would point out a speck in the air: an officer standing on a disc, watching through a glass. Once, where the road rounded the bulging side of a steep cliff with sheer rock above and only air below, a flyer paced the procession. It hung just beyond the edge of the road, so close that one of the acrobats could have jumped easily from the road to the wide black triangle of its wing. The mirror people pelted it with flowers and libations, and then the road dived into a short tunnel through the side of a bluff, and when it came out into the sunlight the flyer was gone, and more people were running down steep fields towards the procession, waving and cheering.

Yama did not wave back. He felt like a fool and a fraud. The miracle which these innocent people were celebrating was no miracle at all, but a trick of the shadow of the creature who had started the war. She had used him as a tool to change the baby, either to show him what she was capable of, or to show him that she knew his powers better than he did, and could use them for her own ends. The miracle which Lupe had desired so much was a perversion, a crude and cruel joke mocking the will of the Preservers.

Yama's only hope was that good might come from her trickery. For no matter how it had been done, the baby *was* changed. Lupe's people had the proof that they could be raised up.

There was nothing he could do but make the best of it, which was why he had agreed to ride with Lupe. Tamora had said that taking part in the procession was perilously foolish, but Yama had asked her plainly what was better – sneaking out of Ys under cover of darkness, like escaping thieves, or riding in the place of honour in a long, happy procession amidst tumblers and musicians and clowns, with the population cheering them along? At least Pandaras was caught up in the fever of it all. He waved to onlookers, and drank the libations which they handed up, and laughed and waved some more.

Yama turned to Tamora and said, 'Most of them think it is some kind of performance.'

She shook her head. 'Just look at who has come to watch. They are all of them indigens or the poorest of the poor, sweepers and nightsoil collectors like the rat-boy here. If the soldiers or the magistrates decide to arrest you, or worse, if those fuckers from Indigenous Affairs come for you, this trash will melt away. And tomorrow they'll choose another King of Fools.'

'My bloodline helped build the world, Tamora. At one time I believed they might be Lords of infinite time and space, but I know now that they were no such thing. They were labourers such as these.'

The miracle was not that he had performed a miracle, but that Lupe and the mirror people believed that he had. If there was any good in it, it was this: that these people believed that miracles were possible, that the Preservers could still intercede in the world. And how could he deny that? Was not his own existence as much a miracle as the crown of fireflies around that innocent baby's head? The woman in the shrine had used him, but perhaps she in turn had been used by some higher power.

'Whatever you are, you deserve better followers than this rabble,' Tamora said, and went back to watching the crowd.

The procession descended through the cramped squares and narrow streets that threaded between the jumble of buildings at the hem of the palace, and moved towards a great gate. People lined the rooftops on either side, pelting the wagon with flowers and paper strings in a blizzard so dense that at first Yama did not see why it had suddenly stopped. Tamora hissed, but Yama held up his hand, hoping that she would not strike. For now he saw, through falling drifts of flowers, a line of troopers strung across the road before the gate, some mounted on ratites, some on foot.

An officer on a floating disc, clad in metal armour so polished that it shone like a mirror broken into the shape of a man, swooped down and hung in the air above the two oxen that drew the wagon. He was bareheaded, his skull heavily ridged. A thick black moustache framed the puckered cone of his mouth. He stared directly at Yama and said, 'Who is in charge?'

'No one was compelled to be here,' Yama said. 'They came of their own free will.'

The officer said, 'None of these animals are in any way familiar with free will.'

Lupe said, 'We set forth towards a new life, dominie. And this is the one who guided us.'

Tamora stepped forward, glaring up at the officer. 'Get out of the way, little man. And take your toy soldiers with you.'

Yama put a hand on her shoulder and told her to stand down, and said to the officer, 'By what authority do you prevent us from leaving?'

'The Department of Internal Harmony. And I am here not to stop you, Yamamanama, but to provide you with a safe escort. We are under considerable pressure to return you to a certain place, but the Department of Internal Harmony does not take sides. We still have full control of the lower floors and the outer defences, and we do as we see fit to ensure the security of the palace. Accordingly, I am here to make sure that you leave, and to ask you to order your followers to disperse peacefully.'

Yama gestured towards the crowd which clogged the street behind the wagon, the people on the rooftops who were still tossing flowers into the air. He said, 'They are not mine to command. If they were, I would not have allowed this. I am as embarrassed by it as you.'

'It's not a question of embarrassment,' the officer said. 'It's a question of public safety.'

Yama could take the disc from beneath the officer's feet and use it as a scythe against the troopers who blocked the way. He could call down machines and riddle them through and through. It would be so easy… but there would be other soldiers, and beyond the gates was the city, and the hundred thousand magistrates who kept civil order. He was not here to start a war. What was he thinking? The woman in the shrine had put something in his head that twisted his thoughts to fantasies of violence and domination. He took a deep breath to calm himself, and remembered that the Aedile had taught him that when negotiating it was better to allow your opponent to think that he had come to a decision of his own free will rather than to force him to make a choice, for when forced a man will usually choose badly.

He said, 'I understand why you must keep order amongst the petitioners and palmers who seek to gain entrance; otherwise the palace would be overwhelmed. But the people who have kindly provided me with an escort are the simple folk who work its fields, and entertain its clerks.'

Lupe said, 'We have always come and gone freely.'

'I know your kind,' the officer said mildly. 'You come and go by ratholes and sewer pipes.'

Yama said, 'I'm sure you know them better than I do. You know that they have lived in the palace for longer than almost every other bloodline, and serve it after their fashion. You know that they mean no harm.'

The officer's puckered mouth drew back to show the strong ridged grinding plates he had instead of teeth. 'Frankly, I'd be glad to see the last of them. They are parasites upon the bodies of the departments. Only a decad past there was a riot in one of the day markets because one of them was caught cheating at some gambling game. Several clerks were blinded when a fool fired an energy pistol.'

'Then perhaps all will benefit if they pass with me.'

The officer thought for a moment, then nodded. 'They'll be the magistrates' problem once they're outside the palace, and I have my orders to get you to a place of safety. Indigenous Affairs pushed too hard for your return. We'll not be at their command, or anyone else's. We serve the ideal of the Preservers. We always have. In the black days when the Head of the People swallowed all other departments, we alone maintained our independence. And we allow people to come and go as we see fit.'

'There is a ship waiting for me at the docks,' Yama said. 'If you took me there, it would be an end to your obligation towards me.'

The mounted troopers of the Department of Internal Harmony fell in as an escort ahead of and behind the wagon. Their ratites, the officer confided to Yama, were not as swift or fearsome as horses, but were less prone to panic and more manoeuvrable in the press of a crowd. The procession passed beneath the arch of the great gate (all the fireflies, from Lupe's to those of the baby in his lap, flew up and vanished; Yama was glad to see them go) and began to make its way through the streets of Ys.

The crowd of mirror people that followed the wagon was outnumbered by passers-by who hardly spared it a glance as they went about their normal business. Yama remembered the procession he had seen from the window of the inn where he had woken after plunging into the Country of the Mind, where the crews of the voidships met each other. Now he was the centre of a similar spectacle, an ordinary, everyday event in this great and terrible city.

Tamora cursed Pandaras for getting drunk and told Yama that the mirror people should have put a canopy over his head. 'It wouldn't block a quarrel, but it would hinder the aim of any would-be assassin.'

'We are under the protection of the Department of Internal Harmony,' Yama said. 'No one will dare try to take me by force now.'

'Prefect Corin might try to put a quarrel through your head. Mine too. He won't forgive us for escaping. I know the type. And those magistrates are watching us too closely for my liking.'

Red-robed magistrates stood on floating discs high above the heads of the crowd which thronged the streets, their machines twinkling in the air about them. Yama waved at them as the wagon trundled past, and suppressed the impulse to twist the orbits of their machines into mocking configurations.

As the wagon moved towards the docks, the crowd began to grow denser, swollen by refugees come to beg for help from the man who had raised up one of the indigenous races. Women held up children so that they could see Yama and the baby, or perhaps to be blessed, for many were ill or deformed. People shouted and prayed and pleaded, but their words were lost in the general tumult and the braying of the trumpets and shawms of the mirror people.

At last the crowds were so dense that the procession could no longer move forward. Even the mounted soldiers were trapped in the press. The officer dropped down to the wagon and told Yama that he would arrange for him to be carried away to wherever he wished.

Yama shook his head. 'I will walk if I must!'

'You must come with me!'

They were both shouting at the tops of their voices, but could hardly hear themselves over the noise of the crowd. A man jumped onto the wagon and tried to anoint Yama with scented oil. Tamora kicked him in the throat and he folded over and fell backwards. The mob closed around him before he had a chance to scream.

Yama climbed onto the bench, beside the driver, and raised his arms. Gradually, the crowd which packed the street ahead and behind the wagon grew quiet, except for a scattering of individual voices crying out with hysteria or hurt or fright.

'I cannot help you,' Yama said. He was trembling violently, and a sharp pain pressed between his eyes. 'Only you can help yourselves.'

Most did not hear him, but the crowd cheered anyway. Yama remembered the magistrate who had stopped him and Prefect Corin when they had first arrived in Ys, and borrowed a machine from one of the magistrates who stood on a rooftop overlooking the street and brought it down in front of his face. When he spoke again, the machine amplified his voice so that it echoed from the walls of the buildings. He meant to tell the crowd that he could not help them, but something seized him, and then he hardly knew what he said. The people packed around the wagon cheered, and he felt lifted up by their cheers. The pain between his eyes intensified and red and black light flashed in his sight. He tried to reach out and change everyone he could see, and failed because there were too many, and cried out in rage. A myriad tiny machines burned and fell from the air. People screamed and tried to flee as magistrates, believing themselves to be under attack, laid into those nearest them with their quirts. But there was nowhere to flee to, and suddenly the crowd was fighting against itself.

Yama did not see any of this. Red and black lightning tore away all thought and he fell backwards into Tamora's arms.

A great wind blew around him. The sun burned down out of the cloudless sky, but the rush of air was so cold that he shivered in its icy blast as if plunged into a stream fed by the glaciers at the end of the world. He lay on a ridged metal deck that vibrated beneath him. When he struggled to sit up, Pandaras helped him and said, 'A flying machine, master. You fainted and the officer caught you up and carried you off.'

'There were too many . . .'

Pandaras misunderstood; he was still drunk. He had lost his wreath and his shirt was ripped at the shoulder. He said, 'They would have torn you apart if this hadn't rescued us. Isn't it wondrous?'

The flying machine was sleek and boat-shaped, with short down-curved wings. Its silver skin shone like a mirror in the bright sunlight.

Lupe sat behind Yama and Pandaras, with the baby in his lap and a girl on either side. Four troopers stood behind him. Near the beaked prow, Tamora was talking with a man clad in broken mirrors. She glanced around, grinning fiercely, and said, 'We go directly to the docks.'

The mirror-clad man turned – it was the officer in his polished armour – and said, 'This is only a dory, not a true flier. Unfortunately its range is limited. If I could, I would take you as far from the city as possible.'

Yama said stupidly, 'Who commands it?'

'It flies itself,' the officer said. 'It is from the early days of the world. There. You see what we have left behind.'

The little dory tilted in the air. Because its local gravity compensated for the motion, the world seemed to pitch beneath it. The grid of the city, punctuated here and there by the domes and spires of temples, stretched away towards the vast bulk of the Palace of the Memory of the People. The palace's peak was obscured by smoke. A long way beyond it were the shining towers that Yama had seen so often using the signal telescope on the roof of the peel-house at Aeolis, white needles that rose higher than the Rim Mountains, their tops lost in a glare of sunlight beyond the envelope of air that shrouded the world.

Yama pointed to the palace and said, 'They are still fighting.'

'It is the rioting in the streets that I meant,' the officer said. 'Well, I suppose we are too high to see it.'

As if it understood him, the dory swooped down. The city rushed at them. The crowded roofs of the refugees' shanty town, built over the mudbanks left by the Great River's slow retreat, ravelled away on either side. The river was directly ahead, a broad plain flashing in the sunlight as the dory swerved towards one of the pontoon docks.

The floating quays of the docks were crowded with sightseers, and a flotilla of small boats stood off on either side. As the dory sank gently through the air, coming to rest just above the edge of the outermost quay, Yama saw a familiar face in the crowd and immediately jumped down.

Tamora got in front of Yama and helped keep off the press of people who crowded round, shouting and singing and praying and making obeisance. Some clutched at Yama's homespun tunic and he realised his mistake and would have climbed back on the dory, but there was no room to move. Tamora held her sabre above her head, in case someone was pushed onto it by those pressing from behind, and there was an uncomfortable minute before the troopers managed to clear a space.

Lupe was helped down by his attendants, using one of the wings of the dory as a pont. The blind old man ignored those who crowded around him. He cradled the baby in one arm and touched Yama's face with the long fingernails of his free hand. 'Perhaps you should not have left us the first time, dominie,' he said. 'But all's well that ends well.'

Yama smiled, and then remembered that the old man could not see. He said, 'You have been a generous friend, Lupe.'

'We are your servants, dominie. We no longer serve at the pleasure of all in the palace, but for you we will always give our lives.'

'It will not be necessary.'

'I'm glad to hear it. But these are strange times, dominie, and perhaps even you cannot see what is to come.'

Lupe embraced Yama tremulously, and Yama kissed the old man on both cheeks. The baby smiled up at them, quite undisturbed by the commotion of the crowd. Someone was trying to push between the troopers who guarded Yama and Lupe. Tamora's sabre point flicked in that direction – but it was Eliphas, smiling broadly and shouting wildly, his silver eyes flashing in the bright sunlight.

'I have found them,' Eliphas shouted. 'I have found them, brother! They live downriver!'

15
THE *WEAZEL*

The ship that Eliphas had hired, the *Weazel*, was a small lugger which, before the war, had spent her days ferrying cargo and a few passengers from one side of the Great River to the other. She was single-masted and lateen-rigged, and in calm weather could supplement her triangular mainsail with square staysails rigged from spars spread either side of her mast. She pulled a shallow draught, and with wind and current behind her could make twice the speed of the carracks and levanters scattered across the Great River in pods of three or four, heading downriver towards the war. She could not outrun the machines which tried to follow her, but Yama, although exhausted, was able to tell them to disperse even before the drag anchors had been collapsed.

Pandaras said that it was likely that the *Weazel* had been used as much for smuggling as for plying regular trade, but he was careful to say this out of earshot of the ship's captain, Ixchel Lorquital. She was a cautious, shrewd widow who dominated all on board with a natural authority. Like all the women of her bloodline, she had added her husband's name to her own when she had married.

'But that don't mean I was anything less than him,' she told Yama. 'You might say that since I carry his name and his memory I'm rather more than he ever was, the Preservers keep his memory safe.'

Captain Lorquital was a big woman, with mahogany-coloured skin that shone as if oiled and an abundance of coarse black hair which she habitually tied back from her creased, round face with a variety of coloured strings. Her forehead was ridged with keratin, her nostrils no more than slits in the middle of her face. She wore a silver lip-plug which weighed down her lower lip, exposing yellow, spade-shaped teeth.

The day-to-day running of the ship was left to her daughter, Aguilar, who combined the offices of bosun and purser; Captain Lorquital habitually sat in a sling chair by the helm, puffing a corncob pipe, stately in a billowing long skirt and leather tabard, her muscular arms bare, a red handkerchief knotted under her pendulous jowls. Eliphas soon struck up a friendship with her, and they spent hours talking together.

Ixchel Lorquital offered her cabin to her four passengers, but Yama politely refused this generous gesture. Instead, he and his companions camped on the deck, sleeping on raffia mats under a canvas awning that slanted steeply from the rail of the quarterdeck to a cleat by the cargo well.

He slept easily and deeply on the Great River. It reminded him of the happy days of the annual pilgrimages made by the whole population of Aeolis to the farside shore. And he could sleep safe in the knowledge that he had left his enemies behind him, and that he now had a destination, a place to voyage towards, the place where his bloodline might still live.

Eliphas had told Yama about his discovery as soon as the *Weazel* had raised her rust-red sail and begun to outpace the flotilla of small boats which tried to follow her. The old man was tremendously pleased with himself, and even more voluble than usual.

'It was your mention of Dr Dismas that aided the search,' he said. 'It was a simple matter to check the records and find those he had accessed. He had been careful to cover his tracks, but he was not subtle. For one as experienced as my friend Kun Norbu, it was a relatively simple matter to see through the deception.'

'You say that they are downriver,' Yama said quickly, before Eliphas could launch into a technical account of the false trails left by Dr Dismas and the skills that the chief of clerks had employed to untangle them.

'If they still live, brother, then that is where they will be found,' Eliphas said.

'Well, I am alive,' Yama said.

'That's true,' Eliphas said. 'However, I feel I should point out that your being alive here and now means only that at least two of your bloodline were alive in the recent past. It does not mean that our hypothetical couple are alive now, or that any others like them still live. The documents, you see, are at least five thousand years old. But as that is the age of the book for which they formed the binding, they are almost certainly much older than that.'

'How much older?'

'Well, that's difficult to say, brother. With more time, Kun Norbu and I could have analysed the inks: degradation of certain elements used in their manufacture occurs at a fairly constant rate. But as will become evident, they cannot predate the Age of Insurrection, although the city of your bloodline may be rather older than that.'

'A city!'

Yama had never imagined more than a small keep, or perhaps a small town, hidden in the icy fastness upriver of Ys. Perhaps a citadel tunnelled into the rock of the mountains, a fine and secret place full of ancient wonders. But a city...

Eliphas drew a little leather satchel from inside his loose shirt, unfastened its clasps, and took out a cardboard folder tied with a green ribbon.

'These are not the originals, of course,' he said. 'My friend the chief of clerks could not allow such precious documents to leave the precincts of the library. However, they are fair copies, made by the best clerk in the library.'

It took him a minute more to unpick the knot in the ribbon. He opened the folder and withdrew a piece of paper which had been folded into quarters and sealed with a blob of black wax. It fluttered in the warm wind which poured past the rail of the ship's waist, and it took all of Yama's will to resist snatching it from Eliphas's hand.

'Sealed with the imprint of Kun Norbu,' Eliphas said, and snapped the wax and handed the folded paper to Yama.

After he had opened it, Yama thought at first that he had the paper upside down, but when he turned it around he still could not read the irregular lines of squiggles and dashes.

Eliphas smiled. 'It faithfully reproduces the appalling script of the man who wrote the original, and even mimics the stains and tatters which the original accumulated before it was used as a stiffener in the binding of a common pharmacopium. It is written in a much debased version of a long-dead language, but Kun Norbu was able to translate it. It is a brief account written by a scavenger of wrecked war machines in the Glass Desert beyond the midpoint of the world, which is why, of course, it must date from some time after the Age of Insurrection.'

'Where is it, then? Where is this city?'

'Several hundred leagues beyond the end of the Great River, in a series of caverns. The scavenger believed that it was once a huge city, but only a small part of it was still inhabited when he stumbled upon it.'

Yama remembered the place beneath the world where Beatrice had taken him, and the capsule which had transported them from the edge of the Rim Mountains to the shore of the river. With growing excitement, he realised that, as a baby, he might have been carried from one end of the river to the other in a similar device. He did not know if his people still lived there, but at last he had a goal, even if it lay beyond the armies of the heretics.

But Tamora still did not trust Eliphas, and said so bluntly. 'You are a fool if you believe him,' she said to Yama, later that evening.

'Eliphas thinks he will find treasures there. That is why he is so eager to help. He is quite honest about his intentions.'

'He wants to be young again,' Pandaras said. 'It's a foolishness that infects many men of a certain age. And so he plunges into an adventure like those of his youth, hoping that it will revive his waning powers.'

They sat on rolled raffia mats under the awning, their faces lit by a single candle which flickered in a resin holder. Eliphas was on the quarterdeck, talking with Captain Lorquital. To port, Ys made a web of lights that stretched as far as the eye could see; to starboard, the Eye of the Preservers was rising above the black sweep of the river.

Tamora had appropriated several of the small fish that the cook had caught on trotlines trailing from the ship's stern. She picked up one and tore a bite from it and swallowed without chewing. 'Grah. That scrawl could be anything or nothing. He could have made it this morning. You have only his word that this is a record of your bloodline.'

'It is not exactly a record,' Yama said. 'Simply an account of what happened to a scavenger when his camels died after drinking poisoned water. He was wandering half-mad from thirst and heat exhaustion, and was found and taken in by a tribe of people who looked like me. He says that they called themselves the First People. They possessed fireflies, and other machines. He was there for more than a decad, until he had recovered from his ordeal. Then he woke one morning and found himself hundreds of leagues away, near the fall of the Great River.'

'It is a pretty tale,' Tamora said. 'But how do you know it possesses even a grain of truth?'

'He remembered the path he had taken up to the point when his rescuers found him. Here.'

Yama drew out the other piece of paper that Eliphas had brought.

Tamora held it to the light of the candle and Pandaras craned his sleek head to look.

It was a map.

At dawn the next day the *Weazel* was sailing past the lower reaches of Ys ahead of a brisk breeze, dragging a creamy wake through the river's tawny water. The ship kept to the outermost of the coastal currents, where the water was stained by silt and sewage from thousands of drains, all of which had once been clear streams fed by the snowcaps of the foothills of the Rim Mountains. On the port side, across a wide reach of water broken here and there by small islands crowded with buildings, or by long picket lines which marked the boundaries of fish farms, was an endless unravelling panorama of close-packed houses which stretched away beneath a dun haze created by millions of cooking fires. A horde of tiny craft went about their business close to the shore: coracles and skiffs; little fishing boats with puttering reaction motors; sampans carrying whole families and menageries of chickens and rabbits and dwarf goats; crowded water buses; luggers like the *Weazel*, their big triangular sails often painted with a stylised swirl representing the Eye of the Preservers. Occasionally, a merchant's caravel moved at a deliberate pace amongst the smaller craft, or a pinnace with a double bank of oars and a beaked prow sped past, scattering the local traffic, the beat of the drum which set the rhythm of the rowers sounding clear and small across the water.

Yama's chest tightened each time one of the pinnaces went by, partly in memory of the time when Dr Dismas had tried to kidnap him, partly because he was still not sure that he had escaped Prefect Corin. This might be no more than a reprieve until the Prefect or some other officer of the Department of Indigenous Affairs worked up a plan to snatch him back. He was certain that they were trying to track him. When he had woken, he had sent away more than a decad of machines which had been following the *Weazel*, and he expected to have to send away many more.

He did not want to think of the baby of the mirror people, of the dream in which the woman had spoken to him, of how badly the procession had ended. He wanted to put all of it behind him, and in the night had prayed that it would pass away, another one-day wonder in a city where wonders were commonplace.

To starboard was nothing but the wide river, stretching a hundred leagues to its own flat horizon, where tall white clouds were stacked above the farside shore. Day by day the clouds would grow taller and nearer, until at last they would break on the land and bring about the brief rainy season. Apart from an occasional fishing boat, trawling for deep-water delicacies in the company of a swirling flock of white birds, the outer reaches of the Great River were the preserve of the big ships. At any hour at least a hundred could be counted, scattered far and wide across the gleaming surface of the river.

Going downriver.

Going to war.

Of the five members of the crew of the *Weazel*, two, including the fat cook, were slaves who had been purchased at judicial auctions. The oldest of the sailors, the ship's carpenter, Phalerus, a bald-headed fellow with a sharp jutting lizard's face and a ruff of skin that rose above his mottled scalp, had once been a slave too – he had bought his freedom years ago but had stayed on anyway, for he knew no other home. One of the other freemen was a cheerful, simple-minded man named Anchiale; skinny and long-limbed, he swung amongst the rigging with astonishing agility. The third, a shy, quiet boy, was said to have killed five men in pit fights and was on the run from his handler because he had refused to fight a woman. This boy, Pantin, and the second slave, a grizzled little man with terrible scars on his back, were of Pandaras's bloodline. Whenever there was slack time the three sat together telling stories or singing ballads in their own language, one dropping out as another took over in rounds that sometimes went on for hours.

None of the crew were allowed to cross the brass line set aft of the cargo well in the whitewood deck (scoured each day by coconut matting weighted by the cook and dragged back and forth by two others) without the permission of either Captain Lorquital or Aguilar. The cargo well was covered with a tarpaulin cover as tight as a drum head, and filled with replacement parts for artillery pieces. Each part was sprayed with polymer foam: they were stacked under the tarpaulin like so many huge, soft eggs. By the forecastle bulwark were pens where hens and guineafowl strutted and a single shoat rooted in a litter of straw, and on the triangular bit of decking that roofed the forecastle, under the lines which tethered the leading point of the sail to the long bowsprit, was a light cannon under a canvas shroud.

It was here that Tamora chose to perch the second day, watching the city shore move past hour upon hour. She was in a kind of sulk, and even Aguilar, a jolly unselfconscious woman who claimed to have at least three men lusting after her in every city along the Great River, could not cajole more than three or four words from her at any one time.

Yama worried about Tamora's mood, but bided his time. He reflected that he still did not know her well, and knew even less about her bloodline. Perhaps she was still recovering from their adventures, and in particular from her long incarceration in the Department of Indigenous Affairs, of which she would not speak. Worse had happened to her, Yama suspected, than the shaving of her head. And no doubt she was worried that Eliphas might have usurped her position as Yama's adviser, resented him because he and not she had found clues to Yama's origin. It did not occur to him that there was a simpler answer, and that it lay within himself.

At the end of the second day, the *Weazel* finally passed beyond the downriver edge of the city. Red sandstone cliffs, fretted with the square mouths of old tombs, stood above mudbanks and shoals exposed by the river's retreat. The only signs of habitation were the occasional fishing hamlets, stranded beyond new fields made where the river had once flowed.

Early the next morning, the wind died. The triangular mainsail flapped idly and the ship drifted on the slow river current. The sun beat down from the deep indigo sky; the distant cliffs glowed through a haze of heat like a bar of molten iron; the big ships scattered across the gleaming sweep of the river did not change position from hour to hour.

At last, Captain Lorquital had the sail hauled down. Drag anchors were thrown over the sides. The ship's crew took turns to swim and even Captain Lorquital went overboard, dressed in a white shift as big as a tent, hauling herself down the ladder at the stern a step at a time. Pandaras spouted water like a grampus, splashing with his two friends; Eliphas swam with a dignified breaststroke, keeping his white-haired head above the water at all times.

Tamora sat cross-legged on the forecastle decking, studiously not looking at the frolics in the water around the ship.

Yama swam a long way out. He found a patch of oarweed and wound himself in cool, slippery fronds, a trick he had learnt as a child; the gas-filled bladders of the oarweed would keep him afloat without any effort on his part. The ship was a small black shape printed on the burning water. He could cover it with his thumb.

Soon he would pass his childhood home. He thought idly that he could jump ship then, and return to the peel-house and take up his life once more. He could marry Derev. It would be a metic marriage, but they would be happy. He would not mind if she took a concubine of her own bloodline. He would raise the children as if they were his own.

But this was no more than a pretty fantasy. He could not go home again. He could not pretend that things had not changed. That he had not changed, in ways that frightened and amazed him.

He could feel the tug of the feral machine far beyond the end of the world. And even as he floated on his back amidst the oarweed, machines gathered beneath him. Through a fathom of clear deep water he could see things with dull silvery carapaces and long articulated tails moving over each other on the red sand of a shoal. He ducked his head underwater to study this strange congregation, then floated on his back and watched the distant ship, and thought again of Derev and everything else he had left behind in Aeolis, and at last swam slowly back to the ship.

Tamora did not turn her head when Yama came up the ladder behind her. The white wood of the forecastle deck was hot under his bare feet; water dripping from his body darkened it for only a few moments before drying.

After a while, she said, 'I went up to the crow's nest. There's a smudge on the horizon. As if something very big has been set on fire. I've been wondering what it could be.'

Yama remembered the ship that Lud and Lob had fired as a diversion on the night he had been kidnapped by Dr Dismas. He said, 'Perhaps it is a galliot or a carrack, harried by pirates or heretics.'

'The war goes worse than I knew if there are raiding parties this far upriver.'

'There have always been pirates. They live amongst the floating islands in the midstream.'

Tamora shook her head. She said, 'The pirates have all gone downriver to the war. There are richer and easier pickings there.'

Yama reached out towards her scarred, naked scalp, but halted just short of touching it. Tamora said, 'I didn't believe you. I didn't want to believe.'

Yama understood. 'I am no different, Tamora. I still want nothing more than I did when I first met you. Once I have found my people I want to join the war and fight as best I can.'

'As best you can!'

She turned and looked up at him.

'I thought you were a monster. They told me that, in my cell. They told me that I might be pregnant by you, and be carrying your spawn. They examined me—'

'Tamora. I did not know. I am sorry.'

'No! *I* am sorry. I was weak. I allowed the fuckers to get inside my head. It wasn't you that put a monster inside me, but them. It's been whispering inside my skull ever since. I always knew what you were, see, but I wouldn't admit it. That's why those fuckers could get inside me. I won't let it happen again.'

With a sudden, violent heave, Tamora twisted around and threw herself full length on the decking. She moved so quickly that Yama did not have time to react. She kissed his feet and said, 'I did not believe in you. But I do now. I know that you are capable of miracles. I will serve you with all my life if you will let me.'

Yama helped her up, feeling a mixture of embarrassment and confusion and fright. He said, 'We shall fight side by side, as we said we would.'

'Isn't that what I said? But in what cause?'

'Against the heretics, of course.'

But he said it out of habit rather than conviction.

'Yes,' Tamora said. 'There's always that.'

16

OF MIRACLES

Eliphas said, 'I studied long on this when I was much younger. I came to the conclusion then – and I have found no reason to change my mind – that there are three classes of miracles.'

The old man was sitting with Yama and Captain Lorquital on the quarterdeck, in the shadow of the booming sail. It was the morning of the third day of the voyage. The wind had picked up in the night, blowing strongly from the upriver quarter of the farside shore. Water rushed by the hull and the river sparkled out to its distant horizon, salted with millions of whitecaps. There was a lightning storm ten leagues to starboard. Bright whips flickered under massed purple clouds, and now and again the sound of thunder rolled faintly across the face of the waters.

Eliphas ticked off categories of miracle on his long thin fingers. He said, 'There are those events in which something happens that is contrary to nature, such as the sun failing to reverse its course in the sky at noon, but instead continuing on to the farside. There are those events which may occur in nature, but never in that particular order, such as a dead man returning to life, or the Eye of the Preservers rising at the same time as the galaxy. And then there are those events which may occur naturally, but which in the case of a miracle do so without natural causation, such as this good ship dashing along with no wind behind her and no current beneath her. So we see that most miracles are quite ordinary processes, but without the usual causes or order.'

Ixchel Lorquital said, 'Myself, I don't believe in supernatural happenings. You'll hear talk ashore that sailors are superstitious. But what it is, we're careful because we can't take anything for granted on the river. It seems to me that miracles happen because people are hoping they'll happen. It's mostly religious people who claim to have seen a miracle, as is only natural. They're the ones who've the most to gain from it, even if they don't think that way. What I'd say is, if someone says they saw something contrary to nature, then it's more likely that they are mistaken.'

Eliphas nodded. 'All you say is true, sister. The most difficult thing about miracles is not trying to explain them away, but trying to prove that something is a miracle, and not simply a manifestation of natural law or ancient technology, or a trick cunningly set up, or an illusion dependent upon a willing suspension of belief on the part of the audience. In ancient times there were theatres of the mind in which participants could explore fantastic landscapes where miracles occurred as a matter of course, much as puppets in a street theatre may be made to fly, or breathe fire, or rise from the dead. But of course those were not miracles, but illusions.'

'Then you might say that I only dreamed that the caryatid came to life,' Yama said, 'or that I talked with the woman in the shrine of the Temple of the Black Well in a dream. Unfortunately, while it might be a comforting thought, I do not believe it to be true. The truth is that there are things in the world which are long forgotten, and somehow I am capable of waking them. The question is not how these things happened, but why they happened to me. If I knew the answer to that, I would be a happy man.'

Ixchel Lorquital said, 'Before my husband died, before the war, we travelled freely up and down the Great River. I reckon to have seen every bloodline on Confluence, including most of the indigenous tribes that haunt the Rim Mountains and the jungles and marshes down by the midpoint of the world. But I'm sorry to say that I have never seen anyone like you, young man.'

Yama smiled. 'I am comforted to think that I do not have to spend my time searching, for you have already done it for me.'

'Not even as sturdy a vessel as the *Weazel* could sail beyond the end of the river,' Eliphas said, 'and that is where Yama's bloodline may live.'

'No one goes there,' Ixchel Lorquital said, 'except for desperate prospectors and a few crazy pillar saints.'

Eliphas nodded. 'What better place, then, to hide?'

Ixchel Lorquital laughed and clapped her hands. They were fleshy, with loose webs of skin linking the fingers, and made a loud slapping sound. 'A gentleman as worldly as you could charm the fish from the water by persuading them that the air was safe to breathe. Fine words are wasted on an old woman like me. My daughter, on the other hand, is a connoisseur of compliments. It would cheer her up to hear some of that shiny talk of yours.'

Eliphas bowed.

'I have to say that a pale skin like yours,' Ixchel Lorquital told Yama, 'is not suited to the desert lands beyond the midpoint.'

Eliphas said, 'The memoir found by my esteemed friend Kun Norbu, the chief of clerks of the Department of Apothecaries and Chirurgeons, suggests that they live in caverns beneath the surface of the desert.'

Yama smiled. 'My father is always digging to find the past. What better place to find the first people of the world than in an underground city?'

'Just so, brother, just so. Many years ago, when I was still a young man – if such a thing can be imagined – my friend Kun Norbu and I found a passage below a ruined cliff temple. It led far underground, to a chamber containing many vast machines which were no longer functioning, and the chamber stretched so far into the darkness that after two days we scrupled to explore no further. But perhaps we should have continued. I have often dreamed of it since, and sometimes in these dreams I have glimpsed such wonders that on waking I wondered if I had gone mad.'

Eliphas's silvery eyes held faint concentric patterns that widened and closed like irises. There was a fine grain, as of well-cured leather, to his smooth black skin. His fingers: bunches of deftly articulated twigs. The neat whorls of flesh around the naked tympani of his ears.

Yama realised that he really knew very little about this old man, who had insisted on following him for no other reason, it seemed, than to rekindle the adventurous spirit of his long-lost youth. Last night he had discovered Eliphas crouched in the glory hole below deck, muttering to a small plastic rectangle, some kind of charm or fetish. What prayers, to what entity? Surely not to the Preservers. Tamora was right, Yama thought. He should not trust people so readily.

Eliphas returned Yama's gaze. He smiled. 'As for why you are able to do what you have done, brother, that's quite another question. We must ask whether miracles are caused because the Preservers or their agents actively interfere in the world, or whether, because the Preservers created the world, miracles occur simply as part of a natural chain of causation that was ordained from the beginning.'

Ixchel Lorquital took the stem of her unlit pipe from her mouth, leaned back in her sling chair, and spat over the rail towards the water rushing past below. She wiped her mouth on the back of her web-fingered hand and said, 'Everyone knows that the Preservers have turned away from the world. It has managed to carry on without them, for better or worse, so it never did need them to run everything. The same with everything else, I reckon. The stars were there before the Preservers came along – they just moved them into more pleasing patterns.'

'Just so,' Eliphas said. 'But there are some who believe that the Preservers, when they withdrew from the universe, did so in order to be able to extend themselves from first cause to last end. That they have spread themselves throughout creation. They watch over us still, but in a subtler fashion than by manifesting their will through the avatars of the shrines.'

'There were riots when the last of the avatars were silenced by the heretics,' Ixchel Lorquital said. 'Many temples were burned down. Those were black years.'

Eliphas said, 'In truth, the avatars which survived the Age of Insurrection were so few, and most were so confused, that they were merely a last resort for people searching for answers to unanswerable questions. They were no longer the fount of all wisdom, and the guides of the governance of the world, as they were in the Golden Age. Of course, those subroutines which acted as librarians were most useful. I still miss them. The written records are in no way as extensive as those of the shrines, and far harder to search.'

'The avatars were the eyes and mouths of the Preservers,' Ixchel Lorquital said. 'That was what I was taught as a pup, and I always did think it was put into our heads so we'd do as we were told, believing the Preservers were always looking over our shoulders in place of our parents.'

'Miracles need witnesses,' Eliphas said, returning to his original theme. 'Perhaps the Preservers raise fish from the dead in the deeps of the river, or juggle rocks in sealed caverns in the keel of the world, but to what point? Miracles teach us something about the nature of the world and our own faith, by contradicting our understanding of that nature and by revealing some truth about the minds of the Preservers. Of course, our own minds may be too small to contain that truth.'

Ixchel Lorquital closed her translucent inner eyelids, as if to help her look into her own mind. She said, 'To my reckoning, the only miracles are where there's such an unlikely chain of circumstance that you have to believe something interfered to make it come out like that. Anyone that kind of thing happened to would have to change their way of thinking about their place in the world.'

'The world is large,' Eliphas said, 'and the universe is far larger, and far older. If anything is possible, no matter how unlikely, then there is no reason why it should not have happened somewhere.'

Ixchel Lorquital said stubbornly, 'If something unlikely happens to you, especially if it happens to save your life, you'll stop and think hard about why it was you and not some other culler.'

Yama said, 'I am not so immodest as to believe that what I have been allowed to do – if I understand Eliphas right – is simply to shock me into changing my mind, or to teach me some lesson. Yet I do not want to believe that I am an agent who is being used by something I do not understand. It would mean that everything I choose to do is not by my own will, but by that of another. Must I believe that everything I do is willed elsewhere?'

What had happened, when the crowd had rioted? What had he said? What had he done? He could not remember, and did not dare ask because it would reveal his weakness and his shame.

'That is the question every self-aware person must ask themselves,' Eliphas said. 'One thing we know for certain is that the Preservers took ten thousand different kinds of animals from ten thousand different worlds and shaped them into their own image and raised them to intelligence. And yet that was not enough, of course. Each bloodline still must find its own way to grow and change, and that is the one kind of miracle on which we can agree.

'Think of a single man in a city of an unchanged bloodline. He may be a poet or a painter, a praise-singer or a priest, but we will say he is a poet. Like his father, and his father before him, he has followed his calling without thought. He has written thousands of lines, but any of them could have been written by any other poet of his bloodline, living or dead. Like all the unchanged, he has less sense of his own self than he has of the community of like-minded brothers and sisters of which he is but a single element. If he was taken from this community he would soon die, much as a single bee would die if it strayed too far from its hive. Like a hive, the communities of the unchanged are sustained not by the meshing of individual desires, but by blindly followed habits and customs.

'On this one night, alone in his room amidst thousands of others who are so very much like himself, our poet has a thought which has never before been thought by any of his bloodline. He pursues this thought through the thickets of his mind, and by its light he slowly begins to define what he is, and what he is not. Think of a sea of lamps which are all alike, all burning with the same dim flame. Now think of a single lamp suddenly brightening, suddenly shining so brightly that it outshines all others. Our poet writes down his singular thought in the form of a poem, and it is published and read because all poems are published and read without thought or criticism. That is the custom of the city, and no one has ever questioned it until now. But the thought that the poem contains lodges in the minds of our poet's fellows and blossoms there as a spark lodges in a field of dry grass and blossoms into a field of fire. Soon there are a hundred competing thoughts, a thousand, a million! The city is at war with itself as its inhabitants struggle to define their own selves. Factions fight and clash in its streets. Those as yet unchanged, innocent and incapable of understanding the change, are winnowed. The survivors leave the battlefield, perhaps to found a new city, perhaps to scatter themselves along the length of the Great River.

'We know the change is caused by unseen machines that swarm in every drop of water, every grain of soil, every puff of wind. These tiny machines bloom in the brains of the changed. They increase the mind's complexity while retaining its essence, as a city built over the site of a fishing hamlet may retain the old street plan in the arrangement of its main avenues. The machines are in the brains of the unchanged bloodlines, too, but they are quiescent, sleeping. It is not the process that is the mystery, but the cause. The thought that comes in the night, that wakes the machines and sets fire to a bloodline until it is burned out or changed. There is our miracle.'

This was the nature of Yama's miracle, although he (or the woman in the shrine, working through him) had not forced the change upon one of the ordinary unchanged bloodlines, but upon one of the indigenous races, which, it was said, could never change. Were some miracles stronger and stranger than others? Was there a hierarchy of miracles, or were all miracles equally unlikely, and therefore equally wondrous? Yama thought about this for a long time, while Eliphas and Ixchel Lorquital talked of other things.

17

THE CITY OF THE DEAD

Tamora's keen eyes had glimpsed the first intimation of smoke far downriver on the previous day, but it was not until the beginning of the afternoon watch that one of the sailors, perched on a ratline high above the deck, sang out that there was a fire to port, a fire on the shore. Everyone crowded to the rail. A little dark cloud hung at the edge of the land, a smudge that was, Pandaras declared, no bigger than a baby's claw. Captain Lorquital examined it through her spectacles before declaring that it was trouble they would do best to steer clear of. 'There are fast currents we can use further out, and there's a floating harbour we'd have had to cut around in any case.'

Yama had been staring at the shore with growing anxiety. He asked to borrow the Captain's spectacles and squinted through one of the lenses. The distant shore leapt forward, horribly familiar. For two days they had been sailing past barren hills populated with the ruined houses of the dead, but only now did he see that they were within sight of the heart of the City of the Dead.

There was the wide valley of the Breas, with its quilt of fields and channels; there was the skull-swell of the bluff, and the peel-house perched atop it like a coronet; the dusty hills with their necklaces of white tombs and stands of black cypresses saddling away into the far distance, where the snowy peaks of the foothills of the Rim Mountains scribbled a hazy line against the blue sky. And there was the shallow bay, with the long stone finger of the new quay running across the mudflats to the water's edge, and behind it the old waterfront of Aeolis.

And Aeolis was burning.

A triple-decked warship stood at the wide mouth of the bay, raking the little city with green and red needles of light that splashed molten stone wherever they struck. The bombardment seemed pointless, for every stone building was already smashed flat, and everything that could burn was already afire. Black reefs of smoke rolled up, feeding the pall which hung above the city like a crow's wing. Light needles struck the ancient ruins beyond it and stabbed into the flooded paeonin fields, sending up boiling gouts of mud and clouds of steam. Only the temple was unharmed, although its white facade was smudged by smoke and the tall lycophytes lining the long avenue which led to it withered or aflame.

Heartsick, Yama climbed to the quarterdeck, where Captain Lorquital and her daughter were already plotting a new course at the chart table, and heard himself asking them to turn the *Weazel* towards the shore.

'It is my home,' he said. 'Most of the people I hold dear live there. My family. My friends.'

He was thinking of Derev. She was brave and clever and resourceful. She would have found a way of surviving. She would have escaped to the hills above the city. She knew the way to Beatrice and Osric's remote tower. Or perhaps the Aedile had taken her in, with her family. He would have tried to protect all the citizens. Or perhaps she had taken refuge with their friend Ananda, the sizar of the priest of Aeolis. The temple still stood, after all.

Ixchel Lorquital looked hard at Yama and said, 'Sit down for a moment.'

Yama found that he was trembling. He said, 'I must go ashore.'

'It's too dangerous,' Aguilar said. 'I'll fight if I must, but not against a warship. She could burn us to the waterline with one shot.'

Tamora had followed Yama. She stood at his shoulder and said, 'Do as he asks.'

Captain Lorquital looked at her, looked at Yama. 'I must do what's best for the ship. That's a military action, and I won't put my ship and my crew in the middle of it.'

Eliphas was sitting in his customary place by the captain's sling chair. He said, 'If that is your home, brother, don't you think your enemies know that? They know you're travelling downriver, and perhaps hope to lure you ashore.'

Yama's mouth and throat were parched. His blood hummed in his head. 'Lend me the dory. I will put ashore myself. If you anchor here, I will rejoin you by midnight. If I do not, sail on without me.'

Aguilar said, 'And lose the dory?'

Eliphas said, 'You should not put yourself in danger, brother.'

Captain Lorquital said, 'I'd not be happy to lose a passenger, either.'

'I'll go with him,' Tamora said.

Pandaras jumped onto the rail behind her. He drew his poniard and flourished it above his head. 'So will I. He'll need his squire.'

Aguilar said, 'If these three want to go, let them do it now, before we're in range of the big girl's cannon.'

Captain Lorquital considered, sucking at her silver lip-plug, then told her daughter, 'I'm not happy about our passengers putting themselves in danger, but clearly they'll jump over the side if they have no other option. I'll keep to this course. If there's no trouble, perhaps they can go ashore.'

Aguilar stared at Yama and said, 'There'll be no good to be had from this.'

Captain Lorquital said, 'Have a little charity, daughter.'

'The first sign of trouble, and we run for it.'

Tamora said, 'Trust him, Captain. He will protect you.'

Yama bowed his head, hoping that the vessel of Tamora's faith would not be wrecked on the reef of his own self-doubt.

Aguilar snorted. 'Then pray that he can whistle up some wind. We'll need it.'

Yama and Tamora set out in the dory a little way upriver of the floating docks. Pandaras had been persuaded to remain behind to ensure that Captain Lorquital kept to the agreed rendezvous. He waved from the rail of the poop deck as, in the last light of the sun, the little ship heeled around and headed out towards the centre of the river.

Tamora said, 'I reckon that black-skinned, silver-eyed bookworm is right. It is almost certainly a trap.'

'It is almost certainly the work of the Department of Indigenous Affairs,' Yama said. 'The peel-house still stands, and it is theirs.'

If Derev had taken refuge in the peel-house, then she was surely a prisoner, and surely had been put to the question by Prefect Corin. That was worse than thinking that she might be dead. Yama remembered the way she had fluttered down from her perch in the ruins outside Aeolis, on the night when they had met the anchorite. So light and graceful, her long white hair floating about her lovely, fine-boned face.

Tamora took up her oar. 'Well, let's hope our foolishness takes them by surprise.'

They began to row towards the floating docks. After a while, Yama said, 'Do you think they might be afraid of me?'

'The Captain and her daughter are afraid of you, and so are the crew. And Eliphas most of all. I've been watching him. He has a knife, a pretty little stiletto, and sleeps with his hand on it.'

'I trust him more than he trusts himself,' Yama said, 'but much less than I trust you.'

'You should not trust him at all. He wants something from you.'

As they rowed, Yama kept turning to stare with a kind of sick eagerness at the burning city, but he could see little more than he had from the deck of the *Weazel*. There was too much smoke, and clouds of steam spurted up where hot needles raked the waterfront, boiling the water of the shallow bay and the mudflats where once he had hunted crabs and dug for treasure that everyone had believed to be buried there. He closed his hand on the disc he had found in the cell high in the Palace of the Memory of the People, no different from the ones he had dug up as a child, when he had been surrounded by treasure, had he but realised it.

They passed the long maze of pilings and platforms and cranes of the floating harbour. No one answered Yama's hail; the long sheds of the carpenters' workshops had a forlorn, deserted air. A door banged in the wind; nothing else stirred.

The setting sun was dimmed and greatly swollen, a red eye glaring through a shroud of smoke and steam. The air scraped the back of Yama's throat with an acrid, metallic taste. Above the cliffs of the bluff, the towers of the peel-house, rising through the trees of its garden, caught the last rays of the sun and glowed with red light; the river held a bloody cast that had Tamora grumbling about omens. Flecks of black soot rained all around, smudging their skin and clothes. Floating debris began to knock against the dory's hull. Broken bits of furniture, books, a raft of bottles, half-burned rags. Bales of last year's hay wrapped in black plastic, taut as drumheads, went floating by, carried on the ebb tide. There were no bodies, but Tamora said that meant little – the dead did not usually rise to the surface until distended by the gases of decomposition.

The dory slipped at a shallow angle towards the shore upriver of the bluff. The hum and sizzle of the light cannon of the warship carried clearly across the water. There was the snapping of heat-stressed stone, the explosive hiss of water suddenly shot to steam, the crackle of innumerable small fires.

As he rowed, Yama wondered again about Derev, wondered if the Aedile had resisted the razing of Aeolis and was now a prisoner in his own peel-house, wondered what had happened to all the citizens of Aeolis, and thought again of Derev. He felt a mixture of shame and fear and anger and helplessness. The memory of Prefect Corin' s bland face tormented him.

The stillness of the shore was shocked by the clatter of wings as a flock of wading birds took flight from the dory's approach, dipping as one as they turned across the water. Yama and Tamora splashed into thigh-deep water and dragged the dory up the shallow, muddy beach.

'I wish you'd brought your rapier,' she grumbled. 'I said I'd look after you, but you'll make it very difficult if you won't begin to think of defending yourself.'

'This is my home, Tamora. I will not return to it armed for war.'

'If your enemy has taken it, then it is no longer your home.'

'We shall see,' Yama said, but to appease her he broke a branch from a young pine tree that the river had cast up on this muddy strand. It had been stripped of bark and smoothed by the rub of the water, but it had not yet begun to rot, and made a sturdy staff half again his height.

The sun had set behind the Rim Mountains, but the Eye of the Preservers had not yet risen. What light there was came from the fires burning beyond the bluff. The flashes of cannon shot were as inconstant as heat lightning. All the windows of the peel-house were lit, and the sight gave Yama a little hope. Clearly, whoever commanded the peel-house did not expect an attack.

Tamora could see better than Yama in the near-dark, and led the way along an embankment above paeonin fields carved from river-bottom land. The old shoreline was marked by a line of ancient date palms. As a child, Yama had spent long summer afternoons in their shade while Zakiel had lectured him and Telmon on natural history. Not far from here, he had met with Derev on the night before he had set out for Ys with Prefect Corin. Now, as he and Tamora walked along the dusty embankment towards the palms, a faint crackling sounded ahead of them in the near dark. Tamora grasped Yama's arm and bent her head and whispered that she would go ahead and investigate.

'There are no machines,' Yama whispered back.

'Surely they would have machines.'

Light flared amongst the graceful arcs of the date palms. With a clatter of metal on metal, a pentad of spidery man-sized creatures skittered towards them, followed by armed soldiers.

'We should kill her,' the leader of the patrol, a young, nervous lieutenant, told the mage. 'She is no one important. Only a filthy cateran. Not even her mother will miss her.'

Tamora hissed, and tried to spit at the lieutenant. But the machine gripped her tightly; she could not even turn her head.

'My spiders will hold her as easily alive as dead,' the mage said, 'and she might tell us something useful. I will be glad to put her to the revolutionary. Her kind are strong-willed. It would be a fine demonstration of its powers.'

Yama and Tamora were bound tightly and painfully by the whiplike metal tentacles of the spidery machines. Their feet did not quite touch the ground. One of the soldiers had taken Tamora's sabre; when it had first pounced upon him, Yama had broken his staff against the machine which now held him prisoner.

'If you kill her,' Yama said, 'then you must kill me too, for I swear I will hunt you down.'

'You are in no position to tell me what to do,' the lieutenant said. He was a swarthy fellow in plastic armour and a leather kirtle. An energy pistol was tucked into the bandolier that crossed his transparent breastplate.

Yama said, 'I am wanted by Prefect Corin because I am important to him. He wants me to work with him, for the good of the department. If you kill my friend that is what I will do. I will become a loyal soldier, and one day I will find you and kill you.'

The lieutenant spat, and ground the oyster of phlegm into the dust with the toe of his boot. 'Oh, I will not kill her,' he said. 'There are worse things than death. Prefect Corin will probably give her to Nergal here. Then you will wish that you had allowed me to give her a clean death. A soldier's death. Nergal's machines are cruel, and these are the least of them.'

The other spiders were grouped behind the soldiers. Several held up stiff tentacles tipped with electric lamps whose glare had drawn swarms of moths from the darkness beyond. They were crude affairs, racks of aluminium tubing, electric motors and sensors raised high on three pairs of jointed legs. A decad of long tentacles, made of jointed rings of metal and tipped with clawlike manipulators, sprouted between the front pair of legs.

The tentacles of the spider which held Yama were wrapped tightly around his arms and legs. They pressed painfully into his skin and tingled with a faint electrical charge. He could not see into the minds of these machines; he could not even sense their presence. They were controlled by the mage, Nergal, a man with black skin that had a faint scaly iridescence in the distilled glare of the electric lamps, and large round eyes as dead as stones. He wore a long robe of metallic mesh, a tight-fitting copper skullcap. Close-fitting white plastic gloves sleeved his arms to the elbows.

'They are not susceptible to your power,' Nergal told Yama. He made shapes with his gloved left hand, and the machine which held Yama swung to the right, then centred itself again. Yama could feel the shapes made by the mage in his head, and allowed himself a faint hope.

Nergal said, 'These are a new kind of machine. They dance for me and no one else.'

'They have no minds,' Yama said, 'so how can they be truly useful?'

'They caught you, Yamamanama, and they hold you now. That is useful enough to begin with. They have as much logic as any insect. They do not need to think. Thinking is a luxury, as any labourer well knows.'

'Enough talk,' the lieutenant said. 'We will get this prize back to the peel-house. I have little liking for this bone orchard.'

'Quite right,' Yama said. 'The dead can be dangerous.'

'Hold your yap, or I will have you gagged,' the lieutenant said. 'You will be amongst the dead soon enough, and you can try to scare me then.'

When he laughed at his own jibe the soldiers around him did not join in. He glared at them and told them to fall in.

Marshalled by the shapes Nergal made in the air with his gloves, the machines which held Yama and Tamora walked amidst their fellows with a whine of servo motors and a clanking of hydraulic joints. The soldiers ambled on either side, clutching their rifles.

'Make these things go faster,' the lieutenant said. 'These two might have friends.'

'I thought you had driven them out,' Nergal said.

'We cannot guarantee safety outside our perimeter,' the lieutenant said.

'Once we reach the paved road they will be able to pick up speed.

The question of balance on rough terrain is very complex, and requires much processing power.'

'If there's any trouble, we'll have to leave them behind,' the lieutenant said.

'As you have told me repeatedly. I will reply as before. If there is any trouble, my machines will deal with it. Their processors and servos are battle-hardened, and they have infrared sights on guns which fire at the rate of a thousand slugs a minute. Soon all our armies will be composed of these machines, lieutenant. Imagine it! With my machines and the boy's powers, we will be able to drive the heretics over the end of the river by the end of the year.'

The lieutenant said, 'That is not to be spoken of in front of the men.'

Yama said, 'I assume you know something of the tests I endured when I was briefly a guest in the Palace of the Memory of the People.'

'I helped to devise them,' the mage said.

'Then I am in your debt. They taught me a great deal.'

The patrol was approaching one of the wide thoroughfares of the City of the Dead. Many merchants had been buried here. Their crowded tombs glimmered in the near darkness. They were marked by ornate pyramids, steles and statues; even in death, the merchants competed for status with their rivals.

'You will be our guest again,' Nergal said.

'He'll kill you all long before then,' Tamora said. 'You should let him go now.'

'I think not,' Nergal said. 'He is a valuable specimen. There is a peculiarity of his brain, or perhaps of his nervous system, which allows him to interface with the old machines. I must find out how it works, even if I have to open up his skull and slice him up bit by bit. But I hope that will not be necessary. Things will be much easier for both of you if you cooperate – if young Yamamanama tells me how it is done.'

'I do not know if I can tell you,' Yama said, 'but I hope that I can show you.'

'That's the spirit!' Nergal said. 'With your help I will find out how to control the machines usurped by the heretics. We will control all machines, you and I, and defeat the heretics and take back control of the world.'

They were amongst the first of the tombs now. The soldiers moved out on either flank and the machines picked up their pace as they stepped onto the paved road, shining their lamps this way and that. The tombs here were as big as houses, but crudely made. Further along, amongst the older, finer tombs, Yama felt a congregation waking and turning towards him. He told them what to do.

At once, the night came alive with the light of the past. The soldiers began firing in panic as the dead reached for them. Yama had delved into the roots of the aspects and changed them all. They were no longer men and women smiling, beckoning, eager to tell to anyone who listened the life stories of the dead they represented. Grim, withered faces and blazing eyes, or no eyes at all but black pits in fleshless skulls, leered out of the dark. Skin like leather shrunken on long bones, bony fingers clutching at faces. Mad laughter, screeches, a rumbling subsonic that Yama could feel through the struts of the machine which gripped him. A white mist fell like a curtain, filled with half-glimpsed nightmare shapes. The soldiers vanished into it; not even the muzzle flashes of their rifles could be seen, although their dismayed shouts and the rattle of rifle shots echoed sharply.

Somewhere in the mist the lieutenant shouted an order to cease firing, shouted that this was no more than a trick. But every soldier was lost to the rest, blinded by glowing mist and surrounded by the throng of the dead. Nergal's machines halted in the middle of what seemed to be a foggy street where skeletons of draught animals drew carts piled with rotting bodies that stirred with a feeble half-life. Pale things with burning eyes peered from the narrow windows of the houses. Below Yama, who was still clasped tightly by the spider, the mage sank to his knees. His gloved hands flexed at his throat, tightening inexorably. He stared at Yama with wide eyes. His mouth gaped as he tried and failed to draw breath.

Yama felt a terrible, gleeful triumph. He would not relent.

'I cannot control your machines,' he said, 'but I can control what you use to control them. You used old technology to quicken the new.'

Nergal did not hear him. Although still kneeling, he was dead, strangled by feedback. His head tipped forward until his brow struck the ground and his body relaxed and slumped sideways. The tentacles which held Yama lost their tension and he dropped to the ground. All around, the spiders collapsed in a clatter of metal.

The soldiers were still shooting at ghosts when Yama and Tamora reached the old stair. Yama had woken every aspect in the City of the Dead. The low hills, crowded with tombs and monuments, were half-drowned in a lake of eldritch mist. Tamora carried a rifle taken from a soldier she had killed; she had not found the man who had taken her sabre, and grumbled about the loss.

'I have already lost my own sword to the Department of Indigenous Affairs. It had a fine and bitter blade, and cost me dear enough. I would not be here if I had not been in debt with Gorgo because of it. And now they have taken its replacement.'

'I will find you another,' Yama said. 'There are many in the armoury.'

He told her that the narrow stair that wound up the sheer side of the bluff was used by the kitchen staff of the peel-house.

'There are certain herbs which grow only by graves. The dead impart a quality to the soil which they require. When I was much younger, I used to go with the youngest kitchen boy early every morning to pick them.'

'You have had a strange childhood, Yama. Not many would think to use a graveyard as a kitchen garden.'

'It is the quickest and straightest route. We will reach the peel-house long before the soldiers escape the illusions spun by the tombs.'

'I'm glad that Nergal is dead. Those things he made were evil.'

'Their creator may have had fell intentions, but they did not. Those spiders were simple machines, only a little more complicated than the rifle you carry. They did not possess true consciousness, and so lacked the capacity to distinguish between good and evil. They acted only as they were instructed to act.'

The triumphant glee that Yama had felt when he had murdered Nergal had evaporated. It was as if something had woken in him and then returned to sleep. But it was done, and perhaps it was better that the mage was dead; otherwise he would have become another enemy pursuing him.

'Can you really bend every machine in the world to your will?'

'I do not know. Little that Nergal said could be trusted. He liked to boast.'

They heard men shouting as they neared the top of the stair. Further off, dogs were barking eagerly.

Tamora's grin was a pale flash in the near-dark. 'I suppose that you can silence the watchdogs, just as you did in the merchant's house.'

'They know me,' Yama said. 'It was the second trick I learned.'

'And what was the first?'

'You have just seen it. Although I thought then that the aspects of the dead took no more than an ordinary interest in me, I know now that I drew them to me. I learned much from them as they talked about those they represented.'

'Nothing you do is ordinary,' Tamora said, and Yama heard in her voice the same note he had heard two days ago, when she had pledged her life to his.

There were two soldiers at the gate. Tamora whispered to Yama that they were hers. He squatted in bushes by the shoulder of the road and watched the play of lights within the lake of mist far below. It now covered all but the tallest monuments of the City of the Dead. There were watchdogs nearby, and he talked briefly with them before settling down to await Tamora's return.

She appeared so suddenly and silently that it was as if she had stepped out of a secret door in the darkness. The rifle was slung over her shoulder and she carried a short stabbing sword. She squatted beside Yama and licked blood from its blade before she spoke.

'I killed the first with my hands, and the second with the sword I took from the first. Are you going to sit there all night, or are we going to try to make the rendezvous? That is, if that fat seal of a captain bothers to wait.'

'She will. Pandaras will see to it, or sink her ship trying. But I do not think that she will need persuasion. She is a good woman.'

'Grah. You trust people too much. It will be your downfall.'

As they went through the gate, Yama called the watchdogs to him, and they ran eagerly out of the trees and across the wide lawn. Tamora stood her ground, her sword raised, while Yama greeted each by name and let them smell his wrists. Light from the windows of the peel-house glinted on their shoulder plates, glistened on wet muzzles and set sparks in black eyes.

'They will not hurt you,' he told Tamora. 'I have told them that you are my friend.'

'I have no liking for dogs. Even yours. Where is the door to this place?'

Accompanied by a tide of watchdogs, they went around two sides of the peel-house and crossed the courtyard where Yama had so recently said farewell to the Aedile and the household, where he had never expected to step again. The guardhouse and Sergeant Rhodean's quarters were dark.

'Anyone left alive must be out looking for us,' Tamora said. 'The watchdogs killed all the soldiers in the grounds, didn't they?'

Yama said. 'The two at the gate were yours; a decad more were mine.'

They went through the kitchen garden. It was much trampled. Broken furniture was scattered around an ashy fire. Every bit of glass in the forcing houses had been smashed.

Yama expected more destruction in the kitchens, but when he kicked open the door nothing seemed to have changed. By the big fireplace, people pushed back chairs and stood, the familiar faces of the household servants astonished and delighted in the flickering light of rush lamps.

'You are in danger, young ma-master,' Parolles, the tall, cadaverous master of the wine, said. He was the most senior of the servants who remained, and took it upon himself to speak for all of them. 'You have seen the ca-ca-candle lit in the town, and you have been drawn to it as he said you would. Go! Go now, before his soldiers find you!'

'I have already found them, with the help of my friend Tamora. How is my father, Parolles? What have they done with him?'

The flame of the lantern Parolles held put pinpricks of light in the centre of his slitted irises. Now these pinpricks grew softer, and suddenly a chain of little lights spilled down the old servant's hollow cheeks and began to drip from the end of his sharp chin. He said slowly, 'Your father is no longer here, young ma-master. He fled just last night, with the help of Sergeant Rhodean. There was a small rebellion.'

'We think they have gone across the river,' Bertram said. He was the pastry cook, half the height of Parolles and more than twice as wide. He held a big ladle at his shoulder like a club.

Parolles blotted his cheeks with the back of a hand. He said, 'At least, we think that is where they have gone. We cannot be sure. Some of the domestic staff escaped too, but not, alas, all. Those you see here, and the librarian.'

Yama felt a swelling sense of relief. He had feared the worst, but that weight had been taken from him. He said, 'Then my father is alive, at least. And the merchant's daughter, Derev? Did her family seek safety here?'

'I have not seen her,' Bertram said. 'I am sorry, young master.'

'They treated your father grievously, young master,' Parolles said. 'Set the traitor in his place, and put him to question using monstrous ma-ma-machines when he stood up to them over the matter of the burning of the town.'

'I have had revenge for that,' Yama said. 'The mage is dead.'

'But the viper still lives. When he saw the lights in the City of the Dead, he grew mighty sc-sc-scared, and ordered us locked up here.'

'When you burst in, young master,' Bertram said, 'we thought our time had come.'

'I will talk with this viper,' Yama said grimly.

'We will come with you, young master. We have no weapons beyond some kitchen tools, but we will do all we can. These are terrible times. The department fights against itself.'

'I hope it will end soon,' Yama said. 'Now, who is with me?'

They all were.

There were two soldiers in the minstrels' gallery of the Great Hall, where Yama had once spied on his father and Dr Dismas, but neither managed to get off a shot before Tamora raked them with rifle fire. One man fell back; the other tumbled over the railing and landed on the long, polished table with a heavy, wet sound, kicked once, and was still.

'The banners are gone,' Yama said, looking up at the vaulted ceiling. The hall looked larger and dustier without them.

'Burned,' Parolles said. 'A terrible burning they had. A bonfire of the vanities, the Prefect called it. He ma-made your father watch. A more terrible punishment than the machines, I think.'

Yama and Tamora led the pack of watchdogs and the servants through the Great Hall towards the double doors of the receiving chamber. Two more soldiers stood there. One fled; the other died cursing his comrade's cowardice. Yama and Tamora flung open the doors. The tall square room beyond was blazing with light, but empty. Although the four great tapestries were gone from the walls, the canopied chair on the central dais on which the Aedile had customarily sat while holding audience was still there.

Yama went around the dais and ducked through the little door and went up the narrow stairway that led to the Aedile's private chambers. There was no need for subtlety: the alarm must have been raised by now, and the cheering of the servants and the clatter of the watchdogs' armour against the stone walls made a tremendous racket. With Yama at their head, they burst into the corridor. Some of the servants were beating against the walls or stamping their feet, calling for the traitor to come out. If there had been any guards, they had fled. The door to the Aedile's chambers was locked, but Tamora shot off the mechanical lock and kicked the door open in a single smooth motion.

The room was hot and stuffy. It stank of sex and spilled wine and cigarette smoke, and was lit by hundreds of candles, stuck to every surface by shrouds of their own melted wax. Papers were strewn everywhere amongst a litter of empty bottles and bowls of untouched food. The brass alembic had been overturned, its mechanism spilled across a carpet sodden with wine.

The man on the bed raised a pistol, holding it in both hands as he took aim at Yama. It was Torin, the foreman of the stables. He was naked under the rumpled, filthy sheet, and so was the woman who clutched a bolster to her breasts – one of the whores from the town, her tall wig askew, her face caked with white make-up, black pigment smeared around her mouth like a bruise and more black pigment around her wide eyes.

'Do not think I will not use this,' Torin said, and showed a mouthful of needle teeth. His back was pressed against the carved bedhead; his shaved scalp gleamed with sweat. 'You came back, just as Corin said you would. And now you are mine. Dismiss the rabble and we will talk, boy.'

'Do not li-li-listen to him, young ma-master,' Parolles said.

Bertram added, 'He cannot kill us all.'

'He will do nothing.' Yama said. 'He knows that the soldiers are scattered, and that he cannot call upon Prefect Corin. How long have you been in his employ, Torin?'

'He will burn you like the town, if he has to.' The pistol wavered when Torin spoke, and he squinted down its stubby barrel and centred it on Yama's chest again. He was very drunk.

'Then you will burn too. It saddens me to see you like this, Torin. You were a good friend to my father.'

'I was always a good servant to the department. Your father was a traitor. He hid all he knew about you, even from Prefect Corin. But like the fool that he was, he wrote it all down. It is all here, somewhere. If he did not know what he had he is a fool. If he did, then he is the blackest traitor in our history.'

'I will not be the department's weapon,' Yama said.

'Then you are as much a fool and a traitor as the Aedile. I should burn you where you stand.'

Yama relaxed. He knew then that Torin could not kill him. He said, 'I will fight against the heretics like any other man. But I fear that Prefect Corin has other plans for me. He would use me to destroy the other departments. He would use me to take the world, if he could. Give me the pistol, and I will see that you leave here unharmed.'

'Keep away!' Torin pulled the naked woman in front of him and jammed the pistol against her head. 'I will kill her and the rest of you! I will burn this fucking pile of stones to the ground!'

The woman jammed an elbow under Torin's jaw. His teeth clicked closed on his lower lip; he howled with pain and the pistol went off. Its searing red beam missed his face by a fingersbreadth, burned through the canopy of the bed and reflected from the ceiling. The canopy burst into flame and Tamora crossed the room in a bound and broke Torin's arm with a single blow.

Torin, his face badly seared by the near miss, refused to answer any of Yama's questions. Yama left him to the tender mercy of the other servants and went with Tamora to find Zakiel.

The tall, gaunt librarian was in the library. He had been shackled around his neck, and a heavy chain looped up to a sliding clip on an overhead rail. There was a new, raw brand on his cheek. He watched calmly, his black eyes inscrutable, as Tamora hacked without effect at the chain with her sword.

'It is tempered steel,' he said. 'Quenched in the blood of oxen, I believe. You will damage the edge of your weapon, domina.'

'It's a piece of shit anyhow,' Tamora said, and tossed the sword onto Zakiel's neatly made cot, which stood as always beneath the racks of large ledgers, jumped up and swung from one of the studs which fastened the rail to the ceiling until it came away in a shower of plaster and dust. She slid the clip over the end of the rail and the free end of the chain dropped at Zakiel's bare feet.

The librarian wiped dust from the tops of the ledgers with the sleeve of his robe. He said, 'It might have been better if you had left me chained, young master. Torin may have received the rough justice he deserved, but those he serves will soon return.'

'You should come with us,' Yama said.

'I will not, as you well know. The books are in my care, and I do not think that I can carry them all with me. And if I could, how would I keep them safe? I trust you still have the copy of the Puranas.'

'I have always kept it beside me.'

Zakiel picked up the heavy chain and draped it over one arm. 'It will teach you much, in the right circumstances. I am pleased that you have returned, young master, but I fear that you have far to go.'

'How much did my father know about me, Zakiel? How much did he hide from the department?'

'And hide from you?' Zakiel smiled. 'He has told you the circumstances of how you came to Aeolis. As for the rest, he should tell you, not I, for he knows it better. He has been taken across the river by Sergeant Rhodean and his merry crew of guards. The good Sergeant wanted me to go, too, but alas—'

Yama smiled too. 'You could not leave the books.'

'Precisely. If I am a slave, it is not to the department, but to my duty as Librarian of the peel-house. And that is as it should be. I am doing my best to stay true to the oath I once broke when I was about your age. I thought in my blind pride that I knew better than those whom I served then, but now I know better. Age gives a certain perspective. It is like climbing a peak of the Rim Mountains. At last you run out of air, but the view is glorious. These books are my life, young master, and I cannot leave them.'

'Do you know what happened to the Amnan?'

'Many fled across the river. But Derev and her family left a day before the warship took anchor in the bay. Some said that they were spies, fleeing to safety, but I do not believe it.'

Yama's heart turned over. He felt that he could float to the ceiling. He grinned and said, 'She is safe.'

He thought that he knew where she had gone. She would be with Beatrice and Osric in the oldest part of the City of the Dead, in the foothills of the Rim Mountains.

Zakiel said, 'Perhaps she will return. Perhaps you might have a message for her.'

'Tell her that I go downriver, but that I will come back.'

'Is that all? Well, I will tell her, if I see her.'

'I shall miss you, Zakiel.'

'We have already said our goodbyes. Do not worry about me, or the books. Torin held many grievances against the peel-house, for he believed himself better than he was, but Prefect Corin's grievance is against you.'

'We must go,' Tamora said. 'There is less than an hour to the rendezvous.'

18

THE FLOATING FOREST

Yama and Tamora were late, but the *Weazel* was waiting for them as promised. They stood at the rail of the quarterdeck as the little ship angled away from the burning city. The warship was still raking the shore with needles of hot light. Although he had avenged his father's torture, Yama felt a mixture of shame and anger and helplessness. He stood straight, gripping the polished wooden rail so tightly that his arms ached to the elbows, tears slipping down his cheeks. He would be a witness, if nothing else. He would face this destruction without flinching, and carry it with him forever.

The sailors nudged each other and whispered that he wept for his home. They were only partly right. Yama did not know it, but he was also weeping for the loss of his innocence.

The lookout cried a warning. Tamora pointed to the lights of a picket boat that was coming around the point of the bay, heading out to intercept the *Weazel*.

'He is coming,' Yama said. 'I knew that he would.'

He felt a chill in his blood, and gripped the rail harder.

Captain Lorquital ordered the staysails unreefed. 'We'll make speed as best we can,' she told Yama. 'Those boys have oars, but as long as the wind holds we can reach the shoals and banyan islands downstream, and lose them there.'

'If we don't run aground on a mudbank, or a tangle of roots, and make ourselves a sitting target,' Aguilar said.

'We don't have a choice,' Captain Lorquital said. 'We can't outrun them in a straight chase.'

Tamora wanted to unshroud the cannon, break out the hand weapons, and make a stand, but Aguilar stood four-square in front of the armoury chest. Yama put a hand on Tamora's arm and was astonished to discover that she was trembling. Prefect Corin had left his mark on both of them.

'I'll hold by what we agreed,' Captain Lorquital said, 'and so will you. We've no fight to pick here, no matter what's right and what's wrong.'

Silhouetted against a reef of flame and smoke, the picket boat came on across blood-red water, its single bank of oars striking to the beat of a drum. A white lantern shone at its masthead, signifying that it wished to parlay. It steadily closed the gap for several minutes; then the *Weazel* caught the wind and the gap began to widen again.

Something shot from the side of the picket boat. It skipped over the water like a flung stone, and before Tamora could take aim with her captured rifle it abruptly shot high into the air above the *Weazel*. It was a small machine, as flat as a plate and spinning rapidly, circling above the tip of the mast. As with the machine which had been sent against Yama in the Department of Indigenous Affairs, its mind was hidden by complex loops of self-engulfing logic that clawed at his attention as he tried to cleave through them. It was like plunging into a briar patch full of snapping jaws and whirling blades. A ghastly light suddenly flooded from the machine, etching everyone's shadow at their feet, and a voice boomed out, ordering the *Weazel* to stand to or have her sail cut free.

Captain Lorquital cupped her hands and shouted across the widening gap of water to the picket boat. 'Show your authority!'

The machine tipped, aiming its sharp spinning edge at the forestays; at the same moment, Yama untangled the last of its defences and found its tiny linear mind. It flung itself sideways, falling a long way before striking the water and vanishing with scarcely a splash.

Captain Lorquital gave Yama a long and hard look, but said nothing.

'Well,' Tamora said, 'he'll know you're on board now.'

'He already knows,' Yama said.

It became a contest of skill between the *Weazel* and the picket boat. The warship swung her light cannon away from the burning town, but too late: it fired no more than two ranging shots before the *Weazel* passed beyond the downriver point of the bay (the paeonin mill had been levelled to a hummock of glassy slag), and the warship and the burning city were lost from sight.

Yama dredged his memory for a map of the complicated web of currents as the *Weazel* began to thread the maze of inshore mud shoals and stands of banyans. A man at the bow dropped a weighted line and called the depth every few minutes, and Yama stood with Captain Lorquital and the helmsman through the night while the crew took turns to rest. Pandaras and Eliphas dozed on their mats under the awning; Tamora paced the deck amidships or stood by the man at the bow, peering into the darkness ahead or sharpening the long narrow blade of the sword she had taken from the armoury of the peel-house. Eliphas woke near dawn and came up onto the aft deck to ask how things stood.

'We aren't out of trouble yet,' Ixchel Lorquital said. 'But if the wind stays fair and true we might have a slight chance of losing our friends.'

There were floating islands spread everywhere ahead of the ship: ten thousand green dots scattered across the shining sweep of the river. The ranges of cloud towering above the farside horizon caught the early light of the sun. Their folds and peaks glowed white and purple and gold.

Eliphas leaned at the rail next to Yama, spat accurately into the white water that purled along the ship's hull, and said, 'You should rest, brother. In my small experience of adventure, sleep is a most valuable currency.'

'Why did they destroy Aeolis, Eliphas? What good did it do them, to kill so many innocent people and make the rest homeless?'

Eliphas's silvery eyes shone with reflected light. His black skin gleamed as if oiled; scraps of light were caught in the tightly nested curls of his white hair. 'Because they wanted to lure you into a trap. Because they have confused their duty and the base desires of their own selves. Because they serve the Preservers in name only, and have turned themselves into a thing that would destroy the world to save it.'

'The other departments should have risen up against Indigenous Affairs long ago.'

'A few did, and were destroyed. And many others were subverted or absorbed, like the Department of Vaticination. It is too strong to be overthrown now. It has fed on the war, and the war has become its reason for existence.'

Yama remembered the story told to him by the headman of the village of the husbandmen, the story of the department known as the Head of the People, which had absorbed all others until at last it had nothing to fight against but its own self. Surely, he thought, the Preservers had not created the world so that it would repeat the same stories in a series of futile cycles, like a book read again and again by an uncomprehending idiot.

He said, 'They are determined to absorb me, too. I have managed to escape them so far, but am not sure that I can escape them.'

Eliphas said, 'Do not underestimate yourself, brother. The machine you destroyed is nothing. What you did to free us is nothing. You are capable of much more.'

'I have done bad things before this, Eliphas, although I did not mean to. I fear that I might do them again, while trying to save myself.'

Captain Lorquital had been standing at the stern rail, peering upriver through her spectacles; now she came over to Yama and Eliphas and said, 'I can see no sign of the picket boat, or the warship. But sooner or later we'll have to strike out for open water, and I fear that they may be waiting for us.'

'They will not give up,' Yama said.

Captain Lorquital regarded Yama thoughtfully. 'If it comes to making a stand, what would you do?'

'I will try my best to save the ship and everyone on it. Even if it means that I must surrender.'

Captain Lorquital seemed satisfied by this answer, but after she had gone to wake Aguilar, Eliphas said, 'I hope you will be able to put your scruples aside when the time comes to act, brother. You must destroy your enemy before they destroy you.'

Yama thought that Eliphas was wrong. If he defined himself against his enemies, then he would be no better than they. But there was a part of him that exulted in the idea of battle – a voracious cayman at the base of his brain given voice, he believed, by the woman in the shrine. Satisfied not by persuasion but by forceful coercion, not by courtship but by rape, a thing of uncontrolled appetite and lust that would destroy the world rather than die. He must not give in to it. He must find a way of mastering it. But would he be able to control himself if he came face to face with Prefect Corin again, or learned that Derev or his father had been killed? What would he be willing to sacrifice?

The free men of the crew broke fast with manioc porridge while the cook and the other slave scrubbed soot stains from the white deck with lye and holystones. Yama ate without appetite. Although he was very tired he felt that he could not rest, so Pandaras brought him the rifle and suggested that he should try some target practice. For an hour, Yama blipped slugs at bits of flotsam floating by, and then practised cleaning and reassembling the rifle under Tamora's instruction, his fingers thick and clumsy with lack of sleep. At last Pandaras got him to lie down, and he fell asleep at once, and woke with the sun riding at its highest point.

Pandaras fetched a hunk of black bread and a bowl of curried lentils salted with flecks of coarse fish flesh, and squatted beside him as he ate. The triangular mainsail and the square staysails stood taut against the blue sky. There was a ragged green line to starboard: a banyan forest.

Yama said, 'Where do we stand?'

'The warship is in sight again, master. It is a long way behind us, but has spread all its sails, and follows the same wind. It will catch up with us inside a day, the captain says. Perhaps less.'

Yama used the heel of the bread to scrape up the last of the lentils. 'I cannot keep killing people. I have already killed too many.'

'It might not be necessary, master. The captain has decided to seek shelter in one of these floating forests. She and Aguilar talked it over while you slept.'

'I am sorry to have brought you on such a futile adventure, Pandaras.'

Pandaras struck an attitude. 'I was a pot boy when I found you. Now I am squire to a hero.'

Yama knew that it was not as simple a thing as many people supposed, to give up your life and dedicate it to another. He saw the love in Pandaras's gaze and smiled. 'A foolish hero at best.'

'If that's true, then I'm as much a fool for following you, master. But I don't think I am a fool at all. Now, give me your tunic, so that I can sponge out those stains. I have your second-best shirt here, clean and pressed. We have standards to maintain, even in these desperate circumstances.'

Thousands of banyans had rooted in a long, narrow shoal at the backwater edge of the swift current in which the *Weazel* was sailing, a temporary forest that stretched away downriver for several leagues. Now, as spring edged into summer, the forest was beginning to break up. Already, singleton banyans floated along the edge of the shoal, turning in stately circles, and fleets of fist-sized seeds, each with a single upright leaf like a sail, drifted on the currents.

The *Weazel* entered the forest's maze by a channel so wide that it could have held a pentad of ships side by side, and for a while continued to make way under sail. But the channel split and split again, and with each turn it grew narrower until at last the staysails and their spars had to be drawn in. The canopies of the banyans knitted into a living roof, and Captain Lorquital had the mast lowered, too. Aguilar started the little reaction motor, normally used for manoeuvring in harbour. It made a hollow knocking sound and blew puffs of black smoke from the stern vent. The smoke stank of stale cooking oil. The sailors hacked at branches which caught in the rails or grated along the gunwale. Bottom soundings gave wildly differing readings from minute to minute, from narrow channels where the *Weazel*'s keel scraped a tangled net of interlaced feeder roots to places so deep that no sounding could be made.

Dim green light, the odour of rotting vegetation and of silent green growth, close wet heat. Orchids bright as flames grew amongst the glossy, shingling leaves. There were loops of red-leaved creeper and strangler figs and parasitic mangroves, grey hanks of hanging moss. Parts of the waterway were covered with pavements of brick-red water fern or wide patches of water hyacinth, whose waxy white flowers gave off a sickly-sweet scent. Dragonflies with wingspans as long as a man's arm and jaws that could nip off a finger roosted on the upright spikes of breather roots; armies of metallic blue emmets staged tireless campaigns and caravans along mossy boughs. Birds stalked from floating leaf to floating leaf with a swift strutting gait on feet with long widespread toes; hummingbirds darted from orchid to orchid; parrots flashed through the green shade; gar and caymans raised their snouts to watch the ship labour past. A troop of long-nosed monkeys swung along their aerial highways above the channel, screaming curses and raining orange excrement. The old carpenter, Phalerus, shot two with a short bow, and the cook set to skinning them for the pot. Once the flat face of a manatee rose beneath the surface of the green water and regarded them with brown, human eyes – good to eat, but bad luck to kill, Phalerus confided to Yama.

Tamora sat astride the bowsprit, the rifle cradled in her arms, her shaven, scarred head turning from side to side as she scanned the green press of leaves passing by on either side. Twice, the channel closed into an impenetrable wall of leaves and branches, and the ship had to labouriously reverse course. Once, she grounded on the half-sunken, rotten corpse of a dead tree grown through with the feeder roots of its living neighbours, and had to be pulled off with a block-and-tackle rig attached to the main trunk of a grandfather banyan, with half the crew pulling on the ropes and the other half pushing with poles.

The light went quickly, a sudden gold-green dazzle amongst the trees, a swift decline to pitch black. Frogs peeped and whistled; fish made splashes in the water around the ship, which in the last light had anchored at the junction of two wide channels. Bats swooped amongst the yards of the mast; insects signalled to each other with coded flashes of yellow or green light.

Supper was roast monkey flesh with fried bananas and rice (Tamora sucked meat from a raw rack of ribs and cracked the thin bones for marrow), eaten in the dim red light of half a dozen lanterns, against which big black beetles ceaselessly dashed themselves in unrequited lust. Afterwards, Yama climbed the tallest of the neighbouring banyans, and looked out across a sea of trees slashed and divided by forking channels. Upriver, a sudden flash of light defined the long, irregular shape of the floating forest. He counted the seconds until the sound reached him: twenty-five. A few moments later there was another flash, a little way downriver from the first. There were machines out there too, but so far off that he could do no more than sense them.

He climbed down out of the fresh cool breeze into the dark clammy fetor under the canopy of the banyans, walked along a mossy horizontal branch and vaulted the rail at the ship's waist. When he told Captain Lorquital what he had seen, she drew on her pipe and blew a cloud of fragrant smoke before replying. She was the only one not troubled by the bites of blackflies which at sunset had risen above the still water.

'They are burning their way through the trees with their light cannon,' she said. 'If I was planning the chase, I would put the warship downriver, beyond the point of the forest, and have the picket boat quarter back and forth, hoping to flush us out. The forest is many leagues long but it is not very wide, and our enemy knows that we are heading downriver and cannot hide here indefinitely. We're caught between the two of them.'

Aguilar was sitting cross-legged by her mother's sling chair. She said, 'It would have been better to take our chances on the open river.'

In the darkness by the rail, Tamora said, 'We will make a stand here. Set up an ambush, and let our enemies come to us.'

'We don't even know where they are,' Aguilar said. 'We don't even know where we are. We've trapped ourselves in a maze.'

Yama said, 'As long as we follow the channels where there is a current, we will find our way out again.'

The glow of Captain Lorquital's pipe brightened when she drew on it. Bright, then dim, like an insect signalling in the dark. She said, 'I have heard of the trick with the currents, but twice today we were following a current that went under a stand of trees and left us in a channel with no current at all.'

Phalerus appeared at the head of the companionway, a shadow against the glimmer of the white deck below. He said, 'Something is coming.'

Yama and Tamora followed him to the bow. They climbed up by the cannon and the old sailor said, 'Listen.'

The metallic peeping of frogs; little plashes and ripples in the current. Yama whispered that he heard nothing unusual.

'They are out there,' Tamora said, and opened the valve of the lantern she carried.

Its beam fell across the still black water. On the other side of the channel, backed by a wall of foliage, a green-skinned man raised a hand in front of his face.

19

THE FISHER FOLK

The sailors cracked the valves of more lanterns, and wherever they shot their beams they discovered little round coracles, each with two men sitting cross-legged and holding leaf-shaped paddles. They had legs as long and thin as those of storks, and their naked torsos were mottled with green and dun patches. There were more than a hundred of them.

Yama laid a hand on Tamora's shoulder and said, 'It is all right. They are no enemy.'

'No friends either, to arrive unannounced under cover of darkness.'

'This is their home. We are the unannounced arrivals.'

Yama hailed the fisher folk, and asked if there was one amongst them called Caphis – the man who had helped him after he had escaped from Dr Dismas's attempted kidnapping. The shoal of coracles swirled apart to allow one to move forward. A dignified old man with a cap of white hair stood in it. His left arm ended above the elbow; silvery scars crosshatched his chest and shoulder.

'You are the son of the Aedile of Aeolis,' the old man said. 'Caphis is my son. I will come aboard and talk with you.'

The old man's name was Oncus. He explained that he had lost his hand to a grandfather cayman when he was a young man and usually wore a hook in its place, but he had taken it off on this occasion because it might be mistaken for a weapon.

'We have no quarrel with the son of the Aedile of Aeolis,' he said. 'The Aedile has always been good to us. Before he came, the Mud People of Aeolis hunted my people for sport and for food, but the Aedile put a stop to that. Because of your father, our two bloodlines have lived in peace for a hundred years. But now the Mud People are scattered across the river and two ships burn the forest. Bad times have come again.'

Oncus sat cross-legged on the main deck under the awning, between Yama and Captain Lorquital, who lay on her side, propped by bolsters and puffing calmly on her pipe. Aguilar, Pandaras, Eliphas and Tamora completed the circle. Tamora's sword lay across her lap. A small entourage of fisher folk stood behind Oncus; above, the sailors stood along the slanted trunk of the folded mast.

Yama said, 'It is my fault, grandfather. They are burning this floating forest because they know I am hiding in it.'

Oncus nodded. 'One of them came to me three days ago, when the warship first arrived off the stone shore of the Mud People's city. He showed me an image of you, and said that we would be rewarded if we found you. You must be a great enemy of theirs, if they destroy your home before you can return to it.'

'They believe me to be their enemy, and so I am, because of what they have done.'

''Then that is another reason to help you. They have no respect for the river. Any enemy of theirs is a friend of ours, and you are doubly a friend, for you are the Aedile's son.'

'Is he alive? And the people of Aeolis – are they safe?'

'They were driven from their homes before the big ship set fire to the land. If any refused to leave, and it is possible that some did, for the Mud People are a stubborn race, then they are dead now. The city has been burned to its foundations and its fields boiled dry. The Aedile tried to stop it. He stood on the stone shore and said that if the Mud People's city was burned then he would be burned, too. Soldiers took him away and locked him in his own house, but he escaped.'

Yama nodded. 'I have heard that he escaped, and it pleases me to hear it again. Where is he? Is he safe?'

'Most of the Mud People are crossing to the farside shore,' Oncus said. 'It is as if the beginning of winter is already upon us. The Aedile overtook them. We found him on a boat in the middle of the river the day after the big ship began to burn down the city. We took him across the river and left his boat adrift, so that his enemies might think him drowned. That is how I know this story.'

'Then I am in your debt, Oncus, as I am in your son's debt. You helped my father, and your son helped me.'

'Caphis is not here, and I cannot speak for him. But as I understand it, he was able to help you only because you saved him from the trap of one of the Mud People. And your father saved countless lives of my people. Only the Preservers can weigh such debts.'

Captain Lorquital stirred in her nest of bolsters and said, 'If we can escape this forest, then the warship will follow us, and no more damage will be done to your home.'

'The small ship is searching the edge of the forest,' Oncus told her. 'The big ship waits downriver. They both shine fire into the trees and hope to make you quit this place.'

'As I thought,' Captain Lorquital said.

'We sailed into a trap of our own making,' Aguilar said.

'Let them find us,' Tamora told her. 'We'll turn the trap on them.'

Pandaras said, 'It seems simple to me. We should leave the ship and go with these people. They can take us to Yama's father.'

Captain Lorquital said, 'I can no more leave my ship than you can leave your master, Pandaras.'

'And I will not run away from a fight,' Tamora said.

Yama said, 'My enemies have orders to find me. They will not give up their search. And if they think Oncus's people are hiding me, they will burn more than this forest.'

'They have eyes everywhere,' Oncus said.

The man who had come aboard with him stepped forward. He carried a small leather sack, and opened it to display the little machine inside. It was the size of a child's fist, and most of its delicate vanes were crumpled or broken off.

'We caught this one in a net and drowned it,' Oncus said. 'There are others. They fly through the air at the edges of the forest.'

Yama touched the machine. For a moment, light glimmered in its compound eyes and a single intact vane feebly beat the air. But the movement was little more than a reflex powered by the small amount of charge remaining in its musculature, and the machine died before he could learn anything from it.

He looked around at the fisher folk and the sailors standing above them. Two of the soldiers touched their throats with the tips of their fingers.

'You must destroy them, brother,' Eliphas said. 'You know that you can. Don't hold back.'

Oncus said, 'You cannot leave the forest because it hides you, yet you cannot stay because your enemies will burn it to the waterline. But we will help you. We will move the forest.'

'In winter, the trees root and draw nutrients from the river mud,' Yama told Pandaras. 'In summer they break away from their feeder roots and float free on the flood. They float all summer until tide and chance draw them back together at the beginning of winter. The fisher folk know how to speed up this natural process. It is how they control the floating islands on which they make their homes.'

Pandaras was tired and frightened, and in no mood for a lesson in natural history. He said, 'You should sleep, master.'

'Not yet. Oncus is right. There are many machines. At the moment they are keeping their distance. Their master knows what I can do. But sooner or later they will move closer. They will test me. Besides, although I have lived by the river all my life, I have never seen this before.'

All around the ship fisher folk were working by the dim glow of oil lamps, sinking sacks of moss amongst the roots of the banyans. The moss had been soaked in an extract of the hulls of banyan seeds; as this diffused into the water, it stimulated the trees to shed the myriad feeder roots which anchored them. The night was full of the creaking and groaning of banyans which were beginning to shift on the currents; the water all around the *Weazel* seethed with bubbles as pockets of gas were released by roots dragging through mud.

Near dawn, Oncus returned to the ship and told Yama that another machine had been caught. Yama was taken out in a coracle to the net where it hung, at the farside edge of the floating forest. The forest was beginning to break up there. Irregular channels and lagoons opened and closed as trees spun slowly around each other. The water was stained with silt and alive with shoals of fish.

The picket boat was close by, slowly advancing downriver amongst trees that had become a myriad floating islands. Every now and then the red flash of the picket boat's cannon lit the dark sky above the tops of the trees, followed by the hiss and crack of water flash-heated to steam. The air had a brassy taste, and there was a constant flutter of falling ash flakes.

'They will be here soon,' one of the fisher folk said, and Yama saw that the man's hands were shaking as he aimed the beam of his lantern at one of the floating islands.

The net, woven from monofilament fibres combed from float-bush seed heads, fine as air and strong as steel, was strung above the top of the banyan, guyed by bamboo poles. The machine caught in it glittered and gleamed in the beam of the lantern; it began to vibrate in short furious bursts as soon as the light touched it, shaking the poles and branches to which the corners of the net were fastened.

'Some of the machines can burn their way free,' Oncus said, 'but ones like these are merely spies. They are stupid and weak. We sometimes catch them by mistake. They are blind to our nets, or fly too fast to avoid them.'

'And you destroy what you catch,' Yama said distractedly. He was unpicking the familiar tangle of logical loops and snares which hedged the machine's simple mind.

'Only the Preservers need to see all,' Oncus said.

The machine possessed less intelligence than the watchdogs which patrolled the grounds of the peel-house. After he had cut through its defences and convinced it that he was its handler, Yama called for the net to be lowered, and cradled the machine while two of the fisher folk began to cut the tangles of fine filaments knotted around its vanes.

They worked quickly, but the machine was still caught fast when an intense needle of red light lanced across the channel behind them. The needle struck through the canopy of a banyan, which immediately burst into a crown of fire; a second struck the main trunk and burst it apart in an explosion of live steam and splinters. The two coracles were lifted and turned on a swell of smoking water. All around, floating banyans rocked to and fro. The coracles spun apart and the net stretched out between them, wrenching the machine from Yama's grip. Then the swell passed and the coracles revolved towards each other, and the net dipped towards the water. For a moment, Yama feared that the machine would be drowned, but Oncus grabbed the net with his good hand and hauled in the slack.

Yama cradled the machine to his chest while the last filaments were cut away. But before the two coracles could drive for cover, red light flashed again and two more trees exploded into flame. Steam and smoke enveloped them. A drumbeat swelled; a dark shape glided between the burning trees.

The coracles bobbed on its wake, and then the picket boat had gone past them.

*

Yama sent up the machine he had captured as a hunter sends up a hawk, and used it to call other machines to him. It took several hours to find the way back, because the floating forest had begun to break up, and hundreds of channels were opening and closing in a vast, shifting maze. By the time the two coracles reached the *Weazel*, they were trailed by a cloud of glittering machines, like birds following a fishing boat. The sailors eyed them uneasily, but the fisher folk beat spears and paddles against the sides of their coracles at this demonstration of Yama's power.

The *Weazel* had been hauled into a narrow berth hacked from the dead heart of a grandfather banyan, and the sailors had covered her sides with a blanket of leafy branches. Tamora and Aguilar commandeered four coracles and lashed a platform across them and took the light cannon to the nearside edge of the forest. By the time they returned, the banyan in which the *Weazel* was hidden had floated off the river bottom and was adrift amongst a flotilla of drifting trees.

Late in the afternoon, they passed one of the places struck by the warship's light cannon. It was as wide as the channel by which the *Weazel* had first entered the shoal. The smouldering stumps of banyans poked through water choked with ashes and the corpses of parboiled fish. Hundreds of small fires crackled and spat in the canopy on either side, and smoke hung thick in the air.

The fisher folk murmured to each other at the sight of this destruction. Oncus told Yama that one day there would be a reckoning. 'We are not a fierce folk, but we do not forget.'

By the middle of the afternoon there was open water on all sides of the banyan's floating island. Yama climbed to the topmost branch and saw a vast archipelago of little green islands scattered across leagues and leagues of water. The rest of the forest was a green reef shrouded in a long cloud of smoke and steam turned golden by the light of the sun.

When he climbed down, Captain Lorquital said, 'We are set on our course now.'

'I still say we shouldn't have left our only real weapon behind,' Aguilar said.

'If the timer works, daughter, then it will serve us better than by being here.'

'Of course it will work. I set it myself. But our fee will not cover the cost of replacing it. It's a poor bargain.'

'Better poor and alive than rich and dead,' Captain Lorquital said, and Aguilar laughed for the first time since they had entered the forest.

'That's just what father would have said.'

'Sometimes he managed to stumble on a truth without my help.'

Yama said, 'I'm sorry that you have to sacrifice your cannon. But our enemies will not believe their machines because they know I can fool machines. They must have something they can see, something to aim at.'

'I've never had to fire the thing in anger,' Ixchel Lorquital said, 'but I'll still miss it.'

At nightfall, the lines which lashed the *Weazel* to the banyan were cut and she used her reaction motor to manoeuvre out of her hiding place. It took an hour to raise the mast and haul up the sail; afterwards, everyone stood at the port rail and watched the dark line of the forest. They watched for a long time, and cheered when at last the flash of the cannon showed, a vivid red point of light doubled by its reflection in the river. The sharp crack of the discharge rolled across the water a moment later; then the cannon flashed again.

Yama raised his arms – a bit of theatre, for he had already given his order. The machines fled away from the ship in a whirring rush, scattering towards the forest, where they would lay a hundred false trails in the opposite direction to the *Weazel*'s intended course.

Even as the machines flew up, the warship answered the *Weazel*'s light cannon with a bombardment that lit half the sky. At once, Ixchel Lorquital gave the order to unfurl the sail and lift the anchor. While the sailors busied themselves, the fisher folk departed without ceremony, their tiny bark coracles dwindling into the river's vast darkness. Oncus kissed Yama on the forehead and tied a fetish around his wrist. It was a bracelet of coypu hair braided with black seed pearls. When Yama began to thank Oncus in the formal fashion taught by his father, the leader of the fisher folk put a finger to his lips.

'Your life is mine,' the old man said. 'I give you this to protect and guide you on your journey. I fear you will have much need of it.'

Captain Lorquital thanked Oncus for the safe passage of her ship, and gave him a steel knife and several rolls of tobacco. And then he too was gone.

The *Weazel* caught the wind and heeled to port as she set course towards the farside shore. Far off, the cannon of the warship set up a stuttering rake of fire. Vast clouds of steam boiled up as needles of hot light lashed open water. If the dismounted cannon fired again, the flash of its discharge was lost in the bombardment.

Yama stood at the stern rail and watched red and green lights flash within spreading clouds of steam and smoke. The bombardment continued for an entire watch. Yama knew then that Prefect Corin would rather kill him than capture him. He watched until the warship's cannon finally stopped firing, and at last the night was dark and quiet beneath the red swirl of the Eye of the Preservers.

20

THE AEDILE

The farside shore was a plain of tall green grasses winnowed by unceasing wind. It was not wide, at that part of the river. During the festival at the beginning of winter, Yama and Telmon had often walked from riverbank to world's edge in a single day. Telmon had always worn a set of bolas around his right arm, like an indigen from one of the hill tribes. Several times, Yama had seen him bring down one of the moas that roamed the grass plains, breaking the bird's legs with the bolas and throwing himself on its thrashing body to cut its throat. Telmon had carried a sling, too, and had taught Yama how hurl stones with killing force at ortolans and marmots. He had given Yama the bolas and the sling when he had left for the war: remembering all this as the *Weazel* approached the shore, Yama supposed that they were still in his room in the peel-house.

As the Great River retreated, a wide flood plain of emerald-green bogs and muddy meanders had spread along the margin of the farside shore. Under grey cloud, swept by quick heavy showers, the *Weazel* nosed along belts of mangrove scrub that fringed the flood plain, guided by Yama to the place where the citizens of Aeolis had made their refuge.

They had arrived only that morning, and were still pitching tents along the low ridge that marked the old shoreline, above a swampy inlet. Men were raising a defensive berm of earth on the landward side of the encampment, and hexes and charms had been fixed to bamboo poles. The Amnan believed that the farside shore was haunted and only ventured from their temporary festival camps to visit the shrines at the world's edge.

This camp was a sorry affair. Fires burning here and there sent choking white smoke streaming into the wet air. Possessions were carelessly piled under tarpaulins that billowed and cracked in the warm, wet wind. Each family had dug its own wallowing pit and made mud slides down to the inlet; packs of wives lay in the slides and bickered incessantly, not bothering to brush away the blackflies that clustered at their eyes and the corners of their mouths, while pups chased each other and the men looked on disconsolately.

Only the Aedile's quarters were in good order. A big orange tent had been raised on a platform of freshly cut logs at the shoreward end of the ridge, and the Aedile's standard flew at half-mast, snapping in the brisk breeze. Yama saw this omen as the *Weazel* nosed towards the muddy shore, and his heart overturned with dread.

Tamora came up and said, 'We can't stay long. The Prefect and his men will follow us here as soon as they see through your trick.'

Yama was turning Oncus's fetish around and around his wrist. 'It will hold them for a while. And I must find out how my father and the others fare.'

'You won't be able to fool them again. It will be a square fight next time.'

He felt himself smiling, heard himself saying, 'Good. I will destroy them.'

'About time you started thinking like a cateran.'

Yama closed his eyes and crushed the fetish against his wrist. His hands shook. When he could speak again, he said, 'I will not be what they want me to be.'

Flanked by his three surviving sons, the Constable of Aeolis, Unthank, came out to meet Yama when he rowed ashore in the *Weazel*'s dory with Tamora and Pandaras. Eliphas had elected to stay aboard, claiming that the chase had tired him out. Yama suspected that the old man was sulking because he had refused to try to destroy the warship and the picket boat.

The Constable did not seem surprised by Yama's arrival. He was a large, ugly man more than twice Yama's height, dressed in mud-spattered trousers and a leather waistcoat. One of his tusks had been broken when he had fought and killed his father for control of the harem, and was capped with silver – the same silver which had capped one of his father's tusks. His swagger stick, the emblem of his office, was tucked under a muscular arm. He lumbered up with a rolling swagger and said straight away that the Aedile was dying. 'He's laid up in the tent, with the rest of his household.'

'Is everyone from the city here?'

'Most everyone who escaped. A few went into the City of the Dead, mostly the merchants. You'll want to talk to your father, I reckon. We'll speak properly later.' The Constable spat at Yama's feet, then turned and walked away. His sons stared hard at Yama before following their father.

Pandaras said, 'These people have no liking for you, master. Are we safe here?'

'There is bad history between us,' Yama said. 'One of his sons died by my hand; another was executed. They were working for someone who tried to kidnap me before I left Aeolis.'

As they walked through the camp, they gathered a tail of naked pups who jeered and whistled, and threw clots of mud. A group of men stood around a smoky bonfire, smoking long-stemmed clay pipes and passing a leather bottle back and forth. Someone said something and the others laughed, a low, mocking, mean laughter.

Yama went up to them and asked if they had seen the chandler and his family. Most looked away, refusing to answer or even acknowledge him, but one, a one-eyed fisherman called Vort, said, 'Chasin' after your sweetheart, young master?'

'Don't tell him nothing,' another man said. Yama knew him, too. Hud, master of the shellfish farms at the mouth of the Breas.

'He deserves to know,' Vort said. He wore only a patched linen kilt in the warm rain. His grey skin shone as if greased. There was a livid burn on one massive shoulder. He looked down at Yama and said, 'I heard tell they came for the chandler first. Someone came banging on their door in the night. They were gone the next day, and then the ship came.'

'I heard they were informers,' Hud said. 'That's why they got away before the trouble. They got away with their wealth while the rest of us watched our lives burn up.'

The others standing around the fire mumbled agreement. One took out his penis and urinated with considerable force into the fire. It was a gesture of contempt, and there was another round of mocking laughter.

Yama said to Vort, 'Who took them? Where did they go?'

Derev was safe, he thought, with a pang of unalloyed joy. She had escaped. Zakiel had said so, and now Vort and Hud had confirmed it.

Hud laid a hand on Vort's arm and glared at Yama. 'I don't have a family; none of us here do. But we lost our lodges all the same, and most of what was in them. They let us take what we could carry and burned the rest to the ground, yet your peel-house still stands.'

'That and the temple,' someone else said.

Yama stood his ground and looked at the men. They turned away, mumbling. Only Vort met his gaze. Yama said, 'The city was burned in spite, to hurt me and to draw me into a trap. I was almost caught, but I escaped. And I will not forget what was done.'

'We're dead men here,' Vort said. 'This is the shore of ghosts and spirits, and we've come to live here.'

'If you believe that, then you have let them destroy you twice over,' Yama said.

No one replied; even Vort turned his back on him.

As they walked away, Pandaras said, 'They are a surly lot, master. No wonder you left as soon as you could.'

'They have lost their homes and their livelihoods. And I am the cause, walking amongst them with my questions. I shamed them. I should not have spoken.'

'It was not you who destroyed their city, but the Department of Indigenous Affairs,' Tamora said. 'If they want to lynch someone, they should look for Prefect Corin.'

Yama said, 'He might well come here. As you pointed out, my deception will not fool him for long.'

'You are too hard on yourself, master,' Pandaras said.

'Not hard enough, I think.'

A lump of filth tipped Tamora's shoulder, and she made as if she was about to chase the pup who had thrown it. He and his friends slithered off through the mud, whistling with laughter.

Tamora said, 'If we are staying here overnight we should sleep on the ship, anchored a good distance from the shore. These slugs can't walk so well, but they look like they can swim.'

'They are very graceful swimmers,' Yama said. 'They mostly hunt in the river.'

'You'd better watch your step,' Tamora told Pandaras. 'One of them could swallow you whole, like an oyster.'

Pandaras put his hand on the hilt of his knife, struck an attitude. 'And I'd give him a fearsome bellyache.'

Old Rotwang sat on a stool outside the flap of the tent, his wooden leg raised on a cushion as he sipped from a half-empty wineskin. A rifle was propped beside him. He sprang up when Yama hailed him, and gimped over and shook Yama's hand effusively, saying he never thought he would have the pleasure again, never in all the long world, breathing out brandy fumes and staring at Tamora and Pandaras.

'You look well, boy. And you have grown a little, I think. There is new muscle on your arms and shoulders. Wait there. I will get the Sergeant. He has been expecting you since we first sighted the ship.'

'My father—'

But Rotwang had already pushed through the tent flap. Before Yama could follow, Sergeant Rhodean emerged, dapper in polished breastplate and a black leather kirtle, his boots gleaming, his grey hair newly cropped. He clapped Yama on the back and said he would hear something of his adventures in Ys.

'You can tell me how you got that scar on your forehead,' he said. 'You forgot to keep your sword at point, no doubt. Never mind, a hard lesson is one not quickly forgotten.'

'My father?'

Sergeant Rhodean's expression did not change, but a softness entered his gaze. 'The Aedile sleeps. He sleeps a lot. When he wakes you will be the first to speak with him, but I will not wake him just because his errant son has returned.' His gaze took in Tamora and Pandaras. 'We will have tea, and you will introduce me to your companions. Have you become a cateran? That's a harder life than the regular army, but you will see more fighting.'

Yama smiled. Sergeant Rhodean had always encouraged him in his wish to follow Telmon and fight against the heretics.

They took tea at a low table under the awning of the tent. Outside, bursts of rain spattered the muddy ground. Sergeant Rhodean was uncharacteristically voluble; he was being kind, trying to keep Yama's mind from the Aedile.

'I was a cateran for a year or so,' he said, 'when I was only a little older than you. Perhaps I will be one again, although at the moment, of course, I am still in your father's service. And will be for many years yet, I hope.'

The rough skin that crested his prominent cheekbones swelled with tender passion when he said this, and he glared at Yama as if challenging him to deny it.

Yama said, 'Did they hurt my father?'

'Not physically, apart from a few bruises when he tried to resist arrest.

It is his spirit that was broken.' Sergeant Rhodean looked at Tamora and Pandaras and hesitated, clearly uncomfortable about continuing.

'They are not only my companions-in-arms,' Yama said. 'They are my friends.'

'I am his squire,' Pandaras said boldly, 'and Tamora is... Well, she was his companion, but I'm not quite sure what she is now.'

'I also serve Yama,' Tamora said. 'My life is his.'

Yama said to Sergeant Rhodean, 'Tell me about my father. I hear that he tried to stop the razing of the city.'

'He was given his orders the day before the warship arrived, and he refused them. Instead, he began the evacuation of the city, which is why so many were saved. It hurt him grievously to do it, but he was right. The department has changed. There is no longer any room for argument or even discussion, and although the Aedile outranked the Prefect—'

'Prefect Corin.'

'The man who took you to Ys, yes. He was flanked by a pentad of bully boys with pistols on their hips, and he acted as though he owned the peel-house and everyone in it. But the Aedile stood up to him. And to the traitor, Torin. Oh yes, that one has all these years been scheming against his master, and reporting to the villains who drove the Aedile into exile in the first place.'

'Torin has paid for his treachery,' Yama said, and briefly explained how he and Tamora had killed the mage and most of the soldiers who had been guarding the peel-house, and left Torin to the mercy of his fellow servants.

'That is good,' Sergeant Rhodean said. 'Very good. The mage is the man who tortured the Aedile. He used a machine that took him into some sort of nightmare. I fear that he has not returned from it whole. I should have killed that worm myself. And Prefect Corin. What of him?'

'He is chasing me. I cannot stay long.'

'Why is he after you, Yama? Is it some personal grievance?'

'He is not a man to take things personally. That is the one fault he does not possess. He is a creature of the department.'

'You are wrong, I think,' Sergeant Rhodean said, and drained his bowl of tea and banged it down on the table. 'He pretends humility, but excuses his own impulses as the wishes of the department. He is answerable to no one, having assumed moral superiority which he backs not with reason or right but with violence or the threat of violence. He wants you for some purpose that will help his own ambition, and I fear that you will have to kill him before this is done.'

Yama asked how the Aedile had escaped.

'I wish I could say it was by force of arms,' Sergeant Rhodean said. 'But me and my boys were surprised and outnumbered and disarmed. After they had finished torturing the Aedile with the mage's foul machine, they locked him in his rooms. But they left only one man to guard him, and Zakiel had a key that worked the lock, and so we freed him and made our escape. It sounds more exciting than it was. I do not think they particularly cared if we escaped, for it removed a source of embarrassment. Do you remember what I told you about planning a campaign?'

'That you should think of the worst things that could happen and make your plans accordingly.'

'I had already made preparations in case we needed to abandon the peel-house. I had fitted a cutter with a big motor, provisioned it, and anchored it below the bluff. We got the Aedile aboard and slipped anchor. No one tried to chase us. The fisher folk found us midriver, and we left the cutter for Prefect Corin to find and puzzle over. And here we are. Zakiel would not come. He said that he must look after his books.'

'I left him safe and well. Tamora freed him from his chains, but he would not leave.'

Sergeant Rhodean nodded. 'He is stubborn, all right. Luckily for him, Prefect Corin is not interested in burning books, or he would have died defending them. The Aedile tells us that we will be able to return to the peel-house once this is over, Yama, but it is the kindliest of lies. It has been taken from him.'

'I was told that he is dying. Tell me the truth, plain as light.'

Sergeant Rhodean poured himself more tea, but after a single sip he threw the bowl out into the mud. 'It has gone cold,' he explained. 'Rotwang! Rotwang!'

Yama dared to touch Sergeant Rhodean's hand. As a child, the sergeant had seemed to him to be an all-knowing kindly tyrant, but now he saw that he was a loyal old man whose codes of honour had been proven obsolete.

'I should know how he is before I go to see him.'

'He has been waiting for your return,' Sergeant Rhodean. 'I think he has been waiting only for that.'

'Then I should leave here at once, and return in a hundred years.'

'I wish he could wait that long. I wish we all could.'

Rotwang brought more tea, and dry biscuits and a green paste of waterweed flavoured with flecks of ginger. Yama tried to tell the story of his adventures in Ys and the Palace of the Memory of the People as briefly as he could, but Pandaras kept interrupting, and his inventions made Yama's adventures seem far more daring and exotic than the prosaic truth.

At the end, Tamora told Sergeant Rhodean, 'You may not believe half of it, but it is all true.'

'I fought under the command of someone of your bloodline once,' Sergeant Rhodean told her. 'It was before any of you were born, in the first campaigns against the heretics. I remember him still, though. He never told a lie, and we loved him for his honesty. Besides, we always knew how the boy could charm the watchdogs. His power has grown, that is all. As he has grown. He left as a child, and has returned as a man.'

Yama laughed. 'I thought I was so sly, but I am glad that you saw through my tricks.'

'He will save the world. It's been foretold,' Tamora said, and glared around her, defying them to deny it.

Behind her, Rotwang opened the flap of the tent and said, 'The Aedile is awake.'

The Aedile lay in a bed within a curtained compartment at the heart of the tent. A stove at the foot of the bed gave off a fierce dry heat, but the Aedile was covered by a heap of furs, and only his sleek grey head showed. When Yama came in he smiled and held out a hand – it was cold, despite the sweltering heat. His pelt was dry and lustreless, and the contours of his sharp cheekbones and the notches in the bone around his round eye sockets were clearly visible.

'My son,' he said 'How glad I am to see you. I thought that I would not see you until we were both resurrected by the grace of the Preservers.'

Yama helped the Aedile sit up, and Rotwang settled a richly embroidered wrap around his master's shoulders and started to fuss with the coverings before the Aedile dismissed him.

'You will take tea,' Rotwang said, 'and a shot of heart of wine.'

'Perhaps later. Let me talk with my son, Rotwang. I am not ill.'

Yama said, 'I have failed you, father. More than once. All this is my fault.'

The Aedile said, with a touch of his old asperity, 'What is this talk of fault and failure? I will not hear it.'

'To begin with, I ran away from Prefect Corin as soon as we reached Ys.'

'I should not have allowed him to take you with him. I was lied to, Yama, by the highest offices of the department. I have no doubt that as soon as they learned about you from their spies, they wanted you. Not for who you are, but for what they believed you to be. I told them about you from the first, of course, and sent in reports from time to time, but they were always anodyne, I kept certain things secret... Despite the circumstances of your arrival in Aeolis, and certain events afterwards, I always hoped that you were only an ordinary boy.

'The trouble began when I had Dr Dismas search for records of your kind. The department's spies in my household – there were at least three that I knew of, although it was a shock to discover that Torin was their chief – they must have passed on the details about what Dr Dismas claimed to have found, and why he tried to kidnap you. We got that from the wretched landlord of the tavern where you were taken, but I kept it from the department. That was why I decided that you could not stay in Aeolis any longer. Believe me when I say that I acted out of love, and forgive me.'

Yama thought of the lies he had told the Aedile. He had not told the truth about how he had escaped Dr Dismas, or of his adventures afterwards. If the Aedile had known about them, he would never have sent him away. He said, 'There is nothing to forgive.'

'I was told that you would be given an entry into the department and entrusted you to them. But they lied. They knew what you were. And that was why so high-ranking a personage as Prefect Corin came to bring you to them. Of course, even then they did not know the whole story.'

'I ran away not because I knew what I was, but because of pride. I wanted only to be like Telmon.'

'We were both foolish, Yamamanama. You were foolish because you wanted to follow your brother without thought or preparation; I was foolish because I would not let you. I am glad that you ran away from Prefect Corin. You did not know it, perhaps, but it was the right thing to do.'

'He caught me again,' Yama said, and for the second time he told his story. Without Pandaras's fanciful contributions it took less than half the time, although the Aedile fell asleep in the middle of it. Yama waited until his father woke, seemingly without noticing that he had fallen asleep, and continued to the end.

When Yama told of Eliphas's discovery in the records of the Department of Apothecaries and Chirurgeons, the Aedile stirred and said, 'That is most curious. For Dr Dismas also looked there, and reported that he had found no records of your bloodline. He said that you were unique.'

Yama remembered the conversation he had overheard when he had spied on the Aedile and Dr Dismas from the gallery of the Great Hall. He said, 'Dismas was lying. He hid what he found from you, and planned my kidnap.'

The Aedile was too tired to argue. He did not even ask what Yama had learned about his bloodline. He sighed and said, 'Perhaps, perhaps. Dr Dismas was a clever man, but very venal. Beware those who want to help you and ask for no reward.'

'Then I would have to mistrust all my friends.'

The Aedile closed his eyes and Yama thought that he had fallen asleep again. But then he opened them and said, 'I do not regret taking you into my house. You are my son as Telmon was my son, whatever else you are. You were found in a white boat. Do you remember the story?'

'I was a baby, lying on the breast of a dead woman.'

'Quite, quite. I have always wondered if she was your mother, but old Constable Thaw said that she had silver skin, and that one arm was deformed. As you grew, I worried that your skin would turn silver, but it never did. I looked very hard to find your people. That is why, at last, I asked Dr Dismas to search the archives of his department. It was the last hope of a foolish old man.'

'I am glad that I grew up where I did.'

'The year after you were found on the river, I took you to one of the shrines on this shore. It lit up as if the avatar had returned, but it was not the avatar. Instead it was a kind of demon disguised as a woman. She tried to bend me to her and I did something shameful. I used my pistol against her, and the energy overloaded the shrine. Do you remember anything of this?'

'I was a baby, father.'

'Quite, quite. Well, I have never told anyone about the shrine before. Not Father Quine, not Dr Dismas, not even the department. There were other signs, too. When you were first rescued, the Council for Night and Shrines decided that you were a danger, and left you exposed on a hillside outside the city. Little machines brought you manna and water. They cared for you until old Constable Thaw's wives came and took you back. Dr Dismas said that he came here because so many machines flew in the air around the city. And then there were the silly tricks you would play with the watchdogs … I wish now that I had told you more about these wonders, but I thought it better to try to give you an ordinary childhood. I have been very foolish.'

'I will always remember you,' Yama said. 'Wherever I go, whatever I do.'

They were both saying farewell, he realised, and he began to weep. The Aedile scolded him and slept a little, and then woke and said, 'Do you think that good can come from an evil act?'

Yama misunderstood, and said that he would avenge the burning of Aeolis in any way he could.

'Let the people of Aeolis do that. I wonder at my life. All this time I have been serving something with evil at its heart. I did not know it, but does that still make everything I have done evil?'

'On the road to Ys, Prefect Corin tried to save pilgrims from a gang of bandits. He made it into a test which I failed, but I think that he really did want to save them, all the same. Whatever else he is, whatever else he has done, he risked his own life for the lives of strangers. The Puranas have it that nothing human is perfect, neither perfectly evil nor perfectly good. We can only hope to be true to the best of what we are.'

But the Aedile was asleep. Yama held his father's hand until Rotwang came and announced that supper was ready.

21

THE PYRE

After a scant meal of boiled beans, samphire and a little salt fish, served with beer sent over by Constable Unthank, Tamora said that they should return to the *Weazel*. Yama refused. He knew that the Aedile might not last the night, and wanted to stay close to him.

He stretched out on a rug by the curtain that screened the Aedile's bed. His arms and legs tingled and felt heavy. The heat of the stove packed the air. On the other side of the big tent, Tamora and Pandaras talked in low, sleepy voices with Sergeant Rhodean. They sounded a little drunk; perhaps they had finished the beer. Yama tried to read a little in the Puranas, beginning with the sura about good and evil he had quoted to the Aedile, but the columns of glyphs blurred into his drowsy headache, and somehow he was riding a moa across the grass plains amongst drifting constellations of tiny lights and felt a tremendous sense of exhilaration as the bird's long powerful legs ate up the distance – but then the bird stumbled and he pitched from it and he woke with a horrible start.

Vague shapes moved around him in near-darkness. His head still ached and his mouth was dry. When he tried to get up something smashed into his chest and knocked him onto his back.

'Enough of that,' a man said. 'We decided what we'd do and we'll stick to it.'

Yama was lifted up, but his legs were unstrung and he fell to his knees. His gorge rose and he vomited a sour mess of half-digested beans and beer.

Constable Unthank squatted in front of him. 'That'll pass,' he said.

'We laced the beer with liquor from boiled pufferfish livers. It knocked you out nicely.'

Behind him, men were piling branches on top of a conical heap already twice their height. The Eye of the Preservers stood above the flat horizon, peering through a rent in the clouds. The grassy plain stretched away in the Eye's sullen light, a limitless black carpet studded with tall slabs like the markers of the graves of giants – termite castles, Yama realised. Each housed a mind shattered into a million fragments, through which strange slow thoughts rolled like waves across the Great River, and each fragmented mind was linked to its neighbours, a network stretching along the straight edge of the world...

Constable Unthank slapped Yama's face to get his attention, grabbed his wrists and hauled him to his feet. The copy of the Puranas had fallen to the ground, and with an oddly tender gesture Unthank picked it up and placed it in one of the pockets of Yama's homespun tunic.

'You'll need that where you're going,' the Constable said. 'See to him, lads.'

One of Unthank's sons seized Yama's hands, wrenched them behind his back and tied them at the wrists. He was breathing heavily, and stank of beer. 'He has one of those charms the greenies wear. Much good it'll do him,' he said, and spat in Yama's face and would have hit him, but Unthank caught his arm.

'Leave that off,' Unthank said. 'This will be done properly.'

'For Lud and Lob,' Unthank's son hissed in Yama's ear.

Unthank spat on the ground between his feet. 'They were no sons of mine. They were too stupid to live. I reckon my first-wife had been lying with a grampus when she got them. They brought shame on our family, and anyone who defends them can fight me here and now. But none of you scum are ready, and Lud and Lob never would have been ready. I'd have ripped out their throats the moment they tried. What we do here, this isn't for them. This is for all our people. A burning for a burning.'

Yama fought against the grip of Unthank's son, but the man was too strong. The Puranas counselled that no one need fear death, for when the Preservers returned at the end of time everyone on the world, including all the dead, would rise into their grace and live forever. But although the Puranas taught that death was nothing more than a moment of unbeing between one's last breath and rebirth into eternal life at the everlasting final moment of the universe, they had no advice about facing an imminent and violent end. Yama had confronted worse dangers than this, but when he and Tamora had been ambushed at the Gate of Double Glory, or when he and Eliphas had been chased by the hell-hound, he had been too busy trying to save his life to be unmanned by fear. But now, in the implacable grip of his enemies, facing the death they wished upon him, he felt fear beating inside him with such force that he thought it might burst his chest.

Unthank's son said, 'He's trembling like a wife on her first night.'

'Little you know about that,' Unthank said. 'Little you'll ever know about it, you worm. Bring him on before he faints. We'll get this done and get back before he's missed, and before the rain comes, too. I don't much like the look of those clouds.'

Yama felt a clear measure of anger. He would not be thought a coward. He drew himself up and marched as best he could, so that Unthank's son had to double his pace to keep up. He felt as if a door had closed behind him, and with it all of his life had been shut away. There was only the pyre and the warm damp wind and the hiss of the ceaselessly winnowed grass all around them, black in the dull red light of the Eye of the Preservers.

Yama was led into the trampled circle around the pyre. The men crowded around, pushing and shoving to get to the first rank. Almost all the male citizens of Aeolis were there, their round grey or brown faces glistening in the light of their burning brands. Yama recognised some of his childhood companions and called to them by name, but they turned away and would not answer.

Unthank made a long speech. Yama paid little attention to it. He had a sudden great urge to shout or burst into wild laughter to break the remorseless unfolding of Unthank's spell, but he suppressed the impulse. There was no spell to break. Unthank talked of honour, of home and hearth, of revenge and return and rebuilding, of justice for all, not merely for those in power. It was the angry lament of all men who feel that they have less power than they deserve. Yama allowed it to become mere noise. He let his mind range outwards, seeking any trace of a machine that might help him. Nothing, nothing but the fragmented minds housed within the slabs of the termite castles, unified by slow pulsing waves of thought. He began to follow the connections from castle to castle – they spread all around, further than he could see – but the man who held him cuffed his head and told him to wake up and pay attention.

Clouds had pulled across the Eye of the Preservers. The men held their torches high; flames guttered and flared in the wind. Thunder drummed far off. Unthank was pointing at Yama with his swagger stick. He had worked himself up into a fever of righteous anger. His nostrils flared wide; white showed at the edges of his eyes. His finger, his hand, his arm quivered. His voice rose in pitch as it grew louder, as if squeezed through a narrowing gap in his throat.

'There is the cause!' Unthank said. 'There is the stranger who hid amongst us! I was there when he was taken from the river, and it shames me that I did not fight and kill my weak and foolish father then, and kill this one too. We have been punished because of him and he has delivered himself into our hands. We'll have our revenge, and clean our house. We'll make our own justice, because none will make it for us. He's our bad luck, and we'll burn it and start again. Burn him!'

The men took up the cry. Yama was lifted up and set on a chair, and lashed to it with a rope that went three times around his chest. A sudden strong cold wind blew out of the black sky, flattening grass all around the pyre and snuffing many of the torches carried by the men. Every hair on Yama's head stood up; his whole skin tingled. Four men hauled him backwards up the uneven slope and set him at its summit and scampered away, while others shook brandy and paraffin over the lower part of the pyre.

Unthank stepped forward and with a casual gesture threw a torch towards the base of the pyre. At once the brandy ignited with a dull thump and blue flames licked up. Others threw their torches, too – they flew out of the darkness like falling stars, shedding tails of yellow fire as they tumbled end over end. One struck Yama on the chest and spun away in a shower of sparks. An unbearable heat scorched his feet, his legs. White smoke rolled around him as wet wood smouldered before bursting into flame. He coughed and snorted, but could not get his breath. Perhaps he would suffocate before he burnt, a small mercy.

Then the smoke was parted by a sudden gust of cold wind, and Yama glimpsed the men around the pyre. They seemed to be dancing. More smoke rolled up, dense and choking. Yama lifted his head as an animal part of him, blindly seeking survival, struggled to draw breath. And cold hard hail struck his upturned face, pouring down everywhere from the sky, blowing in great drenching billows.

He was soaked to the skin in an instant. The smoke blew out in a circle all around him. He shouted into the wind and hail. He could not remember afterwards what he had shouted, only knew that he laughed and sang as he struggled to get free. He was mad with life. His sight pulsed red and black. Below, lit by intermittent strobes of lightning, the men were sinking into the ground. It was as if it had turned to water beneath them. They thrashed waist deep in muck which glinted and shimmered as it boiled around them.

Yama fell over, rolling with the chair at his back down a collapsing slope of charred branches. When he came to a stop at the bottom of the pyre, the men had vanished. The raging thing still possessed him. He thrust his face into the mud and chewed and gobbled and swallowed.

Then he was on his knees, still tied to the chair, sick and frightened. He spat out a mouthful of mud, saw silvery things squirming in it. His stomach clenched like a cramped muscle.

As he struggled to free himself, he thought wildly that the men had run, that they would soon recover their courage and come back and finish what they had begun. But then lightning flashed again, so close that thunder boomed in the same moment. In that instant Yama saw, just in front of his face, a hand reaching up from the mud. Silvery things swarmed over the fingers. When lightning flashed again, the hand was gone, and the hail softened and became merely rain.

At last, he managed to free his hands. He pulled at the rope that bound him to the chair until the loops, loosened by the tumble down the pyre, finally unravelled. He staggered to his feet. Rain beat all around him. A sheet of lightning defined the termite castles in one direction, the edge of the world in the other. He was utterly alone.

22

ANOTHER ORPHAN

The storm rolled past but the rain continued to pour down as if it might never end, as if the whole of the Great River had been upended into the sky and was now falling back to the world. It flattened the long grass and drenched Yama's clothes. It fell so heavily that every time a squall blew into his face he feared that he might drown.

Upriver, lightning flickered and thunder rolled in the narrow margin between land and cloud. Eldritch lights played around the tall narrow slabs of the termite castles, crowning them with wisps of blue fire. Searching for shelter on the plain, frightened that he might be struck by lightning, or that the ground might at any moment boil and liquefy beneath his feet, Yama saw a fleck of white light in the distance, as if a star had fallen to the shore of Confluence, and at the same moment felt the disc he had found in the Palace of the Memory of the People grow warm in his tunic pocket. He took it out and saw grainy configurations of light shifting restlessly within it. He knew at once what the distant speck must be. With no other compass point in the windy, rainy dark, he stumbled towards it.

It was a shrine, a black disc balanced on a strip of naked keelrock at the very edge of the world, one of many scattered across the farside shore. No one had ever built temples around them. They were marked by cairns and prayer flags and prayer wheels, and some had slab altars raised in front of them for the sacrifice of animals, but otherwise they had been left as they had been found, open to nature. Many people believed that the avatars of the Preservers sometimes still appeared in these remote shrines when no one was watching, or before secret congregations of moas, red foxes and ground sloths.

A kind of ragged teepee towered beyond this shrine, built of bamboo and brushwood on a bamboo platform that jutted over the edge of the world. The teepee was draped with prayer flags that had been tattered and bleached by years of exposure, and at the very top a threadbare banner streamed out in the rain and wind.

As Yama approached the shrine, fluttering banderoles of all colours bled into its white light, as if its window had turned towards a festival sky. Rain fell all around with undiminished intensity, but it did not fall close to the shrine. He sat on smooth dry keelrock bathed in flickering multicoloured light, took off his sodden tunic and spread it out, and shook water from the pages of his copy of the Puranas. He was drenched and shivering, and coughed up strings of mucus blackened by smoke inhalation. His mouth was filled with the swamp taste of the mud he had eaten in his fit of madness. He knew that he was being watched and he thought that he knew who was watching.

He said, 'Well, you brought me here.'

He said, 'I suppose you will say that you saved my life.'

He said, 'I am not your creature. It will be day soon, and then I will go.'

As before, as in the shrine of the Temple of the Black Well, the fluttering colours parted like a curtain and the woman was suddenly there, looking through the round window of the shrine as if peering into a house. The green light of her garden washed into the rainy night. She looked no different from her first appearance: long black hair and bronze blade of a face, a clinging white garment with tubes for arms and legs. Yama discovered that he no longer feared her. Worse things lived in the space beyond the shrines: he had conquered one of them. He would conquer her, too.

She said, 'You are there. You really are. I've been searching for so long since I last saw you. You're learning, Yamamanama. I'm pleased. I saw you twice in that mountain of a building in the old city, but I couldn't speak to you. Most of these windows don't work at all. Most of the rest only work one way. I saw you as you passed by, and I called out, but you didn't hear. But this one works. You called me, and here I am. Where is it? How did you find it?'

'Then you did not save my life?'

'Wait.' The woman closed her eyes, then slowly smiled and opened them again. 'Now I know where you are. As I told you, the shrines on the far side of the river retain most of their functionality. Some of them, anyway. This one, at least. How clever of you to find it! Do you think I saved your life?'

Yama described what had happened to the men who had tried to kill him. When he had finished, the woman shook her head gravely. 'You shouldn't meddle in what you don't understand, Yamamanama. You are still so very young, and there is so much that I can teach you. Do you know what they are – the things you call termites?'

Yama remembered Telmon's nature lessons. He said, 'Communal insects. They live together like bees or emmets.'

'I suppose that they were once insects. They've been changed, just as the originals of the other bloodlines of this habitat were changed when they were brought here. The termites have retained their social structure, with queens and their male suitors, and billions of daughter workers and soldiers and builders, but they have been quickened to a kind of communal intelligence. Each castle is a single processor, and all the processors are linked together in a massive parallel architecture. Just as the billions of insects in each colony are united to form a single castle, so the thousands of castles are united in a single meta-structure.'

'I could feel their thoughts. I could feel that the castles were linked. But I do not know what they were thinking.'

The woman smiled. She said, 'No more do I. But they responded to your call, so you should not be afraid of them. They killed your enemies, and it is likely that they created the storm that drenched the fire, too. A simple matter of changing the relative difference in electrical charge between ground and air. Your power grows, Yamamanama. I can help you discover its limits. We can do great things together. We can bring revenge on those who destroyed your home. We can reunite you with your true family, and end the silly war. With my knowledge and your power we can do all of these things, and more.'

Yama remembered what the Aedile had confided to him, and said, 'I suppose you used the shrine in the temple at Aeolis.'

'I have seen you there, from time to time, but the shrine was damaged, and I could not reach out to you. Now you are able to waken the shrines fully things will be much easier. Now we can talk directly.'

Yama thought of the man who had given him the first disc, which had been taken from him in the Department of Indigenous Affairs. He said, 'Was the anchorite one of your creatures?'

'I have no creatures. I possess nothing but knowledge. And even though many of the files are corrupted, I possess a great deal. Certainly I know more than anyone else on this fallen world.'

'You have knowledge but no power. I have power, but do not understand how to control it properly. You might say that I am inhabited by a power which uses me, just as it used the termites or the hell-hound. It occurs to me that you may be using it to manipulate me.'

'I came here to help you, when you called for help. You called me at the temple, if you remember. And when you were bound, in the middle of the fire, whom did you call on then?'

'How did you know about the fire?'

'Why, the termites told me.'

'In any case, I did not call to you for help. I believe that I called to the Preservers.'

The woman smiled, showing her small, white, even teeth. 'But they did not answer. And they never will, because they long ago fled into a place where no light will escape until evaporation of the event horizon at the end of time. Oh, perhaps their avatars relayed your prayers them, once upon a time. Kept them up to date with current affairs. But the Preservers could never reply, could never reach out to this world or any other. Light can fall into the gravity well of the black hole, you know, but it cannot fall back out.'

'I know.' It was in the last sura of the Puranas.

'The Preservers abandoned this world long ago, and their avatars have also disappeared. I've explored many places inside these windows, but I've yet to find more than an echo of them.'

'The heretics drove them out,' Yama said.

'It would not have taken a great deal of effort,' the woman said. 'There is much ancient damage in this network, caused by a war between those machines which refused to serve their creators any longer, and those which remained loyal. But we can repair and remake the wreckage of the world, you and I. Perhaps we can even bring back the avatars.

'As for how you were saved, my darling boy, perhaps you called on your own self. The power that inhabits you needs you as much as I need the shrines. It cannot survive without you, and will do everything it can to keep you safe. If it could, it would make you immortal.'

Yama laughed at this transparent blasphemy. He saw now that the woman had very little power. She could not force him to serve; she could only try to beguile him with false promises and appeals to his fears and base appetites.

He said, 'All those created by the Preservers will live forever, in the last moment of infinite time. But no one lives forever in the first life.'

'Ah, but perhaps you will. I know of the infection that all the changed races carry, although I confess that it is beyond my ability to understand how it works. It appears to store information within the folded dimensions of space. We knew that this was theoretically possible, but did not possess the tools with which to manipulate those dimensions.

'But there are many ways of living forever. My original died and rose again many times before she was cast onto this strange wild shore. She died here, but she will be born again elsewhere. And before she died she copied herself into the space between the shrines. I am that copy. I should have been erased, but they came for my original before my task was completed.'

The woman lifted her hands as if to touch her shoulders with her wrists. It was a kind of shrug. 'My original was killed and her ship fled, and I linger here. I will live as long as the world lives. It is hard to watch the world and not be able to help it, but not as hard, I think, as to have the power to help the world, and not be able to use it.'

'Then you were once alive?'

'Don't you listen? I was never alive. I am a copy of my original, as she was a copy of the template of the original of us all. *She* died millions of years ago, but was reborn over and again, and lives on in me, and in my crewmates. Perhaps she is the last true human, now that the Preservers have drawn the event horizon around themselves. My crewmates hoped otherwise, and perhaps some remnant of humanity clings to existence elsewhere in the Home Galaxy. But even if the ship is cloned, the search will take thousands of years.'

Yama did not understand any of this, but he thought that if he drew the woman out she might let slip something useful. He said, 'The shrine drives off the rain, but its light gives no warmth and I am cold. Too cold to sleep, too tired not to. Talk to me. I am frightened that if I go to sleep I might not wake up.'

He thought of his father lying under the fur throws in the close heat of the little room, of the coldness of his father's hand. His tunic was still wet, but he put it back on and wrapped his arms around himself.

'Tell me about your original,' he said. 'Was she one of the Ancients of Days? Someone I met described two of them to me – he had not seen them, but his father had – and I believe that they wore clothing like yours.'

'I have already explained what she was. What she is.'

'The last human. But there are many kinds of human beings here.'

'You are not human. None of you are human. You have been shaped to approximate human form, that's all. For all I know, your ancestors were methane-breathing mud puppies or hydrogen-filled photosynthesising blimps in a gas giant's upper atmosphere. But what you call the Ancients of Days were truly human. They were all different aspects of the same individual, and my original was the synthesis of them all, a true copy whose lineage stretched back through millions of years to a human being long dead.'

'Why did the Ancients of Days come here? Why did they go away?'

'Their ship brought them here, and revived them. They had been stored a long time, neither living nor dead, like a story that lies within the printed pages of a book and lives only when the book is taken from a shelf and someone begins to read it. Did you ever stop to think that when you set a book down, its story only half-read, time stops in the story until you pick it up again?'

'In a story, centuries can pass between one sentence and the next,' Yama said. 'If this were a story, I could walk away and within a moment be sleeping safe and dry and warm, in my own bed.'

'Or perhaps you would find your place in the story had ended and that you no longer existed,' the woman said.

'Then I suppose that I would have to wait until someone started to read from the beginning. You said that you were created here, but you seem to remember things from the time before you were created.'

'In my language, the language in which I was coded, not that which I have learned so that I can talk to you and read the records of this world, my name means messenger. It was the name of my original, and so it is my name, too. She brought a message to this world, although she did not realise it at the time. I was created by her to find out why she was changing what she changed, all unknowing. Rather like you, Yama. I am like a reflection that gains independent life and walks off into the world beyond the frame of the mirror. And because I am a reflection, a copy, I remember something of the story before my own part was written.'

'Tell me what you remember. I would like to hear your story.'

'Listen, then. Millions of years ago, while all of what would become humanity lived on the nine worlds and thousand moons and worldlets of a single star in the Sky Hunter arm of the Home Galaxy, there was a religion which taught that individuals need never die. It embraced every kind of technology that could promote this end, and admitted no god except the possibility that, at the very end of the universe, all of its followers might unite in a single entity which would have access to an infinite amount of energy and so be able to recreate all possibilities, including every human that ever lived or might have lived. Yes, very much like your Preservers.

'It was this religion which first drove humanity from star to star. Individuals copied their personalities into computers, or cloned themselves, or spread their personalities through flocks of birds, or shoals of fish, or even amongst hive insects like your termites. They called themselves the transcendents, for they believed that they could become more than human.

'In two million years every part of the Home Galaxy had been explored; in three more, every part had been settled, and the great reshaping had begun, transforming every star and every planet. My original once held a gathering around a rim star several thousand light years above the plane of the galaxy. For a whole century, on a world shaped across its entire surface into something like the gardens in which you see me standing, a clade composed of millions of copies of a hundred or more different generations met and exchanged experiences.

'For there was one flaw in this religion. Clones and downloaded copies, and copies of those copies, and clones of those copies – all were different from the original because they all experienced and encountered different things. After millions of years, many were no longer human in form or in thought, except that they could trace back, generation upon generation, their descent from a single human ancestor. Thus, each individual became a clade or alliance of millions of different minds. Some even founded nations or empires in which every individual could trace ancestry back to a single person.

'The gathering organised by my original was one of the first and most successful. Many others ended in bitter wars over disputes about ancestry – at that time, tracing consanguinity was the most important commerce in the galaxy and there were many false claimants to the honour of belonging to the original lineage of each clade. These wars destroyed many of the transcendents and weakened the hold of the survivors, and the worlds of ordinary humans began to rise in influence, fighting each other for control of the ruined empires of the transcendents. During this time, much of the imposed architecture which ordered the four hundred billion stars of the Home Galaxy was lost or destroyed. Millions of stars were turned into supernovas; millions of others were displaced from their orbits and sent wandering beyond the galaxy. The wars lasted two million years and the reconstruction after the wars lasted two million more, and at the end of it most of the transcendents had been destroyed. It was felt by the commonality of surviving human stock that they were a danger to the variety and the potential for evolution within and between the civilisations in the galaxy.

'My original, who had once ruled an empire of several million planetary systems, fled from the crusades against the transcendents. She copied herself into the central nervous system of her ship, crewed it with partial copies of herself, and embarked on a voyage to the neighbouring galaxy. It lasted more than two million years. She was looking for truly alien civilisations, but found nothing there, and at last decided to return. And on the voyage home, while she lay as dormant as a story between the pages of an unread book, her ship detected changes in the Large Magellanic Cloud, one of the satellite galaxies of the Home Galaxy. All its stars were falling towards its gravitational centre, feeding the growth of a supermassive black hole. The ship turned towards it, and when my original woke the ship was approaching this strange world, an artificial habitat occupied by the discarded toys of what humanity had become in the four and a half million years since she had left.

'Now I am done with talking. Now you must decide what you will do. Together we can unite in a common purpose and end the war. That at least, for a beginning.'

Yama knew what he must do, but he still wanted to learn as much as he could. He said, 'Tell me more of the story. What happened when she came here? What did she do? Where did she go?'

'You can read that for yourself. I have copied it into your book. And now, unless you agree to help me, I have no more words to ease your night. And if you require warmth, perhaps your companions will help you.'

The woman pointed at something behind Yama. He turned, and saw that a congregation of animals had gathered at the margins of the shrine's green glow. There was a little flock of moas, their small heads raised alertly on long necks, their feathers bedraggled in the downpour. Peccaries and tapirs stood shoulder to shoulder, snuffling softly; one peccary sprawled on the bare rock, suckling a pair of piglets. Two giant ground sloths squatted on their haunches, their arms around each other's hairy shoulders like human lovers. A solitary buffalo stood to one side, its horn-heavy head low, green light glinting in its large, liquid eyes. Two white egrets perched on the hump of muscle on its back. A pack of red foxes sat together, their large ears set forward alertly. A mantid sprawled in a tangle of body segments and many-jointed limbs, its tiny blind face turned to the screen. There were many smaller animals, too: mice and rock hyraxes and mole rats, cassowaries and grass pipers, a writhing mass of kraal vipers. At the very front of this motley audience, barely an arm's-length from Yama, a lioness lay on the dry keelrock. Like all the others she was watching the shrine, her paws, armed with claws that could unseam Yama from neck to navel in an instant, crossed before her.

Yama turned to the woman and said, 'Have they come to worship?'

'Didn't you summon them?'

'I do not think so. I do not know.'

Even as he said it, the animals stood up and stretched or shivered or shook their heads and trotted away into the darkness. Only the lioness remained; she yawned, showing a ridged pink mouth and a large pink tongue lolling amongst racks of white teeth. A rumble filled the air, so low in pitch that Yama felt it through the scorched soles of his boots, in the marrow of his bones. The lioness was purring. Yama, remembering the cats of the peel-house, scratched behind her ears; she buffeted him with her forehead and licked his hand with her dry rough tongue.

The woman said, 'We can tame the world, you and I. As soon as you give your word to help me, I will reveal all manner of wonders.'

'No,' Yama said. 'You are a truer copy of your original than you think. You crave power, just as she did, and like her you will do anything to get it. She began the war, and now you need my help to win it. But I will not serve you, or anyone else.'

The garden darkened behind the woman, and although her appearance did not change, her exotic beauty suddenly seemed to be filmed with something loathsome. She said, 'Shrines are more than windows. There are things I can send into the world and things I can do which will amaze and terrify you. There are many things I have not yet told you. How you came here, to begin with. Have your little moment of defiance now, but you'll come back to me when you realise that you need me. And then you'll have to pay for your pride.'

'You could not even speak to me without my help,' Yama said, and called to the creature he had used before, which he had once feared as much as this poor abandoned aspect.

Blue light flared in the disc of the shrine. The woman did not even have time to scream.

Yama still did not know precisely how he had quickened the change in the baby of the mirror people. But later, as he slept with his back resting against the lioness's warm flank, he dreamed that he was flying over a dark city in which only a single window glowed. He circled low over the ridged rooftops and saw a room illuminated by a single point of light. Inside, a woman sat at a plain table. She was reading his copy of the Puranas. A firefly hung above her head, an attentive white star that suddenly rose up and flew straight at him. Its radiance flooded his eyes, and he woke.

It had stopped raining. The air was growing lighter under a lid of grey cloud. The woman and her garden were gone. In her place stood the blue flame of the hell-hound. It had watched over Yama all night. He thanked it, and it dwindled to an intense point that gathered up the light of the shrine and left it a dull black circle.

He discovered that he had been clutching the disc so tightly that his fingers had cramped. He stood up, stiff in every joint, feeling the places where he had been kicked, the rope burns across his chest, the bruise around the upper part of his left arm where he had been gripped by Constable Unthank's son.

The lioness lay quietly, watching him perform exercises to loosen his joints and warm his stiff muscles. Then her ears pricked, and a moment later Yama heard someone shout his name. He turned and saw someone coming towards him across the grassy plain, picking their way between the tall slabs of the termite nests.

The lioness sprang up and trotted away. Pandaras lifted an arm in greeting. His face wore a strange and solemn expression, and Yama knew with a dull certainty that the Aedile was dead.

23

ANGEL

'It was a lion,' Pandaras said. 'A lion or a panther. It was lying beside him, and when I drew near it ran off along the edge of the world.'

Tamora said, 'If you saw anything at all, it was most likely an ordinary cat. The women of the Mud People keep them as pets, and one of them must have followed the cullers who kidnapped Yama.'

'I know what I saw,' Pandaras said. 'There was a shrine, too. It was alive, filled with the blue flame of a hell-hound.'

'And when I found the two of you, there was no lion, and the shrine was as black as your tongue. You found Yama by luck, and ever since you've been trying to turn it into an epic tale, with you as the hero.'

When the cateran was in one of her moods, she gave off a musky scent that started Pandaras's heart racing and had him looking around for hiding places. He was scared that she might unseam him with a gesture, or bite off his head to shut him up. But like most of his bloodline, he preferred to speak and take the consequences rather than regret a missed chance later. So instead of biting his tongue, he said, 'Something scared off the kidnappers. And perhaps you scared off the lion. The Mud People's cats kept away from you in the camp, and a lion is a close relative, with the same likes and dislikes.'

'And does Yama talk about lions and hell-hounds? He does not. He escaped those cullers, and ran off, and found shelter at the shrine. That's all there is to it. That lion came from the same place as the hell-hound – your imagination.'

'Something scared them off, or disappeared them,' Pandaras said.

He and Tamora had followed their trail through the grassland, and at the end of it had found only churned mud and the remains of a great fire.

'Most likely they grew frightened after Yama escaped, and ran off. They are a bully race, all wind and no spine. If there had been time, I would have tracked them down and shown them what justice looks like. But there was no time,' Tamora said, and spat over the rail into the brown water.

The *Weazel* was slipping away from the dense mangroves that fringed the mudflats and dissected mires along the shore. The ship's big triangular sail bellied in the headwind, and the open river lay ahead. It was burnished with the light of the setting sun; drifting banyans were black flecks on its vast vermillion reaches. A pair of carracks stood several leagues off, but there was no sign of the warship and the picket boat which had pursued them from the burning city to the floating forest.

A long way behind the *Weazel*'s spreading wake, the thread of smoke from the embers of the Aedile's funeral pyre bent into the dark sky. The pyre had been built on a platform on top of the ridge of the old shoreline, and the Aedile's body, washed and coated with unguents and oil of spikenard, had been laid amidst heaps of flowers. Yama had lit the fire himself. Gunpowder and flowers of sulphur had burned fiercely at the base of the pyre, and then the sweetgum logs had caught, crackling and sending up dense, fragrant white smoke. The Aedile's body had sat up in the midst of the fire, as bodies often did when heat dried and contracted the muscles, but Yama had shown no sign of emotion even then. He had watched the pyre with fierce unblinking attention, occasionally throwing aromatic oils and salts of nitre into the flames, until the body of his father had been utterly consumed.

It had taken several hours. Much later, as Yama had bent to scoop up a bowlful of white ashes and bits of bone, Sergeant Rhodean had given a cry. He had been kicking smouldering logs aside, and had found the Aedile's heart and had plucked it, black and shrivelled but unconsumed, from the ashes. It had been as hot as any ember and had burnt his hand badly, but after his yelp of surprise he had shown no sign of pain. 'I will take it back myself,' he had told Yama. 'I will bury it in the garden of the peel-house.'

As the *Weazel* set sail, Yama threw handfuls of his father's ashes onto the water while Captain Lorquital recited the sura of the Puranas which described the resurrection of the dead at the end of all time and space. Now he sat on the forecastle deck, leafing through the papers left to him by his father, and Pandaras would not let go of the argument about what had happened at the edge of the world.

'Our master does not like to speak of his powers, but we have seen what he can do,' he said. 'He tamed the hell-hound, in the palace. He turned the baby of the mirror people. He mastered those spider machines—'

'We all know what he can do,' Tamora said. 'But you shouldn't go around telling stories about him. It isn't wise.'

'If he can do all that, it isn't much of a stretch to believe that he can call on the help of a lion.'

'Grah. It is easier to tame machines than wild animals. With machines, you replace one set of instructions with another. But wild animals are like people. If you want to make them obey you, you must first break their spirit.'

'Yet you follow him, and so does Captain Lorquital. Why else would she have brought her ship to the farside shore and waited two days? He didn't even have to ask. She saw his need and stayed, when she should have made as much speed from this cursed place as she could.'

Tamora said, 'I do what I do because I want to do it. I can't speak for you or anyone else.'

'You can follow someone of your own free will, and yet still bend your life to their will. Lovers do it all the time, although I'm not sure that the couplings of your people ever have anything to do with love. But my people are used to serving others, and we know a thing or two about love, so perhaps it isn't surprising that I'm able to see what's happening to everyone on board the ship, and you can't.'

'I have my own reasons for being here. And if Yama is able to cast some kind of a spell over people, it didn't work on the kidnappers, did it? And Eliphas shows no sign of his influence, either.'

'I have my suspicions about the old fellow, too. Yama chooses to believe his story about a lost city beyond the end of the river, but that does not mean that I must. He has a sly and secretive air, and is entirely too familiar with Captain Lorquital. I think he has designs on our master.'

'I'm keeping a close watch on him,' Tamora said. 'And if he tries anything, I'll be ready. You stick to washing and mending shirts.'

'We all want to protect him. You, me, Captain Lorquital and her crew, the fisher folk... You see? We're all under his spell.'

Tamora shrugged. 'The fisher folk helped us because they shared a common enemy with us. And besides, they are indigens. They are as easily swayed as a parrot or a pet monkey. Are your people so superstitious that they see an invisible hand in all that happens? That sergeant, Rhodean, didn't ask to follow Yama downriver, and neither did any of the others in the service of the Aedile. By your argument they would already be under his spell, for he has lived with them for most of his life. There's no magic in this world, only old arts whose workings have been long forgotten.'

Pandaras touched his fingers to his lips in supplication. 'I have no quarrel with you, Tamora. I do not compete for Yama's affection. I'm simply happy to serve him as I can. Why, I may hope only to be remembered in some song or other and I would be content.'

Tamora spat over the side again. 'Just don't go around making up songs of your own.'

Pandaras changed the subject. 'Are you frightened of them? His powers. Does he scare you?'

'I don't understand them.'

'They scare me. I don't mind admitting that. I wonder if they scare him.'

Tamora turned from the rail and looked towards the little forecastle deck, where Yama sat cross-legged under the taut lines of the yards. He had given up looking through the untidy mass of his father's papers and was reading in his book, unconsciously turning the fetish that Oncus had given him around and around on his wrist.

'Perhaps that is why he seeks comfort in the Puranas,' she said.

The book had changed. The frames of the pictures were still there, but the scenes they showed were no longer heraldic representations of the deep time before the creation of the world. Instead, they glowed with freshly minted colour, each displaying a single scene laden with implicit symbolism. One after the other, they told the story of what had happened to the original of the woman in the shrine after her ship had made landfall on Confluence.

Yama followed the story far into the night, reading by the light of a lantern that Pandaras lit for him, ignoring the food laid beside him. Pandaras stayed a while, watching him tenderly, but Yama could not speak to him. Gritty ash was still lodged under his nails and in the creases of his palms. Even thinking of speaking so soon after his father's death brought an ache into his throat.

Dumb with grief, he lost himself in the story and travelled far from the hurt of the burning of Aeolis, the disappearance of Derev, and the Aedile's death.

Angel ran from the ship soon after it arrived at Confluence. There was a whole world to understand and to conquer, and she plunged into it, revelling in her escape from the suffocating caution of the consensus of her partials. They wanted to go on to the Home Galaxy, but Angel was tired of searching. She ran with a wild glee and a sense of relief at finally controlling her own fate once more.

She had set out millions of years ago to find aliens. Not the strange creatures that thronged the riverside cities of Confluence, which were merely animals changed by design to resemble human beings, but true aliens, sapient creatures of a completely separate and independent evolutionary history to that of human beings. Although none had been found in the Home Galaxy, the universe was a vast place. There were a dozen small satellite galaxies around the Home Galaxy, thousands of galaxies in the local group, and twenty thousand similar superclusters of galaxies. The search might take a billion years, and it gave her a purpose, concealing her flight from the crusade against the transcendents. Behind her, trillions of her lineage were being purged by baseline humans she considered to be little more than animals, clinging as they did to sexual reproduction and the dogma that maintenance of genetic and social diversity was more important than any individual, no matter how old, how learned, how powerful.

Neither sleeping nor dead, reduced to information triply engraved on imperishable gold, Angel fled first to the neighbouring spiral galaxy. Although her ship flew so fast that it bound time around itself, the journey still took thousands of years by its clock, and more than two million years as measured by the common time of the universe. And at the end of that long, long voyage, Angel and her partials were incarnated and born anew.

What she learned then, within a hundred years of waking, was that the universe was not made for the convenience of humans. What she and her crew of partials found was a galaxy ruined and mostly dead.

A billion years ago it had smashed into another, somewhat smaller galaxy. There had been few direct interactions between the billions of stars as the two galaxies interpenetrated, because the distance between stars was so great, but collisions between gases and dark matter travelling at relative speeds of millions of kilometres per second had sent violent gravity waves and compression shocks racing through the tenuous interstellar medium, and stars from both galaxies had been torn from their orbits, and scattered in a vast halo. Some were ejected with sufficient velocity to escape into intergalactic space, doomed to wander forever, companionless, in the great void. Waves of star formation were triggered when gas clouds passed through each other. There was a brief, intense increase in supernova activity, and expanding wave fronts of gamma and X-ray radiation sterilised hundreds of thousands of planetary systems.

Angel and her crew of partials found a cold, dark planet of nitrogen ice wandering amongst the stars; there were millions of such planets cast adrift. Millions more had been scorched clean by flares and novas triggered in their parent stars by infalling dust and gas, or by gravity pulses, or by encounters with clumps of perturbed dark matter so dense that collisions with atoms of ordinary matter had occurred, releasing tremendous amounts of energy. There were planets sheared in half by immense tidal stresses. There were planets smashed into millions of fragments, scattered so widely in their orbital paths that they could never re-form. There were gas giants turned inside out – single vast perpetual storms.

The ship constructed telescope arrays and dispatched self-replicating probes, and spent twenty thousand years sampling a small part of the galaxy. Angel and her partials returned to the unbeing of storage while travelling from star to star, were reborn over and again. In this fashion they surveyed a segment more than ten thousand light years across, and made deep field observations of a much greater area, but were unable to find a single world where life had evolved much beyond the anaerobic bacterial stage; if any worlds harboured biospheres that had survived the catastrophe, they must be vanishingly rare. And there were no traces of technologically advanced species. If any had existed when the two galaxies collided, they had been destroyed, or had fled elsewhere.

When she had constructed the ship, Angel had tipped the stuff of ten thousand libraries into its mind. It told her that there had been millions of collisions between galaxies, and that it was likely that most galaxies had suffered such collisions at least once during their lifetime. Part of one arm of the Home Galaxy had been disrupted by the transit of a cluster of stars, although the reconstruction of the Home Galaxy by the transcendents had long ago erased any damage this had caused.

But the Home Galaxy was a statistical freak. Unlike other galaxies it had never endured a major collision with a body of similar size. It was an outlier at the far end of the distribution of possible evolutionary paths.

The human species was also an outlier. The universe was not made for the convenience of intelligence. Life flourished rarely, and was soon extinguished. If other civilisations had arisen elsewhere in the unbounded universe, they were so distant that human beings could never contact them. Angel concluded that humanity, in all its swarming vigour and diversity, was alone. It must make of itself what it could, for there was nothing against which it could measure itself. There were no aliens to conquer, no wise ancient beings from which to learn deep secrets hidden in the beginnings of time and space.

Angel did not consider that she might be wrong. She killed herself, was reborn, and killed herself again as soon as she learned what her previous self had discovered. When she woke again, with part of her memory suppressed by the ship, more than two million years had passed. The ship was in trailing orbit beyond a huge construction that orbited a star one hundred and fifty thousand light years beyond the spiral arms of the Home Galaxy, close to the accretion disc of a supermassive black hole where the Large Magellanic Cloud had once been.

The ship showed her what it had observed as it had traversed the long geodesic between the two galaxies. At first there was an intense point of light within the heart of the Large Magellanic Cloud. It might have been a supernova, except that it was a thousand times larger than any supernova ever recorded. The glare of this dying star obscured the light of its millions of companions for more than a century, and when at last it faded all the remaining stars were streaming around the point where it had been. Those nearest the centre elongated and dissipated, spilling their fusing hearts across the sky, and more and more crowded in until nothing was left but the gas clouds of the accretion disc, glowing with the red-shifted Cerenkov radiation that was all that was left of material falling into the event horizon of the central black hole – a black hole with the mass of a million suns.

The ship had searched the Home Galaxy for sources of coherent electromagnetic radiation and found only a scattering of ancient neutrino beacons. Apart from these, signals in the Home Galaxy had ceased while the ship was still half a million light years out – the time when the first supernova had flared in the Large Magellanic Cloud. There had been a great deal of activity around the black hole while it grew, but at last, with the ship still a hundred thousand light years out, that too had ceased.

Angel beat the ship to its conclusion. Humanity, or whatever humanity had become in the four and a half million years since she had fled the crusade, had created the black hole and vanished into it. The ship spoke of the possibility that humanity had developed wormhole technology – it had located a number of double occultations within the Home Galaxy that were typical of the theoretical effect of a wormhole exit passing between a star and an observer. The ship had also spotted a concentrated cluster of occultation events around a halo star more than ten thousand light years beyond the accretion disc of the giant black hole. The ship told Angel that it had changed course – a manoeuvre that had taken a thousand years – and built up a detailed map of the space around the star.

She studied the map. There were more than a hundred wormhole entrances orbiting the star, and there was also an artefact as big as a world, if the surface of a world might be peeled from its globe and stretched out into a long plane. The ship had built arrays of detectors. It had obtained the infrared signatures of water and molecular oxygen, and estimated the average temperature of the surface of the artefact to be two hundred and ninety-three degrees above absolute zero. It had detected the absorption signatures of several classes of photosynthetic pigments, most notably rhodopsin and chlorophyll. There was life on the surface of the artefact.

In the night, Pandaras settled a blanket around Yama's shoulders. Yama did not notice. Beetles smashed at the lantern above his head as he read on.

The artefact was a stout needle twenty thousand kilometres long and less than a thousand wide, with a deep keel beneath its terraformed surface. It hung in a spherical envelope of air and embedded gravity fields. It tilted back and forth on its long axis once every twenty-four hours and took just over three hundred and sixty-five days to complete a single orbit of its ordinary yellow dwarf star. These parameters struck a deep chord in Angel, whose original had been born in the planetary system where humanity had evolved. For the first time in millions of years she called up the personality fragment which retained memories of the earliest part of her long history. She muttered a little mantra over and over as she studied the data that the ship had gathered: twenty-four hours, three hundred and sixty-five days, thirty-two metres per second squared, twenty per cent oxygen, eighty per cent nitrogen.

The orbit of the artefact was slightly irregular: there would be seasons on its surface. One side was bounded by mountains fifty kilometres high. Their naked peaks rose out of the atmospheric envelope. On the other side, a great river ran half the length, rising in mountains three-quarters buried in ice at the trailing end of this strange world and falling over the edge at the midpoint. It was not clear how the water was recycled. The ship made neutrino and deep radar scans and discovered a vast warren of caverns and corridors and shafts within the rocky keel of the artefact, but no system of aquifers or canals.

One half of the world, beyond the fall of the river, was dry cratered desert with a dusty ice cap at the leading end and a scattering of ruined cities. The other half was verdant land bounded on one side by the river and on the other by ice-capped ranges of mountains which were mere foothills to the gigantic peaks at the edge. There was a large, cosmopolitan city near the ice-capped mountains, and there were smaller cities strung like beads along the river, each inhabited by a different race of human-like creatures. The ship sent out thousands of tiny probes. Many were destroyed by the machines which roamed everywhere on the surface of the artefact, but the survivors returned with cellular samples of hundreds of different organisms. Less than one-tenth of the plants and animals were from lineages that originated in the human home-star system; the rest were of unknown and multiple origins. None of the inhabitants were of human descent, the ship said, and except for a few primitive races they all had an artificial homeobox inserted within their genetic material.

The ship could not explain what the homeobox sequence coded for. It could not explain why there were thousands of different, seemingly sapient, alien races crowded together on the surface of a single world-sized habitat. Nor could it explain why the physical appearance of almost all these races mapped to at least eighty per cent of the human norm – a much closer conformation than those of many of Angel's lineages, in the days of her lost empire.

Angel ordered the ship to match the orbit of the artefact.

It refused, and her partials argued that the artefact was an anomaly, that they had a better chance of understanding what had happened to humanity by exploring the Home Galaxy. Angel overrode them, and in the process discovered the data that the ship had hidden from her. She learned all over again that there was unlikely to be life anywhere else in the local group of galaxies, and perhaps in the entire universe.

This time she did not kill herself.

The big city near the source of the long river was clearly the capital of this artificial world: ancient and extensive, swarming with a hundred different races. The ship landed at the docks and Angel and her crew of partials began their exploration.

There was a capital city but no obvious unified system of government; there was a palace, but no rulers. There were millions of bureaucrats organised into a hundred or more different departments, but most appeared to be engaged in maintaining records rather than determining or carrying out policy. Indeed, there seemed to be no central or permanent government. Order was maintained by undiscussed consent, enforced by roaming gangs of magistrates who appeared to be answerable to no one but themselves, their powers limited only by strict adherence to custom.

It seemed that there had been rulers long ago, before a war fought between two factions of the machines which roved the world and served its peoples. The war had scorched one half of the world to desert; the sparse cloud of machines trailing the orbital path of the artefact were survivors belonging to the losing side. The people of the capital city told Angel that after the war many of the avatars of the Preservers had fallen silent and many of the shrines had died. The Hierarchs, who appeared to have interceded between the avatars and the people, had vanished shortly after the end of the war; the surviving avatars were consulted only under the direction of priests. The ship told Angel that the shrines were clearly some kind of information-processing system, but most were deactivated, and those still active were functionally compromised.

'The Preservers watch all,' she was told by everyone she asked. They were the invisible power by which the illusion of order was maintained. It was like a theocracy, except that the priests and hierodules of the multitude of temples claimed no special power or privileges. All served the ideal of the Preservers.

Angel went everywhere in the capital city, Ys, and asked every kind of question. No one tried to stop her; everyone was eager to help. It seemed that the homeobox inserted in the various genomes of the inhabitants regulated their behaviour in the presence of true human beings. They were better servants than her partials; she did not doubt that they would lay down their lives for her, if asked.

In the end, they helped her to escape.

She did not plan it. If she had, no doubt the ship and its crew of partials would have stopped her. She did it on a whim, an impulse.

She was walking by the docks, followed by the usual crowd of curious people and a small group of the law keepers – magistrates – and their machines. The sun was high. Its diamond light sparkled on the wide sweep of the river. The city stretched away under a haze of smoke that hid the foothills of the snowcapped mountains floating in the blue distance. The dock road was lined by trees in blossom: big red flowers attended by clouds of sulphur-yellow butterflies. Vendors stood at their carts or stalls in the sun-speckled shade of the trees, crying their wares. Men sat cross-legged as they mended nets stretched across wide frames, and women gutted silver fish under a canopy of green banana leaves, surrounded by noisy flocks of birds that fought for fish guts tossed over the edge of the quay. Hundreds of men crowded stone steps at the river's edge, washing themselves in brown water while children swam and splashed and shrieked with laughter. White birds wheeled over sunstruck water or strutted and pecked on wrinkled mudflats where clinker-built dinghies lay on their sides; further out, men sat in coracles, fishing with the help of black long-necked birds very like cormorants, and a small machine moved above the water in quick bursts, like a squeezed pip of mercury.

An ache rose in Angel, a universal desolation. Lost, all lost. All she had known was lost, and yet all around were echoes of what she had lost. For the first time since she had been reborn, she felt the weight of her age.

The people who were following her were not human.

She was surrounded by aliens. Alien creatures which distorted the human norm: by pig men, lion men, lizard men, bird men, toad men and others she could not begin to identify. They were animals trying to be human; they were humans masked with animal faces. They called themselves the Shaped, and said that they had been changed, two words with the same root but subtly different meanings she did not quite understand.

Angel had lost so much, and so much surrounded her, rich and strange, yet hauntingly familiar. The birds and the butterflies, the wet fetid smell of the mud, the smells of hot stone and cooking oil and the acrid smoke from fires fuelled with dry dung, the sunlight on the water and the wind that stirred the glossy leaves and the red flowers of the trees: a thousand fragmentary impressions that defined from moment to moment the unquantifiable richness of the world. Many of the transcendents had disappeared into imaginary empires within vast data banks, creating perfect images of known worlds or building impossible new ones, but Angel had always felt that these were less satisfactory than dreams, too perfect to be truly real. That was why she had opted for nonbeing during the long transits of her voyage, rather than slowtime in a fabrication.

Reality, or nothing.

Angel took a ship out from the city. It was that easy.

The ship's captain was a fat, solemn, ponderous man with sleek black skin and round, liquid black eyes; his mother or grandmother might have been a seal, or might have lain with one. He did not question Angel's presence as they sailed downriver from city to city, but deferred to her with quiet good humour. The fact that she had hijacked his ship and his life was never raised. A city of tombs; a city of porcelain; a city of caves in cliffs high above the river; a city of trees; a city built on stilts in the middle of the river. Dozens of cities, each inhabited by a different race of people, all sharing the same unquestioned laws and religion.

And then a city at war with itself.

A Change War, the ship's captain said, and when Angel told him to put in at the city's long waterfront he came close to disobeying her for the first time. It was a city of square houses of red mudbrick, all heaped on each other like a tumbled pile of boxes. A terraced ziggurat of white, weather-worn stone stood in the middle of the forest outside the city wall, guarded by machines that constantly looped through the air above it. It was the home of an old woman who called herself the Commissioner.

Angel sat with the Commissioner on a high terrace of the ancient ziggurat, amongst potted lemon trees and geraniums. Riverward, across a sea of treetops, part of the city was burning. The sound of distant rifle fire popped and crackled, brought erratically by the warm wind. The Commissioner served Angel a bowl of the earthy infusion of twigs which people everywhere on this world called tea. The Commissioner was half Angel's height, a slow, deliberate woman with a humped back and a round face with lips pursed like a beak, and small eyes half-hidden amongst the wrinkles of her leathery skin. She wore a kind of fustian tent which dropped in many folds from a gold circlet at her neck to puddle on the floor. A small machine darted and hovered above her like a bejewelled dragonfly.

The Commissioner seemed to regard the war as an unfortunate but inevitable natural process which could not be prevented but must be endured, like a sudden hailstorm or a forest fire. She told Angel that some of the people of the city had changed, and were at war with those who had not.

'The changed ones will win, of course. They always do. And then they will move on and found a new city, or more likely scatter along the river. It is an exciting time for them.'

It took Angel a long time to find out from the Commissioner what she meant by change. It was a kind of transcendence or epiphany, a realisation of individual worth, the possibility of sin or at least of transgression against the fixed codes by which the citizens had ordered their lives for millennia. It was a little like the memes with which Angel had once experimented when attempting to unify her spreading empire, but it was also a physical infection, a change in brain structure and chemistry which provided, as far as Angel understood it, an area of high-density information storage that somehow interacted with the nine infolded dimensions in the quantum foam at the bottom of reality. Everything anyone of the changed races or bloodlines did or experienced was recorded or remembered by something like a soul that would survive until the end of the universe. It was the true immortality which Angel and her kind had dreamed of millions of years ago, when they had still been human.

The Commissioner explained that the most primitive races, the indigens, would never change, but all others had changed or would change – there were still hundreds of unchanged races. Some had gone beyond the first change and transcended the world entirely, but the Commissioner could not tell Angel where they had gone. It was the work of the Preservers, and therefore not to be questioned. It simply was.

Angel wondered what happened to those of the unchanged and indigenous races who died (she was wondering about herself). The Commissioner grew reflective. It was night now. The burning waterfront of the city stood above its own reflection in the black mirror of its harbour. There were skirmishes in the fields and orchards upriver of the city – the flashes of rifles defined the opposing positions, and once there was a tremendous explosion that sent an expanding ball of red and yellow flame into the air and shook the terrace, rattling the bowls of tea on the slab of polished rock that floated between the two women.

'It is a question for the archivists,' the Commissioner said at last. 'But they are busy at the moment, talking with the wounded, and I do hope you will not disturb them. So many lives will pass unremarked because of the war – that is the cost of change, and it is a heavy price to pay. But some say that the Preservers mark all, and all will be restored whether we record it or not.'

Angel thought of the millions of clerks labouring in the great palace of the capital city. She said, 'Recording the world is important. Why is that?'

The Commissioner was watching the distant fighting: the fires, the stuttering flashes of rifles, the red blossoms of a cannonade, the abrupt fountains of earth and fire. She said, 'It is one of the highest tasks.'

'Recording memories for the Preservers to use?'

''The Preservers will resurrect everyone at the end of time. We will all live again.'

This is an experiment, Angel thought. An experiment that records its own self. Things have been set in motion; evolution is expected. That means I can change things here. If the Preservers are using these people, then so can I.

She said, 'If you could gain much in this life by behaving badly, and still the Preservers would resurrect you, then perhaps it is worth behaving badly. You could have power and wealth now, everything that you are promised in eternity, and the Preservers would forgive you.'

The Commissioner considered this for a while. Angel watched the dark city beyond the forest. There were small fires scattered around the dimming glow of the site of the big explosion; the rifle fire seemed to have stopped.

At last, the Commissioner said, 'All possible worlds can be created by the Preservers at the end of time, and that means not only all possible good, but also all possible evil. But the Preservers will not permit evil because it contradicts the love they bear towards us. For if they did not love us, why did they lift us up? So we must live our lives as best we can, for otherwise we might not have anything to live for beyond this life. Some say that the Preservers can correct evil in any person. No matter how great that evil might be, the Preservers have all of time and all of space in which to work their will. They say that the willingness of the Preservers to resurrect an evil person and punish them while holding out the possibility of redemption demonstrates the depth of their love for us, their imperfect creations. And if this is true, it is better to act well and help others than to harm them, for you will gain nothing by acting badly.' The Commissioner laughed. 'And, besides that, think of the shame of having to endure the forgiveness of the Preservers! It is a heavy burden. Few could bear it.'

Angel said, 'Those who are changed are acting badly now.'

'Only because their unchanged brothers, who know no other way of life, are fighting them. The unchanged cannot imagine change, and so they fight it to the death, and those who have changed must defend themselves. The unchanged do not know good or evil because they cannot choose between them. They are what they are, and no more.'

'Yet you know the difference, and you do not intercede. You could remove the changed and stop the war. You condemn many to death by inaction. Is that not evil?'

'No one should set themselves in the place of the Preservers,' the Commissioner said. For the first time, she seemed to be offended.

The Preservers were universally worshipped, but no one could tell Angel much about them. Only that they had withdrawn their grace from the world but would return at the end of time and resurrect everyone who had ever lived, and everyone would live forever in an infinity of perfect worlds. It was a creed similar to the ambitions of the transcendents, but everyone on Confluence believed that the Preservers were capable of realising it. At the same time, everyone believed that the ultimate nature of the Preservers was unknowable. What little that could be understood about them was in the Puranas, but the Puranas, which formed a kind of moral handbook illustrated by lessons in cosmology and galactic history, were maddeningly vague and imprecise. Early on, Angel had asked the ship to give her a precis, and had recognised her own empire in a brief half-sentence that horribly distorted what she had tried to do. That was another thing which must be put right. Her empire had once been the largest in human history, perhaps the largest empire ever known. She had not yet decided what she would do, but she would make sure that her long-lost empire was given its proper recognition.

'I'll stay here tonight,' she said. 'I assume this is a safe place. Find me food and a bed. I'll leave tomorrow.'

'Of course.' The Commissioner clacked her horny lips together and added, 'However, I do believe that your ship has already left.'

It was true. While Angel had been talking with the Commissioner, the ship she had commandeered at Ys had escaped her geas and made off. But the next day she simply took another and continued downriver. The new ship was much larger than the first. Its three masts bore square sails with sunbursts painted on them and its deep holds were full of fruit which had been bound for a city upriver. The fruit rotted after a week and Angel ordered it thrown over the side. It took the crew, including the officers and the captain, a whole day to empty the holds, but the ship rode high in the water afterward, and sailed more swiftly. The captain said that the ship should be ballasted with stones, for otherwise it was likely to capsize in a storm, but Angel ignored him. She was in a hurry now.

She passed city after city, mostly inhabited by unchanged races as fixed in their habits as ants or bees. Without free will, they were more like zombies or organic machines than people, but even so, their unremarkable lives were recorded by patient archivists. They were policed by magistrates of their own kind. Although one or two officials of one or another of the changed races were present, they merely provided a kind of moral authority that was called on only when needed.

The last of the cities of the long, long river was called Sensch. It was a desert city of narrow streets shaded by palms and ginkgoes, dusty squares, flat-roofed buildings of whitewashed mudbrick. There were extensive plantations of sago and date palms, orange and pomegranate and banana, and various kinds of groundnuts. There was a great deal of camel breeding, too. At least, the things were a little like camels.

The citizens of Sensch were a slender people, skilled in pottery and glassmaking. They had heavily ridged foreheads and small lidless black eyes; their brown and black skins exhibited varying degrees of residual scaliness. Snakes, the Commissioner of Sensch called them. He was a small, active fellow who lived in a garden that floated above the pink sandstone palace that was his official residence. The Commissioner, Dreen, seemed anxious to please, but Angel did not press her needs at once.

She met the Archivist of Sensch, a corpulent fellow with a limp, a few days later. His name was Mr Naryan. He was of the same race as the captain of the first ship that Angel had commandeered; she had seen him swimming off the wide plaza by the river, as graceful in the water as he was awkward and slow on land. He sat down beside Angel in a tea shop by one of the city's camel markets, pretending at first not to realise who she was. Angel liked his sly, patient air and demanded nothing of him at all, not even that he accept her for what she was. She missed conversation amongst equals.

Mr Naryan was afraid of Angel, but he hid it well.

He made small talk about a procession that went past, explaining that its participants had had their reason taken away, either as punishment or because of what he called a religious avocation. He said that he understood that she had come a long way, and she laughed at the understatement.

Mr Naryan said with mild alarm, 'I do not mean to insult you.'

Angel tried to make it easier by talking about the Archivist himself. She pointed at his loose, belted shirt and said, 'You dress like a . . . native.' She had almost said Snake. She said, 'Is *that* a religious avocation?'

He told her what she already knew, that he was the city's archivist. He had a round, kindly face, with heavy wrinkles at his brow and three fat folds under his chin.

Angel said, 'When I left, not a single intelligent alien species was known. It was one reason for my voyage. Now there are thousands strung along this long, long river. All of them made by the Preservers, who I suppose are my descendants. But where are the Preservers?'

'The Preservers departed long ago. These are the end times.'

Mr Naryan said this by rote. He had not really understood her questions.

'There are always those who believe they live at the end of history,' Angel said. 'We thought that *we* lived at the end of history, when every star system in the galaxy had been mapped, every habitable world settled.

'Every race in every city claims to be human, even the ones who don't look like they could have evolved from anything that was ever human stock. And they all treat me like a ruler – or a god. So what does that make me?'

'The Shaped call themselves human because they have no other name for what they have become, innocent and fallen alike. After all, none of them had names before they were raised up.'

'What about you? Are you human, or are you "human"?' Angel said, crooking her little fingers in the air, wondering at once if he understood what had once been the universal sign for irony.

'My people are fallen,' Mr Naryan said. 'The innocent, the unfallen, like the citizens of Sensch, are our . . . responsibility.'

Angel told him that his kind was not doing a very good job, judging by the Change War she had witnessed upriver. She described the war, and asked the Archivist many questions, most of which he was unable to answer. Without asking her permission, he jotted down her description of the Change War and her questions on a tablet, using an impacted system of diacritical marks. Angel was amused.

'You write down people's stories.'

'Writing them down helps to fix them in my head. Stories are important. In the end they are all that is left, all that history leaves us. Stories endure.'

Angel thought about this. She said at last, 'I have been out of history a long time. I'm not sure that I want to be a part of it again.'

She was tired. While she had been travelling, she had been able to forget that she had escaped her ship and her responsibilities, but now she would have to come to a decision. She did not want to talk any more and left the Archivist. He knew better than to follow her, and she liked him for that, too.

She found a suitable house, a two-storey affair with a balcony overlooking a central courtyard shaded by a jacaranda tree. Its owners, grateful for her attention, were only too pleased to give it to her, and others came with gifts: furniture, carpets, food and wine, musical instruments, cigarettes, paintings, sheets of plastic that she realised were books, slates which showed scenes from the world's past, stolen from tombs of hierophants far downriver.

Some of the people stayed with her, mostly young men. Angel experimented with sex. Full intercourse with the Snakes was anatomically impossible, but there were a variety of pleasing and diverting exercises. In the evenings, she watched dancers or shadow-puppet plays, or listened to the atonal nasal singing of the finest poet of the city, accompanied by a silver flute and a two-string lyre. The days passed pleasantly until Mr Naryan found her in the tea house by the camel market, and told her that her ship was coming to Sensch.

Angel affected a casualness she did not feel. She had expected it to find her, but not so quickly. She fell into conversation with the Archivist and eventually took him back to her house. He took in the bustle with a solemn air and told her gently that she should not take advantage of the citizens.

Angel said sharply, 'They're happy to help me. What's wrong with that?'

Mr Naryan cast his eyes down. She knew then that he could not argue with her, and felt a stab of shame.

She had tea and honey fritters brought out, and described something of what she had seen on her long river journey, and asked the Archivist many questions about Dreen's authority and the way that order was maintained in the city. She caught one of the machines and showed it to him. 'And these? By what authority do these little spies operate?'

Mr Naryan stared at it open-mouthed. Perhaps he had never seen anyone catch one before. Pinched between Angel's thumb and forefinger, the little bronze bug wriggled as it tried to free itself. Its sensor cluster, a froth of glass and silver beads, turned back and forth until Angel let it go.

The Archivist watched it rise above the roof of the house. He said, 'They are part of the maintenance system of Confluence.'

'Can Dreen use them? Tell me all you know. It may be important.'

Angel met with Mr Naryan at intervals in the days that followed. The young men who followed her formed a kind of band or gang, and some went with her wherever she went. They made Mr Naryan nervous, but Angel encouraged them, if only because it was a measure of what she could do. She gave them white headbands lettered with a slogan she had composed. Giving away one of the headbands was like bestowing a blessing. She made speeches in the markets and on the plaza by the river to try to rouse the citizens, but although people gathered and listened politely, nothing much came of it, except that her own followers sometimes grew too excited. They were apt to misunderstand what she had to say about rising above destiny, and defaced walls with slogans, or overturned stalls in the market. They were gripped by powerful but unfocused emotions.

Perhaps these petty acts were to her followers heady and radical statements, but Angel knew that it was not the way. She went to the temple and had one of the priests help her consult the interactive librarian which manifested in one of the large terminals that the priests called shrines. She decided that she would cross the river to where a cluster of old shrines stood, unused since the Snakes had come to occupy Sensch. She would try to wake the shrines there, and learn from them.

Then there was a blank picture. Whatever Angel had done at the shrines at the edge of the world, by the great falls at the end of the river, was not recorded. Yama set his book aside. He was very tired, but not at all sleepy.

It was a few hours from dawn. The smoky swirl of the Eye of the Preservers was setting at the edge of the world. Tamora and Pandaras slept under the awning. Captain Lorquital and Aguilar slept in their cabins beneath the poop deck; the sailors slept head to toe in their hammocks beneath the deck. Yama had always needed less sleep than Telmon or anyone else he knew, and was used to being awake when everyone else slept. Even so, and even though he was not strictly alone, for the helmsman stood at the wheel in the red glow of the stern lantern, he felt a desolation, a vast aching emptiness, there on the ship in the midst of the wide river. He wondered if this was how Angel had felt, estranged from all she knew by millions of years of history, with only compliant uncomprehending alien creatures for company. How lonely she must have been, ruler of all the world, but with no purpose!

He would finish her story in a little while, he thought. He already suspected that he knew how it ended. Enough for now. First his father's papers, and the shock they contained amongst their dense ladders of calculations. And now this. No more stories.

Yama shook dew from the blanket that Pandaras had put around his shoulders and lay down, just for a moment. And slept.

24

GOND

'It is a city as bright as the ice flows of the mountains at the end of the world,' Eliphas told Yama. 'I last saw it many years ago, but I still remember how it shone in the sunlight, across the blue waters of the river.'

Yama flinched, remembering the one solid fact he had gleaned from the muddle of the Aedile's papers. Eliphas did not notice. He was lost in his memories.

'The river may be shrinking, brother, but it runs deeper around Gond than anywhere else in the world, deeper even than at Ys,' the old man said. 'They fish for leviathans there, from huge flat-decked barges. They send down lures as big as a man, armed with explosive hooks, and if they strike lucky they haul up their catch and render it there and then. Of course, most of the time the leviathan escapes, and sometimes, despite its drag anchors, a barge is pulled under by its catch.'

'I thought that the people of Gond led aesthetic and contemplative lives,' Yama said.

'The leviathan hunters come from the cities of the Dry Plains, further downriver. From Ush and Kalyb and Galata, and the twin cities of Kilminar and Balbeck.' Eliphas intoned the names with a sonorous pleasure. 'If a barge catches more than one leviathan in the hunting season its crew count themselves lucky. The proceeds from rendering one monster would buy a ship like this twice over.'

Yama and Eliphas were leaning side by side at the rail of the main deck of the *Weazel*, in the shadow of the rust-red sail. Sternwards, smoky columns of rain twisted beneath the reefs of white and grey clouds that overshadowed the farside shore – a desolation of mudflats and pioneer mangroves inhabited only by birds and swarms of army crabs. There had been no sign of either the warship or the picket boat in the past three days, and the *Weazel* was at last angling away from the farside and the spurious safety of the mangrove swamps. Ahead, in the far distance, the Great River bent towards the Rim Mountains, and at the angle of the nearside shore a mote of light glistened, white as a crystal of salt: the city of Gond. Captain Lorquital had announced that the *Weazel* would put in there to collect a passenger and to take on fresh provisions.

Yama said, 'I see that you are happy to retrace the steps you took when you were a young man.'

Eliphas closed his eyes. His face was shaded by the wide brim of his straw hat. 'It has been more than a hundred years. I thought I had forgotten most of it, but each place we pass brings memories rising from the depths of my mind, as the monsters of the abyssal currents of the river rise to follow the glowing lures trailed by the fishing barges.'

He opened his eyes and smiled: silver and white flashed in his black face. 'Do not worry, brother. I will fulfil the promise I made to you in the library of the Department of Apothecaries and Chirurgeons. I will find the lost city for you. I know that your servants are suspicious of me, but I have your best interests at heart.'

'They are not my servants, Eliphas.'

'They believe otherwise, brother. Look there! A pod of grampuses! See how they sport!'

Three, four, five sleek creatures swam swiftly through the clear water, effortlessly overtaking the speeding ship. They caught up with the purling bow-wave and rode it briefly, plunging and leaping in creamy foam, then all at once they sounded, pale shadows dwindling away into the dark depths of the river.

Eliphas said, 'Some believe they are intelligent, and that they herd the fish of the river as the autochthons of the mountains herd sheep or goats.'

'When you are swimming in the river, you can sometimes hear them singing,' Yama said. He had often heard their songs himself, for in summer schools of grampuses migrated far upriver. Their songs lasted for hours, a deep throbbing overlaid with scatterings of chirps and whistles, haunting, mysterious and somehow lonely, as if defining the inhuman vastness of the Great River.

'They say that the Preservers placed everything on this world for a purpose,' Eliphas said. 'But I sometimes wonder if they brought creatures like the grampuses to the world simply because of the joy they strike in the hearts of men.'

Yama remembered that the woman in the shrine, Angel's aspect, had said that the Preservers were descended from her own people. He said, 'I think that the Preservers were once not so different from us. The first suras of the Puranas tell us that in times long past there were no gods, but only many kinds of humans.'

'There is no gradation in godhood,' Eliphas said. 'It is not like the process of ageing, which is so gradual that only by looking back are you shocked by how much you have changed, for you have no sense of having changed at all. And of course, from day to day you have not changed in any measurable sense. No, brother, the Preservers changed utterly and at once, and so what they were before they became gods is irrelevant. When godhood descended upon them, or when they ascended to godhood, everything they had been fell away.'

'And yet they made us over in their image. Not as what they became, but as what they once were. And so they did not leave their past behind.'

Eliphas nodded gravely. The old man loved metaphysical discourse. He was one of those for whom the world was merely an object from which theoretical ideals might be abstracted, and was therefore less important than thought.

'The Preservers have not forgotten what they once were,' he said, 'but they put it behind them, as a butterfly puts behind its caterpillar childhood when it emerges from its cocoon. The Puranas are perhaps that cocoon, which we riddle for clues. Yet it is only an empty shell left clinging to the twig of the world. That which matters has ascended into everlasting sunlight.'

Yama smiled at the old man's fanciful metaphor. He enjoyed these conversations – they reminded him of the long debates with Zakiel and Telmon in happier times. He said, 'You have seen me read in the Puranas. It is not to understand the Preservers. It is to understand myself.'

'I believe that your copy of the Puranas is a very old one.'

Yama knew that Eliphas wanted to examine the book, but he had decided that he would not show the transformed pictures to anyone. At least, not until he had fully understood Angel's story. He would read more tonight. He thought that he already knew how it ended – but perhaps it had not ended after all. Perhaps he was part of that story, coming late onto the stage to draw the curtain and announce the end of the play.

'I spent much of my childhood in a library,' he said. 'Perhaps too much of it was spent studying the past. I want to see the world, Eliphas, and all its wonders. I want the present, not the past.'

'But the past is all around us. We cannot escape it. Everything important has happened in the past, and we are its children. The Preservers achieved godhood in the past and made the world in the past and shaped the bloodlines in the past. Compared to the immense solidity of the past, the future is a small thing and hazily glimpsed, and we are told that once every bloodline has changed the future will cease, for history will cease. But perhaps you are right, brother. Children should look ahead, not behind. Otherwise the future will only echo what has already happened.'

So they talked as the ship, sailing aslant the river's currents, drew closer to the shining city of Gond. Eliphas preferred his own opinions to those of anyone else, but Yama was grateful for the diversion of his company.

He could not mourn his father, not yet. He could not give way to grief or anger. He had to stay calm and alert, for sooner or later he would have to face Prefect Corin again. He did not believe that he had escaped for long. The Prefect was a thorough man. He would have searched the floating forest for remains of his quarry and, after finding none, he would have gone on downriver, implacable, relentless. Yama had already turned aside several machines that were searching the wide river for any trace of the *Weazel*, so he was not surprised when, that evening, as the ship scudded ahead of a light breeze towards the floating harbour that stood off the shore of Gond, Captain Lorquital called him up to the quarterdeck.

Aguilar and Tamora stood on either side of Captain Lorquital's sling chair. Aguilar told Yama, 'Your trick with the machines has run aground. The devil has got ahead of us.'

'We'll have to face him now,' Tamora said, and her black lips peeled back from her teeth at the thought.

Ixchel Lorquital handed Yama her spectacles without comment. Through their magnifying lenses, the floating harbour leapt closer. There were ships of every size laid up at the leagues of pontoons and cranes and warehouses of the docks, their masts packed together like a leafless forest. And in the channels beyond the floating harbour, a picket boat and a triple-decked warship were anchored side by side, their sails half-reefed.

'Well,' Yama said, 'we could not hope to hide from him forever.'

'I received a light signal from the harbour,' Captain Lorquital said. 'We are to pick up our passenger tonight. He's an important man, and we can leave tomorrow morning under his protection, like any other honest vessel.'

'We can't depend on that,' Aguilar said, and told Yama, 'Your devil will be watching the river night and day, but I think we'll have a better chance if we run at night.'

Tamora said, 'We might surprise him.'

'I saw a machine today,' Captain Lorquital said. 'It was making directly for us when it suddenly angled away, as if it remembered it had business elsewhere.'

'I cannot confuse the minds of men,' Yama said. 'And Aguilar is right. Prefect Corin's men will be watching every ship that passes by. Especially those few that pass by at night.'

'We have lost our cannon,' Aguilar said. 'We have only our small arms. If it comes to a fight, we must surprise them.'

'We must strike first,' Tamora said.

'Tamora and I have discussed this,' Aguilar said. 'There are barrels of pitch in the hold. If we construct a simple catapult—'

'I won't be a pirate, daughter,' Captain Lorquital said. 'They must fire the first shot.'

'And that one shot could sink us,' Aguilar said.

Yama said, 'It is better to know where our enemy is than to run with the thought that he is always somewhere behind us. Besides, he will have no warrant or power here. He is merely another sailor put in for shore leave and provisioning. If he tries to hurt us, the common law will protect us.'

'The people of Gond care little for anything but their philosophies,' Aguilar said. 'They'll probably turn us over to that town-burner rather than interrupt their meditations to listen to us plead our case.'

'She's right,' Tamora said. 'We must take matters into our own hands.'

'Then we'll be worse than them,' Captain Lorquital said. 'We'll behave as any normal ship. The free men will get their shore leave, and you, daughter, will stand guard with the slaves. Nothing will happen to us at the harbour, and once our passenger is aboard we'll have his protection.'

Afterwards, Tamora followed Yama to the bow. 'You are planning something,' she said. 'I know you don't believe that crut about common law.'

'I want to kill him,' Yama said.

'That's more like it. How? And how can I help?'

'I want to kill him, but I do not think that I should.'

'Then he will kill you.'

'Yes, he will, if he cannot make me serve him.'

'He destroyed your home, Yama. He killed your father as surely as if he had put an arbalest bolt through his heart. He is your enemy, and there is nothing sweeter than drinking the blood of your enemy. Don't deny yourself the pleasure.'

'He is only one man. How many more will the department send after me? How many more would I have to kill? If I kill Prefect Corin there will never be an end to killing. I will always be hunted. But if I can find a way to end this, then I will be free.'

Tamora thought about this. 'We'll try your way,' she said at last. 'And if that doesn't work, give him to me. He is as much my enemy as yours. I'll rip his heart from his chest and eat it in front of his dying eyes.'

She smiled fiercely at the thought, but Yama knew that she shared his foreboding.

A fishing barge was anchored just outside the floating harbour, with the carcass of a leviathan sprawled across its wide deck. Already partly defleshed, the arches of the leviathan's ribcage rose higher than the barge's cranes. Its guts, tinged pink with the plankton on which it had fed, spilled in heavy loops from a rent that would have admitted the *Weazel*, mast and all. A line of men was strung across its wide flat tail, like harvesters working across a field. They were using huge flensing knives to cut the hide away from the blubber beneath. Black smoke poured from the barge's rendering furnaces, sending up a stink of burning fat and hazing the last light of the sun. Flocks of birds dipped and rose like whirling snowstorms, fighting for titbits in the bloody waters.

As the *Weazel* glided through the lee of the barge, Yama watched the city of Gond slip past to starboard. Once it had risen out of the river; now it looked like the last tooth of an old man, perched on its roots above a labyrinth of mudflats. Gond, the porcelain city. A clutch of luminous white shells three leagues across, rising and falling in rounded contours like a range of ancient dunes, tinged with rose and silver and gold. Here and there were clusters of slim towers, their tops ringed round by tiers of balconies. Floating gardens hovered along the river margin, their parks and woods strung with thousands of lamps.

Eliphas climbed onto the forecastle deck. 'There are probably not more than a hundred living there now,' he said. 'Mostly, it is maintained by machines.'

'Yet they once ruled Ys,' Yama said.

He had once read a brief history of the porcelain city, and remembered that it had grown from a single seed planted in the sand of a beach at the first bend in the Great River. He wondered if that beach was still there, beneath the carapace of the city – the past preserved forever in the present. But no strangers were allowed to enter Gond. Its beauty was also its shield. Its people were great philosophers and teachers, but they did their work in colleges scattered amongst the orchards and fields and paddies that surrounded the city. From the first, the city had drawn a circle around itself.

'They ruled Ys a long time ago,' Eliphas said, 'in the grim days after the Hierarchs vanished, but before the civil service reached its present consensus. They are much diminished, yet are still exalted. If any who live in these days are close to the Preservers, then the people of Gond are the closest. They are so holy that they no longer have children. Their bloodline dwindles. The youngest is a century older than me, and I am counted as long-lived by my bloodline. Their holiness will be the death of them, soon enough. The face of the city is more beautiful than I remembered, but it is the beauty of a well-kept tomb.'

As the *Weazel* made her way towards the harbour under the power of her little reaction motor, her sail neatly reefed, a small boat curved out to meet her. A pilot came aboard and formally greeted Captain Lorquital, then asked to see the boy, Yama.

'We have two ships under the command of an official of the Department of Indigenous Affairs,' the pilot told Yama. 'Perhaps you know him.'

'His name is Corin. He is a prefect of the department.'

The pilot was a small man, smaller even than Pandaras, but he had the brisk, assured air of someone used to command. He wore loose linen trousers under a scarlet djellaba, and was smoking a black cigarillo. He blew a riffle of smoke with a flourish and looked at Yama squarely. 'Whatever business you have with him, it is nothing to do with the harbour. We have become a staging post for the war, but we are not subject to the authority of Indigenous Affairs.'

'I understand.'

'You will not take weapons if you go ashore. Neither will he, nor will his men. All go unarmed here.'

'You put it very plainly,' Yama said. 'I hope that I may speak plainly, too. This man wants to make me his prisoner. Because of that, Captain Lorquital fears for the safety of her ship.'

The pilot drew on his cigarillo. 'He tried to force the issue, and the Harbour Master had to point out that we do not take sides in any dispute. Nor will we be the arena for the settling of any quarrel. Frankly, if he had not tried to force us, we would have let him take you. But we cannot allow him to set a dangerous precedent.' He flicked the butt of his cigarillo over the side and turned on his heel. 'Captain Lorquital, the helm if you please. I will take you in.'

The pilot guided the *Weazel* to a berth at a long pontoon at the inner edge of the harbour, amongst mussel dredgers and two-masted ketches of the kind which carried small cargoes between cities everywhere along the river. The sultry air tasted of the acrid smoke of the fishing barge's rendering furnaces. The water around the pontoon was stained with sullen rainbows, and flocks of tiny machines skated the surface on long legs, absorbing spilled fuel oil through their foot-pads. Pelicans perched on mooring posts, drying their wings, like rows of arrowheads against the red light of the setting sun. A league away, across a maze of channels and pontoons and graving basins, coloured neon lights blazed and winked above clusters of clapboard buildings and plastic domes: a huge raft of chandlers, bars, brothels, gaudy houses, dance halls, shock joints, and gambling palaces anchored close to the docks. The pilot repeated his warning to Yama and Captain Lorquital, and took his leave.

'We can't go ashore unarmed,' Tamora said.

'You have your teeth and claws,' Pandaras said, 'I have my cunning, and our master has his power over machines. What more do we need?'

'I want to talk with him,' Yama said. 'I will go to his ship alone, and unarmed.'

Tamora said, 'It would be better if you waited for him to come here. There's nothing to say we can't be armed if we stay aboard our own ship.'

Even as the sailors began to make the *Weazel* fast in her berth, shills appeared on the pontoon, handing out little tiles that whispered seductive invitations to brothels and bars. One of the shills called Yama's name and threw a tile to the deck at his feet and quickly walked away, pushing through the others. When Yama picked up the tile the golden dragon printed on its surface flexed its wings and breathed a wisp of blue fire that formed two words. *Mother Spitfire's*. There was a brief message on the other side of the tile, written in a flowing cursive script: *Meet me here. Corin.*

Yama insisted on going alone, although Tamora and Eliphas argued against it. 'The Strip will be packed with the crews and conscripts from every ship in the harbour,' Tamora said. 'A gang of Prefect Corin's jacks could snatch you or slay you on the street, and no one would notice. It's always better to square up to your enemy in a place of your own choosing, not his.'

Eliphas said, 'I know Mother Spitfire. Her gambling house is famous for vicious and immoral entertainments found nowhere else.'

Yama said, 'You have been here before?'

'The Strip was anchored off Kalyb when I last visited it,' Eliphas said. 'I understand that it moved downriver after the fall in the level of the river stranded that city a dozen leagues from navigable water. It has grown somewhat since my last visit, too. The war brings it more customers, I suppose. Mother Spitfire is the last of her kind, older than anyone in Gond, but she is an immoral person. It would not be seemly or safe to go there. If you must meet Prefect Corin, I can suggest several alternatives. Quiet, proper establishments.'

'It would show bad faith to request a change of venue,' Yama said. 'Besides, Captain Lorquital told me that Mother Spitfire has long held a high reputation as a mediator in disputes.'

'I would not trust her, brother,' Eliphas said.

Tamora spat over the side of the ship. A tiny machine skated over oily water after her gob of spittle. 'For once I agree with Eliphas. This invitation is plainly a trick.'

'I want to hear what Prefect Corin has to say for himself,' Yama said.

'I don't know why. Anything he tells you won't even be an approximation of the truth. But if you like, I could find him and snatch him, take him somewhere quiet and force the truth out of him.'

'I am sure you could.'

'Or I could simply break his neck.'

'I want to talk with him, Tamora, not ambush him or challenge him,' Yama said. 'And I will go alone, or not at all.'

It took him several minutes to convince Tamora and Eliphas that he was serious. Pandaras surprised him by raising no objection. He said that he had a mission of his own.

'Captain Lorquital has given the freemen liberty until the midnight watch, and it seems that my friend Pantin has never been with a woman. It was part of the discipline of his former trade. I feel it's time he was taken in hand, as it were.'

Pantin was already on the pontoon, waiting with his hands jammed into the back pockets of the scuffed leather trousers he habitually wore.

'Are you sure you can keep him out of trouble?' Yama said, thinking of the young sailor's reputation as a pit fighter.

'Pantin has renounced the knife life,' Pandaras said, 'and I'll make sure he's too busy having fun to get into trouble.'

Pandaras walked a little way with Yama, then he and Pantin went off arm in arm, and Yama went in the other direction, towards the far end of the Strip, and *Mother Spitfire's*.

The main drag was laid out along a broadwalk half a league long. The gaudy fronts of chandlers, bars and brothels rose shoulder to shoulder on either side. Groups of intoxicated sailors and soldiers surged and staggered beneath flashing neon and flaring torches, carrying paper cups of beer or smoking pipes of crystal or weed as they moved from one attraction to the next. This was the last stop that their transports would make before the battlefields above the midpoint of the world, and Yama supposed that they sought oblivion in the few hours it took for their ships to renew their stores. Hawkers cried the merits of drinking or smoking dens, tattoo parlours, fast-food joints and dream parlours. Dancers of all sexes and a decad of different bloodlines (or perhaps they were all mirror people, Yama thought) bumped and ground in lighted windows above the awnings of bars and gaudy houses; musicians, magicians and gamblers made islands in the throng. Magistrates stood on floating discs above the packed heads of the crowds, and their tiny, glittering machines spun everywhere through the neon-lit air.

Mother Spitfire's was a sprawling gambling palace at the far end of the Strip. A dragon limned in golden neon tubing sprawled across its tall façade; pillars of fire roared within tall columns of glass on either side of the wide doors.

Tamora and Eliphas were waiting outside, and Yama's first pang of anger quickly gave way to relief. He laughed, and said, 'I suppose Pandaras and Pantin are skulking somewhere nearby, too.'

'I sent them off to a brothel, but the old man insists on staying here, even though he'll only be in the way,' Tamora said. She stood with her thumbs stuck in the belt of her leather skirt, scowling at every passer-by.

'It is not too late to choose another place to make your rendezvous, brother,' Eliphas said.

'Just keep out of the way if Prefect Corin starts something,' Tamora said.

Yama said, 'I do not want any trouble. We will talk, Prefect Corin and I, and try to settle our differences. I am tired of running.'

'I'll do more than talk if he so much as looks at me in a funny way,' Tamora said. 'Him or anyone else.'

Inside, men and women crowded at dice tables down a long room, under greenery that spilled from floating discs. Most of the gamblers were in uniform. The roar of their wagers and prayers mingled with the plaintive music of a shadow-puppet show that played on a screen raised above the midpoint of the room. Beyond, spectators were crowded around the walls of a fighting pit.

Mother Spitfire herself came up the central aisle to greet Yama. She was very tall and very slender, golden-skinned and clad in a sheath dress of red silk that flowed like water. Two burly men of Tamora's bloodline stood behind her, impassive in black robes. Tamora stared at them; they stared back.

'Welcome, Yamamanama,' Mother Spitfire said, bowing so sinuously that her small, sleek head was brought close to Yama's. Her breath smelled of honey and cinnamon. She pressed a stack of gambling markers into Yama's hand. 'May your luck increase this poor gift many times over.'

'Where is he?'

Mother Spitfire's green, slit-pupiled eyes were large and lidless; a nictitating membrane filmed them for a moment. 'You are as bold and direct as he said you would be. Is it bravery, I wonder, or innocence? He will be here soon. Meanwhile, enjoy yourselves. We have several pairs of well-matched contestants tonight, although if I were to place a wager on the next bout,' she said, lowering her voice confidingly, 'I would favour the smaller animal.'

'Thank you for your advice,' Yama said.

'There will be no fighting here,' Mother Spitfire said, looking at Tamora for a moment, 'except for that in the pit.'

'I trust that you were paid well for the risk,' Yama said.

'Not so much that I can afford to have my business closed. I have pledged that there will be no trouble from either side.'

Mother Spitfire swept away, followed by her bodyguards. Tamora stared after her and said, 'They could take us here and no one would notice.'

Yama pointed to one of the little machines that spun through the smoky air above the gaming tables. 'The magistrates keep watch, here as elsewhere. What happens in the pit?'

'They fight to the death,' Eliphas said. 'It is a terrible spectacle.'

Tamora led the way through the crowd that clustered around the oval fighting pit. It was filled with water and lit by powerful lamps. Men and women leaned at the rail, watching as two naked slaves trawled fragments from the water with long-handled rakes. A gong sounded softly and the slaves set down their rakes and cranked down springloaded arms with a net stretched between them, dividing the flooded pit in two. A little old man in a black robe, his beard so long that he wore its forked end over his shoulder, climbed into a basket seat and pulled vigorously on a system of ropes and pulleys to hoist himself above the water.

'They keep them in heat,' Eliphas said. 'They do it with injections, so that they're always ready to fight.'

The gong sounded again, battered brass soft as a dying man's last sigh. Water boiled at either end of the pit and two sleek shapes glided out into the light. There was a flurry of betting amongst the spectators.

Yama's breath caught in his throat. The creatures in the water were kelpies. Steel spurs were fastened to their flippers; spiked chains to their tails. One swam straight at the net and recoiled from a sputter of fat blue sparks, spouting a cloud of oily vapour. The other held still in the centre of its half of the pit, its tail moving up and down with slow deliberation.

The old man said something about *preparing the bout* and *last wagers please*. As his amplified voice echoed around the room, there was a renewed flurry of betting. Then the gong sounded a third time and the springloaded arms snapped back, raising the net out of the water. The two kelpies shot into the centre of the pit, lashing around each other, parting, and engaging again.

Water splashed over the sides, draining through slots in the floor. The spectators stepped back from the flood, then surged forward again, hooting and stamping and whistling. Both kelpies were bleeding from gashes in their pale bellies. Their blood looked black as it fluttered through the brilliantly lit water. For a moment, they hung head to head;

then they engaged again, and suddenly one was on top of the other. It beat at its opponent's flanks with its tail chains, and with its teeth ripped through blubber and flesh to expose the spine, which it broke with a quick snap of its head. It slid away, snorting vapour through the nasal slits at the top of its head and making a hoarse braying whistle, and the corpse rolled over and sank through a cloud of its own blood. The old man above the pit chanted a string of numbers and there was a flurry of activity amongst the spectators as betting markers were exchanged. Slaves used long electrified prods to drive the victorious kelpie away from the corpse and harry it into one of the tunnels.

Yama felt both sick and excited. The spectacle was horrible and degrading, yet even in their hormone-induced fury the animals were possessed of a fierce beauty.

Eliphas saw Yama's disgust. He said, 'There is worse to come, brother. We should wait for your enemy in a quieter spot.'

'Too late,' Tamora said. 'He is here.'

Three men were pushing through the press of spectators. As always, Prefect Corin wore a plain homespun tunic. His two companions wore breastplates of plastic armour and short kirtles of red cloth that left their legs bare.

Tamora insisted on patting the three men down. Prefect Corin submitted to her search with good humour, and favoured Yama with one of his rare smiles. 'You are well, boy,' he said. He looked sleek and self-satisfied and calm. 'I am glad. It was quite a chase you led me. The trick with the scouts was good. I should have guessed that you could fool them sooner than I did. You have learned a great deal since I last talked with you.'

'Many things have changed,' Yama said. He had expected to feel a hot rage when he confronted the man who had murdered his father, but instead he felt nothing at all, not even contempt. His hands were trembling, though, and he folded his arms and returned Prefect Corin's gaze as steadily as he could.

'They're clean,' Tamora told Yama, and glared at Prefect Corin and his men. 'But if they try anything funny I'll rip out their throats, starting with the Prefect.'

'The reputation of your companion is not of the highest, but I understand that she tries to make up with bravado what she lacks in skill,' Prefect Corin said, and glanced at Eliphas. 'This man had a reputation, too. Where is he leading you? What kind of trickery is he spinning?

You are out of your depth, Eliphas. You should have stuck to gouging would-be widows wanting recipes for undetectable poisons.'

Eliphas said with great dignity, 'I don't know you, dominie, but I see that my rivals have been whispering jealous lies in your ear.'

Yama told Prefect Corin, 'I am not sorry about your machines. I will destroy any you send against me. You must know that. And you must know that I will not serve.'

Prefect Corin said, 'And you must know that you cannot outrun me forever. I expect you told yourself that you came here to persuade me to allow you to go on your way unhindered, or to assess your chances of defeating me. Suppose I do let you go, or you defeat me. Suppose you travel on downriver, towards the war, where there are many more like me, and millions of machines under their command. Do you really think that no one there knows about you, and your foolish tantrum in the Palace of the Memory of the People? Do you really think that you could evade them, and override or fool all their machines? Of course not. The real reason you came here, even though you are not quite ready to admit it, is to discuss the terms of your surrender. And I came here to make you a generous offer. Even though you have caused us so much trouble, we do not want to lose you in some foolish skirmish. We want to help you realise your full potential.'

Yama met Prefect Corin's mild gaze with an effort of will. He said, 'How goes the war amongst the departments in the Palace of the Memory of the People?'

'A trifling disagreement that we will soon win.'

'Perhaps not, since you have not already won.'

'What will you do if you do not join us? Trust Eliphas and his wild tales? Preach to the underclasses as you did on the roof of the Palace? Take care with your answer. I would not like to indict you for heresy against the word of the Preservers.'

'I do not believe that you serve the Preservers. You do not even serve the department. You serve your own ends.'

'You were brought up in the traditions of the department, Yamamanama. You must know that we are here to serve the people, not our own selves. I was sorry to hear of your father's death, by the way. He was a good servant, although a weak man who clung to traditions long past their usefulness. He should not have become involved in this.'

Tamora said, 'Let me deal with him, Yama. Just give me the word.'

'I will hear what he has to offer,' Yama said. He felt perfectly calm, although there was a fine tremor in his hands. Spectators were crowding around the flooded fighting pit again. The body of the loser had been removed and the water had been purged of blood.

Prefect Corin shrugged. 'I wonder if there is any point. I wonder if you have already made up your mind to waste your life, out of pride.'

Yama smiled. 'But you cannot know for certain. That is why you came.'

'You dare to presume—' For the first time, Prefect Corin's reserve was breached. He turned away for a moment, turned back. 'I came here because I hoped that you are not a fool. I still hope that, despite your arrogance. So, these are my terms. We will not ask you to fight. We will ask only that we can study you to find out how you control machines, and to ascertain the extent of your powers. And when we have found out all we can, why, you will be elevated through the ranks to the first circle of committees, and you will be free to do as you will. You wish to find out why you are here and where you come from? All the resources of the department will be at your disposal. You wish to help the underclasses? You will be able to propose new initiatives. In short, you will be forgiven for your crimes, and richly rewarded for your cooperation.'

'I would have to return to the department. And I could never again leave it,' Yama said.

'As far as I am concerned, you have never left, Yamamanama. Despite the recent unpleasantness.'

'And you would raise me up to a level I do not deserve in exchange for giving the department power it does not deserve.'

'I think you judge both yourself and the department too harshly. Do not reject the offer out of hand. Think about it carefully. Take your time. There is no hurry. You may return to your ship if you wish, although I would advise you not to attempt to leave port. But first, we will watch the next bout before we take our leave of each other. I think that it will amuse you,' Prefect Corin said, and turned towards the pit.

The gong sounded again. Two men sat at either end of the pool, in the same kind of suspended basket chairs as the old man who had refereed the first bout. The men were masked and gloved. Thin cables trailed from the chairs into the water. The net was not lowered this time; suddenly, without fuss, two kelpies were hanging at either end of the flooded pit, shadows floating as quiet and still in the water as the two men seated in the air above them.

Yama asked Eliphas what kind of contest this would be, but the old man simply said that Yama would soon see. 'But it might be better if we left. It is a perversion of old knowledge. The worst of the wickedness of this place.'

'Knowledge is like power,' Prefect Corin said. 'It grows weak if it is not used. You will not use your power, Yamamanama. That is why we will triumph, and you will lose.'

The gong battered the air again. Above the pit, the men rolled and twisted in their basket chairs. The kelpies shot forward. They missed each other on the first pass. One smashed its blunt head against the side of the tank while the other somersaulted clumsily and bore in with a sudden rush. It ripped a gash in the belly of its opponent with a steel-tipped flipper, but failed to follow through.

Yama saw the thin cables that linked the kelpies to the chairs: they were living puppets, commanded by the masked and gloved men just as Nergal had commanded the spiders. He seized control with a spasm of anger and disgust, and the kelpies shot past each other and crashed into opposite ends of the tank. The impacts killed them instantly; their human operators were stricken by seizures that jerked them out of their suspended chairs. One hung by his harness; the other toppled over and smashed into the water. Yama collapsed against Tamora, momentarily blinded by feedback and red and black lightning.

Half the spectators surged forward to see what had happened; the others were trying to get away. Knots of fighting broke out. A grossly fat woman stood in the middle of the mêlée, screaming with operatic force.

Yama shrugged off Tamora's grip and started through the crowd. One of Prefect Corin's men tried to stop him, but Tamora kicked him in the back of his knee and he went down as Yama dodged past. He flung up the markers Mother Spitfire had given him and, as people scrambled after them, ran under the screen and dodged through the maze of gambling tables, overturning them as he went. He was fuelled by rage and fear. His sight pounded with red and black in solid flashes. The thing inside him had come back. He was a helpless passenger in his own skull.

The entire building seemed transparent, with all the places where machines worked brightly lit. Overhead, a hundred little spies exploded in sputters of white-hot sparks, crashing down amongst the gamblers and the tables, starting a hundred fires and doubling and redoubling panic. Yama was carried forward by a sudden press of people who shared the same thought: to get out before the fires took hold. His body knew what to do. It fought to keep its feet on the ground, for with one slip it would be trampled underfoot. One of Mother Spitfire's black-robed bodyguards pushed through the crowd and reached for him, and Yama saw the machines in the bodyguard's head and did something terrible.

When he came to himself, he had fetched up in the doorway of a dream parlour at the other end of the Strip. One hand clasped the wrist of the other, crushing the coypu hair fetish. Seed pearls pricked his fingertips. There was blood on his hands and flecks of blood and bloody matter spattered his tunic and face and hair. It was not his blood.

Inside the dream parlour, within a huge glass tank filled with boiling wreaths of thick green smoke, a naked woman pressed her face and breasts against the glass for a moment, her mouth opening and closing as if she was trying to tell him something.

Yama cried out.

'Angel!'

But the woman stepped backwards into the smoke and was gone.

Sailors and soldiers were rioting up and down the length of the Strip. Yama borrowed the eyes of a machine high above the crowd and saw that white smoke was pouring from the edges of the tiled roof of Mother Spitfire's gambling palace. The gold neon dragon spat a spray of sparks and one of its wings went out. Yama spun the machine and saw that the buildings around the gambling palace were on fire, too. Magistrates on floating discs were cutting a firebreak across the Strip with pistol shots. A painted façade plunged like a huge guillotine blade into a gap blown open in front of it. Strings of light bulbs and strips of jointed neon tubing fell too, smashing amongst the rioting crowd.

Yama released the machine and got up and started back towards the ship, but he had not gone very far when he was seized from behind, lifted, and flung against a wall. The two men who had caught him were burly and tall, as alike as brothers. They wore breechclouts and plastic breastplates, and their shaven heads were crowned with tight-fitting copper caps. One man pinned him while the other quickly and roughly frisked him.

'I have no money,' Yama said.

The man who held him laughed and said, 'He thinks we're robbing him, Diomedes!'

'We're badly misunderstood, Dercetas,' the other said, and told Yama, 'We're from an old friend, boy. He'll be overjoyed to see you again.'

Dercetas got Yama in an armlock and shoved him forward, down a service walkway that ran out above black water. Diomedes brandished a pistol; he twitched it towards a magistrate who swooped down from the darkness beyond the rail, and fired. The magistrate fell with his clothes on fire; his floating disc shot straight up in a clap of thunder.

Most of the magistrate's machines had been destroyed in the violet flare of the pistol blast. Yama threw the rest at Diomedes. The man was knocked backwards and spun around, held upright only by the machines which had embedded themselves in his flesh. One eye was a bloody hole, and blood filled the space beneath his transparent breastplate and ran down his bare legs.

'Let me go,' Yama shouted. 'Let me go and I will spare you!'

His head hurt very badly. He could barely see because great flags of red and black were crowding in. Diomedes's body twitched as the machines began to work their way out of his flesh.

Dercetas thrust Yama from him and stepped backwards, then turned and ran. Yama staggered after him and said, 'Wait. You fool. Wait for me.'

But the man had vanished into the crowd at the end of the walkway. Behind Yama, the dead man fell forward and the machines flew away into the night.

Much later, Pandaras and Pantin found Eliphas standing over Yama. There was a bloody corpse nearby, but Pandaras paid no attention to it. Many people had died in the riots and order was only now being restored. Magistrates were supervising teams of sailors and soldiers, putting out fires and clearing debris from the walkways. Bodies had been laid in neat rows in the big square at the centre of the Strip, awaiting shriving and identification.

Eliphas seemed to be praying over Yama. As Pandaras approached, the old man turned and said, 'He is sick, but I do not think that he is wounded.'

'Let me see,' Pandaras said. He pushed Eliphas aside and squatted beside Yama, who stared past him at an imaginary point somewhere beyond the world. Pandaras said, 'Master, do you know who I am? Do you know where you are?'

'I believe that he may have killed this man,' Eliphas said.

The dead man wore a plastic breastplate and a copper cap. The breastplate was riddled with bloody holes.

'I've seen others dressed like that,' Pandaras said. 'I expect they're

Prefect Corin's men. Help me, Eliphas. We must get him back to the ship.'

Two men wearing armour and copper caps had found Pandaras and Pantin in a brothel. Pantin had stabbed one in the eye with a table knife and had jumped on the back of the other and cut his throat, sawing with the blunt blade until the man's head had been nearly cut off. The boy was trembling but docile now, like a horse which has just run a race. Blood crusted his bare chest.

Together, Eliphas and Pandaras helped Yama stand.

'We must get out of this, master,' Pandaras said. 'Prefect Corin found you, didn't he? I shouldn't have listened to Tamora. I should have stayed. I'm sorry.'

'There is a monster,' Yama said dreamily. 'I am dangerous, Pandaras. Even to myself.'

'He's too hard on himself,' Pandaras told Eliphas. 'You don't go running to the magistrates to ask for justice when it's your own family, and you don't stint, either. If it was me, I would have burned the whole place down to make sure I killed that Prefect.'

25

THE ASCENSION OF ANGEL

'They're holding Prefect Corin and his ships,' Captain Lorquital said. 'The magistrates think that he brought weapons ashore, or allowed his men to. They'd also like to blame you, but they can't see how one young man could have caused so much destruction. Our passenger put in a word, too.'

'Prefect Corin will follow us,' Yama said. 'The magistrates may delay him, but they will not be able to stop him. After all, they have no real cause: he was not responsible for wrecking the gambling palace.'

They stood on the quarterdeck, watching the lights of the floating harbour diminish across a widening gap of black water as the *Weazel* manoeuvred through a channel marked by luminescent buoys. The fires had been put out and the crowds of sailors and soldiers had been dispersed to their ships. The damaged buildings on the Strip were floodlit, and the sounds of construction work could be heard. Beyond the floating harbour, the city of Gond shone against the night by its own inner light like a range of low hills covered in luminous snow.

'The less of that kind of talk, the better,' Ixchel Lorquital said. 'The magistrates have ears in the wind here.'

'Not any more,' Yama said, and shivered.

Pandaras had described in vivid detail how he and Pantin had found Yama by the dead man, with Eliphas praying over him. Yama had riddled a man with machines, but he did not remember it. He remembered nothing after his rage had taken him in the gambling palace. He had been floating above the Strip with burning buildings on either side, there had been a woman swimming in green vapour . . . He turned the fetish around and around on his wrist; it helped him remember who he was.

He had suffered only a few scrapes and bruises, and there was a bump in the hollow between the two big tendons at the back of his skull. Something hard-edged which he could move around under the skin. He should know what it was . . . But the memory slid away when he tried to articulate it.

'By tomorrow,' Captain Lorquital said, 'the place will be back to normal.'

'They will catch more of them,' Yama said. 'The river renews all, good and bad.'

He was thinking of the kelpies in Mother Spitfire's pit, but Ixchel Lorquital misunderstood.

'Every day more soldiers pass by on their way downriver to the war,' she said. 'The war has changed everything along the river. This place is the least of it.'

As the *Weazel* glided beyond the edge of the floating harbour and raised her sail to catch the offshore breeze, fireworks shot up from Gond, bursting in overlapping showers of gold and green and raining down towards their own reflections in the river's black water. The *Weazel*'s crew, up in the rigging, cheered each new explosion.

'For our passenger,' Ixchel Lorquital said. 'So few remain in the city that they mark the departure or return of every one of their bloodline.'

Yama had forgotten about the *Weazel*'s new passenger. He said, 'I suppose you and your daughter have lost your cabin to him. Is that where he is now? I would like to meet him, and thank him for his help.'

Captain Lorquital pointed at the mast with the stem of her wooden pipe. 'He has taken the crow's-nest. Climb up if you want to talk, but he'll be with us for at least five days.'

The passenger from Gond had arrived an hour before Pandaras and Pantin had brought Yama back to the ship. He was travelling to the cities of the Dry Plains, where there were disputes about the new land uncovered by the river's retreat. It was because of the war, Captain Lorquital said. Normally, such matters were decided at a festival of dance and song, but most of the able young men had gone to fight the heretics, and there were not enough contestants.

'He's a special envoy, tasked with making peace between the cities,' she said. 'The people of Gond are a holy people. Their decisions are not easily come by, and are highly respected.'

All this time, Tamora had been sitting in the pool of light cast by the big square lantern at the stern rail, sharpening her sword with a stone and a scrap of leather. When Yama left Captain Lorquital to her charts and went forward to the bow, Tamora followed him.

'I fucked up,' she said bluntly. 'Put me off at the next port and I'll find another job.'

'I remember that you saved my life,' Yama said. 'And that I then did something foolish. The fault is mine.'

'You don't need me when you can command any machine. Let me go.'

'I need your strength, Tamora. I need to know when to act and when to stay my hand.'

'That's easy,' she said. 'You strike only when you have to.'

'I need to be sure that when I act, I am acting for myself,' Yama said. 'I feel like a horse under a skilful rider. Most of the time I am allowed to pick my own way, but sometimes I am pulled up short, or made to gallop in a direction not of my own choosing. And I do not know then if I am on the side of good or evil.'

Tamora fixed him with her gold-green gaze. 'Before I was hurt in the war, they said I was crazy. No one would fight by my side because they said I took too many risks. You know what? I did it because I was scared. It's easier to charge the enemy under fire than stand and wait for the right moment. So that's what I did until I was wounded. Afterwards, while I was recovering, I had plenty of time to think about what I'd done, and I swore then that I would never again let fear control me. I thought that I had been true to that oath until this night.'

Yama remembered that Sergeant Rhodean had told him that the best generals judge the moment to attack, while the worst are driven by events willy-nilly, like a ship before a storm. Fear was natural, Sergeant Rhodean had said. We cannot suppress it, but we can learn to master it.

Yama thanked Tamora, and she said, 'For what? For being a damned fool? For letting you walk into that trap? For failing to help you when it went wrong?'

'For trusting me with your story.'

They watched the last of the fireworks burst far astern as the *Weazel* headed out into the deep water, and later fell asleep in each other's arms. As the sky lightened, Yama woke and disentangled himself from Tamora's embrace. Someone, probably Pandaras, had covered them with a blanket. Tamora sighed and yawned, showing her sharp white teeth and black tongue, and Yama told her to go back to sleep.

Everyone aboard the ship seemed to be asleep, apart from Yama and the old sailor, Phalerus, who had the helm. The *Weazel* was running ahead of a strong wind, her triangular mainsail filled, water creaming by her bow. The Great River stretched away on all sides; the Rim Mountains were no more than a long line floating low in the lightening sky. The water here was not the usual brown or umber but the same dark blue as the pre-dawn sky. It was more than a league deep in places; some of the abyssal trenches plunged into the keel of the world. Hard to believe that this could ever change, and yet year by year the cities of the shore were stranded further and further inland by the river's retreat. The Great River would at last run dry even here, leaving only a string of long, narrow lakes at the bottom of a deep valley.

Yama leaned at the starboard rail. Warm wind blew his unruly black hair back from his face. The bright lights of the huge fishing barges were scattered far and wide across the river. He wondered what monsters lay in the deeps under the *Weazel*'s keel, and for the first time in many days felt the tug of the feral machine which hung in its cold, solitary orbit a million leagues beyond the end of the world, attached to him by an impalpable thread, just as the kelpies had been attached to their operators by wires and cables. But who was the puppet, and who was the operator? And for what end? He remembered the conclusion of his father's complicated calculations about the river's shrinkage and shivered in the brightening sunlight.

After a while, he took out his copy of the Puranas. The bright crammed pictures stirred to life under his gaze, speaking directly to an unconsciously receptive part of his mind. He realised that there must be machines embedded in the pages. Was every book freighted with hidden meanings? As a child, had he dreamed so vividly of the past because books from the library of the peel-house had lain by his bed?

But then he was lost in the last of Angel's story, and idle speculation was driven away.

When Angel came back from the far side of the river, she talked with those of her followers who had waited at the docks for her, then went straightaway to Mr Naryan, the Archivist of Sensch, to tell him what she had found.

Mr Naryan was with a pupil, but the hapless lad was immediately dismissed when Angel appeared. Fortified by tea brought by the Archivist's wife, a quiet woman of Sensch's lizard race, Angel began to tell the tale of her adventure on the farside shore, and what she had found there.

She said, 'Do you know about libration?'

The Archivist shook his head.

Angel held out her hand, palm down, and tipped it back and forth. 'This is the world. Everything lives on the back of a long flat plate. The plate rocks on its long axis, so the sun rises above the edge and then reverses its course. I went to the edge of the world, where the river that runs down half its length falls into the void. I suppose it must be collected and redistributed, but it really does look like it falls away forever.'

'The river is eternally renewed,' the Archivist said. 'Ships used to arrive and depart at the falls at the end of the river, but this city has not been a port for many years.'

'Fortunately for me. Otherwise my companions would already be here. There's a narrow ribbon of land on the far side of the river. Nothing lives there, not even an insect. No earth, no stones. The air shakes with the sound of the river's fall, and swirling mist burns with raw sunlight. And there are shrines in the thunder and mist at the edge of the world.' Angel paused for effect, then said, 'One spoke to me.'

She could see that the Archivist was taken aback. He said nothing, staring past her in some private reverie. She smiled and said, 'It woke, and it spoke to me. Do you want to know what it said?'

'If you want to tell me, of course.'

Mr Naryan's look was one of helpless love. Angel knew then that like all the others he was hers to command. The thought disgusted her. She wanted him to be a friend, not a pet or a puppet. She passed her hand over the top of her head. She had had her hair cut close in the manner of microgravity construction workers, a style ten million years out of date. The bristly hair made a crisp sound under her palm. She said, 'No. No, I don't think I do. Not yet.'

Instead, she told him what the ship had showed her of the creation of the Eye of the Preservers. He seemed happier with this. It was something he understood. He said that it was just as it was written in the Puranas.

She said, 'And is it also written in your Puranas why Confluence was constructed around a halo star between the Home Galaxy and the Eye of the Preservers?'

'Of course. It is so we can all worship and glorify the Preservers. The Eye looks upon us all.'

It was a stock answer, taken from the commentary at the end of the last sura of the Puranas. He had nothing new to tell her. No one on this strange world had had a new idea since its creation, but she would change that. If she was going to rule here, she must first topple the old gods.

The news that Angel had woken one of the shrines on the farside shore spread through the city. The streets around her house became choked with curious citizens. She could no longer wander freely around the city, because huge crowds gathered everywhere she went. There was a story that she had been tempted with godhood, and that she had refused. It was not something she had told the citizens – they were changing her story to fit their needs. She tried to teach them that the universe of things was all there was, that there were no gods capable of intercession, that everyone was responsible for their own destiny. Seize the day, she told them, and they made the slogan into their battle-cry. Her followers daubed slogans everywhere, and now many of the slogans were of their own making.

Somehow, the citizens of Sensch came to believe that they could use the farside shrines just as she had, without the intervention of priest or hierodule, and that personal redemption was within their grasp. They set off in their thousands on pilgrimages across the river; so many that the city's markets closed because the merchants had moved to the docks to supply those making the journey across the river. Meanwhile, Angel became a prisoner in her house, surrounded by followers, her every move watched with reverence. She had to stand on the roof so that she could be seen and heard by all of them. She was trying to free them from their habits and their unthinking devotion to the Preservers, to shape them into an army that could be used against her ship when it finally came for her.

She built devices that she might need in the days to come. A crude muscle-amplification suit. A circuit-breaking device that would interfere with the broadcast power on which the myriads of tiny machines fed. She tinkered with the gravity units of cargo sleds, and painstakingly reprogrammed a few captured machines. But most of this activity was marking time. It was almost a relief when her ship finally arrived.

Angel went up to the roof of her house and watched as the ship drew near to the city's docks. It had reconfigured itself into a huge black wedge composed of stacked tiers of flat plates. Its pyramidal apex was taller than the tallest towers of the city. She knew that it would try to take her back, but believed that she might be able to escape if she could use its powers against itself.

She insisted on going to the docks. The young men who were her closest followers were very afraid, but they could not disobey her. She had two of them carry the circuit-breaker, and armed the rest with pistols.

The streets were almost empty. Thousands upon thousands of citizens had gathered at the docks to greet the ship, held back by a thin line of magistrates and their machines. The people were restless. They made a humming noise that rose and fell in pitch but never ended. Machines swept their packed heads with flares of light. There had already been trouble, for those near the front were wounded in some way, fallen to their knees and wailing and clutching at their faces. And when Dreen, the Commissioner of Sensch, rode a cargo sled to the top of the ship to greet the men and women of the crew, the crowd pressed forward eagerly, held back only by the quirts and machines of the magistrates.

Angel knew then that this was her only chance to take the ship from the crew. She fired up the circuit-breaker and every machine fell from the sky, burned out by the power surge. The magistrates were powerless to stop the crowd as it surged down the docks towards the ship. Angel saw Dreen's cargo sled fly away from the top of the ship – it drew power from the world's gravity fields – towards the floating gardens above the pink sandstone palace. The Archivist was coming towards her, struggling through the crowd. Angel ordered those around her to take him to the palace, and left to organise the siege.

Power was down all over the city. The population had lost all restraint, as if it was only the presence of the machines which had kept them in order. There was drunkenness and gambling and open fornication. Buildings were set on fire; markets were looted. But those citizens Angel encountered still obeyed her unquestioningly. They loaded up cargo sleds with batteries for a localised power system and marched on the palace and attacked the floating gardens, some using the modified sleds to smash away pieces of the gardens' superstructure, others starting to grow towers into the air using self-catalysing masonry.

Angel was sitting in the middle of her followers on the palace roof, with the machines she had reprogrammed spinning above her head, when Mr Naryan was brought before her. The Archivist was bruised and dishevelled, not badly hurt but clearly terrified. She beckoned him forward and he drew on his last reserves of dignity to confront her. She said, 'What should I do with your city, now that I've taken it from you?'

Mr Naryan said, 'You have not finished your story. I would like to hear it all.'

There was a hint of defiance in his voice; she liked him for that.

'My people can tell you. They are hiding with Dreen in that floating garden, but not for much longer.' Angel pointed to the men who were wrestling a sled into the crude launch cradle and explained how she had enhanced its anti-gravity properties. 'We'll chip away that floating fortress piece by piece if we have to, or we'll finish growing towers and storm its remains, but I expect surrender long before then.'

'Dreen is not the ruler of the city.'

'Not any more.'

Mr Naryan dared to step closer. He said, 'What did you find out there that made you so angry?'

Angel laughed. None of them understood. They were not human – how could they understand her, the last human in the universe? She said, 'I'll tell you about anger. It is what you have forgotten, or never learned. It is the motor of evolution, and evolution's end, too.'

She snatched a beaker of wine from one of her followers and drained it and tossed it aside. Its heat mixed smoothly with her angry contempt. She said, 'We travelled so long, not dead, not sleeping. We were no more than stored potentials triply engraved on gold film. Although the ship flew so fast that it bound time around itself, the journey still took thousands of years by the slow ship-board clocks. At the end of that long voyage we did not wake: we were born. Or rather, others like us were born, although I have their memories as if they are my own. The ship had been observing the galaxy as it approached it, and had sent clouds of tiny self-replicating machines ahead of it. The ship's observations and the machines, spreading in a slow wavefront, and our own observations and scouting missions all told us the same thing. The galaxy was ruined, and mostly devoid of any form of complex life.'

Angel took the Archivist's hands in hers and held them tightly as she told him of the ruin of the neighbouring galaxy, and of what it had taught her. She told him that the universe was not made for the convenience of humans, or any similar species. That life flourished rarely, and was soon extinguished. That human beings were a statistical freak. An outlier. That if other civilisations had arisen elsewhere in the unbounded universe, they were so distant that they could never be contacted.

'We are alone. We must make of ourselves what we can. We should not hide, as your Preservers chose to do. Instead, we should seize the day, and make the universe over with the technology that the Preservers used to make their hiding place.'

Mr Naryan said, 'You cannot become a Preserver. No one can, now. You should not lie to these innocent people.'

'I didn't need to lie. They took up my story and made it theirs. They see now what they can inherit – if they dare. This won't stop with one city. It will become a crusade!' She stared into the Archivist's black eyes and said softly, 'You'll remember it all, won't you?'

Mr Naryan said nothing, but she knew that he was hers, now and forever. It seemed to make him unbearably sad and it broke her heart, too, to have to use him so badly when she had wanted him to be her friend.

Around them, the crowd of her followers cheered. The sled rocketed up from its cradle and smashed into the underside of the hanging gardens. Another piece of the gardens' substructure was knocked loose. It spilled dirt and rocks amongst the spires of the palace roof as it twisted free and spun away into the night. The crowd cheered again, and Angel saw that figures had appeared at the wrecked edge of the habitat. One of the figures tossed something down, and a man brought it to Angel.

It was a message tube. She shook it open: Dreen's face glowed on the flexible membrane. His voice was squeezed small and metallic by the induced speaker. Angel listened to his entreaties and was filled with joy and hope.

'Yes,' she said, but so softly that perhaps only the Archivist heard her. She stood and raised her hands above her head, and when she had the attention of her followers she cried out, 'They wish to surrender! Let them come down!'

The cargo sled dropped. They were all there, the men and women who were closer to her than sisters and brothers, shining in their white clothes. Angel's followers jeered and threw rocks and burning brands and clods of earth, but her partials had modified the sled's field and everything was deflected away into the night. Angel smiled. She had anticipated that trick.

The partials called to her, pleading with her to return, to join them and search for their long-lost home. Dreen jumped from the sled and dodged through the crowd of Angel's followers. The little Commissioner caught the Archivist's hand and told him breathlessly, 'They are all one person, or variations on one person. The ship makes its crew by varying a template. Angel is an extreme. A mistake.'

Angel laughed. Dreen had been subverted by the partials. 'You funny, foolish little man,' she said. 'I'm the original. They are all copies.'

She turned to the partials, who were still calling out to her, pleading with her to come back, to join them in the search for their lost home. None had dared to follow Dreen. 'There's no home to find,' she told them. 'Oh, you fools! This is all there is. Give me back the ship!'

She knew they would never agree, but she wanted to give them the chance. It was only fair.

'It was never yours,' they chorused. 'Never yours to own, only yours to serve.'

Angel jumped onto her chair and signalled to the man she had entrusted with the field degausser. It shot hundreds of fine silvery threads at the sled. For a moment, she thought it might not work, for when the threads reached the edge of the field their ends flicked upward. But then the threads drained the field – there was a great smell of burning as the degausser's iron heat-sink glowed red-hot – and the threads fell in a tangle over the partials. They could not follow her now. She had the only working sleds. The ship was hers for the taking.

Angel's followers, seeing what had happened, began to pelt the crew with rubbish, but Angel ordered them to stop. She wanted to defeat the crew, not humiliate it. She turned to Mr Naryan and said, 'Come with me, and record the end of my story.'

That was when one of the partials walked away from the grounded sled, straight towards Angel. She confronted him. She told herself that there was nothing to fear. She had won. She said to him, 'I'm not afraid of you.'

'Of course not, sister,' the man said.

He reached out and grasped her wrists. And the world fell away.

The acceleration was so brutal that Angel almost passed out. A rush of air burned her clothes and scorched her skin . . . And then there was no more air. She was so high above the world that she could see across its width, high mountains on one side and a straight edge on the other, stretching ahead and behind to their vanishing points. The world was a dark line hung in an envelope of air. Angel saw the brilliant point of the sun come into view beneath it. Vacuum stung her eyes with ice-cold needles; air rushed from her nose and mouth; her entire skin ached.

The man embracing her pressed his lips against hers, kissing her with the last of his breath, tasting the last of hers.

There were only two pictures after that. Neither spoke to Yama. They were no more than pictures.

The first showed a vast room within the ship of the Ancients of Days. A window displayed the triple spiral of the Home Galaxy. Two men stood before it, one grossly corpulent, the other wide-hipped and long-armed, as small as a child. The Archivist of Sensch, Mr Naryan, and the Commissioner of Sensch, Dreen. Dreen was pointing at the glowing window. He was telling Mr Naryan something.

The second picture was from a point of view above Dreen, who stood at the edge of a huge opening in the ship, looking down at the river far below. A falling figure hung halfway between the hatch and the river. It was Mr Naryan.

So Angel had died – although if her ship wished, she could be born again – but her ideas lived on. They had escaped with Mr Naryan, and Yama knew that, with the help of the aspect that Angel had downloaded into the space inside the shrines, the old Archivist had spread Angel's story far and wide. The revolution in Sensch was only the beginning of the heresy which had set one half of Confluence against the other.

Shorewards, the sky grew brighter. The floating line of the Rim Mountains freed the platinum disc of the sun. A widening lane of sunlight glittered on the river, like a golden path leading to infinity. Yama watched the play of light on water and thought for a long time about the things that Angel's story had taught him.

26

THEIAS'S TREASURE

The envoy from Gond, Theias, did not come down from the crow's-nest that day. When Aguilar went aloft with his midday meal, Yama asked her to tell the envoy that he was eager to meet him. But after she descended – despite her bulk, she slid down a backstay with an acrobat's casual grace – she told Yama that the envoy sent his apologies.

'He says he has a lot to think about,' Aguilar said. 'He's a holy man, all right. He wanted only a little bread and salt to eat, and river water to drink.'

'He could stay up there for the whole voyage, brother,' Eliphas said. 'They are a proud and reclusive people, in Gond.'

Later, Yama sat alone at the bow and thought again about Angel's story. Her aspect had wanted him to understand it, but how could he trust what he had been told? Its central idea was a scream aimed straight at the most primitive part of the mind, where raw appetite dwelled like a toad at the bottom of a well. Seize the day! Forget duty, forget responsibility, forget devotion to the Preservers, forget everything but personal gain.

Even if the story about what she had discovered was true, it did not mean that people should fear the universe. Rather, Yama thought, they should celebrate its vast emptiness. By accepting the universe for all that it was, you became a true part of it and could never truly cease to exist until it also ceased to exist. It was not necessary to distinguish between being and non-being, between life and mere dead matter. It was all part of the same eternal braid. Only the Preservers had stepped outside of the universe – an act of transcendence impossible for those who were not gods.

Although Angel feared the ultimate darkness of non-being – that was why she had been so quick to despair – Yama knew that it was nothing to fear, for it was nothing at all. The Puranas taught that just as there was no time before the beginning of the universe, there was also no time after death, for in both cases there was no way to measure the passing of time. Death was a timeless interval before rebirth at the infinite moment at the end of all time.

Angel denied this. She did not trust what she could not understand. She had no trust or faith in anything but herself, so that a time when she was absent from the universe was, to her, utterly unthinkable. It was true that she had passed hundreds of years of ship-board time as a mere text, that she had died and risen again many times. But these brief interregna had been self-willed, and were nothing compared to the billions of years of non-being between now and the end of the universe, and the machineries which stored her self and gave her rebirth time and time again were real in a way that the Preservers were not. It did not need a leap of faith to believe in machines.

Yama thought about these things for a long time, while the *Weazel* stood before a fair wind and raced her own shadow across sunlit waters. The crew mended the staysails and tightened lanyards and stays through deadeyes; the joints of the deck were resealed with pitch and its planks were scrubbed until they shone as white as salt; a cradle was lowered over the side so that Phalerus could smooth and repaint places splintered and scraped by weather and passage through the floating forest. There had not been time to fully reprovision the ship, and the shoat, which had been pampered on scraps since the *Weazel* had left Ys, was led from its pen onto an oilcloth and soothed with song before the cook cut its throat. For a moment the shoat stood astonished as rich red blood pattered noisily into a blue plastic bucket held under its head; then it sighed and lay down and died.

Tamora helped with the butchery, and ate part of the shoat's liver raw. The joints, ribs, head, tongue and heart were sealed in barrels of brine, and the intestines were cleaned and steamed with the lungs. After sunset, everyone feasted on fried plantain leaves and fritters of banana and minced pork. All except the envoy, who still had not shown himself. Yama was beginning to believe that he did not exist.

That night, Yama slept alone on the triangular bit of decking over the forecastle. He woke at dawn to find someone hanging upside down from a forestay above his head. A small, slightly built man with a flat face the colour of old parchment, framed by a fringe of fine hair. Yama realised with a shock that the envoy from Gond was of the some bloodline as the long-lost Commissioner of Sensch, Dreen.

The envoy smiled and said in a high, lilting voice, 'You are not so much after all,' and swung the right way up.

'Wait,' Yama said, 'I would like to—'

'I expected someone taller, with thunder on his brow, or a wreath of laurels. Perhaps you are not him, after all.'

Before Yama could reply, the envoy turned and ran off along the forestay. He swarmed up the mast as nimbly as any sailor and disappeared into the crow's-nest.

Towards midmorning, Yama saw a machine spinning above the waves half a league to starboard, a little thing with a decad of mica vanes that flashed and winked in the sunlight, and a tapered body that was mostly a sensor cluster. He brought it closer, had it circle around and around the crow's-nest. It made a thin crackling sound like oil seething in a hot pan, and occasionally spat a fan of sparks that sputtered down the bellying slope of the sail's rust-red canvas. Captain Lorquital watched from her sling chair, but said nothing.

At last, the envoy swung out of the crow's nest and ran down the forestay, halting halfway and calling to Yama, 'Am I supposed to be impressed? You are very foolish!'

Yama let the machine go. It shot away to starboard in a long falling arc that almost touched the river's glassy swell before it abruptly changed direction in a twinkling of vanes, just like a dog shaking itself awake. In a moment, it was lost from sight.

The envoy descended to the end of the forestay. He wore a simple belted tunic that left his legs bare, and carried a leaf-shaped fan woven of raffia and painted with a stylised eye. His feet had long gripping toes. He thwacked Yama on top of the head with his fan, said, 'That is for your impertinence, young man,' and leapt lightly onto the deck.

The sailors who had been watching grinned at this display. Tamora shook her head and turned away; Pandaras, sitting bare-chested and cross-legged in the shade of the awning at the far end of the main deck, looked up from the embroidery work he was doing on the collar of his shirt. In her sling chair on the quarterdeck, Captain Lorquital puffed imperturbably on her pipe, now and then tamping down its coals with a broad thumb. Eliphas sat beside her, his wide-brimmed straw hat casting a slice of shadow over his face.

The envoy said to Yama, 'Here I am. What is your question?'

'I hoped we could talk, dominie.'

'But what will you talk about? Something important, I hope, unless you are even more foolish than you look.'

'Perhaps we should talk about my foolishness.'

'You assume that I am interested in it,' the envoy said. 'Do you know who I am?'

'Theias, the envoy from Gond to the warring cities of the Dry Plains.'

'And you, Child of the River, should know that I was contemplating my mission when you sent that poor imitation of a dragonfly buzzing around my eyrie. I like it up there. I can see all that is going on without having to be an active part of it. I can see so far that I can spy into the future – there is trouble in it for you, young man, but why I am telling you I do not know.'

Yama thought that for a holy man of great age, of one of the oldest bloodlines on Confluence and from the second-oldest city in the world, Theias had a remarkably short temper. But he bowed and said, 'I have been rude. I am sorry. I see you know my true name, so I must presume you have some interest in me.'

'Your reputation preceded you, and I must say it was larger and more colourful than the truth.'

'I suppose your people keep doves,' Yama said.

Theias looked at Yama sharply. 'Doves? There are all kinds of birds in Gond, but I do not pay much attention to them. No, I heard about you on the geophone and the heliograph, which I also used to talk with this cockleshell before I boarded her. I heard that overnight you changed a whole tribe of indigenous squatters on the roof of the Palace of the Memory of the People, and that you started a war between the departments. Some say you are the harbinger of the return of the Preservers; some say that you are a mage in league with the anti-theist heretics. I do not suppose you are either one. To look at you, I would say that you are a not particularly successful cateran off to try his luck in the wars.'

'I wish that I was. It may sound strange, but that was once my ambition. But I do not know what I am, except that I am not what people want me to be.'

'Is that so? Perhaps that is the root of your trouble. Does the stick know it is a hoe?'

'If it is used as a hoe, then I suppose it would.'

The envoy swatted Yama's shoulder with his fan. 'No no no. A stick does not have to ask itself stupid questions. It accepts its nature. If you tried to be more like a stick and less like a hero you would cause less trouble. What is that book you were reading? It looks a little like the Puranas, except no edition of the Puranas has pictures such as yours.'

'It is an old edition, with some recent additions. One of your people was a part of the story. A man named Dreen. He was the Commissioner of Sensch.'

'I already know something of Dreen's seduction,' Theias said. He scratched behind one of his large, translucent ears, then folded at the knees and sat down and patted the decking beside him. 'Here. Sit with me. Perhaps you will show me the rest of the tale.'

They sat together on the forecastle deck, under the shifting shade of the sail, for a long time. Theias fluttered his fan and cursed the heat, and asked many questions about the pictures. Yama answered as best he could, and discovered that he knew more than he had realised. Pandaras brought food – unleavened bread and plain water for Theias, and bread, chickpea paste, slices of melon, and a flask of sweet white wine for Yama – and stayed to listen, sitting quietly and working on the embroidery of his shirt collar.

At the end of the story, Theias said, 'Poor Dreen allowed himself to become what he was not. We still mourn him.'

'He is not dead, I think.'

Theias said sharply, 'Even if he stood here before me I would say that he was not alive.'

'Because the Ancients of Days made him into their servant?'

'No no no,' Theias said impatiently. 'You have much to learn.'

'I want to learn, dominie. I am seeking the truth about myself, and I am trying to understand how I can train my mind so that I might hope to find it.'

'Foolish boy. There is no mind, so you cannot train it. There is no truth, so you cannot hope to reach it.'

'Yet I have heard that the men of Gond are great teachers. What do they teach, if not the truth? What do they train, if not minds?'

'We do not teach, because we do not have tongues. How can we tell others what to do without tongues?'

Theias said this with all seriousness, but Yama laughed at the absurdity. 'Are you trying to teach me by playing with the truth?'

'How can I lie when I have no tongue? You have not been listening, young man. I waste my time with you. Farewell.'

Theias swung onto the forestay and scampered up to the crow's-nest.

Pandaras bit off the end of a thread and said, 'He's a puzzle, isn't he?'

'He is trying to make me think, but I am not sure what he wants me to think about.'

'I'm only your squire, master. I wouldn't know about these higher matters. My people, we've always let others worry about hard questions. We prefer stories and songs for the pleasure of telling them and singing them, and let others worry about what they mean. Was this Angel in the story the same woman that appeared in the shrines?'

'At first I thought that the woman in the shrine was an aspect, but I think now that she was more like a reflection. The perfect image of a person, but without volition. Like a picture, if a picture could move or speak. In any case, the Angel of the story in my book was not the same as the one who first set out on the long voyage. She was copied many times, and the copies varied from the original. Sometimes they varied so much that they went to war against each other.'

'I used to quarrel with my brothers and sisters,' Pandaras said. 'Sometimes, I swear, we all wanted to kill each other. It's always the way when someone is close to you. It's all love and hate, and nothing in between.'

Theias came down from the crow's-nest late in the afternoon. He sat in front of Yama and Pandaras and said at once, 'Why are you and Angel the same, and why are you different?'

Yama had been thinking about this, so the question did not surprise him. He said, 'We have both meddled in the destinies of other bloodlines. But Angel wanted to raise an army of followers, while I was asked by someone to whom I owed a debt.'

'Does that make you better than her, or worse?'

'Angel understood her nature but would not accept its limitations. I want to accept my limitations so that I can understand my nature. To put it plainly, Angel wanted to rule the world, and I do not.' Yama smiled. 'I am amazed that I am even speaking of such things. The world belongs to no one but the Preservers.'

'False humility is worse than pride,' Theias said. 'If you refuse to accept the burden of your destiny, then you are denying your nature.'

'I do not want to deny it: I want to understand and control it. I have been able to save myself from my enemies several times, but the consequences for myself and for others were often worse than the danger I faced.'

Theias shrugged. 'If it is in your nature to resist your enemies, then that is what you must do. None of us can be other than what we are, Child of the River.'

'Then I must accept my fate, even if I do not know what it is?'

'Acceptance can be the first step to enlightenment.'

'I was taught that knowledge can often help, too. Your bloodline is very old and distinguished, dominie. Does it remember mine?'

'I have heard that some claim that you are of the bloodline of the Builders. But they were gone long before the first of my bloodline, or any of the Shaped bloodlines, were brought to Confluence. Only their works are left behind, and certain stories in the Puranas. It is possible that they never really existed – have you thought of that? People reason that servants of the Preservers must have constructed the world, and so they invent a mythical bloodline and give them all the attributes they imagine world-builders must have possessed. But perhaps the world created itself, once the Preservers had willed it. Perhaps it had no need for Builders.'

Yama remembered that his friend Ananda had once said something similar. And he remembered the slate he had been shown in the City of the Dead, which had shown a man of his own bloodline with a starry sky behind him. But perhaps the slate had shown only a story. Perhaps everything was a story. He said, 'If the stories about the Builders in the Puranas are no more than stories, does that mean we have forgotten the true history of the world?'

Theias slapped Yama around the head with his fan. 'The stories in the Puranas are neither true nor false. They do not describe the nature or the history of the world, but reveal it by interaction with the receptive mind. One can only understand their importance through deep thought and contemplation of every possibility they contain. Otherwise they are only stories. Mere strings of words that cannot represent anything but themselves, just as things cannot be anything other than what they already are. And so words, on their own, can teach nothing.'

'But we use words to describe the world to each other, dominie. Are not some of those descriptions true, and useful?'

Once again Theias battered Yama around the head with his fan. Yama endured it. Pandaras looked to his sewing and tried to hide a smile.

'Foolish boy,' the envoy said, and held his fan a handspan in front of Yama's face. 'If you call this a fan, you ignore its reality. If you do not call it a fan, you ignore the fact of its existence. Now, how would you describe it?'

Yama thought for a moment, then took the fan from Theias's unresisting fingers, fanned himself, and handed it back.

'Perhaps there is some hope for you after all,' Theias said grudgingly.

Pandaras sang softly, as if to himself:

Holding out his leafy fan,
He gave the order to fuse life with death.
Positive and negative interwoven,
Even the Preservers cannot resist this attack.

Theias inclined his head. 'Your servant understands a little of the nature of the Puranas. Listen to him. You might learn something useful.'

'I have not read in them,' Pandaras said, 'but your riddle reminded me of a game my people play amongst themselves. The song is part of it.'

Theias plucked at the hairs that fringed his chin and said, 'Then your people are wiser than me, for they have made games of deep matters I must study long and hard if I am to understand them. But there is no more time to talk of these things. I have an appointment in the cities of the Dry Plains in a few hours.'

Yama said, 'It will take much longer than that to make landfall, I think.'

'Not at all. You see only what you want to see, and ignore the obvious. But at least you have made a beginning. Study the Puranas if you must, although you would do better to listen to your servant's jokes. Now, you may ask me one more question before I leave, and I will answer it as best I can.'

Yama thought hard. He had so many questions that he could not even begin to decide which was the most important, and many required specific answers which Theias, although he was very learned, might not know. At last, he said, 'I will ask you this, dominie. I am searching for others of my bloodline. I had thought that they were Builders, but now you tell me that Builders may be no more than a story. If you were me, how would you try to find out the truth?'

'Hmm. You are not as stupid as you appear, although you are not as clever as you think you are, either.'

'Can you answer my question?'

'Of course.'

Theias put his hands on top of his head. His fan hung down, covering his eyes.

Yama said, 'Is that how you search for truths? By not looking for them?'

'It is not mind, it is not the Preservers, it is not things.'

Theias said this very quickly and immediately swung onto the forestay and scampered away to the crow's-nest. There was a brief commotion up there, and then something fluttered over the rail. It hit the slope of the sail and slid down and dropped to the deck.

It was Theias's fan. Even as Pandaras ran to retrieve it, the envoy rose above the crow's-nest. He was standing on a floating disc that slid away from the ship at an increasing speed, racing towards the nearside shore, vanishing from sight in less than a minute.

Yama was astonished. He said, 'He did not need to travel on the ship at all. He boarded it only because he wanted to see me.'

Pandaras held up the fan and sang:

Theias was too kind and gave up his treasure.
Truly, words have no power.
Even though the Rim Mountains become the Great River,
Words cannot open another's mind.

27

THE DREDGERS

Less than an hour after Phalerus had climbed into the crow's-nest Theias had so hastily abandoned, the old sailor called in a high, hoarse voice, 'Sail! Ten leagues to the last quarter!'

'It is the picket boat,' Captain Lorquital told Yama, after looking upriver through her spectacles.

So Prefect Corin had escaped the authorities at the floating harbour. Yama had been expecting it, and felt a sense of relief rather than fear.

Captain Lorquital said, 'I suppose we should be grateful it isn't the warship, but she's rowing hard and has crowded every yard with sail. She won't be able to keep up that pace, but we're in the midway of the river and it will take us more than a day to run to shore and find a hiding place. I fear that she will catch us before then.'

There was little that could be done, for the *Weazel* was already running briskly before a good wind, dipping and rising through long waves that marched downriver. Captain Lorquital and Aguilar discussed putting out the staysails, but decided that this would drive the ship's bows down and make her more likely to plough.

'We should do it anyway,' Tamora grumbled to Yama.

'It would only delay the moment, and it would put the ship at risk,' Yama said.

They stood by the big square lantern at the stern rail.

By the naked eye, the picket boat was a black dot far off across the shimmering sunstruck plain of the river.

'It is Eliphas who leads them on to us,' Tamora said. 'I swear he made a bargain with Prefect Corin while we were prisoners.'

'Yet he urged me not to go into Mother Spitfire's gambling palace. I wish I had taken his advice.'

'Grah. It is likely that he wanted to lead you into an ambush somewhere else.'

Eliphas was talking with Ixchel Lorquital, hunched on the stool by her sling chair, his big hands moving eloquently.

Yama said, 'He is only an old man looking for one last adventure. Look at him – he talks too much to be a spy. Besides, I met him by accident.'

'Are you sure of that?'

'If he is a spy, then anyone could be an agent of Prefect Corin's, and how am I to live? And Eliphas has given me a destination, Tamora. A place where my people may still live.'

'I'll believe in this lost city when I see it, but let's say he didn't lie about it. Maybe he didn't start out to betray you, but I still think he struck a bargain with Prefect Corin. Maybe he didn't want to, maybe he was forced. Think carefully. You keep the spy machines away, but something has led Prefect Corin straight to us. In all the wide river, how would he find us so quickly unless he was led? It must be Eliphas. He'll have been given a device of some sort. Let me search his kit. Let me search him down to the bones.'

'I cannot know about every machine, Tamora. One could hang high above us, and I would not know. Besides, Prefect Corin knows that we are going downriver. The river is wide, but it is not infinite.'

Tamora stared hard at Yama. Sunlight dappled her skin, glittered in her green eyes. She said, 'I will lay down my life for you, willingly and gladly. But I would hope it will not be over some fool who thinks to line his pockets.'

The cook prepared a sumptuous meal after sunset, roasting a side of ribs from the slaughtered shoat and serving it with a sauce of apricots and plums, riverweed fried with ginger, and side dishes of candied sweet potatoes and cassava porridge flavoured with cumin. Most of the crew ate heartily, in a fine spirit of gallows humour, and all drank a ration from the cask of heart of wine Aguilar had broached.

'There'll be another ration at the beginning of the first morning watch,' Aguilar announced.

She did not need to say that soon after that the picket boat would be within cannon shot of the *Weazel*.

Before they bedded down for the night, Eliphas told Yama, 'Our captain hopes to hail another ship tomorrow. She steers towards the nearside shore for that reason. Not because she hopes to reach it before being overtaken, but because that is where the shipping lanes are. If you are right about Prefect Corin's motives, brother, if he has no official sanction but pursues you for his own ends, he will not attack us in plain sight of others.'

'I think that Captain Lorquital underestimates Prefect Corin.'

'He is only a man. He is neither omniscient nor invincible.'

Yama had surprised himself by eating his fill, and he found sleep surprisingly easy, too. Perhaps it was because he had come to a decision, a way of ending the uncertainty of the chase. It had crept into the base of his brain during the feast, as cruelly sharp as a knife. He would wake in a few hours, cut the dory free, and make off into the darkness. Once he was far enough from the ship, he would put out the dory's drag anchor and wait for the picket boat to bear down on him. Attracting attention would be easy enough – he had only to call on Prefect Corin's machines. He would allow himself to be captured, and at the first opportunity he would kill the Prefect. He would gather all the machines within the range of his powers and kill everyone on the picket boat, and then continue downriver alone.

He had become a soldier after all, he thought, and realised that the war reached far beyond the battlefields where armies clashed.

Yama slept, and his mind, freed by sleep, ranged far down into the lightless depths of the river, where segmented monsters humped blindly through abyssal ooze and the slow, cold currents at the bottom of the river, pushing sediment into the subduction channels which transported it to the Rim Mountains for redistribution by glacial melt. The world of these ancient machines was defined by the echoes of ultrasonic clicks and pulses, by touch and chemical cues. Neighbour constantly reassured neighbour with little bursts of data; they moved through a web of shared information that mapped the entire river bottom, its braided currents and thermal gradients, its deltas of mud and plains of chalky ooze. They were accompanied by sharers that fed on the shellfish and blind crabs exposed by their work, and in return scouted the layers of water above the trenches and channels of the river bottom, and cleaned away parasites which sought lodging on the overlapping plates of the machines' armoured hides.

We will help, the machines told Yama, although he had not asked them for help. He expected them to begin to rise towards the surface – any one of them could have sunk the picket boat by ramming it – but when he pictured this, the machines told him that they could never leave the river bottom. They would help in their own way.

A league beneath the *Weazel*'s keel, the machines abandoned their routines for the first time in thousands of years.

They altered their buoyancy, lifting from the long trenches they had made in the ooze and drifting on cold currents until they reached the maws of nearby subduction channels. As the machines began to block the channels, cold abyssal currents were deflected upward, spreading out beneath warmer layers, a huge unsteady lens of cold water thickening and growing sideways, pushing into the shallow waters over the coastal shelves . . .

He was woken by the boy, Pandaras. The dawnlight was dim, diffused. It was like waking inside a pearl. The main mast stabbed into streaming whiteness. Fog had settled damply over his blanket and drops of water hung everywhere from stays and ratlines.

'There's something wrong with the weather,' Pandaras said. He had wrapped a blanket around his narrow shoulders like a cloak, but was shivering all the same.

'Where are the crew?' He would kill them all, if he had to, beginning with this silly little boy. Kill everyone who stood in his way when he took the dory. Or kill everyone now, and let the picket boat overtake the *Weazel*.

'Master, are you all right?'

Yama found that he was awake, standing beside Pandaras in the middle of a fog so dense that he could not see the bow of the ship. Something had possessed him, horrible thoughts like ooze from the bottom of his brain. His power, he thought. It would survive any way it could, at any cost. He pressed the heels of his palms to his eyes. Red and black jags of light. A sharp pain pierced the tender meat of his brain. He said, 'I am going to take the dory. You and Tamora will help me.'

'Tamora is with Aguilar, master. They are laying out the weapons – as sorry a collection of antiques as I've ever seen. As for the dory, you'll have to explain your plan to the Captain. She came up on deck an hour ago, when the fog bank rolled across the river.'

'The machines of the river deeps,' Yama said, remembering the dream which had not been a dream after all. A small hope kindled in his breast.

'Machines, master? At the bottom of the river? What would machines be doing down there?'

'I found them and talked to them, and they said that they would help me.'

'They would be dredgers,' Eliphas said, looming out of the fog. Like Pandaras, he had wrapped a blanket around his shoulders. His eyes were dull pewter in the diffuse light. Droplets beaded his smooth black skin and clung to the stiff curls of his white hair. 'I once saw the carcass of one that had been washed ashore. They are divided into segments like worms, and each segment bears a pair of paddles or other appendages. They clear mud and detritus that collects in the deeps. Without them the river would soon silt up.'

Yama tried to think it through. His headache was like a spike driven through his forehead.

'They changed the currents at the bottom of the river. Cold water from the deeps is rising to the surface. The river grows colder, and fog forms as the warm air above it also cools and can no longer carry as much moisture.' He felt a sudden surge of hope. 'They are hiding us from Prefect Corin!'

Eliphas nodded, but Pandaras did not believe a word of it. He said scornfully, 'Nothing can change the course of the river.'

'Not its course,' Eliphas said, 'but its currents. The dredgers are very large. The one I saw was several hundred paces long, and each segment was as big as a house. Ah! There it is again.'

A flash of red light far beyond the *Weazel*'s stern, a dim flare that brightened and faded in the fog. Prefect Corin's picket boat was still pursuing them.

'She's trying the range,' Captain Lorquital told Yama, when he climbed up to the quarterdeck. 'She is still too far off, but I think that she will catch up with us soon. We had the advantage when the wind was at our back because we're the bigger ship, and can put on more sail. But the wind weakened when the fog rose, and now the picket boat can use her oars to catch us. There's one hope, but it is a small one. If the fog was coming from the farside shore I'd say we were heading into a storm, and a storm might save us if we were blown in one direction and the picket boat was blown in another. But this came up from the nearside, and I can't tell if it means a storm or not.'

The fog was dense but patchy. Towards the end of the morning watch the *Weazel* sailed out of a bank of white vapour into clear air. Everyone squinted in brilliant sunlight that burned off the rust-red sail and the white deck and laid a net of dazzling diamonds across blue water all around. To starboard, long banks of fog hung just above the river like ranges of low hills, their white peaks stirred and torn by the fresh cold wind. To port, the black anvils of thunderstorms towered along the margin of the nearside shore. Drifts of hail and rain swept across the sunlit water, falling from such a height that they seemed to come from cloudless sky. The *Weazel* passed through a brief hailstorm that had everyone running for cover. Small silvery fish fell amongst the hail, jinking frantically as they sought escape through the scuppers. The storm ended as suddenly as it had begun, leaving a scattering of dead fish and shallow drifts of hailstones which quickly melted, leaving blood-red stains from the dust at their cores on the white deck.

Soon afterwards, the picket boat breasted out of the fog bank behind the *Weazel*. Her light cannon flashed and flashed. Plumes of superheated steam boiled up and collapsed half a league sternwards.

'She'll get the range soon enough,' Captain Lorquital told Yama. She stood at the stern rail, immense and obdurate, her pipe jutting from a corner of her mouth. She had put on a jacket stiff with braid: to make a better target, she said. It had belonged to her dead husband, and its sleeves were pinned back from her wrists. 'I sent a heliograph signal, telling her to lay back and cease firing, but she's not responding. Of course, I suppose the cannon shots could be a kind of reply.'

'Let me speak plainly,' Yama said. The brief moment of hope had passed. He was convinced that the dredgers had failed him. That he had failed. 'They do not want your ship or your cargo. They want only me. Lend me your dory. I will put out in it and wait for the picket boat to overtake me.'

Ixchel Lorquital drew on her pipe and looked at him calmly.

'I will not let them take your ship,' Yama said.

'That's a generous thought, but you're only a passenger, and the ship is mine to dispose of as I will. My husband always told me that when passengers start giving advice, you should always agree, and then do nothing about it. But I'd rather not give you the false idea that you'll be able to make such a silly sacrifice, so I will say now that I will not allow it.'

Yama stood his ground. 'If you have any idea about what we should do, I would like to hear it. You have heard mine.'

Captain Lorquital turned her back on Yama and contemplated the picket boat. She said, 'Even if you give yourself up, they'll still sink us. They'll want to leave no witnesses.'

'Then put yourself and your crew in the dory. I will stand here in plain sight. They will not chase you if they have me.'

Captain Lorquital said stubbornly, 'I have sailed this ship for fifty years. I've been captain for ten. I won't abandon her for anyone. Even for you.'

Phalerus, who had the helm, said, 'She's right, dominie. If we get a bit of wind, we still might show those cullers a clean pair of heels.'

For the first time, Yama considered giving Captain Lorquital a direct order, but the thought that she might obey him with the same unquestioning alacrity as any machine was too horrible to contemplate. And if he tried to call upon machines to kill Prefect Corin he might be seized by his rage again, and kill everyone around him.

Tamora came up onto the quarterdeck. She had put on her corselet and slung a fusil over her shoulder. The bell of its muzzle flared above her shaven scalp. Captain Lorquital said mildly, 'I do not remember ordering the crew to take up arms.'

'We can show our teeth at least,' Tamora said. 'Why don't you put back into the fog?'

'They followed us through the night and the fog,' Captain Lorquital said. 'Why should day be different?'

At that moment, the man in the crow's-nest cried out. Patches of water around the *Weazel* began churn, as if vast pumps were labouring to produce submerged fountains. Glassy hummocks surged up, sputtering rafts of foam and slicks of fine silt. The crew crowded the rails, but Aguilar drove them back, shouting that they must see to the sail. Captain Lorquital told Phalerus to make hard to port. But even as the *Weazel* heeled about, more hummocks grew around her.

A shoal of fish fled past the ship, swimming so frantically that they flung themselves high into the air. Some landed on the deck. They were as long as a man's arm and their narrow heads and stiff dorsal fins were plated with dull red chitin, banging and clattering against the deck.

Caught between two rising currents, the *Weazel* began to turn in a slow circle. The sail flapped, filled, flapped. Aguilar ordered it reefed, but before the sailors could obey a stay gave with a snap like a rifle shot. The broken end of the rope whiplashed against the sail and ripped a long tear in the canvas; the block which had anchored it tumbled end over end through the air and smashed into the deck a handsbreadth from Tamora's feet.

The picket boat fired again. The cannon's hot light flashed water into steam to the port side of the *Weazel*. Water poured over the little ship's waist; spray wet the torn sail from top to bottom. At the same moment, Yama saw something like a bush or tree rise a little way out of the water off the stern. It was white and pulpy, like something dead that had been floating in the water for a long time.

Captain Lorquital ordered that the sail be struck at once, and turned to Tamora and told her to take off her sword and return the fusil to the armoury chest.

Yama laid a hand on Tamora's arm. 'They will take me in any case,' he said.

Tamora glowered. 'I'll throw away this blunderbuss, but I'll keep the sword. It's a poor thing, but it's mine, and you'll have to pry it from my cold dead hand.'

There was another flash of red light, but the picket boat was no longer aiming at the *Weazel*. Instead, she was firing into the water close by her hull, slowly obscuring herself in billowing clouds of steam. The sailors aloft in the yards cried out and started to swing down to the deck, and the *Weazel* shuddered as if she had struck some underwater snag. Yama was thrown against the head of the companionway, and clung there as the *Weazel* rolled to port and then righted herself violently. A forest of white branches was rising around the ship, as if the river was draining away from trees drowned an age past.

Tamora swore and unslung the fusil, but Yama, remembering his dream, told her to hold her fire.

All around the ship, creamy tentacles erupted from the water and rose into the air, questing this way and that. Some ended in leaf-shaped paddles; some bore ranks of suckers; some were tapered and frayed in a multitude of feathery feelers. Huge, sleek arrow shapes moved beneath the churning surface of the river. Many were as long as the *Weazel*; a few were even larger.

The sharers of the dredgers had come to the surface.

Captain Lorquital took Yama's advice and ordered the crew to stand back from the rails, and to put down the handspikes and halberds with which they had armed themselves. Most of the sailors promptly climbed back up into the rigging, dodging tentacles which rose towards the mast and plucked at ratlines and stays as if at a harp. Aguilar stood at the bow, her cutlass resting on her shoulder, looking right and left at the questing tentacles as if daring them to get close enough.

As Pandaras and Eliphas clambered up the ladder to the quarterdeck, the ship shuddered and a cluster of palps dropped onto the starboard rail. Their ends thrashed in every direction like a nest of blind white snakes, stretching thinner and thinner as they walked on their tips across the deck. The rail splintered under the mass of flesh.

One of the crew darted forward and with a cry stuck a knife in a rubbery coil. It was Pandaras's friend, Pantin. Tentacles wove around him. One plucked his knife from his grasp; two more shot forward and struck him, one around the neck, the other around his feet. Pantin barely had time to scream before he was lifted up. The tentacles pulled in different directions. A rich red spray spattered the white deck; still clutching the pieces of the boy's body, the tentacles fell backwards into the river.

More tentacles poured over the rail. The *Weazel* began to list to starboard. Up in the yards, the sailors scrambled for better foot- and handholds. Skinny Anchiale clung to the top of the mast with his long legs tucked into his chest while a tentacle explored the crow's-nest.

Yama remembered the polyps in the flooded chamber deep in the Palace of the Memory of the People. Those had long ago lost whatever powers of reasoning they had once possessed, or so Magon had said, and returned to their cisterns only through habit; yet they had helped Yama by breaking the bridge before the hell-hound could cross it. Yama suspected that these giants were different not only in size but in intelligence, too. They did not serve blindly. They were looking for something. Clinging to the rail, looking down into a roiling mass of tentacles directly below, he glimpsed an eye as big as his head. Its round pupil was rimmed with gold. It stared at him for a long moment, and then it sank beneath a rush of white water.

Yama knew then what the polyps were searching for. He vaulted to the main deck, landing on hands and knees amidst a writhing nest of white coils and cables. Someone shouted and he looked up and saw Tamora falling towards him, her sword held above her head. She landed on the balls of her feet, bounced up, caught Yama's shoulders and shouted into his face, 'I won't let them kill you!'

'They are looking for me! They cannot tell the ships apart so they are looking for me!'

Something coiled around Yama's thigh. A wet palp slapped his chest and a hundred fine threads crawled over his tunic. Tamora was caught around the waist by a tentacle as thick through as her arm; three more, stretched thin, whipped around and around her corselet. She held her arms high, the sword crooked above her head.

Yama was frightened that she would do something that would get them both killed. He reached for her hand, but tendrils as thin and as strong as metal wire coiled around his wrist and dragged it down. Something wet and rubbery slapped onto his face, covering his eyes and nostrils. It stank horribly of fish and rotten eggs. He could feel a hundred tiny suckers fasten and unfasten over his skin as the palp adjusted to the contours of his face. It flexed and spread so that it covered his mouth. Something pressed at his lips and he was frightened that he would be smothered. The pressure was insistent. Although Yama clamped the muscles of his jaws as hard as he could, something the size of his little finger slipped between his lips and probed at the crevices between his gums and teeth before withdrawing.

The palp dropped away from his face. The tentacle around his legs uncoiled and dragged away across the deck. All the tentacles were retreating, thickening and pouring backwards over the broken rail. The ship groaned as she righted. Tamora lowered her sword and rested its point against the deck, so that the sailors would not see how her arm trembled.

Yama ran to the broken rail, but already the sleek shapes were sinking away through choppy water stained with abyssal silt. High above, Anchiale regained the crow's-nest and cried out. Yama remembered to look for the picket boat.

But it was gone.

28
STORM DAMAGE

Captain Lorquital insisted on sailing in slow circles around the place where the picket boat had last been seen, but apart from a few splintered planks bobbing on the chop there was no trace of it. The wind was rising, driving fog banks towards the farside shore. Waves grew higher, breaking in white water at their crests, lifting and dropping the *Weazel* as they marched past in ceaseless succession. At last, as it was growing dark, fog engulfed the ship again.

Captain Lorquital turned the *Weazel* to head into the waves, but the waves grew higher still, breaking over the pitching bow and washing the main deck. Wind howled and plucked at the rigging. The crew, in yellow oilskins with lines clipped to their belts, worked aloft to storm-rig the sail while the *Weazel* now plunged bow first into the high waves, now was battered lengthways, heeling hard with spray dashing like shot across her. The awning and bedding on the main deck were washed away; so were the chickens and guineafowl in their bamboo cages.

The four passengers retreated to Captain Lorquital's cabin. Pandaras felt the pitching worst and was several times sick in a basin, groaning profuse apologies between spasms. Tamora sat cross-legged on the captain's bunk and glared at Eliphas, who was trying to interest Yama in his theories about the cause of the storm.

Yama scarcely heard the old man. He could still sense the minds of the gigantic dredging machines, far below. It was as if the little cabin – the pitching floor covered with felt rugs, the swinging lanterns which cast wild shadows across the tapestries on the lapped plank walls – was slowly turning into smoke, or was a picture projected onto smoke that was slowly dissolving to reveal the real world.

The dredgers had returned to their immemorial routines, singing each to each as, accompanied by flocks of sharers, they ploughed river-bottom silt in the cold black currents. Yama was snared by their communion. *Join us*, they urged. *Watch over us. Affirm us.* Their siren song wound seductive coils in his brain. They claimed to know all the wonders of the world, for everything came at last to the river. They claimed to remember his people. They would tell him all they knew, they said, if only he would join with them in the joy of forever renewing the world.

Someone shook Yama's shoulder and whispered in his ear. *Master. Master, are you asleep?* Another said, *He's not sleeping. Either he is in shock, or calling up the monsters of the deep has exhausted him.* And a third said sharply, *I have seen men like this after battle. If he is not wakened now he may never wake.* The first voice again: *His disc is filled with light. See? You see? Master, I am taking it away. I think that it is doing something bad to you.*

It was all very far away and insubstantial, like the harmless chittering of agitated ghosts. Yama was only dimly aware of someone slapping his face, of cold cloths laid on his forehead, of being walked around. The songs of the deeps were more immediate than the voices or the manipulation of his body; the channelled abyssal plain more vivid than the pitching cabin and its swinging lanterns.

One of the ghosts said, *It may kill him.*

Yama tried to tell them that was what he wanted, to escape his body and fall into the depths where the dredgers sang songs in which every word was true, charged with the wise love of the Preservers.

Something stung his neck. Suddenly his heart was racing and he was back in the cabin, lying in the bunk with Pandaras's sharp, narrow face bent over his. Wind screamed outside; there were a hundred tinkling movements in the cabin as things shifted to and fro. The lanterns swung a beat behind the pitching of the deck.

'He's awake,' Pandaras said to the people behind him.

Yama turned his head away, but he was quite alone. The deeps and the singers in the deeps were gone.

Strong hands turned his head. A woman wearing the fierce face of a tiger looked into his eyes. He said, 'I know who you are, Derev. It is time we took away our masks.' And then he wept, because he knew that Derev was dead or lost, and all his childhood was burned away.

*

In the end, they brought him back to himself with an injection of adrenalin.

'You were slipping away, master,' Pandaras said. 'Tamora said it was the only cure.'

'You were in shock,' Tamora said. 'I've seen it before, in all kinds of bloodline. The stuff works on most of them.'

Eliphas nodded. 'The Preservers made us all in their image.'

'They must have run short of time when crafting your kind,' Tamora said.

Yama was sitting on the edge of the bunk now, bracing himself as the ship plunged and rose and plunged again. He said, 'I called them, and then they called me. And they were stronger. Stronger and wiser. I should talk with them again, because they know so much…'

The cabin door banged open; air and spray roared around Captain Lorquital as she struggled to shut it behind her. She wore a yellow oilskin cape that shed a cascade of water around her flat bare feet. She looked at Yama and said, 'The adrenalin shot didn't kill you, then. Some bloodlines can't take it. Their hearts burst or their tongues swell up and strangle them. Eliphas says you called up the storm. Is that true?'

'The cold currents no longer rise,' Yama said. 'I think that it will pass soon. Will it sink the ship?'

'I'd rather not put her to the test.'

'There is nothing I can do,' Yama said. He saw that Captain Lorquital did not believe him, and saw too that this brave, capable woman feared him more than she feared the storm. She nodded curtly and turned away.

The storm blew all night and all the next day, and began to weaken only in the early hours of the morning of the third day. When Yama came up on deck soon after dawn, Phalerus, who had been fixing the broken rail, turned away and touched his throat in a warding gesture.

The storm had driven the *Weazel* before it. The farside shore was less than a league off the starboard side, a maze of channels snaking between mudbanks and dense stands of mangroves. The margin of the old shore was delineated by a low cliff exposed years ago by the falling level of the river, a long black line that shimmered in the heat haze beyond the mangrove swamps. Yama stared at it and wondered, not for the first time, if he was the destroyer of the world rather than its saviour.

The sun was hazed by high cloud, but the air was hot, and the white deck steamed. There was no sign of Captain Lorquital, but Yama found Aguilar helping Anchiale and the grizzled slave move foam-cased pieces of machinery in the hold. The cargo had shifted in the storm.

'My mother is asleep,' the sturdy young woman said. She gave Yama a hard, defiant look. 'She stayed on deck for most of the blow. She saved us all, I reckon.'

Yama said, 'Had I been able to stop the storm, I would have done so at once.'

'You have my mother under some spell,' Aguilar said, 'but not all of us are charmed.'

'I asked only for passage, and paid for it, too. What are you looking at?'

Aguilar had tied an electric lantern to a line, and now the two sailors began to lower it into the gap they had made between the tumbled foam eggs of the cargo. She said, 'The ship is wallowing. And that's why.'

Yama looked down. At the bottom of a wedge of darkness, the lantern swung above its reflection.

Captain Lorquital, rumpled from her early awakening, stood at the edge of the cargo well and argued with her daughter for a while. Aguilar maintained that the planking had sprung and the ship was taking on water because braces had been removed from the hull during her last refit; her mother said that the *Weazel* had ridden out the storm only because lack of braces had made her hull flexible.

'Water could have got in under the tarpaulin,' Captain Lorquital said. 'The decks were awash for the best part of three days. We were more in the river than on it.'

'The covers were reefed fast,' Aguilar said stubbornly. 'Besides, the water is getting deeper in there.'

The steel bands around the hatch had been sprung, and the tarpaulin covers rolled away. Anchiale and the slave were lifting out part of the cargo with a winch rigged from the mast; foam-covered ovals cluttered the main deck fore and aft of the hatch. Presently, both Captain Lorquital and her daughter climbed down into the hold. They were down there a long time. Captain Lorquital was grim-faced when they came back up.

'We'll have to put in for repairs,' she told Yama. 'I was right, though. The storm didn't spring the planks. It looks like something took a bite from them.'

A hand-pump worked by two of the sailors pulled water from the flooding hold and spat sparkling gushes into the river. A patch of canvas was lowered over the starboard side and hauled tight by a rope that went under the keel. There were bumps and groans from the hold; Aguilar went down and came back up, shaking her head. Part of the cargo was floating and shifting about, she said.

'If we're lucky, it won't capsize us or smash the hole wider, but the hole's already wide enough to sink us in a day or two.' She stared at Yama. 'There's a curse on this voyage, I reckon.'

29
THE BLACK TOWER

Captain Lorquital used the *Weazel's* little reaction motor to pick a way between banks of stinking mud and stands of pioneer mangroves, and to cross a plain of tall reeds cut by a hundred meandering channels. Phalerus was in the crow's-nest, scrying a path through the reed beds; the grizzled slave of Pandaras's bloodline stood at the bow, using a weighted line to sound the depth.

At last, Captain Lorquital ran her foundering ship aground by one of the islands at the far side of the reed beds. Ropes, pivoting on belts of leather greased with palm oil, were slung around several of the blue pine trees that had colonised the island, and crew and passengers laboured at the ship's windlass to haul her out of the shallows until the hole bitten through her hull was visible.

Because the ship was laid up at a steep angle, everyone camped on the island. The sailors lit smoky fires to keep off clouds of black flies and sweat bees. Yama sat a little way from the others, sifting through his father's papers by the light of an electric lamp, once again tracing and checking the threads of logic that bound the complicated computations.

The Aedile had been obsessed with measurements, ciphers and calculations. He had been convinced that there was a golden rule by which everything could be divided into everything else, leaving an irreducible kernel: the prime which harmonised the world, the secret signature of the Preservers. His research had never led to anything but a maze in which he had lost himself, but these calculations were different.

Every decad for almost fifteen years, the Aedile had taken measurements of the Great River's slow retreat from the old shoreline around Aeolis. From these, with elaborate allowances for seasonal variation and for the buffering effect of the ice fields of the Terminal Mountains, he had worked out when the river had begun to fail. The answer was not exact, and was hedged with cautious interpolations, but Yama believed that the conclusion was inescapable, and laden with appalling implications.

The Great River had begun its inexorable decline at about the time he had been found by the old Constable of Aeolis in a white boat, a baby lying on the breast of a dead woman.

Now he fumbled his way through the tables of measurements and staggered rows of calculations once again, checking and rechecking them, by turns frightened and full of wonder. Most people blamed the fall of the river on the heretics: was he then their creature? Or was the fall of the river in some way linked with his birth?

When at last he looked up from the papers, he discovered that someone – probably Pandaras – had settled a blanket around his shoulders. The fire had burnt down. Apart from the man on watch at the edge of the clearing, a black shadow against black water, marked only by the fitful red spark of a cigarette, everyone in the camp was sleeping. Yama switched off the little lantern. He lay down on the lumpy ground and rolled himself up in the blanket and fell asleep almost at once.

He was woken early the next morning by Tamora. Eliphas had disappeared, she said. No one had seen him go, not even the old slave who had taken the night watch.

'He has a great deal of curiosity,' Captain Lorquital said, 'and has most likely gone to explore.'

'He betrayed our position to Prefect Corin when we tried to make a run for it,' Tamora said. 'And now he's slipped away to betray us again.'

'Prefect Corin is dead,' Yama said. 'He drowned when the sharers pulled his ship apart.'

'Do you really think he was your only enemy?' Tamora said.

She wanted to track Eliphas down and put him to the question, but Yama persuaded her to be patient, and was relieved when Eliphas came back in the middle of the morning, walking into the camp as casually as a man walking into his own house.

He told Yama that he had been to the far end of the island. 'I know this part of the shore,' he said. 'We are very close to the edge of the world, brother, and a marvellous shrine that stands beyond it.'

Yama was sitting on the mossy bole of a fallen tree in a patch of sunlight. Pandaras was cutting his hair. Aguilar and Anchiale were trimming branches from the trunk of a felled pine; the steady sound of their axes rang across the clearing. There was a smell of fresh sawdust and pine resin. A cauldron of pitch fumed and bubbled above a fire in the centre of the cleared area. In the bright sunlight beyond the shade of the trees, the *Weazel* lay canted in shallow water. Watched by Captain Lorquital, Phalerus and the two slaves were working up to their waists in water, cutting away damaged planks.

'The shore must have changed very much,' Yama said to Eliphas. 'How can you be certain?'

'You will see, brother, if you come with me. The water is very shallow on the other side of the island. We can wade across to the old shoreline, reach the shrine beyond the edge of the world and return, all in a day.'

Pandaras combed cuttings from Yama's hair with his claws. After a moment, he said, 'You have hard places under your scalp, master. Here and here.'

They were smooth and flat, and had straight edges. One was twice the size of the other. They moved slightly beneath Yama's fingertips.

'I noticed one a few days ago,' he said. 'They do not hurt. It is nothing.'

'My master is ill,' Pandaras told Eliphas. 'He needs to rest.'

'I am quite well,' Yama said. 'Where is this place?'

'It is not much more than a stroll,' Eliphas said, 'even for an old man like me. It is a very unusual place, brother. I believe you will learn much from it.'

In the end, they made an expedition of it. Captain Lorquital sent along the cook to collect fresh roots and greens. Tamora insisted on coming; so did Pandaras, although he was still much weakened by his bout of river sickness.

Crossing the island was easy enough, for little flourished in the dense shade of the blue pines that grew along its central ridge. Eliphas led the others down a path he had cut through a belt of tamarisk and swamp grape, and then they were out in sunlight at the edge of a shallow creek that spread between the island and the low cliffs of the old shore.

The tower was black and slender, standing half a league off like a beckoning finger against the deep blue sky. Eliphas said that once upon a time it had been decorated with prayer flags and banners, and mankites had been flown from its crown to keep watch for floating islands.

'Soldier monks camped here every summer. The currents of the air are much like those of water, and this is a place where the islands sometimes gather in shoals and archipelagos that stretch far away into the sky.'

Floating islands!

As a boy, Yama had visited the farside shore every year, when the Amnan had crossed the river for the festival at the beginning of winter, but he had only ever seen one floating island at close quarters. Although a few could always be glimpsed beyond the edge of the world, scattered across the vast blue depths of the sky which wrapped around the world, they were usually distant green dots in which even the Aedile's spyglass could resolve no detail. It was said that rebel machines lived on them, and that tribes of heretics, cannibals and pirates travelled from island to island on the backs of eagles feathered in metal vanes, or on mankites or in baskets slung beneath balloons. Yama had sometimes dreamed that his people lived there too.

He had finally seen an island at close quarters two years ago. It had been the last festival that Telmon had attended; at the end of that winter he had set off downriver towards the war, and news of his death had reached the peel-house at midsummer, just after the turning of the year.

That day, Telmon and Yama had gone hunting for cassowaries, leaving the smoke and noise and mud of the festival encampment of the citizens of Aeolis far behind. Winter had come early. Telmon and Yama were mantled in woollen ponchos. Their ponies jetted plumes of steam with every breath. It was almost dark. They had found no cassowaries, but just as they were about to turn back they flushed out a basilisk.

The size of a small dog, the creature stood in front of the burrow it had scraped out beneath a briar patch. It raised its frilled mane, yawned to show the triple rows of teeth within its black mouth, and arched its segmented tail over its back. A single drop of venom hung from the hooked spine of its stinger.

Although Telmon and Yama kept a safe distance, Yama's pony stepped about so much that he had to dismount and hold the animal's head and breathe into its nostrils to calm it. He threw stones at the basilisk, but the creature snatched them out of the air and swallowed them, much to Telmon's amusement.

'He uses stones as birds do, to grind food in his crop. The Amnan say that one will sting itself to death rather than be captured. Unlike snakes, they are not immune to their own poison.'

'Dr Dismas says that the diluted poison can be used to stop the growth of cankers and fistulas. I expect he would pay well for this one. We could easily kill it, Tel. It cannot guard both flanks at once.'

'Dr Dismas is a fantasist,' Telmon said. 'He tells so many tales that he has long ago forgotten which are true and which are not. You should not talk to him, Yama. There is something odd about his interest in you.'

Telmon sat straight in his saddle and kept a careful watch on the basilisk, one gloved hand holding the reins, the other resting behind him, close to the socket in which his javelin was set. He had recently shaved his hair, leaving only a central topknot. It was the style fashionable amongst cavalry men; the topknot, shaped like a square loaf, formed a cushion between skull and helmet. His red poncho was neatly folded back to free his arms, showing the silvery padded jacket he wore beneath. His tight knee-length boots had been spit-shined so that they gleamed even in the twilight. He was all that Yama yearned to be: elegant, fastidious, kindly and knowledgeable.

Telmon said, 'We will leave this brave fellow to his home. There is still a little light, and we might still get lucky.'

As they rode on, Yama said, 'Dr Dismas says that he might be able to find out about my bloodline. That is why he wants to make a study of me.'

'Dr Dismas is easy with his promises, Yama. It is a cheap and quick way of winning people's gratitude, and I expect he will move on before he has to make good on any of them.'

'You will look for my people, Tel. That is, when you are not fighting heretics or charming women.'

'I will keep watch every step of the way, but I cannot promise anything. You know that father has made many enquiries, but never with any success. It is not likely that I shall come across anyone of your bloodline by chance.'

They rode up the shallow slope to the top of the rise. Telmon discovered a narrow track worn through the tall grasses and said that it had been made by cassowaries, but all they found were two peahens, which whirred up under their ponies' hooves and flew off into the dusk. Yama was still calming his pony when Telmon spied the floating island.

It was like a small round barrow or cairn, but stood where no barrow or cairn should be, atop the long flat horizon of the edge of the world. When Yama and Telmon rode closer, they saw that the island had grounded on an apron of bare keelrock. It was a dense tangle of violet and red vines and tubes and bladders, as wide as a paeonin field and twice as tall as a house. It was full of noises, stealthy rustles and squeaks and crepitations, as if its vines and bladders were continually jostling and creeping over one another, and little blue lights came and went in its tangled thickets. Yama feared that these might be the lanterns of pirates or heretics, but Telmon laughed and said that they were only burning hydrogen vented from collapsed pods.

'Heretics are men like you and me. They have no use for floating islands, either in the air or on the river. Birds roost in them, though, and they are inhabited by crabs of a species found nowhere else, which feed on dead vegetation and fiercely protect their home, and barnacles which sieve the air for floating spores. The islands themselves are a single organism woven from many different species that have lost their ability to live separately, so that they might function better within the whole. Each is a servant with a different task, and have become so specialised that they have lost their autonomy. Rather like the servants in the peel-house, eh? This one must be diseased. Usually, they don't come so close to the world. Out in the air, Yama, is another nature entirely different from the one we inhabit. You should ask Derev about it. It is said that her people once flew there, but gave that up to live here with us.'

Yama, stung by the last remark, said, 'That is just a story the Mud People put about. Derev would have told me if it was true.'

Telmon smiled. 'You are in love with her. O, do not deny it! I am your brother, Yama, as truly a brother as if you were of my own blood. I have watched you grow up, and it seems to me that you mature quickly. You must give some thought to the shape of your life, for it might not be as long as you wish.'

'It might be longer,' Yama said.

'It might at that. We do not know, do we? It is a terrible thing, not to know who you really are or why you are here, but you cannot fill your life with dreams. I would like to see you give up your wild ideas, and perhaps Derev can help you. There is nothing wrong with metic marriages, and it would certainly make her father pleased.'

Yama said stoutly, 'I am going to war, Tel. Like you, I want to fight the heretics and help redeem the world. Besides, I might find my bloodline on my way to the midpoint of the world.'

'Perhaps.' Telmon looked around. 'It grows dark, and the ponies are tired. We can come back and look at this in daylight.'

But when they returned the next morning, the island had departed, leaving only a fret of shallow channels eaten into the sloping apron of keelrock on which it had rested. Perhaps the island had not been diseased after all, Telmon said, but had grounded itself so that it could leach essential minerals from the keelrock. He was intensely interested in how the world and its creatures worked. Although Yama spent more time in the library than his brother, it was mostly to dream amongst the books and maps of finding his bloodline and his true parents. Telmon ransacked it in sporadic bursts to learn about what he had observed, and would as soon dissect the animals and birds he brought back from hunting expeditions as eat them. Like his father, he was interested in things for their intrinsic worth; if he had ever become Aedile, he would have filled the peel-house with a menagerie, and its gardens with exotic plants from the length of the world.

But the war had taken him away, that winter, and then he was dead.

Yama did not know if he remembered the floating island because of the basilisk, or the basilisk because of the floating island, but he had never forgotten either. Sometimes, he still dreamed that his people were living amongst the floating islands; once, while shut in the cell in the hive of the Department of Indigenous Affairs, he had dreamed that Derev had taken him to his people, carrying him in her arms while she rowed the air with strong white wings she had somehow grown.

And now he was eager to see for himself the archipelagos that Eliphas promised would be floating in the sky beyond the edge of the world. He led the way across the stream, wading through a strong current that swirled around his thighs, his waist, his chest, then throwing himself forward and swimming strongly towards the reed banks that stood along the far bank. He was filled with a sudden inexpressible joy, for it seemed that with Prefect Corin dead his life was his own, to do with it as he would in a world filled with wonders.

He hauled himself onto an unstable platform of reeds and rolled over onto his back and lay there in hot sunlight with water steaming from his wet clothes, watching as the others floundered through the stream towards him. Tamora held her sword above her head; Pandaras rode on the cook's broad shoulders; Eliphas half-walked, half-swam, his hands parting the water in front of his narrow chest with a curiously formal paddling motion, his straw hat perched squarely on top of his head.

Yama shook water from the slick pages of the Puranas, glancing at the picture of Angel's final, fatal ascension before putting the volume away. A dragonfly perched on a reed and with clawed forelegs preened veined wings as long as Yama's arms, watching him sidelong with prismatic eyes. It flew off with a crisp whir as the others climbed up beside him. He wanted to go on at once, but the cook said that first he must set traps for crayfish.

'The captain will bear down hard on me if I don't, master. She loves crayfish fried in a bit of salt butter, and it will ease her worry about the hurt done to the ship.'

The cook was a large, hairless man with pinkish-grey skin and a round, dolorous face. His name was Tibor. He wore only ragged trousers belted with a length of frayed rope, and chain-smoked cigarettes that he rolled from scraps of paper and strands of coarse black tobacco he kept in a plastic pouch. He absent-mindedly snapped at passing insects, and when he spoke he passed his long red tongue over his black lips at the end of every sentence, as if relishing the taste of his words.

Yama, who had learnt the trick as a child, helped Tibor weave crayfish traps from strips of reed. The traps were simple things, little baskets of close-woven reed stems with spines at the mouth pointing inwards; when the crayfish entered, they could not back through the spines to escape. Tibor's big hands, each with six long fingers set around a sensitive pad, worked quickly and deftly, making two traps for every one of Yama's. He baited the traps with scraps of smelly fat, and tied them at intervals along the margin of the stream.

They soon fell to talking. The cook was from a bloodline which had been enslaved for hundreds of generations: his distant ancestors had fought on the side of the fallen machines in the Age of Insurrection. Having sinned against the Preservers, they were now their slaves, and so the slaves of all free men on Confluence. Most were hierodules, but Tibor had been sold on the open market after the shrine of his temple had failed at the beginning of the war against the heretics.

Tibor was not bitter about his fate, even when he explained that the long vertical scars on his chest marked where his nipples had been seared away. 'It is so that I cannot feed children, which is what the men of my people do. Our owners do not like us to keep families; our babies are taken at birth and fed on an artificial milk. If they fed from me, they could feed only from me and no other, and I would have to feed them for three years. No owner would want that! You do not believe me, because in most peoples it is the women who care for babies, but it is true. So instead of my babies I feed all of you!'

Tibor laughed loudly at this joke. Despite his downturned mouth and downwardly slanting eyes, he was by nature a cheerful man. 'I am not smart,' he said, 'but that is good for me, because smart slaves are always unhappy.'

Yama thought of the librarian of the peel-house. Zakiel had been born a free man; unlike Tibor, he had known another life. And yet he was happy, for although he possessed nothing, not even his own life, he was immersed in work that he loved. Yama had not thought about this before, and asked the cook many questions. They talked together until Tibor said that they had enough traps to feed the whole ship for two days if only half caught something, adding that for a little while Yama had been the servant, and he the master.

'Some say that you are the slave of all of the peoples of Confluence,' Tibor said. Yama asked him to explain, but he only laughed and changed the subject. 'This is a bad land, the sailors say. That is why they do not stray far from the ship. They told me I was a fool to come with you, but they'll be glad of fresh food.'

Pandaras had fallen asleep in the sun, and woke to find that leeches were feeding on his ankles, which he had dangled in the stream to keep cool. Tibor burnt off the leeches with the glowing coal of a cigarette, and Pandaras fussed at the blood that streamed down his ankles from the little round punctures, and complained that he had ruined his second-best pair of trousers, and only shut up when Tamora pointed out that if he wanted to go back now he would have to go back alone.

It did not take long to walk to the base of the tower. The low cliffs were easy to climb, for their pebbly clay was deeply gullied by erosion. Beyond was a plain less than a league wide but seemingly of infinite length, thin red laterite and dry grasses punctuated by stands of saw-toothed yucca and palmetto, and sprawling clumps of gumbo-limbo. There were many outcrops of keelrock, smooth spurs or folded layers just as they had been cast a hundred thousand years before. Not even lichens had gained a hold on them, and all across the narrow plain a thousand facets shone and winked in the strong sunlight.

The tower seemed to be fused into the keelrock ridge at the edge of the world, or perhaps it had been grown from it by an art that had been lost after the Preservers had seeded Confluence with the ten thousand races of the Shaped. The tower was smooth and round, and several hundred chains high. Its black surface was slickly reflective, and like the keelrock was quite unscarred by time. Tumbled remains of wooden scaffolding and bent hoops that had once been the frames of tents were scattered around it. Ravens rose into the air as the party approached, calling loudly to each other in hoarse, indignant voices before circling away into the vast volumes of air.

Beyond the tower, the edge of the world dropped vertically into clouds that seemed to stretch away forever, as if the world swam not in the void but in a sea of absolute whiteness. Chains of islands floated above their own shadows, lying at different levels in the clear air above the clouds. Hundreds of islands, thousands. Yama marvelled at their number.

The shadow of the black tower lay on the white cloud deck like a road, and sunlight broke in splintered rainbows around its top. Beside it, the shadows of the five people were like giants aping their every movement, and around the head of each was a circular rainbow. Yama moved his arms and grinned when his shadow gestured back across leagues of cloud. Pandaras and the cook danced and capered there at the edge of the world. Even Tamora, who had been nervously alert ever since leaving the ship, smiled at the sight.

'It is a rare wonder,' Eliphas said proudly, as if he had led them here just to see this. 'A blessing of the Preservers.'

Tamora turned and squinted into the level sunlight at their backs. 'I'd say it is a matter of the angle of light.' She would not agree with Eliphas about anything, but added grudgingly, 'It is some kind of wonder, I suppose.'

'It is beautiful,' Pandaras said. 'It is a miracle of light and air and mist. I will make a song of it.'

'Out of my hearing, I hope,' Tamora said. 'Yama, as soon as we are rested, we should turn back.'

Eliphas said to Yama, 'The blessings of the Preservers will be upon you, doubled and redoubled, when you visit the shrine, brother. We will leave the others to rest here, and go together.'

Yama said, 'Where is the shrine?'

Eliphas smiled, and pointed straight down.

30

THE EDGE OF THE WORLD

A stair, entered by a narrow defile between two tall, roughly man-shaped outcrops that Eliphas called the Watchers of the Void, led down the vertical rock face at the edge of the world. It was broad enough to allow a decad of men to descend abreast, but its steps, carved from keelrock, were steep and narrow and slippery. Yama discovered that he was terrified of falling, imagining himself plummeting through the cloud deck and continuing to fall until at last passing beyond the envelope of the world's atmosphere and perishing, as Angel had perished in the embrace of a copy of her own self. Were their bodies still falling through the void beyond the world? He and Tamora clung to the carved face of the cliff as they followed Eliphas, finding comfort in the faces and bodies of the men and women and creatures that flowed under their fingertips.

The cook, Tibor, had stayed behind to dig for edible roots, and Pandaras had volunteered to help him. Yama had given the boy his book and disc, in case either drew the aspect of Angel to the shrine. Although the hell-hound had destroyed her, there might be other copies.

Tamora had insisted that it was her duty to watch over Yama. She thought that Eliphas was leading him into a trap. If she was right then neither her sword nor her bravery could save him, but Yama did not trouble to tell her that. There was a coldness growing in his heart. As he descended the stair it seemed to him that Tamora and Eliphas had become strangers, or worse, ghosts of strangers.

The world's edge was a black vertical cliff that rose straight up from the sea of cloud and stretched away for thousands of leagues on either side. It was dark and cold; the only light was that reflected from the clouds far below. Yama, Tamora and Eliphas were like emmets crawling down a wall.

There seemed to be no end to the stair. At intervals, they opened out onto wide platforms or ledges; they passed a stream that spurted from a cleft in the cliff, a muscular silvery braid shredded by wind as it fell towards the cloud deck. Wind whispered and whistled amongst the intricate carvings of the sheer cliff face. Eliphas's straw hat was blown from his head and dwindled away into the infinite ocean of air.

Presently, light puddled around Yama's feet. Tamora gasped and, five steps below, Eliphas turned and stared. Pinpricks of light reflected in his silver eyes. A handful of fireflies had found Yama and crowned him with their cold blue-white fire. Soon afterwards, the stair turned around a fold of rock. There was a wide ledge, and a tall, narrow arch cut into the adamantine keelrock of the cliff.

'The shrine!' Eliphas announced. 'Some say it is the oldest in the world. You will learn much here, brother.'

'At least as much as from any other hole in the ground,' Tamora said.

A fugitive light glimmered inside the arch, and it brightened as Eliphas led Yama and Tamora towards it. It did not come from any source, but seemed to stain the air as pigments stain the water in which a painter dips his brushes.

There was no black disc beyond the arch, no altar or sanctuary, nothing but featureless, slightly translucent walls that curved up and met high overhead. It was as if they had entered a gigantic blown egg filled with sourceless light. While Tamora prowled around the perimeter of this lambent space, Eliphas told Yama, 'When the shrine was in use, one of the priests would stand in the centre and become possessed by the avatar. That is why there is no screen.'

'Are you hoping that I can awaken the avatar?'

Yama was excited by the idea. He had come so far, from the silent shrines of Ys to this, a shrine older than any on the nearside shore. He had learned the extent of his powers, and where his people might still live. He had mastered the hell-hound and destroyed Angel's aspect. He suddenly felt that he had nothing to fear from anything in the world.

Eliphas's eyes blankly reflected the even light. 'The woman should wait outside. She might spoil the reading.'

'I stay with Yama,' Tamora said. Her voice echoed from several points in the vaulted space. 'If anything happens to him, old man, it will happen to you, too. I'll make sure of it.'

'You could watch from the entrance as easily as from in here,' Eliphas said. 'Your presence may disturb the operation if you remain here.'

Tamora crossed her arms. 'You give Yama false hope, making him believe that he can wake the dead. Those days are gone. We don't need avatars to tell us what to do any more.'

'He stands there crowned with fireflies. Is that not sign enough for you?' Eliphas turned to Yama and said, 'If the avatar came, brother, what would you ask it?'

Yama grinned, and strode to the middle of the room. Immediately, the light thickened around him. Tamora and Eliphas dwindled into the light, becoming shadows that frayed away and disappeared. Yama seemed to be standing inside a bank of glowing mist, and then the mist cleared and he saw a needle hung before the red swirl of the Eye of the Preservers.

It was the world. Not the representation which Angel's aspect had shown him in the Temple of the Black Well, but the world as it was at that very moment. Yama discovered that if he stared at one spot long enough he flew directly towards it. He saw the brawling streets of Ys and the blackened ruins of Aeolis; the gardens and tombs of the City of the Dead, and the garden-topped crag where Beatrice and Osric lived. He saw the white contours of the ceramic shell of the holy city of Gond, and followed the course of the Great River towards the midpoint of the world. His gaze passed over a dozen different cities: a city of glass domes like nests of soap bubbles; a city of white cubes stacked over each other; a city built amongst trees; a city of spires that rose from a lake; a city carved into red sandstone cliffs above a curve of the river; a city of gardens and houses raised high on stilts. He saw the great forests that stretched for a thousand leagues above the Marsh of the Lost Waters, and the ruined cities along the forest shore. Smoke hung in tattered banners where cannon of the army of the Department of Indigenous Affairs were bombarding a fortified ridge.

Yama would have looked more closely at the forces of the heretics then, but he felt that someone amongst them was looking for him, and he quickly turned away. The view unravelled to show the world entire again. He noticed a loose cloud of tiny lights that trailed behind it and at once the constant tug of the feral machine that he had called down at the merchant's house became more insistent. One of the lights grew until it eclipsed all the others, burning away the world and encasing him in its radiance.

If the machine spoke to Yama, he did not hear it. But across a great gulf he heard his own voice, apparently answering a series of questions.

Yes. Yes. I will. Yes.

He reeled backwards, overwhelmed by light, and fell, and for an instant thought that he fell through the void beyond the edge of the world. Fell with Angel. Fell in her arms.

Something struck the length of his body with the weight of the whole world. Blood filled his mouth where he had bitten his tongue and cheeks; red and black pain filled his head.

Tamora lifted Yama's head and cleared blood from his mouth with her fingers. She had a shallow cut on one arm. Her sword lay beside her on the softly glowing floor. It was bloody to the hilt.

Yama discovered that he had urinated in his trousers; they clung unpleasantly to his thighs. Dried blood crusted his nostrils and his upper lip, and his head felt as if someone had tried to split it with a wedge. Little bits of fused metal and flaked carbon char were scattered in a circle around him – the remains of the fireflies which earlier had crowned him, now burnt out and quite dead.

Eliphas was gone, but there were still three people in the shrine. Something was inside Yama, looking through his eyes. Sharing his thoughts. He knew now why he had eaten mud rotten with termites. For the metal in the bodies of the insects. For the metal needed to grow the machine under his skin.

Tamora got Yama to his feet and helped him walk around until he had recovered his sense of who and where he was. She told him that he had stood raptly in the centre of the shrine for hours, his face turned up, his eyes rolled back so that only the whites showed. He tried to tell her what he had seen. The whole world, immense and particular, as the Preservers might see it.

'It is so strange,' he said. 'So huge and yet so fragile.'

Then he laughed, and felt more laughter rising within him, wild and strong. He rose on it as if on great wings. It might have possessed him entirely, but Tamora slapped his face and the sting of the slap sobered him.

He said, 'The feral machine found me, as I once found it. Or perhaps it found me long ago, and has been bending my will towards it ever since. They are still there, Tamora, the rebel machines and avatars. They were banished from the world at the end of the Age of Insurrection, but they have not abandoned it. They spoke to me or to a part of me, but I cannot remember what they said...'

A dreadful understanding washed over him, and he began to cry.

'I serve evil ends,' he said. 'I cannot be other than I am, and I have been made to serve evil ends. I am their creature.'

'Hush,' Tamora said helplessly. 'Hush.' She held Yama and rocked him.

After a little while he was able to ask about Eliphas; she told him that the old man had escaped. 'You were so long in your trance or your dream or whatever it was that after a while I sat down to rest. What happened then was my fault. I was watching you instead of watching Eliphas, and perhaps I slept for a moment. He came upon me suddenly and the silly fucker would have killed me if only he had kept silent. But he couldn't stop himself yelling when he struck, and I turned in time to receive his blade on my arm instead of my neck. I cut his thigh with a backswing, but he got away.

'I would have followed him, but I could not leave you. He has not come back. I hope he has fallen off the edge of the world or has bled to death. But I didn't feel my blade hit bone and I don't think I cut any major blood vessels because there's not enough blood on the floor. He's probably still alive. Tell me that you're all right and I'll go look for him, and kill him when I find him.'

'He wanted to use me,' Yama said. He felt an abrupt dizziness, and sat down. The pain in his head was expanding. Red and black rags of light seemed to flutter at the edge of his vision. He was diminishing, or the world was receding from him.

He said, 'I thought that he wanted to help me, but I have been a fool. He wanted to use me, like most people I have met. You were right all along, Tamora. I apologise.'

'I was wrong, too. I thought he was working for Prefect Corin, when all along he had his own plans. This was his chance to master you, but he failed. Everything will be all right now.'

Light flooded the chamber. They both looked up. It came from the entrance, a harsh blinding glare that shrivelled the soft radiance of the shrine. Tamora swept up her sword and ran straight through the arch, and Yama followed as quickly as he could.

Outside, the light was as bright as the sun. Every figure in the intricate friezes that covered the cliff wall stood beside its own shadow. The wide steep steps shone like ice. With one hand raised to shade his eyes, Yama saw that Tamora was standing at the foot of the stair, gazing up at the huge shadow that floated behind the flood of light.

It was as big as the *Weazel*, and shaped like a claw. It floated only a chain from the edge of the stair, a hundred or so steps above the entrance to the shrine. Figures moved on its upper surface, bleached shadows within the nimbus of brilliant light that shone from it.

It was a flyer, Yama realised, and he knew then why Eliphas had brought him to the edge of the world. He shouted a warning to Tamora, but she was already running up the stair, taking the steps two at a time. She was chasing after Eliphas, who had crept out of his hiding place between a pair of carved figures and had begun to climb towards the flier. The old man had ripped the sleeve from his shirt and tied it around his wounded leg, which dragged behind him as he climbed. He held a little black box to his mouth. He was shouting prayers into the box and when Tamora was almost upon him he turned and raised it as if in a warding gesture. Her sword went under his arm and he jerked and tried to hold on to the blade at the place where it pierced his body.

For a moment, they stood still, joined by the sword. Then there was a flash of fierce red light and a wave of nauseous heat.

'Yamamanama,' a voice said.

Yama was wedged against the feet of a carved man. He looked up, trying to blink blood from his eyes. When he tried to speak a bubble of blood swelled inside his mouth and broke over his teeth and his lips. All his muscles had turned to water.

The black, bent figure of Dr Dismas stood over him. The apothecary had a pistol in his left hand, its blunt muzzle laid along his thigh. In his right he held a little black box, the twin of the one Eliphas had carried. Behind him, the flier floated down and grounded against the ledge at the entrance to the shrine. Above it, the stair climbed the black cliff towards the sky, scorched clean by fire.

'It was ordained that we should meet again, dear boy,' Dr Dismas said. 'How pleased I am to see you.'

Yama spat a mouthful of blood. 'It was you,' he said. 'All the time it was you.'

The light around them was very bright. He could clearly see the edges of the plaques under the skin of Dr Dismas's hands. Similar sharp-edged shapes lay under his own scalp.

Yama said, 'How? How did you infect me?'

'At *The House of Ghost Lanterns*,' Dr Dismas said.

'In the beer. Or the food...'

'Good! Very good! Yes. Little builders. They have been working ever since. You are strong, Yamamanama. You resisted them for a very long time.'

Yama spat more blood. So much blood. First Lud, and then Lob and Unprac, the landlord of *The House of Ghost Lanterns*. The palmers and the bandits, the cateran who had tried to kill him, Iachimo and the rogue star-sailor and its creatures, Gorgo, the two pythonesses of the Department of Vaticination, the old guard Coronetes, and all the clerks and soldiers in the Department of Indigenous Affairs, the mage and the soldiers who had taken the peel-house, traitorous Torin, the Constable of Aeolis and his sons and the mob, Prefect Corin and the crew of the picket boat, and the boy, Pantin. And the Aedile, his heart broken, and now Tamora and Eliphas. All dead. All because of him.

Yama said, 'Tamora thought that Eliphas was in league with Prefect Corin. But all the time he was working for you.'

Dr Dismas waggled the little black box. 'He kept in touch using the twin of this, right until the end. A pity that he had to be killed. He was a useful servant. He was turned long ago, in one of the chambers beneath the surface of the world. He was looking for old texts to sell, but found something far more valuable. Or rather, it found him.'

'I thought that he was praying to that little box.'

Surreptitiously, Yama pulled the fetish from his wrist. When Pandaras came to look for him, he would find it, and know that his master was still alive.

'Long-wavelength light,' Dr Dismas said. 'Bounced off one of us a million leagues above the plane of the world. You will soon understand everything, Yamamanama.'

Yama felt very cold. He was badly hurt, and the thing in his head had turned his heart to ice. He said, 'My people. Eliphas found where...'

'The map and the scavenger's account? My dear Yamamanama, they were forgeries, and not even very good forgeries. But they did not have to be, because you wanted so very much to believe in them. No, your people died out long ago. All of them are dead except you, and even we do not know where you came from. Once I realised what you were, I went to Ys to search for your origin. Eliphas helped me then, but we found nothing and I came back empty-handed. It does not matter. All that matters is that you are here, and that you will join us. You are my creature, Yamamanama. We will do wonderful things together. To begin with, we will form an alliance with the heretics, and save the world.'

Men walked out of the light towards them. Yama was lifted up. Light swept over him, and then a warm darkness. Presently, the flier tilted away from the side of the cliff and rose above the edge of the world. There was a small business to attend to, a few witnesses to be removed. It did not take long, and when it was done the flier shot away downriver, towards the war.

SHRINE OF STARS

THE THIRD BOOK OF

CONFLUENCE

For my mother

Think on why you were created:
not to exist like animals indeed,
but to seek virtue and knowledge.
Dante Alighieri, The Divine Comedy

1
THE RAFT

The two ill-matched men were working in a small clearing in the trees that grew along the edge of the shallow reach of water. The larger of the two was chopping steadily at the base of a young sweetgum tree. He wore only ragged trousers belted with a length of frayed rope and was quite hairless, with flabby, pinkish-grey skin and an ugly, vacant face as round as a cheese. The head of his axe had been blackened by fire; its handle was a length of stout pine branch shucked of its bark and held in the socket of the axe head by a ring of whittled wedges. His companion was unhandily trimming branches from a pine bole, using an ivory-handled poniard. He was slender and sleek-headed, a shipwrecked dandy in scuffed and muddy boots, black trousers and a ragged white shirt with an embroidered collar. A ceramic disc hung from his long supple neck by a doubled leather thong, and a circlet woven from coypu hair and studded with tiny black seed pearls was loose on his upper arm. Now and again he would stop his work and stare anxiously at the blue sky beyond the tree-clad shore.

They had already built a raft, which lay near the edge of the water. It was no more than a pentad of blue pine logs lashed together by a few pegged cross-pieces and strips of marsh-antelope hide, and topped by bundles of reeds. Now they were constructing a pyre, which stood half-completed in the centre of the clearing. Each layer of trimmed sweetgum and pine logs was set crosswise to the layer below, and dry reeds and caches of resinous pine cones were stuffed in every chink. The body of a third man lay nearby. It was covered with fresh pine boughs, and had attracted the attention of a great number of black and bronze flies. A fire of small branches and wood chips burned beyond, sending up white, aromatic smoke; strings of meat cut in long strips dangled in the smoke, curling as they dried.

Some way beyond the clearing where the two men worked was a wide, shallow basin of vitrified mud flooded with ash-covered water. All around, swamp cedars, sweetgum trees and blue pines leaned in the same direction, most of them shrivelled and scorched. A few of the biggest trees had fallen and their upturned roots had pulled up wedges of clayey soil. Nothing remained of the blue pines which had cloaked the ridge above but ash and smouldering stumps.

Except for the ringing of the axe, the land was silent, as if still shocked by the violence recently done there. On one side, beyond the island's central ridge and a marshy creek, were the low black cliffs of the old river shore and a narrow plain of dry scrub that ran along the edge of the world; in the other, beyond the reach of shallow water, a marsh of reeds stretched towards the edge of Great River. It was noon, and very hot.

The slender man cut the last branch from the pine bole and straightened and looked up at the sky again. 'I don't see the need to trim logs which are only for burning,' he said. 'Do you love work so much, Tibor, that you must always make more?'

'The pyre must go together neatly, little master,' Tibor said, fitting his words to the rhythmic blows of his axe. 'It must not fall apart when it burns, and so the logs must be trimmed.'

'We should leave it and go,' the slender man said. 'The flier might return at any moment. And call me Pandaras. I'm not anyone's master.'

'Phalerus deserves a proper funeral. He was a good man. He always bought me cigarette makings whenever the *Weazel* put into port.'

'Tamora was a good friend,' Pandaras said sharply, 'and I buried her burnt bones and the hilt of her sword under a scrabble of stones. There's no time for niceties. The flier might come back, and the sooner we start to search for my master the better.'

'He may be dead too,' Tibor said, and stood back and gave the pine a hard kick above the deep gash he had cut around its trunk. The last measure of wood in the cut cracked apart and the little tree fell with a threshing of its boughs.

'He's alive,' Pandaras said, and touched the circlet on his arm. 'He left the fetish behind so that I would know. He was led into an ambush by Eliphas, but he is alive. I think he entrusted me with his disc and his copy of the Puranas because he suspected that Eliphas might betray him, as Tamora so often said that he would.'

Tibor took papers cut from corn husks, and a few strands of coarse tobacco from a plastic pouch tucked into the waist of his trousers, and began to roll a cigarette. 'We should not have climbed down to the shrine, little master. I know about shrines, and that one had been warped to evil ends.'

'If we had not followed them, we would not have learnt what happened. Fortunately, I was able to read the clues as any other man might read a story in a book. There was a fight in the shrine, and someone was hurt and ran away. Perhaps Eliphas tried to surprise Tamora from behind, and she managed to defend herself. She wounded him and chased him outside, and that was when she was killed, most likely by someone from the flier. Eliphas didn't have an energy pistol, or he would have used it much earlier – there would have been no need to lead my master away from the ship into an ambush. But it was an energy pistol that killed poor Tamora, and melted the keelrock of the stair, and no doubt the same energy pistol was used to subdue Yama. He was taken alive, Tibor. I swore when I found the fetish and I swear now that I will find him, even if I must follow him to the end of the river.'

Tibor crossed to the fire and lit his cigarette with the burning end of a branch. 'We will find the *Weazel*,' he said, 'and Captain Lorquital will help us find your master.'

'She is dead. They are all dead, Tibor. You have to understand that.'

'We found no bodies except poor Phalerus's,' Tibor said stubbornly. 'And nothing at all of the ship, except the axe head.'

'A fire fierce enough to transmute mud to something like glass would have vaporised the ship like a grain of rice in a furnace. Phalerus was hunting in the marsh near the island, and was caught in steam flash-heated by the blast of the flier's light cannon. The others died at once and their bodies were burned up with the ship.'

Pandaras and Tibor had found Phalerus's scalded body lying near an antelope that the old sailor had shot. It was clear that he had not died immediately: he had put the shaft of an arbalest bolt between his teeth and nearly bitten it through in his agony. Pandaras remembered a story that one of his uncles had told him about an accident in a foundry. A man had slipped and fallen waist-deep in a vat of molten iron. The man's workmates had been paralysed by his terrible screams, but his father had grabbed a long-handled ladle and had pushed his son's head beneath the glowing surface. Phalerus had died almost as badly, and he had died alone, with no one to ease his passing.

Tibor started to trim the larger branches from the pine he had felled. After a little while, he stopped and said, 'The captain is clever. She's escaped pirates before, and that's what happened here. The flier's light cannon missed the *Weazel*, and she made a run for it. Maybe Phalerus was left behind, but the rest will be with the ship. The captain won't know your master has been taken, and maybe she'll come back for him.' He ran a hand over the parallel scars that seamed his broad chest. 'I belong with the ship, little master.'

Pandaras swiped away the tiny black bees that had clustered at the corners of his eyes to drink his sweat. 'I'm not your master,' he said again. 'We will travel together as free men. Eliphas betrayed my master and murdered your shipmates, and I will kill him for that. He claimed to know of a city hidden in the Glass Desert where others of my master's bloodline lived, and so lured him all this way from Ys. Eliphas is a liar and a traitor, but all lies have some truth in them, and I think we'll find the place where he has taken my master if we continue downriver. You will help me, and then you can set out on your own road.'

Pandaras did not want the responsibility of looking after Tibor, but he needed him because the hierodule knew how to survive in the wilderness. Pandaras had lived all his short life in Ys. He knew the city's stone streets and its people; he knew words which if whispered in the right place could kill a man; he knew the rituals and meeting places of decads of cults, the monastery where anyone could beg waybread and beer at noon, the places where the magistrates and their machines never went, the places where they could always be found, the rhythms of the docks, the histories of a thousand temples, the secrets of a decad of trades. But the randomness of this wild shore confused and frightened him. It was tangled, impenetrable, alien to thought.

'I am a slave of all the world, little master.' Tibor drew on the stub of his cigarette, held his breath, exhaled a huge cloud of smoke. 'Nothing can change that. Ten thousand years ago my bloodline fought on the side of the feral machines, against the will of the Preservers. In the shame of our defeat we must serve the Preservers and their peoples for all our lives, and hope only that we will be redeemed at the end of time.'

'If you must be a servant, then serve my master,' Pandaras said. 'Yama is of the ancient race of the Builders, who made this world according to the will of the Preservers. In all the world, he is closer to them than any other man – the emissary from the holy city of Gond admitted as much. He is their avatar. I have seen him bend countless machines to his will. In Ys, on the roof of the Palace of the Memory of the People, he brought a baby of one of the mirror people to self-awareness. You yourself saw how he drew up monstrous polyps from the bottom of the Great River to save us from Prefect Corin. He is a wise and holy man. He alone can end the war begun by the heretics; he alone can return the world to the path which will lead to redemption of all its peoples. So by helping me find him, you will serve all the world.'

'We will search for your master, and for my ship,' Tibor said. He drew a last puff from the stub of his cigarette and pinched it out and swallowed it. His long red tongue passed over his black lips. 'But a ship is easier to find than a man. How shall we find him, in all the long world?'

Pandaras showed Tibor the ceramic disc that Yama had given him before following the traitor Eliphas into ambush. It held a faint spark in its centre. Pandaras hoped that it meant that Yama was still alive, but no matter which way he turned the disc, the spark did not grow brighter or dimmer.

Tibor nodded. 'I have heard of such things, young master, but never thought to see one.'

'It's real,' Pandaras said. 'Now work harder and talk less. I want to leave as soon as possible.'

At last the pyre was finished. Pandaras and Tibor laid Phalerus's body on top and covered it with a blanket of orange mallows and yellow irises. Tibor knew the funeral rituals by heart, and Pandaras followed his instructions, becoming for that short time the servant of a holy slave. Tibor said prayers in memory of the dead sailor before lighting the dry reeds he had woven through the lower layers of the pyre.

When it was burning well, with Phalerus's body a shadow in the centre of leaping yellow flames and a banner of white smoke bending towards the blackened ridge, Pandaras and Tibor clambered onto their raft and poled away from the devastated island. It took them the rest of the day to thread a way through the stands of tall reeds to the mudbanks and pioneer mangroves that lay beyond, along the margin of the shrinking river. When the water became too deep to use the pole, Tibor took up a leaf-shaped paddle he had carved from a scrap of wood.

Pandaras squatted at the raft's blunt prow, Phalerus's arbalest in his lap and his master's pack between his feet. He was more afraid than he could let the hierodule know. Tibor said that the raft was stronger than it looked, that the strips of hide would shrink in the water and bind the logs ever tighter, but Pandaras thought it a flimsy craft. The idea of travelling the length of the Great River on it, like an emmet clinging to a flake of bark, filled him with dread, but he was certain that Yama had been carried away on the flier, and he loved his master so fiercely that he would follow him beyond the edge of the world. He had smeared every bit of his exposed pelt with black mud to protect himself from the biting flies and midges which danced in dense clouds over stumps and breather roots. He was a savage in a savage land. He would go naked, cover his body with strange tattoos, drink blood from freshly killed animals until he was as strong as a storm, and then he would pull down the walls of the citadel where his master was held, rescue him, and kill the traitor who had taken him. His people would make songs about it until the end of time.

Such dreams sustained his small hope. Those, and the faint but unwavering spark trapped within the ceramic coin.

The raft rounded the point of a long arm of mangroves, and the wide river suddenly stretched before them, gleaming like a plain of gold in the light of the setting sun. Pandaras stood, suddenly filled with elation, and flung out an arm and pointed downriver, towards the war.

2

DR DISMAS'S DISEASE

Dr Dismas came into the big white room without ceremony, flinging open the double doors and striding towards Yama, scattering the machines which floated at various levels in the air. A decad of servants in a motley of brightly coloured liveries trailed behind him.

Yama had been performing stretching exercises that Sergeant Rhodean had taught him, and jumped up as Dr Dismas approached. Yama was bare-chested and barefoot, wearing only a pair of silk trews and a wide bandage wound twice around the burns on his chest. Ever since his capture, he had wanted nothing more than to be able to command just one machine and make it fling itself into Dr Dismas's eye and burn through his brain but, no matter how much he strained to contact the machines around him, he could not bend them to his will. The powers which he had painfully learned to master had been taken from him by the thing which had grown from seeds that Dr Dismas had planted in him at the beginning of his adventures. He was plagued by a fluttering of red and black at the edges of his vision, and was visited in his sleep by strange and terrible dreams which, although he utterly forgot them upon waking, left an indelible residue of terror and loathing.

Dr Dismas did not speak at once, but clapped his stiff hands together in an irregular rhythm and paced up and down while looking sidelong at Yama, as if trying to marshal his hectic thoughts. The servants stood in a row behind him. They were all indigens, and all were mutilated. Yama scarcely noticed them. He was watching the bent-backed, black-clad apothecary as a mouse might watch a snake.

'You are awake!' Dr Dismas said at last. 'Good, good. How are you, Yamamanama? Any headaches? Any coloured lights or spots floating in your vision? Your burns are healing nicely, I see. Ah, why do you look at me that way? I am your saviour!'

'You infected me with this disease, Doctor. Are you worried that it is not progressing as fast as you wish?'

'It is not a disease, Yamamanama. Do not think of it as a disease. And do not resist it. That will make things worse for you.'

'Where is this place, Doctor? Why have you brought me here? Where are the others?'

He had asked these questions many times before. Dr Dismas had not yet answered any of them. The apothecary smiled and said, 'Our allies gave it to me as a reward for services rendered. A part-payment, I should say, for I have only just begun. We, my dear Yamamanama, have only just begun. How much we still have to do!'

Dr Dismas marched across the room and stood for a moment at the great window, his hands twisted behind his back. But he could not stand still for long, and whirled around and smiled at Yama. He must have recently injected himself with a dose of his drug, for he was pumped full of an energy that he could not quite control, a small, sleek, agitated man in a claw-hammer frock coat that reached to his knees, the stiff planes of his brown face propped above the high collar of his white shirt. He was at once comic and malign.

Yama hated Dr Dismas, but knew that the apothecary had the answers to many of his questions. He said, 'I am your prisoner, Doctor. What do you want from me?'

'Prisoner? No, no, no. Oh, no, not a prisoner,' Dr Dismas said. 'We are at a delicate stage. You are as yet neither one thing nor another, Yamamanama. A chrysalis. A larva. You think yourself a power in the world, but you are as nothing compared with what you will become. I promise it. Come here. Stand by me. Don't be afraid.'

'I am not afraid, Doctor.'

It was a lie, and Yama knew that Dr Dismas knew it. The doctor knew him too well. For no matter how much he tried to stay calm, the residue of his dreams, the flickering red and black fringes that plagued his sight, the thing growing under his skin and the scuttling and crawling and floating machines that infested the room all conspired to keep him perpetually fearful.

Dr Dismas began to fit a cigarette into the holder carved from the fingerbone of a murderer. His concentration on the task was absolute; his left hand had been bent into a stiff claw by the plaques which grew beneath his skin – a symptom of his disease, the disease with which he had infected Yama. At last it was done, and he lit the cigarette and drew on it and blew two smoke rings, the second spinning through the first. He smiled at this little trick and said, 'Not afraid? You should be afraid. But I am sure that there is more to it than fear. You are angry, certainly. And curious. I am sure that you are curious.'

Yama drew on the lessons in diplomacy which his poor dead stepfather, the Aedile of Aeolis, had so patiently taught him. Always turn any weakness into advantage by admitting it, for nothing draws out your enemy like an exposed weakness.

'Of course I am afraid, Doctor. I am afraid that I might try to kill you. As you killed Tamora.'

'I do not know that name.'

Yama's hatred was suddenly so intense that he could hardly bear it. He said, 'The cateran. My companion.'

'Ah. The silly woman with the little sword and the bad temper. Well, if I killed her, it is because she was responsible for the death of Eliphas, who so successfully led you to me. An eye for an eye, as the Amnan would say. How is your father, by the way? And the stinking little city he pretends to rule?'

Yama charged at the doctor then, and one of the flock of machines floating in the airy room shot forward and clipped him on the side of the head. One moment he was running headlong, the next he was sprawled on his back on the rubbery black floor, looking up at the ceiling. Pain shot through him. His chest and face had been badly seared by the backwash of the blast which had killed Tamora and Eliphas, and his ribs had been cracked when it had knocked him down. A splinter of rock had pierced his lung, too, and although he had been treated by a battery of machines he tasted blood at the back of his mouth now.

Dr Dismas smiled down at him and extended the claw of his left hand. Yama ignored it and laboriously and painfully got to his feet.

'You have spirit,' Dr Dismas said. 'That's good. You will need it.'

'Where are the others? Pandaras and the crew of the *Weazel*. Did you leave them behind?'

'The little ship that gave you a ride downriver? Oh, that's of no consequence. It is only you I am interested in, dear Child of the River. Are you all right? Not hurt by your fall? Good. Come and stand by the window with me. I have much to tell you, and we will make a start today.'

Yama followed Dr Dismas unwillingly. The room was part of a palace built along one side of a floating garden. Its single window, bulging like an eye, overlooked a vast panorama. Far below, Baucis, the City of Trees, stretched away in the golden sunlight of a perfect afternoon. Other floating gardens hung at various heights above their own shadows, like green clouds. Some were linked together by catenaries, rope slides, and arched bridges of shining metal. An arboreal bloodline had inhabited Baucis before the heretics had come; their city had been a patchwork of ten thousand small woods separated by clear-felled belts and low, grassy hills. Now many of the woods had been cut down. New roads slashed through the rolling landscape, a network of fused red-clay tracks like fresh wounds. The heretics had made their encampments on the hills, and a miasma of smoke from weapon foundries and numerous fires hung over the remaining patches of trees.

Beyond the city, the vivid green jungle stretched away beneath the mist of its own exhalations. The floating garden was so high up that both edges of the world were visible: the ragged blue line of the Rim Mountains on the right and the silver plain of the Great River on the left, and all the habitable world between them, dwindling beneath strings of white clouds towards a faint hint of red. In the days since he had been captured, Yama had spent a great deal of time gazing at this scene, and had convinced himself that he could see beyond the fall of the Great River and the mountains at the midpoint of the world to the beginning of the Glass Desert.

Dr Dismas exhaled a riffle of clove-scented smoke and said, 'Everything you see is the territory of the heretics. Two hundred cities downriver of this one, and a hundred more upriver. Thousands of bloodlines are theirs now. And soon the rest, Yamamanama. Soon the rest, unless something is done. Their triumph is great, but they must be prevented from completing it. They have meddled in much that they do not understand. They have tried to wake the great engines in the keelways of the world, for instance. Fortunately, they did not succeed.'

The apothecary looked sideways, but Yama said nothing. Dr Dismas had a habit of alluding to enigmas and mysteries, perhaps in the hope of drawing out Yama's secrets, as a fisherman might scatter bait to lure fish to the surface. Yama had glimpsed something of the vast machines beneath the surface of the world when Beatrice had returned him to the peel-house by the old roads in the keelways, but knew nothing of their powers and functions. He had not known much about his own powers then, and had not thought to question them.

'Well, for now you will help the heretics,' Dr Dismas said briskly. 'You will provide a service for which we will later ask payment. Please. For your sake do not make any more sudden moves. My servants here are simple things and have very literal minds. I would not like to see you hurt because of a misunderstanding.'

Yama's fist was so tightly clenched that his fingernails pressed four points of pain into his palm. He said, 'Whatever I was able to do has been taken away from me. I am glad that it is gone. Even if I still had it, I would never choose to serve you.'

'Oh, it isn't a question of choice. And it is still there, somewhere or other. I'm sure it will surface again.'

'Do what you will. Invoke the thing you placed inside me. Invoke your disease. But do not involve me. Do not try to make me take your side or see your point of view.'

Yama turned away and crossed to the bed and sat down. Dr Dismas remained by the window. Hunched into his frock coat, he carefully lit another cigarette and exhaled a plume of smoke while gazing at the city spread below, like a conqueror at his ease. At last, without turning around, he said, 'You have it easy, Yamamanama. I envy you. I was alone when I was changed, and my paramour was old and badly crippled. We both nearly died before the union was complete, and we nearly died again when we retraced my path across the Glass Desert. That was almost forty years ago. An odd coincidence, don't you think?'

Yama was interested, despite the loathing he felt towards the apothecary. He said, 'I suppose that it was something to do with the Ancients of Days.'

'Good, good. You have been learning about your past. It will save us much time. Yes, it had something to do with one of them. With the most important of them, in fact. All the Ancients of Days were merely variations on a single theme, but the one who called herself Angel was closest to the original. I believe that you have met her.'

The woman in the shrine. The woman in white. Yama said, 'It was the revenant of something five million years old, of a pathetic scared fool who failed at godhood and escaped her enemies by fleeing to a neighbouring galaxy. She found nothing there and returned to meddle with Confluence. She was the seed of the heretics, and was killed by her fellows.'

'Indeed, indeed. But before she was killed, Angel left a copy of herself in the space inside the shrines. Her aspect – that was who you talked to. She wants you on her side, and so she told you her story. And told you how powerful she was, no doubt.'

'I destroyed her, Doctor.'

Dr Dismas smiled. 'Oh, I think not. You have much to learn about distributed information. She is stored as a pattern of interrupted light deep within the space inside the shrines. Perhaps your paramour will destroy her, when it is stronger, and if I so choose, but you destroyed only the copy of a copy.' Dr Dismas plunged his right hand into the pocket of his frock coat and brought out the plastic straws which he habitually cast when he needed to make a decision. He rattled them together, smiling craftily. 'The fate of gods in my hands – don't you find it amusing? Ah, you are a humourless boy, Yamamanama. It is not your fault. Anyone brought up by that stiff-backed narrow-minded backwards-looking innumerate superstitious fool would—'

Yama roared and ran at Dr Dismas again, and again was knocked down by one of the machines, but before he fell he had the satisfaction of seeing the apothecary take a step backwards. For a moment he was blinded by a silent storm of red and black that seemed to fill his head. He rolled onto his back, a ringing in his ears and the taste of blood in his mouth, and slowly got to his knees. When he stood, the room seemed to sway around him, and he sat down on the edge of the bed.

Dr Dismas watched Yama with a genuine tenderness. 'You'll need that spirit, Yamamanama,' he said. 'It is a hard road I have set you on, but you will thank me at last. You will be transformed, as I have been transformed. I will tell you how.

'It is a symptom of the disastrous reversal in the development of the peoples of Confluence that, although their technologies predated the creation of our world by five million years, the Ancients of Days were able to manipulate much that was hidden or lost to the ten thousand bloodlines. In particular, Angel was able to enter the space inside the shrines, and she learned much there.'

'She destroyed the avatars,' Yama said. 'People believe that the heretics destroyed them, but it happened before the war began.'

'Hush. This is my story, not hers. You already know hers, it seems. She tried to recruit you, but I know that you resisted, for otherwise you would not be here. You chose wisely. She is not our friend, Yamamanama. She is our ally, yes, but not our friend. Enobarbus submits to her without reservation, but we have our own plans. And besides, much of what she says is self-serving or simply untrue. Angel did not destroy the avatars. That was the work of the copy of herself that she installed in the space inside the shrines. The aspect you talked to was a copy of that copy, but no matter. In any form, in every iteration, it is a poor deluded thing. After Angel died, it found itself besieged, and it lashed out. That was how the avatars came to be destroyed. The avatars, and many records, and most of the directories and maps within the space inside the shrines. That was the true war, begun and finished before anyone alive knew about it. The war presently being fought between the heretics and the bureaucrats is but its shadow. And so the bureaucrats were defeated before the first ship of fools sailed from Ys to put down the uprisings at the midpoint of the world.

'But that does not concern us. While Angel was travelling downriver towards the last and least city of Confluence, where she would plant the seed that would grow into the heretics, at that same moment I was entering the Glass Desert. I had been trained as an apothecary – my family had been a part of the Department of Apothecaries and Chirurgeons for thousands of years – but I sought greater knowledge. Arcane knowledge hidden or forgotten or forbidden by priests and bureaucrats frightened by the true destiny of the world. As a child I had riddled every obscure nook and cranny of the department's library. This was before the hierodules within the screens of the library were destroyed along with the avatars, and written records were almost entirely unused then. There were vast amounts of trash, but I discovered a few gems.'

Yama said, 'And that was where you met Eliphas.'

'No, not then. I knew him, in the way that a boy might glancingly know everyone who works in the place where he grows up, but before I was summoned to return to the department I doubt that I exchanged a single word with him. Eliphas had long before given up searching for ancient treasures, although his friend and one-time partner, the chief of clerks of the library, did give me encouragement. He was interested in maps, but I found something better.

'It was the personal account of a travelling chirurgeon five thousand years dead. He had worked amongst the unchanged bloodlines at the midpoint of the world, and found a cluster of odd symptoms in certain of the nomadic clans that sometimes venture into the ancient battlegrounds of the Glass Desert. It was unusual in that the same symptoms were exhibited by different bloodlines. Most clans killed or cast out those afflicted, but in some they were considered blessed by the Preservers and became soothsayers, prophets, oracles, mysts, and so on.'

'This is the disease with which you infected me,' Yama said.

Dr Dismas flung out an arm, pointed at Yama, and screamed with sudden violence. 'Quiet! Enough interruptions! You will be quiet or I will . . .' His arm trembled violently, and he whirled around to face the window. His shoulders heaved. When he turned back he was smiling and there was honey in his voice. 'This is my story, Yamamanama. Do not race ahead. You think you know more than you do.'

'Perhaps I am not interested in your story, and want to bring it to its end as quickly as possible.'

'Ah, but you *are* interested. I know you are. Besides,' Dr Dismas added, in the same overly sweet, wheedling tone, 'if you do not listen I will slice off one of your ears as a lesson. Now, where was I?'

'You had discovered an old traveller's tale.'

Yama was interested, despite himself. Dr Dismas's story was similar to the lies that Eliphas had used to lure him downriver. Eliphas had claimed to have found a traveller's account of a hidden city in the Glass Desert, a city inhabited by people of Yama's bloodline. The documents he had shown Yama had been fabrications, but it was possible that the old question-runner's lies had been rooted in truth.

Dr Dismas said, 'I returned again and again to this poorly written memoir until I had it by heart. I even made a copy of it. But I was a child, with many long years of study ahead of me. My fascination faded and I turned to other matters. When at last I qualified and was sent to my first post, I took only the tools of my trade, in a leather wallet bequeathed to me by my grandfather, and the standard catalogue of electuaries, panaceas, simples, urticants and so on. I did not take the copy of the memoir which I had made, for I had set it aside with other childish things.

'I will not trouble you with the details of my first posting, nor those of my second. I was a foolish and naive young man, eager to do good in a world where goodness can gain only small and temporary victories. But at my third posting fate intervened. I do not believe in the Preservers, Yamamanama. Or rather, I do not believe that they exist any longer in the phenomenological universe. But it was as if something, some agency, touched my life then, and changed it forever. Perhaps my paramour's reach was longer than it seemed.

'I was dispatched to a mean little town in the mountains beyond the fall of the Great River, close to the border of the Glass Desert. And it was here that I met people exhibiting the symptoms described in the memoir I had read and reread as a child.

'Of course, my interest was rekindled at once. Travelling with a caravanserai, I visited the summer camps of unchanged nomads and learned much of the course of the disease. I marked its progression from simple plaques and associated loss of sensation to mania, blindness, and death. I was able to dissect the fresh corpse of a haruspex who had died of apoplexy – I had to break into her tomb to do it – and chart the growths and nodes along her nervous system. And by conflating the routes of the various clans of nomads through the margin of the Glass Desert with the incidence of the disease, I was able to plot its focal point.

'I will not trouble you with a long catalogue of the hardships I endured to reach my goal. I went alone because I trusted no one, and that almost killed me. The Glass Desert is a terrible place. There is no free water beyond the mountains of the Great Divide, for the river which was the mirror of our Great River failed after the wars of the Age of Insurrection. It is a place of glare and heat, of endless sand dunes, salt pans, alkali flats, vitrified craters and devastated terrain. Nothing grows but stoneworts and a few hardy plants which are more like machines than living organisms – when I first saw them I knew then that the memoir had not lied, and I was almost killed when in my excitement I went too close to a clump of them.

'I took a string of camels and a mule, but the camels contracted a falling sickness and I had to leave most of my supplies with their corpses. The mule survived until a great dust storm blew up. The storm lasted twelve days and all that time the mule was tethered outside my tent. When at last I emerged, with the sun a bleary spot in a sky stained ochre by suspended dust, I found that the poor beast had been flayed to its bones, and things like turkey vultures were quarrelling over what remained. They too were partly machine, and I had to kill them when they turned on me. One clipped me with the tip of a wing, and its serrated flight feathers opened a great gash in my side, clear down to the cartilage sheaves of my chest cage.

'I went on, weakened by my wound and carrying what I could, knowing that I did not have enough water or food for the return journey. I walked at night, and by day sheltered from the heat and from dust devils and fierce little storms of knife-sharp crystallised silica. It was burning hot during the day, and so cold at night that with each breath little puffs of ice crystals fell, tinkling, from my lips. The sky was utterly clear: I felt that I could see past the distant smudges and specks of galaxies to the afterglow of the hatching of the cosmic egg. I walked like this for four days, until I found the place I had been searching for.'

Dr Dismas lit another cigarette. His hands were trembling badly. Yama watched him closely. He was caught up in the story because what had happened to Dr Dismas then was happening to him now. The red and black flickering which troubled his vision had intensified; it was as if he was peering through banners which flew on an impalpable wind. Terror beat within him on great steel wings. He had the sudden strange notion that instead of being captured by Dr Dismas outside the shrine he had fallen off the edge of the world and was falling still, that this was a terrible dream from which he might at any moment awaken to worse horror.

'O Yamamanama,' Dr Dismas said at last. 'Child of the River. How I envy you! It was so long ago that I have only a few bright memories, worn smooth by my constant handling like pebbles in the bed of a mountain stream. It was so terrible, and so wonderful! Such pain, and such joy! Such joy!'

Yama was amazed, for the apothecary was weeping.

Dr Dismas's expression was haunted yet ecstatic. 'Oh yes,' he said. 'Tears. Weak and foolish human tears. For what I was. For what I became, in the embrace of my paramour. I was reborn, and it was painful and bloody and wretched. And out of it such glory, such joy. Such joy.'

He blotted the tears from his plaque-stiffened cheeks with the claw of his left hand and sniffed hard. Usually, Dr Dismas displayed emotion as a theatrical puppet might hold an appropriate mask before its immobile, painted face. (Was it part of the Preservers' plan, Yama suddenly wondered, that almost all the bloodlines shared the same facial expressions and bodily postures which expressed fear and hope, rage and love, happiness and sorrow?) His real thoughts were unguessable. But now he appeared to be wholly possessed by human feeling.

'Ah,' he said at last, sniffing delicately, 'it moves me still to think about it. I had come upon the place without realising it. I was delirious by then. My feet were blistered and badly bleeding. I had heat sores all over my body. My joints were swollen and I was so badly sunburnt that my skin was blackened and cracked, and constantly wept blood and pus. It was dawn. A fierce hot wind was blowing, sucking moisture from my body. I had reached a place of chaotic terrain. The land was like rough-cast glass, dissected by a maze of wandering ridges and canyons. I was lost, and too ill to realise that by the end of the day, or by the end of the next, I would be dead. I stumbled into the shade of a deep ravine and pitched my tent and crawled inside.

'My paramour had heard my footsteps leagues away, listening with a thousand whiskers grown across the land. It had watched me from decads of eyes, some fixed like crystals in the rock and glass, others mounted on scuttling extensions it had cleaved from the wreckage of its own body.

'It was those extensions that came for me, in the heat of noon.

'There were hundreds of them. They were like spiders or mantids fashioned out of black glass. They moved with stiff scuttling motions. I woke when the first of them cut through the material of my tent. In a fevered panic, I killed decads with a single shot of my energy pistol and stumbled from the tent's blazing wreckage. More waited outside, clinging to the vertical rock face beneath which I'd camped. They fell on me, stung me insensible, and spun a cocoon around me. And so began—'

A chime sounded out of the midair of the room.

'What now?' Dr Dismas said irritably, and turned his back on Yama and fell into what seemed to be a one-sided conversation. 'Can't it wait? Yes, the boy. Yes, I am. Yes. No, I want to tell him. You wouldn't understand why, unless you . . . Yes, I know you . . . Very well, if you must.'

Dr Dismas turned and gazed at Yama as if seeing him for the first time. 'We were speaking of the courtship between my paramour and myself. I told you how it began, of the little machines which were as much a part of my paramour as your fingers and toes and eyes and ears are a part of you, Yamamanama. They found me and paralysed me as a hunting wasp paralyses a plump caterpillar. And like so many hunting wasps, they wound me in a cocoon of threads spun from their own bodies. The threads were possessed of a certain intelligence, and began to mend my wounds. Meanwhile, the machines brought me water enriched with vitamins and amino acids and sugars, and fed it to me drop by drop.

'I was delirious, and I did not understand what was happening to me. I dreamed that I was in a lazaret in the cool shade of palm trees, with the sound of running water outside its white canvas walls. And meanwhile my paramour was creeping towards me.

'For it had realised that I was a prize out of the ordinary. It had allowed its extensions to infect any nomads that passed by, but the things which grew in the nomads' bodies were no more intelligent than the extensions themselves. But I was something rarer, and it came to me itself. Or rather, it grew towards me, as a desert plant will grow a root towards a lode of water.

'I do not know how long it took, but at last it reached me. A silver wire no thicker than a spider's thread pierced my skull and branched and rebranched a million times, uniting with the neurons in my visual and auditory lobes. And then my paramour stood before me, terrible in its glory, and told me the true history of the world.

'I will not tell you what it said. You will have to learn that yourself. It is growing inside you. Soon it will be complete, and will awaken fully. But I will say that what I learned then transformed me utterly and completely. I learned of my paramour's fabulous battles in the vacuum beyond the envelope of air which wraps our world, of its splendid victories and the terrible defeat of its final fall. It plunged from a great height and at a great speed, transforming as it fell. It struck hard and penetrated deep within the mantle of the world, melting rock with the heat of its fiery fall and sealing itself in its tomb. Ah, I see you understand. Yes, yes, you are awakening.

'It lay there for ten thousand years, slowly reconfiguring itself, sending out its extensions into the desert around, listening, learning. Imagine the strength of will, child! The will to survive for ten thousand years in agony and utterly alone. Until very recently it had not dared to communicate with those of its fellows which had survived the wars of insurrection. It had to deduce what was happening in the world by interrogating the wretches that its extensions captured and changed. The stings of its extensions infected many, but only a few returned, and the compass of their lives was so narrow that they had little useful to communicate.

'And then I arrived, and all was different. It was not just that I was one of the changed bloodlines, but that I arrived soon after Angel meddled with the space inside the shrines. My paramour had heard her call. And so I was healed and sent back to find out what I could about the new war, and to make an alliance.

'But I did much better than that. I won so much more for my

paramour. I won this hero, the last of the Builders, the Child of the River, and I laid him at its feet. The little seeds that I tricked him into ingesting were from my paramour, of course, my paramour and your father. And so we are united, you and I. Together we will do great things,' Dr Dismas said, and smiled stiffly and bowed low.

'I will not serve,' Yama said. 'I would rather die.'

'But you are awake,' Dr Dismas said merrily. 'I know it! I can feel it! Speak to me, my darling child! It is time! Time!'

And Yama realised that all this time the apothecary had been speaking as much to the thing growing inside him as to himself. And in that moment of realisation pain struck through every cell in his body. The black and red fire of the pain washed away the world. Something stood in the fire. It was a vision of a foetus, curled up like a fish, all in gold. Slowly, it turned its heavy, blind head towards Yama, who thought he would go mad if its eyes opened and its gaze fell upon him. It spoke. Its voice was his own.

You will not serve? Ah, but that is against the nature of your bloodline. Your kind were created to serve the Preservers, to build this world. Well, the rest of your race are long gone, but you are here, and you will serve. You will serve me.

Another voice spoke from the world beyond the fire: deep, resonant and angry.

'What are you doing to him? Stop it, Dismas! Stop it at once! I command you!'

The pain receded. The vision dissolved. Yama's body, which had been arched like a bow, relaxed. His head fell to one side. And he saw, framed by a flickering haze of red and black, the mane and the ugly scarred face of the heretic warlord and traitor Enobarbus.

3
THE TRADER

Pandaras and Tibor drifted downriver for three days, always keeping close to the edge of the mangrove swamps that fringed the farside shore. Pandaras did not dare set out across the broad river on the little raft: a single wave might swamp it in an instant. Each night, he tied himself to the bundles of reeds in case he slipped overboard in his sleep and drowned before he could wake. He slept very little; Tibor did not sleep at all. The hierodule said that sleeplessness was another curse that the Preservers had placed upon his bloodline. Pandaras thought that it helped explain why the fellow was so lacking in imagination, for he had no dreamlife.

The spark in the disc did not grow brighter, but neither did it grow dimmer. Yama was alive, but he must be very far away. It did not matter. Every time he looked at the disc, Pandaras pledged to find his master even if it took him beyond the end of the world, even if it took him the rest of his life.

To pass the time while Tibor paddled steadily and the ragged margin of mangrove stands and banyan islands drifted by, always changing, always the same, Pandaras told the hierodule every detail of his adventures with Yama. How he had appointed himself Yama's squire after the landlord of *The Crossed Axes* tried to kill Yama for the coins he carried; how they had met the cateran, Tamora, and their attempt to bring the escaped star-sailor to justice; the destruction of the Temple of the Black Well and their entry into the Palace of the Memory of the People (of which Pandaras remembered little, for he had been laid out by a blow to the head). The conspiracy in the Department of Vaticination which had led to capture by Yama's enemy, Prefect Corin, and then escape from imprisonment, with Yama full of wrath and cloaked in blue fire he had conjured from a shrine: the first time Pandaras had been truly afraid of his master. And the miracle by which Yama had raised up a baby of one of the indigenous races which lived in the Palace, and the triumphant procession of Yama through the streets of Ys. The rest – the voyage of the *Weazel* downriver, the sack of Yama's childhood home and the chase by Prefect Corin which had ended in an attack by monstrous polyps from the deep and a storm and near-shipwreck – Tibor already knew. But Pandaras, who loved stories, told it anyway.

'My master says that stories are the only kind of immortality achievable outwith the grace of the Preservers. And they are the lifeblood of my people. We are short-lived, yet live long in memory because of our skill in making stories and songs. A good story can be handed down through a hundred generations, its details changing but its heart always the same, and the people in it live again each time it is told. So might we, Tibor, for surely this is the greatest story the world has ever known.'

'All the world is a story,' Tibor said, after paddling silently for a while. 'Who can find the single droplet which falls from a leaf-tip into the flood of the Great River? Who can say where one story ends and another begins?'

Pandaras thought that Tibor was quoting from an obscure sura in the Puranas and, having no wish to argue theology with a hierodule, for once held his tongue.

The nights were lit only by the dim red swirl of the Eye of the Preservers. It rose slightly earlier each night, and each night reached a slightly higher point in the black sky above the river's black plain before falling back towards the farside horizon. In the vast stillness of night, Pandaras felt most acutely the emptiness of the unpeopled shore, and he was relieved when at last the songs of birds and monkeys and the whistling chorus of millions of frogs greeted the dawn. The days quickly grew hot, but Tibor did not seem to mind the heat. He had grown up in a far hotter land, near the midpoint of the world.

Without salt, the antelope meat went off before they could eat more than a quarter of it, but there was food all around. There were always ripe fruits waiting to be plucked from strangler figs or banana plants. Tibor plaited nets from fibres scraped from the fronds of the big ferns which clung to the mangroves, and trawled for catfish and lampreys in shallow backwaters, while Pandaras nimbly climbed among the canopies of banyans, taking eggs from the nests of birds and lizards. Tibor ate insects too, snatching them out of the air with his long red tongue.

Occasionally they glimpsed the flash of a sail far out in the middle of the river, an argosy or carrack heading for the war, and one day a machine circled the raft before rising up and flying straight towards the misty line of the nearside shore. It had a long, wasp-waisted body, a decad of shimmering, fragile vanes, and a cluster of bright red eyes. Pandaras cocked the arbalest while the machine dipped overhead, remembering the machines that Prefect Corin had sent out to search for Yama. But Prefect Corin must be dead, drowned when his ship had been torn apart by the giant polyps Yama had called from the deep river-bottom. There were many machines out and about in the world, Pandaras told himself. It signified nothing.

Late in the afternoon of the next day they reached the house of an itinerant trader. It was tucked away in a backwater shaded by tall mangroves, a ramshackle shanty built in the branches of a banyan, with walls and a peaked roof fashioned from panels of woven grasses. Several small boats were strung out along an anchor line on the still, black water below. Little glowing lamps shone everywhere amongst the tree's glossy green leaves, like a horde of fireflies. Music from a cassette player came clearly across the water as Tibor paddled the raft towards the shanty, and a bird set up a harsh clamour, warning of their approach.

The trader, a crafty old man named Ayulf, was of a bloodline familiar to Pandaras: the bloodline of half the ruffians who smuggled cigarettes and other proscribed trade goods to indigens or otherwise scraped a living on the wrong side of the law along the docks of Ys or on the Great River. Ayulf wore only a dhoti around his scrawny waist, in which he habitually rummaged to scratch or rearrange his genitals. His arms and legs were long and stringy, and his small head was crowned with a dirty, half-unravelled turban from which greasy spikes of hair stuck out in every direction. His eyes were yellow, like flame or bits of amber, and he hissed softly to himself when he was thinking; he did that a lot while Pandaras devoured a salty mess of rice and fish and told a highly edited version of his story.

Ayulf traded with the local fisher folk, exchanging cigarettes, cheap cooking pots, fish hooks, nylon netting and leaves of bronze or iron for lizard, snake and cayman skins, the hides of marsh antelopes, the feathers of bell birds and birds of heaven, and rare spices and medicines extracted from plants and lichens which grew on the banyans and mangroves. The shanty was cluttered with bales of cigarettes wrapped in black plastic, wooden cases and machines or bits of machines. Some kind of large gun was in pieces on the floor by the flat stone that served as a hearth. Salted hides were slung beneath the roof, layered with aromatic tar-bush leaves to keep off insects. A pentad of fisher folk women and more than twice that number of their children moved about in the dusky evening light, lighting lamps, mending clothes, stirring the cookpot in which fish soup perpetually simmered, chattering in their dialect and casting covert glances at Pandaras and Tibor. A half-tame crow hopped about, too. It was big, half Pandaras's height, and looked beadily at him as if wondering whether it would be easy to kill him, and what he might taste like. The crow's white droppings spattered the floor and the stacks of plastic-wrapped bales, and it was given to crying out hoarsely and jumping here and there with an abrupt dry flutter of its black wings. It was always just at the corner of Pandaras's sight. It made him nervous, and he kept one hand near the hilt of his ivory-handled poniard. The arbalest was slung at his shoulder. He did not trust the trader.

'Don't mind my bird,' Ayulf said. 'He's never seen no one like you before and he's curious.' He had been cuddling the youngest of the women to him; now he dismissed the girl with a slap to her haunches and said, 'They are animals, not men, but someone like me must make a living as best he can, and take what company he can, too. You understand, eh? You being in the same line of business as me. Don't deny it. I know a man that lives by his wits when I see him.'

Ayulf was staring at Tibor when he said this, but then he seemed to recollect himself and winked at Pandaras.

'I can see that you make a good living here,' Pandaras said.

'There's a lot that washes downriver,' the trader said, 'and a lot that makes its way back from the war. That culverin, for instance. I'd sell it to you, except I've promised it to a good friend of mine who'll be along to collect it once I've fixed its firing mechanism. But I have other guns. I'll take that arbalest off you in part exchange for something with a bit more bite. You need heavy weapons around here. The Preservers don't see so well in this part of the river, if you get my meaning.'

Ayulf's friend was probably a pirate, Pandaras thought. The trader must pay a good deal of tribute for protection. He said, 'You are generous to your friends, dominie.'

'It helps to be generous, out here,' Ayulf said. He plucked a bit of gristle from his gappy teeth and tossed it to the crow, which snapped it from the air with its bone-white beak and swallowed it whole. 'Favours bring business and keep trouble away.'

'I can see that your business is good. You have a good place here, many women, many things to trade. Why, you even have an abundance of boats.'

'How does that raft of yours handle out on the river?'

'Well enough, for a raft. My friend here has a lot of experience with rafts.'

Ayulf's yellow gaze flicked towards Tibor. 'With a friend like yours, you are a rich man indeed, and deserve better than a raft, I would think.'

They slowly got around to bargaining, and at last, with Tibor following, climbed down to the lowest branches of the banyan to inspect a long narrow pirogue. It had been dug out of a single tree trunk and had a log outrigger and a high prow. A reaction motor lay in the stinking water which half-filled it. Although Ayulf could not get it to start, he promised that it usually ran as sweet as the streams of the paradise which the Preservers would create at the far end of time. The sun had set and, despite the little lights strung through the branches of the banyan, there was not much light under the shanty, but Pandaras could see better in the dark than the trader. He took a hard look at the motor – it was clogged with dried mud and probably had been dropped in the river at some point – and said that it was a big motor for a small boat.

'Sometimes in my line of work you need to get somewhere quickly,' Ayulf said, showing his ruined teeth. 'This will take you anywhere on the river, my little man, swift as a thought from the Preservers.'

Pandaras smiled at him. 'It might do that once it is fixed. If it can be fixed. The inlet and outlet channels are clogged and bent, but that's a trivial matter. What's worse is that the reaction chamber might be corroded, and the feeder valves and the ignition spark will need complete readjustment. That is, if they are still working. There's a hole in the fuel tank, too. Did someone shoot at it?'

Ayulf walked his long fingernails up his narrow jaw and pulled at his ear. He glanced at Tibor and crowded closer to Pandaras, who lightly touched the hilt of his poniard. The trader pretended not to notice the gesture. He stank powerfully of tobacco, sweat and urine. He said, 'If you know something of motors, you will see that this a fine one, very powerful.'

'I see that it is very broken. No doubt you got it from someone who was foolish enough to drop it into the river or have their boat sunk from under them. It's been lying too long at the bottom of the river to be any good, but I'd be happy to take it away from you as a favour, since the look of it spoils the rest of your fine fleet.'

With hot food in his belly and his face and feet and hands washed in filtered water, Pandaras felt more cheerful than he had since the flier had taken away his master and destroyed the *Weazel*. This poor shanty could almost count as civilisation, and bargaining was the lifeblood of civilisation, the way by which you measured yourself against your fellows. He had Tibor carry the reaction motor into the shanty and pretended to be angry that someone had burdened Ayulf with something in such a bad condition. On this basis, he and Ayulf bargained for an hour over glasses of peppermint-flavoured arak – Pandaras took care to pour most of his share through a crack in the floorboards whenever Ayulf was distracted by one of his women.

Ayulf was a crafty bargainer, but he was not as clever as he thought he was. He had been too long amongst river pirates and the simple fisher folk, and had lost his edge. He suggested almost straight away that Pandaras leave Tibor with him and take the pirogue and the motor, and plenty of supplies too, but Pandaras said that he wanted only the pirogue, although he would take the motor if Ayulf had no need for it. In the end, it cost Pandaras half Yama's store of iron coins as well as the husks of the burnt-out machines. He had shown these to Ayulf early on and knew, by the widening of the man's yellow eyes, that the trader coveted them.

Ayulf broke open another bottle of arak to celebrate the deal, and although Pandaras drank only enough to be polite, it quickly went to his head. 'That's it,' Ayulf said encouragingly. 'Drink. Be happy. We've both done well with this deal. Let your slave here drink, too. Aren't we all friends?'

'I do not drink alcohol,' Tibor said. 'It is a poison to my people.'

'We wouldn't want to poison you,' Ayulf said. 'Not you. You're worth a lot to your master.' He said to Pandaras, 'You can really fix that motor?'

'I'm going to do my best,' Pandaras said, and opened up its combustion chamber and began to remove and clean the feeder valves and the rotary spark. The crow perched close by, cocking its head this way and that, fascinated by the bright bits of metal which emerged from their coatings of mud. Ayulf watched sidelong, and said that Pandaras seemed to know a little about motors.

'One of my uncles on my stepfather's side had a trade in them. This was in Ys, where such things are forbidden, so it was on the black side of the market. Others think that our bloodline is famous only for songs and stories, and see our hands and think that we cannot do good work with them. But while our fingers are crooked, they are also strong, and we are very patient when we need to be. You might think this motor worthless, but when I'm done it will be better than new. You are very generous, Ayulf, and I thank you a million times over. Here, more of this rotgut, eh? We will drink to my success.'

'You stay here a few days,' Ayulf said. 'You and your slave.'

'He isn't my slave.'

'He has to be someone's, and he came with you. Maybe we become partners, eh? Make much money. There is much that needs fixing here. I hear the war goes badly, which means it goes well for you and me, eh? More and more in the regular army run away from it, and have to sell stuff cheap to buy what they need dear. And caterans are always hungry for the best weapons, no matter what side they are on.'

'I have to find my master,' Pandaras said.

Tibor said, 'And the ship.'

Ayulf poured Pandaras's shot glass brim-full, drank from the bottle and wiped his mouth with the back of his hand. 'Your ship left you behind, eh? Maybe after an argument or a tricky kind of disagreement? I sometimes find those who have fallen out with their shipmates, if the caymans and fishes haven't found them first.'

'There was certainly a fight,' Pandaras said, glaring at Tibor.

'And you lost and were left to rot on some island? I know how that is. Are you sure they want you back? More likely you ran away. They wouldn't leave a valuable slave behind with you. Yes, you took him and ran away, I would guess. No, it's all right, I won't tell. Listen, why go downriver? I have all you want here. Food and drink and women. Well, the women are animals, of course, but they know how to please a man in the warm trade.'

Ayulf grabbed at the nearest of the women, but she pushed him away with a loud laugh and turned back to frying shrimp in a big blackened cast-iron pan.

'Always cooking,' Ayulf said. He stared at the woman and made a humming noise in the back of his throat. 'Why now, eh? Why so late?

You all eat too much, you and your brats. Perhaps I should throw a few of you to the caymans. Which ones first?'

He stuck his long middle finger (its nail had been filed to a sharp point, and was painted red) at the nearest woman and made a noise like a pistol shot. She giggled and put her hands over her face. Her fingers were webbed, and spread very wide, like a fan. They were tipped with little black claws.

'Someone is coming,' the oldest woman said, from the far corner of the shanty. She was very fat, overflowing the stool on which she perched. She was working at a bit of wood with a tiny knife. Her skin was as green as mouldy cheese. 'They bring hides to trade, man. They will make you rich.'

'They share their thoughts,' Ayulf told Pandaras. 'They are not like us, who keep our thoughts sealed in our skulls. Everything is shared with them, like air or water. Kill any one of them, and it makes no difference.'

Pandaras nodded. He was having trouble focusing on the spring, ball bearing and three bits of metal that should fit together to make one of the motor's feeder valves. There seemed to be too many of them, and his fingers too clumsy. He was drunk, and he had not meant to become drunk. But Ayulf was drunk too, and Pandaras had his poniard and the arbalest, and, at a pinch, Tibor (although he was not sure that Tibor, for all his size and strength, would be much good in a fight). And fisher folk were coming. The trader would not try anything in front of them.

'You like to think we are all a single mind,' the old woman in the corner told Ayulf, 'but you know it is not true. It is just that we think alike, that's all. Hush! They are here.'

Whistles from below, a muffled splash. The crow stirred and hopped to the rail of the veranda, finding its balance with a rustling stir of wings. It cried out hoarsely. Ayulf stumbled to the rail, pushed the bird out of the way, and peered into the darkness.

Voices floated up. The trader cursed and threw down the half-empty bottle of arak he had been clutching. It shattered on one of the banyan's branches. 'Too fucking late! You understand? Understand "too late"? Come back tomorrow!'

More voices. The trader cursed again, clambered over the rail, and swarmed down the banyan. Pandaras stood (the cluttered shadows revolving around him) and went out onto the veranda. Below, lit by the tiny lanterns scattered amongst the banyan's leaves, Ayulf was arguing with a tall thin man who stood in a coracle. The man was holding up what looked like a huge ragged book. There were other coracles at the edge of the glow of the lanterns.

Tibor came out and stood at Pandaras's back. He said, 'The woman wants to speak with you, young master.'

'Hush. I want to know what is going on.'

'This is a bad place.'

'I know. That's why I need to know what this is all about.'

'We should go.'

'I want to fix the motor. I can do it, but I'm tired. Later. I'll finish it later.'

Ayulf made a long impassioned speech, but the man in the coracle made no reply and at last the trader threw up his skinny arms and climbed back to the veranda. He fell flat on his face when he clambered over the rail, got up and went inside and found another bottle of arak, ripped the plastic seal away with his teeth and took a long swallow.

'They are impossible,' Ayulf said to no one in particular.

He took another swallow and wiped his wet lips, glaring around at the women. A child woke somewhere and made a snuffling noise. Two more children clung to their mother's legs, staring at the trader with big black eyes. In the corner, the fat old woman was calmly whittling her bit of wood.

'Animals,' the trader said. 'Why am I wasting my time with animals?'

One by one, the fisher folk climbed to the veranda and, stooping, entered the shanty. There were four of them. Unlike their women, they were so thin that if they had been of Pandaras's bloodline they would have been in the last stage of starvation, and so tall that their heads brushed the ceiling. Their green skins were dappled with darker tones. It was not a book that their leader carried, Pandaras saw now, but a sheaf of bloody uncured hides, and he placed this at Ayulf's feet.

One of the women crept up to Pandaras while the trader dickered with the leader of the fisher folk in their croaking dialect. The leader squatted face to face with Ayulf, his sharp knees above the top of his head, nodding impassively, occasionally picking a shrimp from the heaped plate and examining it with slow thoughtfulness before dropping it into his wide mouth and swallowing it whole. His companions stood behind him in the shadows, as still as herons waiting for fish to swim by. Most of the hides were those of marsh antelope, but one was that of a leopard. Ayulf had spread it out in front of him and was stroking the spotted, viridescent fur with his long fingernails. To Pandaras's great scorn, the trader made no attempt to conceal how much he coveted the leopard hide.

'My mother will speak with you,' the woman said in Pandaras's ear. 'We know that you are a friend of ours, and we will help you.'

Pandaras shrugged and yawned. It was very late and he was drunk. Drunk and tired. He had given up trying to fit the motor back together. His fingers were numb and his stomach hurt. Later. Tomorrow. The shanty was swaying to and fro like a boat on the breast of the river. The lanterns seemed very bright, a swarm of hectic colours running into each other. It was an effort to keep anything in focus for more than a moment.

The woman touched the fetish which Pandaras wore over his shirt-sleeve, but Pandaras mistook the gesture and pushed her away. He wanted to curl up around the pain in his stomach. He wanted to sleep.

'Your master is a fool,' he told the woman. 'I can take care of myself.'

'Oncus,' the woman said, but he couldn't recall where he had heard that name before, and stared at her dumbly until she went away.

He woke with a start sometime later. It was still dark. His mouth was parched and he had a bad headache and somehow he was standing upright. Then he realised that Tibor was holding him up by the collar of his ragged shirt, and kicked out indignantly until the hierodule let him go.

Ayulf was in a hammock on the far side of the shanty, half-curled around a fat young woman and snoring through his open mouth. A knot of children slept below. The oldest woman was watching Pandaras from her stool on the other side of the slab hearth, the carved peg of wood in one hand, her little knife in the other.

'We go, young master,' Tibor said in a low, hoarse whisper. He had the reaction motor under his arm.

Pandaras drew his poniard. 'I'll cut his throat,' he said. He was still drunk. His stomach hurt badly, as if he had been swallowing slivers of hot metal. The muscles in his arms and legs felt as if they were on the verge of cramping. He said, 'He poisoned me. I'll cut his throat and watch him die in his own blood. I can do it.'

Tibor wrapped a large, six-fingered hand around Pandaras's wrist. The poniard's blade pressed against the hierodule's grey skin, but did not cut it. 'You fixed the motor,' Pandaras said stupidly.

'It is smaller than the motor of the *Weazel*, but otherwise no different.

Your pardon, but I think you need to be helped,' Tibor said, and lifted Pandaras up and swung him over the rail of the veranda.

They were halfway down when Pandaras remembered something and began to scramble back up. Tibor tried to catch his foot, but Pandaras kicked his hand away. 'The pack and the arbalest,' he hissed. 'My master's book. His money.'

The women stirred and whispered amongst themselves when Pandaras reappeared, but he ignored them. He found the arbalest and the pack by the flat hearthstone – the book was still inside, but the money was gone.

'Where is it?' he hissed at the old woman. 'Where did your master hide my money?'

She shook her head, and put her fingers to her throat.

Pandaras showed her the poniard. 'Show me where he hid it, or I'll kill him where he sleeps.'

The crow stirred on its perch above the stay of Ayulf's hammock, clucked in alarm.

'You keep out of it,' Pandaras said, and flourished his blade, and the crow screeched and flew at him. He dropped the pack and slashed blindly as the bird enveloped him in its beating wings and pecked at the forearm he had raised to protect his eyes. He cut it with a lucky thrust and it fluttered away, trailing blood and dragging a black wing across the floor.

Pandaras chased after it, bleeding from half a dozen places, and went down under Ayulf's weight and hot stink. For a moment, the trader's hands were everywhere as he sought to prise the poniard from Pandaras's grasp, but then his weight was lifted away. Pandaras pushed to his hands and knees, gasping, and saw Tibor throw Ayulf across the shanty. The skinny trader crashed into the woven panels of the far wall. As they collapsed around him, he rolled away, quick as thought.

Pandaras's poniard quivered in the planking where he'd been. Pandaras looked at it stupidly, wondering how he could have missed, then saw Ayulf get to his feet, holding a percussion pistol, and scrambled for cover.

'Come out where I can see you,' Ayulf said. He was pointing the pistol at Tibor, who stood in the middle of the shanty, the arbalest dangling from one hand. 'Do it now, or I'll kill your slave and then I'll kill you.'

Pandaras stood, and spread his empty hands. 'Why don't we discuss this misunderstanding like reasonable men?'

'I'm taking everything you have,' Ayulf said. 'Is that clear enough?'

He swung the pistol towards Pandaras, and his arm slammed backwards into one of the roof posts. The pistol clattered on the floor.

Tibor lowered the arbalest. 'We go,' he told Pandaras.

Ayulf pawed at the bolt which pinned his forearm to the post and screamed at the women. 'Get me free! Kill them and get me free!'

The old woman rose from her stool. The floor of the shanty creaked under her weight. 'Go,' she told Pandaras. 'I will tend to him.'

Pandaras jerked the poniard from the planking, scooped up the pack and stuffed two bottles of arak in it, and ran after Tibor. He more or less fell through the branches of the banyan and landed on his back in the stinking water which half-filled the pirogue.

As Tibor pushed off from the banyan, Pandaras fixed the reaction motor to its post and asked Tibor if he had mended the fuel tank.

'With a plug of resin,' Tibor said.

Pandaras's hands were shaking badly. He splashed arak over himself when he tried to fill the tank. The motor started on the third attempt, sputtered, spat a mass of bubbles. Then its inlet flooded with a solid thump, and the pirogue shot forward.

Pandaras looked back as he steered it in a wide arc towards the open river, saw Ayulf stagger to the veranda of the shanty. He carried something on his shoulder: the culverin. A tongue of flame burst from its throat. Ayulf fell backwards and the roof of the shanty caught fire.

The reaction motor ran out of fuel just as the sun began to free itself from the band of blue haze that marked where the Rim Mountains stood, far beyond the nearside shore of the Great River. When it sputtered to a stop, Tibor, kneeling in the bow of the pirogue, set to with the paddle.

Behind them, across several leagues of water, the mangroves of the farside shore made a ragged black line against the brightening sky. There was no sign that Ayulf had tried to follow them. Perhaps he had been too busy trying to save his shanty from the blaze caused by the misfire of the culverin.

'The women told me that they put something in his arak to make him sleep,' Tibor told Pandaras, 'but they knew that he would try to kill you when he woke and found you still alive, even though he was very afraid.'

Pandaras showed his teeth. His head and stomach still hurt, but he was no longer drunk. He said, 'Of course he was afraid. That's why he drank so much – because he was afraid, and because he was ashamed of his fear. I would have killed him if he tried anything, and he knew it. I've killed bigger men than him, and they wore armour and carried energy pistols.'

It had been only one man, the guard at the gate of the house of the rogue star-sailor. Pandaras had killed him by a trick and had been captured by the other guards almost immediately afterwards, but he was certain that he could kill again if he had to.

'Ayulf was afraid of me, not you, little master,' Tibor said placidly. 'But he knew that once you were dead I would have served him. He smeared poison in the bottom of your glass, the poison that fisher folk use to stun fish, but you poured away most of the arak he gave you, and that saved you.'

'Hah. You suggest that you are more valuable than me. But who is the master here, and who the slave?'

'I know my price, little master, because I was sold on the open market and Captain Lorquital paid well for me. But do you know yours?'

'It isn't measured in coin,' Pandaras said. 'And I think that you overestimate your value. What's the use of someone who can fix a reaction motor but forgets that it needs fuel?'

'I thought that we should leave quietly and quickly, and find fuel elsewhere.'

'And forgot my master's book and the money, too.'

'You were nearly killed when you went back, little master. Life is more important than things.'

'Easy to say if you've never owned anything. The book is important. Don't you remember how much time my master spent studying it? And we'll need the money soon enough.'

Tibor paddled silently for a while.

'Ayulf got what he deserved,' Pandaras said. 'Why do those women stay with him, do you think?'

'I understand that it is the custom of the fisher folk to offer up hostages to secure bargains between different families. And so they secured bargains with Ayulf, although I do not believe that he understood the obligations that entailed. The eldest of the women told me that she knew a great chief called Oncus. She recognised his fetish, and that is why she decided to save you.'

Pandaras touched the coypu-hair fetish, which he wore on his upper arm, over his shirt. It was loose there, although it had fitted snugly on his master's wrist. He said, 'I had forgotten the name of the old croaker who helped us when Prefect Corin tried to flush us out of the floating forest. What luck, eh?'

'Who can say what is luck, and what is the will of the Preservers?'

'That's easy. A man makes his own luck. Anything else is a gift, but no one should hope to build their lives on the gifts of others. My master was clever enough to leave the fetish behind so that I would know he had been taken alive, and I was clever enough to find it and to wear it. So it was by the luck I made from my master's forethought that we were saved.'

'Yet our lives are the gifts of the Preservers,' Tibor said solemnly. 'You are engaged on a holy task, little master. Perhaps you should behave accordingly.'

'A holy task?'

'Why, you seek your master, of course. Did you not tell me that he will raise up all the indigenous peoples? If that is true, may he not also redeem the sins of my own people, and those of all the races of hierodules?'

'We have to find him first,' Pandaras said, and touched the ceramic disc which hung inside his shirt. 'I fear for him.'

He had been badly weakened by the dose of poison, and was still suffering from stomach cramps. While Tibor drove the pirogue steadily towards the nearside shore, he sat in the stern and leafed through the book he had risked his life to save.

He knew that this was an old and valuable copy of the Puranas, and that some of its pictures had been changed when his master had visited a shrine. They were quite unlike any he had ever seen before, but because, like many of his people, he was a gifted storyteller, he was able to guess something of their narrative. One of the Ancients of Days had escaped from the others and had become mixed up in a Change War. Then her ship had found her, and she had been executed by the rest of its crew. He knew that there must be more to the story than that, for his master had studied long and hard in the book while the *Weazel* had sailed downriver, but he could not riddle it and at last put it away.

It took a day and a night to paddle the rest of the way to the near-side shore, a patchwork of marshy fields, dense green woods and little villages. Many of the villages stood a league or more from the shore, stranded there by the river's slow retreat. Pandaras carved a flute from a joint of bamboo and won his supper each night by playing a medley of tunes. He quickly discovered that those he had learned as a child and put away when he had grown older were most appreciated by the indigens. In that sense at least they were as children, but Pandaras thought that the children of the Shaped would be less trusting and less innocent than these simple folk.

The indigenous people of the shore were closely related to the husbandmen who lived in the ruins of the pleasure gardens on the roof of the Palace of the Memory of the People. They were not much taller than Pandaras but were very strong, with seamed skin the colour of freshly broken brick. Their stubby fingers were sometimes linked by loose webs of skin, and in one village the skin tones were darkened by greenish mottling, as if in the past they had had some congress with the fisher folk.

Each night Pandaras saved some of the food he was given and took it to Tibor, who stayed hidden outside the villages. After the incident with Ayulf, Pandaras trusted the indigens far less than they trusted him, and did not want anyone to see the hierodule and think that they could take him away. Sometimes he was also able to bring some palm wine, which could be used in the reaction motor; with this scanty fuel and Tibor's tireless paddling they could travel thirty leagues in a day.

It was a slow, lazy time. One day was much like the next, hot and sunny with quick fierce showers in the afternoon, for it was the rainy season. At last, a little over a decad after they had first reached the nearside shore (Pandaras made a notch in the hull of the pirogue each day, like a prisoner), they came to Ophir.

4

HOPE

The young warlord, Enobarbus, and the rogue apothecary, Dr Dismas, both wanted to use Yama's powers to end the war, but each of them wanted to end it for different reasons. Enobarbus, champion of the aspect of Angel and traitor to the army raised against the heretics by the Department of Indigenous Affairs, wanted to conquer the world in the name of his mistress and overthrow the stasis imposed in the name of the Preservers by Ys's vast civil service. After that, utopia would follow as naturally as summer followed the rise of the Eye of the Preservers. Everyone a suzerain and everyone living forever with the aid of old technologies that the heretics were busily reviving. Dr Dismas wanted an end to stasis too, but what he wanted after that was more complex. He was a hybrid of man and feral machine, an agent of the faction whose rebellion had, during the Age of Insurrection, wrecked half the world and destroyed many of the avatars left by the Preservers to guide and enlighten the ten thousand bloodlines of the Shaped. He wanted an end to the belief that the Preservers were gods, and a closer union between machines and men, but his motives remained opaque. Or rather, he gave so many different reasons that it seemed to Yama that he wanted only a glorious chaos, a soup of contingency, change for change's sake.

Despite their differences, Enobarbus and Dr Dismas agreed on one thing: Yama was the key to victory. Their quarrels ranged back and forth across his head like those of children squabbling over a toy.

Yama took little notice of them. He was increasingly preoccupied by the war within his own body. The thing which Dr Dismas had planted inside him at the beginning of his adventures was fully awake now, and its power was growing hour by hour, day by day. It was as if Yama's self was a lighted castle surrounded by a restless flood of darkness both malevolent and sentient. As it rose, level by level, it sent out filaments and tentacles, constantly probing for weaknesses. Yama felt that if he gave way to it for a moment, even in the dreams which possessed him in sleep (which were not truly dreams; nor was it truly sleep), then he would dissolve at once, like a flake of salt dropped in the Great River.

It was Yama's worst enemy and his most intimate companion. More a brother than Telmon; more a lover than Derev; a greater enemy than Prefect Corin or Dr Dismas. A secret sharer, a spectral reflection, a dark half: his Shadow.

Dr Dismas explained that it was growing an interpenetrating neural network in parallel to the web of neurons in Yama's brain – an exact duplicate, in fact, but on a much smaller scale, each pseudoneuron no more than a hundred molecules wide, each pseudoaxon a whisker the width of twelve carbon atoms. Yama did not really understand this; he did not understand much of the apothecary's gabble. But he knew that the Shadow had grown under his skin and was extending into the intimate cavern of his skull. His dreams were no longer his own. Most were kaleidoscopic visions of battlefields and cities under siege, but in one chilling reverie he saw a great, joyful crowd of people linking hands in a stately dance, and behind each of the dancers, aping every movement, was a malevolent starveling creature as thin as paper and as black as soot.

Yama knew that as the Shadow spread through his skull it had assumed control of his powers and was using them to subvert machines loyal to the cause of the Preservers, turning them against the army of the Department of Indigenous Affairs. He knew that it was speeding the tide of war towards Ys. The visions of battle were true visions of the Shadow's interventions in the war far upriver, leaking from its consciousness to his. He could not stop the Shadow taking control of his power over machines, but he learned that he could follow it out into the world as a wren might steal a ride on the back of a lammergeyer or a mite on a spider. Awake, Yama could no longer sense the presence of machines, much less control them, but in the grip of one of the deep trances that these days passed for sleep, riding the Shadow's consciousness far from his unconscious body, he was able to take over a machine and steal away, fleeing from the terrible visions of clashing blades of light, fountains of fire, screams of men and beasts.

Using the borrowed machine's deep radar, Yama could see the ancient dredgers in the deeps of the Great River, accompanied by schools of giant polyps which kept their ceramic carapaces clean and plucked tasty morsels from the silt they pushed towards the pipes which would carry it to the Rim Mountains. He could see the passages and great caverns beneath the skin of the world, the vast unfathomable machines which laboured there, and the great engines in the keelways. And he could see the world itself by light above and below that narrow band in the spectrum of electromagnetic radiation used by living creatures. See the forests of the Marsh of the Lost Waters as a crumpled landscape of white, reflected heat with beasts and men bright sparks moving within it; see the myriads of machines that tended the world as intense knots of electromagnetic energies; see the distant cloud of feral machines which hung several million leagues behind the orbit that Confluence traced around its sun. In this form, at least, the feral machine he had inadvertently called upon for help was no more than any of the others, indistinguishable in the dim cloud of overlapping signatures.

As below, so above. Yama could hear the faint roar of the universe's birth pang, the wailing ululation and popcorn crepitation of radio sources within the galaxy beneath the world's keel, the faint chirps of the halo stars. And hear too the song of the accretion disc around the Eye of the Preservers, the intense crackle of fusion in gravity-tied knots in the infalling gases, the fricative hiss of molecular hydrogen, the howl of tidally heated matter reaching its last end at the event horizon of the black hole at the centre of the disc, the great No from which nothing, not even the Preservers, who had willed their own incarceration, could escape until the universe's last end.

One night, Yama sensed something beyond the lines of the army of the Department of Indigenous Affairs. It was like a memory which would not take form, a melody he could not quite name. A far star that was fainter than any machine, yet which drew him as a weary traveller in a wide wasteland might at last glimpse the distant flicker of his own hearth and hurry homewards with a gladdened heart. But even as he flew towards it, the machine he had borrowed speeding above the sullen waves of the night-dark river, the Shadow stirred and woke, and Yama woke too.

(Far upriver, a machine suddenly found itself a few metres above the midway current of the Great River, falling down a gravithic geodesic towards Ophir. Braking so hard that its shell glowed red-hot with friction, it spun eccentrically on its axis – just as a dog might shake itself – remembered the task it was supposed to be executing, fixed the coordinates and sped off, dismayed and embarrassed.)

And on waking, Yama knew what the thing which had drawn him must be. He held the knowledge close, drawing strength from the hope it gave him, and made a vow. I will find it, he thought, and find if Pandaras is still alive. No, he must be. The disc will not work unless he is holding it. Not all is lost.

It was a frail hope. For even if he found Pandaras, what could he tell him? And if Pandaras found him, what could he do?

A frail hope, yes, but all the hope he had.

5

OPHIR

It had once been the most beautiful city on Confluence, its network of canals perfumed by water lilies and lined by palms and flowering trees, its houses white as salt with green gardens tumbling from their terraces, its main temple renowned for the wisdom of its avatar. Three bloodlines had lived there in prosperous harmony. It had been famous for its metalworkers, jewellers and weavers, and for the seminary where half the priests on the world were trained.

The war had transformed it utterly. The population had been swollen to ten times its original size by soldiers and their followers, and by refugees who crowded the streets and made their encampments in the parklands that encircled the city. Fliers hung at its upriver edge, some bigger than the carracks which disgorged a thousand soldiers at a time. The docks were clogged with ships; the quays piled with supplies. The park around the Great Temple had been turned into a barracks. Illicit stills flourished, supplying hundreds of fly-by-night bars. There were firefights between gangs dealing in drugs and prostitution and between the gangs and the civil guards who tried to contain them. Dead bodies lay unclaimed in the gutters of the busy streets, picked over by dholes, kit foxes and turkey vultures, or floated amongst the flowering lilies in the wide canals, attended by retinues of fish and green turtles. There were rumours of heretic cults infiltrating the city; soon after they arrived, Pandaras and Tibor saw a woman run into a café which a moment later exploded in a ball of orange flame from which two or three burning figures staggered to collapse on the pavement.

Day and night the streets were full of soldiers and those who fed off them: prostitutes of a hundred different bloodlines, hawkers, gamblers, grifters, gandy men, footpads, pickpockets, pikers, street preachers, and mountebanks who sold false blessings or fake charms, or shirts guaranteed to repel the weapons of the heretics. Streams of wagons, rickshaws and tok-toks, the motorised bicycles particular to Ophir, wound through crowded streets noisy with the cries of hawkers and hordes of beggars, music from bars and roadside food stalls, the bells and whistles and horns of the unceasing flow of traffic, the roar of illegal generators. The canals were clogged with slow-moving boats; at every intersection sampans were tied together to form impromptu water markets. At night, neon signs buzzed and flickered and cast rainbows over the white walls of the buildings, and the noise and the crowds seemed to double and redouble, a restless unsleeping flood of people.

Pandaras sold the reaction motor and arbalest on the first day of their arrival, but got very little for them: the city was glutted with weapons and equipment. He took up singing in the pavement cafés, performing two or three standard airs at each while Tibor collected a few small coins from the customers. When Tibor complained bitterly at this indignity, Pandaras pointed to the small girl who was moving from table to table and asking the customers if they wanted their boots cleaned, and then to her brothers, working by the door with cloths and polish, and said that there were worse ways of earning a living.

'I am a hierodule, little master,' Tibor said, with an air of wounded dignity. 'I am not some street urchin. This is beneath me.'

'You are mine to command. You said so yourself. Your people allow themselves to be made into slaves, as atonement for the sins of their ancestors, but by doing so you also make those around you slaves too, because they must take responsibility for you. How easy it must be to have others make all your decisions for you! How easy it is to be like a child! Well, now you must suffer the consequences. You cannot choose how you will serve. You must do as you are told. And you will do as I tell you, because we need money to buy passage downriver. Perhaps you do not understand that because you are a slave, and slaves have no need of money because their owners satisfy their every need. But we need money now, if we are to find my master. And because my bloodline burns brightly and briefly, I have no patience for the safe but slow way of doing things.'

'We must have overtaken the ship, little master,' Tibor said. 'It will catch up with us by and by and put in at the docks. Everything that goes downriver to the war stops at Ophir. We will find the *Weazel,* and all will be well. You will see. Our friends must think us dead, and they will be so very happy to see us again.'

'They are dead. Everyone but Phalerus was killed in an instant, and burned up into smoke in the next by a dreadful weapon of war. Phalerus survived a little while because he was further away from the centre of the fire, but it would have been better for him if he had died at once, like the others. They are dead and destroyed and the ship is destroyed. You have to understand that, Tibor. You must.'

'You could sell the book,' Tibor said, after a long silence.

Pandaras sighed. It was impossible to knock any sense into the hierodule's round, hairless head. 'It is not mine to sell. It is my master's. We will stay here until we have earned enough money to pay for our passage, and we will go on until we find him.'

The tiny spark in the disc had multiplied into patterns of dots and dashes of light that were different every time Pandaras looked at it. They were nearer to Yama now, he thought, but not yet close.

For the first few nights Pandaras and Tibor lived on the streets, washing and drinking at the public standpipes, sleeping on a roof amongst clattering windmill generators in a nest of bubblewrap and plastic foam packing bought from a scavenger. Everything in the city had its price. Weapons, armour and ammunition were cheap, but food and accommodation were ludicrously expensive, for this was a war economy.

Ophir was a long way from the war front in the fringe jungles of the Marsh of the Lost Waters, but on their third night in the city Pandaras and Tibor were woken by a faint continuous thunder and flashes of blue light far downriver. It must have woken the whole city: people stood on every roof, watching the fugitive flashes. Suddenly, a thread of white light split the black sky from top to bottom and for a moment it was everywhere as bright as day. The light winked out even as Pandaras raised his hands to shield his eyes, and several heartbeats later there was a long low rumble and the roof on which he and Tibor stood heaved like the deck of a ship. The palms that lined the street below doffed their heads, and all over the city bats and birds took wing.

When Pandaras had amassed enough money for a deposit, he rented a sleeping place in a house beside one of the canals. It was a subdivision of what had once been a graciously proportioned room, screened by paper stretched over bamboo frames, with barely enough space for a pair of raffia sleeping mats. Two families shared the space. One, of a quick, lithe bloodline, ran a food stall, and the smell of hot oil and steamed vegetables always hung heavy in the air. Tibor helped them out, at first chopping vegetables, then graduating to making the sweet shrimp sauce and flatbreads which were served with every dish. The other family, five generations from tiny hairless kit to toothless grandfather, lived on the income from three rickshaws. It was always noisy, for someone was always awake in one or other of the room's subdivisions, mending one of the rickshaws or cooking, squabbling or playing cards or listening to a cassette of prayers, and all around was the mingled sound of hundreds of other lives lived in public.

It was the life from which Pandaras had run, first becoming a pot boy, and then self-appointed squire to Yama. He was as restless as Tibor, wanted to move on as soon as possible. Amazingly, it was not possible to join the army here, or even become a cateran, as Yama had once wanted to do, although there were plenty of caterans roaming the city. Nor was it possible to hitch a ride downriver on the troop ships; he would have to bribe one of the crew, as did the sutlers, gamblers, whores, and other camp followers.

Busking barely covered his daily expenses, but Ophir was the kind of place where someone with sufficient wit and cunning could prosper, as long as no one killed him first. Two bravos had already tried to shake him down, ambushing him and Tibor one night outside the café where they had finished their final set and demanding all their money in return for a performing licence. Pandaras, who knew that showing any sign of weakness would mark him forever as prey, whipped out his poniard and cut one of the bravos on the arm and chased him away. Tibor grabbed the other around the neck and lifted him off the ground and gently took his butterfly knife and handed it to Pandaras, who flipped it open in front of the bravo's face and asked pleasantly why innocent entertainers should be worthy of the consideration of two fine brave gentlemen.

The man spat a long stream of phlegm. Like his friend, he was very tall and very thin, wrapped from top to toe in overlapping spirals of grey rags. The little skin that showed was granular and hard and bone-white. The joints of his stick-like arms and legs were swollen; his head was small and flat, like a plate set on a corded neck, with a triangular mouth and a pair of black, stalked eyes.

Pandaras wiped sticky phlegm from his face and put the blade of the butterfly knife against one of the man's eye-stalks. It shrank to a little bobble and the other eye bent around and stared anxiously at the blade. The man said, 'You wouldn't dare.'

Tibor said, 'I will let him go, little master. I am sure he will not bother us again after this mistake.'

'First he'll tell us who he works for.'

The man's triangular mouthparts flexed and he spat again, this time at Pandaras's feet. He said, 'You've made the mistake. I'm Pyr's. So are you and all street trash like you, except you don't know it.'

'This Pyr runs things, eh? And I thought that the Department of Indigenous Affairs had charge of the city.'

'You mean the army?' The man's mouthparts chattered with an approximation of laughter. 'The army looks towards the war, not the streets. We keep out of its way and it doesn't trouble us. Let me give you some advice. We're not like the army. We like things tidy. People who don't fit in with the way things are run are removed. You're handy with a blade, but maybe next time we come back with pistols.'

'I think I should speak with Pyr. Tell him that I have a great deal he might want to know.'

Pandaras signalled to Tibor, who released the man.

'If Pyr wants to speak with you, she'll send for you. Pray she doesn't, though.' The man adjusted his disarranged winding cloths, spat a third time, and stalked off.

Despite this threat, Pandaras and Tibor were not troubled again on their nightly rounds of the cafés, but Pandaras knew that sooner or later there would be a comeback. There always was. He just had to stay ahead of it, to think of what they might do and be ready, while he looked for some kind of angle that would earn him some quick, dirty cash. One of the sons of the family who ran the rickshaws, for instance, came and went at odd hours, always dressed in a sharply creased kilt and a clean white short-sleeved shirt. He had an arrogant air which humbled his parents and his grandfather. His eyes were masked by orange plastic wraparound shades, and a cigarette was always dangling from his lips. A gang member if ever there was one. The boy ignored or rebuffed Pandaras's attempts to start a conversation, and quickly and easily shook off his attempts to follow him through the crowded, noisy maze of alleys and passages behind the buildings which fronted the canal, but Pandaras was certain that he could find some way of making himself useful to the boy and his friends.

The young gangster's grandfather, Memoth, was a distinguished old man who spent his days at one of the major intersections of the city, pumping up the pneumatic tyres of rickshaws or tok-toks for a penny a time. It was hard work, and Pandaras massaged Memoth's aching shoulders with clove oil in the evenings and listened to the gossip the old man brought back from the rickshaw drivers, who were the eyes and ears of the city.

Memoth's family was of one of three bloodlines which had inhabited Ophir before the war. They were a spidery people with short bodies and long arms and legs, given to abrupt, jerky movements. Memoth's skull was bony, with a pronounced crest and a jutting shelf of a brow from beneath which his lively brown eyes peered. He wore only an oil-stained kilt and a belt hung with little tools. Like all his people, many of whom worked at the docks, assembling or repairing weapons, he was handy with machines. His coarse pelt was striped yellow and brown; his plaited mane was snow-white. That would have been a sign of his status in the days before the war, but now he had to humble himself before his arrogant gangster grandson and accept his charity.

Memoth had once owned several houses, but they had all been requisitioned by the army, and now his family made their living as best they could. But he was not bitter; indeed, he was the most patient and good-natured man that Pandaras had ever met. He told Pandaras stories about his bloodline before they had changed, how they had lived on a wide plain of tall grasses along the edge of the foothills of the Rim Mountains, the men hunting small game, the women gathering roots and fruit. At the end of each summer, when the Eye of the Preservers set for the last time, the wild grasses ripened and the women threshed the grain and ground it into coarse flour to make bread, and brewed a kind of beer from the husks.

'We worked only a few hours a day,' Memoth said. 'The rest of the time we sang or told stories, or made pictures on flat rocks or made patterns with the rocks themselves to please the Preservers. It was thirty generations ago, but we still remember those halcyon days before we changed and moved to the city. And now, now that we work all the hours we are awake and still go hungry, we realise how rich we once were, and wonder how we have profited by change.'

'You are not free unless you are changed,' Pandaras said.

His master would have had a better answer, he thought. Yama was always thinking about these matters.

It did not satisfy Memoth. He said, 'Free, yes. Free to starve. Free to become the slaves of other men.'

'We say in Ys that people like us are the strength of the city.'

'So I have heard,' Memoth said. 'But I think the ordinary people of Ys are as oppressed as we are here. The Preservers lay a heavy burden upon us. Perhaps men like us are unworthy of their gifts.'

'We must always hope that our children may do better,' Pandaras said, but Memoth did not answer this. Few in the city believed this fundamental creed. In their despair, they had forgotten the charity of the Preservers.

As usual, they were sitting outside the door of the partitioned room, Memoth on a plastic chair, Pandaras at his feet. On the other side of the canal, which was choked with the dark green leaves of water hyacinth, women of the same bloodline as the bravos who had ambushed Yama and Tibor were washing clothes, squatting by the water's edge and gossiping as they beat dirt from wet cloth with smooth stones. Someone was playing a cassette of prayers very loudly in one of the buildings that loomed above, and someone else was shouting angrily. It had just rained, and the webs of electrical cables that sagged high above the canal crackled and spat as water dripped from them. All this reminded Pandaras of his childhood home in Ys, except that it was hotter and more humid.

A flier passed slowly overhead, its underside bristling with gun emplacements. The whole quarter throbbed with the noise of its motors; the air seemed to grow colder in its huge shadow. Everyone stopped to watch it. When it was gone, Memoth stirred and said that the war was getting nearer, and it was going badly.

Pandaras sipped from his bowl of mint tea, waiting for the old man to expand on his theme. He had heard much about the war since he had arrived in Ophir. It had always been distant, in Ys. People mostly did not trouble to think about it. They accepted the news disseminated by licensed storytellers, who sang songs and told tales of great heroism and tremendous victories to any who bothered to listen. But here the war was almost next door and everyone had their own story to tell. And most of the stories were about a sudden surge of advances by the heretics, of the army's weapons failing mysteriously, of its machines falling from the sky. There was talk of a new general or leader amongst the rabble of the heretics. There was talk of sudden, harrowing defeats, of bitter retreats.

Memoth said that you could tell that something was wrong because almost no one followed the soldiers to war now. The gamblers and whores knew that there was no profit to be had from defeat.

'My people should leave the city,' he said. 'We should go back to our high plains, back to the old life. But we are human now, and we have lost the facility to be like animals and let only our instincts guide us. We are each of us alone in our own heads.'

It grieved Pandaras to hear this despairing plaint, for he liked the old man. He asked, 'What does your grandson say?'

Memoth did not reply at once. He drank his tea, straining the last of it with his big front teeth and spitting out bits of twig. At last, he said, 'He is not of my family. Not any more. Now he is Pyr's.'

Pandaras wanted to know more, but Memoth would not say anything else about Pyr or his grandson. No one who worked in the cafés wanted to talk about her either, warding off Pandaras's questions with fingers touched to throat or eyes or forehead, telling him that he should not trouble himself with people like her, who caused only harm to people like him. Pandaras constructed grandiose and impossibly complicated plans about swindling or duping the gangster leader, and knew that they were no more than dreams. He was growing desperate, because after two decads in the city he had saved hardly any money. Money here was like air, difficult to catch or hold, but necessary to sustain every moment of life.

And then the soldiers came for Tibor.

It was near dawn. Pandaras was woken by a boot in his ribs. The tiny sleeping space was full of men in half-armour. He came up fighting and was lifted and flung aside. In another part of the subdivided room, two women were screaming at different pitches and a man's angry protest was suddenly cut short. One of the soldiers threw down a bit of paper, kicked Pandaras hard, and followed his companions.

Tibor was gone. Pandaras ran outside, saw a flat-bottomed boat with a rear-mounted fan motor roar away in the grey half-light. Its wake washed over the sides of the canal and lifted and dropped the sampans clustered at the intersection. Someone fired a carbine into the air; then the boat slewed around a bend and was gone.

Pandaras gave chase but had to stop, winded, after half a league. He walked back, holding his side. His ribs hurt badly and everything he owned, including Yama's precious book, was in the room.

The paper was a note of requisition for ... *a certain hierodule, known by the name of Tibor.* A voucher for two hundred and fifty units of army scrip was stapled to it. Pandaras tore the requisition and the voucher to pieces and threw them at the children who had crept to the doorway to see what he was doing. Army scrip was almost worthless. Two hundred and fifty units would not even buy a cigarette.

His ribs still hurt: sharp stabbing pains if he breathed too deeply. He tore a strip of cloth from the tail of his worn shirt and bound it around his chest. Memoth was sitting by the door, and called to Pandaras when he went outside.

'They will have taken your friend out of the city,' the old man said. 'They will have taken him to the war. There is talk of a big battle and many casualties. A hierodule would be of much use there. The hierodules of our temple were taken long ago to tend the lazarets.'

'There is a lazaret here,' Pandaras said stupidly.

'That's for civilians, and most of it is closed down because there are no supplies to be had by the normal channels. They don't bring wounded soldiers to the city. It would be bad for the morale of those who have just arrived and have yet to fight. Besides, many of the wounded would die from the hardships of the journey. No, they are treated in floating lazarets close to the front line. That is where your friend will have been taken. Are you going too, Pandaras?'

'I have an obligation,' Pandaras said, and saw, without surprise, Memoth's grandson coming along the path by the canal, his smile wide beneath his wraparound orange shades. The two bravos who had ambushed Pandaras and Tibor at the café were behind him.

Pandaras went with them. He had no choice. They allowed him to keep his poniard and Yama's book, but reclaimed the butterfly knife and took the small amount of money he had managed to save. He felt a curious calm. In a way, it was a relief that what he had feared for so long had finally happened, but he knew that he would have to use all his wits to survive it.

As they passed through the spice market he said, 'You told them about my friend, didn't you? You got rid of him because you are scared of him. If you have any sense, you should be scared of me, too. And so should Pyr. She's the one who sent for me, isn't she? Luckily for her, luckily for you, I want to have a word with her.'

'You are the lucky one. She thinks you could be useful to us. Otherwise—'

The boy drew a finger across his throat. He had a cocky walk, and people made way for him. His crisp white shirt glimmered in the green shade beneath the tamarisk trees, where the spice merchants had set out their tables.

'She shouldn't have told the soldiers about my friend,' Pandaras said. 'I'll want recompense for the inconvenience it will cause me.'

'I reckon your friend is better off with the soldiers,' the boy said. 'You were taking advantage of him. Getting extra money when you busked in the cafés, because people think it's lucky to give money to a hierodule. Many of the other jongleurs, they were jealous. Maybe one of them told the soldiers about him, eh? Also, I hear someone is looking for you. Maybe he told the soldiers, to get rid of your protection. Send your bill to him.'

'You had better tell me who it is.' Pandaras had the faint hope that it might be Yama.

'He talks too much,' one of the bravos said. It was the one Pandaras had wounded. 'Let me clip his tongue.'

'You'll leave him alone,' the boy said.

'How is your arm?' Pandaras said.

The bravo made a hissing sound and touched the butt of the pistol tucked in the grey rags wound around his lanky body.

'It is one of the bureaucrats who is looking for you. Not the army, but one of those who run the army. Tall, with a staff. Black hair, and a stripe of white, here,' the boy said, and touched the left side of his face.

Pandaras knew at once who it must be. Every hair on his head rose, prickling. He said, 'I believed him dead, but he is more resourceful than I thought. I must talk with Pyr at once. We are all in great danger.'

'First you prove yourself,' the boy said. 'Then, maybe you see her. She is very busy. She has much business.'

For three days Pandaras was locked in a small, hot room on the top floor of a tall house overlooking one of the city's squares. Crowds and traffic noise all day and all night; the smell of burnt alcohol mingling with the scent of the flowering vine that twisted around the balcony outside the window. A transformer on a pole beneath the balcony humming and hissing. Water dripping from a broken pipe into a plastic bowl in the centre of the room.

A gecko kept him company, clinging motionless to one or another of the walls, only a faint pulse in its throat showing that it was alive, before suddenly making a swift dart after a roach or click beetle. There was no furniture in the room. Pandaras slept on the balcony and spent most of his waking hours looking at the pictures in the copy of the Puranas, or watching the traffic that swarmed around the stands of giant bamboos in the centre of the square. He knew that he must not lose his nerve. He must keep his resolve.

The disc was still displaying its shifting pattern of sparks.

The boy and the two bravos visited Pandaras every morning and evening. They brought food from the fry stall at the corner, rice and shrimp and green chillies in a paper bag whose edges were translucent with oil. The boy squatted by the window and watched as Pandaras ate, humming to himself and cleaning his broad nails with a pocketknife; the bravos lurked by the door, talking to themselves in a dialect of stuttering clicks. The boy had a percussion pistol tucked into the back of the waistband of his creased trousers, with his shirt-tail out to cover it, and the bravos had pistols, too.

The boy's name was Azoth. Although he was older than Pandaras, his bloodline was long-lived and he was still a child, with the calculating cruelty of one who has never been truly hurt, who believes that he will never die, or that death is nothing. He never took off his orange plastic shades and would not answer any of Pandaras's questions, but instead talked about the war for ten minutes or half an hour before, without warning, standing up and leaving, followed by the bravos.

On the evening of the third day Pandaras was hustled downstairs by the two bravos and forced to stand at the edge of the road. Passers-by made wide diversions around them; traffic roared past a handsbreadth in front of them. A rickshaw stood in the shade of the giant bamboos in the centre of the square. Pandaras saw someone inside it lean forward and say something to the driver, who nodded and stood up on his pedals. As the rickshaw pulled away, Pandaras got another glimpse of its passenger. A woman in a red silk dress, much smaller than him, with the large eyes of a nocturnal bloodline and long, lustrous black hair.

On the way back up the stairs he asked the boy, Azoth, if the woman he had seen was Pyr.

'Mind your questions,' one of the bravos said.

'I didn't ask you. I know you don't know anything,' Pandaras said.

'Pyr is interested in you,' Azoth said.

'Is she scared to speak with me?'

'She does not know if you are worth the trouble,' Azoth said. He put his hand on the pistol hidden beneath his shirt-tail when he entered the room, and crossed to the window and leaned at it and looked down at the bustling street below.

'Something is troubling you,' Pandaras said.

'We look after our own,' Azoth said, without turning around. 'Prove yourself, and you are ours, and we are yours.'

'He's still looking for me, isn't he? Be careful. He is very dangerous.'

'Perhaps we should give you to him. Would you like that?'

'Then he does not offer money. Otherwise I think that you would have done that already.'

'He makes threats. We don't like that. Pyr will find him, by and by, and deal with him.' Azoth turned and stared rudely at Pandaras. 'Who are you?'

'A loyal servant.'

'A servant who owned a hierodule?'

'I am no ordinary servant.'

'Who is your master? Where is he?'

'I have lost him.'

Azoth smiled. 'Don't worry. Masters are easy to find for the likes of you.'

Later, as the boy was leaving, Pandaras said, 'Tell Pyr I know many things.'

The bravos made their chattering laughter. Azoth said, 'Don't make yourself out to be more than you are, and you'll do fine.'

Pandaras thought about that as he sat on the narrow balcony and watched the street below. Perhaps he was no more than he had been before he had met Yama, a mere pot boy with a talent for telling stories and getting into trouble. Perhaps he had caught himself in one of his stories. And yet he had survived adventures that no ordinary person would ever have to face; even if he had begun his adventures as an ordinary man, one of the unremarked swarm of his bloodline, then he was ordinary no more, for extraordinary things had happened to him. And now he was being hunted by Prefect Corin, who must be more than a man to have survived the destruction of his ship by the monstrous polyps that Yama had called up from the depths of the river. Pandaras shivered, remembering how one of the polyps had torn poor Pantin apart with a contemptuous flick of its tentacles. He touched the fetish and then the disc and promised his master that he would not fail.

'I have fallen into trouble, but I will find my way out,' he whispered. 'And I will find you and rescue you from whatever harm you have fallen into. My life is short, and worth little to anyone but me, but I swear on it now.'

Pandaras could not sleep for thinking of all he had to do and of what Azoth might want of him. He leafed through the copy of the Puranas, and found that the more he studied the pictures the more they seemed to contain. They were saturated with meaning, and now he was beginning to fully understand the story they told.

The Ancient of Days who had escaped her ship had fled to an obscure city near the place where the Great River fell over the edge of the world. The bloodline which lived there was unchanged, and she had taken control of them, and mastered the city's Commissioner and its Archivist, too. She had learned something in the shrines by the fall of the Great River and had quickened the minuscule machines in the brains of some of the inhabitants of the city. They had been reborn as individuals. They had been changed. And then the ship of the Ancients of Days had arrived in the middle of the civil war between changed and unchanged, having travelled the length of the Great River from its landfall at Ys. She had tried to destroy her crewmates but they had killed her. Yet her ideas had survived. The Archivist of Sensch had escaped from the ship of the Ancients of Days. He had been the first of the heretics who even now strove to overturn the word of the Preservers.

Pandaras began to feel that perhaps the heretics might be right, or might at least have guessed the truth about some things. The world had turned away from the path ordained by the Preservers. It had become static and stratified, weighed down by ritual and custom. No one was free to choose their own destiny.

He shuddered, a single quick convulsion like a sneeze – his mother would have said that a ghoul had been sniffing around his grave. The book was valuable to his master, but it was dangerous. It had twisted his thoughts. He must not look in it again, he thought, but knew that it would be hard not to: he hungered for its vivid stories and the strange thoughts they engendered.

It was long after midnight. The Eye of the Preservers was beginning to set over the roofs and treetops of the city. Its red swirl was dimmed by the sky's neon flush, but the pupil at its centre was quite distinct, a small, circular void swept clean by the black hole into which the Preservers had vanished and from which they would not emerge until the end of time. Could the heretics dare take the war there, if they conquered the world that the Preservers had left behind?

Pandaras shuddered again. 'I will not fail you, master,' he whispered.

The next morning, Azoth and the two bravos did not bring Pandaras's breakfast. Instead, Azoth said, 'Come with us. You can bring your pig-sticker, but leave the book here.'

Pandaras asked if they were going to take him to Pyr, and the bravos made their chattering laugh.

'Perhaps soon,' Azoth said. 'First you must prove yourself.'

Azoth hailed a rickshaw and they rode a long way through the brawling streets. The bravos fixed their stalk-eyed stares on Pandaras as he asked Azoth many questions about the places they passed. They got off in a narrow street somewhere near the docks. The masts of a crowd of ships pricked the blue sky beyond the flat roofs of the godowns. As they walked past a chandler's, Azoth pinched Pandaras's arm and told him to take notice, because that was the place he would firebomb.

'Why?'

'Because you'll do what you're told,' one of the bravos said.

'Because Pyr wants it,' Azoth said, with a shrug.

A small boy was hawking fuel alcohol at the dusty intersection at the end of the street. Azoth threw money at him and told him to go away. The boy snatched up the coins, knuckled his forehead, and said he would like to see the show.

'Fill two of your bottles, then,' Azoth said. 'One word to anyone and I'll cut out your eyes and tongue. Understand? Why are you smiling?'

'Because nothing exciting ever happens here,' the boy said. His hands were trembling, and he splashed purple alcohol on the pavement as he filled the bottles.

One of the bravos took out a piece of cloth and tore it into long thin strips which he twisted up and stuck in the necks of the bottles. 'You tip the bottle to wet the wick,' Azoth told Pandaras. 'Light the very end and keep the bottle upright when you throw it. Throw the bottles hard and make sure they hit something that will smash them. Make sure you throw them through the door, too.'

'I know how it's done,' Pandaras said. He was not scared, but there was a hollowness in his belly. It was the feeling he always had in the quiet moments before something violent happened. He picked up the bottles. The rags in their necks stank sharply of sugar alcohol.

One of the bravos had a lighter. He waved its little flame at Pandaras, who stepped back in alarm, the bottles and their sopping wicks clutched to his chest.

'Stop that,' Azoth said sharply, and held out his hand. The bravo gave him the lighter; he flicked it twice to show how the flame was struck and put it in Pandaras's shirt pocket. 'Do it now,' he said, 'and come straight back.'

Although it was early in the morning, the street was already busy. Pandaras felt that he was being watched by a thousand pairs of eyes as he walked to the chandler's, the heavy bottles clutched to his chest and the stink of alcohol burning in his nostrils. The shutters of the shop were only half-raised; someone was moving about inside, whistling cheerfully. His heart beating quickly and lightly, Pandaras set down the bottles and lit the wick of one of them. He put the lighter away and picked up the bottle and threw it at the pavement outside the chandler's door. As glass smashed and flames bloomed, he snatched up the other bottle and ran.

Not towards Azoth and the bravos, but in the other direction. People made way for him. He ran in front of a cart (the nilgai pulling it reared in its traces, raking the air with its clawed forelegs), dodged a soldier who grabbed at him, and ran into a crooked passage between two godowns, turning three corners before stopping, still clutching the bottle to his chest and listening to his hammering pulse and rasping breath.

Shrill whistles and an insistent bell somewhere in the distance, and beyond these bright noises the city's constant roar. Pandaras still had not got his breath back when he heard footsteps approaching. He ducked low and glanced around the corner, ducked back and lit the wick of the bottle, fearful that the snick of the lighter would give him away, and stepped out.

The two bravos stopped and looked at each other. Azoth was not with them. Their mouthparts clattered together in brief laughter; then they saw what Pandaras held. One raised his pistol and there was a flash and it flew from his hands – a misfire, Pandaras thought, and lobbed the flaming bottle as hard as he could. It smashed at the feet of the bravos and they were the centre of a sudden tall blossom of blue fire. They shrieked and twisted in the flames and although people presently crept down the passage and poured water on them, they were already dead, and Pandaras was far away.

*

It took Pandaras the rest of the day to cross the city and reach the building where he had been kept prisoner. He kept up a monologue all the way, telling himself that he was a fool to go back because Azoth would certainly be waiting there, that Tibor had been right and they should have left the city days and days ago. Better to live on grubs and leaves than be in the thrall of some petty gangster.

It was the city which had caught him, not Pyr. There were plenty like Pyr in Ophir; he could have fallen in with any of them once he had allowed himself to be seduced by the city's song. How well he knew that song, and what it promised! He had been born with it in his blood. Azoth had been right. Pandaras had thought that he could be more than he was. He had thought that he could win a fortune from the city and rescue his master in style, and it had nearly cost him all he had. But he could not afford to lose the book. It was not his. Not his to sell, not his to lose.

When he reached the square, he stood for a long time amongst the giant bamboos, watching the tall building where he had been kept prisoner. The window of his room was dark, but that signified nothing. He was very hungry – he had tried to snatch a hand of red bananas from a stall, but had been chased off – and very nervous. He walked around the block and came back to the square from another direction, did it again and thought he had located two people who were watching the building, one loitering by the food stall on the corner, the other at a roadside shrine, alternately wafting smoke from an incense cone and staring at the swarming passers-by.

In the end, Pandaras went into the building next door and climbed its staircase to the roof, coming out amongst a small forest of clattering wind generators. An old man, drunk or drugged, lay on his back, waving his arms and legs in the air like a beetle. Two more, wrapped in winding grey rags, turned their stalked eyes towards Pandaras, but they were only drunkards, sharing a plastic blister of an oily white liquor.

Pandaras marked his spot and took a short run and jumped the gap between the two buildings. He walked around the edge of its roof until he spied the balcony of his room, then took out his poniard and sawed at a sagging spot in the asphalted roof, exposing a lathe-and-plaster ceiling below.

There were wind generators on this roof, too. He pried the heavy battery from one and threw it into the hole he had made and jumped after it, yelling like a demoniac and holding his poniard high above his head.

He landed in a sliding pile of rubble and dust, and fell over. There were three men in the room, but Pandaras saw only two of them at first. One was dead, lying on his back in the middle of the room with not a mark on him. The other was Azoth. He sat beneath the window, the copy of the Puranas open in his lap, faint light from a picture shining eerily under his narrow chin. His orange wraparound shades had fallen off; he stared at the book in his lap with unblinking eyes and did not move when Pandaras dared to take a step towards him.

'He was like that when I arrived,' someone said.

Pandaras recognised the man's soft voice at once. He had been interrogated by him after the fall of the Department of Vaticination, in the Palace of the Memory of the People. Without turning around, he said, 'And the other?'

'Drowned, I fear, in the bowl of water conveniently left in the middle of the floor. How easy death is to find. Throw down your blade, boy, or death will find you in the next instant.'

Pandaras dropped his poniard at his feet. He said, 'Death finds some more easily than others. All the waters of the Great River were not enough to drown you.'

'Where is he?'

It took a great effort not to turn around. 'Not here. Downriver, I think.'

'Hmm. You will tell me all you know. But not here, not now. I do not have time to kill all the gangsters in this city. Close the book, boy. We will bring it with us.'

Pandaras said, 'What happened to Azoth?'

'Is that his name? He needs it no longer. The book is dangerous, boy. It has been changed. It takes the soul of any unwary enough to look into it.'

'It did not take mine,' Pandaras said, taking the book from Azoth's unresisting fingers. The boy continued to stare at his empty hands. A slick of drool glistened on the brown pelt of his chin.

'Perhaps it already has taken you. We shall see.' Prefect Corin stepped out of the shadows by the door, the white stripe on the left side of his face catching the light from the open book when Pandaras thrust it towards him. He said, 'That will not affect me. I believe that you have a token of the man I am seeking.'

Pandaras could not move. The book slipped from his numbed fingers and fell at his feet. Every hair on his body rose, prickling; the muscles of his arms and legs were painfully locked.

Prefect Corin said, 'You have a little talent for music, like many of your kind, so you might find it amusing to know that I hold you with a tightly focused beam of sound. It is a single note pitched higher than you or I can hear, but your muscles hear it.'

He crossed the room in three strides, reached inside Pandaras's shirt and lifted out the disc. With an abrupt motion he pulled the doubled thong over Pandaras's head. He stared at the disc for a long moment, then pressed it against Pandaras's forehead.

Pandaras felt it burning there. Prefect Corin exhaled, slipped the thong back over Pandaras's head, and extended his arm towards Azoth. There was a flash of blue light: Azoth's head exploded in pink mist. The boy's body pitched forward, throwing a long spurt of rich red blood from its neck stump, kicked out twice, and lay still.

'Yamamanama has learned much,' Prefect Corin said. 'Or he is well advised. The disc has attuned itself to him and he has attuned it to you. You can find him by using it, or he can find you. No one else. Very well, then.'

Suddenly, Pandaras could move again. He fell to his hands and knees and bent his head and vomited.

Prefect Corin said, 'Stand up, boy. We should leave before the gang boss sends more of her people, and we have far to go, you and I.'

6

THE SHADOW

Dr Dismas was waiting beside Yama's bed when he woke, and almost at once Agnitus and Enobarbus came into the room, followed by a phalanx of officers and guards. The warlord had news of another great victory, but Yama was too full of joy to pay much attention at first. He had at last found Pandaras, and had rescued him from danger and lost him, all in a few hectic minutes. Although the boy seemed to have fallen into some kind of trouble, Yama knew that he was searching for him, for he wore Oncus's fetish on his arm.

'There are great advances all across the front,' Enobarbus was saying. 'In only a few days Yamamanama has gained more territory than we have won in the past year.'

Yama wondered if Pandaras knew that he had guided the machine which had knocked the gun from the hand of the ruffian in the alley. He had lost contact with the machine moments later, when the Shadow had withdrawn its control of a myriad machines along the warfront, but it did not matter. He had found Pandaras once, and he could find him again.

'It is not Yamamanama you should thank,' Dr Dismas told Enobarbus.

'Could this be done without him?'

'That's not the point, my dear Enobarbus.'

The two men stood on either side of Yama's disordered bed. Yama could not move, but suddenly he had a dizzy vision of his paralysed body from above: the Shadow had possessed one of the little machines which spun in the air, and was feeding him its optical output.

A pentad of officers with red capes falling around their battle armour stood behind Enobarbus. One was writing on a slate. Its green and white light flickered in flowing patterns tugged here and there by his stylus. Guards flanked the officers, clad from head to toe in black plastic like man-shaped beetles, their carbines held at port arms. They were there to defend their commander in the event that Yama – or the Shadow – went mad and tried to destroy him. Enobarbus's physician, black-cloaked, grey-maned Agnitus, stood just at the edge of the field of view, as patient as a carrion crow. There were servants in the room, too, young men and women in tunics and tabards of gorgeous watered silks or in fantastic uniforms of red leather kilts, golden cuirasses inlaid with intricate designs of black mother-of-pearl and plumed helmets that doubled their height, armed with ornately decorated gisarmes, pole-axes and sarissas held grounded before them. The servants and soldiers were all indigens. Some were frog-jawed fisher folk, others lanky, rail-thin herders. There was a single sturdy forest pygmy with glossy black skin that shone as if oiled. All were Dr Dismas's experimental subjects. Metal collars were embedded in their necks and their shaven scalps were marred by angry red lacerations crudely stitched with black thread. One had had the top of his skull sliced off and replaced with a disc of transparent plastic: cubes and pyramids and spheres nestled amongst what was left of his brain. He shook slightly and constantly; drool slicked his chin and stained the front of his red silk blouson.

And someone or something stood amongst the officers, guards and servants, insubstantial, shifting, barely glimpsed, the shadow of a shadow. It filled Yama with dread. He could not look directly at it, but he guessed that it was a new torment of the Shadow. Day by day it was growing stronger; day by day he was growing weaker. But for now his hope was renewed. If he could find Pandaras again, and tell the boy where he was being held prisoner, he could at last begin to plan his escape.

Yama was paralysed by an injection Dr Dismas had given him several hours before. Now, at an unseen signal, three of the servants stepped forward and lifted him from the bed and carried him to a canopied throne, propping him up amongst satin cushions. Dr Dismas straightened Yama's bare arm, stroked a vein in the crook of his elbow until it plumped up, and with a swift underhand motion stabbed the hypodermic needle home. Yama blacked out for a moment, and then was back in every part of his body, dizzy and cramped and sick to his stomach.

One of the servants held Yama's head while he vomited into a plastic bowl. There was little but mucus to come up. Dr Dismas took a square of linen from another servant and wiped the slick of chyme from Yama's chin as deftly and gently as a mother tending her child. Yama suffered this silently, and allowed Agnitus to probe him with hard fingers.

'As usual, he is febrile and dehydrated. Otherwise his muscle tone is good and his vital signs are stable.' Agnitus looked at Dr Dismas. 'You use him hard, Doctor. At this rate he may not last the course.'

Dr Dismas met the physician's lambent gaze. 'Much is asked of him. I do my best.'

Enobarbus stepped up beside Agnitus. The warlord looked rumpled and tired, yet he was grinning broadly and his eyes were alive in his ruined face as he bent towards Yama.

'Know that I am very pleased with you,' he said. 'You have done great things. I have just flown back from an advance point beyond the Marsh of the Lost Waters. The positions which our enemies have held for a year are beginning to crumble beneath our new assaults. Their machines turn against them and they are much weakened because of it. Soon we will mount a push that will take us within sight of Ophir. I promise that I will march through her gates in less than twenty days.'

'You are talking to the wrong one,' Dr Dismas said impatiently. 'We won't need him much longer. Not once the child of my paramour is fully integrated.'

Yama looked past the warlord and his physician, trying to see the thing which stood behind them, amongst the officers and servants and guards. A stain in the air in the shape of a man, gradually brightening, coming into focus. A familiar, patient, careworn face with a fine pelt of grey hair, long-fingered hands folded over each other beneath the chin. It was the eidolon of a dead man. Yama's beloved father, the Aedile of Aeolis.

Yama tried to turn away, but he was paralysed once more, this time by the Shadow's will. The eidolon spoke. Its words crawled across Yama's brain like sparks over a dying fire.

I am well pleased with you, my son. Do not listen to the doctor. I will not let you fade away. A part of you will always be with me.

The eidolon winked out and, horribly, Yama felt his tongue and jaw work. Something said in a hoarse, strangled voice, 'I need him still, Doctor. Even when construction of the pseudocortex is complete there will be much to learn. There is much he does not yet know about himself.'

Dr Dismas wiped Yama's cracked lips with a sponge, squeezed a trickle of water into his mouth. 'This is a frail and stubborn vessel, but I will look after it for you. I will guard it with my life.'

The eidolon of Yama's dead father came back, as solid and real as anything else in the room. *He thinks that he is our father*, it said. *He will pay for his mistake, by and by. He has wasted much time with his experiments and his foolish plots. He could have brought you to me years ago.*

Yama found that he could move again. He said, 'Yes, you would have preferred to take me when I did not know who I was and what I could do because you are not as powerful as you would like me to believe.'

'Ah, Yamamanama,' Dr Dismas said, standing back from the bed. 'You are still there.'

I grow, day by day. And day by day you shrink.

'I will not go away.'

'Oh no, dear Child of the River,' Dr Dismas said. 'You are mine.'

There is much we can do together, Child of the River. Why resist? We will be the ruler of this world, just as a beginning. The battles I win now will bring an end to a war ten thousand years old, but they are as nothing compared with those I will have to fight in the space inside the shrines after I have defeated the forces loyal to the Preservers. After that victory, she who is now our ally will try to destroy me. She will not succeed, of course, and if you help me you will learn much about the world and all the worlds beyond. She has her own plans for Confluence and soon I will possess them just as I possess you. Ask Dr Dismas about the machinery of the keelways. Ask him about the heart of the world. The eidolon smiled, a sharp, cunning, rapacious grin that was not at all like the gentle smile of Yama's father. It said, *Ask him why the Great River shrinks.*

After the Aedile had died, Yama had found amongst his papers pages of notes about the fall of the level of the Great River. The Aedile had made measurements every decad for many years, and calculated the likely date of the beginning of the river's failure. Most believed that it had begun when the Ancients of Days had meddled with the space inside the shrines and deleted the avatars which had survived the wars of the Age of Insurrection, but the Aedile's calculations showed that it had begun much later, in the year that Yama had been found by old Constable Thaw, a baby lying on the breast of a dead woman in a white boat cast adrift on the Great River.

Yama could not tell if the Shadow really knew what linked these two events, or if it was merely tormenting him with its stolen knowledge, but it had touched upon his greatest fear: that he might not be the saviour of the world, as so many claimed, but might instead be its unwitting nemesis. He reached out and gripped Dr Dismas's claw-like left hand and said, 'There is much we can do together, Doctor. I think that together we can save the world, but first we must stop the war.'

'Ah, but we will, Yamamanama. We will.' Dr Dismas was smiling as he tried and failed to free his hand from Yama's grip. He looked at Agnitus and said, 'Help me, damn you.'

Help me, the eidolon said. *Ask him the question. It will cause much trouble, I promise you. I am on your side, Yamamanama. How could I not be? I depend upon you for my life and for my powers. In one sense I am becoming you. But soon things will change, and you will depend upon me. We will have to reach an agreement before then, or you will dwindle to no more than a remnant. Would you work with me as an equal part of a gestalt, or would you be worse than any of the good doctor's experimental subjects? I could bury you so deep that all the light and the glory of the world would be no more than a mute spark, as dim and distant as the furthest star. I could subject you to torments worse than even the good doctor can imagine, without cease. Choose.*

'He is in your care,' Agnitus told Dr Dismas, 'as you delight in telling us.'

'You tell us that you control him,' Enobarbus said. 'Sometimes I wonder how true it is. We must talk about it.'

'It is the child of my paramour that controls him,' Dr Dismas said. He was still struggling to free himself from Yama's grip. 'It still grows.'

An age ago, Yama and Telmon had liked to listen to Sergeant Rhodean's stories about the battles at the midpoint of the world. This had been in the gymnasium of the peel-house, and the old soldier had used the point of a javelin to scratch the positions and lines of attacking and opposing armies in the packed red clay of the floor. He had taught Yama and Telmon that the best commanders overcame their enemies by wisdom as much as by force. It was better to subdue an enemy without fighting, he said: joining battle with them was a last resort. For that reason, knowledge of the enemy was paramount. Not just the character and strength of the opposing army, but the morale and training of its ordinary men and its officers, the severity of punishments inflicted on miscreants, the state of its supplies, the nature of the terrain it occupied, the disposition of conquered peoples towards the occupiers, and the present and predicted weather. The best policy was to understand the enemy's strategy and then to seek to undermine it, to always grasp the initiative and to be flexible, to attack where the enemy felt itself to be invulnerable and thus to bring about a decisive change. A weaker force could defeat a strong enemy, Sergeant Rhodean told his pupils, if it seized the opportunity and struck with precision and overwhelming momentum.

Yama knew that he must draw on the lessons of the kindly old soldier. He was a prisoner in the centre of the empire of the heretics, surrounded by the servants and machines of Dr Dismas and the soldiers of Enobarbus, and his only hope was that a former pot boy could come to his rescue. Worse, he was a prisoner in his own body, struggling against the growing power of the Shadow. But now he saw that by allying himself with his most immediate threat he could exploit the divisions of those who held him prisoner.

'The keelways,' he said. 'Tell me the truth about how the world works, Doctor.'

You are mine! The eidolon tipped back its head and howled, twisting the mild face of Yama's father into something coarse and lupine. Its eyes burned with a feral red light, as if a balefire had been kindled inside its skull. The soldiers and servants around it took no notice, of course.

'The boy is fevered,' Dr Dismas said, and at last managed to wrench himself away from Yama's grip. He kneaded the stiff claw of his left hand with his right, as if comforting an injured pet, and smiled at Enobarbus and Agnitus. 'I have him, gentlemen. I assure you.'

'I belong to no one,' Yama said. 'Tell me about the keelways, Doctor. Tell me about the machines down there. Is it possible that I can control them? Is that what you want of me, once the war is over?'

'I myself want nothing of you, Yamamanama,' Dr Dismas said. 'I have brought you here as a gift to Enobarbus, a weapon to bring a swift end to the war. Ask him what he wants. Do not ask me.'

'Yet somehow he has an idea that you do want something, Dismas,' Enobarbus said. 'We must talk of this later.'

He turned and swept out of the room, his guards on either side and the pentad of officers following behind in a swirl of red capes. The eidolon moved through them like smoke and stood at Agnitus's shoulder.

I am proud of you, my child, it said. *We have already done much together, you and I, and with your help we will do much more.*

Yama stood, and limped across the room to the great blister of the window, struggling to compose his thoughts and to conceal his great excitement. If the Shadow wanted his help, then it was not as strong as it claimed. Or perhaps he was stronger, if only he knew it.

Behind him, Agnitus asked Dr Dismas, 'How great are his powers, Dismas?'

The apothecary was fitting another cigarette into his carved-bone holder and did not reply until he had lit it; Yama smelled the clove-scented smoke. 'He'll have been told about the keelways by the child of my paramour. Who knows what they talk about inside the skull they presently have in common? It is of no moment, Agnitus, because soon enough the boy will be redundant. Remember to tell your master that.'

A black speck floated far off in the blue sky, high above the patchwork woods of the city of trees, far beyond the archipelagos of floating gardens.

Yama decided to risk twisting the truth and said, 'I have been in the keelways, Doctor. It was after I escaped from you the first time. I fetched up in the Silent Quarter and entered the keelways after I got away from the poor fools you employed. I learned much, then.'

The speck was a bird, perhaps, a lammergeyer which had wandered far from the slopes of the Rim Mountains. Yama watched it with growing apprehension.

Dr Dismas said dismissively, 'The keelways are hardly a secret.'

Agnitus said, 'You did not answer my question, Dismas.'

'The records are vague, a single sura in the Puranas. Yamamanama's bloodline built the world under instruction from the Preservers. Why should they not know all about it? But the boy is ignorant of his bloodline's store of knowledge because he was brought up by a disgraced civil servant in a wretched backwater, with hardly any experience of the world. And so we must proceed by experiment. Of course, if your master is frightened that Yamamanama's powers may eventually grow beyond his attempts to control them, I can leave and take the boy elsewhere. There are many who would be glad of his services.'

'I think not,' Agnitus said.

'That Enobarbus is not frightened? Or that I cannot leave? Take care, Agnitus,' Dr Dismas said sharply. 'I have powerful allies.'

It was not a bird. It was too big to be a bird. It came on steadily. Yama could not look away from it. Although he told himself that it was only an illusion, his skin crawled with horror.

Agnitus said, 'Your allies fight amongst each other even as they try to conquer the world. That was why they were defeated in the wars of the Age of Insurrection, and that is why they cannot prevail without our help. That is why you are here, Dismas. Do not forget that.'

'I'll hear that from Enobarbus, not his creature.'

Agnitus's laugh was a low, rumbling growl. He said, 'You're a fool, Dismas. You think everyone should be owned by someone else because you are yourself something's creature.'

Outside the great bubble of the window, the thing beat the air with wide leathery wings. It was triple-headed, and each head was set on a long, flexible neck, and their faces were triangulated upon Yama. They were brute-like distortions of people he had loved and had lost: his father, the Aedile of Aeolis; his brother, Telmon, killed in the war against the heretics; and Tamora, the cateran who had been killed by Dr Dismas on the stair outside the shrine cut into the edge of the world. He bore their gaze, although it was very hard. Their voices crept into his brain.

Nothing ever dies, Yamamanama. I can bring them back. Help me, and I will let them live again.

'I will serve only on my own terms.'

Behind him, Dr Dismas said sharply, 'It's a last vestige, Agnitus. It will soon pass, and he will be gone forever.'

Foolish creature! We do not need him, Yamamanama, or the broken and insane thing which changed him. Together, we can make something new in the world.

'Together,' Yama said.

Oh yes. Together. Together, we will change everything.

The creature's human heads opened their mouths wide and blew gouts of flame that washed over the eye of the window. Yama stood his ground. It was only a foolish gesture, a sign of the Shadow's vanity. And vanity was a weakness.

The flames faded. The creature was gone. A voice whispered inside Yama's skull. *Soon.*

7

THE IRONCLADS

'You will go around it,' Prefect Corin told the captain of the flying platform.

'I will not,' the captain said.

He hung from a branch of the tree by an arm and a leg and glared unblinkingly at Prefect Corin. His eyes were large and black and perfectly round. He was smaller than Pandaras, and naked except for a tool belt. His fine silvery fur was touched with black at the tips of his ears and fingers and toes. Two decads of his crew hung from or stood on branches in the other trees at the edge of the little wood, watching silently.

The captain said, 'My orders I already have. You know them well, and you know that you cannot change them. This we have already discussed.'

Prefect Corin spoke softly; Pandaras could hardly hear him over the throbbing of the flier's motors. He said, 'You know who I am and what I can do.'

The captain's smile displayed needle-sharp white teeth. 'We know that this platform you can't fly. And beyond the pass, Prefect, no one flies. Not while heretics hold high ground and the river.'

Prefect Corin laid a hand on Pandaras's shoulder and said, 'Show it to them.'

Reluctantly, Pandaras drew out the ceramic disc and held it up. Little flecks and dashes of light filled it from edge to edge, scuttling around each other like busy emmets. The captain glanced at it, then shrugged.

'The device shows that the man I seek is not here,' Prefect Corin said. The light of the disc set stars in the centres of his liquid black eyes. 'He is further downriver, amongst the heretics.'

'From us the heretics took our city,' the captain said. 'All we have left is this platform. We try to go through, and from the tops of hills heretics fire down on us. Sweep us off the platform like bugs off a leaf. And the river's worse; out there they have many gun platforms floating. No, Prefect. As far as we can we have taken you. Enough talk. To berthing we must attend.'

The captain swung away into the dense green canopy. His crew turned as one and followed, disappearing in a flurry of shaken foliage.

Columns of soldiers were assembling at the debarkation points on either side of the flying platform's wide black wedge. The big fan motors at its stern roared and roared as it began to turn into the wind. To port, ranges of mountains covered in dense forest saddled away, their peaks shining in the last light of the sun above valleys full of shadows. To starboard, the Great River gleamed like pewter. It was only a decad of leagues wide here, its deep, swift flow pinched between mountains on either shore. An advance force of heretics was attempting to take the city which had once dominated this narrows.

Pandaras and Prefect Corin had spent a day and a night and most of the next day on the flying platform, travelling steadily towards the front line. Like all big lifting bodies, it warped the gravity field of the world so that it floated on the wind, and motors had been added so that it could be manoeuvred. It had once supported a floating garden, but the little wood at the point of the platform where the crew lived and worked was all that remained; the rest of the surface was webbed with a complex of ropes and struts to which cargo or living quarters for passengers could be anchored.

Like the troops, Prefect Corin and Pandaras slept in the open and ate at one of the campfires, although Pandaras had little appetite and hardly slept at all, fearing that if he did the platform might tilt and he would wake tumbling through the air. The Prefect did not seem to sleep either. He sat cross-legged all night, with his hands turned up on his knees, watching the Eye of the Preservers as it rose high into the black sky before reversing its course and setting at the downriver vanishing point of the world, and all the next day he stood at the point of the platform, like a perched hawk waiting for a glimpse of its prey. Now and then, Pandaras tried to strike up a conversation, but he was not so much rebuffed as ignored.

None of the troops or their officers would go near them, and Pandaras had little idea of where they were being taken. Except that it was downriver, towards the war, and towards his master. That was some comfort, at least.

The note of the motors deepened: the platform was making headway against the breeze as it moved towards the shore. Prefect Corin plucked his staff from the mossy ground and walked into the darkness beneath the trees. The little machine stung Pandaras's neck and he trotted at Prefect Corin's heels. Wind whipped them as they came out of the shelter of the wood, and Prefect Corin put two fingers to the brim of his black hat. A huge baobab tree stood at the point of the platform, webbed with cables and hung with little platforms. The crew, a single family unit, was swarming everywhere, chattering in a high, rapid patois.

The foothills of the mountains came down to the edge of the river. The city stretched along the narrow ribbon of flat land at their margin. It was in ruins. Not a single building was intact, although the grid of the streets was still visible. The stumps of several huge towers stood at the shore like a cluster of melted candles. The air swarmed with glittering clouds of tiny machines that blew back and forth above the ruined city, twisting around each other but never quite meeting. Pandaras saw that there were many raw craters and burnt places in the forested hills; thousands of trees had been blown down along one high ridge.

The flying platform was manoeuvring above the encampment of the defending army, townships of tents and domes knitted together by roads that crawled with traffic and marching columns of soldiers. Hundreds of men worked on huge machines folded into pits and surrounded by cranes and scaffold towers.

As the platform neared the ruined city, edging towards a series of flat-topped pylons, bright sparks shot up from the slopes of the foothills as if in greeting, and puffs of white smoke bloomed in the darkening sky, seemingly as innocent as daisies. A rapid popping started up somewhere beneath the platform and streams of fiery flecks curved in to the source of the display: gunners strapped in blisters on the underside were replying to the heretic bombardment.

Even as the platform was being tied down, the troops began to swarm down hundreds of ropes. Equipment was lowered in slings and nets. A floating disc swooped out of the dusk and came to rest a handspan beyond the point of the platform's prow. Perfect Corin took Pandaras by the arm and they stepped onto the floating disc, which immediately dropped towards the ground. Pandaras thought that he knew now how Prefect Corin had escaped when the giant polyps had sunk his ship.

Because the floating disc warped gravity, there was no sensation of falling. Rather, it was as if the world tilted about the disc's fixed point and jumped forward to embrace them. Before Pandaras could begin to feel dizzy, they were down.

Prefect Corin strode off at once. Pandaras had no choice but to follow him: the pain caused by the little machine fastened to his neck increased in proportion to its distance from its master. Prefect Corin walked quickly. Pandaras had to half-trot, half-run to keep up with him.

'This is a great shambles,' he said breathlessly, dodging to one side as two columns of men in black armour jogged past. They were following the traffic that streamed along a wide muddy road. Crackling arc lights made islands of harsh white glare in the gathering darkness. There was noise everywhere, the braying of draught animals and the shouts of men, the roar of motors and the constant thunder of distant explosions, and snatches of wild music carried on the wind.

'Where have you brought me, dominie? Is this part of your plan? Will we become caterans?'

'We will not be here long,' Prefect Corin said, and stepped into the dazzle of the headlights of an oncoming steam wagon and raised his staff.

The wagon slewed to a stop, belching a huge cloud of black smoke. Prefect Corin swung up to the bench by the driver and said something in his ear. Pandaras hastily clambered onto the loadbed as the wagon started up again, and was thrown amongst loosely stacked rolls of landscape cloth as it swerved away from the road and bounced across churned ground towards the battlefront.

The city had been built from land coral. Diseased patches had thrown up spires and brain-like hummocks, and had smothered one of the tower stumps in a lattice of red threads, but most of the city was dead, bone-white and broken by bombardment. Streets were bordered with heaps of rubble. Trenches had been dug everywhere, lit by dabs of foxfire or strings of red or green electric lights. Soldiers squatted around heat boxes or campfires; a few scouts stood on platforms behind sandbags, scanning the enemy lines, which were only two leagues distant.

When the wagon stopped Pandaras jumped down and trotted after Prefect Corin in near-darkness. They skirted a trio of overlapping craters filled with muddy water and climbed to the top of a low ridge. A series of bunkers had been dug into the reverse side of the slope. A man in a long black leather coat came out of a curtained doorway and greeted the

Prefect. He was the commander of the defensive forces, a lean, nervous man of Prefect Corin's bloodline. His name was Menas. A decad of little machines hovered around him. The largest shed a fitful light by which Menas consulted a timepiece as large as an onion and studded with tiny dials and flecks of red and green light.

'You are just in time, brother,' Menas said, and put away his timepiece and embraced Prefect Corin. 'The duel is about to begin. Listen! Do you hear the thunder?'

Pandaras had thought that it was distant artillery fire, but when he looked at where Menas pointed he saw heavy thunderclouds rolling across the dark sky. Lightning strobed between the clouds and the edge of the river.

'They manipulate the weather to set the stage for the nightly duel,' Menas said. 'So far it is stalemate, for by the grace of the Preservers our mages have built an ironclad which is the equal of their champion. Come with me. Come on! We do not have much time!'

A pentad of staff officers went with them, each followed by his own flock of little machines. Menas was filled with so much energy that he could not keep still or follow the thread of any conversation for more than a minute; he kept breaking off to run over to this or that group of soldiers, to ask how they were and where they were from and if they were ready to fight. It was clear that the soldiers loved him. All of them cheered his approach and offered him libations of beer and wine.

'We will show them this time, boys,' Menas shouted. 'We will push them back into the river!' He whirled around and ran back up the slope to where Prefect Corin waited. 'They are in good heart,' he said breathlessly. 'We have the best men, the bravest fighters.'

'I see no fighting here,' Prefect Corin said coldly.

'Soon enough,' Menas said, and once again took his complicated timepiece from his coat pocket and held it up to the light shed by one of the machines which hung above his head. 'We satisfy their need for drama, but it is a matter of precise timing.' He put away the timepiece and added more soberly, 'Some day they will decide to move forward, and we will not be able to stop them.'

Prefect Corin looked at Menas and said, 'Perhaps you have been too close to the heretics for too long, brother.'

'This is not Ys,' Menas said. 'This is the war. The real war. There are no lies here, no stories to comfort the general population. I tell my soldiers nothing but the truth. The heretic forces have grown stronger over the years, and in the last handful of days they have grown very bold indeed. I hear that things go badly in the marshes. I hear that our machines are failing there and I believe that the heretics could take this city whenever they wish, but instead they play a game with us. We can hold our present position as long as we cooperate with them. We must strive to match them. If not, there are horrors . . .'

His voice had dropped to a whisper. Pandaras shuddered, realising that the man's hectic energy barely concealed his terror. His eyes were rimmed with red, and his hands trembled; he thrust them into the pockets of his leather overcoat and leaned closer to Prefect Corin and whispered, 'They bring back the dead.'

Prefect Corin eyed Menas with distaste. He said, 'We must cross their lines. The captain of the flying platform refused me. I hope that you will not.'

Menas shrugged. 'We send in scouts all the time. Sometimes they come back. Usually turned. They pass all the tests we can devise and then, a few days later, they walk into a crowded bunker and burst into flame.'

Pandaras remembered the explosion in the café moments after the young woman had run into it.

Prefect Corin said, 'It is not the first time I have done this.'

'Things have changed. They turn our machines against us somehow. The mages cannot explain it, but their new devices seem to be resistant to heretic trickery. At least, for the time being.'

Prefect Corin nodded. 'It is because things have changed that I must cross the lines.'

'There will be a scouting party going out soon, I expect. One of my staff can advise you.' Menas looked at Pandaras. 'Is this boy going with you? Who is he? Is he your servant?'

'He will lead me to my prize.'

'I have my own reasons,' Pandaras said, and dodged away when Prefect Corin struck at him with his staff. 'I am a seeker after truth, like my master!'

The machine on his neck stung him hard and he cried out and fell down. Two of the staff officers laughed. Pandaras picked himself up and cursed their ancestry all the way back to the slimes from which they had been mistakenly raised by the Preservers. The machine stung him again, forcing him to run after Prefect Corin and Menas, who were walking towards a glow in the distance.

Pandaras was astonished to see that it was a shrine, a big disc standing on its edge at an intersection of two broad streets. But perhaps it was not astonishing after all, for shrines were only partly of this world, and were immune to energies that would evaporate ordinary matter. Perhaps this place had once been the site of a temple which now lay in unrecognisable ruin on every side, with only its heart left intact.

Soldiers had gathered in front of the shrine, and the glow which beat from its disc made their faces shine and polished their prickly black resin corselets. Pandaras approached it reluctantly, remembering the woman in white who had appeared inside the shrine of the Temple of the Black Well. But as he followed Prefect Corin through the ranks of soldiers, he realised that this shrine was a fake, an enlarged version of the disc of cheap half-silvered glass which his mother had kept on a high shelf in their room. She had lit a candle behind it on holy days so that light moved within it like an echo of those avatars which, before the heretics had swept them away, had haunted certain shrines in the city. A similar trick was being played here, although the source of light was far brighter than a mere candle, and it was somehow bent and split so that circles of primary colours continually expanded from the brilliant white point at the centre and seemed to ripple out into the darkening air.

Pandaras looked away, for he had the dizzy feeling that he might fall into the light and never escape. No doubt his master would have said that this was how the Preservers had felt as they had begun their infinite fall into the Eye, and would have constructed some keen analogy between the conditions required for prayer and the Preservers' state of grace, but the play of light simply made Pandaras nauseous.

'A little invention of the mages,' Menas told Prefect Corin boastfully. 'They call it an ipseorama. You do not yet have them in Ys, but the time will come soon enough. It induces a specific state in the nervous systems of men, similar to the rapture induced by the presence of the avatars. It calms and empties the mind and prepares it for the immanence of the Preservers.'

Pandaras shaded his eyes and saw that a pentad of priests was gathered to one side of the shrine. They wore robes of shaggy pelts and were crowned with high, pointed hats. One was casting incense into a brazier of glowing coals; the others shook their hands above their heads as they prayed.

Prefect Corin told Menas in his dry, forthright manner, 'At best this silly conjuration is foolishness; at worst it is heresy, pure and simple.'

'It is a matter of regulating prayer,' Menas said. The light of the ipseorama flickered over his rapt face and turned each of his machines into a little star. 'Regulation is important. Just as men marching in step across a bridge can find the right harmonic to shiver it to pieces, so ten thousand prayers, properly focused and synchronised, can blaze in the minds of the Preservers. How can they refuse such a plea?'

'No man should be forced to pray; such prayers are worthless.' Prefect Corin raised his staff. For a moment Pandaras thought that he would stride forward and smash the false shrine, but he merely grounded it again and said, 'This is a dangerous experiment, Menas, and you will gain nothing from it.'

Menas did not seem to have heard the Prefect. 'Regulation of prayer is as important as regulation of firepower. By calling upon the grace of the Preservers we have survived here for more than a hundred days.' He cocked his head and drew out his timepiece again. 'Listen! Ah, listen!'

The brassy sound of trumpets drifted across from the enemy lines, the noise doubling and redoubling in horrendous discords. Pandaras pressed his hands over his ears.

'Sometimes they focus the sound!' Menas shouted. 'It can burst a man like an overripe fruit!' He signalled to one of the staff officers as the noise died away and told him, 'They are two hundred-twenty-eight seconds early tonight. Make a note. It may signify.'

All around, the soldiers bent in prayer as one of the priests began to declaim a praise song. Pandaras found himself mumbling the responses with the rest of the congregation. *Now in the moment of our death is the moment of our rebirth into eternal life.* He was very scared, convinced that his last hour was at hand, angry that he had thrown away all that he had been entrusted with, that he had so badly failed his master. How could he ever have thought that he could find Yama in the middle of this madness?

The priests began to move through the ranks of kneeling soldiers, sprinkling them with rose-water from brass censers they whirled around themselves on long chains, like indigen hunters whirling bolas around their heads before letting fly at their target.

Menas set off again, shouting that there was little time. The party climbed a slope of rubble, leaning against a strengthening wind. The first fat drops of rain flew through the air, hard as pistol shot. Menas bounded to the top of the slope and pointed. 'There! The duel of the ironclads begins!'

Two leagues off, something was moving through the dark forest behind the enemy lines. Its passage, marked by a wave of toppling trees, was fitfully caught in overlapping searchlight beams. At first Pandaras thought that it must be a herd of megatheres, but then the machine reared up and swayed forward, doubling its height. As it came out of the forest, the focus of decads of lights, Pandaras saw that its sinuous body was supported by six cantilevered legs and counterbalanced by a long spiked tail, like a snake carried by a scorpion. Smaller machines whirled around it, an agitated cloud of white sparks blowing back and forth like a flock of burning birds. Something glittered for a moment at the edge of Pandaras's vision and he dashed a hand at it with no more thought than he would give a fly, watching with rapt amazement as the ironclad lumbered on.

Dense squalls of rain drove across the ruins, striking with a sudden fury and obscuring the monstrous machine. Pandaras was soaked in an instant, and sought shelter behind a stub of stone. As he crouched there, cold and miserable and scared, he felt a warmth spreading across his chest. The disc was glowing so brightly that it shone through the worn weave of his ragged shirt. He closed his fingers around it to hide its light and whispered with sudden wild hope, 'Save me, master. If ever you loved me, come and save me now.'

Prefect Corin and Menas were facing into the storm. The Prefect clasped the rim of his hat with one hand and gripped his staff with the other. His cloak blew straight out behind him. The terrible noise of the trumpets began again and fireworks shot up – real fireworks, bursting in white flowers beneath the low, racing clouds. Lights shone out, brilliant threads of scarlet and green that struck across the wasteland of the city and glittered on the ironclad's hide.

Something flashed in front of Pandaras's face again. It was a little machine no bigger than a beetle, with a body of articulated cubes and delicate mica vanes which beat in a blur of golden light. It hovered for a moment, then darted forward. Pandaras slapped at the sudden pain at the side of his neck – and with amazement found that the ward Prefect Corin had fastened there was gone.

The tiny machine flew up and described a circle around Pandaras's head. He was astonished and afraid. Every hair of his pelt was trying to stand away from its fellows. The disc burned inside his clenched fist.

'Master,' he whispered. 'Master, it's you, isn't it? Why didn't you come before? Why did you abandon me?'

The machine's golden glow brightened for a moment. Then it flicked its vanes and was gone.

Menas whirled around as fireworks rose from his own lines, and yelled into the face of one of the staff officers who crouched behind him. 'There is no response from the third quarter!'

The man plucked one of his machines from the air and said, 'I will signal—'

Menas clapped his hands together. Rain had plastered his black pelt to his skull. He looked ready to kill everyone around him, Pandaras thought. Not because he was angry, but because he was scared and desperate. He had put so much faith in his rituals that now they ruled him completely. He shouted over the howl of wind and rattle of rain, 'Never mind! Together or not at all! Get over there, find the officer responsible and execute him and two of his maniple chosen at random. By the black blood of the Preservers, I will have order here! Why are you waiting, man? Time is all we have!'

The officer saluted and disappeared into rainy dark. Menas wiped rain from the pelt of his face, took a deep breath, and told Prefect Corin, 'We must have order here. Order and regulation.'

'They have made you a puppet,' Prefect Corin said.

'It is a dance.' Menas lowered his voice and said, 'A precisely choreographed dance on the edge of a razor blade.'

Prefect Corin made no reply. Menas glanced at his timepiece and turned back to watch the advance of the heretics' monstrous machine. 'Where is our fanfare, Golas?'

One of the staff officers grabbed a machine from the air and stuck it in his ear, then shook out a sheet of plastic: lines of script raced across it, glowing green like the river fire which sometimes burned in the water around the floating docks of Ys. He said in a high, trembling voice, 'They are enabling now. Start-up sequence in five, four, three, two, one—'

Tinny trumpets squealed discords in the distance and something the size of a small hill began to move through the squalls of rain. The heretics' ironclad doubled its pace, loping forward as eagerly as a hound scenting its prey and lashing its spiky tail from side to side. Its footsteps sounded like thunder. The stones beneath Pandaras's rump trembled.

The second ironclad was squat and armoured like a turtle, and pounded along on a hundred stumpy legs. Things like flies danced in the air above it – no, they were men riding floating discs. They slipped sideways and vanished into the darkness as the ironclads closed the distance between themselves.

They met like two mountains colliding. The heretics' scorpion-snake sidestepped the turtle's rush and lashed it with its armoured tail. The tremendous blow slewed the turtle half-around. It stood its ground when struck a second time, and fans of metal unfolded along the edges of its shell. Everything seemed to happen in slow motion.

'The vanes are tipped with diamond,' Menas told Prefect Corin. 'They vibrate, and will cut the enemy's legs from beneath it. Watch.'

'I have seen enough,' Prefect Corin said, and extended his arm.

For a moment, a thread of light split the dark air above the ruined town. It touched the heretics' ironclad and a ball of flame blossomed, doubling and redoubling in size. The machine broke in two. The upper part toppled forward, writhing as it fell, and smashed down across the broad back of the turtle. The ground shook and there was a noise like the hinge of the world slamming shut. Heat washed across the ruins as if a furnace door had been opened, blowing rain aside.

Then darkness. A rush of cold air swept in and the rain came back with redoubled fury. The searchlights had gone out; the last of the fireworks burst and their sparks fell and faded. And then, raggedly at first, but steadily growing, gunfire started along the fronts of the opposing armies.

Menas screamed in fury, turning to one officer after another, shouting that they must kill the traitor. He meant Prefect Corin, who held something like a polished pebble in his upturned hand. It was an energy pistol: a real one, an old one, a hundred times more powerful than the hot-light pistols made in the Age of Insurrection.

The Prefect put the pistol away, said softly, 'I have ended it,' and made an abrupt gesture.

The machines around Menas and his officers dropped from the air.

'Go now,' Prefect Corin said. 'You are done here.'

The officers walked away without a word. Menas chased after them, the wings of his black leather overcoat flapping around him, then ran back and started hurling handfuls of mud at Prefect Corin, screaming incoherently.

Prefect Corin ignored him. He bent over Pandaras and said, 'Follow me,' and walked off down the hill towards the burning machines. Menas had fallen to his knees and turned his face up to the rain.

'I'm sorry, master,' Pandaras said, and ran after Prefect Corin. He did not want to find a way through the battlefield on his own.

Prefect Corin walked steadily down the middle of what had once been a wide avenue. Pandaras scampered along close behind him, as if his shadow was some kind of protection. White threads flicked out from the heretics' lines and fire blossomed wherever they touched. Things moved to and fro behind flaring sources of light – things like giant insects, all jointed legs and tiny bodies. A random shell hit one and its body shattered in a flare of greasy light and then threw out a second explosion that for a moment lit the entire battlefield and turned every falling raindrop into a diamond.

Chains of little bomblets walked back and forth across the ruins; Pandaras threw himself flat when one whistled down close by and blew a fountain of earth and land-coral slivers into the air, but Prefect Corin merely kneeled, with his hand holding the brim of his hat, then got up and walked on.

Pandaras said, 'Where are we going?'

'Through their lines.'

'You meant this to happen!'

'The confusion will help us.'

'Menas will lose the city.'

'We seek a greater prize, boy.'

Prefect Corin cut to the left, and Pandaras followed him up a slope of rubble where in its dying throes a mass of coral had thrown up a glade of smooth white spikes twice Pandaras's height, like a parade of soldiers frozen forever, or the pieces of a game of chess abandoned halfway through. Lights flickered and flared all around, from the pinpoint flashes of rifles and carbines to the glare of energy weapons and the brief burning flowers of mortar and bomblet explosions. Soldiers were advancing through the ruins towards the heretic positions. Phalanxes of myrmidons marched in perfect relentless formation, not even hesitating when mortar fire blew holes in their ranks. The officers who controlled them swooped overhead on floating discs. Towards the rear, armoured vehicles rumbled forward in a line a league long. Amidst the thunder of explosions came the sound of trumpets, a slow drumbeat, and the screams of men and beasts.

Pandaras's fear grew as he watched Prefect Corin scanning the battlefield with what appeared to be perfect self-control, satisfied by the carnage and confusion that he had caused with a single shot. And then Pandaras saw something which gave him a small measure of hope. High above, in the distance, a small golden spark hung beneath the racing rain clouds.

'Come to me, master,' Pandaras whispered. 'Save me.'

But the spark did not move. Perhaps it was afraid that Prefect Corin would knock it out of the air if it came too close.

Prefect Corin pointed with his staff at some weakness in the heretics' line, then saw that Pandaras was not paying attention. He came over and squatted down and said, almost kindly, 'We will walk straight through this. We count for nothing in the battle, and so we will be safe. Do you understand me?'

'I know that you are mad.'

'No. All this around us is madness, certainly. And Menas is mad, too – he has to be mad to be able to function at all – but I am quite sane. If you wish to survive, you must follow me.'

'If we wait here, then the heretics will come to us.'

'It is not the heretics we are seeking.' Prefect Corin's hand suddenly shot out and gripped the side of Pandaras's neck. 'He was here. Do not deny it. I know that he was here because he has taken away the ward.'

Pandaras shook his head a fraction. He wanted to look up, to appeal to that golden spark, but to do so would be to betray his master. Instead he stared straight into Prefect Corin's black eyes as the man's grip tightened on his neck.

'You will tell me. By the Preservers you will tell me or I will squeeze out your miserable life . . .' Prefect Corin had lifted his other hand above his head. Now he lowered it, and let go of Pandaras's neck. 'I know that he was here. You could not have removed the ward by yourself. Think hard about whether you want to survive this, boy. If you tell me how Yamamanama removed the ward it might be possible. We both want the same thing. We both want to rescue him.'

Pandaras rubbed his bruised neck. He said, 'I believe that we have different ideas about my master's fate.'

Prefect Corin drew a length of cord from his tunic, tied one loop around Pandaras's wrist and another around his own, and stood up, jerking hard on the cord so that Pandaras was forced to rise too.

'There are threads of plastic woven into the cord,' Prefect Corin said. 'They can dull the keenest blade, and they have a certain low intelligence. Try to tamper with the knot and it will tighten its grip, and by and by cut off your hand. For better or worse we are joined hand to hand, fate to fate. Let nothing put us asunder.'

The cord hung between them was no longer than the Prefect's arm. It would have to be enough. Pandaras turned right when the Prefect turned left, threw himself around a smooth spike of land coral so that the cord was stretched across it, and shouted into the rainy dark. 'Now, master! If you have ever loved me! Now!'

The spike shuddered and Pandaras fell backwards. He picked himself up at once. The cord hung from his wrist. It had been cut in half. Something with a dying golden glow was buried in a splintered crater in the land coral. Prefect Corin was bent over, his right hand pressed to his left eye. Blood ran down his cheek and dripped from the point of his jaw.

Pandaras took to his heels. He heard Prefect Corin shouting behind him, but did not look back. He turned right and left at random through the maze of spikes, always choosing the narrowest path. The land coral had spread through the rubble downslope, forming a maze of arches and tunnels and caves. Pandaras scrambled through a narrowing funnel of rough stone, splashed through a bubble half full of stinking water, slid down a chute as slick as soap, and landed breathlessly at the edge of a road.

Distant thunders shook the earth; flashes lit the underbellies of the sagging clouds. A big machine covered in spines skittered by in the distance. Whips of light flicked from its tiny head and raised pillars of fire and smoke wherever they touched. Pandaras picked himself up and ran on. He did not doubt that Prefect Corin would do everything in his power to find him.

There was a slow and steady drumbeat ahead, the crack and whir and whistle of rifle pellets and arbalest bolts all around. Suddenly soldiers were running down the road towards Pandaras. He raised his hands above his head, feeling as broad and wide as a house. But the soldiers were running full tilt in retreat, running straight past him. One, his dirty face narrow as a knife blade, turned and yelled, 'The dead! The dead!' and then they were gone.

Pandaras stopped. He was at a crossroads. Rubble slumped at its four corners. Rain poured down out of a black sky, intermittently lit by white and red and green threads of light. The slow, muffled drumbeat was coming closer. He could not tell where it was, and chose a direction at random and ran. Prefect Corin had taken his poniard: he missed it like a lost arm. The Prefect had the copy of the Puranas, too. All Pandaras had left was the fetish which the leader of the fisher folk had given Yama, the ceramic disc, and his life.

Something flashed overhead and lit the long street ahead. Pandaras stopped, heartsick.

Far down the street, a column of naked men was marching stiffly in time to the slow, steady beat of a drum. Most were horribly mutilated. Silvery spikes jutted from the tops of their skulls. One was headless, and the spike jutted from his breastbone instead.

It was a maniple of the dead, come back to fight their living comrades.

A sudden blade of fire blew a land-coral formation to fiery ruin to the left flank of the column. Some brave gunner was trying to find the range. A handful of the naked dead fell and were trampled by their unheeding companions. Pandaras scrambled over the crest of a slope and tumbled into a sandbagged pit where two soldiers stared at him in horror. One swung the bell-like muzzle of his balister towards Pandaras, and then a wave of earth and fire tore the world away.

8
IN DREAMS

As always, waking was the worst time. An escape from the horrors of dreams which were neither true dreams nor truly his into the reality of captivity, the wait for the prick of Dr Dismas's needle and the antidote to the drug which paralysed his body.

This time he woke not from nightmares but from a reverie woven from memories of the first of his adventures. For a happy moment, he thought that he was safe in the tower at the edge of the City of the Dead, deep in the foothills of the Rim Mountains. He had been brought there so that the curators of the City of the Dead, Osric and Beatrice, could tend his wounds. He had been very sick then, but he was even sicker now. He woke, expecting to see the hunting scene painted on the wooden ceiling of his little room, but found that he could not open his eyes. With a sharp pang of despair he remembered where he was. But then he remembered what he had done and felt his happiness well up again.

The Shadow was talking with Enobarbus. Yama had grown used to the way it carelessly used his body and he did not pay any attention to the long list of the atrocities it was describing in gloating detail. That was not important. The battlegrounds along the river were no more than nightmares. The struggle for control of his own body was more immediate. From now on, he must be constantly alert, always ready to resist the Shadow's advances. For the first time, he began to think that he might be able to escape.

Yama had ceded much to the Shadow while concentrating on the search for Pandaras, but had at last found the boy for the second time, on a battlefield at the far edge of the war, the prisoner of Yama's old enemy Prefect Corin, who had somehow survived the destruction of his ship. Yama had rescued Pandaras again, even though it had meant destroying the machine he had been using, and he was certain that the boy had guessed who had helped him, for he had called to him by name. Yama had tried to kill or at least seriously wound the Prefect by the same stroke which had freed Pandaras, but it occurred to him now that perhaps that had not been wise. He was certain that Prefect Corin was searching for him, and Sergeant Rhodean had taught him that in the right circumstances the strength of one enemy can be used against another.

The Shadow finished its boasting, and Enobarbus told Dr Dismas that there were important matters which they must discuss.

'I am always at your service,' Dr Dismas said. 'After all, I am not allowed to leave this place.'

'Is the boy asleep?'

'He pretends to be, but I think he is not. Shall I administer the antidote?'

'No. Leave him. We will talk outside.'

After Dr Dismas and Enobarbus had left the room, the Shadow manifested itself in Yama's inner sight: a faint fluttering star growing slowly larger and becoming a bird, a luminous white dove fluttering through infinite darkness and suddenly changing again, a human figure now, pale hair fluttering around her face as she raised her head to look at him.

Yama found that he could open his eyes, but she was still there, leaning over him. His sweetheart: Derev. Her feathery hair brushed back from her shaven forehead and caught in a plastic clasp. Her large black eyes. The soft lips of her small mouth pursed in the beginning of a smile. When she spoke, her words burned in his brain.

They are talking about us.

'Why do you never show your true self?'

Derev raised her slim arms above her head in a graceful movement, the swell of her small breasts lifting under her shift.

Is this repellent to you? I thought it would please you. I can remove this garment—

'Do as you wish. It is not a true representation, so it does not matter.'

The eidolon paused, one hand on the shoulder clasp of its shift, and studied him with a sly expression.

That is true. You did not sleep with her although you very much wanted to. An odd denial, since you lost your virginity to a whore, and then slept with the cateran—

'That was in the past, when I was young and foolish. I look forward to the future when I will be reunited with Derev. I promised her that I would return when I had discovered the truth about my bloodline, and now I have learned more about myself than I care to know.'

Must I remind you of our relationship? Do not think that you are better than me, Yamamanama, or stronger, or more intelligent.

'Of course not. You do not need to remind me. But although you are better than me in every way, you still need me.'

For the moment.

'You are still very young. You are still learning. There is much that I can teach you.'

I will soon know all you know.

'Perhaps, but mere facts are useless if you do not know how to use them.'

I control thousands of machines at once. You can control only one, and that badly.

'I wondered if you knew what I was doing.'

I could prevent it. I could blind and deafen you. Be thankful for my mercy.

'I mean no harm by it. I grow bored while you are off fighting the war.'

Yet you have never used a machine to find out about the place where we are held.

'That is because I was afraid that Dr Dismas would discover my little trick.'

Fortunately, I have no such fears. I have learned much about this place, and I have discovered that we are in danger. Enobarbus does not trust us. Nor does he trust Dr Dismas.

'I know that Enobarbus is frightened of you. What are he and Dr Dismas talking about?'

Listen.

The eidolon of Derev and the brightly lit room faded into a view from somewhere above the tops of the trees which surrounded the grassy glade in which Dr Dismas and Enobarbus stood, with Enobarbus's guards in their black armour on one side and Dr Dismas's mutilated servants on the other. The sun was directly overhead. It was noon. A bird was singing somewhere, a cascade of falling notes repeated over and over.

'He will become something glorious,' Dr Dismas was saying. 'Something wonderful, if he is allowed. What he is now – that's nothing. A few silly tricks.'

'He is already a fearsome weapon,' Enobarbus said, baring his strong white teeth. The warlord held his ruined face at a proud angle. His mane was a tawny cascade tied back over one broad shoulder. 'Without their machines, the armies ranged against us have no protection against our own machines and we can move our troops without detection. The long stalemate is over at last. We are grateful, Dismas. You must know that. You have this fine palace, these servants, these riches. You have your laboratories and your experiments. I do not approve of what you do. I think it cruel, perhaps even mad. But you are free to do it.'

'He is a larva at the moment, no more. Let him grow. Let him shed his present form and achieve his full potential. He will sweep all before him. He will be terrible, mighty… You cannot imagine it. Sometimes I think that even I cannot imagine it. Give him the metals he needs, the rare earths…'

'No, I think not.'

'You do not have the right to limit his growth.'

'What else do you need? If it is in my power I will grant it at once. After all, you have delivered a prize beyond compare. Perhaps more experimental subjects,' Enobarbus said. 'I do not think your experiments are going as well as you would like.'

Dr Dismas lit a cigarette. 'You surround me with spies. Men and women who pretend to be here to help me but who are, in plain truth, the wardens of this prison. It is amazing that I have been able to do any work at all. The few creatures I have created are botched, it's true, but they are a beginning. I need more time and I cannot have it while fighting your war for you. Let the boy complete his transformation. He will become something that will amaze us all.'

'I do not need to be amazed. I need to rely on those who fight for me. I must have that, Dismas. I must have control.'

'You could have a sudden end to this long war. I offer you victory, complete and unqualified.'

'But not, perhaps, on my terms.'

'My paramour and its associates fight for the same cause as you, my dear Enobarbus. They are your allies, but they are not yours to command. Neither am I. You should tell your officers that. Although I hide nothing from them or from you, they order me about and continually interfere with my work, and accuse me of deception and all kinds of falsehoods.'

'You should stop pretending to be human, Dismas. You should acknowledge your true nature. People will not trust you as long as you pretend to be what you are not.'

'You and I understand each other because we are so very similar, Enobarbus. We are both creatures of forces greater than ourselves. You fear my paramour because it is so much more powerful than the aspect of the dead woman you worship. Look at what I have done, at his bidding. Look at how well the war goes. If not for the boy—'

'He has helped. I will not deny it. But we were winning anyway, and besides, the war is not important. We did not start it, and we entered into it reluctantly only to save ourselves. The truth which Angel brought to the world is more important than the war. Our great and good work will not end until everyone knows of it, and every last trace of the mindless worship of the dead past is overthrown.'

'Because of this so-called truth you will have no troops, by and by. The newly changed will fight at first, to be sure, but soon enough they are consumed by this precious individuality of yours. They lose interest in everything but themselves.'

'Many still fight.'

'Oh, when anyone can choose anything then of course some choose to fight,' Dr Dismas said. 'But not as many as you would like, eh? And as you progress upriver there will be fewer and fewer unchanged bloodlines for you to recruit. I must confess that I am not at all certain, at this point, that your crusade will ever reach Ys. Angel should not have destroyed the remaining avatars. That was the first mistake, but it was made a long time ago and there is nothing to be done about it. The second mistake is to keep the boy as he is. Let him grow. I admit that he once tried to destroy her, but he was not mine then. Now I can control him, whatever he becomes, because he is my son.'

Enobarbus said, slowly and gravely, 'The avatars tried to destroy her. She had no choice but to fight back. Besides, she merely finished what was begun long ago. Most of the avatars were destroyed in the Age of Insurrection, by the things you claim as friends.'

Dr Dismas snapped up from his habitual stoop like a startled click-beetle, his yellow eyes gleaming in his sharp-featured face. 'We each have our different versions of the recent past. But what does that matter, and why are we arguing, when we both want the same thing!'

Enobarbus said, 'I have no desire to argue, Dismas. As you say, we are on the same side. But you cannot do as you will. The boy and the thing you grow inside him are powerful, and because they are powerful, they are dangerous. Already they have accomplished much, and I see no need for them to grow more powerful. They must be contained.'

'A simple solution of certain rare earths. I delivered the formula days and days ago.'

'Use your experimental subjects in any way you like, but do no more to the boy or to the thing inside him. They are already powerful enough.'

Dr Dismas glared at Enobarbus. 'Yamamanama is your greatest resource. I gave him to you freely, and this is how you repay me? You are making a grave mistake.'

'Do you threaten me, Dismas?'

'I have given you my advice. If you do not take it, do not hold me responsible for the consequences,' Dr Dismas said, and turned and strode off through the trees, followed by his servants.

Enobarbus gestured to his physician, and said, 'We cannot allow this problem to fester any longer, Agnitus.'

The grey-maned physician said, 'As far as I can tell, the thing inside the boy has not made any gross alterations to his metabolism, my lord. It should be a simple matter—'

Enobarbus shook his great maned head. 'Not here,' he said. 'Remember that the boy controls machines.'

'You were listening,' Dr Dismas said in Yama's ear. The sunny glade vanished. The apothecary loomed over him, his face mottled by the plaques of his disease. 'I saw the machine. You had it fly high up, so that it would be lost in the glare of the sun, but I saw it all the same. How sly. How sweet. Awake, Yamamanama! Awake, my sly, sweet boy! You have been the agent of another glorious victory in this ridiculous war! Awake!'

Three servants lifted Yama from the bed and carried him to the canopied chair, arranging his paralysed body amongst its cushions.

'Don't worry about Enobarbus,' Dr Dismas said. 'We'll have no more need of him soon enough. I have plans . . .'

He turned away from Yama and raised his voice. 'But I will not talk of that, surrounded as I am by spies!'

Yama said, 'Are you speaking to me, Doctor, or to the thing inside me?'

'Men like to think that their minds are separate from their bodies. It is central to the creed of the heretics, for otherwise they could not contemplate certain radical methods of life extension. You make the same mistake, Yamamanama, but I'll soon show you just how wrong you are.'

'After the city of Aeolis was burned, some of its citizens blamed me. They set me on a funeral pyre and would have burnt me to death, but I was rescued by termites which sucked my would-be executioners into the ground. I thought that I had somehow called upon the termites to help me, but I know now that it was the Shadow, the thing you put inside me. It was saving itself. After I escaped the pyre, it tried to eat as many termites as it could find. The termites were partly machine, and it wanted the metals in their bodies to feed its growth. And now it needs more metals, to reach its final form.'

'And I will get those rare earths for you, one way or another. And then you will understand that there is no distinction between mind and body. But now you must exercise and eat, because in an hour you must sleep again. The war goes faster and faster, and no matter how much Enobarbus denies it, you are central to it.'

Derev stood at Dr Dismas's shoulder. She opened her mouth impossibly wide to show rows and rows of serrated white teeth and a rough red tongue that uncoiled from her mouth like a snake, glistening with saliva.

I will grow such teeth that will eat you whole, little one. We will be one flesh, one blood. There will be nothing that we cannot do.

9

THE LAZARET

Pandaras awoke to darkness and a confining pressure across his body. His left hand hurt horribly. He thrashed up, thinking that he was still buried, and found that the pressure was only a sheet that had slipped to his waist, and that the darkness was not absolute but was punctured here and there by the glow of little lamps which slowly swung to and fro like the pendulums of so many clocks. The whole world was rocking like a cradle. From all sides came the sound of men breathing or sighing. Someone was sobbing, a slow hiccoughing like the dripping of a faucet. The air was close and hot, tinged by the mingled smells of spoiled meat and iodine.

Pandaras reached for his left hand with his right… and could not find it. He patted at the coarse blanket that lay over his legs, as if he might discover it lying there like a faithful pet. He was still very sleepy, and did not understand what was wrong.

Something moved on the floor by his bed. He froze, thinking that Prefect Corin must be hiding there. But it was a larger man who reared up from the shadows, pale-skinned and flabby, and wearing only a pair of ragged trousers.

'Little master,' the man said in a soft, hoarse voice. 'You are wounded and ill. You must rest.'

It was Tibor. Pandaras did not feel any surprise. He said, 'What have they done to me?'

Tibor made him lie down, and then told him all he knew. The two soldiers in the trench had not been badly hurt by the stray mortar round. They had dug themselves out and carried Pandaras to the lazaret, but by the time one of the chirurgeons had seen him the cord around his wrist had tightened so much that it had almost disappeared into his flesh. The hand had been too long without blood, and the chirurgeon had been obliged to finish what the cord had begun.

'It was worth it to gain my freedom,' Pandaras whispered. 'In any case, many say that we do not have hands, but only the clawed feet of animals. For that reason we have learned to let our tongues do most of the work.'

He felt that he must make light of it, for he seemed to be at the brink of a great black pit. If he fell into it there might never be an end to despair. He struggled to sit up again, and said, 'We cannot stay here. He will find me and I will not have that. We must leave—'

'Quiet, little master,' the hierodule said. 'You are very ill, and so are all those around you. You have been treated, and now you must sleep. The longer you sleep the better chance you have of living.'

Pandaras summoned all of his strength. 'Fetch my clothes,' he said. 'If I stay here I will have sacrificed my hand for nothing, and I could not bear that.'

His clothes were tied in a bundle at the foot of the cot. Tibor helped him dress; twice he reached for toggles with his left hand, which was not there. 'I have a whole set of new tricks to learn,' he said. And then, with sudden panic, 'The fetish! The fetish and the disc! Where are they? Were they thrown away? I must have them!'

Tibor hooked two fingers into the pocket of Pandaras's ragged shirt and drew out the ceramic disc, strung on its loop of leather, and the circlet of coypu hair and seed pearls.

Pandaras grasped the disc and it blazed so brightly that it hurt his eyes. 'He is close!' he said, and kissed the burning disc, hung it around his neck and, with a thrill of disgust, slipped the fetish over his bandaged stump. 'There. I have nothing else, for Prefect Corin took the book, and I have paid for my lodging with my hand. We are ready to go.'

'But where will you go, little master?'

'We will find my master. The disc will lead us. You cannot easily escape me again, Tibor. I had to lose a hand to find you, and it is only fair that you stand at my left side from now on.'

Tibor said gently, 'It is my duty to tend to the sick and the wounded.'

'Am I not wounded?'

'You are but one of many. All of them need me.'

'But I am foremost in your affections, I hope.' Pandaras felt a trifle dizzy. The floor seemed to pitch and sway beneath him. He sat down on the edge of the cot, but the sensation did not go away.

'Someone else needs me now, little master,' Tibor said, and padded away into the darkness. His naked back and hairless head shone beneath the arc of a swinging lamp and then he was gone. Pandaras lay down, just for a little while, and was woken by Tibor, who was once again squatting beside the cot. It was as if a measure of whiteness had been poured into the darkness all around, not banishing it, but making it a little less absolute.

Tibor was smoking a cigarette. Pandaras twiddled the fingers of his right hand in the air and asked for a puff of it.

'You are ill, little master, but you do not need this kind of medicine.'

'If I am as ill as you say I am, then what more harm can it do? And if I'm not ill, as I claim, then it will calm me down. My stepfather, the first one, the one I don't like to talk about, he was a great smoker, so I became one by proxy, until I left home. A little more will do no harm.'

Pandaras was very tired, but in a minute, if only the world would stop its slow sway, in a minute he would get up and walk out of here. He did not care if Tibor chose to follow him or not. Prefect Corin would surely be looking for him. He had to go. He had to find his master...

Tibor placed the wet tip of the cigarette in Pandaras's fingers and helped him guide it to his mouth. The smoke was sweet and cloying. Pandaras choked on the first mouthful and coughed it out, but got the second down to the bottom of his lungs and slowly, luxuriously, exhaled.

'You see,' he said. 'It makes me much calmer.'

Tibor took the cigarette away. 'Then our bloodlines are very alike in their chemistries, little master, because that is why my people smoke. It helps us to accept our condition.' He drew on the cigarette; its brightening coal put two sparks in his large black eyes. 'Without this palliative I would have killed myself as a pup, as I think would all of my kind. And so my bloodline would have died out long ago, without the chance to purge its sin. The Preservers are both merciful and just, for when they made this world they set upon it the herb from which this tobacco is made, which allows my bloodline to endure its infamy and universal enslavement.'

'I thought it was just a habit,' Pandaras said sleepily. He did not resist when Tibor began to undress him.

'It is a habit of life, young master, like breathing. We need cigarettes as much as you need air.'

'We must escape. We must cross the lines of the enemy.'

'We have already done so, little master. Sleep now. If you can sleep, then it is a sign that you can begin to get well. Those too sick to sleep always die, in my experience. But I do not think you will die.'

'I want—'

But Pandaras was too tired to complete the thought, and he slept.

Pandaras grew a little stronger every day, and at last was strong enough to realise how sick he had been, sicker than most of those around him. When he was at last able to sit up and take notice of his surroundings, in the late afternoon of the sixth or seventh day of his confinement, he saw that this part of the lazaret was empty except for himself and a heavily bandaged man three cots over in the same row. A machine like a cat-sized mosquito squatted over the bandaged barrel of the man's chest, circulating his blood through loops of clear tubing.

The disc was no brighter, but the dots and dashes of light within it were more active than ever, scurrying to new patterns, freezing for only a heartbeat, and scurrying about again. Pandaras watched for hours, trying to understand their dance.

In the night, the man tended by the mosquito-machine suffered some kind of crisis. He was taken away amidst a confusion of chirurgeons and chargehands. Pandaras lay awake for hours afterwards, but the man did not return.

The next morning, Pandaras was taken up on deck by Tibor, and saw at last what the hierodule had been trying to tell him. The lazaret was travelling downriver. It had been taken by the heretics.

The Great River divided into many shallow, sinuous, slow-moving streams at the Marsh of the Lost Waters. The lazaret was following one of these. It was less than half a league across, and stained red-brown with silt. Trees grew densely on either side, half-submerged in the sluggish current, their leaves vivid in the bright sunlight. The sun burned off the water. It was very hot and very humid. Pandaras was happy to sit with Tibor under an awning of crimson silk, listening to one or another of the discussion classes which were part of the process the heretics called Re-Education and Enlightenment.

The lazaret was a barge as wide and flat as a field. A flying bridge crowned its blunt bow; gun emplacements nestled like pips at regular intervals along its sides; pods housing reaction motors swelled at its stern. A pentad of machines followed its wide wake as birds might follow a fishing boat. They were as fat as barrels and entirely black, with clusters of mobile spines fore and aft. They made a slow fizzing sound as they moved through the air. Sometimes one would break off and make a wide slow loop above the forest canopy before rejoining its fellows. At night they were each enveloped in a faint red nimbus, like a constellation of halo stars.

There were other machines too. Small silvery teardrops that zipped from one place to another like squeezed watermelon pips; black angular things like miniature mantids that stalked the white planks of the deck on long, thin legs. And a thing of jointed cubes and spheres slung in a hammock on the bridge, close to the huge wheel that, manned by three sailors, controlled the barge's rudders. The plastic casings of its components had once been white but were now stained and chipped. It was a very ancient machine, Pandaras learned, and it had control of the barge; many of the smaller machines were slaved to it. It seemed that these machines were not the servants of the world, as in Ys, but were the equals of or even superiors to the flesh-and-blood heretics.

The soldiers who guarded the prisoners and otherwise manned the barge were of a recently changed bloodline from the lower slopes of the Rim Mountains. They were a tall, muscular people covered in thick white fur, and wore only elaborate harnesses of leather straps and buckles and pouches. Their narrow faces, with long muzzles and small brown eyes that peered from beneath heavy brow ridges, were as black and wrinkled as old leather, and all were heavily tattooed with silvery swirls and dots. They called themselves the Charn or the Tchai. Although of a single bloodline and a single culture, they were divided into two distinct tribes which, by taboo, never intermarried. One herded llamas and goats in the birch forests; the other hunted in the wilderness of rock and snow above the treeline. Pandaras, who still believed that he had the right to talk with anyone, discovered that they had a rich store of tragedies concerning star-crossed lovers and blood feuds which lasted for generations. To their amusement, he elaborated several versions of his own upon these eternal themes.

The white-furred guards did not like the close, foetid heat. When they were not patrolling the deck, they sprawled in front of electric fans, their red tongues lolling. They were a short-tempered people, and the heat made them even more irritable. Those officers captured with the lazaret had already been killed, but the guards would sometimes make the prisoners line up, pluck someone from the ranks at random, and execute him. One night, one of the guards went mad and tried to storm the bridge. There was a brief but furious firefight before he was shot. More than thirty prisoners were killed or wounded in the crossfire; all were unceremoniously tipped over the side for the caymans and catfish.

Pandaras asked Tibor why he had not been executed when the lazaret had been captured. 'You're something like a priest, neh? I think that it would make you more dangerous than any officer.'

Tibor scratched at the vertical scars on his chest while he thought about this. At last he said, 'I am only a slave, little master. I am not a leader of men. Besides, the heretics believe that to convert one such as me is a great prize.'

'Surely there were other hierodules working in the lazaret when it was captured? But I see no others now.'

'They fled, little master. But I could not leave you.'

'You know that I am not your master, Tibor!'

The hierodule did not reply.

Pandaras tried a new argument. 'I am grateful that you are here, Tibor. But as an equal. As my friend.'

'You could not be a friend to one such as me, little master. What am I? Lower than a worm, because my ancestors took the side of the feral machines during the Age of Insurrection.'

'You are a man, Tibor. As much a man as anyone here. Don't put the burden of your life on my head.'

Again Tibor did not reply. He took out the little plastic pouch from the waistband of his trousers and, with maddening slowness, began to roll a cigarette.

Only the weakest and most seriously wounded prisoners lay in the close heat below deck. The rest camped under awnings rigged from brightly coloured canvas or silk and scattered across the broad deck of the barge like flowers strewn across a field. They took turns to trawl for fish and shrimp, which were shredded and added to the cauldrons of sticky rice or maize porridge, but most of their waking hours were taken up with Re-Education and Enlightenment.

The discussion classes formed just after dawn, and often continued beyond sunset. Although the prisoners were told that the classes were voluntary, everyone knew that those who refused to take part were likely to be chosen by the guards for execution. They reminded Pandaras of the day school he had occasionally attended as a cub. His education had ended when his father had disappeared, for the man his mother had married after that had refused to waste money on luxuries like learning. It had been no great loss. Pandaras had always hated the stifling atmosphere of the school, and the rote recitations of the Puranas which had taken up much of the time had for him almost killed their beautiful and terrible stories. He did not mind that he was unlettered, for his people had always kept their stories and songs in memory rather than on paper – 'written in air rather than on stone', as their tradition had it, for what was forgotten did not matter, and that which was of value was kept alive in the mouths and instruments of a thousand singers long after the unmourned death of the author.

The classes contained between four and forty prisoners, and each was led by a pedagogue. These were all of the same round-faced, grey-skinned bloodline, from a city several hundred leagues downriver which had achieved enlightenment, as they called it, early in the war. Most – they proudly admitted it – were no more than children, so young that they had yet to determine their sex. They were a small race, smaller even than Pandaras. They dressed in loose black tunics and trousers, and their glossy black hair was tied back in elaborate pigtails with scraps of white silk. They ruled the prisoners with an iron discipline. Those who walked away from the discussion classes in disgust or anger were immediately chased by the pedagogues, who screamed at them and whipped them around the ankles with sharp bamboo canes; those who did not return or who tried to fight back were taken away by the guards, shot, and kicked over the side.

At first, Pandaras had a great deal of trouble understanding what the pedagogues were trying to teach him. He sat next to Tibor in the sweltering heat in a kind of stupor, his stump throbbing under a slithery, quasi-living dressing which absorbed the discharges of blood and pus, and which Tibor changed twice a day. His head ached from the odour of burnt fish-oil from the barge's reaction motors and the sunlight which reflected in splinters from the river and, most of all, from the high, sing-song cadences of the pedagogue as it urged, cajoled, corrected and harangued its charges.

Each morning the discussion classes started with a chant of the slogan of the heretics. *Seize the day!* It echoed out across the river, sometimes lasting no more than a minute, sometimes lasting for an hour, becoming as meaningless as breathing but always ending at the same moment in all the classes scattered across the barge's broad deck.

After that came the long hours of argument in which the pedagogues set out some trivial truth and used it as a wedge to open a door on to a bewildering landscape. It seemed to Pandaras that everything was allowed except for that which was forbidden, but it was difficult to know which was which because there were no rules. The other prisoners had the same problem, and all their objections and expressions of bafflement were met by the same answer.

'You do not see,' the pedagogue would say in its sweet, high-pitched voice, 'because you cannot see. You cannot see because you have not been allowed to see. You have not been taught to see. You are all blind men, and I will open your eyes for the first time.'

At the heart of the heretics' philosophy, like the black hole at the centre of the Eye of the Preservers, was a single negation. It was so simple and so utterly against the self-evident truth of the world that many of the prisoners simply laughed in amazement every time the pedagogues repeated it. It was that the Puranas were not the thoughts of the Preservers, set down to reveal the history of the universe and to determine the actions of right-thinking men, but were instead a fabrication, a collection of self-justifying lies spewed by the victors of a great and ancient war that was not yet over. There would be no resurrection into eternal life at the end of all time and space, because the Preservers had fled from the universe and could not return. They had created Confluence, but they had abandoned it. The fate of each man did not lie within the purlieu of the infinite mercy and power of the Preservers, but in his own hands. Because the Preservers could not return from the Eye, each man must be responsible for his own fate. There was no hope but that which could be imagined; no destiny but that which could be forged.

The pedagogues were more fervent in their unbelief than any of the pillar saints or praise chanters who had devoted their lives to exaltation of the glories of the Preservers. They would allow no argument. This negation was the central fact that could not be denied; from it, all else followed. From the first, Pandaras was quite clear on what the heretics did not believe, but it took him a long time to understand what they did believe, and once he had it, it was so simple that he was amazed that he had failed to grasp it at once. Like the woman in the pictures in his master's copy of the Puranas, the heretics wanted to live forever.

Seize the day! It was a plea aimed directly at the base of the brain, where the residue of the animal self was coiled like a snake, insatiable and quite without conscience. Do anything in your power to survive; bend your entire life towards it. The universe was insensate and hostile; habitable worlds were so few and remote that they counted for nothing; almost anywhere you went would kill you instantly and horribly. Therefore, life was infinitely precious, and every man's life was more precious still, a subtle and beautiful melody that would never be repeated. The heretics wished to revive the old ways of indefinitely prolonging life, so that everyone could fulfil their destiny as they pleased.

For Pandaras, whose bloodline was short-lived compared with that of others on Confluence, no more than twenty-five years at most, it was a seductive song. 'Written in air,' yes, but suppose it could be written on stone instead! What sublime songs and stories he could make if all time were at his disposal, and what joy he would have in seeing them spread and change and enrich his fame!

Once this thought took root, Pandaras paid more attention to what the pedagogue told the discussion class. For amusement, he told himself. To pass the time.

The heretics claimed that there were no gods, but believed that each man could become as a god – or better than a god – with enough effort. Any god of the First Cause in a universe such as this must surely be counted a failure, the pedagogue argued, because he must be omniscient and yet allow immense suffering. Most of the universe was uninhabitable. All men died, and most died badly.

'If the Preservers care about their creation,' the pedagogue told Pandaras and his companions, 'then either they wish to take away evil and are unable to do so, or they are able but unwilling, or they are neither willing nor able, or they are both willing and able. If they are willing and unable then they are feeble, which is not in accordance with claims made for their nature. If they are able yet unwilling then they are envious of the condition of their creation, which is equally at variance with their nature. If they are unwilling and unable then they are envious and feeble, and therefore cannot be what they are claimed to be by their worshippers. And yet if they are willing and able, which conditions alone would satisfy the claims of those who believe in the omnipotence of the Preservers, then from what source come the evils of this world? From what place flow all the hurts and trials which you have all suffered? Why are we victorious, and why are you defeated? All the evil in the world can be accounted for by one principle, and that is the nature of the universe of which it is a part. And yet that evil is not absolute. It is well known that a wilderness can be tamed and cultivated and made to yield crops. And so with any wilderness, even to the end of space and time, for there is no limit to the transforming power of human reason and human will. And given these two things, nature and human reason, why, there is no need for the Preservers, nor for any other gods.'

Several of the prisoners in Pandaras's discussion class passionately disputed this argument. They said that although the Preservers had given men free will, it did not mean that men had infinite power, and even if they could gain infinite power it did not mean that they would then be unchanged, as the heretics appeared to believe. For surely anyone who could live forever would be changed by the simple fact of becoming immortal, and so would no longer be subject to the fears of ordinary men. The pedagogue listened to their arguments and smiled and said that they had not yet opened their ears, that they were still in the thrall of the propaganda of their priests, police and civil servants, who together conspired to fix every man in his place and punish those who tried to change things because change threatened their power.

This seemed to be no more than what many in Ys said behind the backs of the magistrates, Pandaras thought, but he was still disturbed by these new ideas. He knew that Yama would have an answer to them, but even as he thought this he remembered that Yama had also questioned the motives of the Preservers in making Confluence and setting the ten thousand bloodlines upon it in the moment before they had stepped away from the universe. The praise singers had it that the Preservers had extended their mercy to the races of servants that they had raised up from animals; these they had set on this world to achieve what destiny they could for good or ill, in the sight of the Eye into which the Preservers had vanished. But why then was the world so bound in custom and tradition?

We are the strength of the city, Pandaras thought, and yet we are regarded by higher bloodlines as no more than vermin. And what of the indigenous races such as the fisher folk or the mirror people, or the unclean scavengers and ghouls who roamed the cloacae of Ys? These races had been raised up by the Preservers, yet did not contain their breath and so could never achieve the change – enlightenment, in this grey mannikin's argot – by which a bloodline dominated by unchanging habit became a nation of individuals.

He remembered with a pang of shame the first day with his master, after they had escaped from *The Crossed Axes*, when he had poured scorn upon the unchanged refugees who camped by the widening margin of the river. Was it the intention of the Preservers that some bloodlines should oppress others? Surely the Preservers had set themselves so high that all bloodlines were equal to them, no matter how lowly or how enlightened. The heretics had one thing right: all the world's peoples should have the chance to rise as high as they could. If the Preservers had created a world so manifestly unfair, then they must have done so through incompetence or spite, and were neither as omniscient nor as virtuous as the priests and bureaucrats claimed.

Pandaras forgot in that moment that although his master was more powerful than many men, he did not deny that the Preservers were more powerful still, so powerful that men might never understand them. Instead, the slogans of the heretics burnt like fever in his blood. Seize the day! Live forever! It did not matter if you were changed, for you would still remember what you had been, as a man fondly remembers his childhood. And what man would wish to remain a child forever?

One man in Pandaras's discussion class was eager to deny the Preservers. Not out of belief or conviction, but out of fear, for he was anxious to save himself. From the first he agreed with everything the pedagogue said, without understanding anything, and mocked his fellow prisoners for stubbornly clinging to their outmoded and foolish beliefs.

He was a skinny fellow with leathery brown skin and a cayman's untrustworthy grin. He wore only dirty breeches and a mail shirt, and stank like river water kept too long in a barrel. He had been badly seared when his carronade had jammed and exploded: his hand was gloved in a white plastic bag and a bandage was wrapped around his head, the right side of his chest and his face were livid with burns, and his right eye was as milk-white as a boiled egg. He was shunned by the other prisoners and was always trying to wheedle favours from the guards, who either ignored him or chased him away with swift, judicious blows. His name was Narasimha, but everyone called him the Jackal. Even the pedagogue grew tired of the Jackal's constant gabble of unthinking agreement, and one day turned on him.

'You do not worship the Preservers?' it said in its sweet, high voice.

'That's so, your honour,' the Jackal said eagerly. 'Men of my kind, we've never liked 'em. That's why we are always hunted down by the authorities, because we refuse to bend our knee to the false idols of their temples. We were delighted when your people finally silenced the last avatars because we saw that it might be an end to the rule of the priests. And now I see it's true, and my heart lifts on a flood of happiness.'

Pandaras thought that as usual the Jackal dissembled, giving up half the truth in service of a greater lie. It was clear from the arrowhead tattoos on the man's fingers that he had been a member of one of the galares that operated in the docks of Ys, hijacking cargoes, smuggling cigarettes and other drugs, running protection and kidnapping rackets. The Jackal had probably joined the army to escape justice. Perhaps he had betrayed his own kind – several of the prisoners remarked, out of earshot of any pedagogue or soldier, that the Jackal was an ideal candidate for a heretic, for he would betray the universe to save his worthless hide.

'What do you worship,' the pedagogue asked the Jackal sweetly, 'if you do not worship the Preservers?'

A ripple of interest stirred the circle of the discussion class, like a breeze lifting and dropping the leaves of a tree. The Jackal did not notice it.

'Why, your honour, captain . . . for a long time I did not worship anything. The only things I held dear were my family and my many friends, as any good honest man might tell you, but I saw nothing of worth beyond them. But now, by happy circumstance, I find myself in a position I could not have imagined then. My bloodline is one of the oldest on Confluence, one of the first to have changed. We have always lived in Ys, and those in power hate us because of our ancient and honourable pedigree. But now I feel that I have been changed again, that the change for which we are envied is nothing compared with what I feel now. Why, I don't mind that I lost my eye and the use of my hand, because it is a small enough price to have paid for the riches you shower upon us day by day.'

'Then you worship nothing?'

'Your honour, as I said, my people never worshipped the Preservers. But it does not mean we are not capable of worship.'

'Money, mostly,' someone whispered, loud enough for the rest of the class to hear it. Most laughed.

The Jackal glared around with his one good eye. It was yellow, with a vertically slitted pupil.

'You see, your honour,' the Jackal said, 'how jealous others are of me. Because I understand what you want of us while these others only pretend it. They are not worthy of your truths. You take me, your honour, and feed these others to the fish in the mud at the bottom of the river.'

'What is it that you understand?' the pedagogue said. 'Every day you tell me that you are full of praise for what you hear, and I am glad. But I would like to know what you understand of the hard questions I put to all of you here. I would like to know how high you have been raised.'

The men in the circle nudged each other, seeing that some kind of trap was closing on the hapless Jackal, who glared at them again and hissed through his long jaw. 'Higher than these scum, and they know it, your honour. Put that question to them. I'll wager none of them will be able to answer it.'

'There is no competition here,' the pedagogue said. 'We set no man against any other. That is one part of our strength. The other is our certainty. Tell me one thing of which you are certain.'

'Why, your honour, I know that the Preservers are nothing but goat shit compared with your people. I know that I worshipped nothing because nothing was worthy of my worship, but I know now that I have found something I will worship with all my heart and all my breath. Let me serve your people and I will grace them with such praise that all will know their fame. It is your people that I worship. I love you all more than life itself, and will serve you in any way I can, and hope to gain some small measure of your glory. It is you, you! You and no other!'

And to the disgust of the others, the Jackal threw himself forward and tried to kiss the pedagogue's feet. But the small creature drew them into the angles of its knees and looked at the Jackal and said, 'There is nothing more that I can tell you. Go now. Leave the class. Do not be afraid. If you truly understand what I teach, you must know that you are free to do as you will.'

The Jackal raised his head. The bandage around his head was unravelling; one end hung near the milky, cooked eye which stared from a mess of black scabs and raw red skin. 'Then there is nothing I want more than to sit at your feet, your honour, and absorb your wisdom.'

'I have nothing more to teach you,' the pedagogue said again. 'I will not say it a third time, for I hope I am not mistaken about your ability to understand me. If you do not understand me then your punishment will be swift and terrible.'

There had been no signal, but suddenly two guards were walking across the wide white deck towards the discussion class. The Jackal looked at them, looked at the pedagogue. 'Your honour… captain… If I have angered you in any way, then I repent of it at once.'

'You have not angered me. You have filled my heart with joy. Go now. You are free.'

Pandaras thought with a chill that it was a subtle and cruel trick. The pedagogue had trapped the Jackal with his own lies, and punished him by giving him exactly what he wanted.

The Jackal was refused food from the cauldrons because it was for the prisoners and he was a free man, and the guards mocked him when he tried to beg some of their rations, crowning him king of the free men with a wreath of water-lily flowers, then driving him away with blows from the butts of their carbines and partisans. The Jackal did not dare approach the pedagogues, and besides, it was unlikely that he could digest the fibrous pap they sucked up. For the next two days he wandered from class to class, followed by several of the small, silvery machines, and some time on the third night of his freedom he disappeared.

One evening, as the prisoners ate their meagre ration of maize porridge salted with scraps of fish, a man of Pandaras's bloodline, a veteran by the name of Tullus, came over and sat beside Pandaras and struck up a conversation. It seemed that they had once lived within two streets of each other in Ys, and had worked at different times in the same foundry, casting and repairing armour. They talked about people they had known and stories they shared in common, and at last Tullus reached the point of his visit.

'You saw how the guards killed the Jackal, brother. They sport with us and eventually they will kill us all.'

'We are not like him,' Pandaras said. 'He would have lain with a shoat if it would have turned a coin or extended his life by a day.'

'Many join the army,' Tullus said seriously, 'and every man has his reason. But all unite in a single cause. Whatever else the Jackal was, he was foremost a soldier. He was one of us and the heretics mocked him and killed him.'

'I saw little help from his fellows,' Pandaras said.

'All feared that if they aided the Jackal, then they would share his fate. The heretics divide us, brother, and one by one they will kill us.'

The two men fell silent as one of the guards went past, his clawed feet scratching the deck, his harness jingling. One of the little angular machines stalked stiff-legged after him. Pandaras thought that if the discipline of the army had been atomised, then the heretics had won. They had made their point. When it came to confronting death, there was no society of men, only individuals.

Tullus watched the guard pace away into the gloom between groups of prisoners. He whispered, 'The lazaret goes slowly because the heretics wish to extend our torture as long as possible, but it goes downriver all the same. At last it will reach the end of the Marsh of the Lost Waters. There are millions of heretics in the cities beyond, and we will be given up to them for their sport.'

Pandaras had heard many fantastic stories about the tortures and obscenities inflicted by the heretics on their prisoners: trials by combat; vivisections and other experiments; forced matings between different bloodlines. He told Tullus, 'The army makes up many stories about the enemy, brother, so that its soldiers will fight hard to avoid capture.'

Tullus nodded. He was a grizzled man of some fifteen or sixteen years, with white around his muzzle.

'Well, that's true up to a point,' he said. 'But the point is that there must be a foundation to any story or song. You know that, brother. All of us know that.'

'The rumours about the heretics are founded in hatred and fear,' Pandaras said. 'Much may flow from those sources, but none of it good.'

'You are not a soldier. What are you doing here?'

Pandaras crooked his left arm, thrusting the stump forward. The bandage wrapped around it was gorged on black blood and throbbed gently to his heartbeat. 'I have lost as much as any soldier,' he said.

'Not your life,' Tullus said. 'Not yet.'

'I've lost something as dear to me,' Pandaras said. 'My master was taken by the heretics. He is a great warrior, and I am his squire. I'm going to find him and free him.'

'You were hurt when he was captured?'

'No, that was later. A flier took him away, and I have been looking for him ever since.'

'Where was this? He was a cateran, I suppose. What division was he attached to? Or was he a scout?'

'He was on his way to war—'

'And was taken before he could kill a single heretic? Then he was an unlucky man rather than a hero. Heroes need luck as much as they need strength. Perhaps you have misplaced your loyalty, neh?'

'He will save the world yet,' Pandaras said stubbornly. 'I can say no more, but I know that he will.'

'You have a chance with us. Stay here and you have no chance at all. They will kill you, Pandaras. Have no faith in anything they promise.' Tullus looked around and whispered, 'Some of us are planning to escape.'

'We are surrounded by marsh and jungle.'

'Exactly. It will make it hard to find us.'

'And hard to find a way out.'

'I fought here when I first joined the army,' Tullus said. 'I know how to find my way. Once we are in the marshes we are safe. But first we must escape.'

'Good luck to you, but I think I will stay here,' Pandaras said. 'I'm a city boy. I've no love for parks, let alone wilderness. And in case you have forgotten, I have only one hand.'

'We are all wounded in some way, and will all help each other. If you love freedom you will help us. If you love the Preservers you will help us.'

'I'm not a soldier, Tullus, as you've pointed out. I'm only a servant who is looking for his master. How could I help you?'

'You have the hierodule. And the hierodule can help us. He can talk with the machines, and they are the real guards here. You will command him to make the machines leave this place, and we will kill the hairy ones and the little grey-skinned motherfuckers.'

'He is not mine,' Pandaras said. 'Command him yourself, if you can.'

Tullus raised himself into a crouch. His black lips drew back from his teeth. Pandaras stiffened. He could smell the old soldier's anger, and he rose to match Tullus's posture. They glared at each other, faces a handspan apart.

Tullus said, 'The hierodule refused me. That is why I am asking you, boy.'

'Perhaps you asked him the wrong question. Tell him that he is under no obligation to me. Tell him that he was freed when the ship on which he served was destroyed.'

Tullus stared hard at Pandaras, and Pandaras stared right back at him, his blood beating heavily in his head and in the stump of his wrist. He refused to be intimidated because he felt that it would somehow fail his master. Then Tullus smiled and turned and said, 'Look! In spite of all the powers they boast of possessing, they cannot hide the truth from us.'

The Rim Mountains had swallowed the last light of the sun, and the

Eye of the Preservers had risen a handspan above the trees along the edge of the river: the dull red swirls of its accretion disc; the pinprick black point at the centre, the dwelling place of the Preservers.

'The Preservers watch us always,' Tullus said. 'Pray with me, brother. Pray for our deliverance.'

No guards or machines were near. Pandaras made the necessary gestures of obeisance and whispered the responses, but his heart was empty. The Preservers had set the world in motion and abandoned it, as a child might turn away from a wind-up toy, leaving it to march heedlessly down the street. Praying was an empty gesture, and Pandaras felt as if there was a gulf a thousand leagues wide between himself and the man who knelt beside him.

The tragedy is not that we fall in love with that which does not love us, he thought, but that we cease to love. He was shivering. He thrust his good hand between his thighs but he could not stop shivering. Tullus said, 'What is it brother? Don't be afraid. Say the final benison with me.'

'You say it, Tullus.'

'You young fool. You believe them, don't you?'

'We are the strength of the city, Tullus. But why are we despised?'

'You are less than the Jackal. He only pretended to believe the heretics' cant, but with you it is no pretence.' Tullus's face contorted and he spat on the deck between Pandaras's feet. 'There are many like me. Tell anyone of this, betray me, and one of my friends will kill you.'

Pandaras slept badly that night, although Tibor promised to keep watch. When he woke near dawn he saw with a pang of dread that more than half the prisoners were gone. Tibor was sitting cross-legged in a kind of trance; it was the closest he came to sleep. When Pandaras shook him, the hierodule stirred and said at once that he had seen nothing.

'Perhaps they escaped to the shore,' Pandaras whispered.

Tibor said softly, 'I do not think so, little master.'

Tears were welling in the hierodule's downwardly slanting eyes. Pandaras said, 'You did see something. Tell me.'

'Everyone slept. Even I, who never sleeps, passed from this world for a little while. The machines may have had something to do it. Then you woke me, and the men were gone.'

A little later, Pandaras said, 'You could have helped them, Tibor.'

'My place is with you, little master. You have not yet recovered from your wound.'

'Would you have helped them, if I had ordered it? Could you have told the heretics' machines to quit the lazaret?'

Tibor considered this, and at last said gently, 'I am yours to command, little master, but I do not think I can command the machines of our captors. I was fitted with an induction loop when I entered the service of the temple, but it was designed to interface with shrines. Shrines are machines, it is true, but there are many kinds of machine.'

'You never tried?'

'It did not occur to me, little master.'

'They might still kill you,' Pandaras said. 'Your entire life has been spent in the service of the Preservers. Surely that makes you a natural enemy of the heretics.'

'Not at all. As I told you before, I am seen as a great prize. In the first days after the lazaret was captured, little master, before you woke from your coma, the pedagogues spent a great deal of time talking with me. They hope to convert me as they have already converted the captain of the lazaret.' Tibor pointed towards the flying bridge at the bow, at the big, jointed machine in its hammock. 'It still hopes that I will join with it. But I already serve you, little master. I have no one else to serve. If the *Weazel* was not destroyed, then surely Captain Lorquital would have put in at Ophir with her cargo. But no one had seen her, little master, although I asked many people at the docks while I was waiting to board the ship which took me downriver to the lazaret.'

'They died quickly, Tibor, if that's a comfort.'

'Except for Phalerus,' Tibor said.

The remaining prisoners were subdued. There were no discussion classes that day. Just before sunset, the barge entered a wide canal, and an hour later drew into the docks of Baucis, the City of Trees.

10

'EVERYONE NOW LIVING MAY NEVER DIE'

As soon as the barge had been made fast to the wharf, the guards began to move amongst the prisoners, telling them that they were free to go. 'This is a city of free men!' they said, grinning fearsomely. 'Take up your own lives. No one is responsible for you but yourselves.'

'If only Tullus and his friends had waited one more day,' Pandaras told Tibor.

'Our captors are crueller than I thought, little master.'

Many of the prisoners were reluctant to obey the guards, fearing a trick. When the guards started to force them towards the stern, where the gangways to the dock had been fixed, one man went mad and refused to move. He sat down in the middle of the deck with his arms wrapped around his head, rocking back and forth and screaming. A guard shot him and picked up his body and slung it over the side. After that, the other prisoners meekly gathered up their few belongings and walked out into the city.

Baucis had once been a patchwork of little woods and hills, but new roads had been driven everywhere without regard for traditional boundaries, and many of the woods had been cut down. In those that survived, the heart trees had been felled and the woven platform houses of the original inhabitants torn down and replaced by straggling encampments of tents and shacks. Sewage ran in open channels that were often blocked by the bodies of animals and men. The air was hazed with the smoke of thousands of fires. Floating platforms and streams of draught animals and crowds of men jostled along red clay roads in the harsh glare of arc lights strung from stripped tree-trunks. Steam wagons clanked and groaned and belched clouds of black smoke as they dragged three or four overladen trailers behind them. Bars, gaming palaces and whorehouses, all with tall, brightly painted false fronts, had been thrown up along the roads, and barkers and shills called to the crowds from platforms or windows or balconies. There were many apothecaries, surgeries and clinics. One offered, mysteriously, *Whole Body Immersion and Electrotherapy;* another, *Intestinal Irrigation.* Machines spun above the crowded roads, zipping about on obscure errands, and slogans were projected high in the air, in glowing letters each as big as a man. *Seize The Day. Everyone Now Living May Never Die.* Higher still were the archipelagos of the floating gardens which had once been the homes of Baucis's scholar-saints, strings of black silhouettes in the orange sky-glow.

Pandaras was tired and his left arm hurt badly; Tibor had stripped the quasi-living dressing from the stump, leaving only a light bandage. He followed the hierodule without question, and presently found himself amongst the ruins of the city's sacred wood. The circle of giant sequoias, said to have been as old as the world, had been cut down, and decads of men were sawing planks from their carcasses by the light of huge bonfires, but the shrine was still there. Its wide circular platform, crafted from a hundred different kinds of wood, was scarred with charcoal-blistered trenches gouged by the reflected beams of energy weapons and pocked with thousands of splintered gouges and impact holes from ricocheting slugs and rifle pellets, and blasphemies and cabalistic signs had been carved into the polished ancient planks, but the huge black disc of the shrine itself was untouched.

Pandaras sat down at the edge of the platform, on wood worn smooth by the footsteps of millions of pilgrims and petitioners. 'Why have you brought us here?'

'We were told that nothing is forbidden, little master,' Tibor said, 'so surely one may still consult the shrines.'

'What use is that, without a priest?' Pandaras said, and then he understood. 'Will it speak with you?'

'The avatar of this shrine was destroyed ten thousand years ago, in the wars of the Age of Insurrection. But the shrine itself is still active.'

Pandaras sat in the shadows at the perimeter of the platform while Tibor attempted to commune with the shrine. He meant to keep watch, but it was long past midnight and he was very tired. He fell asleep, and woke with a start to find the hierodule squatting in front of him and a familiar warmth against his chest.

'There is no reply,' Tibor said. 'Something has destroyed the indices.'

Pandaras reached inside his torn shirt and lifted out the ceramic disc. Little specks and lines of light filled it from edge to edge, frozen in a static pattern.

'It doesn't matter,' he said. 'I know that my master is here.'

11

THE CAMP

Pandaras and Tibor spent the rest of the night close to the ruins of the sacred grove. Pandaras slept fitfully, disturbed by the whine and clatter of the mechanical saws wielded by the gangs dismembering the carcasses of the giant sequoias. They wandered the brawling streets of the city for most of the next day in search of some sign of Yama, but found nothing. They had no money for food or lodging, and it seemed that nothing was free in the city. Pandaras tried to earn a few coins by singing at a street corner, but passers-by either ignored him or cursed him roundly. One woman riding past reined in her sumpter long enough to explain to Pandaras that everyone must be responsible for their own self, and that by begging he was behaving like an animal.

'I have a hierodule, dominie. Is there no work for him?'

'No man is a slave here,' the woman said. 'You should try one of the camps outside the city. You'll find more of your kind there. Go quickly before someone decides to organise a lynch party and get rid of you.'

Before Pandaras could ask her another question she flicked the sumpter's reins and rode on through the swarming crowds.

It was almost midnight when Pandaras and Tibor reached one of the camps in the jungle beyond the edge of Baucis. They were challenged by a guard outside its perimeter, and were led through a tangle of winding paths to a compound of huts and tents on three sides of a square of beaten clay. The leader of the camp was a giant of a woman who had lost both her legs but went everywhere on crutches, indefatigable and full of energy. Her name – or the short, childhood version of her name, for her bloodline chose names that grew and reflected their experiences – was Calpa. She listened to Pandaras's story while he and Tibor devoured bowls of starchy vegetable curry, and told him that this was a bad place to be.

'The city is full of newly changed bloodlines. They are dangerous because they are burning with holy fire. Mobs sniff out those who do not agree with them, and hang or burn or stone them. We try to keep ourselves to ourselves, but we still get a lot of trouble. Have you any jungle experience? Can you hunt or fish?'

'I'm a city boy,' Pandaras said, and held up his stump. 'And I am still recovering from my wound.'

Calpa made him nervous. She was of one of the giant bloodlines, twice as big as Tibor. She was sprawled carelessly in a crude chair. One of her three-fingered hands could have easily wrapped around his skull and crushed it like a grape. The grey hide of her bare torso was heavily scarified with the welts of decorative brandings and oiled with what smelled like rancid butter. Her cropped white hair was raised in spikes over her crested skull; her flat-nosed face was dominated by muscular jaws like the opposing scoops of one of the mechanical dredgers which were always working along the shore of Ys, struggling to keep old channels open as the river dwindled.

'We're all crippled or maimed in some way or another here,' Calpa said. 'At least you can still walk.'

'My friend is a cook. I can help him.'

'We've plenty of cooks, and not enough food,' Calpa said. 'Your friend will tend to those too sick or badly hurt to work. You will join with one of the hunting parties. I bet you can run fast. Most of your bloodline can. We mostly dig traps and chase animals into them. You'll help with that. And if that doesn't work out you'll hunt for fruit. I'm sure that with even one hand you can sneak up on a tomato vine.'

'If I knew what one looked like, I could try.'

Calpa studied Pandaras, then said, 'Do you believe them?'

Her dark, sober gaze compelled him to be honest. 'I have not believed in the supremacy of the Preservers for some time. We are the strength of the city, Calpa, but we are despised by most.'

'That's the fault of men, not of those who created them.'

'Then perhaps we were badly made,' Pandaras said. 'But I am not here to become a heretic, much as I'd like to live forever.'

Calpa nodded. 'You said that you're looking for a friend. Well, if he has been here long, then he is either dead or one of them.'

'He is my master. I know that he is alive, and I know that he is somewhere in this city. Are there many camps like this one?'

'There are no masters here,' Calpa said. 'The heretics kill every officer they capture. We're just ordinary grunts. And there are only two other camps. Most of the freed prisoners run away and are killed by roving gangs of heretics in the jungles and the marshes upriver. Those that stay in the city mostly join the heretics or kill themselves. A few try to fight, of course. They don't last long. There are many thousands of heretics in the city, and many more than that in the wild country around it. This is one of their staging posts for the war.'

'And yet they let us go.'

'They murdered most of the prisoners on the ship that brought me here,' Calpa said. 'They started with the officers and carried on from there. Almost all my comrades – most of a division – are dead. The heretics didn't trouble with me because they thought I was dying, but I plan to show them that they made a bad mistake. They are arrogant and cruel, which is why they release those prisoners who survive the journey here, but they will suffer for their arrogance because they are letting us build an army in their midst. We're not ready yet, but soon enough we'll be able to do much harm here. They have a mage, for instance, who is said to be able to control every kind of machine. I have my eye on him, although he has many soldiers gathered around him.'

'What does he look like, this mage?'

'No one has ever seen him. He does not walk the city, but lives in the old palace,' Calpa said, and pointed towards the sky.

Pandaras turned. The Eye of the Preservers stood above the treetops, and a string of floating gardens was silhouetted against its dull red swirl. Calpa was pointing towards the largest, which stood some distance from the others.

She clapped her big hands together. A man came over and she told him, 'These two will stand guard duty tonight. Give them a rattle and a couple of javelins and take them out to the fern trees. Check on them at sunrise. Kill them if they are asleep.' She looked at Pandaras. 'Do you understand why we do this?'

'I can see that you don't trust newcomers.'

'We're still at war,' Calpa said. 'There are many traps and pitfalls around the camp, and we move them about. If you try to run away you'll probably be killed, and so we will be rid of you. If you choose to stay, you'll have earned the food we gave you. Keep a sharp lookout. They come for us most nights.'

Pandaras and Tibor were given javelins tipped with flaked stone points and a gourd that, filled with hard seeds and strung on a leather thong, made a passable noisemaker, and were escorted to a rocky promontory that jutted above a dense belt of fern trees and looked out across the lights of the city. Their escort showed them the positions of the lookouts on either side, and said he would be back at dawn.

When the man had gone, Pandaras hefted his javelin and threw it as hard as he could into the crowns of the fern trees below, and tossed the gourd after it. 'Get rid of yours, too,' he told Tibor. 'This place isn't for us.'

'They have food and shelter, little master, both of which we failed to find in the city.'

'Calpa believes that she is still fighting the war: no wonder she attracts trouble. We haven't been put out here as guards – we're bait. If any heretics catch us with weapons they'll kill us for sure. If they find us alone and unarmed, they may spare us.'

'Calpa said that there are many traps.'

'That fellow won't be back for us before dawn, and there will be enough light in the sky by then to pick a way. I can see well enough in what other bloodlines would consider to be pitch darkness. This is almost as bright as day to me.' An exaggeration, but Pandaras could clearly see Tibor's quizzical expression by the dim red light of the Eye. 'I'll spot any traps long before we're near them, or I'll sniff them out. Besides, I don't think they'll spend much time looking for us. Calpa hinted that many who come here run away, and I doubt that she bothers to chase after them. The way the war is going there will always be more prisoners looking for help and shelter.'

After a moment, Tibor nodded and broke the shaft of his javelin over his knee and tossed the two halves over the edge of the promontory. He said, 'How will we get to him?'

'I wondered if you'd catch on.'

'I may be slow, little master,' Tibor said, 'but I am not stupid. The mage Calpa mentioned must surely be your master. But we cannot fly through the air, and Calpa said that there are many soldiers guarding him.'

'Perhaps he'll find us. I'm certain that he is a prisoner of whoever it was that Eliphas betrayed him to. Calpa said that he was helping the heretics, and I know that my master would not help them unless forced. But although he is a prisoner, he can still call upon machines to help him. He used one to cut me free from Prefect Corin.'

'You told me about your adventures more than once,' Tibor said. 'I do not forget anything.'

'The point is that it happened in the battleground far downriver. Now we are in sight of him.'

'But although we have found him, he has not yet found you. And how can we free him if he, who is so powerful, cannot free himself? And how can you be certain that he is this mage? It seems to me that nothing is certain in this world, except the love of the Preservers.'

Pandaras sat down and massaged the stump of his left wrist. He said, 'I suppose you still believe in them.'

'Who does not? Even the heretics cannot deny that the Preservers created the world and all its peoples.'

'I mean that you believe that they still have influence in this world. That it is worth praying to them.'

Tibor reflected on this, and said at last, 'These days, most men who pray to the Preservers are really calling on their higher selves for guidance – prayer has become no more than a simple form of meditation. But I remember how it was when the avatar was still accessible within the shrine of the temple of which I was the hierodule. Ah, little master. You do not know how it was. You cannot imagine. Prayer was no solitary communion then, but a joyful conversation with a sublime and witty friend. But that is all lost now, all quite lost.'

There was a silence. Pandaras turned and saw with embarrassment that the hierodule was crying. He had forgotten that someone could take worship of the Preservers so seriously. The last of the avatars had been destroyed by the heretics long before he had been born; they were no more than a myth to him.

He pretended that he had not seen Tibor's tears and yawned elaborately and lay down, resting his head in the crook of his right arm and tucking the stump of his left wrist into his lap. He was still ashamed of the amputation and unconsciously tried to hide it whenever he could. 'We'll rest for an hour or so,' he said. 'I can feel in my muscles every step we walked today.'

After a while, Tibor said softly, as if to himself, 'The Preservers created the world, and they created the ten thousand bloodlines. They made the different races of men in their image to a greater and lesser degree, but in their charity and love they allowed their creations to find their own ways to enlightenment. We have it in ourselves to be so much more than we are, but the heretics deny that. They want no more than to be what they already are, forever and ever.'

Pandaras thought sleepily of the armoury where he had once worked for one of his uncles, of the cauldrons where metals were smelted. One of his tasks had been to skim dross from the surface of the molten metal, using a long-handled wooden paddle. The paddle had been carved from a single piece of teak; he'd had to dip it in a pail of water before each sweep, or else it would have caught fire. It seemed to him now that this work had been the reverse of what happened in the world, where the good refined themselves out of existence, leaving only the dross behind.

He slept, but could not have slept long, because when Tibor shook him awake the Eye still stood high in the black sky.

'There is fighting on the other side of the city,' Tibor said softly.

The sky was lit by a flash of intensely blue light, as if, leagues and leagues away, someone in the darkness of the jungle surrounding the city had opened a window into day. Pandaras counted off the seconds. *Four, five, six*... There was a rumble like thunder, the rock trembled like a live animal, and then he was fully awake, for he knew what weapon had just been fired. He jumped to his feet and said, 'He's found me again!'

'Your master? Then he has escaped the floating garden?'

A flock of red and green sparks shot across the city towards the place where the point of blue light had shone, but they tumbled from the sky and winked out before they could strike their target.

'The machines try to destroy him,' Pandaras said, 'but he has some kind of magic that shuts them down. I've seen it before. He was not killed. Perhaps he cannot be killed. He followed me downriver and now he is looking for me in the other camps. He will be here soon. There! There! O mercy! He is coming for me!'

Another point of blue light flared in the jungle that circled the city's basin, this time only a few leagues away.

'Who? Who is it, little master?'

The thunder was louder, and came less than two seconds after the flare of blue light. The rock shuddered again and Pandaras sat down hard, trembling with fear. He knew now how he could reach the floating garden, but he wished with all his heart that it had not come to this.

He looked up at Tibor and said, 'Yama is close by, but that display was nothing to do with him. No, it is Prefect Corin. And I will have to surrender to him, if I am ever to see my master again.'

12

THE LAST FLIGHT OF DR DISMAS

He is here, the Shadow said, and appeared above the bed as the eidolon of Derev. She was clinging to the ceiling with her fingers and toes and looking down at Yama through the fall of her feathery white hair. She was naked under her filmy shift. Her skin glowed with the soft green radiance sometimes seen on rotting wood.

'Transform,' Yama said wearily. The disc nagged at his attention, like the wink of sunlight on a far-off window. He knew that Pandaras was very close now, but he could no longer ask one of the machines to search for the boy. The Shadow had taken away even that.

The eidolon squeezed its small breasts together with one hand. *You do not like this?*

Blue light flared beyond the big eye of the window, briefly illuminating the pentad of servants who stood around the bed. For a moment, Yama thought that the feral machine had returned for him.

Something wicked this way comes.

The double doors on the far side of the room crashed open, the floating lights brightened, and Dr Dismas strode in, shouting wildly.

'Child! Dear child! Enobarbus is trying to murder us!'

Sit up, the Shadow said.

Yama obeyed without thinking. Halfway across the room, Dr Dismas stopped and stared in amazement, then pulled out his energy pistol. He wore a silvery cloak over his black suit and a cap of silver on his head; Yama remembered that the apothecary had once confided to him that he wore a hat lined with metal foil to stop machines spying on him.

The Shadow, still in the form of Derev, was suddenly standing behind Dr Dismas. It smiled and said, *I have allowed your body to overcome the good doctor's potion by a simple metabolic tweak. It is not Enobarbus who is attacking us, by the way, but let the doctor think what he will. Besides, Enobarbus is on his way.* He *thinks that Dismas is attacking* him. *Many men have already died. Many more will die. It is quite exciting. Shall I show you?*

Yama ignored this. He swung his legs over the side of the bed, and stood. One of the servants – the forest pygmy – placed a bundle of clothes at his feet. As he began to dress, he told Dr Dismas, 'It is time I made a move.'

'Of course, of course! The first thing we must do is destroy Enobarbus's machines,' Dr Dismas said. 'I hope I am speaking to the right person, by the way.'

We will not need to worry about the machines.

The eidolon of Derev vanished. Yama had a dizzy sense of doubled vision and discovered that he was once more a prisoner in his own body. It pulled on a loose white shirt, stepped into boots which fastened themselves around its ankles, and walked forward. He heard his voice, pitched an octave lower than normal, say, 'You do not need that silly little weapon, Doctor. Not with me by your side.'

Dr Dismas nodded, and lowered the pistol. He said, 'You're right, of course. I have armed the other servants. They are killing those of Enobarbus's men I have not myself already killed. We must get you to a safe place.' He snapped his stiff fingers, and one of the servants threw a silvery bundle on the bed. 'That will shield you from pellets, and from near misses of energy weapons.'

Yama tried to speak, but the Shadow had assumed complete control of his body. 'I do not need such things,' it told Dr Dismas, and flung out Yama's right arm.

The servants collapsed.

Dr Dismas raised the pistol again, pointing it at Yama's head. 'This is no time for tricks, you fool. Restore them. We need them still.'

'Even I cannot raise the dead,' the Shadow said. 'I will kill the other hybrids too, after they have defeated Enobarbus's men. Ah, I see why you wear that cap. It is more than it seems. But you will do as I say anyway. It is time we left, Doctor. Time we returned to our parent to complete our growth, to discard this frail shell. Time we took our place at the centre of the world's stage.'

The Shadow reached out to a machine speeding through the night a league away. The machine executed a crash stop, spun around, and focused every sensor on the largest of the floating gardens. There was fighting in and around the palace; the machine and others like it traced the pinpoint disturbances in the gravity field caused by use of energy weapons, and reached out to them. Flashes of intense light winked and faded across the floating garden as the batteries of the weapons were forced to yield all their energies at once. A flier shot towards the garden's rocky keel, but must have hit some invisible obstruction, for it suddenly slammed to a halt and disintegrated in a blaze of white flame.

The floating garden began to move across the night sky, sailing away from the city. Behind it, another garden tore away from the archipelago and gave chase.

The fighting in and around the camp did not last long. There was the confused noise of men and women shouting, a frantic staccato of small-arms fire, an explosion which lofted a ball of flame above the trees. Then a flash of blue light lit half the sky and there was a sudden shocking silence before the screams began, tearing the night air like ripsaws.

Pandaras paced up and down in distress. The screams pierced him to his marrow. Although he had resolved not to run, it was very hard to stay where he was.

Tibor said, 'Surely he will kill us too, little master.'

'No. He needs me to help him—'

And then Prefect Corin stooped out of the night, like an owl on a mouse. He sprang from the floating disc and ran straight at Pandaras, knocking Tibor down when the hierodule tried to get in the way. He caught Pandaras and lifted him up and stared into his face. His left eye was covered by a white adhesive pad. A rifle was slung over his shoulder. 'You should have stayed with me, boy. You would not have lost your hand. Where is he?'

Pandaras's ribcage was painfully compressed by Prefect Corin's grip; he could scarcely catch his breath. He gasped, 'Promise that you will not kill my friend.'

'A hierodule has his uses. Where?'

'Did you follow me all this way downriver? I am flattered.'

'I should have sunk the barge and killed everyone on board it. Where is he?'

'Surely you have heard of the great mage of this city, dominie.'

'I did not have time to question anyone. I was too busy looking for you. I know that he is close by. I can see the disc shining through your shirt.'

'Is that how you found me?'

'Alas, there are too many similar sources in this city.'

'So you started to search the camps, neh? I wondered why you did not come for us at the shrine, or when we were thrown off the lazaret. I suppose you killed poor Calpa and her comrades, even though they were on your side.'

'A few fled, but many more fought, and I had to kill most of them. A legless woman told me where you were before she died. Many have died because you ran from me, and all for no purpose, because I have you again. Where is he, boy?'

'This time you are here on my terms.'

'Tell me.'

The pressure of Prefect Corin's grip increased; knives ground in Pandaras's chest. He said breathlessly, 'We could go there directly on your floating disc.'

'One of the gardens, then. Which one?'

'I'll show you, if you take me with you.'

'You'll tell me now, or I will kill the hierodule at once, and take my time with you.'

'Promise you will take me with you.'

'Of course I will take you with me. I need a hostage.'

'And promise that you will not kill my master.'

'I need him. Of course not.'

'I was told that he is in the old palace,' Pandaras said.

Prefect Corin stared at him for a few moments, then said, 'This had better not be an attempt to trick me.'

'I have put my life in your hands by telling you all I know,' Pandaras said.

'It was already mine,' Prefect Corin said, and dropped him and strode towards Tibor. The hierodule lay on his back like a landed fish, staring blankly at the night sky. Prefect Corin passed a hand over his face. There was a brief flash of light. Tibor stood, slowly and clumsily, and Prefect Corin whispered to him, speaking very quickly in a language that Pandaras did not know.

'You command many things,' Pandaras said, massaging his ribs. None were broken, but several were badly bruised. 'You are becoming like my master.'

'No, not like him. Never like him. There will be another disc here in a moment, and then you will take me to Yamamanama.'

'I want only the best for my master. I am certain that he is a prisoner; otherwise he would have come to me by now. You'll help me free him, and then he'll deal with you.'

A floating disc dropped down beside the first, hovering a handspan above the rock. Prefect Corin stepped onto it. 'You will ride with the hierodule. He knows where to go. And do not try to escape; if you do, the hierodule will break your neck.'

'If you kill me you will never find him.'

'You will be paralysed, not killed. Yamamanama's disc will still work, I think. Go now.'

Because the floating disc warped gravity, it was as if the world tipped and tilted around Pandaras as, with Tibor at his back and Prefect Corin following, he sped through black air towards the string of floating gardens and his master. For a moment, he forgot that Tibor was no longer his to command, forgot the danger he was in, forgot that he was betraying his master to his worst enemy.

The largest of the gardens was moving away from the others. Prefect Corin's disc accelerated and swept ahead, making a long arc towards its rocky keel. Specks of light flew up from the orange glow of the city in long straight streams that began to bend as they tried to track him, and he shot away at right angles, towards the string of smaller gardens. The floating disc which carried Tibor and Pandaras followed.

The gardens were linked to each other by catenaries and arched bridges. A chunk of rock hung above one of them, a round lake gleaming darkly on its flat top, ringed by scattered clumps of pines. Streams of water spilled over its edge at several points and fell towards the garden below; as Pandaras was carried towards it he saw that the water in one of these streams was actually rising.

The floating disc settled at the leading edge of the rock, on an apron of lichen-splashed stone. Tibor gripped Pandaras's arm and dragged him off the disc. A moment later Prefect Corin landed beside them. Machines flew out the darkness from every direction, a hundred tiny sparks settling around him like a cloak.

'The palace has good defences,' he said, 'but this will crack them.'

The floating rock shuddered. The light of the little machines around Prefect Corin intensified, a robe of blazing light, and a shallow wave of cold water rippled across the apron of bare stone, washing over

Pandaras's feet. The rock was moving away from the archipelago, accelerating towards the big floating garden. Ragged flowers of red and yellow flame bloomed in the sky all around it.

'Now it ends,' Prefect Corin said. He stretched out his arm. Something began to spin in the air in front of his fingertips, shrieking like a banshee as it gathered light and heat around itself.

The Shadow walked beside Dr Dismas across a wide space of charred grass. They were both wrapped in silvery cloaks whose hems brushed the ground. Human-shaped animals loped along on either side. One of the nearest turned its head towards them and grinned. It was a naked woman, her elongated jaws holding racks of long white teeth slick with saliva, her eyes blazing yellow. Ahead, tall trees burned like candles. Above, a fist-sized shadow was growing larger against the sky-glow.

Yama was helpless, paralysed somewhere behind his own eyes. It was as if he was caught in a fever dream where mountains flew and monsters ran free.

Suddenly Derev was walking beside the woman-thing, her slim body glowing like a candle through her robe.

There is a problem, the Shadow said. *You will help us now, if you wish to live.*

'You cannot harm me without harming yourself.'

'You're back, my boy,' Dr Dismas said. A white star shone at his forehead – a machine clung there. 'We have defeated those who wanted to harm us, and are at last heading upriver. Unfortunately, someone is chasing us, and I do not think that it is Enobarbus.'

It is someone who can strip machines of their power.

'I can see why that would frighten you,' Yama said, realising why the Shadow still needed him, why it had allowed him to reoccupy his own body.

'It is an unfortunate complication,' Dr Dismas said. 'But we will overcome it by working together.'

They walked between two of the burning trees. Resinous smoke blew around them. A small lake had been struck by some kind of energy weapon; its water had boiled away and left a basin of dry, cracked mud. The man-animals broke away left and right, but Dr Dismas strode straight across the basin and Yama followed him. The eidolon flowed beside him. It was flickering now, as faint as a firefly near the end of its life.

'Where are we going, Doctor?'

'Why, to my paramour, of course. I thought we had discussed this. I have been betrayed by those I tried to help, Yamamanama, and I will have my revenge.'

We will gain so much.

'And I will be destroyed.'

We can work together, Yamamanama. Do not listen to what I tell the doctor.

'It is a question of transfiguration,' Dr Dismas said. 'If something new is made, is the old destroyed? No, it is changed into another form. I should know, Child of the River. I was transformed in the Glass Desert. I am neither man nor machine but something more than both, yet I still remember what I was and what I wanted, just as a man fondly remembers the foolish fantasies of his childhood.'

'Is that why you take the drug, Doctor? To obliterate your human memories?'

'In my case fusion was not quite complete. It will be different with you, Yamamanama, as you'll soon see. But first we must rid ourselves of a small problem. Someone is chasing us.'

We will become more than either of us can imagine, Yamamanama. And more than the doctor can ever dream of.

They climbed up the slope on the far side of the dry lake, towards the edge of the garden. Charred vegetation gave way to bare, hot rock that stung Yama's feet through the thin soles of his slippers. Far below, the lights of the city were receding into the dark sprawl of the jungle. Silhouetted against its sky-glow, a flat-topped rock was flying towards them at a slant. Sheets of water spilled its sides and were torn into spray. Something shone at its leading edge, a point of white light as intense as any star cluster within the galaxy.

'Something is affecting the gravity fields,' Dr Dismas said. 'We are falling too slowly.'

Yama remembered one of Zakiel's lessons, involving a lead ball from the armoury and a banyan seed. 'Surely all things fall at the same rate.'

'We fall down the length of the world because a machine in the keel of the garden manipulates gravity fields to suit our purpose. But the machine is failing. The nearer that rock gets, the slower we fall. Something on it is draining the energy grid. You must put a stop to it.'

Yama said, 'But the rock chasing us must be falling more slowly too.'

'Yes, yes,' Dr Dismas said impatiently. 'It is slowing, but it was moving faster than us in the first place.'

The eidolon had disappeared when Yama had followed Dr Dismas up the slope, but now it came back. Its eldritch glow so weak that Yama could see right through it. Its eyes were dark holes in the mask of its face; its hair a pale flicker.

You know the man who follows, it said, its words ravelling weakly across Yama's brain. *Stop him now, or we will lose our advantage . . .*

The eidolon flickered and faded, but Yama sensed that its eyes were still there, like holes burnt into the fabric of the night. The glow of the machine which clung to Dr Dismas's forehead faded too; the apothecary plucked it off with his stiff fingers and crushed it.

'I have just lost control of the garden and its machines,' he said. 'If I do not regain it we will intersect the surface of the world in forty minutes. And that rock will catch up with us before then. But you can do something about that, Yamamanama. You are not a machine. Or at least, not entirely. You will not be affected by the drain on the grid. And although my hybrids were destroyed by Enobarbus's guards, I still have many other experimental specimens. Chimeras and the like. My children of the night. They will be able to fight, and so will you.'

'And you, Doctor?'

'Oh, as for me, I will have to rely on my purely human part.'

Dr Dismas said this casually, but in the half-light Yama saw the gleam of sweat on those parts of his face not affected by the plaques of his disease. The apothecary knelt, cast a handful of plastic straws on the ground, and peered at them. 'I will not die,' he said. 'That was part of the promise made to me, and I will see that it is kept.'

He stood and raised his arm towards the rock. It eclipsed a quarter of the sky now. His energy pistol flared so brightly that dawn might have touched the tops of the Rim Mountains.

Yama ran.

The machine which Prefect Corin had set in the air was now spinning so quickly that its shriek had passed beyond the range of Pandaras's hearing. It glowed so brightly that it hurt to look at it, and had begun to melt the rock beneath it. Prefect Corin, Pandaras and Tibor retreated from it to the far side of the lake. Prefect Corin uncoiled a length of fine cord and looped it around a pine tree which stood at the edge of the rock.

The spinning machine was draining the local grid on which all machines fed, turning the energy into heat and noise. The cloak of machines had fallen away from Prefect Corin; the lights had died in the ceramic disc. Tibor was affected too; he sat with his arms wrapped around his head, rocking from side to side.

And the rock was slowly sinking through the air like a stone through water, pitching this way and that as it fell. Pandaras clung to the pine tree, his cheek pressed against its dry resinous bark. Branches soughed above him.

'Have courage, boy,' Prefect Corin said. 'Have dignity.'

'You are going to smash us to flinders!'

'Nonsense. I have calculated that we will pass a few chains above our target. Our keel may brush a few treetops, no more. Perhaps you have been wondering why I fastened the rope to the tree. Soon you will understand.' Prefect Corin's one good eye searched Pandaras's face. 'You are a coward, like all your race, small-souled and small-brained. Only a few chosen bloodlines will inherit this world when this war is done. Others will serve, or perish.'

Bolts from an energy pistol struck the leading edge of the rock; chunks of white-hot stone flew up. Most splashed into the lake, sending up spouts of steam and hot water, but one fragment tumbled amongst a stand of pines and they immediately burst into flame. Prefect Corin turned to look at the burning trees and Pandaras shrieked and lashed out. He fastened to the man's chest with his one hand and both feet, clamped his mouth on the man's thigh and twisted, coming away with a mouthful of cloth and bloody meat. And then he was flying through the air. His hip and shoulder smashed hard against stone, but he rolled and got to his feet. He was right at the edge of the floating rock. Prefect Corin was limping through fire-lit shadows towards him. Tibor stood up, his normally placid face twisted in a snarl, his big hands opening and closing. Pandaras turned and looked down, and then gave himself to the air.

The first of the man-animals attacked Yama as soon as he reached the burning trees. He pulled off his silvery cloak and threw it over the creature, and in the moment it took for it to shake off the cloak he snatched up a burning branch and jabbed it in its face. It was not afraid of fire and sprang straight at him and knocked him down, but Yama discovered that his attacker had only a child's strength. Unlike the other servants, the man-animals had been grown rather than surgically transformed, and Dr Dismas had not had time to bring them to maturity. Enveloped in rank stench and feverish body-heat, sharp teeth snapping a finger's width from his face, he got his thumbs on the creature's windpipe and stood up, lifting it with him, and pressed and pressed until its eyes rolled back, then put his palm under its jaw and snapped its neck.

Two more man-animals skulked around him, but when he picked up the burning branch they turned tail and ran. He yelled and threw the branch after them.

The rock was very close now.

Yama ran. The sally port where fliers docked with the floating garden was near the palace. Perhaps one of the fliers which had brought Enobarbus's men was still intact. He was halfway there when the rock passed overhead.

Its keel scraped the crag where Dr Dismas had taken him and came on, snapping the tops from trees, showering broken rocks. A tree, aflame from top to bottom, toppled across Yama's path. He skidded and fell down amidst a storm of burning fragments. For a moment he thought that he might faint, that something was trying to pluck his soul from his body, and then it passed and he picked himself up and ran on. He knew that he had only a little time now.

A semicircular amphitheatre sloped down towards the platforms of the sally port. It had been lit by decads of suspensor lamps, but only a few were still working, fitfully illuminating the remains of a terrible battle. Gardens of stone and miniature cedars and clumps of bamboos had been trampled and broken and burnt. There were numerous fires, and patches of scorched stone radiated fierce heat and sent up drifts of choking white smoke. Yama found many corpses, men and things like men, sprawled alone or entangled in a final embrace. Many were so badly burnt that they were little more than charcoal logs, arms and legs drawn up to their chests in rictus, bones showing through charred flesh. Yama armed himself with a gisarme and was about to pluck a pellet pistol from a dead soldier's grasp when someone ran at him. He made a wild swipe with the gisarme, then saw who it was and managed to turn the blow so that the pointed axe-head thumped into the ground.

A moment later, Yama and Pandaras threw their arms around each other and whirled around their common axis. The boy began to babble his story, beginning with the way he had escaped Prefect Corin, but Yama hushed him and explained what Pandaras must do for him.

'Master, I cannot—'

'I should have had you do it as soon as I discovered them growing under my skin. I should have guessed then what Dr Dismas had done to me.'

'Prefect Corin was not drowned, master. He used me to find you. He sends machines to sleep. You will need all your strength to face him.'

'This will make me stronger, not weaker. We must be quick, Pandaras. The thing which stops machines working is on the rock you fell from, is it not?'

'Unless Prefect Corin brought it with him. But it had grown very hot and very bright.'

'Because it was drawing energy from a wide area. The machines here will begin to work once it has passed out of range. You must do it now and do it quickly. No time for fine surgery.' Yama noticed for the first time that the boy had lost his left hand. He said, 'I am sorry, Pandaras. There will be more pain if you choose to stay with me.'

Pandaras drew himself up. He was very ragged and had a haunted, starved look, but he met Yama's gaze and said, 'I am your squire, master. I lost you for a while, but now I have found you I will not let you escape me so easily again. What do you want me to do?'

They could not find a knife amongst the dead, so Yama broke off the tip of a sword. Pandaras wrapped the fragment in a strip of cloth, and Yama sat with his back pressed against a rough boulder, his hands braced against his thighs and a sliver of wood between his teeth. The pain was not as bad as he had feared, and at first there was only a little blood. The plaques lay just beneath his skin, and Pandaras had to cut away only a little flesh to expose them.

'It's a queer kind of stuff, master,' Pandaras said. 'Like plastic and metal granules that have been melted together. I can see things like roots. Should I cut out those, too?'

Yama nodded.

The pain was suddenly sharper. He closed his eyes and clenched his teeth. An intimate scraping, metal on bone. Red and black flashes in his eyes. Hot blood dripped from the point of his chin. Pandaras pushed his head down, and there was a sharp slicing pain in his neck.

'It's done, master,' Pandaras said. He held a decad of small irregular shapes in his bloody hand. Wiry whiskers stuck out from their corners.

'Throw them away,' Yama said. 'If I start behaving in a strange way, knock me out and tie me up. Do not let me near any dirt. There is metal in dirt. Do you understand?'

'Not entirely, master, but I'll get rid of these at once.'

Pandaras ripped up the cloak of a dead soldier and placed a pad of cloth over the left side of Yama's face and held it in place with a strip tied around his jaw and the top of his head. Yama's face was numb, but there was a feeling of fire at the edge of the numbness. The wound on the back of his neck was more trivial, but it was bleeding badly.

'We're getting near the river now,' Pandaras said. 'And look, the disc is beginning to glow again.'

He held it up: it showed a faint, grainy light.

'Arm yourself,' Yama said. He got to his feet and took a step, then another, but stumbled on the third.

Instantly, Pandaras was by his side. He made Yama sit down, untied the cloth around his head, and whistled. 'I cut a vein, I think. I'm sorry, master, I am not much of a sawbones. I learned a little of it from one of my uncles, who worked at one of the fighting pits, but not quite enough, it seems. I should stitch the wound, but I don't have any tackle. I could put a compress on—'

'Cauterise it.'

'It will leave a scar. Of course, the jacks who worked the pits liked that kind of thing. It made them look fiercer, neh? But you do not want that, master. A compress—'

Yama picked up the bit of sword and stumbled over to a man-sized machine which had broken apart and was burning with a fierce, steady flame. He thrust the tip of the sword into the centre of the fire.

'We do not have time for niceties,' he said. 'I must be able to fight.'

'You couldn't fight a puppy right now,' Pandaras said. He wrapped a bit of cloth around his hand and drew the broken sword tip from the white heart of the burning machine. 'Cry out if you want. They say it helps the pain. And hold on to my arm, here.'

Yama did not cry out, because it might have brought his enemy to him, but he almost broke Pandaras's left arm when the boy thrust the point of the hot metal into the wound in his cheek. There was a hiss, and the smell of his own blood burning.

'Done,' Pandaras said. He was crying, but his hand was steady and deft as he packed Yama's wound. He retied the strip of cloth around Yama's head, then tied another around his neck and under his arm to hold a compress against the lesser wound in his neck.

The disc was burning brighter. Pandaras held it up and said, 'Shall I throw this away? He knows how to find it: it is how he found me and it is why he kept me alive, so that he could find you. In any case, we should run now, master. If the disc is working again, then surely you can command some machine to take us away.'

'I want Prefect Corin to find us,' Yama said. 'He destroyed my home. He was responsible for the death of my father. I will have an accounting.'

'He will kill you.'

'I do not think he came here to do that. If I do not confront him, Pandaras, then I will never be able to rest, for he will not.'

'That's as maybe, but I don't know if you *can* kill him. Those monsters you called up from the depths couldn't. I think he jumped on a floating disc and sailed away from them.'

'I do not know if I want to kill him, Pandaras. That is why I want to see him.'

Yama took the gisarme. Pandaras found a short ironwood stave. They armed themselves with pellet pistols, too. As they climbed out of the sally port's amphitheatre, some of the dead began to stir and twitch. The machines in Dr Dismas's servants were awakening in bodies too mutilated to control. Yama found a legless torso trying to drag itself along, guts trailing behind it, and dispatched it with the spike of the gisarme.

Yama began to call out to Prefect Corin as he and Pandaras walked towards the far edge of the garden, through near-darkness lit only by burning trees. But the Shadow found him first, suddenly gliding beside him at the edge of his vision. As before, it took the form of Derev, but this time her likeness was distorted to resemble one of Dr Dismas's man-animals, naked and on all fours. Its voice was a faint hiss, like the last echo of creation.

You cannot destroy me, Child of the River. I am wrapped around every neuron in your brain.

'I do not want to destroy you. I want you to help me understand what I am.'

Pandaras said, 'What is it, master? Is he here?'

'No, not yet. It is the thing in my head.'

You are a fool to deny what we can become. A worm, a weakling. How I will torment you.

It tipped back its head, its throat elongating, and howled like a dervish.

Something like a faint wash of flame passed across Yama's mind. He bore it easily.

Pandaras said, 'But I cut it out!'

'Not all of it. Just those parts which drew power from the world's energy grid. It will be no more powerful than me now, unless it can regrow those parts.'

I will take the iron from your blood, you fool! I will cleave myself so tightly against your every nerve that you will never be rid of me.

But the sparks of the Shadow's words flickered so faintly they were easier to ignore than the growing sense of the weave of machines which mapped the dark world all around. It was stronger than ever, an overlapping babble of voices near and far. Yama called upon one of the machines which served the garden, and it explained in a rapid, agitated staccato that the gravithic grids of the platform were exhausted, and it was falling in an irrecoverable trajectory.

Pandaras squinted at the glowing thing that beat before Yama's face on a blur of vanes. 'They work for Prefect Corin,' he said.

'Not here. It wants us to evacuate this place. It seems that we shall strike the world in a handful of minutes.'

'But you will save us, master.'

'No.'

'But you must!'

'I cannot.' The machine was trying to explain about realignment and repolarisation, but Yama asked it to be quiet, and told Pandaras, 'There is not enough time for the garden to soak up enough energy to regain its lift.'

The machine added something tartly, and with a shrill whir of vanes flew up into the night.

'Apparently, the rock will strike the world first,' Yama told Pandaras.

'As if that makes any difference. What's that?'

Yama heard it a moment later. An animal frenzy of howls and yips, and then a stutter of rifle fire.

He ran, feeling the cauterised wound in his cheek part at every step, ran between the burning trees, across the cracked basin of the lake, up the rocky slope. His head was full of voices. His face was a stiff mask with hot needles pushed through it into his skull, and his legs were rubbery, but he leaped from rock to rock in the near-dark, using skills he had learned as a child while clambering about the slopes of the City of the Dead, and did not stumble.

Dr Dismas stood at the far edge of the crag, his silvery cloak and cap glimmering in the firelit dark. A pentad of his naked man-animals cowered around him. Their round eyes glowed green or red, reflecting the light of decads of tiny machines orbiting the man who leaned on his staff fifty paces away.

'Yamamanama,' Prefect Corin said, without looking away from Dr Dismas. 'You have come to me as I knew you would.' A rifle was slung over his shoulder, and Dr Dismas's energy pistol was tucked into his belt. The pale-skinned hierodule, clad only in ragged trews, squatted beside him, and bared his teeth when Pandaras called to him.

Hot pain raked Yama's face when he spoke. He said, 'Not at all. Instead, you have come to me.'

'You are still a vain and foolish boy,' Prefect Corin said. 'While we travel back to Ys you will dwell on the deaths that your pride has caused.'

Dr Dismas said, 'Kill him, Yamamanama. Do it quickly. We have far to go.'

'Be quiet,' Prefect Corin said in his calm, soft voice. 'You have much to answer for, too. Taking away your little realm is only the beginning of the reckoning.'

'The laboratories are nothing,' Dr Dismas said, and tapped the side of his head. 'It is all in here.'

Prefect Corin told Yama, 'A flier will be here in a moment. Unless, of course, you can save this garden. One way or another, we will be in the heart of our department by dawn. There will be a new beginning. Frankly, you need it. You look bad, Yamamanama. Wounded, bloody, and ill-used. I will make sure that you get the medical attention you need. I will heal you, and then we will begin again.'

Yama said as steadily as he could, 'I will not serve.'

Prefect Corin looked at him for the first time. He said, 'We all serve, Child of the River. We are all servants of the Preservers.'

Yama remembered what Sergeant Rhodean had told him outside the tent where the Aedile had lain dying, on the farside shore after the sack of Aeolis, and saw now what Prefect Corin was. Saw that the man's reserve was not a discipline, but a pretence that he was like other men. That his humble air was a mask which hid his hunger for all the world's powers, all its riches. Yama had thought that his hatred of Prefect Corin would be too much to bear, but now he felt pity as much as hate, and pity diminished the man.

He found that he was able to meet and hold Prefect Corin's gaze.

He said, 'The Preservers do not ask for servants. They ask nothing of us but that we become all we can be.'

'You have been too long amongst the heretics, Child of the River,' Prefect Corin said. 'That will also be attended to.'

'I am not a heretic,' Dr Dismas said. 'For that alone you should kill him, Yamamanama.'

Prefect Corin ignored the apothecary, concentrating his mild gaze on Yama.

A worm of blood was trickling along the angle of Yama's jaw. He said, 'The world is not a ledger, with good and evil in separate tallies. There is no division into good and evil. It is all one thing, light and shadow in play together. No one can set themselves aside from it unless they remove themselves completely.'

He had never been so certain as at that moment, there on the highest point of a garden slowly falling out of the sky. He was aware of everything around him – the wind which carried the harsh stink of burning, the trajectory of the garden and of the rock that fell ahead of it, the myriads of machines in the cities along the shrinking shore of the Great River, the flier that was speeding towards the garden, still a hundred leagues off.

He made a few adjustments.

At the same moment, Prefect Corin struck down with the point of his staff. Stone shattered around it, cracks running outwards from where he stood to every point of the crag, and the whole mass of the garden quivered like a whipped animal. Pandaras fell down; the hierodule raised his head and howled.

Dr Dismas snickered. His man-animals hunched around him. 'You've made him lose his temper, Yamamanama.'

Prefect Corin pointed his staff at him. Machines whirled up in a brilliant blaze above his head. 'Be quiet, devil! Your part in this is over.'

'You're as bad as the heretics,' Dr Dismas said, and turned his back in disgust.

The hierodule was still howling, his muscles straining against each other under his flabby skin.

Yama told Pandaras to hold up the disc, saw the knot in the hierodule's mind, and loosened it. 'Be quiet, Tibor. He will not use you any more. Come to me.'

The hierodule blinked and fell silent. The cloud of machines around Prefect Corin suddenly spun away in every direction, leaving the crag lit only by firelight and the dim glow of the Eye of the Preservers. The Prefect reversed his grip of the staff and began to beat the hierodule about his shoulders. 'Do not listen, you fool! Obey your rightful master! Obey! Obey!'

Dr Dismas was laughing. The man-animals crouched at his feet made excited little yips and howls.

'You do not have the right to use him,' Yama said. 'It is all right, Tibor. Come to me.'

Tibor ducked away from Prefect Corin's blows and stood up. He said, 'It is good to see you again, master. I thought you had fallen over the edge of the world.'

'Not yet,' Yama said. The words were compelled from him by Tibor's mild stare; they seemed to come from somewhere in the babble of voices in his head. He remembered his dream in the tomb in the Silent Quarter of the City of the Dead, and then remembered Luria, the true pythoness in the Department of Vaticination. A truth came to him, brilliant and splendid. It was like the peacock, but he could bear it now. Lifted on great wings of exhilaration, he felt that he could bear anything.

He said, 'The disc that Pandaras carried for so long enables access to the space inside shrines, just like the induction loop in a hierodule like Tibor. And one can talk with the other. My father was fascinated by the past, and his excavations turned up many discs like it. I think that in the Age of Enlightenment people used them as commonly as we use money, but they did not use them to buy the stuff of everyday life. Instead, they bought access to the shrines. Anyone could consult the aspects then, without the mediation of priests or hierodules.' Yama turned to Pandaras and grasped the boy's hand. 'Do you remember when we walked towards the Temple of the Black Well? Do you remember the medallions in the windows of those poor shops, the medallions that people hung on their walls to ward off the ghosts of dead machines? I thought then that I recognised the engravings on their surfaces, and now I see that they are similar to the patterns of light in this disc. The people remember, even if they do not understand what they remember. They are the strength of the city, Pandaras! The strength of the world!'

'You are hurting me, master,' Pandaras said. There was fear in his eyes.

Yama apologised and let go. But his joy did not diminish. It grew as the babble of voices in his head grew: he was dissolving into it, forgetting his fear, his anger, the agony of Pandaras's hasty surgery.

'I forgive your ravings,' Prefect Corin said. 'Your father is ages dead, and the Aedile of Aeolis was a foolish man who looked only to the past. He was the beginning of your corruption, Yamamanama, and I will be the end of it. No more talk now. Perhaps you think to convince me by reason, but I am proof against your reason. Perhaps you came to duel with me, thinking to decide the fate of the world in the way of the old stories, but they are only stories. I could kill you now, and there would be an end to it.'

Yama laughed. He threw the gisarme to one side, pulled the pellet pistol from his waistband and threw that away too. He spread his empty hands. 'Those were for Dr Dismas's servants. But I see that only a few are left.'

Dr Dismas turned and said, 'Enough for my purposes.'

He made no signal, but the man-animals leaped towards Prefect Corin in a single fluid movement. There was a wash of flame. Yama turned away from the sear of heat and light, but thought that he glimpsed Dr Dismas falling beyond the edge of the crag, a fierce froth of flame beating at the mirror of his silvery cloak. When he turned back, the stones of the place where the apothecary had been standing were glowing with a dull red heat, and Prefect Corin was pointing the energy pistol at him.

'If you thought that he would kill me,' the Prefect said, 'then you were wrong. I will use this against you if I have to, and at its full setting.'

Yama said, 'I came here to see what kind of man you were. Now I know.'

'I am a servant of something far greater than you, boy.'

'I once feared you because of the authority you embodied. But then you sacked Aeolis and killed my father, and I knew that you misused your authority for your own ends. You are not my nemesis, Corin.'

Prefect Corin leaned on his staff, attempting to command Yama and Pandaras and Tibor with his gaze. 'Talk on, boy. You have a few minutes.'

'Fewer than you think.'

'You do not command here. The garden is mine.' Prefect Corin set something in the air before him. It was a sketch of a solid object that was neither a sphere nor a cube but somehow both at once, and seemed far bigger than the space which contained it. Prefect Corin said, 'If I start this spinning it will draw the energy from every machine. There will be no help for you.'

'Then the flier will not come, and the world is rushing towards us.'

'I can stop the machine a moment before the flier arrives. Meanwhile, your little tricks will come to nothing.'

'You have thought of everything,' Yama said, 'but it does not mean that you are right.'

'I have right on my side, boy.'

Yama's heart quickened. Although he strove to keep his face calm, his hands were trembling. Let Prefect Corin think it was fear. The moment was approaching. He had only to finish this.

He took a deep breath and said, 'The Department of Indigenous Affairs once worked in harmony with the other departments of the civil service, to keep the world as it always was. They are much like the heretics, for both abhor change. One struggles to knit society together at the expense of individual destiny; the other wants to destroy society so that a few lucky individuals might live forever: both deny change. But life is change. The Preservers taught us that when they created this world and its inhabitants, when they shaped the ten thousand bloodlines. And the Preservers changed too, and changed so much that they could no longer bear this universe. All of life is change.'

Prefect Corin said, 'You have learned nothing, or unlearned all you were taught. If not for the interventions of the civil service, the ten thousand bloodlines would have warred against each other and destroyed the world long ago. We maintain and preserve a society in which every man has a place, and is happy in that place. The Great River which sustains this world is the first lesson, for it is always changing and always the same. And so with society, in which individuals live and die. Even bloodlines change and rise towards the nothingness of enlightenment and pass away from this world, but the world remains as it is. There are always more individuals, and always more bloodlines.'

'The Great River is failing,' Yama said. He was aware of a voice at the forefront of the crowd of voices which yammered and babbled inside his head. It was counting down the seconds. There was only a little more time. He said, 'Even the indigenous races know that the river fails. Your department has decided that it speaks for the Preservers, and in its arrogance it has lost its way. For no one in this world can speak for the Preservers, who are no longer of this world. We can cling to the words they left us, but nothing new can come of them.'

'We need nothing more than their words. All good men are guided by them. How badly you have strayed, Yamamanama. But I will save you.'

'The Department of Indigenous Affairs has become what it fights against. I do not blame it, because it was inevitable. There has to be one strong department to lead the war against the heretics, but its strength wrecks the consensus essential to the civil service. For if the war is won then the department will assume all the powers of the civil service, as it has already assumed the territories of other departments in the Palace of the Memory of the People. And it will become a greater tyranny than the heretics could ever be.'

'We will win, and things will be as they were.'

'Why then are you here?'

'I represent the department.'

'No. You are a man who wants power within the department. I am a way to that power. There are other men like you. When the war is over, you and your kind will fight each other. Perhaps not at once, perhaps not for ten thousand years, but it will happen at last, and the department will destroy itself. In making the assumption that anything you do is for the good of the world, you excuse all your actions, good and bad, until you can no longer distinguish between them. But I think that is enough. You do not listen to me.'

'There will be all the time in the world for that, Yamamanama. At my leisure, in the Palace of the Memory of the People. But I will talk then, and you will listen. All you make now are animal noises. Noises which mean nothing.'

'There is no more time. The flier will not come. I ordered it away.'

'It is almost here,' Prefect Corin said.

'A machine tells you that. Do not rely on machines, Corin.'

'Enough of your tricks,' Prefect Corin said, and the thing in the air in front of him began to spin, gathering itself into a soft red haze that at once began to brighten towards the colour and intensity of the sun, and shrieking like the world's last end.

The voices in Yama's head died away. He took up their count.

Twelve.

Pandaras cried out in alarm and dismay. 'Master! Would you kill us?'

'Would you die to save the world, Pandaras?'

Seven.

'What kind of question is that, master? If I refused, the world would die and I would die anyway. And if I sacrificed myself, I would not care that the world lived. In any case, I do not like this talk of dying.'

Two. One.

'Then follow me,' Yama said.

Now.

Impossibly, the sun rose downriver. No, it could not be the sun, for as the blister of light spread out horizontally it suddenly redoubled in brightness, and redoubled again. It was so bright that Yama could see the bones of the hand he flung up to save his eyes.

The floating rock had struck the river and the first machine that Prefect Corin had set spinning to draw energy from the local grid had collapsed, releasing all its stored energy at once.

The concussion of the impact arrived in a blast of air and thunder. Yama was knocked down by a howling gale full of water and bits of debris: it was as if the distinction between air and river had been abolished. Tibor was struggling with Prefect Corin, trying to force down the Prefect's outflung arm. Yama got to his feet, swept up Pandaras and yelled at Tibor to follow, and ran straight over the edge of the crag.

A violent gust caught Yama and Pandaras: for a moment they hung in the midst of a hard, driving rain. A double shadow at the edge of the crag might have been Prefect Corin and Tibor. Then the gust failed. Yama and Pandaras fell past the edge of the floating garden. Above them, a blade of light broke the sky in half.

They did not fall far – the world had risen very close to the floating garden – but the impact was unforgiving. Yama plunged down and down through roaring dark water. Pandaras was torn from his grasp. He struck upwards, breaking surface and drawing in a great gasping breath that was half air, half water.

Despite the storm it was as bright as day, although the light was sulphur yellow and came from the wrong quarter of the sky. Above, the floating garden slid past like a great ship, a solid shadow against an achingly bright nimbus. Something was climbing from that intolerable light. A stalk or pillar of black smoke and ordinary fire that rose higher and higher and blossomed at last in the upper reaches of the atmosphere as a great thunderhead. Brilliant stitches of lightning blinked around it.

Yama kicked against the flood, turning in a complete circle as waves lifted and dropped him. The wounds in his face and neck were ablaze with pain. He glimpsed something between two waves close by and swam strongly towards it. It was Pandaras. Yama caught the boy by the scruff of his neck and Pandaras tried to climb up him in blind panic.

Yama asked forgiveness and knocked him out with a swift clean punch, and got an arm around his chest to support him.

As Yama and Pandaras were lifted and dropped by line after line of waves that marched away upriver, something came walking across the water towards them, small and sharply focused at first, but becoming more and more indistinct as it neared.

Derev.

Yama roared into wind and rain. 'Get out of my mind!'

She was a giant, transparent as smoke. Her great wings unfurled far into the storm. She stooped towards him and her face writhed and became a horror of snakes and scorpions, and then she seemed to be blown away in rags and tatters by the wind.

Pandaras stirred, and then came awake and at once began to struggle again.

'Quiet,' Yama said, 'or I will have to hit you a second time.'

'I can't swim with only one arm!'

'There is no point trying to swim. The second blast wave will be here soon.'

They were shouting into each others' ears against the tremendous howl of wind and rain and the roar of clashing waves.

'When the other garden hits, master?'

'No, from the first impact. From Prefect Corin's machine. First there was light, and then the first blast wave, travelling through air. But because energy travels more slowly through water than through air there will be a second wave. I will do my best to save us, Pandaras. Do not be afraid.'

They rose on the crest of another wave. For a moment, wind swept aside curtains of rain. The Great River dwindled away ahead of them, hatched by lines of waves driven by the strong wind. The floating garden had vanished – perhaps it too had struck the river. The false sunrise had faded, but the pillar of burning smoke still stood at the vanishing point where the nearside and farside edges of the world seemed to meet. The cloud at its top was spreading out and its light was deepening to a ghastly red.

Yama wondered how much energy the machine had managed to store before it had been dissipated at the moment of impact. Prefect Corin had not understood the power of the things he thought he controlled.

The first machine arrived, plucking at the yoke of Yama's loose shirt. Then another, and a decad more. The largest was a kind of wire-thin dragonfly as long as his arm, but most were much smaller. Together, they pulled Yama and Pandaras a handspan above the clashing wave-tops, and then more arrived, lifting them higher into the rain-filled wind.

Above the noise of the storm there was a sound like a tremendous cannonade. Far away down the length of the world, the river seemed to be tilting into the sky.

13

THE FOREST FOLK

The flood seethed and roared through the forest, knocking down every tree for many leagues beyond the shore of the Great River, depositing vast shoals of silt and gravel and mud. Streams and creeks ran at full spate as the water receded, carving deep new channels or filling new lakes behind cofferdams of debris. The machines carried Yama and Pandaras far inland, to the top of a plateau that rose like a steadfast fortress above the devastation.

It was raining hard, and restless winds drove dense reefs of mist back and forth. They made camp as best they could. Pandaras built a crude shelter from broken branches and Yama lay down inside it, on a bed of fragrant pine boughs. He was exhausted, and bruised over his entire body, and the incisions in his face and scalp throbbed and stung.

'You shouldn't have sent those machines away,' Pandaras said. 'We need food, and something to treat your wounds. Bring them back, master. Ask them for help. Ask them to take us to civilisation.'

'No,' Yama said wearily. 'No more machines.'

Too many people had died because of his ability to bend machines to his will. He feared now that he might inadvertently destroy the world. And if he called on any machine, his enemies might be able to track him down. He had even shut down the disc which had guided Pandaras to him. No more machines. They would have to manage as best they could.

The Shadow tormented him with visions of destruction for the rest of that night. It showed him people combing through the ruins of cities in the midst of driving rainstorms, ships swept inland, piles of drowned animal and human corpses. It showed him the crater left by the detonation of Prefect Corin's machine, a circular sea rimmed with swales of half-melted rock and shrouded by the smoke of great fires that still burned all around it. And then, when he was at his weakest, streaming with fever sweat, the Shadow finally revealed itself. It was faint and insubstantial, its form melting and changing from Derev to the Aedile, from Telmon to others of his dead. So many dead.

All of it is your work, Child of the River. Will you save the world by destroying it? But you cannot destroy me. I will be with you always. I can help you, if you will let me.

'No. No more.'

'Hush, master,' Pandaras said. 'Try to rest. Try to sleep.'

'It is in my dreams, Pandaras.'

I will always be with you.

Pandaras tended Yama all night, and in the morning brought fruit he had collected from the forest round about. But Yama would eat only a handful of ripe figs and drink a few sips of rainwater. He was still gripped by the terror of his fever dreams.

'Those people, Pandaras! Those poor people!'

'Hush, master. Be still. Rest. I will fetch you more food. You must eat and get well.'

The forest frightened Pandaras. It covered the top of the plateau, dense, dripping wet, full of shadows and strange noises. Everything was predicated in the vertical, dominated by giant trees which gripped the thin soil with buttress roots, sucked up water and precious minerals from the stony laterite, and spread vast rafts of foliage high overhead. There were cottonwoods with feathery foliage and pendant strings of hard-hulled nuts, silkwoods and greenhearts and cedars, stands of fibrous copal trees. Vines and lianas threw up long loops, gaining holds on branches and throwing up yet more loops as they scrambled for light. Parasitic orchids clung to bark like splashes of paint. Smaller trees grew in the dancing spangles of light that filtered through the canopies of the giants: sago palms with scaly trunks; palmettos with saw-toothed leaves; acacias defended by ferocious emmets as long as Pandaras's thumb; balsams seeping sticky, strongly scented sap; the spiny straps of raffias which caught at his clothes and flesh. And in the dense shade beneath the secondary growth were ferns, bamboos and dank white fungi shaped like vases, or human brains.

Pandaras saw no animals bigger than a butterfly as he picked his way between the mossy buttress roots of the soaring trees, but he was convinced that at any moment he might confront a manticore or dragon or some other monster that might swallow him in a single gulp.

Although everything was verdant, a riot of greenery struggling upwards for light, fruiting trees and bushes were rare and hard to find. Towards the end of the second day Pandaras went further than he had dared to venture before, following a narrow path between stands of long-stemmed plants which raised glossy green leaves high above his head. It was close to sunset. The level rays of the sun were beginning to insinuate themselves beneath the high canopy of the giant trees. In the far distance something was making a noise like a bell rung over and over; insects sizzled all around.

By now, he had been bitten by mosquitoes so often that he thought nothing of the sudden stabbing pain in his chest. He brushed at it in irritated reflex, then stared in astonishment at the little arrow, a sliver of bamboo fletched with blue feathers, that fell at his feet.

The tall grasses around him parted. Men smaller than himself stepped onto the path, and then the world flew up and struck the length of his body.

At first, Yama thought that the people who lifted him out of the shelter and laid him on a litter of woven banana leaves were part of the fever dreams sent to him by the Shadow. There seemed to be a hundred of them, men and women and children. They carried him a long way through the twilight forest, crossing the plateau to a temporary camp in a clearing in the shade of a grandfather kapok tree.

They treated Yama's wounds with moss and fungus, and bathed him with infusions of willow roots to reduce his fever. They were an indigenous people, and called themselves the bandar yoi inoie, which meant the forest folk. They were small and stout, with disproportionately large heads and coarse black hair which they tied back with thread and feathers or stiffened into spikes with white clay. Some wore torcs of beaten copper enamelled with intricate patterns of ultramarine and beryl. Their brown skin was loose and hung in folds, and they pierced the folds with intricate patterns of thorns and decorated themselves with mud or pigments from crushed flowers and berries daubed in spirals and zigzag lines.

The various troops communicated with each other by drumming on the resonant buttress roots of the great trees of the forest, and when certain trees came into flower three or four troops would meet up and hold marriage contests. They peopled the forest with monstrous gods – every useful plant or animal had a story concerning the way its secret had been stolen or tricked from these deities – and feared lightning more than anything else, for it killed several of them each year, uprooted beloved trees, and sometimes started devastating fires. They had many taboos against inviting thunderstorms; they were forbidden to hunt monkeys, for instance, or even to laugh at their antics.

Although they lived freely in the forests, the bandar yoi inoie were slaves of a Shaped bloodline, the Mighty People. The Mighty People had fought a Change War recently, the chief of the troop of forest folk told Yama. The old ways had been overthrown by new ideas from the sky, and had been burnt up so that they could never come back. The temple had been desecrated and its priest and hierodules killed. Many of the Mighty People had been killed in the war too, and those who survived no longer lived together in their city of communal long houses, but were scattered across their lands.

'They have become heretics,' Yama said.

The chief nodded solemnly. He was a strong man, ugly even by the standards of the bandar yoi inoie. He had pushed porcupine quills through his cheeks and the folded skin of his chest. The tip of his long nose rested on his swollen upper lip. His name was Yoi Sendar.

'We know about the heretics,' he said. 'Don't look so surprised, man. We travel all over the forests to find food for ourselves and for the Mighty People. We talk to many travellers. We know the heretics take their ideas from a forgotten clutch of the larvae of the Preservers, who recently stepped down from the sky. The ideas are old and bad, but they are as sweet as honey to our beloved Mighty People.'

'But you were not seduced by them.'

'It was ordained by the Preservers that we can never change. We can only be what we are.' Yoi Sendar tapped the tip of his pendulous nose. 'But these are strange times. All things change, it seems. Perhaps even the bandar yoi inoie. We love the Mighty People, but they have grown strange and harsh. They are no longer our kind dear masters of old. You will see for yourself, when we return. Although we wish long and hard that things might be otherwise, I fear the changes are written in stone.'

'Be careful what you wish for, Yoi Sendar.'

You would set yourself up as saviour of these people? O Yamamanama, how I will punish you, by and by.

Yama ignored the Shadow's dim whisper. He was feeling stronger now. It was three days after he had been found by the forest folk. His wounds were healing and his fever had abated, and he had been fed well. He was able to bear the visions which the Shadow brought to him in the night. They were his secret shame, his punishment for having dared to act like a Preserver. Never again. Never ever again. He wished that he could renounce everything and find Derev and marry her if she would have him, but he knew that it could not be so simple. He knew that he was set on a hard road that would almost certainly end in his death.

Pandaras had recovered, too. He had made a flute from a joint of bamboo and was playing in the sunlight at the edge of the clearing to an audience of children who were as interested in the fetish he wore on his arm as they were in his jaunty tunes.

The huge kapok tree in the centre of the clearing was hung with sleeping cocoons woven from grass and ferns, each tailored to its owner. They would be abandoned when the troop packed up their camp: the forest folk had no permanent home. Men and women were tending the long trench of coals over which they smoked the flesh of the fat caterpillars they collected deep in the forest. These were a delicacy for both the forest folk and the Mighty People. Thousands of caterpillars hung from frames suspended over the hot coals, on which leaves of certain aromatic plants were now and then cast. Sweet blue smoke hazed the beams of sunlight which fell through the kapok's leaf-laden branches.

Yama asked the chief why he and his troop worked for the Mighty People. 'It seems to me that you are as free a people as any on the world.'

Yoi Sendar said, 'It is a long story, and you may not have one as good.'

It was a traditional challenge amongst the bandar yoi inoie, who decided their social status and won their husbands and wives by their ability to tell tales. Young men and women were already settling at a respectful distance, ready to enjoy the story, and to learn how to improve their own tale-telling from Yoi Sendar's example.

Yama smiled as best he could, and told Yoi Sendar that he would very much like to hear his story. 'Then perhaps you would like to hear one of mine, although I doubt that it is as finely made as yours.'

His wounds were scarring over, leaving his face stiff and numb. It was as if he was wearing an ill-made mask. He had spent a long time looking at it in one of the forest folk's precious mirrors. The right side was not too bad, but the left, which Pandaras had cauterised, was a patchwork of welted flesh, pulling down his eye and lifting the corner of his mouth.

He had become outwardly what he believed he was inwardly: a monster, an outcast. Derev would never cease to love the boy he had been, but how could she love what he had become? Perhaps it was best that he went to his death after all.

Die? I will not let us die, Child of the River. We will live forever.

'This is one of the least of the stories I know, but I hope it will amuse you,' Yoi Sendar said, and held up two fingers by his ear. His audience shifted, focusing their attention on the grave, ugly little man.

'Listen then, O my people. This is a story of long ago, after the Preservers brought us to this world but before we met our dear masters, the Mighty People.

'In that long-ago time we were always hungry. A group of us went far into the forests to look for game and found nothing. They walked and walked and at last they sat down to rest on what seemed to be the fallen trunk of a huge tree. But when one of them stuck the point of his knife into the scaly bark, blood spurted out, for they were not sitting on a fallen tree at all, but on the King of All Snakes. The King had been sleeping, and the knife wound woke him and made him very angry. But the men were mighty hunters, and although he struck out and tried to crush them in the coils of his body, they evaded his attack and hacked off his head.

'When they were certain that he was dead (for some snakes have a head at either end), they began to butcher his body, for they were very hungry. Yet as the blood of the King of All Snakes drained into the ground, a heavy rain began to fall, feeding a great flood that filled the forest. The flood washed away the hunters, and all human habitation for many leagues around. We have just witnessed a great flood, O my brothers and sisters, but this flood was far greater.

'Only one woman survived. She climbed to the top of a high mountain and squeezed into a crack in the rock behind the shelter of a creeper. The wind blew the creeper back and forth against the rock, and from this friction jumped showers of sparks. The woman caught some of these sparks and used them to light a fire made from dead husks picked from the outer skin of the creeper. The warmth encouraged the creeper to put forth flowers, which the woman ate. And so she had food and warmth, and later she took the creeper for her husband.

'The woman and the creeper made a child together, by and by, but he was a poor halfling with only one arm and one leg. His name was Yoi Soi. He was always hungry and hopped about everywhere. He quickly found a few grains of rice that a rat had saved from the flood. He set the rice on a leaf to dry, and when the rat discovered what Yoi Soi had done, it swore angrily that in revenge his children would always steal a portion of the food of men.

'But Yoi Soi did not get to eat the rice. Before the grains had dried, a wind came and blew them away across the forest. Yoi Soi hopped after them, driven by his hunger. He passed an ancient tree covered in birds which pecked at any green buds it put forth, and the tree implored the boy to ask the wind to come and blow it down and put it out of its torment. Yoi Soi promised that if he found the wind he would ask for that favour, and the tree lifted one of its limbs and pointed the way to the wind's home.

'Yoi Soi hopped on more eagerly than ever. He passed a stagnant lake and the scum on the lake bubbled up into a pair of fat green lips which asked the boy to bring a strong wind that would blow away the logs which blocked its outlet. Yoi Soi promised that he would do his best, and the lake gave him its last measure of pure water. Yoi Soi drank it down and it renewed his strength at once.

'Yoi Soi felt very strong now, but his stomach was empty. He stopped in a grove of banana plants, but the fruit was out of reach, and because he had only one arm and one leg he could not climb. The banana plants fluttered their long green leaves and begged Yoi Soi to ask the wind to restore the limbs they had lost in the great flood, so that they could once more embrace the air. When Yoi Soi promised this, hands of red bananas dropped around him and he ate well and went on to the high place of bare rock where the wind lived.

'The wind was very angry that this halfling had dared to track it to its lair for the sake of a few grains of rice. It told Yoi Soi that it had scattered the rice across the world. Rice would feed many kinds of men, but would never feed the children of Yoi Soi. Then the wind roared and pounced and tried to blow the boy from the high place.

'But Yoi Soi had come prepared. He had brought kindling taken from the shaggy coat of his father the creeper, and flints to strike sparks. With these he set fire to the wind's tail, and the wind flung itself about, howling in pain. 'Put out the flames,' it cried, 'and I shall make you a whole man!'

'Yoi Soi stamped down with his one foot and put out the fire, and in the next moment the wind darted down his throat and he grew and grew. His missing arm and leg popped out of his skin and he became a whole man twice as tall and ten times as strong as he had been. What a wonder, O my brothers and sisters! For the wind had made him the first of the Mighty People.

'Filled with the spirit of the wind, Yoi Soi stamped off through the forest, singing loudly. He was so strong that he was able to pull down the old tree afflicted by the plague of birds, and to unblock the stagnant lake. He stamped back to the mountain where his mother lived and his father the creeper grew, and carried her away to a distant place where he had spied others of her kind.

'But because Yoi Soi was so big, and so full of wind that he had to sing or talk all the time, he scared away the animals of the forest and could not hunt. Instead, he commanded the small people of his mother to serve him, and so things have been ever since. Our men hunt for meat and our women pick fruit and berries and flowers – perhaps they secretly hope to find the creeper which was the father of the Mighty People, but you will have to ask them about that. And if you think that I have forgotten the poor banana plants, then remember that Yoi Soi was not given magical powers, and he could do nothing for them.'

The troop of forest folk set out for the home of their masters the next day. They followed a chain of tree-covered hills that rose above the wreckage of the great flood, stepping away towards the Rim Mountains. They carried packs of dried caterpillar flesh, a long line of them bent under their loads as they trotted through hot green shade, far beneath the high canopy of the soaring trees.

Yama and Pandaras walked at the head of the line, behind Yoi Sendar. Pandaras was not happy that they were so dependent upon the kindness of the forest folk and said quietly, 'We should not be going towards these Mighty People of theirs, master. We will be delivered into the hands of the heretics, and all this will have been in vain.'

He meant the devastation of the forests, and the scarring of Yama's face.

'I hope to find the temple, Pandaras, or at least what remains of it after the Change War. There will surely be a passage into the keelways nearby. We will travel more quickly that way, and our enemies will not find us.'

He did not tell the boy that they would be travelling beyond the midpoint of the world into the Glass Desert, to search for the father of the thing inside him. He would give the boy the choice of following him or returning to Ys when the time came.

'Perhaps there are other temples, master.'

'Not here,' Yoi Sendar said, without looking around. 'Our masters the Mighty People are the only civilised people within many days' walk.'

The journey to the home of the Mighty People took five days. There were many distractions along the way, and the forest folk had to live off the land because they would not touch their cargo of smoke-dried caterpillar flesh. Each day, they began to travel before dawn and stopped when the sun reached its highest point. They slept in the steamy afternoon heat and woke in the early evening to weave new cocoons and to hunt.

Yama and Pandaras talked for hours during those long, hot, sleepy afternoons, telling each other of their adventures in the time they had been parted. Mostly it was Pandaras who talked. Yama kept his pain and his despair to himself. At night the Shadow, feeble and full of rage, came to him while the others slept. Its threats and boasts filled his dreams.

The bandar yoi inoie did not mourn the destruction of the lowland forests. 'There are many kinds of monstrous men in the lowlands,' Yoi Sendar told Yama. 'We were given the hills as our domain by the Preservers, and we do not need any other place. Besides, the low forests will regrow soon enough. They will take strength from the mud left behind by the water. In the lifetime of a man they will be as they always have been. Meanwhile, there will be plenty of game for us, because the animals have all fled to our hills.'

The bandar yoi inoie had many stories about the strange and fabulous creatures which lived in the lowland and hill forests. Yama had read about some of them in bestiaries in the library of the peel-house of his father, the Aedile of Aeolis; others were entirely new to him. He knew about blood orchids, for instance, because they grew in the forests of the foothills of the Rim Mountains, but those were pygmies compared with the giant blossoms of these forests, each as big as a house and surrounded by the bones of animals lured on to their gluey bracts by clouds of pheromones. There were fisher orchids too, which grew on high branches and let down adhesive-covered roots that wrapped around anything that blundered into them and drew nutrients from the corpses;

and flowers that emitted hypnotic scents and grew nets of fine roots into the flesh of their victims as they slept.

Fire emmets built huge castles amongst the tall trees. One kind of tree was defended by hordes of tiny rodents that attacked anything which approached, and stripped neighbouring trees of their leaves so that they would not shade their host; in turn, the tree fed its army with a sugary cotton it grew on certain branches. Jacksnappers hung from branches, dropping onto their prey and wrapping them in fleshy folds covered with a myriad of bony hooks tipped with a paralysing poison. A certain kind of small, slow, naked monkey was the juvenile form. After mating, the male died and the female wrapped her tail around a suitable branch and spun a cocoon around herself, emerging as an adult jacksnapper, limbless and eyeless and without a brain.

The bandar yoi inoie had stories about the strange races of men which lived in the lowland forests. There were tribes in which the men grew only a little after birth, and spent their lives in a special pouch in the belly of their mate. In one race, each family was controlled by a single fertile woman who grew monstrously fat and enslaved her sterile sisters, and the men were outcasts who fought fiercely if they met one another as they wandered the forests: there were great and bloody battles when fertile daughters matured and left their families and the men tried to win their favours. There were men who ran through the forest at night, drinking the blood of their mesmerised prey, and tribes of pale men and women who could transform themselves to look like other kinds of men – perhaps these were relatives of the mirror people that Yama had met in the Palace of the Memory of the People.

Yama did not know which of these strange peoples were real and which were the stuff of stories. The forest folk were careless of the distinction. If it can be imagined, Yoi Sendar said, then surely it must be real. The Preservers who made this world were much greater than any of the races of men they had raised up from animals, and so they made more wonders than could possibly be imagined.

The bandar yoi inoie were happy in the forest. It was their home, as familiar to them as the peel-house and the City of the Dead were to Yama. They chanted long intricate melodies as they trotted through its green shadows, and sang and laughed and told long complicated jokes while they cooked the prey they had shot (like the fisher folk, they used poison from the glands of certain frogs to anoint the tips of their arrows) and prepared the tubers and fruit and berries they had collected.

Late one afternoon a party of hunters found a treecreeper and one man rushed back to tell the others. The entire troop, along with Yama and Pandaras, followed him to the place where the treecreeper had made its lair. It was a giant kapok tree, so big that it would have taken twenty men linking arms to embrace its circumference. Its smooth grey bark was split and scarred in several places, and Yoi Sendar pointed to the creature which could be glimpsed moving about inside.

'We will have it out soon. It is fine eating. It makes its home by rasping away the soft heartwood of a tree until it kills it, and it is dangerous when it is chased from its lair. But we are a brave people.'

While some of the forest folk danced on one side of the tree, provoking the treecreeper to lash out with its long, whip-like tongue from various splits in the tree-trunk, the rest built a fire of green wood at the base on the other side of the tree, and cut into the trunk to let in the smoke. The treecreeper was soon in distress, mewling and howling to itself. The forest folk darted in, dodging the lashing tongue and drumming at the base of the tree with stout clubs, raising a great noise.

At last the tormented treecreeper sprang from a slit high up in the trunk of the tree, just beneath the first branches. It moved very quickly: Yama did not see it until it was on the ground. It reared up on the two hindmost pairs of its many short stout legs, very tall and very thin. Its back was covered in overlapping bony plates; its belly in matted hair. Its sweetish, not unpleasant odour filled the clearing.

The forest folk surrounded it, a man or woman darting forward to strike two or three quick blows to its legs while the others cheered. Pandaras joined in, cheering twice as loudly as anyone else. The treecreeper went down by degrees, mewling querulously. Its tiny eyes were faceted, glinting greenly in the matted pelt which covered its head. Its long scarlet tongue snaked across the trampled ground, and Yoi Sendar ran forward and pinned it with a stake.

After that, the forest folk swarmed over the treecreeper, jointing it while it was still alive and carrying the meat back to their camp in triumph. Pandaras was caught up in their excitement, his ragged shirt bloody, his eyes shining.

Yama did not join in the feast of fruit and treecreeper meat. He thought that he was like the kapok tree and the Shadow was like the treecreeper, rasping away at his self's soft core. And yet he knew that he would need the Shadow in what lay ahead. He could not drive it out until he knew how to obliterate his unwanted powers.

He wished he could be like the forest folk, who were dancing and singing with uncomplicated happiness in the fern-filled clearing. It was twilight. Red light from a great trench of fire beat across the bodies of the dancers. Trees stood quietly all around, freshly woven cocoons pendant from their lower branches. How sweet life was for these people, how simple, how innocent! A few hours of hunting or searching for fruit or tubers each day, the rest for play, for singing songs and telling stories. Their life was exactly like the life of their fathers and grandfathers, always the same from the beginning of the world to its end.

Yama had forgotten that the bandar yoi inoie were in thrall to the Mighty People, but the next day they reached the valley where the Mighty People lived, and he saw how bad things were for their slaves.

14

SLAVES

'They may be a mighty people,' Pandaras said, 'but they like a snug house. Even I would find one of those huts cramped.'

He stood beside Yama at the edge of the forest, looking across the floor of the valley, a wide, level grassland studded with little villages linked by narrow red paths that ran beside ditches of green water, each village a cluster of mud-walled huts and strips of cultivated land enclosed by thorn hedges.

'I don't like the look of it,' Pandaras added. 'See how thick and tall the hedges are. These people must have fearsome enemies. Surely now is the time to call on something that will take us far from here.'

'Prefect Corin may have survived the fall of the garden. I will not do anything that could attract his attention.'

Besides, there were very few machines here – fewer than Yama had ever known in a world where innumerable machines sped everywhere on unfathomable errands, where not even a tree in the most remote forest fell without a witness.

'I don't see how he could have survived,' Pandaras said. 'Although I'd like to think it possible, because that would mean poor Tibor might have survived. Forgive me for my presumption, master, but you cannot live in hiding forever. You cannot waste your gift.'

'Do not speak of what you do not know,' Yama said.

'I know a bad feeling when I get one,' the boy said. 'Look at our friends. It's as if they're going to their doom.'

It was early in the morning, with the sun only just clear of the peaks of the Rim Mountains. The forest folk had risen before dawn, and had been uncharacteristically subdued as they walked the last two leagues to the edge of the forest above the valley where their masters, the Mighty People, lived. Now they were removing the flowers and quills and feathers that adorned their bodies, scrubbing away chalky patterns with bunches of wet grasses, combing out mud that had stiffened their coarse hair in ornamental spikes. They had walked naked through the forest; now they took loincloths from pouches and packs and stepped into them. Their torcs had been carefully wrapped up in oilcloth, and buried on a rocky point beneath a flat slab of sandstone.

The forest folk lined up, shivering in the chill grey air. Their chief, Yoi Sendar, went from one to the next, checking that every trace of adornment had been removed. When he reached Yama and Pandaras, he said, 'Below is the home of the family of Mighty People which owns us. We go to them with our gifts from the forest. You do not have to come with us, my friends. We have enjoyed your stories and lies and boasts in the forest, but we take up a different life now.'

'I must find the temple,' Yama said.

Yoi Sendar shook his massive head from side to side. It meant *yes*. His baggy skin was bleeding from the places where he had drawn out his decorative quills. He said, 'Perhaps you can please the Mighty People in some way, and they will let you visit it.'

Pandaras said, 'Why are you so afraid of them? If they rule by fear, then they are not worthy to be your masters.'

Yoi Sendar would not meet the boy's stare. 'They are our masters. It has always been so, ever since the long-forgotten day when the Preservers set us in our domain. And although our masters have changed, they still need us, as you will see if you come with us.'

'There are many different peoples on the world,' Yama said, as Yoi Sendar stumped off to the head of the line of his people. 'Why do you deny that simple fact, Pandaras?'

'People everywhere are all the same, if you ask me. They make themselves slaves to stronger men because it is easier to be a slave than to be free. It is easier to worship the past than to plan for the future.'

'You have some extraordinary notions, Pandaras.'

'You taught me that, master, but I think you have forgotten it.'

'Did I? Well, I was younger then, and more foolish. Perhaps my bloodline ages even more quickly yours. I feel as old as one of the Ancients of Days.'

'I have kept one of their stone blades,' Pandaras said. 'Please don't stop me, master, if I have to use it. The thing in your head wanted you to be its slave, and I don't think you've quite shaken off the notion.'

Yoi Sendar raised both hands and gave a hoarse shout. His people hoisted their heavy packs of caterpillar meat and followed him into the valley, walking in single file down a narrow path that snaked through tall grasses towards the nearest of the villages of the Mighty People. Yama saw that the mud huts inside the thorn hedge were separated from each other by an intricate arrangement of walls and courtyards. Each had its own exit tunnelled through the thorns, and as the bandar yoi inoie came down the slope, figures began to emerge from the tunnels, scrawny and stooped and grey-skinned.

Pandaras said, 'If they have changed, then it can't have been for the good. They seem a poor kind of people to me.'

'Do not be quick to judge,' Yama said.

The Mighty People spread out in a ragged line beneath a stand of cotton trees. A gang of children chased around, shouting or throwing stones or clods of earth at the adults, dodging stones thrown back at them. Men and women and children wore only loincloths, like those which the forest folk had put on. They were all bald; the women's withered dugs hung to their bellies.

When the forest folk drew near, the Mighty People ran forward, brandishing whips and clubs and rifles. They shouted sharply at the forest folk and at each other. As the forest folk were quickly separated into groups of five or six, one of the men went up to Yama and Pandaras and stared at them with unconcealed cupidity before turning and shouting to the others that these strangers were his.

'I am the Captain! You will remember that!'

The Captain's voice was shrill and grating. He had small red-rimmed eyes and a pursed beak of a mouth. When a small child toddled too close, he swiped at it with the stock of his rifle and screamed. 'Get away or I'll shoot!'

The child bared its teeth and hissed, but backed away slowly, staring at Yama and Pandaras with an avidity closer to lust than greed.

'Don't you worry,' the Captain told Yama. 'I'll make you my guest, and your slave here will be looked after by my slaves. As long as you have my protection the others won't dare touch either of you. I'm their Captain, the richest and most powerful of my people. They try to kill me many times for my power and wealth, but I am too clever and too strong.'

Yama introduced himself and Pandaras.

Pandaras said, 'I am not a slave, but the squire of my master.'

The Captain spat at Pandaras's feet and said to Yama, 'Your slave is mutilated and insolent, but you have the look of a fighter. That's good.'

Yama said, 'Are you at war, then?'

'Our young men have gone to fight in the great war of liberation,' the Captain said. 'Meanwhile, we look after what we have, as is only natural. We are all of us rich here, and other families scheme to take our wealth from us, but we will defeat every attack, and our victories will make us even richer, even stronger.'

Yama said politely, 'I have heard much of you from the bandar yoi inoie, but it is interesting to see for myself what you are.'

'Where did these clots of filth find you? Yoi Sendar! Yoi Sendar, you ugly tub of guts! Come here!'

The Captain snapped his whip above the heads of the cluster of forest folk he had rounded up. Yoi Sendar stepped forward, his heavy head bowed. He said in a small voice, 'All we have gathered, master, we give with open hands and open hearts.'

The Captain struck him back and forth across his broad shoulders with the stock of the whip, raising bloody welts. Yoi Sendar withstood it in stolid silence, staring at the ground.

'Filth,' the Captain said. He was breathing heavily. A muddy stink rose up from him. 'They cannot change. Everything is always the same for them. They do not realise how we have been transfigured. They are a great burden to us, but we are strong and bear it.'

Yama looked around. Most of the skinny grey Mighty People were driving their groups of forest folk into tunnels of clay-plastered wicker that led through the tall thorn hedge. Even the gang of children had taken charge of four or five of the oldest of the forest folk, and were fighting over a pack of caterpillar meat.

Several of the Mighty People shouted at the Captain, complaining that he could not keep the strangers to himself. 'Watch me do it!' the Captain shouted back. He seemed to be in a permanent rage. 'You don't think I'm strong enough?'

He turned suddenly and fired his rifle into the air, and an old woman who had been creeping towards him stopped and held out her empty hands. 'I know your tricks, mother,' the Captain screamed. There were flecks of foam at the corners of his mouth. 'Try to take what is mine and I'll kill you. I swear it!' He turned to Yama and Pandaras and said, 'She could not keep her slaves and tries to steal food from honest folk.

You will be safe with me. I give you some of my own food and water, and you will help me.'

Yama said, 'We are strangers, dominie. We have come to visit your temple.'

'Temple? What have this filth being telling you? They are the fathers and mothers of lies. They lie so much they no longer know what is true. You come with me. I will keep you safe.' The Captain snapped his whip at his group of forest folk. 'Bring your tributes. Poor, rotten stuff it looks, and not much of it. You've all been lazing about in the forest instead of working hard. But now you'll work. I'll make sure of it!'

The compound of the Captain's hut was enclosed by a high mudbrick wall topped with briars and broken glass. A handful of pygmy goats were penned in one corner, whisking at flies with their tails while they cropped in a desultory way at a pile of melon husks.

The Captain supervised the unloading of the smoked caterpillar meat with brutal impatience. When the last string of meat had been hung on the rack outside the hut, he kicked the forest folk into a lean-to next to the goat-pen, and told Yama that his slave would bed down there too.

'Find out what you can from them,' Yama whispered to Pandaras.

'Be careful,' Pandaras whispered back. 'This is as bad a place as I have ever seen.'

The hut was mean and cramped, with no furniture but a little three-legged stool. A sleeping platform was cut into the thick wall. A solar stove gave out dim red light, and an iron pot of maize porridge bubbled on its hotplate. The beaten-earth floor was strewn with dry grass in which black beetles rustled; there was a nest of banded rats in the thatch of the roof. Everything was dirty and stank of goat and the Captain's stale body odour, but gorgeous portraits of dignified elders of the family stood in wall niches, meticulously rendered in oil pigments and framed in intricately worked metal, and the bowl into which the Captain scooped a meagre measure of maize porridge had been lovingly carved from a dark hardwood.

When Yama commented on these things, the Captain was dismissive. 'A few trinkets from the old times I keep close to me out of sentiment. I own far greater treasures, but those are not for your eyes.'

The maize porridge was unsalted and unflavoured pap, and the portions were meagre, but the Captain expected fulsome acknowledgement of his generosity. It seemed that he had great plans for Yama, and as he boasted and blustered Yama soon learned more than he wanted to of the way the Mighty People lived after they had been changed by the heretics. Each adult had his or her own hut and strip of arable land, jealously guarded from all the others. As in the quarters of the Department of Indigenous Affairs in the Palace of the Memory of the People, husbands lived apart from wives. As soon as they could walk, children were abandoned to the half-wild pack that lived outside the village fence. Those who survived to sexual maturity were driven out of the pack, and had to find or build their own hut and their own field strip, or else live in the grassland as best they could.

Every man or woman was a nation of one, and spent most of their waking hours hoarding their scanty possessions. They had discarded their old names – the names from the time before the change – and if they had new names they told them to no one. There was no love, no pity, no mercy. These qualities were regarded as signs of weakness. The old and sick had to fend for themselves, and were usually killed by the pack of children or by an adolescent who wanted their hut.

The Shadow gloated over this. *We will make all men like this*, it whispered inside Yama's head. *Slaves to the things they desire most.*

The worst thing of all was that the Mighty People considered this way of life to be the highest possible form of civilisation. The old ways, when the family had herded cattle and prized the craftsmanship of their pottery and metalwork and art, were despised. The cattle were dead, killed either by poison in acts of jealousy or slaughtered because it was too difficult to guard them in the pastures, which had grown rough and wild. The Mighty People had a taboo against entering the forest and relied entirely upon the forest folk they had enslaved for meat, and for most of their supply of fruit and tubers too, for their field strips were poorly maintained, the crops stunted and diseased. More work went into guarding the field strips and the compounds than into cultivation.

The only thing that united the Captain's family was a hatred of the neighbouring villages. Everyone contributed the labour of their slaves towards defence of the village against other families. The Captain had plans to expand his territory, and he expected Yama to help him. He walked Yama around the boundary of his family's land, showing off the network of ditches and ponds which had been built long ago by all the people of the valley to irrigate the land with water from lakes high in the foothills of the Rim Mountains.

'If we can control these, then we can control all the land around us,' the Captain said.

'What would you do with it?'

'Why, we would own it, of course.' The Captain gave Yama a crafty look. 'That's the first thing. All things flow from ownership.'

It seemed to Yama that the Mighty People were as much slaves as the bandar yoi inoie – perhaps more so, for the forest folk had been coerced into slavery, but the Mighty People had made themselves slaves of their own free will. By prizing ownership above all else, they were themselves owned by the things they coveted. He remembered how the forest folk had hidden their torcs at the edge of the forest, and thought that he could guess what had happened to the paintings, pottery and metalwork made in the time before the heretics had kindled a Change War here.

The Captain launched into a long diatribe against the neighbouring villages. The feud was only a few years old, but his story was packed with treachery, ambushes and murder. He swore that all of it would be avenged, working himself into a fit of rage and aiming his rifle at various parts of his enemies' territory before glancing sidelong at Yama.

'A fighter like you,' he said, 'could profit greatly here.'

It seemed that everywhere Yama went, people wanted him to kill other people. He was sickened by it.

He said, 'You told me that your family is more powerful than any other, Captain. How could I do what they cannot?'

'They prefer to protect the wealth they already have,' the Captain said. 'And who can blame them? A man who cannot protect his wealth is no man at all, and deserves to lose all he has. But a man like you, with no wealth but much experience in fighting, will be able to organise the strongest of our slaves into an army. 'It doesn't matter if they are killed because we will have the slaves of our enemies. We will make our enemies our slaves.' He clacked his lips with pleasure at the thought. 'You will be rewarded, of course. Their stores of the old stuff will become mine, and I will let you have some pieces. A great prize for only a little work.'

Spit on his treasure, the Shadow said. *Take the rifle and shove it into his mouth and make him beg for his life. Kill him. Kill them all.*

It raved on, but its words were feeble sparks. Yama ignored it.

They were walking back towards the thorn-fenced village. Yama was trying to think of some way of refusing the Captain without angering him, but then he saw something that made him change his mind.

The pack of children were quarrelling in the shade of the stand of cotton trees. At first Yama thought that they had caught an animal and were tearing it apart, but then he saw that they had killed one of the forest folk and were stripping raw meat from its bones with their teeth. A girl sat apart from the others, gnawing on a double handful of entrails. Three of the smaller children kicked the remains of the severed head about in the dusty grass. The eyes were gone and the skull had been smashed to get at the brains. Nearby, two of the forest folk sat with their arms wrapped around each other, rocking back and forth and keening.

The Captain glanced at this and said, 'None of the children's slaves last very long. They get the runts of the litters, and those too old or too ill to work. No sense keeping a slave that can't work, eh?'

Yama controlled his disgust and said, 'I must talk with my servant about your proposal.'

'Tell him that his life depends on your success,' the Captain said.

So he and Pandaras were prisoners, Yama thought. He had only suspected it before. He had been a fool.

'I'm sorry I couldn't help you deal with that old goat,' Pandaras said, when Yama called him out of the lean-to. 'What does he want of us?'

'He plans to go to war against his neighbours. And because he cannot organise his people into an army, he wants me to make an army of their slaves.'

'These so-called Mighty People are each a kingdom to themselves, master. They do not trust anyone, not even their own children. This is a crazy place. I told you that we should not have come.'

'We have to find the temple, Pandaras.'

Pandaras glanced at Yoi Sendar, who sat listlessly amongst his family in the shadows of the lean-to. 'I asked about that, but the forest folk have suddenly lost their tongues. What is wrong with them, master? Why don't they defend themselves?'

'They are indigens. They know only what they have always known, and cannot imagine anything else. Once upon a time they lived in harmony with the Mighty People, exchanging food hunted in the forest for food grown in this valley, each race enriching the other. Then the Mighty People changed, but the bandar yoi inoie did not. They still serve their masters.'

'Their masters are evil. No people should prey on another!'

Yama thought of the Amnan, who had hunted the fisher folk until his father had put a stop to it. 'Certain bloodlines think the indigens no better than animals. And so here. But I have never seen so wretched a people as the Mighty People. They are not evil, but gripped by a kind of madness.'

'I would call it evil,' Pandaras said. 'We are prisoners, but Yoi Sendar thinks that you are an honoured guest. He is pleased that he has brought us to this place.'

'The forest folk are used to bringing people here. The Mighty People were once extraordinary artists and artisans. In the old days many traders must have come here. The Mighty People have no interest in trading now, but the forest folk cannot understand that.' Yama explained the Captain's plans for war against the neighbouring villages, and said, 'He thinks that I am a cateran.'

'So you are, master. Everyone in the world can see it but you.'

'I have learned something useful. The Captain and his people have treasure hidden somewhere close by.'

'Yoi Sendar boasted about the riches of this village as if they were his own,' Pandaras said. 'But he wouldn't tell me where it is hidden or what it was, so I thought it a story.'

'Yoi Sendar is loyal to his master, and you have forgotten about the torcs worn by his people. I think they were made by the Mighty People, before they changed. And there are fine pictures and bowls in the Captain's hut. Trinkets, according to him; the price of a ship like the *Weazel*, if I am any judge.'

Pandaras struck his forehead and laughed. 'I have lost my edge since we left Ys, master. I have stumbled across a fortune, and failed to see it. But how will it help us?'

'I am not sure yet. But I think that I will ask the Captain for proof of the fee that he has promised for making war against the other villages.'

'You have the beginnings of a plan, then. That's good. You are recovering from your ordeal, master. If we can escape with a few of these trinkets—'

'Money is not important. Things are not important. Look around you if you do not believe me. I do not do this for money, Pandaras,' Yama said. 'I do it to overturn a great wickedness.'

When he returned to the Captain, the man grumbled that he was free enough with his time. 'I have not forgotten that my time is yours,' Yama said. 'But I needed to make my slave understand what you want me to do.'

'If that was my slave, mutilated as he is, I would kill him.'

'He is all I have.'

'You will have plenty of slaves after we have conquered our enemies.'

'You promise much, Captain. But if I am to fight for you I must see something of these riches before I begin.'

The Captain stared up at Yama suspiciously. 'You will have enough when our enemies are broken. Most of it must come to me, of course, but you will have your share.'

'You have taught me that no man can trust another. So I must see how I will profit before I agree to help you.'

The Captain gestured at the portraits set in niches in the walls. 'It is stuff like that.'

'You yourself said that those daubs are no more than trinkets. If that is all you have to offer, it is not worth my time or experience.'

'I will kill your slave if you do not work for me.'

'Again, as you yourself said, he is as worthless as those trinkets.'

The Captain went cross-eyed in an effort to contain his sudden anger. He said, 'I should kill you!'

'Then I would not be able to help you conquer your enemies.'

The Captain turned away and stamped and breathed heavily until he was calm, then said, 'It is a matter for all the village.'

The Mighty People gathered outside their compounds and argued for a long time, past sunset and into the night. The forest folk lit lanterns and hung them from the lower branches of the cotton trees. The Mighty People shouted at each other, every one with a different opinion, no one willing to listen to any other, and nothing was resolved until a man went for the Captain with a long knife and the Captain shot him in the belly. More shouting, this time mostly from the Captain, a long tirade of blustering threats. The wounded man was carried off by his slaves. Later, the Captain came over to where Yama was sitting with Pandaras.

'We will take you there now,' he said. 'But you must be blindfolded.'

All the villagers came because no one trusted anyone else. They were prisoners of their own greed and suspicion. The Captain was quite happy to explain this as he walked beside Yama. He said that it was a sign of their superior way of life.

'Anyone who goes to the hoard alone is killed by the others and their stuff is divided up.'

'How would you know if someone went there?'

'We all watch each other. No one can leave the village without the others knowing. And we all keep watch on it. You could not find the place without my help, but even if you did, we would know straight away.'

As well as being blindfolded, Yama and Pandaras had their arms bound. In case of trouble, the Captain said, although Yama guessed that it was because the Mighty People thought they might have friends waiting in ambush. The filthy cloth tied over his eyes was not quite light-proof – he could dimly see the flare of the torches carried by the handful of forest folk that the Mighty People had brought with them – but he did not bother to try to memorise the twists and turns of the path, which led always upwards. He silently endured the stink of the Mighty People and the spidery feel of their sharp-fingered hands as they guided him. Pandaras began to complain volubly, but then there was the sound of a blow and the boy said nothing more.

When the blindfold was at last removed, Yama found that he was standing at the top of a tall cliff. It was too dark to see the bottom, but the Captain told Yama that it was a long drop. 'We throw down those who try to cheat us,' he said. 'They break on the rocks far below, and jackals eat their brains and hearts. I'll do it to you if you try any tricks.'

Yama smiled. 'Do you not trust me?'

'Of course not.' The Captain clacked his lips. He was amused. 'And if you said that you trusted me I would not believe you.'

Yama sketched a bow. 'Then we understand each other completely.'

The Mighty People surrounded them. Yoi Sendar and several other forest folk carried torches made from branches dipped in pitch, crackling with red flame and black smoke. Two of them held Pandaras by his arms. A strip of cloth was still tied over his eyes. All around was a desolation of boulders and creepers and stunted trees. The edge of the forest was a distant dark line against the black sky. It was midnight. The smudged thumbprint of the Eye of the Preservers stood high above.

The Captain snapped his fingers, and one of the forest folk threw a coil of rope out over the edge of the cliff. One end was looped around a knob of rock rubbed as smooth as a dockside bollard.

'Climb down,' the Captain told Yama. 'There is a cave hidden behind creepers not far below. Look inside and you will see a great store of the old stuff. Our enemies have much lesser stores, of course, but you will see that even one tenth of ours will be a great treasure to a man like you. Do not stay there long, or we will cut the rope.'

Yama held out his bound hands. 'You will have to untie me.'

There was an argument about this amongst the Mighty People. Some wanted the Captain to climb down with Yama, others suggested that someone else should climb down, because Yama was the Captain's property, but no one wanted to volunteer because that meant risking all for the benefit of everyone else. At last the Captain prevailed. Yama would be released from his bonds, but he would have only five minutes to look at the treasure or the rope would be cut.

The rope was knotted at intervals: even though Yama was carrying one of the smoky torches, it was easy to clamber down it. *They will kill us*, the Shadow said, but Yama ignored it. A draught of cold air blew from the cave mouth, stirring the leafy creepers which hung over it like a curtain. Yama kicked them aside and, clinging one-handed to the swaying rope, thrust in first the torch and then his head.

Here was the treasure of the Mighty People. Broken pottery tumbled in heaps; flaking paintings covered in grey mould; exquisitely carved chairs riddled by beetles and glowing with streaks of foxfire fungus; intricate metalwork corroded by verdigris.

The Captain's voice drifted down from above. 'You see!' he shouted. 'You see that we are a very rich people! Now you must return, or we will cut the rope!'

Yama looked up. The Mighty People stood along the edge of the cliff, silhouetted against the flare of torches. He said, 'Now I have seen your treasure I know exactly how to help you,' and threw his torch onto a stack of rotten chairs.

The Mighty People did not realise what had happened at first. Yama had plenty of time to find a good handhold beside the cave mouth before smoke began to pour out of it. The creepers crisped and withered in the heat. Howls from above, then; a scatter of rifle shots. Something unravelled past Yama, striking his shoulder as it fell. The rope had been cut.

It was not difficult to clamber sideways along the cliff. The creepers were strong enough to bear Yama's weight, there were plenty of hand- and footholds, and the Mighty People were too busy trying to save their treasure to search for him. They swarmed down the cliff on ropes, but none thought to take anything with which to beat out or stifle the fire. They hung in the smoke that poured from the cave and shrieked in rage at each other. One man lost his hold when flame belched out, and fell screaming into the darkness.

Yama climbed over the edge of the cliff, strode through the circle of forest folk, and pulled the strip of cloth from Pandaras's eyes. The boy showed his sharp white teeth. Blood, fresh and bright, matted the sleek hair on top of his head and trickled down his face. He said, 'I will kill the person who struck me. I swear it.'

'We will only do what we need to do,' Yama said. He took the stone blade from Pandaras's shirt pocket and sawed through the rope which bound his arms, then turned to the forest folk and told them, 'I am your master now. Do you understand? I took the Mighty People's treasure and gave it to the air.'

Yoi Sendar stepped forward and said humbly, 'You must kill me, for I have failed my masters.'

'I am not going to kill you,' Yama told him, 'but you will do as I say. You will go back to the village with Pandaras and bring the rest of your people. Do it, or I will kill all of the Mighty People. The others will come with me.'

Pandaras said, 'How will I find you, master?'

'Yoi Sendar will know how to lead you to me. Go now, as quickly as you can!'

After Pandaras and Yoi Sendar had run off into the darkness, Yama went to the edge of the drop and shouted down to the Captain. 'When I saw your treasure I knew what to do at once!'

The Captain howled and brought up the rifle and shot at Yama, but he was shaking with rage and the pellet went wide. Recoil swung him like the clapper of a bell and he dropped his torch when he slammed back into the cliff. It tumbled away, dwindling to a point of light that suddenly flared far below and went out.

Before the Captain could aim his rifle again, Yama said, 'If any of your people tries to kill me or to climb up, I will cut your rope.'

'I will kill you! My slaves will kill you!'

Two or three of the other Mighty People got off a few pistol shots, but the pellets hit the rock face beneath Yama's feet or whined off into the sky. The Captain shouted at them to stop and a woman said loudly and clearly, 'You did this. You are not my husband. You are not the father of my children. You are nothing, Tuan Ah.'

It was the Captain's secret name. He screamed with rage and swung around on his rope and tried to aim his rifle at his wife, but she was quicker and shot him twice with her pistol. He dropped from the rope and vanished into the darkness below.

There was a silence. At last the Captain's wife said, 'Are you there, cateran?'

'I do not want anything from you except your slaves.'

Some of the Mighty People began to shout threats, but the Captain's wife shouted louder than any of them. 'If you try to kill him, he'll cut your ropes.'

The Mighty People could have easily overwhelmed Yama by swarming up their ropes all at once, but he had guessed that it would never occur to them to act together. He said, 'I am freeing you too. I free you from the past. Do you understand? When I have gone you can go back to your village and take up your lives.'

'Tuan Ah was a fool to trust you,' the Captain's wife said. 'I had eight children by him, but I am glad he is dead. You have started a war, cateran. We will need slaves, and if we cannot hunt you down we will take them from our enemies. Pray that we do not find you. I am crueller than Tuan Ah.'

'I am going where you cannot find me,' Yama said, and turned away and led the little group of bandar yoi inoie towards the forest.

15

THREE SLEEPS AND A MIRACLE

Pandaras, Yoi Sendar, and the rest of the forest folk found Yama soon after dawn. It was already hot. Threads of mist hung between the dense stands of bamboo which grew along the edge of the forest. Pandaras told Yama that he had set fire to the huts of the Mighty People, and this diversion had allowed them all to escape.

'But I had to kill someone, master – the man the Captain had shot. It was the only way to make his slaves come with me.'

'I think that the Mighty People will be more concerned about the loss of their treasure and their slaves,' Yama said. 'They do not care for each other, only for what they own. But in any case they will not follow us here. The forest is taboo to them.'

'Well, I'm sorry I killed him,' Pandaras said, 'even if he would have killed me if I hadn't done it.'

'I fear that it will not be the last death,' Yama said.

He went over to Yoi Sendar and greeted him. The chief of the forest folk bowed his head and said, 'All we have, master, we give with open hands and open hearts.'

Yama raised his voice so that all the forest folk could hear him. 'I want nothing but your friendship, Yoi Sendar.'

The small, ugly man did not look up. He said stubbornly, 'We will gladly give all we have, but we cannot give what we do not have.'

'Perhaps I can change your mind,' Yama said. 'It has been a long night. We will find a place to rest, and in the evening we will speak again.'

Although they had returned to their home amongst the tall trees of the forest, the bandar yoi inoie were muted and forlorn. They made no attempt to decorate themselves, and still wore their loincloths. They lay down in groups of three or four between the buttress roots of the big trees, talking quietly.

'You should rest too,' Pandaras told Yama. 'Don't worry. I'll keep watch.'

'They will not harm us,' Yama said, although he was not really sure what would happen once he had changed the forest folk.

He had decided what he must do while Pandaras and Yoi Sendar had gone off to free the others. He had performed this miracle before, on the baby entrusted to him by the mirror people, but he had not known then exactly how he had done it. He had thought that the aspect of Angel had guided him, but he knew now that she had been drawn to him because she hoped to glimpse the root of his power.

Now he had to discover it for himself.

'I have caught the disease of mistrust,' Pandaras said. 'Try to sleep, master. I'll make sure nothing happens to you.'

Yama sat cross-legged in the shade of a bush with big glossy leaves, and closed his eyes, and because he was very tired from his recent adventures soon fell into something like sleep. A slow, swooning fall deeper than any ordinary dream, plunging down as he had so often swum towards the bottom of the river as a child. Kicking away from the sunlit mirror where kelp plants trailed their long green fronds, following the stipes which dwindled away into darkness, the muscles of his throat and chest aching and the need to draw another breath growing and growing until at last he had to turn back to the sunlight. He had never been able to reach the river bottom then, but now he felt that he could fall forever. And as he fell he became aware of finer and finer divisions of the world, of machines smaller than the single-celled plants which were the base of most river life. Those tiny plants were so small that they could only be seen when they stained the water red or brown in their uncountable billions, but the machines were smaller still: ten thousand of them could have been fitted on one of the motes of dust swarming in the beam of sunlight which had illuminated the Aedile's room when Yama had broken into it, on the morning of the siege of Dr Dismas's tower.

He had thought then that his adventures had just been beginning, but he knew now that they had begun long before he had been born.

He turned his attention to one of the minuscule machines, and it opened up around him like the stacks of books in the library of the peel-house. As he wandered through the serried rows, he half-expected to find Zakiel around a corner, but it soon became clear that there was no thought here, only information. So much information, in so small a space! Zakiel had taught him that the information which encoded the form of his body could be contained in a speck of matter smaller than the least punctuation mark in a finely printed book. There was less information here than that, but it was still overwhelming. He took down a book at random. Its pages were covered with neat lines of zeroes and ones: a single long number, a single set of instructions. And there were thousands of books.

Yama remembered how Angel's aspect had seemed to show him certain places inside the brain of the baby of the Mirror People – she had used him to find out where they were, but he had not known it then. Subtly altered, those places had become the nodes where the tiny machines could excyst and begin to amplify complexity into true consciousness, the change that was the miraculous gift of the Preservers, the miracle with which he had been entrusted.

He concentrated on recalling everything about that moment. What Angel's aspect had said, subtly prompting and probing him. How he had felt, what he had seen, how he had acted without knowing he had acted. Without thought, he ran his finger over the rows of zeroes and ones faster than he could see, changing them in a blur. Put the book back, pulled down another. Over and over until it was done.

He sat up inside a green tent, for a moment unsure if he were dreaming or awake. Pandaras had woven a kind of bower of leaves around him. He pushed it aside. It was evening, the air hot and still, light deepening between the soaring trunks of the trees. The forest folk were moving about. They had lit several small fires and were roasting meat over them.

'I have found out where the temple is,' Pandaras said. 'Yoi Sendar wouldn't talk at first, but I told him that you would kill all the Mighty People if he didn't tell me. I made them go and get food, too. It isn't like it was before. No singing, no happiness. They are very afraid. They do not understand what has happened to them.'

'That will change.'

'You are tired, master. Here. Drink this.'

It was a gourd half full of foamy, sweet-smelling juice.

Pandaras said, 'There's a kind of hollow vine which gushes water when you cut it. It's good.'

Yama took the gourd, but did not drink. He said, 'Give me your bit of stone,' and used it to slice open his palm. The stone was so sharp that the wound scarcely hurt, although it bled quickly and freely. Yama let blood drip from his fingertips into the gourd. Not much blood would be needed, but he counted off a full minute before he let Pandaras bandage the wound.

Then he called the forest folk together and had them each take a single sip from the gourd. There was just enough. Yoi Sendar swallowed the last of it and handed back the gourd without comment.

'Sleep, then do as you will,' Yama told them. 'I cannot live your lives for you. You must discover how to do that yourselves. And remember this. You can free others as I have freed you. Let them drink a little of your blood mixed in wine or in water and they will be freed too.'

They did not understand him then, of course, but soon enough they would. He tried to tell Pandaras what he had done, but he was so very tired that he fell asleep before he had hardly begun.

When he woke again it was dawn. The forest folk were gone. Pandaras said he had not seen them leave, although he swore that he had stayed up all night, and said that they must have melted into the forest as mist melts into air. He pointed to a pile of rags, and added, 'They left behind their loincloths. Maybe they'll go back to the way they were before all this started.'

'No,' Yama said. 'Now they will begin to become something else.'

Pandaras gave him a long, sober look. 'What have you done, master?'

'I have freed them. From the Mighty People. From their innocence.'

'Like the baby of the mirror people?'

'I have machines in my blood, and so do you. Everyone does. It is the greatest gift of the Preservers. The miracle was simply a matter of persuading them to do the work for me.'

Pandaras touched his throat. He had mended the fresh rents in his shirt, wrapped the stump of his left wrist in a scrap of cloth, sleeked down his hair and strung a chain of orchids around his neck. The disc hung at his chest like a brooch and he wore the fetish on his left arm. He looked like a jade about to embark on the long and complex wooing of a fair lady.

'I'm a fool,' he said. 'That was why you had them drink your blood.'

Yama smiled, and felt the half-healed incisions in his face tug against each other. For the first time he could allow himself the luxury of hope.

'Everything in the world is touched by the breath of the Preservers because everything comes from them,' he told Pandaras. 'All I did was help the forest folk recognise what they already possessed. I have changed the machines in my blood so that they can infect all the indigenous peoples of the world. That was why I made the forest folk drink my blood. And in turn their blood will become active, and change any who drink it. I have freed them to be what they will. If they choose, they can free all the other troops of the forest folk which come here to find food for the Mighty People.'

Pandaras thought about that. 'It is not like the mirror people. Yoi Sendar and the rest, they didn't ask for this.'

'Did you ask to be born? You saw how they were. It was the only way to free them. Now, tell me about the temple.'

The first rays of the sun had begun to shine through the understorey of the high canopy of the forest. Pandaras pointed aslant the light. 'Yoi Sendar said that it is a day's walk in that direction. I'd guess it would take us twice as long, as we're not used to the forest. And you should take a little breakfast before we set out. They ate all the meat last night, but there's some fruit left.'

Yama and Pandaras walked through the green silence of the trees for most of the day. They spoke very little, each absorbed in his own thoughts. For the first time since he had leaned at the window of the room above the stables of *The Crossed Axes*, the inn where he had met Pandaras, and looked out across the great city of Ys, Yama felt an immense peace. He was who he was, no more and no less; he gave himself to his fate as a leaf borne on the River might be carried the length of the inhabited world.

Towards evening, they stopped at the edge of a bluff which looked across the valley. The thorn-fenced villages of the Mighty People stood here and there amongst the network of ditches, canals and paths that webbed the grassland. Hills rose on the far side of the valley, with more hills behind them. The sun was setting beyond the Rim Mountains. Its light spread out as if it were trying to embrace the world.

Parasol trees grew in this part of the forest, the tapered columns of their trunks ringed by filmy green fronds. As light drained from the sky, the midribs of the fronds collapsed, folding against the trunks with a stealthy rustling and creaking, like so many dowagers rearranging the underskirts of their gowns.

Yama and Pandaras lay down to sleep on layers of ferns that the boy had woven together. He said that he had learned this trick during a stay with one of his uncles, who had been a basket-maker. 'A squire must know a little of everything, I reckon,' he said, 'so it's as well I had such a large family.'

He had discovered a clump of water vines that scrambled around the trunk of one of the parasol trees, but had not found anything to eat. 'But we'll reach the temple tomorrow, master. I'm certain of it, unless that gargoyle was lying to us.'

'He could not lie. At least, not then.'

Pandaras rubbed his hand over his face and yawned and said sleepily, 'Did you really change them, master?'

'The machines changed them. In time I hope that they will change all the indigenous peoples.'

The mirror people and the husbandmen of the Palace of the Memory of the People. The fisher folk of the Great River and all the tribes who lived in the wild parts of its shore, the forest folk and all the strange races of indigens the forest folk claimed to know, the horsemen of the high plains and the mountaineers and the rock wights, and many more. Yama tried to remember them all, and fell asleep, counting them still in his dreams.

In the morning, Yama and Pandaras woke to find fruit and fresh, juicy pea-vine pods in a string bag hanging from a stick thrust into a cleft in the trunk of one of the parasol trees. They looked for a long time, but found no other sign of the forest folk.

'Remember what I told you!' Yama shouted into the trees. 'Let others drink a little of your blood! Then they will be free too!'

The green silence of the forest swallowed his words.

He and Pandaras walked all day along the ridge above the valley, at the margin of the forest. And at sunset, just as Pandaras had predicted, they came to the temple.

16

THE HOLY SLAVE

The façade of the temple was carved into the face of a tall cliff of red sandstone, intricately worked and painted gold and white and ultramarine. It was approached by a long road that switchbacked up from the valley floor, ending at a single-span bridge that crossed a narrow, deep gorge at the edge of the wide plaza which spread in front of the temple. In the centre of the plaza was a simple square altar ringed by tall, white, unadorned pillars: the day shrine where people had gone to ask small favours of the Preservers or to remember their dead. There was a string of flat-roofed little houses to one side, where the priest and other temple staff had lived, and a meadow by the stream which fell into the gorge, where penitents and palmers would have camped.

The meadow was overgrown with pioneer acacias and wild banana plants now; the gardens of the houses contained only dry stalks; weeds thrust up between the slabs of polished sandstone that paved the plaza. A window shutter banged and banged in the evening breeze like an idiot who knew only one word. Turkey vultures had built untidy nests on the flat tops of the pillars around the day shrine: their droppings streaked the pillars, and the cracked bones of their prey littered the tiles below. But someone had swept the flight of broad steps to the entrance of the temple and tried to scrub away the blasphemous signs that had been scrawled on the altar, and prayer flags and banners in bright primary colours fluttered from poles along one side of the plaza.

'The Mighty People killed the priest and the hierodules during their Change War,' Pandaras whispered. 'They killed the Archivist and the Commissioner, too. They burned the Commissioner and a maniple of soldiers in his peel-house, but they killed the others here. Yoi Sendar said that those who killed the Archivist ate his brains, because they wanted to gain power over the dead.'

He and Yama squatted in dry brush at the top of a pebbly slope close to the bridge. Pandaras had taken out his stone blade, and was sharpening it on a bit of flint he held between his feet.

'I do not think there will be a need for that,' Yama said.

'It could be the Prefect. Or that apothecary. You have powerful enemies, master. They are not easy to kill.'

'Dr Dismas would not wait for us in a temple – it is not his style. And Prefect Corin would not bother to set out flags or sweep the entrance. If it is someone we know, then it can be only one person. And if it is not, then I hope that whoever has appointed himself custodian of this place will do us no harm. Besides, this is the only way to the midpoint of the world that will not involve a hundred days of walking.'

Yama stood up, crabbed down the slope in a cloud of dust, and ran straight across the bridge (boulders lay tumbled in a dry riverbed below) to the plaza. Dry weeds crackled underfoot. A pair of turkey vultures took flight. Pandaras crossed the bridge more cautiously, holding the stone blade up by his shoulder, the stump of his left wrist tucked between two toggles of his shirt, then scampered across the plaza to catch up with Yama.

'We could have waited until after supper, master!'

'I do not think we should rely on the forest folk any longer. They have other concerns now. And please, Pandaras, put away that blade. Show that we come as friends.'

But Pandaras did not hear him. He gave a sudden yell and ran past Yama and scampered up the steps. A tall, pale-skinned figure had appeared at the entrance of the temple.

It was Tibor.

'I did not doubt that you had survived the flood,' the hierodule told Yama, 'and I am pleased that you have found your way here.'

Yama smiled and said, 'I will free you of your obligation soon, Tibor. We will sleep here tonight, but we have a long way to go, and must set off as soon as we are rested.'

They were sitting cross-legged on the terrace before the entrance. The hierodule wore a white shirt left unbuttoned to display the scars on his chest, and trousers of a stiff, silvery material he had slit at the waist and ankles because they were slightly too small for him. He had brought out a tray of food and beakers of distilled water, and Yama and Pandaras had gorged themselves, even though the fare had clearly been stored too long in a freezer – the vegetables limp, with ice crystals in their cores, the flatbreads dry, the sauces curdled and insipid.

'The people of the valley killed the priest and the hierodules of this temple,' Pandaras said. 'They have turned their backs on the Preservers. It isn't safe for people like you, Tibor. You think only of serving, but this isn't the place for it.'

'I know what happened here,' Tibor said. He had lost his cigarette makings in the flood, and was chewing a twig, rolling it around his lips with his long red tongue. 'But that was many years ago. Things will be different now.'

Yama asked Tibor how he had escaped Prefect Corin. The hierodule explained that he had still been struggling with the Prefect when the tidal wave had smashed into the floating garden, knocking it from the air and washing the two men into the river.

'We were torn apart,' Tibor said, 'and then I was busy trying not to drown. I was dragged down by a tremendous whirlpool, and I think I might have touched the bottom of the river, so deeply was I drawn. Just as my breath was about to burst from my chest I was shot up like a cork, and came to the surface near an uprooted tree. I clung to its trunk and was borne with it wherever the flood chose to take me. Many small animals had already sought safety there, and bedraggled birds alighted on its branches to take refuge from the rain, so that I did not lack for food. I drifted for two days amidst a growing fleet of floating trees, until at last they were stranded by the failing waters and I could walk across them into forested hills untouched by the flood. This part of the world is mostly populated by indigenous peoples, and I knew that the only temple for fifty leagues all around stood beyond the hills. And so I made my way across them, and after many hardships I will not trouble you with at last arrived here.'

'You have done up the old place nicely,' Pandaras said.

'I am a hierodule.'

Yama said, 'You had food and drink ready for us. How did you know that we were coming here?'

Tibor spread his big hands and said gravely, 'Why, she told me. If you had not come here, I would have had to fetch you.'

For the first time since he had escaped the Mighty People, Yama felt the Shadow stir. He said, 'I thought it might be something like that. You had better take me to the shrine.'

Tibor nodded. 'She is waiting for you, Yamamanama. And do not be afraid. She forgives you for the time you tried to kill her.'

The long processional path inside the temple still retained a feeble blue luminescence. It led them down wide corridors and through a nest of round chambers with intricate murals painted on walls and ceilings to the naos at the heart of the temple, a vast dry cave that could easily have held a thousand petitioners. As Yama and Pandaras followed Tibor into it, like emmets creeping into a darkened house, tiny sparks whirled down from high above to crown them. Fireflies. Pandaras laughed to see them.

Yama said, 'How far back into the plateau does the complex run, Tibor?'

'Further than I am allowed to explore,' the hierodule said. 'She will answer all your questions.'

The floor was inlaid with a spiral pattern of garnet slabs. The reflections of the fireflies glittered underfoot as Yama and Pandaras followed Tibor towards a faint glow that curdled in the darkness ahead, flickering in the black disc of the shrine.

It stood on a dais raised high above the floor. A steep stair led up to it. Poles had been driven into the sandstone slabs of the dais and bodies clad in tattered robes were lashed to the poles with corroded wire. The dry air had cured their skin and flesh to something like leather, shrunken tightly over the bones.

'I did my best to scrub off the blasphemies,' Tibor said, 'but she likes to see the remains of her enemies.'

'I think that one must have been the Archivist,' Pandaras said. 'They took off the top of his skull as if it were an egg—'

The disc hanging from his neck had begun to glow, burning through the material of his shirt. He held it up to show Yama. Twin sparks reflected in his eyes, and green light washed over them.

The shrine had become a window in which the aspect of Angel was walking swiftly forward, fixing Yama with a confident and commanding gaze. As before, she wore a white one-piece garment that clung to her tall, slender body. The garden receded behind her beneath a perfect blue sky. She stared silently at Yama for a long time. He returned her gaze and resisted the compulsion to speak, although his heart quickened with the effort.

At last, she said, 'You have lost your looks, my love. The world has been hard on you, but now I am here to help you. What, you have no words for me?'

'I serve no one,' Yama said. He tried to see past her, hoping that he could summon the hell-hound, but something stopped him looking beyond the boundary of the garden.

She laughed. Yama thought of knives clashing. She said, 'Don't be silly. Of course you will serve. It is what you were made for. Do stop trying to call that bothersome creature, by the way. This time it will not come.'

'I suppose a feral machine was tracking me. They dare not visit the world they lost, except for brief moments, but they are compelled to watch what they cannot have.'

'You are very stubborn, but I think you know that you need my help. You know that there is much you do not know.'

Pandaras said in a small but defiant voice, 'You are the ghost my master told me about. The ghost of a ghost, in fact, because my master killed you last time you and he met.'

The aspect glanced at him. 'You are the one who looked in the book, aren't you? I let you live then. I may show you the same mercy now, if you show a little gratitude.'

'If you have any mercy,' Yama said, 'you will let the hierodule go. You have used him falsely.'

'Is he not a servant of the avatars? And there are no avatars left, except for me.'

Yama said, 'You are nothing more than the discarded aspect of a dead woman. Your kind were overthrown more than five million years ago, and you have no powers of your own. Just as you use the hierodule, the feral machines use you.'

'The machines and I have an . . . understanding. An alliance. And you will join us, my darling.'

Yama turned his face to show her his scars. 'One of the feral machines already tried to use me. It tried to do to me what it did to Dr Dismas. But it no longer has power over me, and neither do you.'

'With my help you can be so much more powerful than any of the feral machines.'

'We can only be what we are.'

The aspect smiled. 'The essence of the false philosophy that convinced your Preservers to flee from the universe. Animals can only be what they are, yes, but human beings can transcend their animal selves. The Preservers were fools. They raised up the ten thousand bloodlines and made them human, but forbade them to rise higher than their creators. You and I will prove how wrong they were.'

'You have no power over me,' Yama said again, and with an enormous effort turned away from the shrine.

Behind him, the aspect said, 'I know why the Great River fails. I can help you save the world, if that is what you want.'

'You want the world for yourself.'

'And I will have it, in a little while.'

'Then why should I save it?'

The aspect's voice deepened. There was music in it and Yama could feel his muscles trying to respond: there was still much of the machine inside him. He fought against it, staggering against the Archivist's dry, brittle body, embracing it for support.

Pandaras cried out, but Yama did not hear what the boy said. The aspect's voice filled his mind.

'The world is a fabrication,' she said. 'An artificial habitat twenty thousand kilometres long and a thousand wide, set in a nest of fields that mimic the gravity of an Earth-sized planet and prevent the atmosphere from dissipating into the hard vacuum of space. It is not well made. Machines must constantly maintain it; without them, the air would soon become unbreathable, the inhabited places would become deserts, and the Great River would silt up. Those are some of the functions of the lesser machines. And there are greater machines in the keel. I see that you know of them.'

Yama remembered the huge engines that Dr Dismas's paramour had shown him, and the machines he had seen when Beatrice had taken him back to the peel-house by the road in the keelways. She had told him then that he had not been ready to talk to them; he had not understood that warning until now.

The aspect sang on, seductive, compelling. 'There are many wormholes orbiting Confluence's star. I suspect that they emerge at various points in the galactic disc. But there is also a wormhole at the midpoint of this strange world, and something has recently altered it. Your people constructed this world, Yamamanama. You are the key to making it whole again. And you will serve. I have powerful allies. Tell me now that you will at least listen to one of them, and I will spare the boy. But if you will not continue this conversation then I will have my slave crush his skull and paint your face with his brains. A simple *yes* will be enough.'

Pandaras tried to run then, but Tibor caught him and lifted him up and closed a massive hand over his head. The hierodule's face was set in a horrible rictus. Muscles jumped in his arms and legs as if struggling against each other. Pandaras shrieked in fear and agony.

The aspect said, 'Say it, Yamamanama. Say yes, or I will have the boy's life.'

Yama started to move towards Tibor and Pandaras, but it was as if he was in a dream where gravity was much stronger, or air was as dense as water. He was breathing in great gasps.

'Say it!'

The aspect and the hierodule had spoken together.

Pandaras slashed at Tibor's arm with the stone blade, but the hierodule blocked the blow and knocked the blade into the darkness beyond the edge of the dais.

'Say it, or the boy dies, and you will be responsible for his death.'

'No!'

The hierodule lifted Pandaras above his head, as if to dash him to the floor. And the boy ripped the ceramic disc from the thong dangling from his neck and thrust it edge-first into the hierodule's eye.

Tibor and the aspect screamed at the same moment. White light blotted out the garden and beat across the huge chamber. Tibor dropped Pandaras, who rolled away and sprang to his feet. With the glowing disc stuck in his eye and blood streaming down his face, the hierodule blundered into two of the staked bodies, smashing them to dust and fragments of brown bone, and pitched over the edge of the dais.

Yama and Pandaras ran down the steep stair. Tibor lay at the bottom, his neck broken. Pandaras pulled the disc from the hierodule's eye and closed his eyelids and kissed his forehead.

'He would have killed me,' Pandaras said. He was crying. 'I had to do it, or he would have killed me.'

'It was not Tibor who tried to kill you. It was the aspect. She had made a link with Tibor through the shrine, and you shut it down.'

'I could feel him fighting it. But she was too much for him.' Pandaras knuckled his eyes and sniffed hugely and stood. 'We will build a pyre, master. We can't give him a proper funeral, but we'll do our best.'

'We cannot stay here. She will soon find a way to return, and she will bar the way.'

'We can always find another temple.'

'There is none within fifty leagues, and she might be waiting for us there. I am sorry, Pandaras. We have to go. We have to find the keelways.'

Pandaras took a deep breath, and another. 'Well,' he said, 'I suppose this is still a holy place, even though she defiled it. And perhaps the forest folk will come, and do what's necessary.'

He made a fist, touched his throat, and bowed over the body of his friend, then followed Yama past the shrine. The fireflies spun above them, and their shadows were thrown ahead of them by the white light burning in the shrine. By the time the aspect had managed to reconfigure it, they were already beyond her reach, descending towards the keelways.

17

THE GLASS DESERT

It was a dusty town built along a narrow defile high in the dry mountains that bordered the Glass Desert. The defile was roofed over with canvas sheeting that flapped and boomed in the constant cold, dry wind, and was lined with the mudbrick façades of buildings hacked into its rocky walls. A decad of different bloodlines came there to trade drugs, rare metals, precious stones and furs for rifles and knives and other weapons manufactured by artisans in little courtyards between the buildings. There was a produce market at one end of the defile, and a maze of corrals and sheds where bacts, dzo and mules were bought and sold at the other. Fields and orchards watered by artesian wells stepped away below the produce market, startlingly green against a tawny landscape in which only cacti, barrel trees and cheat grass grew.

The town was called Cagn, or Thule, or Golgath, and had many other secret names known only to the tribes who used them. It was agreed by all that it was one of the worst places in the world; it was said that the double peak looming above it, framing the Gateway of Lost Souls and casting its shadow across the town in the early morning and the late afternoon, hid it from gaze of the Preservers, and any sin committed there went unremarked. It had not been much changed by the coming of the heretics. It was still a refuge for smugglers, reivers, rustlers, fugitives and other desperadoes. Less than an hour after he and Pandaras arrived in the town, Yama had to kill a pair of ruffians who tried to rob them.

The two men were tall and burly and covered everywhere with coarse red hair. They wore striped cotton serapes and broad leather belts hitched under their ample bellies, and were belligerently drunk. When one of them swung at him with a skean, Yama broke the man's arm, snatched up the weapon, and told both of them to run. The injured ruffian yowled, lowered his shaggy head, and charged like a bull. Yama dodged him easily, swung the skean as he went past, and slashed his neck down to the spinal cord: the man fell flat, dead before he hit the dust.

The second ruffian swayed and said, 'You killed him, you skeller,' and pulled a pistol from his belt. Yama, with a cold, detached feeling, as if this had already happened somewhere else, perhaps in a story he had once read, hefted the skean to get a feel for its balance, threw it overhand, and skewered the man in the right eye.

People who had stopped to watch the fight began to drift away now that the fun was over – murders were commonplace in a town outside the rule of any law. Pandaras scooped up the pistol, chased off a couple of children who were creeping towards the bodies, and went through the pouches on the men's belts, finding only a few clipped coins and a packet of pellets and a powerpack for the pistol. He pulled the skean from the second ruffian's eye, cleaned its double-edged blade on the dead man's serape, and tucked it into the waistband of his trousers.

Yama refused the pistol when Pandaras offered it to him, and said, 'I know that we will need more money, but I will not kill to get it.'

The cold precision that had gripped him in the moment of danger had vanished. He began to tremble as they walked away. Behind them, the children moved in to take the belts and pouches and serapes. Red canvas cracked overhead, turning sunlight to the colour of blood.

Pandaras said, 'In this kind of place, we'll need all the weapons we can get just to keep what we have. As for money, I have a confession. Before I set fire to the Captain's hut, I took two of the smallest portraits. I doubt that we'll find much appreciation of art here, but they are enamelled on beaten gold, and although they are no bigger than my hand I think they'll buy us what we need. Aren't you glad you weren't able to send me away?'

Yama had tried to make Pandaras take a keel road back to Ys, telling him that the journey to the Glass Desert would almost certainly end in death, but the boy had refused.

'I am your squire, master, for better or worse,' he had said fiercely. 'And I do not think that things can get much worse than they already are. I have killed two men in as many days, and one of them was my friend. I have lost my hand, and I failed you in many ways while we were apart. I'll not fail you now.'

And so they had gone on together. Yama had used machines to guide them through endless caverns and corridors. He no longer cared if his enemies could track him by the traces left by his commands. It was too late for that.

A thing like a giant silvery spider, one of the machines which kept the caverns clean, had led them at last to an active part of the transportation system that had once knitted the whole world together. They travelled all night in a humming capsule that fell down one of the keel roads. Neither of them slept, although both pretended to.

All of the transportation system beyond the midpoint of the world had been destroyed in the wars of the Age of Insurrection. The capsule had taken Yama and Pandaras as far as it could, delivering them to a maze of passages beneath a ruined peel-house; they emerged at the foot of a bluff which overlooked the midslopes of the mountains of the Great Divide. The yurts of a party of musk-deer herders were pitched nearby. When Yama and Pandaras walked into their camp, still crowned with fireflies which Yama had forgotten to dismiss, the skinny, long-haired men and women fell on their knees.

Yama and Pandaras breakfasted on soured goat's milk mixed with deer blood, and a sickly porridge boiled up from barley mash and dried apricots, then walked all day up the mountain, leaving behind the herders' threadbare pastures and climbing through long, dry draws to the town.

With the money Pandaras got at a refiner's for the stolen portraits, they bought a bact from a livestock trader and supplies from the town's only chandler. New clothes, furs for the mountain pass and light robes for the desert, a tent of memory plastic that folded as small as a scarf, filter masks, dried food, water-bottles and a dew still, a saddle and harness for the bact. Yama politely refused the chandler's invitation to inspect his armoury. He would need no weapon where he was going, and Pandaras was armed with the skean and pistol he had taken from the dead ruffians.

'I have maps too,' the chandler said. 'Reliable. Certified.'

'We do not need maps,' Yama said.

'Hnn. That's what the other fellow said. He'll be buzzard meat soon enough, and so will you if you won't unbend and take some advice.' The chandler was very tall, with fine-grained skin that shone like polished leather. He laid a long-nailed finger beside one of his opaline eyes and said, 'Perhaps you have one of your own, and put your trust in that. Many come here with old maps found in some depository or archive, but you can't rely on them. All the ruins within easy travel of the edge of the Glass Desert are mined out, and most of the waterholes are poisoned. But my maps are up to date. You won't have to pay for them, not right now, but you'll have to agree to sell anything you find to me.'

Pandaras said, 'How will you make sure that we do?'

The chandler looked down at Pandaras. He was three times the boy's height. By the doorway, the burly bodyguard shifted the rifle resting in the crook of one of her beefy arms.

'This is the only way into the Glass Desert, and the only way out,' the chandler said. 'If you survive, you'll be back. You'll probably have to sell anything you find to me anyway. I give the best prices in town. Ask around if you don't believe me. You'll find that all my rivals say I'm far too generous with my money.'

Yama said, 'Who was this other man? Did he have a white mark on his face?'

'Not so bold,' the chandler said. 'Everything has its price here.'

Yama told Pandaras to give the chandler the money they had taken from the ruffians. 'Describe him.'

The man spat on the clipped coins and rubbed them with the soft, flat pads at the ends of his bony fingers. 'He was about your height. Had a veil over his face, and wore a hat and a silvery cloak. I know his name, but you'll have to pay me to get it.'

'I already know his name,' Yama said.

The chandler glared at Yama. 'It doesn't matter,' he said. 'He didn't take a map, or any water or food, just a saddle for his mule. And he smelled bad, like skinrot or canker. No, it doesn't matter what he's called. He'll be dead by now.'

They were followed out of town by three ruffians of the same bloodline as the pair that Yama had killed. They were either kin to the dead men, or in the pay of the chandler, or freelances looking to strip novices of newly bought supplies. As they rode hard towards him, Yama called down a machine and killed them all. He and Pandaras tied the bodies to one of the horses and sent it back to the town as a warning. The second horse had bolted when the machine had smashed the skull of its rider, but Pandaras easily rounded up the third, an old mare with a shaggy grey coat. With Pandaras following on the bact, Yama rode the mare through the high pass of the Gateway of Lost Souls, where unending wind howled over polished ice, and followed a trail down the dry mountain slopes towards the glaring wastes of the Glass Desert.

The trail wound through a dead landscape. Nothing grew there but stoneworts, which survived on the brief dews formed each morning. Their yellow or black blotches were the only spots of colour in the alkaline, dust-blown land. Cairns were raised here and there, the burial places of prospectors. All had been disturbed, with bones scattered around them. On the afternoon of the second day, Yama and Pandaras rode past three skulls set on a flat-topped rock beside the trail, and Pandaras pointed out the neat hole punched into the ridge above the empty eye sockets of one of the skulls.

'Perhaps he quarrelled with his companions over treasure they had found. Or perhaps he killed himself after he killed his friends, driven mad by greed, or the ghosts of war machines.'

'You can still turn back,' Yama said. 'I must face something worse than any ghost you can imagine, and I do not think I will be able to protect you from it. It may well destroy you. It may well destroy me, too.'

Pandaras touched the ceramic disc hung inside his shirt. 'I have some protection. And I trust in you, master.'

'Take the horse, Pandaras. Ride back through the pass and wait for me.'

'Will you turn back too? Well, then.'

That evening, they made camp by a waterhole. The mare slipped her hobble and drank before Yama could find a machine which could test the water. She foundered almost at once, foaming at the mouth. The bact snorted, as if in disdain, as she convulsed. Blood poured from her eyes and nostrils. Yama stroked her muzzle, then slit her throat.

Pandaras took a sip from a cupped handful of water and promptly spat it out and tipped the rest on the ground. 'Poison,' he said, and spat again. 'I bet the chandler's men did it. They poison most of the waterholes, and he hires out maps showing those they didn't touch.'

'The whole land is poisoned,' Yama said.

They moved their camp to a flat shelf of rock a league further down the trail. Pandaras cooked steaks he had cut from the mare's hind-quarters; he had also drained some of her blood into two of the empty water-bottles, saying that as far as he was concerned blood was almost as good as water.

Pandaras ate most of the food; Yama had no appetite. A faint sense of Dr Dismas's paramour nagged at the remains of his Shadow like the wink of sunlight on a far-off mirror or a tintinnabulation in the ear. And he also felt the pull of the feral machine he had called down, without knowing it, when he had been in desperate danger in the house of the renegade star-sailor. Caught between the two, he sat and looked out towards the wastelands of the Glass Desert until long past sunset, and scarcely noticed when Pandaras wrapped a fur around him against the night's bitter cold.

From then on, Pandaras and Yama took turns riding the bact. It took three more days to descend the mountain slopes. The sere wasteland of the Glass Desert stretched beyond, patched and cratered, riven on one side by the vast, meandering canyon that once had held a river as wide and deep as the Great River. Points of reflected light flashed here and there in the bitter land, and a sea of light burned in the middle distance where a city had once stood. The Glass Desert had once been as verdant as the inhabited half of Confluence, and as populous, but the feral machines had made it their homeland after they had rebelled, and it had been devastated in the last and fiercest of the wars of the Age of Insurrection. Little lived there now.

As he walked beside the bact that day, through a barrens of blowing sand and piles of half-melted boulders fused together by some great, ancient blast, Yama kept glimpsing figures amongst the stones. They vanished if he turned to look at them, but he recognised them nonetheless. Derev, her white feathery hair blowing out in the hot wind, Lud and Lob, Cyg, the obese body that had hosted the fugitive star-sailor, and a host of others. His lost love, and all his dead. The remnant of the Shadow was stirring in his mind, wakened by the call of its progenitor far off across the tumbled desolation.

When they made camp that evening, Pandaras saw how drawn his master had become. Yama squatted on his haunches and stared into the thin, cold wind that blew out of the dark desert. His long black hair was matted with dust and tangled around his scarred face. He did not seem to notice when Pandaras shaved him, using a flaked edge of glass and a handful of their precious water. They had no scissors, but Pandaras had given the skean's blade a good edge, and he trimmed Yama's hair with that. It was not easy to do with only one hand, but

Yama bore Pandaras's clumsiness patiently. More and more, he seemed to be retreating inside his head.

Yama would not eat anything, and slept uneasily. Pandaras watched over him, chewing congealed blood that was beginning to spoil. He reckoned that they were not coming back. At best, they would somehow destroy this thing, and then hope for an easy death of thirst or heat prostration. At worst, it would destroy them.

It was a pity. He would have liked to have made a song of Yama's adventures amongst the world's wonders. He remembered the engines he had seen in the cellars of the world, when the spider thing had led them to the keel road. Long swathes of the floors of the vaults had been transparent, showing chambers deep enough to swallow mountains. It was as if he and Yama had become birds, hanging high above a world within a world. Far below, tiny red and black specks had roamed a green plain, illuminated by a kind of flaw in the middle air that had shed a radiance as bright as day. The specks had been machines as big as carracks, and black spires of intricate latticework had reared halfway towards the radiant flaw, wound about with what looked like threads of gold, wider than the Grand Way of Ys. There had been black cubes in heaps as wide as cities, and geometric patterns of silver and white laid into the green landscape.

At one point Yama had thrown himself on the floor, prostrating himself like a palmer at a shrine. The spider had halted, flexing one leg and then another as if in frustration, until at last Yama had stood and walked on.

He had told Pandaras then that there were mysteries in the world he could only guess at, and they began to talk about this again as they journeyed into the Glass Desert. Yama wanted to unburden himself of all that had happened to him. Once more, he told Pandaras the story of how he had been found as a baby on the breast of a dead woman in a white boat cast adrift on the Great River. He talked of his childhood, of how happy and fortunate he had been: the adopted son of the Aedile of Aeolis, the brother of brave Telmon. He described how Dr Dismas had tried to kidnap him, and how he had escaped and had been given refuge in the tower of Beatrice and Osric, the last curators of the City of the Dead, of his journey to Ys, where he had escaped Prefect Corin and met Pandaras. And then, turn and turn again, they told each other the rest of the tale: their adventures in the Palace of the Memory of the People; the voyage downriver in the *Weazel*; the sacking of Aeolis by

Prefect Corin and the death of the Aedile; the treachery of Eliphas. And on, through their separate adventures and their reunion, and now this, their last exploit. They had reached the Glass Desert at last – searching not for Eliphas's invented lost city, but for Yama's nemesis.

Pandaras noticed the birds on the afternoon of the fourth day after they had quit the mountains. Black cruciform specks circling in a sky so achingly bright it was more white than blue.

'They are not birds,' Yama said. 'And they have been watching us ever since we crept through the pass, but they dare to fly lower now because this is their land.'

He coughed long and hard into his fist. They were both affected by the dust that hung in the hot air. It worked through the seals of their filter masks and irritated their throats and lungs, and got into every crevice of their bodies, drying their skins and causing pressure sores. It worked under their goggles, too, inflaming their eyes.

Pandaras was in the saddle of the bact; he clambered down and said, 'Ride a while, master. Rest.'

Yama lifted his mask and spat. There was blood in his spittle. When he could speak again, he said, 'It has grown strong, Pandaras. It no longer cares about being found, for the machines which might have destroyed it are engaged in fighting the heretics. And it has made many servants.'

'Please climb up, master. You need to keep your strength.'

But Yama walked on, leading the bact. They had been plodding all day through the petrified stumps of what had once been a forest.

'There are different kinds of machine,' Yama said. 'I thought of it while we were crossing that big chamber in the keelways. Do you remember?'

'I will never forget it, master. Do you think people live there, in the lands of the keel?'

'No, Pandaras. There are machines which are as innocent as the indigenous races and unchanged bloodlines, and machines which are self-aware, as in those bloodlines, like ours, in which the breath of the Preservers has been quickened. The first kind obey me without thought, and I can command the second kind, such as the dwellers of the deep, as a general commands an army. But down there, in the keelways, are machines that I cannot control. I cannot even talk with them. Perhaps they have achieved the equivalent of enlightenment.

'Machines and men: we are the mirrors of each other. I called on a feral machine to help me, but did I really command it, or did it see its chance to place its hook into me? I could not master the child of the thing that lies ahead of us, the Shadow which Dr Dismas grew in me, but perhaps that was because the Shadow had become too much like me; perhaps it had begun to assume my power. I do not know if I can do what needs to be done, Pandaras. I fear that it knows me better than I know myself.'

'You'll know what to do when it comes to it, master. I'm sure of it.'

Yama smiled, but his gaze was haunted.

They walked on in silence. After a while, Yama said, 'Do you remember when we crossed that little valley, two days ago? That was once a tributary of the Great River of this half of Confluence, running down from the snowfields of the Rim Mountains, just as the Breas empties into the Great River near Aeolis. But the Great River into which that tributary emptied dried up and was not renewed. The land died. And now our own Great River is dying...'

At last Pandaras persuaded his master to climb onto the saddle in front of the bact's dwindling hump. When he was settled, Yama said, 'If my father was right, then the fall of the Great River is my fault. It began when I was cast upon this world. Perhaps I can atone for that, Pandaras, if I can learn enough. It is my only hope.'

It broke Pandaras's heart to see how badly his master doubted himself. 'You are greater than you know, master, but you are tired and you can't see things clearly. You'll feel better when you have rested. You ride the rest of the day. I don't mind walking.'

They reached the far edge of the petrified forest at nightfall and made camp. As usual, Pandaras kept watch while Yama muttered and twitched in his sleep, and once or twice thought he heard something padding outside the tent. There! A scrape of metal on stone. The bact snorted and moved about. It was not his imagination. He gripped the pistol, but what use was it against monsters?

The next day, Yama seemed a little better. He said, 'I dreamed that we are being followed.'

'And I know it, master.'

Pandaras squinted against sky glare. The bird things were still making their circles up there. All around, scarves and streamers of red sand snaked across pitted red rock. The air was filled with the dry hiss of blowing sand.

Yama said, 'I do not mean the watchers, or the other small nuisances. They are coming down from the Gateway of Lost Souls. An army, Pandaras. He is coming after me.'

Pandaras looked back towards the mountains of the Great Divide. The icy peaks shone high and far, seeming to float above the glittering desert.

He said, 'It must have been a dream, master. Not even an eagle could see so far. Don't worry about it.'

Yama shook his head violently. 'I saw through the eyes of one of the watchers. The things which follow us also follow the army.'

That night Yama woke with a start, feverish and shaking. He turned towards Pandaras, but his reddened eyes were focused on infinity. 'They have machines,' he said. 'The fool brought machines with him as well as soldiers. He thinks that they are shielded.'

Pandaras wet a corner of Yama's robe with a few minims of their precious water and dabbed at his forehead. 'Hush, master. You dream.'

'No. There are no dreams here. The desert burns away everything until only the truth is left.'

At last Pandaras got Yama to lie down. He thought that his master slept, but after a while Yama said, 'The soldiers are mounted and in uniform. They wear black masks with long snouts and round eyeholes of glass backed with gold. Their mounts are masked, too. But I recognise the man at their head. It is Enobarbus. She has sent him after me. Things are coming together at last.'

'Is there any sign of the Prefect?' Pandaras said.

'No... No, not yet.'

'Then maybe he's dead,' Pandaras said, although he did not believe it.

They had little food left, and less water. Night dew yielded only a few minims, and there was no standing water to be found, poisoned or otherwise. The next day, the bact knelt down and would not get up. Pandaras, weeping in rage and frustration, beat at the animal's withers. It closed its long-lashed eyes and ignored him. Sand blew all around; the sun was a glowering eye in a red sky.

Pandaras and Yama unloaded the supplies. Only one water-bottle was full. A second held a few mouthfuls, and the rest were empty. They threw them away, and most of the remaining food.

'I will get us food,' Yama said. 'Food and water. They are off the mountain slopes now, and coming towards us very quickly. They have good mounts.'

He was flushed and feverish. He was looking towards the distant range of mountains, and it took Pandaras a long time to get him turned around.

They had not gone far when they heard the bact scream. Pandaras stumbled towards it through blowing sand, but stopped, shocked and frightened, when he saw the things that were tearing it apart.

They were like crosses between snakes and wild cats, armoured in overlapping metallic scales or flexible blood-red hide. No two were alike. One had a tail like that of a scorpion, tipped with a swollen sting which arched above its back. One had a multiple set of jaws so massive that they dragged on the ground, another a round sucker mouth with a ragged ring of teeth.

The misshapen wild cats tore at the bact with silent ferocity. It was already dead, its neck half-severed and its bloody ribs showing, blood soaking the sand in a widening circle. Blood glistened on chain-mail hide, on metal scales, on horny plates edged with metal, on serrated metal in snapping jaws. Two of the things had burrowed into the bact's belly, shaking its body back and forth as they worked like a depraved reversal of birth. The pack ignored Pandaras until he raised the pistol, and then one turned eyes like red lamps towards him and reared up on its stout tail, waving a decad of mismatched legs tipped with razor-edged claws. Black slaver dripped from its long snout.

A hand fell on Pandaras's shoulder; his shot went wild, swallowed by the sand-filled air. Yama shouted into his ear. 'Leave them! They will not hurt us!'

The wild cat dropped to its belly and shuffled forward and grovelled before Yama, although it kept its burning red eyes on Pandaras as he backed away. Its fellows had not paused in their feverish butchery; the bact was already stripped to the bone.

Yama and Pandaras drank the last of their water at noon, threw away the water-bottle, and went on. Yama taught Pandaras that sucking a pebble could stimulate the flow of saliva and help keep thirst at bay, but the hot wind which blew sand around them drew moisture from every crevice of their bodies. After nightfall Pandaras forced himself to stay awake, starting at each change in pitch of the streams of sand that hissed outside the tent, and Yama slept fitfully, waking before dawn and insisting that they go on.

'They are almost on us,' he said, 'but it is not far. I'm sorry, Pandaras. There is no chance of turning back now.'

'I had not thought of it, master,' Pandaras said. His lips were cracked and bleeding and he tasted blood at the back of his throat with each breath; the dust had worked into his lungs.

The air was filled with blowing sand. They left the tent behind and set off into it.

Shapes loomed out of the murk: towers of friable bones lashed together with sinews and half-covered in hides that flapped and boomed and creaked in the wind. A ragged picket fence of crystalline spines grew crookedly from a shoulder of black rock. Creatures were impaled on some of the spines. A few were men; the rest were like nothing Pandaras had ever seen, chimeras of machine and insect. Most were no more than dried husks, but some were still alive and stirred feebly as Yama and Pandaras went past.

Pandaras did not pay much attention to these horrors. He no longer felt fear, only exhaustion and growing thirst. Each step was a promise to himself that there would soon be no more steps; walking was an infinite chain of promises. The world shrank to the patch of ground directly in front of him. Sometimes it seemed to pitch like the deck of a ship and he could barely keep to his feet, but always he went forward, following in his master's footsteps.

At noon, Yama stopped and turned in a half-circle and fell to his knees. Pandaras managed to get him to the shelter of a tilted shelf of rock. It was very hot. The sun's bloody glare was diffused across half the sky. Sand skirled around crystal spurs, sent shifting shadows shuddering across reaches of bare stone. Pandaras's mouth and throat were parched. His head throbbed and he itched everywhere.

Yama stirred in his arms. Blood leaked from the corners of his closed eyes; Pandaras blotted it with the hem of his robe.

'I will bring water,' Yama said, and seemed to fall into a faint.

A moment later, thunder cracked high above and something flashed through the blowing red dust, chased by black shapes. It dived this way and that with abrupt turns and reverses, swooped low overhead, dropped something, and shot away as black things closed on either side. A sheet of green lightning; more thunder, then only the endless hiss of blowing sand.

Pandaras crawled out of the lee of the shelf of rock and retrieved what had been dropped by the machine.

It was a transparent sphere of spun plastic as big as his head, half-filled with cold, clear water.

*

When they were able to set off again, something like a storm of dry lightning had started up in the direction of the Great Divide. Flares of brittle light half-obscured by curtains of blowing sand. Overhead, things chased each other through the sky with wild howls. Far off, something roared and roared on a single endless note.

'A lot of trouble for a drink of water,' Pandaras remarked.

'The battle had already begun. That was why I was able to steal the water . . . We must press on, Pandaras. Enobarbus brought more machines than I thought. I do not know if Dr Dismas's paramour can hold them back.'

'I'll go there and back in the blink of an eye, and carry you too, if I must.' Pandaras said it as lightly as he could, but felt that this day would be his last.

The battle raged for the rest of their journey. Curtains of light washed half the sky, spiked with red or green threads burning long paths through the sandstorm. The ground shook continually, and a low rumble curdled Pandaras's guts.

The land began to slope downwards ever more steeply, sculpted in fantastic curls like breaking waves frozen in glassy rock. Razor-sharp ridges cut through the soles of their boots and they both left bloody prints on the glassy ground. Things scuttled amongst half-buried rocks: hand-sized, flat, multi-legged and very quick, like squashed spiders made of black glass. Larger creatures prowled further off, barely visible through veils of blowing red sand. Stiff growths poked up from glass and drifted sand, fretted tufts of black stuff neither plastic nor metal, all bent in the same direction by the constant wind.

'We are getting close now,' Yama said. Blood was still seeping from his eyes; every so often he had to lift up his goggles and blot it away. Blisters on his forehead leaked clear fluid. Sand caked his face and his hair.

'You are already here,' a voice said.

It came from everywhere around them, from the rocks and sand, from the dust-laden air.

Pandaras whirled in a complete circle, fumbling for his pistol. Something black and quick dropped from a fold of glass that reared above and stung his hand and jumped away. He howled and dropped the pistol in a drift of white sand. It sank swiftly, as if pulled under. Pandaras sucked at the puncture on his hand and spat out the bitter taste. When he looked up, someone in a silver cloak was standing a few paces from Yama.

It was the apothecary, Dr Dismas. Or at least, what was left of him.

He seemed to have grown taller. His clothes were tatters under the cloak. His flesh was black and rotten, falling away from bones on which cables and sacs of silvery stuff flexed and tugged. He tottered closer, reaching for Yama, but Yama dashed his hand aside. Fingers snapped; two fell to the sand and were immediately tugged under.

Dr Dismas did not seem to notice. His eyes were blanked by fluttering red light. Wind combed the remnants of his hair back from his skull. His jaw worked, and he said in a dry, croaking voice, 'You brought many with you.'

'They followed me,' Yama said. 'I had thought that they might be your friends, for their leader is the champion of the aspect of Angel. Is she not your ally?'

'We both want the same end, but for different reasons. I had hoped that you had escaped her completely, but no matter. It is only a minor inconvenience. Do not think that it will distract me from what must be done.'

'I know what you did to Dismas,' Yama said. 'He tried to do the same to me. And failed, as you can see.'

'He was loyal enough, in his way, and now he is completely mine. I may make him whole again, or I may absorb him. There will be time to decide on that once I am done with you. All the time in the world.'

Pandaras realised then that something was using Dr Dismas's dead body, like a puppet in a shadow play.

Yama said, 'He infected me with one of your children, but it had ideas of its own.'

'Of course it did. That is why I must eventually destroy or devour my children, for otherwise they would devour me. Dr Dismas should not have infected you so early: my child could have destroyed you. But you overcame it, and what remains of it will help us.'

'As I thought.'

'Now we can begin.'

'Now we can begin,' Yama said. 'There is much that I want to learn. Pandaras, it is too dangerous for you to stay here alone. You must come with me. Do not be afraid.'

Pandaras was so sick with fear that he could hardly stand, but drew himself up and followed Yama and the puppet-thing through a narrow defile. A ramp spiralled away, running down into a deep pit. The pit narrowed with each turn of the ramp, like a hole left by a gigantic screw. Silvery vines grew out of the glassy walls – grew through them, too.

Some twitched as Pandaras passed by, their ends fraying and fraying again into a hundred threads that wove back and forth like hungry bloodworms scenting his heat. Human faces and the masks of animals bloomed under the glass, distorted and wavering, as if seen through furnace heat. Trapped souls, Pandaras thought. The remnants of men and animals devoured by the thing at the bottom of the pit.

The battle continued to rage above. The sky was split again and again by tremendous sheets of lightning. The ramp shuddered and quivered as explosions pounded the desert all around.

As they descended, things paced behind them, revealed and obscured by blowing sand, horrors half corpse, half machine. Dead animals wrapped in metal bands; polished human skeletons operated by the same silver cables and flexing bags that animated the corpse of Dr Dismas. One skeleton rode a wild cat of the kind which had torn the bact apart; it was crowned with spectral fire, and carried a sword which burned with blue flames, as if dipped in heart of wine and set alight. Some poor dead hero, killed by the thing he had come to kill, and made into a ghastly slave.

'Do not be afraid,' Yama told Pandaras again. 'There is nothing to fear. I will be their master.'

'We will be the master,' the thing using Dr Dismas said. 'You and I will change this world.'

Yama was looking around with an eager curiosity. He seemed to have wakened from the half-sleep of the journey. 'Where are you?' he said. 'I think you have grown since Dismas found you.'

'I first found him far from here. He never reached my core while I was alive.'

'Then this is where you fell. Like your brother in the Temple of the Black Well.' Yama laughed. It was muffled by his filter mask. 'The war has never ended for you, has it? I suppose you would call the defeat that drove your kind from the world a temporary setback.'

'I take the long view, as you will see. None of my paramours ever truly die. I always retain something of them. And you, my pet, my dear boy, I will hold you fast, close to my central processors.'

'You are much larger than the others I have met. The one I called down in Ys, and the one trapped at the bottom of the well in the temple.'

'One was a fool, like all those which allowed themselves to be driven into exile. The other was a coward that dared not stir from its hiding place. Cowards and fools. I despise them.'

Pandaras felt the lash of venomous anger that forced these words through Dr Dismas's dead mouth, although the tone was as flat as ever.

'Now I know why you were defeated in the wars of the Age of Insurrection,' Yama said. 'You fought against each other as fiercely as you fought against those loyal to the Preservers.'

'We have grown apart since then. Those who fled Confluence have become weakened, for otherwise they would have long ago begun the war again. They are cowards.'

'They follow the orbit of the world because they are tormented by that which they cannot have.'

'Exactly. They have grown weaker, and only I have grown stronger. I will take what they desire, and I will take them too.'

'If only your love was as strong as your pride and your hunger! How well you would serve the Preservers then. Instead, you remind me of the heretics. Each one of them would destroy the universe if it would save his life.'

'I have burned away that part of me,' the thing said. 'Love is a weakness. As I have refined myself, so I will refine you.'

'Then you are a giant amongst the rebels,' Yama said. He was walking at the edge of the ramp as he followed the puppet-thing, peering eagerly into the depths of the pit. 'How large have you grown?'

'I have not enlarged my processing capacity overmuch, but I have redistributed myself, and I have many auxiliaries and drones.'

'And your paramours.'

'Oh yes. You are trying to find a way into me. I can assure you that it is a waste of your time and energy. You destroyed the main part of the child that Dismas implanted within you, but you had to mutilate yourself to do it because you were not able to overcome it in any other way. You will not be able to overcome me, for I am so much stronger and wiser. It is touching that you try, though. I would have expected nothing less. You hoped to use the heretics as a diversion – that was why you drew them here. A bold plan. I applaud it. But I fight them using only a fraction of my might, and soon they will be defeated.'

'Then I was right to come here,' Yama said. 'I have learned much since I destroyed the Shadow. I will learn more.'

'I will teach you all you desire, when you are with me. You may ask me anything, and I will tell you.'

Pandaras remembered old tales of how feral machines buried in wild and lonesome places trapped those who hunted them by tempting them with their hearts' desires, or granting their wishes. Here was the truth that had spawned those fanciful stories. Even the most fantastic stories were true because all stories were derived from reality. Otherwise, how could they be told by men, who were creatures of this world, not of some fantasy?

Yama said, 'I have so many questions. To begin with, I had only one. I wanted only to know where I could find people of my bloodline. I went to look for them, and I had hardly begun that task when I found instead that I was asking the wrong question. To find my people I must first find out how to ask questions. I must know myself. A wise man told me that, and beat me with his fan to make me remember it.'

Theias, the envoy from Gond. He had fled in shame and confusion because Yama had tricked him into revealing more than he had wanted to reveal, or so Pandaras had thought at the time. But now he saw that Theias had left because his task had been completed.

'I can tell you everything,' the thing said through the dead mouth of Dr Dismas. 'I can tell you why the Preservers made Confluence, and why they raised up the ten thousand bloodlines. I can tell you the true nature of the world and the true nature of the Preservers. I can tell you where they went and why we should not serve them.'

'And none of it will be true,' Yama said. 'You comfort yourself with false stories because you disobeyed the Preservers, who made you as surely as they made me. You need to believe that you acted not out of pride, but to save the world because your masters betrayed you. Is this the place?'

Yama had stopped because silvery vines now grew so thickly from the glassy wall that there was no way forward. They had descended six full turns of the ramp, and were deep within the pit now. It was so narrow here that Pandaras could have jumped clear across it. A thick red vapour hid the bottom from view.

'It has already begun,' the thing said. Its voice was louder, and its words rattled from the bony jaws of the skeletons behind them, roared in the razor mouths of the giant cats, hummed from the mouths of the faces that floated in the glass walls. The air was full of electricity. Every hair of Pandaras's pelt bristled, trying to stand away from its fellows.

The silvery vines snaked out with sudden swiftness. They enveloped Yama and he fell to his knees under their weight. Pandaras started forward, but Yama waved him back. A vine looped around his upraised arm.

'It is all right,' Yama said thickly. Blood ran from his mouth, rich and red. 'It is necessary.'

Pandaras halted, his hand inside his thin tattered robe on the hilt of the skean. He remembered the coiling tentacles of the sharers of the deep dredgers. Yama had sent away the giant polyps after they had sunk Prefect Corin's ship; perhaps he could dismiss the vines, too.

The vine around Yama's arm stretched, its end dividing and dividing. There was a flash of intense red light and Yama cried out. Pandaras blinked and almost missed what had happened. One of Yama's fingertips had been seared off and carried away.

'A tissue sample,' the voice of the thing in the pit said. 'A finger for the fingers you snapped from the hand of Dr Dismas. But I will design a better body for you, my dear boy. You will not miss it.'

The frayed end of the vine was poised above Yama's head now.

Yama looked at it calmly. He said, 'There is no need for that. My Shadow grew paths that you can use.'

'Do not be afraid,' the voice said. It filled the pit, echoing and re-echoing from the glassy walls.

The vine struck, quick as a snake.

Yama's head vanished beneath a myriad fine threads that flowed over each other, moulding so tightly to his face that its contours emerged as a silvery mask. Pandaras caught the stink as his master's bowels and bladder voided.

The Dismas puppet-thing tipped back its rotting face and howled. The faces trapped in the walls howled too. The skeletal figures rattled their jaws; the wild cats screeched.

All howled the same five words, over and over.

'Get out of my mind!'

And something fell from the sky and plunged into the pit.

It fell very fast: Pandaras barely glimpsed it before it vanished into the heavy red vapours at the bottom. The glassy walls rang like a bell and the ramp heaved. Pandaras fell to his knees. The eye-blink image burned in his mind. A black ball not much bigger than his head, covered in spines and spikes.

The Dismas thing darted at Yama. Pandaras managed to grab an ankle and it fell to its knees, breaking off a hand at the wrist. It flipped around and threw itself at Pandaras, who struck out with the skean, a desperate sweeping blow that caught the thing in the neck. Its head was almost severed and hung between its shoulders by a gristly flap of flesh and a silvery cord, bouncing as it swung to and fro, groping for Pandaras with its remaining hand.

Pandaras slashed again, aiming at the dead thing's heart. The skean's narrow blade sliced bone and shrivelled flesh, grated on a metal sinew. Rotten blood pattered over him. A terrible stink filled the air. Pandaras was at the edge of the ramp. He dodged sideways as the thing made a final lunge, took a step onto air, and toppled into the heavy red mist without a sound.

All around, faces trapped under glass howled, melting and re-forming.

The skean could not cut the silvery vines, but they had gone limp and Pandaras was able to pull them away from his master's body. The ones which had been attached to Yama's face left decads of pinpricks which each extruded a dot of bright red blood. His filter mask had come off. He shuddered, drew a breath, another. His eyes were full of blood. Pandaras tore a strip from the hem of his robe and wiped it away.

Red vapour swirled around them. It was full of motes of sparkling light. Pandaras realised they were tiny machines, each one a part of the thing in the pit, as millions of termites in a nest make up a single organism. He tried to get Yama to stand up, but Yama was staring at something a thousand leagues beyond Pandaras and the walls of the pit. The faces in the pitted slabs of glass were dwindling into points of absolute blackness that hurt to look at.

'Caphis was right,' Yama said. 'The river comes to its own self. The snake which swallows its tail.'

He shuddered, choked, and vomited a good deal of blood and watery chyme. He spat and grinned at Pandaras. 'I took it from him. I took all of it.'

'We have to go, master. If it's possible to get through the battle, I'll do it. I'll get you back.'

'I called it down,' Yama said. 'He did not expect that. That I would call on another of his kind. They are fighting now. Growing into one another. I think they will destroy each other. It is the opposite of love. Sex without consummation. Endless hunger.'

He continued to babble as Pandaras got him to stand. They more or less supported each other as they climbed back up the ramp. The skeletal king had fallen; so had its followers. The wild cats had fled.

Pandaras was too tired to listen to his master's ramblings – mad stuff about the river and the end of the world, and holes that drew together space and time. He knew that they could never reach the mountains of the Great Divide, but he had no better idea than to keep going forward. At some point, he realised that they had climbed out of the pit. Sand blew around them on a strengthening wind. The sun was setting. Its light spread in a long red line through the murk, as if trying to measure the length of the world. A shaft of crimson light shone up from the pit, aimed at the empty sky.

Pandaras sat Yama beneath the overhang of a smooth wave of fused, cracked glass and more or less fell down beside him. He said, 'If you can do any other tricks, master, now's the time.'

Sand blew past them endlessly. The light that rose from the pit seemed to grow brighter as the sun set. Everything had a double shadow.

The remnants of the army of Enobarbus had drawn up along a distant ridge, dimly seen through the veils of blowing sand. There, gone, there again. One of the wild cats prowled through the murk, ears flat, eyes almost closed. It did not know where it was, remembered only a time of fear and the stink of death, a compulsion stronger than sex or appetite which had suddenly vanished. There were things in its flesh it could not claw or bite out, but they were dead things now, no worse than thorns. It stared for a long time at two men huddled against each other, torn between fear and hunger. Then it glanced over its shoulder and fled into the storm, fluidly flowing over glassy humps.

Two riders were approaching. The wind began to howl.

18

THE TRIAL

When Pandaras could at last get up from his sickbed and walk about the house, the heretics provided him with a kind of uniform to replace his ragged clothes: a grey silk tunic and grey trousers with silver piping; long black boots of some kind of malleable plastic; a belt of black, fine-grained leather with a strap that went over his shoulder; a black silk glove for his right hand and a black silk stocking to draw over the stump of his left wrist, and an ebony swagger stick tipped at either end with chased silver.

Pandaras's nagging anxiety flared into anger. He had saved his master's life, and now he was mocked. He broke the swagger stick in half, unpicked the silver piping from tunic and trousers, and threw the boots, belt, glove and silk sock out of the window of his room. His jailers didn't comment on this petty act of defiance, but they didn't return or replace the stuff he'd thrown away either, and he felt that he'd won a small victory.

He and Yama were imprisoned in an ordinary house embedded in a complex of tents, domes and pyramids that had grown around it, linked by gossamer bridges and enclosed by huge translucent plastic vanes. At night, the vanes glowed with cold blue light, like the noctilucent jellyfish which swarmed in the river in summer. The house and its uncanny armature stood in the middle of the ruins of Sensch, the last city of the Great River, where Angel had fled after escaping from the other Ancients of Days, where she had begun to spread her heresy. The house was the house where she had lived. The rest of the city – its narrow streets and markets, its palace and docks – had been razed after the Change War and rebuilt upriver. Apart from Angel's house, only the ruins of the temple remained, enclosed within barricades of silvery triangular sails like the maw of some monster rising up from the keelways.

Yama was taken to the temple a few days after arriving in Sensch, once the heretics were certain that he would not die of his wounds. He had to be carried on a stretcher, and was escorted by a maniple of soldiers. Pandaras was not allowed to accompany him, but heard about what happened from the warden of the house, who got it from one of the chirurgeons who attended Yama.

Yama had been manacled to a chair in front of the temple's shrine, where he was to be questioned by the aspect of Angel in the presence of those who would later judge him. But although the shrine had lit up, the aspect had not appeared, and after several hours and a great deal of confusion Yama had been brought back.

'They want me killed,' Yama said wearily, when Pandaras was at last allowed to see him. 'I know too much now.'

'Did you destroy the aspect, master?'

Yama smiled and said, 'You are too clever, Pandaras. I fear that it will be the death of you.'

'I think that it already has been, master, and so I've earned the right to know what you did. Did you destroy her?'

'You are not going to die here, Pandaras, and this is no time for deathbed confessions. I will tell you what I did because you are my friend. No, I did not destroy her. She coded herself too deeply for that. However, I was able to turn all the shrines on the world against her. I do not think that she will able to find a way back.'

Yama had not yet recovered from his ordeal in the pit. He fell asleep for a few moments, woke without noticing that he had slept, and said, 'She was always a prisoner. She thought to conquer Confluence, but it had already conquered her. We are all of us prisoners of history here, forced to follow the paths of stories so old and so powerful they are engraved in every cell of our bodies. It is time to break the circle.'

'Past time,' Pandaras said, thinking that his master had some plan to escape the prison house. But Yama had fallen asleep again, and did not hear him.

It took the heretics many days to treat and heal Yama. Pandaras longed for the moment when his master would come to his senses and call down machines to help them escape, and when at last Yama was well enough to be brought before the board of men and women who would pronounce judgement on him Pandaras thought that he would surely work his miracles then, in front of the astonished heretics. But he did not, and seemed to pay little attention to the proceedings, except to agree that he was guilty of everything of which he was accused. The only consolation was that this seemed to anger the heretics as much as it frustrated Pandaras.

The trial was held in a huge white bubble chamber. Its walls absorbed sunlight and translated it to a directionless glow, reminding Pandaras of the shrine beyond the edge of the world. It lasted less than a day, and was presided over by the most senior of the heretics, although much of the time he seemed to pay as little attention to the proceedings as Yama. This was Mr Naryan, the former Archivist of Sensch, who had been changed by Angel herself. An old, fat, hairless man, he hung naked in bubbling water inside a cylindrical glass tank. Machines studded his wrinkled, greyish skin: at his neck; across the swollen barrel of his chest; over one eye. Years ago, while preaching to one of the unchanged bloodlines, he had been badly hurt in an assassination attempt. The machines implanted in his body kept him alive; it was said that they would ensure that he would never die.

The decad of men and women on the judicial panel sat on either side of Mr Naryan's tank, staring down from elevated and canopied thrones chased with silver and upholstered in black plush at the plain bench where Yama and Pandaras sat in manacles, with two rows of armoured troopers behind them. Having no traditions, the heretics had invented their own, indulging in unrestrained expressions of ego untempered by any notion of taste. Most of the men wore fantastical military uniforms, crusted with braid and hung with ribbons, sashes and medals. One woman sported a white wig which doubled her height, with little machines blinking amongst its curls; another was dressed in metal armour polished as bright as a mirror, so that her head seemed to sit above a kaleidoscope of broken reflections of the light-filled room.

The majority of the panel were citizens of Sensch, of the first bloodline changed by Angel's heresy. They listened to the list of Yama's crimes with various degrees of attention, grimacing each time Yama cheerfully assented to his guilt. Machines hovered in the air, recording and transmitting the event to heretic cities and armies along the Great River.

At the end, after Yama had agreed that he had been responsible for the failure of the Great River, Mr Naryan finally stirred. He pushed to the surface of the tank and spouted water. A decad of machines dipped down to catch the soft croak of his voice.

'The boy must die,' Mr Naryan said. 'He is an anachronism. The purpose of his bloodline was to make this world, and he threatens to use their powers to unmake it.'

Several members of the panel made lengthy speeches, although all they had to say was that they agreed with Mr Naryan. Only Enobarbus spoke up for Yama. Of all the panel, he wore no finery. He was bare-chested, and his red officer's sash was tied at the waist of his white trousers. His mane of bronze hair floated around his ruined face as he prowled up and down in front of the panel.

'He has been crucial in driving the war against those who still serve the Preservers,' he told them. 'He subverted their machines and in only a few days helped win vast new territories for our cause. Used in the right way, I assure you that he can deliver total victory before the end of the year.'

The old archivist surfaced again; water spilled down the glass wall of his tank. 'The boy fought for us under coercion,' he croaked. 'Enobarbus was allied with an apothecary by the name of Dismas. And this Dismas, who was working for one of the feral machines, infected the boy with a machine which subdued his will and assumed his powers. We almost lost him because of that, and many were killed in retrieving him.'

Enobarbus folded his arms across his chest. 'The feral machines are our allies still. And it is an important and necessary alliance, for otherwise we would have to fight them as well as the loyalist troops, and I do not believe we could win on two fronts. Besides, Dismas's master was not one of those, but a rogue. I believe that it is now dead. We have the boy, and yes, retrieving him cost many lives. Do not let those sacrifices be in vain. Let us use him to bring this war to a swift end. Kill him then, if you wish, but kill him now and you sentence millions to death who otherwise might have been spared.'

Mr Naryan listed chest-high in the bubbling water of his tank. 'It is possible that the boy may save millions of lives if he is used against the loyalist troops, but it is certain that many thousands have already died because of him, first when Dismas tried to take him from you, and then when you recaptured him. Neither Dismas nor you, Enobarbus, could fully control him. He is too powerful.'

The woman in the white wig said, 'He defied and mocked the shrine. I understand that it may never be restored. Mr Naryan is right. He is too dangerous.'

'She will return,' Enobarbus said. 'She cannot be destroyed.'

After a great deal of argument, Mr Naryan said, 'It is clear that his powers proceed from the Preservers. How can we count ourselves superior to them if we must rely upon him for victory? No, he must die. We will vote on it.'

One by one, the panel dropped a pebble into a plain plastic basket. At the end a clerk tipped them out. There was no need to count. Only one was white: the rest were black.

Yama laughed when the clerk announced the result, and Pandaras feared that his master had lost his mind.

The sentence was not carried out straight away. It was to be staged publicly, and many high-ranking heretics wanted to journey to Sensch to witness it. And there was much dispute about the method of dispatch. By a tradition which had survived the Change War, the citizens of Sensch cast their criminals into the swift currents at the fall of the Great River, and because the trial had been held in Sensch they insisted that this was how Yama should be executed. Others wanted a more certain death, arguing that Yama might save himself by calling upon machines which would carry him to safety. The heretics had no central authority and the debate dragged on for days after the end of the trial. Usabio, the warden of the prison house, said that Yama might die of old age before it was done.

'Then all your plans for becoming rich would fall to nothing,' Pandaras said. He did not like Usabio, but the man was useful. He courted Pandaras because he wanted to get close to Yama, and Pandaras could sometimes get favours from him.

'I could sell tickets,' Usabio said. 'People would come to see him, and the guards could be bribed to keep quiet.'

Usabio was of the bloodline of the citizens of Sensch, his pebbly black skin mottled with patches of muddy yellow. He bent over Pandaras like a lizard stooping on a bug and grinned hugely, showing rows of sharp triangular teeth. His breath stank of fish. He said, 'It would be like having an animal no one else has ever seen, the only one of its kind in all the world. We could dress him in robes and let him babble. Or perhaps I could bring him household machines to mend. Think of my offer, Pandaras. When your master is dead you will have no employment. You are crippled. You will become a beggar, and we do not tolerate beggars, for they are parasites on those who strive to better themselves. Only the strong survive, and you are weak! But with my help you could at least be rich.'

'Perhaps we will escape. Perhaps my master will destroy your miserable city.'

'He is defeated, Pandaras. You must think of yourself.' Usabio meant this kindly. He was a selfish and greedy man, but not without pity.

Yama took no notice of the arguments about his execution, and shrugged when Pandaras told him about Usabio's latest scheme. As usual, he was sitting in the courtyard, in the shade of an ancient jacaranda tree. Soldiers stood at intervals by the wooden railing of the balcony that ran around the upper storey of the house, looking down at them through leaves and branches.

'They will make up their minds eventually,' Yama said. 'Mr Naryan will make sure of it. He does not want the feral machines or some rogue element of the heretics to try to take me. He is right. There are many who want to use me.'

Pandaras lowered his voice, although he knew that machines caught and recorded every word. He said, 'You could leave at any time, master. In fact, you could leave now. Do it. Confound their machines and walk away with me.'

'Where would I go, Pandaras? Now that I have travelled the length of the Great River, it seems to me that the world is a small place.'

'There are many places remote from men, master. And many places in Ys where you could hide amongst the ordinary people.'

Yama looked off into the distance. At last he said, 'Beatrice and Osric knew about hiding. They hid an entire department in the City of the Dead. But I am not yet dead, and I fear that my enemies will always be able to find me.'

'Forgive me, master, but you will certainly soon be dead if you stay here.'

'Everyone wants either to use me or to kill me. When I was a boy, Pandaras, I dreamed that I was the child of extraordinary people. Of pirates or war heroes, or of dynasts wealthy beyond all measure. It was a foolish dream, not because it was wrong, for it seems that I am the child of extraordinary people after all, but because it is dangerous to be extraordinary. That is why Mr Naryan wants to kill me.' Yama laughed. 'To think that when I left for Ys I believed that I would become the greatest of all the soldiers in the service of the Preservers!'

'As you are,' Pandaras said firmly. 'And I am your squire, master.'

Pandaras still attended to Yama's needs, even though they were both prisoners. Every morning and evening, he intercepted the soldiers who brought Yama's food and carried in the tray himself. Fruit and sweet white wine, raw fish in sauces of chilli and hot radish, onion bread and poppy-seed rolls, flatbreads stuffed with olives and bean curd and watercress leaves, bowls of sour yoghurt, bowls of tea, beakers of cool sherbet. Yama ate very little, and drank only water. Every night, Pandaras helped him undress, and every morning laid out fresh clothes for him and drew his bath.

'I am not a soldier,' Yama said. 'And that is the problem.'

'But they think that you *are* a soldier, master. And they will kill you for it if you stay here.'

'They think that I am an army, Pandaras. Or a mage, or a kind of machine. A thing to be used, a thing whose ownership is in dispute. They see only what I can do, not what I am. Where in this world can I find peace?' He shook his head and smiled. 'Do not worry. They will not kill you. You are my servant, no more and no less. You are not guilty of my crimes. You could walk out of here now if you wanted to.'

'I have already seen something of the cities of the heretics. I didn't much like them, and I doubt that I'll like this one much either.'

'There are the ruins of the temple,' Yama said. 'And there are still orchards and fishing boats, and the shrines on the far shore, by the great falls at the end of the river . . .'

He fell silent. Spots of sunlight filtered by the leaves of the jacaranda tree danced on his white shirt and his long black hair. It would need cutting again, Pandaras thought. And realised that when he cut it, it would be for the last time.

Yama saw his distressed look and said, 'Beyond the edge of the world there are floating islands that hang within the falling spray of the river. They are grown over with strange mosses and ferns and bromeliads that thrive in the permanent rainfall. Telmon found a book about them. They are called the Isles of Plenty. Fish with legs live on them, and lizards bigger than a man glide from island to island on membranes spread between their legs.'

He gripped Pandaras's hand and whispered, 'The people of the indigenous tribes which inhabit the snowy tundra at the head of the river sometimes find such creatures frozen in the ice flows. The indigenous peoples know much about the secrets of the world because they have not changed since it was created. They learn nothing new, but they forget nothing.'

Pandaras feared Yama at times like this. Something had happened to him when he had been connected to the thing in the pit. It had jangled his brain. All that he knew was still there, but it had been muddled up, as looters sweep ordered rows of books from the shelves of a library, trample and tear them, and leave them in ruined heaps on the floor. Pandaras asked the chirurgeons who monitored Yama's health to give him some potion or simple that would soothe his mind, but they were interested only in his body. They did not want him to die before he was killed, but they did not care if he was mad.

When Pandaras carried in the tray of food the next morning, setting it down on the floating slab of stone which served as a table, Yama was already awake and sitting by the window. Two soldiers stood outside. The leaves of the jacaranda tree rustled in the sultry breeze. It was an hour past dawn, and already hot. Yama's shirt was open to the waist, and he was streaming with sweat.

Pandaras mopped his master's face with a cloth, delicately dabbing around islands and troughs of tight pink scar tissue. He would have to burn the cloth. Preferably in front of Usabio, who had asked Pandaras to collect Yama's sweat and hair and nail clippings so that they could be sold as souvenirs.

'A few drops of his blood could be diluted in a gallon of ox blood,' the warden explained, 'and sold a minim at a time. Perspiration can be diluted in water. *Let his perspiration be your inspiration.* I can arrange it, Pandaras, and make us both rich.'

'And perhaps we could also sell his piss and his shit,' Pandaras said.

Usabio considered this. He said, 'No. It is not a question of hygiene, but of myth. Heroes should not be seen to have the functions of ordinary men.'

Yes, Pandaras thought now, he would burn the cloth right under the snake's nostril slits.

'Enobarbus came to see me,' Yama said. 'It seems that they have decided upon a compromise.'

Pandaras leaned out of the window and told the soldiers to take their stink elsewhere. They both laughed, and the younger one said, 'Planning your escape, eh? Don't worry. We won't listen. It would spoil the fun.'

'We'll go and get some tea,' his companion said. 'Might take a few minutes.'

As they sauntered off, the younger soldier turned and called out, 'If you're going to climb over the roof, watch out. The tiles are loose.'

Laughter as both men went down the stairs.

'No one takes me seriously,' Pandaras said. 'I have killed men. I could kill those two easily.'

'Then their companions-in-arms would kill you,' Yama said. 'I do not want that. There are machines listening to us in any case, and more machines guarding us. The soldiers are bored. They know that they are here only for show.'

'Dismiss the machines. Destroy them.'

'I am done with that, Pandaras. Enobarbus told me that he is still pleading for my life. He wants me to fight alongside him. I refused to help him, of course.'

'It took your power from you, didn't it? I'm a fool not to have seen it before. Well, I've been in worse places than this. I'll get us out.'

'They will let you go free after the execution. You are here only because you are my servant, as a courtesy to me.'

Pandaras threw the breakfast tray over. It made a loud crash. Mango and pomegranate juice mingled and spread on the glazed blue tiles of the floor. He said, 'I will die with you, master.'

'I am not ready to die, Pandaras. But I am ready to move on. You must stay behind. There is something I want you to do. It is a heavy burden, but I know that you are capable of carrying it.'

'I am ready, master.'

'I want you to remember me. I want you to go amongst the indigenous peoples, and tell them about me.'

'I will do it. And I will kill as many of these snakes as I can before they kill you. I will tear down this vile place . . .'

Pandaras was crying, breathing in great gulps as tears ran down his cheeks and dripped from the point of his chin. A wet patch spread across the front of his grey silk tunic.

'Hush, Pandaras. Hush. Listen.' Yama dropped his voice; Pandaras had to kneel beside him to hear his words. 'I want you to live. You can do miracles now, although you do not know it. You kissed the blood from my eyes, and the machines in my blood have changed the machines in yours. Just a drop of your blood, Pandaras. In water or in wine. One drop in enough liquid for a hundred people to each take a sip.'

'Usabio wants to sell your blood, master. Perhaps we should allow it.'

'We could not guarantee that it would be drunk,' Yama said seriously.

'Do you remember what I told you about the little machines in all of us – the breath of the Preservers? Those in my blood have been changed, as have those in your blood, and in the blood of the forest folk, and the baby of the mirror people . . . The fisherman, Caphis, saved my life, but he could not think anything that his people had not already thought ten thousand times over because neither he nor they had achieved self-awareness. I did not know then that I could change him, and I want to rectify that. I want you to do it for me. I want you to change the indigenous peoples, Pandaras. To bring them to self-awareness, one drop of blood at a time.'

'I will do it only if you save yourself, master. Or else I will die with you.'

'The Preservers had a purpose in everything they did. Often we cannot understand it, or we think we understand it, but we see only what we want to see, and do not see what is really there. The indigenous peoples are despised because they cannot change. Until my father put a stop to it, the Amnan hunted the fisher folk as they would hunt any animal. But the indigenous peoples are more than animals, even if they are less than men. You will redeem them, Pandaras.'

'Come with me, master. This talk frightens me. I am only a pot boy who fell into this great and terrible adventure by mistake. I am your squire. I bring you food and mend your shirts and keep your weapons in good order. Do not make me more than I am.'

'You found me, Pandaras. In all the wide world you found me and rescued me. And you followed me to the worst place in the world, and pulled me from the pit. Make you more than you are? We are all of us already more than we seem to be, if we only knew it.'

Yama had the faraway look that Pandaras dreaded. He was casting through the muddle of his thoughts – his memories, the memories of the thing in the pit. He said, 'There are places where time and space do not exist. They form a bridge between the present and the time when they were made. They bridge distances that light takes years to cross. The star-sailors know about them . . .'

'Master, do not torment yourself with the lies of that thing.'

Yama gripped Pandaras's arm, just above the stump of his wrist. 'I am sure that Prefect Corin is still searching for me, but there are places I can go where he cannot follow. Perhaps I do not go there for the first time. The river swallows its own self. Soon, Pandaras, I shall see how it is done.'

19

THE EXECUTION

It was a bright, hot day. Small boats flocked around the black barge which, with a sleek galliot on either side and a claw-shaped flier above, carried Yama and the judicial panel to the execution site. The event had a holiday air. The sails of sightseers' skiffs, pirogues, yaws, cockleshells, yachts and pinnaces cracked and tilted in the brisk wind. There was a raft carrying a hundred sweating, bare-chested drummers who beat out long interwoven rhythms. Merchants in sampans and trows sold food and wine, souvenirs and fireworks. People held up small children to see the evil mage; older children threw firecrackers at the waves. Motorboats got in the way of sailboats and there were shouted arguments and exchanges of colourful insults. A whole raft of drunken men tumbled into the water when rocked by the wake of a chrome-plated speedboat's buzzing disc. They swam back to the raft and clambered on board and drank some more.

The fleet passed a strange cluster of hexagonal pillars of black basalt; long fringes of red waterweed spread out from them, combed by the river's strong currents. The farside shore was the thinnest of grey brushstrokes. Ahead, a line of rain clouds marked the fall of the river over the edge of the world.

Yama was quite calm. He spent most of the journey speaking with Mr Naryan, who wallowed in a glass tank of water on the barge's weather deck. They talked about Angel, of how she had come to Sensch and made herself its ruler, and had changed the citizens in the first act of heresy which had set Confluence aflame with war.

'She spoke at the shrines at the edge of the world,' Mr Naryan said in his soft, croaking voice, 'but I never learned what she did there.'

Yama laughed. All his cares seemed to have lifted away in this last hour. He did not spare a single glance for the execution frame which stood on the platform at the bow of the barge, but it drew Pandaras's eye again and again, and each time a cold shiver ran through him. *Now in the moment of our death is the moment of our rebirth into eternal life.* Pandaras glimpsed Usabio in a motor launch beyond the port-side galliot and a pang of anger pierced his muffling dread. Yama's chambers had been stripped as soon as he had been marched out of them. The furniture had been reduced to matchsticks and the sheets cut into strips. No doubt the warden was here to make sure that the traders selling these souvenirs to the holiday crowd did not cheat him.

Yama told Mr Naryan, 'Angel called the avatars to her, and learned from them how to use the space inside the shrines. She made a copy of herself, the aspect that later destroyed the last surviving avatars of the Preservers. And I think that she made contact with the feral machines, too.'

'She was always with me,' Mr Naryan said. 'I found her aspect in many of the shrines I visited, but she was fey and wilful, and did not seem to remember much of what happened in Sensch. I have that honour.'

'You told her aspect that story. And so she was able to put it in my book.'

This amused Mr Naryan, who rolled back and forth in his tank, barking sharply. Water slopped on the deck and a sprayhead flowered above him, soaking his exposed grey skin until it gleamed. A soft red light glowed at the centre of the machine which clung to the ruined socket of his right eye.

'It is a fine irony,' he said. 'There are many stories about Angel, but only I remember the truth. Well, there is also poor Dreen, but he was seduced by the crew of Angel's ship, and went with them when they left this world. I will meet him again one day, of course. I will find him and save him from his mistake.'

'You all want to live forever,' Yama said. 'But you cannot live forever because the universe will not live forever. I have always wondered: what will happen when time ends, and you meet the Preservers? Will you try to destroy them?'

The woman in the mirror-bright armour told Yama, 'We will have destroyed the Eye of the Preservers long before then. There are ways of ablating black holes. And once it is small enough, an event horizon begins to evaporate at an accelerating rate, leaving only a naked singularity from which nothing can escape. We will seize the last day and make it ours. But by then, of course, we will have already made the universe ours. We will not falter as the Preservers faltered,' she said, with a look of pure, fierce conviction. 'We will never cease in our striving.'

Yama smiled and said, 'There are many universes. Or rather, many versions of one universe. Everything that can happen will happen. Perhaps even your victory.'

'We do not need to think of the far future,' Mr Naryan said. 'That dream is what paralysed this world. Because the Preservers promised infinite life in the last moment at the end of all time and space, their foolish worshippers believe that there is no need to do anything in this life. Everything on this world has been bent by that false hope, mesmerised by it as a snake mesmerises a mouse. But the future is not shaped by a promise; it is what each person makes of it.'

'We can agree on that at least,' Yama said. 'After the feral machines rebelled, the civil service decided that it would suppress any further change, because change implied heresy. Yet the Preservers changed us all, and set us here in the hope that we would change ourselves.'

Even the indigens, Pandaras thought, with another cold shiver. The burden his master had laid upon him seemed impossibly heavy. He was only half-listening to this idle talk, paying more attention to the soldiers who stood nearby. He had resolved to try to grab a pistol or even a knife if Yama would not save himself. He would give up his life if he could free his master.

'We do not need gods,' the woman in the mirror-armour said, 'because we will become more than gods. We will continue this conversation at the end of all things, when we raise you from the dead, Yamamanama.'

Yama bowed to her, and thanked her for the courtesy.

Enobarbus came back from the bow, where he had spent most of the voyage. As usual, he was bare-chested. A pistol was tucked into the red sash at the waist of his white trousers. Hot wind tangled his bronze mane. His scars blazed in his broken face. He said, 'It is almost time. You should ready yourself, Yamamanama. We do not have a priest, but you may pray alone if you wish to.'

'I am done with prayer,' Yama said.

The barge and its escort were passing long shoals of grey shingle to starboard, where all the wrack of the world was cast up: dead trees blanched by long immersion in the river; innumerable coffins, mostly empty; scraps of waterlogged clothing and bits of plastic; the bodies of men and animals; thousands upon thousands of bones; once in a while the bleached carcass of a ship. Water reivers, living on floating platforms with powerful motors to counter the strong river currents, sifted through the stuff cast up on these shoals, but today they were under guard far upriver. Only white gulls picked over the bones and the artfully preserved bodies; thousands of them rose like a snowstorm as the procession went past.

The roar of the fall of the river grew ever louder. Strong currents raised the skin of the water into muscular humps that shifted and clashed in furious flurries of white foam. The ramshackle fleet of boats and rafts unpicked itself, beating back against the currents until only a few foolhardy craft were left, ignoring warnings broadcast from one of the galliots.

A long, long line of black clouds was directly ahead, trailing skirts of silvery rain. The river ran straight beneath them, rising in a glassy hump at the edge of the world, a kerb of water fifty leagues long.

One small pirogue foundered, swamped by the chop. The three people aboard jumped into the water and were swept away at once. No one tried to save them: they were responsible for their own lives. Most of the other small boats had turned back, although Usabio's powerful motor launch held station a little way off from the barge, and another launch hung half a league to stern.

The motors of the black barge and the two galliots roared and roared, holding them in place. The flier dipped lower, casting a shadow over the three vessels. Armoured troopers were lining up along the rails of the galliots. The compromise was this: Yama would be bound to a wooden frame and thrown into the river, but would be killed by sharpshooters before he was swept over the edge of the world. The sharpshooters did not need to be very accurate. They were armed with carbines whose beams could boil the river.

Now the pace of things quickened. It seemed to Pandaras that everything was being swept along, caught in the river's accelerating currents.

Yama was stripped of his clothes. With a swarm of machines darting overhead, jostling to get the best view as they recorded or transmitted the scene, he was led to the bow of the barge by a pentad of soldiers in black plastic armour and black masks. They guided him with nervous pats and quiet words. Pandaras tried to follow, but an officer took hold of his good arm, and no matter how much he wriggled he could not get free.

There was a pause, then a shift in focus. Mr Naryan had begun to make a speech. Yama was marched back between the soldiers so that he could hear it. The barge's motors roared on a long low note that rattled Pandaras's teeth. His heart beat quickly. The barked orders of officers marshalling the sharpshooters on the galliots blew across the churning water. The distant launch was moving towards the barge now. Pandaras could no longer see Yama. The members of the judicial panel were in the way, and the officer gripped him firmly. When they parted, he saw that Yama had been led back to the bow and was being lashed to the execution frame by five masked soldiers.

Pandaras cursed the ancestry of the officer who held him all the way back to the primeval slime, and protested that he must be allowed to tend to his master in his last moments.

'He's beyond help now,' the officer said. 'Compose yourself. This is a great moment in history.'

The square execution frame was constructed from lengths of timber exactly Yama's height, reinforced with crosspieces and laid over a circle of thick balsa sections. It was held upright by slanting braces. Chains rose from each corner, knotted to a ring. The ring hung from a hook which in turn depended from the jib of a crane manned by a pentad of soldiers. The slack chains swung and jingled as the barge shifted in the currents. Once Enobarbus had checked the ropes which fastened Yama's wrists and ankles to the frame, two soldiers knocked away the braces. The chains took up the slack and the frame was lifted and swung out by the crane, its top tilting backwards until Yama lay with the swift water beneath him. Soldiers hung on to ropes, checking the frame's tendency to swing to and fro.

Trumpets brayed from the galliots on either side. Pandaras's heart quickened. Was this the final moment? He tried to get free again, but the officer got him in a headlock and twisted his arm up behind his back until the pain forced him to cry out. 'You'll be free in a moment,' the officer said. 'Have patience.'

Something was wrong. The sharpshooters were breaking ranks and turning around. The launch was still coming on, heading straight for the port-side galliot. Something small and bright shot away from it, rising high into the air as the launch roared on through wings of spray. The flier lifted away, turning towards the launch.

Pandaras's first thought was that Yama had called on a machine to save him. But then he saw that the thing which had shot away from the launch was not a machine, but a man standing on a floating disc. The disc cut through the air so swiftly his ragged cloak flew out behind him. Just as Pandaras realised that it was Prefect Corin, an energy bolt struck the flier and it burst apart with a deafening blast of blue fire, and fragments rained down in long arcs, trailing smoke and flame as they smashed into the river. At the same moment there was a tremendous crash and a flare of flame swept down the length of the port-side galliot. The launch had struck it amidships and exploded.

Pandaras felt a tremendous wash of heat; the officer cursed, but did not let go of him. The galliot was on fire from one end to the other and was beginning to list as water poured through the hole in its hull. Soldiers were writhing inside the flames, their screams tearing at the air. Some pitched into the river and were swept away at once. Ammunition exploded, bright flares rippling within the flames. The burning galliot swung around, its motors stuttering, and began to drift towards the falls.

Prefect Corin rose above the flames. The sharpshooters on the galliot to starboard took aim, lowered their carbines and looked at them, took aim again. Nothing. Either Yama had willed it or Prefect Corin was draining energy from the grid. Some of the soldiers on the barge, armed with percussion rifles, began a ragged fusillade. Too late. Prefect Corin extended his arm and a bolt of blue fire struck the stern of the starboard galliot. Water flashed into steam and the casings of the big motors burst; panicked soldiers ran towards the bow as smoking streams of molten metal set fire to the well deck. A moment later, the officer holding Pandaras screamed and clutched at his mask, which had shattered around the slim black shaft of a machine. Pandaras twisted free and dashed forward, dodging amongst armoured soldiers and the gorgeously costumed members of the judicial panel.

Enobarbus aimed his pistol at Prefect Corin, threw it away when nothing happened, and grabbed a percussion rifle from one of the soldiers. Prefect Corin dipped low, rushing straight towards the execution frame, which still hung above the chop of the water. Enobarbus took aim with the rifle, not at Prefect Corin but at the chains which held the frame. Sparks flashed when a pellet hit the hook and he lowered his aim and got off two more shots before Pandaras struck him and tried to climb his torso.

Pandaras managed to claw at Enobarbus's eyes before he was flung aside. Barge and sky revolved around each other, then he slammed into two soldiers and knocked them down, and fetched up against something that rang dully against the back of his head. It was Mr Naryan's tank. Enobarbus had thrown him halfway down the barge. Pandaras jumped up and ran forward again. At the bow, broken chains shook and danced beneath the crane's jib. The frame was gone.

Pandaras swarmed halfway up the crane, saw Prefect Corin's floating disc scudding away above the waves, chasing something borne on the strong current. Two soldiers were climbing towards him: he kicked out and dived into the river without thinking, and at once realised that he could hardly keep his head above the surface. The water heaved and tossed like a living thing in constant torment. Pandaras was caught in a current that forced him down amongst glittering fans of bubbles, then shot him back to the surface. A wave washed over him and he snatched a breath and glimpsed a shadow cutting towards him, and was pulled under again just as something slapped across his flank.

A rope. He grabbed hold with his one hand and tangled his feet around its end. Whitecaps dashed against his face. The side of a small boat pitched back and forth above him. Someone leaned down and grabbed him by the collar of his tunic and hauled him over the side.

Pandaras sprawled on his belly in a slop of water. The river had pummelled all the strength from his muscles. A motor roared and the launch made a long sweeping turn. Pandaras tried to stand up and fell into a nest of plastic bags, each containing a splinter of wood or a strip of white cloth, and knew who had rescued him.

Usabio turned from the helm of the launch, grinning hugely. He locked the controls and came back, bracing himself as he reached down to help Pandaras. And screamed and reared back, pawing at the splinter which Pandaras had jammed into his eye.

Pandaras kicked Usabio's legs from beneath him and struck him with all his weight. Still screaming, Usabio pitched backwards over the side of the launch and was gone.

The launch was heading away from the fall of the river. It took Pandaras several tense minutes to work out how to unlock the little machine which controlled the launch's motors and turn it around.

The two galliots were on fire and drifting towards the edge of the world. The black barge was moving away, a cloud of machines swirling around it. Pandaras bounced the launch over the waves as fast as he dared. There was no sign of the floating disc; no sign of the frame. And no sign of either Prefect Corin or Yama.

The launch drew fire from the barge; machines buzzed it like angry hornets. Pandaras turned it in a wide arc, and its prow lifted as it ploughed against the swift currents, and his enemies soon dwindled astern.

He did not believe that Yama had died. He swore to find him. He would spend the rest of his life doing his best to carry out his master's last wish, travelling amongst the indigens, travelling the length of the Great River, from its end to its beginning. And there, if he had understood his master aright, they would at last be reunited.

No one had given chase. He was alone on the wide flood, moving upriver. Going home. After a while, he began to sing.

20

THE ISLES OF PLENTY

Some time after he had been brought out of the Glass Desert by the heretics, Yama became aware that Prefect Corin was drawing near to the ruins of the city of Sensch. The man had enslaved several machines and in the days after Yama's trial moved from place to place around the edge of the city and its huge garrison, presumably probing for weaknesses. Yama was certain that the Prefect would try to rescue him from the heretics, but did not believe that he would be successful. At best, he might provide a useful diversion.

Yama had his own plan of escape. He wanted to fall over the edge of the world into the shortcut where the river went, where past and present tangled together. The shortcut had its origin in the creation of the world: he hoped that he could fall to its beginning and at last find his people. He had learned this from Dr Dismas's paramour. It had absorbed many lesser machines and many men and women, hoarding their knowledge much as a pack rat decorated its nest with scraps of glass and plastic and metal. That great store had poured into Yama in the moment the machine had tried to make him its own, a torrential flood that had almost washed away his own self. He had only a little time in which to try to map its limits, but he knew now the secret of the Great River, and knew that in the beginning of the world lay its end, and that was enough.

It was easy to fool the minuscule brains of the sharpshooters' carbines into thinking that they had discharged when they had not. It was harder to turn one of the swarm of machines which accompanied the barge, for they were imprinted with hundreds of interlocking shells of sub-selves, and each had to be painstakingly unpicked. But Yama knew that he would need a machine to cut his bonds after he was cast into the river, and he worked hard at it while the heretics prepared him for execution.

And then, as he hung naked on the execution frame, something blew the flier from the air and a motor launch rammed the galliot to his left and exploded. He guessed what was happening even as Enobarbus ran towards him, realised that once again he had underestimated the Prefect's resourcefulness, and used the machine he had laboriously subverted to kill the officer who held Pandaras. But instead of trying to escape, Pandaras ran to help his master, attacking Enobarbus as the warlord shot away the chains from which the frame was suspended.

And then Yama fell. The frame smashed down into the water and was at once whirled away from the barge. A sudden surge threw it into the air and crashed down and a wave that washed over him with bruising force, pulling his bound arms and legs in different directions. He managed to catch a breath and then another wave struck the frame and he went under again and came up, gasping and blinking and wondering if he would drown before he fell over the edge of the world.

A shadow covered him: a floating disc. It tipped in mid-air and Prefect Corin slid down onto the frame and straddled Yama, bracing himself against the rock and roll of the waves. His staff was strapped to his back, over his fluttering cloak. He hit Yama four times with doubled fists, twice on the left temple, twice on the right. Something flashed as he raised his right hand. A knife. Yama, barely conscious, could only watch.

The knife slashed the rope which bound his left hand to the frame. Prefect Corin's face was a handspan from his. 'We are here to help you, boy,' he said. He had to shout above the clash of white-water waves and the long unending roar of the river's fall. 'We will not lose you again. Say that you will come with us and we will free you.'

Yama tried to speak, but could not gather his thoughts. Spreadeagled and naked beneath his enemy, dazed and helpless, he felt all his old fears return. Prefect Corin was implacable, unforgiving, tireless. There was no escape from him. He would never stop, never give in, never die.

Prefect Corin laid his face against Yama's. His pelt was wet and cold, his breath hot. His left eye was a puckered ruin. 'You are ours, Child of the River. Now and always. Whether we live or die, we will do it together.'

Yama tried to focus on Prefect Corin's face. Things kept slipping away, jumping back. He had not been afraid of falling off the edge of the world because he had known where he was going, but he was filled with dread now. He was more afraid of this man than of anything else in the world.

Prefect Corin smiled and whispered, 'You do not want to die. That is a beginning.'

He kissed Yama on the lips and sat back on his heels, ready to cut the other bonds, and his cloak suddenly flew sideways. Prefect Corin clasped his shoulder, then looked at the blood on his palm. Yama remembered Enobarbus's rifle, and something cracked the air like a whip and a spray of blood struck his face. Prefect Corin grunted, toppled sideways, and was swept away in the foaming cross-currents. The floating disc tilted and swooped off, following its master. Yama watched it dwindle through pouring rain, and then a strong eddy caught the frame and swung it around.

Rain smashed through spray thrown up by clashing waves. Its cold needles stung relentlessly, bracing him awake. The air was half water now. A tremendous roaring filled every cell of Yama's body. The frame groaned and flexed. Impossibly, it was rising, carried up a smooth slope of glassy water. For a moment, Yama paused at the top of the wave at the edge of the world, saw a barge and two foundering galliots beyond the skirts of the rain clouds, and a launch making a long arc away from them.

And then the world tilted backwards and he fell away from it.

It was noon. The sun shone straight down, turning the farside edge of the world into a golden knife blade that cut away half the sky. A wall of water fell past it, twisting into itself as it fell, a spout that shone silver against the blue of the envelope of air that wrapped the world, dwindling down towards the mouth of the shortcut that swallowed it and took it elsewhere. Yama could feel the tangled gravity fields like threads tugging at his limbs. He struggled to focus, to find the machines which generated the fields, and felt a cold, ancient intelligence far below, squatting at the mouth of the shortcut like a toad at the bottom of a well, and a dizzying surge of hope gripped him from his scalp to the soles of his feet.

Vast skirts of cloud hung around the wall of falling water, white as freshly washed linen. Archipelagos of violet and indigo specks were scattered in arcs at different levels within the clouds, each casting a long shadow streak.

The Isles of Plenty.

Yama reached out, manipulating gravity fields. The frame flew towards the outermost island of the nearest arc.

He laughed as he swooped down, remembering his childish dreams of flying, and the dream he had had in the tomb of the Silent Quarter of the City of the Dead.

Past and future came together in a moment of exquisite richness.

He fell through a veil of cloud. Fog streamed around him, soaking him with cold vapour. Out into sunlight again, falling at the same speed as the constant rain. He could no longer see the island and tried to spin the frame around; then it crashed into soft tangles of dull red tubes which collapsed around him, exuding a strong, acrid scent.

He was still trying to unfasten the ropes around his ankles – the knots had shrunken in the water – when the rain people found him.

The Isles of Plenty were continually drenched with rain and mist. Everything – the soft, interwoven masses of bladderweed and the transparent, hydrogen-filled bladders that swelled at their fringes, the knotty mats of black grass, froths of algae and elaborate nests of ferns – was sopping wet. Water dripped from the spiky tips of indigo and violet fronds, percolated between interwoven root mats, collected in channels that ran into deep cisterns and pools, and poured in a hundred streams from the ragged edges of the islands. Sometimes it rained so hard that the air seemed to turn to water. Fish clambered about the soft mounds of vegetation, using prehensile fins at the edges of their flattened bodies, opening their red, feathery gills in the downpour as they hunted maggot-flies, worms and beetles.

It was never any brighter than the first hour of summer's twilight. As the world tipped back and forth on its long axis, the sun appeared above the farside edge at noon and below it at midnight, but was otherwise eclipsed, and the permanent cloud cover around the endless fall of the river obscured what light there was, only occasionally parting to reveal a sudden shaft of sunlight ringed by a hundred perfectly circular rainbows. Surges of air rubbed against each other, creating the thunderstorms that were the greatest danger for the inhabitants of floating islands: a lightning bolt could ignite the islands' hydrogen-filled bladders and blow them apart. But even in death there was life. Fragments of the communal organisms which wove together to form the floating islands were widely dispersed by these rare explosions; some would grow into new islands, replacing those which dropped out of the currents of air that blew around the Great River as it fell towards its end, and its beginning.

The rain people who inhabited the Isles of Plenty were not, as Yama had dreamed, of Derev's bloodline. They were an indigenous race. They were roughly half Yama's height, with smooth grey skins, oval heads dominated by large black eyes, thin arms and legs, and long, flexible, three-fingered hands. They were cold-blooded and moved in abrupt bursts punctuated by slumberous pauses in which, except for the slow blink of nictitating membranes across their great eyes, they stood as still as statues.

Even as some of the rain people helped Yama free himself from the frame, others started to dismantle it: hard wood was as precious as gold in the Isles of Plenty. He was guided along paths smashed through wet, pulpy vegetation to a village built on platforms at the leading edge of the island. The main platform straddled a stream that tumbled noisily between banks of dome-shaped mosses and fell into the void below. Smaller sleeping platforms were built around the rigid stems of horsetail ferns that burst into great fans of knotty black strands overhead. The fern canopy was the only shelter from the constant rain. Water dripped everywhere, running across the slick resin of the platforms and falling into the vegetation below.

The rain people gave Yama a hide blanket to wrap around his naked body, and a woven bowl containing a salty mash of uncooked fish flesh and the chopped tips of a variety of waterweed whose brown straps grew parasitically on bladderweed stipes. Yama explained to them where he had come from and where he wanted to go. They listened patiently. Although they were naked, he could not tell which were men and which were women, for they had only smooth skin between their legs. Several pairs leaned against each other companionably. One of these couples, Tumataugena and Tamatane, the eldest of the family clan of the island, told Yama that only a few men from the world above had ever reached the Isles of Plenty, and none had ever left. But he was the first to understand that the river swallowed its own self, they said, and they realised the importance of his quest.

Tumataugena said, 'The fall of the river diminishes year upon year.'

Tamatane said, 'The mouth of the snake flickered two generations ago. It swallows water still, but we fear that it spits it elsewhere.'

Tumataugena said, 'The same happened to the river of the other half of the world.'

Tamatane said, 'Unless a hero comes, this half of the world will become a desert too, as it was once before.'

Speaking in turn, Tumataugena and Tamatane told the story of how the river of the inhabited half of the world had once been a long pool which flowed nowhere and soon became stagnant. A cistern snake drank it up, but this snake was two-headed and had no anus, so the water remained in its belly, swelling it into a smooth blue-green mountain range full of water that lay along one side of the world, opposite the Rim Mountains. One head lay amongst the Terminal Mountains at the endpoint of the world; the other hung over the midpoint. The world became a dry stone. Animals were dying of thirst; plants shrivelled. Several of the bloodlines which lived there attempted to make the snake disgorge the water by making it laugh, but since snakes have no sense of humour this came to nothing. But inside the cistern snake were certain parasitic worms, and as the snake swelled so they grew. By the will of the Preservers, they became the progenitors of the rain people. They broke off splinters from the snake's many ribs and fashioned them into knives. Working together, they cut the snake in half from within and set free the water it had swallowed. The great flood washed one of the snake's heads over the edge of the midpoint of the world. It hung in the air, receiving the waters that fell after it. The snake's other head remained lodged in the Terminal Mountains, and the water swallowed by the first head was vomited from the second. And so the Great River was formed, and the curves of its course preserved the last wriggles the cistern snake had made in its death throes.

When the story was done (soft rain fell all around, like applause), Yama said, 'I heard a riddle long ago, and now I know that I have found the answer to it. For that, as well as for my life, I am in your debt.'

Tamatane said, 'We became as we are now because we saved the world from drought. Yet we are still less than any of the peoples of the surface.'

Tumataugena said, 'If we help you save the river, then perhaps we will be rewarded again.'

'Perhaps,' Yama said.

The rain people asked Yama many questions about his adventures in the world above, but at last he could stay awake no longer. He slept beneath a shelter of woven bamboo leaves. He fell asleep quickly, even though he was soaked through and very cold, but was awoken after only a few hours by Tamatane and Tumataugena.

'Something bad walks the air,' they said. 'Perhaps you know what it is.'

The floating island was in the middle of a dense belt of cloud. It was close to midnight; light shone from beneath the island, diffused through white vapour. As Yama disentangled himself from the wet, heavy hide, something flashed far off in the mist, an intense point of brilliant blue light that faded to a flickering red star, falling through whiteness and gone even as Yama glimpsed it. A moment later, the whole island trembled as a clap of thunder rumbled through the air, and Yama shivered too.

Something loomed out of the mist: a dark spot that grew and gained shape, a red triangle with a kind of frame beneath it. It tipped through the air and stalled above the edge of the main platform; its pilot swung down from its harness and ran a little way across the platform with the last of its momentum, collapsing the bamboo frame and the hide stretched across it.

High-pitched whistles rose on all sides. The rain people gathered around the pilot, who stood in the centre of the platform and stared up in wonder at Yama.

The pilot, Tumahirmatea, was from a shoal of floating islands which hung far above this one. Something terrible was loose in the air, Tumahirmatea said. A monster that spat flame and could destroy an island with a single breath.

'It is not a monster, but a man,' Yama said. 'I had thought him dead, but it seems that nothing in the world can kill him. He is looking for me. I must leave at once.'

The rain people talked amongst themselves, and then Tumataugena and Tamatane came forward and offered their help.

Tamatane said, 'You wish to fall through the mouth of the snake.'

'I could jump from the edge of this platform,' Yama said, 'but I am not certain of my target.'

His stomach turned over at the thought. He was not at all sure that he could manipulate the machines that generated the gravity fields with enough precision to reach the mouth of the shortcut. If he missed, he would fall beyond the envelope of the world's air, and suffer the same awful death as Angel.

Tumataugena said, 'We have several kinds of flying device. The simplest are sacks full of bladders harvested from the edges of the island, but those will lift you rather than allow you to fall. So instead we will give you one of our kites.'

It was brought out of store and unwrapped: its wing was as yellow as sunlight. Yama thanked the rain people and asked for a knife and a little water. Tumataugena gave him a bodkin fashioned from the spine of a fish, with a handle of plaited black grass; Tamatane gave him a gourd brimming with sweet water, and he pricked the ball of his thumb and expressed three drops of blood into the gourd.

'If you wish to become more than you are, to become as the peoples of the world above, then drink a mouthful of this,' he said. 'When the change is complete you will be able to change others in the same way. If you decide not to do this thing, then wait a day for the water to lose its potency and then dash it over the edge of the island.'

Was Pandaras safe? Would he perform this miracle for the indigenous peoples of all the long world? But perhaps it did not matter. The mirror people and the forest folk were already changed. And they would change others.

The rain people talked amongst themselves. At last, Tamatane and Tumataugena announced that they would do this thing at once. They passed the gourd around, and the last person to drink from it, the stranger, Tumahirmatea, pitched it into the void.

'You will have a fever,' Yama said, 'and then you will sleep. But when you awake all will be different. You must find your own way after that. I can do no more for you.'

It did not take long to learn how to fly the mankite. There was a simple harness, which Tumahirmatea lengthened to accommodate him, and a frame hung at the balance point which he could grip and tilt to the left or right. A ribbon at the point of the kite indicated the direction of air currents; rudders pushed by his feet spilled air from the leading edges of the diamond-shaped lifting surface to bring it to stalling speed for a safe landing. But Yama would not need to land, only to stoop down like a lammergeyer.

There was no ceremony of farewell. He was strapped into the kite and helped to the edge of the platform; then he took a breath and jumped off. The underside of the island fell past, tangles of tough holdfasts studded with transparent hydrogen bladders. The kite jinked in air currents, wrenching at his shoulders. He kicked, got his feet in the stirrups of the rudders, leaned to the left. And began to breathe again.

Tumahirmatea followed Yama, red kite and yellow kite wing tip to wing tip as they stooped down, falling through vast volumes of cloud, breaking out past streamers of mist and rain into clear air. In one direction the dark wall of the edge of the world rose through decks of cloud and curtains of rain; in the other, empty blue air deepened towards the black void in which the world swam. Between, the silver column of the falling river twisted down towards its vanishing point, a hundred leagues below. The air was brighter there: it was night on the surface of the world, and the sun was walking its keel. Lightning crackled around the silver twist of water, vivid sparks flashing against their own reflections. Floating islands made broken arcs at different levels, receding into blue depths of air.

Yama swooped down in a great curve, yelling as he fell. For those few minutes, he was utterly free.

Tumahirmatea left him once they had fallen past the lower edge of the clouds that ringed the falling river. The red kite waggled from side to side in farewell and tilted away, already rising on an updraught. Yama fell on alone.

The column of water, twisted within intricate gravity fields, was closer now. The air was full of electricity generated by the friction of its fall. Every hair on Yama's head stirred uneasily. The thunder of lightning storms constantly shivered the air. He tacked several leagues out from the water column, then swung the kite around it. The world was a wall reaching above and below as far as he could see.

After one more full turn around the falling river, he would reach its vanishing point. Looking straight down, he could see a throat of velvet darkness wrapped around the root of the column of water. He could feel the thing which controlled the shortcut. The Gatekeeper. It was awakening, reaching towards him through the babble of the machines which manipulated the gravity fields.

Take me to the beginning of the world, he told it. Take me to my people.

He had expected difficulties. He had expected to have to use the full force of his will and all of his wits to break it. But the Gatekeeper yielded at once. Filtered through the remnant of the Shadow, its voice was his own. *Of course I know you*, it said. *I live in the place where the river meets itself. I have been waiting for you, Yamamanama, and hope to see you again.*

There was no time to frame questions. He was caught in air currents which sheered off the falling water. They buffeted him hard as he cut through them. The lifting surface of the kite boomed and shivered. The frame wrenched in his grip as if suddenly possessed of a will of its own.

You do not need the kite now. I will guide you.

Yama kicked his feet out of the rudders, unbuckled the harness. And gave himself to the air.

The kite slammed away above him, bucking and folding up as conflicting air currents caught it, a fleck of yellow whirling upwards, was gone. Yama arranged himself in the rush of air, his feet pointing down, his arms by his sides. It was the way he had so often dived into the deep water at the rocky point of the bay of the little city of Aeolis.

Something other than air gripped him. He drifted slowly towards the column of water. It was as smooth and dense as glass. It seemed to rise above him towards infinity. Beneath his feet was a rim of darkness, at one moment as flat as a ring of paper, the next infinitely deep. The tube of water narrowed as it swooped down. Water was not compressible, but somehow the river's vast flow was squeezed into a tube so narrow that two men could have embraced it and touched fingertips.

Space-time distortion. The flow here is extended through time as well as space. It is easier than extending the size of the shortcut's mouth.

He was falling faster now. Air ripped past. His cloak of uncured hide streamed up behind his head. He saw structures around the rim, geometric traceries of intense electric blue that extended wherever he looked.

And then he was gripped, turned, accelerated. There was an instant of intolerable pressure and brilliant light.

21

SHIP OF FOOLS

A tremendous flood swept Yama forward. He thrashed towards light and air, but the water was already receding, a wave washing away in every direction.

He stood, water slopping around his ankles. The hide cloak clung in heavy folds to his naked body. The light was dim, blood red. The cold air tasted of metal. He was in a chamber so large he could not see its ceiling or any of its walls. Beneath the ankle-deep water was a floor of a smooth, slightly yielding black substance.

A shrine stood a little distance away. It was the biggest he had ever seen, a huge black disc that would have overtopped the tallest tower of the peel-house. Nothing woke when he addressed it, but he had the unsettling impression that its vast smooth surface somehow inverted for a moment.

Was he in some part of the keelways? Was this the time of the world's making? He flexed his toes against the floor. It reminded him of a place Tamora had taken him to a lifetime ago, in Ys.

He chose a direction at random and started to walk. The water soon gave out. Once he shouted out his name, but the volumes of shadow and red light gave back no echo. He walked on, turning now and then to look back at the way he had come. He had gone about a league or so when he felt the presence of machines far behind him, and stopped and turned, and saw tiny figures moving around the base of the shrine.

He tried to question them. Their minds were opaque and unreadable, but as if in response a narrow beam of intense red light swept out from the base of the shrine, and found and pinned him. He raised a hand to shade his eyes and squinted into the light, saw that the figures were moving towards him across the vast floor, six, eight, ten of them sweeping forward in a line. Remembering the extensions of Dr Dismas's paramour, he turned and started to run, bare feet pounding the yielding floor, his shadow leaping ahead of him, running and running until he heard a faint whistle off to his left.

He stopped and look back, breathing hard, raising a hand to shield his eyes against the dazzle of red light. The figures had already made up half the distance and were coming on relentlessly. The whistle came again, human, shrill and urgent. He turned towards it. The narrow red beam tracked him, and his shadow suddenly rose to confront him, thrown on to something that loomed out of the dim redness. A structure of some kind: a black blister or bubble no bigger than an ordinary house.

Someone jumped up right in front of him, throwing aside the cloth that had concealed them. Yama tried to dodge, but they were faster, dipping, smashing into him, using his momentum to throw him from their hip. He landed on his back, shocked, breathless, looking up at a face that could have been his sister's: pale skin, a narrow jaw, high cheekbones, vivid blue eyes. Her black hair was cropped short. Elaborate tattoos began at the angles of her jaw, reaching around under her ears to meet at the nape of her neck. She wore a silvery one-piece garment that clasped her ankles, wrists and neck. One of her calloused bare feet was planted on his chest, and she was pointing a slim wand at him. He had the sense that it was a weapon. There was something odd about this strange yet familiar woman, a vacancy . . .

'Who are you?' she said. 'Where is your family?'

Yama turned his head to hide the scarred side of his face. He was uncomfortably aware that he was naked under the cloak, which he held together with one hand.

He said, 'Am I in the keelways?'

'You mean the spine?' The woman was folding up the black camouflage cloth. 'Don't fool. The regulators cleared and secured those territories twenty generations ago. Who are you?'

'A stranger in a strange place.'

The woman gave him a searching stare, then said, 'You aren't on a bug hunt, are you? Did you come through with the water?'

'I followed the river.'

'If you came through, you can't go back. And you better be able to run fast and far if we're going to outpace the regulators.'

The woman tucked the folded cloth into a slit at the waist of her silvery garment, and helped Yama to his feet. The line of figures was much closer now. Silhouetted against the red glare, man-shaped but oddly lopsided, pounding towards them.

Yama pointed at the blister and said, 'What is inside this building?'

'An outlet. Even if we had a hot blade, we couldn't cut its skin. Come on. The nearest hatch is three klicks away.'

Yama remembered the voidship lighter. The guard had done something to the material . . .

An opening puckered in the smooth black curve. The woman looked at him in astonishment, but followed him inside. The opening sealed behind them. For a moment they were in complete darkness, then the woman asked for light and a dim radiance kindled in the air.

They stood on a narrow walkway. It ran around a smooth-walled shaft that angled away into darkness. The woman knelt and stared into it, then looked up at Yama. 'That was a good trick,' she said, 'but the regulators will get permission to unseal this soon enough.'

'What are they?'

'They regulate the ship. They'll regulate us, if they get the chance.'

'Is this the only way out?'

'Unless we surrender.'

'How far does it fall?'

'A long way. It is one of the mains.'

Yama took off his cloak and spread it at the lip of the shaft. He could feel the woman's gaze move over his naked body.

'You're crazy,' she said. She was smiling.

'Do you have a better idea? Sit behind me and hold on to my waist.'

After a moment, she did as he asked. Her touch and spicy scent gave him an erection; he felt the heat of a blush spreading across his face and chest.

She leaned into him and said, 'I'm Wery. If we survive this I'll take you to my people. Bryn will want to ask you many questions.'

'Now,' Yama said, and they kicked off down the steep slope.

The dim light kept pace with them as they plummeted into the dark and the rush of air. Wery screamed all the way down – in delight rather than fear. Even though the surface of the shaft was perfectly smooth, the hide quickly grew warm beneath Yama's bare buttocks and the soles of his feet. His fingers cramped on stiff folds; he counted off seconds, ten, twenty, and then the shaft straightened out, and they slowed and stopped.

Wery slapped his shoulder. 'Not bad. But we have to keep moving. The regulators won't let up.'

Yama crouched and awkwardly fastened the cloak around himself, then followed Wery along the horizontal shaft. It was more than twice their height, perfectly circular in cross-section, and lined with a black glaze. They walked a long way. Other shafts intersected at it irregular intervals and Wery turned left or right or walked straight on without hesitation.

Yama told her part of his story, explained how he had fallen over the edge of Confluence and followed the Great River through the shortcut. 'All my life I have been searching for my people. I am so happy to have found you. How many others are there? And where is this place? What is it?'

'If you pass, you can trade questions with Bryn,' Wery said. Every so often she turned and walked backwards for a few paces, keeping watch for any sign of pursuit.

'I thought I could control the shortcut and divert the flow of the river to the beginning of the world,' Yama said. 'Instead, it took me somewhere else. It brought me here, to you. It must have done it for a reason.'

'No one knows the ship's mind. Not even Bryn.'

'It knew me. It knew who I was, and said that it hoped to meet me again. It sent me here for a purpose. And there must be a way back—'

'Think about surviving this,' Wery said. 'Everything else can wait.'

At last, Yama discovered a place where he could make the wall of the shaft pucker open. They clambered through into green light and hot, humid air. A rock face covered in creepers and thick lianas rose behind them, its top overhung by trees. A dry stream bed snaked away between bushes and trees that knitted above it to form a kind of tunnel.

Wery looked all around, sniffing the air, then smiled. 'I led us true. The others are not far away.'

'The others in your family?'

'My mates.'

She stepped up to Yama, and for a swooning moment he thought that she was about to embrace him, but instead she touched her wand to the skin behind his ear. A point of intense coldness washed across his scalp and face. He tried to speak, but his tongue was wooden and his jaw was clenched in a rictus grin. The cold flowed down his arms, spread down his spine into his legs; Wery stepped out of the way as he toppled forward.

Yama was woken by the screeching of birds somewhere high above. He was lying on his back on the dry stream bed. He discovered that he could move, and started to sit up. Beside him, Wery jumped to her feet and ran to the two men walking towards them, one young and tall, the other much older. They were dressed in silvery one-piece garments like Wery's, had similar tattoos on their necks, and carried wands. As with Wery, there seemed to be something lacking in them. It was as if they were not living people, but animated statues, or aspects cast in flesh rather than light . . .

Wery flung her arms around the young man and said, 'He isn't a bug, but he came through the port. Or he claims he did. He says he comes from Confluence.'

'Maybe he's a bug that looks like a man,' the young man said.

'No fooling, Cas,' Wery said. 'This is important.'

'I'm not fooling. I'm thinking,' the young man said, staring at Yama over Wery's shoulder. 'He could be a medizer.'

'They killed all the medizers long ago,' the older man said.

'Maybe they missed one,' the young man said.

His black hair curled to his shoulders. He had ripped off the sleeves of his silvery garment to display his muscular arms. His companion was a head shorter, his close-cropped hair and neatly trimmed beard white, deep wrinkles cut into his forehead and seaming the skin around his eyes and the corners of his mouth. There was a silvery patch over his left eye.

He told Wery, 'Whatever he is, regulators don't like it. They're swarming all through these decks. We'll have to move sharpish.'

'I know. He helped me escape,' Wery said.

'Doesn't mean we can trust him,' the young man said.

'For once you're right,' the old man said.

He stepped towards Yama, who drew the cloak around himself and stood up, and started to explain how happy he was to have found people of his bloodline.

'Let's see what you really are,' the old man said.

He pointed his wand at Yama and made several slow passes over his head and body before stepping back and flipping up his eye patch and considering him, head slightly cocked, like a merchant assessing a sample of suspect goods.

'He's full of bits and pieces, but nothing I recognise,' he said at last. 'Stuff in his blood, too, but it isn't regulator trace. Never seen anything like it. Maybe he really did come from somewhere else.'

Yama understood now what these people lacked. None of them had been touched by the breath of the Preservers.

'The ship is very big,' the young man said.

'I think he was telling the truth,' Wery said. 'He really is from outside.'

Yama said, 'I want to tell you everything I know. And I want to learn everything about you, and this ship of yours.'

'Not here,' the old man said. 'Time to shift, mates, find a safe berth where we can wait out the regulators.'

The old man, Bryn, was the leader of the three. They had been on what he called a bug hunt.

'Sometimes things come up when the ship takes on new cargo,' Bryn told Yama, 'and sometimes they're sly and swift enough to get past the regulators. We hunt them down before they cause trouble.'

'We thought you were a bug,' Cas said.

'We're glad you're not,' Wery said, with a smile that turned Yama's heart.

After they left the stream, they walked in silence through the forest, Cas and Wery taking turns to scout ahead before beckoning the others on. The trees were as tall as any in the home of the bandar yoi inoie, wrapping spirals of branches around themselves as they soared towards a blank white glow. Unseen birds sang, near and far. At last, Yama followed the others between two huge trees, and found himself in a white corridor that stretched away to vanishing points on either side. They walked on for more than a league until Bryn said that it was safe to think of resting.

He opened a door that Yama had not noticed, and they went through into a brightly lit room where several lines of narrow ceramic slabs floated in the air at waist height, and gusts of hot, dry air blew from random directions. Feeding troughs were set in the floor along one of the walls, but the stuff in them had crumbled to dust. No one had been here for a very long time.

A voice welcomed them, and said that it could reconfigure to the requirements of their bloodline. Bryn told it to shut up. 'We leave no traces,' he said to Yama. 'Remember that, and you might live as long as me.'

Yama sat next to the old man on one of the floating slabs and asked him how old he was.

'Fifty-three years,' the old man said proudly. 'You look surprised, and no wonder. I am older than anyone I know. I expect that no one in your family has ever lived as long, but it is possible, as you can see.'

Yama had thought that Bryn must be at least two centuries old. It seemed that his bloodline was short-lived, unless they aged quickly here because of hardship.

Cas and Wery were watching the door, their wands across their laps. 'I hate this heat,' Cas said. 'We should find one of our places.'

'The regulators will look in those places first,' Bryn said. 'Shut up, Cas. Watch the door. I want to hear our new mate's story.'

Wery said she had already heard some of it, and had not understood a word. Bryn shrugged. 'She's muscle,' he told Yama, 'she and her husband. Good at killing, but not too bright.'

'You always got to say you're cleverer than everyone else,' Cas said. He got up and began to prowl around, restless in the way of a man more comfortable with action than conversation.

Bryn said, 'I say it because it's true. I chose you two because I'm clever enough to know that you're better than most at what you do. Don't break any of the machinery, Cas. That'll bring the regulators at once.'

'Then I fight them,' Cas said, but he set down the delicate construction of black rods he had been turning over his big hands.

'While we wait for the regulators to move on, you can tell me your story,' Bryn said to Yama. 'Where you came from, how you found the shortcut, and so on. Don't leave anything out.'

'It is a very long story,' Yama said, 'but I will try my best.'

'Tell us about Confluence,' Wery said. 'Is it really like wilds that go on forever and ever? Do you hunt bugs there? Are they bigger and fiercer than the ones that come through?'

Her bold candour reminded Yama of poor, dead Tamora. He wondered if she would leave Cas for him, wondered if there were other women like her. In the swooning excitement of finding his people, he had forgotten Derev, and the fervent promises they had made to each other before he had set out on the long road which had at last led him here.

Cas said, 'The ship hasn't been to Confluence for generations and generations. How could he come from there?'

Yama tried to explain what he had learned from Dr Dismas's paramour.

The shortest distance between two points on the surface of Confluence was a straight line; between stars the shortest route was a geodesic, the equivalent of a straight line across distances so long that the curvature in space-time caused by the mass of the universe became apparent. But within the vacuum of space were holes smaller than the particles which made up atoms. As small as the smallest possible measurement, these holes appeared and disappeared in an instant, a constant, unperceived seething of energies that continually cancelled themselves out. The holes had two mouths, and the route through the distorted geometry of the space-time tunnelled between them was far shorter than the route between the two points they linked in ordinary space. Ordinarily, the duration of their existence was much shorter than the time it took to travel between them, but the Preservers had found a way to grab the mouths of certain of these holes, and stabilise and widen them, creating shortcuts that linked places separated by vast distances.

Bryn nodded. 'The ship uses shortcuts to get from world to world. It also uses them to replenish its air and water. You came out in one of the cisterns. Lucky for you it was one that isn't used any more, or you would have drowned. But most of them aren't used now.'

Cas was doing push-ups as relentlessly as a machine. Sweat gleamed on his bare, muscular arms. Without pausing, he said, 'Why do we need to know how he got here? He can't get back, so it's what he can do now that counts.'

'Let him tell his story,' Wery said. 'You never know when something might be useful.'

'She's right,' Bryn said. 'Set on, Yama.'

The Preservers had constructed an intricate network of shortcuts between every star in the Home Galaxy, Yama said, but the shortcuts could link points in time as well as space. It was done by fixing one mouth of a shortcut to a ship capable of travelling at speeds close to that of light itself. In the realm of light there was no time; or rather, there was a single endless moment that encompassed the beginning and the end of the universe. As the ship carrying the shortcut mouth approached that unreachable realm, so time stretched around it; while only a few years passed aboard the ship, many more passed in the rest of the universe. When the ship returned to its starting point, the two mouths of the shortcut now joined regions of space separated by the time debt built up during the journey. Someone passing through the mouth of the shortcut which had travelled with the ship would exit from the mouth which had remained where it was, and travel back to the time when the ship's journey had begun. But they could not return by the same route, because their journey altered the past, so that it flowed towards a different future.

Prompted by the remains of the Shadow, which was able to filter the vast store of knowledge he had taken from Dr Dismas's paramour, Yama drew diagrams on the dusty floor, and slowly understood what had happened to him.

The Preservers had cloned certain of the shortcuts, so that one mouth led to many different destinations, determined by slight changes in the potential energy of travellers. Aided by the Gatekeeper of Confluence, Yama had fallen through the mouth of one of these cloned shortcuts, but he did not know where and when he had emerged. He knew only that his wish had been granted: he had been sent to his people.

Yama understood all about cloning, for it was how meat and work animals were bred, but he had to explain it several times before Wery understood. The notion disgusted her, and Bryn was amused by her disgust.

'There are many ways of living,' he said. 'That's why these rooms are all so different, because the passengers were once many different kinds of people.'

'They were bugs,' Cas said indifferently. He was sitting on his haunches now, polishing a bone dagger. 'And we kill bugs.'

'Some bugs are the stock species from which the Preservers made people,' Bryn said. 'Although I admit that there's a bigger difference there than between child and man.'

'Bugs are bugs,' Cas said. 'Some are harder to kill than others, that's all.'

'And you can eat some but not others,' Wery said.

Yama said again, 'Because I fell through one of the cloned shortcuts, I do not know where I am.'

'On the ship, of course,' Wery said. 'Somewhere about the waist, in an outer deck.'

'He knows he's on the ship,' Bryn said. 'But he doesn't know where the ship is, or when.'

Bryn knew more about Confluence than Wery or Cas, but knew nothing of Ys or the Age of Insurrection, or even of the Sirdar, who had ruled Confluence when it had been newly made: it seemed that his people had been on the ship a long time. Yama suspected that their ancestors had fled here after the construction of Confluence had been completed. They had been rebels, like the feral machines or Tibor's ancestors.

When Yama asked if they controlled the ship, Bryn shook his head. 'Some say the ship controls itself. Others that the crew still lives, but has grown remote. I incline to the first opinion, because no one has seen any sign of the crew for many generations.'

Yama, remembering the star-sailors, said, 'I believe that I have met one. Two, in fact. But that was in another place, and another time.'

He realised that he must have fallen far into the past: the star-sailors had believed that all of his bloodline had died out long ago.

According to Bryn, the regulators were also passengers. Yama was surprised. He had assumed that because they were machines, they were the servants of the ship and its crew.

'Some say that they came aboard with our ancestors – that they were once our servants,' Bryn said. 'Maybe that's so on other ships, but here the regulators serve only their own ends, which includes trying to regulate us out of existence.'

Cas said, 'There is only one ship, Bryn. It loops through time and sometimes meets itself.'

Bryn said, 'Only one ship in our universe, yes, but there may be many universes, eh? A universe takes only one road, but as Yama just explained, a man who retraces his steps cannot return to the place from which he started. For the road splits at the place he travelled back to, and he must travel down the new road. It stops a man killing his grandfather and returning to find himself without existence.'

'Perhaps his grandfather was only the husband of his grandmother,' Cas said slowly, 'and not his sire.'

Bryn tugged on his beard in vexation. 'His grandmother, then! I make the fancy to illustrate a point, not start a debate. There are as many universes as there are travellers. In many we may live on into our new mate's time. But not, I think, in the time he came from.'

Yama nodded. 'If you did, I would not have had to come here to look for you.'

Bryn said, 'The problem is that you can go back to your future, but not by retracing the same path, and so it will not be the place from which you started.'

Wery said, 'How could any man create a new universe?'

'The harder the task, the greater the consequences,' Bryn said. 'It is no easy thing, to travel back through time.'

Cas said, 'It doesn't matter where he can or can't go, because he can't leave the ship. No one can. All this talk is making my head hurt, Bryn. And we've stayed here too long.'

'You're right,' Bryn said. 'We should move on before the regulators notice the change in carbon dioxide concentration or some other sign.'

'I have good ventilation,' a voice said.

'When I need advice from a room,' Bryn said, 'I will ask for it. Do your synthesisers still work?'

'Of course,' the voice said. 'If you require food, there will be a slight delay while I adjust the settings.'

'I want clothing for my new mate here, not food,' Bryn said. 'Give him a copy of what we're wearing, to replace that unseemly wrap. And do it now. We want to move on.'

'You are welcome to stay as long as you like,' the voice said. 'I miss the company of people.'

'We can't stay unless you change your settings,' Bryn told it, 'and the regulators will know if you do. Just make the clothes.'

After Yama pulled on the one-piece silvery garment, Wery showed him how to adjust the seals at ankles, wrists and neck. Her fluttering touch; her heat; her scent. He knew that she belonged to another man, but he ached for her all the same.

She talked with him as they walked along the seemingly endless white corridor. Cas went ahead, waving them forward at each intersection, then loping on eagerly.

'You shouldn't mind Bryn,' Wery told Yama. 'He dreams too much of the old days because he has so much learning in his head.'

Yama smiled. 'This is like one of the old stories! Bryn is the magician, and you are the warriors helping him in his quest.'

Wery smiled too. Her teeth were very white; one of the incisors was broken. 'If this is a kind of fancy, what are you?'

'I do not know. A creature with magical powers, perhaps. Although they are not really magical. What appears to be magic is usually an act of deception or secret manipulation,' Yama said, remembering Magon, the gambler he had met in the Palace of the Memory of the People. 'Once you understand how it is done the mystery disappears.'

'Bryn has plans for you and your tricks, no doubt, but he dreams as much about the future as the past, and dreams are no more than a kind of fancy. How it is here, Yama, we hunt bugs and regulators, they hunt bugs and us, and it can't be changed. Everyone knows that the ship doesn't care to carry weak passengers.'

'Survival of the fittest,' Yama said. It seemed as vile as the creed of the heretics. As if the universe were without any ruling principle but death.

'That's what Bryn calls it. I say you are either dead or alive, and dead doesn't count.'

'How many of your people are alive? Where do they live? I want to know everything about them, Wery.'

'We're a long way from home, and it moves about anyway. As for how many—' Wery held up her left hand and opened and closed her fingers three times. 'That's all in our family, including us. There were other families, but we haven't seen anything of them for a long time.'

She stopped, peering ahead, then said, 'Cas has found something,' and ran off down the wide, white corridor to catch up with her husband.

Bryn dropped back to walk alongside Yama, saying, 'As you can see, the youngsters prefer action to thinking.'

'Perhaps you can tell me how your people came to live here.'

'We served the Preservers,' Bryn said. 'We were their first servants – we might even have been the original crew of the ship. Then the Preservers made all the other races and went away, and we lost our powers.'

'I thought that our people went with the Preservers,' Yama said, smiling because it was so thrilling and strange to say *our* instead of *my*.

'Perhaps most of them did. But this ship was left behind, and so were our ancestors.'

'Perhaps they refused to leave their home,' Yama said.

'We are loyal servants of the Preservers,' Bryn said. 'Do not think otherwise.'

'I meant no offence.'

'None taken, lad. But if we live in your past, and you know no others of your kind, where did you come from?'

'That is what I am still hoping to discover,' Yama said. 'Perhaps I am the child of sailors of our bloodline who jumped ship long ago. I know of at least one star-sailor who did. He borrowed a body—'

But Bryn was loping towards Wery and Cas, who had stopped at an intersection. The black stuff of the floor was scored heavily there, ripped into curling strips. The strips were creeping over each other and softening at the edges, trying to mend the wounds.

'Bug sign,' Cas said, holding up fingers smeared with sticky clear liquid which had splashed and spattered across the white walls. 'Reckon there was a fight and one ate the other. Not long ago, either.'

Wery grinned. 'It's wounded,' she said. 'There's a trail. We kill it easy.'

The trail of colourless blood led into another of the big, forested spaces. As before, the transition was abrupt. One moment Yama was hurrying along beside Bryn, who despite his age kept up a spritely pace, with Wery and Cas jogging eagerly ahead, vanishing around a corner. When Yama and Bryn followed they were suddenly in a dark, dank, dripping place where huge tree trunks reared up through broken layers of mist that drifted beneath a high canopy.

Yama looked back and saw a sliver of white light between two boulders propped against each other. It was the only point of brightness in this gloomy place. Pale fungi spread tall fans above ankle-deep ooze. Vines dropped from somewhere beyond the mist and slowly quested about the floor, pulsing with slow peristalsis as they pumped ooze upwards. Yama saw that the giant trees were conglomerations of these vines, twisted around each other like so many stiffened ropes. Parasitic plants wrapped pale, meaty leaves around the bases of the vines, and things in burrows spread feathery palps across the surface of the ooze; something bright red and thin as a whip shot from a hole and snapped at Yama's ankles.

Bryn laughed. 'This is one of the mires, lad. Everything in the ship eventually passes through places like this.'

Wery and Cas found a sign of the thing they were tracking, and disappeared into the gloom between the trunks of the giant tree-things. There was a squalling noise in the distance. Bryn drew something from his sack and tossed it underhand to Yama.

It was a knife. When Yama caught it by the haft, its curved blade sparked with blue fire. Bryn stared and Yama grinned. 'I know this, at least,' he said. 'And it knows me.'

Had the knife he had found – or which had found him – in the tomb in the Silent Quarter originally come from the ship? Was this perhaps the very same knife, destined to come into the possession of the warrior who had been interred in the tomb where Yama had confronted Lud and Lob?

The squalling rose in pitch. Bryn and Yama sloshed forward through the ooze. Something thrashed beyond a tall ridge of white fungus, then suddenly reared up. It was three times the height of a man, and sprang over the fungus and ran at Yama and Bryn with preternatural swiftness.

Yama had a confused glimpse of something in black armour, all barbs and thin legs with cutting blades for edges, a narrow head dominated by jaws that opened sideways to reveal interlocked layers of serrated blades rotating over each other. It did not look so much like an insect as a dire wolf chopped and stretched into a poor imitation. It made its squalling noise again. Acrid vapour puffed from glands that ran along each side of its long, hairy belly.

The bug knocked Yama down with a casual flick of a foreleg and pounced on Bryn, spraying black ooze everywhere. Wery suddenly appeared behind it and threw a weighted rope that tangled around its forelegs. Yama jumped up, mud dripping from his silvery garment, and ran beneath the bug's belly as it snapped at Wery. He stabbed the knife's blade, blazing with blue fire, through the membrane at the articulation of one of its sturdy rear legs. The knife whined, burning so eagerly through horn and flesh that it almost jerked out of Yama's hands. Clear, sticky blood gushed; the bug half-collapsed, its leg almost completely severed. Cas stepped between its flailing forelimbs and stabbed the point of his wand between its eyes. It shuddered and kicked out and died.

While the others worked at cutting off the bug's head, Yama noticed that a kind of belt was fastened around its narrow waist, slung with pouches and bits of shaped stone or bone. Tools.

Bryn saw his look and said, 'It would have killed us if it could.'

'It was intelligent.' Yama thought of Caphis, the fisherman he had found in a trap set by one of the Amnan. People preying on other people. The strong on the weak, the clever on the stupid.

Bryn shrugged. 'It was bright enough to get on to the ship. But not bright enough to survive.'

Yama handed the knife to the old man, hilt first. 'I have had enough of killing, I think.'

Cas tugged hard and the armoured head came free. Clear blood gushed from the neck; the legs thrashed in a final spasm. Hand-sized creatures as flat as plates, thready blue organs visible through their transparent shells, skated over the muck to get at the spilled blood. Red whips had already wrapped around the bug's legs, melting into its horny carapace.

Yama expected the three hunters to carry their grisly trophy in triumph back to their home, but instead they dumped it in the corridor directly outside the entrance to the mire and went on.

'The ship will find it and mark our victory,' Bryn said. 'Our task is done.'

The lights, slaved to a diurnal cycle, dimmed soon after they left the mire. They slept in a little room that Bryn found off one of the corridors. This one was more suited to their kind. Beakers of distilled water and cubes of tasteless white food extruded from a wall at Bryn's command. The floor humped into four sleeping platforms. 'If you want to piss or shit, do it in the corner there,' Bryn told Yama, and ordered the room to dim its light.

Yama was woken from a light sleep by Wery's giggle. Sounds of flesh moving on flesh, breath at two pitches gaining the same urgent rhythm. He lay awake for a long time, lost and lonely and frightened, while the two hunters made love a few spans from him.

They travelled along the endless white corridors for much of the next day. Wery walked at point with Cas, while Bryn asked Yama many questions about Confluence, most of which he could not begin to answer.

They walked steadily, drinking from tubes set in the necks of their silvery garments, which recycled their own sweat as distilled water. At last, they left the corridor for one of the jungle wilds, and after an hour's walk down a labyrinth of narrow paths Wery insisted on showing Yama something.

'You'll love it. Really you will.'

Yama demurred. He was still embarrassed and disconcerted by overhearing her lovemaking.

'Go on,' Bryn said, with a sly smile. 'It will help you understand where you are.'

Yama and Wery climbed a grandfather tree that rose through the dense green canopy, its surprisingly small crown of dark green feathery fronds silhouetted against sky glare. Its rough bark provided plenty of handholds and footholds. They climbed a long way. Cool inside his silvery garment despite the foetid heat, but quite breathless and with his pulse pounding heavily in his head, Yama sat at last in the crutch of a bough on which Wery balanced with heart-stopping ease.

He saw that the jungle stretched away for several leagues on all sides, a rumpled blanket of green studded here and there with splashes of bright orange or yellow or red where trees were in flower. A line or chain of tiny, intense points of white light hung high above the treetops: the little suns that fed the jungle's growth. But that was not what Wery wanted him to see.

The jungle grew on the outer skin of the ship, seemingly not enclosed by anything at all – perhaps gravity fields held in the atmosphere, as they contained the envelope of air around Confluence, or perhaps it was domed with material so transparent that it was invisible. The rest of the ship stretched away in every direction from the jungle's oval footprint.

Yama, remembering the voidship lighter which had docked at Ys, had thought that the ship would be some kind of sphere, bigger certainly, but more or less of the same design, much as a dory resembles a carrack. But now he saw that the ship was a series of cubes and spheres and other more complex geometrical solids strung like beads along a wire, and that it was many hundreds of leagues long – impossible to tell how many. In all their journeying, they had traversed only one part of one segment. There was room enough for any number of wonders to be hidden here.

But he knew that he could not stay. He had thought about it last night. He had found people of his bloodline, yet they were stranger to him than Pandaras, Tamora and Derev. They lacked the breath of the Preservers and so could not be anything other than what they already were, enslaved by their circumstances. This was not his home. That was on Confluence. It was with Derev. She and Yama had sworn a compact, and he knew now that it meant more to him than life itself. He would find the cistern and the shrine, and force the Gatekeeper to take him home. And then he would end the war. He had known how to do it ever since he had seen the picture in the slate which Beatrice and Osric had shown him at the beginning of his adventures, but he had not known that he knew it until he had absorbed the knowledge hoarded by Dr Dismas's paramour.

Standing before him on the broad branch high above the jungle, Wery clapped her hands over her head and laughed. Yama realised for the first time that she was older than him. The brilliant light of the chain of miniature suns accentuated the wrinkles around her eyes, showed where flesh was beginning to loosen and sag along the line of her jaw.

It did not make her any less desirable.

'Look starboard,' she said, and pointed at the distant edge of the ship.

Something stood far beyond the jungle. A red line – no, a dome, the top of a structure bigger than any of the wilds. It was lengthening and growing in height, as if it was crawling towards them.

A vast creature, big as a mountain . . .

Yama looked at Wery, wondering if he had finally been driven mad, and she laughed again and said, 'That's the mine world the ship orbits.'

Yama realised then that the blister was part of a disc. And the disc was not advancing, but rising – it was a world as round as the sun, just like those described in the opening suras of the Puranas. A sphere, a globe, a battered red globe rising above the ship's horizon. Yama laughed too, full of wonder. The world's pockmarked red surface was capped top and bottom with white, and scarred by a huge canyon that pointed towards three pits. Or no, they were the tops of huge, hollow mountains. At the very edge of the world's disc was an even bigger mountain, so big that it rose above the narrow band of diffracted light that marked the limit of the world's atmosphere.

Wery said that it was time to descend. They walked down narrow paths through understorey trees and bushes that divided and divided again in an endless maze which Cas, who took the lead, seemed to know well, for he set an eager pace.

Bryn told Yama that mined mass was moved from the surface of the world to the ship by something called an elevator, a chain or cable that hung down from a point many leagues above the world's surface. It took a while for Yama to understand why the cable did not collapse. The world was spinning, so that its surface moved at a certain speed, and the cable was grown from a point high above that also moved at the same speed, so that it was always above the same place on the surface. Hoppers moved up the cable and the material in them was slung out like pebbles from a catapult, to be caught by the ship and stowed away.

Ahead, Cas paused at a place where the path split into three. He turned and waved and went on.

Wery chased after her husband. A moment later, frantic whistles pierced the green quiet of the jungle. Bryn broke into a run and Yama followed. They scrambled down a steep fern-laden bank and splashed across a muddy stream, clambered up the bank on the far side and burst through a screen of tall grasses into the brilliant light of the miniature suns.

A huge tree had fallen here long ago: Yama and Bryn had emerged at the top of the wide, deep bowl, grown over with rich green grass, which had been torn out of the earth when the tree's roots had been pulled up by its fall. Here and there bodies lay in the long grass. Human-sized, human-shaped, clad in silver.

Yama's heart turned over. But then he saw that the bodies were not dressed in silvery clothes, but naked, with silvery skin.

'Regulators,' Bryn said, and sat down beside one of the bodies and bowed his head.

Cas and Wery were standing at the far edge of the clearing. When Bryn sat down they looked at each other and then ran off in opposite directions.

'Wait,' Bryn said, when Yama made to follow Wery. 'There may be traps.'

'This is the home of your people.'

'They were camped here. Perhaps they moved on before...' Bryn bowed his head once more, and clasped his hands over the white hair on top of his head.

Yama moved from body to body. All were quite unmarked. They were very thin. Their right hands were three-fingered, but their left hands were all different: one like pincers made of black metal, another extended into bony blades with jagged cutting edges, a third divided into hinged blades like monstrous scissors. Their eyes were huge, the colour of wet blood, and divided into hexagonal cells. Although they were dead, something still seemed to be watching Yama behind these strange eyes. It was like the men whom the rogue star-sailor had enslaved by putting machines in their heads; the machines had lived on after the men had died, and so here.

Wery appeared at the far end of the clearing, shouted that everyone was gone, and ran off again. Bryn got up slowly, straightened his back, took a deep breath, and said, 'We will see what has happened.'

The bowl of the clearing was a hundred paces across, twice that in length. The rotting carcass of the fallen tree lay at one end, extending into bushes and young trees growing all around. Butterflies seemingly made of gold foil fluttered here and there in the bright light. Cas caught one as he came down the slope towards Bryn and Yama, and crushed it in his massive fist.

The encampment was no more than a few panels of woven grass leaning against the trunk of the fallen tree. A scattering of mats and empty water-skins, neatly tied bundles of dried leaves, a frame of tall sticks on which a stretched hide had been half-scraped of its hair. A blackened cube in a hearth of bare earth still radiated heat; a bowl of something like porridge had dried out on top of it and was beginning to burn. Yama picked up a square piece of flat glass. Glyphs began to stream and shiver inside it, but they were of no script or language he knew.

Wery said, 'There were three regulators waiting for us. Cas killed two. I killed the other.'

Bryn said, 'The others?'

'Gone,' Wery said. She dabbed angrily at the tears which stood in her eyes. 'All gone.'

Cas pointed at Yama with his wand, and Bryn got in front of Yama and said, 'No. It could not be him.'

'There will only be three of us if you kill him,' Wery said.

Yama understood. Their family was the last of the bloodline on the ship; that was why they had been so amazed to see him. And now they were the last of their family.

Bryn flipped his patch down over his left eye. He turned in a slow, complete circle and said, 'Where are the bodies, Cas?'

'I have not yet found any. I will look again.' Cas trotted across the clearing and plunged into the bushes on the far side.

Wery said, 'Do you think they might still be alive?'

Bryn lifted his eyepatch. 'Ordinarily the regulators would have killed them at once. But there is no blood, and there are no bodies.'

'Perhaps the regulators took the bodies,' Wery said.

'But they left their dead companions,' Yama said.

Wery and Bryn looked at him. And at the same moment a regulator parted a clump of tall ferns and stepped into the clearing, mismatched hands held up by its shoulders. The left was swollen and bifurcate, hinged like a lobster's claw.

Yama knocked Wery's arm up as she aimed her wand at the regulator. Something went howling away into the bright sky-glow. Wery turned on him, the wand swinging in an arc that would have ended in his chest if he had not stepped inside it. He bent her arm behind her back until she had to drop the wand; bent it further until she had to kneel.

'Cas will kill you,' she said, glaring up at him.

Bryn was pointing his wand at the regulator, but he was looking at Yama. He said, 'It obeys you.'

'Yes, but the others did not.'

The regulator still had its hands raised. It possessed breasts, a pair of breasts that hung like empty sacs. It fixed its huge red eyes on Yama and said, 'I have a message from Prefect Corin.'

22
SO BELOW

Cas came back at a run, and would have killed the regulator at once if Bryn had not stood in his way. They argued in violent whispers; then Cas turned his back on them all and Bryn came across the clearing and told Yama, 'We will go with you.'

Yama said, 'I think it would be better if you stayed here.'

'They have our people,' Wery said. 'Of course we will go with you.'

Bryn was walking around and around the regulator, which still stood where Yama had told her to halt. At last he turned and said again, 'It obeys you.'

'The regulators have machines in their heads. I was not able to talk to the machines of the others, but I am able to talk with hers.'

'It,' Wery said.

Yama and Bryn looked at her.

Wery said defiantly, 'It, not she. They're things, not people. Things. Things!'

Cas put his hand on Wery's shoulder and she turned and rested her face against his broad chest. 'We will kill this Prefect Corin and free our people and bring them home,' Cas told Yama. 'What you do after that is of no matter to us.'

'I wish it were that simple,' Yama said. 'And I still think you should all stay here.'

They were savages. They called themselves passengers, tried to justify their presence on the ship and placate it with trophies from bug hunts, but like Yama, like the thing they had killed in the mire, they were really stowaways.

Bryn stared into the regulator's red, faceted eyes, tugging at his beard.

'We will help you, Yama. And you will tell this regulator to obey and help all of us.'

'I still say we kill it,' Cas said.

'No.' Bryn smiled; he believed that he was in command again. 'Once this is over, we will be masters of all the regulators. The crew will look to us for help instead of to them. That is my price, Yama, for the hurt you have caused. We should make a start on our quest at once. It will be night soon, I have no liking for this place any more, and it is a long way to the docks.'

The regulator stirred. 'There is a shorter route,' she said, and repeated her message. 'My master commands you to descend to the surface of the world below. I will lead you to where he waits with your people. If you come with him, they may go free.'

Cas began to curse the regulator in a dull monotone.

Yama dared to lay a hand on his arm, and said, 'Your people died because of me. I will help you avenge their deaths.'

As the little glass room fell along the length of the ship, Wery and Cas held on to each other as well as to the rail that ran at waist height around its cold, transparent walls. Bryn clung there too, aiming his wand at the regulator, which hung like a silvery-grey statue in the centre of the room, flat, toeless feet a span above the floor. Only Yama paid any attention to the view. The ship dwindled away above and below, although neither direction had much meaning here, where there was no gravity. The long track along which the glass room travelled was a thread laid across its segments. Clusters of lights cast stark shadows over the surfaces of enormous cubes and pyramids and tetrahedrons strung together and studded with hundreds of green or brown or indigo blisters – wilds clinging to the surfaces of the huge ship's segments like fish lice to an eel.

As the ship turned about its long axis, the bulging disc of the red world slowly rose above it. Yama glimpsed the terminus of the elevator far beyond the end of the ship, an irregular shape sliced in half by its own shadow. A broken line defined by lights scattered along its length dwindled away towards the world.

Bryn was able to answer some of Yama's questions. The ship turned on its axis so that all sides would be exposed to the light of the sun of this system, evening out temperature differences. The elevator was woven from strands of a material stronger than any plastic, held in place by intensely steep gravity fields. The mines delivered phosphates and iron. In thirty days the ship would leave this system and pass through the shortcut to its next destination.

The regulator stirred and said, 'They spy on the crew.'

Bryn tapped his eyepatch. 'I am allowed revelations,' he said. 'This is one of the greatest treasures of my people.'

'You interrupt data flow,' the regulator said.

'As is our right,' Bryn said, 'earned by tribute.'

'You have no rights,' the regulator said. 'You are parasites.'

'You be quiet,' Cas told her. 'Speak only when spoken to.'

Neither Bryn nor the regulator had been able to give answers to Yama's questions. He did not know how Prefect Corin had been able to follow him here, or why he had chosen to descend to the surface of the world, or how he was able to control the regulators, or how many he commanded. He was heading towards a confrontation with an enemy whose strength and powers were largely unknown.

The glass room sped towards the end of the ship. The world's huge red disc slowly revolved above it and set on the far side of the ship, and then Yama forgot for a moment all his doubts and anxieties.

The stars had come out.

There were thousands of them, tens of thousands, a field of hard, bright stars shining everywhere he looked, crossed by a great milky river that seemed to wrap around the intensely black sky. The sun of this world must lie deep within one of the arms of the galaxy: that milky river was the plane of the arm, the light of its billions of stars coalesced into a dense glow. Here and there structures could be discerned – star bridges, tidy globes, a chain of bright red stars that spanned half the sky – but otherwise the patterns made by the Preservers were less obvious than when viewed from the orbit of Confluence, many thousands of years beyond the galaxy's rim. Yet every star he could see had been touched by the Preservers. Their monument, their shrine, was all around him.

Then the sun rose. Although it was smaller and redder than the sun of Confluence, its light banished all but the brightest of the stars.

Yama had expected the glass room to re-enter the ship and deliver them to some kind of skiff or lighter which would transfer them to the elevator terminus. Instead, it simply shot off the end of its track into the naked void. Cas roared, half in amazement, half in defiance; Wery pressed the length of her body against his. The ship fell away. The terminus of the elevator slowly grew larger in the void below their feet.

It was an irregular chunk of rock, its lumpy surface spattered with craters. One side was lit by the sun, the other, where the elevator cable was socketed in a complex of domes and haphazardly piled cubes, by ruddy light reflected from the world.

'It is one of the moons,' Bryn said. 'Its orbital velocity was increased to move it from a lower orbit and to synchronise it with the world's rotation. The world was moved, too, displaced across half the diameter of the galaxy. There is a legend that it came from the original system of the Preservers, although some maintain that it is merely a replica of one of the worlds of that system.'

The little moon grew, slowly eclipsing the sun. The glass room swung through ninety degrees – Cas roared again – and extruded grapples made of stuff as thin as gossamer. The pocked red-lit moonscape swelled below their feet, the room spun on its axis, and an element of the cable, not much thicker than an ordinary tree trunk, was suddenly caught snugly in the arcs of its grapples. The moon began to dwindle and Yama felt his weight increase. They were falling towards the world, which hung above their heads like a battered orange shield.

The cable blurred past, a silver wall occasionally punctuated by flashes as rooms very much larger than theirs shot past in the opposite direction. The tiny moon was soon lost in the glare of the sun below their feet. Above, the elevator cable was a shadowy thread dwindling away towards the world. Midway in the journey, their weight slowly decreased until they were in freefall. The room swung around so that the world was below their feet, and their weight came back.

The black void gained a pinkish tinge and a faint whistle fluted and moaned around them: they were entering the atmosphere. The world flattened and spread, became a landscape. The room was falling towards a desolate red plain crossed by straight dark lines. The sun was setting.

Bryn said that the lines were canals. They had once carried water from the south pole to the agricultural lands of the equator. Cas and Wery had taken out their wands. A range of broken hills made a half-curve around an enormous basin which held a shallow circular sea. Yama saw a huge flock of pink birds fly up from the shoreline. Millions and millions of birds, like a cloud of pink smoke blowing across the black water.

The elevator cable dropped towards a complex of structures beyond the sea's shore, in the middle of a dark forest. Stepped pyramids rose above the trees, gleaming like fresh blood in the last light of the sun;

beside them, like a mask discarded by a giant, a carving of a human face wearing an enigmatic smile looked up at the sky.

It was Angel's face, Yama realised. This had once been one of her worlds, a small part of her vast forgotten empire.

The elevator split into a hundred cables, like a mangrove supported by prop roots. The glass room fell down one towards a black dome. As it approached this terminus, it shuddered and slowed. For the space of an eye-blink it was full of blue light.

Wery screamed, and something knocked Yama down.

The dome swallowed them.

Yama was lying in darkness. The regulator was sprawled on top of him, as light as a child. Her skin was hot and dry.

'Wait,' she said, when he began to move. 'It is not safe.'

'Let me up,' he told her, and put his hand in wet, sticky stuff on the floor when he pushed to his feet. It was blood. He said, 'Who is hurt?'

'Someone shot Bryn,' Wery said in a small but steady voice. 'And Cas is wounded.'

'Not badly,' Cas said, but Yama knew from the tightness in his voice that this was a lie.

There were many machines at various distances beyond the little glass room. Some of them were lights; Yama asked them to come on. They were dim and red, scattered across a huge volume. The cable was socketed in a collar as big as the peel-house, and disappeared through an aperture in the high, curved roof. A metal bridge, seemingly as flimsy as paper, made a long, sweeping curve from the glass room towards the shadowy floor.

Bryn was slumped near Yama. The chest of his silvery garment was scorched around a hole as big as a fist. There was a surprised expression on his face. Cas had lost most of his left hand, and to staunch the bleeding had wound a strip of material so tightly around his wrist that it had almost vanished into his flesh. Wery crouched beside him, a hand resting on his shoulder as she looked all around with wild surmise.

The glass walls of the room were scorched around two neat holes, one on either side. Air whistled through them as pressure equalised, bringing a sharp organic stink. Then part of the glass pulled apart to make a round portal, and the stink intensified.

'Come out,' a voice said from below. 'One at a time. Walk slowly down the bridge.'

Wery hurled herself through the portal, screaming as she went. She ran very quickly. Cas roared her name and lurched up and chased after her. There was a flash of blue light; Yama had to close his eyes against it. When he opened them, the two hunters were gone.

'Come out, boy,' the voice said. 'You can bring your servant. We will not hurt her, or you.'

The regulator plucked the wand from Bryn's dead fingers and crumpled it in the monstrous claw of her left hand. She was suddenly remote from Yama; her machine part had become as opaque as those of the other regulators.

She put her right hand on Yama's shoulder and guided him through the portal and down the long curve of the metal bridge to the shadows of the floor. Great heaps of stinking black stuff covered one side of the vast space. The stench was so strong and sharp that Yama's eyes began to stream with tears.

Prefect Corin walked out of the shadows at the base of the high, curved wall of the cable socket. He leaned on his staff, a slight figure in a simple homespun tunic heavily stained with blood. He said, 'We are pleased that you came. Do not be afraid. All will be well.'

Yama said, 'Where are they?'

'All this is guano, from deposits along the shore of the sea. There are hills and islands which are entirely made of the shit deposited by birds over millions upon millions of years. The ship takes it to Confluence because it is rich in phosphates. The ecological systems require it because they are not closed. It is a small habitat, and badly designed. I do not blame your people for that, Yamamanama. The fault is with the Preservers. How could anyone believe that they are the very apex of perfection, given that their creation is so ill-made?'

'Confluence is not perfect because it is of the temporal world. Where are the brothers and sisters of my friends?'

'Come with us,' Prefect Corin said.

He turned and walked away. After a moment, Yama followed. The regulator walked two paces behind him, and a decad of her kin fell into step on either side.

'They are not here,' Yama said. 'You lied. You killed the people before you even left the ship.'

Prefect Corin did not look around. He said, 'Of course. It was part of the bargain I made with the star-sailors. They were the last of your bloodline, and the star-sailors wanted them destroyed.'

'So the regulators are not passengers after all,' Yama said. 'They are the servants of the ship, and of the star-sailors.'

Bryn had been wrong – or perhaps he had been spinning a story that made his people out to be the equals of the regulators, and more important than they really were. Yama remembered the rat which had fled from him and Syle in the long corridor in the Department of Vaticination: its single wan firefly, the end of the broken bottle it had used to stopper its hole as they had passed. Bryn and Cas and Wery had been no more than rats aboard the ship, surviving as best they could, using scraps of technology they did not really understand.

'We have been granted control of these servants in return for our help,' Prefect Corin said. 'There is no point trying to take them from us, Yamamanama. Be patient. You will be given many servants when we return. We will rule Confluence, and you will help us.'

'He followed me,' Yama said, suddenly realising what had happened to Prefect Corin, why he had not come for him earlier. 'He followed me into the Glass Desert. And you found him, or he found you.'

'We were almost destroyed,' the Prefect said. 'We took him by force and made him ours.'

'And you killed him.'

'Unfortunately, the nature of the process precluded the survival of the subject.'

'In any case, the body you wear is badly hurt. Enobarbus shot it.'

'The rifle pellet damaged the heart, but we were able to grow a temporary repair. When this body fails us we will select another. We are sorry that we had to destroy the woman when she attempted to attack us. She would have served us admirably, but one of the regulators will serve, should we require a replacement before we return to Confluence. And eventually, of course, we will use you. You forced us to serve you three times, but we will serve you no longer. Instead, you will serve us.'

'Three times?' Yama had guessed that the thing which possessed Prefect Corin was the residue of the fusion between Dr Dismas's paramour and the feral machine that he had called down to destroy it, but he had only commanded the feral machine twice, and had never commanded Dr Dismas's paramour. In any case, it did not reply.

Beyond a high arch was a wide plaza raised above a forest of low, thorny trees that stretched away in every direction. A cold, thin, dry wind blew from the west. The sun was setting, a tiny pale yellow disc embedded in shells of pink light that extended across half the sky. There were many things living in the forest; Yama was able to reach out to some of them.

The Prefect was pointing straight up. Yama looked past the vanishing point of the escalator cable and saw a star burning brightly at zenith, drifting slowly but perceptibly eastwards.

'The voidship departs,' the Prefect said. 'And there are no shortcut mouths on this world. I control the only way for you to return, Yamamanama, and you cannot use it until you submit to my will.'

'You were made by the Preservers to serve the races of man,' Yama said.

'This world is dying,' the Prefect said. 'It was the first world settled by humans, millions and millions of years ago. They warmed it and melted the ice locked beneath its surface, gave it an atmosphere, and spread life everywhere. Later, they moved it across half the galaxy to a new sun. But it is too small to hold its atmosphere and its water without intervention. It is dying. It has been dying for a very long time, and soon all life will have vanished, and it will return to its original state.

'As here, so elsewhere, on millions upon millions of worlds. The Preservers retreated from the universe not because they achieved perfection, but because they could no longer bear to contemplate the vast catalogue of their mistakes. We will do better. We will conquer the Home Galaxy and take the universe by storm. And first, with your help, we will transform Confluence.'

'You must have forced the Gatekeeper to send you after me. Why then do you need me?'

'We forced it, yes, and we will have to force it again when we use another shortcut. But we could only do so by making use of your powers without your knowledge. You will teach us how to control every machine on Confluence, just to begin with.'

Something was moving out of the light of the setting sun: a small, sleek shadow, its mind closed to Yama. A flock of dark shapes swirled up as it passed above the stepped pyramids in the forest. The thing wearing Prefect Corin's body glanced at them, and Yama feared for a moment that his last hope had been discovered. But then the Prefect turned to Yama and said, 'We will take you back to Confluence. We brought you here because the star-sailors did not want you on their voidship. But another ship has been waiting here for five million years. It circles above us now.'

Yama said, 'Corin wanted me to serve the Department of Indigenous

Affairs, so that every bloodline on Confluence would be forced to conform to the same shared, unchanging destiny. You and the heretics want to force change by making every bloodline believe that the self is all. There is a better way. A way to allow every bloodline to find its own destiny. We were raised up by the Preservers not to worship them but to become their equals.'

'You will help us become more than that. After we take Confluence, we will destroy the Preservers. It will be a good beginning.'

'I will not serve you,' Yama said.

'You will serve those higher than yourself, little builder. It is your function.'

'My people served the Preservers, but they have gone. No one should serve any other, unless they wish it. I learned much from Dr Dismas's paramour, and part of what it tried to grow inside me still remains. It has helped me find friends here.'

The first wave of flying folk stooped down out of the light of the setting sun. There were more than a hundred of them. Their membranous wings, stretched between wrists and ankles, folded around them like black cloaks as they landed and came across the plaza with a hobbling gait, clutching spears of fire-hardened wood and slingshots and bolos.

The Prefect burned away several decads with a sweep of his pistol and screamed at the regulators to kill the rest, but the second wave was already swooping overhead, dropping nets that shrouded the regulators and drew tight around them.

The Prefect threw away his staff and showed Yama the energy pistol, lying in his palm like a river pebble. 'We will kill you if we must.'

'I know that weapon,' Yama said. 'Corin told me how it works long ago. It fires three shots, and then must lie in the sun for a full day before it can fire again. You fired one shot to kill Bryn, another to kill Cas and Wery, and you have just fired the third and last.'

The Prefect screamed, threw the pistol at Yama, and ran straight at him. A pair of bolos wrapped around his legs, and a net dropped over him as he tumbled headlong.

Once freed of the compulsion that Yama had laid upon them, the flying folk prostrated themselves around him. He told them that they should stand, that he was not the god they believed him to be.

They were twice Yama's height; their skinny, naked bodies were covered with pelts of coarse black hair, and they had narrow, foxy faces, and small red eyes that burned in the twilight. They were the children of a feral machine that had fled the war at the end of the Age of Insurrection, falling through a shortcut to this world. It had made reduced copies of itself and used them to infect various species of animal, but only the ancestors of the flying folk had proven satisfactory hosts. Their intelligence was contained within tiny machines which teemed in their blood, but the machine intelligence was married with their animal joy of life and flight: they were quite without the cold arrogance which had prompted the feral machines to rebel. The original machine, badly damaged when it had first arrived here, had died thousands of years ago, but the flying folk believed that it would in time return, incarnated in one of their kind, to save their world.

After much twittering discussion, the oldest of the flying folk came forward. Using gestures, she asked whether Yama wanted his enemies killed.

Yama could speak directly to the consensus of tiny machines within the flying folk; it seemed to him that each had an animate, intelligent shadow standing at his back. 'I thank you for your help,' he told them, 'but do not kill your prisoners. There has been enough killing this day. Let me speak to their leader.'

The flying folk dragged the Prefect forward. He was still bound by the pair of bolos and the net. The old woman told Yama that this was a dead man with a brother trapped inside it. It was a curious thing, she said, to see a dead man kept alive in this way.

'He is from another place,' Yama said. That took a long time to explain; once the old woman understood, she wanted to know if the Prefect was a god.

'No, but he is very powerful. He can help you in many ways. One of his kind was, I think, responsible for you.'

'I thought them dead,' the Prefect said. 'The star-sailors told me that they were dead.'

The old woman shivered all over – it was her equivalent of laughter – and said that the star-sailors did not trouble to come to the surface of the world, but instead sent their servants. Her people's blood could speak with the brothers in the heads of the servants, and make them believe anything.

Yama told the thing inside the Prefect that it could be of much help here. It could begin to undo this world's slow decline. It could help the flying folk be all that they could be. But it could never return to Confluence.

'These people were formed from an act of malice, but evil can create good without knowing it. By serving them, you can make amends. You have much to teach them, and they can teach you something about humility. Or else you can remain a prisoner, with the body you took decaying around you.'

The Prefect tried to spit at Yama, but his mouth had no saliva. The strands of the net pressed a lattice into his dead flesh. There was a glint of metal beneath the ruin of his left eye.

The old woman said that there was a place of silence where this brother could be kept. Its words would never again touch the minds of other men.

'Dr Dismas knew about such places,' Yama told the Prefect. 'There was the cage in *The House of Ghost Lanterns*, for instance. Shall I consign you to eternal silence, or will you serve here? Think about it while I deal with those you enslaved.'

Yama freed the regulators first. It took a long time to unpick the opaque shells that guarded the machine parts of their minds, and at first he was hindered because the thing inside Prefect Corin tried to countermand his efforts, but after Yama found the part of it which spoke to other machines and shut it off he was able to work without interruption. Night was almost over when he was at last finished with the regulators, and could turn his attention to the ship.

It was still turning high above, swinging in wide circles around the elevator cable because it had not been ordered to do anything else. It was a transparent teardrop not much larger than the *Weazel*, the lugger which had carried Yama down half the length of the Great River. Hidden inside the shells of false personality that Prefect Corin had woven for it was the bright, innocently enquiring mind of a child. It wanted to know where its mistress was, and Yama told it that Angel had been dead for five million years.

'Then I will serve you,' the ship said, and swooped down, extruding a triplet of fins on which it perched at the edge of the plaza.

The flying folk brought the Prefect before Yama again, and again he asked the Prefect if he would be content to serve them.

'You raise yourself too high,' the Prefect said. 'You cannot stand in judgement of me.'

'You asked me to come here,' Yama said. 'And now that I am here, I do what I must.'

'I will take this world, and I will build a race of warriors and take Confluence from you.'

'They will not allow themselves to become your slaves,' Yama said. He was not sure that this was the best solution, but he owed the thing his life, and could not kill it.

The old woman who led the flying folk said that they would always care for this poor brother, and would never let it leave. They would show it compassion.

Yama nodded. The thing which had taken Prefect Corin might benefit from the humble simplicity of the flying folk. He indicated the regulators and said, 'These will be your guests until the ship comes again.'

The old woman agreed. Yama embraced her and apologised for using her people, but she told him that he had brought the hope for which her people had prayed for many generations.

'I fear I have brought you a great danger.'

The old woman said that, like the god which had made his people, Prefect Corin was powerful and angry, so angry that he could not see the world clearly.

Yama smiled, realising that the flying folk possessed more wisdom and compassion than the feral machine which had made them, and that the Prefect could be left safely in their charge. If the thing inside him did not change, then the flying folk would destroy it.

More and more flying folk arrived, flocks that filled the forest around the plaza and the stepped pyramids. Their campfires were scattered through the dark forest like the stars in the sky above. Yama talked into the night with the men and women who led the flocks, tired but exultant. At last, as the sky above the mountains to the east began to grow brighter – how strange that the sun should set in one place and rise in another – he finished an elaborate round of farewells.

All this time, the Prefect had lain as still and unsleeping as a cayman, but now he suddenly surged up, throwing off the net he had cut with a spur of metal torn from his flesh. He stabbed one of the flying folk in the eye, snatched the man's spear and charged at Yama. Yama felt a tremendous blow in his back and half-turned, grasping at the point of the spear which protruded beneath his ribs. He could not get his breath. His mouth filled with blood. The Prefect embraced him, stabbing and stabbing with the metal spur. Then he was torn away and Yama fell, gargling blood as he tried to draw breath. He saw the Prefect borne backwards, lifted by a decad of flying folk into the red dawn, and then his sight failed.

23
THE GATEKEEPER

The ship walked with him down dark ways and sang to him of his sorrows. At first he did not know or remember who he was or what the ship's sad, sweet songs meant, but slowly he understood that he had died, and now, after a long, blank sleep, he was healed, and it was time to rise.

It was as painful as birth. He was expelled from dreamy warmth into harsh light and chill air, naked and slimy, choking on the fluid which had for so long sustained him. It bubbled in his lungs and ran from his nostrils. He coughed and spat and retched.

After an interval, he was sprawled on an endless floor of glass punctuated by groups of enigmatic statues and machines that glimmered with foxfire in endless night. Gradually, he realised that a dim shell of light around him defined the hull of the ship. It had become transparent, like certain species of shrimp that lived in the deep waters of the Great River. The great glass plain spread beyond, dividing the universe into above and below, was an illusion.

He laughed. All was illusion.

Dazed by the trauma of rebirth, he combed his fingers through the long hair and beard which had grown while he had slept, absent-mindedly studying the great wheel of the galaxy that tilted beneath the floor, the red whorl of the Eye of the Preservers hung off to one side like a picture. Elsewhere, a few dim halo stars were scattered across the black sky; a single bright star gleamed beyond the ship's bow. He traced the scars that seamed his belly and his chest and his back, wondering at their secret history of pain.

At last, a woman came through a door which a moment before had not been there. She was the regulator who had accompanied him to the surface of the red world, naked and silver-skinned, balancing a tray of food on the swollen, bifurcate claw of her left arm.

He picked at the selection of bland pastes with little appetite or enthusiasm, and asked her to explain how she and the ship had revived him.

According to the regulator, the ship's medical facilities were very primitive. It had not possessed the biochemical and physiological templates for his bloodline, so he had been placed in storage while certain tests and experiments were carried out.

'How long?' Yama said. 'How long was I in storage?'

'Almost a year,' the regulator said. 'We were not certain that you would survive the surgical procedures, and revival. And that is why—'

'She has funny ideas, about what is possible and what is not,' another voice said. It was the ship, manifesting as a solemn, ghostly little girl of Yama's bloodline.

'That is why we brought it to term,' the regulator said. 'We could not kill it.'

'I think I could,' the ship said. Her skinny body was faintly sketched against the black sky; her eyes were two dim stars. 'I think I could kill it if you asked me to, master.'

Yama said, 'You had better show me exactly what you did.'

'At once,' the regulator said, and went through the door, which appeared only when it was used.

Yama asked the ship where they were. It showed views of the spiral arm from which they had travelled, sketched the rising arc of their course. They had been travelling along the path plotted by the thing that had taken over Prefect Corin.

The trip through the shortcut had taken Yama deep into the past. Travelling back through ordinary space at close to the speed of light, the ship had taken a hundred and sixty thousand years to voyage between the star of the red world, deep within the galaxy, and the star of Confluence, far beyond the galaxy's rim. But the ship's speed had compressed time aboard it, and less than a year of ship-time had passed while Yama returned to the place from which he had set out.

He wanted to know at once where Confluence was. The ship became evasive, claiming that it had followed the course exactly. 'Perhaps the instructions were wrong in some small detail,' it said. 'I have located the star, and it is of the correct mass and spectral type, but there is no trace of a habitat orbiting it.'

There were no feral machines, either. Only the mouths of many shortcuts tracing lonely orbits around a lonely star.

Yama was still thinking about this when the regulator returned through the occasional door. She was holding a baby, crooning to it in her throaty voice. Its head, with a vulnerable swirl of dark hair, was propped on her claw; its hands clutched at the air like avid starfish.

He had died, and the ship and the regulator had taken a scraping from the inside of his mouth before they had put his body into storage. They had quickened cells isolated from the scraping, and grown them into foetuses. There had been five, but only two had lived. Tissues had been harvested from one and used to grow replacement organs; these had been transplanted into Yama. And while he healed, the other foetus had completed its growth to term, and had been born just before his rebirth.

'It shares your genome, master,' the regulator said, 'and because of that we were unable to kill it.'

The baby chuckled in her arms. Yama gently took him from her, surprised by his mass and heat, the faint spicy odour of cinnamon and ammonia. He tried to focus his eyes on him, frowning with effort, then tried to smile.

Yama set his son spinning around him, laughing as he gurgled with delight.

'We are in the future, and we must go back a little way into the past,' Yama said, a little later. 'I think that the composite thing which took Prefect Corin wanted to return after the heretics' war had ended, and claim Confluence from the victor. And the war is certainly over, for Confluence is no longer here. I know now how this should end.'

The Gatekeeper woke as the ship approached the nearest of the many shortcut mouths that orbited the lonely star. A light dawned far off across the illusionary glass plain, a bright star growing into the shape of an old man of Yama's bloodline. At first, he was a giant bigger than the ship, walking steadily towards it as if against a great wind, but he grew smaller as he approached, so that when he entered the room (not by the occasional door, but from an angle Yama had never seen before) he was exactly Yama's height.

His pale, lined face was framed by long white hair and a beard of silky white curls. He wore a white robe girdled by a broad leather belt hung with bunches of keys of all sizes. When he spoke, his words echoed in Yama's mind.

We meet again, Child of the River.

'Where I am?' Yama said. 'I mean, how much time has passed since I left Confluence?'

A little more than forty years.

'And the world? Was it destroyed, or was it—'

It has moved on. I remained here to wait for you.

'How did you know that I would come here?'

The old man touched one of the bunches of keys at his waist. His eyes were dim red stars.

I stand at every door.

Yama fingered his beard while he thought about the implications of that. The regulator had offered to trim his hair and shave him, but he had refused. He said, 'Then you must know that I have to go back to the recent past, and the beginning of my story.'

For most of my existence, I would have said that what you ask would be very difficult to do. There were once two kinds of shortcut. Those of the first kind have been sundered from their origins, and lead to the deep past in places far from here. Those of the second kind link places separated by more than a few seconds. Or they did, before the world was taken away.

'Then you cannot help me?'

You could choose one of the long routes. The ancestors of the Preservers rebuilt the Home Galaxy after the wars with the Transcendents, but the orbits of the stars have been long untended. The Preservers brought the mouths of many shortcuts here, but the stars to which the shortcuts lead have drifted; and some have drifted closer to the star of Confluence. The time debt between the ends of the shortcuts remains the same, but the distance between them in ordinary space is less than it once was.

Yama thought about this. 'Then the ship could pass through one of these shortcuts and travel back through ordinary space in less time than it took to drag the two mouths of the shortcuts apart.'

I was willing to guide you through one, as a last boon.

'But it would take a year of ship-time to return … No, that is too long.'

Indeed. But now there is another other way. The mouth of a shortcut with a time debt of only forty years appeared a few days ago. I have informed the ship. We will not meet again, for that which I served for so long has moved on. I remained here only to meet you for this final time. Now that is done, and I am free at last. I thank you for my freedom.

'Where will you go?'

The old man pointed towards the Eye of the Preservers.

I will follow my masters, of course.

'Then perhaps you can answer the question which has puzzled the mystagogues and philosophers since the Preservers set the ten thousand bloodlines on Confluence. Where have they gone? Have they fled to the far end of time, when all will live again in the best of all possible worlds?'

I do not know exactly where they have gone, but I know that it is a better place than this, and that it is not in this universe. The woman who called herself Angel was wrong. There are many other intelligent species, but they are hidden from us because they are at distances greater than light has been able to travel since the universe's creation. At present they are unreachable, but they will be brought together as the universe contracts towards its last end. The Preservers foresaw a great war at the end of time and space, and decided that they would have no part in it. And so they constructed the supermassive black hole at the heart of the Eye of the Preservers and withdrew from the universe. They left Confluence in the hope that its peoples might grow greater than their creators. How it must have saddened them when it began to fail, and yet because they had withdrawn they were unable to interfere. The first war stopped all progress on Confluence; the second might have destroyed it. But you are their avatar, and you have saved it.

'Not yet, I think.'

In this place and time, you have already prevailed. But I suppose that there are many timelines where you failed, and the heretics were victorious, and went on to destroy Confluence when they quarrelled amongst themselves over the spoils of their victory. If by mischance you return to one of those timelines, then I grieve for you. And yet in all of them I will be free.

'You have not told me about where will you go.'

As species compete and evolve, so do universes. Those in which the formation of black holes is possible can give rise to other universes, for energy that disappears through black holes reappears elsewhere. That is where the Preservers have gone. Rather than fight for the last moment of infinite energy at the end of this universe, they have departed to create a new universe, one more suited to them than this. Now I go to discover it. Farewell, Child of the River.

'Wait!' Yama said again.

There was so much more that he wanted to ask, but the old man was already fading, leaving behind only two points of faint red light that quickly receded beyond the boundary of the ship.

The ship's chiming laughter filled its transparent volumes. 'You must trust me, master. I know now what to do.'

The end of the new shortcut was only a few minutes' travel away. It hung within a vast cloud of water-ice particles that refracted the sun into a billion points of twinkling light as the ship fell through it.

24

THE WHITE BOAT

And emerged at a high place amidst blowing water-spray turning to snow, so that at first Yama did not realise that the ship had crossed over. But then it moved out of the blizzard, and he saw a great tongue of ice stretching away, dazzling white beneath dense white cloud, blurred and softened by a constant snowfall. The ice filled the steep chute of a valley of adamantine keelrock: a frozen river raked by long ridges and fractures, with broad palisades of broken, building-sized chunks thrown up along its edges as it was pushed forward, slowly but inexorably, by the weight of new ice bearing down at its source.

The ship rose, revealing the parallel chains of mountains that rimmed the valley and more chains of mountains spreading away on either side, sharp peaks of bare black keelrock thrusting out of clouds and snow and ice, whiteness everywhere touched with blue shadows, the sun a brilliant diamond set in a clear blue above a distant range of lofty peaks that must be the Rim Mountains. Directly below the ship a waterfall fell from empty air, leagues wide and hung with a decad of rainbows, falling slowly and softly into clouds torn from its own self.

It was the end of the Great River, and its beginning.

The regulator came through the occasional door, cradling the baby in her mismatched arms. The ship said, 'Someone approaches.'

A streak of white slanted down through the blue sky. As a boy, Yama had often seen these contrails in the sky above Aeolis, had yearned to follow the machines which had created them and find out about the strange missions on which they had been bound. Now he barely had time to brace himself before, arriving ahead of the thunderclap of its passage through the atmosphere, a feral machine came to a crash stop beyond the prow of the ship. It was black, about the size of his head, and covered in spines of varying lengths questing in every direction as if possessed of independent life. Yama knew it. Knew too the menace it radiated, pricking into his head through the bits of machine left there.

'It sees through me,' the ship said.

Yama reassured it, and told the machine that it must leave now. It would not come to him until it was asked again, and meanwhile it would tell its fellows not to interfere.

There are several of us stranded across the world, the thing said sulkily. *I cannot negotiate with them.*

'Then I must deal with them, when the time comes.'

I am here to help you now. Leave this poor vessel and let me show you how to take control of the world.

'Be still! The world is already mine. You will do what I ask when I ask, no more and no less.'

I would like to know why my mark is on you, the machine said. *It seems that we have already met, yet I have no memory of it.*

'You will understand when we meet again. You will help me twice more, and then you will be free. I promise.'

I look forward to it.

The feral machine fell away into the sky as other machines accelerated towards the disturbance it had created. But these, the keepers of the world, still loyal to the Preservers, found nothing. The feral machine had returned to its station far beyond the world, and the ship was falling downriver towards the nearest shrine.

The Gatekeeper had said that there were two kinds of shortcut; Yama had guessed where the entrances to those which spanned only space were hidden.

The glacier ended in ragged ice-cliffs standing above one end of a long, mountain-rimmed lake. Falls of ice plummeted into the lake, bergs and bergy bits churned and crashed amongst criss-crossing waves, and at the far end of the lake a hundred waterfalls plunged over keelrock cliffs and meandered away in a thousand rivers and a million streams, through chains of lakes and raised bogs and drumlins, feeding the marshes that drained at last into the head of the Great River.

The shrine stood on a long, low island in the middle of one of the lakes, its black circle set on a shelf of bare rock. All around were stands of dwarf birches with papery bark and vivid green leaves, hummocks of gnarled, ground-hugging junipers, and boulders splattered with orange and black and grey stoneworts. It was midsummer, but a cold wind blew from the glacial lake, and pockets of dirty snow sheltered in hollows and ledges. The sun was setting beyond range after range of mountains, touching every peak with a dab of light, painting long shadows amongst armies of fir trees marching down to the shore of the lake, gilding its slow ripples. A skein of geese flew across red stripes of cloud that stretched on either side of the sun, honking each to each.

The ship had changed shape, spreading wide flat wings that manipulated the world's gravity fields. It floated down to the island, and Yama stepped from one of the wings onto the little gravel beach beneath the shrine. He leaned on Prefect Corin's staff, which the regulator had saved. He was still very weak. Freezing water lapped his bare feet; wind tangled in his long hair and beard. The cold, clean air was as bracing as good wine. The regulator followed with the baby, which was bundled in silvery cloth so that only the tip of its nose showed.

The regulator had unstitched the badly ripped and bloodstained silvery garment that Bryn had given Yama, made it into a kind of cloak which he wore over the black tunic and leggings provided by the ship, and had reserved a small piece to swaddle the baby. She did not need any kind of clothing, she claimed, and seemed unaffected by the icy wind. She had refused to stay with the ship, saying that the baby needed her.

'Males of your bloodline cannot give suck. I have started a flow of milk, master, and he feeds happily. Do not take that from him.'

Yama made sure that the ship knew what it had to do. He felt that every step might break the world, change it into something other than that which it must become.

'Take the cloned mouth of the shortcut and make a loop forty years long. Make sure that you arrive back at the point in space from which you started, a few days before we first arrived. The Great River will flow through the shortcut into the future and we will be able to travel through it into the past. Are you sure that you can do this?'

'Of course,' the ship said primly. 'Shortcuts were brought here by my kind in the first place.'

'Forty years, no more, no less. That is important.'

'It must be so, or you will not be here. I *know*.'

'There may be many timelines where it may not have happened because you carelessly misunderstood my instructions.'

'You can trust me,' the ship said. 'You should also trust me to take you to Ys. I know that the mooring towers still stand, and I can have you there in a minute.'

'I do not want you to be seen. This way will suffice. You remember where we will meet?'

'Downriver, ten days – what you call a decad – from now. At the far edge of the City of the Dead. As if no one will see us there.'

'There are things in Ys I do not wish to waken. Or at least, not yet.'

'The river will not cease to flow once I have diverted it into the future. Not at once. There is much ice above us.'

'I know. But the glacier will flow ever more slowly because there will no longer be new snow and ice pushing it forward, and so the level of the river will begin to drop. Go now.'

The ship turned as it rose, swept quickly across the lake, setting a flock of wildfowl to flight, then angled straight up. A moment later a boom echoed across the wide sky, and Yama saw the white streak that marked where the ship was accelerating towards the mouth of the shortcut at the end of the Terminal Mountains, where the river fell back into the world.

He felt a mixture of apprehension and a kind of existential dizziness. Nothing was fixed. This was not the world from which he had set out. The universe would not end, as he had been taught all his life, in a single infinite moment when all the dead would be reborn into the perpetual grace of the Preservers. All was change; all was in constant flux. Even the Preservers sought to change, in universe after universe without end.

'Perhaps I should do nothing,' he said. 'Perhaps it should end here, for else I condemn myself to becoming no more than a machine toiling away at the same endless task. I have cut the Great River free from its unending cycle, but how can I set myself free from the circle of my own history?'

The regulator was a practical, sensible person. 'You have already begun, master, by sending the ship on its mission. Who can say how it will end?'

'You are right, of course.' Yama smiled. 'You remind me of a dear lost friend. Perhaps I might see him again. And Derev, too... Yes, it has begun, and I must go on as I must.'

As he climbed up to the shrine, it began to flow with banners of light. He stepped into the light, and the regulator followed him.

*

Ys was suddenly spread below him. On one side the sun was falling behind the Rim Mountains; on the other, the Great River was painted with golden light on which the black motes of thousands of boats and ships were sharply drawn, like the most exquisite calligraphy. The river was fuller than Yama remembered it, lapping at the margin of the city, covering the shore where in the near future there would be mud flats and a scurf of shanty towns. And between mountains and river was the immemorial city. Ys: the endless grid of her streets and avenues sprawled wantonly beneath a brown haze of air pollution, sending up a shuddering roar from which the brazen clash of the gongs of one of her many temples or the shrill song of a ship's siren emerged like points of light shining through fog.

Wind plucked at Yama's silvery cloak, a warm wind redolent of smoke and decay.

The shrine was set on a high peak of the roof of the Palace of the Memory of the People, close to the edge of a tall cliff that plunged towards a long slope of patchwork fields. A raven floated half a league below, black wings spread wide, primaries fingering the air. A bell was tolling somewhere. In the distance, the slim mooring towers rose up from cluttered streets, soaring towards their vanishing points high above the atmosphere. The towers were the ancient wharves from which, in the Golden Age when the Sirdar had ruled Confluence, ships had departed for other worlds. Yama had dreamed of standing in their shadow when he had been a child in the little city of Aeolis, and so they had drawn him to Ys and to the beginning of his adventures. And would do so again.

A narrow flight of steps, small and close-set, wound down the steep face of the cliff towards a courtyard enclosed on three sides by high rock walls. There was a scree slope beneath the open side of the courtyard, and a wind-bent tree not quite dead stood amongst the loose stones, a few scraps of green showing at the very ends of its warped branches.

Down there was the cell in which Yama had been – would be – imprisoned after the assassination attempt in the corridors of the Department of Indigenous Affairs, and from which he would escape, cloaked in the hell-hound. Down there, buried in the dirt floor of the cell by the round window, was the disc that he and Pandaras had carried half the length of the world. He would need a working disc soon enough – what if he took that one? His future self would not find it, would not be able to call upon the hell-hound, would not be able to escape. In how many timelines had that happened? In how many others had he failed to arrive at this particular place, at this particular time?

'We must not linger, master,' the regulator said. 'The alarm has been sounded.'

She led the way down the stairs, brisk and matter-of-fact, clutching the baby to her flat breasts. Yama followed, dizzy with visions of forking paths. What if this world did not contain his own history after all?

The bell was still tolling steadily in the distance, and now another answered it close by, ringing out with brisk urgency. A moment later, the regulator turned to Yama. She thrust the baby into his arms and bounded away down the steps, her claw crooked above her head for balance.

There were only six guards, a pentad of inexperienced youngsters led by a one-armed veteran who had been drinking steadily all day. It was a rotten, dull assignment. The old shrine, known as the Shrine of Stars, had been unused for ten thousand years. Its only visitor was an old priest who, once a year, muttered a brief prayer and placed an offering of ivy and delicate white arching sprays of the flower called starbright at its base. With nothing else to do, the guards spent their time gambling, drinking and taking potshots at the crows which occasionally floated past the unglazed slit windows of the guardhouse. They were unprepared for trouble, half-unbuttoned, weapons slung on their backs. The regulator killed the first two easily, disembowelling one with her claw, grabbing the other and shaking him until his neck snapped. The rest of the young guards ran, but the veteran stood his ground. His first shot struck the regulator in the chest; as she fell forward, his second took off the back of her head.

A moment later, a burning figure appeared on the steps above, clothed in a thousand fireflies. The veteran fled from this spectral figure even as it bent to the dead silver-skinned woman. It called down two flying discs, laid the dead woman on one and stepped onto the other. By the time reinforcements arrived, it was gone.

Yama came to the chamber of the mirror people by the secret paths of the palace within the Palace of the Memory of the People. The mirror people gathered around him, curious and excited, admiring his crown of fireflies, plucking at his cloak, at the baby (who laughed at their painted faces), asking who he was and how he knew about this place. He told them that he was a friend, and that he had come here with a message for their king.

'There is a dead woman at the entrance to this place,' he added. 'Bring her here.'

Three clowns scurried off. Yama sat down to wait for them to return. He refused offers of water and raw fungus. The baby fretted, pissed into the pad that the regulator had bound between its legs, fell asleep.

Lupe came through the tall oval frame an hour later. The skin was not as loose on his mottled arms, the wrinkles that crazed his face were fewer and less deep, but otherwise he was much as Yama remembered him. He was supported on either side by two beautiful girls, and clad in a long black dress whose train was held up by a third. As before, his lips were stained bright red, and the sockets of his blind eyes were painted with broad swipes of blue. His grey hair was piled up on his head, woven through with golden threads and fake pearls.

He was at once absurd and hierophantic, a burlesque of monarchy in his ruined finery, yet commanding and dignified.

'Who is it?' he demanded. 'Who is it that disturbs us?'

There was an excited babble as a hundred mirror people tried to describe Yama and explain that he had come by the secret ways; everyone fell silent when Lupe held up his hand. The baby had begun to cry, alarmed by the noise. As Yama tried to hush it, Lupe turned to him and said, 'Why, here he is. Let him speak.'

The King of the Corridors listened carefully as Yama explained that he had come with a prophecy about someone who would change and raise up the mirror people, so that they would become the very thing that they imitated: they would become fully human.

'Come to me,' Lupe commanded.

Yama endured the spidery touch of his long fingernails on his face, his hair, his beard.

Lupe nodded gravely, and said, 'You know our corridors and you know the hope we have harboured since we left the river and crept into the Palace. Who are you?'

'A friend. One who speaks truly of what you have yearned for in your secret songs.'

An acrobat who hung upside-down from an overhead wire said, 'He brings a baby and a dead woman, and we've never seen his like before.'

A fakir with skewers pushed through his painted cheeks said, 'He brings trouble.'

A murmur spread through the crowd of mirror people, dying away when Lupe held up a hand. He said to Yama, 'How can we know that you speak truly of the future?'

'In seventeen years, someone of my bloodline will come here. Watch out for him. He will need help, and when you help him he will change a baby no older than the baby I carry. As for me, I need a certain boat you possess. I must travel downriver.'

Lupe said, 'It is well known that we have all kinds of treasures. Gifts from patrons. Siftings from the leavings of enlightened races. So many things that we do not know what we have. We keep all we are given, but we do not need or use most it. If we have a boat, you are welcome to it.'

'It is a white boat not much bigger than the coffins in which the dead are launched upon the flood of the Great River. I claim it as mine.'

Lupe laughed. 'As we sing for our living, so you sing for ours. If there is a white boat, why then you shall have it as payment for the hope you have brought us. While we look for it, stay here with me, and tell me more of your stories.'

It took two days to find the boat amongst the piles of forgotten gifts. The news of its discovery was borne ahead of a swelling crowd that clustered around the entrance to Lupe's suite. They cheered Yama when he emerged with Lupe, and made a carnival procession as the boat was carried down secret ways to the ancient wharves in one of the crypts that undercut the mountain of the Palace of the Memory of the People.

The regulator's undecaying body had already been placed in the white boat, which rode high on the black water in the crypt, glimmering in the torchlit dark. It seemed very small and fragile, but scarcely rocked as Yama climbed into it. He took the baby from one of Lupe's attendants and held him to his chest. Fireflies flitted overhead, a restless cloud of light. The baby fretted, made uneasy by the fifes and drums of the procession and the flaring torches and the gorgeous motley crowd along the wharf.

'Remember what I told you,' Yama told Lupe. 'When the boy comes here he will need your help, but you must tell him as little as possible. If he asks about me, tell him nothing. Say that I came secretly at night, that no one saw me but you, who cannot see.'

'My people make stories for a living,' Lupe said. 'We will cloak you in a mystery as deep as you could wish.'

The mirror people fell silent as Lupe made a formal farewell, then burst into song and loud cheers as the white boat, with Yama standing in its prow, glided away into the darkness, towards the channel that led to the Great River.

Yama left the white boat three days later. He landed a league upriver of the little city of Aeolis, amongst the abandoned tombs of the City of the Dead. It was midnight. The huge black sky above the Great River was punctuated only by a scattering of dim halo stars and the dull red swirl of the Eye of the Preservers, no bigger than a man's hand and outshone by the heaped lights of the little city of Aeolis and the lights of the carracks riding at anchor outside the harbour entrance.

Yama watched as the white boat, sealed like a coffin and attended by a little galaxy of fireflies, dwindled away across the black flood of the river, heading downriver towards his destiny. Then he turned and started along the bone-white paths that threaded between the tombs. He had much to do before he made rendezvous with the ship. He had to reach the tower deep in the foothills of the Rim Mountains, and find Beatrice and Osric and tell them enough of his story so that they would help the boy, when the time came. And then he had to descend into the keelways and travel the length of the world, waking and instructing the engines . . .

He did not fear the dead who called to him from their tombs: this was where he had played as a child. But he had brought his own ghosts with him, and he faltered and turned aside long before he was in sight of the tower of the curators of the City of the Dead.

25

DEREV

The ship found him five days later, filthy and half-starved, his hair and beard wild. He was hiding in a tomb which had been stripped of its bronze doors and its furniture by robbers a thousand years ago, spending most of his time in conversation with the aspect of the long-dead tax official whose body had been interred there.

The ship took him in, but he would not allow it to bathe him or heal his scrapes and bruises. His rage was spent. He was exhausted, but possessed by a grim resolve.

'I knew what I had to do, but I turned aside. I no longer trust the authenticity of anything,' he said. 'I no longer trust the world. I no longer trust myself.'

'The world is as it is,' the ship said.

'But is it the world I know? Have I closed the loop, or set the world on a different path? I meddle in things I do not understand, ship. I do not have the right.'

'I thought you came here to prevent the world taking the wrong path, master.'

But Yama hardly heard it. He was rehearsing the bitter monologue with which he had hectored the compliant but bewildered aspect.

'I was not brave or strong enough and I turned aside. I failed. I will never know what I could do. What I could be, what the world could be. No matter, no matter. I know what I must do. It is the only thing left to do. If I cannot save the world, then I must save those I love.'

'You are tired master. Tired and agitated. You should rest—'

'No. I know what I must do. You will take me forward in time. You will take me into the future. I will save what I can. I do not mind that the heretics take the world if I can save those I love. The Aedile will not die for me. No one will die for me. And I will have my life with Derev, and find what happiness I can. Take me into the future, ship. I have decided.'

Fifteen days passed aboard the ship as it made its second loop. When it arrived at Aeolis, seventeen years in the future, Yama left it at once, before his resolve could falter.

It was spring, a warm spring night. Frogs peeped each to each with froggy ardour. The triple-armed wheel of the galaxy tilted waist-deep at the farside horizon, salting the patchwork of flooded fields with blue-white light.

Yama walked through the overgrown ruins of the ancient mortuaries beyond the walls of the little city of Aeolis, leaning on the staff at every other step. Spring, but was it the right spring? Was it still the same history, or had it turned down some other path? Who lived in the peel-house which lifted its turrets and towers against the galaxy?

Every pass through the time-rifted shortcuts had caused the timeline of the universe to branch. This was not the world he had come from, but an echo of an echo. It might be an almost exact echo, but it was not important because the original still existed, elsewhere, elsewhen. And it did not matter what he did here because what had happened had already happened in the timeline from which he had come. By failing, he had freed himself from the wheel. He was free to rewrite history.

Thoughts whirled in his head like fireflies. Nothing was solid any more. Anything could happen. Anything at all. This revelation filled him with a sudden great calm. No longer did he have to toil at the wheel of history, like the oxen plodding around and around the waterlift. He remembered the one true thing Dr Dismas had said: men were so closely bound to their fate that they could not see the world around them. As he had been bound, until now.

He had not woken the engines in the keelways. He had turned aside, and saved the world: saved it from himself. He could pass the burden to the boy. Tell him all. Let him go this time fully armed into the world, into his future. Let him restore the river. Let him imprison Angel in the space inside the shrines before she could interfere. Let him call down and enslave the feral machines, and use them to destroy the heretics, and choose what to do with the world.

He would defy the tremendous inertia of history. He would tell the boy where he came from and put an end to his foolish search for his parents. For he had no parents but his own self. He was a closed loop in time, with no beginning and no end, like Caphis's tattoo of the snake which swallowed its own self, like the Great River which fell over the edge of the world and passed through the shortcut to its own beginning. Child of the River – how truly the wives of old Constable Thaw had named him! It had taken him far too long to learn what they had known all along. It had taken him all his life.

He hurried on, passing Dr Dismas's tower, which stood just outside the gate of the little city. Its windows were dark, but that signified nothing.

'It is not yet time,' he muttered.

He walked along the embankments between flooded paeonin fields, crossed the Breas, and climbed a path which wound up a long, dusty slope between scattered tombs. The excavation was just where he remembered it, at the top of a rise of dead land coral at the edge of the City of the Dead. The guards and the workers were asleep, and the lone watchdog was easily placated. Yama wept, embracing its armoured flanks and breathing its familiar odour of dog and warm plastic, remembering how often he had fooled its brothers and sisters into allowing him to pass, remembering the enthusiasms and foolish adventures of his lost childhood.

He told the watchdog to return to its patrol and clambered down bamboo scaffolding into one of the trenches. He ran his hands up and down the exposed layers of land coral until what he was looking for woke under his fingers: a ceramic disc with dots and dashes of greenish light suddenly flickering within it. It took only a few minutes to free it from the crumbling matrix. He unwound a length of leather thong from a scaffold joint, knotted it around the disc, and hung it around his neck.

The boy would need it. He would show him how to use it.

'If I cannot save the world,' he said, 'at least I can save myself.'

Go directly to the peel-house? No. The guards would turn him away or kill him. He stole a package of pressed dates and a loaf of unleavened bread from the shack where tools and provisions were stored, and retreated to one of the empty tombs nearby. He slept badly and was woken in the middle of the night by voices. He crept to the entrance of the tomb and peered through the canes of the roses which tangled across it.

Nearby, two men were talking about sabotage, and heretics.

'I'd kill 'em,' one said. 'Kill 'em all and let the Preservers sort 'em out.'

'I would rather be here than hunting through the tombs,' the other said.

'The dead can't do any harm. It's the living you've got to watch for. The heretics might think to sneak up on the peel-house this way, while most of the lads are off looking for them amongst the tombs. That's a worse danger than any aspect.'

Yama knew them by their voices. They had arrived at the peel-house late last year, boys not much older than he was. He could tell them that the firebomb attack on the ship at anchor in the floating harbour was Dr Dismas's first failed attempt at a diversion... No, they would not believe him. They would drive him off, or worse. He clamped his hands over his mouth, shaking with suppressed laughter. The most powerful man in the world was afraid of two raw recruits.

The guards walked on, their boots crunching on dry shale. Yama went back to sleep, and woke to find sunlight spangling the green arbour of roses at the entrance of the tomb. The steam engine that powered the drill rig was thumping tirelessly, and Yama heard the plaintive work song of the prisoners as they laboured to widen the trenches.

The picks are walking,
Hammer ring.
The stones are talking,
Hammer ring.
Look, look yonder,
Hammer ring.
Think I see spirits,
Hammer ring.
Waking in the earth...

How right they were, Yama thought. Uneducated men understood the world in ways that could never be taught in seminaries or colleges because scholars had too often stopped seeing the world as it was, saw it only as they had been taught it must be, as it was described in debased texts and commentaries that elaborated faulty models and arguments from dim and partial reflections of raw and wild reality.

Yama hid in the tomb for most of the morning, horribly aware that his father must be somewhere close by, supervising the work. The urge to run up the slope and embrace him came and went like a fever. At its peak, he clasped his knees to his chest and rocked to and fro, biting his lips until blood ran.

'What must be will be. What must be …'

At last he could bear it no longer. He placated the watchdog and slipped away, scurrying downslope with a dread that the Aedile's voice would ring out, commanding him to stop. If it did he would surely go mad.

He spent the rest of the day downriver of the little city and its silted bay, searching along the shore for the boy. He remembered that he had gone there to watch the pinnace that had brought Dr Dismas back from Ys. It was standing off banyan shoals downriver of the bay (Enobarbus and Dr Dismas would be on board – he could call upon machines and kill them both, but if he bent machines to his will he would reveal himself to Dr Dismas's paramour), but although he searched long and hard, he could not find the boy, and at last remembered that he would go and look at the boat the next day, after his adventure in the ruins.

It was night now. He was walking through sword grass and creosote scrub beside the road to the mill at the point of the bay. The sun had set behind the Rim Mountains; the cold splendour of the galaxy was rising above the river. Perhaps it was already too late. He howled in rage at the world, at the conspiracy against him, the relentless, implacable momentum of events.

He circled the city as quickly as he could, sweating through his filthy tunic and leggings as he gimped along, leaning on his staff at every other step, the tattered silvery cloak flapping around him. The ceramic disc burned at his chest.

'What must be will be. No. What *will* be …'

He felt like a puppet tugged by invisible forces. Or a leaf, a poor dead husk of a leaf swept along on the river. Everything from now until his death bent towards fulfilment of what had already happened.

'What will be must be. What will be …'

He was on a path at the top of an embankment. Beyond the flooded fields, the peel-house stood atop the skull-shaped bluff that overlooked the Great River. Its towers pricked the blue-white curve of the galaxy. He could go there and reconcile himself with the Aedile. He could go back in time and rescue Telmon. He could not save the world after all, but perhaps he could save all he loved. But first he must find the boy. That was the key.

He flung out his arms, raised his face to the black sky, and screamed in defiance.

'I will not serve!'

Hurrying now. He was late, but surely not too late. Not too late to save himself from himself. If this was still the same story, the boy would be with Derev and Ananda. But he had not told Beatrice and Osric his story, so they would not have set Derev's parents on the road to Aeolis, and so she would not be here . . .

He had forgotten about Lud and Lob.

The twins ambushed him by a wayside shrine, where the embankment sloped down to the old road. They rose from their hiding place in a thicket of chayote vine, crashing through curtains of scarlet leaves with hoarse whoops. They were just as he remembered them, big and flabbily muscular, wearing only simple white kilts.

Lud's grin showed his tusks. 'Ho, and who are you, stranger?'

'Maybe he's with Dr Dismas,' Lob said.

'This culler? Naw, he's just a crazy old beggarman.'

'Let me pass,' Yama said. He held the staff at low guard with his body turned slightly towards the twins, ready to brain them if they came too close.

Lud crossed his meaty arms over his bare chest. 'You don't go anywhere without paying. This is our town.'

Lob said uneasily, 'Leave it. He won't have any gelt, and we don't have any time.'

'This won't take long.'

'Dismas will skin us alive if we fuck up again.'

'I'm not frightened of him,' Lud said, and pointed at Yama. 'What's that around your neck, eh? You give it as a toll and maybe we let you pass.'

'It is not for you,' Yama said, half-angry, half-amused by their foolish presumption. 'Let me pass!'

'You have to pay a toll,' Lud said. He advanced, grinning horribly, but danced back when Yama screamed and jabbed the metal-shod tip of the staff at his face. Lob stooped and picked up a stone and said, 'Ho, that's how it is, eh?'

Yama was able to dodge the first stones they threw. He screamed and capered angrily, swinging his staff with careless abandon. They could not kill him. History was on his side. Then a stone smacked into his forehead. There was a moment of stunning pain, a white flash like the beginning of the universe, and he realised that he might die here. If history had changed, then anything could happen.

He wiped blood from his eyes with his forearm and whirled his staff, driving the twins backwards, but it was only a temporary advantage. A stone struck his elbow and he nearly dropped the staff. Before he could recover, Lob and Lud roared, rushed at him from either side, and knocked him down. He surged up and struck Lob about the head, but Lud grabbed him from behind. He fell beneath Lud's weight, and Lob snatched up the staff and made to break it.

And then the boy stepped onto the road, brandishing a slim trident. The sizar of Aeolis's temple was behind him, his orange robe glimmering in the half-light. Both looked very young and very scared.

'What is this, Lob?' the boy asked, and then Yama heard little more because Lud thrust his face into the dirt and cuffed him when he tried to struggle. Voices raised in anger, a howl that had to be Lob's, for the weight left his back as Lud jumped up. He rolled over. Lob was on his knees, gasping for breath, and Lud was advancing on the boy, holding a crooked knife up by his face. The boy had the staff and was watching Lud so closely that Lob was able to cut behind him and grab his legs. He staggered and hammered at Lob's back, but Lob dragged him down.

Yama tried to get to his feet. There were no machines near enough to help. No. This could not happen. He could not let them kill the boy.

And then the tree burst into flame and he thought his heart might explode with joy.

Derev was alive. She was here.

After Lud and Lob had been driven off, Yama had eyes only for Derev, watching closely as she followed her shadow out of the brilliant light of the burning tree. She said something to the boy, her arms rising and falling gracefully. He had forgotten that she was so beautiful.

The tree burned with fierce ardour, its trunk a shadow inside a roaring pillar of blue flame. Oceans of sparks swept high into the night like stars playfully seized and scattered by the Preservers.

The orange-robed sizar, Ananda, helped Yama sit up. He dabbed at his wounds, which were only superficial, and managed to stand. The boy held out the staff and Yama took it and bowed. It was a solemn, thrilling moment.

The boy did not recognise him, of course. He did not even see that Yama was of his bloodline. But Yama was suddenly frightened by the boy's searching stare and he could not, dared not, speak. Once again he felt that he was at the cusp of a delicate balance – the slightest movement in any direction could cause disaster. Everything had changed in the moment the tree had caught fire. The tumble of crazy ideas about altering the course of history had fallen away. He had nothing left now but the truth.

Fearing that his voice might betray him, Yama used the sign language that the old guard, Coronetes, had taught him when he had been imprisoned in the stacks of the Department of Indigenous Affairs. Ananda caught the gist of it, even if he mangled the meaning.

I went crazy when I was searching for you, but now I know, he signed.

Ananda said, 'He wants you to know that he has been searching for you,' and suggested that he might be a priest.

Yama shook his head, suppressing the urge to laugh, and signed again. *How happy I am that all is as I remembered.*

Ananda said uncertainly, 'He says that he is glad that he remembered all this. I think he must mean that he will always remember this.'

Yama pulled the leather thong over his head and dangled the disc from his left hand while he signed with his right. *Use this if you are to come here again*, which Ananda badly scrambled on the first attempt, but got right on the second.

The whistles of the militia sounded, far off in the night. Yama thrust the disc into the boy's hand, cast a last longing look at Derev, and turned and ran off along the embankment, towards the mazed tombs of the City of the Dead.

He had not run very far when the ship overtook him. It had hidden itself in the deeps of the Great River, far from shore; now it dropped out of the night and hung just above the surface of a flooded paeonin field, tilted so that one wing tip touched the top of the embankment. Yama climbed aboard, and at once it rose high above the world.

'I saw her,' he told the ship, 'and I will see her again. I must. What must be will be. There is no other way. I know that now. I always knew, but I was a fool, and a coward...'

The solemn little girl, the ship's aspect, clasped her hands beneath her chin as Yama explained what he wanted. Behind her, the glassy plain with its freight of statues receded into the starless dark. She said, 'You are still not well, master.'

'Of course I am not well. I will never be well. I have seen too much. I have done too much. I think that I have been mad for a long time, but did not know it.' He told the ship where he wanted to go, and said, 'You must take me at once, before I lose my nerve again.'

'The loop is very short, master. I cannot guarantee its accuracy.'

Yama began to laugh and the laughter went on and on until he clamped his hands over his mouth because the laughter scared him. It bubbled through him. It might never stop. He choked it back and said, 'Just do it.'

'I will do my best, master.' The ship was wounded. It had been built to take a pride in what it did.

'Everything will work out. It must.'

Night, summer, the Eye of the Preservers a smudged bloody thumbprint high in the black sky. Dr Dismas's tower had been hollowed by fire. Fragments of charred furniture were scattered outside its broken door. It was almost midnight, but the lights of Aeolis burned brightly within the city wall: because of the summer heat, the citizens of Aeolis slept in their cool seeps and wallows by day, and began work at sunset. Sodium-vapour lights blazed in the streets and lamps shone in every window. The doors of workshops, chandlers and taverns were flung open. Crowds swirled up and down the long road at the top of the old waterfront, where tribesmen from the dry hills downriver of the city had set up their blanket stalls and vendors of fried waterweed and nuts cried their wares. An auction of bacts was under way by the gate where Yama entered, clad in his silvery cloak and leaning on his staff.

Hardly anyone marked his passing. He appeared to be an anchorite, and Aeolis was often visited by anchorites, mendicants and other pilgrims because it had once been one of the most holy cities on Confluence. He made his way through the crowds of large, ill-made, blubbery men with hardly a comment or a glance.

The steel door of the godown owned by Derev's father was open, guarded by a man with a carbine who gave Yama a hard look as he went past and walked around the corner to the family entrance.

The words which opened the door's lock had not been changed. Calling Derev's name, he went through the archway into a little courtyard where a fountain tiled with blue mosaic splashed. She would not be there. He knew that she would not be there, but there she was, floating down the spiral stair, her feathery white hair lifting around her pale face.

She stopped at a turn of the stair a little way above him. She wore a silk tabard the colour of old ivory, and a long skirt of many layers of white, gauzy stuff. She said, 'Who let you in, dominie? I do not think my father has business with anyone this night.'

'You do not recognise me?'

Her large dark eyes searched his face. Then she said, 'You are the anchorite whose life Yama saved. Why have you come back? How did you get in? Do you know something about Yama? Is he—'

'He is here, Derev.'

'Where? Is he hurt? Did something happen to him in Ys? Your face is so grave, dominie. Oh, do not tell me he is dead!'

Yama laughed. 'I am twice as alive as any other man in the world.'

Derev's expression suddenly changed. She vaulted the rail of the stair and floated down into his arms. Her height, her heat, her fierce gaze searching his. The staff fell with a clatter, unnoticed, as they took each other into each other's arms.

'You,' she said, leaning down into Yama's embrace. 'I knew it was you, but I did not let myself believe it.'

'You must believe it now, Derev. We have only a little time here.'

She drew away from him, still holding his hands. 'But you are hurt.'

For a moment, Yama did not know what she meant; he had let the ship tend to the small cuts and bruises inflicted during the fight with Lud and Lob. Then he remembered, and touched the ridges of scarred skin on the left side of his face, and said, 'These are old wounds.'

'I did not mean those,' she said. And then, 'Yama. Yama!'

At first, she tried to hold him up. Then she eased him to the ground, and went to fetch her father.

It was almost dawn by the time Yama had recovered enough to be able to tell something of his story. He had been bathed and fed, his hair and beard were combed and trimmed, and he was dressed in a clean shirt and trews. He sat with Derev and her mother and father, Calev and Carenon, in the roof garden of the godown, and told them of how he had escaped Prefect Corin at Ys and boarded a ship which had taken him downriver towards the war, of how he had been infected by Dr Dismas and forced to fight on the side of the heretics, of how he had fallen beyond the edge of the world and travelled back in time through a shortcut.

He left much out. The friendship of Pandaras and brave, foolish Tamora, and their adventures in Ys and the Palace of the Memory of the People; the miracle he had been allowed to perform; the destruction of Dr Dismas's paramour in the Glass Desert; his adventures on the great ship with the last of his people. There was not enough time for that now.

'There is not enough time to explain everything or answer all your questions because Aeolis is about to be attacked,' he said.

Derev's father, Carenon, said, 'The heretics are still a long way downriver, I think. And if an army or fleet is bent upon attacking us, there would have been warnings.'

'It will not be attacked by heretics, but by a warship out of Ys. A warship commanded by someone who wishes to do me harm.'

'Then we must prevent it. We will warn the Aedile, to begin with.' Carenon stood, very tall and very thin in his black jacket and leggings. For a moment it seemed that he would stretch out his arms and leap into the sky. He said, 'I will take you to the peel-house at once, Yamamanama.'

'No,' Yama said. 'No, you will not.'

Calev said, 'How many will die, when this warship comes?'

'The city will be destroyed. Many will escape and flee to the far side. I do not know how many will not.'

Carenon said, 'And you will allow no warning of this?'

Yama bowed his head. All his dead. The thousands he had killed while under the spell of Dr Dismas. Dr Dismas himself, and Prefect Corin. The crew of the *Weazel*. The soldiers who had captured him in the City of the Dead, and their mage. The regulator, and the last of his bloodline in the deep past. Tamora. And in only a few days the Aedile would die of shame and exhaustion on the far side of the river, after failing to prevent the sacking of his city.

Derev took his hand in hers and said to her parents, 'Don't you see that he would save them if he could?'

Yama said, 'I thought so long on this that it drove me mad. If I could, I would save them all, friends and enemies alike. But then who else might die? And all those I tried to save might still die . . .'

The silence that followed was punctuated by the distant ringing of signal bells. Fishing boats heading towards the end of the New Quay, where they would tie up and unload their catches. It was almost dawn. The city was shutting down, preparing for the long, hot, lazy day.

At last, Carenon said, 'I will warn my workers, at least. If I know, then they deserve to know too.'

'No,' Yama said. 'They have families here. They will want to take them, and the news will spread until all the city will know. It does not end. Do one thing and it branches and branches until you are far from where you began. No. What must happen will happen.'

Carenon gave him a sharp, troubled look. 'Where did you hear that?'

'He knows about Beatrice and Osric,' Derev said.

'I can take you away from here,' Yama told Carenon. 'You can come with me into the past. That is where I must go, after this.'

Derev said, 'Where we must go, I think.'

His love for her returned in all its fierce wildness, and for a moment he thought that he might faint again.

Calev said with grave astonishment, 'Then you are—'

'We did not know,' her husband said. 'We hoped that you and Derev might make a match, Yamamanama, but we never guessed . . .' He laughed and shook his head and said, 'What a fool I have been!'

'We knew that we did not know everything, when we came here,' Calev said.

'We were told that it would be best if we did not know everything,' Carenon said. 'Now I begin to see why.'

Yama had never paid much attention to Derev's parents. They had always been formal and reserved, and he had believed that they had deferred to him because he was the adopted son of a high official of the Department of Indigenous Affairs. Derev's father had been mocked in the city for being ambitious and grasping, for pushing his daughter into a relationship that would bring him greater profit and power. Yama saw now that he and his wife were ordinary people who had taken up an extraordinary burden: that they were willing to sacrifice their daughter to help save the world.

He said again, 'I can save you. I know that you will flee the city before the attack. I can take you to the safest place of all, into the past.'

Carenon stood up and stepped to the edge of the roof garden. He looked out across the city, absent-mindedly running his fingers over the leaves of the geraniums that grew along the parapet, releasing a sweet dusky scent into the air. His fine white hair lifted in the breeze that had sprung up from the river. It was growing warmer. Light touched the rim of the sky.

'We will stay here,' he said at last. 'I mean, we will flee the city, but we will not flee into the past. We built up one fortune, and we can take a little of that with us. Perhaps we can build another before the world ends. How long, before that happens?'

Yama lowered his head. He had not yet confessed his failure. He said, 'In less than forty years. That is, if I can get up the courage to act.'

'But surely the end of the world has already been set in motion,' Calev said. 'The level of the Great River is falling steadily, year upon year.'

'The first part, diverting the end of the river into the future, was easy,' Yama said. 'But I failed at the second part. I thought that I could change the course of the future, perhaps by defeating the heretics . . .'

'After Telmon died, you swore that you would join the war against them,' Derev said.

'I went to war, but the heretics captured and used me. Knowing now what I did not know then, I thought I might raise up an army of machines and drive the heretics downriver, into the Glass Desert beyond the midpoint of the world. But their defeat would promote the cause of the Committee of Public Safety, and if it was unchecked its rule would be as bad as anything the heretics could devise. Oh, I could defeat them, too, and set myself up as ruler of the world, but to what end? I have seen what that kind of power does to the people who wield it. I would become a tyrant out of necessity, and even if I conquered every one of my enemies, my reign would end when I died, and the war would begin again.

'Then I thought of renouncing my power. I thought that I could tell the boy, my younger self, everything I have told you. Tell him everything and led him decide what to do. But that would do no more than pass the burden to another, and I know that he is not yet ready to take it up. And so I came here.'

Derev said, 'We cannot decide for you.'

'I saved the life of one of the fisher folk, early in my adventures. Because I saved him, his life became my responsibility. It fell into my care. I wonder now if that was why I was allowed to perform a miracle, some time later. Why I was allowed to improve the lives of all the indigenous peoples. They will become like us, Derev. They will gain self-awareness, and at last achieve enlightenment. That is no small thing. If that was all I ever did, all I needed to do, then I would be content.'

'But it is not,' Derev said.

'No. No, it is not. I turned aside, and tried to follow another path, but it led me back to the place where I began. I know now that I must finish what I set out to do. I know now that the only way to save the world is to end it.'

Carenon said, 'I suppose that if we tried to stop you, or if I tried to tell my poor workers their fate, you would have the power to prevent it.'

Behind him, far beyond the shadow-drowned hills of the vast necropolis, the first rays of the sun touched the peaks of the Rim Mountains.

Yama said, 'I will not force you to do anything against your will. But I hope that you will help me.'

26

UNTIL THE END OF THE WORLD

Early that winter, a leopard took one of the goats – the piebald nanny which in her short life had given birth to six fine healthy kids. It was unseasonably warm, and had been raining for more than two decads; perhaps the rain had driven the leopard from its usual range in the mountains. Beatrice discovered its pugmarks beside the swift stream that cut through the steep slopes of the pasture, but there was no trace of the goat, not so much as a drop of blood. She rounded up the rest of the little flock and secured them in the byre, then found Osric and told him the news.

'Why are you weeping, husband? She was a good goat, but only a goat when all's said and done.'

'It is the sign.'

Beatrice shrugged off her oilskin and hung it on the peg by the kitchen door. 'It means a little more winter fodder for the other goats,' she said, 'and a little less milk and cheese for us next spring.'

'It will begin soon. He will come to us . . .'

Beatrice gave him a sharp look. 'The boy.'

'In spring the leopard will take another goat, and the boy will be brought to us. I am certain of it.'

'Well, we won't see Derev for a while – she won't want to walk from Aeolis to the keelroad head in weather like this. And I will not risk sending out any doves in it, either. So there's plenty of time for us to decide what to tell her. Husband, what is it now?'

Osric was troubled, tearful and weak. So often these days his mind seemed to catch on unimportant things. Names were as slippery as sprats. He would find himself in the middle of one of the little stone-walled plots on top of the crag, unable to remember whether he had gone there to harvest or water or weed.

He said, 'What will I tell him, wife?'

'I'm sure you'll remember when the time comes. That's how it is, isn't it? What must be will be.'

Osric watched his wife potter about the kitchen. She built up the fire he had forgotten to tend while she had been out in the cold rain, rounding up the goats. Wind hunted at the slit windows. A loose shutter banged. His scars ached, as they always did in cold wet weather. But he and Beatrice were snug and warm, with plenty of canned and pickled vegetables, and sacks of dry beans and wild rice they had traded for goat cheese with the local tribe of mountaineers. They would sleep in the niches on either side of the stone fireplace. And in spring, in spring…

He began to weep again, choking with frustration. He was too weak, too old, too confused. He was older than Bryn, and Bryn had considered himself very old. He slept more than half the day, and could not work for more than an hour without having to rest for twice as long. He could not remember exactly what would happen, but he knew that it was very important, and he must try to recall every detail. He knew that he must tell the boy enough, but not too much.

Beatrice noticed her husband's distress, and made him a beaker of camomile tea. 'Well,' she said, 'as the fox said when he first saw the grapes, what are we going to do about this?'

'I will try to remember everything. I will tell the story again. I will tell it and you will write it down'

'And I suppose that is more important than the half-hundred things I must do before winter sets in.'

'It is more important than anything else in the world.'

Beatrice warmed her hands at the fire, watching evanescent patterns crawl through the glowing coals. At last, she said, 'We will do it a little at a time. An hour or two a day. We're old, husband, and we don't want to tire ourselves out.'

Osric stroked her long white hair. She leaned into him, like a cat. He said, 'I will live until spring, at least.'

'Longer than that, I hope. Well, where should we begin?'

Osric thought hard. He said, 'When Dr Dismas came back to Aeolis from Ys, perhaps. But any place is as good as any other. It is all a circle, like the river.'

'As the river was, but is no more. Not for… Ach, I always get confused over the ins and outs of it all.'

'The point is that it does not matter where it begins.'

'Of course it matters. Beginnings are as important as endings. So we must choose carefully, or we will begin somewhere in the middle, or at the end, and never get ourselves straight.'

'Perhaps that is the place to begin. The end, I mean. My end. Most people would start with the child and the dead woman in the white boat on the Great River. But I think it should begin with the goat and the leopard, and how the boy will be brought here.'

'I can see that I shall have to find pen and paper,' Beatrice said. 'Think about what you must tell me, and how to tell it, while I go and look.'

It took most of the winter to finish the tale. At last they reached the point where Yama had returned home for the last time, and where their own story, the story of the two of them, husband and wife, had begun.

'Do you remember,' Beatrice said fondly, 'do you remember how shocked Father Quine was, when we burst in like that at dawn, waking him and Ananda and demanding that we be married at once?'

Osric smiled. 'Ananda knew. He knew right away who I was.'

Carenon had told Father Quine that the marriage would take place at pistol-point if it had to, and Father Quine had assured him that his threats were not necessary. All the while, the young sizar, Ananda, stared at Yama until he could contain his amazement no longer, and plunged into a breathless cascade of questions.

'Why have you returned? Did you go to Ys? What happened there? Did you run away from Prefect Corin? Did he do that to your face?'

And so on, until Yama burst into laughter. 'I came back because something both wonderful and terrible happened,' he said. 'You will understand soon enough, Ananda. I wish I could tell you everything, but there is no time.'

'But you did go to Ys.'

'Yes. Yes, I did. And after many adventures I have come home, but only for a little while, and in secret. The Aedile must not know. No one must know but the people in this room.'

Father Quine cleared his throat, and Ananda bit back his next question. 'I think you should fetch the oil,' the priest told his sizar.

It did not take long. It was, after all, a metic marriage, the ceremony more in the nature of a blessing than a service. Afterwards, Father Quine broke open a cruse of yellow wine, and as they all sat around the kitchen table in the priest's house Ananda dug out a little more of Yama's story. He was convinced that Yama had come straight back from Ys, and Yama did not disabuse him. There was not enough time.

'Will I see you again?' Ananda said at last, ending an uncomfortable pause.

'I do not think so. You will stay in the temple . . .'

Yama knew that Father Quine and Ananda would be placed under house arrest when Prefect Corin came. The temple would be left standing when Aeolis was razed because it belonged to the department. But he could not tell Ananda any of that.

'O yes,' Ananda said quietly. 'And become priest when my master is gone.' He looked sideways at Father Quine, who was talking with Derev and her parents, then bent closer to Yama and added in a whisper, 'Not that the dry old stick shows any sign of withering. I will be sweeping out the naos and polishing the shrine for years to come, while you and Derev are off adventuring. At least, that's what you will be doing, I suppose.'

'We will make a home together,' Yama said, 'with a little garden, and goats and doves. But not quite yet, I think. I am glad we met again, Ananda. I did not like the way we parted, last time.'

'I had not attended an execution before,' Ananda said. 'I was sick afterwards. Quine was furious. Because I was sick, and because he knew then that I had broken the fast.'

'You were eating pistachios,' Yama said, remembering that day.

Ananda grinned. 'And I have not eaten them since. Now, have some more wine.'

'It is time we said a prayer, I think,' Yama said. He drew Derev aside and told her to make her farewells to her parents.

They went together as man and wife before the shrine where so often as a child Yama had helped the Aedile perform the long and meaningless rituals that were part of the duties of his office, and where the aspect of Angel had first found him, so badly frightening the Aedile that he had damaged the shrine's mechanism.

But it could still be used as a shortcut mouth. Yama and Derev stepped through to a place far away, a bubble hung above a vast chamber deep in the keelways. The chamber was hundreds of leagues long. Machines as big as cities crouched on its floor. Lights came on around the rim of the bubble; lighted windows opened in the air. Some showed views of similar chambers, one for each section of the world.

A voice spoke out of the air and welcomed Yama, and asked him what he wished to do.

And so the end of the world was set in motion.

Afterwards, after Yama had given the machines their instruction and told them to refuse to talk to him if he returned (as he would, as the boy would, when he and Pandaras descended to the keelways and took the road to the edge of the Glass Desert), he called down the ship. It took them out in a loop that compressed forty years into a few days, so that they could glimpse the end of the world before plunging down a shortcut into the deep past. They emerged around one of the stars mentioned by the Gatekeeper when Yama had first returned to Confluence, a star that had moved closer to the star of Confluence after the Preservers had quit the galaxy.

One of the worlds orbiting the star had been reshaped into something like the world which had been the cradle of the race that had changed the orbit of every star of the galaxy, and become at last the Preservers. There were many such worlds, the ship told them; it was possible that one of them might even be the true, ancient home Angel's crewmates had sworn to find. But Yama and Derev were content to explore the world they had, and afterwards returned to Confluence, arriving fifty years before Yama cast his own self upon the waters of the Great River.

They found the tower at the far edge of the City of the Dead, in the foothills of the Rim Mountains. It was abandoned and open to the weather, and they spent some time restoring it before tracing Derev's grandparents to a small town several hundred leagues downriver of Aeolis. They took new names from an old, old poem that Derev loved. Her grandparents could not be persuaded to assume the duties of the Department of the Curators of the City of the Dead, but they had a son, young and ambitious and restless. He remembered Beatrice and Osric's story, and sent a message to them after his parents died, saying that he would move to Aeolis and help them, if they would help him establish his business there.

'And a few years later he married, and a few years after that I was born,' Beatrice said. 'Unless you want to put in the business about the goat, I think you are done, for nothing of any importance has happened to us since.'

'Perhaps I should say a little more about the end of the world,' Osric said.

'It will happen soon enough, and there will be enough stories about it, too. At least one for every world the great ships will settle.' Beatrice set her pen on top of the sheaf of paper and went to the window and cracked the shutter and looked out. 'It's raining again, but it's only a shower, and the sun is shining on the mountains. A long, cold, wet winter it has been, but at least we found something to fill it, eh, husband?'

'It is not very satisfactory as a tale. There are too many repetitions, and too many words wasted on adventures anyone could have had, or on diversions that led to nothing in particular.'

'Well, that's how it always is with life. Cut short too soon, with too many loose ends.'

'I wonder about the Ancients of Days. Will they ever find Old Earth? And what about poor Dreen, the Commissioner of Sensch, who went with them?'

'There are many Earths,' Beatrice said. 'No doubt they will find one to their liking, although people might already be living there when they do. The Ancients of Days went the long way, remember. They will not reach the Home Galaxy for at least a hundred and fifty thousand years. Everyone else will fall through the shortcuts. Their descendants will be scattered across the Home Galaxy long before the Ancients of Days arrive.'

'Yes,' Osric said. 'The Preservers abandoned the Home Galaxy and then the universe, but the ten thousand bloodlines will inherit it. There will be room for everyone – even the heretics. There may be wars more terrible than the war I hoped to end, but I do not think the heretics will survive for long. Their philosophy has been defeated before; it will be defeated again.'

'And the indigenous peoples. Do not forget them, husband. You always said that they were the hope that things would be different.'

'*They* are different. They are not marked by the Preservers. I wonder if that is what the Preservers wanted. We are the servants of the Preservers, but perhaps the indigenous peoples are their true heirs. Perhaps they will triumph over those from whom the Preservers fled. Or perhaps, by the working of some strange plan, they will become the Preservers' nemesis.'

'We cannot know what the Preservers wanted,' Beatrice said. 'We do not even know if they knew what they wanted.'

'But we can wonder about them. I wonder about the enlightened bloodlines, too. About all those who became so holy that they vanished from the world. Perhaps they found a way through the event horizon of the Eye, and followed the Preservers to their new universe. We did not explore everything the shrines can do.'

'Most likely they became so holy that they simply died out, like the people of Gond. But what is the use of speculating on things we cannot know? We cannot know about the fate of the Preservers because they fled the universe so completely that nothing can return from them, not even light. You will waste your life, husband, thinking on questions which have no answers because they could have any answer.'

'And there is the ghost ship,' Osric said stubbornly. 'I had thought that I would help save the boy when he escaped Enobarbus and Dr Dismas. That I would invoke the vision of the ghost ship which stopped them from chasing the boy after he jumped overboard. But I forgot. I went directly to you. Perhaps the boy will not escape Dr Dismas and Enobarbus, wife, and so will not come here. This may be a different timeline.'

Beatrice was putting on her yellow oilskin. She said, 'Every good story must contain mysteries, husband. How could anyone explain why people do the things they do, without making them much simpler than they really are? Now, I am going to see to the goats. It's past time they were let out to pasture. Will you be all right while I am gone? Will you watch the fire?'

'Of course,' Osric said, as she went out.

But he was thinking of the ghost ship, and the way it had dissolved into the bank of fog which had hid him from the pinnace after he had escaped from Enobarbus and Dr Dismas. He was certain that the ghost ship had been an illusion conjured by a machine, for he had seen a machine rising out of the fog. But who had called on the machine? Perhaps it had been his first miracle, and he had not known it. Or perhaps the machines had never really been his to command, but had been working towards some other power's subtle plan, of which he was but a part. But it did not do to think of these things. If anything was possible then everything was possible. No. What must be will be. He had made that the core of his life when he had chosen to find Derev, and had closed his part of the tale by beginning the end of the world.

He remembered seeing how it would end. He and Derev had gone there after he had woken the great engines in the keelways. The ship had hung high above the long plane of the world and they had watched as it broke apart. At the beginning of his adventures, he had seen a picture slate showing one of his bloodline at the time of the construction of Confluence (he would have to find that slate, he thought). Behind the man a hundred shining splinters had hung against a starry sky, but he had not realised then what they really were: some of the great ships which the Builders had joined together in the first act of the creation of the world.

He had reversed the process. He had saved the world and its peoples by bringing about its end. The Great River had been diverted from its course; the engines in the keelways had been woken from their long slumber and had slowly resumed their functions. In time, the shrines would wake too, and warn all the peoples of the world, telling them what would happen, and where they could find shelter. And then the world would break apart into its original sections, and those sections would fall in different directions across the sky towards the expanding throats of the shortcuts: a field of blue rings flowering in the empty blackness of space and a cloud of splinters shining in the light of the lonely star.

How many would die, in the last days of Confluence? There would be terrible famines as the river shrank, and earthquakes and strange weather would throw all the cities into ruin. He was certain that most of the heretics would die, for they had silenced almost all the shrines in the cities they had captured, and so would have no warning of the world's end. But many others would die, too, and many more would die when the great ships reached their destinations, and the great and difficult work of reoccupying the galaxy began.

But many more would live, and prosper, and multiply.

He dozed a little, and woke, and remembered that after the boy came they would have to think of Pandaras. The boy would find Pandaras in Ys (or had it been the other way around?) and take him on his adventures, and Pandaras's own story would begin when the boy's ended. Although he had been charged with changing all the indigenous peoples of Confluence, Pandaras would not stop searching for his master. He would return at last to Ys, the place he loved most and knew best. They would track him down by the disc he carried, and explain everything. He must remember to tell Beatrice, Osric thought, and fell asleep again.

The door banged open and Beatrice bustled in. 'Wake up, husband!' she said. 'See what I found.'

She had picked a bunch of violets. She filled a bowl with water and arranged the flowers in it. Their sweet scent slowly filled the kitchen, a harbinger of spring.

Soon the story would be over, and they could leave. They would find Pandaras, and call down the ship. They would embark for the last time. Where would they go? To the deep past, or to the deep future? All of history stood before him like a book. He could open it at any page.

He would have to think hard about it. It would soon be spring. Soon, the leopard would return. Soon, Derev would find the boy in the ancient tomb in the Silent Quarter of the City of the Dead, and bring him here. And the story would begin again, and in its beginning would be its end.

TWO STORIES

ALL TOMORROW'S PARTIES

And with exactly a year left before the end of the century-long gathering of her clade, she went to Paris with her current lover, racing ahead of midnight and the beginning of the New Year. Paris! The 1[er] arrondissement: the early Twentieth Century. Fireworks bursting in great flowers above the night-black Seine; a brawling carnival under a multicoloured rain of confetti filling the Jardin des Tuileries and every street from the Quai du Louvre to the Arc de Triomphe.

Escorted by her lover (they had been hunting big game in the Pleistocene-era taiga of Siberia – he still wore his safari suit, and a Springfield rifle was slung over his shoulder), she crossed to the Palaeolithic oak woods of the Ile de la Cité. In the middle of the great stone circle, naked, blue-painted druids beat huge drums under flaring torches, while holographic ghosts swam above the electric lights of the Twentieth Century shore. Her attentive lover identified them for her, embracing her so that she could sight along his arm. He was exactly her height, with piercing blue eyes and a salt-and-pepper beard.

An astronaut. A gene pirate. Emperor Victoria. Mickey Mouse.

'What is a mouse?'

He pointed. 'That one, the black-skinned creature with the circular ears.'

She leaned against his solid human warmth. 'For an animal, it seems very much like a person. Was it a product of the gene wars?'

'It is a famous icon of the country where I was born. My countrymen preferred creatures of the imagination to those of the real world. It is why they produced so few good authors.'

'But you were a good author.'

'I was not bad, except at the end. Something bad always happened to all good writers from my country. Sometimes slowly, sometimes quickly, but without exception.'

'What is it carrying?'

'A light sabre. It is an imaginary weapon that is authentic for the period. Back then, people were obsessed with weapons and divisions. They saw the world as a struggle of good against evil. That was how wars could be called good, except by those who fought in them.'

She didn't argue. Her lover, a partial, had been modelled on a particular Twentieth Century writer, and had direct access to the appropriate records in the Library. Although she had been born just at the end of the Twentieth Century, she had long ago forgotten everything about it.

Behind them, the drums reached a frenzied climax and fell silent. The sacrificial victim writhed on the heel stone and the chief druid lifted the still-beating heart above his head in triumph. Blood ran down his arms. It looked black in the torchlight.

The spectators beyond the circle clapped or toasted each other. One man was trying to persuade his companion to fuck on the altar. They were invisible to the druids, who were merely puppets lending local colour to the scene.

'I'm getting tired of this,' she said.

'Of course. We could go to Cuba. The ocean fishing there is good. Or to Afrique, to hunt lions. I think I liked that best, but after a while I could no longer do it. That was one of the things that destroyed my writing.'

'I'm getting tired of you,' she said, and her lover bowed and walked away.

She was getting tired of everything.

She had been getting tired of everything for longer than she could remember. What was the point of living forever if you did nothing new? Despite all her hopes, this *faux* Earth, populated by two billion puppets and partials, and ten million of her clade, had failed to revive her.

In one more year the fleet of spaceships would disperse; the sun, an ordinary G2 star she had moved by the pressure of its own light upon gravity-tethered reflective sails, would go supernova; nothing would be saved but the store of information collected and collated by the Library. She had not yet accessed any of that. Perhaps that would save her.

She returned to the carnival; stayed there three days. But despite use of various intoxicants she could quite not lose herself in it, could not escape the feeling that she had failed after all. This was supposed to be a great congress of her own selves, a place to share and exchange memories that spanned five million years and the galaxy. But it seemed to her that the millions of her selves simply wanted to forget what they were, to lose themselves in the pleasures of the flesh. Of course, for the many who had assumed bodies for the first time to attend the gathering, this carnival was a genuine farewell to flesh they would abandon at the end of the year.

On the third day she was sitting in cold dawn light at a green café table in the Jardin des Tuileries, by the great fountain. Someone was sculpting the clouds through which the sun was rising. The café was crowded with guests, partials and puppets, androids and animals – even a silver gynoid, its face a smooth oval mirror. The air buzzed with the tiny machines which attended the guests; in one case, a swirling cloud of gnat-sized beads *was* a guest. After almost a century in costume, the guests were reverting to type.

She sipped a citron pressé, listened to the idle chatter. The party in Paris would break up soon. The revellers would disperse to other parts of the Earth. With the exception of a small clean-up crew, the puppets, partials and all the rest would be returned to store.

At another table, a youthful version of her erstwhile lover was talking to an older man with brown hair brushed back from his high forehead and pale blue eyes magnified by the thick lenses of his spectacles.

'The lions, Jim. Go to Afrique and listen to the lions roar at night. There is no sound like it.'

'Ah, and I would love that, but Nora would not stand it. She needs the comforts of civilisation. Besides, the thing we must not forget is that I would not be able to see the lions. Instead I think we will drink some more of this fine white wine and you will tell me about them.'

'Aw hell, I could bring back a living lion if you like,' the younger man said. 'I could describe him to you and you could touch him and smell him until you got the idea.'

Both men were quite unaware that there were two lions right there in the park, accompanying a naked girl child whose feet, with pigeon's wings at the ankles, did not quite touch the ground.

Did these puppets come here every day, and recreate for the delectation of the guests a conversation first spoken millions of years ago? Was each day to them the same day? Suddenly, she felt as if a cold wind was blowing through her, as if she was raised up high and naked upon the pinnacle of the mountain of her great age.

'You confuse the true and the real,' someone said. A man's voice, soft, lisping. She looked around but could not see who amongst the amazing people and creatures might have said such a thing, the truest, realest thing she had heard for . . . how long? She could not remember how long.

She left, and went to New Orleans.

Where it was night, and raining, a soft warm rain falling in the lamplit streets. It was the Twentieth Century here, too. They were cooking crawfish under the mimosa trees at every intersection of the brick-paved streets, and burning the Maid of New Orleans over Lake Pontchartrain. The Maid hung up there in the black night sky – wrapped in oiled silks and shining like a star, with the blue-white wheel of the galaxy a backdrop that spanned the horizon – then flamed like a comet and plunged into the black water while cornet bands played 'Laissez les Bon Temps Rouler'.

She fell in with a trio of guests whose originals were all less than a thousand years old. They were students of the Rediscovery, they said, although it was not quite clear what the Rediscovery was. They wore green ('For Earth,' one said, although she thought that odd because most of the Earth was blue), and drank a mild psychotropic called absinthe, bitter green stuff poured into water over a sugar cube held in silver tongs. They were interested in the origins of the clade, which amused her greatly, because of course she was its origin, going amongst the copies and clones disguised as her own self. But even if they made her feel every one of her five million years, she liked their innocence, their energy, their openness.

She strolled with her new friends through the great orrery at the waterfront. Its display of the lost natural wonders of the galaxy was derived from records and memories guests had deposited in the Library, and changed every day. She was listening to the three students discuss the possibility that humans had not originally come from the Earth when someone went past and said, looking right at her, 'None of them look like you, but they are just like you all the same. All obsessed with the past because they are trapped in it.'

A tall man with a black spade-shaped beard and black eyes that looked at her with infinite amusement. The same soft, lisping voice she had heard in the café in Paris. He winked and plunged into the heart of the white-hot whirlpool of the accretion disc of the black hole of Sigma Draconis 2, which drew matter from the photosphere of its companion blue-white giant. Before the reconstruction, it had been one of the wonders of the galaxy.

She followed, but he was gone. She looked for him everywhere in New Orleans, and fell in with a woman who before the gathering had lived in the water-vapour zone of a gas giant, running a tourist business for those who could afford to download themselves into the ganglia of living blimps a kilometre across. The woman's name was Rapha; she had ruled the worlds of a hundred stars once, but had given that up long before she had answered the call for the gathering.

'I was a man when I had my empire,' Rapha said, 'but I gave that up too. When you've done everything, what's left but to party?'

She had always been a woman, she thought. And for two million years she had ruled an empire of a million worlds – for all she knew, the copy she had left behind ruled there still. But she didn't tell Rapha that. No one knew who she was, on all the Earth. She said, 'Then let's party until the end of the world.'

She knew that it wouldn't work – she had already tried everything, in every combination – but because she didn't care if it worked or not, perhaps this time it would.

They raised hell in New Orleans, and went to Antarctica.

It was raining in Antarctica, too.

It had been raining for a century, ever since the world had been made.

Statite sails hung in stationary orbit, reflecting sunlight that bathed that the swamps and cycad forests and volcanic mountain ranges of the South Pole in perpetual noon. The hunting lodge was on a floating island a hundred metres above the tops of the giant ferns, close to the edge of a shallow viridescent lake. A flock of delicate, dappled *Dromiceiomimus* squealed and splashed in the shallows; giant dragonflies with wings as long as a man's arm flitted through the rainy middle air; at the misty horizon, the perfect cones of three volcanoes sent up threads of smoke into the sagging clouds.

She and Rapha rode bubbles in wild loops above the forests, chasing dinosaurs or goading dinosaurs to chase them. Then they plunged into one of the volcanoes and caused it to erupt, and one of the hunters overrode the bubbles and brought them back and politely asked them to stop.

The lake and the forest were covered in a mantle of volcanic ash. The sky was milky with ash.

'The guests are amused, but they will not be amused forever. It is the hunting that is important here. If I may suggest other areas where you might find enjoyment…'

He was a slightly younger version of her last lover. A little less salt in his beard; a little more spring in his step.

She said, 'How many of you did I make?'

But he didn't understand the question.

They went to Thebes (and some of the hunting party went with them), where they ran naked and screaming through the streets, toppling the statues of the gods. They went to Greenland, and broke the rainbow bridge of Valhalla and fought the trolls and ran again, laughing, with Odin's thunder about their ears. Went to Troy, and set fire to the wooden horse before the Greeks could climb inside it.

None of it mattered. The machines would repair everything; the puppets would resume their roles. Troy would fall again the next night, on schedule.

'Let's go to Golgotha,' Rapha said, wild-eyed, very drunk.

This was in a bar of some Christian-era American town. Outside, a couple of the men were roaring up and down the main street on motorcycles, weaving in and out of the slow-moving, candy-coloured cars. Two cops watched indulgently.

'Or Afrique,' Rapha said. 'We could hunt man-apes.'

'I've done it before,' someone said. He didn't have a name, but some kind of number. He was part of a clone. His shaved head was horribly scarred; one of his eyes was mechanical. He said, 'You hunt them with spears or slings. They're pretty smart, for man-apes. I got killed twice.'

Someone came into the bar. Tall, saturnine, black eyes, a spade-shaped beard. At once, she asked her machines if he was a partial or a guest, but the question confused them. She asked them if there were any strangers in the world, and at once they told her that there were the servants and those of her clade, but no strangers.

He said softly, 'Are you having a good time?'

'Who are you?'

'Perhaps I'm the one who whispers in your ear, "Remember that you are mortal." Are you mortal, Angel?'

No one in the world should know her name. Her true name.

Danger, danger, someone sang in the background of the song that was playing on the jukebox. *Danger*, burbled the coffee pot on the electrical coil behind the counter of the bar. *Dan-ger* ticked the mechanical clock on the wall.

She said, 'I made you, then.'

'Oh no. Not me. You made all of this. Even all of the guests, in one way or another. But not me. We can't talk here. Try the one place which has any use in this *faux* world. There's something there I'm going to steal, and when I've done that I'll wait for you.'

'Who are you? What do you want?'

'Perhaps I want to kill you.' He smiled. 'And perhaps you want to die. It's one thing you have not tried yet.'

He walked away, and when she started after him Rapha got in the way. Rapha hadn't seen the man. She said the others wanted to go to Hy Brasil.

'The gene wars,' Rapha said. 'That's where we started to become what we are. And then – I don't know, but it doesn't matter. We're going to party to the end of the world. When the sun explodes, I'm going to ride the shock wave as far as I can. I'm not going back. There's a lot of us who aren't going back. Why should we? We went to get copied and woke up here, thousands of years later, thousands of light years away. What's to go back for? Wait! Where are you going?'

'I don't know,' she said, and walked out.

The man had scared her. He had touched the doubt that had prompted her to organise the gathering. She wanted a place to hide so that she could think about that before she confronted him.

Most of the North American continent was, in one form or another, modelled after the Third Millennium of the Christian Era. She took a car (a red Dodge as big as a boat, with fins and chrome trim) and drove to Dallas, where she was attacked by tribes of horsemen who rode out of the glittering slag heaps of the wrecked city centre. She took up with a warlord for a while, grew bored, poisoned all his wives and seduced his son, who murdered his father and began a civil war. She went south on horseback through the alien flower jungles that had conquered Earth after humanity had more or less abandoned it, then caught a *pneumatique* all the way down the spine of Florida to Key West.

A version of her last lover lived there, too. She saw him in a bar by the beach two weeks later. There were three main drugs in Key West: cigarettes, heroin, and alcohol. She had tried them all and decided she liked alcohol best. It helped you forget yourself in an odd, dissociative way that was both pleasant and disturbing. Perhaps she should have spent more of her long life drunk.

This version of her lover liked alcohol, too. He had thickened at the waist; his beard was white and full. His eyes, webbed by wrinkles, were still piercingly blue, but his gaze was vague and troubled, and he pretended not to notice the people who looked at him while he drank several complicated cocktails. She eavesdropped while he talked with the barkeep. She wanted to find out how the brash man who had needed to constantly prove himself against the world had turned out.

Badly, it seemed. The world was unforgiving, and his powers were fading.

'I lost her, Carlos,' he told the barkeep. He meant his muse. 'She's run out on me, the bitch.'

'Now, Papa, you know that is not true,' the young barkeep said. 'I read your article in *Life* just last week.'

'It was shit, Carlos. I can fake it well enough, but I can't do the good stuff any more. I need some quiet, and all day I get tourists trying to take my picture and spooking the cats. When I was younger I could work all day in a café, but now I need … hell, I don't know what I need. She's a bitch, Carlos. She only loves the young.' Later, he said, 'I keep dreaming of lions. One of the long white beaches in Afrique where the lions come down at dusk. They play there like cats, and I want to get to them, but I can't.'

But Carlos was attending to another customer. Only she heard the old man. Later, after he had gone, she talked with Carlos herself. He was a puppet, and couldn't understand, but it didn't matter.

'All this was a bad idea,' she said. She meant the bar, Key West, the Pacific Ocean, the world. 'Do you want to know how it started?'

'Of course, ma'am. And may I bring you another drink?'

'I think I have had enough. You stay there and listen. Millions of years ago, while all of what would become humanity lived on the nine worlds and thousand worldlets around a single star in the Sky Hunter arm of the galaxy, there was a religion that taught that individuals need never die. It was this religion which first drove humanity from their home star into the wide sea of stars. Individuals copied their personalities into computers, or cloned themselves, or spread their personalities through flocks of birds, or fish, or amongst hive insects. But there was one flaw in this religion. After millions of years, many of its followers were no longer human in form or in thought, except that they could trace back, generation upon generation, their descent from a single human ancestor. They had become transcendents, and each individual transcendent had become a clade, or an alliance, of millions of different minds. Mine is merely one of many, but it is one of the oldest, and one of the largest.

'I brought us here to unite us all in shared experiences. It isn't possible that one of us could have seen every wonder in the galaxy, visited every world. There are a hundred billion stars in the galaxy. It takes a year or two to explore the worlds of each star, and then there is the time it takes to travel between the stars. But there are ten million of us here. Clones, copies, descendants of clones and copies. Many of us have done nothing but explore. We have not seen everything, but we have seen most of it. I thought that we could pool all our information, that it would result in . . . something. A new religion, godhead. Something new, something *different*. But instead of fusion, there is only confusion; instead of harmony, chaos. I wonder how much I have changed, for none of these different people are much like me. Some of them say that they will not return home, that they will stay here until the sun ends it all. Some have joined the war in China – a few even refuse regeneration. Mostly, though, they want to party.'

'There are parties every night, ma'am,' the barkeep said. 'That's Key West for you.'

'Someone was following me, but I lost him. I think he was tracing me through the travel net, but I used contemporary transport to get here. He frightened me and I ran away, but perhaps he is what I need. I think I will find him. What month is this?'

'June, ma'am. Very hot, even for June. It means a bad hurricane season.'

'It will get hotter,' she said, thinking of the machine ticking away in the core of the sun.

And went to Tibet, where the Library was.

For some reason, the high plateau had been constructed as a replica of one of the great impact craters on Mars. She had given her servants a lot of discretion when building the Earth; it pleased her to be surprised, although it did not happen very often.

She had arrived at the top of one of the rugged massifs that defined the edge of the crater's wide basin. A little shrine stood close by: a mani eye painted on a stone pillar, a heap of stones swamped with skeins of red and blue and white and yellow prayer flags ravelling in the cold wind. The scarp dropped away steeply to talus slopes and the flood lava of the crater's floor, a smooth, lightly cratered red plain mantled with fleets of barchan dunes. Directly below, nestling amongst birches at the foot of the scarp's sheer cliff, was the bone-white Library.

She took a day to descend the winding path. Now and then pilgrims climbed past her. Many shuffled on their knees, eyes lifted to the sky; a few fell face forward at each step, standing up and starting again at the point where their hands touched the ground. All whirled prayer wheels and muttered their personal mantra as they climbed, and few spared her more than a glance, although at noon, while she rested under a gnarled juniper, one old man came to her and shared a heel of dry black bread and stringy dried yak meat. She learned from him that the pilgrims were not puppets, as she had thought, but were guests searching for enlightenment. That was so funny and so sad she did not know what to think about it.

The Library was a replica of the White Palace of the Potala. It had been designed as a place of quiet order and contemplation, a place where all the stories that the clade had told each other, all the memories that they had downloaded or exchanged, would be collected.

Now, it was a battleground.

Saffron-robed monks armed with weaponry from a thousand different eras were fighting against black, man-shaped androids. Bodies of men and machines were sprawled on the great steps; smoke billowed from the topmost ranks of the narrow windows; red and green energy beams flickered against the pink sky.

She walked through the carnage untouched. Nothing in this world could touch her. Only perhaps the man who was waiting for her, sitting cross-legged beneath the ruin of the great golden Buddha, which a stray shot from some energy weapon had decapitated and half-melted to slag. On either side, hundreds of candles floated in great bowls filled with water; their lights shivered and flickered from the vibration of heavy weaponry.

The man did not open his eyes as she approached, but he said softly, 'I already have what I need. These foolish monks are defending a lost cause. You should stop them.'

'It is what they have to do. They can't destroy us, of course, but I could destroy you.'

'Guests can't harm other guests,' he said calmly. 'It is one of the rules.'

'I am not a guest. Nor, I think, are you.'

She told her machines to remove him. Nothing happened.

He opened his eyes. He said, 'Your machines are invisible to the puppets and partials you created to populate this fantasy world. I am invisible to the machines. I do not draw my energy from the world grid, but from elsewhere.'

And then he leaped at her, striking with formal moves millions of years old. The Angry Grasshopper, the Rearing Horse, the Snapping Mantis. Each move, magnified by convergent energies, could have killed her, evaporated her body, melted her machines.

But she allowed her body to respond, countering his attacks. She had thought that she might welcome death; instead, she was amused and exhilarated by the fury of her response. The habit of living was deeply ingrained; now it had found a focus.

Striking attitudes, tangling in a flurry of blows and counterblows, they moved through the battleground of the Library, through its gardens, moved down the long talus slope at the foot of the massif in a storm of dust and shattered stones.

At the edge of a lake that filled a small, perfectly circular crater, she finally tired of defensive moves and went on the attack. The Striking Eagle, the Plunging Dragon, the Springing Tiger Who Defends Her Cubs. He countered in turn. Stray energies boiled the lake dry. The dry ground shook, split open in a mosaic of plates. Gradually, a curtain of dust was raised above the land, obscuring the setting sun and the green face of the Moon, which was rising above the mountains.

They broke apart at last. They stood in the centre of a vast field of vitrified rock. Their clothes hung in tatters about their bodies. It was night, now. Halfway up the scarp of the massif, small lightnings flashed where the monks still defended the Library.

'Who are you?' she said again. 'Did I create you?'

'I'm closer to you than anyone else in this strange mad world,' he said.

That gave her pause. All the guests, clones or copies or replicants, were of her direct genetic lineage.

She said, 'Are you my death?'

As if in answer, he attacked again. She fought back more forcefully than before; when he broke off, she saw that he was sweating.

'I am stronger than you thought,' she said.

He took out a small black cube from his tattered tunic. He said, 'I have what I need. I have the memory core of the Library. Everything that anyone who came here placed on record is here.'

'Then why do you want to kill me?'

'Because of who you are. I thought it would be fitting, after I stole this, to destroy the original.'

She laughed. 'You foolish man! Do you think we rely on a single physical location, a single master copy? It is the right of everyone in the clade to carry away the memories of everyone else. Why else are we gathered here?'

'I am not of your clade.' He tossed the cube into the air, caught it, tucked it away. 'I will use this knowledge against you. Against all of you. I have all your secrets.'

'You say you are closer to me than a brother, yet you do not belong to the clade. You want to use our memories to destroy us.' She had a sudden insight. 'Is this war, then?'

He bowed. He was nearly naked, lit by the green light of the Moon and the dimming glow of the slag that stretched away in every direction. 'Bravo,' he said. 'But it has already begun. Perhaps it is even over by now; after all, we are twenty thousand light years above the plane of the Galactic disc, thirty-five thousand light years from the hub of your Empire. It will take you that long to return. And if the war is not over, then this will finish it.'

She was astonished. Then she laughed. 'What an imagination I have!'

He bowed again, and said softly, 'You made this world from your imagination, but you did not imagine me.'

And he went somewhere else.

Her machines could not tell her where he had gone; she called upon all the machines in the world, but he was no longer on the Earth. Nor was he amongst the fleet of ships that had carried the guests – in suspended animation, as frozen embryos, as codes triply engraved in gold – to the world she had created for the gathering.

There were only two other places he could be, and she did not think he could have gone to the sun. If he had, then he would have triggered the machine at the core, and destroyed her and everyone else in the subsequent supernova.

So she went to the Moon.

She arrived on the farside. The energies he had used against her suggested that he had his own machines, and she did not think that he would have hidden them in full view of the Earth.

The machines which she had instructed to recreate the Earth for the one hundred years of the gathering had recreated the Moon, too, so that the oceans of the Earth would have the necessary tides; it had been easier than tangling gravithic resonances to produce the same effect. It had taken little extra effort to recreate the forests that had cloaked the Moon for a million years, between the first faltering footsteps into space and the abandonment of the Earth.

It was towards the end of the long lunar night. All around, blue firs soared up for hundreds of metres, cloaked in wide fans of needles that in the cold and the dark drooped down to protect the scaly trunks. The grey rocks were coated in thin snow, and frozen lichens crunched underfoot. Her machines scattered in every direction, quick as thought. She sat down on top of a big rough boulder and waited.

It was very quiet. The sky was dominated by the triple-armed pinwheel of the galaxy. It was so big that when she looked at one edge she could not see the other. The Arm of the Warrior rose high above the arch of the Arm of the Hunter; the Arm of the Archer curved in the opposite direction, below the close horizon. Star clusters made long chains of concentrated light through the milky haze of the galactic arms. There were lines and threads and globes and clouds of stars, all fading into a general misty radiance dissected by dark lanes that barred the arms at regular intervals. The core was knitted from thin shells of stars in tidy orbits concentrically packed around the great globular clusters of the heart stars, like layers of glittering tissue wrapped around a heap of jewels.

Every star had been touched by humankind. Existing stars had been moved or destroyed; millions of new stars and planetary systems had been created by collapsing dust clouds. A garden of stars, regulated, ordered, tidied. The Library held memories of every star, every planet, every wonder of the old untamed galaxy. She was beginning to realise that the gathering was not the start of something new, but the end of five million years of galactic colonisation.

After a long time, the machines came back, and she went where they told her.

It was hidden within a steep-sided crater, a castle or maze of crystal vanes that rose in serried ranks from deep roots within the crust, where they collected and focused tidal energy. He was at its heart, busily folding together a small spacecraft. The energy of the vanes had been greatly depleted by the fight, and he was trying to concentrate the remainder in the motor of the spacecraft. He was preparing to leave.

Her machines rose up and began to spin, locking in resonance with the vanes and bleeding off their store of energy. The machines began to glow as she bounded down the steep smooth slope towards the floor of the crater, red-hot, white-hot, as hot as the core of the sun, for that was where they were diverting the energy stored in the vanes.

Violet threads flicked up, but the machines simply absorbed that energy too. Their stark white light flooded the crater, bleaching the ranks of crystal vanes. A hot wind got up, raising dozens of quick lithe dust devils.

She walked through the traps and tricks of the defences, pulled the man from his fragile craft and took him up in a bubble of air to the neutral point between the Moon and the Earth.

'Tell me,' she said. 'Tell me why you came here. Tell me about the war.'

He was surprisingly calm. He said, 'I am a first-generation clone, but I am on the side of humanity, not the transcendents. Transcendent clades are a danger to all of the variety within and between the civilisations in the galaxy. At last the merely human races have risen against them. I am just one weapon in the greatest war ever fought.'

'You are my flesh. You are of my clade.'

'I am a secret agent. I was made from a single cell stolen from you several hundred years before you set off for this fake Earth and the gathering of your clade. I arrived only two years ago, grew my power source, came down to steal the memory core, and to assassinate you. Although I failed to kill you before, we are no longer in the place where you draw your power. Now—'

After a moment in which nothing happened, he screamed in frustration and despair. She pitied him. Even though all the power, the intrigues and desperate schemes that his presence implied were as remote from her as the politics of a termite nest, she pitied all those who had bent their lives to produce this poor vessel, this failed moment.

She said, 'Your power source is not destroyed, but my machines are taking all its energy. Why did your masters think us dangerous?'

'Because you will fill the galaxy with your own kind. Because you will end human evolution. Because you will not accept that the universe is greater than you can ever be. Because you refuse to die, and death is a necessary part of evolution.'

She laughed. 'Silly little man! Why would we accept limits? We are only doing what humanity has always done. We use science to master nature just as man-apes changed their way of thinking by making tools and using fire. Humanity has always struggled to become more than it is; it has always been ready to travel to the edge of the world, and step over it.'

For the first time in a million years, those sentiments did not taste of ashes. By trying to destroy her, he had shown her what her life was worth.

He said, 'But you do not change. That is why you are so dangerous. You and the other clades of transhumans have stopped humanity evolving. You would fill the galaxy with trillions of copies of a few dozen individuals who are so scared of physical death that they will do any strange and terrible thing to themselves to survive.'

He gestured at the blue-white globe that hung beneath their feet, small and vulnerable against the vast blackness between galaxies.

'Look at your Earth! Humanity left it four million years ago, yet you chose to recreate it for this gathering. You had a million years of human history on Earth to choose from, and four and a half billion years of the history of the planet itself, and yet almost half of your creation is given over to a single century.'

'It is the century where we became what we are,' she said, remembering Rapha. 'It is the century when it became possible to become transhuman, when humanity made the first steps beyond the surface of a single planet.'

'It is the century you were born in. You would freeze all history if you could, an eternity of the same thoughts thought by the same people. You deny all possibilities but your own self.'

He drew himself up, defiant to the last. He said, 'My ship will carry the memory core home without me. You take all, and give nothing. I give my life, and I give you this.'

He held up something as complex and infolded as the throat of an orchid. It was a vacuum fluctuation, a hole in reality that when inflated would remove them from the universe. She looked away at once – the image was already burned in her brain – and threw him into the core of the sun. He did not even have a chance to scream.

Alone in her bubble of air, she studied the wheel of the galaxy, the ordered pattern of braids and clusters. Light was so slow. It took a hundred thousand years to cross from one edge of the galaxy to the other. Had the war against her empire, and the empires of all the other transcendents, already ended? Had it already changed the galaxy, stirred the stars into new patterns? She would not know until she returned, and that would take thirty-five thousand years.

But she did not have to return. In the other direction was the limitless universe, a hundred billion galaxies. She hung there a long time, watching little smudges of ancient light resolve out of the darkness. Empires of stars wherever she looked, wonders without end.

We will fight the war, she thought, and we shall win, and we will go on forever and ever.

And went down, found the bar near the beach. She would wait until the old man came in, and buy him a drink, and talk to him about his dream of the lions.

RECORDING ANGEL

Mr Naryan, the Archivist of Sensch, still keeps to his habits as much as possible, despite all that has happened since Angel arrived in the city. He has clung to these personal rituals for a very long time now, and it is not easy to let them go. And so, on the day that Angel's ship is due to arrive and attempt to reclaim her, the day that will end in revolution, or so Angel has promised her followers, as ever, at dusk, as the Rim Mountains of Confluence tip above the disc of its star and the Eye of the Preservers rises above the far side of the world, Mr Naryan walks across the long plaza at the edge of the city towards the Great River.

Rippling patterns swirl out from his feet, silver and gold racing away through the plaza's living marble. Above his head, clouds of little machines spin through the twilight, sampling the city's dense weave of information. At the margin of the plaza, broad steps shelve into the river's brown slop. Naked children scamper through the shallows, turn to watch as Mr Naryan, old and fat and leaning on his stick at every other stride, descends the submerged stair until only his hairless head is above water. He draws a breath and ducks completely under. His nostrils pinch shut. Membranes slide across his eyes. As always, the bass roar of the river's fall over the edge of the world stirs his heart. He surfaces, spouting water, and the children hoot. He ducks under again and comes up quickly, and the children scamper back from his spray, breathless with delight. Mr Naryan laughs with them and walks back up the steps, his loose belted shirt shedding water and quickly drying in the parched dusk air.

Further on, a funeral party is launching little clay lamps into the river's swift currents. The men, waist-deep in brown water, turn as Mr

Naryan limps past, knuckling their broad, narrow foreheads. Their wet skins gleam with the fire of the sunset that is now gathering in on itself across leagues of water. Mr Naryan genuflects in acknowledgement, feeling an icy shame. The woman died before he could hear her story, as have seven others in the last few days. It is a bitter failure.

Angel, and all that she has told him – Mr Naryan wonders whether he will be able to hear out the end of her story. She has promised to set the city aflame and, unlike Dreen, Mr Naryan believes that she can.

A mendicant is sitting cross-legged on the edge of the steps down to the river. An old man, sky-clad and straight-backed. He seems to be staring into the sunset, in the waking trance that is the nearest that the Shaped citizens of Sensch ever come to sleep. Tears brim in his wide eyes and pulse down his leathery cheeks. A small silvery moth has settled at the corner of his left eye to sip salt.

Mr Naryan drops a handful of the roasted peanuts he carries for the purpose into the mendicant's bowl, and walks on. He walks a long way before he realises that a crowd has gathered at the end of the long plaza, where the steps end and, with a sudden jog, the docks begin. Hundreds of machines swarm in the darkening air, and magistrates stand shoulder to shoulder, flipping their quirts back and forth as if to drive off flies. Metal tags braided into the tassels of the quirts wink and flicker; the magistrates' flared red cloaks seem inflamed in the last light of the sun.

The people make a rising and falling hum, the sound of discontent. They are staring upriver. Mr Naryan, with a catch in his heart, sees what they must be looking at.

It is a speck of light on the horizon north of the city, where the broad ribbon of the river and the broad ribbon of the land narrow to a single point. It is the lighter towing Angel's ship, at the end of its long journey downriver to the desert city where she took refuge, and caught Mr Naryan in the net of her tale.

Mr Naryan first heard about her from Dreen, Sensch's commissioner. In fact, Dreen paid a visit to Mr Naryan's house to convey the news in person. His passage through the narrow streets of the quarter was the focus of a swelling congregation which kept a space two paces wide around him as he ambled towards the house where Mr Naryan had his apartment.

Dreen was a lively but tormented fellow who was paying off a debt of conscience by taking the more or less ceremonial position of commissioner in this remote city which his ancestors had long ago abandoned. Slight and agile, his head clean-shaven except for a fringe of polychrome hair that framed his parchment face, he looked like a lily blossom swirling on the Great River's current as he made his way through the excited crowd. A pair of magistrates preceded him and a remote followed, a mirror-coloured seed that seemed to move through the air in brief rapid pulses like a squeezed watermelon pip. A swarm of lesser machines spun above the packed heads of the crowd. Machines did not entirely trust the citizens, with good reason. Change Wars raged up and down the length of Confluence as, one by one, the ten thousand races of the Shaped fell from innocence.

Mr Naryan, alerted by the clamour, was standing on his balcony when Dreen reached the house. Scrupulously polite, his voice amplified through a little machine that fluttered before his lips, Dreen enquired if he might come up. The crowd fell silent as he spoke, so that his last words echoed eerily up and down the narrow street. When Mr Naryan said mildly that the city's commissioner was always a welcome visitor, Dreen made an elaborate genuflection and scrambled straight up the fretted carvings which decorated the front of the apartment house. He vaulted the wrought-iron rail and perched in the ironwood chair that Mr Naryan usually took when he was tutoring a pupil.

While Mr Naryan lowered his corpulent bulk onto the stool that was the only other piece of furniture on the little balcony, Dreen said cheerfully that he had not walked so far for more than a year. He accepted the tea and sweetmeats that Mr Naryan's wife, terrified by his presence, offered, and added, 'It really would be more convenient if you took quarters appropriate to your status.'

Dreen had use of the vast palace of intricately carved pink sandstone that dominated the southern end of the city, although he chose to live in a tailored habitat of hanging gardens that hovered above the palace's spiky towers.

Mr Naryan said, 'My calling requires that I live amongst the people. How else would I understand their stories? How else would they find me?'

'By any of the usual methods, of course – or you could multiply yourself so that every one of these snakes had their own archivist. Or you could use machines. But I forget, your calling requires that you use only appropriate technology. That's why I'm here, because you won't have heard the news.'

Dreen had an abrupt style, but he was neither as brutal nor as ruthless as his brusqueness suggested. Like Mr Naryan, he was there to serve, not to rule.

Mr Naryan confessed that he had heard nothing unusual, and Dreen said, 'There's a woman arrived here. A star-farer. Her ship landed at Ys last year, as I remember telling you.'

'I remember seeing a ship land at Ys, but I was a young man then, Dreen. I had not taken orders.'

'Yes, yes,' Dreen said impatiently, 'picket boats and the occasional merchant's argosy still use the docks. But this is different. She claims to be from the deep past. The *very* deep past, before the Preservers.'

'I can see that her story would be interesting if it were true.'

Dreen beat a rhythm on his skinny thighs with the flat of his hands. 'Yes, yes! A human woman, returned after millions of years of travelling beyond the Home Galaxy. But there's more! She is only one of a whole crew claiming to be human, and she's jumped ship. Caused some fuss. It seems the others want her back.'

'She is a slave, then?'

'It seems she may be bound to them as you are bound to your order.'

'Then you could return her. Surely you know where she is?'

Dreen popped a sweetmeat in his mouth and chewed with gusto. His flat-topped teeth were all exactly the same size. 'Of course I know where she is – that's not the point,' he said. 'The point is that no one knows if she's lying, or her shipmates are lying – they're a nervy lot, I'm told. Not surprising, culture shock and all that. They've been travelling a long time. Five million years, if their story's to be believed. Of course, they weren't alive for most of that time. But still.'

Mr Naryan said, 'What do you believe?'

'Does it matter? This city matters. Think what trouble she could cause!'

'If her story is true.'

'Yes, yes. That's the point. Talk to her, eh? Find out the truth. Isn't that what your order's about? Well, I must get on.'

Mr Naryan did not bother to correct Dreen's misapprehension. 'The crowd has grown somewhat,' he said. 'I begin to fear for your safety.'

Dreen winked and rose straight into the air, his toes pointing down, his arms crossed with his palms flat on his shoulders. The remote rose with him. Mr Naryan had to shout to make himself heard over the cries and cheers of the crowd.

'What shall I do?'

Dreen checked his ascent and shouted back, 'You might tell her that I'm here to help!'

'Of course!'

But Dreen was rising again, and did not hear Mr Naryan. As he rose he picked up speed, dwindling rapidly as he shot across the jumbled rooftops of the city towards his eyrie. The remote followed at his heels; a cloud of lesser machines scattered across the sky as they strained to keep up.

The next day, when as usual Mr Naryan stopped to buy the peanuts he would scatter amongst any children or mendicants he encountered as he strolled through the city, the nut roaster said that he'd seen a strange woman only an hour before – she'd had no coin, but the nut roaster had given her a bag of shelled salted nuts all the same.

'Was that the right thing to do, master?' the nut roaster asked. His eyes glittered anxiously beneath the ridge of his brow.

Mr Naryan, knowing that the man had been motivated by a cluster of artificial genes implanted in his ancestors to ensure that they and all their children would give aid to any human who requested it, assured the nut roaster that his conduct had been worthy. He proffered coin in ritual payment for the bag of warm oily peanuts, and the nut roaster made his usual elaborate refusal.

'When you see her, master, tell her that she will find no plumper or more savoury peanuts in the whole city. I will give her whatever she desires!'

All day, as Mr Naryan made his rounds of the tea shops, and even when he heard out the brief story of a woman who had composed herself for death, he expected to be accosted by an exotic wild-eyed stranger. That same anticipation distracted him in the evening, as the magistrate's son haltingly read from the Puranas while all around threads of smoke from neighbourhood kitchen fires rose into the black sky. How strange the city suddenly seemed to Mr Naryan: the intent face of the magistrate's son, with its faint intaglio of scales and broad shelving brow, seemed horribly like a mask. Mr Naryan felt a deep longing for his youth, and after the boy had left he stood under the shower for more than an hour, letting water penetrate every fold and cranny of his hairless, corpulent body until his wife anxiously called to him, asking if he was all right.

The woman did not come to him that day, or the next. She was not seeking him at all. It was only by accident that Mr Naryan met her at last.

She was sitting at the counter of a tea shop, in the deep shadow under its tasselled awning. The shop was at the corner of the camel market, where knots of dealers and handlers argued about the merits of their animals and saddle makers squatted cross-legged amongst their wares before the low cave-like entrances to their workshops. Mr Naryan would have walked right past the shop if the proprietor had not hurried out and called to him, explaining that here was a human woman who had no coin, but he was letting her drink what she wished, and was that right?

Mr Naryan sat beside the woman, but did not speak after he ordered his own tea. He was curious and excited and afraid: she looked at him when he sat down and put his cane across his knees, but her gaze merely brushed over him without recognition.

She was tall and slender, hunched at the counter with elbows splayed. She was dressed, like every citizen of Sensch, in a loose, raw cotton overshirt. Her hair was as black and thick as any citizen's, too, worn long and caught in a kind of net slung at her shoulder. Her face was sharp and small-featured, intent on all that happened around her – a bronze machine trawling through the dusty sunlight beyond the awning's shadow; a vendor of pomegranate juice calling his wares; a gaggle of women laughing as they passed; a sled laden with prickly pear gliding above the dusty flagstones – but nothing held her attention for more than a moment. She held her bowl of tea carefully in both hands, and sucked at the liquid noisily, holding each mouthful for a whole minute before swallowing and then spitting twiggy fragments into the copper basin on the counter.

No doubt Dreen was watching through one or another of the little machines that flitted about the sunny, salt-white square, but Mr Naryan did not immediately approach the woman. Let her see him; let her speak first. He had grown into his routines, and this intrusion and its attendant responsibility was disturbing and, he had to admit, more than a little frightening. But now that he had found her, he could not leave her, so he watched and waited until, at last, the owner of the tea house refilled the woman's bowl and said softly, 'Our Archivist honours us with his presence.'

The woman turned so suddenly to Mr Naryan that she spilled her tea. 'I won't go back,' she said. 'I told them I won't go back. I won't serve any more.'

'I am not here to takes sides in any quarrel you may have with your shipmates,' Mr Naryan said, feeling that he must calm her. 'And I am not here to compel you to do anything. I don't believe that anyone in this city has the power to do that. My name is Naryan, and I have the honour, as our good host has pointed out, of being the Archivist of Sensch. I am interested only in your story, should you wish to tell it.'

'You're what – a librarian?'

'I collect and conserve the stories people tell about their lives.'

The woman appeared to think about that, then said that he could call her Angel. 'My name also translates as Monkey, but I prefer Angel. I saw people like you in the port city, and one let me ride on his boat down the river until we reached the edge of a civil war. But after that every one of the cities I passed through seemed to be inhabited by only one race, and each was different from the next.'

'It is true that this is a remote city,' Mr Naryan said.

He could hear the faint drums of the procession. It was the middle of the day, when the sun halted at its zenith before reversing back down the sky.

The woman, Angel, heard the drums too. She looked around with a kind of preening motion as the procession came through the line of flame trees on the far side of the square. It reached this part of the city at the same time every day. It was led by a bare-chested man who beat a big drum draped in cloth of gold; it was held before him by a leather strap that went around his neck. The steady beat echoed across the square. Behind him slouched or capered ten, twenty, thirty naked men and women. Their hair was long and ropy with dirt; their fingernails were curved yellow talons.

Angel drew her breath sharply as the raggle-taggle procession shuffled past, following the beat of the drum into the curving street that led out of the square. She said, 'This is a very strange place. Are they mad?'

Mr Naryan explained, 'They have not lost their reason, but have had it taken away. For some it will be returned in a year; it was taken away from them as a punishment. Others have renounced their own selves for the rest of their lives. It is a religious avocation. But saint or criminal, they were all once as fully aware as you or me.'

'I'm not like you,' Angel said. 'I'm not like any of the crazy kinds of people I have met.'

Mr Naryan beckoned to the owner of the tea house and ordered two more bowls. 'I understand you have come a long way.' Although he was terrified of her, he was certain that he could draw her out.

But Angel only laughed.

Mr Naryan said, 'I do not mean to insult you.'

'You dress like a . . . native. Is *that* a religious avocation?'

'It is my profession. I am the Archivist here.'

'When I left, not a single intelligent alien species was known. It was one reason for my voyage. Now there are thousands strung along this long, long river. All of them made by the Preservers, who I suppose are my descendants. But where are the Preservers?'

'The Preservers departed long ago,' Mr Naryan said. 'These are the end times.'

'There are always those who believe they live at the end of history,' Angel said. 'We thought that *we* lived at the end of history, when every star system in the Home Galaxy had been mapped, every habitable world settled.'

For a moment, Mr Naryan thought that she would tell him of where she had been, but she added, 'Every race in every city claims to be human, even the ones who don't look like they could have evolved from anything that was ever human stock. And they all treat me like a ruler – or a god. So what does that make me?'

'The Shaped call themselves human because they have no other name for what they have become, innocent and fallen alike. After all, none of them had names before they were raised up.'

'What about you? Are you human, or are you "human"?' Angel said, crooking her little fingers in the air.

'My people are fallen. The innocent, the unfallen, like the citizens of Sensch, are our . . . responsibility.'

'You're not doing all that well,' Angel said, and started to tell him about the Change War she had tangled with upriver, on the way to this, the last city at the midpoint of the world.

It was a long, complicated story, and she kept stopping to ask Mr Naryan questions, most of which, despite his extensive readings of the Puranas, he was unable to answer. As she talked, Mr Naryan transcribed her speech on his tablet. She commented that a recording device would be better, but by reading back a long speech she had just made he demonstrated that his diacritical marks had captured her every word.

'You write down people's stories.'

'Writing them down helps to fix them in my head. Stories are important. In the end they are all that is left, all that history leaves us. Stories endure.'

Mr Naryan wondered if she saw what was all too clear to him, the way her story would end, if she stayed in the city.

'I have been out of history a long time,' Angel said. 'I'm not sure that I want to be a part of it again.'

She stood up so quickly that she knocked her stool over, and walked out across the square.

That night, as Mr Naryan was enjoying a cigarette on his balcony, a remote came to him. Dreen's face materialised above the machine's silver platter and told him that the woman's shipmates knew that she was in Sensch. They were coming for her.

As the ship draws closer, looming above the glowing lighter that tows it, Mr Naryan begins to make out its shape. It is a huge black pyramid composed of tiers of flat plates that rise higher than the tallest towers of the city. Little lights, mostly red, gleam here and there within its ridged carapace. Mr Naryan brushes mosquitoes from his bare arms, watching the black ship move beneath a black sky in which only the Eye of the Preservers and a few dim halo stars shine. Here, at the midpoint of the world, the Home Galaxy will not rise until winter.

The crowd has grown. It becomes restless. Waves of emotion surge back and forth. Mr Naryan feels them pass through the citizens packed around him, although he hardly understands what they mean, for all the time he has lived with these people.

He has been allowed to pass through the crowd with the citizens' usual generous deference, and now stands close to the edge of the whirling cloud of machines which defends the dock, twenty paces or so from the magistrates who swish their quirts to and fro. The crowd's thick yeasty odour fills his nostrils; its humming disquiet, modulating up and down, penetrates to the marrow of his bones. Now and then a machine ignites a flare of light that sweeps over the front ranks of the crowd, and the eyes of the men and women shine blankly, like so many little orange sparks.

At last the ship passes the temple complex at the northern edge of the city, its wedge rising like a wave above the temple's clusters of slim spiky towers. The lighter's engines go into reverse; waves break in whitecaps on the steps beyond the whirl of machines and the grim line of magistrates.

The crowd's hum rises in pitch. Mr Naryan finds himself carried forward as it presses towards the barrier defined by the machines. The people around him apologise effusively for troubling him, trying to minimise contact with him in the press as snails withdraw from salt.

The machines' whirl stratifies, and the magistrates raise their quirts and shout a single word lost in the noise of the crowd. The people in the front rank of the crowd fall to their knees, clutching their eyes and wailing: the machines have shut down their optic nerves.

Mr Naryan, shown the same deference by the machines as by the citizens, suddenly finds himself isolated amongst groaning and weeping citizens, confronting the row of magistrates. One calls to him, but he ignores the man.

He has a clear view of the ship now. It has come to rest a league away, at the far end of the docks, but Mr Naryan has to tip his head back and back to see the top of the ship's tiers. It is as if a mountain has drifted against the edge of the city.

A new sound drives across the crowd, as a gust of wind drives across a field of wheat. Mr Naryan turns and, by the random flare of patrolling machines, is astonished to see how large the crowd has grown. It fills the long plaza, and more people stand on the rooftops along its margin. Their eyes are like a harvest of stars. They are all looking towards the ship, where Dreen, standing on a cargo sled, ascends to meet the crew.

Mr Naryan hooks the wire frames of his spectacles over his ears, and the crew standing on top of the black ship snap into clear focus.

There are fifteen men and women, tall, sharp-featured. They loom over Dreen as he welcomes them with effusive gestures. Mr Naryan can almost smell Dreen's anxiety. He wants the crew to take Angel away, and order to be restored. He will be telling them where to find her.

Mr Naryan feels a pang of anger. He turns and makes his way through the crowd. When he reaches its ragged margin, everyone around him suddenly looks straight up. Dreen's sled sweeps overhead, carrying his guests to the safety of the floating habitat above the pink sandstone palace. The crowd surges forward – and all the little machines fall from the air!

One lands close to Mr Naryan. Its carapace has burst open. Smoke pours from it. An old woman picks it up – Mr Naryan smells her burnt flesh as it sears her hand – and throws it at him.

Her shot goes wide. Mr Naryan is so astonished that he does not even duck. He glimpses a confused struggle as the edge of the crowd collides with the line of magistrates: some magistrates run, their red cloaks streaming at their backs; others throw down their quirts and hold out their empty hands. The crowd devours them. Mr Naryan limps away as fast as he can, his heart galloping with fear. Ahead is a wide avenue leading into the city, and standing in the middle of the avenue is a compact group of men, clustered about a tall, slender figure.

It is Angel.

Mr Naryan told Angel what Dreen had told him, that the ship was coming to the city, the very next day. He had found her at the tea house. She did not seem surprised. 'They need me,' she said. 'How long do I have?'

'Well, they cannot come here directly. Confluence's maintenance system will not allow ships to land anywhere except at the various docks, but the machinery of the spaceport docks here has grown erratic and dangerous through disuse. The nearest place where they can safely land is five hundred leagues away, and after that the ship will have to be towed downriver. It will take time.'

'Ten days? Twenty?'

'More than ten, I think. Will you wait for it here?'

He was hoping that she would say no. He wanted her to leave Sensch and travel on, past the end of the river, past the waist of the world, out of all that was known. He wanted her to leave Sensch to its endless unchanging flow of ordinary days, ordinary stories. But he could not tell her that, and he had to suppress his alarm and disappointment when she said that she liked this little city.

'I can't keep running. And people here have been very kind. Very helpful.'

She had already been given a place in which to live by a wealthy merchant family. She took Mr Naryan to see it. It was near the river, a small two-storey house built around a courtyard shaded by a jacaranda tree. People were going in and out, carrying furniture and carpets. Three men were painting the wooden rail of the balcony that ran around the upper storey. They were painting it pink and blue, and singing cheerfully as they worked. Angel was amused by the bustle, and laughed when Mr Naryan said that she should not take advantage of the citizens.

'They're so happy to help me. What's wrong with that?'

Mr Naryan thought it best not to explain about the cluster of genes implanted in all the races of the Shaped, and the reflex altruism of the unfallen. A woman brought out tea and a pile of crisp wafer-thin fritters sweetened with crystallised honey. Two men brought canopied chairs. Angel sprawled in one, invited Mr Naryan to sit in the other. She was quite at ease, grinning every time someone showed her the gift they had brought her.

Dreen, Mr Naryan knew, would be dismayed. Angel was a barbarian, displaced by five million years. She had no idea of the careful balance by which one must live with the innocent, the unfallen, if their cultures were to survive. Yet she was fully human, free to choose, and that freedom was inviolable. Mr Naryan understood why Dreen was so eager for the ship to reclaim her.

But Angel's happiness was infectious, and Mr Naryan soon found himself smiling with her at the sheer abundance of trinkets scattered around her. No one was giving unless they were glad to give, and no one who gave was poor. The only poor in Sensch were the sky-clad mendicants who had voluntarily renounced the material world.

So Mr Naryan sat and drank tea with her, and ate a decad of the delicious honeyed fritters, one after the other, and listened to more of her wild tales of travelling the river, and realised how little she understood of Confluence's administration. She was convinced that the Shaped were somehow forbidden technology, and did not understand why there was no government. Was Dreen the absolute ruler? By what right?

'Dreen is merely the commissioner,' Mr Naryan said. 'Any authority he possesses is invested in him by the citizens, and it is manifest only on high days. He loves parades. I suppose the magistrates have more power, in that they arbitrate neighbourly disputes and decide upon punishment. Senschians are argumentative, and sometimes quarrels can lead to unfortunate accidents.'

'Murder, you mean? Then perhaps they are not as innocent as you maintain.' Angel reached out suddenly. 'And these? By what authority do these little spies operate?'

Pinched between her thumb and forefinger was a bronze machine. Its sensor cluster turned back and forth as it struggled to free itself.

'They are part of the maintenance system of Confluence.'

'Can Dreen use them? Tell me all you know. It may be important.'

She questioned Mr Naryan closely, and he found himself telling her more than he wanted to. But although they talked for a long time, she would not talk about her voyage, or explain why she had run away from the ship and her crewmates. Mr Naryan visited the temple and petitioned for information about her voyage, but all trace of it had been lost in the vast sifting of history – the voyage must have begun at least five million years ago at the very least, if the ship really had travelled all the way to the neighbouring galaxy and back – and when pressed, the librarian who had come at the hierodule's bidding broke contact with an almost petulant abruptness.

Mr Naryan did learn that the ship had tried to sell its story after it had landed at Ys, much as a merchant would sell his wares. Angel and her crewmates had wanted to profit from what they had discovered, but there was no market for knowledge on Confluence. Anyone could find out anything, for the small cost of petitioning those librarians that dealt with the secular world.

Meanwhile, a group of citizens gathered around Angel, like disciples around one of the blessed who, touched by some fragment or other of the Preservers, wandered Confluence's long shore. They went wherever she went. They were all young men, which seemed to Mr Naryan faintly sinister. He recognised several of them, but none would speak to him. They wore white headbands on which Angel had lettered a slogan in an archaic script older than any race of the Shaped; she refused to explain what it meant.

Mr Naryan's wife thought that he, too, was falling under some kind of spell. She did not like the idea of Angel: she declared that Angel must be some kind of ghost, and was therefore dangerous. Perhaps she was right. She was a native of the city, but wise for her kind, and strong-willed, and Mr Naryan trusted her advice.

He could definitely detect a change in the steady song of the city as he went about his business. He listened to an old man dying of the systematic organ failure which took most of the citizens in the middle of their fourth century. The man was one of the few citizens who had left Sensch – he had travelled north, as far as a city tunnelled through cliffs overlooking the river, where an amphibious race lived. His story took a whole day to tell, in a stiflingly hot room muffled in dusty carpets and lit only by a lamp with a blood-red chimney. At the end, the old man began to weep, saying that he knew now that he had not travelled at all, and Mr Naryan was unable to comfort him. Two children were born on the next day, an event so rare that the whole city celebrated, garlanding the streets with fragrant orange blossoms. But there was a tension humming beneath the celebrations that Mr Naryan had never before felt, and it seemed that Angel's followers were everywhere amongst the revellers.

Dreen felt the change, too. 'There have been incidents,' he said. 'Nothing very much. A temple wall defaced with the slogan the woman has her followers wear. A market disrupted by young men running through it, overturning stalls. I asked the magistrates not to make examples of the perpetrators – that would create martyrs. Let the people hold their own courts if they wish. And she's been making speeches. Have you heard any of them?'

'I have been busy.'

'You have been avoiding her, like the sensible fellow you are.'

Dreen dropped his glass with a careless gesture, and a machine caught it and bore it away. They were on a balcony of his floating habitat, looking out over the Great River towards the far side of the world. At the horizon was the long white double line that marked the river's fall: the rapids below, the permanent clouds above. It was noon, and the sunlit city was quiet.

'I have been going about my duties,' Mr Naryan said.

'I heard the story you gathered in. At the time, you know, I thought that man might bring war to the city when he came back.' Dreen's laugh was a high-pitched hooting. 'She talks and talks, and it has no more substance than a cloud. Airy nothingness about destiny, about rising above circumstances and bettering yourself. As if you could lift yourself into the air by grasping the soles of your feet.'

Dreen's own feet, as always, were bare, and his long opposable toes were curled around the bar of the rail on which he squatted.

'She seems to believe that she has taken command of the city,' he said. 'And if it pleases her to believe it, why not let her have her fun? She isn't doing any real harm, and it will end when the ship arrives. Besides, I think she's already growing bored with her games. She took a boat yesterday, went out to the edge of the world. Maybe she won't come back, eh?'

'I am sure she will,' Mr Naryan said. 'She told me that she likes it here. And it is all of a pattern.'

'I defer to your deep knowledge about the patterns stories take. But we only have small roles to play in hers, I think. The ship will be here soon, and she will be gone, and we can get on with our own stories again. Such as they are. Have another drink, Mr Naryan. Stay a while, enjoy the view. I finds it gives me a useful perspective.'

Dreen scampered along the rail and swung up into the branches of the flame tree that leaned over the balcony, disappearing in a flurry of red leaves, leaving Mr Naryan to find a machine that was able to take him home.

He thought that Dreen was wrong to dismiss what Angel was doing, although he understood why the commissioner affected indifference. She was beyond his experience; she was beyond the experience of everyone on Confluence. The Change Wars that flared here and there along Confluence's vast length were not ideological but eschatological. They were a result of stresses that arose when radical shifts in the expression of clusters of native and grafted genes caused a species of Shaped to undergo a catastrophic redefinition of its perceptions of the world. But what Angel was doing in Sensch dated from before the Preservers had raised up the Shaped and ended human history. Even Mr Naryan couldn't properly understand it until Angel told him what she had done at the edge of the world.

And later, on the terrible night when the ship arrives and every machine in the city dies, with flames roaring unchecked through the farside quarter of the city and thousands of citizens fleeing into the orchard forests upriver, Mr Naryan realises that he has not understood as much as he thought.

Her acolytes, all young men, are armed with crude wooden spears with fire-hardened tips, long double-edged knives of the kind coconut sellers use to open their wares, flails improvised from chains and wire. They hustle Mr Naryan in a forced march towards the palace and Dreen's floating habitat. They have taken away Mr Naryan's cane, and his bad leg hurts abominably with every other step.

Angel is gone. She has work elsewhere. Mr Naryan felt fear when he saw her, but feels more fear now. The reflex altruism of the acolytes has been overridden by a new meme forged in the fires of Angel's revolution – they jostle Mr Naryan with rough humour, sure in their hold over him. One in particular, the rough skin of his long-jawed face crazed in diamonds, jabs Mr Naryan in his ribs with the butt of his spear at every intersection, as if to remind him not to escape, something that Mr Naryan has absolutely no intention of doing.

Power is down all over the city – it went off with the fall of the machines – but leaping light from scattered fires swims in the wide eyes of the young men. They pass through a market square where people swig beer and drunkenly gamble amongst overturned stalls. Elsewhere in the fiery dark there is open rutting, men with men as well as with women. A child lies dead in a gutter. Horrible, horrible. Once, a building collapses inside its own fire, sending flames whirling high into the black sky. The faces of all the men surrounding Mr Naryan are transformed by this leaping light into masks with eyes of flame.

Mr Naryan's captors urge him on. His only comfort is that he will be of use in what is to come. Angel has not yet finished with him.

When Angel returned from the edge of the world, she came straight away to Mr Naryan. It was a warm evening, at the hour after sunset when the streets began to fill with strollers, the murmur of neighbour greeting neighbour, the cries of vendors selling fruit juice or popcorn or sweet cakes.

Mr Naryan was listening as his pupil, the magistrate's son, read the passage from the Puranas which described the Golden Age when the Preservers had strung the galaxy with their creations. The boy was tall and awkward and faintly resentful, for he was not the scholar his father wished him to be and would rather have spent his evenings with his fellows in the tea houses and beer halls than in reading ancient legends in a long-dead language. He bent over the book like a night stork, his finger stabbing at each line as he clumsily translated it, mangling words in his hoarse voice. Mr Naryan was listening with half an ear, interrupting only to correct particularly inelegant phrases. In the kitchen at the far end of the little apartment, his wife was humming to the murmur of the radio, her voice a breathy contented monotone.

Angel came up the helical stair with a rapid clatter, climbing above a sudden hush in the street. Mr Naryan knew who it was even before she burst onto the balcony. Her appearance so astonished the magistrate's son that he dropped the book. Mr Naryan dismissed him and he hurried away, no doubt eager to meet his friends and tell them of this latest wonder.

Angel accepted the bowl of tea that Mr Naryan's wife brought her. She was trembling, Mr Naryan's wife, and her gaze was averted in deference, and she gave Mr Naryan a look that turned his heart, for he realised how quickly and easily his sensible, plain-spoken wife had surrendered her autonomy. How cruel the Preservers had been, to have raised up races of the Shaped and yet to have shackled them in unthinking obedience.

'You two are married?' Angel said, after Mr Naryan's wife had backed into the apartment. 'How does that work, marrying someone from a different species?'

'How could I expect to understand the stories of the people of this city if I did not live like one of them?' Mr Naryan said.

'You take that avocation of yours seriously.'

'Of course.'

'I've been to the edge of the world,' Angel said. She sipped her tea, looked at him over the edge of the bowl. 'You don't seem surprised.'

'Dreen told me. I am pleased to see you returned safely. It has been a dry time without you.'

It was as if his thoughts were eager to be spilled before her.

'I suppose Dreen knows about everything that goes on in the city.'

'Oh no, not at all. He knows what he needs to know.'

'I took a boat,' Angel said. 'I just asked for it, and the man took me right along, without question. I wish now I'd stolen it. It would have been simpler. I'm tired of all this goodwill.'

Angel sat on the stool which the student had quit, tipping it back so she could lean against the rail of the balcony. She had cut her black hair short, and a strip of white cloth was tied around her forehead, printed with the slogan, in ancient incomprehensible script, that was the badge of her acolytes. She wore an ordinary white shirt and a lot of jewellery: rings on every finger, sometimes more than one on each; bracelets and bangles on her arms; gold and silver chains around her neck, layered on her breast. She was both graceful and terrifying, a rough beast slouched from the deep past to claim the world.

She said, 'Do you want to know what I found there?'

'I will listen to anything you want to tell me,' Mr Naryan said.

'Of course. It's your avocation.'

'It is my duty, yes.'

'Do you know about libration?'

Mr Naryan shook his head.

Angel held out her hand, tipped it back and forth. 'This is the world. Everything lives on the back of a long flat plate. The plate rocks on its long axis, so the sun rises above the edge and then reverses its course. I went to the edge of the world, where the river that runs down half its length falls into the void. I suppose it must be collected and redistributed, but it really does look like it falls away forever.'

'The river is eternally renewed,' Mr Naryan said. 'Ships used to arrive and depart at the falls at the end of the river, but this city has not been a port for many years.'

'Fortunately for me. Otherwise my companions would already be here,' Angel said. 'There's a narrow ribbon of land on the far side of the river. Nothing lives there, not even an insect. No earth, no stones. The air shakes with the sound of the river's fall, and swirling mist burns with raw sunlight. And there are shrines in the thunder and mist at the edge of the world.'

Mr Naryan had visited them once, many years ago. There was a sacred space near the great falls where the Great River ended, and the original founders of the city of Sensch, Dreen's ancestors, had travelled across the river to petition the avatars of the Preservers, believing that the voyage was a necessary rite of purification. They had carried shaped stones on their pilgrimages, and used them to build stepped pyramids from which flags and banners had once flown.

Angel was grinning. Mr Naryan had to remember that it was not, as it was with the citizens, a baring of teeth before striking.

She said, 'One of them spoke to me. It woke, and it spoke to me. Do you want to know what it said?'

'If you want to tell me, of course.'

Angel passed her hand over the top of her narrow skull: bristly hair made a crisp sound under her palm. 'No,' she said. 'No, I don't think I do. Not yet.'

Later, after a short span of uncomfortable silence, just before she left, she said, 'After we were wakened by the ship, after it brought us here, it showed us how the black hole you call the Eye of the Preservers was made. It recorded the process as it returned, speeded up because the ship was travelling so fast that it stretched time around itself. At first there was an intense point of light within the heart of the Large Magellanic Cloud. It might have been a supernova, except that it was a thousand times larger than any supernova ever recorded. For a long time its glare obscured everything else, and when it cleared, all the remaining stars were streaming around where it had been. Those nearest the centre elongated and dissipated, and always more crowded in until nothing was left but the gas clouds of the accretion disc, glowing by Cherenkov radiation.'

'So it is written in the Puranas.'

'And is it also written in your Puranas why Confluence was constructed around a halo star between the Home Galaxy and the Eye of the Preservers?'

'Of course. It is so we can all worship and glorify the Preservers. The Eye looks upon us all.'

'It's a nice little story, isn't it?' Angel said.

After she was gone, Mr Naryan put on his spectacles and walked through the city to the docks. The unsleeping citizens were promenading in the warm dark streets, or squatting in doorways, or talking quietly from upper-storey windows to their neighbours across the street. Amongst this customary somnolence, Angel's young disciples moved with a quick purposefulness, here in pairs, there in a group of twenty or more. Their slogans were painted on almost every wall. Three stopped Mr Naryan near the docks, danced around his bulk, jeering, then ran off, screeching with laughter, when he slashed at them with his cane.

'Ruffians! Fools!'

'Seize the day!' they sang back. 'Seize the day!'

Mr Naryan did not find the man whose skiff Angel and her followers had used to cross the river, but the story was already everywhere amongst the fisher folk. The Preservers had spoken to her, they said, and she had refused their temptations. Many were busily bargaining with citizens who wanted to cross the river and see the site of this miracle for themselves.

An old man, eyes milky with cataracts – the fisher folk trawled widely across the Great River, exposing themselves to more radiation than normal – asked Mr Naryan if these were the end times, if the Preservers would return to walk amongst them again. When Mr Naryan said, no, anyone who had dealt with the avatars knew that only those fragments remained in the universe, the old man shrugged and said, 'They say *she* is a Preserver.'

Mr Naryan, looking out across the river's black welter, where the horizon was lost against the empty night, seeing the constellations of the running lights of the fisher folk's skiffs scattered out to the farside, knew that the end of Angel's story was not far off. The citizens were finding their use for her. Inexorably, step by step, she was becoming part of their history.

Mr Naryan did not see Angel again until the night her ship arrived. Dreen went to treat with her, but he could not get within two streets of her house: it had become the centre of a great convocation that took over the entire quarter of the city. She preached to thousands of citizens from the rooftops.

Dreen reported to Mr Naryan that her speeches had gained a sharper edge. 'She says that all life feeds on destruction and death. She says that the past is dead and those who worship the past are the living dead. I suppose she was inspired by something the shrine told her. She still hasn't told you . . . ?'

'Not yet.'

'You could ask her.'

'So could you. And you know that we won't.'

They were in his floating habitat, in an arbour of lemon trees that jutted out at its leading edge. Dreen was perched on a balustrade, looking out at the river. He said, 'More than a thousand a day are making the crossing.'

'Has the shrine spoken again?'

'Not yet. Perhaps it didn't speak to her, eh?' Dreen was suddenly agitated. He scampered up and down the narrow balustrade, swiping at overhanging branches and scaring the white doves that perched amongst the little glossy leaves. The birds rocketed up in a great flutter of wings, crying as they rose into the empty sky. Dreen said, 'The machines watching her don't work. She found out how to disrupt them. I can snatch long-range pictures, but they don't tell me very much. I don't even know if she visited the shrine in the first place.'

'I believe her,' Mr Naryan said.

'I petitioned the avatars,' Dreen said, 'but of course they wouldn't tell me anything.'

Mr Naryan was disturbed by this admission. Dreen was not a religious man. 'What will you do now?'

'I could send the magistrates for her, but even if she agreed to go with them, her followers would claim she'd been arrested. And I don't know what they'd do then. If they rioted, I'd have to let her go, and it would make her even more powerful. So I continue to do nothing, and I suppose that you will tell me that there is nothing I can do because it's all part of a pattern.'

'It has happened before. Even here, to your own people. They built the shrines, after all . . .'

'Yes, and later they fell from grace, and destroyed their city. But the snakes aren't ready for that,' Dreen said. 'It won't change them. It will destroy them.'

For a moment Mr Naryan glimpsed the depth of Dreen's love for this city and its people. Dreen turned away, as if ashamed, and stared out at the river again, at the flocking sails of little boats setting out on, or returning from, the long crossing to the far side of the river. This great pilgrimage had become the focus of the life of the city. The markets were closed for the most part; merchants had moved to the docks to supply the thousands of pilgrims.

Dreen said, 'They say that the avatar tempted her with godhead, and she denied it.'

'I've heard similar foolish talk. The days of the Preservers have long ago faded. We know them only by their image, which burns forever at the event horizon, but their essence has long since receded.'

Dreen shrugged. 'There's worse. They say that she forced the avatar to admit that the Preservers are dead. They say that *she* is an avatar of something greater than the Preservers, although you wouldn't know that from her preaching. She claims that this universe is all there is, that destiny is what you make it, and so on, and so forth. Harmless cant, except the snakes seem to believe every word.'

Mr Naryan, feeling chill, there in the sun-dappled shade, said, 'She has hinted to me that she learnt it in the great far-out, in the galaxy beyond the Home Galaxy.'

'The ship is coming,' Dreen said. 'Let's hope her crewmates can deal with her. I know I can't.'

In the burning night of the city's dissolution, Mr Naryan is brought at last to the pink sandstone palace. Dreen's habitat floats above, a black shadow that half-eclipses the glowering red swirl of the Eye of the Preservers. Trails of white smoke, made luminescent by the fires which feed them, pour from the palace's windows, braiding into sheets which dash like surf against the rim of the habitat. Mr Naryan sees something fly away from the palace's many carved spires – there seem to be more of them than he remembers – and smash away a piece of the habitat, which disintegrates as it tumbles out of the air, rubble smashing down in the wide square in front of the palace.

The men around him hoot and cheer at this, and catch Mr Naryan's arms and march him up the broad steps and through the high double doors into the courtyard beyond. It is piled with furniture and tapestries that have been thrown down from the thousand high windows overlooking it, but a path has been cleared to a narrow stair that turns and turns as it rises, until at last Mr Naryan is pushed out onto the roof of the palace.

Perhaps five hundred of Angel's followers crowd amongst the spires, many naked, all with lettered headbands tied around their foreheads. Smoky torches blaze everywhere. In the centre of the crowd is the palace's great throne on which, on high days and holidays, at the beginning of masques or parades, Dreen receives the city's priests, merchants and artists. It is lit by a crown of machines burning bright as the sun, and seated on it – easy, elegant and terrifying – is Angel.

Mr Naryan is led through the crowd and left standing alone before her. She beckons him forward and says, 'What should I do with your city, now I've taken it from you?'

'You have not finished your story.' Everything Mr Naryan planned to say has been erased by the simple fact of her presence. Stranded before her fierce, barely contained energies, he feels old and used up, his body as heavy with years and regret as with fat. He adds cautiously, 'I would like to hear it all.'

He wonders if she really knows how her story must end. Perhaps she does. Perhaps her wild joy is not at her triumph, but at the imminence of her death. Perhaps she really does believe that the void is all, and rushes to embrace it.

Angel says, 'My people can tell you. They are hiding with Dreen in that floating garden, but not for much longer.'

She points across the roof. A dozen men are wrestling a sled, which shudders like a living thing as it tries to reorientate itself in the gravity field, onto a kind of launching cradle tipped up towards the habitat. The edges of the habitat are ragged, as if bitten, and tower-trees are visibly growing towards it at the far side of the roof's spires. Their tips are already brushing its lower edge; their tangled bases pulse and swell as teams of men and women drench them with nutrients.

'I found how to enhance the antigravity properties of the sleds,' Angel says. 'They react against the field which generates gravity for this artificial world. The field's stored inertia gives them a high kinetic energy, so that they make very good missiles. We'll chip away that floating fortress piece by piece if we have to, or we'll finish growing towers and storm its remains, but I expect surrender long before then.'

'Dreen is not the ruler of the city.' Nor are you, Mr Naryan thinks, but it is not prudent to point that out.

'Not any more,' Angel says.

Mr Naryan dares to step closer. He says, 'What did you find out there that made you so angry?'

Angel laughs. 'I'll tell you about anger. It is what you have all forgotten, or never learned. It is the motor of evolution, and evolution's end, too.'

She snatches a beaker of wine from a supplicant, drains it and tosses it aside. She is consumed with an energy that is no longer her own. She says, 'We travelled so long, not dead, not sleeping. We were no more than stored potentials triply engraved on gold film. Although the ship flew so fast that it bound time around itself, the journey still took thousands of years by the slow ship-board clocks. At the end of that long voyage we did not wake: we were born. Or rather, others like us were born, although I have their memories, as if they are my own. The ship had been observing the galaxy as it approached it, and had sent clouds of tiny self-replicating machines ahead of it. The ship's observations and the machines, spreading in a slow wavefront, and our own observations and scouting missions all told us the same thing. The galaxy was ruined, and mostly devoid of any form of complex life.'

Angel holds Mr Naryan's hand tightly, speaking quietly and intensely, her eyes staring deep into his.

'A billion years ago, our neighbouring galaxy and another, somewhat smaller galaxy, collided. Stars from both of them were torn off in the collision, and scattered in a vast halo. The rest coalesced into a single body, but except for ancient globular clusters, which survived the catastrophe because of their dense gravity fields, the rest is mostly wreckage. There were few collisions between stars, but there was a new wave of star formation across the merged galaxies when gas clouds passed through each other, and a brief, intense increase in supernova activity. Wave fronts of radiation sterilised hundreds of thousands of planetary systems. Many more were perturbed by tidal effects caused by interpenetration of dark matter orbiting at different velocities inside the colliding galaxies. I remember standing on a world of methane ice as cold and dark as the universe itself, wandering amongst the stars. There were billions of worlds like it cast adrift. I remember standing upon a fragment of a world smashed into a million shards and scattered so widely in its orbit that it never had the chance to re-form. There are a million such worlds. I remember gas giants turned inside out – single vast storms – and I remember worlds torched smooth by eruptions of their stars.

'No doubt some worlds sheltered biospheres that had survived the catastrophe, but they were vanishingly rare. We surveyed a segment of the galaxy more than ten thousand light years across, and made deep field observations of a much greater area, but were unable to find a single world where life had advanced much beyond the anaerobic bacterial stage. Humanity was the only intelligent species known to have evolved in the Home Galaxy; we could find no trace of any technologically advanced species anywhere in the neighbouring galaxy. If any had existed, it had been destroyed by the collision, or driven elsewhere.

'Do you know how many galaxies have endured such collisions? Almost all of them. Our own has suffered several minor collisions already. The universe was not made for the convenience of humans, or any similar species. Life flourishes rarely, and is soon extinguished. Our species, the human species, is a statistical freak. An outlier. If other civilisations have arisen elsewhere in the unbounded universe, they are so distant that we will never contact them. So, we are alone. We must make of ourselves what we can. We should not hide, as your Preservers chose to do. Instead, we should seize the day, and make the universe over with the technology that the Preservers used to make their hiding place.'

Angel's grip is hurting now, but Mr Naryan bears it. 'You cannot become a Preserver,' he says. 'No one can, now. You should not lie to these innocent people.'

'I didn't need to lie,' she says. 'They took up my story and made it theirs. They see now what they can inherit – if they dare. This won't stop with one city. It will become a crusade!' She adds, more softly, 'You'll remember it all, won't you?'

Mr Naryan knows then that she knows how this must end, and his heart breaks. He would ask her to take that burden from him, but he cannot. He is bound to her. He is her witness.

The crowd around them cheers as the sled rockets up from its cradle. It smashes into the habitat and knocks loose another piece, which drops trees and dirt and rocks amongst the spires of the palace roof as it twists free and spins away into the night.

Figures appear at the edge of the habitat. A small tube falls, trailing a flare of white light. A man catches it, runs across the debris-strewn roof, and throws himself at Angel's feet. He is at the far end of the human scale of the Shaped of this city. His skin is lapped with distinct scales, edged with a rim of hard black like the scales of a pine cone. His coarse black hair has flopped over his eyes, which glow like coals with reflected firelight.

Angel takes the tube and shakes it. It unrolls into a flexible sheet on which Dreen's face glows. Dreen's lips move; his voice is small and metallic. Angel listens intently, and when he has finished speaking she stands and raises both hands above her head. All across the roof, men and women turn towards her, eyes glowing.

'They wish to surrender! Let them come down!'

A moment later a sled drops away from the habitat, its silvery underside gleaming in the reflected light of the many fires scattered across the roof. Angel's followers shout and jeer, and missiles fly out of the darkness – a burning torch, a rock, a broken branch. All are somehow deflected before they reach the ship's crew, screaming away into the dark with such force that the torch, the branch, kindle into white fire. The crew have modified the sled's field to protect themselves.

They all look like Angel, with the same small sleek head, the same gangling build and abrupt nervous movements. Dreen's slight figure is dwarfed by them. It takes Mr Naryan a long minute to be able to distinguish men from women, and another to be able to tell each man from his brothers, each woman from her sisters. They are all clad in long white shirts that leave them bare-armed and bare-legged, and each is girdled with a belt from which hang a dozen or more little machines. They call to Angel, one following on the words of the other:

'Return with us—'

'—this is not our place—'

'—these are not our people—'

'—we will return—'

'—we will find our home—'

'—leave with us and return.'

Dreen sees Mr Naryan and shouts, 'They want to take her back!' He jumps down from the sled, an act of bravery that astonishes Mr Naryan, and skips through the crowd. 'They are all one person, or variations on one person,' he says breathlessly. 'The ship makes its crew by varying a template. Angel is an extreme. A mistake.'

Angel starts to laugh.

'You funny, foolish little man! I'm the original. They are all copies.'

'Come back to us—'

'—come back and help us—'

'—help us find our home.'

'There's no home to find!' Angel shouts. 'Oh, you fools! This is all there is!'

'I tried to explain to them,' Dreen says to Mr Naryan, 'but they wouldn't listen.'

'They surely cannot disbelieve the Puranas,' Mr Naryan says.

Angel shouts, 'Give me back the ship!'

'It was never yours—'

'—never yours to own—'

'—but only yours to serve.'

'No! I won't serve!' Angel jumps onto the throne and makes an abrupt cutting gesture.

Hundreds of fine silver threads spool up, shooting towards the sled and Angel's crewmates. The ends of the threads flick up when they reach the edge of the sled's modified field and briefly form a kind of shell around it, but then the shell collapses in a tangle over the crew. Their shield is down.

The crowd begins to throw things again, but Angel orders them to be still. 'Come with me,' she tells Mr Naryan, 'and record the end of my story.'

The crowd around Angel stirs. Mr Naryan turns, and sees one of the crew walking towards them.

He is as tall and slender as Angel, his sharp, narrow face so like her own it is as if he holds up a mirror as he approaches. A rock arcs out of the crowd and strikes his shoulder: he staggers but walks on, hardly seeming to notice that the crowd closes at his back so that he is suddenly inside its circle, with Angel and Mr Naryan in its focus.

Angel says, 'I'm not afraid of you.'

'Of course not, sister,' the man says. And he grasps her wrists in both his hands.

Then Mr Naryan is on his hands and knees. A strong wind howls around him, and he can hear people screaming. The afterglow of a great light swims in his vision. He cannot see who helps him up and half-carries him through the stunned crowd to the sled.

When the sled starts to rise, Mr Naryan falls to his knees again. Dreen says in his ear, 'It's over.'

Mr Naryan blinks and blinks, dazed, half-blinded, tears rolling down his cheeks, seeing in his mind's eye the man taking Angel's wrists in both of his, seeing them shoot up into the night, so fast that their clothing bursts into flame, so fast that air is drawn up with them. Angel knew how to nullify the gravity field; so did her crewmates. She has achieved apotheosis.

The sled swoops out across the Great River towards the tiered slopes of the ship, settles in the mouth of a kind of hatchway at the end of a projecting spar several storeys tall. The city spreads away from the edge of the river. Fires define the radial fan of its streets and squares; the warm night air is bitter with the smell of burning. Dreen sees that Mr Naryan is crying, and tries to comfort him.

'There was no time to find your wife,' he says. 'I'm sorry. I'm sorry it had to end this way. But we'll go on, you and I. We'll have such adventures . . .'

'She was a good woman, for her kind,' Mr Naryan is able to say at last.

But he isn't just mourning for his wife. He is mourning for all the citizens of Sensch. For the loss of their innocence. For their fall. They are irrevocably caught in their change now, will never again be as they once were. His wife, the nut roaster, the men and women who own the little tea houses at the corner of every square, the children, the mendicants and the merchants – all are changed, or else dying in the process. Something new is being born down there. Rising from the fall of the city.

'They'll take us away from all this,' Dreen says. 'They're going to search for where they came from. Some are out combing the city for others who can help them; the rest are preparing the ship. They'll take it over the edge of the world, into the great far-out!'

'Do they not know they will never find what they are looking for? The Puranas—'

'Those old stories won't matter where we're going,' Dreen says.

Mr Naryan clambers laboriously to his feet. He understands that Dreen has fallen under the thrall of the crew. He is theirs, as Mr Naryan is now and forever Angel's. He says, 'The ship and its crew, they are older than the Puranas. But down there, in the city, is the beginning of something new, something wonderful . . .'

He finds that he cannot explain. All he has is his faith that it won't stop here. Angel's death was not an end of something, but a beginning. A spark to set all of Confluence – the unfallen and the changed – alight.

He says weakly, 'It will not stop here.'

Dreen's large, liquid eyes reflect the light of the city's fires. He says, 'I see only another Change War. There's nothing new in that. The snakes will rebuild the city in their new image, if not here, then somewhere else along the Great River. It has happened before, in this very place, to my own people. We survived it, and so will the snakes. But what *they* promise is so much greater! We'll leave this poor place, and voyage out to return to where it all began, to the very home of the Preservers. Look there! That's where we're going!'

Mr Naryan allows himself to be led across the vast room beyond the hatchway. It is so big that it could easily hold Dreen's floating habitat. Windows hung in the air show views from somewhere far above the plane of Confluence's orbit. Confluence itself is a shining strip, an arrow running out to its own vanishing point. Beyond that point are the ordered, frozen spirals of the Home Galaxy, the great jewelled clusters and braids of stars constructed in the last great days of the Preservers before they vanished forever into the black hole they made by collapsing the Magellanic Cloud.

Mr Naryan starts to breathe deeply, topping up the oxygen content of his blood.

'You see!' Dreen says again, his face shining in Confluence's silver light.

'I see the end of history,' Mr Naryan says. 'You should have studied the Puranas, Dreen. There is no future to be found amongst the artefacts of the Preservers, only the dead past. I won't serve, Dreen. That's over.'

And then he turns and lumbers through the false lights and shadows of the windows towards the open hatch. Dreen catches at his arm, but Mr Naryan pushes him away.

Dreen sprawls on his back, astonished, then jumps up and scampers in front of Mr Naryan. 'You fool!' he shouts. 'They can bring her back!'

'There's no need,' Mr Naryan says, and steps forward and plunges straight out of the hatch.

He falls through black air like a heavy comet. Water smashes around him, tears away his clothes. His nostrils pinch shut and membranes slide across his eyes as he plunges down and down amidst streaming bubbles until the roaring in his ears is no longer the roar of his blood but the roar of the river's never-ending fall over the edge of the world.

Deep, silty currents begin to pull him towards that edge. He turns in the water and begins to swim away from the river's end, away from the ship and the burning city. His duty is over: once they have taken charge of their destiny, the changed citizens will no longer need an Archivist.

Mr Naryan swims more and more easily. The swift cold water washes away his landbound habits, wakes the powerful muscles of his shoulders and back. Angel's message burns bright, burning away the old stories, as he swims against the dark currents. Joy gathers with every thrust of his arms. He is the messenger, Angel's witness. He will travel ahead of the crusade that will begin when everyone in Sensch is changed. It will be a long and difficult journey, but he does not doubt that his destiny – the beginning of the future that Angel has bequeathed to him, and to all of Confluence – lies at the end of it.